The Chronicles of Julian, the Hospitaller
A Medieval Novel

The Chronicles of Julian, the Hospitaller
A Medieval Novel

Eduardo Bernardi

Higuma Limited
2018

First Printing: 2018

A catalogue record for this book
is available from the National Library of New Zealand.

ISBN 978-0-473-43697-1

Higuma Limited
161 Ridgeview Rd
Redwood Valley, Richmond, 7081, New Zealand

Cover design: Vittorio Bernardi
Image on page 577: Augusto Bernardi

Ordering Information:

Special discounts are available on quantity purchases by corporations, associations, educators, and others. For details, contact the publisher at the above listed address.

U.S. trade bookstores and wholesalers: Please contact Higuma Limited,
Tel: (+61) 7 3048 8594 or email higumaltd@gmail.com.

Hugs and Kisses

to Giuliana, Vittorio & Augusto

*Thank you. Without your support and patience,
I would have never achieved this dream.*

Contents

Valley of the Serchio & Lunigiana
circa Anno Domini 1000
Genova
Luni
Luna
Apuane Alps
Pietrasanta
Camp Majore
Ligurian Sea
Pisa

Apennine Mountains
Serchio River
Montefegatesi
Barga
Controne
Corsena
Fornulo
Lima River
Chifenti
Menabla
Traghetto
Mutianum
the Hospital
Oiecimo
Bertangna
Pescaglia
Partigliano
Ottavo
Anchiano
Tempagnano
Sesto
Lucca
Tassignano
Serchio River
Rome

Acknowledgements

It would be an understatement to mention Gustave Flaubert's *La Légende de Saint Julien l'Hospitalier*, Jacopus de Voragine's *Leggenda Aurea* and Ítalo Calvino's *Fiabe Italiane* as major sources of inspiration for this book, but I should mostly say that this story sprouted from a conversation I had with Andy Carse, from Welland, Ontario, at a lovely lunch in the winter of 1999, at The Mill restaurant, in Cambridge (Ont). When I told Andy about the legend of the Ponte del Diavolo, from the place where my great-grandfather had come from, he said that I had right there all the elements for a medieval novel. Interestingly enough, as I developed the range of characters, I later came to find that I was much more involved in this tale than I could ever imagine.

This has been a work of passion. I must thank most of all, my wife Giuliana and my boys Augusto & Vittorio, for their tolerance to my insistence and isolation during the writing hours; and my mother Cidinha, for believing in my passion and supporting the making of this story.

I had tremendous help from a willing and passionate crowd, including my sons, who spent exhaustive hours reading parts of the story for me; Gigliola Del Carlo, Francesco, Giuliano and Paolo Bernardi, from Valdottavo; Manuela Pucci, Laura Giannoni and Laura Magnani, from Borgo a Mozzano; Pio and Chiara Burlamacchi from Bagni di Lucca, Angelo Frati from Colognora; Massimo Bertolucci from Lucca; Nancy Lamensdorf, from Basking Ridge; Lázsló Bajnók, Nóra Jákoi and Tímea Juhász, from Budapest; Giovanna Gianola, from Bologna; Ruth Mazo Karras, from Minessota; Edward Peters, from Pennsylvania; Michael Jecks, from Dartmoor; Paul Gartland and Colette Cosgrove from Ponte a Serraglio; Andrea Pieroni, from Bra; Erika Bartoli, from Montefegatesi; Forest Sheely, from Toledo, Ohio; Werner Haberl, from Vienna; Reza Abdollahi & Fifi Zaefarian from Palmerston North; Mihaela Ranga, from Melbourne; and the young hunter who had lost his *segugio* in Isola Santa (and whose name unfortunately I never got).

And a heart full of special thanks to four angels: the first two are Angela Amadei and Veronica Baccetti, respectively from the libraries of Bagni di Lucca and Borgo a Mozzano. I have always wondered how Karl May and Jules Verne managed to write their stories without travelling the world or surfing the internet. Those authors must have had angels like Angela and Veronica helping them, with such a passion for their work that made life so much easier when visiting a library. The third angel of course is Giuliana, for putting up with my uncountable writing hours. And the last that I am eternally grateful to is my own and very powerful Guardian Angel, who's been patiently and gracefully watching over my back. She was so skillful and kind, giving me a second chance on a rainy evening in Borgo a Mozzano. *Mille grazie!*

Note to the Readers

It is not easy to think of medieval times without having our imagination flooded by images of crusaders, knights, crossbows, jousting, heraldry; Dominican and Franciscan friars; witch hunters and witch trials; and the classical representation of the Devil as Old Nick, with goat limbs and a goat face. But at the turn of the first Millennium of the Christian Era, none of these themes had yet been properly brewed from the plot of history or folk lore. This particular early period of the middle ages has lost most of its memory beneath fundamental changes on the making of Christendom over the following centuries. This was a time in limbo when all of Christian Europe still used the Roman algorisms and there is limited knowledge left of the regional structure of spoken languages. I have thus taken complete freedom to punctuate my narration with regional terms and names which may appear on its Latin, Italian, other non-English or English shapes. With no editor reviewing this book, the choice has been mine, according to my own judgment for the sake of veracity, charm or fluidity of text above consistency. Besides, there's a good chance they could mask some of my appalling misuse of prepositions.

For example, I have often chosen the local term for many items, such as Tevere (over Tiber), or old names for localities, as Mutianum (over Mozzano). Neither the spelling nor the terms may necessarily be the specific word utilised by the inhabitants of the described locations a thousand years ago. Still, on the other hand, except for the German who became Bishop Giovanni of Lucca, I have favoured the English versions such as John for the popes' names, over Johannes or Giovanni; and for the main character I prefer Julian over Julien or Giuliano; in both cases probably due to their universality.

With few exceptions, the modern system of patronymic family names had not been well established at the turn of the first Millennium in Italy – the Family of the Suffredinghi, for example, a branch of the Cunimundinghi that are active characters in this story, was only called as such more than a hundred years after being solidly established in that area. However, for ease of understanding, I will use family names whenever needed, but hopefully not too abusively.

For such a considerable amount of words in different languages and dialects, I have included a glossary at the end of the book, but I advise you to use it only when really in need, for I fear that words nearby could be spoilers to the plot.

Although I do mention the locality of Mutianum (Mozzano), the bridge was known earlier then as "Ponte di Chifenti", referring to the village at the junction of the Lima and the Serchio, called Coflenti during the IX-X centuries, but which I will simply use the current "Chifenti" so it will not be confused with other similar names. On the same manner, I changed the name of current Corsagna to Bertagna. The village of Corsena remains as Corsena. Most villages and parishes mentioned in the valley of the Serchio still exist, except for the parish of Santa Giulia, in Controne. A thousand years ago this church was not located exactly in any of the hamlets known later as "Controne", but in a mountainside right above Bagni di Lucca (Corsena), where today lies the cemetery of Pieve di Monti di Villa. It should also be understood that the river Serchio of a thousand years ago, before so much construction and deterioration of the geography around its banks, had a very different ecology than what is seen today.

This is a work of fiction, but many of the characters are historical, such as the German emperors, the French nobility, the Roman Patricians, the Tuscan Margraves and the Lombard Cunimundinghi family. The genealogy of the Theophylacts, the Tusculans, the Obertenghi and their association with the courtesan Theodora and her daughter Mariozza is as accurate as possible, broadly based on Lindsay Brook's, although not all historians will agree with my version or dates presented in this story. The liaisons of these families with different popes, whether through bloodline or through amorous affairs, is quite precise, during a period of the Church of Rome known as the Papal Pornocracy. Although the specific lewd acts described on these pages are fictional, those pontiffs were indeed known, reported and remembered for engaging in them. Each of the popes described as committing a diversity of highly un-priestly sins, with the exception of verbal abuse, has been accused of doing so historically. All other characters, including deities, are strictly fictional, except the Devil, who personally confirmed to me that it was all real.

The Thorn on the Countess's Side

Lucca – Tuscany, sometime at the end of the 11th Century

'We all know exactly what startled that horse,' said old Albertazzo with a snort. 'The pope must have been saved by angels from falling into that pit, as the poor beast had inhaled the putrid breath of Hell!'

'You are indeed a bad thorn, my cousin,' the contessa Matilda said to the old man, after shooting a quick glance down to the pope, who snored obliviously, resting his head on her lap. 'No wonder they call your people the Malaspina. You have survived all your kin, outliving even your castle, which sinks into a fetid swamp while the bad thorns endure on the brush. Unpleasant as a prick, yes, but now, in my bedchamber, please keep your nastiness out of my house and spare the Most Blessed Father from your delirious thoughts.'

The Marchese D'Este Albertazzo had little respect for his much younger cousin, the contessa, whom he was paying a visit after learning of the riding accident with the pope. Dressed in a rather discreet dark blue robe over his vest, Albertazzo was bald and toothless, but slim, quite agile and extremely alive up on his head for his nearly centenary age. Surely the old thorn still enjoyed the company of young, beautiful women, but not of his cousin Matilda. People said she was formidable, but to him, the contessa was no more appealing than a warty toad. Yes, Matilda was powerful, ruling over all lands of Northern Italy, so much that he had been forced to pledge his allegiance, negating his earlier support for the German emperor. This was not the first time that Albertazzo had moved his loyalty according to the swing of power between pope and emperor. Malleability was part of his old-age survival. But that scandalous adoration of the contessa for the bishop of Rome, to the point of entertaining carnal commerce with his blessed flesh, that just sickened him.

Albertazzo was not particularly sympathetic towards the wounded pope, who had been carried to Lucca on a bullock cart. Lightly bruised, Gregory VII was perfectly fine. The pope had no broken limbs, after all they were just too stubby to snap, even as he was majestically hurled backwards at the Bridge of Chifenti. Everyone knew the pit was a passage into hell. The pope and the contessa had ridden around its edge many times before, as they crossed the bridge, heading to their love nest at the thermal baths of Corsena.

The filthy pair! The marchese could not help but retch with nausea at the thought of that dwarfish, arrogant pontiff fornicating with his cousin like a badger every time he came for a papal visit to the baths. Brushing those obscene thoughts off his mind, Albertazzo concentrated on his knowledge of that bottomless pit where the accident happened.

'I am not being delirious, Matilda,' he said with a forced grin. 'Everyone knows the devil dug that pit when Julian was alive.'

'Julian? The saint?' she smirked. 'We have had a saint but I miss the knowledge of any relics. Saints and devils! They are all lies.'

Albertazzo waved a hand. 'Who cares whether you believe it or not, anyway?'

'I do!' grunted the pope, lifting his head so suddenly that he bounced his large nose on her breasts. 'If there's been a saint, then we must find the relics.' He seated himself straight up next to the much taller Matilda, holding her long hand with his freckled short fingers, and his feet hanging high above the floor. 'Perhaps we could finally manage to have that pit closed.'

'Then, let me just ask you a question, Matilda,' said Albertazzo. 'How many years has it been since you have sent for the locals to cover the hole?'

The pope and the contessa looked at each other. 'Over four years,' she answered.

Albertazzo shook his head. 'That pit is the thorn on your side then. That hole. It is now you two who must ask yourselves, how come the task has not been fulfilled yet? How many more lives will you waste on the job?'

Matilda narrowed her eyes. 'Even you believe that, don't you old cousin? The devil! Yes, that simple task to cover the pit with soil and stones took more than a just few days to be completed. When we knew the stones would disappear as they dropped into the gap, never piling up at the bottom, I did order a group of stonemasons down the pit with a miner. Regrettably, they have never returned to see the sunlight again. In spite of this loss, nobody tells me anything. The villagers never mention what caused the hole or even who built the bridge.'

'The devil did!' Albertazzo said, with a hint of triumph. 'Those were the times of Julian, the Hospitaller. I was alive then, but I wasn't there to see it happen.'

'Nobody saw anything.' Matilda said, shrugging with resignation. 'They know nothing of Julian… or devils.'

'They know there has been something terrifying about that bridge, but they hide it behind their ears. Still, there is someone who can tell it all,' said the marchese. 'It is our cousin Lando Delle Rocche, from the forest of Ottavo. A true storyteller, just like his father.'

'Well, I don't have much time for any son-of-a-wench cantastorie,' the contessa said, using the local word for the storytellers. 'I want facts.'

Albertazzo chuckled 'Lando knows all the facts. His father Bernardo was a witness when it all happened. Not only was Bernardo the first to meet Julian, but also the last to see him. The story lives on through the next generation.'

'No story as such should live on,' grunted the contessa to herself.

'Well, then let's call for this cantastorie!' suggested the pope, his eyes sparkling. 'Who knows we could even locate the relics?' And he turned to Albertazzo 'Old man, you may not be such a bad thorn at all.'

They say the best remedy to overcome a trauma is to talk about it. But the people from that stretch of the valley found an easier route to put behind them the terror they had seen in that morning: Hellmouth surfacing from that pit and spreading its maw wide on the Bridge of Chifenti, spewing hordes of demons, the legions of Satanas, into the dark waters of the river Serchio. Now they just refused to acknowledge that it had ever been there. In a matter of years, it was all forgotten. And not even their fear of Countess Matilda's crushing swords would stir them into any recollection.

Nevertheless Lando Delle Rocche was ready to tell her about it. As the last remaining child of Bernardo Delle Rocche who had stayed behind, Lando was tending the family lands on the eastern side of the Apuane Alps, while his brothers and sisters had all left to the cities of Lucca, Pistoia and Genova. For a unique opportunity to have noble ears listening to his stories, he went alone, but left his lands well-guarded. With a rough sheepskin coat, only the spots of the fine l'onza fur hat gave Lando a touch of elegance as he journeyed through the day down to the city. The francesca axe that he carried was a clear warning that Lando was a warrior to be reckoned with.

Lando knew the contessa despised the lack of refinement of that cunning branch of the family. Not surprisingly, she was asserting her power by receiving him while sitting up on the highest chair in the hall, lavishly dressed on her bright red silk robe, rimmed with the plated fine furs of dozens of small creatures, carefully folded around her cowl and sleeves.

'Where are the relics, Lando?' Matilda solemnly asked him, as soon as he entered the hall.

Lando made no secrets that he liked that kind of attention, appreciating that both his powerful cousin the Marchese D'Este Albertazzo, and Pope Gregory VII were on the palace too. He knew that Gregory was a great man, in spite of his minute dimensions and the suspected condemnable liaisons with Matilda.

'The saints' relics?' Lando said slowly, taking his hat off and kissing the faces of the countess and the pope, in that order. Savouring his moment with a contained grin behind his behaved lips, Lando was suddenly distracted by a fourth person sitting next to the contessa. An inconspicuous long-necked cleric, with parchment and a quill on his hands.

'Who's the goose?' Lando asked Matilda, pointing unceremoniously to the cleric, who did not move a muscle on his face, but swiftly scribbled something while shuffling his parchment rolls.

The pope gasped irritably and Matilda clenched her jaws. 'I would have expected you to recognise Liutprando, Bishop of Cremona. The bishop would welcome some respect, as we all would appreciate too. He will be here to take any relevant notes on your tales.'

'Everything is relevant in my –'

'The relics!' interrupted the contessa. 'We were asking about the relics.'

Meanwhile the bishop of Cremona was already frenetically writing.

'Oh, the bones!' said Lando with satisfaction. 'Those bones are long, long gone. But before they were found, they had been kept by the marabbecche, deep in the waters of the river Serchio.'

The countess shivered at the mention of the marabbecche, the water goblins of the Serchio. Before the suddenly fragile-looking Matilda figured something to say next, the pope stepped in. 'Who took them? And where to?'

Lando cleared his throat and licked his lips, taking random, slow strides across the hall. 'This was on the year just before my father died. A rich pilgrim that had arrived from the East came to the town of Mutianum, accompanied by his wife and a large committee. When people in Mutianum and the Traghetto heard about his reason for being there, the pilgrim was advised to seek my father, in the castle of Rocca.'

'I remember your father well,' said Albertazzo. 'Bernardo Delle Rocche was a good -.'

'Oh, you old man,' the pope hissed with annoyance, 'do let the Messere Delle Rocche tell us his story!'

Lando continued, unaffected. 'My father told me that the pilgrim he encountered at the riverbank was a robust square-shaped foreigner, one of those northerners with no distinguishable neck and a long white beard hanging from his leathery face. He had a short-bladed sword sleeved in his scabbard and he rode a cart with excellent horses, accompanied by a well-chosen team of trustworthy Lucchese escorts. The wife on the cart was very silent. She had most of her face covered in veils, perhaps hiding scars or signs of an old age. They had come to retrieve Julian's body, and they were prepared to pay generously for it.'

'But who was such man?' the contessa asked.

'He had come all the way from the Holy Land, allegedly making the journey as a spiritual fulfilment, a final step in his wife's redemption.' Lando raised a hand halting his listeners from asking questions, and continued. 'But as soon as they had crossed the walls of Lucca, they were duly informed that there had never been a body. And they found a peculiar general reluctance do speak about those days, especially the circumstances in which Julian disappeared.'

'Did they know this Julian in life?' asked the pope.

'My father asked him that too. But the pilgrim just warmly rested his hand on his wife's shoulder. He said something unintelligible to her and she raised the sleeves of her tunic to reveal just part of her arm.'

'And what was it?' asked the pope, the contessa and the marchese, altogether.

'According to the pilgrim, it was "God's punishment on the filthy!"' Lando said, with an enigmatic grin across his face.

There was a brief silence from the three, all looking as stupid as groupers hooked out of their hidings. But the pope was not as amused as Lando.

'You are not going to play games with us, Messere Delle Rocche,' Gregory said with irritation. 'My time here is short and precious. If you can contribute to us finding the relics, do carry on, but if you —'

'Pardon my interruption, Beatissimo Padre' Lando said, raising a very careful finger. 'But perhaps you should know that while the teams raked the riverbed, the pilgrim told my father what he knew of Julian, and on his turn, my father told him all about the saint. And did you know that those relics were first dug out of the dark waters as soon as my father finished telling the whole story to the pilgrims? On that very moment, the marabbecche let those bones go. That was the first miracle of the Julian's relics.'

'A miracle?' asked the pope with a sceptical and formidable nose.

'The whole story?' Matilda asked hurriedly. 'What whole story? About Julian sending a dog across the bridge?' she sniggered.

'Oh, my cousin,' Lando said, pausing to appreciate Matilda with amusement, 'do you really think the devil can be that much of a fool? Julian too was far cleverer than that. The bravest man ever to step on these lands. He did much more than dare to deceive the Devil. Julian, my dear…Julian defied God!'

The pope went white, as if all blood had hidden under the thick vests he bore. But before he opened his mouth, Matilda declared, with very little patience escaping through her grited teeth 'We have a pit to fill up and relics to find. Perhaps we can get another miracle out of it. And very little time to hear your story.'

'Then you better extend my stay here, for this may take longer than you would expect,' declared Lando, grinning deviously. 'For now, just send us some food and wine.'

He was not even finished when Matilda was roaring to the palace household to bring them the most immediate banquet they could put together. Then, returning her cantankerous gaze to Lando, she ignored their kinship and groaned, as if to a servant, 'This better be good.'

Book 1: To Lucca

Julian of Mans

" Réjouis-toi, ô mère ! Ton fils sera un saint! "
(Rejoyce, oh mother! Your son will be a saint!)
Gustave Flaubert - La Légende de Saint Julien L'Hospitalier

None of the *cantastorie*, as the storytellers were called then, seemed to know precisely in what tongue the Devil had spoken to him, although they could swear it was forked, black, and glistening with poisonous spit. Whether Julian, Julien, Giuliano, Julião, Julius, Juliano, Juluan or any other variant was the original version, it must have been spoken on those French tongues that said *oïl* for yes. A name that was solemnly uttered at the baptismal font. It would have been then still a *piscine* - fairly large basin lined with marble, locked with a lid and occasionally refilled with holy water blessed by the bishop. He would have divided its mirrored surface in the shape of a cross, signed it with the crucifix, cast some droplets from its four imaginary parts to each of the cardinal points and breathed on it to expel evil as he dipped the Paschal candle into it. Its wholesomeness would even be more purified after the pouring of the oil. But still under the power of the Devil, as any unbaptized soul would be, the baby Julian must have been presented to the deacon wrapped in linen blankets and covered with a veil. We know his parents would have used the finest to hand their precious Julian to Bishop Avesgaud at the Benedictine abbey of Saint Bertrand in Le Mans.

The baby was then uncovered and held by the bishop, and roared as loud as he could, three times, as he felt the gelid embrace of the Holy Water - *Holy Water*, which with time and frequent dipping of infants who were never bathed due to superstition, became stale and unclean, and cleansing him from the grips of the Evil One. Holy Water lying on stone that would never see the sunlight. It made his newborn thin skin shrink and raised the fair down on the back of his neck.

Julian, that one day would be the *Hospitaller*. Not a devout or a hermit, neither a martyr or a powerful preacher, but someone like most of us, with weaknesses and passions, and whose life, times and his dealings with the Devil this tale is all about.

'It's a boy! Oh Emma, my dear, it's a beautiful fair-headed boy' she heard the midwife say.

Awaking from the most excruciatingly painful night that she had ever been through, Emma savoured the news warmly and she was handed a robust baby boy, with dark eyes and fair skin. Emma watched him open his eyes wide to fix a liquid gaze at her face. She embraced him dearly against her breast. A heavy drop of tear splashed gently on his forehead.

In that moment, she already knew that her little baby would never be considered as successor to the vicomté.

Those were times when the kingdom of the Franks was reduced to a patchwork; a broken feudal mosaic with only a tiny area around the city of Paris enduring direct ruling by the king. His father descended from a Vicomte Hubert du Mans, who had picked up the pieces of the city left by the last invasion of the Norsemen and started the local dynasty of feudal lords. Emma's only child, yes, but from a first marriage with her older sister Widenoris, his father had already sired Raoul, who would be III one day, and also Geoffroy, Yves, Hubert, Eudes and Odile. Widenoris had been a robust mother, but did not survive to see her only daughter, Odile. Upon her sister's tragic death, Emma fetched a wet nurse for Odile and discreetly but rigidly kept the household of Raoul on the pace. For the time that her sister shared a life with Raoul, Emma knew that he had been a good husband to Widenoris. Unlike most men, he never beat his wife, not even for discipline, and treated her with attention and utmost respect. Emma had always dreamed of a husband such as Raoul, but it had been her sister who'd found one. In that situation, while mastering the household of her dead sister, Emma saw herself getting older, approaching the stage when she would probably be considered an old bride, for she was already seventeen winters of age.

Raoul also had grown to admire the determination of the young red-haired girl. Admiration quickly turned into an uncomfortable infatuation, filling the Vicomte with guilt for the shameful thoughts towards his sister-in-law. The more Raoul craved Emma, the more he tried to avoid her, never daring to look straight into her eyes. As his children were being educated, on the arts of warfare, hunt, working the land and the beasts, learning music, religion and the prodigies of the saints, Emma used her care for Odile as an excuse to be closer to the Vicomte.

Raoul only opened his heart to Emma when, after months of intolerable evasion, she demanded that he look in her eyes, just once. Tears of shame washed over his, before he finally defied guilt and faced the woman he had come to love. Emma's face was like an open summer sky, and her comforting smile made the Vicomte fall into her arms.

They were blessed in wedding by Bishop Avesgaud, two years after the death of Widenoris.

When little Odile reached her third birthday, her young stepmother became pregnant. The new baby would bring a cart full of joy to the manor in le Mans. Raoul would watch Emma's belly for hours while she rested at night, each ripple of flesh that waved across her womb filling him with delight and pride.

On observing the embarrassing gayety of their father, Raoul's grown children promptly agreed and announced that if a male was produced, he should be educated to carry the staff of the shepherds of souls and serve God with his best. Neither of the parents objected to it.

So in that brief instant of consciousness, when Emma happily panted with Julian in her arms, she outlined determined plans for the boy: not overthrowing his siblings or venturing into the liaisons that were such common dirty play among the noble families of that kingdom, but only the best of infancy - academic education, religious studies and especially participation in the daily life of serfs in the borough. From that he would be able to extract respect, discrimination, common sense and accountability, and above all, he would be exposed to the most ample and unlimited love from his parents, for sentiments should nurture the heart and compassion for a servant of God who wants to climb high. The ultimate aspiration for her baby, Emma knew, would be the bishopric of Mans.

'Julian shall be his name,' sighed an exhausted Emma, covered in sweat and panting on her bed, as she moved the newborn to her breasts. 'The name of the saint who brought the true faith to Mans will elevate his spirit,' she continued as she cuddled the tiny head of the baby.

The baby finally found the source of nourishment and crunched into it. The stinging but somehow rewarding pain made Emma bite her lip. She shut her eyes but still had the spirit to give Raoul a quick glance. 'My beloved son, ravenous little bear cub! And he definitely knows what he wants ... just like his father.'

Julian would run to his parents' bed in the mornings and throw his arms around Raoul's neck, covering the vicomte's hirsute face with kisses, and spending precious moments hugging his Emma, telling her about his dreams, just touching her cheek with his, burying his face in her long red hair. His cheerful and generous personality earned him the respect and affection of all his siblings and the servants of the citadel of Mans. A golden birth had not at all corrupted the gentle youth. With humble spirit, he received the best instruction from itinerant Tuscan, Jewish and Mozarab masters in arithmetic, geometry, astronomy and music, the arts of the quadrivium. Julian was also starting to be exposed to the arts of the trivium - grammar, dialectics and rhetoric - thanks to a number of abbeys flourishing in region. Curious and talented, with a captivating warmth, he even gained a careful but genuine respect of his masters.

Besides the passion for his family, Julian enjoyed games with swords, hunting and archery, being dexterous with the weapons, much to the embarrassment of his brothers, dedicated swordsmen who had never wasted their time in the learning of letters and books.

At fourteen, around the turn of the *Millenium*, Julian was the most handsome of Raoul's children. His fair curls had long changed into a dark, almost black crown of hair, typical of his father's side, which he wore short and clean. He had also the same heavy eyebrows, the firm jawbones and the walnut eyes of his brothers. From Emma's proud side, he was blessed with a long face, straight nose and tall stature, which at fourteen gave him a noble presence, even if not completely fleshed as a fighting warrior. He stood handsome and firm, snatching away thrills from the maidens and drawing sighs from some of the friars who ached to see him bishop one day.

On the thousandth year of our Lord, Julian could see enough reasons to celebrate the occasion. The bishopric had been quite discreet about portents and the year slid by smoothly, with hardly any ominous demonstrations of fear of prophecies. As the *Anno Mille* progressed, Julian believed and insisted that the vicomté should rejoice with the first Millennium of the coming of the Redeemer, and nothing better would to it than to commemorate the town's Feast of the Nativity of Our Lady.

'Why do you suggest such a celebration, child?' enquired his amused confidant, the bishop Avesgaud. They were both sitting on a patio of the abbey, outside the cloistered area. Heavily leafed blackcurrant bushes that had slowly grown for at least one hundred years were hiding the two from pilgrims and monks who transited in prayer and contemplation through the southern portico. Sticking out of a stone slab above the door, five sculptures struggled to detach themselves from their base. An almighty Jesus Christ had his arms open, but disappointingly in a lazy, seated position. But around him, the evangelists stood out in a crescent, ever watchful of every word uttered across the bushes. Saint Mathew was carried by an angel and Saint John had an eagle at his feet. Saint Luke sat astride a bull and Saint Marc rested his hand on a lion standing at his side.

Julian inhaled the fresh air with gusto for, regardless of rain or sun, stars or clouds, cold or heat, he always favoured the open air over dank, gloomy interiors. He looked at Avesgaud with a warm interest. He knew the respected bishop was well aware of his disdain for the term 'child'. However this annoyance would vanish when it came from the lips of the bishop. Not that Julian feared the cannon, but he knew that his friend wrapped a sense of provocation in the warmth of fondness. The bishop took a special pleasure in discussing all kinds of matters with that bright young relative of his sister, from private theological debates to the best hound breeds for hunting; from administrative strategies on the land, to rhymes and silly games of words.

'This is the thousandth year,' explained Julian. 'Now look at what is happening all around, but in the Maine. What have we heard of so far, during the last period of the 999th year of our Lord and the first months of this year? The riots in Tolouse; the hysteria in Brussels; the massacres in Spain; suicides in Brittany; werewolves in Verdun. Confusion is breaking out across the land. Don't you think it could be happening here?'

'How can you keep reckoning of all these facts?' interrupted Avesgaud.

'How can I not?'

'Do your brothers worry about these issues too?' the bishop asked.

Julian shrugged. 'Why should they?'

'Well, aren't they inheriting the vicomté?' said the bishop.

'Then isn't that the answer for your previous question?'

'Do you think this unrest that surrounds the God-fearing world is no matter for lords?' The bishop looked at Julian deep in the eyes and was just about to say something when he swallowed and continued. 'But then, with disgrace and desperation sweeping several corners of the land, why should we celebrate?'

'Can't you understand my point?' asked Julian.

The bishop slapped his knee and said with a wide smile, 'Are you trying to play a *questions only* game?'

Puzzled, Julian paused with an empty expression until his face brightened. 'What do you mean by that?'

They both exploded with laughter.

Regaining his composure, Julian continued. 'The reason I think we should celebrate, Father Bishop, is that our parish has not suffered from these horrors of the Millennium. We have survived. Satan has not been unbound, and will never be – those Satan tales are nonsense, anyway. It's about time we tell the populace that there is not such a thing as the Devil.'

'Hold on, child. Be very careful with your thoughts! These ideas of yours are always dangerous.' He stood up for a while, scanning the bushes to see if no one else was near. Sitting back with a more relaxed face, the bishop continued with a warm smile. 'I must confess, they are very interesting! However, you *must* shut your stupid little trap. Don't you *ever* discuss these judgments of yours with anyone else from the abbey, or from the religious orders, or indeed with anybody at all.'

Julian laughed. 'I could not be less afraid of the Beast, and I'd challenge Him to a duel.' He shrugged, raising an eyebrow. 'These threats of yours do disturb me. I thought I could speak freely with you, as we are almost blood brothers.'

'True, and I love you with all my heart, child! That is why I let you spill out these blasphemies without regard to the punishment that you'd usually deserve for such perverted unGodly thoughts. Don't you *ever* dare the Devil again!'

Julian squeezed the bishop's hands between his with honest affection.

'Listen, child,' the bishop said, throwing glances to the sides, 'I have a confession to make to you, and please, only to you.' He looked up to Christ and the apostles on the portico and lowered his head. As his voice was reduced to a whisper, his face darkened. 'Sometimes I fear that the Devil is not really an angel, as the sacred words make him to be. The apostle John called Lucifer the prince of this world. But we hear so many names for the Devil; Demon; the Adversary; the Slanderer; the Spoiler; Beelzebub, the Prince of the Devils; the Enemy, Satan. Others call him Perdition; a murderer or a liar from the beginning; the Prince of the Power of the Air; Son of the Morning; the Great Dragon or that Old Serpent. But we have also heard through dark whispers in our church, that before the early times of the bible; before God called Abraham to leave the city of Ur behind; far from the lands where Ham saw the nakedness of Noah; in the land of Shinar, which would see the erection of Babel, where the great whore, the mother of all harlots was shown to Saint John, there was only darkness, and the Devil was already known to exist. It was called Tiamat. The book of Genesis tells us that *terra autem erat inanis et vacua et tenebrae super faciem abyssi*, meaning that the earth was unformed and void, and darkness was upon the face of the deep. The abyss, Julian! That is what it is! So frightening. We are told that God's creation was performed out of nothing, as opposed to an eternal, shapeless matter. But was it? Wasn't the Devil this primordial state of matter? The emptiness, the natural disorder and the darkness? And God shaped it into some time of *unnatural* light?' And the abbot's eyes wondered into some sombre memory. 'Tiamat...'

'Chaos', said Julian, quite matter-of-factly. 'The abyss. The Greeks called it χάος.'

'How do you know these things?' the bishop asked, half-awakening from his state of acknowledgment.

'Astronomy. Do you forget that I am being trained to be in your place one day?'

'Dangerous fields of study, Julian,' said Avesgaud. 'You'll end up like me.'

Julian shrugged. 'Anyway, we have all the reasons in this world to celebrate redemption, this gift of God to humankind, and disregard this stupid concept of Satanas. So nothing better than the feast –'

He was cut off by Avesgaud. 'First you would have to convince me that there isn't a Devil. Not an easy task.'

Julian was adamant. 'These ideas are so much outdated, Father Bishop. Not even the pope in Rome is heard of talking about the Devil anymore. He's never been heard to mention the Beast.'

'And that really worries me, Julian. I've heard all kinds of stories about this new pope of ours, Sylvester. Even though we should be so glad to have a Frenchman on the throne of Rome, there are tales that he is interested in sorcery and that he can speak to animals. These are indeed dark times.'

'My uncle, I think it is you forget yourself now,' Julian declared with a mischievous smile. 'These are stories! Folk dejecta! No more true than scary tales of forest ogres that our parents tell us. You are the bishop of Mans. You read books and talk to scholars. You travel the world. You have the knowledge!'

'You are right, Julian,' sighed Avesgaud. 'But this seat that I occupy is nothing more than a burden. I wish I had your enthusiasm for life ...' He looked suddenly very tired, and waved a hand. 'Go and talk to your father. We could indeed make it a bigger feast than usual on this thousandth year of Our Lord.'

The bishop received an affectionate hug from Julian, who flew back home. With a certain envy for the boy's fervour, he watched him galloping back to the castle. *I wish you were never born to be a bishop, Julian. What a waste for a good man.*

'Of course,' grinned Raoul, agreeing a little reluctantly with Julian's idea. 'However, for such a delight ...' He snapped his fingers as if calling a servant. '... a great gathering is needed. There are only three months to the Feast. Someone had better get those hounds in the woods or we'll be having cabbages for the celebration!' He tried to slap Julian amicably on the bottom, but his son was already flying to the kennel.

Julian had acquired a taste for hunting and an enviable respect for the game. For the last three years, he had been supervising the care of a cry of hounds that a merchant had smuggled into Le Mans, all the way from the kingdom of Englaland. These beasts were not anything like the clumsy brachets of the Frankish counties. On the contrary, they were magnificent. Strange hounds, tall and slim, with small ears folded back against their long necks. Unlike the legendary heavy lymers from St. Hubert's abbey in Luxembourg, these had a poor sense of smell, relaying better on their sight. They were very docile and had a sweet nature, with a straight snout and alert eyes that called for compassion. The Saxons in Englaland called them *grighunds*, meaning 'Greek hunter dogs'. Specially attached to the blue male, Julian spent his time with all of them, cuddling their arched backs vigorously and whispering words of encouragement.

Julian called for the chasseurs' party to leave on the next day, an hour before sunrise. They attended vespers and offered a prayer to St. Hubert in the chapel, asking for nothing less than plenty.

At supper, all of Raoul's kin were overly excited about the big celebrations the Vicomte was going to throw at Le Mans. Bishop Avesgaud had been invited to join them for the meal, which was quite common, for he was considered indeed as part of the family. His sister Gothefride de Belleme was married to Raoul III, Julian's oldest half-brother. Women sat separately, with their embroidering pastimes decoratively resting on their laps, elegantly waiting for the men to finish eating. From a distance, the ladies did hear and occasionally participated in the conversation that was carried out at the table, but as delicate, charming creatures, they would never allow themselves to eat - such an inelegant and messy activity - in the presence of the men.

'Maybe we should have a company of actors and musicians performing from the castle walls!' exclaimed Yves.

'And jugglers and acrobats,' shouted Odile from her chair, at the corner of the hall.

'Or maybe hold a race,' suggested Hubert.

'And lots of whores!' said Eudes, triumphantly. All the men exploded in generous laughter, while the women smiled shily.

'What we need, when you think of it,' said the bishop, pretending to ignore the joke, 'is a major draw of goods and visitors to this area.'

'Yes! If we attract more merchants than we would on a normal feast of the Nativity of Our Lady,' said Raoul, the son. 'We can enlarge the name of the fair, establishing a mark that will stay with our feast for the following years.'

'We can even have better control on the gambling,' said Geoffroy. 'Races, dogfights, cockfights and wrestling should pay us not only the space rental, but also a fraction of the bets'.

'We can make sacks of gold,' said Odile, 'by betting on Julian with his sword against any challenger who'd be silly enough to dare!'

Another burst of laughter muffled the comment of the Vicomtesse, who said she found nothing funny about that. She looked at her precious son, so handsome, his brown eyes lost on the tapestries of the hall, oblivious to all of them as he thought of something else, probably dreaming of a hunt or a cavalcade on the fields of other lands. She loved him so dearly that even the thought of his daydreaming disturbed her.

Anxious about the hunt, Julian retired to his room much before the discussion had started to cool down, but not without kissing each member of the family good night. He hugged all his brothers and sister and they kissed each other on the faces. He did the same to his parents after taking their blessing by kissing their hand. Long after, Julian would think that he would not have done it so carelessly, had he known the events that would change his life on the next day.

The Chaos of the Deep

Rome – Anno Domini 997

'Look, there is an ass on the cart!' shouted the children.

While those youngest of Romans watching the parade giggled at the sight, most of Rome's population was terrified.

In the castle of Sant'Angelo, the mercenaries had already called Crescentius. The noble had not slept all night. That fortress was his last grasp of a dream that was crumbling into dust. Now, early in the morning, the mob was roaring outside the walls.

'So, the rumours are true,' said Crescentius Numentanus to no one in particular. The patrician nimbly descended the dark stairs, following the soldier to a narrow window on the castle wall. From the protected view Crescentius, who was known in Rome as the *Marble Horse*, saw an interminable flow of people moving constantly across the bank of the Tevere. Among the mass of curious folk trying to get a glimpse of the scene filled with soldiers of the emperor, mountebanks and jesters, he saw the figure on the bullock-cart.

'Oh, merciful God! What have they done to him?'

John Philagathos of Piacenza was wearing only a belt, standing naked with open arms, his wrists firmly tied to two poles on the top of the oxcart. He was not fully aware of his surroundings. A guard was prepared with a pail of cold water to wake him up in case he fainted. On the top of John's head, a crown with two fake ears depicted him as an ass. From the back of his belt, a mock ass tail with a bell had already been snatched out by an excited harbinger. His face was a mess of dried blood and burn marks. Although the humiliation clearly meant little to him, he looked as if he just wanted to die.

But God would deny him even that wish.

The spectacle was terrifying. Such a circus around a miserable figure of a man was already a sign of the end of times. What were people going to suffer at the turn of the Millennium if in Anno Domini 997 that kind of humiliation was already being forced onto a man like John Philagathos?

The Romans did not appreciate it. Now anything could happen once they had seen their pope being paraded through the city dressed up like an ass.

On the previous day, it was early morning when the Italian-Greek John Philagathos, later considered by Christendom as *antipope* John XVI, had been chained and taken to the emperor.

A tall young man, Emperor Otto III was just eighteen when he re-entered Rome to expel John XVI from the papal seat. When the prisoner was presented to him, Otto was sitting on an improvised throne in St. Peter's basilica, wearing a simple white robe and a mantle that was thrown around his shoulders, on the classic ancient roman style. He stuck his long neck out, haughty, the arteries bulging as he carried the weight of a heavy gold crown that adorned his blond curls. By his side, a middle-aged man wearing all the highest-ranking clerical attire of the time sat more comfortably on another solid chair and looked at the prisoner with curiosity. The thin line of his mouth drew a subtle grin as the captive roared his indignation.

'How can this be? I demand an explanation!' The shouts of the destitute pope echoed through the rather dark interior of St Peter's basilica, erected on the fourth century of the Christian era by Emperor Constantine on top of a necropolis where Peter the Apostle was believed to be buried.

'You mean you were not expecting a conflict?' asked the young Emperor Otto with a cynical smile. 'How do you explain the armed resistance then? Why did you leave the Lateran? And what were you fleeing from?'

'Of course there was a conflict!' grunted the imprisoned pope, between clenched teeth. 'My loyal guard will respond appropriately to any threat sensed to the Pontiff. I had to take refuge in the south as your soldiers ravaged the Lateran Palace and all of Rome.'

'You are not the Pontiff!' rasped the emperor. And he pointed to the man on his side. 'This man who has taken the oath required by the constitution: His Holiness Gregory V is the pope!' The figure did not make an effort to confirm the allusion, but stared defiantly at Philagathos, immovable.

John tried not to give Gregory the pleasure of acknowledgement. 'I was elected by the people of Rome, and the ministers of the Holy See all approve and anointed my selection. I have sworn to the emperor too. And the emperor is now telling me I am *not* the pope?' He finally pointed an arthritis-crooked finger to Gregory V, still without looking at Otto. 'That man over there, he is not just a joke. He is a farce. He is *your cousin*, for Jesus Christ's sake!'

Otto started, 'The Holy Father Pope Gregory is the best qualified-'

'Nonsense,' spat John. 'Has Your Highness already forgotten who I am? Well, let me refresh your memory. I was made the abbot of Nonantola by *your* own father. I have authentically risen to the see of Piacenza, which was then turned into an archbishopric. I commanded *your* very own Highness's mission to Constantinople, to find *you* a bride that would double the size of the lands that *you* claim.'

'You betrayed me,' shouted the emperor in an embarrassing high-pitched squeak. 'You and I well know it. No one else than Crescentius Numentanus and his so-called Roman patricians created this farce. I just had to turn my back around to the German lands and they were already putting the true pope to fly from Rome. And you, so naively, became their puppet, their *burattino*, as they say. This miserable Crescentii family has been plaguing Rome for at least four generations. But since then our latest Pope Leo has given the emperors, starting with my grandfather, the privilege to veto any new pope to be consecrated. The Crescentii insist on electing their popes before the death of the legitimate occupier of the Lateran. It's about time we stop the harlots or Rome interfering in papacy...'

'When you were bathed in holy water,' said John with forced patience, 'I swore to God and to your parents that in the name of God I would care for you. Unfortunately you don't seem to be familiar with the holy sacrament of baptism, or with the concept of loyalty, so the valour of a vow has no meaning.' His voice trembled with rage and despair. 'It is just sad to think that the man who has me prisoner is the son of my good friend Empress Theophano; I'm shattered to realise that this same man who wants to strip me from my rightful mitre is my own godson.'

'You betrayed the Sacred Roman Empire,' said Otto bluntly

John chuckled. 'You are very optimistic to call it an *empire*, for what anyone can sense is just a poor amalgamation of states, some unhappy, some un-ruled and some independent. Besides, there is nothing Roman about a Tedesco – a German –

emperor who dresses up in sheets just like a sodomite and who appoints another Tedesco to occupy the highest seat of Rome. Do you know what happened when other Tedeschi were elected to be the pope? It turned out to be a *woman!*'

'That is not true. That was never true!' said Gregory from the emperor's side.

'And finally,' barked John, ignoring the remark, 'even your blind pretension cannot hide the fact that there is nothing even close to *sacred* in your deliberate, nepotistic and selfish ruling. No, do *not* use the word sacred for this hoax. How dare you call your short vision sacred? How can you not see that I, only I who was your godfather and your loyal servant could be the best link between your Empire pretensions and the Romans?'

'Enough,' said the emperor. 'As the head of this Sacred Roman Empire, I will determine the extension of the reach of secular rule. I will determine who occupies the seat of Rome as I would do to any other archbishopric. And you, impostor …' He stood up triumphantly and pointed to John. 'You shall never again see the glory of the Sacred Roman Empire. For the rest of your short life you will be praying that you were dead.'

The other pope was still impassible, immovable. Only his eyes moved between John and the emperor.

'So it must be true…' spat John with disgust, looking at Otto from head to toes. 'You really are the Devil, aren't you? I never thought that Satanas would be coming in the shape of a brat.'

'Take him away!' cried Otto.

As the guards dragged John to the front door, he shouted with all might that he could still gather, taking advantage of the basilica acoustics. '*And he laid hold on the dragon, that old serpent, which is the Devil, and Satan, and bound him a thousand years … and when the thousand years are expired, Satan shall be loosed out of his prison!*'

In the dungeons of the basilica, next to the catacombs where the Apostle who brought the message of the Christ could have been buried, John howled in agony and begged for death as both his eyes were gouged out with a hot iron rod. While he was still raving with pain among the tombs of the faithful and devotees from many centuries before who gathered to discuss messages of peace from the Nazarene, a guard pulled out his tongue with pliers as another cut it off with a pair of scissors. His lips were trimmed off and his nose was snatched out with nippers. Later on that same day, while agonising on grounds not far from the crypt of St. Gregory I, the Great, John lost both his hands to the blade of an axe. He would never see, talk, or write again.

Still in the cathedral, the young Emperor Otto confided to the ever-attentive Gregory. 'I did not like that final speech.' He got closer to the pope, whispering 'Those *Satan* matters …what kind of discourse was that?'

'Just a reference to the words of St. John's Revelations about the coming of the Millennium,' explained the pope, vague and matter-of-factly.

The young emperor wrinkled his nose. 'Well, I don't like it!' He sat back on the throne 'You know, people may talk.'

The silent Gregory V smiled mysteriously. He finally moved around the throne, stretched his legs, cracked his knuckles and sat in a very comfortable position. He looked at the emperor with a devious smirk and said softly, 'Actually, that turns out to be a very useful idea!'

Pope John XVI, henceforth called an antipope, blind, with no lips, tongue, nose or hands, survived the shock and the bleeding, and still lived for another 13 years, in the monastery of Fulda, in German lands. A few months after he was paraded as the ass-pope through the city, the emperor's troops raided the castle of Sant'Angelo, where the last resistance to the Emperor Otto was sieged. For more than a week, Rome saw the birds feasting on Crescentius Numentanus's body, the Marble Horse dead, impaled on a mast on the red walls of the city battlements. His eyeless head was stuck on another pole.

Nevertheless, the biggest news, which was quickly and efficiently spread across the lands of the empire, was that of *the antipope announcing the coming of the Beast.*

Gregory V had seen the best opportunity of a spiritual and material enrichment of the church at all levels if humankind was to face the perspective of Satan being released after one thousand years in captivity.

Those were not the words of antipope John Philagathos, but the lines of Saint John, the Divine, on his book of Revelations. Exactly the same wording, copied and read by the keepers of the faith throughout Christendom.

Fuelled by Rome, the omen quickly took shape and body, reaching the far corners of known Christian lands with its dark shadow, from the abbeys of Hibernia to the monasteries in Syria. The Revelations were undeniable: the Antichrist was coming.

Alarmed by the prediction, desperate souls flocked to the temples, hoping those shrines of safety would spare them from the arts of the Enemy. In the race for absolution entire villages were abandoned, with people donating all their material goods to the clergy. Abbeys, monasteries, chapels, priories, all kinds of nunneries, any category of churches and cathedrals, basilicas, all got their shares of contributions from the desperate faithful. Herds and flocks were directed to the church; a colossal supply of grain; fields were passed into religious hands; manors, castles and multitudes of servants. Parents offered their healthy and ablest children as oblates, rather than the crooked and monstrous. Nobles and even merchants bestowed their richest treasures to buy a privileged seat for key witnesses at the Final Chapter. Never, in a thousand years of history, had the Christian church made so much with so little effort in such a short time.

The consequences, however, extended much beyond any imaginable reach of the religious limbs. False prophets and soothsayers appeared, offering redemption in exchange for total delivery. Men with the gift of words predicted the day of the last judgement. Holy men, saints who gathered crowds of believers, but mostly hordes of the discredited. Battalions of the desperate, willing to give up on their riches, their families, children and lives, defying the organised men who spoke for God and raiding their temples in the name of a true model after the Lord Christ, cleaning the land from sin and evil. Holy men who purified women by spurting their sacred seed in their wombs. Sages that foresaw darkness, but who had the powers to save immaculate children from Satanas by introducing them to unbounded love. Farmers, shepherds, artisans, stewards, smiths, soldiers, cartwrights and merchants, even the noble, the religious and the lettered, but mostly mothers, women and their children, mortifying their bodies, taking their own lives to meet paradise through martyrdom, rather than waiting for the impious who would desecrate their temples or for the final verdict.

Tear-drawing stories abounded of messiahs leading the people off their lands towards collective suicide. Countless families left their possessions behind and wandered aimlessly through deserts and forests, until cold or hunger slowly harvested each of their miserable lives. Lazarettos that were emptied, with lepers taking to the towns, hoping to spread their filth and pestilence at that very end of times. Those that had been called the wicked and the heathen, as the liberation of the Antichrist approached, stampeded out of their forest dens and village dungeons, invading and pillaging, doing as they pleased, for no forgiveness could be expected nonetheless. Iniquity also erupted spontaneously into religious houses. Nuns and monks would frequently succumb to a frenzy of indecency and blasphemy, often drawing others into it or spilling their smut out of the orders' gates.

Men re-created the Devil as they wanted.

The predictions of Saint John had been true. Chaos did reign, but was afterwards controlled, and never defeated. Humankind, as always, survived but never learnt from its own deeds. As men endured, Chaos also survived.

In general though, this had been the most profitable and efficient magnet of attention for Christianity.

Pope Gregory V accomplished the spread of his wrong throughout Christendom, but never lived to savour the fruits of his venom. An invasive case of *lues venerea* started in his shameful parts and spread as fast as the news of the last days, consuming his whole body until the ultimate breath, drawn a year before the advent of the Millennium. He was buried in the sacristy of Saint Peter's, not far from the same dungeon where John Philagathos was disfigured.

Those were the strange ways of God.

The Ogre's Nightmares

A.D. 1000

In the darkest corner of an oaken thicket in a duchy that sits now in a country called France, the ogre was getting ready.

The boy and girl both shrieked with terror. They knew there was nowhere to run. The ogre would bring them back just as he had done before. The bushes would close around them, the trees would make the shadows darker, the ravens would denounce them and the boar would find them. They had attempted several times before, but they were now tired. They were giving it up. The ogre just seemed to know his way too ably in the darkness of the forest. He was either a friend of the creatures or a master of them.

Nico looked at the two terrified victims and rejoiced with their fears by making those bristly noises every time he ran the stone along the rough blade. He gave them a bitter grin as he thought of his own terror. He thought of his nights. His nightmares. Now he felt better about doing what he was about to. He was soon going to get rid of his bad dreams. No more voices. Just the soothing visits of the stranger. Nico looked at the children and smiled.

The village had been nearly empty, as folk had sold their belongings and donated it to the church. But it had not been difficult to fetch the boy out of a night camp on a forest clearing. The stranger had told him where to find them. Nobody saw the ogre coming and going. A stolen provision sack under his left arm counterbalanced the weight of the boy, whom he had silenced with a thump on the nape. He kept the boy in his den for two days, before going for the girl. Providentially, the boy was too young to understand most of those horrendous matters the ogre had told him.

The girl was much more of a problem. In his rusty reasoning, Nico had never thought of a girl reacting like a beast.

She was very young, but courageous and daring. Her father was gone and now her sister had only her to help tend the sheep. She needed bravery especially when required to get some stranded ewe near the old house. That place terrified her. She could still hear her father warning them about the forest and the ogre. He would never exaggerate when describing what the villagers had found in that house and the atrocious things the ogre had done to his own parents. She would think of her father's wide-open eyes as he cautioned them again and again.

So, in that early evening, when she heard the bleat of a lamb that would not leave the ruined walls, she armed herself with reason and marched towards the dark piles of stones and rubble. *The ogre is not there*, she thought. *There is no ogre. He is deep in the woods, living with the beasts. He would not come here. No, not after his awful crime!*

She looked at the weeds, spreading their vines over the walls, desperately trying to cover the corruption of the place. She did not want to find anything except her stranded lamb.

The bleating was getting desperate, and the descending darkness was making the skies more visible than her surroundings. There is no ogre. Nobody can survive for years in the forest. There is nothing more than ruins of a burnt house here. Fire has cleansed all malice from this place.

Almost choking from desperation, the girl finally exhaled with relief as she spotted the lamb at the edge of the woods. She ran for it, for all that mattered was to release the poor creature which seemed to be caught between two trunks, and leave the dreadful place to join her sister.

She was not even near the lamb when she started to scream.

The devil took many forms in those days of the tenth century of Christendom. He was the Enemy, but the identity of the enemy depended on the lips that spoke of it.

On the passing of the Millennium, there were those who saw the Devil as in impersonation of the pain and destruction that any enemy hordes could bring with them. The child king Alphonse V of León saw the Devil leading the Cordovan armies of Al-Andaluz against the last Christian bastion of Iberia. For insular Anglo-

Saxons, orphaned by the invaders from the boats, the Devil had the shape and features of their new Viking leaders. For the Lombards, the Devil could look like the Saracen pirates from Sicily or even as the citizens from competitor states that rivaled in commercial and productive activities of their homes. On the Sacred Roman Empire, many were the fingers pointed at the enmity between papacy and the emperor or even between ruling clans of Rome. Every major player would have been said to be the Devil at some point. And most peasants from the uncountable kingdoms, counties, viscountcies, earldoms, duchies and so many other vassalages, probably had a very well-defined vision of the Devil, which must have had the reminiscence of their lords and suzerains. Old Nick crossed paths with knights, abbots, bishops, monks, saints and kings. His features were often disguised, for learned men would have refrained from being tempted by the proposals of an unmasked Devil. Incubi and succubi haunted the herd of God during bad dreams, leading them into wrongdoing, creating thus a reason for burning on eternal flames. So yes, perhaps Satan's hands were indeed free after all. The Devil was unbound and his presence was felt across the land. He had not slept at all, and possibly never been constrained. From the times when the Eden was young, when this earth and the heavens had just been created, the Devil was already old and active, for out of his nature God created. God separated, God distinguished, God illuminated. The Devil was originally just the dark face of the deep. Chaos.

The ogre never liked to get any close to the village, but the stranger assured him that this would be the best way. The bad dreams and the voices, he thought. The ogre just longed for an end to them. The stranger had told him how to attract the girl, but there was never any prediction that the child would fight and scream, attracting her big sister to rush to her aid. The ogre let the small girl go and prepared himself for the blow from the shepherd's staff, which came swinging with full force towards his head.

Nico thrived in the darkest core of the forest, sharing his makeshift shed with the wild boars. As a young lad, he had lived with his parents in the house which was now in ruins. Due to his unfortunate appearance, he was never allowed to accompany his family to the village church, for such an abomination would be offensive to God. The local parishioner constantly spoke of evil forces that had moulded that unnatural child. The coming of the beast, the prophecies, all indications that the ogre's own family were to be blamed for brewing that wrong. The ogre heard it all. Nothing the priest said was ever missed, and it must have been true. He did something about it, but for some unexplainable, incomprehensive reason even to himself, he knew he had done wrong, very wrong. And this wrong had forced him to exist away from people.

He survived on mushrooms, roots and nuts, eventually catching some animal with his own hands, always sharing the meat with his friends the boars. Nicolas had been his name, but none had he now, except for some villagers who would swear they had seen Nico Cochon – 'Nico the pig', running somewhere in the forest, or even fornicating with wild sows in the shadows of the woods. He had succeeded in the woods for those few years, more like an animal than as a hermit, away from a humankind that would never forgive his crimes. His lifestyle, if one could categorise it as such, made him think less and less about his deeds, until one day he did not think about them at all. Nico Cochon lived happily digging roots and truffles, sometimes sneaking food or curiosities from voyagers and always retreating to the darkest corner of the woods, where he had assembled his shed. Such was his life when they came.

In the beginning it was only their voices. They would scream in his dreams, scorning him, sometimes asking him to liberate them from eternal suffering. They would laugh at his misery and clammer for his attention. They whispered wrongdoing in his ears, and roared blameworthiness for his faults. They would mock his parents' tones and replay the tragic day when he had taken care of them. They reminded him of that.

Then he started to see them. They came with the darkness, roaring as they flapped those ugly wings and tormented him with malice and violence. They would get into his dreams and take him back to other times. They licked his ears with their filthy tongues and shrieked with hate while flying around his den. Night after night they tormented the ogre, until one dreadful day, after so many nights without sleep, so many restless and fearful hours of darkness, under bright moons or violent storms, and especially after so many, many days and nights without uttering a single word, mimicking the sounds of the wild, howling after slaughtering a beast, snarling at an approaching predator, grumbling to the herd or grunting when relieving his own accumulations, Nico the pig finally opened his brown-toothed mouth to speak.

The ogre spoke to them. He begged for mercy and asked for their leave, to be abandoned in peace. Such demonstration of flimsiness just drove them wilder. It made them more numerous and more terrifying. Whilst fear can warp the spirits of the sane, it can straighten the ways of the wicked. Horror was then becoming a mental exercise for the tormented Nico Cochon, who concluded that the only power capable of ruling over such forces would be the supreme will.

He spoke to God.

Nico was not the pig any more. He was just a conscious Nicolas, rueful of his unmentionable sins, sincerely asking for forgiveness and release from that evil. He thought of his parents, the words of his father thanking God for their daily provisions, or the *sweet*… yes, he actually thought of the *sweetness* in the voice of his mother on his side, looking at the stars and expressing gratitude for another day and asking for protection especially for him on the next. Somehow the awareness of his deed filled him with sadness, not for what he had done to them, but because he missed their presence. Nobody to protect him. He just laid on the dry leaves and offered himself to God. No more nothing. No more living with the pigs, no more living like an animal. Punish me the way you want it. *Beat me, kill me. Just get me out of this life.*

But God did not attend to his plead.

It was an exercise of denial and self-depreciation in face of his helplessness, leading to a simplistic but very obvious assumption: If God does not listen to me, somebody else will. Someone who would be there to do what He was not able to. Someone who had already made the ogre do things.

The stranger came in silence, smooth, as if floating through the woods, never disturbing the bed of leaves, or startling the boars that rested among the enormous roots embracing the ogre's den. Nico Cochon was delirious in his dreams, being dragged by the creatures which hysterically screamed evil and corruption in his ears. As soon as the nightmares saw the stranger they left the ogre, screeching as they flew in all directions, evaporating in the moist air of the forest like a friar's lantern fleetingly dissolves in the night.

The ogre sat up astonished, watching the stranger approaching delicately on the tip of the toes. Such a silky walk had those small and delicate feet. The stranger was the most beautiful woman the ogre had ever seen. She could have been a peasant's wife, but Nico had no recollection of seeing such a beauty before. Strangely, her rags were only held together around her long legs by vines and flowers that grew greener and more luxuriant than the season would allow for the rest of the forest.

She glided towards him and smiled gently, as she touched what had once been his lips with her soft finger. Her long brown hair caressed the tip of his ears. The stranger smelled of something long forgotten, maybe of the forest, but definitely not of common folk. A pungent aroma of herbs that Nico could not identify.

The ogre did not move. The sensation was very good, especially after the demons' torments of his dreams. The stranger spoke words of the woods and the animals. She made him feel at ease and opened her legs, sitting delicately around his body. Her breast came sweet and full into his mouth, and she let the ogre suckle a silvery milk that sent shivers of cool solace. As the icy flashes reached his groin, he held her body up as he clenched his teeth on her nipple. She produced a malicious grin and wrapped her legs around him, arousing his most beastly instincts to the point of drawing blood from bite. Her skin was slick as if of shiny metal. Delicately, she disentangled herself from his grasp and leaned on the ground, turning her back to the ogre. She knew how Nico Cochon was used to doing it. As he pumped furiously, Nico heard through the moans the reassuring words of the stranger, promising to be back and keep the nightmares away. And she also asked him to do things. Strange things.

He lay exhausted, never seeing the stranger leave, and soon he had already forgotten about the things she had requested.

On the next night though, the demons came more furious than ever, and again, in his dream, Nico pleaded for her intercession. This time a different stranger came to frighten them away. The imps disappeared as a woman with a long black mane floated towards the den. A red and purple dress draped in gold hung from her hips. Her torso was bare, oily and magnificently pulsing. A copper tiara tied the long locks around her crown. The ogre never said a word. He was feeling better, freed from the nightmares. He noticed this stranger had a thick layer of paint on her face: green circles around the eyes and a muddy white paste that accompanied all the curves of her features. She extended her arms to him and grinned, releasing the same herbal fragrance as the day before. Then, Nico knew it was she. This time they copulated as the ogre suckled that honeyed milk which poured of her engorged teats. Her lips and tongue softly rubbed his ears as she reminded him of his duties.

They were strange tasks that the ogre only fully understood as the stranger came back with a different appearance but the same request, night after night. The demons would leave him in peace at her arrival, and she said that the nightmares would be gone forever if he did just that one thing.

Borbála is Bleeding

A.D. 1000

A pair of black, crooked, goat horns adorned his helmet. He had a wolf skin around his shoulders and a collar of boar tusks decorating the abundant black hair on his chest. The eyes were of an uncommon dark yellow, savage, squeezed against fine, long eyebrows by the high cheekbones, an indication that his people had come from far, from the east. The heavy tips of his moustache fell to the sides of his mouth, braided in a mixture of sweat and grease. He held the baby with a tight grip, as if unaware of the child's bellowing. A simple fox skin was wrapped around the newborn.

As he came to the top of the hill, the sun was already casting amber beams through the eastern clouds. Cold tears were rolling down his face, as he raised the child above his head and shouted with all the strength of his wide lungs:

'Oh dear God! Thank you for such a great gift!' He exploded with laughter and tears. 'Thank you for peace! Thank you for Istvan, our king! But most of all, thank you for *this* Istvan of mine, my beloved son, and for the righteous future you have held for him!' He looked at the baby and hugged him, ripping out more shrieks from the tiny creature. In that unique moment of privacy, he looked warmly at the child and cooed, 'We will be a Christian nation, my beloved Istvan - a Christian nation!'

He sat down and embraced the baby, covering him with his wolf skin. He wept for a long time, as the child quieted down, synchronising his sobs with the father.

The man was Ferenc, chief of the Osi, one of the one hundred and eight clans among seven tribes of the Magyar who had lived for centuries in rivalries and skirmishes with neighbours, spread across the plains west of the Carpathian range, almost all the way to the Adriatic Sea.

The baby Istvan was one of the thousands of other babies of the Magyar tribes named Istvan, all honouring the duke who had brought the Western ways to his country, securing their distinctiveness for history. Fenrec's clan had been Christian for many generations, which was leading the region towards an identity crisis, separating it from some of the other clans of his tribe, until the Duke's victory over a pagan revolt established Christianity as the religion to be followed, by the rule of will or by the sword.

Ferenc looked at his land. To the west of the hill, the village. To all directions, the roads. His father had decided to settle on those crossroads. It was a prosperous zone, and allowed his people to trade with travellers and caravans. Scouts were always ready to alert the tribe of voyagers, traders and their cargo, much before they'd reach the intersection.

Ferenc started to descend, still talking to his baby. In his mind, he was planning the structure of the church to be built on the top of that hill. Four deep holes had already been dug to insert the massive logs they'd bring from the northern mountains for the foundations. He wanted it to be the longest hall of all constructions in the region. In a few days he would get the villagers to be sent for the logs, but they were now ready to greet the caravan of Abbot Astricus, on his journey to see the Holy Father in Rome. As long as foundations were started, he thought that it would satisfy Astricus, the duke's envoy.

As he was considering all these perspectives, he hardly noticed one of his men, who was coming up the hill as fast as he could.

'It's your wife, Ferenc,' he said, panting.

'What is it with Borbála?' said the chief, already handing the baby to the messenger.

'The midwife and the shaman are trying everything, but she's still bleeding.' He swallowed and wiped the sweat that was stinging his eyes. 'It looks like she's not going to make it'.

But Ferenc never listened to this last part. He was already stampeding down the hill.

The howling wind would not dry up the folds of scarlet skin encompassing those deep yellow eyes. Yellow eyes that could scan the land with accuracy for expanses vaster than any conceivable for human capacity. Yellow eyes that could spot its prey. Eyes that could watch men on the land, going on about their little human deeds, so irrelevant to it. Eyes that would spot death and sickness, the carrion that were so vital to it.

Its name was Turul, the bone-crusher, worshipped by generations of men.

Its talons were sharp and arched. The black feet were covered in tough, shining reptile leather. The black feathery horns drew a strange white crown half around its head, continuing down in a black beard that divided its white face, growing from the lores, all the way down, past the nostrils, to hang in tufts on the side of the powerful mandibles.

Turul would inspire fear and admiration when it opened the huge silvery black wings and casted its magnificent shadow on men. People would fear that if Turul was on the heights, anyone could expect things falling from above, to smash bones. They hated to think that the wedge-tailed Turul could suck their bone marrow out.

Turul was hungry. Its thick neck arched down to focus on the lonely shed, north of the village. It could well search the yard for new carcasses or bones. Its yellow eyes focused on the frail figure of a man, coming out of the cabin. The huge creature dove down, sweeping back its long wings, reminiscent of a colossal falcon, making the wind whistle with awe, as it cut through the air like a falling sword aimed at the man, leagues below on earth. As it got nearer, the burning hum called up the attention of the man, who turned around just as Turul spread its wings over to a halt and brought down the legs, covered with a thick layer of honey-coloured feathers, spreading open its long talons. The man raised his right arm above his head and Turul, the lammergeyer, softly perched on it.

Béla was already an old man. The *táltos* – shaman of the village – now lived on his own. Offerings from the dwellers to the táltos had never been much generous, especially since the father of Ferenc, the chieftain of the Osi, had confirmed that all the families should follow the new religion. Béla had grown up during a time when the old religion, the worship of Turul, had dwindled against this new faith that venerated a crucified man, sweeping through the Ongurs, all the way to the peoples of the eastern Black Sea. Béla had been prepared to be a counsellor, a spiritual leader, a healer of body and spirit. He learned the old ways from his father, the táltos before him. But the new religion took the people away. Most were not interested in the old traditions, but in the medicine only. Béla was ordered by the chieftain to learn the Christian faith, for there were no priests in the clan, and some still professed the old beliefs. Several missionaries and monks had been through their lands, and many spent time with the táltos, speaking of this God, supposedly much more powerful than Turul, his god. Not that Christianity was something new for him. Béla had grown up in a world of dual religion, his father always warning him about the dangers of that weak Christian god – *weakling* – for Turul would never let himself be tortured and crucified. *How could they adore him?* The táltos had given up on its understanding, but not Ferenc. The chieftain insisted that Béla practiced only medicine and administered the holy sacraments of baptism, communion, marriage and death rites. Béla's knowledge of the world of the dead, on how to send the deceased to the afterlife, was denied and left to oblivion. Those were days when law had already prohibited the Ongurs to bury their people with treasures, weapons and other utensils that would be useful in the afterlife. Béla knew the glorious days of the táltos only through tales from the elders. His world was of isolation, merely a repository of medicinal herbs that the villagers would come for in time of need.

It had only been six years before when, already a widower, Béla came across a caravan of traders coming down from the Balkans. Among other merchandise, they brought birds - falcons from Syria, lanners from Egypt, merlins and kestrels from Greece, sparrowhawks, alphanets and booted eagles from Barbary. Old Béla tried in vain to exchange what he thought a reasonable amount of silver for one of those birds, for this was the once-in-a-lifetime chance to have a Turul for himself. He needed a Turul to remind the villagers of their old god. Those táltos of the past had often kept goshawks, buzzards or other raptors as a symbol of Turul. However, since the days of Géza, father of duke Istvan, the capture of hawks had been limited to the clan of Árpad. A disturbance of a nest could be punishable by death.

So insistent was Béla that the falconers in the caravan decided to sell him a young bearded vulture from Byzantium, whose hysterical and insistent shrieks were creating a major nuisance to the other birds, of much higher value. The yearling was covered in dark brown feathers, already with those black feathery tufts hanging on the sides of its powerful beak. The bright-red eyelids were stitched closed with a thread. A young Greek sparviter from the caravan spent some time instructing Béla on the care for the lammergeyer, on how to replace the stitch with a hood, on leashes, jesses and bells, but the táltos hardly understood a word, except that he should feed the vulture with bones.

For the first few days, the clumsy and frightened bird was left on a leash outside Béla's shed, fed by bones that the táltos broke with an axe. As the months passed, not only Béla, but most of the villagers developed a special affection for the vulture, which still grew even bigger. It became accustomed to the children, who would come with bones from the slaughters. Its bristly thick neck would extend down for their little fingers so they could rub his nape. Other táltos came from neighbouring villages to discuss the identity of Turul. Flooded with jealousy, most of the other shamans would, in the end, despise and dismiss the unique creature with a statement that the real Turul must have had been a mere *sólyom*, a falcon, anyway. Béla however, knew that this bird was sent as a message by the real Turul. The old man was starting to benefit from a popularity that he had never experienced or ever hoped to enjoy during his long forty years of life. He became more daring in talking about the old ways, even challenging the guidance of Ferenc. He would brag about his medicine and cures, attributing them to the knowledge of the old religion and hardly to herbal power and knowledge of human anatomy. He saw the direction of the tides changing with the increased attention he was given with the company of his gigantic pet. That was until the lammergeyer started to express one of its natural behaviours.

Turul would take flight and the villagers appreciated the watchfulness of the magnificent bird. However, no one had expected that the lammergeyer would carry huge pieces of bones to those heavenly heights and drop them on the expectation that they would smash into pieces, exposing the delicious marrow that the bird thrived on. As the land was marshy and the soil was soft, the smart creature knew it had to drop the bones on solid ground, which was restricted to the roads or the village. Soon the táltos was receiving complaints from disgruntled travellers who were startled by dropping femurs or from villagers who were afraid of being hit on the head. Béla promised that never again would he feed the vulture with any form of whole bone. Still, Turul would thieve from backyards and drop them to explode on village grounds. Now, on a sudden turn of events, the táltos was facing his lowest level of popularity ever, and the promise of eviction from the village if he did not kill or get rid of the bird.

When Turul perched on Béla's arm early in that summer morning, his mind was already rushing through the alternatives he had in life. As an old man, he would not be able to build shelter anywhere else. But as a táltos, he needed some type of confidence that he had only seen since his acquisition of Turul. Other villages around were Christian too. Those that were not, had their own táltos already. He could only stay, and he would not let the bird go.

He scratched the bird's neck delicately. Turul gave a purr of satisfaction. Looking around his cabin, the horse skull on top of the ridge beam, the bone debris scattered around the yard, Béla did not notice the woman who came running in. It was Turul who gave him a soft kick and looked at the visitor, with a warning shriek. Soon they both recognised the village midwife.

'Béla, Béla,' she cried with haste. 'It's Borbála. She is bleeding and I cannot stop it. She needs you'.

Béla left the vulture on the ground, dove inside his cabin and came out with a leather bag, a wine skin and clay pots. He ran to the village with the midwife, as fast as he could. He knew this was his only chance to stay in the village – now they needed him – only if he could prove he was the sole chance for the chief's wife to stay alive.

The flow of blood continued, slowly, but insistently.

Borbála had lost all the colour she had once proudly displayed on her beautiful face. The bluish grey of her skin was a bad sign. Her lips were cracked, trembling as Ferenc tried to pour some more hot nutmeg infusion between them. The long black hair was stuck together in sweaty tongues, plastered around her neck. An acrid odour arose from the palliasse where she lay.

Béla and the midwife replaced the rags constantly, but didn't observe any improvement. The táltos had already anointed Borbála's parts with a plaster of honey and heather, but that had only made the flesh around her womb swell. It did not staunch the bleeding.

'I want to see my baby,' Borbála tried to mumble, but nothing came out of her lips. Ferenc understood the plea in her eyes and left to fetch little Istvan.

As Béla observed the chieftain holding the baby in front of his dying woman, he realised how his own life too was crumbling apart. He thought of the woman he once had and the baby that had gone with her, making his heart heavy with pain. But so many years later he was still alone, missing company, affection, humanity. He was a loner, and that could not be changed. Even his knowledge of the old ways, which could have brought people closer to him, was undesirable within the new religion. His only friend, Turul, was also repudiated by the village folk now. Béla had only this last chance to be recognised for his medicinal knowledge, or else he knew he would be sent away, banished, forever an outcast.

And slimy as an eel, the opportunity was just slipping through his bloody and trembling hands now. There was nothing he could do. Borbála was still bleeding, and vanishing.

While Ferenc rocked the baby back to the wet-nurse, Béla instructed the midwife to put some pillows under Borbála, to keep her head down. 'Let's bring her hips higher up.' And he almost let it slip out loud by saying 'Maybe in this way we can delay her death.'

Thick dark blood had welled from a slit on the abbot's temple as he still moaned in pain.

Many leagues to the North, just a few miles from the great Zala lake, Abbot Astricus was being bled by the chief physician from Mons Sacer Pannoniae. They had left the abbey two weeks before, but the journey was being delayed by the abbot's predicament of headaches and nausea. An Italian brother examined the black humours of the abbot's blood and concluded that maybe a clove of garlic should be inserted into the cut. But the German physician insisted that the incision was sufficient to reduce those crises of *hemicrania* which they all knew afflicted the father abbot from time to time.

'And if it still gets worse,' confirmed the German physician, 'we should wait for a full moon and apply a brazen iron to the temple. That should drive the peccant essences away.' Just as he said it, the monk was spluttered with blood across his face as the abbot stood up with force on hearing the prescription.

'Imbeciles! You are going to kill me before my headaches do it. I need healing, not torture! I must be treated, not exorcised! Care for me, not for the disease.' Moaning with pain, he pressed the back of his hand against the slash on his temple which still bled profusely. 'Now somebody bind this wound up before I bleed to death! But not you two,' he growled, pointing to the two physicians. 'You get away from my sight. Go and find out what are the medicinal powers of this muddy lake that people talk so much about. And quick! We have a whole nation of savages waiting for us to make them Christians. And a king waiting for a crown!'

The physicians instructed a lay brother on the staunching of the wound and how to spice the grease to apply on the cut.

There were about a score of Benedictines travelling with the abbot to Rome. They had travelled in tranquility, escorted by a strong battalion of soldiers from the duke Istvan – Stephen – who was born Vaik, son of Géza. Those religious brothers had been living together for no longer than four years, on the newly founded abbey of Mons Sacer Pannoniae, right where it was believed to be the birthplace of Saint Martin of Tours. Now, as abbot of the first Benedictine abbey in Magyar lands, Astricus was on a mission to meet the Holy Father in Rome. But unfortunately, the abbot's crisis of migraines called for several halts during that initial part of the journey. Even if carried on a chariot, he'd heave and vomit copiously, roaring with nausea and demand a pause. A messenger from King Stephen had arrived a few days before with the offer of a court physician, which the abbot had declined. Now, still agonising with the excruciating pain on his head, he watched the physician monks leave by horse and regretted that he had refused the other choice.

A thundering clatter of hooves on the other side of the camp called for his attention. A messenger was arriving, with a roll of parchment.

After the abbot read it, he sighed deeply.

The other brothers were just reading part of psalm one hundred and nineteen, for while waiting on the abbot's health, they had resumed the celebrations of the divine office. When the final prayer concluded the Terce, they settled for a meal. Shaken by the urgency of the message, Astricus decided that this was the moment to keep on going with the journey. He would send someone to fetch the physicians and they would all raise camp and leave.

He tried to stand up. He was glad to feel that his legs were still in strong shape. Firm on the ground, he breathed deeply and looked around, the smiles drawing across those faces who were watching him standing. But the pain increased, pressing his skull like a boulder, drawing a dark curtain across his vision, so intense that the abbot could not feel his legs any more. When Astricus hit the ground, he did not lose his wits. His vision returned, to watch the brothers hurrying to help him, as he kept thinking how tragic that situation was. The delay was unacceptable.

The message had come from Benedictine brothers at Danzig, where the Duke Boleslaus of Poland was also sending a committee to the pope, to petition for the crown.

If I do not reach Rome in time, Istvan will lose the crown, the emperor's approval, and his kingdom could fall into disgrace. Dear God, help me. You don't want your new children to fall back into war, do you?

'How far is the committee with Abbot Astricus?' asked a desperate Ferenc to one of his warriors.

'I hear they are being delayed by the abbot's health. They should not be here before three days,' the warrior said with sincere regret.

Ferenc punched the wall of his own house with a furious hopelessness. His knuckles emerged bloody from the hole dug through the mortar.

'But I also learned,' continued the warrior, trying to pacify the chieftain, 'that there is a caravan of Bulgars coming from the mountains, probably still a day of distance.'

Ferenc turned to the warrior. With flames in his eyes he grunted between grated teeth: 'Fly! Fly to the Bulgars and bring me a proper physician.'

As the warrior left with haste, Ferenc spoke to himself, but loud enough for everyone in his hall to hear 'Bring a physician before my wife dies, in the filthy hands of this …this incompetent… this … this *táltos*!'

Béla said nothing. He was asking for the old Gods to keep Borbála alive, at least until another physician came. Then, she should better die.

The Den

The seductress had brought the ogre the taste of the flesh. After so many years spent with the beasts in the woods, Nico found solace in his visitor.

Their encounters had been more intense, and more terrifying were the dreams when the visitor was not there. The demons would roar incessantly in Nico's mind, tormenting him with unbearable pain, only to leave when the visitor would shoo them away. As the moments of carnal pleasures were becoming scarcer, the ogre pleaded for the visitor to stay, forever. That was when she started to instruct him on the devious task.

Nico had never been particularly fond of other people. Since he ran into the forest, he had raped two or three travellers, mainly nuns who were on their way to or from le Mans. And that was enough to make people aware of his evil existence. Everybody knew about Nico Cochon, the forest ogre.

Search parties had been raised, the hue and cry. Mastiffs, harriers, kenets and lymers were sent into the woods, but never had anyone come with the prey. Beaters and drummers invaded the forest, horns were blown and the game was driven out, but never the ogre. Into the darkest and thickest core of the forest, some had gone, but less returned. Those who made it told of supernatural beings - hags, goblins, ghosts, werewolves and ogres who lived with the forest beings, inhabiting hollows and ponds, dragging the forest intruders into their dark dens and eating them alive. No, but not Nico. He had never gone that far. At least not until the stranger had told him to do it.

The children tried not to look, not to listen, not to believe, but they understood. Although Nico was not articulate, but mumbled his words through grunting and groaning, both his captives were well aware of the painful horizon ahead. They wanted to wake up from that bad dream which was dragging for days. To get away from fear and hunger, thirst and insanity. They had lost any idea of who they were or why they were there. They could just see the rusty blade, now with a shiny edge which was getting wider at every new scrape of the stone. They could see the ogre – the bad dream man – looking at them and telling them how they would see him split them open, pull their hearts out, and watch him eat them.

But much worse, much more tormenting or horrifying than the thought of being butchered by that horrible creature, was the vision of those eyes behind the ogre. Those yellow eyes.

The stranger was now with him, more prominent, increasing in size, growing in power as Nico was about to slaughter his hostages. It watched the ogre with its yellow eyes, the deep and dead yellow of fire; a cold fire that swallows away the light and brings darkness all about it. Not a woman any more, the stranger had grown stronger arms and longer legs. It had gained height, so that it could watch the children while standing behind the ogre. It could also tear their souls apart with its eyes. While they still shrieked as the ogre was getting prepared, the stranger grew its torso, thick and hairy, with long feathery wings, while its head swelled in size, carrying a large black mane around an old feline face. Nico felt the fetid breath of the stranger and turned around. The horror of the sight made him drop the blade.

A lion. A gigantic black lion, dark as chaos, with a pair of thick curved wings growing from its shoulders and sharp points facing forward. It stood huge on its hind legs, much taller above the ogre. Crowning its feral dark features, the yellow eyes drew the air out of Nico, but told him that there was no escape from what he was about to do. The steam of its breath hissed the words for the ogre to go on.

Numbed by terror, Nico picked up the blade and turned to the children. He could see his own horror in their eyes. They screamed. He untied the boy and held him by the neck. A wild boar rushed past the den, disappearing just behind the ogre and the visitor, pushing through the dry leaves with a loud blare.

Had the ogre turned around to look at the boar as the scared animal rushed by, the events that followed could have turned out differently for him.

A sharp, high-pitched howl broke through the woods, followed by a crackle of barking and shuffling of bushes. The grīghunds had scented game. Julian just had to let go off the reigns a little and his steed knew exactly the direction where it came from. With its nostrils steaming through the thick morning forest air, the horse climbed a slope of dry leaves and dove into the woods after the cry. Julian controlled his mount with subtlety to avoid the lower branches, thorny bushes on his face and clothes, or to protect his knees from being crushed into a trunk passing by his path. He had been so well trained in horsemanship that most mounted chasseurs would find difficult to keep up with his pace and dexterity.

He was at ease with the bow as he had sleight of hand and firmness with the sword. These skills were partly result of the regular steps through the education of noble children. Although it was public that Julian's destiny would be the under the ceilings of the bishopric, he had been instructed on the arts of war, as any of his half-brothers had before. And for their amazement, they noticed that even a priest-to-be could be as sharp as a cavalier should have been.

They ventured deeper into the forest and Julian failed to notice that the beaters and chasseurs had lost sight of him. The barking of the hounds was getting louder, perhaps closer. He had not seen the cry yet, but by their insistence and long tortuous way, he knew it could not have been a hare or a fox or a wolf, and not even deer, be it red, fallow or roe, for these would have taken a straighter line of escape. But the cry changed the tone all of a sudden. The barking became briefer, with quick yowling, intermingled with lower pitched howls. The game was cornered.

He needed to get to the cry soon, otherwise the prey would charge against the dogs. With bow and arrow in the left hand, he quickly approached the clutch of trees where the noise seemed to come from, but a shriek of pain broke through the growling, and soon the barking was back again, moving deeper into the darkness. Julian knew that he had lost a dog. No single hound could be a match against a cornered wild boar.

The beast panicked. Julian finally saw it through the dark green beams that arched around his way. The boar darted through the ferns of a steep slope into a huge crater in the forest and, tireless, climbed up again to the rim, disappearing over the other side. The hounds came after, diving into the crater, and by the time they were out of it, the boar had left onto a different direction. Confused by the scent and with the prey out of sight, they hesitated with shy movements, their thin snouts gently touching each other. They looked around, searching for Julian. But he was not there. He had been long gone, on the track of their prey. His prey.

He had hunted boars before and seen dogs slashed by ferocious tusks. But of this new cry he had never lost any.

The boar flew further into the heart of the forest, where nobody would ever dare to go, where it was believed that hags and ogres were likely to snatch travellers from their wanderings and devour them in their filthy lairs. Julian followed, avoiding thick vines and branches that in this darkest part of the woods could be there just waiting to break his neck at the slightest distraction. But he had only one thing in mind: the slain blue grīghund he had seen minutes before. The boar had opened a gash from the dog's breast all the way to its mandible. It was still shaking when Julian spotted it.

With the boar located, Julian came closer and closer. The forest was thick with moisture. Misty and dark, it was just as well that the beast was exhausted, for only a bit further on, Julian would have lost it into that sea of gloom. It was cold, and the pig now walked slowly to a huge oak, puffing steam through its muzzle. Julian dismounted and prepared the bow. His mount paralysed. A well-trained horse, used to the tricks of the chase. He could stare at the boar now, maybe just less than thirty alders ahead. It was looking straight at him. Its eyes wide open, ready to face a deadly blow of a charging arrow or to use its last strain of energy to down its pursuer.

Julian's shoulders were tense as rock. For his sake, he had to move slowly and precisely. He could smell his own sweat, mixed with the intoxicating stench of the forest floor. So intense and repulsive it was in those woods that he almost felt the sensation that it emanated of something as a human latrine. It felt wrong. He just wanted to kill the boar and get out of there. As quickly as possible. He inserted the arrow onto the string and he raised the bow. The beast was panting, gazing back at him, just like Julian was aiming at it.

Suddenly a light breeze blew over Julian's face, bringing the perfumed herbal smell of something rancid, nauseous, but that Julian could not precisely recognise. His horse neighed nervously and the boar disappeared once more through the trees. He scanned around the unsteady horse for vipers, but found nothing wrong.

Then his soul congealed as he heard a shriek through the woods. A child's cry. It must have been a child. No other forest beast could scream like that, at least not the ones he knew. He waited and heard nothing more. Maybe it could have been the boar attacking his dogs again. He waited in silence, but now the breeze was diving from the trees, still bringing that fresh herbal scent. The shuffling of leaves rose too loud for him to hear that sound again. He advanced a few steps and was about to return when another of those yelps was heard through the wind. He looked ahead where it came from and, deep in a dark den behind the huge roots of the same oak where the boar had rested, he saw it. His blood froze, for it was a beast that he would never forget.

It was dark. Darker and blacker than anything that he could have imagined. It stood tall on its two legs and had a thick mane of black long hair covering its torso. He could not see its face, but from behind the head was like that of a bull, with a pair of horns shaped like a lyre, pointing forward. It breathed loudly, a guttural growling that rumbled through the wind, which was getting fiercer. Julian had never seen a lion, but he thought this beast could be one. He never expected however that lions would be black and stand on two legs, and never dreamed, in his worst nightmares, that they'd be so terrifying. The woods around him felt very wrong.

As gelid fingers of terror wrapped around Julian's ankles, he found he could not move his legs. The vicious grunting of the beast and the forest wind deafened him. Only an arrow could save him from that presence. Swiftly he slid it down from the quiver and prepared the shot. A storm of dead leaves flowed through the woods, and covered Julian, making it difficult to focus of the beast. Still, invoking the name of Saint Hubert and the Blessed Virgin, he drew the arrow back as fast as he could, and with an unwavering hand on the bow, pointed its tip firmly to the monster. When certain of the aim, with an explosive sigh, he let the string go.

Vicomtesse Emma felt the pang in her stomach, as if a sword had crossed her body. A lump came up to her throat. With eyes wide opened scanning the dim hall, she realised that there was still daylight outside. She must have slept from exhaustion after the long hours of waiting and the disappointments of returning parties with no news of Julian. With some difficulty to stand up from a wooden chair after such a long sleep, Emma ignored the pain in her joints and ran up to the window, pulling the heavy tapestry to the side. The cold fresh air hit her face with mockery; such happy weather on an autumn afternoon entering the musty domain of a broken family, broken by what seemed to have been a tragedy.

Emma watched the empty road winding its way through the low hills out to the west. The path that curved northwest, to Fougéres, passing through the great dark forest where Julian had disappeared. She could see the orchards and fields of wheat, and the cruel woods beyond. How cruel it was to have taken her baby away. Her little bear cub. How could it have done that, when so many other cubs, pups, chicks, kits, foals, calves, brockets, staggards and leverets, all kinds and sizes of defenceless babies were going through the woods every day? Why would God take away her very own baby cub, Julian? Why would He do it to her? How could He do it to the ever good Julian? No, it could not be that; she had tried to convince herself so many times during those days; it was impossible, for Julian was a skilled swordsman and hunter. There was nothing that could have hurt him. Even if his mount had been injured, by fall or by an adder, which was not a beast of those woods, anyway, Julian would have come out alive.

Nevertheless, the dangers of the hunts were not unknown. Emma knew that at a hunt's final stage, a hart could kill a man and its mount. A boar was capable of the same destructive force or much worse. It had not been many years since news came of the death of Robert, one of the sons of Geoffrey Grey-tunic of Anjou, slashed from top to bottom by the tusks of a ferocious *synguler*. Hunters had been known to be attacked by ravenous wolves during the curée. The packs would be attracted by the blood of the quarry, mixed with bread by the chasseurs and given to the hounds. Emma knew nothing about wolf attacks recently. And that was not what had happened to her boy. That, she knew.

She had already thought about bandits. Yes, groups of outlaws would surprise travellers and rob them of everything, dumping their bodies in the woods. No limits to what they could do, until they'd be driven out of one's lands by force, or else have their necks hung by tight ropes on the gallows, to public view. But it had been already two days since that horrible evening when the desperate beaters and chasseurs returned to inform that Julian was not to be found, and still, no hearsay surfaced on any marauders around the Vicomté or its environs. Those devils were difficult to track, but they would usually leave tracks of terror, and none had been found.

Why did that path have to be so empty? In a few weeks it would be busy with the crowds, arriving for the fair. But now Emma did not want to see anyone, except a search party arriving with Julian, alive.

Earlier parties had returned empty-handed. The extra horse, taken for Julian, repeatedly came back un-mounted as it had left. Emma spent those nights on her own, for Raoul had gone out with the hue-and-cry. Nights of dark dreams. Nights that opened her soul to fears of devilish deeds.

She had heard the stories of a forest hag, hiding in hollows or in pools, who would devour hounds, one by one, until she could finally snatch at the chasseurs and eat their entrails. Or the Ogre Nico, who had killed his own family and now lived in some forest, sleeping with the pigs. Or worse, it could have been one of those loup-garou, the werewolves. She could still remember, as a child, hearing the news about werewolves' attacks to the villages around the forests of Verdun. Ghost stories! Hags, banshees, *loup-garous*, *sanguisugae*, ogres, *wodewoses*, lemurs, shadows, ghosts! Yes, they must have been imaginary stories, just to put fear on children, so they'd grow up taking the righteous ways, rather than acquire un-Christian habits.

While thinking for all these reasons *not* to believe something bad had occurred to Julian, Emma hardly noticed when a group of mounted men appeared at the point where the road vanished around the hills. As they approached, a subtle cloud of dust was raised, awakening the Vicomtesse from her daydreaming and making her heart almost explode with apprehension.

Forgetting her head net, Emma flew downstairs to the patio, laughing and crying with a strange mixture of joy and fear. By the time the household noticed, the Vicomtesse had already crossed the gates, breathless with the burst of the run, followed by the long flame of her red hair, furiously flickering on the dimness of the afternoon. Villagers watched the lady of Mans, racing by their simple places, most taking pity and praying that she would meet a happy disclosure for her plight. Long behind her came her maidens, Odile and a couple of squires, calling upon her to slow down and wait.

Emma held her skirts as she ran past the houses that edged the western side, gasping for air and trying to discern who the mounted figures on the horses were, still far away crossing the fields against the setting sun. The cold wind that blew from the wheat washed her face with force, muffling the cries of the household following her. She could already discern the men-at-arms on the front horses.

Where was Julian?

She sped up her chase, startling some of the riders at the front of the party who noticed their lady coming towards them on the distance. They opened the way and called to the rear of the company. Emma then saw that the man on the last horse was Raoul.

Marching just in front of him was an un-mounted horse.

Emma's heart sank and she stopped suddenly, wheezing and moaning, her throat dry with dust. So much exhaustion for another day of exasperation. The wait would be longer.

As she tried to recover her breath, among red strands of hair, sweat and dust that stuck to her face, sobs of desperation started to choke her. Tears filled her eyes while a bloated wail was about to burst through her face. Why would God test her like that? She could not support it. She tried to keep herself together as Raoul approached on a gallop, carrying a stern face. Then she looked again at the mounted company coming behind her husband and verified for the empty horse that would come last. Except that the saddle was not empty.

Raoul tried to warn the Vicomtesse about something, but his wife had been deafened by her own screams, as she ran to the cadaver that was stretched across the saddle.

The Gran Putanna

A.D. 897 – About one century before our story

With the exuberant papal vestments looking rather heavy for his tiny stature, Pope Formosus sat clumsily on the throne as the crowd of deacons, cardinals and guests looked at him, amused. His eyes did not move to scan the spectators or to focus on the man who furiously spat accusations at him. The pope's hands were immovable, loosely hanging outside the arm rests of the wooden throne, whereas most of the *curiae* were holding kerchiefs to their disgusted noses. A young deacon, standing shyly next to the pope, was matter-of-factly accepting all the insults which were directed to Formosus.

This synod was taking place at the Lateran palace, the pope's residence. Its state of conservation was still more reliable than the neighbour basilica of the Holy Saviour, which had been abandoned to a calamitous condition. Huge gashes in the roof welcomed not only rainwater in, but also the sunlight to rot the wooden structure that still kept what was left of the ceiling, hanging dangerously above some improvised scaffolding. Walls were broken and scraped, new mosaics had been left undone for a long time. Officials of the See looting the palace and the basilica had become commonplace with the intense succession of popes since the death of Emperor Charlemagne. Rome had been left orphaned, forgotten by the break of the empire and by the never-ending battle between Italian city-states. Especially for this synod, makeshift regal adornments and ecclesiastical paraphernalia had been brought in from other churches and mansions.

Sitting quietly at the bottom row of a side tribune, surrounded by men-at-arms and not at all unnoticeable to any of the male's eyes in the audience, was Agiltrude, the formidable widow of Duke Guido, of Spoleto. Wearing rather flamboyant attire for the occasion, she was in the spring of her thirties, with her long blonde curls flippantly escaping from her wimple, and her bosom heaving generously from her chemise's neck opening. Agiltrude's feral eyes and the tremulous chin muscles holding her clenched jaws could not hide her rage, which seemed to want to explode from her glorious breasts, but the slight curve on the one side of her usually hard lips gave away the immense pleasure she was taking on witnessing the occasion.

Next to Agiltrude was a very attractive young couple, proud of their youth, hardly paying attention to the proceedings, but just beaming to anybody they thought worthy of a fruitful friendship. Their eight-year old daughter was sitting comfortably in the lap of a handsome thin-haired deacon, Sergius, on the opposite tribune. Thrilled with excitement to be the centre of attention for that attractive grown-up on splendid attire, the enchanting Mariozza Maricuccia was engaged in a revealing conversation with the cleric, who was completely dedicated to his young company.

'So why are they saying these things about Pope Formosus?' she asked with a fairy expression, squeezing the shine out of her violet eyes, clearly aware of the bedevilment they had on adults, especially men.

'They are accusing Formosus of not being worthy of taking the throne which was once occupied by St. Peter himself,' explained Bishop Sergius, without a drop of condescension, looking at her eyes as if talking to an adult. 'When he was a cardinal, just like I should have been a cardinal if it wasn't for him, the pope did something he was not supposed to.'

'I know what a cardinal is,' said Mariozza with a purposeful bored air. 'But what did Pope Formosus do that was so wrong?'

'As a bishop, not only was he too ambitious to become a pope, which is a sin, for papacy is a gift and burden that the chosen one must humbly accept; but he also left one See where he had a commitment, to another, of Rome. That is unacceptable!'

Mariozza looked puzzled. 'Did he change from place to place on his own or was he send by the pope then?'

'You are a very smart girl indeed,' said Sergius with some surprise, allowing a contagious smile to draw across his face. 'Let's be honest here, between the two of us,' and he got closer to whisper in her ear, his lips brushing against Mariozza's silken black hair, making her giggle with delight. 'His main sin was to crown Arnulf, of the Franks, as emperor in Rome; three years after having already crowned Guido of Spoleto, the husband of Agiltrude.'

They both turned their eyes to the magnificent widow, who was still glaring at the pathetic figure of the accused pope. Cardinal Sergius continued with his whisper, now touching Mariozza's ears. 'And not happy with this treachery, he helped Arnulf drive Agiltrude out of Rome.'

'Back to Spoleto?'

'Horrible, isn't it. Banned from Rome, which she most cared for.'

'That is why she is so glad now that Pope Formosus is dead? And she brought us all here to watch this stinking, fly-ridden cadaver being accused by all these people?'

'Yes, that is why she is so happy with the current pope. Stephen VI sent to dig out the corpse of Formosus after ten months and brought it here for this synod, making all the wrongdoings of that pope public.'

Mariozza looked at the new Pope Stephen and saw only a rabid look on his face, as the pontiff kept reading more and more accusations to the stiff carcass seated in front of him. She cringed and hugged Sergius, throwing her arms around his neck. 'He is scary, this new pope. Scarier than the dead one. How come the Duchess Agiltrude is not scared of him?'

'I am sure it's Pope Stephen who fears her and organised this theatre to please the widow. She is a very powerful woman.'

'Men *fear* the duchess?'

'Worse, my dear Mariozza. Men *desire* her!'

'Yes,' she said excitedly. 'I have heard people say that she is one of the most desired women of all the Italian lands. What does that mean?'

'It means they want her in their beds.'

'You mean they want to fornicate with her?'

Sergius looked into the deep violet of Mariozza's eyes. 'Child, you just will not stop surprising me! You are indeed a well-lettered young woman. Yes, it means they want to fornicate with her. Or better, as lovers say, to *make love* to her.'

Mariozza considered it and said, very close to his face, 'When I grow up, I want to be as powerful and beautiful as the duchess. I want men to desire me too.'

The well-groomed deacon thought for a moment, waiting for the goose bumps on his skin to smooth out. He glanced at her parents, who nodded and waved their hands to their precious little girl. He knew them well, the origins of Theophylactus, from Roman nobility and the splendid Theodora, who had been a professional seductress. Her radiant beauty would surely be freshly repeated in the daughter. Turning to Mariozza, he smacked a soft kiss on her cheek.

'You *are* already very desirable, my dear, very desirable!'

When the synod was over, the cadaver had three fingers snatched from its right hand, symbolising the unacceptability of any of the blessings and offices Formosus had given since leaving the see of Porto, and nullifying any ordinations he gave throughout his papacy. The corpse was stripped of its vestments and ordered to be dragged through the city. Many Romans saw this unnecessary demonstration as a bad omen. The rotten skeleton was thrown into the Tevere. On the next day, a hermit found the corpse down the current. He handed it to deacons who had received holy orders from Formosus hands, so they could give him proper burial.

On this same day, those Romans who transited around the great equestrian statue of Emperor Constantine on the Lateran hill were startled by a massive thunder: the roof of the basilica of the Holy Saviour had completely collapsed.

Seven years and six popes later, it was the time for cardinal Sergius. He managed to throw in prison Pope Leo V, who had just been elected one month before. That was done with the help of a deacon named Christopher, a follower of the condemned Pope Formosus, and who became Pope Christopher. It was soon Sergius's turn to rise to the throne of St. Peter, by changing loyalties and tossing Christopher in the dungeons, next to Leo. Pope Sergius III then arranged for a few soldiers to go down into the dark, fetid cells of the Lateran and have the warden twist a rope around the necks of both men, until they would stop breathing.

By this time, Mariozza Maricuccia, blooming at fifteen, was the most powerful and spectacular woman in Rome. The girl had already been Sergius' lover for a long time. The talk of the city centered on the precise age Mariozza would have had when Cardinal Sergius started to instruct her on men's weaknesses and guide her through the abilities she should develop to get the world on its knees before her.

At seventeen, while mounting the pontiff on his purple silk bed linens, her sculptural features illuminated by the sun from a magnificent summer morning, Mariozza stopped her gallop and said casually, 'I carry a child inside me. It's yours.'

The pope lifted his head and torso, resting on his elbows.

'How do you know it's mine?'

'I *fucked* you, for the Devil's turd!' And she started rocking her hips back and forth, languidly, her clean face opening into a ferocious smile. 'Like this … and you spilled your seed inside me.'

'Yes, but you fuck others too,' the pope said, matter-of-factly.

'There are those that I should, those that I can, and those that I need.'

'Which one am I then?' asked the pope.

Mariozza started bucking up and down more strongly. 'You are a different one. You are the one that I love, the one that I want and the one that I *must*.' And she accelerated her hips even more, back and forth. 'You are my best friend, you are my brother, my father, my child, my husband, my lover. You make me feel so deliciously indecent that I feel I am fucking the Devil himself!'

As she felt Sergius was about to throw his head back and enjoy the explosion of ecstasy, she jumped out of him, stood up on the bed and spat in rage. 'But if you will not believe me when I say I know the child is yours, you may not be worthy of this filthy heat that still burns in me. Use your hands or any other whore to conclude your pleasure. Forever!'

The flabbergasted pope stroked his precocious baldness and watched her leave the room, naked, dragging her clothes behind. The most beautiful bottom he had ever seen.

'Shit,' he thought.

A.D. 928 – Rome, somewhere underneath the city.

The prisoner had been dragged down through dark corridors, tumbled over hard steps, leaving thin tracks of blood on the slippery bricks. Semi-naked and cold, choking from the ever more fetid air, his vision was already blurred by pain, and it had to repeatedly adapt from the complete darkness of the tunnels to the bright yellow flames that dripped at every new gallery they entered.

At the end of a passage, when the prisoner had already lost his senses, one of the *custodes*, the roman guards who held him, produced a large iron key from a pocket on his belt and unlocked a well-concealed door. Two paces beyond it, a heavier door was secured with a thick latch. Once opened, they rang a bell that hung outside the third door.

They heard it being unlocked from inside and, when it opened, out of a thick mass of the most nauseous reek of filth that hit them like a boulder, a very large, almost amphibian white face appeared from the darkness.

'W-Who are you?' asked the *custos*, almost stuttering from that ghostly sight.

'I am the King of the Darkness' answered the man, his breath stinking like a dead elephant. He was wearing a greasy patchwork of rags, which left his naked arms out, long, strong, but white as a cadaver. His face was muscular, well shaven with big eyes that shrunk as they were lit by the torch and enormous, swollen lips, which slithered sideways as if they wanted to swallow both custodes and prisoner at once.

'The password is correct,' the custos said. 'You are Cicero, right?' Without waiting for an answer, he helped the other custos push the prisoner onto the hands of the warden. 'This is Johannes, and today is the thirtieth day of May.'

The toadish warden nodded and held the unconscious prisoner with one of his arms, and with the other hand he clamped his fingers around the prisoner's jawbone, so hard that the pain awoke the man to his misery.

'Who are you?' asked the prisoner in sheer disbelief.

The warden pulled him close to his bulgy eyes. 'I'm King Cicero. Welcome to my kingdom.'

The prisoner wanted to cry in horror, but he was too exhausted for that. Instead, he only gave in to somnolence again.

'Stop crying like a baby' Cicero said, calmly. He sat on a small empty barrel by the door, in utter darkness. 'You've done nothing but cry and retch and scream and vomit…Pull yourself together, for Christ's sake.'

There was a moment of silence. Finally a sonorous sob came from the cell, followed by a shy voice. 'Who are you'?

'I told you already. I am King Cicero and in my kingdom it is me who asks the questions.'

'I'm sorry,' said the prisoner, returning to his sobbing.

'You better tell me now something about you,' the warden said, with little patience 'I do like to get to know my subjects.'

'Don't you know who I am?' the prisoner said, much more alert.

'Oh, no, my dear Johannes. Don't get too excited. I haven't allowed you to ask questions yet. Just tell me a little bit about you.'

The prisoner ran to the door and spoke clearly though the slot on its top, moaning and sighing at every other word that came out of his desperate mouth. 'I am Pope John X, Bishop of Rome.' He swallowed for a second and continued. 'Yes, I am the pope, your pope! I am very powerful and influential. Take me out of here and I will cover you in riches.'

Cicero giggled. 'If you're really the pope, who I fear you could really be, for I have heard the news from outside, you can do a lot better than that. Get a hold of yourself to start with. Are you a bishop? Then behave like one, and not like a prostitute!'

He heard the prisoner hissing 'Prostitute…it was her! That *putanna*! That *gran putanna*!'

'Great prostitute?' Cicero asked. 'You must be referring to Mariozza Maricuccia, of course.'

'That harlot!' The prisoner seemed to have regained full power over his voice. 'May her filthy womb rot with a thousand devils inside!'

The warden smiled with his massive eyes only. 'Now, just wait, just wait, Johannes! This is no language fit for the apostle of Christ. You do want to convince me that you are, I mean, that you were the heir of Saint Peter, don't you. So do calm yourself and tell me about Mariozza. I have been hearing about this fascinating woman for so long…'

'And how would you know of her?' asked the prisoner.

'Oh, Johannes, you will soon learn that you should keep quiet when I say it is only I that asks the questions in my kingdom. But Rome is full of whispers and that I have many sources from the world outside, pretty much every day and night. I know what happens there, but nobody knows what I do here. The main fountain of information comes from my subjects, who enter my kingdom and generously share their stories with me, making my burden more bearable through this eternal stink and darkness. And you may want to know why they talk so freely with me? Because I want them to. Because I am King Cicero! And in my kingdom, it is I who decides ultimately if my subjects will lever leave this place. And the only way out is by the door to the *cloaca maxima*, yes, the sewers of Rome. Most will be eaten by rats before the light of day sees their corpses, anyway. But they do talk to me, and I award those that I like accordingly. And they also appreciate these exchanges, carrying a more bearable existence when they hear others talking. Right now, there are dozens of cells around these corridors listening to our words. Maddened faces. Many of them have become little else than beasts, rolling on piles of their own excrement and throwing their meagre seeds away at the faintest mention of a woman –'

A few yells and yaps were heard from down the corridor, as from a pack of jackals.

Cicero smiled silently again. 'As I was saying, I knew of the young Mariozza since the times she was the lover of Pope Sergius, so many years ago. He gave me the privilege of meeting bot Leo and Christopher, the previous pontiffs. Interesting men. But that Sergius was implacable. Within a month he ordered both bishops to be strangled. Who would think of that? A pope ordering the execution of another!'

The prisoner babbled a few disconnected sounds and started to weep.

'Do not despair, Johannes!' Cicero said. 'You still have a chance to redeem yourself.'

'I am in pain, in horrendous pain,' the prisoner moaned, but then his voice went dry 'But I can tell you whatever you want to know.'

'Well, then perhaps you should pick up from the latest news I had. I do know that Mariozza Maricuccia had conceived a son, Johannes! Yes, your name.'

'He is a useless, spoiled brat!' the prisoner yelled. 'John must be eighteen now,' he explained, now with a calmer tone, 'Mariozza's oldest boy. Yes, he is the son of Pope Sergius III, the putanna's first lover.' Although Mariozza shared the sheets of the pontiff in the Lateran while he was alive, she still lived in her parents' palace.'

'Theophylactus, the count of Tusculum, and his beautiful wife Theodora,' the warden said.

There was a long pause of silence, and a sigh. The prisoner said, 'Yes.'

'Something tells me that you know these two well,' the warden said. 'Especially the stunningly beautiful Theodora, as she is still described, in spite of her old age. *Senatrix* and *vestararissa*, the keeper of the papal treasure, and now made *patricia* of Rome. As if it wasn't enough that her husband Theophylactus is the vestararius, in addition to *judex, dux, consul et senator*, having climbed as much as any layman could in Rome. You are particularly well acquainted with Theodora, aren't you?'

'If I haven't had the courage to confess my sins to God to this day, I won't do it to a prison warden.'

'Of course you wouldn't, Johannes. Then you cannot be Pope John X. I hear that he was an insignificant cleric, made archbishop of Ravenna thanks to the insatiable Theodora, who would repeatedly harbour him between her legs under complete connivance of her husband Theophylactus. Bishop John made a daughter in her, who was also named Theodora, and which had been born when Pope Sergius was still alive. So you cannot be the father of young Theodora, can you? She seems to be well on her way to harlotry, just like her half-sister Mariozza and their mother.'

'I was certainly not any insignificant cleric. My father was Pope Lando.'

'Correct, Johannes, you seem to know well about who you claim to be. And do correct me if I'm wrong, but I remember that at the death of Pope Lando, Theodora arranged for this John to be elected, so that she could keep her lover nearby. But tell me, her daughter Mariozza, was raising young John and she continued to have sexual delights with several adventurers who came into the city. There's word that Mariozza repeatedly tried to replace her mother Theodora as the love of the pope. How as it then? If that pope is really you, did you succumb to Mariozza's attempts? Sharing a bed with mother and daughter would have been the carnal wishes of many men of Rome.'

Another wave of yaps and screams arose from the darkest entrails of the dungeons. Some of those grunts were maddening loud.

The prisoner hissed 'Your insolence does not fail to surprise me, warden. I will not answer to that disgraceful nature of questions. I know nothing about that family of strumpets, shameless whores.'

'You should know indeed, as they inhabited the brazen rooms of the Lateran, and one is your daughter' said the warden.

'Theophylactus is dead!' said the prisoner. 'As so are the harlots not in the Lateran any more. That was so many years ago. Your stories survive for too long inside your memory, Cicero, while they have been long forgotten outside these walls.'

The warden chuckled. 'Do not underestimate your king, Johannes. I know it all. I know that Mariozza raised her son John among half of Rome's whores in her palace at Isola Tiberina, and everyone remembers when hordes of Saracens tried to break open our city gates with their battering rams, while Rome's princes pounded theirs between Mariozza's legs. Except for you, of course that's if you are the pope. You had yours inside old Theodora, and quite wisely allied yourself with Alberic of Spoletto to expel those Saracen raiders from papal lands. How could anyone have missed that you ingeniously married Alberic with Mariozza, while expelling her old mother from the Lateran? Nobody can forget. Or how stupid you were to crown Alberic's very fiercest rival Berengar of Friuli as the emperor!'

The prisoner yelled 'I could not leave the power completely under the Theophilactii family and Alberic's, so strongly united.'

'*Shit stupid*, that's what you were,' Cicero said, for the first time with a note of annoyance on his voice. 'A *pope*! How many men and women and children died when Tuscany and Lombardy rebelled against Berengar? All because of you. And how many more had their blood and heads trampled by the hooves of the Ongur mercenaries when Berengar brought them from the north to help him? Monstrous savages that stayed in Italian lands when even Berengar was murdered. You may fuck with Rome's whores but you don't touch Rome. Alberic was even more stupid than you on trying to use the Ongurs for his own power. He was lynched and dismembered by the people of Rome, and –'

'And the Holy See finally rid itself of that gran putanna Mariozza Maricuccia,' said the prisoner.

'*That's* what I want, Johannes! I want to hear your own side on these episodes. I want to know what went through your head when you made your own brother Peter the vestararius of the papal treasure as soon as you saw Mariozza a widow again. Is it true that you forced her and her two boys to see the mutilated remains of Alberic? Wouldn't it be too much for little Albericus to see his dad in pieces?'

The prisoner only grunted.

'And how did it feel Johannes, to still have the putanna around? Three years, Johannes. Three years of Peter plundering Rome's treasures while Mariozza prepared her vengeance. Did you actually think her blood was thin enough to accept her humiliation and bow to your rule? Oh Johannes…'

Now the prisoner seemed to initiate an anguished weep. 'My wounds…the pain is so intense…'

'Yes, I know Johannes. There's plenty of reasons for crying once Mariozza married Guido of Tuscany. That's when it all went wrong for you.'

The sobs increased with those words 'Please let me out of this filth!'

Cicero's voice was unshaken, carrying the casual tone. 'I never had the pleasure to meet your brother Peter, for I heard we was taken immediately from the treasury room and butchered in front of your own eyes in the Lateran.'

Weeping turned to a wail. 'God, almighty God, help me!'

'But perhaps you should consider him lucky, Johannes,' Cicero continued, his voice now raising to a tone of command, 'for if Peter was as uninteresting as you show yourself to be in this moment, he would not like the treatment he would get from Cicero, king of the underworld. And God is not here to help you.' He finished by punching the cell door with his fist.

He had left a few paces already when Johannes voice was heard from the cell. 'Cicero, please wait! Can I ask you a question?'

'Johannes? You talk? What do you want to know? Talk.'

'Have you ever allowed anyone to leave this place?'

Cicero smiled in the darkness. Surely night creatures would have marvelled at his massive lips framing a toothless grin. 'Yes, I have, Johannes, but only those that I admired. I can tell you that when Pope Sergius had both his predecessors Leo and Christopher imprisoned, it was a matter of weeks before I received instructions to through their corpses down the sewers. I had no problems strangling Leo, but Christopher was such a pleasant company that we spent a few years developing a unique camaraderie. I trusted that Christopher could spend the rest of his days in silence if I showed him the way out. I believe he still lives, as a monk.'

'Is that what I have to do to gain your trust?' Johannes said, 'Just talk to you?'

Cicero's voice came out icy 'You've had your question already, Johannes. Now shut the fuck up.'

Johannes was in utter pain. He had little account of how many days it had been since he was thrown in that cradle of darkness and filth. Cicero had been silent, his voice only occasionally heard talking to other cells far away down the corridors. But the pots that were slipped through the slit on his door had been many already. Initially, Johannes cried and screamed in protest, for someone must have vomited on his pot. After a few days he gave in to hunger and agony, understanding that whatever was given to him was to be regarded and treasured as food. Johannes did think of God initially, but in a short time his prayers had been mostly interrupted by delirium, daydreams with erotic encounters with Theodora, or engineering a plan to rape and kill the putanna Mariozza one day.

The door opened after a rusty slip of the latch, and a bright red fire appeared through, the first light that hit his eyes since he had been brought in.

'It's time to go, Pope John X!' he heard Cicero's voice say.

Johannes thought the blinding light could have been indeed God's answers to his humble prayers. He forced his eyes opened to praise that saving angel, but instead he devised a monstrous white figure covered in a few pelts fixing the torch to a wall slot, and quickly turning its massive arms to him, grabbing onto his neck. He had no chance to react to the white demon. While struggling to breathe, Johannes felt no pain, but just utter fear.

Looking at the Cicero's bulgy eyes inflated with sheer madness while the warden slowly and pleasurably tightened the grip around his neck, Johannes had a last impression that his own eyes must have been looking pretty much the same.

Fear

Le Mans – A.D. 1000

For many years after that prophetic arrow shot, Julian would still struggle with visions of the beast's yellow eyes, bellowing in an ear-shattering din which turned into a human cry, and looking back at him through the storm of leaves as soon as his arrow sliced through its hairy back. Eyes that were intensely yellow, but not bright or shining, although they would have been seen from any distance in the darkness. That was a yellow that consumed light, rather than emanated it. They were as dark as the forest, but the intensity of the yellow could burn through its wood.

He saw those furious lanterns turning to him just for a second, as the leaves stormed around him, blocking his vision. Then the beast was not there anymore. As the leaves fell with a sudden stillness that loaded the forest, he just saw a man dragging himself through the dead leaves, coming towards him. Not a hairy beast with paws or a dark mane, but a man. And the tip of his arrow was showing through a gap opened in the man's breast.

Julian was filled with horror. It could not be. He did not see a person. He had seen an animal. A beast. Not a man. He had meant to shoot an animal.

He had shot a man.

'Merciful God,' he sobbed. 'Help this poor soul' and he went running to help him.

The man came stumbling with his hands stretched towards Julian. He was dressed in skins and rags, probably a shepherd or hermit that lived in the forest. It would hurt even more in Julian's heart if he had wounded a holy man. As they got closer, Julian noticed that the man's face was horribly disfigured. Not with pain, he sensed, but with hatred.

'*You!*' howled the man, as he approached Julian.

'I am sorry … I did not mean … let me try and get…' stuttered Julian, and then he saw something which confused him even more: a little girl disappearing behind a tree. Looking further, far inside the woods, at the edge of the visible tree line, he saw the figure of a boy running away, hopping frantically between the trunks as if the ground was burning hot.

This vision was also immediately brushed aside when the man fell in front of him with a grunt. A thunderous grunt, so loud and powerful that it felt like a dragon had been awaken. It made Julian fall to his knees.

The man raised his face to look at Julian. Dead leaves were stuck to his brow and beard. Mud and moss covered his distorted features. He pointed a long-nailed fat finger at Julian and uttered in the most unbearable voice, a grave and rumbling tone that emanated from the darkest corners of the forest, from the bowels of that filthy soil.

'You!' he roared. Julian doubted that it could be a human voice. He was listening to a wizard or ogre who spoke with the furious laments of hell.

'You will pay for this!' the roaring continued. 'I put a curse on you!' As he said this, the branches and trees seemed to lean back, away from that horrendous voice that spoke so wrongly. Tears sprung from Julian's eyes as he heard the terrible words.

'You will live through misery and pain, and what has been my doom will be also yours. The ones that you hold most dearly, father and mother …' Julian tried to cover his ears, but the howling was too fierce and loud. '… father and mother, will have their blood spilled by your own hands'.

'NO!' cried Julian, from the top of his lungs, pressing his head so strongly that the pain and the horror made his knees bend.

'There is no escape,' insisted the ogre. And his voice rose to a chorus of shrieks and screams. 'You are doomed to live through blood, until you kill them and meet us later, in suffering, just as this bestial soul is doomed to meet *us*, IN HELL, NOW!'

His face fell on the ground.

'And Daniel said that the first beast was like a lion, and it was lifted up from the earth, and made to stand upon its feet like a man, and a man's heart was given to it!' proclaimed a holy man in rags, ferociously spitting some of his learned biblical words at all the customers who were breaking their fast at the tavern.

'Damned soothsayer!' hissed Julian between clenched teeth. 'I wish he'd shut his filthy trap. I cannot concentrate on writing.'

My beloved Father and Mother,

I pray that one day you will forgive me for what I have done, but I fear that you may never understand or accept. It fills me with sorrow and pain the idea that I must leave you and not come back. If for a long time or forever, I leave that to the hands of God.

I am sorry that I have never returned to Mans, to your arms, or that I have never sent any word of what it has been of me. I am sorry that I heated up the flame for the feast but was not there to celebrate. I am sorry that I may have caused grief when the moment for the fair was one of joy.

Many were the things that happened to me since the day I went into the woods. The day when innocence was lost along with my scepticism. The day when I became part of the evil that afflicts our souls, but which I had never felt touching mine until then. I do not want to describe the wrong that fell upon me, but I must tell you that it drags me to another direction, away from you, for I have found that I can do harm, and no ill do I wish to those which are most dear to my heart.

Father, my tutor and master, you have granted me your heritage and you have set the righteous example to me and to my brothers and sister. Be strong and care for them, for not only they need your guidance, your joy and your flame, but also they will be looking upon your justice and piety on your noble duty as the lord of Mans.

Mother, delight of my heart, keeper of our home. There will not be one day, until the end of mine, when I will not be thinking of your warm smile and they blue sky of your eyes. They will be watching over me, protecting me from evil and harm, even though you may not be knowing of my whereabouts. Please kiss my father and my brothers and my dear sister as many times as you can, every day, every night, for somewhere else I will be wishing I was doing that. When they return your love, try and see it as me adoring you too.

'And the fourth beast shall be the fourth kingdom upon earth, which shall be diverse upon all kingdoms, and shall devour the whole earth, and shall thread it down, and break it in pieces!' continued the prophet.

'Just shut up, will you?' said Julian loudly.

The soothsayer paused for a while as other voices supported Julian, but a woman's tone came out louder. 'Sinners! Wicked heathens! Just let his holy man warn us of the coming of time. This could be our last chance to repent before we are burnt forever in the fires of hell!' And he continued. So did Julian.

'When I made this hasty decision to go away from you, from my family, my love, from where my heart is rooted, I even considered a confession to my dear friend, the Father Bishop Avesgaud. But knowing Raoul's brother-in-law as I do, I fear that the father bishop is too good of a man to be restrained by the secrecy of the confession, by a rule of the mother church. No, Avesgaud is man of flesh and blood, who loves you and me too much to keep such a terrible secret to himself. It would not be fair of me to share this with him. Just tell him that forever I will think of our last conversation, by the abbey's southern patio. It was about the Devil. And I was wrong.

Father and Mother, such a careless son may not be worthy of being worried about, but in case you are concerned about my physical and spiritual health, do not worry, for I am well…

That was a lie, Julian thought, but he kept on writing.

'… I have sold the horse, which by now you know was the bay stallion. Sorry, I could not get a fair price, but what I have will keep me well fed for a long time. I am a grown man and I can fend for myself.

May the Lord always be gracious to you, after I have been so ungrateful. I do not understand why bad things happen, but I just do not want them to happen again. If you wish to remember me in your prayers, please ask for the protection of my guardian angel. I will need an angel to guide me for the rest of my life.

With my deepest love,

Julian.'

He read it again and was not satisfied. But there was no time to waste. He rolled down the parchment and shoved it into his bag. Except for the annoying soothsayer, his *religieuses* companions had already left the inn at Matins, when it was still dark. But Julian had been so tired that he let them go without him. At breakfast, he had finally sat down to write that note to Raoul and Emma. Other guests seemed surprised or shocked to see such a young traveler with quill and parchment, writing down as if he were a monk. That was unusual, if not at all suspicious. As Julian was scribbling line after line, he looked around the tables and saw them all vigilant, very aware of him. He reckoned that probably no one else at the inn would be literate, and for his own safety and discretion, it would be better to leave.

The road south of Limoges carried on for many leagues, dug through a thick dark forest that covered most of a day's travel. Julian hoped that this time he would again find warm company with the religious group that he had accompanied since leaving Poitiers. If he did not catch up with them, he would dearly miss the company of Martino, Bernardo and especially Louise.

Never leaving his bow, he crossed the southern gate of Limoges and hurried the pace. The sun was already shining high on the southeast. Some oxcarts, mounted companies, other travellers and shepherds crossed his way for the first hour, through meadows and planted hills. When he approached the looming forest, no one else seemed to be coming from it. Looking backwards he also noted that nobody followed him. It would be a lonely day through the woods.

The way was dark and silent. Except for jays or pigeons that occasionally startled a traveller by bursting into flight, only the cawing of crows in the distance broke the stillness of the woods. The cold air that blew through the road brought more dead leaves down to cover the ground.

Julian thought that probably a week before he would have been very afraid of walking through an unknown path in a dark forest in lands far away. But somehow he had felt different since the day he had killed a man. Of course there was the misfortune, the shame, the disgrace and regret. For that he needed penance.

There was the fear, the beast, the surprise, the horror, the voices, the curse and the doubt. For that he needed time, distance and answers.

And then, there was this empowerment, this vigour, this courage and thrust that pushed him to keep going, so he could get the distance and the time, for one day, maybe through penance, to find the answers.

He thought of that ominous day when his life started falling into shambles, when he had fled the ogre's den right through the west side of the forest. The dead ogre could not tell him anything else. Desperately trying to find answers for the inexplicable event, for signs of the disappeared beast or those glimpses of children, Julian just kicked through some utensils in the filthy den. Nothing but the sickening stench of pigs, manure and an uncomfortable herbal scent.

He ran back to his horse and galloped for hours, through the forest and fields, crossing roads and hedges, fording rivers and avoiding towns. They only stopped when the bay stallion refused to continue, by a time when the sun had already set and a cloudy autumn sky was sheltering the land. Lost and hungry, with his face stinging with the cuts from branches that whipped at him during the career, tired and hopeless, Julian dismounted on a grassy meadow and fell into a deep slumber.

Shivering and aching, he opened his eyes in the middle of the night, trying to re-capture the reasons why he had been left behind in the darkness. Heavy thundering clouds made it so black that nothing could be distinguished. He desperately groped his way through the grass to locate his horse, which he could smell, but not find. The constant rumbling from the cloudy ceiling tormented the stillness and it was made even worse as a torrential rain started pouring, hitting Julian's cold body like sharp stones. He could not hide, but shield himself under his thick cape as much as its size allowed. The downpour soon evanesced, leaving hanging in the distant darkness two tiny yellow lights. Julian stood up and got excited. Now he should definitely touch around to find his horse. Those lights seemed to be from fire, not too far from where he fumbled on the meadow.

But when the roaring clouds sent a bolt of lightning down, the luminosity revealed what those faint yellow flames were, making Julian's legs turn to water, and his stomach turn to stone: A large black creature, standing on its hind legs, walking away from him, its yellow dead eyes seen through the back of its enormous horned head.

Julian tried to scream but no air came out. He was only jerked out of his sleep. The darkness was complete and there were no lights any more. No beast.

But it had indeed rained. After being repeatedly tormented by the beast's eyes, which invaded his thoughts and trances, recapturing every detail of that day, he surrendered his heart and body into a profound sleep.

Julian woke up with the first rays of sun warming up his hair, to find himself not far from the jolly trickling of a river.

A cold bath made him feel less filthy, although he could not erase the fear, the bitter memory of those odious words from the ogre: '*the ones that you hold most dearly, father and mother, will have their blood spilled by your own hands!*'

That was a threat, just a scare. Not an omen. That was not a prophecy!

Still, aimless with doubt and fear, he kept following the river as it calmly bent south. By mid-afternoon Julian faced the turreted silhouette of a major castle, which he learned from some boys who were herding their cows into shade, to be from the town of Angers.

Julian was ravenous. He needed to go into the walls, but judged it unwise to spend much time through Angers, for he did not want to draw attention. His father paid vassalage to the Comte d'Anjou, which was a constant source of tension and careful liaisons, for not only a formidable warrior was the Comte, but better known as an implacable and ruthless lord.

A beaten crowd of religious people in their grey tattered cloaks was about to enter through the gate. Pilgrims probably, thought Julian. They were men and women, pulling carts and trolleys. Looking tired, if not miserable from their march down to Angers, they carried a sedan with a large wooden crucifix, covered in banners and tapestries.

'I fear that this may well be the end of humanity!' harangued an old man with a charcoal black-staff that ended with an image of the slain Christ on top. 'Few are the just who will enjoy the power and the glory of the earthly kingdom of Christ, after His imminent return and the resuscitation of the deceased saints and martyrs'. While some women got down on their knees and crossed themselves with flowers or inhaled the aromatic fag from burners, others would uncover silver boxes from their rags and kiss them repeatedly. Some of the wanderers were not patient enough to stay and listen, so they just continued through the gate. That was when Julian blended in.

Once past the walls and into the fetid alleys, detached from the pilgrim crowd, Julian tried to get food in exchange of some useless utensils he carried, but he did not succeed. He finally found a goldsmith shop where he offered for sale a gold medallion that hung on a necklace, which had been given to him by his mother. The goldsmith was very distrusting, demanding a story behind the medal, obliging Julian in the end to identify himself as being from the vicomté of Mans. He also learned that Julian had been lost during a hunting trip and would have to spend the day in Angers before heading home on the next day. After what seemed to Julian like an endless tale of sorrow and tragedy on the consequences of such exchange, the goldsmith gave him a sack of silver pieces, probably not worth a quarter of the medallion's value. Before leaving the shop, Julian thanked the goldsmith for his discretion and asked the ever suspicious man to keep his presence in Angers a secret, alleging that his accidental stray away was an embarrassment to himself and his father.

On the following morning, while devouring a rather clear turnip soup at a contemptible tavern, Julian considered the odds of following the road south. Poitiers would be another two days on horse. He would try it. Perhaps he could go through the sacrament of confession in Poitiers, find someone who would listen to him, someone he could tell his story to. Then, he could try Limoges. Depending on how much his silver coins would last, he could go all the way to Toulouse, perhaps finding some work in the city, a burden on his back to make him forget the other on his heart.

Toulouse … Julian had never dreamed of even getting to Poitiers. But thinking realistically, the sack of silver would not feed him for long. He started to realise the big mistake he had made on trying to sell his medallion. The same medallion which, right now, as he slurped the last broth of his soup, was dangling in front of his face, shining the window sunlight on its solid gold.

'Do you recognise this fine piece of jewellery, young man?'

Julian had taken some time to understand that it was *his* medallion, hanging right ahead of his eyes, but as soon as he heard those words being uttered, he startled, almost falling back from his bench.

'Whoa!' the man said with a smile, glancing quickly at an armed gang that stood behind Julian. 'Let's calm this foal down before we have him fenced!'

Julian was speechless. The rough hand holding the medallion belonged to a tall man, his shadow blocking the daylight to half of the tavern. Probably no more than thirty years old, he dressed as a noble, obviously the commander for the other man-at-arms. His beaked nose and dark skin gave him an exotic appearance, accentuated by his raven black hair and a pointed beard which shone reddish on the sunbeam that entered the inn. He had a fiery smile and eyes of a hawk. It was those eyes that made Julian understand the situation he was at and recognise the man. He needed to give some very credible and careful explanations, for he was now face to face with no one else than Foulques Nerra, the *Black Falcon*, Comte of Anjou.

The Cheated Bukhari

"anno autem nono Osee cepit rex Assyriorum Samariam et transtulit Israhel in Assyrios posuitque eos in Ala et in Habor iuxta fluvium Gozan in civitatibus Medorum…"

(In the ninth year of Hoshea the king of Assyria took Samaria, and carried Israel away into Assyria, and placed them in Halah and in Habor by the river of Gozan, and in the cities of the Medes). 2 Kings, 17:6

The brown-bearded man rested the parchment on is lap and examined his guest with curiosity. 'Are you sure this is the same *Habor* that you are talking about?'

'None other', responded the smiling visitor, speaking a broken but still understandable Greek. 'I cannot read the Latin version from the *Sepher M'lachim*, but I know it tells the story of my people, descendants of the Nephtalites.'

Everybody in the hall was looking at him, although few understood Greek. He had those small blue eyes, rather close to each other, held up high on his face by the solid cheekbones. The thin beard gave him a fragile appearance, looking actually older than he really was. He was dressed up just like a Tuscan merchant, wearing a cap as large and as colourful as his original kippah.

'Nephtali? Well you wouldn't be a *Jew*, then.'

'Certainly not, that's well noted of you. I am an Israelite, although since I arrived in Damascus everybody has been calling me a *Iouda* or *Yahudah*. Well, if I understand properly the story that my father tells me, the Yahudah should be only the descendants of the tribes of Judah and Benjamin, and all the Israelites that returned to the Holy Land'.

'Very true', observed the other man. 'So, when did you start learning Greek?'

'Five months ago, when arriving in Damascus with a caravan of Iouda.'

'Remarkably good, then! What else have you to amuse me?' Although his tone sounded falsely joyous, almost mockingly, the brown-bearded man was indeed interested in that visit, for he was not only a scholar himself, but also likewise a foreigner to those lands. He was actually the first French man to occupy that position and he sought to make a difference. 'So you are of extremely generous heart, you are a physician and a reader of the Holy Scriptures, but most of all, you are a man from the east!'

'At your service!' completed the Israelite. He could sense he was gaining ground.

The man on the throne handed his parchment to one of the many pages who assisted him and stood up, coming down the steps towards the visitor. The hirsute face gave him a coarse look of a peasant in regal vestments. The pointed nose became even redder as he smiled to the visitor, asking very close to his ears, almost whispering.

'Do you know the numbers, my son?' His curiosity was contagious.

'Mathematics? I certainly do,' said the visitor, 'The great al-Khwarizmi came from my lands.'

'Then, I think we should spend some time together! There's actually someone I think you should meet...'

That was how Immanuel Ben-Malachi, the Bukhari Israelite had, in less than two years, from fleeing his homeland with nothing in hands, gained the favours of Gerbert of Aurillac, the man who many believed to be a wizard, to talk to animals. The man widely seen to be the Antichrist incarnated. At the turn of the first Millennium, Gerbert was sitting on the throne of Rome, being known throughout Christendom as the Most Holy Father Sylvester II, the pope.

Immanuel had come from Bukhara, capital of the kingdom of the Samanids, far beyond the Levant and the Persian kingdoms. Bukhara was across the Caspian Sea on the Silk Route to Cathai. Although they were seen as unbelievers in a Muslim nation, the Israelites of Bukhara benefited from the protected status of *dhimmi*, which conferred them the right to study and profit from the arts and culture that flourished during the Samanid rule of the region.

Immanuel's family had vineyards, making very popular wines among the *kafirs* in Samarkand. Shy but inquisitive, the boy Immanuel did not find himself fitting into the wine trade. And as the firstling of a numerous family, he was entitled to choose his fortune and decided to study the arts of medicine, which offered him more interesting challenges than living among his brutish younger brothers.

During his academic years he met a Muslim Bukhari named Ibn Siná, founding a solid camaraderie. They both turned their attention to deciphering actual malign powers that were behind infections and pestilences, taking also good advantage of their masters' knowledge of herbal baths, ointments and elixirs.

When Turkic invaders from Kashgar started a series of raids to Bukhara, Ibn Siná, who had been until then the physician of the Samanid monarch, called for Immanuel and warned him about the restricting regime and the age of unrest that those invaders were likely to grant the Israelites. The young but already solicited physician invited his friend to join him on a trip to the great city of Baghdad. Despite the protests of his family, which believed that there could be a milder future under the new rulers, Immanuel decided to go with Ibn Siná.

Many were the adversities that their caravan came upon during their unique journey south-west, crossing deserts and mountains, coming upon fierce bandits and hostile villages, but nothing had appalled Immanuel more than their arrival in village whose name has been forgotten.

That was when he saw just a sample of the vastness of the power of death.

The village was on the cold northern border of the great desert and it had been partially destroyed by mudslides from recent torrential rains. In addition, the dwellers were raided by a horrid plague, which invaded them with demons, causing delirious madness. It burned under their skin and consumed their limbs with rot, to the point of severing them from the body, falling off to a ghastly demise. Uncountable men, women and children suffered from atrocious blights and whole families were decimated by such evil, causing a calamity that disrupted the entire region. The well supplied caravan stayed for a while, with Immanuel and Ibn Siná tending the ill and helping with incineration of the putrefied limbless corpses. As precautious as learned men of sciences that they could be, both recommended all the unaffected survivors to wear a scarf and protect their breathing parts. The maleficence would get anybody who had been invited to a villager's home, even the ones who had not laid down with local women. Whatever caused it was strangling the vessels that carry the humours through the body, as they surreptitiously observed in cadavers, for local Islamic law would not allow them to examine the dead.

Having little more to learn, Ibn Siná resumed his journey to Baghdad, but Immanuel could not leave the suffering behind, preferring to stay in the village.

One of the villagers, who had lost his family, blamed the affliction on the black rye. He insisted that rye with black-comb was the cause of that disgrace, which they should have listened to him and starved for a while. Immanuel did not dismiss the opinion. He knew about black kernels, which should be avoided when grown on wheat, but in Bukhara that had never happened to the harvest. After searching around, he found a loaf of spoiled rye bread and, in the silos of the empty houses, some grain with the strange black growth. From one of the desperate villagers, he bought a goat and fed it with the grain and the bread. It was with amazement and expectation that, in a couple of days, he saw the putrefaction take place in the goat's legs and teats. The beast was rotting long before taking its last breath.

The journeying Bukhari may have led the villagers to near famine, but he indisputably hindered the spread of the disease. It was only the ones who did not listen to his warnings about the corrupted rye that still fell to the fire.

Holy Fire.

That was how some of the Jewish merchants in a passing caravan on its way back to Damascus, had called the misfortune. These merchants were commonly known as Radhanim. They told him that a similar plague was named by a strong religious sect in the west, as Ignis Sacer, which meant Holy Fire. It had recently swiped whole populations north of the Black Sea. One of the Radhanim mentioned that in Eastern Kingdoms, very small bits of black rye were given to cure headaches and to stop post-partum bleeding. It all seemed to make physiological sense to Immanuel. He kept some of the tiny black combs and, not having anything else to do in that God-forsaken village, left with the Radhanim to the west.

In Isphahan he came across Ibn Siná, who showed him the academy of medicine and the court hospital. The Bukhari thanked him, but decided to leave to the west. He was fascinated by all those wonders described by the Radhanim, prodigies like the great city of Damascus, the Holy Land, and the far empires of Byzantium and Rome. Rapid changes in the world were making more countries into Christian nations, the sect they had repeatedly mentioned. And what was so intriguing about this creed he had heard about? A doctrine that had been originated with a Jew.

Immanuel mounted on the back of a donkey and decided to go along with the merchants, heading to Damascus. It was an unusually fast trip, crossing deserts, mountains and seas as swift as animals walked or the wind blew.

Less than a year later, Immanuel Ben-Malachi, the Israelite from Bukhara, speaking a trader's Greek much better than most peddlers, would be involved in helping a man become the first king of his country.

That was just a day after almost losing his life under a pile of stones.

God was with him that day.

But months before, Immanuel was struggling to explain to the fat skipper of a Syrian ship that he had been fooled into believing the journey led to somewhere else:

'But this is *not* Rome!' he shouted at the man's face.

The skipper just ignored him, as if that little iouda was nothing more than one of the flies that furiously swarmed over the filth on board. With a contained fury but unlimited annoyance, Immanuel looked at the skipper. He saw that massive confusion of muscle and fat, ready to explode through a thick leathery hide, tanned and cured by many decades on sea and covered by rebellious patches of curly black hair. He reminded Immanuel of a sheepskin so full of water that it would transpire through the pores. In spite of the rough appearance, so far the skipper had always been quite decent to Immanuel, especially during the first part of the trip, when the iouda had inevitably succumbed to seasickness. Nevertheless, at this final stage of the journey it appeared that he was filled with nothing but foul dishonesty, and Immanuel felt entitled to be loud.

Taking a deep breath, on a theatrical display of patience gathering, the skipper decided it was going to be the tenth and last time he would say that same phrase in Greek, for he knew the iouda understood that quite well.

'Change in plans.' Said the skipper very articulately, 'We do not go to Rome. We'll be docking here in Dalmatia and, as soon as we fill the ship up, we return to Syria.'

Immanuel cursed. He realised it was useless to argue. They would not turn the ship around to take him to Rome. He had been deceived, trapped as a mole. His money gone, paid for a trip to Rome that may have never existed on the plans for that ship. A journey that felt much worse than crossing the deserts of Persia and Syria altogether. A journey on sea.

He had vomited his feet out for the first few days on board. *Oh God almighty, why do you have to make me feel so weak? Is that just for the sake of contrasting my frailty with your power?* Even after emptying his stomach, a false sensation of stillness would betray him. It would not soothe him for long, for in less than an hour he would again have surrendered to a queasiness that made his inside want to come up. This felt as the worst physical misery that his frail body had ever encountered. He came to a point of believing that nothing else would matter, for a slow and painful demise due to nausea was going to catch him anyway. Under a sick trance, when he actually wanted to die, Immanuel pulled out some flame of force that was still burning inside his frail body and managed to do what the sailors were telling him to. Look at the horizon and observe it swaying up and down, following the same rocking motion of the ship.

Whatever spell was on that magic, it worked. And after all, when he thought of it, it did make sense, for the body is at peace when some inner perception that distinguishes the swaying agrees with what the eyes see.

In a few days, he eventually improved to the point of being cheerful and establishing a healthy camaraderie with the seamen. He told them about things of his far away Bukhara, and they told him of many wonders elsewhere. Several of those men talked about their devotion to the Son of God. That same man who had changed a large part of the world since he had come a thousand years before. This gave the Jew something else to consider, for all he could think so far was how naïve it was of him to be tricked into paying for that trip. He regretted his role, for they all must have thought him nothing but a fool. An idiot who would be paying to help with the sick, treat the wounded and still not get his gold's worth. Nothing but a cheap, or better, a lucrative servant who was constantly cleaning the deck from human waste that not even seagulls seemed to be interested in.

But Immanuel never despaired. He calmed down and breathed deeply. *Think!* He always had a way to look at the worst circumstances and squeeze the sweetest juice out of them. He'd survived the labyrinths of Damascus without being mugged or assassinated for his purse. And indeed the whole trip from Bukhara had been quite dangerous. He could have died of thirst or cold in the desert, or killed by bandit tribes. He saw himself alive at the ship. At least they hadn't thrown him overboard. He *would* get to Rome. It was not a mob of thugs that was going to prevent him to get to his destination. To his destiny.

The Bukhari had thought well. So well that the skipper did his best as they docked in Tragurion, a small but busy Dalmatian port where ships could berth in a protected quay. They slipped the ship between two smaller vessels with dark men in black turbans and painted faces that shouted curses at them. At least that was what Immanuel had figured. To him their talk sounded as ducks squawking on flight.

A crowd of hungry and readily volunteers immediately flooded into the ship, offering their prompt services and already grabbing anything that could be removed from it. Now it was the skipper's turn to roar curses. He vainly tried to push the intruders out, but it felt like chasing moths out of a torch. To get their attention he held one of those men by his arms and legs and threw him out of the ship, back on the quay. As the others saw it, they jumped out into a safer ground, away from the reaches of that mean commander.

The skipper finally saw them all out and shouted for their attention. He spoke in Greek that they should follow the instructions of his immediate on unloading. 'And if anybody creates any problems' said the skipper 'I'll see to it that the troublemaker is skinned and thrown into the sea.' That sent a serious shudder of terror through the volunteers, who wanted to provide help for the sake of some bread and oil in return. He nodded to his immediate and the working started.

The skipper negotiated the port taxes with the local officer and turned to Immanuel. He told the iouda to stay at the ship. Then, he disappeared for the whole day.

Immanuel had a feeling that the skipper was indeed going to help him, rather than sell him as a slave, right there or on a different port. But perhaps he was not as sure as he was hopeful.

Night fell and the ship was empty of its cargo. Part of the crew had left for a tavern, as the rest stayed to guard the ship. Not much of value was left, but those beggars could sneak in and snatch anything they could carry, just for a chance to have something. As the seagulls dedicated their last shrieks, perched on the ships masts, a dark silence fell on the quay. Only the noise from the taverns could be heard from a distance.

A shout broke through the early night. 'Iouda!' The skipper was calling.

The Bukhari jumped into land to meet the plump figure who was quickly approaching.

'We must hurry,' said the skipper. 'Come with me.'

Immanuel followed him with difficulty, through very dark alleys, not much different from what he had seen in Damascus. But the houses soon ended, and he found himself into open darkness, stepping onto a non-paved road. He smelled the trees and cow manure. The stenches of the town were being left behind. They were into farmland. The night could not be any blinder. Just a few flickering lights were seen in one or two houses in the distance. A chicken cackled far away, probably disturbed in its coop. The skipper kept hurrying him.

'Where are we going?' Immanuel asked, 'We are out of the city already!'

'Just follow me!' said the skipper, 'There's no time to waste.'

After what felt like a long time running in the darkness, just following the sound of the heavy strides in front of him, Immanuel heard mixed noises of people and horses. The smells of bonfires and animals and food and excrement became more intense, and they soon reached a large gathering of people who were in full activity.

His eyes, much better accustomed to the darkness, devised a battalion of horses and riders in the middle of the field. Tents were being pulled down with a massive movement of people. He slowed down. Everything started to make sense. He was going to be taken to those nomads. The skipper had made a great deal with him. Immanuel was going to be a slave.

He stopped just as the skipper was entering the circle of tents and horses. If he followed behind, this would be his end. He heard the amiable voice of the man who was supposed to take him to Rome but instead was about to sell him as a slave to a caravan in Dalmatia: 'Come, Immanuel, I broke a great deal for you!'

That was it. He knew the tone. He turned around and started running. Just running, as Nephtali the antelope, on escape, back to the port, to a safe area, to the city, he did not know where. And so dark it was that he must have been out of the road.

'Where are you, iouda?' he heard the skipper thundering though the darkness. But that darkness was his only escape. His only chance. He prayed for God, and also for that son of him, the Messiah that many had talked about.

And as he thought of the misery of ending his life as a slave, he never knew how abruptly could the ground in the darkness change without warning to a stampeding beast. His foot was violently kicked back as it hit a solid rock, and he felt the ground blasting against his face.

The Black Falcon

At Saint Bertrand, in Mans, a horseman handed the reins to one of the boys who always rushed to visitors approaching the Abbey's gate. A brother came hurriedly, recognising the rider as a man of Raoul.

'We have news for the bishop,' cried the horseman.

'Bishop Avesgaud is busy now, I can pass him the message,' the brother explained.

'I'm afraid not,' said the rider, wiping the sweat from his brow. 'I should speak to the bishop personally.'

'What I mean to say,' explained the friar with a careful smile and a lower tone of voice, 'is that the bishop is purifying his body at the *reredorter.*'

'In this case,' said the rider, understanding the intrusive nature of his intermission, 'I had better wait.'

The reredorter was behind the monk's lodgings, strategically located at the lowest side of the Abbey, where the waters of the creek had already entered and left the kitchen and laundry. Bishop Avesgaud was resting his body, heart and soul. Comfortably seated on one of the several round apertures along bench that sided the back wall, the bishop's naked bottom was being refreshed by the cool breeze that blew along with the merry creek below.

This was a peaceful moment of rest during those that had been nightmarish days. Ever since the disappearance of his favourite 'nephew', the bishop had to battle with desperation in order to comfort Emma, not due to a dutiful obligation to the mother-in-law of his sister, but to the dear closeness he kept them all to his heart. While Raoul and most of the children had been out with the searching parties, poor Emma was hardly able to eat. She had to be forced into sipping some broth, through arguments of a sure positive outcome for the searches, that Julian would be back to see her, rather than through a simple reason for survival, for Emma on her own would not make it. The finding of the dead ogre had been a dark omen. The vicomtesse had initially thought the cadaver on the horseback had been of her cub. But then she saw, with a different kind of horror, the features of the creature: And she noticed the strange smell.

Regardless of the conditions – yes, the monster had been killed by one of Julian's arrows, which was true, so it could mean the boy was alive – but the stories told about the whereabouts of the corpse were bone-chilling. Avesgaud was too late after he helped those exhausted men tend the horses, when he arrived at the dinning hall. He saw the sickened face of Emma listening to Hubert and Eudes, oblivious to the damage they were doing to their stepmother's future sleepless nights, describing with detailed gore the conditions of the ogre's den.

'Do *not* continue, you two! Can't you see that the lady is about to faint?'

The family accompanied Avesgaud to the abbey for a special prayer at vespers. As the last chants were finalised, the bishop rode the shaken vicomtesse back to the castle, to tend to her needs as the search resumed with sunrise. As the morning unfolded without news of young Julian, Odile insisted that the bishop went back to the abbey for a rest. She would watch over Emma for the rest of the afternoon.

Now, resting his tired arse at the fresh autumn breeze and having rid his body of the weight from those sweet meats that Raoul so much appreciated, Bishop Avesgaud hurried himself to receive the messenger.

'Most Reverend Father,' said the messenger as he kissed the coolness of the freshly washed ring on the bishop's hands. 'The Vicomte Raoul has just received news which left yester noon, all the way from Angers.'

'Good news?'

I am not to judge them, Most Reverend Bishop,' answered the messenger with apparent humility. 'It is for sure though that the young lord Julian has been seen alive in Angers, two nights ago.'

'Jesus Christ be praised!' burst the bishop, falling on his knees.

'However,' continued the messenger 'there is more to it.'

'Dear Lord! Go on, deliver it.' The bishop grunted, standing back and crossing himself.

The Black Falcon slammed the door and showed Julian to a leather chair at the castle. He pushed a tray of dried fruits and a jug of wine to the boy and sat himself on a higher seat. His face was now grave, making Julian shiver with anxiety.

'Go on,' he said dryly, 'tell me what is happening.'

'N-nothing grave, my Lord,' babbled Julian, as he schemed a credible explanation. 'I have only been separated from my party during a hunt, confused during a dark rainy night and lost as I followed the course of the river to find myself back on the track.'

'Not good enough, Julian of Mans,' retorted the Comte, through clenched teeth. 'You have been crossing my lands at no previous advice. You have looked into my fields and my people. You have entered the heart of my realm without the proper acknowledgement. You have hidden from me and asked for a concealment of your name!' He punched the solid table with a dry thud. 'Did you see those fanatics outside? Did you see the fury in their eyes? These are evil times, Julian. So now tell me - what kind of devilish deed are you hiding from me?'

'I swear, my Lord, in the name of ...'

'Do *not* swear or blaspheme in my house, young man,' intervened the Comte. 'Besides, the value of your word is unknown to me. As your father's word may also be. Just speak.'

Julian tried to look deep into those quick raptor eyes. Although the hall was fairly large and quite empty, with just two large windows that allowed light and some warm draft inside the stone chilliness, Foulques Nerra's eyes were constantly moving, searching around, making the Comte fully aware, always, of his surroundings. It did not help on Julian's intention to display frankness, but he had no alternative but start, otherwise the Black Falcon could make matters even worse.

'My Lord,' started Julian, sweat running down his forehead. 'I am very afraid. I went out for a hunt on the forests west of Mans, for that game, as you well know, is entitled to the house of Mans.' He measured the level of patience of the Comte, which, by the way he bit his inner lip, seemed to be very low. He continued fast. 'Anyway, I was training a new cry of grīghunds for our celebrations of the Feast of the Nativity of Our Lady, for which you must have been informed of and we are looking forward to have your presence there. I did not have on that day any relative with me into the forest. Just a small party of beaters and chasseurs.'

'And why not?'

'I was the only one who was excited enough with the whole affair – the feast, the hunt, the hounds. So, to be shorter on this tale, as the cry picked up a scent, I was driven further deep into the woods, to the darkest corner of forest I had ever seen. There I got lost and entangled into thorny brambles and had to leave my horse and walk. I heard strange noises and cries, as if they were from children. I was suffocated by foul smells and driven deeper into the forest by the only open tracks through the thick foliage, until I found myself into complete darkness. There, I must have dreamed awake. Dreams of a large black beast with eyes of fire, standing on its two legs and looking at me. I apologise for the ridicule my Lord, but I am indeed scared. Scared of all these stories people are telling about Satanas, about the coming of times.'

'Enough!' said the Comte raising a hand. 'But how did you get to this land here?'

'I got out of the forest probably through the wrong end. I drove across the black night, under rain and cold, until I lost my senses. I had no idea where I was when I awoke yesterday, so I just followed the river down to see myself in Angers. Please forgive me if I tried to be furtive, but I did not want to be an embarrassment to my father, neither raise any suspicions of an unannounced visit.'

'Your story, Julian,' the Comte said finally with steady eyes, which gave his weather-worn face some humanity, or better, some humour. 'Your story is so naïvely pathetic that I start to believe its veracity. Tell me one more thing: what latest do you know of the Comte Thibauld, of Blois'.

'*Who?*' Julian asked, with the most genuine puzzlement on his face.

'Comte Thibauld, of Blois,' repeated Foulques Nerra, very articulately this time.

'I do know of him, my Lord, but we have no relations to Blois, for our loyalty lies with Anjou. I know nothing of him.'

Very well,' said the Black Falcon after a long pause. To Julian he seemed to be fairly satisfied, at least for the moment. He stood up, throwing his heavy chair back. 'So, where is your horse then, Julian of Mans?'

'At the tavern where we met…where you met me.'

'Fine. For this evening, you are my guest, so please enjoy my hospitality. Tomorrow we get your mount and you ride with me back to Mans.'

That was the only thing Julian did not want to hear; and what he planned to do on the next day would certainly cause the house of Mans a great deal of difficulties.

'Bishop Avesgaud!' said a surprised Comte Foulques Nerra coming to the front patio of the castle in Angers, as the dust-covered religious unhorsed next to a crestfallen Vicomte Raoul. 'I don't recall having sent for *your* presence here'.

'With all respect, my lord, you need not to worry about the tenacity of your young memory, neither do I require any summon of yours for me to come when I feel necessary,' answered the plump bishop. He hastily passed the reins to a standing groom and kissed the face of the Comte as a sign of equity, instead of showing the back of his right hand for the expected kiss on the ringed fourth finger. 'And before you ask, neither has the good Vicomte Raoul here asked me to ride with him. He actually insisted I did not come at all, probably because he thinks I'm just a bit on the heavy side for these long rides.'

Foulques Nerra brought the anxious visitors into the hall, where cold cuts where already displayed at a central table. After helping himself with some sliced tongue, he pushed the trays towards Vicomte Raoul and asked him to speak.

'My Lord, I come here for news about my son,' started Raoul, respectfully lowering his eyes. 'He has been disappeared since –'

'You came here because *I summoned you*!' interrupted Foulques Nerra, with a visible impatience.

Raoul lowered his gaze for a second. 'Indeed, my Lord, I would not have failed your call, but it is still true that my heart is heavy with anguish for my son's disappearance. Only when you become a father yourself, will you indeed reckon the pain of such loss,' said a teary eyed Vicomte.

Bishop Avesgaud, fretful about the tension building up between lord and vassal, intruded subtly as he took a cup of wine from a server. 'Julian is a wonderful young man who has built himself an enormous place in my heart, just as much as he did in his parents' and his siblings'.' He noticed Comte Foulques annoyance but made a point to ignore it, avoiding eye contact and continuing with his part. 'He went out for a hunt into the thick western woods of Mans, trying out a cry of hounds the Vicomte has been breeding for two years. The dogs caught a scent and dashed into the denser part of the forest, with Julian behind.' and he sighed with genuine sorrow 'That was when he had last been seen.'

Comte Foulques Nerra was about to confirm it was the same story he had heard from the boy himself, but he preferred to withhold the information. 'So bizarre, isn't it?' he remarked with sarcasm. 'And then he appears in Angers, does not announce himself, mocks my hospitality and steals himself away in the still of dawn.'

'All I can do, my lord,' started Raoul, who was dying to ask all questions about Julian 'is to apologise …'

'Tell me if anything unusual happened before his disappearance,' the Comte said without heeding attention to Raoul. He added a threat: 'I usually know about things which are not initially told to me.'

Raoul and Avesgaud looked at each other. The bishop gave a slight nod, as the Vicomte started: 'On our second day of searches, at the very darkest spot in the forest, we found the body of a hermit that had been known to have disappeared many years ago. Not really a hermit, but an …' He cleared his throat nervously. '… an ogre.'

'Are you kidding me?' said the Comte, a devilish white smile ripping though his hawk-like dark face, 'an *ogre*?'

The bishop jumped in: 'People called him an *ogre* since the times, a decade ago, when he murdered his family – peasants – and took refuge into the forest. He was never found by the hue and cry but, once in a while, travellers told of an ogre stealing supplies. So we are not talking about a hermit as an anchorite, a holy man, but more of a God forsaken beastly creature who's sought refuge away from man, living with other animals.' The bishop paused and finally added, 'This body we found, partly eaten by the forest pigs, had been trespassed by one of Julian's arrows.'

'Now, let's put a pause here,' intervened the Comte, raising a hard hairy hand. 'This is very complex. I do not remember any story of a murdered family in Mans.'

'Again, with all respect, my Lord, the tragedy was indeed communicated to you,' Raoul said with a loud gulp. 'We received several visits of your *bailli* to investigate the circumstances of the massacre, but no more traces of the murderer were found.

The bishop completed the tale. 'After that, the occasional apparitions reported by hunters or wanderers were regarded as ghosts, never the monster himself.'

'Nevertheless,' Foulques insisted, 'here is a murder that has been left unsolved, for the accused has never been caught. And now he surfaces out of oblivion, murdered by a weapon which belonged to your son. Indeed, if this ogre had killed his own family, young Julian delivered the righteous punishment, but if not, we have another murder whose perpetrator is on the loose.'

Raoul was about to say something, but the bishop noticed his blood-infused eyes and held his hand firmly, to do the talk instead. 'First of all, my dear Comte, the fact that one of Julian's arrows was in the ogre, does not mean it was put there by Julian himself.'

'Agreed!' shouted the Comte with a loud slap on the table, without letting the bishop finish. 'but the fact that he ran away does not help his cause, or does it, Vicomte Raoul?'

'Not at all, my Lord, not at all…' said a sweaty Raoul, with lowered eyes. 'But I would thank the Lord Jesus Christ and the Virgin Mary and all the blessed saints if I heard from your own lips that my boy is safe and healthy.'

The bishop observed how the Black Falcon studied his vassal with calm. The state of a desperate soul was the best condition on an adversary or ally to lose a negotiation. Raoul was a broken man, completely at Foulques mercy for the news of the disappeared son. Lord of a vast area and a loyal ally, Vicomte Raoul had the potential to increase the contribution of Mans for the Comté. The young Julian had been a fool. He should have returned back home after shooting the hermit, only reporting it under confession. God would care about him. The hungry dark forest would care for the remains and not a living soul would ever know of the fate of the miserable creature. But no, either if succumbing to a prudence or fear, he fled the scene. His naiveté would cost his father dearly.

'All in its time, my dear Vicomte, all in its time,' the Comte said with a reassuring smile, which suddenly turned into a rapturous grin as he added, 'but first let me know how you are dealing with your friend, the Comte Thibauld, of Blois.'

'My friend?'

The distraught vicomte only heard about the good health of his son after re-affirming his loyalties, making a full report of his neighbour and opponent, the Comte Thibauld of Blois, listing his vassals and army capacities and sealing new and very high tallies to Comte Foulques Nerra with a jug of wine.

Later in the evening, emissaries returning from Rennes informed they had lost track of Julian. The young man had apparently never been seen on his way west.

Avesgaud saw Raoul almost putting his stomach out of his mouth.

Echoes of Pornocracy

Rome - A.D. 932

The castle Sant'Angelo had been given this name centuries before, when the pope had a vision of the archangel Michael on its top. Michael had his sword in hand to bring the plague to an end, what the pope and the dying people of Rome had been praying for. The sword that the archangel fought Satan and his demons with. The sword that cast the dragon from heavens onto earth.

If the Holy Archangel was to come down to the castle on that evening of celebrations in the year of our Lord of 932, he would have seen some of the hatred, envy, treachery, greed, lust, sedition, vanity, lies and arrogance that the dragon seeded through mortal men. Especially among those who were heading the Church of Rome.

Mariozza entered the hall dressed in a splendid celestial blue dress, the silk so well wrapped around her figure that, more than showing the shape of a mature bride entering her forties, it recalled to most guests that the lucky groom was marrying one of the most desirable bodies in the city. Her beautiful face shone imperiously through the veil, violet eyes brightly gazing at all those present in the hall of the castle, telling them that this deity of beauty and desire was still the goddess of Rome. She carried a large wimple that allowed the loose bundles of apparently unkempt black hair to caress her shoulders. And like the so admired duchess Agiltrude, that she had never forgotten since those days of learning to be a woman with cardinal Sergius, she made sure that the lights of the hall reflected on the smooth skin or her formidable breasts, wildly kept inside her blouse by the lock of a brooch, at the very bottom of her chemise collar.

On the celebration of her third wedding, Mariozza was the picture of elegance and carelessness, matron and girl, dame and harlot, and yes, the obvious angel and devil. Only two men in the room were not lusting after that extraordinary woman. And Pope John XI, her son, was not one of them.

John was five years old when his father, Pope Sergius III, died. He grew up on the hamlet that Mariozza had at Isola Tiberina, used to see different men, young and old, entering and leaving the house for pleasurable diversions with his mother. The fabulous Mariozza would not make private some of the sensual games she engaged with her visitors, often attacking her lovers during meals, mounting them on the floor or paying them caresses under the tables, always oblivious to the eyes of the servants or of her son. John was well aware that Rome saw his mother as a slut. He also knew that his grandmother Theodora was a beautiful woman, then the lover of Pope John X. Two whores, desired by men, so he learned. And so did he learn to desire them.

As soon as Mariozza noticed that the almost teenaged John was pursuing peeks of her adventures with men, she organised that her son was properly brought into manhood by hiring a brothel to join the household at the island. Young Albericus came later, from Mariozza's second marriage, but her third son Adalbert was removed from his mother and taken to Tuscany, where his father Guido had been brought up.

Soon after recovering from giving birth, Mariozza had Pope John X, the man who had fathered her half-sister Theodora, arrested and suffocated in prison. She orchestrated the installation of two more consecutive popes with very brief pontificates and finally managed to get her young John on St. Peter's throne.

Pope John XI took an easy way through his pontificate, concentrating on his diversions with women, as he let his mother run the power and authorities of the city.

Now, after Guido of Tuscany had also died, Pope John XI had managed to annul the marriage of Hugo of Provence, Guido's half-brother, so he could wed his mother with Hugo. Even though the Roman church would not accept that a widow would wed her brother-in-law, there was nothing that would stop John from making his dear mother happy. As he blessed their union in the chapel of Sant'Angelo he admired her radiant beauty and tried to concentrate on the sacraments, struggling not to think how much he still desired her.

One of the men who was *not* thinking of Mariozza's beauty was the groom, Hugo of Provence, king of Italy. The rough nobleman lusted for power, but hardly took notice of women, so arrogantly missing the differences among those weak creatures, daughters of Eve, not even among those whose fame and beauty crossed lands and countries. Sure, they were just as desirable as ordinary whores, but he had had his share of them all. If Mariozza ruled Rome, Hugo despised the Romans and lusted for power over them even more. Now that he had already had pre-marital commerce with her, which was enough, he would rather lay with the other bitch, the much younger sister Theodora. But for that evening, Hugo would mount Mariozza as he had done many times as a bull would do in a cow, a *filthy cow*. And he would be ready to beat her very hard if she annoyed him about anything.

The other man was Albericus, Mariozza's son. Now a strong young man of sixteen, he was not at all impressed with this new stepfather-to-be, that fat old king of Italy.

Albericus' status as Mariozza's heir, already threatened by the omnipresence of his half-brother, the pope, was now even on a thinner edge as this rude old man was entering the family. The least that he could expect was that Hugo would probably have him sent to a monastery, to spend the rest of his life in seclusion, if not to be murdered by some horrible means.

As he looked at the groom's relatives, Albericus saw someone who made him think about his only chance to get through the grim scenario as a survivor. The chance which would commit the new stepfather into his own future. The chance that would make Albericus an even more inextricable part of Hugo's family. Not only the king's stepson. But also to be his son-in-law. The king's daughter, little Alda of Provence was a pretty maiden of seven-years old – by old Roman standards it was already at a good age to be engaged and get married.

As the celebrations broke through the Roman night, Albericus constantly tried to get the attention of his new stepfather Hugo for a private conversation. The king of Italy was however constantly surrounded by his personal guard, if not by Mariozza's or the pope's attentions. Not an unnoticeable figure among the hall, the handsome Albericus attempted several times to interfere into Hugo's conversation, making comments of his own, but the old man was just too invasive himself, conducting the action and constantly ignoring the intrusions, only to his new stepson's greater annoyance. The chance for a private conversation came by a moment when Hugo, having already vomited his first round of meats and wine, was returning to the table for some more food.

'Have an apple, my king. It will make you feel better,' suggested Albericus, almost blocking the king's way with his offer.

Hugo shoved the youth to the side. '*Fuck off!* Let me through. I need some more goose fat.'

'Well, then have some more wine,' said Albericus, aware that the king would not appreciate any suggestion for staying healthy or sober.

Hugo stuck his stubby fingers into a bowl of fat and dug out some pieces of cold meat. He trusted the greasy piece into his mouth and turned around, facing the handsome Albericus, who was holding a jug of wine and offering him a goblet.

'*Why* do you care about me, boy?'

'Because I think we can be good friends,' answered Albericus, never losing his smile, although he hated to be called *boy*.

'You don't attract me as a friend,' said the king without returning his smile.

'But surely I would attract you as an ally,' insisted Albericus, now stumbling to maintain the grin.

'What the fuck are you talking about?' asked Hugo with sincere puzzlement.

'Listen here,' called Albericus, now excited that he had caught the king's attention. 'The ideal alliance between us would be sealed if I could wed your daughter Alda. In this manner, both Rome and ...'

'Wait there, boy,' said Hugo grabbing Albericus shirt by the neck. 'Who the fuck do you think you are to propose yourself for my daughter? She doesn't need a little shit like you. Neither do I, least your mother. Now get the fuck out of my way, for I have got to mount my whore – isn't that, my dear Mariozza?' he asked as the beautiful Mariozza came frolicking from the latrine, beautiful, but also inebriated with the excess of food and wine. She laughed stridently at the sound of dear Mariozza and turned around to wriggle her bottom at the fat king's crotch.

Hours later, as Hugo of Provence was snoring, his arms thrown about other sleeping guests in the hall and Mariozza, still vibrant with delight, was letting herself be fondled by some of her other guests, a shout of alert awoke them all. The Castle was being invaded by Roman militia, commanded by the young Albericus.

In a few minutes, a large basket with a heavy load was lowered to the ground outside the walls of Sant'Angelo. Dressed in a woman's garment, Hugo, king of Italy, jumped out of it, seeking refuge into the Roman night, while most of his men were having their throats slit by the Roman militia. By dawn he was already gaining his way outside the city battlements.

Besides having the bulk of Hugo's guards trespassed by his lances, Albericus entered the fortress in command, only to find his vexed mother roaring insults at him. The pope also showed up to support Mariozza on protest against such affront to the family and unnecessary blood spill. Cheerless, Albericus realised that Hugo had not been caught, although the household of Provence, including Alda, were in his possession.

The purple ink that Mariozza had used to bring out the line of her eyes for the ceremony was washing down her face by tears of revulsion. As she indignantly watched the young Albericus helping himself with a glass of wine, she heard a muffled turmoil behind her. She turned to see three of the militia men grabbing the pope, one with a strong hand clasped around his face, dragging him away. Mariozza's scream did not last long, for another hand covered her mouth and others grabbed at her arms and legs, lifting her from the floor. The last thing she saw in the castle hall was her son Albericus, calmly watching her and the pope being dragged out by his giggling guards, down to the dungeons.

That was the first night of Albericus's twenty two years as Prince of Rome.

Rome – A.D. 954

The physicians advised the ailing Albericus that he would probably not survive until the next day. On hearing that, the *vestararius pontificalis, senator et princeps Romanorum*, so desperate about his last hours, summoned all leaders of Rome to see him at the Isola Tiberina.

Riding down the *Via Sacra*, a Roman patrician held his horse side by side with a senator's, both heading to Albericus hamlet.

'What do you think?' asked the patrician. 'Will the Prince impose his son on us?'

'Of course he will,' sighed the senator. 'Albericus knows he hasn't very long to live, and wants to guarantee that his son Octavianus secures the title of *princeps* and maybe even the pontifical chair.'

'Should we support this? And should the people of Rome?' asked the patrician.

'Let's look at it from this perspective,' the senator said without looking at the patrician. 'Albericus has ruled Rome for twenty-two long years, preserving our glorious city from attacks of Saracens, Franks and other neighbouring cities. He rid us of the shameless rule of his mother, that slut Mariozza Maricuccia of Tusculum, locking her up at the Sant'Angelo dungeons until she dwindled to death. If we compare the stability of this period with the chaos that preceded it, I quite honestly think we should be very grateful to the princeps.'

'Oh yes: Marozia!' said the patrician, mispronouncing her name. 'I do remember being told stories about her. The gran puttana. But now times are not different. This Octavianus,' the patrician said with abhorrence, 'his lifestyle is highly condemnable. How can we put up with a sodomite at the throne of Saint Peter?'

'He is just a young man,' said the senator. 'What age is he now - seventeen? Of course he may be impressed by the muscular presence of some stablemen, grooms or soldiers. Frankly, which man has not been attracted by the male physical profile? But Octavianus will shape up, I think. He already bears the burden of a bishopric. Maybe better choose him than start a feud among you patricians and put us on the grill for siding with one party or the other. If you want to keep all parts of your body intact, you should be very careful!'

'They say he entertains incestuous relations with his mother Alda,' the patrician insisted.

'Princess Alda is *not* his mother,' explained the senator plainly. 'When Octavianus was born by a concubine of Albericus, princess Alda was still thirteen. She had been married to Albericus since the age of eleven. She never bore him any offspring, though. Some say that the impetus of Albericus ruined her womb too early before she developed her body properly to bear children. So, how can you blame the poor girl? Yes, it is known that she does entertain carnal relationships with her stepson, but again, a woman in her late twenties and a young man of seventeen – that is an invitation to sensuality!' and he chuckled as he kept his eyes on the approaching ruins of the Colosseo.

The patrician was not amused. 'Even if we have to accept Octavianus as princeps, are we supposed to support his installation on the Lateran too?'

'I expect that Albericus will demand that we swear or promise the election of his son to the papacy as soon as Pope Agapitus dies. That could be a problem,' said the senator, with a grim face.

'Is Octavianus going to be present at this summoning today?' the patrician asked.

'I wouldn't expect so,' dismissed the senator. 'I hear he is spending these days on a hunting lodge in Tusculum, with Princess Alda.' and he pointed excitedly at an alley on his left side. 'Look, *that* is the spot is where the pop*ess* Joan is supposed to have given birth to a child!'

'The *woman pope*?' asked the patrician, crossing himself. 'I've heard the story, but I thought it was not true.'

'I think it was! They say it happened in the times of our great-great-grandfathers,' said the senator, with a shine in his eyes. 'That is why the popes never use this Via Sacra, the shortest way to go from the Lateran to the Vatican hill.'

'Well, it makes sense and I do not blame the pontiffs!' the patrician said with a disgusted face. 'Thanks to God and the Holy Blessed Virgin Mary that in these times that we live, such hideous deeds of Satan do not stain our Mother Church with shame!'

'Indeed', said the senator, crossing himself piously 'indeed!'

And they rode down past the Colosseo.

In that evening, the Roman nobility elected Octavianus the new princeps Romanorum and, defying a 450 years-old cannon that no pope could ever be elected while his predecessor was still alive, they all sworn to the dying Albericus that, as soon as the Most Holy Father Agapitus expired, Octavianus would be elected to the seat of Saint Peter.

Rome – A.D. 964

The Lateran palace was silent.

Only a dark cowled figure walked down the corridors, quietly, avoiding some of the inebriated pilgrims who had fallen asleep on the divans or the marbled floors. The pope was dressed in a monk's garb and did not want to alert anyone to his escapade. Pope John felt really good that night. Octavianus he was born, of princeps Albericus of Rome, before accepting the burden of the pontificate and, for the first time in history of papacy, changing his name. Octavianus was now John, the twelfth of that name to occupy Saint Peter's throne.

He felt very powerful, and not only because on that same day he had mounted a gorgeous pilgrim from France. Yes, she had indeed been a wild mare, kicking and bucking as he held her fists tight and entered her. But he had seen worse, who had to be held by his grooms as he blessedly joined his holy flesh to theirs, and they'd become one in the eyes of God. After a few times of submission to such a sublime ecstasy, most of the pilgrims that were chosen, nuns or villains, sometimes even noble women of distant lands, they would all submit peacefully to the unique experience of sharing flesh with the pope. His enemies, including the ungrateful emperor, whom he himself had once crowned, accused him of kidnapping pilgrims and transforming the Lateran into a *bordello*, a *lupanar*! That was preposterous. No pilgrim in full awareness of the privileges of sharing the holy flesh had ever stayed in the Lateran against her will.

Pope John cut through the warm air of the roman night, crossing to the stables, feeling more vigorous than ever before. How many other men on Christendom enjoyed those privileges that the princeps and Holy Father held? At twenty seven years of age, he could choose a virgin for his bed, and he could kill his enemies with his own hands.

He was tranquil now. It had been three months since he had been re-instated on the Lateran. Three months since the end of his banishment.

In December of the previous year, as Emperor Otto's troops entered Rome, Pope John had to flee. Otto then organised a synod in St. Peter's, where two scores of Italian, French and German bishops accused Pope John of simony, perjury, sacrilege, adultery, profanation, blasphemy, incest, and murder. Among many others, the charges included mockery of holy orders, necromancy, gambling, invoking or toasting to the name of Satan, arson, kidnapping, torture, violation of holy virgins, bawdiness and incest, with his mother and sisters.

That was the second time the emperor had launched accusations against Pope John. The first time had been when imperial troops intercepted correspondence from the pope to King Berengar, king of Italy, which unmasked treachery of the pontiff John against Otto. The emperor sent the accusations to Rome and demanded that the pope defend himself by dispatching two bishops to deny the charges or two champions for a debate. John ignored the request. In a few months later he was driven out of Rome.

This second time he sent to the synod a hand written sentence, excommunicating all participants, including the emperor, if they dared to elect and install another pope. On reading the atrociously spelled Latin note, the bishops cracked up in laughter and motioned for the election of a certain Leo, a *protoscrinarius*, a layman, to replace John as the pope. Infuriated with the imposition of that impostor Leo, the Roman nobility manifested their support to John, and after a fierce battle, they chased both the emperor and Leo out of the city. Back in Rome, Pope John had dedicated time and efforts over the last three months to concede a fair punishment on all the clergy and citizens who had backed the emperor, or the election of Leo.

Early on that morning, John had himself, with only one strike of the *falchion* - the square-ended sword - separated the head from the body of the protoscrinarius who had accepted to be Leo's notary. The pope felt a mix of joy and lust as he drenched his hands in the blood that gushed from the notary's stump. It had been a clean, straight cut. The neck felt soft as he brought the sword down with a snort.

The pope had tried himself with the falchion on many of the necks of scores of clergyman and Roman citizens who had been Leo's supporters. They had been handed in to John by his loyal followers as he returned to Rome in triumph. To make sure they would all savour the fear of their fate, he made all of them watch as one by one were decapitated. There were still a dozen to be dealt with, but he would take them one at a day.

As he entered the stables, a young groom came with the saddled horse. The pope mounted with ease. The groom put his hand on the pontiff's thigh and asked, 'Should I accompany you, Beatissimo Padre?'

'No need for protection. The way is open, and I do not go far.'

'I did not mean to guard you ...' said the groom caressing John's leg.

'No, my dear,' the pope said with a smile, holding the groom's chin. 'Tonight I serve the spiritual needs of another lost soul.'

He galloped through the Lateran alleys, crossing dark streets and ruined marketplaces, all the way to the Esquiline hill. At the front of a large villa, a man signalled and he followed him through a dark garden. Leaving the horse at the stable, the man took the pope through a back door and conducted him to a large marble and bronze-lined room, which shone bright with the light from a myriad of candles. The door shut firmly behind the pope.

Many of the walls were all covered in carpets. A large bed was prepared with brown silken covers, but nobody else was inside the room. The pope had a flash of desperation, thinking that he had fallen to a cheap ambush. He saw a carpet withdrawn to the side and a beautiful woman appearing from behind it. John smiled with relieve and plunged into her arms. They undressed quickly and silently while their mouths explored every surface of their bodies. As they rubbed their sweated skins against each other, John could still smell on his own body the musky scent of the pilgrim he had taken on the morning. And the lines of his hands were still brown with the blood from the notary. These were trophies of the hunt that he savoured for as long as he could. He was the master and he liked to see and feel it.

He positioned the woman on the bed, right in front of a mirror and, as he possessed her body, he carefully watched her face. Was it pain or pleasure? Or was it the joy of bodily communion with the pope, or maybe the vengeance on the cheated husband? She was not young, but still a gorgeous woman. He would watch her plump body glistening in front of him and switch his eyes to the mirror, where he saw himself muscular, long black hair caressing his shoulders, so handsome, so powerful, illuminated by the light of candles. That was when he saw another man appearing in the mirror, right behind him.

After that, he never saw anything else.

The woman screamed with horror, watching her husband bringing the candlestick holder again and again on the fallen pope's head. Blood sprayed on the husband's face, as he grunted with rage *'May Satanas take your perverted soul, now!'*

Campfire Stories

Anno Mille

The horse was tired, but Julian kicked his spurs in to gain some ground into the road, leaving a light layer of dust on most peasants who were melancholically bringing their grain carts to the city. The sun was already bringing some warmth into the gelid walls of Poitiers. Julian preferred not to look excessively back into the burg. He had rounded the walls by the western side, at a fast but discreet pace, avoiding the watch and attention. He gained distance from Poitiers with a sigh of relief.

A few miles to the south, he caught up with a large group of religieuses. They were mainly nuns, perhaps two scores, a couple of friars and a few peasants.

'Do you journey with us as this fine steed of yours rests, young man?' a friar said, approaching the rider and raising a frank smile towards Julian. A welcoming greeting, enough to make Julian dismount and give his horse a reasonable rest at a slow pace. The friar was a tall, handsome dark haired and olive skinned man, probably on his late twenties or early thirties. His accent was southerly, not of those who say *Oc* for *yes*, but more foreign, non French, perhaps from Italian lands.

'Good morning, friar,' Julian replied. 'Where do you all head?'

'With a few exceptions, we all go to Rome.'

'Holy Year or End of the World?' teased Julian.

'That is a good question, young man" said the friar. 'Many of my fellow travellers still search for an answer. Some of these ladies are too confused to know why we head to Rome. And there is a young man here, just over your age, who's making them even more confused. Bernardo's been telling them silly stories.'

'What would you say then?' Julian asked at ease, and ignoring his last sentence. He dismounted and strolled calmly side-by-side with the talkative friar. 'Holy Year or End of the World?'

'For me, I am on a different mission. I go to Rome as an obligation of my order. I have just been *sent away* from of an abbey in the Kingdom of Englaland ...'

'*Sent away*?' asked Julian, without concealing a giggle.

'Sounds funny, doesn't it? A friar been sent away!' he hissed. 'Well, you wouldn't...what was your name again?'

'Julian,' he answered without thinking.

'Julian, I am Martino, from Rome. So, Julian, you young-well-educated-northern-man-heading-south-of-Poitiers-on-a-fine-steed-that-seems-to-have-been-on-a-chase-all-night.' He waited for Julian to absorb his perspicacity and added, 'You would not even believe what I have seen this year!' And when Julian finally bit the bait, with pleading eyes of curiosity Martino said, 'But I'll only tell you after you tell me *your* story. Where do you come from? Where do you go?'

Julian, couldn't help but stutter and babble, before asking with uncertainty 'Do I really have to tell you *now*?' There was something in this religious man that reminded him of his dear Bishop Avesgaud. A clear kindness in his face, honest eyes and a generous smile. This man seemed to give away no pretensions or malice.

The friar grinned. 'Take it easy, Julian, my friend ... I suppose I am not wrong in considering you *my friend*, Julian.'

And with the hair on the back of his neck standing up, Julian said heartily, 'Not at all, my friend, you are *not* wrong.'

Martino smiled. 'So let's not hurry, Julian. You must be a runaway, correct? No shame on that. I am a constant runaway.'

'You run away from what? From whom?'

'From my own humanity,' said the friar. 'Every single day, since I took the cowl.'

'How come you tell me that, friar? You have never seen me before.'

'And maybe I will never see you again, but what is wrong with admitting failures?'

Julian was silent for a while, thinking about an appropriate answer, but the best he could come up with was, 'I hope we do see each other again, anyway!'

Martino tapped Julian on the shoulder, a very non-northern gesture that the young man was not familiar with, but a heart-warming touch, which lead the boy throughout the day walking with the group. The friar told him about the land of Englaland, where the sun always shines. 'That is above the heavy clouds of rain, of course,' he said, 'which are there covering the skies, every-single-fucking-day!'

Julian was not familiar with the swearword the friar used, probably from his own dialect, but he was pretty certain of its blasphemous meaning. He also started to understand, as he listened to the friar's stories, what Martino had said about constantly running away from his humanity. This was a man so unlike the ideal shape of a religious, and still just the same as any person of good, not likely the horribly corrupt monsters that often clerics were said to be. Julian's good friend Bishop Avesgaud quite often transpired his humanity, through tears, smiles or friendly words, but being a God-fearing mortal, he was still a prisoner of his principles. Martino, on the other hand, behaved like he had a God-granted freedom to doubt. He questioned everything he was supposed not to, instead of just accepting them. Yet, he still struggled to believe, to have a reason beyond that would tell him how to behave, rather than just doing it because someone tells you to, or just for the sake of the principle.

After telling Julian a strange feat of a brother in his order who had flown like a bat from the abbey's tower, the friar singled out the individuals who were going with them, describing each one briefly, as if preparing Julian to join a team. He was a good observer, slightly humorous, but never disrespectful, with a buoyancy that Julian felt quite comfortable with. He paid special attention to the nuns, teasing Julian about the virginal womanhood. But he sighed deeply as he referred to the young novices. Poor preys of destiny and misunderstanding. Victims of poverty and of God himself, who had put them into families that could not afford to feed one more hungry mouth.

As they rested after a quick meal, Martino told Julian very bluntly that he had been sent to those far lands of Englaland ten years before, after having a love affair with a nun in a monastery in Tuscany.

'Caterina was her name...' he said with a smile as his eyes focused somewhere above.

'Is she dead?' asked Julian.

'Oh no, I hope not!' the friar said with a startle. 'She ran away, back to her *borgo*, probably...but this is the last I heard from her. She is probably married these days, with someone who I surely envy as the luckiest man in the world.'

'You still love her!' Julian said with a radiant smile, 'even after eleven years!'

'Julian, distance and time are no enemies of love. Betrayal, deceit, lies and pretence, yes, those can destroy love.' The friar picked some dried meat from his teeth. 'And I am no specialist in love, as you can see by my attire – a religious – what do I know about love if not for the type that comes from God? But I think it applies for any type of love.'

They stood up and followed the rest of the group, at the very rear. Martino went on. 'However, this love that I came across, when I met Caterina, or better, Sister Caterina, it can survive the wear of the years and the oceans, mountains and deserts that separate two souls. Indeed, it was … do you mind if I tell you?'

'Of course I don't,' said Julian. 'I'm quite keen to hear it!'

'Anyway, I was called into this nunnery to deal with some disturbed souls. Young foolish girls who had been negatively influenced by an old sister taken in by that religious community. Caterina had fallen into sensuous games with another young novice and I was asked to counsel them.' He gulped discreetly and smiled to himself. 'Well, little was I prepared for the challenges that the Lord would put ahead of me. Temptation, yes, indeed, but hardly from the devil, for only God Himself could conceive such pleasures upon this earth. Caterina won me over the other girl, Antonia, and the lust that involved our bodies soon turned into love. We met surreptitiously at every new session, until it became painful to leave each other's warmth. But before we were to conclude plans about our future, on how to get away and live forever with each other, our affair was unveiled and I was immediately sent to the lands of Englaland.' He sighed. 'But maybe this was better for both of us. I grew as a religious, but maybe still not as a man. Unfortunately, hardly do I know of Caterina.'

'This is terrible,' exclaimed Julian, 'to be sent away from the people we love…'

'It is, Julian my friend, it is. But what about you? Where, or who are you running away from?'

Julian did not have the time to stop his lips from uttering softly: 'From the people I love…'

Martino squinted his light brown eyes and tried to suppress a smile of amusement. 'Go on,' he said. 'Tell me your story, if you can bear it.'

Julian took a deep breath. *Oh, what the hell…* And he told Martino everything.

After being told exactly what had happened, the friar chose to wait and maybe raise questions on another occasion. Rather than censoring Julian, Martino wondered in silence, thinking of what possible reasons God would have to make the young man either fabricate such a preposterous story or actually believe he had seen the Devil.

Once upon a time, in a little village in Auvergne, a poor rabbit hunter took his son down to the pond to catch yellow perch. As they bathed the bait for hours under a cloudy warm day, frogs kept croaking in a way that bothered Gerbert, the boy. He started to notice that he could understand the frog in conversation.

'Can you hear that?' Gerbert asked his father.

'Frogs croaking? Of course I can,' answered the impatient hunter.

'I mean, can you understand what they're saying to each other?' the boy said.

'I don't know. They are frogs…' said the father without a smile.

'But I can,' said the son. 'It is something about the miller's daughter, the ill one! They say her hoiste is still here, inside the pond.'

'What do you mean her hoiste? The poor girl is simple. She doesn't even take communion: Where are you getting these ideas from?'

As Gerbert tried to explain the story being unfolded by the croaking of the frogs, his annoyed father gave him a good beating and they returned home without any fish. A few days after, as his father was off to set some traps, the boy slipped out and ran to the pond, where somehow he managed to ask the frogs the whole story. They gathered around and told him that six years before, the miller's daughter, still a young girl, was probably tempted by the Devil to avoid swallowing the Eucharist at communion. She hid the loaf of the oblation in her vests, came to the pond and threw it in its deep green waters. In that moment she fell ill and was found unconscious by the pond banks. Gerbert was astounded to see how the frogs were so well aware of the miller's daughter, a poor soul who had been suffering from dementia ever since he knew of her. 'We think that maybe she should take the discarded bread to wake up to the world of the living again.' the frogs added.

'Do you still have the loaf?' asked the boy.

The frogs dived and quickly came back with the hoiste, untouched by time, smelling a sweet scent of freshly baked dough. Gerbert took the bread and ran to the mill, finding the miller's wife tending for her sick daughter. He shyly offered the bread to the woman, lying that this was from his mother for her ailing daughter. The miller's wife took the warm loaf and suspected of the sudden outburst of generosity from the rabbit hunter's family. She even asked the boy if he had not stolen the loaf from the church. Gerbert would not leave before she'd had fed the loaf to her daughter. He was afraid the mother would take it for herself. As soon as the daughter feebly munched the first portion that was pushed between her broken lips, she woke up from her eternal dream and asked her mother politely for some water. The miller's wife fell to her knees and praised the Lord, but Gerbert was already hurrying back home. His parents learned of his good deed by the miller himself, never sufficiently thankful, but that still earned Gerbert a good beating for his arrogance in talking to animals.

A few months later Gerbert overheard the conversation of some jackdaws that chattered quite loudly while searching for critters on a ploughed field. 'There goes that boy,' said one 'from the rabbit trapper that sells his wife to the parish priest. The poor thing!' Another Jackdaw quickly intervened. Shut up! He can understand the languages of animals!'

Gerbert went home and did not find his mother there. So he ran to the church and, at the back door, he was somehow not surprised to encounter the fat old priest saying a rather sweet farewell to his mother, kissing her on the lips. The mother was very surprised and nervous to see Gerbert there. At night he received the rightly punishment by a memorable beating from his father and, on the following week, the local priest arranged for a travelling teacher to take him away. Far away.

Gerbert was taken to Spain. On the way, while staying overnight in a village, dogs outside would just not stop barking. He heard the dogs talking about a band of marauders preparing to attack the village. So he warned everyone and, although many were sceptical about his visions, they armed themselves and at the end of a fierce battle they drove the marauders away.

The teacher was utterly impressed and took Gerbert to the best of schools in Spain. He grew up in religious life, received his ordinances and returned to France. On a pilgrimage to Rome, one day, Gerbert found a trapped dove. He released the poor bird from the string entangled on its legs and the dove expressed its gratitude by saying, 'Hurry to Rome. The pope is ill, and he will be dead in a few days.'

Gerbert got to Rome as fast as he could. As he got there, the pope was already dead, and crowds gathered around the Lateran palace for the flight of the dove. This is how they chose popes: they released a dove from the Lateran and the next pope would be the man on whose head the dove landed.

Needless to say, the dove was the same that had been released by Gerbert, and it landed on his head. As he was acclaimed by the crowd, an old man looked at Gerbert and fell on the ground with a stroke. As the new pope rushed to the man, he recognised his father, who asked for forgiveness for having him sent away. The pope forgave him and the hunter died in peace.'

'What was his father, the rabbit hunter, doing in Rome, Bernardo?' asked one of the nuns.

'Bernardo, you should stop with these stories' said brother Martino with a grave face.

'Not even this one? This is absolutely innocent!' Bernardo winked to Julian. 'And very true!'

'No, it is not innocent at all!' continued Martino. 'It speaks of witchcraft and stupidity. What a wonderful system the choice of a new pope that you came up with. A fucking pigeon!'

Some of the nuns turned their faces in shame as they heard swearwords from the friar, but others giggled. Martino pleaded with them. 'My sisters, this man is a very good storyteller. But please do not believe the things he says. They are all made up.'

'How can he say that about me?' Bernardo said, elbowing Julian amicably.

Brother Martino continued. 'And watch for his stories of doom. There is no end of the world. The Devil has not been released. Actually, there is no Devil at all!'

'So then who's convinced the miller's daughter to hide the *hoiste* and throw it in the river?' asked another nun.

Martino just shook his head in hopelessness as Bernardo and Julian exploded in laughter. He waved them good night and warned the nuns not to visit Bernardo at night for any favours he might have suggested.

Julian was still giggling when he was cut short by the bitter memory of the discussion he had had with Martino that afternoon, two days after he had told the friar his story.

'My friend, I think we should talk about what happened on that forest and your flight from your family,' Martino had said.

'I'm not sure I want to talk about it,' Julian answered bluntly.

'You are afraid, aren't you?'

Julian nodded, without looking at the friar.

'Julian, I cannot explain what happened, and I do believe in what you saw and what in you heard. But listen to me: not for the sake of the crucified Christ, neither for the sake of any saint or martyr who has died defending their beliefs, but just for the sake of everything which is sacred to you, your mother, your father, your family, please re-consider this whole matter. How can you be sure of those words in the forest? What accreditation has a demented man, or an ogre, if you prefer, to say sooths?'

'Indeed!' snapped Julian with pain, 'for the sake of everything that is dearest to my heart, I *must* stay away! I heard the voice, and it did not come from the ogre. I have seen the beast again. One knows the Devil when he sees Him.'

'Julian, whatever you saw was a creation of your own mind. It *must* have been a product of your own bad dreams.'

'My bad dreams are a product of what I saw.'

'There is no Devil, Julian, simple as that, unless it has been brewed by our own desire. Look at these pathetic youngsters listening to Bernardo's spooky stories. I have seen wonders, Julian, and they are only God-related, although quite often referred to as a devilry or witchcraft. I have seen a man fly, Julian ...'

'I certainly wish it was an apparition concocted by my fears, Brother Martino,' said Julian, without paying attention to Martino's story, 'but they were not there before this encounter. So, please, let us be for this evening. I do not want to think about it.'

'Just think about how much you are hurting yourself and the hearts of your loved ones. That's what a true devil would want,' said Martino before covering himself with a blanket. 'Good night, Julian'.

As he tried to sleep for hours, Julian was tormented by doubt. His new friend the friar seemed like a man of reason, displaying the same scepticism towards the personification of evil as Julian had always done before. This is how Julian wanted to be, but his destiny had been tossed towards another direction. Dizzied by thoughts, his eyes could not just rest and let his mind slip away into slumber. Watching the rustling from the blue crowns of the trees around him in the clear night, Julian tried to see his situation from an outsider's perspective and observe the ridiculousness of it all. Maybe, he thought after all, there could be a misunderstanding. Maybe the words were vain, and the threat was none existent at all.

He was intending to talk to Martino on the next day and re-discuss his plans. He felt easier and was about to doze-off when some movement on an old oak to the north of the clearing caught up his attention. He rested on his elbow, trying to fix onto the tree crown, guessing what sort of novel bird would be moving the great branches. Nobody else at the camp seemed to be awake in that moment. The fires had already been extinguished. He looked once more at the swaying branches, and was about to cover himself again, believing that it had only been a disturbance of nature by a gust of wind, when he saw the big black shape moving behind the leaves. No bird was that, for it moved with arms and legs.

A huge man was climbing through the branches.

But he *knew* so well that it was not a man on the moment the air around him froze and the enormous creature stuck its black head out and stared at him with yellow eyes of fire.

As Julian's ears picked up its low guttural whisper, shivering with horror and fright, he reached over to Brother Martino, not too distant, without losing sight of the terrifying dark mass.

'Martino, wake up, Brother Martino.' He shook the friar, still fixed on those demoniac eyes staring at him from behind the leaves. 'It's here, brother! It has followed me!'

Martino was awake in seconds, but so was the creature gone when Julian pointed at the oak. Only the branches where swaying then.

Brother Martino made a huge effort to comfort Julian, who was very disappointed for not having been able to show the friar what he had seen. Martino would be there for him, as a friend who helped light the fire and stay awake with him until the break of down. But what Julian did not see was the colour on Martino's skin, which had turned to whitish green, for his stomach had turned inside out. Indeed, the friar had seen nothing on the tree, but he had sensed its powerful volume moving around the camp, the most wrong presence he had ever felt in his life. He still did not believe in a devil, but he heartily believed in Julian's fears now.

The Physician

'You silly sod!' was the first thing Immanuel ben Malachi heard. 'Time to wake! We must go.'

The Bukhari tried to understand where he was and what had happened to him. Why there was so much pain on his face.

He'd heard a voice talking something foreign, but he could understand. Oh yes, the skipper? No, it was a different voice than the skipper's, but it was also in Greek, mixed with the sound of a thousand donkeys that seemed to be screaming at his ears. Immanuel felt that a heavy stone must have been resting against his face, or as if somebody was sitting on it. He tried to open his eye and the first thing he saw was his nose. No stones or nobody sitting on it. Just his nose, as large as ever. And the pain that glowed, pulsating fiercely through it.

'Your horse is ready. Come! You're riding with us tonight.'

There were some torches nearby. By the freshness of the cold air on his nose, Immanuel knew there were no tents sheltering him. It was hard to get his eyes to stay open, but he could devise a clear side of the sky, where darkness was by now being broken through by a purple aura. That must had been hours since he had fallen on his face, but it only felt like the blink of an eye. He also noticed that the clang of metals had suddenly ceased. Only the shuffle of hooves and the constant barking of dogs muffled people's voices.

'Come on, hurry up!' said the voice, and Immanuel was shaken by the arm. A man with a torch was smiling at him. The man was small, just like himself. With a thick black beard and black eyebrows that met on top of a majestic nose. Both his teeth and his eyes were large and beautiful. He was wearing a white tunic with a rope as a belt and leather boots. Covering the bald spot on his head there was a blue skullcap. Immanuel thought that the man actually looked very Israelitish.

'Silly man', he said to Immanuel. 'Almost got yourself killed last night.'

'I hit my foot…' answered the Bukhari with a trembling voice.

'Yes, I know it, but we did see that you tripped towards the opposite direction' said the man. He helped Immanuel to the horse and let him mount it. 'What did you think you were doing?'

'But who are these people?' asked Immanuel. Better aware of its surroundings, he controlled the horse, admiring its gait. Unlike the huge thin beasts he saw in Persia and Syria, this was a small bulky pony, much like the horses he was used to in Bukhara. He looked around and saw this immense cloud of dust blocking the few lights that danced around the darkness. The torches were being carried around by horsemen.

'These are Bulgars!' said the man. 'They come from a distant country, as I do. They formed this caravan of merchants that will go all the way to Acquisgranus, the seat of the Roman Empire. Isn't that where you want to go? The Roman Empire? That skipper arranged with them to take care of you all the way, as long as you service them with your medical abilities! Now, what exactly did you think you were doing when you ran away?'

Immanuel's nose still hurt badly and he was very confused, but managed to tell the truth. 'I thought the skipper was going to sell me as a slave.'

The man could not help but break into laughter, and said something aloud which triggered laughs from others. 'You silly, frightened thing!' said the man, with a smile so white that Immanuel could see very well in the darkness. 'Nobody would want you as a slave. We are wise merchants, but this time we only carry spices, some deplorable quality silk, animals, leather, shoes, pelts and especially marten furs. I carry holy relics from Syria and Greece. And we also trade good horses, mules and women – companions of flesh!'

'Slaves, you mean…'

'Nah, not slaves,' dismissed the man 'these are dames who like what they do – they are free to come and go. We are just agents to find them generous masters. But do not be afraid: you know, that skipper from the Syrian ship that you came with organised that you'd join us along the hard journey to Acquisgranus, paying with your services, if needed.'

Immanuel was invaded by an embarrassing sense of ridiculous. In spite of the pain, he looked at the man and they both laughed. The caravan was taking one direction. They were going north.

The tone of the eastern sky was red now, and the man looked quite familiar to Immanuel. The Bukhari kicked his horse closer to that man's and asked. 'Are you a Jew?'

'Funny you asked,' he answered, making a wise face 'For many have asked the same to me before. But no, I am not iouda nor Syrian. My name is Procopius. I am just Greek. A Christian. I follow the man who was crucified as the king of the *Juddahs*. I follow Jesus, the Son of God!'

Immanuel stayed silent, with a certain disappointment at the answer. But also with a thousand questions brewing to ask the Greek.

'What was that you just said?' the Greek Procopius asked, riding through a narrow path on the valley incrusted in the Dinaric Alps, right behind the pony of the Immanuel Ben-Malachi, the Bukhari.

'Nothing with you.' Immanuel answered. 'I was just cursing. I would do it in Greek too if I knew the swear words.'

'That should not be a problem,' Procopius said. 'I can teach you some interesting ones. But why are you so crabby?'

'What do you expect?' Immanuel grunted. 'I keep getting told that the group I travel with heads to Rome, but suddenly it's revealed that I am on the way to somewhere else. First they dock me in a Tragurion port, which was no doubt far from Rome. Then they mount me on this caravan that is heading to...where?'

The Greek looked up for a second, trying to think or the itinerary. 'Well, our way goes through the main markets of Istropolis, Prague, all the way to Mainz and Acquisgranus.

'None of which are Rome, as I have learned!' said Immanuel, 'I've been fooled once more. Wouldn't you be upset with such disrespect too?'

Procopius lost his smile for a while and said irritably 'Honestly, I do not recall anyone among these Bulgars promising you anything about Rome. Indeed Acquisgranus is the seat of the Holy Roman Emperor, but definitely a month or two north of the great city. It must have been that skipper of your ship who either brought you in here to get rid of you as a whining nuisance or perhaps an honest misunderstanding of him.'

'Misunderstanding?' the little Bukhari was almost yelling. 'An experienced sailor does not know where this Rome is?'

'Well, we can always set you en route with another passing caravan that comes across us.' Procopius said. 'Pilgrims, mostly, they will likely be. But I doubt the Bulgars will let you go that easy. Your medical knowledge has been precious, especially on dealing with our livestock.'

'Yes, a passing caravan...' Immanuel wondered. 'But when could that be? How can I know I could trust those too?'

'That, I cannot guarantee. Here in this caravan you are among friendly people. But be aware that Juddahs are not particularly favoured in Christian lands.'

Immanuel dropped his shoulders. 'People of my race do not seem to be liked anywhere.' He turned around to see Procopius on his mule. 'What sort of problems do Christians find with us Israelites?'

Procopius gritted his teeth on one side of his mouth and lowered an eyebrow over his wide eye. 'It's not all of us Christians who have problems with people of your race. I think the rationale is that the Jews are perceived as those who did not accept Jesus Christ as the Messiah. By this denial or refusal, they led him to his condemnation and death.'

'But that does not make any sense at all! First of all, if the faith started in Judea, it could only be passed to new recruits from the mouths of Jews themselves. So the first Christians must have been Jews, correct? Then, if I understood precisely what you've been patiently telling me about this creed, the Lord Jesus Christ died to redeem the sins of men. How would He have died with all that suffering, bearing the weight of humankind's wickedness, if it wasn't for some criminal condemnation? Without the disapproval of some disgruntled Jews, he would never have achieved the Lord's heavenly plan. And third, the best thing, in my opinion about Christianity, is tolerance. It is the Christ accepting the wicked, the impure, under the protection of his arms. It is compassion and forgiveness. Where are the Christians finding their forgiveness towards the Juddahs?'

The merchant sighed. 'Christianity is a sensible faith, Immanuel, but Christians are only humans. Do not expect sense from Christians, for a change. When things are not well, it is often a better feeling to blame someone else. Jews are often the target. To this day, in some cities far in the Frankish countries, when Easter is celebrated...'

'So the Christian Easter, as in the remembrance of the Christ's death?' Immanuel asked.

'Exactly. Death and resurrection.' Procopius completed. 'Well, in some cities, during the ceremonies of Easter, they still grab a poor Jew to be beaten with a stick every year.'

'That's monstrous! No better than what I would expect with the Qarakhanids in Bukhara.'

'Is that the reason you left?' Procopius asked. He looked at Immanuel nodding and raised his lower lip and swayed his head to the sides. 'It won't be any better on these lands.' Then he changed the subject. 'Were you from a family of physicians?'

'No, not at all. My family was into wine making. We sent it to the kaffir kingdoms out in the east.'

'Farmers? Not many Jews are allowed to own land here.'

'Oh, this is just getting worse...'

'But tell me Immanuel Ben-Malachi' the merchant said 'if you grew grapes, could you grow mulberry trees in Bukhara as well?'

'No, no! For silkworms? No.' Immanuel dismissed with a condescending smile 'Bukhara has always been too dry for the white mulberries, I'm afraid. We were never into the silk activity, although most caravans came through to get silk from the eastern kingdoms.'

'Silk is indeed very precious here' Procopius said, looking quickly to both sides. 'As precious as gold!'

'And why don't they produce it here?' asked the Bukhari?

'They would if they knew the secret!'

'Secret? What secret? It's pretty straightforward: Feed the worms with mulberry leaves, boil the cocoons to unroll the silk threads, and keep breeder moths in a dry place. Everyone knows!' concluded Immanuel.

Procopius shushed him, waving with both hands. 'Nobody knows the details, neither the points you listed,' he said. 'In addition, these people have not the worms.

The secret has only travelled as far west as Constantinople. Even there we are hardly allowed any freedom on the manufacture, weaving, dyeing, trading or even wearing of silk fabrics. As a merchant, I must deal with minor goods of little value for my survival. Constantinople keeps the Bulgars and other neighbours happy and calm by giving them these crumbs of trade. The great city sends smaller merchants like me as a pose of respect and equality of commerce. But what can I do? I cannot trade any silk. I am not of the right blood to be part of a public guild of silk traders, neither a rich enough to afford association with a private guild. Can I buy pieces of silk in my city? I cannot even wear the accursed fabric! Neither am I in any guild of silk manufacturers or purple makers. I cannot buy murex shells from any fishermen or trade with processed purple dye. And there would be a revolution if I was seen wearing any purple pieces on my attire. Constantinople creates an aura around its people to be envied and craved. But that city also welds the links that keep you chained away from this aura.'

Immanuel had lost his concentration on listening to the Greek. He was still thinking about the silk. 'It sounds to me like a case of not asking the right persons and offering the right price.'

'That could well be the situation, Immanuel Ben-Malachi! But I would advise you not to dwell into this dangerous grounds. No matter what you say, you are a iouda for us, and especially in Rome, you will have to think about survival, before dreaming of anything else.'

'How will they know I am a Jew?'

Procopius chuckled. 'Look at yourself in a good mirror, Immanuel! Even if reputation and bad news did not travel, you would be betrayed by your own self. However, if you ever would convert, everyone would know you only as a has-been Jew.'

'Conversion? As in becoming a Christian? Does that make any difference?'

'I deal with many Jewish bankers and many converts throughout many lands. It does seem to help when needed.'

Immanuel though for a while.

'In this case,' he said, 'I'd have no problem in converting.'

'Very impressive!' Procopius said. 'Good progress! You have even lost your bad temper of a while ago.'

'That is only until they come to me with another sick horse. Just wait.'

But the Bulgars did not bring any other sick animal or person to Immanuel for the next seven days. They had already left the rocky Dinaric Alps behind. Fording rivers and thundering over old wooden bridges, they entered an extensive forest that carpeted an infinity of hills, where gigantic deer with towering antlers dwelt, with plenty of succulent boars and shy bears making an unfortunate encounter with the caravan. Arriving on the market town of Gradec, they made a few exchanges and followed journey on the second day. Some twenty leagues to the northeast, on a flat marshy terrain, the caravan was interrupted by a local rider, arriving from the opposite direction. After a brief discussion, a couple of the leading Bulgars came to the back to see Immanuel.

'The rider comes from the village at the crossroads, five leagues ahead. We expect to be there by night, but he urges us to send our physician with him on gallop.'

'What is the problem?' Immanuel asked.

'He says the chief's wife has delivered a baby, but she does not stop shedding blood. They fear she will be dead before tomorrow. Quite frankly I don't think it is worthwhile to waste our horses in such –'

But he never finished the sentence, for Immanuel Ben-Malachi had already dug his heels on the flanks of his pony, which exploded into a gallop to follow the rider.

'Please help us! I will give you anything,' Ferenc begged. 'The richest of my treasures!'

There was no smell of birth in the house, although a baby howled nearby. Its sweet, musky, milky scent had been overwhelmed by the stench of blood.

The body lied still, cold, spread as a boneless corpse. Her face was of a waxy stone grey, with lines of green lye growing off the wrinkles. This could hardly remind Ferenc of what his wife Borbála used to be a few hours before she entered labour.

Looking shyly to the other people in the room, Immanuel Ben-Malachi approached the palliasse. The chief Ferenc opened way for him, strangely by grabbing an older villager who sat next to the woman and tossing him out of the house. This was followed by an animated sequence of shouts and words that Immanuel could guarantee were not flattering.

'Who was that man?' Immanuel asked, startled.

They explained to him that this was the local medicine man, the táltos. He was supposed to be an expert in midwifery too, but failed to stop the bleeding, so far. Ferenc spat on the floor on talking about it.

'Maybe he should be here to help...' Immanuel said.

'It's your job now. The táltos is useless,' Ferenc said, looking desperate at the body that was once his wife. On seeing Immanuel's speechlessness, he kneeled in front of the tiny Bukhari. 'Please make her live!'

Immanuel swallowed with difficulty and touched the skin of Borbála. She was scarily cold to the touch. He felt her pulse. Borbála was still there.

'For how long has she been bleeding?'

'Since late this morning' a midwife indicated.

'I'm surprised she is still alive,' Immanuel suggested, 'and the blood is still trickling...' It was the moment when he normally would have dropped his shoulders and said: We did all we could. Now we can only wait for God, on his mercy and wisdom, to make his decision. But given their conduct towards their own medicine man, Immanuel would not be expecting any God-like mercy from this people if he failed to keep that woman alive. And moreover, willingly or not, he had accumulated quite an amount of knowledge during that past year. Perhaps this would be the time to test the power of black comb. It had led to rotten limbs and madness, but as the Radhanim affirmed, maybe in a reduced amount it could bring anyone ready to depart back from the gates of death. He searched through his satchel and withdrew the vial where he had kept the poison. Holy Fire. He would try a couple of those tiny black stems.

'Do you have any broth?' he enquired.

'We do have it, but she is not swallowing.'

Immanuel would only need enough to wet her tongue, mixed with the powdered stems. He had no idea if that would be enough, but at that stage, nothing could go worse than death.

He placed the drop on her tongue and lifted her chin to shut it. Borbála had barely the strength to keep her mouth closed. Her eyes were vague, cloudy. For what seemed like an eternity, Immanuel kept his hand holding Borbála's chin up until his arm tired. He released it and her mouth fell open again. Another shallow spoon of broth was placed in her mouth and he raised her chin again. Borbála choked, spraying the broth on Immanuel's face. Calmly, he reached over to the broth and tried to place some of it again in her mouth, this time with less.

Many villagers watched, from behind Ferenc. Immanuel could hear only the wind and the horses snorting outside. The baby must have been sleeping.

Borbála did not gag the broth out this time. He checked the bleeding. It did not seem to have changed. But maybe it was too early. Once his arm was again in pain, he asked for another shallow spoon. The Bukhari was prepared to repeat that procedure all night.

In that cold autumn morning Turul raised its massive wings in alert. The lammergeyer was ready to take flight as it could easily devise the goat horns over the tall dry grass of the swamp. Horns that came on a straight line towards the yard. When Ferenc stormed out of the bush like a boar, roaring out Béla's name, Turul's wings beat down, effortlessly raising the vulture onto the safety of the sky.

Although he did not get much sleep, after being expelled from Ferenc house, the táltos came promptly out of his shed to greet the chieftain, but the countenance he saw did not seem to bring any good news. With blood-infused eyes, Ferenc grabbed him by the neck and clenched his fist, ready to strike a blow that would break the old man's jaws into pieces.

But the chieftain held it for a while, looking at the terrorised face of the táltos. His fist tightened.

'No, Ferenc, don't do it...' Béla squeaked.

The chieftain released the táltos, throwing him on the floor, among the bone splinters from Turul's meals. Ferenc kicked him on the side, again and again, making Béla moan and cry with pain.

At last, when the beating had ceased, the old man finally said, with his mouth full of dust. 'How is Borbála? Did she survive?'

'Get out of here!' Ferenc shouted imperiously.

Béla opened his eyes better to stare into the chieftain's. *What did that mean?*

'Get out of the village and never come back! You are banned!' Ferenc repeated.

'Banned?' asked Béla aghast. 'Why would you do that? What have I done to deserve it?'

'You are a fraud.' Ferenc said. 'We do not need you here.'

'But Ferenc, my life is here. This is where I was born and grew up. You have always known me and I have always known you and your family. I saw you coming out of your mother's womb and I raised you to be the man that you are! *My life is this village!* I have ridden our crops from plagues and birds, I have scared storms away, I have soothed the moods of uncountable spirits and saved so many lives. I tended for the sick and I cured the wounds in magical ways. I have brewed for the entire village, I have the remedies, the ointments, the herbs and the powders for all ailments. I have prepared restful herbal baths on the hot springs and determined our best days to sow and harvest. Ferenc, my world is here!' he implored.

'Not anymore,' Ferenc spat. 'When the time came for you to do something really meaningful other than witchcraft, you failed.' He turned around. For him, the discussion was over. As he entered the bush, he shouted to Béla. 'Three days. You have three days to pack your things and leave us forever.'

'Ferenc, women die on delivery all the time!' he screeched 'There is nothing that can be done in these cases!'

But Ferenc did not answer. Béla only saw the goat horns on the helmet disappear behind the tall grass. But in that moment of utmost desperation, it all occurred to him at once.

'It was the medicine man, wasn't it?' Béla shouted. 'That Greek medicine man! He told you to get rid of me! Pay not heed to him, Ferenc! He is no better than me. He could not save Borbála either!'

His screams just faded into the distance. Bruised and still sitting on the floor, all that Béla could hear was the shriek of Turul, coming from high above.

Back at home, Ferenc looked at Borbála. She snored loudly on a clean palliasse. Istvan, the baby was on the wet nurse's care. There seemed to be life still coming up on his horizon.

'You should take a rest, Immanuel' he suggested.

The Bukhari sighed. It had been the longest night he could remember, since some of those cold desert slumbers. The bleeding had stopped, and with the utmost patience, he managed to slip some broth into Borbála's throat. Now she seemed to have recovered a bit of colour, suggesting improvement.

His joints ached when he stood up. Wondering where the Bulgars had camped or if they had waited for him at all, Immanuel approached the sunlight that came through the door. It hurt his eyes, but he needed the rest and some fresh breath of air. He was glad to see his pony was still there. It had been taken care of. And just casually, he overheard Ferenc telling him in Greek, from inside the house. 'I will be getting your generous payment soon, Immanuel Ben-Malachi. And by the way, I have banned Béla from this village.'

'The shaman?' Immanuel asked, completely forgetting about the treasures promised by Ferenc.

'Yes, he has three days to leave us.'

'*Why?* What has he done? Don't you need a medicine man here?'

'He has done nothing. That is the fault. If it wasn't for you, I would have lost my Borbála.'

'Nonsense...' said Immanuel. 'Nonsense! He is probably good and knows a lot. Can you afford to live from medicine that comes with the caravans?'

'Maybe you should stay with us, Immanuel.' Ferenc said with a grin, totally unconcerned.

Immanuel ignored the comment and asked 'Where is the shaman now?'

'Hopefully packing. His home is in the swamp. The northwest path takes you to his shed. But don't go in there, for you can get lost and drown into those lecherous quagmires. '

But Immanuel had already disappeared.

Strangely, the yard outside Béla's hut was littered with crushed bones. A fetid stench attracted myriads of flies that kept the boggy land around the hut under a constant hum. Immanuel called for Béla. Nobody answered. He dared to enter the spacious hut.

Once inside, there was no doubt for him that this was the office of a true medicine man.

There were alabaster flasks and glass phials with oils and spirits, ceramic pots with powders, dried mushrooms and crushed leaves, vessels with seeds, chopped stems, petals, odd looking grains and what appeared to be desiccated diced meats. Immanuel recognised a number of herbs, but marvelled at the experience of smelling, seeing or touching many others. Tied to the roof beam, drying as they made themselves available for any medical or magical emergencies, were Arabian ginger, long radish stalks of devil's helmet, valerian roots, dried gentian, and the magic tuber that Immanuel knew as the love plant of Rachel and Jacob, and that the Moslems knew as djinn's eggs, and that he later learned to be called in Christendom by *mandragora*. Piled on the corners were iron ploughs, sickles, shovels, axes, picks, shears, mattocks and all types of hoes, but some of them were strangely hanging from the ceiling. This was certainly a place of magic but with a considerable amount of herbal knowledge and natural sciences. He wondered how the folk of Ferenc would survive without the aid of that man. Such an unpremeditated stupid idea indeed had been that banishment of Béla. Unfortunately, there was nothing Immanuel could obtain from that hut without the presence or the aid of the old táltos. He left the hut, to almost gag in terror as a monster stood on the patio outside.

Immanuel leaped back at the sight of the enormous feathered creature, which seemed to ignore him as an edible organism. Immanuel had seen the hunting eagles and falcons that the nomads from northern desert would sometimes bring for exhibitions in Bukhara, but nothing as massive and terrifying as that lammergeyer. He carefully stepped back to detour around the hut when another fright shook his soul, for someone was standing behind him. He turned around to get a glimpse of the sun-dried face of the shaman, who was strangely smiling at him. But Immanuel could not figure out the reason, for a sharp pain exploded on the side of his head and he sank into utter darkness.

Coriander, Milk and Honey

Once upon a time, deep in a valley of the Tuscan lands, a husband and wife who lived in a house next to the befane were expecting their first child. The befane were hags who were seen mostly at night, with their heads covered with a scarf, for everyone knew that a long beard grew from their napes.

As pregnant women are often succumbed by unusual cravings, this wife had a particular preference for the beautiful coriander that grew on the befane's vegetable garden.

'What is that?' asked one of the nuns.

'Coriander is a herb that some Eastern people put in their food,' explained Bernardo. 'But just let me continue with the story.'

The woman asked her husband to go and fetch her a bunch of coriander at daylight, but the good man knew of befane's evil nature and strongly advised his wife to stay away from that garden. Besides, he said, who would want to use that repulsive herb on food, anyway? The craving however was too intense. So the woman sneaked into the garden one day and took off a bunch of coriander for her soup. The flavour was soothing and she did the same on the next day.

The befane, aware that someone had been entering the garden, set watch for the third day. They buried themselves next to the coriander patch, just leaving their big mushroom-sized ears out, to detect the unwanted visitor. The expecting wife sneaked in again for the coriander, but this time she was caught. Terrorised by the grip from the befane's claws, she saw the hags coming out of the earth, with a long-fanged smile on their faces, so she offered them anything in exchange for her release. They let her go, but demanded that if the baby was to be born a girl, she was to be called Coriandola, because of the herb she had been stealing, and if a boy, Coriandolus. The wife quickly agreed with that, but the befane had one more demand: They made her promise that when the child was grown, she would give it to them!

The husband was so disgusted by his wife's bargain, and he blamed her for such imprudence. When their beautiful baby girl was born, they immediately saw the fanged faces of the befane at their window. Coriandola, she became.

As the years passed, the couple hardly ever saw the befane again. But on a certain night when Coriandola had grown into a young woman, mother and father were surprised by the strident shrieks of the befane, who invaded their house and snatched Coriandola from their care, forever.

Coriandola worked as a slave for the befane. One day her caretakers decided that the girl should perform harder tasks. So she was given a piece of rag and shown into a coal-black room, which was supposed to returned milky-white clean at sunset, or she would become the befane' dinner.

On that afternoon, as the vile befane slept loudly, Coriandola was visited by the priest Mamilian, a distant cousin of the befane. He saw the girl crying of hopelessness and asked her what was the problem. She told him about her fate for that evening, and the impossible task of cleaning that room into milky white. Mamilian thought a bit and advised the girl to use the seed of a holy man to rub on the walls and make them white. As Mamilian himself was a priest, he offered to give her his seed and quickly instructed Coriandola on how to extract it from him. Soon walls of the room all shining, milky white.

The befane were surprised to see she had completed her task, and none had yet suspected of a visit and advice from their own cousin. So, for the following night, they asked her to go up to the mountains and bring them back a jar that Pandora kept inside her womb.

Pandora was a hag whose cave was shut by a big marble gate and guarded by a pair of colossal black dogs and a greedy old hermit. Coriandola was terrified just to think of Pandora's name, least to steal the jar from the hag's womb. When desperation seemed to start to corrode the girl, cousin Mamilian showed up again, this time as a bishop. Coriandola told him of her new designated task and if she did not bring them the jar, the befane would devour her. Mamilian again suggested that Coriandola extracted some of his holy seed. The young lady did it with pleasure, as he carefully advised her how to use it on her journey. Walking up to the mountains, she came across a hermit, with his fingernails entangled in his beard. The old men avidly asked her for alms, or else he would abduct her to his burrow. But quickly she gave him some of Mamilian's holy seed to grease the beard. Following that, she filled a pot with some more seed and gave it to the two giant black dogs at the gate. At this point, she poured some more of Mamilian's seed onto the gates' hinges. At the cave, Coriandola touched the belly of Pandora with her fingers smeared into the remaining seed of Mamilian, drawing the sign of the cross. Pandora fell unconscious to the ground and the skin on her womb opened into a cross, where the holy seed had dug through it, revealing a beautiful pewter jar. Corindola, so flabbergasted with the sequence of events, grabbed the jar and ran away as fast as she could. Pandora soon recovered from her unconsciousness and asked the gate to shut close, keeping Coriandola inside. The gate answered that, thanks to the girl, it could now swing its doors freely, without friction, so it refused to obstruct the way. Then Pandora warned the guard dogs about Coriandola running away. But the dogs, happy and well- fed, ignored the hag's screeches. Lastly, Pandora blasted with all the strength of her lungs, offering many riches to the hermit if he brought Coriandola to her, but the old man, now with a well combed beard, was so proud that he never paid attention to her appeals.

Back at the befane's place, where they were still soundly asleep, Coriandola arrived with the pewter jar. On noticing that there was still some liquid inside the jar, Coriandola poured it out through the window, but to her horror, instead of liquid, a host of tiny little men fell onto their backyard, screaming and cursing, quickly scattering through the vegetable patches. She tried desperately to put them back, but they were very elusive and she had grabbed only a few. Frantically crying, fearing that the befane would devour her if all the tiny people were not back in the jar, she was about to panic when cousin Mamilian showed up. 'What have you done?' cried Mamilian in surprise, seeing the little men scurrying all over the garden.

In tears, Coriandola explained that the little people spilled from the jar.

'But why did you pour it?' asked the befane's cousin.

'Most reverend bishop, remember that this jar came from Pandora's entrails. I was afraid there would be blood or other humours in the jar!' she explained.

'Never mind,' said the bishop thoughtfully. 'Let me explain what you should do to get these little people back together before the befane wake up.'

So he instructed her to join his holy flesh in sacred communion, right there in the garden. Very piously and with a bit of joy, Coriandola complied with his instructions and as they reached the holy communion with the angels, the little people gathered around to pray, and they were delicately put back into the jar. All of them.

The befane woke up, ready to eat a failed Coriandola, but they were surprised to find Pandora's pewter jar, with all of its contents. More surprised even were they when they saw their cousin Mamilian.

'You have not been here to help that girl, have you, Mamilian?' the oldest befana asked.

The bishop assured them that he hadn't. But he overheard them confabulating, deciding that they would devour Coriandola in a soup on that same day, no matter what. Mamilian ran to the girl and advised her to prepare a fire for the cauldron and ask to go out of the house to fetch more logs for the fire. She did as he told her, hearing the befane cackling with laughter when she left the house to fetch more logs. Outside, Mamilian quickly pulled her by the hand, across the garden, taking Coriandola to a hidden shed which was locked. With a key he had produced from a pouch on his vests, he brought her into this dark shed lit by candles. The bishop explained that each flame held the life of a befana. Coriandola quickly blew all the candles, extinguishing the flames. She ran to the house and found all the befane already stinking dead.

On the same day she left the valley with Mamilian. They went together to Sicily where they got married and lived happily ever after.

'Bernardo, how can you tell these people such a stupid, senseless, silly, confusing and blasphemous tale?' Brother Martino asked, as he saw the mesmerised faces of the nuns and pilgrims, and Julian hiding behind, shedding tears of laughter.

'Come on, it is not too bad,' reasoned Bernardo. 'And it is a true story!'

'True, Bernardo? Really?' Martino looked furious. 'A jar with people inside. What did the befane want with a pewter jar? And who is this Mamilian? Is it *Saint* Mamilian, of Palermo, that you are talking about, Bernardo?'

'Yes, he was later canonized,' Bernardo answered shyly.

'It's just bits and pieces that you collect from your excrescences here and there and you put them together, don't you?' insisted Martino, his face close to the storyteller.

'Well...' started Bernardo.

'*For what?*' asked Martino, leaving the campfire as the nuns all watched him retire in fury. 'What is the purpose of this nonsense? I just cannot understand.'

Bernardo just stood there, looking at the ground, thinking aloud. 'Maybe people should learn that coriander is not to be eaten...'

One of the older nuns stood up severely and looked at Bernardo. 'Well, if it was not Saint Mamilian of Palermo, then who was it that helped Coriandola though her ordeals?' As she finished the question, they all heard a blasphemous curse coming from the side of the camp where brother Martino had retired to.

After selling his horse, Julian continued on the road south, together with the same group who grew fond of him, as he learned to enjoy the company of, among others, the friar Martino and Bernardo, the storyteller.

Bernardo Delle Rocche had grown up as a shepherd. He was from a wealthy but rather eccentric family holding their lands somewhere in the Tuscan mountains. Bernardo, like his father, was taught to read and write, gaining his education in the monastery of San Michele, in Pesa and seeing the world on his pilgrimage to the homonymous monastery of Saint Michael, in France. Now, on his return journey to finally take the landwork upon his shoulders, tend to the herds of sheep and conduct the wool trade that his family thrived on, he had met Brother Martino on the way, establishing a close camaraderie. The friendship grew stronger as the travelling group swelled with the presence of the nuns. The unusual, rather interesting and certainly stimulating female presence triggered in Bernardo his cantastorie side.

In Bernardo's homeland, cantastorie were the storytellers. Heralds and minstrels that hopped from town to town, living from their generous memory of history and tales, sharing their knowledge to every village in the most entertaining way, through poetry or ballads, theatre or jokes. But Bernardo descended from the Obertenghi family, nobles of the Ligurian coast and certainly not minstrels. However, his grandfather and father had passed to him an inherited talent to create and tell stories, a gift to gather a small crowd around them, to hear their unforgettable accounts, granting them all the nickname of cantastorie.

Keeping still the appearance of an adolescent, young Bernardo had firm muscular legs, which could have been more generously fleshed for the mountain life in Tuscany. With a fairly tall built, but not yet towering, sunlight could reveal a violet tinge to his disarming brown eyes. Bernardo had a generally well-tanned complexion, with a mixture of an angled Lombard head with a proud Roman nose. His easy smile was always accompanied by a couple of mischievous dimples that deliciously shot up to his cheeks.

Once the larger group of religieuses had joined them on the road south, Bernardo was quick to find young company for the night under his blanket. Although Brother Martino condemned vehemently Bernardo's tales of the Beast unleashed and the end of days to be happening in that Anno Mille as a lure to final deliverance of some devout women, he was not particularly opposed to the nocturnal activities of the shepherd. Still, he did have a few stern conversations with Bernardo and the girls who had liaised with him. As Martino had shared with Bernardo words on his own affair with a religieuse and the true love he still had for her, Martino could not put himself in a position of condemning young men and women on the bloom of discovering love.

'I hope it is true, honest love!' he rasped at Bernardo.

'It is, Brother Martino! From the bottom of my heart, for *all* of them!'
The friar tried not to change his expression, but the side of his lips curled up.

Julian was awakened in the middle of the night, this time not by a demon, but most likely an angel. A sweet, young angel, climbing languidly under his blankets.

His hands embraced the tiny body of that angel, caressing it, feeling its sinuous shape and all of its smooth young skin. As soon as the angel's lips touched his, Julian knew her name. A name of little relevance for the story of the Bridge of Borgo a Mozzano, but yes, her name was Louise, or Luiggia, as Bernardo had been calling her.

A bright-eyed novice into the wedded life with Christ, Louise was seeing the world for the first time as she journeyed from her abandoned monastery on that Anno Mille pilgrimage to Rome. Trails joined into paths and these became roads, joining others into main routes throughout the farms and forests of France. Crossing their chosen ways with other expeditions, learning of privation of the flesh, self-denial, fasting and mortification stories from other pilgrims, discovering newly built churches, they prayed at every new calvary on the crossroads. Sister Louise was enchanted by the diversity of life, the human encounters, all that was so much shun away from her during those full sixteen years of her life.

Bewitched by the novelties, confused with the differences and afraid of the unknown, Louise gave in to her desires, built up as the sisters gathered to hear Bernardo's stories and debated in whispers the mysteries of love and men. She saw a blessing anointed by heavenly rays onto those who had shared a night with the cantastorie, with their cloudy eyes wandering through white heavens and a constant smile decorating their young faces. When the heat of fear, uncertainty and desire seemed to burn up her body, she decided to share her affliction with that handsome and gentle Julian, innocent, young, maybe a chance in a lifetime to be acquainted with the power of love.

Together in that journey of discovery, protected by the intimacy of the blankets, Julian and Louise were confused and eager, quickly lifting fabrics and mutually exposing their skins, burning at a touch, crawling away and leaving a track to be branded again by an embrace or a caress. Legs were hastily intertwined as lips opened wide in delicious agony. They tried and missed, helping each other in a mutual acceptance of their innocence, pulling themselves against one another strongly, all the way into a perfect and delightful plunge, wet and profound, freezing their bodies for a brief eternity of bliss and accomplishment, a tender complicity that allowed them to slow down and extend the embrace, to fully release the endearment built up by their deliverance. The sounds outside were closed to them. There were no more darkness or forest, or nuns or friars; there was no more cold or discomfort, no smouldering embers on the fire and no wind to shake the trees. Only the light of the stars were with them, emanating from their hearts, burning from where they united.

With subtle contortions, tightening or releasing their grips, Julian and Louise detected each other's limits. They moved slowly to expand the frontiers further, on an enchanting pace that gradually increased to a luscious trot, accelerating their breathing and digging their heels and nails into each other's flanks, finding themselves instantly in a frantic gallop that took them away from the world of the living, halted only by a tender but exhilarating explosion, as if a large amphora of milk and honey they'd be carrying across a bridge had suddenly burst, relieving the carriers from that burden, filling them with its perfume, allowing the precious content to spill, losing itself into the happy waters of the creek.

Limp in each other's arms, Louise and Julian were sitting on a bridge in Heaven, quietly enjoying the view of that creek, hardly knowing that around the next bend those waters would be plummeting into the mouth of Hell.

Furore in the Abbey

A.D. 989

Eleven years before, in Rome, the bells of the Lateran church were calling for complines, as the thin but faithful mob entered the gates and quickly passed into the cool interior of the basilica. At the peak of Roman summer, evening services were a great excuse to protect oneself from the scalding heat. Nobody in the crowd that crossed the central nave towards the choir noticed those two people behind the bars, hidden in the darkness of the side chapel of St. Paul and St. Dionysius.

Accustomed to the shadows, Bishop Claudio of city of Pozzuoli looked grievously at the tender features of the young nun in front of him and talked very softly, almost in a whisper.

'You may not see who's there on the walls, Sister Antonia, but you are under the scrutiny of the Apostle Paul and his disciple Dyonisius, the Aeropagite. As witness of God, these two martyrs are watching us from their decapitated heads, to verify the imposition of the penance on those who confess and to admit them into the gates of heaven, purified through the gateway of reconciliation. Paul holds onto his two keys of the church, passed down from Peter, who was entrusted with them by the Lord Himself.'

Sister Antonia did not seem to be listening. Her eyes were wandering into nothingness, thoughts that could be leaving a shameless smile on her lips.

Bishop Claudio continued in a hissed whisper. 'Do you trust and believe that as the Holy Father's *nomenclator* I have judicial power as a representative of Christ, the judging of the living and the dead, to absolve and to condemn those who sin after baptism? And do you believe that without confession there is no entry into paradise?'

Now Sister Antonia lost the amusement on her face but still forced a grin to the bishop. 'Father Bishop, I may be only nineteen but I have enough knowledge to be confused. I always thought that Dionysius, the Aeropagite, bishop of Athens, was a different person than the Dionysius who was decapitated in Paris, after surviving the grilling, torture and beasts.' She watched the puzzlement build up on the bishop's face and continued, 'But anyway, as far as your capacities and entitlements are concerned, I do trust that you hold the power to inflict on me whatever you feel or conclude is the best for me. I believe that you may do everything among your reach to demonstrate to others your trust in the written laws and traditions of our church. I also think that you have no idea of what God really wants from us, if anything at all.'

'Sister Antonia,' the bishop said, calmly hardening his voice, 'I will pretend that I did not hear these blasphemies against the holy mother church. And now that you have shown yourself to be a very bright girl, tell me exactly what happened in Santa Maria Lei Giudice.'

'I have heard this request many times over these last few days. And the consequences have been of immense pleasure for me and for my inquisitors. Therefore, I am quite glad that we are now hidden in darkness, so that the bodiless heads of Saint Paul and Saint Dyonisius will not be able to see what you do when I spread my legs wide open …'

The bishop gasped. 'Try to concentrate on the episode with Sister Caterina, and cut short of your devilish daydreams,' he said.

The nun obediently declared 'It is quite simple then. Sister Caterina and I have been engaged, over the last few months, on a process of self and mutual discovery,' Antonia said ending with a shiny smile.

'You uncovered your nakedness to your sister in God then, is that correct?'

'Yes! Just as she shared her nakedness with me. As you may well know, father bishop, the intensity of passion and pleasure achieved through the embrace of naked bodies, the broad touch of the skin, the contact of lips and eyelashes, hair and tongue, is incomparable to the supposed bliss achieved by prayer or chanting, which in my view is mostly inexistent.'

'Your views, Sister Antonia, are of little relevance to this matter, given the altered state of your crooked soul,' said the bishop with a sweaty face. 'Your sin is grave. Your vows are broken; you uncovered your nakedness to your sister as she did to you; lying together as a woman would do to a man. Your filth covers you in shame, as it does to the whole mother church.'

'Of course, this is how you see it, father bishop,' explained Antonia, lifting her hand to touch his knee. 'But the same mother church that harbours and protects many brothers in God of you and I, brothers who shared these moments of paradise with me as I was interrogated. Vigorous young men who felt the moisture and tenderness of my flesh as they entered me with their beautiful hard cocks, spurting me with their tasty seed, which comes out of an indescribable state of blessedness…'

'Enough of this smut, young woman!' intervened the bishop, taking his leg away, for the hand caresses of Sister Antonia had become painfully pleasurable on his thigh. Outside on the main nave, chanting attracted the public's attention.

'No, father bishop,' she insisted, 'I can *never get enough of it*. Nobody can. Look at these,' she said as faint light from the nave shone a pale honey-coloured reflex on the shapes of her exposed bare breasts. 'See them? *Feel* them! Yes, give me your hand here. Yes, feel them softly, cup them. Makes you feel good, doesn't it? Let me feel you too. Oh yes!' she giggled, 'it *does* make you feel good! Father Bishop, what an endowment!'

'Satan of a thousand years, leave me be!' grunted the bishop with fury, slapping her hand away. 'I will not be led away from the path of righteousness by your lewd tricks. Cover yourself! Aren't you afraid of the Lord's revenge? It is written that He shall punish those who engage into immorality, sensuality and commit abominations, for they shall surely be put to death, and their blood shall be upon them.'

'Father Bishop,' Antonia said with a recovered composure. 'I respect your knowledge of the Old Testament and your virtue in abiding to the Leviticus. The trials of our material world must be indeed an endurance for an extremely fascinating and charming man like you. How many ordeals and temptations must you have been through? I would suppose that the most glorious women in Rome and Napoli must have fallen at your feet, offering themselves to you. You came from the *Diocesis Puteolana* in Pozzuoli, right? What makes you dark-haired man so handsome and attractive? Is it your soft, apricot scented skin? How I love to feel it. Please, let me do it. Let me touch your most reverend face.' The bishop was paralysed as her fingers touched his shaven chin. 'Yes, this is so tender,' she continued, 'compared to the hardness I felt a minute ago. You have the face of a boy. You are sweating like one too. No need to perspire so much, for I know by your wisdom and knowledge that you are a fully grown man. I can see it in your built. I can even smell it in your sweat. Yes, apricot mixed with the smell of man's seed. I can even taste it from my fingers. It is coming through your sweat.' And she drew her face closer, her nose almost touching his 'But why should you keep it inside? Even if you don't bring it out, you know it explodes on its own during your dreams of sensuality, right? So, you cannot stop the dreams. Why keep it only in your sleep then? Open your eyes, father bishop and let me share my youth with you. Let us both be nineteen now.'

Her lips drew a track across his face as they finally met his, which were moist and receptive to her challenge. She giggled once again as her hand reached under his alb. They raised their vestments and Sister Antonia mounted a rendered Bishop Claudio with force.

'Here, take them in your lips,' Antonia said raising her blouse. '*She* always mentioned that we must extract heaven from our nipples, as blessedly as Saint Agatha's own breasts.'

'Whore!' the bishop moaned as he was muffled by Antonia's naked torso. 'Why do you have to drag me into the fires of hell with you?'

'Not into hell, but up with the angels, mounted on a cream-coloured horse,' Antonia declared as she rocked on the bishop's lap. 'Oh, you feel so big, my horse. You are such a stallion! I knew *she* had told me about men of this size, but I never thought…'

'Sister Antonia,' said the bishop in trance, firming his fingers deep around her hips as he thrust with energy, 'we were here for a confession! What am I doing? I am a sick man. You have passed your illness onto me. An abscess is forming in my conscience; it is tormenting me and it will give me no rest . . . I must confess, and in confession we'll let the pus come out and flow away.'

'Yes, confess that you love it! Confess that you feel closer to the angels now than you have ever experienced. That is what *she* always told me: Making love is the best way to feel closer to God!' Antonia closed her eyes and threw her head back, bouncing still with more energy.

'*Vade retro, Asmodeus!*' hissed the bishop as he pushed her back. 'Do not touch me any more!'

'Of course not!' Antonia sizzled without hesitation 'You touch me instead. Come and hold my hips. Take me from behind, the horse that you are. This was *her* favourite fashion of doing it!'

'So your lover sister Caterina liked to do it this way, right? Do you like it?' Bishop Claudio moaned as he entered her again, digging his fingernails in her swaying hips.

'No!' said sister Antonia

'You don't like it?' asked the indignant bishop.

'Of course I love it, but I said no about sister Caterina. I have not been referring to her. I have been referring to the gran puttana, the old woman!'

'Who?'

In the many years that he lived thereafter, Bishop Claudio forever regretted the moment when he asked who the old woman was. Every time he had to relieve his demonic lust with the help of a courtesan, the bishop's mind and body would lament that he never finished what he started with Sister Antonia in the chapel of St. Paul and St. Dionysius. At the mention of the gran puttana, he'd composed himself quickly and called the custodes to take away that succubus impersonating Sister Antonia. She should tell her story to the pope himself.

Soon after, the young woman was put into a filthy cell at the palace dungeons, where two weeks later she died of fever.

Many hours after compline, as night time muffled the small burg of Santa Maria Lei Giudice, the old abbess was desperate to talk to her guest. The plump head of San Giovanni Battista's Abbey had already reached her sixties, still healthy as a true mother, but nonetheless thirty five years younger than her guest, whose identity only she was aware of, but whose value only those who remembered her would understand. The abbess had just received the news through a very small window at the thick door that separated the cloistered sisterhood from the outside world. A messenger from Lucca had insistently banged on the door until she decided to leave the collective warmth of the dorter and face the cold. Bad news were those indeed, for now the world of sin and iniquity outside, or worse: Rome had come to learn of the name and relevance of the professed sister who still lived within the walls of San Giovanni Battista.

The abbess cruised through the dark corridors of the old building to reach the dormitory cell of her guest and she prayed that they would not come for the poor creature on the following morning. She broke through the door, considering the waste of all those cautionary actions, two decades before, by having moved her guest from the dorter, expecting that this would keep the old fox from contacting and talking excessively to the younger novices which occupied the collective dormitory, the most vulnerable members of the cloister. Their innocence should be protected at all costs. And if virtuous, their righteousness would carry these young women through the paths of prayer, fasting and ascesis, simplicity and vigils, taking the solemn vows into the exemplary life of the followers of Santa Maria, Santa Ana and the martyrs Sant'Agnese and Saint John the Baptist, all for the service to God.

Yes, those who did not befall into foolishness were much better than the abbess herself, which was too mellow and sensitive to the pains of mortification, too flimsy to resist to the honey of temptation, regardless of the shape of the enemy, especially when it came as a dear friend.

Feeling through the darkness of the small cell and reaching for the pallet, she found the old woman's bony shoulder and shook it.

'Wake up, you old bag! Wake up!'

The dead weight just stayed still and snored louder.

'Stop pretending, you silly bitch, I know you are awake'.

Again, no response came from the guest. As the abbess turned around to reach for tinder, she asked solemnly while she worked on starting a small flame: 'Marozia, oh Marozia daughter of Theodora! Marozia, you gran puttana! Are you still among the world of the living?'

A sound came from the palliasse. A long and exhausted sigh, followed by a harsh moan 'Still having trouble pronouncing my name, Mother Abbess?'

The abbess turned around with a lit lamp and uncovered the old woman, pulling her up by the arm to a seated position. 'You must wake up immediately, Marozia.'

Marozia was the name that Mariozza Maricuccia had turned into a few generations later. She had been the oldest inhabitant of that abbey, and not yet taken the vows. Not less than a constant burden on the life of the cloister. The light revealed an incredibly handsome face for a centenary woman, deviously smiling at the abbess.

'What is it this time, Mother Abbess?' Mariozza asked as she seated herself energetically and quickly tied a cap around her carefully kept grey hair. 'Are you perhaps interested to know how to make a man cry with pleasure by just using one of your fingers?'

Her extraordinary appearance would have been a constant source of annoyance and humiliation for the round abbess, if it had not been for the friendship they developed for three decades. While the abbess saw herself getting older and bigger, she saw her friend ageing at an irritating slower rate. Mariozza stood up youthfully, her slim figure a contrast to the abbess's volume. Mariozza shot her luminous violet eyes into the abbess's and continued, 'or would you rather find out who are the descendants of the man with the largest ...you know what ... that I ever laid with?'

'You are indeed a cretin, Marozia' said the abbess in disbelief. 'By the chopped head of San Giovanni, please shut your filthy trap up and let me tell you what is going on.'

'Why don't we just go round to the warmth of the calefactory so we can talk with –'

'Enough!' cut in the abbess. 'Marozia, my dear. By our friendship. Let me start, please.'

Old Mariozza had not seen the abbess like that for many years. For very long as well she hadn't heard a sweet word from her friend. She saw the pouches on the abbess's eyes filling with liquid, and fear transpiring on the rosy face. Understanding started to dawn on Mariozza.

She asked, 'They are coming for me, right?'

With lips tight, the abbess only nodded, letting out streams of tears, before bursting onto Mariozza's opened arms. 'I am so scared,' she said, sobbing.

'Don't be afraid then. I should be the one who should be scared,' said Mariozza as they embraced each other.

'I'm so sorry, so sorry. Please forgive me,' said the abbess. 'Such a fool I am. I should never have let those two…'

'Listen,' interrupted Mariozza, with the usual power she could exercise at ease, 'there is nothing to regret. You did what you had to do, or else I would have expected that not a drop of decency would have been left in your soul. On the other hand, this is all to be blamed on my foolishness during all these years. Please, stop crying, Mother Abbess.'

'You call me *mother*,' the abbess said with a chuckle, 'but indeed I should be the one treating you as if you were mine, not only because of your age, but for having nursed me through these decades of pathetically trying to dedicate my life to God.'

'We don't want do discuss that now, do we?' Mariozza said. 'You have dedicated your life to God. So have I, always dedicated my life to one of the places where God lives – in me!'

'We must get you out of here!' the abbess said after recomposing herself. 'The messenger is still outside. He is sent from a friend'.

'Get out of here?' Mariozza asked calmly. 'So that they come and don't find me and they will destroy this house, and probably rape all of the women?' She turned around and sat down on her bed. 'I don't think so, Mother Abbess. They would find me anyway.'

'Of course we must get you out of here,' the abbess insisted.

'Please, I am just too old to be running around, to be hiding more than I have done for over fifty years. My time has come. The gates of hell are opened for me.'

'Don't you say that!' the abbess said with awe. 'God knows you. God has been with you at every moment of your long life, bringing you out of your wicked ways, into rectitude, into honesty, prayer.'

'Prayer, Mother Abbess? You know I only pretend. Our recited prayers are rubbish. I do try to converse with God but, given my poor obeisance to a Christian way of life, He still refuses to talk back. But God has given me a good life. I have had power, luxury, riches and endless pleasures. I have had the chances to meet all men I wanted. Who else in this world has learned the art of fornications with a pope? Of course, popes, like most men, prefer to leave their marks in virgins who don't have anything better to compare with, but these maidens are usually thrown away after being passed through. However, Pope Sergius just could not get enough of me. He loved when I was wearing …'

'There you go again, Marozia! Don't be an imbecile. Few people today know there was ever such Pope Sergius. He's been dead for many generations. Your son pope is also dead. So is your grandson pope, thanks to the good Lord and hopefully burning in hell, and dead are your two nephew popes. Should I remind you that the bishop of Rome is now John XV, and he has no connections to your family, or your sister's descendants? Marozia, men are coming for your neck and you are still delirious about your filthy adventures with half the men of Rome? Wake up for once in your life! You are not the *gran puttana* anymore. You are a defenceless centenary woman, a walking cadaver forgotten in a cloister in Santa Maria Lei Giudice. Come, get your things and we will leave'.

'I am *not* leaving, Mother Abbess.'

'What are we to do? Do we just watch them come and take you to their dungeons in Rome once again? Never!'

'I honestly don't think they will bother to take me back. They will finish with me here. But there is one last thing I would like to do.'

'Oh Christ crucified. So please tell me, what is it?'

The abbess heard carefully what Mariozza wished, sad to know that she was soon going to lose her friend, but glad to find out the wish was not too difficult to fulfil.

She would send the messenger to leave to Lucca immediately.

The Calvary in the Forest

Julian woke up to be bathed by Louise's sunny smile. He packed quickly and silently shared some fruits and bread with Bernardo and Martino, watching as the nuns giggled and cooed on the other side of the camp when Louise talked to them. What was the secret that amused them so much that Louise could not share with him?

Bernardo went to say something but he saw Martino's eyebrow shooting up warningly. The friar tensed his body as a cat, ready to strike if the shepherd opened his mouth to make any remark about the night activities in the camp.

Julian and the group walked for half a day, through fields and villages in the rolling country towards Limoges. Stopping for prayers and readings, the progress was slow, particularly uncomfortable and rather painful for Julian, due to the distance he had maintained from the adorable Louise all the time. Whenever he looked at her, she had a serene face rested in prayer, or a fresh young beam on her beautiful countenance, sharing a few words with other travellers or nuns, making Julian's heart cringe with envy and yearning. He could not find the way to approach her. After what happened during the night, his life would never be the same, and he needed to be with her, to be talking to her, to capture all her words and looks, to know how she was feeling and what she felt for him. He wanted to be next to her, to say comforting words, to protect her. But Louise was far away that morning. What had he done wrong? Anything he had said or done? Was he not good on their lovemaking? Didn't it feel as special to her as it was for him? Was it anything he did not say or do? As if being away from his family did not torture him enough, that agony of separation and doubt from a new loved one tormented him for the first part of the day.

After the sixth hour, Bernardo was walking next to Julian.

'Hey, Luiggia!' the shepherd suddenly yelled to the back of the group. 'Come over here and walk with us, I have a question to ask you.' He saw Julian gasping with nervousness as the young novice hurried her pace and approached the pair.

'Yes, Bernardo,' she said shyly, after darting a quick look at Julian.

'Tell us, Luiggia' he said, including Julian on his us. 'Had you ever, in your most savage dreams, thought that you would be travelling so far and seeing such different places?'

'I have not been visited by any savage thoughts or desires, Bernardo,' she said with decorum, gazing at the road that sloped up ahead of them, but the shepherd had already walked away to the back, to join another group of pilgrims. She continued with a devilish grin, looking straight inside Julian's eyes, 'It was only last night that I was carried through a wild, but heavenly dream.'

Julian found himself beaming with Louise. They walked together, holding a conversation that neither ever wanted to end.

Limoges rose at the horizon at the end of the day. The religieuses went all to the Abbey of Saint Martial, where they would be given a warm meal and safe shelter for the night, women isolated in a dedicated area. Aching with the idea of separation from Louise, Julian boarded into an affordable tavern. On that night, Martino came to him for a cup of ale.

'Julian, do *not* lose yourself into this daydreaming of yours,' the friar said in his commanding baritone. 'Louise is a novice who will take the vows and forever be secluded by her order. You cannot drag this girl away from her destiny and expect to give her anything better, or even if partially as good. You are a runaway, you're too young and you have nothing for your own self.' He saw the face of Julian melting into disappointment, but preferred to carry on. 'Bernardo is irresponsible enough to give them a good ride through the pleasures of the flesh, always risking the possibility of ruining their spiritual lives, but he can take care of his own. His heart is made of the stones of the Apuane Mountains and it will not be disturbed by any amorous reveries.' He called for another round of ale. 'But you, Julian, you are a puppy, not ready for this world on your own. Return to your family and forget your nightmares. Whatever is haunting you will not be deterred by your escape. Within your kin you will be someone and you will be able to choose your destiny.'

Julian shook his head and snorted. 'Go back to them and fear every new day? When I could be causing their deaths?'

'At least,' Martino said, 'you should write to your family. Tell them what has led you to disappear. Talking about it works in the same way as the sacrament of the confession. This will help you dissipate your fears.'

'If I write to my family, they will search for me.'

'Another good reason to do it, Julian. Let this be on God's hands. Trust Him.' He tapped the young man amicably, with his typical caress on the shoulder. They both raised their cups and gulped down some freshly brewed ale.

Julian woke up on a dark field, where he heard the sobs of a woman crying under a tree.

'Louise?' he called.

She stopped her weeping. There were many rocks he'd had to step onto to get to the tree. It was dark still, but he saw the woman sitting there. Her face was covered by long hair. As he withdrew the hair from her face, he saw the yellow eyes of fire. The flames that burned deep into the chaos, calling for his soul. A face with no features, as dark as the beginning.

It grunted like a pig. 'The ones that you hold most dearly!'

Julian woke up again in a dark Tavern sleeping side by side with many travellers. It took hours for him to fall into slumber again.

He had written his letter but never delivered it. He carried the rolled parchment in his satchel, ready to be sent to Mans as soon as he would be arriving in Toulouse. He would have to find an abbey that would be happy to dispatch it to Saint Bertrand, to the hands of Bishop Avesgaud for a reasonable fee.

But now he walked southwards, through the dark forest of Limousin, where no villages were erected and the sunlight seldom warmed the ground, even if in the nakedness of winter time. On any normal cold morning during summer, with the tree coverage at its maximum thickness and heavy with moisture, his lungs would be gladly and thankfully filled with fresh forest air. But once again, a foul wind seemed to blow in from the interior. The more he walked deep into the forest, expecting that it would thin out for the other side, the stronger was the sense of wrong and the darkness that surrounded him.

There were no taverns or people travelling through that part. On some of the hilltops, where the forest thinned like a cobweb and allowed for more light to expose the brown musty world of the woods, a few timber calvaries stood lonely where other paths crossed by. These were prayer sites, marking the spot with their ghastly crucified figures, poorly sculpted and covered with moss, manure and lichens, sometimes serving as a perching site for owls or for the sinister crows that scanned the pilgrims' waste. From the confusion of footprints and debris left behind, Julian noticed that these calvaries were compulsory stops for any group of dedicated pilgrims that ventured through that darkness.

Julian did not feel the necessity to pray. That wooden Christ, with his mouth open wide, had only half a head. The rest had been chipped away by time. Little dignity was left on that piece of timber. The hands seemed to have grown into branches after the sculpture had been set in that cold, forsaken place. This did not bring up any thoughts of the presence of God, but surely confirmed His absence. In addition, the noisy crows kept croaking, including one particular individual who seemed to giggle like a child. That gave Julian cold chills on his spine. He left the calvary in a hurried pace and was startled by the crows that rose together to flight on a collective caw. Here again, another bird seemed to be screaming like a woman in terror.

As the birds disappeared behind the dry canopy, Julian lost the air in his lungs, for the screaming continued, and it came from the road ahead of him. He started running towards the sound, as fast as he could. And the screams seemed to run from him too. They would not stop.

Many weeks later, on his way back from Rome, a pilgrim walked with a group through the woods of Limousin. They were still about a mile south of the ghastly calvary with the half-faced Christ when he contemplated the fresh graves that stood quiet and lonely on the side of the track. In addition to tiny dry hellebores, with their petals sadly prostrated, keeping company to the unfortunate souls that rested in the musty soil, the trees were laying their share of dignity onto the mounds, by letting their red and yellow leaves tenderly slide through the forest air and rest comforting on them. Not a name, not a story for them. What evil would have befallen so many? Only the crosses stood mute, refusing to tell the tale to the passers-by.

The pilgrim looked from one grave to the next and quickly prayed for each of those souls. He asked for divine intervention on their achievement of a peace that they probably deserved, if not in that serene sheltered corner of the forest, then maybe at least that those souls could rise above the canopy and enjoy the company of the angels in the open skies of heavens.

Out of the forest floor behind the graves, a rolled tube of parchment clearly stood up from the leaves. This was not a fallen cross, thought the pilgrim. He shook it from the dried leaves and opened the roll. Although moisture had damaged part of the text, the script was still visible and perfectly readable. A letter from one of the deceased. After reading it, the pilgrim decided that the people that those words were meant for were now to be sought. He hoped to find them somewhere along his route.

The travellers continued on, following the path north. The pilgrim gave a last glance at the crosses. One day, those rudely connected sticks would be only standing out of a thick, soft mattress, where the squirrels played and badgers shuffled around in search of berries. And they would eventually break down and disappear, as their rich woods joined the bodies below them, back into ashes, back into dust.

The trees formed a deep, dark gorge in the forest, like long pointed teeth of a frozen beast, a giant ready to munch the bodies that littered its black tongue. Julian found a scene of horror on the path to the screams. Dead pilgrims, with their heads bashed, others moaning or howling with pain, from broken limbs or ribs, or from deep gashes that bled through their habits. His legs started shaking when he recognised the familiar faces of some religieuses who wept in disconsolation, but only one name sprang up to his mind.

Louise.

Was she safe? Julian had to find her.

He ran along, verifying the wounded and the dead, looking at agonised faces, some of them giving up on the pain; some desperate, begging for his help; some dark, unknown savage features that were of not the pilgrims' from his recollection; or only half of some faces, like the Christ on the Calvary a few minutes before. But Louise was not to be found.

At the end of that path of carnage, a ferocious fight still carried on. A hairy forest man, likely a bandit or a new produce of the end of times, was desperately swinging his *francesca*, the throwing axe with an arched head commonly used by the Franks, at two men who surrounded him, one with a cudgel, the other with a sword.

Brother Martino and Bernardo Delle Rocche.

They were both bleeding from battle, but furiously fighting against that cornered weasel. Julian was quick to string his arrow, distracting the bandit for a second, which allowed for Martino to swing the sword on a vertical arch and hit the bandit on the arm. The strike was dry and the sword bounced back. It had hit the bone. The man shrieked in horror and pain, looking at his arm, before the cudgel from Bernardo knocked him to the ground. Groaning with pain, he still tried to stand up, but Julian had already let the string go. The arrow entered right in the middle, just below the ribcage, climbing up his chest. He dropped paralysed on the forest floor.

'Where is Louise?' screamed Julian to both men, before they could even acknowledge or understand his presence there.

They did not answer, but ran back to the battleground, quickly checking the wounded and the dead. They came back to Julian.

'There were no more than six or seven of them!' Bernardo said, panting. His face was a mass of blood and soil. 'We must have gotten four of the bastards.'

'They came to kill, and to take the women,' Martino said, leaning his body down to rest, holding his knees. 'No forest robbers these are, for they should know we carry no riches. These are savage men that could –'

A chilling scream of terror broke down deep into the forest, above the wail of the wounded.

'Luiggia!' Bernardo said. He shouted her name again, as loud as he could.

She screamed again. Clearly southwest.

The three of them plunged into the darkness of the woods, foaming with rage, growling for revenge, swiftly slipping through the old trunks that blocked every new yard ahead of them, jumping over logs and breaking through bushes, blindly trying to sniff the unsniffable and spot the unspottable. Julian, Martino and Bernardo were opening the distance from each other. They could still hear her screams, but her voice seemed tired, far away. Anger kept Julian still running on his feet, for his body, just about to explode, did not seem to be able to withstand the exhaustion. The terrain lowered into thicker bush, but they fought their way through the brambles up to a point where Julian saw no more branches on his face, and nearly no more ground under his feet. He was balancing himself at the edge of a deep gorge, with a creek rumbling somewhere in the bottom.

The feeble shout came from across the gorge. 'Julian!'

His blood curdled from boiling in that instant, bringing his bow forward with a strung arrow ready to be shot. There she was. Not standing on her feet but on a vertical position. Naked and wet, beaten, filthy with soil and leaves, the contrasting white of her skin was a sickening signal of the brutality of the forest and its people. A trembling hand held her chin and the glittering blade of a knife could be seen under her neck. Looking at him with helpless eyes, she tried to scream again, but her chin was held high. She only moaned, limp, wordless. Behind her, the maddened face that gritted his teeth as he looked at Julian. He was but a boy, probably not older than Julian himself, but his wide open eyes revealed his savagery. He growled at Julian and pressed the knife further against Louise's neck, mumbling something in a different dialect that sounded to Julian like, 'Give up. We're at the end of times!'

Julian's arms were tense, pulling the string back, bending the bow to its maximum. His hands and fingers were almost as firm as he wished them to be. Julian could aim at the bandit's face. The arrow would pin that monster to the tree, right through his eye. He could make sure that Louise would not be harmed; that in no circumstances at all the arrow would get any close to her face or body. But as he was ready to release the string, his memory started an inconvenient game of murmurs. A malicious voice, cold and vile, whispered into his ears from inside of his head: *The ones that you hold most dearly... will have their blood spilled by your own hands.*

That was surely what the Devil wanted, then. That was his game, but Julian was not about to play it. While keeping his eyes on the bandit's, Julian sighed and relaxed his arms, slowly lowering the bow. He was *not* going to miss the shot and slay Louise with his own arrow. The devil would not make him commit this error.

And surely the devil must have known what to do, for the bandit opened a wide brown smile and Julian watched, bewildered and voiceless, when the knife was pressed in and pulled to the side, pouring a red wet curtain over the whiteness of Louise's fragile body.

Julian could only howl in horror.

The bandit took flight into the woods, but he was met with the heavy blade of a francesca, coming straight into his face. As Bernardo hacked the young bandit to death, Julian still screamed and screamed, for Louise was slowly rolling down on the forest ground, coated with a cake of blood and rotting leaves, stopping by the edge of the chasm. One very white arm hung lifeless above the ignoring creek that kept rumbling at the bottom.

Julian did not even notice the herbal stench that the forest exhaled.

Nothing else mattered to him.

The Sacrifice

Maledictus vir coram Domino qui suscitaverit et aedificaverit civitatem Hiericho in primogenito suo fundamenta illius iaciat et in novissimo liberorum ponat portas eius fuit ergo Dominus cum Iosue et nomen eius in omni terra vulgatum est

(Cursed be the man before the Lord, that rises up and builds this city, Jericho; with the loss of his first-born shall he lay its foundation, and with the loss of his youngest son shall he set up its gates. So the Lord was with Joshua; and his fame was throughout the entire land.) Book of Joshua, 6: 26-27

A voice was uttering a language that he could not distinguish the meaning. These were clear, well-articulated, but unknown words that followed each other into long sentences that made no sense at all. And other voices spoke too. All jabbering at the same time, very energetic and loud. Surely an argument was going on, but it soon faded again, blending into the buzz that tolled on his eardrums, squashing Immanuel's head against the dirt and rocks.

Slowly wrestling the hammering pain that confused his senses, Immanuel realised his legs could not move. He opened his eyes, but nothing more than lose earth covered them. On trying to wipe it off, another discovery: his hands were also tied. That would be it. Immanuel Ben-Malachi knew this would be the inglorious end of his journey out of Bukhara and pretty much into this life. This was an unexpected and horrendous fashion to be thrown upon the gates of death.

He waited until there were enough tears under his tightly-shut eyelids to wash some of those stinging grains off. It was not of much help. His eyes opened for less than a second, before a new cascade of soil filled them with agonising dirt. Only one thing Immanuel distinguished clearly: he was stuck, deep in the bottom of a hole and the voices were coming from people above, outside, on the surface.

'Oh, look at him...the *Greek* medicine man is awaking from sweet slumber.' Béla said looking down into the hole. 'It's probably better if this valuable medicine man sees what his destiny has reserved for him, after such a valorous deed.'

'Béla,' said one of the other two men, 'I must insist, this is not a good idea after all. Let's just bleed a chicken, as we always do.' They stood with the táltos around the hole where they had thrown the tiny medicine man in. One of the four holes already dug for the church foundations on the cleared top of the hill just east of Ferenc's village. No one else was around.

The mason continued 'Our people have not practiced these sacrifices during our generation and I doubt that our parents have, or even you, Béla.'

On hearing that disbelieving remark, feeling as powerful as he had never felt before, Béla swung around and looked at the man with an expression of bewilderment.

The man continued, in spite of Béla's hostile face. 'Ferenc will see it as no more than an abomination, no matter how noble the ulterior motive may be. He would surely have us all pay dearly for this insolence.'

Béla asked imperiously 'You call yourself a warrior? Do any of you understand the significance of this moment? We have the only hill in this region, doubtless the home of a spirit, a *lidérc*. Now as the Duke Istvan orders every village to have a Christian temple, Ferenc wants to build ours on it. Not a house or a shed for livestock, as a simple chicken or a salamander would probably suffice. How many times haven't we bled a chicken under the foundations of a new house? Haven't we always appeased the needs of the local spirits?' Both men nodded with acknowledgement. Bela continued 'But no! This is not sufficient. Now Ferenc wants a church! A full temple to a different God. Nothing less than insult and indignation are certain to come our way. And so will be the eternal spells of bad luck. The almost-death of Borbála is probably a good demonstration of the upset mood of the lidérc. How can we expect the owner of this hill to accept such affront if we do not offer it a little sample of our personal pain? In exchange for a temple, we must be hard and generous. Nobody could be more valorous than this medicine man that has valiantly saved the life of our dear Borbála. Ferenc will finally see how seriously I take the construction of his temple, and with the utmost respect. We embrace the new religion, yes, but that does not change how our world works, and much less how the spirits reason. They will be pleased with this offer. Yes, sometimes we must do a bad thing to achieve good results.'

The masons had their mouths hanging open.

'Hey, you above there! Get me out of here!' Immanuel shouted.

The táltos spun his head and looked down to the tied man inside the hole. 'Now the Greek is yelling something' he said with annoyance. 'What is it? Can any of you two understand?'

Both men shook their heads, now turning livid with panic. 'I'm telling you, Béla. We should *not* kill this man!' one of them said with trembling voice.

'Nonsense!' the old shaman said. 'All we need is to roll down a large rock ...there is one! You two, please help me carry that rock to this edge here. We will drop it on his head and it will be all over in the blink of an eye.'

One of the men turned around and ran away, down the hill, straight towards the village. Béla froze with rage for a second, finally exploding into a roar of insults. Words of rage that made the other mason moan with fear, running away after the first.

'Cowards!' Béla spat.

Helpless, he walked to the solitary large rock he had spotted and tried to the limits of his strength to roll it. It was a rather flat boulder and Béla struggled hard to lift one side. Maybe he could topple it and repeat the procedure, all the way to the hole. The weight would squash the medicine man immediately. With all the strength of his arms, Béla was able to detach the stone from the soil, and stretching his legs up with agonising pain on the joints, he lifted the disc and released it on its other side with a heavy thud.

The thump was obviously heard by Immanuel, whi started yelling. 'Béla?' he cried. 'Are you there? Please let me out of here! There must have been a misunderstanding!'

The táltos ran back to the hole and sputtered on the tied man. '*Fucking Greek!* Shut your loud mouth and just wait for death.' He dragged his feet across the ground and spilled more earth on Immanuel's face. As his victim growled with agony, Béla continued 'If I had the heart I would have you interred bit by bit, with no more than handfuls of sand. I do hate you for your success over my failure, for your reward over my punishment but I am just not that kind of person. The lidérc of this hill will savour the value of your blood and the pains I will have to go through to drag that boulder to your head.'

Immanuel heard it all, but did not understand a word. He tried to open his eyes again. Béla was no longer seen around the edge looking down on him. The Bukhari stayed still to listen for voices. A distant shriek of a bird of prey was heard. Then, Immanuel's heart chilled, for the strange thump was felt again.

And again, and again, and again, and again.

Immanuel shouted with all his lungs as the sequential thumping continued 'Béla, please do not be an imbecile. I need your help. I want your knowledge. I am here to help you! Do not do whatever you are planning to do with me, please!'

Finally, at the last thump, which felt and sounded as close as above his head, some more soil fell on Immanuel's face. Looking up, he distinguished the side of what looked like an enormous boulder at the edge of the hole. It pulsated with the táltos's exhausted panting. Immanuel's eyes were now clean, with tears of fear and sadness. Such a long journey was ending on a very stupid and undignified manner, knotted with ropes inside a hole, to be squashed like a melon under an ordinary stone. There was obviously nobody to help, except maybe a superior force. But Immanuel's God would not help him from that fate, he was sure. He knew quite well the cruel nature of his God. So he tried to appeal, inside his heart, to the God of the Christians. That frail crucified man that, according to Procopius, would be always there for him.

Béla gathered his last remaining forces to lift the rock for one last time. His dried, broken face was washed in sweat from the rolling of the boulder for all that distance. He contracted his muscles with pain but also with a smile, for this would be the end of it. The boulder felt as heavy as ever. As he brought it to a vertical position, something caught up on the side of his view, distracting his attention.

And he dropped the stone.

Ferenc made sure nobody could see him going inside his chamber. Borbála was sleeping outside, on the couple's room, tended by an elderly village woman. Two wet-nurses alternated with the voracious baby Istvan. The chieftain looked outside through the slit on the leather that covered the window. All was calm now. The Greek tradesman had gone back to the Bulgar camp. In mid-afternoon, the yard in the centre of the village was practically deserted, except for a few children that played, sitting on the mud. Only the horse that had brought Immanuel remained tied to the trough, swinging its tail to drive away the late summer flies that pestered it.

The chieftain shut the leather curtain tight and lit a candle. He placed it in front of a rusty cross, knelt down on the richly decorated, but worn carpet and made a prayer. After thanking the Lord Jesus Christ for interceding through the medicine man, he stood up and withdrew the carpet. Bringing the candle closer, he used his hands to break through some moist, polished soil, removing a thick layer and exposing some flat stones. He carefully lifted the slabs and placed them on the side. A flat surface appeared on the flickering light. Ferenc released the corners from soil and lifted a thick wooden board, revealing an opened box buried in his floor. He brought the candle nearer to the box and suddenly his face was bathed in light, for it was multiplied by the reflections on gold.

Ferenc was a hard ruler, but never ruthless. He inspired loyalty, with no need to demand it. He enjoyed life such as it was, as a farmer, hunter and trader. But mostly, he savoured every bit of the land he lived upon. Whether riding a fiery horse through the winter woods or dipping himself with Borbála into pools of naturally steaming waters spiced with invigorating salts and herbal concoctions prepared by Béla, or hunting wolves and stags with his short bow, he envisioned nothing less than a pleasant age ahead of him, teaching his Istvan about himself and the old tales of his ancestors, while Borbála waited in their warm bed, fresh and magically scented with powers that could take him through the most pleasant journeys a man could be blessed with. As the judge of all disputes upon his land, Ferenc exercised justice and was rightly acknowledged by the Osi people as being a man of remarkable generosity. Surely kind enough to always fulfil his promises of gifts, grants, arrangements and rewards.

Such as the promises made to Jesus Christ his Lord for the life of his beloved wife and to the miracle man who had been sent to save her, the Greek physician Immanuel Ben-Malachi.

The gold was old and it had only been touched a few times, one of them for a particularly magnificent ring for Borbála. But as a jewel of creation that could not be made more magnificent by gold or gems, Borbála kindly refused to use such a rich ornament, even for the chief's wife. Ferenc could have lived and died without the treasure, he thought, but there were always times of emergency. His father had probably never touched it either. The dishes and brooches and buckles and goblets, diadems and necklaces and bracelets were said to have been passed through more than twenty generations, from the times of the great Attila. Of diverse styles and probably different origins, there was nothing known of any item's history or even their real value. He just gave it little value when compared to life with Borbála and his son Istvan.

He chose the dagger.

'Where is Immanuel Malachi, the Greek medicine man?' Ferenc asked one of the villagers.

'That little man? We have not seen him for a while.'

After a brief search, it was clear Immanuel was not to be found around the village. But his horse was still there, so he could not have returned to the Bulgars' campsite. Ferenc followed the track through the marshes, all the way to Béla's house, hoping that Immanuel had not fallen and disappeared into a quagmire. By the untouched state of Béla's shed, no doubt the bitter and failed táltos was still around, but the chief failed to find him to ask if Immanuel had been there or walked by. Ferenc returned to the village, yelling out to his people to hurry and start a search party to find Immanuel.

As the villagers gathered around to hear his appeal, they were startled by a sweating horse charging into the central yard where they assembled, carrying a young man wearing the tonsure and the vests of a religieux. Hopping out of the horse before it stopped, he shouted in the Magyar language, for all to hear. 'We need the physician!'

Ferenc pushed through the crowd, irritated by the stranger's interruption but still cautious and respectful to the religieux habit. He made sure the dagger he had picked from the treasure was well hidden inside his pants. 'And what haste is such that makes you storm into our grounds without a respectful introduction?'

The monk gave a disdainful look at Ferenc. The helmet with the goat horns probably indicated Ferenc was a chieftain or the táltos. He inclined his head quickly in deference to Ferenc's imposing attitude and said with unhidden impatience 'I follow the caravan of Abbot Astricus, from Mons Sacer Pannoniae, envoy of the Duke Istvan, our king. We are on our way to Rome, to collect his crown. But the Abbot is gravely ill, and the trip could be ruined if we do not find a remedy for his ailment. The Bulgar physician is urgently needed'

Ferenc had stopped frozen. 'The duke? The abbot? The Bulgar physician? You mean the Greek? For the love of Jesus Christ our Saviour, we need the medicine man!'

The monk rolled his eyes. 'That is what I came for. The Bulgars have told me he has not returned to their camp yet. And they do not want to raise camp without the physician in the caravan. I was told by a fat Greek that I would find him still around here.'

'He disappeared!' Ferenc squeaked. 'I was asking my folk to start searching, but I am afraid he could have drowned into a quagmire on this side of the village, towards the house of our táltos.'

'A táltos?' the monk's face lightened, 'then maybe that will do. The abbot refuses to be tended by our own physicians.'

'Our táltos? Oh, forget it. He is useless.'

A murmur of the crowd broke the conversation. The mob opened to let a third man enter, drenched in sweat, and panting his lungs out. The exhausted mason stood in front of Ferenc. 'It's Béla,' he said with difficulty. 'He is on the hill with the medicine man, the Greek.'

Ferenc's eyes inflated like plums. 'What the f —', but the mason interrupted already with the answer.

'I think the táltos wants to honour the construction of our church with a sacrifice of the medicine man.'

With a long, painful growl, Ferenc charged against the crowd, pushing all villagers away from his passage, leaped onto the religieux's horse and dashed out towards the hill. With the monk trailing behind, Ferenc arrived at gallop on the summit to indistinctly discern at a distance old Béla lifting a large stone on a vertical position, at the edge of a foundation hole.

When Ferenc roared for the táltos to stop, the old man dropped the stone.

Că vrem să glumim

Şi să te zidim

Nici că mai ridea

Ci mereu zicea:... Agiungă-ţi de şagă

Că nu-i bună, dragă, Zidul rău mă strînge

Trupuşoru-mi frînge, Copilaşu-mi plînge

Viaţa mi se stinge

(We want to play a joke, And wall you up. No longer did she laugh; But kept on saying:....Stop playing the joke. The bad wall presses me; It is breaking my body; It is making my child weep)

Ancient Romanian ballad - compiled by Leon Leviţchi

Many leagues to the east of the Ferenc's village, beyond the dark forests of the Carpathian mountains, some Magyar tribes had settled in a place rightly named Erdö-elve, which meant nothing else than *beyond the forest*. The Latin name for the region obeyed a literate translation for Erdö-elve: Transylvania.

Ballads tell us of the construction of the tall fortress of Deva, in Transylvania. The local master masons all agreed that, to ensure the protection and unsurpassablility of the fortress's walls that would tower above the village, a considerable sacrifice should be offered to the spirits of the hill. It was settled among them that the first of their wives that would come to bring the daily meal on the following morning would be walled within the foundations. Among all of the masons, only one respected the pact and did not forewarn his wife. When she showed up on the hill, he had to calm her, telling her it was only a joke. She found out too late it was for serious.

And on the hill at Ferenc's village, south of the great lake Zála, a foundation sacrifice was offered to the modest Christian hall planned for the site. The victim was squashed under a large flat stone. After Ferenc was satisfied with the offer, he ordered his masons to erect one of the poles on this firm base.

The Lioness

They had not seen each other for three weeks, since the family had split. With offspring already independent, something was changed: they had both lost interest on family, or even on their mutual company. And now, at the end of the day, after a hard day's work on gathering and feeding, they were among the hundreds of others who stood there, waiting for the late afternoon drink.

She took her drink next to him, not noticing his presence at all. Everybody just looked the same. It was as if they had never raised a family together. The memories were somehow lost among the priorities of survival. He was well aware of his surroundings. Aware of her, of the blue circles around her eyes, of her chestnut-coloured breast, just above the gleaning white of her belly. She looked just like him and everyone else. Nevertheless, he noticed something which brought back a strange memory: the way she communicated, her voice, the movement of her head, the black lines on her front. As the remembrance, the recognition, started to make sense, his senses were alerted by a commotion far away, where the signal for danger had been raised by a few hundred. As he prepared to flee, he saw the arrow head explode out of her breast and coming straight to break through his own. The life went out of him on the same second that his partner was also dead.

'*Lucky me*,' though Julian with a certain glee, thrilled that his arrow had pierced through two of those pigeon-like creatures, 'but, who's ever going to believe this was possible?' As he walked to the edge of the water whole, among the thousands of other birds that flew around on a deafening chorus of *ga-ga-ga*, he wondered if there was ever going to be anyone else who he could share these small things of life with. The role that family and friends played was needed, but the real ones were lost, maybe forever. Those had been very lonely days. Frightening days.

Julian yanked the birds out of the still good-to-use arrow, trying not to think of Louise in the forest.

This tragic reminiscence would make his stomach turn, and his state of heath could not afford another night of hunger. *Ga-ga-ga*, they continued, settling on the other side of the water whole. Two more arrows flew through the dusk, and Julian doubled his initial catch.

A well-fed and rested Julian returned to the pond at the break of dawn, garnering six more birds, before most of the flock disappeared from the clearing crimson landscape, probably off to some recently harvested field, where they'd be provided by spillage. As he came back to the main road, it had not been one hour when he heard noises, some considerable commotion around the hill slope. He carefully left the path and walked through the trees, approaching the clearance where the noise had come from.

A few dozen pilgrims, the usual road rabble, gathered around a provisional camp, which, by the look of the banners and men-at-arms, demonstrated high lineage. Among the voices that echoed up to the woods where he stood, Julian could hear an energetic shout, speaking a basic Latin, familiar to him, but on a strange southern accent. '*Cibum iam non habemus manducare! Intellexistis?*' said the deep male voice. 'We have no more food! Do you understand it?'

Julian looked at his string of dead pigeons. Those birds could certainly be too much for him before spoiling into rot, so why not to share with those people in need? As he descended through the path and came into view, men-at-arms quickly mounted and galloped towards him, which made him instantly regret his decision for sharing.

'Who are you, why do you bear weapons and what do you carry there?' said the first rider on a similar Latin, halting his horse just a couple of feet from Julian, raising a cloud of dust between them. The man had the same strange accent as the other voice he had heard. Although his request was firm, his face was clear of ill, making the words, to a certain extent, courteous. The dignity on his stare made Julian more at ease, inviting him to give the man an answer.

'I am…' And he paused. Julian had not yet thought of a name. He surely knew that *Julian of Mans* would not be appropriate, maybe denouncing his escape once again, taking him into a torment of mind. He had to prevent being sent back to his beloved family at all costs. For all those days since he had fled from the Angers, he hadn't had a need for identification, except for friends. Those were gone east, so now he lived with himself without a name. He desperately required one. 'I am…*Hubert of Liège*,' he elaborated on a badly rehearsed tone, as he presented the stringed birds on his grip 'my bow I use for hunting, and I came to offer these pigeons to your lordship'.

'Well… Hubert of Liège,' the same horseman said with a rather condescending smile. 'You have a different bulk from the throng that surrounds our camp. If you are indeed who you are, I must make myself known. I am Alberto Azzo, from Toscana. We are into a friendly land, and this is indeed a demonstration of this country's generosity. Your offer of these *calandrini* you caught arrives surely at a time of need. Come down to the camp with us, Hubert of Liège, and meet my family. We are on our way home.' He walked his horse next to Julian, through the other mounted men that observed them pass.

Approaching the cluster of tents, Julian saw the mob of pilgrims, who watched with curiosity the arrival of the stranger. They were peasants, monks, nuns, beggars, probably former hermits and anchorites, pregnant women carrying snotty-nosed children, a few idiots and a dwarf. Still, in face of their hopeless and apparently empty lives, they had a certain dignity and satisfaction on their expressions. The same tranquillity that Julian had read on Alberto Azzo's countenance.

The horsemen dismounted and accompanied Julian to a tent where a large mid-aged man came to greet them with forthright smile 'So, who do we have here this morning?' Julian immediately recognised the powerful voice he had heard at from the top of the hill.

'My father', started the horseman who had brought Julian to the camp, with a subtly raised eyebrow, 'this is …Hubert de Liège, who comes to offer some calandrini of his own kill to share with us.' Then, turning to Julian: 'Hubert of Liège, you may make your offer to my father, Lord Oberto II, Marchese of Toscana.'

The handsome man who faced Julian was tall but not too wide. His silver hair, beard and moustache were cut short and all his teeth seemed to be perfect as a horse's, except for a slight pink staining. The red woolen tunic looked as being of the highest value, but not fancy. But what mostly caught Julian's attention were his violet-coloured eyes, which seemed to reflect against the sunlight from any angle one would look at them.

'My lord,' bowed Julian elegantly 'I have already broken my fast this morning, but here are still six fat pigeons, which I offer as a token of friendship, for the sake of free passage.'

Lord Oberto looked fixedly at the birds for an instant, but turned his fascinated stare to Julian, which lowered his eyes, incapable to meet the explosion of light which emanated from Oberto's violet glare. 'Hubert of Liège, right? Free passage!' Lord Oberto reached Julian's chin with his finger and pulled it up, so that the youth stared at him in the eyes. 'Well, Hubert of Liège, I do find it a bit disturbing that someone will ask us for free passage, for we are the strangers, visitors in this land. We came through and we return in peace. We are the ones who have been granted free passage in this land. And so should you have been given, for surely you look as a young man from northern lands, and Liège, as it may be as you say, is not part of this county.' A dreadful silence surrounded them as Lord Oberto paused and turned around towards the tent, giving his back to Julian. Scores of people just gazed wordlessly. Even the children from the camp and the pilgrims, were watching the visitor. Suddenly Oberto turned again and almost hopped in front of Julian, with an inquisitive smile asking 'Is the old Rathier still holding the bishopric at Liège or has he gone to meet his creator?'

Julian sweated with embarrassment and fear. He could not elaborate anything to say. Oberto waited a while and finally sighed. He put his hand on Julian's shoulder and said 'come with me into the tent, my son…'

Although afraid and helpless, the grip on his shoulder was reassuring enough for Julian to keep himself together. He followed the lord into the tent. They sat down as the noise outside resurrected to the usual campground bustle. After taking a comforting goblet of wine, Julian listened as the Tuscan asked him very carefully 'Is there anything else you should be telling me?'

Again Julian lowered his gaze and sighed. He closed his eyes and said 'No...' And than, looking into Lord Oberto's eyes, he asserted with conviction 'Not yet!'

'Never mind,' the Lord Oberto said immediately, 'whenever you're ready, my son.' And he was about to leave when Julian suddenly asked.

'You do not trust me, my Lord?'

'Hubert of Liège,' said Oberto with a chuckle, 'I do not know if this is how you have always been called. This is just a name as... *Nobody of Arsehole* could be. Whatever your real name is, I think we understand each other. Well, at least I trust that there's trouble with you and indeed, you do not trust me yet. Where you came from, what you are doing here, where you go, that is your problem. I hope you can make it to your destiny. You seem to have a strong heart, for I can tell by the way you approached the camp, free of ill on your face. I am hoping that this earnestness goes all the way into your heart. And indeed, thank you for the birds. By the way, these are not pigeons and much least calandrini, for sure. They are sandgrouse.'

In this instant, Alberto Azzo burst into the tent 'My father, the birds have disappeared. I think Clarissa has slipped them into the hungry rabble again.'

'Oh, by the devil's balls, that rascal! I cannot believe she's given them even *that!*' cursed Oberto as he darted out of the tent, in a language that Julian could not quite understand, but still with a certain and very perceivable theatrical note to his exclamation.

'Sorry, it's...my sister,' Alberto explained with a crooked smile at Julian's surprised face, 'she has probably passed your birds to those people. People in need, she says.'

As they came outside, Julian was staggered to have found lord Oberto in the middle of a small gathering, arguing loudly with no one else but a child. Barefoot standing on a chest, the young woman wore a long simple tunic which was rather dirty, from grass and mud, dust and soot. The very young Clarissa stared impassibly at her father, as he scolded her with a forced fury. Her small lower lip firmly locked over its upper partner. The full jowls were as soiled as her dress, and a glorious long dark brown hair cascaded carelessly around her shoulders. Julian noticed that she was confirming with a serious defiance the questions lord Oberto was throwing at her. The father sent someone into the mob, probably trying to find what had been made of the birds. And as he continued to interrogate the not yet twelve years-old girl, Julian understood it all when Clarissa, still wearing the same serious determination on her face, suddenly turned to point her finger at Julian, making the whole group look, as she said 'He can do it!'

Julian never noticed that the father was holding his glee as he turned to face him. Oberto smiled as soon as Clarissa could not see his face any more. The Tuscan lord asked Julian: 'My son, are you a good hunter?'

But Julian was paralysed by the vision of Clarissa's eyes. The moment she turned to point at him, her face was unveiled from her long mane, revealing a pair of eyes that met his' and easily took the breath out of his lungs. Julian was not yet sixteen and had seen very little of the world around Mans, being as illustrated as an interested boy of good birth can be in the wonders of the world. As soon as his vision was pierced by Clarissa's eyes, which were as strikingly bright as her father's, but not violet, he was blinded by a rainbow green. In a few days he would be able to look closer and detect many more colours than she would ever accept, but right then, his mind was invaded by enormous animals which raced through the forest, beautiful creatures with those wild eyes. Enormous cats, with manes and stripes, tigers, lions and leopards, animals that looked into the eyes of prey to stun them, wolfs. Animals that were devouring his stomach and roaring with thunder, almost muffling Lord Oberto as he asked once again: 'Are you a good hunter, my son?'

Julian fell from his visions with a painful thump, as Clarissa impatiently crossed her arms, waiting for the answer to her father's enquiry. The whole group was watching Julian as he babbled, without turning to Lord Oberto, 'I am the best hunter that there's ever been in le M…' but a flash of light from Clarissa's glare cleared his thoughts and prevented him from revealing his hoax.

'The best in *Liège*, right?' asked Oberto with sarcasm, acknowledging the group 'and do you know where to find more of those sandgrouse?'

'I certainly do, my lord. Hundreds, by a waterhole, not more than an hour, walking back to the east.'

'Well, I do not have any fowlers in this party, but if you would have the time, Hubert, would you like to take some of my bowmen to this field of fodder?'

'I would heartily do it sir', he answered, without avoiding a glare at Clarissa, which to his disappointment was not looking at him anymore. She was nodding and smiling to her father, as if saying: 'See? I told you!'

Alberto designated two hunters to accompany Julian, a partial cry of *spaniels* he had acquired during his visit to the west and an extra horse for the boy. They came back three hours later, when the camp had been raised and the caravan was all set to head east. The quarry string had no more than two sandgrouse hanging from it.

'It is not the best time of the day yet.' Julian explained, as his eyes carefully scanned for Clarissa through the large dusty amalgamation of horses, carts and people. 'We…you should go back for dusk and dawn, as the sandgrouse must be swarming back at the pond'. To his disenchantment, the girl was nowhere to be found.

'Well, come with us then, Hubert of Liège,' suggested Lord Oberto, 'I am sure that your affairs out west can wait for another incursion into your alleged hunter's paradise. You would like to stay with us, wouldn't you, my son?'

And Julian couldn't find a reason not to.

They both kept at the rear of the troop, right behind the throng that followed the carts. Lord Oberto rode at Julian's side, carefully watching the crowd, to keep an eye on his daughter. Clarissa was gleaming, floating easily through the mob, talking to every single pilgrim, smiling to each miserable oblate, chattering with the mothers, carrying toddlers, soothing the pain and exhaustion of cripples and calling for the company to halt if there was a need from anyone in the walking group. She could become a nuisance, but Oberto seemed to take pleasure on the ease that his precious daughter found among those people and the authority she had on the entire group.

'Why do these people follow you?' Julian enquired.

'In reality, they do not follow us. They follow the way to Rome. Pilgrims which go to see the majesty of the seat of Saint Peter once in their life and, if they are lucky, they can get a peek at the holy aura of the bishop of Rome himself.' Oberto said it all without hiding a bit of his sarcasm. 'Oh, yes,' he said with a sigh 'if they only knew what I know about the Holy See and the families of Rome…' but he recovered the composure and continued 'nevertheless, what keeps them travelling with us is Clarissa, as you can see. This girl is a source of light for their dark existences. Her fairy ways, her sunny smile, her touch, makes the painful journey much lighter for their spirits and broken bodies. In addition, she keeps them well fed and keeps my hunters twice as busy.'

'Do you also go to Rome?' asked Julian, intrigued by Oberto's comments but without taking his eyes off the lord's daughter.

'No, no! There is nothing to be done in that horrible place,' dismissed Oberto. 'We stay in Luna, by the town of Luni, where I call home.'

'*Luna*? Moon?'

'Our home,' explained Oberto with a dreamy air. 'You should come with us to Luna. Quite modestly, it is the finest castle in all of Christendom. Luna! As white as the moon'

Julian accompanied Lord Oberto's stare to an imaginary point in the cold blue sky. It looked just like the horizon he would see while lying on the lawn outside the castle at Mans. On this very instant, an image of Viscountess Emma appeared in front of his vision, offering her open arms for a formidable hug. These home and family reminiscences invaded his soul, breaking his heart into dust, which escaped though his lips as an audible sob of desperation.

Lord Oberto pretended he did not notice the emotional outburst. Without really knowing the best fashion to react to this, he rode in silence next to the boy for another few minutes. His face was grave with frank concern for the boy, who was obviously suffering from wounds of a troubled soul. But the Tuscan lord's heart was light, for it had been told by his eyes that the boy who claimed to be Hubert of Liège, although protecting himself with a false name, was somehow dressed in virtue and most likely, for Oberto was never wrong about people he read, free from any ill intentions.

Finally, after a prolonged period of uncomfortable silence between the two riders, he patted Julian amicably on the shoulder, before taking of for the front of the cavalcade. Hardly did he know that loneliness would only make Julian's anguish heavier, squashing the boy much faster.

Among the walking crowd that silently dragged ahead of his horse, Julian saw the dark haired child turning around and taking a careful look at him. This was the first time, since he had been blown away by her beauty, that Clarissa actually acknowledged him at all. Julian waved at her, waiting for the natural response.

Clarissa did not react for a long time. She just kept walking, looking back at him with a serious expression, making him sweat generously before turning her head back to the front, but not without breaking into a shining smile at Julian.

Quite strangely, all he wished in that moment was to stay longer with that caravan.

At mid afternoon, Julian and the two archers had to leave the road for the water whole. He did it with difficulty and a strange longing, as the day dragged on and they waited for the sandgrouse to return. The archers spoke little of Provençal, but the youngest, Pietro di Filippo, a young man who was no more than two years older than Julian, excelled in other communication talents and entertained Julian for the whole journey. Julian was able to pick up some information on their dealings through those lands. Lord Oberto and his party had left on spring, been all the way to a place in Gallecia that they called *urbe Compostella*, a name which was becoming popular for the *civitas sancti* Jacobi. One would have assumed that this was a pilgrimage to visit the place of rest of Saint James the Great, but Julian could gather that the reason behind the visit to the sanctuary was for commercial dealings. The wife of Lord Oberto, Lady Railenda, had stayed at their castro in Tuscany, with an older daughter, Bertha, and a daughter in law, Adela, who nursed a young son from Alberto Azzo. The family apparently had several manors and castles throughout a vast piece of land. Julian could not help but see his family's viscountcy dwarfed by the tales of the archers.

They caught up with the pitched camp at evening, much further to the northeast, where the path turned to Tolouse. They arrived at an easy gallop, the spaniels tiredly panting at their rear. With his eyes discreetly scanning the camp, trying to find Clarissa, Julian smiled and sang along with his companions, bringing with them a total of at least three scores of fat sandgrouse. The archer Pietro, for his impressive total of twenty eight birds, was nicknamed the *calandrino*, for everyone still insisted were just ordinary larks, except the Lord Oberto and Julian. Pietro was flattered by the title, but he insisted his luck owed to Julian's generosity, which allowed him always to have the first shot.

'Congratulations, my son!' toasted Lord Oberto looking at Julian, as the roasted sandgrouse was being gulped down, washed with generous servings of wine. His eyes seemed to Julian that they could lighten the clearing as well as the fire that drew red waves on his jovial face. 'Listen you all! This is official: I have invited Hubert of Liège here, which has provided us with this delicious feast, to go along with us all the way to Luna.' That snatched a few oohs from the gathering, but he continued 'and do you know what? He's accepted!' They clapped and cheered, for Julian's frankness had already subtly conquered their hearts.

'Does it mean, my father', intervened Alberto Azzo with a grave and loud voice from the other side of the fire, carrying a stern look which froze Julian, but soon changing into a generous smile as he completed 'that you have already chosen a tamer to subdue our little lioness?'

As the crowd roared with laughter, Julian could feel his legs going numb, for all his blood had converged into his face. By the throbbing that he felt, even if he had been wearing a cowl, his blushing would have been shamelessly perceptible. At least to his minor embarrassment, Clarissa was nowhere to be found to hear those tasteless jokes, hopefully too busy with serving some sandgrouse to the pilgrims. But part of Julian also wished that those were not jokes.

And it was not over. The little crowd quieted down as Azzo continued 'What will the lady Railenda say to this? She, who's been studying a match for Clarissa since before the little lioness was out of her womb. Will Hubert of Liége prove his heritage to be allowed to conquer the little beast?'

An uncomfortable silence followed before lord Oberto thought it out: 'If not, than he can be Nobody of Arsehole and I still could not care less!' And that was again followed by another explosion of laughter.

Julian tried to smile, but he felt extremely out of place at the moment. He had probably made a big mistake on having felt himself quite comfortable among those foreigners. That was obviously not the best way to go. He considered turning around again to southwest, the opposite direction on next morning. He would politely express his gratitude and leave them. Then, among goblets being filled, jokes being sung and himself feeling more and more inadequate, the glowing face of Clarissa emerged in front of him, catching him by surprise.

'He called you Nobody of Arsehole' she said with a broken Provençal and a devilish smile on her lips, adorned by her delicate left eyebrow, raised much higher than the right one. The reflexes of flames danced on her face.

'Yes, I heard it!' said Julian without smiling back 'and that was not funny at all!'

'Don't you understand?' she said as the irony was washed out of her face, so mature sustaining the smile with compassion now. 'You should feel very special. That means he really likes you!'

But before Julian could ask Clarissa if she also approved him, she'd disappeared again through the camp night.

The Gift

One-hundred-years-old-Mariozza waited, sitting straight on her palliasse, wearing her grey hair elegantly bundled in a bright blue silk dimple. Her livid face was lightly whitened by chalk powder, which disguised some freckles. Cosmetics would never be found in the cloister, but Mariozza had this talent for ordering the unusual at a nunnery and getting it, for the sisters would do the unattainable to please their dearest company.

It had been two nights since the abbess came with the news of the pope knowing her whereabouts. No doubt they were coming for her. The long fight between the emperors and the Roman patricians was leaning towards the German boy who had inherited the empire. None of Mariozza's descendants were on the pontifical throne anymore, and neither were her sister Theodora's grandchildren. Now, Roman nobles and the high clergy where being courted by Crescentius Numentanus, the Marble Horse, the same whose head, eight years later, would be stuck on a pole, its empty eye sockets watching Rome from the city battlements. But at this day, the

Marble Horse did not know his great-aunt was still alive, hiding in a forsaken nunnery on a dry hill just south of Lucca. Mariozza had been forgotten by time, her story had been erased or twisted by hatred, but she was kept alive by the care of friends and admirers she gathered during her exile, and stayed unexplainably young by the extraordinary power she carried inside.

Regrettably, Crescentius' enemy had come to learn she was still alive and influential, even if only within the silent walls of the cloister. To keep Mariozza quiet, Pope John XV, who had been hand-picked by the emperor, was sending for a committee to meet her - to make sure she was definitely dead, as she should have been generations ago.

As quick footsteps approached, the light that came from the windowed corridor was blocked by a sister that hurried in through and bowed to Mariozza's majesty. 'He's here. He's coming.'

She disappeared and, a moment later, the small figure of a boy appeared at the door. He wore a richly embroidered purple cape fastened on the shoulder by a silver brooch. The cape was so long that it dragged on the floor, completely hiding the boy's legs.

'Come in,' Mariozza suggested, even though she did not fancy seeing that boy. He had nothing to do with the wish she had confided to the abbess. 'Please come in, do not be afraid!'

'Why should I be afraid of an old hag?' said the boy with a stiff upper lip, stepping carefully inside her room. Following him, a large man-at-arms stood by the door, in a shiny breastplate and a magnificent helmet.

'Because I am old! And that is bad enough!' Mariozza cut with dryness. 'I am so much more ancient than all of those dry crooked trees you see outside. I am older than this religious house, where the walls have lived their life and are about to lay down to rest. Older than your mother Empress Theophano, and older than your grandmother Adelaide of Burgundy. Yes,' she said triumphantly, with violet beams from her eyes, 'I saw that woman that many praise for her charitable life when she was still a tiny defenceless baby. That was just before my tragic third wedding, when my churlish son had me imprisoned. Then I was forever sent away from the life I had fought with my skin to gain. May the devil be still biting at his soul.'

'You indeed sound like an old woman,' smiled Otto the little emperor, 'but you do not look like a hundred years old. Actually I wouldn't say you are older than my grandmother, the Empress Adelaide.'

'I will take that as a compliment, you charming man,' she said with a forced smile, which still had an enchanting power over any audience. 'But I am indeed a lot older. I'm aged enough to be her grandmother. By the way, has she come down with you?'

'No...' Otto answered with a visible disappointment. 'It is my mother who is bringing me to Rome, and she does not want me to be around with Empress Adelaide. Mother says she is a mad old grouse.'

'Of course! Your mother Empress Theophano is caring for you. And why has she not accompanied you to this religious house?'

'She stayed in Lucca. She didn't bother to come out of our way just to see an old whore like you,' said Otto, with a daring lip.

Mariozza's face did not change or move a muscle which, to a perceptive speaker, would have betrayed her control. For a moment, she regretted not having reacted, but thinking better, she must have been overestimating the acuity of that ten year-old little shit. She gave a quick look to the menacing figure of the guard at the door and continued to the emperor: 'And why have *you* come to see me?'

'I just wanted to see this harlot that they told me about last night. I had never heard of you before. I was told about your lewd habits and indecent life, of laying down with popes, breeding your caste and your mother's into more antipopes, sons, grandsons, nephews, all the scum that fills Rome with corruption. I was on my way to Rome when they told me you were alive, and near. So just wanted to see you before you die.'

'Then, are you going to have me killed?' Mariozza asked, making an effort not to smile, or it could seem to the boy as a challenge.

'I could well have my men put you through their swords, but this is a lower service, for the men of Rome. They should be arriving at any time.' Otto was about to turn around when he raised a finger. 'And one more question,' he said, 'how come you are still alive, and free?'

Mariozza smiled, this time with a glitter in her eyes 'It's never late to make friends. Mine was a king. His name was Cicero. King Cicero let me live and walk out of the dungeons.'

'Cicero? I never heard of this king...' and he turned away, leaving Mariozza sitting at her cell in the back of the cloister of San Giovanni Battista, both visitor and host un-amused.

'Well, bring me the abbess,' said Mariozza after a few minutes of silence, as she walked with difficulty outside. 'The child I wanted to see was definitely *not* this little cunt.'

The most powerful woman in her age was about to die.

And she was well aware that Death was coming.

Late, indecently late, but still in time, Death would snatch her swiftly from an existence that had been forgotten by those who knew of her, what she had done and what was left after her.

Mariozza sat up on her deathbed. She held her lips tightly shut, as if she could see her soul slowly escaping through the vapours of her breath.

She thought of the day when the corpse of Pope Formosus was condemned during that insane synod. When she envisioned grandiosity for herself. And she was right. She had been greater than any of the empresses through her lifetime. No other woman in Christianity had held such power as she had. There was Cleopatra, of Egypt with control over the emperors of Rome. But she had been Mariozza of Tusculum, Mariozza of Rome, the Great Mariozza. Senatrix et Patricia. Lover of popes and mother of many others, aunt of the houses of Tusculum and Nomenta.

Not poisoned by an aspis, nor dying in the full bloom of her age, Mariozza reviewed her life with apprehension, noting anxiously for the first time the vainness, the futility and the cruelty of it all. She wondered whether there would be still any time left ahead of her. A few hours, maybe, but she was ready to leave the extravagance of her passion behind, for another to use it in a more compassionate fashion.

'How come they did not bring their child?' Mariozza asked, making no effort to hide her annoyance.

The abbess rolled her eyes. 'Marozia, my dear,' she said, 'just be happy that the *marchese* and the *marchesa* did actually bother to come at your request. And maybe you will feel better when you see them.'

The Lord and Lady of Tuscany asked for the abbess's excuse and entered the room.

Mariozza's breathing accelerated, but she held herself firm. Only her eyes were not able to contain the flood of tears that ran down her face. The youth and power! The life that she had once held in her heart and that now vanished by the minute from her old body. It was the most radiant, if not beautiful couple she had ever seen. They were vigorous and mature, entering the precinct with an elegant respect, a noble humility, and making themselves at ease, a captivating carelessness that made Mariozza quiver with passion.

Having arrived from Lucca riding her own black horse as an amazon from war, in respect to a house of prayer and worship, the lady of Tuscany wrapped her wimple with light movements of her arms, carefully tucking her hair in. A magnificent mane of golden brown hair that insisted on cascading around a nice oval-shaped face with prominent full-cherry lips and a lightly snubbed reddened nose, giving the impression that she had been upset by the flowering birches during haying season. As the lady performed that natural motion to diffuse her femininity, so appropriate for a married woman of those times, she delicately turned the head to the side, looking at Mariozza with striking eyes that seemed to the centenary Roman woman to be the precious blue of the Ligurian Sea under a particularly sunny sky. Her skin was of the whitest marble, a truly polished daughter of the Apuane, with a shape and sheen that reminded Mariozza of the most delicate and intriguing sculptures that had survived in Rome from the glorious imperial times: Venuses, naiads, nymphs, nereids, dryads, muses and sirens, with their glorious curves and movements that drove men to wreck their ships, their hearts, their lives. At no more than twenty four years of age and having borne two children, the lady of Tuscany was a vibrant woman of Mariozza's like, and even more, for she was bloated again with a child. Wonderfully blushed and ballooned with fertility, a vibrant success of her partnership with her husband, the Marchese of Tuscany.

Mariozza could not manage to disguise a sob when the eyes of the marchese stared into hers. A glittery violet sunrise, contemplating the elegant farewell of a still shimmering violet sunset. A mutual and silent recognition of kinship on seeing each other's glimmering irises, as if contemplating their own reflections. Mariozza could distinguish the traces of her beloved Guido. The marchese had certainly a mixture of roman and Lombard blood. His equally oval face was framed by a well-formed beard, cut short as his hair was, a sign of independence and singularity, which only a nobleman of birth and heart would dare to do. If his hair was black or brown, Mariozza could not yet decide, but it was starting to show some silvery shines, which only added to the appeal or colours matching the well-tanned leather of his face. With a respectful bow, he smiled carefully, keeping his full lips under control, covering a magnificent grin of straight and gleaming teeth, not of the white Ligurian marble of his wife's skin, but more of a pinkish Egean stone, an exotic secret, a hidden trace of a man who enjoyed the gifts that nobility had provided for.

Mariozza swallowed her exultation and asked, 'Do you know who I am?'

A couple of shiny, plump, rose apples jumped on his cheeks as his lips once again held tight, keeping a smile under control. Sparks showered by his eyes were not concealing the laughter that danced on his heart. 'I know of Mariozza of Tusculum and who she was, my lady, but I would find it a true miracle if you are who you claim to be, for ageing does not halt for any good Christian that I have heard of and the dead do not come back to life, not since the Christ, one thousand years ago.'

'It is a miracle then,' said the abbess with wet eyes, as she stood watching.

Mariozza was still blown away by his charm. My blood! She wanted to scream out loud with pride. What a man I have bred! So much power, so much enchantment. Four generations and I am there, right in him, into his skin, into his heart! Her eyes were as flooded as the abbess's.

'You do seem to know your matters, marchese, for indeed, in the bloom of my age I have always been called Mariozza as you pronounced it. But generations passed by and I withstood its cycles. Time twists and changes the words as it twists our spines and changes our faces, so Marozia seems to be the name everyone calls me now, from that unfortunate *Tedesco* kid, the future emperor, to this fat old abbess here that endured my obnoxious presence in San Giovanni Battista during all these years.'

The abbess turned around and left the room, sobbing desperately.

The lady of Tuscany watched with a raised eyebrow. 'Death seems to be at your doorstep but you don't appear to review your minor sins. Did you notice you have just offended the abbess?'

Mariozza extended her hand to the marchesa. 'Come here, my child.'

The lady of Tuscany warmed her face into a hearty smile and stepped in to hold the old woman's feeble hand.

'I apologise if my manners with the abbess offend you,' Mariozza said, 'for we have grown careless of decorum as the years dragged our decaying carcasses through the lonely corridors of this monastery.' She opened a rare, frank smile to the Tuscan lady. 'Trust me, my child, that the reason for emotions has less to do with offense and more to do with love.'

The marchesa wrinkled her chin in a sympathetic smile and extended the other hand to hold Mariozza's with both of hers.

Mariozza continued. 'Thank you so much for having attended this old crone's last wish. My call to you must have sounded preposterous,' and she chuckled on seeing the marchese nod. 'However, if you trust me that I am indeed your great-grandmother, marchese, do allow me to do one decent thing. One decent thing that I feel I can still do in these last moments of my very long life.'

'We have nothing to object, as we are nobody to have words over you,' the marchese said.

'Even if that was true,' Mariozza said with an effort, for she felt weaker by the minute, 'you still have your ears and your presence to grant me if you well wish. I would be deeply honoured if I had them.'

The marchese swallowed and said, 'They are yours. What do you want to tell us?'

Mariozza sobbed but managed to say, 'I just want to give my blessing to the daughter that your wife carries here.' And she caressed the bloated belly of the marchesa.

'*Daughter?*' the Tuscan couple asked in unison, as the marchesa retracted her hands in an involuntary reflex. 'How do you know we'll have a girl?'

'I don't know how I know it!' Mariozza moaned with desperation, her hand extended to try to touch the marchesa, tears pouring down her still incredibly handsome face. '*I just seem to know it!*'

That evening, in the independent Lombard village of Santa Maria Lei Giudice, a few hours after the Lord and Lady of Tuscany left the San Giovanni Battista monastery to reach Lucca for the night, a troop of riders arrived in haste and banged the doorknockers of the same monastery.

Pope John XV had sent those soldiers by strong suggestion of the young Otto III and his mother Theophano. There were cries of horror as the door was opened and they stormed into the building.

Old Mariozza knew when to die. Her soul calmly watched from a distance as the soldier looked at her body on the bed and, oblivious to its lifeless state, pressed a pillow around her face. A peaceful face that held an eternal smile of fulfilment.

The First Bear

As they entered Toulouse through the southern gate, Alberto Azzo came to discreetly ask whether Julian would accept the invitation to join the family at the hospitality of Comte Guillaume Taillefer or if he would rather stay with the horsemen and men-at-arms at the barracks. Julian bit his lip at the thought of missing an opportunity to stay not only in decent lodgings, but especially with a smaller group, where Clarissa would invariably go. Unfortunately, the risk would be too much if he was again exposed to the any lord, even if this had been far from the Maine. Indeed he was in any manner aching to have a chance to be with that enchanting child, over and over, but the decision to never be out in the open again made the young nobleman decide for the barracks. Alberto Azzo accepted Julian's choice without comments.

But Lord Oberto turned his horse around and joined Julian on his pace. 'Hubert, my son. My family and I are guests of Comte Guillaume Taillefer. If you are really who you say you are, you should be welcome to accept the Count's generosity, but yet you again choose to hide behind your lame story. Now listen here: I do not want to do anything which goes against the will of the man who holds the highest power in this land.' He looked gravely at Julian 'So you must promise me, Hubert, that you are not sought after by this man'.

'My Lord,' Julian said with a nod of his head, 'this man does not know me or why I am here. My tale is hidden in my heart and no one else should unveil it. My story is not from this land, and I can swear to God that no connection it has to this place. Go and enjoy your lodgings, for I am not deceiving you or putting you into shame in the eyes of …' and he hesitated a little, before finally gasping 'in the eyes of God!'

Before reaching the palace, they stopped by an inconspicuous but well-guarded and solid house. The men quick and expediently unloaded many chests from the carts and, after the last casket had been brought in, only Oberto and Alberto Azzo entered the house, for its proprietor was a banker. Raymonde Burle descended from an old Jewish family of bankers that had come from Englaland. There were Burles into banking activities throughout Spain, Portugal, France Italy and Flandres. Even though the family had supposedly converted into Christianity, the inevitable grudgers around a prosperous activity would grow resentful and have no hesitation on spreading rumours that conversion was only for the outside appearances, for deep inside they still maintained their wicked hearts very un-Christian.

Outside the bank, the load of the caravan was being re-arranged to leave another two empty carts to the banker. The pilgrims had to continue on their way, to cross the bridge in order to reach the eastern gates. Upon bidding farewell to Clarissa, many wept, as others howled that they would not leave her company. She held back tears and hugged every single one, encouraging them to accomplish so gracious a mission on their own.

Two horses had already been freed from the empty carts, and the least resolute of the pilgrims had disappeared from view when Julian saw a lonely Clarissa walking down the tidy lane to a thick stone wall that edged the river. She sat there, carelessly tossing pebbles at the water. Julian approached, picked a stone and threw it further into the river. Clarissa turned to stare at him with such an inscrutable expression and the usual ferociousness in her eyes that Julian could hardly guess if she was thanking him for the company or hating him for that intromission in her brief retirement.

'Is there any way I can help?' babbled Julian?

Clarissa drew a faint condescending smile with her small lips and raised one eyebrow. 'How can you help me then?'

'You tell me how…' suggested Julian, as he leaned his elbow on the wall, next to where she sat.

Clarissa never said anything. She just kept looking into his eyes, silent and deep, for a long time, something that Julian had never experienced before. He felt desperately tempted to look away, so powerful were those beams, but at the same time it was the one of the most soothing sensations he had ever felt. There it was, just over two weeks before this day, it had been the devil that looked into his soul with dead yellow eyes. Now his heart burned by being stared into through his own eyes. It opened his body, heart and soul to that glittering rainbow gaze that could only come from heaven.

For many times Julian tried to say something. He wanted to tell Clarissa how powerful a creature she already was. Without looking away, more than once he chose the words, opened his mouth, but nothing came out of it. No intelligible sound, but gasps and sighs. Meanwhile, she watched all these attempts without taking her eyes from his. Julian felt as if no ground was sustaining his feet. The wall under his elbow was also inexistent. The only thing that touched him is his dreamy floatation was the realisation of the inadequacy for being infatuated for an eleven year-old girl. *I must tell her*, he decided, but again, his lips would contort to say something but the air had been out of his lungs for minutes already. Besides, why break such a magic moment with words? The silence felt indeed uncomfortable, but the eye contact was the best feeling he had ever had, raiding like an angelic horde through his body. Clarissa did not hide that she noticed his struggle, and raised one eyebrow, pressing her lips to hold her laughter in.

It was on this moment that the spell was broken by the shouts of the troop, which were being joined by Clarissa's brother and father. With all his strength, Julian furiously hurled another pebble at the water, as the girl was already trotting back to the carts.

At early evening, as he huddled around the fire with the riders at the Comte's palace barracks, Julian was surprised by the apparition of Clarissa, bringing in a tray of salted meats and mushrooms. He was the first one on his feet.

'That is so sweet of you, Lady Clarissa. You actually thought of me?' asked him.

'Of course I had you in my thoughts', said Clarissa with a firm smile, 'I had all of you in my thoughts!'

And Julian blushed with shame for not containing his disappointment, while all the riders shared that special treat from the child lady of Luna.

After days of a long and slow ride east, Julian came to learn of the dealings of Lord Oberto in Gallecia. Clarissa told him that the banker in Toulouse had a relative in Lucca, in Tuscany, where the riches from lord Oberto could be safely withdrawn when they finally would have arrived. The travel was not done on ships due to the infestation of the Ligurian Sea with Saracen pirates from the Slingers' Isles. However, transporting gold through land could hardly be a better bargain. Banks were a comfortable, safe and rather cheap option for movement of riches. The family had ridden westwards together, carrying relics of saints and martyrs, a light and precious cargo, which only the studied minds would be able to identify, and usually of no value for forest thieves. The king Alphonse V, of Leon, an enthusiast of relics who was engaged into war against the Muslim Al-Andaluz caliphates, utilising those powerful objects to lift the moral and inject thicker blood and courage into his Christian armies. He paid generously for the genuine relics that lord Oberto brought form Tuscan lands and Rome.

'Genuine?' Julian asked impressed. 'Where does he obtain them?'

'Well, I am not really sure,' Clarissa answered with lips pursed. 'He gets them from Rome and other corners. Perhaps some are home-made. I personally think they are all fake. But then, he is not taking money from the poor, but from princes and kings. And I do trust that the fashion on which the revenues are spent by my father are far more honourable than if the money stayed with the greedy relic hunters.'

'And what makes you think your father uses the money on a more decent manner?' Julian asked rather carelessly.

'Well,' Clarissa smiled raising one eyebrow, her eyes blindingly shining with rainbow colours 'I have a fairly good idea of how much I can influence that old badger!'

They rode together more often now. Clarissa spent more time with him, making the journey sunnier for his soul. She would ask about his home, his family, and there was nothing he could hide from her. She soon found out about his real identity, his real name and lineage. In a few days she knew by heart all his siblings, relatives and friends. Clarissa's presence had the magic power to bring anything out of Julian. They'd sit away from the rest of the group for meal breaks, or for the fire. Talking, laughing, feeling happy. They would rest at each other's eye stare, a sensation that brought Julian out of a cruel world, soothing him and rocking him into a dreamland, compensating for the lack of warmth for being away from the fire, the explosion of colours from her eyes involving him, and inexplicably breaking and unlocking all secrets he tried to hide. Simply enough, he started to realise that Clarissa dominated the keys to his heart.

And desperately enough he had not even a clue about where the keys for hers could be.

She did tell him about herself too. Clarissa talked as if she had lived an entire full life. Her friends, every mischievousness they had done within the walls of Luna, or the visits to Pisa or Lucca. Their houses and their parents. Their names and their favourite games, so many things that Julian ached to have been part of. Clarissa knew exactly if she had told Julian about something already, not tolerating that he would have forgotten about it, or mixed this friend that could suck wine from his nostril with the other that could throw her up like a feather in the air. But no matter how special that relationship continued to develop at each day of the journey, how many jokes he had carefully dared to play at Clarissa, how many games and tricks he taught her, or how many laughs they shared, there was something that made Julian feel that Clarissa did not consider him also as part of his friends.

The large group of travellers took the path east, sometimes with a glimpse of the bright sea reflexes by their right shoulders, other times deep into the stony valleys. Lord Oberto ordered a party to the chalk hills, by the cave mouths where hermits produced a precious milk curd. Julian was not surprised to feel reluctant to leave the Clarissa's company behind, but he made the effort to accompany the men. They found the caves abandoned. Not destroyed, or devastated by raiders, but empty of life. The monks had probably left on their final wanders due to the rumours of the Millennium and the Beast. Some of the said curd however was still there, and the men took license to carry it all. Julian was not too impressed with the tart, salty flavour, probably from a blue substance that had been inserted inside the cheese, but he was glad to be back with the main party and tell about his short trip to Clarissa, who adored the blue treat from the caves. Seeing Clarissa enjoying a meal side by side with the men made him wonder if all Lombard women had equally no qualms about the messy habit of eating in male presence. It should be inelegant, as he had been brought up to believe, and he tried to convince himself. But he had to admit that her gracious handling of cheesy bits, much better than a boy would have done it, was just awfully cute.

When they were about to reach the busy port of Zena, called Genova by Oberto and his group, Julian had already made a decision. He verbalised to Clarissa his incontrollable infatuation.

Clarissa was speechless for a while, keeping her mysterious eye stare still strong, not uttering a word. Finally she said 'Julian, I am only eleven,' and waited for a symbolical moment to allow it to sink in. 'Maybe we should give some balance to this friendship, then. Tomorrow we go to the bishop's house for three nights, I think. You stay with the troops in the barracks, right? That will give you some rest from me. Better for you.'

'You want distance from me?' asked a nearly panicking Julian.

'Did I say that?' said Clarissa enigmatically.

'So you would prefer that we stayed together, right?' Julian asked, trying to hold her hands.

She withdrew them quickly, avoiding the touch, and finalised 'Perhaps you don't notice it, but it is all to protect you'.

'From whom? From you?'

'From yourself, of course!' and she stood up to join the others at the fire, the way she seemed to like ending conversations with Julian.

'Let me tell you about protecting someone from myself! Clarissa, come here for a while! Clarissa, please!' Julian bellowed, but she had already disappeared among the carts, horses and the crowd.

On his third day in the enormous port city of Zena, without catching even a glimpse of the brown-haired heiress of Luna, Julian finally found a good reason to get Clarissa from the bishop's house for a stroll down the city. She came to the door accompanied by Lord Oberto, who delivered his daughter with a warm smile but many advices and warnings for the two youngsters, to watch for cutpurses and common port ruffians. Clarissa was looking radiant, with a washed face and the hair bundled into a charming knot, giving her a more grown up appearance.

'Where are we going, Julian? I mean, Hubert,' Clarissa asked, as the two walked from the gate. 'I thought I had told you that we should be away from each other for these days, so we could be…'

'The hell with that,' interrupted Julian. 'I wanted to see you badly, especially after last night, when I went down to the market at the harbour. I saw something that I thought I really wanted to share with you. That is where we're going, Clarissa.'

'What is in there?' she asked, already showing some excitement.

'A bear, Clarissa! A live bear. Brown and big. Hairy and mighty as I always heard bears would be!'

Clarissa smiled shyly and did not say anything. But the brightness of her eyes could not hide the moment of satisfaction. Unfortunately it only lasted until the instant they saw the chained beast.

While Julian marvelled at a creature of tales he had only heard about, Clarissa pitied the sad beast, seated with exhaustion on a corner like a discarded puppet. Its hair was matted and dirty, with naked patches revealing scars and playgrounds for scabies. An old rope tightly winded around its face as a muzzle, with the tongue partially bitten out of its lips, giving the bear an idiotic appearance. The cloudy brown eyes looked into Clarissa as she approached, but the beast did not move. A constant flow of tears met with dust on the sides of its eyes, attracting the flies that hungrily surrounded it. The bear breathed with difficulty, with its bony shoulders leaving a greasy mark on the wall as they slowly moved up and down. The owner slept on its side unaware of the children who watched his artist.

'Let's leave, Julian!' urged Clarissa.

'You don't like it?' Julian asked dismayed. 'You should see it dancing.'

'This is the most degrading display of cruelty I have ever seen, and truly one of my greatest disappointments.' She continued hurrying her pace, out of the market. 'Yes, thank you for trying, but I hated it. I still think bears are noble beasts, but I just cannot put up with the idea of a creature so humiliated as that one. Sorry!'

She went back inside the bishop's house as quickly as they had reached it, leaving Julian alone on the windy morning.

For the next day, already riding out of Zena, they avoided each other constantly. Julian thinking that she did not want to see him, and Clarissa thinking that because Julian was dodging her, she should stay away. Hardly had she known that this was what could break him into smaller pieces.

Late in the afternoon, as they rode through a vast wooded area, after passing by a small but raucous crowd of pilgrims headed to Rome, Clarissa inexplicably came back to ride on his side, at the very rear of the company. She was tender as Julian liked, her smile lightening the tunnel which cut through the trees.

'You were avoiding me these days' started Julian.

Clarissa seemed surprised 'Oh, you actually want to talk about it? I thought it was you who were shunning me.'

'Of course not!' Julian said. 'I'd never want to keep away from you.'

'Maybe you should consider it. Keep in mind that we're getting closer to Luna. To my home and my mother. To my future.' Clarissa explained with a hurt expression. 'Maybe we should be protecting you from further disappointments.'

'You know nothing about protecting me, Clarissa.' Julian intervened, with a bitter taste on his mouth.

'Excuse me then' she snatched with a disgusted expression, 'In this case, I have nothing to talk to you.' And she kicked on her mount to catch up with the rest of the troop, already coming out of the thicket.

Julian realised his stupidity and inadequacy. He saw clearly the horizon ahead, where he'd be eternally hurt by watching Clarissa growing, being courted, being engaged and marrying someone else. He would see her moving away with a loving husband who'd care for her like the angel she was, or maybe being dragged out by an oppressor fiancé who would treat her as a wench and just use her womb to make children. Any which way, it seemed it would be worse than death for him. Much better it would be to go away. To leave them right now. To never get to Luna.

'Clarissa, Clarissa, wait!' he shouted. He caught up with her and handed her the reigns. 'Here, take it. The horse belongs to your household. I am leaving now.' He unhorsed and held her hand, as she silently watched him with liquid rainbow eyes. 'I go now, Clarissa. I do not want to say farewell to your father and brother, it would be almost as painful as not having said goodbye to mine as I did. Neither a word I want with the men from Luna, who treated me as a brother. Please just tell them when I'm long gone. I do not want too many words to you, who treated me as…well, I don't know what you make of me. You can deny that we had a special friendship to each other, full of tenderness and sympathy, but even if you believe it, that does not change the truth. Just keep it forever that I love you'.

And he ran back to the woods.

Clarissa thought of it as being no more than a fit of nerves. She held back her tears and struggled against looking back, riding slowly behind the caravan.

Julian was still running fast, seeing the trees enlarge ahead, entering deep into the shadows when a few steps ahead of him, a huge dark animal came from behind an oak and stood on its hind legs. As no more air came out of his lungs and his soul froze, he saw those dead yellow eyes he knew, as lanterns of fire in the pitch blackness. He tried to run, or to look back to Clarissa, but he was paralysed by horror. As he heard the voice of the ogre coming out through the beast's fangs, he was finally able to let a scream explode out of his lungs.

Clarissa turned around immediately. She had indeed expected some antics from Julian, to call up for attention, but that was no acting. That howl was filled with terror.

'Help!' she cried, and kicked into a gallop towards the woods.

The horse puffed hard as she approached Julian at a desperate speed, seeing him lying on the road ahead but, much worse, just behind him, a dark mass of fur, a conic-shaped mount of about three feet high, as a miniature volcano, erupted itself around the whole surface, with the flow disappearing under its base. Clarissa lost her voice as she too tried to scream, for the furry shape was a mount of rats that kept exploding from its top, squeaking wildly as they got closer and closer to Julian's body.

She jumped from the horse as it still made to reduce the gallop, rolling down the dust, stopping on the side of Julian. She held his face, warm still, which sent a wave of relief through her body, making her shiver with apprehension. The mass of rats was boiling, getting already close to his feet. With all the strength she could gather, Clarissa dragged Julian's soft body by the arms, trying to create some distance from the furry mound of black rodents, their naked tails entangled as furious worms in a cup, their eyes popping out of their faces as they screeched at her. As the other riders were still approaching, her father, her brother and the rest of the men, she realised they would be too late. A large black rat jumped out of the entangled mount and grabbed onto Julian's leg. Another jumped onto his foot, and another and another. Clarissa was roaring with fury as she let Julian's arms fall and kicked through the mount, spreading rats across several paces away, with their plump bodies making drumming sounds as they fell on the ground or hit the trees. She kept kicking though it, as the mount thinned into a few dozen animals that quickly scattered away. The swordsmen were fast to split open the rats which were eating though Julian's clothes. As the last creature was smitten, a strange herbal odour infested the area.

The dead silence of an ended battle was broken by human shouts and cries that emerged through the woods when a group of pilgrims appeared from the road down the forest, in an apparent state of frenzy. The leader, a bearded man with a wide-eyed bony face, carrying long and thin wooden cross conducted the way, chanting prayers and calling onto the angels to grant redemption to all sinners on earth. Others behind wept and dragged themselves on their knees digging their fingernails into the road and rubbing the soil and dust on their faces. Some other people danced around, simulating indecencies and spitting blasphemies.

Clarissa, Alberto Azzo, Oberto and his men helped to load the still unconscious Julian onto his saddle. When the crowd got closer, they heard: 'Oh you harlots, all of you daughters of Eve' the cowled man was crying with fury 'Jezabels born in filthy sin and grown under the shadow of Baal. Oh, you seeders of luxury, fornicators of Abbadon, repent from your grime and smut, for the Prince of Angels is about to come down and incinerate you all. The archangel will appear once again from the Gargano, dressed in all his majesty and glory, holding the shield with the cross that triumphed in Sipontum and the sword that expelled the progenitors from the Eden, leading a celestial army to burn all iniquity from the dirty face of this world.'

Clarissa interrupted him. 'Devils! You bastards. You brought in the rats, didn't you? How could you have done that to him? You people from hell!' and she started towards them with a blind fury, but Alberto Azzo was fast enough to follow her in time, snatching his sister with an arm and bringing her quickly back towards their father.

'Oh rats? What about rats?' grunted the precher man, making all his followers freeze to pay attention to what was coming next. Suddenly his face lit 'Yes! The rats!'

'No Clarissa, no,' Alberto said, as he contained her irate arms, 'let's leave these horrible people behind. These fanatics are dangerous'

'Call us what you want,' continued the madman and the words came out as a river of poison from his tongue 'but the rats will come with the toads and the basilisks, with the foxes and the cats, with the badgers and the eels. They will spurt from your mouths and your arseholes, vomiting flies and shitting maggots as they eat their way into your entrails. The rats will wash the land with plagues and pustules, imprisoning corruption into boils. They will rape you as you sleep into fetid luxurious dreams…' and at this stage the crowd broke out into frenzy again, with some going back into prayers and others into indecent dancing, raising their skirts and holding their shame out.

Clarissa left at gallop with the troop in pack, still looking at the fanatics, but already fearing that they had nothing to do with Julian, and perhaps neither with the rats.

Julian woke up from a nightmare, where he could not stop seeing the yellow eyes out of the dark face behind him, but any time he turned around they were not there. He could just 'see' them behind his head.

As he opened his own eyes, he found himself on a cart, with Clarissa smiling as she saw him coming back to the world of the living. Tears were running down her face.

'I am glad you are back, Jul…Hubert,' she said with a good deal of control, after wiping the tears from her cheeks. 'You are safe, on the way to Luna with us.'

At night, as Clarissa watched a fast-recovering Julian sip the last remains of a rich broth, she asked 'What exactly happened there?'

'Ah, Clarissa.' Julian said shaking his head, 'this is part of my story. If I had told you of it, you would have thought me insane'

'Julian, we all saw the rats! My father said it was a *rat king*, but it was still somewhat un-natural.'

'Rats? What do you mean by rats?'

As Clarissa described him what she saw, Julian was appalled to learn of the phenomenon. And she was more aghast to find that it was not the mount of rats that had put him out of conscience.

She had never doubted his fears. Something was wrong and maybe it was just that accursed year. The year would end and the devil did not make its appearance. And Clarissa would live on to take Julian to Luna.

She would live on to see angels and miracles.

And the devil coming out of the mouth of hell.

Nepotism

Gaeta, by the coast of the Principality of Capua, two days south of Rome. A young monk entered the shack with a respectful bow of his head. He made the sign of the cross and a brief prayer, looking apprehensively at the hermit. The holy man was prostrated with open arms, face on the stone floor, humming something unintelligible. The monk kneeled carefully and whispered something to the hermit.

'I don't want to see him,' the hermit grunted.

The monk bit his lip and thought for a while. He got closer and whispered a few more words to the hermit.

'When I finish my prayers, then,' the hermit said.

The young king, Emperor Otto III, was waiting outside with his ensemble. Now at twenty-one, he had managed to replace his dead cousin Gregory V with another pawn of his on the throne of St. Peter – the former archbishop of Ravenna and Rheims, Gerbert of Aurillac, now Sylvester II. The German king's crushing victory against the Crescentii in the Castle of Sant'Angelo already felt distant and comforting. Nevertheless, that Roman family seemed to be continually able to resurrect from the ashes and produce another nuisance. Anyhow, the king should not be wasting his concerns with it. He was in Gaeta for spiritual matters.

The scorching sun made him unfold his mantle to improvise a hood, as none of the umbrellas held around him seemed to reduce the baking effect. Gathering patience, he exercised humility and waited for another hour in silence. He couldn't but notice that the surroundings were surprisingly clean and tidy for a hermit dwelling. He arrived in Gaeta hearing wonders about the sea caves on the cliffs, but he was instead taken to a monastery on top of the peninsula, with a humble hovel built on its backyard especially for the hermit.

After having waited for another agonising hour, the young king Otto smiled when a contrived hermit appeared at the shack's entrance. The king felt flooded with a divine bliss, for Nilo da Rossano was not just any hermit. He was a living saint.

They prayed together inside the shack, for a long time, venerating a wooden image of the crucified Christ. The king's party waited back under the shade of the monastery, where monks brought them some refreshments. After praying for long enough to symbolise a trial for the king's endurance and serenity, the hermit asked.

'Do you repent?'

There was a brief pause of silence. 'I surely do, oh beatissimo Nilo,' the young emperor moaned with eyes shut tight.

'Easy to admit,' the hermit said 'but what are you repenting from?'

'From everything!'

'What do you mean by *everything*? That is even easier...' He cleared his throat. 'I'm afraid, my son, that you do not know what I am talking about.'

'And now you make me even more afraid!' Otto said.

'I refer to John Philagathus of Piacenza.' Nilo said firmly. 'Do you repent from the monstrosities afflicted on him?'

The young king gagged and answered with a trembling voice 'You do appreciate the circumstances of the conflict, don't you, beatissimo Nilo? The immense wrong that my Godfather had done.'

'Of course I do.' The hermit rasped. 'You should be well aware that I condemned the Crescentii for the raid on Gregory V and the faux election of Philagathus. But once the legitimate pope was restored, there was no need for that abominable action. There is a mutilated man, a piece of meat who cannot see, speak or write. He can only pray for forgiveness and a chance for relief of his suffering in the Kingdom of God. Now you...' He pointed his finger at Otto's face. 'You would be further away from eternal damnation if you had had him killed instead.'

Again the king stuttered. 'Would my salvation be nearer if I rid Philagathus out of his misery? I can send someone to Fulda and...'

With the scarred back of his bony hand, the hermit slapped the king on the face. 'You fool of a Tedesco! So much for the *wonder of the world*!' he scowled. Nilo da Rossano was referring to the term that had been recently utilised to describe the young king, especially among the German clergy, who had brought him up. But Nilo had a different outlook. His dry mouth was foaming, spitting words like a thunderstorm. 'Do not even dare to think of that, you monster! If the beast is to be among us this coming year than you are the Antichrist that we all fear. Do not act upon others, but upon your heart. You must find your own path to salvation, Otto, if there is any at all. Repentance, prayer, contrition! Penitence! Be forgiving and you will be forgiven. Spread the word of Christ! Throw away the crown and embrace the religious life. Join a monastery.'

The king held his slapped side. He was breathing deeply, horrified. There was a silence for a long time, while he looked at the hermit's lines of fury, behind a thick white mat of hair and beard. Finally Otto said 'Beatissimo Nilo of Rossano. I am taking advantage of my regal powers to spread the word of the Christ. I want to see a united church together in worship of God – the Father, the Son and the Holy Spirit.' His blue eyes floated as air. 'I intend to see Rome and Byzantium under the same faith, under one spiritual and terrene ruler. I plan pilgrimages to the tomb of the blessed saints in the land of the Poles, to the land of the Magyars, and guarantee new bishoprics in these pagan realms. I want to extend my hand to their dukes and grant a crown to Istvan, of Hungary, ensuring that his people are finally united under a Christian king. I will bring the relics of Charlemagne and the skin of Saint Bartholomew to Rome, and I will –'

'By the wounds of the tortured Christ!' the hermit interrupted, pleading to the cross. He turned to the king. 'Nonsense. All nonsense. It is you who must set the example. You want unity? Then unite with the Crescentii. Forgive them and ask for their forgiveness. Then you should renounce the royalty and take the cowl, joining the monastic life. From forgiveness, commiseration and contemplation you may be granted salvation.'

'The Crescentii would never talk to me.' said the king. 'They cannot forget the head of the Marble Horse on top of a spike.

'They will go to you if you call them.'

'They will not trust me.'

'You must seek a meeting with Crescentius's wife. Mention my name and she will trust you.'

'Stephania?' said the king.

'No, not Stephania.' said the hermit. 'Stephania is Crescentius Numentanus's widow. Forget her. She is a cheap harlot, from what I hear. I am talking about Theodora, the wife of John Crescentius. She is a pious, virtuous woman, who has been actively involved on commissioning the construction of the monastery in Frascati, near Tusculum. Theodora can manoeuvre well through the greedy interests of the Crescentii from Rome and their Tusculani branch.

'Wasn't Theodora the mother, or grandmother of John Crescentius? Theodora, the sister of Marozia? I met Marozia once when I was a kid...'

'Of course not! Where have you been all these years, Otto? Don't you know that there is an infinity of Theodoras in Rome? Besides, stop your daydreaming. You never met Marozia. That prostitute was dead and burning in hell many years before you were born.'

Otto decided not to argue. 'I will try then to meet this woman and seek reconciliation with the Roman patricians.'

'She will come to you on my name,' Nilo said, 'but do not be deceived or distracted by her charms. Theodora is a woman of legendary beauty'.

Otto, the young king made his decision. 'I will meet Theodora, and if I achieve union with the Crescentii, I will then join a monastery and take the cowl.'

'Then follow your heart and go with God, my son! I will need some penitence to get past my outburst of rage.'

When Otto was leaving the shack after another hour of prayer and silence next to the saint, he heard the last words from Nilo da Rossano. 'Do not seek me again, unless you have already taken the cowl.'

But King Otto III could not think of anything else but Theodora.

Camping with his army outside Rome, Otto waited eagerly for the answer from Theodora. In spite of the discretion he exercised by enquiring about the Lady Theodora, the description arrived more than frequently embellished with accounts of her beauty, intelligence and piety. A tall, mighty woman, already a grandmother, but still looking on the climax of breeding age. Her curves and volumes, they said, could bend the holiest thoughts, and she was favoured by the Lateran to hold talks with the pope. Theodora was often seen with uncovered head, her auburn hair waving at the ugliness of Rome, and with the eyes of an angel she raised the Romans to a pleasant level above the clouds. The Romans always forgave her faults, even though she made them feel so small when she was around.

The answer came in one day.

We will see the king of the Germans at the Crescentii palace, by the Forum Boarium, at the port. The king of the Germans must enter the city from whichever gate he chooses. He must be walking, unarmed and on his own. Only under these conditions will the Crescentii talk.

There was no signature. There was no proper greeting or salutation. As always, the Romans never referred to the emperor as such, but as the king of the Germans.

Otto was outraged. That was no way to treat the Consul of the Roman Senate and People. As a *Servant of the Apostles* and a *Servant of Jesus Christ* he knew he deserved some deference even if from the enemy. The emperor of the World could not suffer such humiliation from those rude Romans. Throwing the parchment in to the fire, Otto raised the camp and followed trip north, back to Germany.

Pope Sylvester II was anointing a new bishop.

Struggling to balance the rather small tiara on his large hirsute head, the pope kneeled down and laid both hands on the head of the prostrated bishop-ordinand. '*Accipe Spiritum Sanctum, quorum remiseris peccata, remittuntur eis; et quorum retinueris, retenta sunt.*' The words echoed through the Lateran church. Sylvester headed to the altar and grabbed a newly bound book.

'Raise, John Theophylactus.' He ordered.

The bishop stood up and received the book. His face was delicate, handsomely designed, edging the feminine.

The pope continued. 'With these Holy Scriptures you will feed the flock of Christ which is committed to your charge. Guard and defend them in Christ's truth, and be a faithful steward of his Holy Word and Sacraments.'

From the shadows of the columns, a cardinal came forward with lowered eyes and handed to the pope the *manicae* - the episcopal gloves. Theophylactus put them on and bowed to receive the *crux pectoralis*. Sylvester placed the delicate wooden chain with the cross around the new bishop's neck, and kissed his face on both sides.

Then, there was an uncomfortable wait. Both man facing each other. The bishop did not move.

Sylvester clicked his tongue. 'You may go now, Bishop John Theophylactus,' the pope cordially advised, almost in a whisper.

A beautifully designed eyebrow shot up. 'That's it?' the bishop asked with undisguised loathe. His womanly pitch never surprised anyone who would expect a female voice to come out of those delicate lips.

'You are suitably consecrated.' The pope insisted, still in good spirit.

'What about my ring? A mitre? Crozier? Pallium?' demanded the young bishop. 'Am I a real bishop or what?'

'Ah, *soberbia!*' Sylvester said laughing, more to himself than to the bishop. With a giant claw clench, he grabbed Theophylactus firmly by the arm and walked slowly with him along the central nave of the almost empty church, towards the entrance door. 'You are an ambitious and intelligent young man, but there are a few household issues that maybe I should make you aware of. They mainly relate to the finances of the Lateran Palace.' He continued, calmly hissing through a grin. John Theophylactus fruitlessly tried to untangle himself from the grip, but he was obliged to hear it all. 'As far as an episcopal ring is concerned, I have already organised for your brother Albericus and all of those who elected you for this bishopric of Porto to donate a ring to you. They can use your father's Episcopal ring. Gregory was a generous bishop and I expect your brothers' generosity will surely be as vast as their piousness in indicating you to be a pastor of Christ. And as your electors are all related to you or subjects to your family, you can take advantage of this intimacy and request the ring of your dreams, I mean, of your wishes. The *pallium*, my young John Theophylactus – Bishop Theophylactus – will not be ready and consecrated till next year. There have not been enough *pallia* since the days when my predecessor Gregory V ordained so many bishops, archbishops and cardinals, and may his soul rest in peace. In heaven, of course. But be at ease, my son. We will dutifully collect wool sheared on the feast of Saint Agnes, which is only next year, so you will have to wait with the rightly dignified patience, for only by the feast of Saint Peter and Saint Paul, in June, I will bless them all. You should be receiving your anointed pallium soon after. Finally, in terms of a crozier and a mitre, they just do not fall on the top of our priorities right now. Our few artisans are totally dedicated to the manufacture of a crown and other regalia to the future kings of Hungary and Poland. All efforts are dedicated to the support of these Christian nations of the north, rather than to feed our own humble vestments with ornaments. I hope you understand.'

They stopped at the door. A full blue morning with a gelid breeze waited with a lively market outside. Pigeons flew around the statue of Emperor Constantine. The pope stretched open his grin even more, bringing his fuzzy beard forward, almost touching the face of the young bishop. 'As you can obviously notice balancing on my head, after more than a year on Saint Peter's office, I never bothered to order a mitre made for my head size.' He finally released the bishop and tapped him amicably on the shoulder. 'If you want to be a Cardinal one day, think of it. And forget the regalia.'

John Theophylactus brushed his shoulder dismayed. 'I am going back inside!' he said determined. 'I will pray to the Lord. I will pray that He understand this!'

'As you wish!' The pope turned his back on the bishop and started walking back towards the altar. 'Try praying for yourself, I suggest!'

Just over a year before, a smart old Frenchman named Gerbert of Aurillac, now Pope Sylvester II, had been surprisingly elected as a reasonable compromise between Roman Patricians and the emperor.

On his first meeting with the successors of Crescentius Numentanus, of the powerful Crescentii family, the pope again surprised them all by receiving the dreadful thugs of the Crescentii, including the leader John Crescentius — later called the first - his son John II Crescentius and some of the Crescentii cousins, including one from Tusculum in his own papal office. Sylvester was unguarded and unarmed.

The tall doors of the papal office were discreetly closed from inside by members of the family.

As they all sat around the fabulously polished oaken table, old John Crescentius started the meeting by referring to their Tusculani branch of the family, demanding that their relative John Theophylactus be made a Cardinal immediately. When the pope rebated this exigency, all of a sudden the members of the committee exploded into loud complains thrown at Sylvester, all at the same time, questioning, charging and claiming an absurd variety of demands, hammering the pope's ears on a strategy that must have often worked to get the quick, desperate agreement on the original plea.

'Listen here,' thundered the furious pope, above all squawking that had broken lose. 'Stop this fucking Sicilian market!'

A freezing dead silence fell like a boulder on the office, an effect expected by Sylvester. They had taken high offence by his comparison, rather than by his choice of adverb. He continued. 'Your nephew will not be made a cardinal in a day...'

'Cousin!' interrupted Crescentius with a grave face. 'He is a cousin, not a *nepos*.'

'Whatever!' said the pope. 'Nepos or not, Theophylactus is hardly a squeaker and he will not be a cardinal in just one day. If you wish me to arrange favours for your family, I may be able to accommodate. But that means we will all execute them on my way, not as in a haggling group of guinea fowls. And my way is within the ways of the Roman Catholic Church... whenever possible. You really want me to raise John Theophylactus to Cardinality right now? I must be very careful with my choice of words here, for I know well what you represent, oh mighty John Crescentius. But I am also very sorry, for I represent the Church of Rome. You will have to wait more than a couple of months to see your nephew a cardinal.' He stood up and firmly conducted the patrician by the arm, dragging the whole entourage to the door. 'If you want me dead, it will not be so difficult, you can do it with a snap of your fingers, and one of your monkeys will cut me in two. But that would be stupid and you know that. It could take another large toll on you, on your family and on Rome, for the German king will not take it very smoothly. And you do not want to be raking the streets of Rome to pick up the dead just because a spoiled brat has not been ordained cardinal within a day, do you?' Sylvester pushed every single one of them out of the office, including the son John II Crescentius, whose feet seemed to be stuck to the floor. 'So, for the benefit of all parties,' Sylvester framed an amicable smile, 'I suggest you get all your men the hell out of here, send my regards to your lovely wife Theodora and leave the young Theophylactus with me. Then, depending on how he behaves, I can even make your nephew a cardinal. Not in one day. But maybe one day.'

'He's a cousin!' corrected Crescentius, just before the door was slammed on his face.

He turned around to a staggered group of open mouthed patricians and relatives that accompanied him. They were not used to see the ruler of Rome being treated with such unsubserviently manners.

Frowning his chin, Crescentius lifted his lower lip almost up to his nose and, with raised eyebrows he said quite lightly 'By the *sedes stercoraria*! This pope has got a major pair of testicles! I quite like him!'

And they all dropped their shoulders, relaxing, except the young John II Crescentius. He cleared his throat with a raucous noise and spat on the marble floor. 'This pope is an insolent bastard, that's what I say.' He dragged the phlegm with his foot across the slab, producing a filthy, glossy band. 'I never liked this Frenchman, from the first day that I saw him. His affected accent, his manners are staining the soil of Rome. He's a sorcerer, they say. I wouldn't be surprised, given his behaviour towards us. Others say he is the true Antichrist, which has finally risen.'

'What a load of excrement!' His father said with a surprised face. 'How can you talk so much nonsense? *Honora patrem tuum et matrem*, the book says. And please do it so by not embarrassing me. Neither your mother, for this man holds your mother in high regard. If it wasn't for her, young Theophylactus would never have had a chance to be consecrated, in spite of being elected.'

'I care shit for that girlie face Theophylactus and the Tusculani.' The young Crescentius said. 'And less for this pope. My mother disgusts me for ever associating with him. He's a filthy old man and I still hold that he's the true Antichrist!'

The papal factotum respectfully interrupted Pope Sylvester and his one guest. They were merrily talking at a well provided dinner table, next to a generous fireplace high on the third floor of the Lateran.

'Beatissimo Padre, excuse my intromission. It is the bishop of Porto, John Theophylactus, who kindly asks for an audience with your guest.'

The Lady Theodora was ready to protest, when Sylvester interrupted, with a pleasant grin. 'Please, I make no objections.'

Theodora dropped her shoulders and smirked back. She indicated with those long fingered hands that the factotum could send her cousin in.

As they waited, the pope continued their conversation 'So you are not at all related to the famous Theodora, mother of Marozia?'

'Sometimes I wish I would be, as my husband is Theodora's great-grandson. If it is in the blood, I would probably find no abhorrence on the corruption and brutality that floods this city! But what can I do? In Rome of these days, out of three women of my age, one is called Theodora!'

'And the other two are Stephania and Marozia!' cracked Sylvester. They both laughed and drank some more wine.

Theophylactus entered, irradiating beauty, but curling his full cherry lips, as if some particular scent in the dining hall was disturbing his nostrils. The pope meant to leave.

'Please stay!' Theodora begged the pope, with a heavenly smile and eyes like a silver blue lake.

'I'm sure that the bishop wants to talk to his cousin in private.' Sylvester said.

'The Beatissimo Padre is correct...' admitted Theophylactus, with a trembling voice. Theodora lost her smile.

When they were both left alone, a much more confident Theophylactus sat at the table, verifying the dishes and sniffing the goblets. He helped himself with some wine and dried fruits. The lady Theodora watched him with amusement and irritation.

'When you've finished eating, you can share with me the important reason why you sent the pope away from his own table, to kindly grant you this audience with me'. Theodora said.

Theophylactus asked her something. Mumbling.

'Only when you've finished eating!' she said with a voice of steel. 'Your mouth is full. I could not understand a word.'

'Aren't you disgusted with yourself?' he repeated, after a painful gulp.

'What do you mean?' Theodora said. 'Just be careful with your words, Theophylactus, for my time in here is not dedicated to you and your beautiful face. And my husband will not tolerate that you insult me.'

'I'm talking about this frolicking, these vain dinners, these intimate encounters.' protested Theophylactus. 'I enter this room and I see you two giggling like a couple of children. Is my cousin aware of what is going on here?'

'I am not sleeping with the pope, if that is what you are interested in,' she said. 'I probably would if I was not a married woman and the pope not a celibate man, but this is how God has put us together. So, for your information, I respect my husband, my matrimony vows and the Beatissimo Padre's holy vows. He is an honourable man, an enthralling creature with a brilliant mind and fascinating knowledge, who has always treated me with the utmost respect, a degree of deference that I have never gotten before. We have private dinners, Theophylactus, because I want it and so does the pontiff. I am the only member of the Crescentii that the Beatissimo Padre will tolerate negotiating with. Maybe you don't even know, but it was I who convinced the pope to accept your election to the bishopric of Porto, after so many bad memories left by the administration of your corrupt father. Your brother Albericus, with his bullying barrel belly, would not have achieved much with his charm or threats.'

Theophylactus cackled. 'Of course you are! The Holy Father is saintly indeed, by the spilled blood of Jesus, but still a man of flesh and bone. The Crescentii are sending him a temptress, for they know the reputation of popes. He's fallen for you.'

Theodora lowered her eyes and chuckled. 'If Pope Sylvester II lusts for me,' she said still looking down, 'I will be thoroughly honoured and humbled, although he seems to have hidden this bodily desire very well. I have seen his powers of sharing, his feelings, his compassion, his intensity and his passion. And I just love that!'

'You love him, don't you?'

'As we all should, Theophylactus...' she said. 'Now, if you don't mind me asking, my dear handsome cousin. In addition to accusing me of being a whore, what else in the name of our Lord Jesus Christ do you have to tell me?'

Theophylactus drained his goblet. He was going to wipe his meaty lips on the sleeve, but thought better after seeing a linen towel. His face reached closer across the table. 'You realise I have not been properly treated as a bishop by the Holy Pontiff, don't you?'

'Oh my dear God!' Theodora held her head with both hands. 'By the liver of Saint Basil, are you still talking about the ring?'

'Well, that is certainly one of the issues...'

'This is your problem!' she yelled. 'Go to your relatives in Tusculum! They are rich. They should be able to fix it all. Slap their faces with your manicae. But don't come to me or to the Crescentii in Rome. And least to the Beatissimo Padre, who has been far more than accommodating on your ordination.'

Theophylactus slammed his fist on the table. 'The pope refuses to present me with the regalia or even to discuss a cardinalate. He has commissioned a crown, Theodora, a full jewel-encrusted gold crown! Now the Lateran cannot provide to its own bishops but it can provide for some barbarian king of the Magyars. That is utterly unacceptable!'

'You have no idea how long is your road to be ever a cardinal, do you?' Theodora said. 'If you want to cover your delicate neck from the chill of the Lateran with a lavish orphrey-rimmed *cappa*, please do it so by your own merits. Forget the regalia and prove yourself a loyal servant of the Christ. Be a defender of the Holy Word of God and a shepherd of the people. This is the best help that I can give you, Theophylactus. Grow up to be a real man, we'll all forget that novice nun face of yours and a cardinalate will be on its way.'

John Theophylactus made light effort to bow his head and said nothing, sailing out of the room with the pomp of a swan. In a few minutes, Sylvester was back. He bent his old body to calmly feed a couple more logs to the fireplace and filled up the goblets.

'Still he complaints and demands...' Theodora said.

'I wouldn't expect otherwise' Sylvester said with a shrug.

'Absolutely hopeless.' she said. 'It will just not grow into a respectable episcopate.'

The pope thought for a second. 'Maybe I should try to influence him with good company. I could put Theophylactus under the tutorship of Cardinal John Fasanus, another cousin of your husband. No evil in that.'

'How cruel can you be?' Theodora moaned. 'Fasanus is a jewel among pebbles. He is the only member of this family that I can actually spend my whole day with, without wishing some family tragedy. I'm sure my husband would find this a brilliant idea, for Fasanus has not been too supportive of the family interests. But my John Crescentius will be actually hoping for Theophylactus to influence Fasanus. Spending time with Theophylactus could be indeed torture for the poor man, worse than being poisoned or skewered by his own cousins!'

'Nah! Fasanus is a grown-up, who has been distant from the family for a while. He can survive Theophylactus unscathed. In addition, your husband's nepos is not that bad! He is a decent green cherry that could still turn out to be red and sweet.'

Theodora cackled with laughter! 'I just love when you refer to Theophylactus as my husband's nephew. They both hate to hear it.'

Sylvester opened a mischievous smile. 'There's little amusement a man in my age and position is entitled to have. I know Theophylactus is a cousin, but I do enjoy seeing the annoyance on your husband's and your son's faces.'

'You are too audacious. Just watch what you eat!' she warned with a grin.

And they both laughed along.

The Convert

The evil spirit was exorcised by a breath upon the face.

The abbot reached over to a small box held by a deacon and grabbed a pinch of salt, that was placed into the mouth.

'For the salvation of your soul, in the name of the Father, the Son and the Holy Spirit,' the abbot carefully dipped the goblet into the creek and lifted some of its crystal clear water, 'I baptise you Istvan, son of Ferenc'. He slowly poured a trickle down onto the baby's forehead, making the tiny creature holler with might. The sign of the cross was drawn on the forehead and chest. This only increased the power of Istvan's howls. With his face lined down with tears, Ferenc passed the little one onto the wet nurse's care. She wrapped the grubby body with skins and shawls.

The gelid water was up to his knees, but abbot Astricus, still smiled as he now turned to the other side. He dipped the goblet again and said. 'The Kingdom of

God shall be yours to enter too, as you are reborn of water and the Holy Spirit. You are God's proof that Istvan should get his blessing and crown to be our king and that we deserve to get our own Episcopal sees. You came to us as *God among us* and *God among us* you remain. No other name you need, for yours is the same name as our Saviour's. You have honoured His name by saving this mission to Rome and by mimicking His compassion on your mercy to this wicked man, releasing him from his deserved doom. In the name of the Father, the Son and the Holy Spirit, I baptise you, Immanuel, *God Among us*.' The frigid water trickled down from the tips of Immanuel's thin moustache. He smiled shyly as his little blue eyes moved fast.

On the bank, many villagers, soldiers and deacons watched. Abbot Astricus and the other officiating deacon were helped out of the creek by the monks of Mons Sacer Pannoniae.

Immanuel, was not really sure of what this ceremony meant to his heart. To his thoughts, compassion came naturally. He found the preached creed of those lands and the teaching of the Messiah, based on forgiveness and acknowledgement to God consistent with the words he heard through his upbringing, on the coming of the Messiah and salvation of the God's chosen people. Conversion, to Immanuel, was just one shape to adaptation. More than the icy water that ran through his thin hair, what occupied his thoughts most was the invitation of the abbot to follow with him to Rome. Rome? The real Rome? The abbot just nodded his head, not sure about what Immanuel had asked.

Now with his feet freezing cold in the creek, Immanuel meant to step out onto the bank after the abbot, when two hands were immediately extended to help him. One was the hand of Procopius, the wide-eyed Greek merchant, who bore a formidable smile. The other was the callused and spice-scented hand of Béla, the táltos of the village. The still incredulous old Magyar looked at his saviour with liquid eyes.

Before they could say anything to the new convert, both men were brushed away by a solemn Ferenc, who came to Immanuel with a rowdy clearing of his throat.

'Immanuel Malachi, the father abbot is correct to call you *God among us*. You are small in stature, but your brief visit to our village has washed us with a blessing as vast as the Lake Zála. You have saved my wife Borbála from certain death, when nobody else could. On the next day, for incomprehensible reasons and with an unmatched spell of Christian mercy, you have begged me to spare the life of this despicable táltos,' he grunted on saying that word 'even though the old vulture would have comfortably crushed you under a rock. Not happy with your display of kindness, or with a bit of fear of your homeless situation and uncertain future, you promised me to take Béla along, for a life of redemption on your side. And to crown the glory of your presence, you cured our father abbot from the spells of hemicrania that kept him from proceeding to Rome. Immanuel, you have the dagger of Attila that I gave to you as a token of my eternal gratitude. Now I want you to have another small treasure, sent by my ever-so-thankful Borbála.' He withdrew a small object from inside his fur coat and handed it to Immanuel. 'Keep it safe and hidden with you. Just like the dagger of Attila may protect you, this may help you one day. Borbála and I wish the best of luck to you.'

When Ferenc withdrew back to the village, following the abbot and soldiers who were preparing for the continuation of their journey, Immanuel was left alone, looking at his gift. Procopius and Béla came back to him, the Greek's eyes almost popping out of their orbits as he saw what Immanuel's held.

'Don't let anyone see it!' the Greek said.

'Procopius, you are the expert merchant here.' Immanuel said, ignoring the advice and showing him the sculpted piece. 'What worth would this be?'

The Greek looked at the medal for a long time, holding it with care and flipping it to appreciate the richness of details on both sides, especially the figure with the laurel wreath holding a T-shaped object with a bird perched on it. He raised his upper lip and both eyebrows, saying assertively to Immanuel. 'I would have no particular interest in the gold, but the sardonyx carving is precious. It is worth as much as you want!' And before Immanuel could have said anything, Procopius completed with a contagious smile 'and please, at least be ambitious this time.'

Weeks later, already long parted from the merchant Procopius, the Bukhari Immanuel rode next to Béla on their way to Rome. Abbot Astricus was still troubled by a couple of mild attacks of hemicrania, which had been efficiently restrained by the new convert, without any delay to the trip.

Immanuel discussed herbs and cures with a surprisingly pleasant and willing Béla. Before leaving Ferenc's village forever, they had hurriedly visited the táltos' hut and filled two bags with any ingredients that he thought were important or that the Bukhari found interesting for further discussion. Language was a difficulty. Béla knew some limited Greek, the offices and hours of the day were often read and celebrated in Latin, but many of the abbot's caravan, especially the soldiers, only spoke the Magyar language. Still, at every new intervention that Immanuel attended to – especially at monasteries and abbeys, where the sick were tended to, an inflamed debate on disease, medicine and cures would follow, including The Bukhari, the táltos and the frustrated physician of Mons Sacer Pannoniae.

When arriving in Istria, Immanuel suddenly asked the táltos 'Béla, would you have killed me under that rock for a sacrifice'.

'Of course I would have, *fönök*.' He had been using that deference title to address Immanuel ever since the Bukhari had saved him from the blade of Ferenc. 'I was blinded by rage and envy. Why I dropped the stone to my side and not towards the hole, I don't know. But be asured, regardless whether we believe in a different religion or not, the foundation sacrifice still works.'

'Hard to believe, I find.' Immanuel said. 'You are such a good decent man, with a vast knowledge on...'

'You may call it stupidity!' Béla suggested. 'It happens to a lot of people.'

They heard a shriek high above.

'This vulture of yours does not miss you from sight!' Immanuel said. 'We were buried for three days in the darkness of that massive forest, and after that it had no problem spotting you again.'

'Turul always knows where I am.' Béla said with a smile. He will be forever thankful to you for saving this ignorant táltos from execution by Ferenc, with Attila's dagger. Your act of compassion, fönök, could only have been...'

'You may call it stupidity.' Immanuel said with a shy smile.

They spotted the outline of Rome after thirty three days.

Immanuel's dream was fulfilled, but only to certain extend, for the great city, the eternal Rome, was a depressing amalgamation of ruins, rotten buildings and shabby houses, perhaps the most untidy and filthy place he had ever seen. Any angle of places such as Damascus, Isphahan and even Bukhara were more pleasant to the eye and proudly sporting more glory than the grime of Rome.

As soon as they entered the city, Immanuel and Béla were ready to leave.

However, Abbot Astricus had a crown to collect and a kingdom waiting in Hungary. And he would thankfully acknowledge Immanuel's help on the mission, by introducing the new Christian to Pope Sylvester II.

On Ferenc's village, Borbála was watching the baby Istvan, who suckled vigorously from the wet nurse. Outside, a large lamb bleated, helpless with cold and fear. As the only feeble warmth of the day descended with the sun behind a thick bundle of purple clouds in the mid-afternoon, Ferenc calmly walked up to the hill. He stood at the edge of the hole where he had found the good physician Immanuel tied down. The frosty wind blew across his face as he remembered how his hand with the dagger was held up by the tiny Immanuel, with unbelievable strength, begging him to spare what was left of the miserable life of the vile Béla.

Ferenc made a brief thanksgiving prayer, one of the many scores he had privately uttered for the birth of Istvan, the coming of Immanuel and the recovery of Borbála. When the eastern wind paused for a second, so did the lamb. Ferenc overheard the bellows of baby Istvan, down below in the village. The chieftain was flooded by a warm feeling and desire to run down to his family. Still, he raised the lamb and swiftly inserted the knife into its neck, piercing to the other side and bringing it down, opening a large gash that rained with blood. The bleating weaned quickly as the blood splattered over the bottom of the hole. When Ferenc finally released it, the dead lamb crushed inside the hole. The boulder was easily rolled to squash the offer to the spirit of the hill.

Ferenc ran down to the village, eager to spend that long cold night with his family.

The church on Ferenc's village was quick and efficiently built. It would last for many decades. The lidérc of that hill was satisfied with the spillage of blood.

In the name of God, Amen.

I, the banker and trader Battista Burle, with a long tradition of loans, commerce, honesty, piousness and Christian dedication towards the community of Lucca, the Marca Januensis and the Holy See, on this thousandth year of our Lord, send my best greetings to the Beatissimo Padre Sylvester II and ask for his most apostolic blessings.

On the same manner that my father reported to those who conducted the affairs of our Mother Church on his time, we have arduously tried acknowledging to the apostles of Christ that have previously occupied the throne of Saint Peter, some of them with a pontificate too short to receive this rather unimportant notice, I will humbly present to the Beatissimo Padre an account of the affairs of the Holy See with the Burle House of Trade. It has taken us exhaustive strains to complete the information that you receive in this book of accounts compiled especially to the Beatissimo Padre, a full acknowledgement which will be appreciated by your most generous tesserarius.

I must point out to the Beatissimo Padre that the members of the noble Lombard family of the Cunimundinghi, faithful landlords of the eastern bank the valley of the Serchio, have indebted themselves to amounts which exceed the funds that this house of trade can sustain. Their guadia on our care has subsequently increased to more than one hundred heredia of the old roman thermal station of Val di Lima in Corsena, on the north-eastern confluence of the Serchio and the Lima. This property belonged originally to the Church of San Martino in Lucca. It was ceded by the bishop Teudogrimo to the Viscount Fra Olmo, of the Corvaresi family. The property passed to Fra Olmo's sole surviving sister, Lucia, who is married to the neighbouring Cunimundinghi, Fulcardo, the nephew of Bishop Gherardo. Now, as part of the Cunimundinghi guadia, it has been promptly transferred to papal lands as traditionally were the wishes of your pontifical tesserarius in relation to guadiae. This manoeuvre shortens the path for the concession to return to its original owners, namely the Church. This land has unfortunately a high price and it has not been properly worked on, making it useless for a launeguildo, which would concede full and permanent transference to the Holy See. On glorious times, the thermal baths of Corsena, are said to have served privileged families of the Roman Empire. Over centuries, the miraculous terme healed pain and fatigue, providing soothing composure to patients and tourists who travelled from all corners of the Empire. Presently, the baths are in a pitiful state of conservation and a full renovation operation is required to recover their functionality and re-establish their splendour.

As the baths of the Val di Lima of Corsena remain at Your Holiness' entire service and usufruct, I take the freedom to humbly propose a complete reconstruction of all the thermal pools and re-establish a bath station for cures and soothing. This station would become not only a meeting point for the noble families of Lucca and along the valley of the Serchio, but also a resting stopover for the thousands of wealthy pilgrims that pass through these lands on their way to Rome.

Knowing also that the times are dire and the moneys to invest in such an enterprise could be of secondary precedence for the interests of the Holy See, I dare to propose my own personal investment – of the Burle House of Trade – on the renovation works. The project will drain a heavy investment from our meagre funds and it may take years to materialise, but it will generate interesting revenues for the Lateran treasury. Once the baths are ready to be utilised, proceeds from the visitors should be equally divided between the Holy See and the Burle House of Trade, who has taken onto its responsibility the full burden of investment on the reconstruction.

As I may be able to save some moneys and mobilise certain funds, I still lack in the expertise of Roman baths. Therefore, all I ask from the Beatissimo Padre is to send to our region the expertise of a reliable physician, a specialist in thermal baths. One that is fortunate to receive your full trust.

On a different and much more personal matter I should also let the Beatissimo Padre know that my single heiress Elvira has long passed the age of marriage and I cannot see any prospect of a good Lucchese young man taking her into a wedded life. Not only have we Lucchese a particular bad spell of only women born of her generation, but Elvira has also been somehow unfortunate in terms of physical endowments. I do expect to have male heirs, but I cannot wait for young Lucchese boys to grow to the age of marriage before I have new apprentices for my office. I should make it clear that your specialist in terme will be most welcome if a single man of marriageable age.

Finally, I am certain that, as a man of knowledge and piety, the Beatissimo Padre will indeed praise this initiative to re-establish the thermal station to sooth the pains of pilgrimage and cure some of the illnesses of the faithful that have not been covered by the unsurpassable power of prayer, relics and true miracles. That is in addition to half of the revenue that will be coming annually to the funds of the Mother Church at no cost. The papal debts, obviously driven by the generosity of your predecessors, have reached alarming rates and this revenue will be a welcoming filler to reduce the unavoidable voids on the finances of the Holy See.

Asking for your apostolic blessing, from your faithful servant, Battista Burle.

Signum ms.† suprascripti (Battisti)qui hunc libellum fieri rogavit.

† Petrus not. dn. imp. rogatus teste subs.

† Ego Johan rogatus ec.

† Ego Hubertus not. dn. imp. ec.

† Tempertus not. dn. imp. post tradit. ec.

When the translator had finished pronouncing the Latin to Greek version and the names of the scribe and witnesses, he discreetly retired from the papal office. Immanuel did not understand it all, but now he saw himself under the gaze of the three sumptuously dressed men left with him. Both Pope Sylvester and Cardinal John Fasanus held an amused smile on their faces. But Immanuel noticed that the third person, the bishop with a womanish face, held up a doubtful eyebrow and the nostrils of his prominent nose appeared to have caved in, as on a permanent sniff. He seemed to regard Immanuel as if he was a particularly unpleasant type of vermin.

The oppressing silence was finally broken by the pope 'This is our man!' he said with glee, looking at the other two, as if a witnessing a prodigy or miracle. 'You are perfect for this endeavour!' he said to Immanuel, who shrugged with a yellow smile.

'Can you do it, Immanuel?' asked Cardinal Fasanus, who had lost his smile.

'Do what?'

'Can you recover the baths of Val di Lima?' The cardinal was serious but still courteous to that foreign visitor.

Immanuel protested. 'I don't know this place! I ignore what the conditions are. I have no idea what this person means by recovering the baths.'

The Bishop Theophylactus sniggered, with a rather attractive face. 'This man has obviously no grasp on what you are talking about.'

'I do know what we are talking about' Immanuel corrected. The bishop swung around and starred at him in astonishment, clearly insulted by the Bukhari's interference.

Cardinal John Fasanus raised a diplomatic hand and asked 'Let me put it in this way, Immanuel Malachi: You do understand about medicinal baths, don't you?'

'That would be correct to say.' Immanuel cautiously dared to answer, in spite of the hateful glare the bishop Theophylactus had shot him.

'And would you at least make an assessment of this place, under apostolic request of the Beatissimo Padre?'

'I would, certainly,' he said with a humble bow of his head.

That was enough for the Cardinal. He smiled and verified for the reaction on his superior. The pope could not hide his unceasing amusement with the convert from Bukhara. He scratched his hirsute beard with a loud gritting noise and asked 'What else do you plan for your life, Immanuel?'

Immanuel thought for a few seconds. It seemed to him that he had never asked himself that question before. And he had not. After a long wait that made the pope lean forward on his seat and the bishop change the weight on his legs on an obvious signal of utter impatience, Immanuel finally said 'I want to establish myself somewhere where I can practice my medicine. Somewhere where I can live peacefully among other Christians. Where I can find a wife to raise children, and maybe we could have other activities, as farming animals or growing crops. Béla, the old Magyar, could help me with his knowledge too.'

'Then, Tuscany is your place!' assured the pope.

'If I may,' the young handsome bishop interfered, visibly annoyed, 'The offer of this banker Battista Burle is not too attractive. First of all, we all know that baths are a place for iniquity, and that bathing is no good for the health.'

Cardinal Fasanus cackled 'Nonsense. Only if one bathes with the filthy will he acquire a pestilence. Baths are healthy indeed.'

'That is very true', said the pope. 'One contracts an illness in an orgy, not in a bath.'

Theophylactus ignored that and continued. 'Then, the Beatissimo Padre should not be accepting only half of the revenue with the baths. Three quarters to the Lateran is a more dignified share. As to specialists, there should be local physicians that do understand the nature of thermal baths, such as in Acqua Pisanae, for example.'

Fasanus was even louder this time. 'Sure, we send a Pisan to help the Lucchese and we have war.'

'If not from Pisa, then a good Christian from Baiae or Anticoli di Campagna, which have sprouted generations of specialists in their thermal waters'.

'Nonsense,' said the pope, ignoring the impertinent bishop and turning to the cardinal 'There is nobody in Christendom who is less committed than this good man. Baiae, Anticoli or any of the hot springs in this peninsula are absolutely decadent, totally run down, probably in no better state than these baths at Val di Lima. There are Tedeschi specialists in Acquisgranus, for example, who could be able to help, but I don't think your family, Theophylactus, would appreciate such move to plant a man of the emperor in the lands that are to be returned to us one day.'

The seat of the Holy Roman Emperor, Acquisgranus – Aachen – was blessed by boasting the hottest known thermal springs in the continent. The pope was referring to the Crescentii, the permanent enemies of the German kings in power. Bishop Theophylactus had been pushed into the Lateran by a descendant branch of the Crescentii that was now lodged in the Roman town of Tusculum, where his great-grandmother Theodora had come from.

The pope continued 'Immanuel has embraced the Christian faith in his heart, more deeply than any God-fearing Italian who was born without a choice. He will be an uncommitted option for a cheap investment that may generate revenues to pay up our debts in the future. The Holy See seems to owe Battista Burle a good quantity of interests, and his offer sounds like a reasonable compromise. We should arrange for an escort *decuria* of custodes to take Immanuel Malachi and his companion to see the banker Battista Burle as soon as possible.' He turned to the cardinal and snapped a finger, saying 'John, please organise for a letter to present this man to Battista Burle.'

And holding Immanuel's shoulder, he conducted the Bukhari outside of the office. 'My good man, congratulations. You now have a place with what you whished for, and that will include a bride. But come with me. We have no more than a couple of days before you go. Let's discuss numbers.'

Theodora's eyes sparkled with excitement and she watched the pope and his guest, a tiny man from a faraway land, play with a piece of chalk and a well-polished board. They were writing their strange symbols and discussing the most diverse methods to perform simple arithmetical operations, which supposedly took an infinitesimal time as compared to the normal numerical operations with the current Roman algorisms. They were discussing the uncountable possibilities of Arabic numerals over the clumsy, limited Roman system.

١ ٢ ٣ ٤ ٥ ٦ ٧ ٨ ٩

Immanuel would look at those numbers and say. 'They are indeed similar, but you seem to be missing a zero.'

Sylvester agreed with excitement. The pope would call Theodora to the board and show her the magic of those symbols, involving the spellbound woman into the rationale, taking her through the addition, subtraction and multiplication steps, but she could not grasp it yet. Nevertheless, while doing a good parallel with Roman algorisms, Theodora noticed the results with those novel Arabic numbers were precise and incredibly faster. She did understand the basic concept of enumeration using the new symbols, though.

The pope excused himself and left them alone for a while.

Theodora looked at the rather tiny Immanuel, who was humbled by her stature and powerful beauty. She tried something in Greek. 'You are a physician?'

Immanuel smiled and nodded.

But that was as far as she could produce a conversation in Greek. Still, she said 'The pontiff is very excited with your visit. He's a lonely man. I wish I could also join the conversation of you two.'

Miraculously, Immanuel seemed to understand and courteously answered on his basic Greek. 'If we ever meet again after this, I promise we will be talking with each other in your language.'

Theodora even giggled with delight as they broke that barrier, and soon the pope stormed in again, bringing with him a couple of square plates. One metal plate with a number of round beads pinned to it and a larger wooden one, with loose polished beads sitting on parallel deep grooves. The Crescentii lady noted 'Good, so you brought us an *abakos*. I know I shouldn't admit to it, but I can operate one.'

Her remark was filled with caution, for the knowledge of numbers was frowned upon and seen with suspicion by most common people of their times. It was a familiarity reserved for merchants and accountants. Both the Frenchman and the Bukhari ignored the comment, the former because he was a man of science and dismissed it; and the latter because he did not understand a word.

Sylvester handed the metal plate to Theodora. 'You can work our abakos with our Roman system. I will work the Arabic numeral system on this abakos. Give me a sum!'

Theodora quickly grabbed the chalk and stood up in majesty, writing down an operation with extensive numbers on the board. Both the pope and the lady started frenetically to flick the beads in their abacus boards. Immanuel observed the pope's board, studying its principle. The pope was ready in no time. The Crescentii lady opened her silvery blue eyes wide. She paused for a second, mesmerised. The pope waited for her to finish hers and they conferred the results. Both correct. Theodora thought for a bit and wrote a new operation. Once again the pope finished his results much earlier, and when she was finished they again matched the final results.

'Maybe it's you that makes the difference, as a faster operator in your abakos, and not this Arabic numeric system.'

'That's a fair argument,' Sylvester said. 'We'll swap it then. I operate the roman abakos and Immanuel will operate the Arabic one. Do you trust me that I will make it as fast as I can?'

'I'm not sure if I do' she said with an impish grin of complicity, 'but let's give it a go, anyway.'

Sylvester gave the board to Immanuel. 'Are you familiar with it?'

'There's a tiny difference, I think.' the Bukhari said.

'Yes, the zero is missing here, but it's this empty column.' explained the pope. 'I have used this system for many years, since my instructions with the Arabs and Bishop Atto, in Vicus Ausonae. This board itself I ordered later from a shieldmaster in Rheims, who claims the beads are made from the horns of the giant auerochs.'

None of those words meant much to Immanuel. He paused for a while and said, assuring 'No problem. I can operate it!'

'Theodora, can you say the numbers in Greek? Can you give us an operation to perform?'

As Theodora dictated the numbers, the additions, subtractions, multiplications and divisions, both men ferociously attacked their calculation boards, until Immanuel stood up quickly and walked to the writing board, drawing a repeated symbol.

ϧ ϧ ϧ

Sylvester was still flicking his beads back and forth when Immanuel calmly returned to his board. The pope finally sighed and said with a smile. 'DCLXVI! Exactly!' He was radiant when he verified Immanuel's symbols. Turning to Theodora, he casually asked. 'Did you do that on purpose, Theodora? Do you know the symbolic relevance of this number?'

Theodora pursed her lips for a while, opening wide with her beautiful eyes in total ignorance.

The pope smiled. 'It says on the revelations of Saint John that six hundred and sixty six is the number of the Beast.'

Theodora laughed! 'Well, the story I hear is that now, the Anno Mille, is the year of the Beast. And we also keep hearing that you are the Antichrist incarnated.'

'They should calculate better then,' Sylvester dismissed with a snort, 'for the Devil is supposed to be unbound after a thousand years after the Christ's death!' and he finished with a chuckle.

During the next five days, while abbot Astricus was on his way back to Magyar lands, carrying the crown presented by pope Sylvester II, the Bukhari Immanuel and the pope discussed numbers and medicine. Their enthusiastic meetings were often accompanied by Theodora, who managed to leave her husband to deal with their rebellious son and his annoyance on the pope's interest for diabolical sciences and the influence on his mother. Nobody would ever calculate or foresee, but this brief acquaintance between Immanuel and the Crescentii lady would have deep influence on the future destinies of the popes and Roman families, involuntarily extending and designing an alternative path to this period of the church that was later known as the Pornocracy.

With a good supply of black comb, hurriedly purchased by the pontiff's factotum from the apothecary stalls at the charlatan's market, the abbot Astricus made his way back to *Lacus Pelso*, the great Zála Lake, on a smooth and peaceful journey with no crisis of hemicrania affecting him, thanks to the assistance of his physicians. The abbot carried with him a crown. A flat and wide band of silver to encircle the head, edged with beaded gold wire and pearls, with an enamel image of the Almighty Christ, surrounded by the standing eleven disciples. A gift from the apostle of Christ to strengthen the mighty power of Christianity, protect the newly created dioceses and expand the borders of His kingdom.

Immanuel Ben-Malachi, the new convert who travelled to Lucca with his Hungarian shaman friend never understood the dimension of his assistance to the abbot Astricus. At the turn of that year when the Beast did not break loose from hell, in the monastery of Mons Sacer Pannoniae, King Istvan received his crown from the radiant abbot. Less than a century later, both men would be revered as saints. And in another hundred years, this Roman crown given by the pope would be disassembled, re-mounted and attached to the top rim of a Greek crown. Even though it lost the images of James son of Alpheus, Simon with its delicate silver saw engraved on the enamel and Judas with a bright flame burning around his head, the newly built crown was richly decorated by talented byzantine artists and composed into a harmonious set. For over a Millennium, it would become the most powerful object and symbol of Hungary.

During the short pontificate of pope Sylvester II, Western Christendom finally was shaken awake from the impracticability of Roman algorisms, as the pope made official the use of the Arabic system of numerals. A century later, few scholars had adapted to this strange but fabulous method of enumeration.

The Allure of Luna

Julian could see the tower. His chest felt about to explode when Clarissa's face touched his cheek as she precisely pointed to him where he would single out the white presence beyond the mists.

The white castle of Luna stood to the southeast of the town of Luni. After the difficult mountain passes in Aùla, or from the hills behind the port of Il Poggio, pilgrims and travellers walking south down the Via Francigena, the road that led from France to Rome, would rejoice at the first sight of the tall shiny tower, much beyond the small castle of Sarzana.

Luna, as Julian saw it in his times, was a new, unimaginable world. Reason would suggest that the more fortified a residence was, the more hidden and brutish the fortress would turn out to be. But Luna defied this logic.

The castle had been initiated by Lord Oberto's grandfather, Adalbert II, the Margrave of Tuscany. Adalbert was the son of the infamous Mariozza Mariccucia, with her first husband Guido of Tuscany. When Adalbert decided to reconstruct the small manor of Luni, he had enough lands and vassals to be dedicated to the exploration of the white marble quarries on the mountains right above them. Those excavation sites of the Apuane Mountains had been stale, forgotten for immemorial times, but it was believed they had originated much of the Roman wealth of the classical imperial era.

The original manor of Luni was entirely razed to the ground, the low motte flattened and all the land around it was drained. Most of the old stones were used to fill the new marble curtain wall, erected high and steep, white and shining as no Christian had ever dreamed of before. Gigantic walls as tall as five lengths of arms, which is higher than a line of five men standing on top of each other's head. Lord Oberto said that nobody knew how deep the walls entered into the ground, but there was talk of many lengths of an arm, the same distance as from the surface to the top of the merlons on the battlements. Those walls covered a vast pentagonal area and, rather than facing the timidly-walled town of Luni at its northwester side, they faced southwest, with its own solid barbican opening towards the south branch of the Via Francigena that took them to Lucca. The five corners of the curtain wall were projected forwards in diamond-shaped bastions. These were massive, solid structures, with very high embrasures on its flat top, where archers could position themselves in safety to protect each of the walls on their sides. Julian was surprised by the abundance of arrow loops along the walls and on the top half of the five bastions. In those times, it was believed that such long slits would weaken any wall, but the Margrave of Tuscany did not seem to be aware of that.

'We Lombards are hard-working diligent people, but our engineering is lousy,' said Lord Oberto to Julian. 'You don't see castles like that anywhere else because most of us Longobardi, Tedeschi, Franchi, Visigoti, Magiari, Alemanni and so many others have ignored the existence of Roman engineering. But not my family. There are still very good engineers in Rome, if you ever need one.'

The eastern wall of Luna, facing the first hills soaring towards the Apuane Alps, was edged by a rather narrow strip of land beyond the wide moat. A flat corridor of grass which was limited on its other side by a thick hedge of dry thornbush. Those brambles had been planted in a distant past, but died from the poor drainage of the soil. The hedge skirted a rocky outcrop of difficult access, if not for a steep stairway that led to a couple of terraces, or detached outworks, equally protected by a parapet and merlons. A small garrison made constant camp on that outcrop. Such detached bastions were inexistent in any other fortress in western Christendom.

And no matter how powerfully a titan could ram them, the curtain walls of Luna would never cave in. Whereas the ramparts stood vertically outside, on their inside a soft slope towards the keep made them immeasurably thick. Most of the domestic buildings were erected against this slope, on several layers, vertically and horizontally. There were stables for a score of horses, two large granaries, a forge, a kitchen, an armoury, a poultry coop and a shed for any small herds brought into the walled grounds, a small orchard and a couple of gardens. Blacksmiths, carpenters, masons, cooks and servants lived mostly in their workshops, but there were extra lodgings for even a small militia of men-at-arms. The lowest part of the bailey was the rim around the keep and the paths towards the two opposite gates, which would prevent the bowl from flooding under the worst deluge.

The keep stood triumphantly in the middle, the actual residence of the Obertenghi family. It was only initiated by Oberto I, when Adalbert was already dead. Seven and a half lengths of an arm, it was white and smooth, a tall cubic structure with rounded corners, a giant marble column that dared to go higher than anyone had ever ventured to go in all of Christendom. It stood sovereign above a rather low motte, where a wide set of stairs soared from the rim and straightened onto its heavy, but rather small front door. Next to the keep, attached to its back wall, between two other doors that allowed for supplies to be brought into the main kitchen, a narrower tower stretched itself towards the skies continuing to ascend once the keep gave up on it. The tower with its spiralling stairs was finished by Lord Oberto II, Clarissa's father. It was stopped when it stretched out to the same height as twice the measure of the keep. Oberto topped it with a small room, with two narrow windows, facing southeast and northwest. The room was never used as a lookout, for the sentries occupied their posts at the top floor of the keep. The magnificent white ensemble of keep and tower was the most spectacular vision of the Via Francigena, leading pilgrims to elect the gnat-ridden swampy road over the pleasant valley of the Serchio, beyond the Apuane.

Luna was unique in its colour, its height and its defiance. And in three generations that it took to be completed, it emptied the coffers of the Obertenghi, obliging the marchese to venture into his own merchant dealings.

Not only the magnificence of Luna had blown Julian away, but the local ways were as different from his home as if from a world of dreams. The weather was different, the plants were different, the food was different and some of the traditions would have been just unthinkable where he had come from.

To begin with, Julian was utterly embarrassed to participate in excessively frequent baths, when the men of the keep were collectively dunked into wide hot water vats placed in the kitchen and received a vigorous scrub from the servants. It had initially seemed unnecessary, as the regularity of baths in the Maine would have been one for every dozen that he received in Luna. However, his body started to learn to differentiate between bathed, which provided a fresh, sensual feeling of renewal, and...dirty, which could be the only description of the sensation opposed to bathed. After a while, he realised that there was a natural inner craving for that process and he started to enjoy the baths and the cleanliness and purity of his body that they provided. The women bathed even more frequently, which made them more pleasant to look at, even to smell the perfume of their hair, just like rich ripe cherries, ready to be plucked and… well, devoured.

Julian was growing. Of course he kept a good memory of what women looked like and how Louise had felt. He did not know or ever wondered how it worked inside him, but at some point he did become aware of their attractiveness or lack of it. Women were to be loved...or not, at least that's what he had known so far. But once he had fled the French lands and gone to that new part of the world where he had taken refuge, he saw them taking a more active role in men's lives. Women in those lands sat at the table to eat side-by-side with the men, they enjoyed food and hunting, they rode their horses wildly over the dusty roads and they were indeed queens of their own castles. Women in those lands, Julian came to realise, were to be loved, admired, followed, understood, respected, desired, envied and, quite often, feared.

The queen of the castle was no other than Railenda of Lombardy, Marchesa of Toscana. On the evening they had finally arrived, Julian's first vision of the Lady of Luna was at the top of the stairs, a golden apparition catching the last rays of the sunlight. Still trying to absorb the enormity of the castle and its crushing beauty, Julian looked down, terrified at the perspective of meeting Clarissa's mother. After a day crossing the cool marshes of the Lunigiana in winter, Julian stayed at the bottom step while Clarissa went up to greet Railenda. Mother and daughter hugged in silence, an intense exchange of forces, a precious touch to regain after such a long time apart. Railenda looked at Clarissa from head to toe and pressed her lips hard, smiling with pride. But the clear blue ocean of her eyes filled, as if regretting every second of not being with her daughter during her uncountable adventures for that year. Railenda shot a sudden glance over Clarissa's shoulder, towards Julian, who immediately looked down again, before Oberto and Alberto Azzo finally reached to greet her. When they had exchanged more hugs and kisses with the other women of the house and with Alberto's young son, they all turned to Julian.

Clarissa pointed down and said his name for the first time. 'This is Julian, of Mans. He will stay with us.'

Even the hammers ceased to beat on the anvils around the keep. When an excruciating silence engulfed the inner yard of Luna, only the cool sea breeze kept blowing and hanging objects tinkled in workshops far away. Julian could see his own knees shaking. He knew that Oberto and Alberto Azzo had finally learned of his name, but above all, that formidable woman was staring down at him, waiting for him to react. The cry of a seagull was heard, far beyond the walls. Julian bit his lips and realised that the longer he kept his head down, the more implacable the Lady of Luna would be on him. He raised his face and saw her standing alone at the top of the stairs, with relatives around. And his knees went even softer.

Railenda was no less than a goddess incarnated. With a fabulous figure, she was superbly dressed for the occasion. A dark blue woollen tunic closely fit to her body, fitting snugly around her breasts, with a leather belt with metal tassels around her waist and sitting comfortably over generous breeding hips and suggestively raising from side to side as she walked. The tunic opened wide like a trumpet from her elbows, exposing a naked forearm. Perhaps because of the arrival of her husband, she had made it a special occasion, for those arms would have been usually covered by a tight linen chemise. The tunic was long, clinging to her thighs and calves, just widening again around her ankles, to drag itself behind her as the receding waters of the tide. A light wimple, perhaps of silk, rolled suavely around her proud neck and covered the back of her head. Railenda had a rosy face, with a rather tall and ample forehead, adorned by dark golden strands that escaped from her wimple. The head adornment for married women hid very little of her exuberance. With wide square jaws and a round chin that gently pronounced itself at the tip, she was smiling. Those were honest burning lips, well designed, bearing the same pink copper that shone from her smiling cheeks. It was a tight smile indeed, contained and closed, but amused, curious and stretching wide, between a pair of pleasing long dimples, making her fabulous cheeks float higher, like shining apples under her eyes. Even though she had been raised up on the mountains of Lake Como, Railenda had been shaped by the seaside land of Lunigiana where she had come to live. Mostly of a marbling gleam to her skin, sometimes she could be coloured like a dazzling sunset over the white hills, but always imposing a towering figure just as the powerful keep of Luna did. Her wide eyes had a liquid blue, a sample of the Ligurian waters under the sun, flowing bright and refreshing, under a pair of long chestnut eyebrows. That comforted Julian, almost as the most frank smile Railenda was about to open. Her eyebrows were pulled up in the middle towards a very human crease in her forehead, and descended towards the sides, angled in an unmistakable compassionate manner.

'Julian?' asked Railenda. 'I had been told me that our guest would have a different name,' she said, biting her lip with mischief. She extended a well-fleshed arm with a caring open hand, opening also a deliciously refreshing smile. 'Welcome to Luna, Julian.'

Julian almost fell on his knees.

Railenda had learned of Hubert de Liege by reading messages sent from Zena. They came in tiny rolls of parchment attached to pigeons' legs. The birds had been bought over generations from Byzantine merchants, who shipped them from Damascus. They were housed and bred in a columbarium on top of the keep, next to the neck of the tower. In addition to the columbarium, the roof supported a full flower garden and a holm oak, which had been carefully planted on a thin layer of soil. The tree had grown sufficiently to provide a cooling shade in agreeable spring days. The garden was one of Railenda's favourite places, where she could enjoy the country view and, to Julian utmost astonishment, read! Julian had thought that Clarissa knew the arts of reading only because of her unconquerable insistence, but this was a common trend of Italian nobility, where women could indeed read. When Clarissa was not spending time with Julian, Railenda would sometimes call him to join her on the garden. They equally enjoyed those moments, where they could discuss common readings, where she told him of Lunigiana and of her native land, and where she asked him about his. Julian went in little detail on his family and least on his dreams or any of those nightmares. It seemed a faraway world, making itself more distant with the passing of every day. Railenda knew there was a part of his life which had been hidden deep in a dark place. She hardly ever asked. That's verbally, to say the least, for she had little qualms about giving him that tight, intrigued smile, opening wide those seducing drops of blue sea, almost breaking through his shell and bringing out the anguish that tightened around his heart.

'I feel sorry for him' she once confessed to Oberto.

'Sorry?' he said. 'Just because he's infatuated with our Clarissa?'

'No, you silly!' she smiled. Than her lips lost the joy and only her eyebrows maintained the compassion 'It's the pain he carries inside. Whatever happened? Why did he run away?'

Oberto sighed. 'Whatever it was, I don't think it was a crime. Give the boy some time. It will come out one day, like a boil finally bursting to heal. But I do think that Clarissa already knows it.'

Railenda laughed 'Now *she*'s the best secret keeper in the world. We won't find it out through that one.'

Of the people in Luna, Julian had always found a soothing company with Railenda. While Clarissa challenged his senses, Oberto challenged his knowledge and Alberto challenged the resilience of his muscles, it was Railenda who provided the heart-warming comfort that Julian needed once in a while. Sitting with Railenda where the sea breeze blew freely through the white and pink rockroses put him at peace. Like Clarissa, Railenda had the power of a Goddess, but in a tamed manner, contained and mellow, perfectly adjusted to bring Julian at peace with himself.

Upon Julian's arrival, Railenda was quick to transfer him from the hall, where guests normally slept, to one of the rooms above, with its own window, chest and mattress. She did treat him as son, but still as a man, unlike his mother that was still calling him a cub by the time he fled. And although he was ashamed of having done so, Julian caught himself comparing Railenda with his mother in more than one occasion. There was no helping it: in a very short period, Railenda did learn to love Julian like a son, and he soon loved her like a mother. It just took them too late to ever express it one day.

Two more women lived in Luna in the times when Julian lived with the Obertenghi. The Obertenghi were, of course, the family that Oberto descended from. Although family names were still not consistently repeated across generations in those times, some families were known collectively by the name of their heads or famous ancestors.

But back to the women, Alberto Azzo's wife was Adela, a robust, wide-hipped Ligurian woman who was passionate for Luna, as opposed to the noisy streets of her native Genova. From a rich family of merchants, Adela had been chosen by Alberto himself, smitten by her beauty, over any pre-arrangement between noble families or strategic alliances. With a rather long face, firm chin, an elegant neck and a generous volume of wavy black hair contrasting with her white skin, she had almond-shaped brown eyes, firm eyebrows, perfect teeth and a long, powerful nose that would make men bow in respect at the sight of her commanding presence. When Adela was around, Julian struggled to stare elsewhere than at her superb chest: a set of spectacular bouncy breasts that magically floated above an unbelievably thin waist. The omnipresence of those well-irrigated mounds would certainly explain, if anyone ever survived to know, why her son would live strong enough to see the age of one hundred years. But then, five year old son Albertazzo was still being reared to be the Lord of Luna one day. When Albertazzo was out, being instructed by the men of Luni, Adela would often engage into the coops, granaries and kitchen, supervising servants, guaranteeing that a fresh meal in Luna was a memory to be kept to heart, only to be swept away by the next one. Like all women in those lands, Adela cooked well and ate well. Her presence was particularly stimulating to the appetite and she smelled of thyme, rosemary and roasts. Somehow Julian could never dissociate the glorious food in those lands from the inspiring presence of Adela.

Bertha was the second child of Oberto and Railenda. She had been promised to marry Odalrico Manfredo, son of Manfredo I, Marchese of Torino. Julian was again surprised to learn how late women got married in Italian lands. French women were being wedded at fourteen, but in Tuscany, Liguria and all of Lombardia, men were even forbidden to take into marriage women younger than eighteen. But at Julian's arrival in Luni, Bertha still had two more years to wait before her wedding. Now, if anyone could imagine whether Railenda could have been a less beautiful woman in her teens, they only had to look at Bertha and see exactly how stunning the lady of Luna would have looked a couple of decades before. Courteous and shy, Bertha had bright gold hair, which was usually carefully braided around the sides of a colourful face. Her wide eyes with great turquoise blue gems took after Railenda's Lombard stock, innocently lighting a face that was bound to be forever girlish. With ample cheeks topped by a light streak of freckles that crossed over a small rounded nose, Bertha's skin had a healthy tan that was loved by the Ligurian sun, blushing easily like a ripe peach even when a distracted bumblebee buzzed by. Bertha would dream of her future husband and the daughters they would have. She divided those flowery visions with a distracted Clarissa, who always had a smile to share back, in spite of a raised eyebrow of amusement. Bertha loved babies, children and animals. She would melt at the mere sight of dogs and puppies. Her blue gems would grow brighter while she cooed and made sweet sounds of adoration. Or else she would giggle like a dove when she fed the ducks by the pond and watched the warblers bending the reeds. Luna had always been in love with Bertha. Even the local marble masons knew that the rock was much softer when Bertha walked by.

She had little notion of the most appealing explosion of changes that had taken shape in her body. But no matter how well-behaved were the cuts and designs of her tunics, the wayward fabric always managed to disobey its purposes and sensuously cling to her curves, whether under the gusty spells of the Tramontana breezes or the sweaty heat of the Sirocco winds, always revealing the intense fervour that slept under those muscles. And like a bright sculpture made from a basket of fruits – lush, red, ripened fruits - Bertha smelled of plums. So enticing and invigorating was her fragrance that a magic change took place on living things when she timidly walked around the grounds of Luna. Women would smile, boys would straighten up, men held their bellies in and inflated their chests, and little girls would sigh. The timid Bertha was often pulled by the hand by the young indomitable Clarissa to play outside, when they'd take off their boots to run around the gardens or on the grass near the moats. While Clarissa ran like a boy, Bertha's magic steps were careful and light, leaving the ground with a swift caress, but almost treating it back with respect when she flexed her long legs, on a musical movement that even made the marble of Luna hold its breath, to finally step down again and touch it from her toes. It was firmly believed that freshly pressed olive oil tasted better after Bertha went out for a morning stroll and many people in Luna could swear they were able to see the grass growing longer and more lush after Bertha had stepped on it.

When Julian courteously bowed to Bertha at their introduction, he hardly noticed her extraordinary attributes, or even that she was a young woman of his own age. It took him the next two years to appreciate her beauty and enjoy her quiet company. But there was just no space inside of him for anyone else. He was just filled up to his veins with Clarissa.

And it only took Oberto and Railenda's oldest daughter a very furtive glance towards Clarissa's face. Bertha clearly understood that she could never allow herself even to think about the young visitor. The flames in Clarissa's eyes were so fierce that Bertha realised her little sister would spit them out like a dragon as soon as anyone raised a finger to take Julian away from her.

Then, of course, there was Clarissa, the youngest of the marchese three children.

One day, Julian would see that girl as a strange composition of the most extraordinary beasts of divine creation.

But not so soon.

During those first years in Luna he just could not even begin to describe how Clarissa differed from anyone else, except that she seemed to be growing by the day, and towards only one direction: up. With the agonising perspective that he would never have a chance to hold Clarissa for himself, Julian secretly prayed to God that her growth never took the direction towards those fabulous shapes of her mother. The milky whiteness of her lengthy feminine features were still a raw version of what Railenda's rosy voluptuousness had turned out to be.

Boyish, but suave, rough, determined and full of fire, Clarissa ran free like a wild creature of the woods, indomitable, beautiful and fleeting, so difficult to get a good glimpse of, impossible to hold on to. The fearless girl was the owner of her own small nose. She went wherever she decided to, she did whatever she wanted and she saw whomever she intended to. In one way or another, she always got what she wanted. And from Julian, of course. It just was too easy for Clarissa to get Julian to do things, to obey her, a blind obedience that she did not prize as much as he would have thought. But father and mother were not falling so easy to her commanding charm. Oberto avoided confrontations and Railenda often resisted longer, but they both ended up accepting her wisdom or her pleads. Not that Clarissa was any whiny, spoiled brat. If she detected unfairness, she would work for justice, but if anyone went all the distance to upset her, she would take revenge. And she knew so well that the most savage revenge would be to ignore their existence from this world. She would shut the doors from her kingdom. She could hurt indeed, but without raising a finger. Finally if she was ever seen to be pouting, she was just being plain cruel.

Nobody could ever remember Clarissa raising her voice or being mean. Clarissa was simply the most generous creature that they had ever known. And to anyone that would madly fall in love with such creature, having to share her with the rest of the world would be no less than infuriating. Anyone with a heart flooding with Clarissa would be naturally oozing jealousy through all of his pores. But she could not tolerate jealousy. The punishment was to give herself even more intensely to the rest of the world.

Such a young girl, but carrying the power of an army in her gaze. Her lower lip could make Julian's legs bend when she pouted and her absence could make him turn into dust. But the silent summer pastures of Clarissa's eyes could lift Julian from the ground and nurture him into a floating state of comfort and eternal happiness. People in Luni said the rainbows in the region always started from the castle, emanating from the light of her eyes. The feast of colours she had taken after Oberto, although his eyes were predominantly violet, while hers were green. The dark, chestnut hair had obviously been stolen from his side too, Julian could tell. But Railenda had given her the seductive powers of which she still managed with a crushing result, whereas her mother could soften them.

Once Julian dreamed that he was holding on to the shoulders of a walking giant that stepped over miles and miles of land. He held on to the giant's long brown hair. The giant was Clarissa. Julian never wanted the dream to end. He was safe, close to heaven, and he could smell her scent, all for himself. Clarissa had the sweet smell of milk.

When Julian's horse thundered through the drawbridge, the rider could immediately feel the cool air that water and stone raised, as opposed to the muggy heat of the travelling path.

The treacherous moats of Luna were only finished in the times of Lord Oberto I. They had been dug into different depths, with concealed pits and deep chasms, palisades and boulders. The level of water, equalled with the swamps and lagoons in the region, would only allow for safe boating for one person on a light paddling craft.

Julian rode into the stables and impatiently cared for the horse's first needs until a servant offered to take over. Grabbing his present for Clarissa with precious care, he ran up the stairs of the keep and pushed the door in.

The Groom

Many years ago, an old merchant and banker from Lucca went on a journey to sell precious goods to the bishop in Gallecia. He entrusted the family business in Lucca to his young son and his pregnant daughter-in-law. Unfortunately, in those times, one of his debtors, the head of a rich Lucchese family - of which I should not be naming here for obvious reasons - was a cruel, unscrupulous man, who seized the opportunity to get rid of the merchant and erase the debt from the records. The young merchant was sequestered by the debtor's thugs, dragged out and locked into the tallest tower in Lucca. Looking through the lone window that eyed the city from its top, he saw his housed being sacked. This was his end, he thought, and probably the same to his wife and the unborn child she carried. Desperation filled him with images of his father in urbe Compostella, piously adorning the relics of St. James the Great with riches brought from Lucca. He fervently prayed to the apostle of Christ to save him from that imprisonment and give him back his merchandise and, even more precious, the accounting books. Waking up in the middle of the night, he faced an apparition. Diffused by a divine light which emanated from its heart, there stood a man with no head, carrying a dead head in his arms. A voice inside the merchant's heart told him to step out through the window and go home. Looking out, he saw that the window was strangely on ground level with the streets. The merchant swiftly jumped onto the paved ground and looked back to see the tower, which had bent, leaning itself down all the way to allow him escape. The light inside the window was suddenly gone and the giant brick building immediately straightened up to its majestic rigid position. He reached his house to find all the merchandise piled up inside, and a man bringing back the last bale of wool, who told the merchant that they had all seen the ghost of St. John, the Baptist at his lord's palace. The ghost ordered them to give back all that had been stolen, the lord to pay his debts and never to pursue the merchant again, for he had been divinely released from imprisonment. When the first son of the young merchant was born, he named him after St. John the Baptist.

'This is an interesting but unbelievable tale, shepherd.' Immanuel said.

'But wait!' continued the storyteller with a devious grin. 'I am not finished!'

The old banker finally returned from Gallecia to see his son prospering in trade and loans, now with an enlarged family. On hearing the story of his son's imprisonment and release by an apparition, the banker thanked God and St. James for the help and justice. He also laughed on everyone's ignorance for the assumption that the headless ghost was that of St. John the Baptist. 'That was for sure St. James the Greater', reassured the banker. 'Like the Baptist, James was also decapitated!'

'Well done.' Immanuel said with grace. 'I am not sure if I understand it all, and I hope my old Magyar friend has captured some of it.'

'I did, fönök. I did.' Said Béla reassuringly. He waved his arm on the gesture of the tower leaning to the ground, accompanied by an almost toothless smile.

'Your friend picks up quickly' said the young shepherd. He imitated Béla's gesture, saying condescendingly 'Yes, tower!'

Sided by cypress hedges and walking through dried cucumber-scented fields of dry borage shrubs, they soon walked over the hill's edge and the towers did start to show themselves ahead of them. This time the shepherd pointed to the city and exclaimed with a genuine joy. 'There! There is Lucca! Those are the towers I was talking about!'

Whereas Immanuel opened a wide smile, charmed by the magnificence of the city down the valley and the towers that proudly rose from inside its walls, Béla frowned, devising that amalgamation of buildings with sceptical eyes. While Rome seemed like a huge dead carcass to the táltos, Lucca looked to him like a very live beast, cornered inside its fenced area, ready to strike at any time.

'I can just see them leaning down...' said Immanuel with a raised eyebrow. He turned to the shepherd. 'What about you? How can a shepherd know so much? Where did you learn Greek?'

'I am just not a shepherd yet. And I am a free man' he said proudly. 'I was educated at the abbey of San Michele, in Pesa.'

'Pisa?'

'No, Pesa!' He looked at both impassive foreigners, who obviously made no geographical acknowledgement of the place or to the strangeness of him being formally educated. 'Last year, I accompanied my abbot on pilgrimage to the abbey of Saint Michael, in Normandy. Now I have finished my education, and just returning to begin my herding. My family, we are descendants of Adalbert II, Margrave of Tuscany. We own land on the western bank on the valley of the Serchio, north of Lucca and we have some serfs who tend areas for my gain and their own, of course.'

'And what brings you here, south of Lucca?' Immanuel asked.

'I accompanied a friend who came from France to this hamlet of Santa Maria Lei Giudice, right where I came across your party. My friend was looking for a woman, but we did not find her.'

'Pity.' said Immanuel.'

'He is heartbroken, but he follows on to Rome. It's another long tale, but I am sure you are not prepared to hear it.'

'Thank you.' Said Immanuel courteously, relieved to be spared from another fantasy. 'Do you go into Lucca with us?'

'I would be honoured, but I go straight through, to the western side of the wall. I stay with the priests of San Donato. Then I return to my lands, to see my family...'

'Your wife and children?'

'No, I have not settled with a woman yet. Too young for that!' he said with an apologetic smile, before drawing breath and changing to a more serious countenance. 'I go see my parents and take onto the herds and the land.'

Immanuel reached into a satchel attached to his horse's saddle and pulled out a map.

The young storyteller was quick to locate what he wanted on the chart. 'Here it is!' he said, pointing to a spot on the map. 'I live on these lands. Across the river is land owned by the Cunimundinghi, including the old baths at Corsena, where you told me you'll be going. So why don't you come straight through and travel with me on the next day?'

'We do have to stop at Battista Burle's bank, in Lucca, and I don't know how long we will be.' Immanuel explained.

'Of course! You had mentioned that already, hence the tale I told you. Are you selling merchandise? Buying anything?'

'I can only sell my services' Immanuel said with a shy smile. 'I have nothing on me, but papal letters and my will to settle and improve the conditions in this Corsena. Recover the baths.'

'That will be a strenuous job. I have seen those baths and they are in absolute ruins. Anything that has once been there is buried under rubble and weeds. And that was when I was only a small child.'

Immanuel made a small gesture with his hands. 'I have nothing else to do, other than be dedicated to my craft, with the help of Béla and the Holy Father in Rome.'

'And what does Battista Burle have to do —'

'I think I am being sent to marry his daughter!' Immanuel conceded, interrupting the obvious question. He rubbed his hands nervously, with a sad smile. His tiny blue eyes were moving hastily to the sides.

The young shepherd was silent for a while, searching for the best words. He looked up to the sky and noticed that a bird was still gliding high above. It had been around since he had left Santa Maria Lei Giudice that morning.

'You are a lucky man, then!' he said, composing an agreeably framed smile.

'Is she a beautiful young woman?' There was still a flicker of hope into his heart.

'I don't know. I have never seen her. But I know she is the only daughter. It means your children will inherit the Burle bank! You do have a star shining upon you!'

Immanuel quietly lowered his eyes.

They were crossing some of the ploughed spinach fields, olive groves and farmsteads, stables and coops on the southwest of the city. Soon they entered the town outside the walls, a whole village huddled along the battlements, with a mixed variety of construction, from miserable sheds to solidly built houses.

'These are the *vellutini*', the shepherd explained, as they crossed the strip of windowless shacks, where worn women tended cauldrons steaming with interesting aromas that blended into the stench of stagnant water, dogs sniffed the dejecta accumulated outside the doors and a good number of children played in the mud. 'They are mostly ignorant free peasants that have come to the city seeking better luck. With no place to live *intramuri*, inside the walls, they have still developed into an intrinsic part of the local economy, squeezed on this narrow land between the walls and the marshes around. Indeed one can obtain many services among the vellutini, as well as goods, and precious information. It is said that Lucca could not live without them these days. You will find that the term vellutini is the local Lucchese slang, from the times when the first families to install themselves *extramuri*, outside the walls, were Sicilians, referring to their velvet patch that grows on their head in place of real hair!' He laughed generously.

Immanuel was not amused. He was not even paying attention to the shepherd, but staring fixed at the western gate. That's where the shepherd would leave them, at the square-fronted new church of San Donato, a twin construction of the monastery of Santa Maria Ursimanni, by the inner side of the gate. Immanuel and his party would follow on to enter Lucca.

'I think I am a bit nervous' he confessed.

The shepherd halted seemed to understand the significance of the moment for that man, travelling in from so far. He tapped Immanuel on the shoulder. 'You should not worry, good man. Battista Burle is very rich, but he is known for being a generous and amicable merchant. Burle is himself from a foreign family that came to Lucca few generations ago. The Lucchese are friendly folk and they heartily take in foreigners like you, far better than they seem to tolerate the vellutini, or accept the peasants up and down the river valleys, such as me, or even more than respect any noble families extramuri, such as the marchese's or the Filippi. But you? You will be welcomed.'

But Immanuel was still not listening. His eyes were set on an invisible point beyond the gate. There, inside those walls, he would find the woman to be his and a piece of land to work on. The frail little convert who had endured so much during that past year was now shaking on his legs.

'When you come to Corsena,' said the shepherd, already retiring from their company with an amiable bow, 'get the local folk to let me know you have arrived. I will come down to welcome you and your friend. And your wife too, of course. My name is Bernardo. Like they did to my father, folk in the valley will be calling me Bernardo From The Rocks.'

They waved farewell, but Bernardo came quickly back to them for a last remark.

'And do ask Battista Burle about the tale I told you, you know, the tower that leaned to the ground? Yes it was Battista's father who was visited by the ghost of St. James.'

Battista Burle was a much taller and larger man than Immanuel feared he would be. Even sitting at the desk in front to the standing Bukhari, who had just arrived out of nowhere, with a letter from the pope and a suspicious old Magyar on his side, the banker raised one eye to look at Immanuel's own on the same level, as the other eye seemed to be still verifying if he had understood the message of Sylvester II correctly. The facial expression was expanded by the volume of Battista's eyebrows, which looked to Immanuel like a pair of restless porcupines. The Bukhari arched one side of his upper lip, but the rest of his face could not smile accordingly.

The office was exuding a warming mixture of fragrances of spices, leather, woods and wine. Parchments and quills littered Battista's worn desk, lit by a wide shaft of dusty sunlight that sprouted from a small window high on the wall. The window could be shut from inside.

Battista Burle now dropped the letter and squinted at Immanuel, curling his lips as if catching a particularly bad whiff while trying to focus. 'Come closer', he said in clear Greek, 'into the light, please'. Immanuel dared to lift his trembling foot from the floor and shyly stepped into the beam. Battista leaned back on his chair, still holding the papal letter, dropped his jaw and, with his mouth hanging open like a lion's, examined his soon-to-be son-in-law for what seemed to be a long, long time. Finally, he said. 'A *Giudeo*?'

Immanuel cleared his throat and began. 'That is quite true, but I was baptised into the embrace of our Lord Jesus Christ by the Most Holy Father, confirmed by the Beatissimo Padre as they call him here...'

'Please, please, please!' interrupted Battista, 'I know! I know that part.' He waved the papal letter. 'It's all in here and I understand it well.' He leaned over, resting his elbows on the desk, with joined hands touching only by the tips of the fingers. 'Immanuel Malachi, you are probably looking at the only soul in all of Lucca that has ever heard about Bukhara. See?' He waved around an open hand with his palm up, casually indicating some rolls of fabric behind them. 'I sell silk! Not of good quality and neither as much as I wanted. And I believe it comes from your part of this world. Many *Giudei* there?'

Immanuel missed the question. He was still looking at the silk bundles and rolls that hid in the dark back of the room. The distraction did not seem to annoy Battista, but rather amuse him. Looking back at the banker, the Bukhari was ready to apologise for his rudeness when he captured Battista's sympathetic nod. Immanuel turned back to the silk bundles and felt the fabric with the tip of his fingers. Béla stood unmoved, with his eyes staring at some point beyond the window, as Battista leaned back on his chair and just watched.

'How much do you pay for silk?' Immanuel asked.

Battista gasped, straightened his body with a clumsy jolt and cleared his throat. 'Listen here, young man,' he said with annoyance, 'you may come into my trade house with a letter from the pope praising your worth.' He held a forced smile, but the serenity in his eyes indicated that he was not taking it too seriously. 'I may have to lay my trust on these references to employ you to recover the *bagni* at Corsena. You are a foreigner, a highly questionable candidate and I may be obliged to consider wedding my daughter Elvira to you, but that does not mean that I will share any secrets of my trade with you.'

The Bukhari dropped his gaze in silence, holding his skullcap on his hand, casually waving an imaginary insect from his face. Finally he shook his head, brushing off the embarrassment and said with modesty. 'I wish to take no secrets from you, Battista Burle. But as you are to be my father-in-law, I thought I could share with you one of mine.'

Battista remained immovable, contained on his chair, looking with a screaming silence at the daring young man, but he was betrayed by one side of his face, that twitched. Realising the subtle facial movement had given away his curiosity, he chuckled. 'Smart man! Smart man you are, Immanuel Malachi. It's tempting to ask you to indulge me, but I will refrain from the... discomfiture, even if the only audience to witness is your old Magyar friend, here.'

'As you wish.' Immanuel said with an elegant head bow.

The banker abruptly stood up, looking at the window. 'The hour is late and there is much to be talked about. You come with nothing, if not for a letter from the Beatissimo Padre. Well, stranger, let me tell you something: for me, that is not enough'. He extended his arm and courteously led them both out to the warehouse, which opened to the street. 'Elvira is my only daughter, and I could care less if she died a virgin – actually I think that was her mother's wish – against marrying a nobody, even if this nobody was a protégé of the good Lord Himself.'

Immanuel made to step out to reach the pack on his donkey, left tied to one of the front posts. 'I have values!' he added with certain desperation on his voice. 'There's something here that perhaps I should show you.' But his arm was held by the banker.

'Please, please, Immanuel Malachi. All in its time!' Battista spoke with a patronising attitude and he did not let Immanuel open his pack. He switched the expression to a serious transaction-like tone. 'You have not seen Corsena yet and I want to hear your opinion on the baths. We should make our way up the Serchio tomorrow. I will feed you and your escorts, and we leave tomorrow morning.' The banker observed the movement of people up and down the street and casually mentioned 'You will have a chance to see my daughter at supper.'

Immanuel just allowed his chin to slowly drop. He raised his tiny blue eyes to the large banker, expressionless. Battista looked back and barked 'And do wipe that stupid expression off your face, because I am already regretting giving you any attention at all'.

It was of no help.

When Battista was turning around to leave, Béla jumped towards Immanuel to whisper something, quite nervously.

'What is your friend mumbling about?' grunted Battista, with a luxuriant eyebrow raised.

With a lowered gaze and one foot dragging an arc on the dusty floor, Immanuel explained 'We met a shepherd on our way to Lucca. A silly boy, really. He told us of a story... a story of a banker locked in a tower and...you know, just a stupid story, honestly. He told us that the banker saw a ghost and the tower leaned over to the ground to let him out. Do excuse my friend here. Béla actually wants to know if there is any truth in this story.'

Battista remained motionless, as if something was building up inside, but it only ended with a twitch on one side of his face. 'A shepherd?' he finally asked, 'Who told you that story?'

'A young man called Bernardo. Bernardo From The Rocks, maybe?'

'Ah!' exclaimed Battista almost with a smile 'The boy is back already? Well that explains.' The banker turned to Béla and measured him from head to toes. He squinted and said with gravity 'Old man, our world is not for us to explain and you probably know that, being a man of medicine and magic. You hear stories about my family before you meet me and I hear tales about you ahead of our acquaintance. Word is that you are watched by an enormous eagle, and I should respect this prodigy if it is true. Now, this Bernardo Delle Rocche is from a smart family of storytellers. Believe me and believe him. All that he said was true. The tower, Saint James, ghost, everything.' And he wrapped up with a contained smirk 'It is embarrassing still, to know that my father mistook the very St James that he had prayed for someone else. Or else I would have been named Giacomo Burle.'

Her face was plain. Round and flat, it had not been granted by nature with any lines, curves or features that could have made it more interesting. It reminded Immanuel of a raw *laffah*, the flat wheat bread. Her almond-shaped eyes would have been beautiful if they were not malpositioned. Far apart from each other and hidden behind pouches that were too fat and dark for comfort, they dropped to the sides on a melancholic angle with her nose. Her narrow straight nose. A bony line almost flattened against the disc or her face. The mouth? Immanuel could not really find anything wrong with her mouth. The thin, but protruding upper lip lined a stubborn and rather charming mouth that would have been gracious if inserted on a different face, or maybe if it ever smiled. But smiling was not on Elvira's nature.

Immanuel tried not to, but his eyes did lower to the body to verify her shape. No particular curves or volumes that indicated she would be a good breeding mother. There was a volume, of course, but nothing that called onto a mate.

'What do you think?' Battista asked.

'Does it actually matter what I think?' Elvira replied shortly, without changing her expression of either heartfelt piousness or utmost boredom. She did not seem to see her father raising his gaze to a superior power above, begging for the necessary patience to deal with his daughter.

'Well, why don't you think it this way?' Battista suggested, widening a grin that did little to cover his annoyance 'is this a man you can spend the rest of your life to live happily with?'

With no more than her eyes, Elvira measured Immanuel with unhidden disdain, but she did not meet his gaze. Still looking at the Bukhari with her permanently frozen uninterested expression, she asked her father 'Can he only speak Greek?'

Battista exhaled, with a feeling of relief. 'I am sure he speaks other languages of the East too, but no, I don't think he masters Lombard.' He turned to Immanuel and grunted in Greek 'You must learn our language.' Back to Elvira, Battista insisted 'Will you be happy if you can at least communicate?'

'If not joining a religious community, as it is not of your wish, I will be satisfied with resigning to a simple life, dedicated to growing children and servicing God.' She let out a subtle sneer and finally looked at her father. 'Happiness is a blessing which is achieved naught but after our corporeal life.'

Battista sighed. 'I should never be surprised by your attitude, but it still startles me how much worse than your mother you turned out to be.' With a sudden renewed mood, rubbing his hands, he changed to Immanuel, who had not opened his mouth all the time since Elvira had joined them at the dining table. 'That does it for me, I mean, for her. For me, in reality, it does not suffice. I want to see what you make of the bagni. Only then will I have an opinion on whether I should marry Elvira to you or not. As for you,' he gazed into the Bukhari tiny blue eyes, and pointed bluntly to his daughter, who observed with a cantankerous face 'this is what you get. Nothing more, nothing less. If you don't like it, make yourself aware that the door is open. Just pick-up your eagle-man and get the hell out of my sight. If you take it, you are welcome to follow me tomorrow to Corsena and later I decide.'

Immanuel resigned with a nod, but before the banker disappeared inside the warehouse, he halted Battista, speaking for the first time without being addressed to. 'Battista Burle, I will go with you, I will care for Elvira and you will not regret granting us your blessing. But I need you to do me a favour or you will most certainly regret not having helped me if you resolve to.'

Battista raised an inquisitive, invasive, if not shocked eyebrow. 'And what favour might this be?'

'Do you own many fertile lands?' asked Immanuel.

'A little bit here, a little bit there...' the banker said with pursed lips.

Immanuel nodded, now with a certain condescension, as if that was exactly the answer he was expecting. Battista was stung by a drop of admiration, for he realised they indeed spoke the same language.

Immanuel continued 'And as a merchant, do you have a vast network of contacts in different countries?'

Battista said matter-of-factly 'Anywhere you want, Immanuel.

'Then I have something that might interest you. But for your participation, at this stage, you will have to help me write a letter'.

Battista once again was paralysed, looking in silence at the man who was willing to marry his daughter. And again he was betrayed by the twitching on one side of his face. He closed his eyes and raised a solemn finger, choosing his words for a second, before saying 'Immanuel Ben-Malachi of Bukhara. As your mysteries, enigmas and surprises build up by the minute, let me tell you of a secret which is quite not a secret, but well known throughout Lucca. The Burle have been trading for many generations. But only for three or four have we been converted to the Christian faith. Like most of the merchant families in this city, the Di Cunizi, the Rapondi, the Filippi and the Kalonymos family that left for German lands, the Burle were also Giudei.'

Immanuel contained a smirk. 'Then...will you do me this favour?'

While staying for a few weeks at a foundry village south of Acquisgranus, before his journey back to Constantinople, the Greek merchant Procopius received a visit from a young Flemish, an associate in Nijmegen of the Burle house of trade. The Flemish brought him a sealed letter. When Procopius opened the parchment and read those lines written in Greek and Latin, much in a merchant's confusing code, he had to hold off a smile. He read it again and a third time, before asking the young Flemish to wait for him to write his response, to be sent back to Lucca.

Procopius's lines were settling the beginning of a deal, a simple plan for a gift to the emperor in exchange of a secret.

A gift that would establish a symbolic position of the emperor as a direct descendant of the old Caesars of classic Rome. Mounted on a cross, it could survive more than a thousand years as symbol of the Sacred Roman Empire.

The secret the Greek merchant would be sharing would allow the launch of Lucca into the top of Christendom's economic pyramid, forever enriching the city, its families and merchants, transforming the small Lombard settlement in a repository for riches which would finance the wars of Europe for the following four centuries.

Procopius knew his acceptance of the deal would make him a rich man. What he did not know was the vast and deep lines that this idea of his would carve in the profile of Lucca, Tuscany and all of Western Europe. Neither could the Greek calculate that, after major expansion and success for his personal business, the letter would signify the definitive doom for him and his family.

Leviathan

The moats around Luna teemed with life. Not only the snails, frogs, newts and a variety of fish and eels that were hidden under the surface, but one could observe the inhabitants of the moat even from the battlements of the castle. There were flashes of blue, emerald and purple, of coots, gallinules and moorhens, carefully stepping on the lilies with wide-reaching toes, as larger swamphens nervously flicked their white tails, scavenging the grasses of the green banks for fat snails. Ghostly little egrets stood still, gazing the sunny mirror of the moat, patiently waiting for their minnows to swim by in the shallows. On the dark waters, noisy pochards, teals, pintails, grebes and widgeons were swimming, diving and dabbling, and often flapping their wings in loud displays of their unmistakable duckishness. If walking by the castle walls, one would hear the booming and clicking and buzzing and wheezing of bitterns, night herons, woodcocks, snipes, harvest mice and water voles, forever invisible behind the thick forests of tall reeds. And by the eastern walls of Luna, known as the backside, the moat was rather shallow, separating the fortification from that narrow meadow and a thick hedge of dead thorny trees, an unused area which became feeding grounds for seasonal battalions of stilts, curlews, plovers, dotterels, oystercatchers, sandpipers and shovelers, all stabbing the land, digging their long beaks deep into the ground for quick morsels. The thorny dead hedge was an ugly sight, but perfect hiding area for many of these birds and it had occasionally been used for nesting by rabbits, gulls, cormorants, wood pigeons and terns, which laid their eggs under its protection. Clarissa could recall a couple of years before, when a pair of black storks that yearly fed on voles and frogs on the bank nested on top of the tallest of the thorn trees. But now, a pair of sparrowhawks stood guard on that site.

Lord Oberto strictly forbade any hunting within a two mile circle around the castle and the town of Luni. Although waterfowl was not considered noble game, the marchese and his ancestors had been led to believe that keeping the birds around considerably diminished any odds of the inhabitants contracting swamp fever.

Whereas Clarissa would take Julian to enjoy the views of the castle's environs, Alberto accompanied him to faraway marshes where they exercised some bow and arrow, mainly on the abundant mallards and coots. Although the most prized of their game was the woodcock, its reclusive habits, shy nature and camouflaged cover made it very difficult to find among the reeds. Mostly, the Obertenghi were happy to occasionally feast on coots, which were abundant in the marshes of the region. In his native Maine, Julian knew those black birds as *foulques*, which never ceased to remind him of that daunting Foulques Nerra, who preferred to be known as a *falcon*. But in Luna coots were, more comfortably for Julian, known as *folaghe*.

The sun had hardly set its first lights out when Julian left Luna that morning to visit one of the northern marshes. A maze of paths around thickets of reeds, lakes, and treacherous quagmires, the hunting area was well guarded by surrounding villages, and fairly safe from bandits, who would not dare to enter the labyrinth and never find their way out again. Careful with his steps, Julian gained ground with silent feet, which still scared away mice and snake-like skinks that were about to come out for their first sun rays, hurriedly slithering under the grass instead. In every pond Julian walked by, frogs still delivered their last furious croaks before disappearing behind a splash, and crickets with tired legs rubbed their last chirps of the night. That cool air was precious in the middle of summer, buffering well the marshy smell of decay, not so pungent at that time of the day, but blended instead with the salty western breeze, bringing up a sweet, fruity scent of seashells and softly allowing for the waving tall grasses, heather, cork oaks, rockroses and amaranths to spread their fragrances along the path.

Julian had never felt as safe as he was, even in the middle of that warren, and neither so invigorated and full of life, even in spite of being so far away from where he had come from. Except that he wouldn't have felt it this way if Clarissa had not been with him. Or, to better describe it, Julian had been guided, directed and guarded the whole time, from Luna to the centre of the swamp, by a cheerful and diligent Clarissa.

Dressed as a boy, with her long brown hair bundled under her shirt, carrying a length of rope over her shoulders, she indicated the path and let Julian lead the way, with his bow and arrow on hands. The trail coiled through a series of lakes and marshes where a multitude of game paraded in the early hours of the day.

'Actually, the marshes are not that difficult to explore,' she said quietly, as they advanced through galleries under the giant grass and rockroses. 'There are some tall thickets that we can easily recognise, with pines and poplars to the west, or willows to the east, cork oaks to the north and maritime pines behind us, in the south. We are getting closer to the centre, where a large elm tree reigns. The whole reputation of this area as a maze is more to keep strangers away. Let pilgrims stay on their path, says my father.'

Julian had stopped, crouching behind an abundant area of reeds. He strung an arrow and waited, wordless. Clarissa could only see a warbler singing on a swinging reed, until a flock of coots appeared swimming in line from behind the thicket.

When she saw the muscles on Julian's arm thicken as he pulled the string, she lightly tapped on him on the shoulder.

'What is it Clarissa?' he asked, relaxing the bow, not a bit disappointed with missing that opportunity, but delighted with every single time she touched him.

'Julian, we have a couple of hours here before the sun gets too hot. You should know that when you shoot a coot, it must be plucked immediately and taken back as soon as possible to be dipped in vinegar.' She raised an eyebrow. 'Kill those coots now and we will have to return to Luna. Adela would not like to receive coots that went off already.'

Julian smiled and suggested 'Let's find a place to sit. There'll probably be some ducks there.'

They sat for hours, soothed by each other's gaze, often silent, just listening to the sounds of heaven. Julian never wanted that to end.

They returned to their horses and rode back to Luna, bringing a pair of shelducks and a string of six coots. Clarissa insisted in taking the horses back to the stables, so Julian could show the birds to the women of the castle.

Railenda quickly called Adela to appreciate the beautiful colours of the shelducks, which they had never eaten before. From their bright red beak to white and chestnut body, pink feet and dark green head, Railenda mentioned that they looked like heavenly creatures. The proud Julian had to agree, just to himself, that it did feel like he had been to heaven, to have Clarissa on his side. Adela took the coots to the kitchen and yanked their skins out, telling the servants to dip them into vinegar. In this moment, her husband Alberto Azzo broke through the front door.

'Julian, do you want to see a true demon?' he asked in a hurry. He did not wait for an answer, but rushed up the stairs to see Lord Oberto, disappearing behind another door. It felt to Julian as fast-as-lightning, but enough to stir an uncomfortable heat in the cool marble interior of Luna.

The Lady Railenda stood up from her chair, covering her mouth as if repressing an incautious curse. 'A demon?' asked she. 'Did I just hear my son mention a true demon, Julian?'

But Julian was lost for words. Especially due to Alberto's perplexing grin. The young Lord of Luna asked him the question with a childlike lividness across his face. What could make him refer so lightly to demons?

Alberto soon came back from conferring with his father. 'Let's go, Julian,' he said.

The Lady Railenda immediately walked to stand behind Julian, holding his shoulders with trembling, but protecting hands. Holding onto Julian's shoulder also helped her stop from shaking. Julian had grown taller than she was. That young, sweet stranger that they brought home one day, with foreign manners and a big heart, eager to learn, dying to please.

'But what devilry is this?' she asked her son.

'Oh mother, it's a Leviathan!' Alberto said. 'A sea monster that destroys ships and devours men. But nothing to worry,' he said, on seeing Railenda's eyes opening wider, 'This Leviathan is dead, washed up by the village of Amelia, at the river mouth. Come Julian, I am certain that you have never seen a demon before. Even my little sister is looking forward to see it. She's on the stables, re-saddling two other horses for you two. You will ride after the men-at-arms.'

'And why would you take the armed men with you?' asked Railenda, while Julian leaped out through the front door, forgetting about demons and only thinking about the ride with Clarissa.

'Oh, my mother,' said Alberto, 'that's because a demon brings trouble with it. It seems that one of the villagers has already been killed in a local fight for the meats.'

They rode under the high sun, a score of men-at-arms, crossing the village of Luni, bathed by the hot, humid Sirocco wind blowing from Southeast.

'The Sirocco in June?' said Alberto, turning his face against the wind and smelling the air. 'Just until last night we had the Ponente, the sunset wind, blowing against us. This is unusual,' he spat and curled his lip, 'the Sirocco brings dust, diseases and death. The Leviathan is already at work.'

Clarissa raised both her eyebrows and laughed. But Julian said nothing.

In little more than half an hour, trotting through a winding path that coiled through a vast extension of marsh, and under an increasingly thick flock of seagulls and crows, they arrived on a fishing village at the mouth of the river Magra. A large man dressed in religious attire awaited for them. In spite of his weight, he was rather young, with a livid face and a thick pair of black eyebrows that joined above this thin nose. He was visibly impatient, mounted on a fine courser ahead of the villagers. That was Bishop Filippo, who had his castle built on the hills across the river, a couple of miles up the current. They dismounted and courteously greeted the bishop, who did not bother to leave his horse, more for laziness than arrogance.

'There has been a death?' Alberto Azzo asked.

'No, not yet,' answered the bishop. 'He is still alive. It's one of local fishermen, who was gutted open by a lance.'

'But by whom?'

'A group of boatmen who seemed to have followed the monster to our shore,' said the bishop. He frowned and looked at the thick flock of crows flying above them, before turning to Alberto again. 'We don't know where they are from. Maybe they are Saracens. These villagers here were only beginning to butcher the creature when the strangers arrived in a few boats on the surf and immediately attacked them.'

'The monster is dead?' Everyone turned back to look at the young man with long black hair who had asked the question.

The bishop paused again and said 'Yes...young man! The monster has been killed.'

'His name is Julian,' Clarissa said, mischievously smiling with pride. 'You should know it by now, Reverend Bishop. Julian has been living with us for two years already. He attends the masses you celebrate at our chapel.'

While Alberto shook his head in embarrassment and the bishop tried to understand whether he had been forgetful or if the girl had been too insolent, a man came through the small crowd of villagers and handed a piece of cloth to Alberto.

'We were cutting the monster's horns, my lord,' he said. Alberto opened the cloth to find a relatively clean, ivory-looking cone. Bigger than his own hands, it had a glossy cream-coloured surface and a dark, bloody, open base.

'Horns?'

'Yes, my lord. The monster has a couple of rows of these horns.'

'Looks like a tooth to me!' Everyone turned to look again at Julian.

'You could be right, Julian.' Alberto said, wrapping the horn in the cloth and throwing it to him. 'But we'll only find out when we see it.'

The crowd opened way and a putrid stench hit their noses.

'It's surely the devil!' Alberto said with enthusiasm.

But Clarissa turned to Julian and said 'Smells like fish to me.'

At the beach, they could devise the colossal body lying on the sand across the river mouth, with a small crowd and canoes beached around it, and the thickest swarm of birds circling above. The dead monster was a dark brown, long, conic shape, larger than a house, with its thickness much higher than a man, ending in a tail fin, broader than the boats that waited for them.

'So where's the head?' Alberto asked.

Julian and Clarissa looked at each other too and shrugged. The creature surely looked headless.

'It was already missing as it came, my lord,' said the same villager. 'Those men are pulling contents from the monster through an opening at the front.

Alberto filled the boats with as many men-at-arms and armed villagers that he could, and rowed across. For safety precautions, Clarissa stayed behind with the bishop. On the other side, under the screaming birds, the foreign fishermen were visibly tense. They stopped their work on the open gash at the front and jumped with their harpoons in hand, placing themselves in a semi-circle around the monster.

'What is that they're taking from the front?' Alberto asked with disgust as they rowed. Nobody answered. It was a foamy-looking white material, which was being filled into barrels. The stench was definitely fishy, but dead rotten, especially from the thick loops of gut that had been pulled out of another gash alongside the body. Alberto was the first to jump out of the boats as they beached. With sword in hand, he told the archers to stand a good few paces behind, in guard, while he approached the strangers.

Those were obviously from foreign lands. One could not tell exactly their age or whether they were naturally dark-skinned, as seamen have always a leathery look to their faces. They were dressed in rags, holding onto strange harpoons with barbed edges and long-bladed spears. Two men made to approach. One walked in front. He was thin, short and chestnut-skinned, carrying no weapons, but with incredibly large hands for his size. With a rather amicable smile on his face, he had no hair, but a long black moustache that seemed to be greased down in two long slugs around his prominent chin. The other man was taller and of stronger built. Although his skin was as brown as the first one, it was livened by a bright cherry tone to it. His face was covered with a long white, silvery fur and his blue eyes shone from deep crevasses. He had a short, one edged sword on his hand and a thin bundle of rags covering his head. Both man were barefoot.

Alberto advanced with his sword down, dragging the tip through the sand. 'What are you doing here in these lands?' he asked. Above him, the screaming and cawing of the birds was deafening.

The smaller man came forward 'We are fishermen,' he said, in a strange fashion of Latin.

Alberto hesitated, before shouting back to his men 'Julian, come forward, if you can! We may need you here if things cannot be understood.'

Julian approached shyly, more intimidated by the stench of the gutted monster on the beach than by the prospect of a skirmish. As he had no weapons, he preferred to stay a few paces on Alberto's rear-guard, holding on to no more than the cloth with the beast's horn.

'So, you are fishermen,' said Alberto with clarity to the small man, 'and you mean to convince me that you caught this Leviathan?'

The short man raised both of his black eyebrows 'Is that what you call it?'

Alberto frowned. 'Well, that's what we think it is. What would you call it then?'

'Different names. We are from different lands. I am from the County of Portucale,' he bowed lightly, almost letting the courtesy slip in, 'and in Portucale we call it *phallaine*. Greek seamen told me it's a Greek name and that it means...' he paused to smile cynically, 'it means a swollen phallus!' he giggled with a yellow smile, 'but we are men from many lands in these boats of ours. We sail from the port of Daniyya. My friend here would call it a...' and he said something unintelligible to the northern-looking man with the white fur, pointing to the monster on the beach.

'*Búrhvalur*!' the furry man answered with a sure groan.

Alberto turned quite apprehensively to Julian, who promptly explained his own version of the bits that he had been understood, except the last exchange. Alberto seemed furious.

'What is this nonsense? I am not here to discuss the name of a fish,' he said, 'but to find what gives you the right to wound one of my local men.'

The two fishermen exchanged a few words and the Portuguese man answered 'We caught this animal and followed it to these shores.'

'You fished it out of the water?' Alberto was visibly irritated, with fingers uneasy at the sword hilt. 'I cannot believe it,' he said.

With a patient sigh, the fisherman explained, using his disproportionately large hands to better demonstrate his words 'We had been following this monster for weeks. It was lanced with a harpoon, one of those spears there, which was tied to a few inflated goatskins. Once the monster was speared, our boats just followed the float until it gave up in exhaustion. In generations of fishermen, many of us have tried to kill a phallaine, but this is the first ever that we have managed to recover. So when the phallaine washed up here, we were quickly cleaning these shores from its body when a hostile local attacked us – and we only defended ourselves.'

Alberto Azzo heard Julian's version. Then, he stuck his sword vertically on the sand, resting both of his hands on the tip of the hilt. 'Had you not injured that man, we would probably be happy if you took this demon with you, to never come back here again. But the mistake was yours. Now I suggest you turn back to your boats and leave this land.

Another brief argument broke between the Portuguese and the hirsute fisherman.

'Your proposal' said the Portuguese, 'is rather unreasonable, if I may say, given our efforts to defeat the monster. If I could suggest a fair share of the catch, once you can claim the ownership of this piece of land, while we the creature is obviously ours, we suggest you can keep all the meat, while we take only the intestinal contents and the *sperma*.'

With a quick shake of his head, Alberto tried to brush his understanding off. 'Julian, please repeat to me what he said. I have to concentrate when he speaks. Now tell me if I am mistaken or does it really sound like an abomination?' While Julian confirmed the words of the Portuguese, Alberto made a face, scraping his tongue with the upper teeth, on a blunt demonstration of disapproval. 'You filthy Saracens!' he said, spitting on the sand. 'Is that what you are taking? Sperm and shit of this demon? And you still dare to offer us its unholy meat? A monster that you call a *phallus*? You will poison us all while you perform whatever vile desecration your gods have come up with. No!' he rasped, now raising the tip of his sword towards the fisherman, 'I will not tolerate that offense. Return to your boats and take nothing with you. We will burn this monster and you will not have it.'

With a patronising shake of his head, the Portuguese started 'I should remind you that we do come from Daniyya, but we are not all Mohammedans...'

While he talked, the large fisherman with the silver fur raised his short sword and advanced towards Alberto, who was paying attention to the Portuguese. Julian had little time to intervene with a yell, but his arms somehow behaved on their own, gathering all the strength they could and throwing the beast's horn on the large fisherman. It hit him with a loud knock on the face, right on the cheekbone, delaying the strike before he ever got to Alberto. With an enraged red rim around his blue eyes, the northern man stopped and stared at Julian, growling. But once Alberto had turned around in time to face him, the man hesitated for a second, not knowing which one of them to attack. He decided he would cut Julian down first.

With his one-edged sword raised, at the second leap he gave towards a terrorised Julian, the northern fisherman felt a painful thump on his back and saw the hard blade of a long sword slipping out of his belly. His legs faltered and he fell with his face on the sand.

The Portuguese man was unmoved. He had just raised a commanding hand to the other fishermen around the sea monster. They stayed where they were. It was only when Alberto turned to him, now holding a blood-covered blade, when the Portuguese spoke. 'Stupid man from the north, he was. But now we are even,' he said, raising his large chin between the thick, black moustache. 'I strongly suggest you allow us to take at least the intestinal contents and the *sperma*. And if you will not eat the meat, we can take it all.'

Alberto Azzo was panting. His fury could be seen through the redness of his face. 'We did not need to be killing each other here. Just go now. Leave us or we will be obliged to push you back into your boats.'

The Portuguese bowed, not courteously, but carefully. He made to leave but said to Alberto, gazing deep into his eyes. 'That is a big mistake. We only wanted the fish. The *saqlabi* of Daniyya will not like it.'

'Who?' Alberto asked.

'The *Musetto*. You probably now him as the Musetto. The great commander of Daniyya.'

Alberto pointed his sword at the Portuguese man. 'Tell your Musetto that I am shitting a pile of dung for him, as big and stinky as this Leviathan of yours. Now leave immediately, before I start to take your threats more seriously. You can take this dead man with you if you want, and do take those barrels of semen that you have filled as well.'

Only when the fishermen were already breaking through the waves with their boats, Alberto Azzo turned to Julian and thanked him. 'We need to find you a good sword, Julian', he said, 'one day you may need it.'

Clarissa never crossed the river to see the monster. She appeared to be furious, but for another reason.

'I did not ride here to see a man being killed, especially by my own brother.' They were slowly riding back to Luna.

'But the monster was fabulous,' said Julian with enthusiasm. He rode next to her. 'We could not see where the head was, for it had already been butchered by the Saracens. What you saw was only the tail. It had such a large...' He paused for a second. Clarissa giggled. Suddenly Julian was as red as a plum, '...you know what...' he said, 'the male thing!'

'Yes, I know!' Clarissa said, mocking a serious countenance. 'The male thing.'

Julian paused again for a second, in shock, but walked courageously over his hesitation. 'Well, it was huge, longer than a boat, and it was covered with those horns...' He frowned and looked down. 'But actually,' he considered, 'maybe those were indeed teeth, and what I saw was only his mouth, as some of the locals suggested. But if it was his mouth, how come it stood right under...' he scratched his head, 'under the part where the semen is stored?'

Clarissa laughed again. 'If it's a demon, Julian, it cannot make any sense, can it?'

That was the first one ever caught in Ligurian waters. The large sperm whale was known by the Saracens to be a source of precious oil and wax, which was believed to be the whale's sperm. Moreover, they valued the substance that came from its intestines, known by the eastern peoples as *anbar*. The material was valued by many cultures for its sweet perfume, its burning resinous scent, its invigorating flavour and its medicinal powers. Anbar was collected from the sea, or found washed on beaches. Seamen would not perfect the art of whale hunting for a long time, and only to find out that anbar still needed to be bathed in salt water, under the sun, for months, before it lost its sticky redolence. The same word - anbar - would be used for the golden resins that arrived in Bizantium with the Norsemen, around that same time.

As for that whale, it was still believed for long that the monster was no more than a tail full of sperm and oil. The Ligurian name *côa d'êuio* – tail of oil – caught on for a long time.

Once the fishermen had disappeared from the horizon, Bishop Filippo magnanimously decided that no villager should eat from that accursed flesh, for which he was quickly praised by Alberto Azzo. The colossal carcass was left for the birds to feast on and, during the following weeks, the villagers of Amelia had to inhale the most putrid fumes of the dead monster, a stench that even reached as far as the lengths of Luna itself. Birds of many kinds joined flocks of seagulls and crows on cleaning the carcass from its decaying flesh and maggots. Locals reported that the demon attracted the most strange creatures, including a griffin, which took with it one of the smaller bones to the infinite heights. The rotting remains even persuaded the crows to change their nesting grounds, as crows often do, to the hills on the western bank of the Magra River.

Years later, those crows would be roosting on a cross, with Julian's effigy on it.

The Golden Thread

The three riders took off as early morning pilgrims were coming out through the Northern gate of Lucca. The bridge of San Frediano rattled as the men crossed it on their horses unhurriedly, towards Monte San Quirico, accompanied by a small troupe of servants and a couple of men-at-arms. Although the large Battista Burle rode on his smooth palfrey, a distinguished ambler of Roman stock, he was nonetheless annoyed by the idea of having to travel on that rather tiny beast all the way to Bagni. Immanuel Malachi, not missing a stone of the early winter scenario that opened in front of him, was on a finely bred mule, which should probably have been carrying the banker instead. Béla, the táltos, silently riding on a hard gaited rouncy, was very happy to see the intimidating towers of Lucca left behind, the smoking city watching him go. High above them, almost out of sight, Turul glided peacefully.

'I notice that there are very few vellutini on the Northern side of the wall.' Immanuel mentioned as he looked back at the still green meadow across the river.

'They'd be there building their shacks and littering the whole place with shit if we wouldn't keep them away.' Battista grunted.

'So are these lands yours?' asked Immanuel.

Battista answered with the expected head nod to the sides, with his eyes closed. 'Well, mine and some associates'. We share it equally.'

'And why is it not planted?' the Bukhari asked. 'Too swampy?'

Battista pursed his lips. 'Actually this is not a swampy part of this city. The land here is firm. This is where San Frediano opened a new course for the river.'

'A holy man?' Immanuel asked excited. 'I saw beautiful pictures of holy men in the churches in Rome.'

'Yes, most certainly a holy man, San Frediano was.' Battista said, relaxing his face with warm smile. 'This was the time when the Serchio ran through the city, infesting Lucca with its feverish waters. Frediano, who was the city bishop, drew a new course for the river over the northern side of the walls. This river bed that you see now was singly dug by the bishop Frediano, who dragged a hand rake on the ground and the Serchio followed its track.'

'That's very impressive!' said a bewildered Immanuel. 'Only with a rake?'

Battista chuckled. 'Even if the story has been changed or exaggerated, the fact that Frediano did rid the city of swamp fevers and organised for the Serchio to run through this area must have deserved him the title of holiness.'

Their ride soon turned northeast, up along the riverbank. A good number of smoke-spewing vellutini shacks accumulated on subtle slopes at their far left. Their population was used to bring the pilgrims into the city, offer themselves as guides, local experts, sell them relics, souvenirs and occasionally pick a pocket.

Immanuel observed the dark, agate-black waters of the river, foaming at every step and stone in that grey winter morning. As if guessing what the Bukhari was staring at, Battista explained 'Just wait until the clear dry days of summer, and you will notice that the Serchio water carries a beautiful intense green.'

'Like *coriander*?' Immanuel asked, startled with himself, for he had no idea on how that thought came up to his words.

Battista turned to him. 'Did you say coriander?'

Immanuel babbled. He had never thought of coriander as a reference for greenness before. He did not even know how that word came up to his tongue in Greek.

The banker continued 'We do bring some coriander to these lands, but the herb does not seem to be too comfortable with our colder weather. I particularly like the warm nuttiness of the dried seeds, but I find the fresh weed repellent.'

Immanuel was still mesmerised with that sudden utterance of his. Rubbing his lips with his thumb, he changed subject.

'Serchio? Is that the name of the river?'

Battista inhaled some of the cold clear breeze that blew down the valley, ready to display his knowledge. '*Auser* was the name they gave to this river during the ancient time of the Romans. Right here next to where we ride, the Auser divided between its main branch, going further South and entering through town, which does not exist anymore, and a smaller branch that flowed through the same location as this main riverbed that we crossed. This smaller branch was called the *Auserculus*, as we love the use of diminutives in this part of the world.'

'Auserculus…*Serchio*?' Immanuel deducted.

'Precisely!' said Battista, just raising a visibly bushy eyebrow and looking straight ahead onto the road.

With the dark waters of the Serchio giggling on their right they braved the winding path and the insistent greenness of the hills which came down from the heavily snow-packed mountains to meet it. The cold stony road was an alternative stretch of the Via Francigena, a pilgrimage route that funnelled travellers from the western part of Christendom, all the way into Rome. Pilgrims that could be coming from France or Germany, and even as far as Canterbury, were to follow that path down the Serchio alternatively to the Ligurian coast, through Luni and Massa. In particularly critical times, as we will find further down this story, this was the only opened route for pilgrimage south through Lucca.

To enter the valley, past a narrow gorge where the village of Sesto rested on the opposite side, the road had to climb up a few hills to the west, before diving again into the bushy banks of the Serchio. Battista explained the ease of Roman names and distances in the valley, where *Sesto* was the sixth mile from Lucca, Wald *Ottavo* was the eight and *Diecimo* was the tenth. It did not help much for Immanuel or Béla, none of which any familiar with either Roman miles or with the ordinal numbers in Latin.

Passing by several smaller paths that climbed up the side valleys to reach other villages, they greeted pilgrims, rode through sheep and pigs that were being brought into the market and they drooled at the inebriating aroma of roasted chestnuts that was spewed from one or two chimneys along the way. Battista Burle pointed across the Serchio, to a fortified hamlet on a rocky hilltop. 'That is Anchiano, where the Lord Cunimundinghi of those lands lives.'

'Does he own this side of the river as well?' Immanuel asked.

'Not really. We are entering into lands that the Cunimundinghi have lost, or better, conceded, to the Obertenghi. The family of Bernardo Delle Rocche.'

'The shepherd!' Immanuel exclaimed, finally with a sunny smile. Battista acquiesced with a polite grin.

It was still before noon, after they had passed through the forest of Ottavo, the parish of Diecimo and a thin strip of a village called Mutianum, when they reached what looked to Immanuel like a God-forsaken, but tidy cluster of shacks.

'This is the Traghetto, where we cross to the Eastern bank.' Battista explained. 'Now we just need to find Old Testa.'

Before Immanuel could ask anything, a hoarse, cantankerous voice, cut loud through the air like a rattle, speaking a merchant's Latin with a heavy Lombard accent. '*I'm here! What the fuck do you want?*'

It came from behind them. Immanuel turned around to face the mossy, leathery features of an old man who kept leaping his gaze from him to the táltos, with undisguised hostility. Besides giving the clear impression that in a not-too-distant future his chin was going to meet his forehead, Old Testa looked like something which had been dipped into the river for a long time and then left out to dry in the sun for just as long.

Battista Burle swiftly unhorsed, to the clear relief of his palfrey, and fearlessly approached Old Testa. He despised the ferryman and his family for being the type of people like the vellutini, who kept a *glirarium* at home. These *gliraria* were large ceramic containers where they kept dozens of dormice, breeding and fattening, so they could harvest the squeaky creatures once in a while for an occasional snack. Now the banker brought his hands upwards, not too far from his face and from Old Testa's, with his thumbs joining the other fingers, releasing them all as he started '*Ma che cazzo* do you thing we want with you, Old Testa? We want to cross! And *now!*'

Old Testa grunted something unintelligible and brought them down to the ferry, a large square punt that would fit a small bullock cart. Still, only two horses and a few people could cross at a time. They put Batista, Immanuel, the palfrey, the mule and a few servants on the first ride. While he poked the bottom of the river with his pole, Old Testa kept staring at the Bukhari as if he was ready to attack him. On the next ride, now with Béla, a man-at-arms and their rouncies on the ferry, Old Testa did not spare the strange looking Magyar with the filthiest of his vocabulary. But the táltos did not make it an easy deal for the ferryman. In his native Magyar language, he was also hissing the most abominable curses a táltos could utter towards a living being.

An old, abandoned building, covered in vines and weeds, stood across the road on the other side.

'It's an old hospital.' Battista explained, upon noticing how Immanuel observed. 'Pilgrims don't stop by here. Maybe they never did. Everyone calls it the hospital, but who knows what it was? There is no use to it, for it stands across the river.'

'If you had a bridge here,' Immanuel suggested 'the hospital would hold pilgrims, on the way to Rome, maybe stopping by to dip themselves in the thermal baths'.

'That would make sense!' Battista said with a puff, as he gracefully mounted the palfrey. 'But it doesn't look like there was ever a bridge here.

Under the watchful eye of Turul, they rode further North through a small village called Chifenti. At the village tavern, they were served a light meal of cold meats, lamb soup and wine. The owner, a handsome young man called Amadeo, was very welcoming to Battista, who he knew fairly well and, quite naturally, to his guests.

'Amadeo has just got married!' Battista explained to Immanuel, tapping the young innkeeper on his back.

The Bukhari warmed up his face and smiled with his little blue eyes, bowing his head elegantly to Amadeo. The innkeeper heartily took the compliment and left them to finish their meal.

'A nun!' Battista said with the side of his mouth, both his caterpillars raised.

'A religious woman?' Immanuel asked, noticing the excitement on Battista.

'Yes!' Battista said with a mischievous smile 'You know, this is the Thousandth year of the coming of our Lord Jesus Christ among us. The Anno Mille. Many said and believed this was the time when the Devil was to be returning from his captivity.

Amadeo's wife was one of the thousands of nuns who left their house of prayer and came on a frenzy to Rome, to free themselves from damnation. Many freed themselves from religious life too, and never went back to their monasteries.'

'I did hear about the Anno Mille in my travels. Immanuel considered aloud. 'Some even say that Pope Sylvester could have been this devil. I personally find it hard to believe. He is an educated man, courteous and compassionate. Nothing that I could find evil.'

'Ignorance is evil!' said Battista. 'And it is ignorance that makes people scared of the unknown and accuse the pope of devilries. We should all be thankful that such a brilliant mind is warming the seat of Rome with his holy arse. For sure not the devil, and if anything else he carries upon his shoulders, it's divinity.'

From Chifenti, they left the Serchio and took the small path east, along the Lima, a smaller river of cheerful gelid waters that could be forded at several points. In less than a mile, they crossed it to reach the hamlet of Corsena.

Immanuel smelled the air 'Are we near the baths? I can smell brimstone.'

Béla noticed the scent too. 'Good for the skin, fönök!'

They were received in a well-kept manor, where a few villagers tended to the horses and brought their packs inside. Battista walked up the hill with Immanuel, Béla and the men-at-arms. They found their way through wooded chestnut slopes and beaten bushes of thyme, avoiding the cool creek crevasses, which were covered with sea-buckthorn, still with their beautiful blood-coloured berries.

'Here it is!' Battista said, after arriving somewhere that seemed to be in the middle of nowhere.

Immanuel tried to capture the joke, but he realised there was none. Behind the stems and straw of the lianas and brambles, the Bukhari spotted the reddish tinge of bricks, moss-covered stones and the mounds of crumbled walls. Those were the baths.

Leaving the path and venturing himself through the dry bushes and weeds, he walked through the ruins. Luckily, with many leaves gone for the winter, there was a glimpse of a past time, a miserable display of what forgetfulness can do to the creations of God and men. Stale water pooled up in several spots. Stepping through the bushes, Immanuel's feet dipped into liquid. Not cold as he feared at that time of the winter, but quite tepid. Béla was right next to him. The táltos crouched to smell and taste the water.

'Don't drink it, Béla! Time could have poisoned it!'

The táltos did not understand and walked over to a different puddle to touch it, smell it and taste it again. He hurried back with some of the water ladled in his crooked hand and an almost toothless smile on his face. 'Not only good for the skin, fönök, but also good for the bones!' They kept exploring the pitiful thermal station until they could hear a trickle. Pushing straw to the sides, they snatched bushes from the soil and lifted heavy networks of stems and dried leaves, until they found a spout, coming out of a wall. The spout was fat with a rocky white deposit around it, leaking a dribble of warm water.

Leaping over the weeds and pools, Immanuel went back to Battista. 'Béla was right! The water is good for the skin, for drinking purposes and for rheumatism. It still runs, nice and warm!' His face, for the first time to Battista, looked almost as young as he really was.

The banker was immobile for a few seconds, until one side of his face twitched. Looking very gravely at Immanuel, he asked 'How long can you take to recover these baths and have a thermal station here?'

'If it's no better than what we see here, maybe twenty years.'

'Can you make it to five years?'

'I am already counting my time spent on the mulberry trees.' Immanuel said. 'So if we squeeze it as much as possible and if I have plenty of help, that's a total of ten years.'

'Ten years is good then!' Battista said. 'I will provide you with all the help that you need. And we can also plant on that area north of the wall in Lucca.'

Immanuel opened a smile, doubting Battista.

'My associates will not be able to refuse it.' The banker said with an undisguised voracious grin.

On the next morning, on their way back across the Serchio, Old Testa seemed to be even more hostile to the foreigners. When all had been ferried, Battista delivered one last message to the crabby old man. 'Old Testa, this man here, Immanuel Malachi, will be my son-in-law. He will be the lord of those lands in Corsena. You will be attentive and courteous to him, to my daughter and to Béla, this man here. Any complaints and I will make sure that the Obertenghi have you scorched out of here. You may join the vellutini in Lucca, feast in your dormice and live like the pig you mean to be.'

The ferryman grunted to himself and swallowed a few curses. As the riders faced the road south, from the Traghetto, Immanuel looked at the river, the abandoned hospital across it, and said. 'Forget the ferryman. It's a bridge that I can see here. I still think someone should build a bridge across it.'

Battista just nodded. 'Maybe one day...'

By spring of the year One Thousand and One, before travelling down to Rome once again, the young Emperor Otto gave himself a present. A large silver cross, covered in gold, richly adorned with filigrees and encrusted with pearls and precious gems. But the most impressive feature was the jewel in the centre. Instead of the image of Christ, Otto's cross extraordinarily had a cameo of the Emperor Augustus. This large medallion, acquired at any cost through a Greek merchant, by what came to be a very large sum of gold, was beautifully carved in sardonix. With the folds of his mantle and the laurel wreath sticking out in a rich tan, the young Augustus had the Jupiter eagle on a standard held by his right hand.

The Greek merchant was correct when he suggested the cameo could symbolise the fusion between the Roman emperor and the Christ, a direct aspiration of Otto, which was to drag the old Roman Empire through the idea of Christ the King into his very own Holy Roman Empire. When Otto heard of the possibility to acquire this cameo, he did not measure any efforts or sums. The Greek said it came from a Magyar village, from a treasure which had belonged to the great Attila, the Hun.

The radiant Emperor Otto, delighted with his cross, took off to Italy, where he never came back from. While the official news referred to an attack of swamp fever, after losing to a rebellion by Romans and retiring to the noxious Ravenna, the monks who embalmed the royal cadaver to be carried back to Germany noticed the sores of lues venerea spread over his body.

The cross would survive as a strong symbol of the Holy Roman Empire. Due to a later detail on its base, a rock crystal seal of Emperor Lothair II of Lotharingia, this potent object would be forever known as the Lothair's Cross.

On the summer of the same year, a pregnant Elvira of the Burle et Malachi received a horseman at the entrance of the manor in Corsena. The messenger informed that her husband Immanuel was being called to see his father-in-law in Lucca. Urgently.

Immanuel took off on that same day, to arrive at the Burle house of trade on the early evening.

In spite of his customary grave eyebrows, Battista was luminous with excitement!

'The ship came directly from Constantinople. Procopius did as he promised!' He brought Immanuel into a hidden corner of his warehouse. 'Look at these. They all arrived by bullock carts. Rather cheap merchandise to travel like that, but nobody seemed to notice. I cleaned this corner only for us.'

There were a few piles with dozens of bundles of wood. Perhaps a hundred, and visibly of all kinds and cuts. A good number of different timbers, filling up the warehouse with the aroma of shavings from a freshly carved boat. Large beams, twigs, poles, stakes and wedges, all bundled together in groups of the same wood and shape.

'Do you know what these are?' Immanuel asked, raising his little blue eyes to the height of Battista's.

The banker walked around the piles and started his review. 'Well, these tiny yellow poles are certainly sandalwood. Quite expensive material, given its oily fragrance. The large beams could be cedar from Syria or Fez, I wouldn't know, and so could these sticky juniper twigs. Look at the grains on these stakes. It could be elm from across the river, but believe it or not, it came from Byzantium. Those vermillion cross sections are *brazili*, precious dyewood from the Levant. This olivewood is probably from Jerusalem, again, who knows? And these oaken wedges are only cheap pieces. They could be originated from carpentry shops not far from Procopius's house of trade, in Constantinople. There's northern pine, willow, spruce, some useless birch burls and God knows what else are those twigs and some many of these others.'

'How do we start then?' asked Immanuel. 'Do you recognise any mulberry branches?'

'No. I have mulberry branches brought in, for this stage of the business, and he has sent us none.' Battista then pulled up a large piece of parchment form under a book. 'But this letter came from Procopius a few weeks before. There's a just a plain description of some of the woods that we see here.'

Battista re-read the letter several times for Immanuel, translating the merchant's code, written in a mixture of Greek and Latin, with other words that seemed to be from Germanic, English and French languages. The text was simple, listing some of the woods and their utilities, but nothing indicated where the merchandise was. After giving up on finding a code, they cut open the ropes, unwrapping the bundles to see if a secret box would have been hidden inside. But if there had been a box, they were not able to find it.

Next, they examined every single piece. A servant came in to bring them more light and something to eat. Each cut of wood seemed to be clean. No hollow areas, no hidden crannies. They switched then to investigate the twigs and the rough poles, but the bells of Lucca were already sounding the Matins. Battista suggested they rested, to continue the investigation on the next morning.

'Battista Burle! Oh, Battista Burle! Why does a man of your stock sleeps up to the third hour of the day?' The shouts came from outside, from the busy street, waking up the guest Immanuel with a strange feeling of impotence. He could not open his eyes against the hot sunbeam that pounded his face. He had slept well over dawn. 'Battista Burle!' The voice continued. 'Wake-up, you big fat Burle for you have an important visitor here. Me!'

'Oh shut your mouth, Fraolmo di Cunizio!' That was Battista's voice, gurgling cranky from the window next to Immanuel's room. A sound clearing of throat was heard, but no spit followed it. 'Isn't an old man like me entitled to sleep until late?' he bellowed.

'Battista Burle, you are not an old man, you fat pig. I have been up before sunrise and I am not young. Get yourself presentable and meet me in your office.'

'I should throw my chamber pot on you, Fraolmo di Cunizio!'

Those yells were heard by busy passers-by and residents across a full block of Lucchese buildings. Immanuel was sure that even the highest towers of the city had heard them. He tried to sleep over a bit more, but his mind was still trying to decipher the secret of the shipment, while the voice of Fraolmo di Cunizio kept shouting inside his head 'Battista Burle! Oh Battista Burle!'

Burle.

Immanuel jumped out of bed. He had to wait until his father-in-law had ended his morning assembly with the insistent Fraolmo di Cunizio.

'What does the name *Burle* mean?' Immanuel broke in when Battista was finally free.

Battista's porcupines slipped down to meet on top of his nose. The sovereign banker definitely did not appreciate being surprised like that.

'Just say it, you stubborn fool! What does Burle mean?' Immanuel insisted, impatient and unimpressed with Battista's theatrics.

Now both porcupines jumped to the top of his forehead. After the shock, he sighed and said with undisguised grumpiness. 'It's a word from the kingdom of Englaland, where my ancestors had sat their trade. It refers to an unusual growth on certain trees, creating deformed shapes...'

'We have those woods in the shipment, don't we?' Immanuel almost shrieked with excitement.

Battista looked at him with doubt. 'We do, they are birch burls...'

'And Procopius used the English word, didn't he? What did he say about the burls?'

Battista lazily stood up to go and retrieve the letter from its hiding place, but before stepping further he knew the answer. 'I do know what he said. He said the burls have the right grain to be shaped into a woman's breast. A nipple.'

'*Papilla mamaria*, in Latin, right?' Immanuel asked.

'That is correct' Battista said.

'And how do you say moth, or butterfly in Latin?'

'*Papilio*' Battista said, and let his chin fall.

They rushed to the warehouse.

Sitting on the floor, they peeled the bark off the burls and found the waxy plugs. Immanuel scooped a thick waxy plug out and turned the burl upside down. Battista's eyebrows almost disappeared behind his head when he saw a bluish grain pouring onto his son-in-law's open palm, overflowing it and dropping on the floor. Tiny little disc-shaped particles that silently settled like heavy dust. And among the bluish grains, looking much closer, Immanuel noticed speckles of black furry soot. Some of those speckles seemed to move.

'Oh Lord almighty!' the Bukhari said, in Hebrew. 'Look at these larvae here. They've hatched already!'

Battista stood up from his knees and almost collapsed like a tree, but he recovered his balance and roared to his servants outside 'The mulberry leaves, bring in those mulberry branches!'

This day when the silkworm arrived would change the history of Lucca forever.

The Rat

As he turned around the hill, finally heading down to the port, the Ligurian Sea opened again in front of him, not quite as turquoise blue as he had seen in the morning. Now in the later hours of the afternoon it held a silvery shine with honey flickers. The large ship could be seen with its sails raised. An adapted dromon, as most of Byzantine merchants preferred to use, for the advantage of a generous cargo space and the safety of fast oars on those dangerous seas.

Immanuel Malachi's stomach twisted with nausea thinking of his sea fare two years before. He was now hoping that, besides the short river crosses on Old Testa's ferry, he would never ever have to go onto a boat again. Now he was only expecting to meet the unloaded cargo at Battista Burle's storage house in that port of il Poggio. Riding on Battista's best palfrey, Immanuel followed with difficulty the young rider from Luna, a handsome man with long black hair who had been courteous enough to accompany him to the faraway harbour. The slim rider was dwarfed by the massive size of the courser he rode, probably a choice of the marchese for wartimes.

Tied to Immanuel's saddle, the large mule from Battista's herd diligently followed, with a good number of full sacks that bumped lightly on its back.

Approaching the end of the harbour, they entered a well hidden but busy cluster of houses. The visitors were covered in shadows and had their senses invaded by smells which were more pungent than the vellutini's. Dealers had their carts filled with heavy loads, carried by slaves and servants, while blatant haggling buffered the diffuse rumour of the animals. Among the streams of human and beast dejecta that ran along the alleys, there were piles of coal, bundles of fabrics which had been brought for the nearest ports; up on the tables there were dried and salted meats from Sicily; cheeses from Dalmatia; figs from Mālaqa, Al-Laqant, Daniyya and Turtusha, African honey, olive oil; there were smaller vessels unloading skins of wine; fresh fruit from Genova; seal skins and blubber, dried mackerel, dolphin entrails, garfish, squids; salted anchovies, sardines, herring, tuna, gurnard and conger eels, all with their smelly brine oozing out of pressing pine boxes; wide boards with salted bottarga, which was flathead mullet roe from Ligurian marshes; freshly caught rock octopuses, cuttlefish and flying squids; a dripping crate with slimy Roman morays, so offensively decomposed that few dealers would be interested to go any near it; spiny lobsters and mantis shrimp from Gorgona, still snapping their tails frantically; baskets with Sicilian shells called Saint Peter's Ears, whose meat was despised for being too tough, but with a valuable internal surface decorated with wavy lines across the iridescent mother-of-pearl; bags full of recently raked clams; the diamond shaped turbots looking suspiciously to their left and the fish named after sandals, the soles, staring terrifyingly to their right; dinghies full of breams and mullets; in addition to a couple of particularly odorous fish, strangely named *pandora* and *diavolo di mare*, all to be taken in baskets to the market in Lucca.

Quite inconspicuously, Immanuel rode through the crowd followed by the young rider all the way to a cabin at the end of an alley. Empty bullock-carts were resting outside. As soon as the rider from Luna knocked on the door, a strong, large woman came out. She was dressed like a peasant, but held her head high. Her greasy wimple covered a wiry mane of grey hair. Bushy eyebrows reminded Immanuel of his own father-in-law. She observed both men and the three mounts with unconcealed suspicion.

'Is this the warehouse for the Burle House of Trade?' asked the young rider.

The woman nodded.

'This is Immanuel Malachi, of Corsena,' he said, pointing to the Bukhari. 'He came for your consignment.'

Immanuel jumped from his palfrey and started unloading the mule.

'And who are you?' asked the woman.

The rider opened a handsome sunny smile and bowed. 'I am Julian, of Mans. I am sent by the Marchese Oberto, to accompany Immanuel on his way from Luna.'

She yanked her face towards the door. 'Come in then. The wood is here.'

A number of delicate wooden boxes were laid side by side on the floor. Immanuel lined them with young mulberry leaves from the bags he had brought. He turned onto the deformed burls that had been thrown somewhere behind the piles of more attractive looking wood.

'How did you know they were here on these pieces, Immanuel?' Julian asked.

'We have received silkworm eggs last year, and they were all in these birch burls as well.' Immanuel said as he popped another wax seal out and poured the bluish grains on the boxes and covered them with a linen screen lid. 'The eggs were already hatched by the time they were in Lucca, unlike these.'

'So you had silkworms? Do they turn into beetles?' Julian asked.

Immanuel instinctively looked to the sides. He could trust Julian, for not only some other bankers, but the lord Oberto himself had contributed to that revolutionary enterprise. 'The larva grows and they weave a beautiful cocoon made of silk. After a few days, a moth comes out of the cocoon. These moths should be left to mate and lay more eggs and when the worms grow they will make a new cocoon. If we boil these cocoons we can pick up the silk thread and unroll it completely.'

'And what happens to the larva, or the moth inside?' Julian asked.

'Dead! Well, it's boiled alive.' Immanuel said, without taking his eyes of the precious eggs that he carefully laid in the boxes.

Julian observed closely the disc-shaped eggs. 'So do you have enough moths from last year?'

While closing the boxes with their linen netting, Immanuel lifted his face for a second to look at that innocent young man. He laughed warmly, sighed and said 'Julian, it's not overnight that Lucca will learn to master a secret that's been kept hidden from us for centuries. Last year I lost all the larvae because they were already weak and the leaves were too tough and dry. Unfortunately, we do not have the opportunity to listen and learn from others' mistakes. So we will have to learn from our own.' He closed the last box and wiped his hands on one of the empty sacks. 'But only the good Lord knows what awaits us this time. Anything could happen throughout the life of these tiny creatures before they grant us what we want. We will pray for their survival...'

He went out to harness the mule to one of the carts. When Julian joined him to help, Immanuel continued. 'And if not, we can still pray that we get a few more shipments from our friends in Constantinople.'

The cargo was accompanied back to Lucca, on Julian's first visit to the city. Riding the courser that Clarissa had elected for him, he followed Immanuel's slow progress on Battista's palfrey, side by side with the mule. The cart was not too heavy with the leaves boxes and some other merchandise that was sent by Procopius. But for Julian's utmost annoyance, the pace preferred by Immanuel was the slowest possible, to minimise any disturbance to the precious worms.

Julian missed Clarissa badly.

Two years before, upon arriving in the Lunigiana, the high tower of Luna had impressed the young Julian coming from Mans, as it did to any traveller that saw it. But nothing had prepared him for the magnificence of the dozens of towers in Lucca. Following the pace of many pilgrims, they had left by early morning from the hospital of San Michele in the village of Contessora and, in less than one hour the towers rose superbly in front of their eyes. Crossing the dark waters of the

Serchio at the bridge of San Pietro, Julian had no eyes for the river which would change his life one day. He was just hypnotised by the straight, tall, red-coloured buildings, erected proudly by the very people he was about to meet. Approaching the city through a road that cut an area of poor, stinking shacks, Julian noticed that the city walls were not that high, and not nearly as magnificent as those of Luna. Of course they encompassed a much broader area, of which Julian could never make the entire circle, but they stood probably no higher than four lengths of arms. The red-bricked wall changed its direction alternatively in every spot where it was interrupted by turrets and ramparts, bastions placed forward in a manner that a city garrison could easily defend the walls on both sides. The result was that, to a flying bird high above, the shape of the circling wall must have looked like a many-pointed star. Invaders would have to brave a rather wide, black moat that could not be too deep, given the soft nature of the swampy terrain, but probably treacherous enough to swallow many incautious victims in its black, dead waters, quagmires and quick sands.

Looking to the sides and pulling the mule further ahead faster than it actually wanted to walk, Immanuel looked uneasy in that stretch. 'This is the vellutini area,' he whispered, throwing glances to the sides. 'I don't trust these people.' And just before they reached the drawbridge Julian learned why.

A large man appeared out of nowhere and stood in the middle of the way, raising his hands and asking them to halt. Before a proper answer was formulated, he held on to the reigns of Immanuel's palfrey and the mule's, dragging them both into a side alley behind the church of San Donato, just outside of the wall, out of the vision of the gate towers. Only Julian followed Immanuel after the stranger. And in that instant the area was deserted. Not a soul seemed to be around them anymore, except for the noxious fumes that rose from the moat. The man was not tall, but still a strong, solid man, probably in his thirties, with a flat, stony face and quick eyes that never stopped and never gazed. His greying hair was cropped short around his quickly balding head.

'What do you take there?' he asked firmly, after Julian joined them.

'None of your business!' declared Immanuel.

'None nah nah neeness!' the man mocked Immanuel's accent, with his tongue out. 'Speak like a man, you little foreign shit.' He walked around the cart, looking at the boxes and hopped on to the back, which made the harness pull up tighter. The mule grunted with irritation. Julian observed it all unmoved and quiet, as Immanuel was.

'What the fuck are these?' asked the man, looking through some of the wooden boxes he'd opened.

'None-of-your-business!' This time it was Julian who said it. Slower, more articulated and much firmer.

The man raised his gaze, startled by Julian's intervention. 'Another foreigner here?' he said, 'Battista Burle is surrounding himself with a colourful array of ladies. And who the fuck might you be, young man?'

'I am Julian of Mans, guest of the Count Oberto, Marchese of Tuscany.'

The man narrowed his eyes, barely looking at Julian, but to all the surroundings. The mention of the marchese had made him suddenly aware of an extra weight to that cargo. 'Nah,' he waved a dismissing hand, 'you foreigners have nothing worthy of tolls.'

'Tolls?' said a dismal-looking Battista Burle. 'What kind of taxes would a vellutino expect anyone to pay?'

'That is not what he was there for' said Immanuel. 'All I know is that he opened our boxes and let us go, as soon as our young Julian interfered. The man just wanted to spy on us, I think.'

Battista pulled two chairs and made them sit in front of his desk. He called a servant and sent for refreshments. His office was as dark as always. The volume of wood, fabrics, leather and metal in the room provided great insulation from winter, and in summer it kept a cool hideaway from the midday sun. The boxes with the silkworms had promptly been taken to a room in the back of his house of trade, where they were cared for by a couple of Sicilian women. Back at his comfortable chair, Battista heard from Immanuel and Julian a precise description of the man who had approached them.

The banker leaned back on his chair. 'It must be Eleuterio, a scoundrel who lives by the western gate. I cannot believe that he would have the bile to do that. Foreigners?' he said, more to himself than to the others, 'he is a *Sicilian*, for the blood of the crucified Christ!' Battista stared at his desk, holding the sides of his lower lip, 'but that brute is too simple to be so bold. He must be acting on someone else's command.'

Immanuel leaned forward 'Do you have any enemies?'

The banker made a clicking sound with his tongue, while his massive eyebrows seemed to meet down, just above his nose. 'I'm sure that some of my debtors could consider themselves as potential enemies,' he said, throwing both of his hands up, 'but I cannot believe that my clientele would venture into any low games with rascals such as Eleuterio. Not their style, I suppose.'

'The other bankers, perhaps?' suggested Immanuel.

Battista curled his lip and tipped his head to each side, eyebrows shooting up. 'Well, indeed the Gualteri and the Orsetti have been hostile to my family in the past generations, but we are in very good terms now. Most bankers have common interests, and we are all together in our silk enterprise. Except for the Pisans, but I don't think the Pisans would get their dirty arses deep into hot water for acting among our vellutini.'

'Any grudges?' Immanuel insisted. Julian only listened. They had both taken a goblet of wine from the servant, who slipped in with a tray.

Battista waited with his eyes for the servant to leave. 'If I think of it, yes, there is a grudge,' he said, now with the gravest of his voice. They could hardly see his eyes, so darkened had they been by his eyebrows. 'Gottefredo di Antelmo,' he said, baring his teeth. 'Gottefredo is a low crook from Tassignano, who lives from exorbitant tolls, protection, petty crime, threats and extortions. He owns large expansions of lands, south of the Cunimundinghi, including the eastern Serchio road from Lucca to Sesto. The man thinks himself a merchant and banker and has recently dared to express his wishes to join our guild.' Battista giggled, almost like clearing his throat. 'Gottefredo even requested for an official application, which was indeed granted, but the membership was unanimously refused.'

'He is not aware of our endeavours with silk, is he?' asked Immanuel.

'No, I don't think Gottefredo would understand how big this could be. But we should not underestimate him. He is a dangerous man. I will talk to the guild about this.' He put his hands on his knees and stood his large weight up. 'Meanwhile, let's care for young Julian here. You must be hungry.'

Julian stood up too and bowed his head 'Thank you for your hospitality Messer Battista, but I should be on my way back to Luna.'

'Of course you won't,' Battista said amicably, 'or else you will kill that horse.' He put his hand around Julian's shoulder and brought him to his patio, where the courser was being cared for. 'No Julian, you will stay with us, resting and eating, so that you can gallop your way to the white castle tomorrow, fresh and renewed.'

Immanuel followed, saying 'We must thank the Lord Alberto Azzo for recommending Julian to accompany me. Such lovely company and helpful voice.'

'We surely will, Immanuel,' said Battista, 'you do not have to remind me of that. Meanwhile Julian and I will go to see our other boxes that came from Constantinople.' He winked to Immanuel. 'Maybe our young man will find something special for someone special. That's of course if there is *that someone special.*'

On the next day, Battista was early to see Julian away. 'I will have two riders follow you to the edge of the city. You don't really want to have any other surprises among the vellutini. I know you can take care of yourself but, for the womb of the Virgin Mary, you are unarmed! If you ever need a good sword of Lucchese steel, do let me know, and we will find you the best one. Now farewell, young Julian.'

He galloped through the city alleys, reaching the western gate in a few minutes, carrying a bag on his saddle. The two riders followed him past the vellutini and turned around. Julian had even forgotten they had been with him. He was only thinking of Clarissa.

On a large manor outside of the city, Eleuterio waited on the outside patio, under the shade of an oak, feeling the crackling of acorns from the previous autumn breaking under his boot. Away from him, the front door opened slightly, and a small white face appeared behind it. Eleuterio rushed to see the same servant woman who had received him a few minutes before, looking at the visitor with a mixture of despise and fear.

'You must wait,' said the servant. 'Messer Gottefredo will see you shortly.'

Eleuterio waited for another half an hour. Meanwhile, two tall young men with long beards came out of the house. They acknowledged Eleuterio, with a silent nod and rode out on their bulky horses. A red beard and a blonde one. Eleuterio knew they were the Genovese brothers, from Sesto. Men to be respected.

Soon after, he was finally called in. Gottefredo of Antelmo waited for him in the main hall. This was the only manor where Eleuterio had ever been to. Although he had always expected rich people's houses to be somehow cleaner and tidier, he saw no difference, comparing to most of the shacks he knew around the vellutini. This manor smelled of stale food and urine. The centre of the floor was covered in deer hide and some other pelts. There were a couple of full-bellied cats sleeping under the table, while a battalion of dormice explored the alleyways and slopes created by a large amount of bones and decaying food that were accumulated on the corners. A servant's child was sitting by the wall, gnawing on an old bone, while mice walked freely around her. Another child, probably the lord's son, sat on a woman's lap, suckling voraciously from a large, flabby breast. Eleuterio couldn't help but stare at that child, who seemed to be probably five or six years old, anyway too old to be suckling milk. The woman was dressed in dirty rags, rocking the boy diligently. She smiled courteously at Eleuterio, exposing a pair of brown gums lacking several teeth. He did not know if that was the mother or just a wet-nurse.

'Gorgeous, fat teat, isn't that?' asked the lord.

Eleuterio was a bit startled, and just nodded shyly. Gottefredo sat on a bench, leaning back with his elbows on a table where some roast had been carved. He was a man of medium built, pretty much of Eleuterio's size, but sporting a much more prominent belly. With a handsome, well-designed face, Gottefredo spent little time grooming a generous brown beard that covered the apparent weakness of a small chin. His blue eyes were faster than Eleuterio's, and he had a ravenous smile. 'Wouldn't you like to suck on those too?' he asked, studying the Sicilian as he stood in the middle of the hall.

Eleuterio smiled, but could not figure what to say. Finally he pointed to the boy 'Your son?'

Gottefredo grinned with satisfaction. 'Yes, that's my boy! Hadn't you seen him before? His name is Antelmino, after my father.'

'He takes after you!' said Eleuterio, finally putting some of his true character on the inflamed grin he opened.

'Thank you Eleuterio! I will take it as a compliment. Now seat yourself next to me and tell me about Battista's son-in-law's trip to the coast.' But before Eleuterio started, Gottefredo grabbed a piece of bone, turned his body around and threw it on the child sitting by the wall. The child roared in pain as the bone hit her forehead, while Gottefredo yelled even louder 'Get your shitty arse out of there and find your mother to bring us some wine.' Back to Eleuterio, he said 'Carry on! I don't have all day for you.'

Eleuterio stuttered a bit before starting. 'They returned with boxes full of freshly cut green leaves. Mulberry leaves, I think, and I have a very good guess about the reason, my Lord.' He waited with a drop of sweat on his forehead for Gottefredo to ask for more. But as the lord did not move a muscle on his face, he proceeded 'It's silkworms, my Lord. They are bringing silkworms in to Lucca!'

Gottefredo pursed his lips and kept immovable. He sat straight up. 'Silkworms? Creatures that make silk? You mean these people are planning to produce silk here? That will be something! They will never get the secrets from the East!'

'Well, the secret is only about silkworms. If you have them, it's not too difficult to produce silk.'

'How can you be so sure, Eleuterio?' Gottefredo lifted his foot to plant a soft kick on Eleuterio's shin. 'What do you know about silk?'

'Everyone knows how to make silk in Sicily,' said Eleuterio.

'Then, tell me everything you know about it,' Gottefredo demanded.

After Eleuterio finished sharing all his thoughts on silk production, Gottefredo rubbed his hands 'We will have a few things to do, my friend.'

'You mean me too, Messere?' Eleuterio said, not too enthusiastic about whatever was coming.

Gottefredo held on to the Sicilian's shoulder and shook it amicably 'Of course you're in it, Eleuterio. Up to your bones!' he said, with a feline grin. 'Just make sure you don't spill it out, understand? You really cannot even start to appreciate how sad your life would become if you told anyone else about this.'

Eleuterio was weeping quietly, while a few insistent embers burned their last flames over a small hearth nearby. Tears were drawing clean tracks across his soot-layered face. But the pain that made Eleuterio cry like a baby was not only bulging from his shoulders any more. Much more than that, pain was a thick jelly of torment that crushed all of his body, from his heavy head that leaned towards his chest, making his neck and shoulders move forward on an unnatural state of paralysis, to his toes, that were suspended above the dirty floor of the dungeon. Eleuterio was hanging from a *strappado*. His hands had been tied around his back and he had been hoisted from his wrists. During the interrogation process, they had jerked the rope a few times, guaranteeing that the joints of his shoulders had been dislocated. He was shaken out of his nightmares of pain, sometimes with a good beating on his face and others with buckets of cold water. Now he just waited in that hot, smoky room, for what appeared to be the worst still to come. He suspected it was dark outside, and he hoped his family had been left untouched.

Three floors above Eleuterio, a group of men discussed the information they were able to snatch out of him. One candle burned shyly on a small table in the middle, but the men were all distant, sitting by the walls, subtly hidden in the corners, their faces concealed by gracious darkness that did not clearly reveal their role in that long session of interrogation. The wide-bodied man who sat nearest to the candle spoke. He approached his face towards the flame, drawing huge shadows on the ceiling with his eyebrows. His voice was low and very grave. Battista Burle was dealing with a serious crisis that had threatened the union of the bankers in the Lucchese guild.

'He has told us very little, besides the fact that he is guilty of the crime,' said Battista.

'Isn't that a sufficient confession?' one of the men asked, from the shadows. 'Now, he must pay.'

'We don't need a confession, Dino,' Battista reasoned. 'We need to know who sent him to do it. And I fear that we may kill him before he tells us.'

'But isn't that obvious? We all know who it was. He must have been paid by Arab merchants to destroy those mulberry trees. There's plenty of these Saracens that come alongside in our ports, from Livorno to Genova.'

'Not so clear, Bartolomeo,' Battista said. 'There are those of us who think it could be a vellutini revenge on their exclusion from our city, or from that rich flat where the mulberry trees are planted. Or it could be no more than a vendetta on those burglars of Monte San Quirico, whose heads are still pinned to the Gate of San Frediano, or even just the envy of our neighbours, the Pisans. Others among us think it is surely a Byzantine plot, as always perpetrated through this Sicilian contingent of the vellutini. But I personally think it is Gottefredo di Antelmo who's behind this. The bastard is making us pay for having despised him all of this time.'

'Gottefredo? That rapist?' Bartolomeo laughed for a second. 'Gottefredo is too simple to even learn what those shrubs are and what we had intended to use them for.'

'Whoever it is that orchestrated it, makes little difference,' said the man previously identified as Dino. 'We know it was Eleuterio himself that chopped those trees down last night. Now quite simply, he should pay for it.'

'But pay with what?' Battista asked, raising both of his hands in front of him, with all fingertips joined in each. 'Eleuterio is a vellutino. And one of the worse ones. We always assume this mob outside our walls is just made of scoundrels, when most are hardworking freemen. Their poverty is indeed helpful to us, for our charity enables us to achieve the so-desired heavens. But this Eleuterio is surely a rogue. He is a lazy, coward villain. He can offer us nothing in compensation for our loss.'

'Does he have any kin? Children?' asked Dino.

'What do you expect?' Battista snorted 'He is a Sicilian, for the Blessed Virgin Mary! I'd be surprised if there's less than a dozen more rascals.'

Bartolomeo stood up 'Then here we have it! The offender can never compensate us for our loss, but we could take he and his family in slavery. The city would certainly approve this.'

'No!' said Battista, raising his voice louder than the rest, 'No matter how attractive this prospect is on the short term, Eleuterio will not become anyone's slave. Neither will his family. Eleuterio has desecrated our investment in silk. We do not want much publicity in this endeavour. As far as anyone else is concerned, those are only trees from an orchard. Much sooner than we expect, we will need the vellutini and their knowledge to help us produce proper silk and good dyed fabrics. Taking his family in slavery would be a fair resolution for compensation, but it would wake up the attentions towards our mulberry trees. Besides, we cannot start a war against the vellutini. We need them.'

Dino gasped. 'So do you intend to just let Eleuterio go?'

Battista sighed and stood up, making the room a bit darker.

'I never said that! On the opposite, we must submit Eleuterio to a new session of torture. Perhaps with more pain we can elicit an accusation against the true instigator. Then, because he has committed a crime against this guild, he will need to die.'

'Don't waste your time, Battista' said a new voice from the dark corners. 'Eleuterio is afraid for his children, which he had with only God knows how many wenches. He values this offspring, and the instigator party must have made sure that if he spills anything, it is his dormouse-eating children that will be punished. We can pluck his arms out and kill him with pain, but you know well that these people have a tough skin. He will not tell us anything else.'

'Then, I trust your advice, Rafaello. If we will not have any proof to accuse the party who instigated Eleuterio to commit this crime, we are indeed helpless, but we do not make any more noise about it. We must care for our remaining mulberry trees, each one of you reinforcing protection for your own orchards. We have some moths already, but not many eggs yet. I've already sent message to my contact in Byzantium for another shipment.'

'And what about my losses?' Bartolomeo asked.

Battista lost his patience and said through gritted teeth 'This is a risky endeavour, Bartolomeo. If we want to produce our own silk, we are not only breaking through a secret. We are defying a whole empire. Now if you cannot see a few paces ahead of your eyes and only worries about those few trees that you had paid for, I will be happy to pay for your loss, to buy your investment and to deserve your silence.'

'I'm with you, Battista' said Rafaello.

A general murmur of approval was heard across the room. Bartolomeo only accepted the sale of his share when Dino also demonstrated interest in leaving the enterprise. When the figures were agreed upon, Dino and Bartolomeo courteously left the room, as an uninterested and silent party. Battista continued. 'And as for that stinky felon hanging in our dungeons?'

Rafaello promptly answered 'I have the boat organised already. My men will take care of him.'

Battista smiled with satisfaction 'Then make sure the crayfish eat it all!' He turned to all the others and asked 'Does anyone here doubt this could have been instigated by Gottefredo Di Antelmo?'

They all accepted the possibility. 'Then we must watch that pig.' He said. 'We should double our strategies to keep Gottefredo away from our financial interests. To keep him away from our city. I still have the feeling that he could act on a different front to spoil our enterprise.'

The Hangover

'Lando Delle Rocche, will digress as much as our patience allows for , but you will not tell us what was the gift that Julian had for Clarissa?' the contessa asked. 'The Beatissimo Padre is about to return from the prayer of *Terces* at the bishop's Palace. He will be more than ready to hear the continuation of —'

'And you don't pray yourself, my cousin Matilda? And goose Liutprando's tail feathers are nailed to that seat of his?' It was early morning, and while Matilda was already sumptuously dressed, the bishop of Cremona appearing ready and tidy,

Lando looked scruffy as a rat. The cantastorie had been awoken by the contessa's household after a late night out, which revolved around the central city market.

'I have already attended the *Lauds*, when you were probably not even back from your nocturnal journey of excesses. So do put yourself together and continue the story.'

'I will get there, great contessa, I will get there!' said Lando, as he hurriedly helped himself with some cold pork at the table. Old Albertazzo observed everything in silence, sitting at the other end.

Lando felt tired and confused. 'My head still hurts…'

'Shame on you!' the contessa said, with hard lips and no trace of amusement in her eyes. 'And shame on me, for unfortunately we share some of this same Tuscan blood.'

Lando looked at all dishes at the table and asked 'I don't suppose you have fried canary, or some fresh owl's eggs, do you?'

'You must be mad!' said the contessa, curling her lips. 'So you do believe on the witchcraft you tell us about, don't you? Owls eggs…' she sniggered. 'A hangover is God's punishment on the weak. You need penitence, and not a fried canary.

'All he needs is a good serving of pork fat, raw yolks and honey,' said old Albertazzo, with a frail voice from the other side.

This annoyed the Matilda further 'You probably know well about these mundane vices, don't you?'

'Well, it would seem that to get to my age one would certainly know about staying alive, Matilda.'

The countess impatiently waited for Lando to gather as much food as he could in his hands and for Albertazzo to slowly move from the dining table.

'Is your sweetheart back from his meeting already?' Albertazzo asked Matilda as he passed by her. Somehow he regretted as soon as it came out of his lips.

'Your suspicion insults me, my cousin. You mock my love for the Beatissimo Padre just as that Bishop Theophylactus doubted his cousin's wife Theodora.'

Albertazzo smiled toothlessly and said with unhidden disdain 'I am no Theophilactus, that's for sure, and you are certainly not a Theodora, at least not on the way that Lando described her.'

'But as Theodora did love the Apostle of Christ, so do I, with all my heart and mortal soul.'

'Different reasons and different times, Matilda.' Albertazzo said. 'That was Pope Sylvestre, so long ago.'

'My love for Pope Gregory surpasses any urges of the flesh, as he is the very person who has convinced me to give up on the idea of joining a monastic house.'

Albertazzo was ready to protest when, for his relief, he noticed the pope was already entering the palace hall. He held onto his words and kissed the papal ring after the other three had done it.

The contessa could not hold from informing the pontiff. 'Lando has a hangover from his late night of depravity.'

'Well, then you should go to Corsena,' Gregory said. 'The best remedy is a hot bath followed by a cold plunge. Then, if we could get any of those meaty thistle flowers that grow in Sicily, -'

He was interrupted by a visibly annoyed Contessa Matilda. 'Rubbish, Beatissimo Padre. It's all rubbish.' She warmed a smile and held on to the pope's hand. 'Everyone seems to be a specialist in hangovers. But what Lando really needs is repentance, penitence and, for the next time, abstinence and decorum.'

Gregory opened his mouth in surprise and raised both his hands in rendition. Matilda noticed and, quite ceremoniously requested: 'Lando Delle Rocche, we are all ready to hear more. Perhaps you could start by cutting short your lies and telling us what it was that Julian brought to Clarissa.'

Lando still had his mouth full before he could start.

Book 2: The Warrior

The Sphinx

Lucca – A.D. 1002

'What kind of creature is that?' Clarissa asked. She was holding a terracotta vase which she had been given after the young rider returned from accompanying Battista Burle's precious silkworm cargo back to Lucca.

The vase was a simple cylinder, slightly slanted to the side, leaning on the back of a meticulously sculpted creature. It had a woman's face, with the head and chest of a lion, and large wings on its shoulders standing opened, wrapped around the vase. It had hooves on its hind legs, and the tail of a bull. The piece was carefully painted under a glossy coating, in beautiful icy white and a raspberry tone to the beast's hair and mane.

'I don't really know,' said Julian, shrugging his shoulders. He was just pleased by watching the colours in her eyes, as she appreciated the novelty of that vase. There was nothing in the world that made Julian happier as being alone with Clarissa. She had grown taller in those two years, to a slim, but still boyish figure, just starting to sprout the shapes that would make her look even more formidable one day. Her brown hair was still kept lose, a silky curtain, now longer than ever, caressing her shoulders, concealing her waist. To his utmost happiness, Julian had been taken into Luna as a family member. He was at ease with the Obertenghi. Their affection could make him forget of past fears and a different life. And moreover, he was particularly delighted with every second he could spend near Clarissa.

Cravings to be with Clarissa, and only with her, only him and no one else.

Julian would cringe with jealousy when other noble young men came to Luna and distracted Clarissa's attention, especially the handsome Pietro di Filippo, whom they called the Calandrino. Getting each day closer to marrying age, Clarissa was always generous to dedicate time to visitors, playing with frank laughter, even dancing enthusiastically with them when entertained by musicians. Julian elected not to measure her dedication to other young men and compare it to the treatment he received. Jealousy made him blind to the fact that Clarissa never seemed to treat them any better than the special care she had for him. She showed no interest in any talk of marriage, and her parents made little efforts to bring the subject up. To his peace of heart, Julian had no knowledge of any other boy that she had taken to that highest tower. Their daily getaway was an undisturbed stay onto heaven, where they could sit and look into each other's eyes while the sun rushed over the sky.

On that afternoon Julian had returned from Lucca with the vase in a bag. He found her by the stables, playing with the servants' children. Even though he had been hurrying her with the notion that the bag contained a present, Clarissa took her time to send those kids away. That was the most irritating thing about Clarissa. She often seemed to be this generous, silvery angel of ice, floating above the petty feelings of possession and selfishness which heated his own heart. As for Clarissa, she was slightly amused on realising that Julian was already biting his lips with impatience when they entered the castle. They climbed to their usual hideaway, up on the tower, where they could watch over the Ligurian blue waters, miles away by the coast, through a window narrow enough where both had to squeeze shoulders. Julian's favourite place in the world.

'Battista Burle told me this vase came in a Constantinople shipment,' Julian mentioned, trying to concentrate on finishing what he had started to say. One thing that annoyed Clarissa was when he began telling her something and lost himself into another story, or just evaporating his words as he stared into her eyes. 'Battista was grateful for my help to his son-in-law, that man Immanuel. He told me that this vase is perhaps made by ancient people of Holy Land. This creature must be some type of...' he hesitated to say the word, '...demon?'

Clarissa dropped her gaze from the ceramic piece. She softened her face and lightly touched Julian's hand. The blasting warmth of her touch comforted him, suggesting she was no ice princess, but full of flames inside. Julian's fingers hesitated, before a spark of fear made him regrettably decide to not hold hers. 'But I think it is an angel,' said she, distractedly withdrawing her hand. 'Look at its beautiful wings,' and her eyes exploded in a festival of colours, when she turned to Julian with an impish curve in the corner of her lips. 'This will be my angel.'

Jealousy kept whispering malicious words on Julian's ears. And it was up on that same tower when he finally ceded to the venom, making his first big mistake of expressing distrust.

Clarissa was watching the sun drop its last rays over the Ligurian sea. The burning slice quickly disappeared behind the very thin coopery strip of ocean that she could devise from the tower. The green tip of the sun that she loved to see before it plunged into the ocean was never so bright before. She was ecstatic.

Julian sat on the mattress, staring at the floor, ignoring Clarissa's enthusiasm.

'Clarissa, when I described you that Leviathan on the beach...' he started shyly, but took a decisive intake of air. 'How do you know about...the *male thing*?'

Her face went dark. 'You must be kidding, right? Tell me you do not think me an idiot, please.'

Julian stared at her dark silhouette against the twilight sky. Even at the worse of her humour, nobody could not look any better. 'Was it Pietro di Filippo, the Calandrino?' he asked.

'Julian, stop it right there. I don't want to know how jealous you are or how much of a sinful harlot or whatever it is that you think that I am.'

Quite blinded by his possessiveness, Julian ignored her. 'Pietro is already getting near his expected age to get married. He is a very handsome young man. Has he been telling you things, Clarissa?'

'I warned you Julian!' she hissed. 'Just...don't talk to me anymore.'

When Julian realised the dimension of his mistake, Clarissa had already left the tower.

She did not speak to him, looked at him, or even acknowledged his existence for an agonising several weeks to come.

He was so glad those long weeks were spent with a new distraction, which made him tired enough to fall asleep as soon as he lied down. Or else, he knew he wouldn't have been able to sleep, or eat, or live. He would have died.

'Hold me firmly, Julian' said the blacksmith, extending his sweaty open hand. 'Now try to pull me towards you, using just the strength of your arm, without stepping back'.

Julian obeyed. With hands as big and leathery as goatskins and sweaty muscular arms sprouting from the sides of his oiled apron, the blacksmith could be an intimidating figure if it was not for his warm brown eyes and an assuring smile. With an undefined olive colour, his glazed face had the Greek beauty of Roman statues, with a straight nose, delicate lips, a carefully-trimmed beard and an ample forehead, adorned by a well-greased cover of silvery hair. His command was so firm and inviting that nobody could have refused. Neither the Virgin Mary, nor the Devil.

'Good!' said the blacksmith when Julian steadily pulled him. 'Very good!'

With twisted lips puzzlement, Julian looked at Alberto Azzo.

'That will give Caligero a more realistic notion of your true capacity,' said Alberto.

'But I am not a grown adult yet. I still expect to get taller and stronger.'

'And you will,' said Caligero, the blacksmith. He rubbed the sweat from his forehead with the back of his hammer hand. Behind him, the bright flames of a forge emitted heat waves that made Julian and Alberto frown as they listened to him. 'Julian, you are one of those deceiving long leggers. Most among your type are fragile young lads, who could be toppled in the blink of an eye by a shorty. You have long limbs, yet you will have the strength to keep a sword straight, to swing it far. The sword I will forge will not be for your use today or this coming week. It will be a weapon for your life. You may find it rather heavy when it's fresh, but I know how much more you will grow – and that will be enough to enable you to master it swiftly one day.'

Julian had a light of understanding on his face, but it darkened quickly and his gaze dropped to the floor. 'I will not be able to pay for it,' he said.

Alberto tapped him on the shoulder. 'Do you really think I brought you to Lucca for your sword and expected you to pay for it?'

'But I insist! I should be able to work for –'

'Forget it, Julian!' Alberto cut. 'Just enjoy this gift as a heartily retribution from all of our family.'

Julian made an effort to smile back. No matter how much the idea of handling a sword excited him, how much it made him feel powerful and attractive, he did not think Clarissa would have approved of the sword. Moreover, she hadn't talked to him for days. Alberto had noticed Julian's helplessness, roaming aimless around Luna like a headless goose. Oberto blinked to his son and they decided to send the boy out on their first opportunity to come to Lucca again.

They came straight to Caligero, by far the best of the blacksmiths in all of Lucca. Caligero was a Sicilian. He left as a child, with a large contingent of Christians that abandoned Sicily since total Arab dominance, gathering in slums around the towns, particularly Lucca, Pisa and Genova. Caligero's family were blacksmiths who had supplied receding Byzantine troops in the island, finding a good opportunity to sell their trade in those new lands. Yet, in spite of destruction of churches, restrictions on the worship and display of Christian symbols, Arab rule in Sicily turned out to be more benevolent to the smallholders, progressive to farming and stimulating to commerce. Many Sicilians had gone back after a few decades and a constant exchange of migration was still occurring. Even Jewish communities in Lombard lands had also found a more welcoming environment under Arab rule in the island.

Caligero's sons had returned to Sicily. Many of these returning children from Lucca and their descendants who remained in the island were to be called forever Lucchese. They provided a bridge of knowledge and experience between Sicily and Lucca, which would push the Tuscan city ahead of its rivals especially when the production of silk took a more relevant role.

Specialised in weapons, Caligero had taken a privileged standing among Tuscan society. In a time when western swordsmiths had not yet mastered the right steel to make long swords, Caligero's forges could produce longer swords than any other blacksmith would dare, with a blade that would resist well in the battle before bending or breaking. Most swords in Christianity were no longer than a forearm and the quality of the steel and craftsmanship could be a reason for embarrassment to any Arab or Byzantine swordsmith. With their long, curved saif swords, firm and virtually unbreakable, Arabs had variants of jokes about the brute Christians spending most of their time in battle stepping on their bent iron weapons to straighten them. Caligero and other Sicilian swordsmiths at the turn of the first Millennium were just being introduced to these differences and incorporating new techniques in their craft. This would make a dramatic difference on the eternal struggle of western armies against the Arabs.

'How much are you willing to pay for this sword?' Caligero asked with the side of his mouth, after pulling Alberto by the arm to a corner distant enough from Julian.'

'We have little gold, to tell you the truth, but my father and I have enough relics in our journey to Gallecia to raise our reserves at the local bankers. And if not, we should have sufficient grain and oil to trade.'

'I'm asking this because I have just received these.' He raised the cover from a large leather pouch on the floor and pulled out an ingot. 'This is the best steel that the swordsmiths from Damascus have used for centuries. It is brought from savage lands beyond the great deserts. Magic steel, that is forged, wrought and folded with a mixture of different iron ores and a special coal, made of dried fly agaric mushroom, the *uovo malefico*.'

Alberto examined the ingot closely, a beautiful dark grey with bluish silvery streaks, bands and mottles that had found their way around the surface, as streams of flowing water or woody grain.

'My father has a few daggers made of it,' he said. 'It's the most powerful steel I have seen.'

'Indeed, I have made those for Lord Oberto, but now I have large ingots to cast a full sword,' Caligero said, passing the piece to Julian. 'That's thanks to some interesting loads from il Poggio that Battista Burle has been getting from Constantinople.' He winked at Julian.

Julian looked guiltlessly at Alberto and shrugged, not too sure if the younger lord of Luna knew of Battista Burle's main import. It was almost a year and a half since the first arrival of silkworms and Caligero had been instrumental in recruiting some Sicilians to grow the worms, boil the cocoons and spin the threads.

'Master Julian, come back here after a month,' the Sicilian said. 'It was good you came now, for there are no re-adjustments for such a sword.'

They left Caligero's workshop mid-afternoon. Alberto planned to spend the night in Lucca to leave early on the next day. He was eager to show a little bit of the city to Julian.

There were over a dozen master blacksmiths in Lucca, clustering their steamy workshops with coppersmiths on the western side of the city. They were fenced enclosures, with a constant transit of *carbonai*, coal makers carrying in massive bags of chestnut tree charcoal and selling them for a pitiful price. Although the environment of casting metal was brutal, from heat and soot and the never-ending hammering of metal against metal, the personal untidiness of blacksmiths was not transferred to their products. The internal walls of some of these workshops were carefully lined with pans, cauldrons, bowls, jam pots, shields, knifes, skewers, sickles, axes, scythes, shears, ladles, spades and shovels, hammers, nails and pegs. These were mostly for the city folk and landowners, as peasants worked mainly with wooden tools. Some were specialised in harnesses and others in intricate material such as locks, chains, hinges and keys and others, as Caligero was, in warfare, displaying battle axes, swords, shields, spears, body plates and helmets. Alberto and Julian walked back through the narrow alley squeezed between the city wall and the steam-spewing workshops. Once they came to the inner side of the Western Gate, at the church of Santa Maria Ursimanni, they turned east, towards the city centre, and stopped by the church of San Benedetto and the Duke's Palace to their right, where they had been staying overnight. A group of ratcatchers was calmly leaving the city with their booty to sell at the vellutini. Julian watched the group with a mixture of amusement and disgust. The rats were hanging from their hands, entwined at the tails.

Alberto noticed Julian's interest. 'Would you like to see a little bit of Lucca?' he asked.

The question helped awake Julian from his disturbing vision. 'Well, yes!' he finally said. On his first time in Lucca, Julian had quickly ridden in for the precious load on Immanuel's cart and fled immediately out for the heartache to see Clarissa.

Following the main street eastwards through a colourful crowd of locals and pilgrims, strolling unhurriedly by several workshops with carpenters, shoemakers, saddlers, ropers and furriers, Alberto was patient while Julian took his time to watch, speeding their pace only to avoid the nauseous smell of the tanner houses. Lucca was well provided with wells, with a strict control on their use, supplying the centre and most of the city intramuri with clean water, while the extramuri region had only a few of them, relying mostly on the Serchio resources. The inhabitants of intramuri were also obliged to hire *raccoglitore* to clean the cesspits and privies and take the material out of the city. They performed their duties at night, to spare the pilgrims from exposure to the filth, but the price was not too cheap, for the vellutini usually charged the raccoglitore exorbitant tolls to allow them to dump the human excreta from the city, whether it was in the stinky moats next to the walls or far away on the fields.

The vestiges of old roman fortifications, pierced and broken into by streets, passages, styles and gates, almost blended into the buildings. The residential constructions were two or even three-storied, and many of the larger mansions had towers losing themselves into the heights, cylindrical brick giants that proclaimed the wealth of its owners. Julian kept looking up at their grandiosity, constantly apologising as he bumped into the passers-by. There were throngs of pilgrims in this area, as well as more men-at-arms standing still, watching the crowd and guarding the safety of goldsmiths, reliquaries, tailors and bankers. Lucca had about fifty churches within the outer walls in those days, disputing every square foot of space and rubbing elbows with monasteries, hospitals, taverns, workshops, warehouses, residences and administrative buildings.

They stopped briefly by the hospital of San Silvestro, the oldest *xenodochium* of more than a dozen of these guest houses functioning in Lucca, providing accommodation for pilgrims and the needed. Travellers arrived at such hospitals with an empty stomach and tired legs and very often they exited with an empty stomach, tired legs, but a renewed face of contentment. At San Silvestro, the healing baths facilities had been abandoned for long, being in no better state than the ruins at Corsena. The hospital had a loyal range of benefactors and it was one of the few that did provide to its guests full boarding, always with a good meal. Alberto told Julian that the secret for a good xenodochium was to be run by a well-organised hospitaller, giving full dedication to a well-supplied house.

Julian could recognise few of the languages, dialects or accents spoken by the pilgrims. Mostly they had in common the tired features, determined eyes and strong feet. Alberto took Julian around the relatively small church of San Michele at the old Roman forum and they headed north, towards the gate of San Frediano. A few blocks further, when the street started bending to the northeast, the crowd ahead of them opened up the way, standing tight against the buildings. An altercation seemed to have broken and a man came running in the middle of the street. People shouted insults and tried to spit at him. Alberto pulled his sword and stretched it out, stopping the man at its sharp tip.

'I am not a leper!' the man protested.

Julian only noticed it then. Dressed in filthy, bloody rags, the man's face was a mass of purple lumps and the skin was broken in several places.

'How do you explain your pestilence then?' asked Alberto, unmoved.

'This is not a sickness!' he begged. 'I have been robbed and beaten.'

Alberto kept the sword firmly pointed at the man's neck 'Explain it more!' he demanded.

The man sighed and knelt in front of Alberto, in respectful submission. 'I am from the north. Brescia is my city. I have done this pilgrimage to Rome before and it has conceded many divine graces to my soul. I felt the need to redeem further transgressions and decided for a new journey. Unfortunately punishment was the price for my redemption, as I was taken by surprise a few miles south from the village of Fornulo. They took everything from me, and I am lucky to be alive.'

With a curl of his lip, Alberto finally withdrew his sword. 'If your story is true, then you deserve justice. Go find a hospital and clean yourself. San Silvestro is probably your best chance. They are not associated with any churches. You don't really want to be declared a leper by any religieux that finds it suitable, do you? Now, just walk down this road, go west after the church of San Michele. When you're clean and cared for, find our *balivo* and complain to him about the robbery and beating.'

'Will you walk with me, Messere?' he begged.

'No! I happen to have a guest' his eyes shot at Julian for a second, 'who does not want to waste his –'

'Oh, it's no trouble to me.' Julian interrupted.

'Oh yes, it is!' Alberto said, now looking irritated at Julian. 'It is indeed much trouble to your plans, young man. And to mine.' He turned to the man and said 'You are on your own.'

When the Bresciano disappeared on a race around the bend, Alberto told Julian 'I could not trust him…'

How different from his sister, Julian thought. He rejoiced quietly at the thought of how Clarissa, fierce as a lioness, would have defended that poor wronged man from further harm, taking him by the hand to the hospital. Julian missed her.

The street curved northeast around a disarranged group of low buildings. Alberto pulled Julian through a small alley and they entered this wide-opened space, mostly a flattened area surrounded by a wall of houses completely circling it. In this circle, an intimidating number of people circulated through small stalls, as some yelled out their merchandise, others sang songs about the freshest produce and most haggled vigorously for a better deal. The smell of bakeries and roasted chestnut was an efficacious invitation for the hungry visitor to purchase more than the actual need or to enter a tavern. Butchers covered in sweat hung their chops, sausages, belly and boar heads on hooks and, behind a dead row of upside down pheasants, thrushes, blackbirds and wood pigeons, rotting for several days already under the late summer heat, fowlers tossed limp ducks and old hens into boiling pots flooded with wet feathers. The rather unpleasant odours that were raised from the gutted animals was smothered by delicious scents of the riverside and the meadows, from fresh and dried bunches of thyme, winter savoury, calamint, spinach, caper flowers, borage and some of the earliest mushrooms of the fall. Julian and Alberto walked past the egglers, with their baskets filled with shiny white eggs popping out of the straw and, on their side, oynters and wine sellers had carts piled with amphorae and barrels, unfolding themselves into pious gallantries, selling oil and wine to several groups of visiting clerics. Julian saw an endless influx of servants and slaves, bringing bags of grain from the alleys, on a seemingly unorganised fashion that he wondered how merchants kept a good account of the trade. The spaces between the stalls was much narrow than out on the streets, with everyone bumping shoulders, satchels, bundles and packs. Groups of dust-covered children held on to Julian's hands, touching him all over, looking for pockets or purses, while opening innocent smiles on their snotty faces. A few women, young and old, exchanged glances with him, while mutely drawing words with their lips. Standing in the middle of that crowd, Julian realised that the blacksmith was probably right: he was already taller than most people, probably cutting an interesting figure with his long features and the long black hair, rather unusual for the region. The proximity with the mob still made Julian uneasy, as if any of those faces that would turn hostile or scorn at him, as if he would not be surprised to see those yellow eyes of fire on the first unfriendly passer-by that raised his gaze to him.

When they had completed the circle around the open market, Alberto pulled Julian by the arm and they slipped into the coolness of a tavern. It smelled of vinegar and sweat, and the outside light came in only through the door. Both had to wait a while before their eyes got used to the darkness.

'Well, isn't that the mighty Alberto Azzo of the Obertenghi?' a woman's voice said. With loose wavy black hair falling on her shoulders, she did not wear a wimple of a married woman and, in Julian's opinion, she walked like a man.

'Scolastica!' Alberto said, opening his arms. They hugged like old friends.

Julian was shocked. The woman was a wench and Alberto Azzo seemed to know her well. He had seen dozens of wenches before, but they were just women that one could not really trust. Women that one would better not look into their eyes. And he had little time to react when Alberto introduced him to Scolastica as a friend, almost like a brother: she came to hold on to his face and kissed his cheeks.

At a first glance, there was little in Scolastica which would have any appeal to Julian's eyes. With enormous hands and thick hairy arms not unlike the blacksmith, Scolastica was wearing one of those clinging tunics that could not conceal a prominent barrel-shaped belly and a rather narrow and completely flat behind. Her chin was only a tiny lump out of the baggy bulge that raised from her collarbone to her lip. The face was probably too large for the size of her body and the space between her eyes and her mouth was just too broad. But to be fair, in spite of the darkness of her working environment, her skin had that healthy tan of Lucchese mixed stock, a vigorous light brown, streaked by roguish freckles just in the right places. When she sat on Alberto's lap with a rather lewd wiggle, Julian was so shocked that he almost fell from the seat he had just taken. Not that he was particularly surprised by the behaviour of a wench, but rather by the ease in which Alberto accepted that intimacy. He wondered if Alberto had been entertaining adulterous delights with that woman, he who was so fortunate to have Adela on his life, to enjoy unimaginable adventures in her wondrous body in their intimacy, *how could he be enticed to entertain sensual commerce with that ugly woman?* Julian was so distracted by these considerations that he almost missed what Scolastica and Alberto were talking about. When the contents that they had been discussing dawned on him with bright, blinding rays, he finally snapped '*Stop!*'

But for the sake of clear understanding, here is the dialogue that Julian had basically missed.

When Scolastica made to sit on Alberto's lap with a brazen rub of her flat behind, she said 'I was just talking about you last night, darling.'

'Bragging to your friends again?' Alberto asked.

'No, silly. It was your cousin who was here. He mentioned that he hadn't seen you for a long time too.'

'Which cousin?' he asked, 'Bonifacio, the duke? Julian and I were at Bonifacio's palace last night.'

'No! I'm talking Bernardo. Your cousin Bernardo Delle Rocche.'

'Oh, Bernardo, of course!' said Alberto 'I miss him. Bernardo has been back from the northern lands already for a few years, but I have not seen him. He is tending all of the lands of his parents –'

'*Stop!*' Julian cried.

There was an awkward silence in the tavern. Julian was close to apologise to the patrons, but he preferred to just ask 'Did you just mentioned Bernardo Delle Rocche? A young man who's returned from the north a few years ago?'

'Yes,' Alberto said with a question on his face. 'My cousin. Why do you ask?'

Scolastica brought them wine as Julian told his story, of joining a group of religieuses in their march south of Poitiers, skipping the part of Louise, but not missing to mention the tales told by Bernardo and the allure that he stirred among some of the nuns. He told them of the attack in the forest of Limoges and of Bernardo's heroism in defeating the assassins. Julian saw Alberto and Scolastica's faces lighting up as they recognised Bernardo's character on every single depiction of those adventures. In this moment, Julian was momentarily distracted by Scolastica's smile. She had a rather narrow set of squirrelled lips, and although her teeth were not straight, they seemed to be healthy as a young girl's. Scolastica's sincere brown eyes nearly disappeared into slits when her cheeks squeezed them up, increasing their distance from her mouth and withdrawing any balance that the face could have had. And somehow, it was still an attractive smile. Its clear honesty was refreshing and filled Julian with assurance and vigour. He could start to appreciate how that woman could be, after all, vaguely attractive.

Almost lost in such considerations of desire, Julian re-captured the thread and finally said, 'I never thought I would hear about this Bernardo again.'

'Well, he is indeed my second cousin, owning a vast extension of lands behind the Apuane snowy peaks that we see from Luna, descending for miles towards the Serchio river,' said Alberto.

'And he should be still in Lucca these days.' Scolastica said.

'But how is that possible?' Alberto said. 'Our common cousin is the Duke Bonifacio, but the good duke has not mentioned Bernardo during our stay.'

Scolastica laughed. 'Bernardo certainly would not be staying with the duke. I wouldn't be so sure if Bonifacio would approve of his lifestyle,' she said. 'Since he has come back from the north, Bernardo has visited Lucca quite often, obviously looking for the amorous adventures he cannot find on the mountains. But he has never been known to pay for it. There are enough widows, wives, daughters or even nuns, brides of Christ, with a craving for a good man between their legs, and so many of these will fall easily to his charming stories.'

Julian nodded, not sure if he should laugh at that.

'He often stays with the monks of San Donato, by the western gate, or in one or two houses that his family maintains in Lucca,' Scolastica said.

'Julian, would you like to find Bernardo Delle Rocche?' asked Alberto.

But he did not need to wait for an answer. Julian's face was lighting up the whole tavern.

'No! Bernardo Delle Rocche has not been here for two days!' said a long, warty nose that stuck out of a small hatch on the back door. 'Leave us in peace. We are conducting the *Vespers*, reading the scriptures, if you don't mind.'

Alberto apologised and the hatch slammed back into place. Julian was rather disappointed.

'Well, we tried,' Alberto said. 'Perhaps you can come and spend some time with Bernardo in his own lands one day.'

They crossed the moat bridge at the eastern gate, back towards the duke's palace. A starry night had already unrolled itself over the city, now even more interesting under the flickering lights and the shadows produced by a still moving crowd. They could see the puffs of steam invading the blacksmith's alley down by the church of Santa Maria Ursimanni.

'Are the lords searching for Bernardo Delle Rocche?' a voice asked.

They both turned to the person who had asked it, a religieuse with her face half covered by her cowl.

'How would you know?' Alberto asked, shaking his head in disbelief. 'We have only crossed over from San Donato. Do you have any under-the-moat connecting passages or something?'

The nun lost the tension on her face and laughed, frankly amused. 'No, we hear this not from San Donato. Those men have little good words to share with us. Bernardo has given up staying with them. It was hours earlier that we knew you were after the Obertenghi shepherd.'

'Scolastica?' Alberto asked.

The nun did not answer. The street torches burned bright. She only kept a slightly enigmatic smile on her face, and lights of amusement dancing in the slits of her eyes. They could see she was young, of good stature, probably in her twenties. Of very white skin, a generous wide mouth of happiness, with shining meaty lips and a pair of prominent rosy cheeks plumping out of her face like apples. No man would need to guess that the shape of her body behind the folds of those robes could inspire nothing else than the idea of breeding.

'Where can we find Bernardo then?' Julian asked.

With feline eyes, the nun measured young Julian from head to toe, never losing that smirk on the side of her lips. 'Are you a relative? Where's that accent from?' she asked, staring now deep into his black eyes, leaving her mouth slightly ajar.

Alberto answered with blunt irritation 'No, I'm the relative! Julian here is a friend. Now can you tell us where to find Bernardo?'

She rolled her eyes and looked back at the monastery, before saying 'Bernardo came at vespers and left with one of our sisters. I expect they'll be back by complines...' she paused, never losing her smirk, '...at least that's how I do when I escape with him.'

'How many of you go out of the monastery with Bernardo?' Alberto asked, indignant.

'And what will you do with the number I tell you? Serve us all?'

Alberto spat. 'Julian, if you want to wait for Bernardo, you wait. I will not stay here to be a witness of this shamelessness. Good night sister.'

'Actually, I would really like to find Bernardo Delle Rocche,' Julian said, shyly.

Warming up with a smile, Alberto Azzo just said 'You know the way. You can take care of yourself. Just watch for this young woman – she's engaged to Jesus – and find your way back to the palace. We're one block of houses from here.'

When he had disappeared around the corner, the nun slowly walked around Julian. Her face glowed with the lights of the blacksmiths down the alley. 'I can keep you company if you want. I can show you the city. We'd need to dress up as pilgrims for that, but I know places where we could be at peace. Just the two of us.'

Julian bit his lip and grinned. 'Thank you for your company, but I will wait for Bernardo right here on this corner.'

'As you wish, young man,' she said with a sway of her hips. 'It could be a few hours before they return. Seat yourself,' she pointed to a low brick wall that surrounded the garden on the side of the monastery. 'Nobody will condemn you for seating. Neither God, nor Santa Maria, or the saints of the gospel, or the abbess...or me!' She entered the garden and disappeared in the darkness. Julian heard the door closing in the monastery, somewhere behind it.

He waited for hours, immobile, watching the thinning movement of people, vellutini leaving the intramuri and the last pilgrims arriving on the opposite direction, rushing up to find a hospital before the hour of complines. Behind him, a garden of hedges, probably a small maze, concealed the front of the main church of that monastery. The building was cubic, almost identical to San Donato outside the walls, just a few paces from them, across the moat. With a thatched roof, there were little adornments, except for the stone cross above the entrance and the rim around the building, where a lion, and eagle, a bull and an angel had been roughly sculpted. The animals of the gospel, Julian knew it. He did not know why Luke was associated with a bull, or John with an Eagle, Mark with a lion and Matthew with an angel. Perhaps it would be obvious for those who read the gospels, but not as clear to him. Maybe if he could ask someone like his uncle Avesgaud.

No, he would never see him again.

'It's getting cold, and they are not back yet.'

It was the nun speaking. She was back in the garden, behind Julian. The last fires of the street were burning down, but he noticed those brown eyes, glowing like embers under her decisive pair of straight blonde eyebrows. Her lips were still ajar, thick and moist, and a tongue was suggestively playing in the darkness behind them. 'Come here, Julian. I have something for you.'

Sightlessly, Julian obeyed and they entered behind the edges.

'Nobody can spot us here,' she said, pulling him by the hand to a very dark area, where the only thing they could see was the top half of the church wall reflecting the garrison lights and the starry sky above.

'What about the guards at the gate. Do they know when –'

His words disappeared, muffled by her lips, thick and hungry, immediately pressing against his, offering him a muscular, wet wrestle that gave him little time to react.

'You like it, don't you?' she asked, panting.

Julian could feel her breath entering him. 'Yes, of course I do,' was all that he could say.

She kneeled in front of him, and in a few seconds his head was thrown back, inhaling the cool air of the night, with the steam of the forges, the steel sizzling under water, the glistening sweat, the fruity scents of olive oil, the spices, the wine and the human filth. Julian opened his eyes, and saw the stars above him, shining brighter as he was drawn further into warm waters. His gaze lowered to the church wall, where four creatures stared with their mouths gaped at him.

'I need you to fuck me,' she said, standing and moving over to a corner, raising her robes.

But Julian was still paralysed by the horrified stare of those creatures. The eagle looked at him furiously, a desperate angel cried with pain, a lion with curled lips of disgust and anger, and a bull ready to charge for kill.

'Come and take me!' Her voice was angry. Julian's gaze dropped to the dark corner of hedges where the nun had leaned upon. He could see her whiteness, shining like the moon from her firm bottom and strong legs. There was a ravenous part of his body that drove him towards her, but his eyes returned to the sculptures at the rim.

It was Clarissa.

Of course! Those creatures blended together into the monster of her vase. Eagle's wings, lion's chest, bull's legs and a human face. It was Clarissa's angel, watching him, ready to bring all the bricks of that church down on him.

'They are only stones,' the nun said, standing next to him.

Julian did not know how long he had been there, paralysed, looking at those animals. The nun had obviously given up. Her voice was calm, contained, but with a chestnut bitter-sweetness to it. He noticed that she was re-composed and that two tears had managed to find their way down around her plump cheekbones.

'I'm so sorry,' was all that he could say, while quickly composing himself.

The nun could not look into his eyes. She sighed and said 'We are wedded into this life, not chosen by so many of us. An eternal repetition of prayer and self-sacrifice. Most of us will conform, give in and give up. We all adapt somehow, and many lose the notion of our weaknesses or the very reason why we are told to abstain from certain pleasures. But there are few of us who need a reminder of our fragile humanity. We crave to still be real women, to be held by men. To feel desired and loved.'

'Desired?' Julian asked, knowing well that there would be nobody else to receive more of his love and desire than Clarissa. 'You probably do appreciate the immensity of your beauty and the fascination you exert upon men.'

'Well, I did feel the fascination in you, to begin with. You were ready.'

'And I would have taken you like a wolf' Julian said, 'except that a larger force kept me from doing it.'

'Because I am married to Christ?' she laughed, bitterly. 'Are you afraid of His jealousy? Who's this Christ but a feeble, dying husband that assures us wives that all our suffering and misery is not nearly as painful as the tortures He endured because of His own words; that our deprivation will meet our real bodily needs, certainly irrelevant as compared to our noble spiritual aspirations; and that our mortification leads us higher upon the steps to heaven? *That* Christ does not touch my face, I cannot feel His lips, and my breasts do not know His caresses. He does not hold me by the waist and He is supposed to live in my heart, but I would rather have a man inside me in a different manner…' she wept quietly.

'It is not that, either' Julian tried to explain. 'Believe it or not, the only woman that I have ever had before was a nun too.' He realised he was talking about long-gone Louise to a stranger. A stranger as strange as Louise herself had been, but probably someone who could keep it locked and mute, forever. 'But that has passed…' he finished, 'the fact that held me is that I already have someone.'

The nun wiped the tears with her sleeves. She smiled to herself. 'I should have known. Young, handsome, virile. A devilish temptation. How could you not be engaged, promised? It is you who must be seeing me as the Devil, now a defeated temptation.'

Julian was ready to disagree. He wanted to say that there isn't such a thing as the Devil, but he could not believe in that any more. Besides, someone arrived in the darkness, standing quietly but shivering next to them.

The nun held Julian by his arm and said 'I beg you not to tell anybody of this. The pain and humiliation that we would suffer could far surpass those of Him,' and she pointed to the stone cross above the door, before disappearing through it with the other figure that had arrived.

Julian ran out and jumped the stone wall. The only fire on was the garrison at the tower, but he saw a pilgrim walking hurriedly towards the city centre.

'Bernardo Delle Rocche! Is that you?'

The pilgrim stopped and leaped to the shadow, completely secluded by darkness. 'Who is it that wants Bernardo?' he asked.

'It's me, Julian. I am Julian of Mans.'

The pilgrim appeared again under the light. '*Julian?*' He flung his cowl back 'Julian, is that you?' He ran back towards Julian with his arms opened 'Oh dear Lord, how much better could this night get?'

But Julian could hardly recognise him.

Betrayal

East Rome (Byzantium) - 6512 Annus Mundi

The year of 6512 AM in the Byzantine calendar, calculated from the creation of the world, was equivalent to the year 1004 AD from the Roman calendar established since Julius Caesar's time. Not a particularly special year to be remembered in the history of Constantinople and its people. Not a bad one either. Life just carried on in the centre of the Eastern Empire, waking up every day with the cries of the seagulls, and seeing the night roll up its stars under the merry songs of the Bosphorus taverns.

The ship sailed smoothly, carried by the northerly wind of the Bosphorus, taking Procopius past the views of the churches of St. Stephen, St. Saviour and St. Lazarus, with the palaces of the first hill towering above them. Finally, as they turned westwards, the lion and the bull statues guarding the sea gate of the Boukoleon palace were a comforting familiar view to Procopius. From the ship, he saw the large *Varangoi* guards, faithful giants standing at the palace walls in their shining scale cuirasses, watching the sea for any danger or foe that could threaten or harm the emperor. Those brave Norsemen had been visiting the waters of the Black Sea for several years already. They came in long, dragon-shaped boats, in expeditions that they called *viking*. Now, the emperor had hired their service to be the highest guard in Constantinople, envied by the local battalions and feared by pretty much everyone else.

Behind the buildings of the Boukoleon, a multitude of smoke and steam columns dispersed itself with the wind, rising from the blacksmiths, coppersmiths and glassmakers district. Procopius saw the smaller harbour where the murex shell dealers brought their products from the islands. He himself had a smaller ship which used that selected pier. Looking ahead, an increasing density of ships and boats indicated that they would soon be approaching the much larger Harbour of Theodosius. Once again, one more adventure was over, and Procopius was finally getting home.

The trip had not been as long as his long journey to Acquisgranus, four years before. Trebizond was no more than two weeks journey by sea. Procopius had already been many times to that Black Sea port. He was not licensed to trade in silk fabrics, purple fabrics or buy raw silk from the Far East. But in the Trebizond market, he could obtain excellent deals for the metals, ceramics, dyes, oil, sugar and meats that he brought from Constantinople. The revenues would buy him good quality slaves for a bargain, besides the cheap access to honey, wax, furs and steel ingots that travelled from the east. Most of the men and women available in those markets were sturdy, resilient people from upriver on the northern shores. They named themselves *rhos*, which meant rowers in their own language. Giants of fair skin, from their size and make, it was believed the rhos were norsemen, some type of Varangoi that had been expelled from their homeland and created their own nation. In Byzantium they were just referred to as *sklábos*, which meant slave. In the

206

future, most people from the regions of the rhos would be known by the westerns as *slavs*.

Procopius would make another small fortune with the sale of those healthy slaves. But above all, he would be able to rest for some time, as his sons had become deeply involved on the trade. Right now, his oldest was already financially prepared to afford the selected acceptance into the private guild of purple makers. This would expand their business to a dimension where no more personal trips would be necessary. Procopius was getting tired.

And the more tired you get, the less alert. He still had to be very careful. The last of four shipments to Immanuel Ben-Malachi was still being prepared. That brave convert was probably weaving the first fabrics of silk on his third year of receiving the goods, so he would not need any further deliveries of eggs in the future.

Treason was a crime punished by death. Much more than the thrill of the misdemeanour, there was a certain self-congratulatory sense of achievement when Procopius thought of his ingenious strategy to breach the walls protecting the system. He knew the gravity of the offense, of course, however consequences of that breach were perhaps overrated in his opinion. Constantinople would survive, he thought, but most importantly, he had been able to reciprocate the opportunity that Immanuel had opened to him. And now, all he had to do was to dispatch his next ship to Genova. For the Christ Almighty, he just could not wait for that moment of relief, when the last pieces of wood with silkworm eggs to leave his ship reached the shores of Liguria.

After that, nothing else to worry about.

Jumping onto the firm stones of the paved pier of the busy Theodosius Harbour was a reassuring feeling of security. A servant of his store was waiting at the docks with a horse. Procopius had a brief conversation with one of the harbour offices about taxation on the merchandise and left orders for his skipper to mind the boat and feed the slaves properly, until later in the afternoon, when they would unload. Now he just wanted to go home and see his family. He made to leave the crowded harbour area, which orbited around a gigantic public warehouse, containing hundreds of storage chambers for grain.

Then he heard his name being called.

An imposing figure, mounted on a well-bred horse, towering alone on an empty space of pavement where nobody dared to go any near, seemed to be looking directly at Procopius. With a thin, blonde beard and an icy stare, the man was wearing the bright red tunic of the Varangoi guards. Procopius pretended he did not hear it, still carrying on with the slow gait, partly hoping that the man had not called him, but someone else, as *Procopius* was surely not an uncommon name.

'Are you Procopius, the merchant of Makros Embolos, by the cistern?'

Procopius heart sank as he heard that voice again, in that slow, pompous accent, typical of the Varangoi. He tried to turn his head to the guard on a casual manner, but did it just too quickly, revealing a tension that should not be uncovered in anyone above suspicion. 'Yes, that's me. How can I help you?'

'Are you riding home, Procopius?'

'I am. I have just returned from Trebizond. Long trip. Apologies if I don't have much time for you.'

'Then I will ride with you, if you allow my company.'

'Of course!' Procopius put on his best smile of tolerance, shaping a friendly wedge inside his beard.

The guard rode next to him, tall, straight, and disturbingly silent, as they went up the hill, leaving the thickest core of the crowd, where minor warehouses of grain had been privately erected. The street climbed over the slope through a wide area of bakeries, under a delighting aroma of toasted wheat. The guard wore no weapons and had his head partly covered by a tight cowl. Procopius was sure the man was wearing a metal cuirass under those fabrics. The tunic had a patch at breast height, with an embroidered peacock in blue. Procopius noticed the cotton pants with wool bands wrapped around the legs under the knees; the gold banded cuffs, the tunic's gold embroidery and the velvet fabric with purple rims, the most valued and controlled colour in all of Byzantium. A public display of purple denoted high ranking, whether political, social, commercial or military. To worsen the intimidating facet of matters, these mercenaries were hardly seen riding horses. A tall horse and a taller man made Procopius look up with the sun on his face, as he was spoken to.

'Do you know who I am?' the guard broke the silence.

'From your gold, your purple, and your patch, you must be an officer of the Varangoi.'

'My name is Farlo, and yes, as you can see, I am a personal employee of the *Basileus Autokrator*,' he said, using reverently the latest titles conferred to the emperor of the Eastern Roman Empire. They never used the word Byzantine or Byzantium. People of the Eastern Roman empire called themselves *Rhomaioi*.

'I must confess that it does stir my curiosity to figure out what could an officer of the Varangoi want with me,' Procopius said, with a firm, well-humoured countenance.

Farlo smiled to himself, without looking at Procopius. The merchant's stomach churned, but he kept calm, now staring at the guard with apparent curiosity. Farlo had a large set of jaws, where this thin buck beard hung from, a rather disproportionally small nose and the high cheekbones of a tracker, squeezing the thin slits of his blue eyes under a shaggy pair of blond eyebrows. Finally the guard said 'You know, Procopius? In addition to being the personal guard of the Basileus Autokrator, we the Varangoi deal with breaches in high security matters that threaten the wealth and power of our state. Cases of treason. '

'Anything I can help you with?' asked Procopius, praying to God that no drop of sweat escaped from his skullcap towards his joined eyebrows, betraying his nervousness. 'I am only but a small merchant, associated basically with the guild of –'

'Can you read this?' the guard extended a hand, producing a worn piece of parchment that had been withdrawn from some hidden fold in his tunic. It hung for a second in front of Procopius's face, but the merchant was expedient to grab it.

'It's Latin.' Procopius said, immediately as he looked at it.

'I suppose it is,' said Farlo, still calm. 'I don't need the knowledge of reading in my trade. But you should know that this letter came from our Sicilian provinces.'

'Actually,' said Procopius, appearing to be genuinely intrigued, holding the letter at a distance in front of his wide eyes, 'this letter seems to have originated in Lucca, in the Marca of Tuscany. It dates from two years ago,' He pressed his lips in helplessness, 'but I am not too good in understanding Latin.'

Farlo gently turned to him 'You are indeed correct. This letter was originated in Lucca.' He said with a spark of amusement. Yet, his voice was still icy cold. 'Do you know what it says?'

Procopius read the letter through, carefully. By the top of the hill, both riders came to a large intersection with the main road to the emperor's palace. They turned their horses east, towards the Theodosian Forum. Once he read the signature, a name that he did not recognise, Procopius made a mental note of it and extended the letter back to Farlo. 'It seems someone has received silkworms in Italian lands.'

Farlo seemed amused. At the slow pace of their horses, he rested both of his massive hands on the front of his saddle and asked Procopius. 'And do you know who could be doing that?'

The merchant thought for a while, pressing his index finger against his lips. That stopped him from any shaking. 'Well, it shouldn't be too difficult to figure,' he finally said, capturing the guard's attention. 'Lucca has a large population of Sicilians. These are mainly Christians who are leaving a land dominated by Islam. They are reasonably good dyers, weavers and spinners, working on wool and on the silk fabrics that the merchants bring from the island. There are Sicilian blacksmiths that have even brought Damascene steel to that land of barbarians. If you want my opinion on it, I would suggest starting an investigation with the silk producers and silk merchants of Sicily. The quality of the product is pitiable. Nothing that would threaten our wealth. But yes, I think it could easily be from Sicily. Those Arabs have nothing even close to our strict control on the production and movement of precious goods.'

Farlo nodded with a smile. 'Interesting,' he said, 'very interesting!'

They were passing by a large fish market across the forum. The catch was always fresh, with heavy penalties on any slimy stall or produce that reeked of dead fish.

'Actually,' Procopius started, renewed by the salty aroma of fresh seafood, eager to end that conversations and get home, 'I would begin by verifying who this alleged author really is. I do send ships to Pisa, Lucca, Genova, but I have never heard of this Gottefredo.'

The Varangoi nodded. 'We have indeed already verified with the merchants in our foreign quarters. None of the Genovese, Venetians or Amalfitans knew of this name, but a few of the Pisans do recall a Gottfrid Anselmsson. Apparently he is a low-life lord from Lucca.'

'I wouldn't be surprised,' said Procopius, disguising his relief as much as he could. They were passing now by the meat market. He could hear the cleavers chopping through bone of sheep, goats and oxen. A butcher was shaving a dead pig.

'It's is probably nothing serious to be trusted,' Procopius added.

'You are right, it does sound like a cheap vendetta.' Farlo said, and waited until they were away from the sound of cleavers on wood, but soon they were crossing through a loud herd of pigs that were being taken to the market. The riders made a left turn, under the gate of Makros Embolos, on a straight avenue that sloped down directly to the Venetian quarters, at the northern shore. 'However,' Farlo continued with a grin, 'there is no reason why he should send this letter to Sicily, to accuse a local merchant of betrayal, is there, Procopius?'

The merchant had the impression that this blond giant Farlo could see right through him, that the innuendoes of disloyalty were no more than an amusement.

'Well, perhaps he wants the supplier to stop sending the silkworms to Lucca.'

'Again I agree with you, Procopius,' said the guard punching the air with enthusiasm. 'But perhaps one detail that I should add is that the Sicilians have already silently investigated and they concluded that it is none of them. This is why this letter has taken all of two years to reach the shores of our city. The traitor is among us.'

'How dare they accuse a local merchant of such low practice?' Procopius said, cursing and spitting on the paved road. 'You can never trust these Sicilians, that's what I say!'

'But you must understand our point of view, Procopius.' Said Farlo, with an apologetic face, only betrayed by the sarcasm in his eyes. 'We do need to investigate.'

'Well, do it then,' he said with undisguised annoyance. 'I will order my crews to enquire in Lucca where the silk is leaking from.'

Just after passing by a large public cistern, they were arriving at Procopius's house. A three-tiered building that stood next to his store, surrounded by an ample façade with porticoes and columns, where much of his merchandise was displayed.

Procopius could not see anyone in the shop. He made to dismount, but Farlo managed to stop him just by touching his shoulder with a large hand. 'Tell me a little bit more about you, Procopius,' he suggested, still mounted on his horse, 'How is it that you have made your fortune? Dealings in Acquisgranus? Lucca?'

Procopius swallowed a lump that seemed to bulge in his throat. 'With all due respect, Farlo, the tone of this conversation has turned towards a direction which makes me feel rather insulted. Is anyone actually suggesting that I could be –'

Another Varangoi appeared out of the door from Procopius store. Large and wide, he did not display any purple on his vests, and he wore the conical helmet of the guards, covered in blue velvet, as opposed to Farlo that only had the red cowl. He had the cuirass on a scale pattern, shining in the sun as a wet fish, iron scales alternated with gilded ones. His cloak had a patch too, but it had an embroidered raven.

'Procopius, this is Kari.' Farlo said.

'Ah, so finally, this is the famous Procopius?' said Kari, without a courtesy bow of his head. He had the strong accent of the Varangoi. His face was a mass of leathery white skin, with wide nose, bright red lips and a circle of brown hairs from his eyebrows to his chin. And unlike Farlo, this Kari held on to the typical long-handle axe of the Varangoi. 'Maybe you should take a look at this, Farlo,' he said and disappeared inside.

'Where is my family?' Procopius asked, almost shrieking.

'Just hold firm there, Procopius. Your family has been taken for interrogation. It will all will be back to normal once you prove your innocence.'

Procopius started weeping 'Please don't hurt them…'

A piece of wood rolled out from the door. It was a bulky lump of a branch, known by many as a burl. Kari came after, flying like a devil, holding his axe with both hands behind his back, stopping only to swing it fully and crash the blade against the pavement, chopping the hard burl into two perfect halves, as one would do to an apple.

'Stop shaking, Procopius' Farlo said, now with a voice even colder than the winter in his homeland, 'or your horse will get tired.'

Kari picked one of the halves and poured something from it in his hand. He showed the granules to Farlo.

The officer turned his face very close to Procopius's and bared his teeth like a wolf. 'I cannot understand betrayal, little man.' He spat. 'You are well aware of the penalty for traitors, don't you?'

'Please leave my family alone,' the merchant sobbed. 'They know nothing about this. Take me instead and apply the full punishment.'

'Too late!' said Kari, with an actual smile on his wide red lips. 'We've blinded them already. It took some pain, but they were the ones who told us about these,' and he poured the silkworm eggs over the wind that blew from down the street.

'Actually, my good Procopius,' Farlo said, watching the merchant's eyes growing even bigger in his panic-stricken face, 'we will spare you from the eye-gouging. We will grant you the privilege to see what happens to your family before their skins are paraded side by side with yours around our city. Treachery against the emperor. Treachery against Constantinople.'

Procopius made to vomit, but Farlo's heavy fist came much faster, full on his face. The merchant fell from the horse and everything became black. Blacker than the bile that flooded his stomach.

He woke up in a dark, cold and extremely fetid cell, with the desperate members of his family around him, crying and howling from pain. They had all been blinded, and they waited for a slow death reserved to traitors, probably on the following day.

On the next morning, guards of the palace dungeon found only Procopius alive. The merchant had used his family's own garments to spare them from further suffering. He killed them with silk.

In Lucca, nobody learned of Procopius public humiliation, torture and execution. They only noticed that those shipments of wood from Constantinople had stopped, forever.

The Crypt

Both the duke and Alberto were asleep.

Duke Bonifacio was a first cousin of Lord Oberto. He had taken over the dukedom of Lucca only a few years before, on the sudden death of his nephew Ugo. As opposed to the immense power that his yet unborn daughter Matilda would have one day, Bonifacio enjoyed no more than a symbolic rule over Lucca and very little power to take important decisions. The duke and his reduced army that protected the city were supported and heavily sponsored by the local bankers and the richest families. He collected duties on notary activities, banking, gaming, prostitution, salt, flour mills, bakeries and wine. This provided not only for a good living, but also for the maintenance of the local garrison. His new palace had been built outside the old roman walls, across the church of San Benedetto, in a much more spacious area than any available space in the old centre.

Julian and Bernardo entered the palace main hall, heavily scented by the smoke of oil lamps and old food. Carved bones were still left on the table. No dogs were around to clean the scrapes, for they were sleeping at the duke's bed chamber. Bernardo lit a few more lanterns and Julian went across to the kitchen, where many of the servants normally slept. He woke one of them up for service.

Once well-provided with a flagon of fresh wine, they told each other their stories.

Something had changed. Although Bernardo still had the same captivating charm of a cultured storyteller, he spoke with more assertion, he drank with more gusto and he truly spoke more like a ruffian. Little physical resemblance remained of the rather personable Bernardo From The Rocks, called the shepherd, son of rich Obertenghi landowners, that Julian had met before. This new Bernardo had metamorphosed into a true farmer, a shaggy appearance of a man of the mountains, as unruly as a wild barbarian. His hair had grown savagely into a wizened mat, which often stuck out in thatched locks and ropes, like a giant starfish or octopus had stuck to his head. The dimples were hidden behind a short shaggy beard. The Apuane mountains had made him thicker outside and the lordship had made him harder inside. But the hypnotic sparkle in his violet eyes was now an obvious sign for Julian of Bernardo's common ancestry of Lord Oberto.

'I never, ever thought I would meet you again! And now, look at you: living with my relatives!' Bernardo said, wiping the wine that dripped from his lower lip. 'My dear God! You are actually sharing the same roof with my delicious cousin Bertha! Oh, Berta that golden temptress…' he sighed and ripped a ravenous gaze. 'Tell me, Julian: have you had a chance to dip your bread into that broth yet?' When Julian smiled and shook his head embarrassingly, Bernardo continued 'I saw Bertha when I returned from Saint Michael, and by the red blood that runs in my veins, dear Lord Jesus, she was such a meaty temptation to moral disorder. I have since increased the frequency of my solitary sinning, staining my chastity with no regard at all to continence.'

'Chastity Bernardo?' Julian laughed. 'By taking the nuns and widows and wives and maidens of Lucca out for a ride on your lap, you seem to be crossing the boundaries of decorum in every possible direction.'

The shepherd waved him away 'I am no more than fulfilling their real need. But it's just a phase, you know, Julian. I am getting less used to this city, and the more I live in my lands the more I like those valleys and mountains. You see that I am growing my hair as an *omo salvatico*, a wild man, already. And if you look away for a while, when you look back you shouldn't be surprised if I'm living in a den, with the wild boars.'

Something twisted around in Julian's stomach. He was glad that it lasted but a brief moment, for Bernardo was quick to return to what seemed to be his favourite subject 'But I would give it all up in exchange for the heavenly privilege to taste the honey of Bertha's skin. You are such a lucky bastard to see her every day!'

Julian smiled to himself. 'Bertha is already promised to the young marchese in Torino, Odalrico Manfrido, and no, Bernardo I would not ignore that!' he said, with his deep eyebrows high on his forehead. His face unwounded, allowing his gaze to travel through the cold cuts and bones on the dirty table, slowly dispersing its focus to an unknown place by a window, out on the night beyond. He hesitated for a moment before saying 'I have instead become very close with Alberto's youngest sister, Clarissa.'

A rather longer than expected silence followed, while Bernardo pressed his lips and poured some more wine for both. The shepherd's eyes could be lighting the whole grandiosity of that palace hall. He raised his goblet and said 'This is to you, Julian! May the angels always carry you under their wings.' He drank it in one gulp and so mimicked Julian, but still with a raised eyebrow. Bernardo waited for the wine to irradiate through to his skin and said 'Julian, I am proud of you!'

'Why?' Julian asked. 'There's nothing but a friendship there.'

'I have only seen Clarissa when I left for Saint Michael. She must have been nine or ten years old then, but this girl blew me away with her presence. Such fire! Bertha is indeed a goddess, but Clarissa, well, Clarissa *is God* herself! I would not even dare to appreciate what it will be of Clarissa when she grows to be a full woman. She will be all the creatures together, the forces of earth, the air and sea, and everything indicates that she will be divinely beautiful.' He moved to the edge of the bank, leaning comfortably against the wall. 'So Julian, if it is you among anyone in this world of ours that has a chance to be with Clarissa, take it heartily and never let her go. You will be indeed with God. And you know what? You will be God,' he giggled quietly, the joy lingering into an inebriated snore.

Julian's eyes were still lost in the night beyond. It was too late when he realised he was saying to Bernardo 'I know exactly what you mean.'

But Bernardo was snoring deeply already.

They spent the next day visiting the southern part of the city, where the weavers, tailors, dyers, wool and fabric traders had their workshops and exercised their commerce. Julian was surprised to see a number of simple one-wheeled carts pushed by people, instead of pulled by beasts. The contraption could withstand a heavy load and all one needed to do was to lift it by two handles and push it, guiding it for short distances between stalls and workshops.

A congestion of oxen and yokes and carts carrying high piles of fleeces clogged the smaller alleys that gave into the larger cathedral square, by the *duomo*, the cathedral itself. Fleeces of good clip, rancid bundles that were flooding into Lucca, taking advantage of the off-season buys. As the oily wool could not be dyed properly, it was pressed and dunked into barrels with boiling salted water. According to Bernardo, Roman, Jewish and Muslim traders fought for the barrels of that putrid yellowish wool wax, which some people knew the secret of refining to mix with olive oil. The resulting concoction was an ointment sought after by noble women, to keep their skin soft and gleaming for the allure of love.

'In fact, the whole world of trade is full of secrets.' Bernardo explained, as they leaned against the cathedral wall, giving space to a passing herd of black sheep. Newly grown, those fleeces were still green in that season, stubbornly squeezing through the alley, marching towards the eastern gate, with their new owner yapping proudly at their back.

As the bleating faded in the distance, Bernardo continued 'Silk production in particular has been the worst of them. An infernal maze of locked doors and secret keys to open them. Only a selected few have the knowledge and the keys. But Lucca has conquered it. Over these last two years Lucca has been able to break through Constantinople's hegemony in silk production by starting a humble orchard of mulberries on the northern side of the walls and up the Serchio valley, across my lands.'

'Silk comes from mulberries?' Julian asked, with a seriously serious face.

'No,' Bernardo said, clearing his throat and re-starting on a rather patronising tone, 'the whole difficulty is apparently that silk is a thread produced by a caterpillar that feeds on mulberries.'

Julian paused for a while, with mystified eyes, until he could not hold the pretend anymore and started laughing. Now it was Bernardo, who looked puzzled and particularly silly, with his matted locks pointing in all directions from his head. 'Why the laughter, may I ask? You don't believe me?'

'Of course I do, Bernardo, but you never knew that I was the first person who saw those silkworm eggs with Immanuel Ben-Malachi, when they were smuggled into il Poggio. I rode into Lucca with Immanuel, to bring them personally to Battista Burle.'

Bernardo shushed him, waving with both hands. 'Nobody knows the details, neither the people you listed.'

'Battista lives nearby.' Julian said. 'I had been to this part of the city.'

'Oh, I do know he lives just over there,' Bernardo said, pointing to a large warehouse across the square and throwing fleeting gazes to the sides, 'And I suspect that, for a long time, Battista wanted me to marry his unwedded daughter. I was not interested though. In fact, I met Immanuel on my way from a southern village, before he came to marry Elvira Burle. Thinking of Elvira's face, I can just sigh with relief. Let's go' he said to Julian, pulling him against a crowd of pilgrims that approached the cathedral, 'we should pay Battista a visit.'

The banker had little time for the indomitable Bernardo From The Rocks, but he gracefully expressed delight on seeing Julian again. 'I hear that Caligero is making a sword for you. That good man's the one I had in mind for it. I did mention that I would be happy to pay for it, but apparently Alberto Azzo has unsheathed his gold faster. Therefore, it will be my pleasure to organise for a good swordmaster.'

Bernardo jumped in. 'And it will be his honour to accept it,' he said, before Julian just prepared to kindly refuse.

With the cooler breeze of September enlivening the already busy warehouse, Battista invited them to sit by the front windows of the top floor. They were given wine and hot pastries filled with salty Pisan spinach and a cheese made of boiled whey, adequately named *re-cotta*, which meant *cooked again*. Outside, the crows circled above a raising murmur of the throngs on the cathedral square.

Battista sighed. 'Pilgrims, cripples, beggars,' he said, curling his lips, tapping his fingers at the edge of the window, 'they say that these crowds bring plenty to the local trade. I doubt it. This rabble is in Lucca for the hospitals we have, and there's little they leave behind, except the contents of their bowels. Blessed are the souls who care for them, for I just could not. Personally, I keep away from their filthy fingers and fetid breaths.' He turned to his two guests. 'But don't mistake me for a mincing tenderfoot. I deal with hard working men around me all time and their smell is one of a task fulfilled. But pilgrims, they smell of laziness, which is a different thing altogether. Attending masses with them, mingling with their reek, is my burden, my painful path to follow the steps of the Christ.'

Bernardo rolled his eyes, while Battista stared back at the cathedral. 'Perhaps I should show our basilica to Julian,' said the shepherd. 'It is an old building but I hear that there are some new riches in it.'

They thanked Battista and left the House of Burle.

'Why did you accept the offer of a swordmaster in my name?' Julian asked as soon as they crossed the door.

'Because it has been offered, Julian. Don't refuse it if there is no cost. You have already paid for it with your kind gesture of accompanying Immanuel ben-Malachi in his secret mission. Now if you think you do not need a lesson for a new sword, just wait and make up your mind after you've had one.'

They stepped into the busy basilica's square, at the thinning shadow of the church, to the east.

'Do you know how to use a sword, Bernardo?'

'No, but I can use the bow, the lance and the *francesca*, as you know.' He thought for a second and added 'and I will use a sword if needed. Yes, I was instructed in the ways of the Christ, but you have seen that I can be unforgiving and vengeful as God himself.'

The cathedral was an old building with several extensions to the sides and towards the back. It held a flat brick façade with rather simple columns, unadorned, except for inner narthex and the portico, where a band of white marble bricks and lunettes was being laid along the old wall. In addition to the activities of the stonemasons, a noisy crowd of pilgrims exchanged their different coins by the local *soldi* with merchants and changers stationed along several benches and tables spread throughout the portico. A large piece of parchment had been fixed to the red bricks, with faded letters advising the traders to be honest and conscientious in their dealings, and reminding pilgrims to trust the protection of the local clergy.

'One wonders what the Christ would do to these traders in the house of His Father…' Bernardo said.

'Mind your own fucking business, shepherd!' groaned a merchant who overheard him.

'I wish someone minded yours!' Bernardo was quick to say and made him a rude gesture, before grabbing Julian's wrist and quickly pulling him through the main doors.

They stepped into the smoky darkness, much more silent, where only a murmur of pilgrims in prayer was suspended above the candlelight. They both kneeled on their right knees and crossed themselves in reverence to an altar that must have been lost in the shadows somewhere across the central nave. The church interior accumulated nocturnal temperatures to cruelly share them with visitors that stepped into the bare stone inside.

'It is so cold in here!' Julian whispered.

'Only those who have their hearts warmed by the flames of faith will make their way through the path to heaven.' Bernardo was quick to say. He saw Julian's face surprised at him and grinned, adding 'At least that's what they say. I'm sure they would make warmer churches if they were capable to. They have been talking forever about a new cathedral. Who knows if we'll ever see a bright new building on this ground…'

'I'd imagine that such influx of silver and gold would pay for a new basilica,' said Julian.

'It would indeed if our clergy ever followed at least a few of the steps of the Christ. But our Bishop Gherardo is too busy, accumulating lands for his children, Fulcardo and Sigifredo.'

'You mean these two are Bishop Gherardo's sons? Aren't the high clergy discouraged from marrying or maintaining concubines?'

Bernardo laughed. 'Et tu, Brute? You seem to be taken back by the fact that Bishop Gherardo has a woman and children, much more than the fact that he uses church funds to build up riches for his family. Let a man be a man, but being honest, above all.'

Julian pursed his lips in a humorous countenance 'Actually, I never thought of it in that way! But thanks for that, Bernardo.'

They walked down to the entrance of the even darker crypt of San Martino, descending the long stairs through a narrow corridor. A silent crowd blanketed by total blackness descended, a mantle of the faithful touching each other for balance. Julian could see nothing. Smothered by the dense flow of bodies, choked by the stale air, thickened by the musty smell of age, he walked ahead with Bernardo holding onto his shoulders, carefully feeling each new step down, going deeper into the ground.

Bernardo approached Julian's face and whispered in his ears 'Just like descending the stairs into *Hellmouth*!'

Julian's hair stood up on its base on hearing that. He was ready to panic and turn around when a flicker of a glow appeared between heads and cowls below on his field of vision. They were finally released into the crypt.

He was so tense that he did not pay much attention to Bernardo as they slowly walked with short steps along with the mass procession through the ghastly display of relics. Bernardo described how San Regulus whose bones laid there, had walked carrying with his own head under his arm after being decapitated He pointed to the casket containing the relics of the Irish Bishop Frediano, who diverted the course of the Serchio River by dragging a rake over the ground. In all their glory, those pieces of cadavers, clean bones, dried muscles, wrists, and even a foreskin, were eerily displayed with ribbons, sleeved by metal rings or inserted in silk-lined silver boxes. There was a toe of Santa Giulia, of which the rest of the skeleton had been transferred to Brescia; a skull fragment of Saint Pantaleon, who had survived the most unspeakable forms of executions before converting all his would-be slayers and choosing to join Christ in heavens; and many parts of other holy men and women, who had chosen to abstain from all comforts of life or to declare their faith before the blades of heathens. On hearing how a particular hermit monk had refrained from eating and kneeled in prayer on top of broken stones until his skin had grown over the fragments, Julian almost vomited. He needed to be rescued him from that dungeon, urgently.

Clarissa!

The thought that she would not be at his side made his head swirl. Nauseated with so much pain and death in that stuffed dark crypt, so sick from Bernardo's detailed description of sufferings and tortures adding to his asphyxia, Julian opened way through the crowd to climb the stairs back into the church.

He arrived for some air next to a cluster of lit candles. 'The *Hellmouth*!' he panted, catching up his breath and looking at Bernardo with certain disgust when the shepherd approached him. 'Such a sickening thought! Where did you get this idea from?'

Bernardo scuffed Julian's black hair with a jolly smile on his face 'Hellmouth? Do not take it too seriously my friend. It is just another story to scare us sinners and make us aware of the sufferings in hell.' He tapped Julian amicably on the shoulder. 'Come and take a seat.'

They sat on a bench facing an unlit chapel, perhaps where a forgotten saint was hiding its own bones among the shadows. Bernardo continued 'There has been much talk about Hellmouth in the northern lands. A dark, terrifying concept. I saw many renditions of it by some of Christendom's best miniaturists in the monastery of Saint Michael, before we met. The Leviathan that swallowed Jonah. The *aspidochelone* – viper turtle – a gigantic fish, as big as an island, whose mouth is the gateway into hell. Oh, those pictures! One can see the maws that spew the hordes of hell, inflicting the most painful tortures upon the condemned souls of this world's sinners.'

'Bernardo,' called Julian, interrupting the enthusiastic cantastorie. 'We saw a Leviathan weeks ago.'

'Excuse me?'

'We saw a giant monster. A dead fish, bigger than a house, washed up at the beach by the mouth of the Magra River.'

'Who's we? Where? In Luni? Tell me more!'

Now it was Julian that smiled at the distressed shepherd. 'At the village of Amelia. I went with Lord Alberto Azzo and Clarissa. A stinking carcass being disputed by a group of foreign fishermen. A rotting monster, perhaps only half of it, with something sticking out which I could not understand if it was its jaws…' he paused and looked around to see if any pilgrim was near, '… or its penis.'

'Christ almighty! What an abomination!' Bernardo exclaimed, with s spark on his eyes. 'And they butchered it?' he asked, curling his lips.

'No,' said Julian, 'the bishop forbade the locals to touch it. The carrion must be still there.'

Bernardo stood up, almost tripping backwards. 'Then, I must go and see it.'

'What?' Julian yelled, following him to the door.

'Yes, I cannot miss this opportunity in a lifetime to see the *aspidochelone*. The *Hellmouth*!'

'But it is a rotting mass of meat and bones, Bernardo.' Julian held him by his sleeve. 'Now you are the one taking it too seriously. It's definitely not worth a trip to –'

'I must go! Julian, you can find your way around here, can't you?' He held Julian's hand. 'See you some day. Hopefully when I return you're still in Lucca.' And he disappeared through the never thinning crowd of pilgrims that filled the square.

'Will you return to Luna with me?' Alberto asked on the next morning as they broke their fast rather early. Horses were being saddled outside.

Julian lowered his gaze towards a bowl of milk and bit his lip, thinking of the anguish of being in Luna, so close and so painfully distant to Clarissa. Alberto waited patiently, wearing a frown of genuine concern. That sweet smell of milk… Julian ached to go with him, but he had to be strong. If not know, when would he be? He could not make a decision.

'It's Clarissa, right?' Alberto asked.

Julian nodded, slow and carefully.

'Leave it be, Julian.' Alberto finally intervened. 'Whatever the bitterness has been between you two, it will be over one day. Stay in Lucca for this month before you get your sword. The duke will be more than happy to lodge you.' He snatched a large lump of precious wheaten bread and stuffed his mouth, dumping the rest in his satchel, getting up to leave. He pointed a buddy finger to Julian. 'Distract yourself from my sister, young man! Train your skills, find yourself more to do, and don't waist too much time with Bernardo Delle Rocche chasing local girls, please. Especially *nuns*!'

'Thank you, Alberto!' sighed Julian, with half a smile. The other half of his mouth did not smile for not having been able to make his own decision.

Up and Down the Serchio

A tidily-clad negro presented himself at the Duke's Palace that afternoon: 'Messere Battista Burle requests to speak to Master Julian, at his house of trade.'

Julian accompanied the negro to the banker's office, never exchanging a word with the slave.

'I have been made aware that you plan to stay in the city for a month, my dear Julian.' Battista said, after snapping his fingers for an immediate mug of hot wine for the visitor.

'Waiting for my sword, messere.'

'Any plans on how to spend your time in the city?'

Julian pursed his lips and shrugged.

Battista rubbed his hands. 'Well, then I would like to offer you to perform some activities for me. You are a trustworthy free young man, filled with bravery and gifted with common sense. I have men of many skills that work for me. They are busy these days. They are mostly loyal, some of them are instructed, some are brave but lack any reason and others such as Merula, the good negro that fetched you at the palace, have all the good features of a great assistant, but they are not free. I could use you for some menial tasks and you can take as long as you need to accomplish them. I will pay you with good silver. Not as high as I would to a banker or a noble, but never as low as I would to a servant. I'd call it a fair deal, for you will have a unique chance to collect the experience that none of the simple folk in Luna, including the Obertenghi, ever will.'

Behind Battista, Merula was standing quietly by the door and, even from that distance, Julian noticed that for the first time he was staring straight into his eyes. The negro had a reassuring half smile as Battista spoke and threw a sneaky glance towards the banker, before returning to Julian and nodding encouragingly.

'Will you take it, my dear Julian?' Battista asked, with both of his enviable eyebrows raised, trying not to be annoyed by Julian's brief distraction.

Julian straightened up and accepted without blinking.

'Good,' Battista said, rubbing his hands, 'now let's discuss a few issues here.' But he suddenly stopped and raised a decreeing finger towards Julian's face 'And before anything else, never, ever shrug as you did before, Julian. It makes one look weak.'

Early on the next day, Merula came to the palace with a harnessed horse ready for Julian. Battista had lent Julian a shortsword to be carried during these trips.

'Have a safe ride, Master Julian,' the negro said, with an honest grin on his face. 'But please remember not to cross the Serchio at Sesto. You must wait until you get to the Traghetto, past the village of Mutianum, and cross at the ferry.'

'I have understood, Merula. Thank you for your help and your advice yesterday.'

The negro smiled shyly 'I did nothing Master Julian. Messere Battista is a good man.'

Julian rode to the northern gate and crossed the Serchio on the bridge of San Frediano. Leaving the vellutini dwellings, he headed towards the hills. The road was never less busy as it distanced itself from the city. There were pilgrims and peasants travelling on both directions, large groups of monks, nuns, families bringing their children and their elders, cripples and beggars, riders on horses or mules, bullock and donkey carts filled with produce heading down to Lucca, and herds of sheep and goats destined to market. The path came down back towards the Serchio at Sesto, the sixth mile from Lucca, where richer families used the ferry for the cross. Most of the movement though, continued on the western side of the winding river, following it through the forest of Ottavo and the villages of Diecimo and Mutianum. There were crowds on both sides of the ferry cross waiting for their turn to take the raft, which was conducted by a crabby old man. Julian was advised that the castle on the top of the northern cliff above them as the Rocca, where the family of Bernardo Delle Rocche made their residence. He knew Bernardo would not be there, as the shepherd was probably on the coast, examining a mass of rotten meat and bones.

After almost two hours waiting for his turn, he paid the fare to the unfriendly ferryman while they crossed to the eastern bank, where dozens of other carts, beasts and carriers with loads of olives, grapes, wine, coal chestnuts, *farro* and cheese waited to make their way across.

'Rather than waiting so long for your turn, why don't you follow this eastern road south and cross it in Sesto, which is much less crowded?' Julian asked one of the men who lined up.

'The road south of here on this side is too dangerous,' said the man. 'Many have been attached by robbers and even murdered. Besides, when we get to Sesto, the rogues at the castle of Moriano demand outrageous prices for the ferry.'

'Then why not carry on without crossing, always on the eastern bank?' Julian reasoned, 'You will get to Lucca with no need to cross the Serchio.'

'Oh, that is even worse. The swamps to the south of Sesto belong to Gottefredo di Antelmo, a man who does little to encourage transit through his lands. We're better off waiting for a day here rather than venture further south.'

Riding another mile northwards through a tunnel in the forest that covered the steep eastern margin, Julian came to the village of Chifenti, where the river Lima met the Serchio. He went to the tavern for some bread and wine.

The taverner Amadeo gave him further directions. 'Young man, if you want to find Immanuel Ben-Malachi, you should perhaps ford the Lima right here at its mouth, over to Fornulo. Then, just ride upstream along the northern bank of the river towards Corsena. Ask anyone along the mulberry trees on the slope and you may find him. There will be a number of streams, some cool and some steaming hot, as the baths are being renovated. If you come to a bridge crossing back to this side, ride up on the opposite direction and you will find the manor.'

Julian thanked him and made it to Fornulo, turning towards the path on his right before entering the village. The road meandered between the jolly cold waters of the Lima, coming down from the Appenine mountains, and the thick forests of chestnut and beech that covered the hillsides. Rows of young mulberry trees were clustered near the streams, with newly erected long sheds nearby. Several people walked past Julian, raising friendly but cautious gazes. They carried baskets of chestnuts, bundles of coal sticks, bags of chestnut flower. The transit was mainly between a number of *metati*, the slow roasting old sheds, short buildings that were found alongside the path and scattered through the forest.

It was mid-afternoon when Julian came to the manor and was coldly greeted by a flat-faced woman, dressed in modest garments. She carried a baby in her arms, and another in her belly. Next to her a snotty red-haired little girl held onto her tunic.

'What do you want?' asked the woman, raising her voice to the tone of a landlady.

'I look for Immanuel Ben-Malachi' Julian promptly answered, suspecting that she was not a servant.

'And where are you from?' she asked, even louder now, after noticing the slight accent to his words.

'I was sent by Battista Burle, the banker at –'

'You will find my husband on that direction,' she interrupted, pointing towards a path that went west alongside the foggy forested slope, 'by the baths.' Julian thanked her and took the pointed direction, understanding now why Bernardo Delle Rocche never wanted to have anything to do with Elvira of the Burle.

He found the unmistakable Immanuel carrying bricks towards an area of construction that produced generous clouds of steam. The Bukhari was livid with happiness to see the young Julian again.

'You have grown even taller!' he said with satisfaction, and proudly introduced Julian to all the locals who were helping him, including to an old foreigner who had arrived together with him from the north. Julian joined the workforce for the rest of the day, talking to Immanuel as they worked, learning more details of the baths renovation, silk production and the region's flow of produce into Lucca.

He spent the next two weeks in the region, lodged at Corsena, pruning mulberry trees, working with the chestnut gatherers, making coal, roasting chestnuts, emptying and loading metati. They were so many vigorous activities from dawn to dusk and he caught himself several times daydreaming of sharing all those menial tasks with Clarissa, feeling the warmth of her presence nearby, listening to her cooing sounds as she played with children, smelling her sweet scent of milk, enjoying her colours as she looked at the scenery. Sometimes he had to shake his head or dunk it into cold stream to brush those longings off for a little longer.

Julian accompanied Immanuel across the villages, and they included a visit to Controne, where he spend the day with the recently appointed parishioner of the region: his friend Father Martino.

'Immanuel is right,' Martino said as they looked down from the church cemetery perched in the heights of Controne into the fog-covered valley of the Lima, 'that ferryman Old Testa can be a threatening figure, and everyone is afraid of him, that's why there are no other ferries around. Only a proper bridge across the Serchio could solve the strangling problem of the ferry. But so far there is no justification, unless we could have the nobility of Lucca interested in visiting the baths when they are concluded. But from the other side, Bernardo Delle Rocche is not ambitious enough to demonstrate any interest in a bridge. He gets his silver from the ferry and is quite happy with his wild life in the mountains and his raids into the feminine population of Lucca.'

Julian learned that Bernardo was back in his lands. He arranged to meet the shepherd in his manor in Wald Ottavo. There was only one thing Bernardo wanted to talk about.

'It was not the Hellmouth…' Bernardo said with disappointment, interrupting Julian's discourse about the need for a bridge. 'I don't think it could be it. Just a mass of shit, so large that it could have been a Leviathan indeed, and maybe big enough to be an aspidochelone, but how could the legions of hell be in there?'

'Bernardo, wake up!' Julian said with a frown of concern 'You are talking about some absurdity while I am trying to speak to you about a real need of a bridge across the Serchio.'

'Sure my young friend, I know I know, but I must confess my deception on seeing that dead creature. The illustrations of Hellmouth are much more impressive. In the end, I really wanted to see the devil.'

Julian felt a shiver, like a dark shadow had fallen over him. Now he badly needed Clarissa to be next to him, to protect him with her wings.

'No interest in a bridge?' Battista grunted. 'These people cannot see any further than the tip of their own noses. No wonder they will be forever peasants.'

Julian was back in Lucca, reporting to Battista all he saw on the progress of the baths, on the state of silk production and on the need of a bridge. He also confirmed that Immanuel had no suspicions whatsoever about who had ordered the uprooting of the trees by the northern gate and also that the Bukhari had never received any more news from Procopius, the Greek merchant.

The banker was more than happy to hear from that fresh, independent point of view but made no secrets about his frustration with the ferry.

He offered Julian another job for the next two weeks, and this time Julian would take a shipment to be embarked at the port of Pisa. This was just a façade for a subtle, but much more important mission.

Before leaving with Merula, Battista gave a few pieces of advice to Julian. 'One can never trust these Pisans. Do not be too direct, do not be blatant, do not be perceptible at all, but be careful.'

It was a rather silent ride across the hills with Merula on his side, driving the cart. Uncomfortably quiet. Julian could not figure whether Battista would approve if he engaged in much conversation with his slave. Julian had always related well to servants and even slaves in Mans, but particularly slave ownership was priced by the owners and many did not like their slaves to cultivate any association outside their household, except for anything to do with a designated task. Merula was respectfully silent and only answered a few questions that Julian asked regarding the places they passed and the mission they hoped to accomplish.

On that clear day, the city of Pisa could be seen from the hills south of Lucca, but as the travellers descended further south, the smoke from the grey buildings was shrouded behind a vast extension of marshlands. Julian found the area not unlike the marshes of Luna, but upon arriving through the very modest and thinly guarded northern gate, he appreciated the complex system of canals which had been dug around the place, allowing an easy system of transportation throughout a city that also lived from trade, and which was just as large as Lucca.

Definitely more humble, with no ostentatious towers, and certainly uglier than Lucca, Pisa seemed to quietly conduct a smooth flow of trade as boats and rafts diligently moved through the waterways. These canals brought in waters of the Serchio, still called by the old name of Auser, by the Pisans. The river was continuing its course southwards from Lucca, along the western edge of Pisa. There, by the south-eastern corner, it joined the larger river Arno, which came from the eastern city of Florence. Further west, not more than three miles, the Arno invaded the Ligurian sea.

They found a tavern and left one of the horses, all at the instructions of Merula. As soon as they arrived at the city port, by the Auser river, Julian saw the silent slave disappearing behind a street-wise visage, a new Merula that constantly wore a generous smile across his lips, weaving a network of information, hopping and shuffling the floor like the blackbirds he had been named after, easily transiting and actively finding his way through the crowds, boats and the piles of merchandise in a neighbour city that felt far from where he had come from.

'I will leave some of the crates here,' Merula said when he came to see Julian, who had just stood, watching. 'You will take the rest to the other port by the –'

'What do you mean the other port?' asked Julian.

'Pisa has three ports,' Merula explained, very respectfully and without a hint of patronising, 'Or perhaps they're all just a very long one. There are these city docks here by the Serchio; another port about a mile down this bank, right at the confluence with the Arno; and the main Porto Pisano, a large extension of firmly built docks for ships coming from across the vastness of the sea. It extends from a village called Grado all the way along many villages to the town of Livorna.'

Julian just nodded. He had never heard of such places.

'When you get to the next port, by the confluence with the Arno river' Merula said, 'look for merchants and buyers for our wool. Do not sell all of it, and do not worry much about prices, for it's not the best clip. The credit obtained will justify your roaming through the ships and the development of precious contacts, as I do now. Go all the way to Porto Pisano and Livorna, if needed.'

They unloaded part of the crates and bundles and Julian happily drove the cart to the next port, leaving the negro behind. Julian quickly found that he was looked upon with a certain suspicion for having brought his wool from Lucca. Although both cities fed a fierce rivalry between them, Pisa and Lucca had never engaged into any aggression against each other. But that was what Julian was there to find.

The merchants were mostly uninterested in his product, but he was quick to find a boat from Sicily. Upon being approached, the skipper looked at him from head to toe, before saying 'I don't know what you're talking about. I have never met any Procopius.'

This was the same answer for the next days, from Sicilians, Greeks, Jews and even the few Saracens that ventured into the port, mainly from the island of Sardinia, none of them admitted to know or have known the merchant Procopius in Constantinople. They were dodgy, suddenly turning grumpy at the enquiry, refusing to even consider talking about Constantinople or who that Procopius could have been.

It was after a week or more that Julian took a night stroll along the docks near Livorna, finding a drunk sailor who spilled it all out. 'This ship used to belong to a Procopius, of Makros Embolos. Poor man!' he said with slurred words, 'One day he disappeared with his family, just like that, into thin air!' and he opened his hand like a flower exploding in bloom. Then he curled his lips, 'But on the next day their skins were seen stretched out in canes under the sun, a public display of the price paid for betraying the Basileus Autokrator, our emperor.'

And the sailor knew nothing more and could not confirm whether this was the same Procopius.

Back in Lucca, when Julian and Merula reported their meagre findings, Battista made a grave shadow over his face with lowered eyebrows. 'This is serious,' he grunted, 'It could have been well our Procopius. But we'll never know where the information about his affairs with us would have come from. The Pisans? The vellutini? Gottefredo di Antelmo?' He sighed with helplessness. 'I wish I knew, so we could inflict our justice upon the accused.'

He offered Julian more gold for another week in Pisa, further investigating the possibilities of a local tattle teller and the true identity of the traitor. But Julian gracefully declined.

'Tomorrow I get my sword!' he said, thinking only of being back in Luna.

'Then go, and I will not forget to organise for a swordmaster.' Battista said, and gave him his farewell.

Perhaps Julian was fortunate, for a week after, the inconvincible Battista sent Merula to research the matter further and try to find the rat. But a few days later the banker would be shattered by the news that his good negro was found with a slashed throat under a pile of rubbish on a Pisan dock. This infuriating affront would trigger a battle of accusations that would escalate in what was to be known as the first communal war between Lucca and Pisa.

From the Forges of Efestu

Julian was back in Caligero's workshop, exactly one month after.

'Are you ready for something which will change the rest of your life?' Caligero asked with a livid grin, wiping sooty hands on his leather apron.

Julian waited, sitting on one of the three-legged seats. When the blacksmith returned, Julian only needed a glimpse of the piece he carried to comprehend the reason for the anticipation.

It was a weapon made for giants.

Even though that sword was still sheathed, and Julian knew well that scabbards were indeed longer than blades, that length was just surpassing reasonable dimensions compared to anything that Julian had ever seen before. And the hilt sticking out was almost as long as his forearm.

Julian's legs started to feel a bit wobbly. He stuttered before finally saying 'I don't think I will be able to master such a long –'

'Be patient, Master Julian.' Caligero interrupted, extending his open palm. He took a seat in front of Julian. 'Julian, your people must be like Lombards: too stubborn to accept any novelties, too thick to learn a new skill. Just let me present you this masterpiece of swordsmithing before you think of any inadequacies.'

Closing his eyes for a second, Julian took a deep breath and dropped his shoulders.

Caligero suggested 'So first, why don't I start by telling you about the scabbard?'

Julian observed the well-oiled sleeve, a dark brown leather that looked fresh, certainly still exhaling those strange reeks of tannins imbedded in the hide. Near the hilt, below a metal sleeve, a mark was engraved, some type of symbol:

'What is that?' Julian asked, pointing his finger to the burnt seal.

Caligero grinned even wider. 'Good question, Master Julian! This is the mark of my swordsmithing. It is a *trisceli*. Three legs united by the hip. It is the symbol in my native Sicily. They say that Efestu, the old pagan god of blacksmiths, who made his living in our volcano called Mungibeddu, had three legged seats and tables that moved on their own, to help him serve the gods with the best of his art. Today, the Saracen rulers in my Sicily forbid us the use of this symbol, which they allege to be blasphemous.'

'But I can proudly bear it!' Julian said, shrugging, and immediately thinking of Battista's advice.

'And may you slay many Saracens with that!' Caligero added with a shout, slapping Julian amicably but so strong that he almost toppled the young man from his seat. 'Anyway, I should tell you that this sheath is still perfumed by the treatment with oil of sea veals, which together with a period soaked in rusty water, gave the leather this brownish tint. The natural colour of the hide is dark grey. This material is from my best stock of Sicilian bufalu tanned hide.'

Julian just raised his eyebrows.

Caligero understood it required an explanation: 'Bufalu is a local ox in Sicily. Black, hairy and with a big, fat belly. They are rounder than pigs, with thick and malleable hide, better than oxen and goats', and the females produce a rich milk that makes the most heavenly fresh cheese.' He sighed with undisguised nostalgia, but quickly brushed it off 'So, the leather is bufalu and also the tip of the scabbard is lined with bufalu's horn, inside, which is the same material as this beautiful piece outside!' he pointed to an arrowhead-shaped shell of four inches length that enclosed the end of the sheath. 'The piece is lined with birch, which will give it firmness at this stage. In time the leather will harden and shrink as the wood chips will thin.' He turned the sword to a vertical position and leaned its tip on the floor, leaving the hilt in front of Julian.

'Now look at this wonder, Master Julian. The hilt is unique! I was able to use the same piece of steel to make the blade and the tang, the metal bone inside it, without having to weld them together. They deserved different treatments, but that was possible – it just took longer than normal. This tang will make the blade stand firm above your grasp, never snapping off the hilt, no matter how powerful the strike. And once I slipped the crossguard through and fixed it, the tang was encased by wood and horn, and finally wrapped with calf-skin leather, for a better grip and softness at every blow. And the pommel,' he pointed to a rough steel sphere at the tip of the hilt, 'quite the contrary of most pommels, which are hollow and riveted around the pointed end of the tang, this one has its own protruding pin that rivets into a hollow end of the tang.'

Now he held the sword with the hilt upwards, both hands on the scabbard, like raising a cross in front of Julian's face. 'This, Julian, is a crossguard that stretches out wide like you have probably never seen before, a true symbol of the faith for our Christ. You will notice that this alloy is not the same Damascus steel, but not to worry – this steel from Carinthia will be just as hard and resilient. You see, most hilts are not really suitable to guard your hand from an opponent's blade, but all they do is prevent the swordsman's hand from sliding upwards onto his own sharp blade. This bar will give your hands protection against all blades and provide you with more balance and grip, as it is a rather heavy base to this long blade.'

'And now', he said with an irresistibly handsome grin, 'your blade!'

He slowly pulled the sword out, unsheathing a wonder of bladesmithing which would initiate trends, help change the history of sword fighting and disappear from existence before another thousand years. It came out gleaming, powerful and proud, longer and more spectacular than any other sword used by the largest men in Christendom. Caligero kneeled on one knee and lowered his head, courteously presenting his masterpiece, lying straight across his hands.

'Master Julian, this is your sword!' he said with awe.

Julian's face shone with the light reflected on the blade. It was not the silvery white shine of new steel, but a dark grey. Perfectly polished, designed with a grain of wavy hairlines, irregular and so close to each other like mother-of-pearl lining of Saint Peter's ears.

He grabbed onto the hilt and lifted it, not concealing a slight jolt of his arm.

'Surprised? Lighter than you expected?' Caligero said with a grin. 'Damascus steel! It does feel light, in spite of the actual size and the solid appearance.'

And solid it looked, as if that whole dark blade had always existed as such, being created from divine touch in that deadly shape from the beginning of times. The blade was lean, with a smooth fuller, silent, the concavity playing with reflexes and concealing treasured lines of magic and a secret formula in wrought iron. Equally dark and displaying those thin wavy silvery lines, reflecting all colours as it moved, the edges were menacingly sharp, with little indication of any grinding. Julian moved the sword through the air, cutting it with a silent swoosh, as Caligero gracefully moved backwards, away from reach.

'You can use a sword, Master Julian. That I can tell.'

'Certainly, but never as such…' he said, firming his grip on the hilt.

'You can probably thrust, strike and cut with a normal sword. But now you will need to re-learn it all.'

'And why should I have to re-learn? Why couldn't I just use a normal sword?'

Caligero held on firmly to Julian's shoulder and jerked it up with a thrust. 'Julian!' he said looking into his eyes. 'You don't want to be just average, do you?' He didn't wait for the answer. 'I made the best sword ever, and by Saint George and Saint Michael, you will be the best swordsman in Christendom to raise it proudly under your grip.'

Julian clenched his jaws and felt a wave of tingling swoosh over his skin. He had the feeling that Clarissa was touching him.

Upon his return to Luni, Julian did not feel any less bitter than a handful of olives plucked from the trees alongside the road. Surely the initial reception was warmer than he could ever dream of, as he was taken with a long hug by Lord Oberto and the Lady Railenda, the latter making his legs suddenly very weak after the whole day traveling, and with skin tingling kisses by Bertha and Adela.

Alberto Azzo was impressed with the craftsmanship of Julian's sword. 'Caligero is surpassing himself,' he said. 'He's worked a masterpiece of swordsmithing. Strange, the colours, the waves in between, the cross bar…it's obviously a guard, not a bad idea, but I wonder how much weight it adds to the weapon. I have never seen a sword as long, and reasonably light, but by the first blood of the Virgin, this is sharp!' He tried a few swings of it, pretending an attack on an invisible army, holding it as he had always done with his much shorter Nordic style of sword. Quite satisfied with his dissatisfaction, he gave it back to Julian's eager grip. 'Too heavy and clumsy for me, and just as well,' Alberto said, 'or else I too would have to order for myself a better one. But do practice with it, Julian. It will not be easy, but if you master it one day, you could harvest through the enemies' swords like a reaper on wheat.'

But there was something else that he could not master. And that, of course, was Clarissa.

She had not much acknowledged his presence back in the castle. Not a word, or even a quick glance to alleviate his stomach from heavy stones. Clarissa's life and routine just continued happily through those long, dragging days, when she would be out in the morning, visiting the houses through the castle grounds, the workshops, the farmers outside, going to the city, bringing food and visiting a nearby hospital, or entertaining visitors back in the castle. For Julian, it could always feel even worse, as when the handsome bachelor Pietro di Filippo popped in from Sarzana, oozing his charm over all the Obertenghi, or for instance when the Lombard goliards came to play their strange but vigorous music to the house of Luni, beating on cat's skin drums and squeezing goat's stomachs under their armpits into pipes and flutes. He hated the sound of that animated drone, thinking that Bertha, Clarissa and the other women would be dancing with the boys and he would not, to those debauched, vagabond songs, mockery and amusement that he ached to be sharing with her.

It had been that same jealousy that had caused that rift in his friendship with Clarissa. And the wider the distance she kept, the more he was poisoned by wariness.

A full week of rejection back in Luna was burden sufficiently heavy for Julian to drop his shoulders and give it up. He stopped practice with the sword, waking up late but not getting up, nailed to his mattress as the sun rose high, dragging his feet as his eerie, downcast appearance stepped down to the hall. Noticeably eating poorly throughout the day, he was grabbed by an annoyed Lord Oberto, who pulled him to the door, stepping outside.

'Julian we demand nothing of you to live with us,' Oberto growled, 'Be who you really are, for you have been picked, and it was not by me. Now make yourself worthy of it!'

'What do you mean by that?' Julian implored, eyes wide open with puzzlement.

'I mean that a beaten, defeated man will not conquer anything. Stand up! Raise your head and fight. We need you.'

Julian could not yet even entertain any thoughts of confronting Clarissa face to face, but at least he could recover his composure. In a timely manner, it all came together when the swordmaster arrived from Lucca.

Gudibrando was a Bolognese who trained the Lucchese garrisons on swords and lances. He had been sent to Luna for a couple of weeks by the banker Battista Burle. A man with shortly cropped blond hair and beard, and with a rather wide body, Gudibrando was not fat, but rather fit and of indeterminate age. His brown eyes were alive, sheltered by expressive eyebrows, ready to provide a friendly countenance, if not for the rock-firmness of his thin lips, which drove away any affability. Wearing the cape of an officer, fastened at his neck with an iron buckle and a sheathed short sword by his waist, he arrived with an air of suspicion and impatience, which with time people came to realise was his every-day face.

Julian tried to ignore when Gudibrando clicked his tongue sequentially, in clear disapproval as soon as he saw the new sword. Alberto Azzo and Oberto were nearby the stables, when the newly arrived swordmaster unsheathed the sword Julian had brought and gave it a few swings. 'It's light indeed, much flimsier than one would dream of, but the length is nonsense. It's not a fighting sword.' He handed it back to Julian and held on to the reigns of his horse. He turned to Oberto and said 'Messere, I must apologise, but this is a ridiculous travesty of a weapon. I will ride back to Lucca. Battista Burle can keep his money.'

Before anyone could say anything, Julian was quick to throw in 'That's very good. I could see he was not up to it. I will ask Battista to send a real man next time.' He had not even finished the sentence when Gudibrando turned in a swoosh of his cape and there was a sword's sharp point raising Julian's chin to face the swordmaster.

Alberto's blade was out as well, pointed at Gudibrando. 'You touch Julian, and you are touching my brother!' he shouted. Oberto held onto his son's arm and begged for calm.

Gudibrando went silent with fear for realising he had offended the marchese, but it was Julian again that broke the impasse, with a grin of triumph still as the sword was touching his chin 'That's the speed that I want you to teach me. You can do it. We all know you can!'

The swordmaster lowered his weapon and said defiantly to Julian 'Your sword is preposterous! Too long, these stupid Sicilians want to make themselves more than they are these days. Green as you are, you will lose your grip at the first strike.'

'Try me,' said Julian, still with a grin.

'Well, why don't you try me instead? Strike me and I'll show you what happens.' Gudibrando said, sliding his sword back into the scabbard and inviting Julian with all of his fingers. Lord Oberto and Alberto Azzo stepped back, opening a wider circle for Julian to move.

Julian did not wait. He pulled the sword and brought it down in an arc, aiming for the kill. As expected, Gudibrando had drawn his sword and raised it on a side arc to deflect the blow. The explosion that followed was less foreseeable, for Gudibrando ducked to spare his scalp from a close shave when a piece of metal flew to the side like a deadly disc, just missing the necks of Alberto and his father. Startled by the blast, both Julian and Gudibrando paused and held their swords in front of their eyes to verify for the damage. The swordmaster held a hilt with the typical half-moon pommel beneath, a shortguard above his fist and only half a blade sticking up. Julian's blade was unscathed.

The training started immediately.

For weeks, Julian was made to exercise his sword to sequential moments of utmost exhaustion. Gudibrando was the expected stern master, initially challenging Julian with hammers thrown at him, but once the master realised some of those tools were chopped in two as Julian deflected them, he found iron bars and stones to viciously hurl at the apprentice. As for an adaptation to the longer weapon, he made Julian use a second hand to guide his sword, often holding it by the long hilt under his right hand and sometimes holding it at the base of the blade, to drive a blow in more forcefully.

Time went by rather fast and Julian hardly had a chance to see Clarissa. The sun would not even settle behind the sea and he was already dropping asleep. After a short night, he would wake up to Gudibrando's slaps, to abuse his blistered hands by carrying buckets of water around the grounds before the break of day.

Lord Oberto asked Gudibrando to stay over for longer. The swordmaster stated his price and dedicated the following week to help Julian use his sword on a horse. By the last day, Julian had a final test. He would ride off to the southern hills and return in full charge.

Gudibrando explained. 'We are testing your defensive reflexes. When you gallop along the western moat, I will be shouting at the children along the path. As we have always done, they will be hurling wooden sticks and iron bars at you. You must protect yourself and the horse. You don't really want your horse to be harmed in any manner. Protect it zealously, for those kids are brutal. Lord Oberto and Lord Alberto Azzo will be watching from the ramparts.'

Julian left through the main gate, while a group of village children were instructed by Gudibrando from the wall, to place themselves alongside the road.

Looking back towards the walls, Julian could see a few heads watching from the parapets. Oberto, Railenda, Alberto, Adela, little Albertazzo and even Bertha were there. He just could not find Clarissa.

Arriving at a lush strip of olive trees edging a grape orchard, Julian turned around and faced north, waiting for Gudibrando's flag. The white castle stood indifferently ahead of him, dreamlike, grandiose but peaceful. Julian had to force himself to imagine that it was surrounded by hordes of the enemy, a hostile mob of blades threatening the lives of the Obertenghi and, most of all, terrorising the lively eyes of Clarissa.

But the hillside was empty, except for a shepherd that drove his cows down the slope to his left, rattling the bells under their necks. Seagulls cried far below, the beating of hammers still came from over the walls of the castle, lambs bleated on the mountain slopes far to his right and a general murmur of life rose from the town of Luni further ahead. No enemies. He would be fighting a farce, but why not? Even when he had no idea for what or for whom he was doing that.

The flag waved.

Julian passed his hand on the blade to cut through his blisters, to perfect the grip. He dug his heels into the palfrey's side, never knowing that one day he would be repeating it, from the same place by the olive trees, but for real.

By the moment the first stick was thrown at him from the reeds, Julian could hear the puffing of his tired horse and feel the sweat on his calves. It was not the best charger he had chosen for this exercise, but he felt uneasy about taking a good steed of Alberto's. He had ridden into the path next to the western moat, between Luna and the southern orchards of Luni. It was quite simple to part in two that stick, with a swift whirl of his sword. The next wooden pole came quickly, whizzing across the air like a giant dragonfly, on Julian's left side. Although using only one hand still wasn't as easy as it would have been with a lighter, short sword, Julian swatted the projectile out preventing the horse from detecting the change in his balance. While readying the blade back to his front, an iron bar flew directly towards them. Julian let the bar knock his sword quite low on the blade, near the crossguard. The impact almost made him hit his own face with the sword, but he saw the bar flying back to where it came from. And he could not miss hearing a dry thud and a thin whimper of pain shooting from the reeds.

Julian pulled the reigns with violence, halting the palfrey with an anguished moan. He sheathed the sword and leaped to the ground, running back to the thicket of reeds, even under the roaring voice of Gudibrando, who was throwing curses from the wall and ordering him to return to the horse and continue the charge. Stepping into the thicket, Julian found the boy, unconscious and with a disturbing amount of blood oozing from his face. He picked the boy up and carried him on his arms, running back towards the South Gate.

'He failed.' Gudibrando barked, throwing his flag down on the moat, while the village children were cautiously leaving their hiding places along the path outside. The Obertenghi were ignoring him, all leaving to rush down the stairs towards the gate. 'The boy is a failure,' the swordmaster shouted at them, 'he'll never be a swordsman.'

'Oh yes he will!' a feminine voice yelled, muffled, far away, probably from a bad daydream, somewhere inside Julian's brain. He brushed it off with a quick shake of the head and tried to stick a thick finger into his ear, to unplug that inconvenience out.

'Julian will be the best of them,' the voice continued, faint but furious, 'now get down and help that child, you failure!'

Gudibrando looked around but he only saw Julian entering the gates carrying the wounded boy. The Obertenghi were there to help him rush the child into their care. It was only when the corner of his eye caught a glimpse of the tower that he noticed the window. A child's face was looking at him. Perhaps not a child, but a teenage girl. And she was furious. He felt a sudden wave of pain in his joints and an overwhelming blanket of tiredness wrapping around him. The girl in the tower still looked at him, and finally said, in that same voice: 'Go!'

He obeyed diligently, rushing down the stairs.

A white moon of late September had sown its blue light over the Ligurian planes and now it sprang up, crawling along the ridges of the Apuane Mountains. A slim, tall figure cut a black silhouette against the night light through the southeast window at the top of the tower.

'The boy will recover.' Clarissa said. She was staring at the clear night outside. Quietly sitting on the palliasse, Julian could not take his eyes of her heavenly shape, a powerful presence made ethereal by the rays of moonlight shooting up into the room, escaping from around her shoulders. Clarissa continued 'He lost a few teeth and they say he broke his nose. His parents are thankful that we are caring for him.'

'I will cease sword practice,' Julian said, lowering his gaze to his own feet.

Clarissa turned around to stare at him. 'Why would you?' she asked. Julian raised his head to be marvelled by her eyes, colours shining bright in the moonlight, like night flowers stubbornly blooming in the gloom.

'That useless Bolognese swordmaster has thankfully gone back to Lucca,' she said, 'but you must continue your practice. No matter how much I hate it, that sword could be of use to you one day. Maybe Alberto could train you, but with wooden swords. He would not dare fight against you and that weapon,' she chuckled.

Julian was staring at her in utter disbelief. She giggled more at his dropped jaw and shocked expression. Julian looked to his side, to the sword placed on the palliasse. He grabbed it by the scabbard and carefully drew the blade completely out, with a smooth rasping sound. The steel shone blue against the moonlight, but moving it on different angles in front of his eyes, Julian could not see the coloured sparks of Clarissa's gaze on it. 'Do you want to hold it?' he offered to Clarissa.

Slowly closing her suddenly darkened eyes, Clarissa sighed. 'Something tells me that I should never touch that sword, Julian. I feel that if I ever had the need to use it, it would be my only and last, and you would never see me again.'

With one more disappointment in his heart, Julian re-sheathed the sword and tossed it on the palliasse. Clarissa watched him with a fond smile and some colour returning to her eyes. She dropped her shoulders and came closer to ruffle his long hair. 'I missed you, Julian' she said, almost as if letting it escape. Her fingers knitted with his hair. 'I hate to think of what happened to you when we were separated. Actually…' she paused for a blink of her eyes, 'I hate to be away from you.'

The feeling of her fingers in his hair irradiated through his body, like the refreshing drops of much wanted rain after a drought of years. The warmth of her touch answered all his questions, quenched his thirst and cured all his ills. He knew he was well and at the only place in the world where he should be. From his seated position, his knees dropped to the floor and his arms embraced Clarissa around her hips, pulling her close to him.

'I missed you too, Clarissa,' he moaned, hugging her tight. 'For every painful moment of these weeks, I missed you dearly.'

Clarissa struggled to keep her lips together, feeling the sting of salt in her eyes, making her somehow weak, powerless and impotent for not being in charge. But she allowed them to run lose. They were happy tears. Dropping her stiffness with her shoulders, Clarissa let those shiny tracks rush down her face, washing her with a happiness for being free, for freeing herself to be delivered into arms that could only offer her pure love.

Both of her hands were now caressing Julian's head, enfolded under her growing breasts, comfortably warming her belly, her fingers digging deep trenches into the long blackness of his hair.

Julian clinched firmly to her cuddle, pressing his head to listen close to the sparks of the fire in her heart. He hugged deeply to that enchanting substance of femininity, his hands firmly holding on to that smooth, subtle curve that had he profoundly missed to observe over those weeks, artfully growing below her waist as Clarissa came closer to become a woman.

Alone with Clarissa on the tower top, Julian never wanted to wake up from it. His eyes were tightly closed but he was certain of its truthfulness. Her loving touch on his skin, her cooing sound, her soft firmness in his arms. It was all true, and agonisingly delightful. He dared to open his eyes, finding the vase he had brought to Clarissa sitting on a small chest next to the palliasse, the only other object in that chamber. Clarissa's angel. It was more alive than ever, with all colours of the rainbow, tiny specks of light shining around its wings, around the walls. Julian looked up and the lights on the walls disappeared as Clarissa smiled at him. Her eyes were those watery gems of green, waves of blue and sparkles of gold. She touched his face, feeling the contour, every trace of its surface. Then she turned her own face to the window, to the moonlight. It was not only when Clarissa moved her head and her tear fell on Julian's eye that he was swamped by a downpour of intense love. It was the moonbeams reflected from her eyes, filling once again the whole chamber at the tower of Luna with the bright coloured sparks of her rainbow light.

The Vulture

Old Béla had been thinking of Attila's dagger. Questions were bursting into his head as flashes of pain exploded in his bowels. It had already been three years since his protector Immanuel had disappointed him. Heavy, dark years. How could Immanuel have done it? Why did he have to bring *her*?

It had all started fifteen years before.

The life Béla had been given by Immanuel in Bagni de Corsena had been not only infinitely better than banishment from Ferenc's village, but far superior than any time he had known since the days of living with his woman. Seasons danced ahead of his rejuvenated eyes as he helped the seemingly fragile but resilient Immanuel with the monstrous task of having the baths cleaned, unclogged, rinsed, drained, scrubbed, re-built and finally re-filled. New walls were painstakingly raised by stonemasons and carpenters from Corsena and from above and below the Lima and the Serchio valleys. At the request of Immanuel, they utilised not only new stone, but as much as possible the residue and what could be saved of the not too glorious days of the roman baths.

Those valleys were a miraculous breath of fresh air into Béla's life. How could the world be so kind to him, after all the boredom and the mistakes of his first life? It was hard to believe, but delightful to accept. As opposed to the stagnant waters and silent creeks of his native village, now he could savour every moment of hearing the river's eternal giggle, not far below his cottage, night and day. The world he was waking up to every morning was filled with a rewarding work, with milestones to be gained and seen. His days were spent learning the local names and words for everything he could point his old crooked finger at. All the plants and seeds and berries, some old acquaintances and others new to the táltos. He would pick up the terms while receiving instructions about the baths, discussing plans, giving orders, carrying, cutting, building, seeing patients, caring for the sick, delivering babies, learning with Immanuel, teaching his skills, dreaming of the baths. He breathed the water fumes night and day. And the vapours of these springs were different, pungent and lively, somehow much more stimulant than the baths of his village.

Béla rejoiced on the flavours of Corsena. Eating had become a pleasure, rather than a survival exercise. The forests provided essences and textures that he had never dreamed of before. Immanuel had built and taught Béla how to use a device of his native land, a contraption that he called a tagh tir. It was a covered metal pan with a funnel top that, when the contents were boiled, channelized its vapours into a pipe that cooled the fumes and transformed them back into liquid. Potent wines were made from boiling residual wine pomace in their tagh tir, and the bottles became highly valued in Lucca, Rome and even Acquisgranus. Béla, with his cures, potions, midwifery and brews became a popular figure among the locals, from the nuns of the community of San Salvatore up the hill; to the new abbess of San Giovanni Battista, who would come for a few visits; to the diligent boys of Immanuel and Elvira. They all took pleasure on his thirst for knowledge and appetite for their humble, but superbly tasty dishes. The language was not difficult to be learned. In less than a year he was communicating well, joking with the locals and taken into their lives, but never losing his exotic accent, the strange medicine man from the land of the Magyars.

Initially, the people of Corsena cordially accepted Béla's presence, but with an inevitable parochial reservation. Some were kind enough to show him the secrets of the land, as to where to pick the best autumn mushrooms, right under the oak trees. It was after another five years that the villagers explained to the táltos that he could actually harvest firmer mushrooms under fir and beech trees instead, although the old man had quietly deduced that by then. He also learned with experience that the most delicious ones were found under the abundant chestnut trees, but the locals only shared that secret with him after ten years.

But the best of it all was his freedom to be with Turul. Béla could give Turul all the bones and carcasses the lammergeyer wanted, for the whole world around them was carpeted in mountains and rocks. The vulture would soar away from view, high across the clouds, smashing the bones on a bed of rocks where neither shepherd, nor even Bernardo From The Rocks would know. Turul's table was his own; a cemetery of shattered bones where even the occasional *camoscio*, the chamois, wouldn't dare approach the stench of decay. A happy, lusciously feathered Turul made a contented Béla. He had been accepted as a cheerful company, a dedicated builder, a prized midwife, a successful physician, a cherished soothsayer, a fortunate curer and much more, a precious aide on raising Immanuel's children.

In the end, Béla was a happy man, he reckoned. It would be a sweet tail end for his existence, before moving to *Túlvilág*, the other world. If only it had not been for this last year, when happiness started to melt away, as his destiny got closer and closer to the depths.

Béla delivered several babies through Bagni, all the way down the Serchio to Mutianum, Diecimo and up the valley to the environs of Barga. Although not comfortable with men in midwivery, the locals did tolerate his presence and were usually thankful for that. After a few years, the skills learned from Immanuel were added to his own old-Magyar's craft, making him the most popular midwife in the valley.

Immanuel was invariably busy with the mulberry trees in Lucca, so Béla came back to the Burle et Malachi house for the succeeding deliveries but he avoided the child Maria Maddalena as a blind crayfish would avoid the sunlight.

The children had been twelve. So far.

Maria Maddalena was conceived at the consummation of matrimony. She came to the world with her legs first, almost killing her mother. Nobody thought Elvira would bear any more offspring after that difficult child. But soon she was inflated again and, named after the saint his grandfather should have been, Giacomo came into this world, easy as his smile. He was followed by Francesco, Piero, Domenico, Malachia, Tomaso, Mira, Matteo, Cara, Muscatta and the baby Girolamo. The folk of Bagni saw these kids growing to much stockier bulk than their fragile *ebreo* father, or the diminutive, grumpy and always pregnant again Elvira. Locally known as the *Burle et Malachi* children, some were handsomely dark, such as Giacomo, Francesco and Domenico, with thick eyebrows and a generous smile. Others were fair and gigantic, like their grandfather Battista, with eyes green as birch leaves, auburn hair and their faces punished by freckles, like those of Maria, Piero and Malachia.

Béla had proudly helped Immanuel deliver them all into the world. He was there on the first birth, tending Elvira through the exhausting and somehow awkward labour of Maria. The old táltos knew the portents of feet-first births and an unusual gelid shiver embraced him as the baby drew her first shriek. But the strenuous attention and care needed for the mother, including the use of black comb syrup, made him give less consideration to the augury.

For the following months Béla was mainly occupied with the thermal constructions, keeping distance from Immanuel and Elvira's home. When sunny Giacomo was born, smooth as a puppy, and later when brawny Francesco came into light, baby Maria was being tended by a local wet nurse and Béla did not see her. It was only when the táltos was hurriedly called in for the deliverance of Elvira's fourth offspring that a red-haired child entered the room where the mother agonised during labour and Béla immediately knew there was something wrong about that child. It was sickening. His stomach churned at the presence of that lovely freckle-ridden girl, innocently looking at him with pale grey eyes, while his own watered. He was forced to swallow back the vomit that filled his mouth.

The girl Maria was unaware of the effect that the old man believed she was causing. When the next to be brought out into this world, which would be Piero, was in due time, the táltos ran away back to the coolness of his shed. He was scared that night. Scared of his senses, scared of the girl. There was some wrong on her presence and, for the first time in his life, the old táltos was seeing more than the effects of nature in this world. He knew he must have been seeing and feeling something from beyond, probably a *lidérc* from the world of ghosts or *Ördög* himself, from Hell.

At Domenico's birth, the táltos was nauseated when Maria showed up. He yelled for someone to take her away and the whole procedure was ten times as tense as it normally would have been. He also noticed then that nobody else seemed to sense the wrong in that girl.

That was except for Divina, the innkeeper's wife. In those days, Divina came to the táltos with a common request. Her baby Ginevra was already four months of age, but the child had not stopped bellowing since the day she had come to this world. The torment to the parents was now unbearable, and they felt that now Ginevra had stopped growing. Divina was certain that there was sorcery there and she came to the táltos to ask for a *cimaruta*, a spring of rue. While Ginevra kept howling with tears, Divina explained carefully to Béla that the little Maria Maddalena of the Burle et Malachi had put the evil eye on her daughter at the birth, and that a cimaruta to put into the baby's mantles should help. The táltos had a stringy bone of a red deer heart that Bernardo Delle Rocche had given to him. He asked Divina for a strand of her hair and tied the bone around the tiny wrist of the hollering Ginevra. In that instant, the baby quieted down, opened her bright brown eyes and drew a contagious smile across her face. Ginevra grew up to be a normal girl from that day.

Maria Maddalena would have been seven or eight on a fresh spring morning that Béla remembers well, when she walked up from the manor to the táltos shed. She just wanted to see Turul up close.

Béla was still inside, distilling some herbal extracts, when he felt a sickening twist on his stomach. He heard a shriek outside and jumped to the door, only to see Turul taking flight and leaving a ribbon of vomit falling behind it. A stone dashed past it, just missing the bird. The red haired girl standing outside had obviously hurled it. As soon as the old man helplessly yelled Magyar curses at an unperturbed Maria, he noticed that clear evil taking cover behind her eyes, and Béla felt the sickness in his stomach immediately cede. The girl gently apologised for the stone and calmly walked down the track to the baths. And this time, even if very briefly, as a quick shadow escaping from the corner of the eye, the táltos noticed how folds of bark on the chestnut oaks frowned back as she passed by, with creases and wrinkles moving quickly to the other side of the shafts.

A táltos would have been traditionally and ideally a chosen member of a community, normally due to physical or mental deformities, which were believed to allow them to speak, see and listen to the other worlds. But like most surviving táltos, on the days of the new Christian religion, Béla had no six digits on his hands or feet, he was no midget or dwarf, not a cripple or a nut-head or a retard. He had no visible disability and no choice but to become a táltos. To follow the craft of his father and his grandfather and the ancestors of his grandfather. He was a learner. Except for delirious dreams or inebriated illusions where he thought he would see other worlds, Béla had basically learned how to read the signals of nature. How to interpret it and use it. He had learned how to sniff the winds from different directions, before any leaf was moving. He knew the right colour for the wisent grass to be harvested. If fire salamanders barked at noon, he would grab a sieve and jump out of his shed into the creeks and waterfalls. He would be prepared to protect his crops if a harvest owl, the turnip moth, flew around his candlelight on any summer night when white lilies would be particularly fragrant. Trees and rocks would tell him where to sow, where to gather, where to hunt. People, animals and plants gave him the indications of what was needed for their bodies if they were diseased. But he also knew too well that not always a treatment succeeded to a satisfactory outcome. Now, for the first time in his life - and the táltos had no idea of his exact age - within his senses and completely sober, he was seeing something else other than signals of the upper world. He could swear for his life or his dear Turul's that the bark did curl around the chestnut tree trunks as Maria Maddalena passed by.

Later on the same day, Immanuel came to the shed to ask about what happened. Apparently Maria had only told part of her story at home, and Elvira was furious with the old Magyar. Immanuel patiently heard the actual facts from Béla — except for the parts where the tree barks curled around the trunks — and he quickly returned home, quietly advising little Maria to stay away from Béla and his vulture. Immanuel then proceeded to placate the ire of his wife.

Surely Maria was her mother's favourite and grew up to be a smart girl. Tall, red-haired, with strong features, and perhaps just a bit too thin on the lips. There were those who were often enchanted by her charm.

And those who saw it all.

Maria Maddalena did her minimum to tend to her brothers and sisters as they grew in the Burle et Malachi house, always in agreement with her mother's ways — the law at home. Most of Immanuel's sons were generally afraid of her. Maria Maddalena was egoistic and dominant. She humiliated her siblings whenever she could and never acknowledged guilt, but passed it to others. The imprint of Maria's hand would often be seen on the face of other children.

Giacomo had been the first to confess to Béla. 'She is cruel', he had whispered. But the other daughters Mira and Cara just accept it as her nature. They loved her as a normal elder, just as the leading child of the family. They always saw the good in Maria, all the way into their final days. Her tiny mother Elvira, of course, wasted by the intensity of motherhood, still always protected Maria with all her claws, growing onto herself like a she-wolf if any accusation was tossed on the daughter. And Immanuel…he preferred to keep his thoughts to himself. He was aware that his daughter could be a difficult person to be liked.

Béla knew that Turul could see it all. He would hear the screeching and cawing, the shrieks of the vulture, flying away and regurgitating with a croak at the gracious approach of the red-haired girl. The lammergeyer would keep its distance, away for a few days, floating serenely above the Apennines. Béla missed the vulture's wheezy coos, with solitude carving a deep scar of melancholy into his heart.

A bleeding wound that would be dug even deeper by the hand of Maria.

The Fools' Tower

A tired visitor passing though the village of Chifenti would need to locate a pile of barrows, handcarts and the filthiest rubbish to find a shelter behind it, with wine, food, local gossip and, if very lucky, comfortable warmth between a good pair of strong legs. Amadeo, like many innkeepers, believed that a signboard was not needed for a tavern, for even in winter the heat of conversations and laughter around the tables invariably leaked to the alley outside.

No further recollection lodged in Amadeo's memory other than growing up in that inn, bringing firewood to the furnace, cleaning up after customers, pushing the old straw outside and observing the grown-ups taking pleasure from the wavy conduct of wenches, who helped in serving and kept the clientele coming. He would watch his parents engage in welcoming visitors with freshly brewed ale, warm wine, and a meagre serving of oil, cheese, farro pancakes, chestnuts, an eventual sausage or cold roast and a thick soup that had the power to transform all rancid and decayed ingredients into fresh again. As a teen, a young and tall Amadeo would bear any insult from idiosyncratic voyagers, nonsense from drunken novices or humiliation from rude soldiers. It was worth the pleasures of living among those incredibly smart and voluptuous women who got from him what they rarely did from those who paid for their caresses.

When the first Millennium approached its end, Amadeo saw an eruption of emotions on people's lives, as characters never before seen in the tavern paraded through those regions, displaying some of the most singular and disapproving behaviours. They all came to the inn, of young and old, searching for salvation or craving to savour some of the proscribed pleasures before the end of times. Even the sceptics of the last days used such omen as an excuse for their thirst to lay with a woman. The backrooms at the tavern were busy as ever.

Pilgrims came through Chifenti on their redemption march towards their last days, to be in Rome. Many crowded the tavern for the food and drink, as others preached energetically against shame, iniquity and any nameable abominations. Amadeo kept peace and order within the chaos of festivity and calamity, dispensing a bare assortment of blows on folks who disturbed the flow of affairs. And indeed, a handful of prophets who took condemnation in their own hands woke up in the alley, with their broken teeth scattered around the stony ground. Such displays of housekeeping were warmly applauded by the regular patrons, and quite often by the pilgrims.

Amadeo noted that a number of monks and priests had become habitués of the back door. On the approach of those last days, he knew sacred votes were being broken, especially Chastity. Even a stinking hermit or two would come from the caves up on the hills showing some unusual property to offer in exchange for delicious wickedness. Lovers rented rooms, and wives took revenge on their cheating husbands. Nuns came in from their abbeys and paid for lodgings, entertaining visitors for some fiery nights, carnal delights before the coming of judgement. Christians were fornicating as never before.

Sleek as an eel and succinct as the Serchio, the year 1000 came and went. It was so brief and uninteresting for the folk at Chifenti, so fast that most did not notice. No beast. No last day. The sun was still rising on the east. Every single day, even if behind the clouds. Life just continued.

The orgy ended, for it seemed that ordinary existence would persist. A bitter awakening.

Revellers and sinners sighed and looked at themselves in shame. It was the turn for contriteness. Repentance embraced those who hadn't fallen to it before. Penitents flowed to Rome, as others tried to return to collect the shatters of life that they could find. Although scores of pilgrims still passed through Chifenti, the movement of hips in the tavern slowed down, almost to a halt. That was with the exception of Amadeo, who had married a stray nun on the year 1000. The tiny and fragile Divina had been lost in place and mind when she showed up at the inn and Amadeo took pity on her. As she recovered reason, her heart was gained by the young innkeeper. The relationship that blossomed was highly criticised, even by some of those who engaged into the most lewd habits when expecting the coming of the last days.

And nine years later, a miracle happened on the life of Divina and Amadeo, when the girl Ginevra came into this world, bringing joy to Chifenti. All, except for one person. From the moment the greasy baby was squeezed out of Divina's womb, the neighbourhood rejoiced with the birth of Ginevra, but this one person felt nothing else, but a sickening mixture of despise and hate. Divina could see it revealed through the grey eyes of the girl Maria Maddalena.

Carpo's upper lip was swollen. A big streak of blood splattered on his dirty rags. Although he had become a master of oblivion and escape, at that corner of the road north of the Traghetto, he just had never had the time to flee. Carpo was used to beatings, but that did not make him tolerant to it. Carpo was not smart either, but you wouldn't have to be a very smart person to see what was coming. The exploding pain on his lip and the devious smiles on the boys' faces could tell him well. He knew that in a short time, not only blood would he be tasting, but the hard gritty humiliating flavour of earth and dust. He started to pray.

'Haven't we already told you that you should not be groping for your crumbs here?' said the older boy, holding a large stone on his hand. 'You can startle the pilgrims with your appearance, *Spatola*!'

That was the name everyone called him. Most did that, anyway, for if it hadn't been for a few good souls, he would probably have had forgotten his real name by now.

'I asked you a question, Spatola. Answer me!'

But Carpo did not say a word. As always.

Like a silent, wounded mouse in a nest of weasels, Spatola could do no more than pray. He prayed in silence, as people laughed at or abhorred his words. He knew that prayers were done on a different language. Words that he did not understand, to a God that he was not allowed to worship, as Carpo was kept out of churches and chapels, shushed or forcefully pushed through the doors.

He learned. Of course he was used to hear the strange words chanted to the spirit God, and Jesus Christ and many saints that he knew nothing about. The words, the pictures on the banners, on the church walls. He saw the sculptures on the portals of the chapels. Angels. The winged creatures that all the others, villagers or pilgrims, seemed to ignore. He prayed to these angels and other things. Perhaps the good things were God that only he could try to figure. Perhaps the true angels were any of those villagers who could treat him as a person, and did not force him to live as a rat, scavenging and begging his way along the riverbank onto the pilgrims' route. The fact that he was kept outside life in general was very clear to him and to everyone else: Spatola, they all knew, was simple. And quite simply, he was the village idiot.

That boy with the stone pestered the poor Spatola around the village on a daily basis, offering him beatings and humiliations, nothing undeserving for a village idiot. The boy smiled a set of pointed yellow teeth as he raised his hand to throw the stone. Spatola had to hold on to his insides, so he did not dodge when the stone came as fast as a falling star. The boy must have guessed that Spatola would duck, so the stone was aimed a bit to the left side of Spatola's face. The idiot felt the air-splitting hum of the rock past his cheek and heard the dry thump behind him, followed by a shriek of pain. He turned around to see a bigger boy, who had been hit on the nose. All the other boys exploded into laughter.

The boy yelled in horror for his bleeding nose. 'You devil!' he cried.

Spatola hoped that this would ease his affliction and the boys would be distracted at each other. He got out of the way between his two assailants. And just before he felt an excruciating bust of pain on his neck that threw his face to the road, he heard the voice of the boy getting near: 'That was because of you, Spatola!'

He was now on the ground, his nose and mouth being rubbed against the stone and dirt of the Via Francigena. The boy sitting on his back and holding his head must have been no more than eleven or twelve. But Spatola could not do anything. Although he was quite strong for his age, he was, after all, only seven years old.

Life on the road to Lucca was usually a bit less unbearable than in the village. Spatola endured abuse from grumpy Old Testa to get to the path of the pilgrims. He just waited there, impassively. His blank face was a clear sign to anyone that came to find him across the road, but the reactions triggered among those who travelled to Rome or back from their achieved pilgrimage could be always a new surprise. Pilgrims had mixed reactions to village idiots. Many were caring souls who heartily helped the poor creature that begged for little. But quite often some would scourge him severely for interrupting their holy duties and expel that unnatural creature from their path.

Spatola had known little of his mother. When she was dead, he had hardly uttered a word yet. Without any relatives or interested guardians, from house to house they fed and raised him, offering clothing and shelter, sometimes as a guest, sometimes as a member of the family, but most often as no more than just another beast that would eat the leftovers with the chickens and pigs on the backyard. He would get care and attention from Divina and Amadeo at the inn, but he was duly advised to stay away from the public eye, for patrons had often expressed disgust by the retard around their tables or circulating near the palliasses or the stable. And lately, with the birth of Ginevra, little time had the innkeepers to care for the orphan.

At the Burle et Malachi house Spatola would have a guaranteed meal and place at the stable in winter nights. Giacomo and his father Immanuel had even brought him into the kitchen a few times, but he had two good reasons to stay away from there. One was Elvira Burle. Spatola had never seen her smile. Elvira would charitably feed him as she turned her pious eyes to the highest heights, as if to make sure she was being observed. They both avoided each other's stares. And when Elvira had any upset with one of her children, or altercated with Immanuel about anyone else in the village she would, from one moment to another, and with an unbelievably stone heavy-hand, smack Spatola out of her way like an insect. The child would disappear into the stables, crying quietly not to disturb anyone.

But the other reason to stay away from the Burle et Malachi was much stronger, for it involved constant pain, torture and humiliation. It had a name that made Spatola's hair stand whenever he heard it: Maria Maddalena.

The sun was high on the valley, and Spatola felt his whole body covered in soreness. With his face pressed against the ground, he was kicked in the head, arms, ribs and especially between his legs. Spatola was a sturdy young boy and that was nothing that he had never experienced before. Still, it was excruciating pain.

He ached much worse than he could bear at all and, still, nobody was expected to appear from around the road or across the river and just stop them bashing him. Not a travelling soul...

That stretch of the Via Francigena was now their kingdom. Like a troupe of excited monkeys, those boys were laughing and yelping as they kept beating him. Spatola had thought this would be a better place than the back alleys of Chifenti, where those boys would chase him too. Except for the itinerant pilgrims that occasionally came up and down the river road, few of the villagers ventured across the Serchio routinely. No one to disperse them, no one to succour the village idiot.

Spatola slowly tried to get himself up, lifting the heavy boy with him, but others came quickly to tumble him back.

'Wait, stop!' someone shouted.

'Who said that?' snarled the boy on sitting on the idiot's back.

They all went quiet. Spatola sighed with relief for the interruption on the blows. Although his head felt broken and bruised, he could still discern the talk and his ears rested on the rock to feel the approach of pilgrims. It felt like a whole herd of pilgrims would turn around the hill. All the boys looked towards the northern side, waiting for the pilgrims to appear.

'I said that!'

They all turned around to face the river, where the voice had come from. That was no pilgrim. While his torturers smiled with relief, Spatola's spirit froze with fear.

It was Maria Maddalena coming from the river bank.

'We can have better plans for Spatola!' she said with an icy smile.

On that moment, the pilgrims showed around the curve.

Walking hunched in a hurried pace, gripping firmly to his cane at every new stride, he kept his head covered in a cowl, even at the heat of summertime, avoiding glances to the sides, where the city folk could be staring back at him. He looked up and the sky was empty, just with the bright sun screaming at his eyes. No sign of Turul.

Béla did not appreciate his visits to Lucca. The big city was still a hostile environment to the old Magyar. The inhabitants eyed him with suspicion, as if everything was wrong with that foreigner.

Not a beggar and neither a pilgrim, his gait was furtive, hiding. Some knew about his deals up the river, others knew about his vulture. And many could sniff sorcery. And poor old Béla, as soon as he crossed the bridge of San Frediano, entering Lucca from its northern gate, could not distinguish any odours of nature but the city reek of filth. The smells were too pungent, confusing. They made his stomach jolt and his eyes sting. He knew he was being watched. Tall buildings with their lonely windows, the incredibly high towers of Lucca looked down at him in disapproval, giants that Béla dodged with his swift walk, but that would startle him with their enormity around the next corner. If those firm monsters could bend to the ground under the command of a mere Christian saint, they would easily squash anyone under their bricks if they knew of his beliefs. The sooner out of the city, the better.

At the end of an exhausting day, Béla had already done his tasks. The messages to Battista Burle were delivered at his house. Sheltered from the strangeness of the city into a different, more amicable universe, Béla spent the rest of the day lost in the maze of Burle's merchandise, protected from the gaze of Lucca's towers by the warm shadows and odd scents of a merchant's office. A bank. The old Magyar moved quietly through the young officers who helped Battista load, receive, record and maintain the stock. They would hardly notice Béla running his finger with care on the velvety surface of leather that was softened with fish oil from Bremen; or observing the complexity of the magnificent harnesses from Poland; or mischievously digging his hands into oily wool on piled up fleeces from North Africa and Englaland; or bravely touching the rolls of silk, which gave his skin a strange, uncomfortable feeling. He admired the shapes and materials used to make different chests and boxes, the bottles of perfumes, wines and oils, the bags of spices and the most fantastic swords that Christian Italy had ever seen, made by Lucchese swordsmiths. Béla would then sit on a hidden corner and watch with amazement the officers with their goose feathers and quills moving about parchments and scrolls, and tablets being repeatedly market and erased with chalk batons.

Béla's visits were timed to avoid a Wednesday overnight, when Battista Burle had his evening meetings with the other bankers, normally at Fraolmo Di Cunizio's hall. Otherwise, the big old banker Burle knew that the strange associate of his son-in-law, in spite of the limited control of the Lombard language, was the most trustworthy man to be delivering messages or goods. Battista would take the terrified táltos into his modest manor and treat him with a warm meal and a clean palliasse to spend a comfortable night. He was very well aware that his guest could not wait to be leaving early on the next day, hurrying the first step of an eight-hour walk to the village of Corsena.

The young mulberry trees on Immanuel's orchard and the buildings behind the walled city of Lucca now watched Béla crossing the bridge. He was rested and hurrying his steps out of those threatening giants of brick, before the sun bathed the Serchio with its welcome morning warmth, rising from the eastern clouds.

Béla left Lucca with letters and small packages to Immanuel, with the quick intent to be in Bagni much earlier before sunset. His legs would tell him the times to stop and rest, or when to stroll down to the river bank for a refreshing drink. His senses welcomed the return to the natural world, away from the city fumes, from the smell of alloy metal and the stench of human decay.

Many pilgrims would have been expected to cross his way, but during that morning not many had shown their pious faces on the Via Francigena. He looked up and there was still no sign of Turul.

When Béla was less than a mile from the forest of Ottavo a numerous group of monks appeared on the road, passing by him zealously praying. Some of those fairly large men were muttering their chants under the rhythm of their own steps. Others had their eyes closed and touched the back of those who guided them. Two of them were conducting a silent heard of chestnut-coloured cows, which clumsily tried to keep to the path. They had mostly ignored the small presence of the táltos, who had courteously greeted them, except for a younger, novice-looking one, who exchanged a friendly smile with him. Béla watched the score of men pass by, with those coming behind the group, probably a few lay brothers, pulling charts with straw, bundles, religious objects, a few piglets and, curiously enough, a little boy with his hands and feet tied by a rope.

Spatola!

Béla recognised the village idiot and yelled for the band to halt. What came after was an indescribable clash of cultures, languages and immediate interests, where the Magyar tried desperately to tell them that the boy belonged to his village and the pilgrims tried to convince Béla that they knew it well, and they wanted to help by ridding the burg off that unnatural creature. The táltos had no perfect control of the Lombard or Latin and, shocked to see little Spatola tied like a beast on the back of the cart, he mixed words, stuttered and babbled to tell those visibly annoyed men that they should not be taking the boy with them.

Neither the monks had the serenity to explain to that inconvenient old foreigner that the idiot boy had disturbed their prayers by attacking other children about a league and a half back on the road. It was through the loose, mixed-up, desperate jabbering of Béla that the younger, novice-looking man with the friendly face, recognised some terms of his native tongue. He rushed to the táltos.

'Can you speak *Magyarul*?' asked the young man.

'I can, yes!' Béla almost yelled. He had never spoken his language since the days after leaving the lands of Ferenc. 'Are you a Magyar yourself? Can you help me here with these people? You cannot take this boy with you!'

'My name is Anton', he said calmly. 'I come originally from Pannonhalma, but I was sent for my studies in Břevnov. However –'

'Hurry up, Anton!' Interrupted one of the monks. 'If you speak the language of this man, do put him back on his way and let us go forward.'

'This old man tells us this child should not go to the city with us, Reverend Prior.' Anton answered. 'I was probably right back then, when I thought we shouldn't have –'

'Nonsense!' the man Anton had referred to as prior cut short. 'Tell this foreigner we will haul this unfortunate creature with us to where it can be dealt with. To the city's *Narrenturm*.'

Anton turned to Béla. 'Old man, listen to me. We are on a pilgrimage from Fulda to Rome. The villagers back on this road, I mean, some of the village's children told us, in very good Latin, that this poor creature was a nuisance to the local folk. It should be taken with us to Lucca. To be left at the...what my brothers are calling the *Narrenturm*.'

'What's that?' grunted Béla, who could not stop staring at Spatola's face ridden with tears. 'I have never heard this word before. The villagers told you *that*?'

'This is their Frankish word used for those towers in the city where the mentally insane are locked up or hung in a cage. The villagers told us to get rid of him. The assumption, among us, is that the city would have its own Narrenturm.'

'There isn't such a thing in Lucca!' protested Béla. 'How cruel! It sounds to me like a foreign monstrosity.'

'Let us go, Anton,' cut the prior again. 'Leave this man. We still have to pay our prayers to the Holy Relics of St Regolo in Lucca, before the last office of the day.'

And the group resumed the march south.

'I am so sorry, I cannot help anymore,' said Anton as the lay brothers hastened to herd the cows together and follow the monks. He bid Béla farewell and accelerated his pace to catch up with the others.

'Wait!' shouted Béla, rushing behind Anton. 'Leave the child here with me!'

'I cannot,' said Anton. 'We somehow 'promised' to the villagers that we would —'

'But then,' interrupted Béla, 'You should go and see the merchant Battista Burle in Lucca. You must see him as soon as possible. Now pay attention here: he operates a house of trade on the northern facade of the cathedral square. The first manor on your right, as you leave the duomo. It has a walled courtyard on the right side. Tell the banker Battista of our encounter here — he knows me - and that he should organise for Spatola, this poor boy, to be brought back to our village of Chifenti. I am sure he will reward you adequately for this.'

'Do I get him to fetch the boy at the Narrenturm?' asked Anton.

'That is foolish!' protested Béla. 'There is no such place.'

'Very well, then. And what do I refer to you as?'

'My name is Béla.' He was already panting from tagging along the swift pace of the monks. 'I came to these lands with the caravan of Astricus of Pannonhalma.'

'The abbot?' Anton stopped.

'The same...' smiled the old man, a bit shyly.

'Were you also from Pannon—'

'No,' Béla was quick to interrupt him. 'I came more as a prisoner. I was the táltos of a village, south of the great Zala Lake. But you can ask Burle about my story, if you speak good Latin or Lombard, or Greek. Now, you better speed or you will miss your brothers.'

'Farewell, Béla! I will arrange for Burle to send this boy back to you.' And he ran to catch up with the monks.

'Have a safe journey,' Béla shouted 'And please untie the poor creature. He is harmless'.

'What is his name again?'

'Spatola is his name.'

In that very moment, Béla heard the shriek of Turul flying high. The old táltos was showered with a delicious bliss and continued his stride to Corsena, forgetting to shout back his last question to Anton. Who had sent poor Spatola to Lucca?

And the quick run to pull alongside the other monks made Anton forget about telling Béla something that would have changed the destiny of both, and the following facts narrated on this story: that it had been a lovely young girl, with a very articulate Latin, which had handed the idiot to them. A young lady with sweet grey eyes and fiery red hair.

When Béla arrived in Chifenti, he was received at the tavern with a refreshing serving of wine, before resuming the walk to Corsena, where he would deliver his messages to Immanuel. The tired táltos told them all about the incident during his journey back.

Nobody could recall such an episode and some wouldn't believe it had been locals who had sent the village idiot away.

Béla paid special attention to the reactions of Elvira or Maria Maddalena, but there weren't any.

Two days later, a messenger arrived in the busy tavern, bringing by the hand a filthy, snotty, blank-faced boy. The messenger was asking for Béla.

At sunset, the táltos came to fetch the boy.

'In old times, it was those unfortunate children, idiots, cripples, dwarfs or monsters, who were brought up to be the táltos – that is the medicine man in our villages.' Explained Béla to Divina, at the tavern's kitchen. 'Now I can keep Spatola around and teach him my craft.'

Divina saw no sense in what Béla was saying. She changed subject. 'I've already asked Carpo – remember Béla, he has a name – whether it was the girl Maria Maddalena who sent him with the monks to Lucca. But he has not answered.'

'What do you say, Spatola?' she asked again, 'Was it Maria Maddalena?'

The boy looked down.

'He must be afraid to tell us, but I am sure it was her,' said Divina. 'She is evil.'

And the child Ginevra was walking by, completing 'Maria is a witch!'

Fire and Death in the Rock of the Calvary

It was on the same day that Ginevra had been born from Divina and Amadeo, but far away across the middle sea, in the fresh heat of the Holy City of Jerusalem, when a very large crowd wearing black scarves piled up on the atrium of the Rock of the Calvary. They were trying to squeeze themselves into the crammed basilica with the rest of pilgrims. They were waiting for a miracle to happen.

In the courtyard of the basilica, holy men prayed for such miracles. Humming in disagreement their chants in Greek, on this special occasion they were not adorned with the sparkling gilding they would have worn at home, but rather soberly dressed, with black robes scarves and belts, and the long mossy beards to their chests. A sea of dark fabric, amongst which mitres and staffs popped up like remnants of a shipwreck. There were bishops, deacons, presbyters, archpriests, hegumenos, archimandrites, primates and metropolitans, many of which had come from churches, monasteries and caves from all corners of Christianity, from far away as Lybia or the Caspian Sea, Bulgaria, Ethiopia and Alexandria. It was not a church council, but they were all assembled, waiting for a miracle to happen.

In the glorious Anastasis, the rotunda of the Resurrection, the very heart of the Church of the Holy Sepulchre, beams of light from the cupola cut through dust and fumes. Standing there, seven men waited for the miracle to be materialised. They prayed to the Father, the Son and the Holy Spirit. They prayed to the Virgin Mary and all the saints, those that God had made known to us and all though their glory and virtue. They prayed in silence, watery red eyes from the smoke of candles, several hours of vigil and weeks of travel. Arsenius, the patriarch of Alexandria and his Coptic rival Zacharias prayed side by side; and so did the Elias and the Syriac Ioannis bar 'Abdun, both of Antioch, enemies in doctrine and dogma. They were watched by the powerful Sergius, patriarch of Constantinople. Two other men were standing away, respectably whispering to each other.

'It is ready', said Nicodemus, the keeper. 'You should go now into the *kouvouklion*!' he said, pointing to a small door in the edicule, a stone chapel inside the large rotunda. 'I have closed the vent to prevent a draft when you open the front door. The flame never endures for too long locked into the icon.'

'That is good', grunted the young Seraphim, bishop of Jerusalem, as his fingers combed the well groomed black beard. He hesitated a bit before disrobing, calmly folding his vestments and giving them to Nicodemus. Although the Rotunda was cold, he sweated. Walking slowly and ceremoniously towards the chapel, Seraphim felt as if naked, showing open palms carrying only the key, crossing in front of the holiest gathering of church men that had ever visited that sanctuary since the times of Emperor Constantine. Seraphim carried the burden of assisting on the miracle for that special day. A day when disagreements were left out of Jerusalem. A day where major schisms were forgotten and all the men who had taken holy orders filled the courtyard and rubbed elbows as they motioned with the sign of the cross. A hazy morning of frankincense, candles, and expectations, after a late night of wine and discussions, of doubts and fears. Fears about the destiny of the very Christian church.

The news from Alexandria had been the worst, but not unexpected. So dangerous had been the situation that Arsenius and Zacharias had both escaped from the Alexandria port on a small vessel, surprisingly tolerating each other presence throughout the whole crossing. That was the first time in more than four hundred years that the Coptic patriarch of was entering the Church of the Holy Sepulchre. In this case, they had no choice, but to be both on the same side. The threat to their church was now fiercer than ever, and it was coming from only one man. The man who ruled the all lands from Fez, to Mecca, including the Holy Land. The Fatimid caliph Abu 'Ali Mansur Tāriqu l-Ḥākim, entitled *Al-Hakim bi-Amr Allah* – 'Ruler by God's Command'.

Bishop Seraphim knew well how times had changed. The previous caliph had been a generous monarch. Now, Jerusalem and the whole province of Syria had no more a Jewish Governor and the caliphate had no more a Christian vizier. The current caliph Al-Hakim had hammered down humiliations onto Christians and Jews, even though his mother was a Christian herself: the sister of Patriarch Orestes. Tax collectors had been particularly heavy on the Church, imposing black scarves and belts as a distinguishing sign onto all faithful and, the worst of all, the consumption of wine was banned, including from their religious rites. Initially, many Christian communities had ignored the obligation, taking wine secretly at the celebration of mass, but break-ins by Al-Hakim militias would easily convert into slaughter if any intoxicating drink was to be found at the ceremonies. Al-Hakim had recently converted several churches into mosques and halted constructions of new ones. He dismantled the hospital and library for Christian pilgrims, which had stood in Jerusalem for four centuries. His distaste for the Christian faith was blunt, and nothing seemed to openly annoy him any more than Christians' stories of miracles and prodigies.

As a bishop of the church in Jerusalem, Seraphim was likely to be elevated to the rank of patriarch, with the approval of the heads of Alexandria, Antioch and Constantinople but, under times of Fatimid rule in Jerusalem, not a moment had been convenient since the death of the last patriarch Orestes, the caliph's uncle.

Ever since, each bishop who had gone into the kouvouklion to get the holy fire had perished to diseases or natural causes. But now Seraphim was a rather young and strong man. He would probably be the best chance for a new patriarch. He just had to help with that one small miracle. And hope for a bigger one.

At the door of the chapel, Seraphim made a quick prayer and unbolted it. He pushed the door open and quickly slithered into the kouvouklion, slamming the iron panel behind him to prevent that any of the patriarchs saw reflections from the icon lamp that Nicodemus had earlier slipped inside.

The bishop did not expect to find himself in total darkness. In the cold and muffled interior of the kouvouklion, Seraphim was in total peace with God, in the most sacred location of Christendom. The Father would bring him comfort and solace in that niche. The Son would guide his feet probing the floor, and his hands groping his way through the squeezed compartment. The kouvouklion that encased the very remnants of the cave where the Christ Himself had been buried. And finally, behind what he felt and knew to be the burial couch, he touched the marble case where the icon lamp from Nicodemus would be, the flame that the Holy Spirit would keep alive and help him light the other candles and come out into the Anastasis covered in all of God's glory. He pulled the case open but surprisingly saw no light. He was still in darkness. A cursory scream came out of his mouth when his fingers touched the still warm wicker of the lamp. The very own lamp which he was expecting to bring out with the holy fire. He'd screamed because the flame had died away.

Outside, no one heard anything. The patriarchs had been chanting a *Kyrie eleison*. They all looked towards the cloudy cupola of the Anastasis, expecting to catch a glimpse of the divine blue light that descends into the Kouvouklion. But there was nothing to be seen.

Nicodemus, watching from a distance, looking at the images and icons, many of them carved in wood by himself, was beginning to feel uncomfortable with the extended wait, but he soon heard the screech of the iron door. Drenched in sweat, a livid Bishop Seraphim emerged from the kouvouklion carrying twelve candles lit with the Holy Fire.

That was no more than what Nicodemus had expected. He smiled and turned around to open the doors into the courtyard, announcing the miracle.

When night fell onto the holy city, Nicodemus hurried the last pilgrims out of the basilica one hour before curfew, as the other bishops and guest priests minded the Anastasis and swept the floor. The patriarchs helped Seraphim, who had spent the rest of the day prostrated on his knees, back into his lodgings for a deserved rest. They convened quickly after the last service, unanimously agreeing that on the next day Seraphim should be anointed as the patriarch of Jerusalem.

Nicodemus was utterly satisfied. The keeper had dedicated more of his sweat to the church than to the upbringing of his own daughter. But it was worth it, he thought. In an instant, the miracle had been talked about in all of Jerusalem. Thousands of candles were lit with the Holy Fire, the fire that does not burn. Celebrations were conducted in the basilica, the faithful praised the Holy Fire and many were cured from boils, lameness, blindness, possessions, idiocy and many other ailments or aberrations. The faithful's hands were passed through flames of Holy Fire without having the skin burned or singed. On the city gates, hundreds of pilgrims were seen leaving the city with new bandages on their hands. Nicodemus also knew that faith was not always solid enough to protect sinners' flesh from Holy Fire.

Many militias of Al-Hakim learnt about this Passover's successful miracle which, just as in the previous years, led to several pilgrims returning to warn Nicodemus about possible revenge against the bishop. This was not a surprise. The only thing that Nicodemus was not expecting, and that intrigued him as unusual, was the manner in which the bishop Seraphim emerged from the kouvouklion with the lit candles: he was laughing incessantly, almost to the point of being hysterical.

Midnight office was celebrated without the presence of Seraphim. By the time they sat down to quietly break their fast after the morning service at the patriarchate annexed to the basilica, Nicodemus noticed the despicable look that Sergius of Constantinople gave towards the empty seat, where Seraphim should have been sitting.

The keeper rushed out to get Seraphim. The bishop had been so exhausted that he must have missed his hours of liturgy. But worse, on the very day when he would be anointed, this was at least discourteous to his guests. Nicodemus hurried up the stairs thinking how Seraphim was completely spent after bringing out the Holy Fire. It was a secret that only Nicodemus and the person to go into the kouvouklion would know. A secret to be kept forever.

Nicodemus opened the door of Seraphim's compartment to find the bishop still lying, staring blankly at the ceiling. His throat was cut from side to side.

If Seraphim, bishop of Jerusalem, had known that an assassin acting in the name of Al-Hakim was planning to pay him a visit on that night, he would not have waited until the next day to tell Nicodemus about the miracle he had seen. How the candles had miraculously burst into flames, lighting spontaneously right in front of his eyes.

'He's calming down!' someone shouted over the confusion of voices and the struggle of bodies. It was very dark and crowded.

'Never mind. Just don't let him go!' another voice warned, before being shushed by others.

Greek words and whispers.

Nicodemus gave in, curling down his fragile body until he felt the bishops' grasps loosen up naturally. He did not want the built-up passion inside his heart to burst through his head. No tears yet. He could not afford them. He needed to pipe it down. And this was the very last second for this opportunity, before renouncing his past and giving up on the work of a lifetime.

His face relaxed. He released the jaws. The eyelids lowered, calmly. Nicodemus sighed and, just as he expected, he felt the bishops release his arms.

Now it was the time. His legs exploded!

In the blink of an eye, he was running as fast as he could, breaking through the sunny alleys of Jerusalem.

Nicodemus fought against the crowd, but he still gained ground. The wave of human bodies made it impossible for the bishops to catch up and retrieve the keeper back to their hideout. That mob had stampeded from the very point in the Holy City where Nicodemus was running towards: the Church of the Holy Sepulchre.

It had been half a year since the assassination of bishop Seraphim. The culprit was never caught, given the pitiable help of the investigation authority, not appointed by the governor, but by Al-Hakim himself. Rumours about this Fatimid caliph's recent actions had arrived in Jerusalem with the most gruesome details, as accounts of sheer madness, such as an order for all dogs in Egypt to be slaughtered. Or how he had himself amputated the limbs of women in his palace, or executed relatives, viziers, governor workers and so many other officers of his legions. Many tales came across as exaggerations to the most sceptic ears, but his hostility towards Christians soon became a painful and terrorising reality. His militia had destroyed Christian temples in cities along the coast, from Ascalon to Georgiopolis, including the most beautiful gem of them all, the church of Saint George, at the gate of Dagon. The marauders had killed deacons and priests, pilgrims and monks, sparing only those who watched the destruction in obedient silence. After the walls had been razed to the ground, which took sometimes days of fire and massive efforts, the thugs presented an authorisation for destruction, signed by none else than the caliph himself. And as if this was not revolting enough to make Nicodemus heart burn with fury, he heard that the remaining Christians on these cities had been advised to abandon their beliefs or suffer further consequences. Hence the sudden congestion of Christian refugees in Jerusalem.

Now the enemies of Christ were entering the Holy City with a profane clamour, going for the Holy Sepulchre. While Christians scattered around, pouring out of the eastern gates, the bishops recoiled into their secret refuge. The basement had been long prepared for this unavoidable event and they dragged Nicodemus, his daughter and their families with them. Yet, the keeper was not going to let the thugs take away into their filthy claws everything he lived for. He was not going to go into hiding with the bishops while the pigs of Al-Hakim pillaged the temple and took away with them every single stone and tile. *Damn the cowards and the weaklings!* He was going to stand at the entrance of his beloved temple and resists the invaders. That church belonged to his Lord and no one else. The bastards would first have to cut him down before they'd be allowed to touch the building. And the Christ would certainly help him. *The Christ that resurrects and lights the miraculous holy fire!* Nicodemus knew that God would keep His almighty powers for this moment of intervention. God's very last instant to defend the dignity of His dead Son's resting place. *This God of mine*, thought Nicodemus, *is the God of Creation, Judgement and Restoration. He is the God of the last days. Much more than a God just for lighting candles.*

As Nicodemus got closer to the church, the commotion was hotter. Families ran in all directions with their possessions and beasts, among the bellows of lost children and the cries of women and men.

The sky suddenly became dark.

He looked up and saw an evil that made him fall on his knees. A thick smoke was covering the city. Too late. The Church of the Holy Sepulchre was burning.

The venerable icons, the statues, the redemption-granting cross…*Why would they burn everything?* Some of the most precious iconography had already been hidden since months, but the church was still a temple where the faithful would congregate to venerate the saints and the Holy Family. They came to wreck these symbols of the true faith, which Nicodemus had so carefully crafted with his hours. With his years.

The icons, the chapels, the statues, the care for the walls and the floor and the columns were all a product of the keeper's utmost love for the true faith. Now, realising that the flames of Al-Hakim were consuming his dedication into ash, he saw a parade of every single piece of his craft rushing through his mind in a blinding spark, almost exploding his heart with the sorrow of loss. All details, repairs and sculptures; icons of the incorporeal angels; the gold and silver of the glorious Theodokos, the Holy Virgin Mary; the colours of the most divine and most famed Evangelists and Apostles, as the delicate pictures of Philip and Aristobolus; the Prophets Haggai and Zephaniah, who spoke of God; the victorious Martyrs, the Alexandrian fathers Cyril, Clement and Anastasius; the dignity of the three Cappadocian fathers; the simple iconic images of models of coenobitic life, as Macarius, Anthony and Euthymios, and other Fathers of the Desert; and many more venerable images that adorned the chapels and niches of the interior. Gilded wood was fire fodder for the enemies of Christ, but for Nicodemus they were pieces of his heart. He needed to save them. His life would be nothing without those pieces, so he might as well offer it for their sake.

He turned around the last corner and was almost thrown backwards by the horrific scene. Behind the patriarchate outside wall, the church roared in fire.

Strangely, the wide street was empty. But then Nicodemus saw the ropes and he understood the deviousness of it all, just in time to save his life, for in a few more steps he would have been crushed. From the windows of the patriarchate, high on the fourth floor, long thick ropes were stretched all the way down, tied to horses' harnesses. The beasts were being wildly whipped by excited men dressed in armour. They yanked the ropes at once, making the whole lateral wall dislocate, exposing the skeleton of the sober patriarchate, and slowly tumbling down on the street with a quake, like a broken giant being tripped by minnows.

Nicodemus hardly had the time or the air to scream horror and vengeance. He just saw the barrier of dust raise as the wall collapsed, thinking that this would be the best time to cross in front of the militia without being noticed, all the way to the front of the church, so he could reach the entrance atrium. As the men of Al-Hakim howled cries of victory, Nicodemus quickly ventured into the dust, among the debris of the patriarchate wall. So passionate was the keeper about saving his lifetime work that he never saw the roof of the patriarchate, which had dangled for a while, sliding down after the wall, to collapse on top of him.

For a second, Nicodemus just felt an excruciating heavy thump on his head and regretted being there, thinking about his daughter. And then he felt nothing else.

The Leopard…

The dark clouds exploded with thunder, heavy and bulged with a raging storm ready to rip out. At points across the moving horizon, their black lumps touched the tips of the waves.

'She will leave us,' assured the captain. 'The storm will not break down on us.'

Julian felt his stomach floating inside him, as the toy-sized ship swayed from the tip of a mountainous swell to a deep valley between colossal walls of water. Next to him, Buonaccorso did not move. His still body was a miserable spread out on the deck, furiously beaten by the mighty slaps of sea water that pounded the ship. His eyes were opaque, as grizzled as the sky. A trickle of vomit and salt water oozed through the corner of his open mouth.

Julian was holding on to the chains next to the rudder post, the only firmness that he could hold on to. The one single source of hope, indicating that the liquefied world he was lost into would be eventually put back together. He tried to reach towards Buonaccorso, whose arm was entangled in ropes and goat skins that they had both inflated for safety purposes. Julian's hand was a few inches from Buonaccorso's. He could not reach to his friend without letting the chain go.

'Leave him!' cut the captain, the only man standing on the deck. His voice sliced through the thick wind that ravaged the sea. 'Any man that does not make it in shape will be thrown overboard. Whether leopard or lamb, we cannot afford to carry corpses on this ship.'

Buonaccorso's lips moved. He turned his head to face Julian. His eyes were still as cloudy as the ceiling above the seas. His lips moved and a thin rasp came out of them. 'I will kill this bastard if I survive this!'

Julian sighed and looked at the captain. He was also smiling.

The ship was tossed again, up to the crest of a titanic wave, where it waggled alarmingly, before zooming down its back, half burying its prow on the next mountain of water.

'Hold on, Buonaccorso!' Julian tried to look tranquil and cheerful as he shouted. 'The storm will go away, the captain has just confirmed. We had already seen land when it caught us. It's only a delay, Buonaccorso! We will soon unfurl the sails and reach safe shores. We will accomplish the mission, if not for heavenly glory, at least for the sake of our friend, the Pheasant!'

'How did we...' mumbled Buonaccorso.

'What?' Julian shouted through the whistling wind.

Buonaccorso lifted his torso and rested on his elbows. After a misty struggle, his eyes were finally able to focus on his friend. 'How did we come to end up here, Julian?' He managed to smile.

It would have sounded preposterous if they had described that situation to each other. Two semi-dead cavalry soldiers, one of them, the Pavese Leopard, confined to the damp and swaying deck of a Greek ship, lost in the sea. But Julian could think well of what had happened.

Julian had met Buonaccorso while still in Luna.

The Lombard Buonaccorso, the '*Pavese Leopard*', with his well-groomed silver beard and deep, but benevolent eyes, was a good-hearted mid-aged man, with a tough skin and a woody voice. His mottled cloak accumulated dust from a vast array of stories and episodes from life as a man-at-arms.

As a young idealist with little to expect from life in Pavia, Buonaccorso walked to the city of Milano, where he offered his services to Archbishop Arnolfo II da Arsago. There was hardly had any role in protecting the city or the safety of its burgers. Instead, Buonaccorso served his lord on skirmishes against communes such as Lodi and Cremona, supporters of the German emperor.

But Buonaccorso's heart was bigger than that. He was a fearless combatant, with sword and lance, on horse and on foot, dreaming of a hero's life. When dedicated to a mission, he would systematically slide his blade deep into necks and limbs, never minding the gushing or the cries of horror, but he found loot particularly disgusting, plunder for payment was but a technicality, and rape unacceptable. Survival and booty should suffice for a professional soldier, but as more assignments appeared on the horizon, less purpose could he devise behind them. Bullying communes much smaller and defenceless than his native Pavia, was clearly not held to his heart as the quintessence of heroism. By the turn of the Millennium, with pilgrims leaving the cities and madness exploding across the monasteries and churches, Buonaccorso left Milano and rode east, arriving in Venice in February, where he bowed loyalty to the local Doge. There, away from his Lombardy and fighting against a real enemy, he could finally see a cause.

Buonaccorso was in one of the six ships that Pietro II Orseolo, the Doge of Venice, dispatched to Pagania, along the Dalmatian coast, to free up the Adriatic Sea from lawlessness and piracy. They were offered ardent opposition by seditious bastions of piracy in defiant isles. Through these bloody clashes and painful sieges,

Buonaccorso build up a reputation for his ferociousness, becoming known among prisoners and survivors, to the utmost annoyance of the native Venetian soldiers, as the *Venetian Lion*.

'Not the lion!' one of the incensed soldiers strongly suggested. 'Maybe another beast, for Buonaccorso is not Venetian. Anything but a lion, please.' And nobody thought it unusual, for Venetians claimed the image of lion as their own. Together with the ox, the eagle and the angel, the lion was one of the four evangelists' symbols. St. Jerome had associated the lion with Mark's gospel, a roar in the wilderness. Mark's relics, stolen by a group of Venetian merchants from Alexandria, had been carefully wrapped with pork and lard and concealed under a church in Venice.

One scarlet evening, after a fierce battle in the island of Lagosta, a small group of armed Venetians approached Buonaccorso. 'Definitely, you are *not* a lion', said a soldier heading the group.

For a moment Buonaccorso believed they had turned hostile against him, the single Lombard in the Venetian company. Had they forgotten how bravely he had conducted himself, with the utmost loyalty to their Doge? But he saw them opening a collective smile and presenting him with a fruit of their loot: a worn-out cape made of a tanned animal skin. Most of the surface was still covered with a well-preserved fur. A pale, almost white colour with clearly distinguishable black spots.

'You are now the *Pavese Leopard*!' they all shouted together.

Some of those soldiers insisted the fur cape was actually made from the hide of local spotted dogs. But as none of these creatures were seen alive during their campaign, the comments were dismissed.

Followed by his fame, Buonaccorso returned to Pavia with a good treasure. In the Pavese diocese, traditionally loyal to the emperor, he became a professional soldier at the orders of Bishop Guido Corti.

He was called in by the old bishop for an audience. Guido received his guest over a rich lunch. He briefed him about the sensitivity of the issue. As they munched on some pungent-flavoured slices of chamois leg, the bishop explained what had happened, twenty years before, to the man who had been his predecessor.

'You probably know that in those times, the bishop of Pavia, Pietro Canepanova, was chosen by the German Emperor Otto II to occupy the seat of Rome, even if this choice was not blessed by the Crescentii family of Rome.' He reached for a small tray 'You should try some of these broiled thrushes, Buonaccorso. They were baked after a day's marinade in vinegar and thyme.'

'Thank you', said Buonaccorso, reaching for the tray with the tiny braised birds.

Bishop Guido continued, 'Like all roman families, the Crescentii do not approve of the so-called Ottonian privilege, where no pope can be consecrated –'

'— without the blessing of the emperor!' concluded Buonaccorso.

'Right!' said Guido, 'The Crescentii had already deposed the previous pope, Benedict IV. They elected their own candidate and had Benedict strangled in prison. So, when our Canepanova took the name of Pope John XIV, he had pretty much nobody in Rome to support him. That's except for the emperor's family, who had been installed in his pontifical palace. So when Otto II returned from Ravena shivering with a bad spell of swamp fever, the pope came to offer him the last rites. Well, the pontiff was holding the still-warm red-bearded corpse on his arms while the rest of the German family was hurrying to flee Rome, taking with them the three-year-old Otto, the next.'

'So how long did the Pietro Canepanova survive on his papal throne afterwards?'

'All the way through six months, Buonaccorso! The Romans soon elected another pope and disappeared with the poor Pietro. You will hear that the Marble Horse himself grabbed the screaming pope by the throat and gouged his eyes with his own hands. But this is rubbish. We have solid gossip from Castel Sant'Angelo telling us that the pope never lost his eyes. He actually endured for several days in those filthy dungeons, believing that he was being given poisoned dishes every day, compliments of the Marble Horse. So he never touched them.'

'And what is to learn from this?' Buonaccorso asked, 'it still seems that even after the beheading of the Marble Horse, nothing has improved in the affair between the Romans and the tedesco empire.' He poured more wine on both goblets.

'Not much, my good man,' the bishop said. He emptied his goblet with one gulp and wiped the cold grease from his fingers in a linen towel scented with vinegar. 'That is exactly the reason,' he continued, blinking an eye and shaking a finger towards Buonaccorso, 'why I have called for the Pavese Leopard. I need your help.'

'And what do you want me to do?' said Buonaccorso with an eyebrow raised, before lifting his goblet.

'You will help us snatch the Iron Crown from Ardoin, our king of Italy.'

The *leopard* dropped his goblet, spilling the wine across the marble floor.

Pope John XVIII received Buonaccorso at St. Peter's, where he had been the Cardinal Priest before taking the papal tiara. Nobody else was in the large hall. Buonaccorso looked at the paintings and decorations, to verify for eyes moving on the portraits, or walls furtively sliding, hiding secret passages and ambushing assassins. He was rather intrigued by the fact that the pope was dressed in a simple white robe. Pope John took on those sandals of Peter in a rather humble fashion. A first cousin of John Crescentius and a good friend of Crescentius's wife, the Lady Theodora, his name was John Fasanus.

'You must understand, Buonaccorso,' the pope said with a beautifully spoken and clear Roman, a dialect not usually clear to any Pavese, 'that we have not had a peaceful pontificate in Christendom for at least thirty years, since the good Pope John XIII, former Bishop of Narnia.'

Buonaccorso never even knew there was a place with such a name. He let the pope continue.

'Neither my cousins the Crescentii nor the emperor seem to favour Ardoin of Ivrea as a king of Italy,' said the pope, with a condescending frown which pulled his Roman patrician features into a contagious smile. But then he sighed, looked to the wooden floor and raised his eyebrows, saying 'We hope that the Lombard people will recognise God's preferences and submit to His choice. Too much blood has been shed already on these Italian lands. The German king's troops are coming toward Pavia. They have taken Trento and the next station is Verona.'

Buonaccorso confirmed 'We hear that families are fleeing from the way, leaving only the fighting-aged men to face the German troops. Women and children have been found aimless on the country roads, victims to the prey of bandits, marauders and rapists.'

'Damn those stupid people!' said the pope. 'If they would just deal with the Germans on a better way...'

'They do see the Germans as a threat to their king' Buonaccorso said.

'Ardoin of Ivrea is *no* king!' said the pope. 'He is a cruel, ruthless, uneducated pig, who makes friends through the blade of his sword. An excommunicated little shit of a margrave, whose thirst for power among the Lombards has lead him to personally beat to death Varmondo, Bishop of Ivrea, and worse, he set fire to the cathedral in Vercelli, locking and burning Bishop Pietro alive in it.'

'Then, I suppose such a man does not deserve to be the king of Lombards' Buonaccorso said humbly.

'And he won't be!' John XVIII snapped. 'The king of Italy should be anointed by the archbishop of Milano. And if he doesn't do it, I will lay myself the Iron Crown of the Lombards on the head of Henry II.'

'Should we make haste then, Beatissimo Padre?' Buonaccorso asked.

'We will be on our way to Pavia the day after tomorrow, Buonaccorso!' the pope said with a smile. 'Will you be my guardian angel in this mission?' He asked, swiftly hurrying his feet to humbly show the Pavese soldier to the door.

'Heartily, Most Holy Father.' Buonaccorso bowed before leaving.

In the 1004 year of the passion of our Lord Jesus Christ, a large committee was travelling north alongside the Ligurian Coast. Among the congregation of church dignitaries, a number of roman patricians and nobility from the Papal States, Spoleto, Capua and Amalfi, plus four hundred soldiers on horse, the committee was headed by nobody else than the bishop of Rome, Pope John XVIII.

On their way to Pavia, they stopped in Liguria to overnight in the white castle of Luna. While soldiers camped on the environs, guests were accommodated in the village and a few were courteously lodged inside the marble wonder of Lord Oberto.

After a session with the pope at the eating hall, Lord Oberto met with his family in a smaller room next to the stairs to the white tower. One extra member was present. The eighteen-year-old Julian of Mans.

'We cannot pretend we are small or insignificant,' said the marchese without looking at anyone specifically. He sat on a short square stool, as the rest of the family accommodated themselves on large oaken chairs on the side of the single window. 'Not only Rome but also the emperor would expect this *marca* to support Henry's coronation.'

'Well, I am not supporting it, my father.' His son Alberto Azzo said, 'Neither should any of us Obertenghi.'

The Lady Railenda rolled her eyes. She was ready to open her mouth in protest when her husband raised a hand of a compromising but wise pause. 'It is just not that simple, Alberto', the patriarch said. 'You may have your individual reasons for —'

'Individual reasons?' gasped Alberto.

'Just let me finish, my son, will you?' Lord Oberto said calmly.

'I'm sorry. Carry on, please.'

'Thank you,' continued Oberto, 'You may have your individual reasons for disagreeing, but as we expected, tonight we have at our door the mightiest powers of Christendom, probably together in arms for the first time in a generation. And surely they are only requesting, just cordially asking for our sympathy on this holy cause. They do not want military support, no men-at-arms, no horses, nothing more than the logistic support to conduct the committee all the way to Pavia... and,' he cleared his throat 'a representative of the family to witness the coronation. Wait, wait! We can decline or refuse, but then it would not take long for us to face the unnecessary consequences. And we won't need Rome or the emperor against us. It will be cities across the whole marca that will be on their feet to rebel against us, from Genoa to Milano, from Pisa to Ferrara. And who's going to help us? Ardoin? Don't kid me, please! What about my son-in-law the Marchese of Torino? Would Odalrico Manfrido come to this part of the world to support us? Well, he is a generous man and a good husband to our Bertha, but there would be battles for a lifetime before he arrived here with his men. He is not stupid. And neither are we.'

There was a pause.

'May I speak now?'

'Please, do speak Alberto' said his father with a frank stare of shiny violet.

'We must oppose this farce not only for my sister Bertha and her husband, who are on Ardoin's side, but also for *the other* Bertha, Ardoin, wife, our cousin. Bertha is an Obertenghi whose husband is rightfully the king of Italy, but we will support a usurper of the iron crown? This crown of the Lombards means so much to the history of this family.

Lord Oberto was pressing the bridge of his nose with his fingers. 'Alberto, let me tell you why we are called the *Longobards*' he said.

'We all know it well, my father!' the handsome Alberto explained with a frown. 'Please spare us from this pain'.

'Well, maybe our dear Julian here does not know.' The marchese said, pointing to Julian, who was shyly trying to tell him that he had heard it too. Protests broke from all the family as Lord Oberto continued, ignoring them. 'Let me tell you, Julian. Our people probably never had a name of our own, but if we did, nobody knows. Not a nation, neither a kingdom, we were identified as an entity only by other people, those who had mastered a proper language and recorded it through writing. The long beards — *longobards* — the Italians called us, as our ancestors invaded these lands, all the way from the North, probably running away from our original home.'

'And your point is...?' hurried Alberto.

'My point is that this iron crown of the Lombards should not mean a world or heaven to us, Alberto. It is a ring of iron, with some gold and jewels around it, nothing more. It has no bearing on who we are. What we do, yes, has great effect on our lives and future. Our family is who we are, our faith, our love for each other, our good times, our principles of compassion and our very unique ways to survive in this world. We are not our ancestors. Now this Pope John XVIII seems to me to be a man of reason. I trust my sense and my testimony. Now, who cares if the king of the Lombards or the king of Italy is a Lombard or a Tedesco? I have heard little of new Emperor Henry, but I do know that, on the other hand, Ardoin of Ivrea cares shit for his people, his allies or his relatives. My niece is obviously married to an idiot!'

'I can't believe we are supporting Henry, my father...' Alberto said, shaking his head.

'Alberto, my son,' said the marchese, 'You have my blessing to choose your own path. The path of this house, however, is already chosen. Not by me or by anyone else in particular, but by these very delicate circumstances themselves.'

'You *will* support Henry?' Alberto asked in disbelief.

'Not only Henry, Alberto, but we are supporting the pope, Rome and most of the cities between here and Ivrea. It represents safety and stability for us. But if you want to support Ardoin, you may go. It is foolish, I tell you, for he most certainly will not reward you for that. But be aware that Henry will surely be bitter about this. Do as you want, my son, but do not be deceived by false morals of honour and bravery. Don't die for a silly cause. I did not raise my children to die in a stupid war. There is no glory in death. When we die, we are all the same, be it in heaven or in hell. Just as the saints and martyrs, we are dead, just plain, rotten dead, fodder for worms, common bones that we buy and sell. In heaven, martyrs and heroes sit next to those who died from age, from swamp fever or those who were smitten when they were running from the enemy. That is the wonder of Christianity, Alberto. Those who are not us will become us, so they do not desire to be us during this existence. Very convenient.'

Alberto rested his elbows on his knees, looking at the floor. He released a long and sonorous sigh before saying. 'Thank you, my father. I will do no more than defend an ideal that I believe. But may I know which one of you will accompany the papal committee to Pavia? You will?'

The lady Railenda stepped in 'I will go!'

'That is not decided yet' said Oberto, trying to hide his annoyance. 'We will soon be talking about it. I certainly do not want to go, but –'

'But I do!' interfered Railenda with a cynical smile. 'I am entitled to participate in such a historical ceremony, even if my husband is too grumpy to do that!'

'I am not finished, Railenda!' grunted Oberto.

'And I have just started, my dear' Railenda said.

'I am talking about Alberto, oh Goddess of Impatience! I am not done with our son yet.'

Alberto was laughing with the others. With bright blue gems in her eyes, Railenda crossed her arms and smiled 'Please carry on, then.'

The lord Oberto stood up with pomp, his shadow towering over the wooden door behind him. 'Alberto, go with God to fulfil your heart. The moment is dangerous for both parties, but it will be much harder for you. You have my blessing and utmost prohibition to be anywhere near Pavia during the next two weeks.'

'That is understood, my father. Is that all?'

'Not really,' said Oberto scratching his beard 'you should also leave Adela and your son Albertazzo here with us. For their safety.'

Adela could not hide a smile of relief on hearing that. She tenderly embraced the boy who was sitting on her lap. Hardly would she know that her boy would one day become the Marchese d'Este, and live to see one hundred years, as much as his great-great-great-grandmother Marozia, the great whore of Rome!

The conversations that followed were on the decision of who would go to Pavia. Thinking of his dexterity with a sword never seen in those times, Julian heroically declared himself available to escort anyone who went with the committee.

They called the commandant of the papal committee into the meeting. A tall Pavese soldier named Buonaccorso. He confirmed that the population of Pavia was said to be a fervent supporter of Ardoin, but they were not expected to throw any hostilities at the visitors. He also assured them that in spite of the pope's small army, the emperor's guards counted on the thousands. 'Still, the safety of your family and others which are accompanying us to Pavia will be a priority.'

The lady Railenda repeated her interest to participate in the coronation ceremony in Pavia. Buonaccorso looked around the room and stopped at Julian.

'You, young man. Are you versed in battle fare?'

'Yes, my lord. I am skilful with the arrows and the sword.' Julian said standing up.

'I am not your lord, young man. I am just a soldier. Can you ride?' Buonaccorso asked with a certain amusement.

'Like a wart on the horse's back.'

'And may I know your name?'

'I am Julian, of Mans, in the land of the Franks.'

'France? Such a far-away foreigner here in this family meeting?' asked Buonaccorso.

'Julian of Mans is one of our finest swordsmen. He is family for us' explained Lord Oberto. 'An excellent young man. Just as one of my sons'.

They all nodded around the room, including Clarissa. Julian's eyes felt inconveniently wet.

'Well, would you like to escort the Lady Railenda to the coronation of King Henry as king of Italy in Pavia?' asked Buonaccorso with a charming grin.

'Yes!' babbled Julian, who was too busy trying to keep his heart from exploding out of his chest.

But the soldier wanted more firmness. Loudly he asked. 'Will you Julian, be the Guardian Angel of the Lady Railenda of the Obertenghi during this trip to Pavia and back?'

'With all my heart, my lord. I will protect the Lady Railenda as my own mother!' Julian proclaimed. Something behind his soul made it tremble. He was not very sure why.

'Well I hope I am being a good mother to you, Julian.' Railenda said with a sweet grin, touching his cheek with the back of her fingers. Julian could only smile shyly, hold her hand and blush from the tears that streamed across his face. The gallant Buonaccorso could not help but notice the flashing of colours on the eyes of the extraordinarily beautiful Obertenghi's daughter, Clarissa, who observed it all with a pretended coldness. Her eyes revealed the fire inside though.

'What about you, young woman?' Buonaccorso asked Clarissa. 'Will you be going to Pavia with your mother and young Julian too?'

The fifteen-year-old sniggered. 'Me? To a coronation? Thank you, but *no*!'

If they could only dream that Julian would end up on a stormy day, on a ship so far from Luna, perhaps then they could have had the faintest idea of how disastrous that coronation would be.

…The Witch…

Béla's major disappointment came after Immanuel called him in for the deliverance of the thirteenth child. Heart-breaking it was indeed, but no one was surprised that Elvira did not make it. The tiny woman had born and bred enough progeny to populate the entire valley with the generations to come, to the slow and fatal cost of her health. Dry, hard-lipped, cantankerous and of stout heart, completely devoted to stern Christian ways, Elvira's physique had deteriorated to a point that Béla started to see her as a feeble, desiccated weed, ready to be crushed under the hands and feet of one more spawn who, not unexpectedly, survived. Little Benedetto was healthy as a horse.

Immanuel mourned Elvira as a dedicated husband should have done, and old Béla respected it from a distance. But not long after the priest had come for the requiem rites, when the soil on top of Elvira's body was still fresh and musty, Immanuel walked with Béla down the road to Chifenti.

'Béla, my friend, you have been a loyal helper, a valuable teacher and an endless source of knowledge for me.'

'Nothing that would fill a thousandth of your heart, fönök.' Béla said, with a smile on his eyes.

'Save your niceties, old man,' grunted Immanuel after a deep tired sigh. 'As you know, my children are growing and many will take on our work here. The land is big and the men will tend it.'

Béla was patiently following up the lines of Immanuel with the typical slow nods when one hears a foreign language. He was not apprehensive, only rather expecting no more than an inevitable session of reminiscence. But then Immanuel ventured into an undesirable ground.

'You are wise and you know about cures, about the land and its resources, you know all about midwifery, more than most barbers we have seen. But your years have passed by and you never had children of your own to transfer this craft down to.' Immanuel looked at the old táltos to measure his reaction. He could sense the tension building up. 'Therefore, I would ask you to take one of my children as an apprentice'

'I already have Spatola, fönök…' he said shyly.

'Carpo is a fool, Béla, you know that. Don't make another one of yourself if you do not accept it.'

'That is exactly the point, fönök. He has the right touch to feel nature…'

'Please!' interrupted Immanuel, calmly. 'Do this for me, my friend. I need you to take one of the Burle et Malachi to learn your craft.'

Béla stopped and dropped his shoulders. With eyes closed he asked 'Which one?'

'The oldest.' Immanuel said.

The táltos face brightened up. 'Giacomo? Heartily, fönök, heartily! I will immediately start to teach him all the knowledge, the cures, the plants, the nature, the spirits, I can have little Carpo help me for the…'

'Not Giacomo, my old Béla… Giacomo is the oldest son. He is already learning the trade of his grandfather in Lucca. The other boys will be needed for the silk production. I want you, Béla, to teach Maria. Yes, to pass all your craft down to Maria Maddalena. She is the oldest. The woman that Elvira would like to see as the midwife for this valley. The cleverest woman in Corsena and Chifenti. Maria will be your apprentice.'

Immanuel had just spoken and he turned around to see the táltos frozen on the way, as if he had seen a thousand ghosts.

And so it was that for the next three years Maria Maddalena followed up the craft of Béla. This was the end of Carpo as an apprentice. The daily presence of Maria was enough to keep the idiot away in Chifenti, if not more often begging across the Serchio.

Béla got older and grumpier, never fully trusting the girl, but always deceived by an evil that would hide behind Maria Maddalena's eyes. Sometimes he would catch a glimpse of it when she exploded with anger or frustration for not getting things right, or when she slipped out verbal cruelty on the world around her.

But Maria was a good learner and a dedicated apprentice, with the only obstacle to a better instruction being her own arrogance. Several times Béla sent her back home, never to return, but he was convinced to take her back by a pleading Immanuel, who wanted to fulfill his dead wife's wish. The táltos knew that at least Turul was smarter than himself and Immanuel. The vulture just kept a good safety distance from Maria.

But there were those times when Béla would forget how he disliked Maria Maddalena, ignoring how she behaved towards goodness and disregarding everything he sensed of the girl. He knew Maria could be deceiving, but her apparent thirst for knowledge was enough to trigger his starvation for tutoring. Maria was quite good at asking the right questions at the right place and time. The enthusiastic táltos would leave his grumpiness aside and carefully bring his treasures into the light of his face. Sharing had turned into an unbearable passion. Maria was smart enough to snatch from him the supernatural world, the spirits, beings that her mother called devils, from an area that she was strongly advised to stay away from. The girl had been sent there to learn medicine only, that is the arts of curing and midwifery, but certainly to stay away from the any wickedness associated with witchcraft.

Master and apprentice, however, were ravenous. Béla for sharing his lore, from practical tips which would be useful for midwifery, to superstitious gibberish that made no sense to anyone else, except for Maria Maddalena. And she devoured all of his secrets in secret.

Even in wintertime, a woman cannot be given any brew on a daily basis if she is with child, or else she may bear a monstrosity. She should better drink goat or cow's milk. However, for the purpose of a smooth deliverance, a good goblet of strong wine may ease the pain. When you read the entrails of a chicken, do not think of it, neither of your fingers inserted in the guts of the bird. Just think of those who are around you but you cannot see. Let them carry you to a world where you understand the portents. You may pray to God, to the Christ and the Holy Spirit, or to any of the Christian saints, of course, for they should work in the same manner as the spirits of the milk lake in heaven, where the angels bathe in. If you see worms in the intestines, it will be no augury neither a distraction. A stench of rot indicates that you need another chicken. And do not eat the first one. Prayers can be powerful. They can make your hair grow faster while you stand under the rain. They can increase the amount of butter from new churn, or speed the curdling of milk. Prayers can help you expel worms from a cow or a child, dry a sty on the eye and mend wounds or broken bones. They work better as the cocks crow at dawn, or as things are poured. While you pour soup on a plate or wine in a goblet. Prayers are powerful by the river rocks, where water pours through the crevasses, singing with the frogs day and night. Cooked grain can be poured on the spot where someone you are praying for is expected to walk on. Illnesses can be understood and driven away while you pray and pour hot tin on the ground. For reversing the power of a prayer, simply pray them backwards. Iron is a powerful element, for both healing and damnation. The metal should be sharp and polished for the cures. It symbolises birth and renewal. The old rusty iron will bring pain and morbidity for those who are pierced by it. Keep iron shovels and pitchforks in front of the house during a storm, for it will prevent lightning from striking. Iron is a good charm against witchcraft and bad prayers. A horseshoe usually works. Stay away from copper and gold for midwifery. These are metals for war and death. Never cut the umbilical chord with any knife that has been used to kill an animal or man. This will surely cause the child to die from malefic pestilences. Instead, keep the mother under a cobweb and bathe the child in milk before sunrise, giving the milk to a dog afterwards. That wards off any evil eye.

Evil eye.

Béla would study Maria. She acted normal. She was probably normal. Or else her grey eyes of innocence would hinder perfectly any wrong in her soul. Maybe she was just a child.

And on, master and apprentice would go, teaching and learning.

For sowing a good crop, pour a few drops of a nursing mother's milk on the seeds. Fingernail clippings mixed with the seed will keep the crows away from the harvest. Carrots and parsnips should be planted when the moon is underground, whereas gourds and grains with the waxing moon. You can tell the weather by the extent of the moon's halo, by the colours of the clouds when the sun sets.Spiders should not be killed. They bring good luck. A powder from the desiccated emerald-coloured blister beetle could cure many aliments when mixed with vervain and burned as incense. It could also be given to men for a long-lasting... but painful erection.

Maria Maddalena giggled, just as a child would.

On rainy mornings, when Turul was gone for its daily soarings, inside the coldness and through the fumes of the dark medication shed, the curved little figure would athletically hop from amphora to beaker, his hands hurriedly juggling vials and pots, through powders and balms, ointments and syrups, wines, creams, honeys and ciders. He would bring up bunches of dried herbs and name every single one, instructing on the best date for harvest and the most appropriate manner to dry them. He would get Maria to help him assorting berries, petals, thorns, fibres, roots, to produce a range of healing and magical goods, from kitchen spices to itching powders.

There were rose hips for scurvy; lard with powdered oak galls to rub in the bottom of one who is suffering from piles; stems of white lilies to reduce fever, or yellow to stop incontinence; bouquets of daisies for treating the pains in the joints, or for infusions which will clean the urine; poisonous hemlocks, which had to be well differentiated from medicinal fennel and parsley; dried *scacciadiavoli*, the devil banisher, bloomed in the summer solstice for Béla, or the day of Saint John for the locals, and burned on the skin for scaring away the evil sprites that may attack the humours of an innocent victim; sprigs of oregano for cough relief and prickly milk thistles to alleviate liver ailments; bunches of sage with a thousand properties on them; yellow alpine monkshood, probably the most efficacious repellent for werewolves; posies of marigold, which heal pustules in the skin and, if harvested in February, the month of *Emese*, the mother of the Árpád family, it makes a wonderful tea that definitely cures the heartaches...

'Heartaches?' interrupted Maria. 'Those that will kill people making their faces blue?

'No, child. I speak of the pain of love', and he saw the disappointment on Maria's face. 'But for that other one,' he stirred through contents of a wicker basket and brought up a short ceramic bottle, 'here is something for very heavy people who suddenly stop breathing, drowning in their own blubber. Their pulse goes so fast to pump the thick blood that it may burst the heart into pieces. It is a wonderful concoction that your father got from a bishopric in the land of the Saxons, many moons north of the Alps Mountains. Just one sip and the blood will be as thin as water. The secret here is concentrated syrup of woodruff, yes the scented stellina, the same that we find around these hills. A phenomenal action! With this we restored an immense German pilgrim which collapsed in Chifenti a few years ago. Perhaps you don't remember that, but the woman was smothered by her own obesity, and a few spoonfuls of this syrup restored her to a better condition in a few days.'

'What about that fat Bishop Rodilando whose life my grandfather saved in Lucca? Did that have anything to do with this concoction?'

'Exactly this one!' Béla answered with a lit face. 'Bishop Rodilando was not too old, but he is now well, and forever thankful to woodruff syrup sent by your family. He has since been taking a few drops of this syrup on a regular basis.'

Béla's radiance could light up the walls of his shed.

'And that is all it is in this brew? Woodruff?' Asked a suddenly much more interested Maria.

'Nonononono! Not only that! It is also mixed with a purified holy *capelli della nonna*, grandmother's hairs, the sweet scented oats that I have once seen big wild bulls grazing on. I have some of it here with me, sent with this syrup.'

'Holy grass? Capelli della nonna?'

'Indeed holy, this grass has been spread over a church floor and stepped on by pilgrims on a saint's day. But where is the name?' With a hurried trembling hand, he searched through a number of leather pieces and parchment inside a velvet bag. 'Ah, here it is. I cannot read it. Can you read, child? I know you can.'

'*Sc. Willehadus... primus episcopus Bremae*', mumbled Maria with little keenness, her mind elsewhere.

'That's the one!' snapped Béla. 'A holy feast that adds to the miraculous action of this herb. But behold! No more than one sip. If much more is taken, the poor soul could fall into...'

...and he stopped at this moment, when Maria's eyes shone towards him with a cataractic grey, freezing the air into his lungs. The rotten silence was muffled by heavy raindrops on the puddles outside.

'Could fall into what, Béla?' Maria asked with a dry voice, with her gaze slowly moving through the entrance door.

The táltos never finished the sentence, He just hustled through his precious belongings, mumbling and shaking his head, hopelessly pretending a senility which had never really taken his thoughts. He put the cork back into the flask. Maria watched him with a thin straight line on her lips, except for one corner, which incautiously curled up.

...and the Iron Crown

Travelling north through a pleasant part of the Via Francigena, Julian and Railenda rode with Buonaccorso to Pavia, invariably engaging into long discussions on the empire and the See, on conquests and defeats, saints and demons, on good and evil. They were honoured to share the company of Pope John XVIII, or better, John Fasanus as an ordinary, jovial man and a particularly inept rider. Pope John defined himself as a 'pheasant perching on a horse'. From the humblest servant, to his custodes, patricians, roman deacons, religieuses and accompanying women, the pontiff never demanded or tolerated them to use the customary third-person treatment when directing the word to the bishop of Rome. He was more comfortable with a 'you'. Calm and extremely patient with the willing priests that travelled with the committee, John did not lose his patience with their clumsiness since being outside the walls of the Lateran Palace. He addressed the ladies with a discomforting charm and Julian was fortunate to witness energetic debates on the Mother Church and its role on men, sparkled between his beloved Lady Railenda and the bishop of Rome.

'Lady Railenda, you remind me so much of a dear cousin I have in Rome, the lady Theodora, of the Crescentii.' The pope noted with airy eyes. 'The charm, the sharpness of mind, the delighting beauty...'

'Oh, please, stop it!' she said, 'I'm hating her already!'

The pope smiled cordially for a few seconds, but changed his countenance to add 'Unfortunately Theodora has lost her will to live, since the deaths of the two men she loved, a few weeks apart from each other.'

'Of course, that Lady Theodora, how could I not make the connections? I have heard about her liaisons with pope Sylvester...' Railenda said.

'Nothing sinful, please do not misjudge any of them. They had utmost respect for each other's positions and vows. Theodora loved and respected her husband too, although she was well aware of the wasps' nest she was into. The pope died a few weeks after John I Crescentius, her husband. For these suspicious deaths, allegedly by poisoning, she blatantly accuses her greedy son, who's now ruling Rome.'

'And where is the poor Theodora?' Railenda asked. 'Why has she not accompanied you in this trip then?'

'As I mentioned, she lost all mirth. She has joined a monastery.'

'Oh, the unfortunate soul!' Railenda said, 'a religieuse. That is indeed losing the will to live.'

It baffled Julian that her vigorous and nearly-blasphemous remarks could be uttered to His Holiness under the most serene and cheerful tone without any indignant rebuff or accusations. It reminded Julian of his times and disputes with the bishop Avesgaud, in Mans.

Julian would brush off the memories quickly. That was in a different life...

As the cavalcade came across pilgrimage groups to Rome, to the horror of his most pious attendants who soundly snorted with disapproval, the Holy Father would frequently dismount and greet the pilgrims personally, praising their cause and laying a humble blessing on them, many times sharing with the feeblest a pouch of fresh water or a few loaves. While sitting around a lunch fire with Buonaccorso or sharing a goblet of wine with the noblest guests journeying with him, the Beatissimo Padre talked about the joy of travel and the blessing of pilgrimage. One of his suggestions developed around the protection of pilgrimage routes and holy sites. But that was already when they were nearing Pavia, so they could discuss this on another time, after the coronation.

The committee was arriving at one of the largest gathering of soldiers the marca had ever seen. There were a few Genovesi, Veronesi, Bolognesi, Milanesi, Capuani, but mostly Germans, camping through a vast area outside of the city, having tramped over precious farmland. On a wider circle, many of the elder, women and children of Pavia camped on improvised shelters and farmsteads, afraid of what was to happen in their city, which still upheld loyalty to Ardoin. The pope left a number of troops to secure the safety of that rabble.

Julian and the Lady Railenda entered the gate on the morning of the fifteenth day of May of the year of our Lord of 1004, riding with Buonaccorso, the pontiff and his entourage towards the Royal Palace.

Necks turned around restlessly, looking for familiar faces, but all they saw were the worn stones of Pavia. The city was unusually still, empty of life, with windows closed and doors shut. After the violent incursions of Henry and his troops on his way to Pavia, most of the Pavesi had either left or locked themselves up inside, afraid of the devastation the German soldiers could cause.

The German sovereign met with the pope for a quick, cordial and mostly public trade of niceties on a neutral ground: the royal palace *atrium*. Buonaccorso was standing next to an impatient Pope John XVIII when the bells of the ninth hour rang and Henry II majestically entered the hall. A tall, square built man with an abundant brown beard and airy blue eyes, Henry would have been a handsome figure, if it wasn't for the pock marks that ravaged his skin. He smiled angelically, before floating towards the corner where the pope waited with his committee. Buonaccorso could not help but notice the pope's lips pursed into a thin smirk as Henry humbly kneeled to kiss the pontifical ring. John gestured for Henry to rise and they embraced, exchanging a kiss on the faces.

'How is your good wife, Her Majesty Queen Kunigunde?' the pope asked.

Henry paused for a few seconds on a frozen smile. His eyes focused at nothing. 'The Queen is well, Beatissimo Padre. She waits for my most quick return. Has the Beatissimo Padre met the Queen?'

'Not personally, not. But her devoutness and piety has made fame across Italy. Do send her my dearest greetings and apostolic blessings'

Henry nodded with the same frozen smile. The pope found some discomfort under that stare, so he turned to the *factotum* and grabbed a package that the deacon ceremoniously held. 'I want to present to Your Majesty a special gift in honour of this event. Here is a Book of the Holy Gospels which belonged to the blessed Pope Adrian III.' He handed to Henry a large and thick volume bound in leather with enamel and gold filigree. The front cover was surrounded by a flat, delicate chain made of swan-shaped silver and gold links. The emperor's face shone as it beamed rays directly from heaven. The smile was still frozen, but now the pope could see that Henry was genuinely fascinated by the gift. John continued. 'Not only the illuminated manuscript is lavishly decorated by the best illustrators of Constantinople, but you will also notice that some pages will have ink marks and notations of the blessed Adrian himself. The pope was carrying this book of Gospels with him a hundred and twenty years ago, passing by Nonantula, when he left this vain corporeal life of ours to join the saints and martyrs on their altar, next to Jesus Christ our Lord. The abbey was desecrated soon after by Magyar raids, and it was only five years ago that this book of gospels returned to Rome, presented to Pope Sylvester II by King Stephen, of the Magyars. As your majesty has surely learned, the reason for the blessed Pope Adrian to be in Nonantula was no more than a stopover on a trip to Worms. He had been invited by the then Emperor Charles, called 'the Fat', to join him in Worms for a dietas.'

Henry seemed to be in bliss. 'I will respectfully bring the book of Gospels of the blessed Pope Adrian II with me, as a symbol of the pontifical presence in Aachen.'

The pope asserted with a handsome roman grin of satisfaction. 'It comes with the blessings of the Archbishop Varino, of Modena and Nonantula.' He was thrilled that Henry did not want to talk about any conflicts with the Crescentii or any of his plans for his kingdom of Italy. No requests, no acquittals. It was bound to be a journey for pure enjoyment.

Henry cordially gave his arm to the pope and they slowly walked to the other corner of the impressive atrium, where his entourage unravelled some other presents. 'This glorious book of gospels from the Beatissimo Padre comes indeed to crown these other marvels I received yesterday and this morning from the other guests. He reached to lift a heavy beaded collar, 'Look at the craftsmanship this marble rosary, presented by the charming Lady Railenda.' With the smile carved on his face, he waited with those unfocused blue eyes until the pope made a flattering remark on the gift. Then he carried on, like a spoiled prince on his birthday: 'The Beatissimo Padre will certainly note the richness of details on this ivory reliquary I got from the archbishop John of Bologna. It contains the toes of St. Petronius. Or this ornate chest presented by the bishop Isembardo, of Capua, containing the sandals used by St. Vitalian. The Montechi Family of Verona sheltered me during my visit, and they gave me this exquisite crucifix with gems. See how the light shines through the alabaster bleeding heart of our Lord Jesus Christ? Now look at this. The Archbishop Leone Orso, of Amalfi, brought me this beautifully embroidered banner, woven with gold and some of the strands of hair of St Andrew Apostle. Alfano the archbishop of Benevento, gave me this beautiful glass cruet, containing the ashes of St Barbas. Yes, many relics, Beatissimo Padre, but not just!' The emperor suddenly paused, his smile widened into a mischievous grin and he spun around on the tip of one foot, making his cloak open in bloom, flashing a scarlet light on everybody's eyes. 'This beautiful red cloak that I am wearing is made of silk! Yes, from the orient. It was a gift from Rodilando, Bishop of Lucca. See how it shines? And do feel its smoothness, Beatissimo Padre. But how silly of me! Please do accept my apologies for my misjudgement. I am sure the Beatissimo Padre does have vast areas of silk on his wardrobe.' The pontiff only smiled condescendingly as he shook his head. Henry continued, unstoppable. 'I am not so used to this luxury. This cloak mesmerised me so much that I could not help but wear it immediately. It is held by this magnificent gold fibula, sent by the old Bishop Lupo of Spoleto, whose advanced age disallowed him to travel to this blessed event. Lupo says in a letter that this fibula is believed to belong to old Umbrian tribes, before the empire.'

'Isn't that something?' giggled the pope. He could not be more satisfied, with such a smooth, easy and absolutely vain meeting. And it was even a short one. Henry's factotum reminded him of the need to schedule a longer audience with the bishop of Rome over the next day. New bishoprics in German lands would be on the agenda.

But the audience was soon over and they were all rushed out of the atrium. News of the arrival of Arnulf of Milano confirmed the coronation for that evening. The palace started to immediately regurgitate its guests out into the streets, following a cloudy blue-eyed king Henry, still with a frozen smile on his face, in procession to the church San Michele Maggiore. A new king of Italy would be crowned.

The strangely hurried procession was clogged at the entrance of the enormous church. While Julian waited next to the Lady Railenda, he watched how the empty streets were now well populated with German soldiers. Behind the dirty but still flamboyant yellow colour of Henry's army, Julian noticed for the first time a few faces of the first Pavesi.

They did not appear to be rejoicing with the usurper's coronation.

Buonaccorso stood next to the pope while a young German deacon pompously opened the ceremony, listing the anointments coming from German ecclesiastical authorities to this new engagement of Henry II.

Strangely, when Buonaccorso expected such ceremony to be respectfully attended in silence by all guests, a constant mumbling by all attendants smothered the priest's tenor voice, who continued impassively. '...and also the blessings from Egilbert von Moosburg, bishop of Freising, representing, Abraham of Görz that so zealously served his majesty during the early years; the blessings of Bernward von Sommerescheburg, bishop of the Cathedral School of Hildesheim; the episcopal blessings from Gebhard, bishop of Regensburg; from Heinrich von Rothenburg, count-bishop of Würzburg; from Megingoz von Lechsgemund, archibishop of Eichstätt; the blessings from Libentius, archbishop of Bremen; from Eribert, archbishop of Cologne; from Ludolf, archbishop of Trier and from Wilgis, archbishop of Mainz; in the name of our Lord the Father, of Jesus Christ His Son and the Holy Spirit.'

The serene pope, sitting on a non-prominent throne at the transept, watched with a contained amusement. 'This is a cauldron of jackals, Buonaccorso,' he said Turn your back to them and they will bite your tail.'

'I am afraid I do not understand the alliances, conflicts and difficulties between the Beatissimo Padre and the emperor.' said Buonaccorso.

'First of all, Buonaccorso, he is not an emperor. Not yet. He is only the king of the Germans, and now, as he receives the Iron Crown, he will be the king of Italy. That is the reason for my presence here. The papal blessing will make it indisputable. Only then can the king travel to Rome and be crowned by the bishop of Rome, me, as *Imperator Augustus Romanorum*. Do you understand the difference?'

'Clear as water, Beatissimo Padre.' Buonaccorso was still trying to behave elegantly, paying attention to the ritual, but the collective buzzing of the audience was totally muffling the Milanese archbishop, who helplessly tried to officiate the coronation with his faint voice.

Although the thick sandstone walls isolated the church from the outside world, a clamour could be heard outside. Behind the soothing curls of incense, Archbishop Arnulf picked up the crown presented on a richly embroidered pillow by his brother, the bishop of Brescia. The old Milanese held the Iron Crown of Lombardy with trembling hands. He laid it on the head of the man who knelt in front of him. A vitreous grin shone on the countenance of Henry II, now king of Italy.

The clamour was louder outside. Now they could hear the words. 'Ardoin! Ardoin, King of Italy!'

Sitting a couple of rows from the front, the Lady Railenda froze. She noticed that, for the first time since she had seen the king, the smile on his face was gone. It sent a shiver through the attendants. Railenda held Julian's hand firmly. He used his other to stroke hers, on a calming motion, as the shouts of 'Ardoin' increased outside.

'The clamour won't bother him,' Julian whispered, 'It's just the stupid rabble that does not know any better.'

But Railenda could not take her eyes from the king's face behind the fumes on the transept. It would not surprise her if the crown started to melt. She squeezed Julian's hand. 'Please stay with me, Julian.'

A voice inside Julian's heart said '*I will, my mother!*'

A German soldier entered the church in a rush, crossing the nave to kneel in front of the king. Before Henry could say anything, a rotund man advanced from the back to talk to the soldier, and then to the king. It was Bishop Guido Corti, of Pavia, Buonaccorso's former lord. After a small exchange of words, the bishop rushed out through an empty corridor that was opened by the guests, between the king and the front door. As the large oaken door was partially opened, the deafening noise from outside escaped into the sanctity of San Michelle.

'Ardoin! Ardoin, king of Italy!'

'What will happen now, Julian?' asked an anguished Railenda, digging her fingers into his arm.

'The Pavese bishop will calm down the mob,' said Julian, embracing her shoulders and dearly trying to believe in his words. 'You have met the king this morning, Lady Railenda. You have seen his sweet nature yourself.'

Railenda whispered in Julian's ears 'That airy smile. I don't like it, neither do I trust it. A wolf in the skin of a lamb'.

Suddenly a sharp crack exploded above on the western wall, showering pieces of an alabaster window over some of the guests in the back, as a large stone flew along the nave, landing on the empty path in the middle. The guests watched the bread-sized projectile sliding across the marble slabs, dragging its way towards the centre of the church, to stop with a thump on the first altar step where the king was now standing.

'*Ginoug!*' Henry grunted: Enough! And as he was opening his mouth again, all attendees turned to the front door as it was cracked open, leaking another good number of German soldiers inside. One of them was helping the fat Bishop Guido, now with stream of blood dripping out of his nose.

'They stoned me!' he shrieked.

The pope was standing open-mouthed, with Buonaccorso alert on his side. As soldiers swarmed around the king, they both heard his sobbing voice commanding 'Stop the rebellion! Do whatever is needed. Call the troops from outside the wall!'

A stream of soldiers ran from behind the altar towards the front door, against a screaming mass of guests that was trampling towards the back.

'Stay with me!' Julian shouted to Railenda.

'Follow the king!' the pope yelled to Buonaccorso. 'And let's get the Lady Railenda and Julian out of here!'

They battled together through that tragic night when Pavia was burned to the ground, with its men, women and children, massacred by the German troops.

Weeks later, with no healing from the pain and horror that followed him, Julian left Luna behind and sought refuge behind more battles and violence.

Buonaccorso, disappointed and tired of fruitless campaigns, retired from the life of a soldier. He joined the monastery of San Aristo, in Rome.

The Landlady

Fulcardo Cunimundinghi came a week too early for one of his inspection visits to the baths. This year, as his wife Lucia was to have their first child, he would ride on his own to Corsena. The villagers had been warned of the visit by a menacing Maria Maddalena. The fifteen year-old bared her white teeth at every single villager and worker at the baths. They were told to put on their best behaviour during the visit and they should better clean up anything that would meet the eyes of a visitor, or else they would have to deal with her. This felt rather strange for some of them. Her father owed nothing to the Cunimundinghi. On the contrary, the debt the lords of Anchiano had towards the Burle et Malachi had grown on these ten years of the baths.

Immanuel's daily affairs gave him little time to consider his position in the centre of a triangle of properties, debts and equities between the Cunimundinghi landlord, the pontifical curia and his Lucchese father-in-law investor. But the Bukhari would never lose the notion of this delicate balance between the factions he was forced to keep with his sweat and reason. The baths in Corsena had been very profitable, offering a luxurious exercise that became the latest, extravagant fashion among prosperous families of Lucca and Pisa. Proceedings were remitted to the papal strongbox, with the Burle et Malachi retaining fifteen percent. The Cunimundinghi saw no limits to the use of the baths, and their debt to the pope and to the baths swell to a desperate condition.

The Bukhari was ready and waiting for the visitor early in that morning. His daughter was nowhere to be found, but he made sure that all the other children had washed and put clean clothes on. They came down to the bank of the Lima and saw a couple of riders approaching from the road to Chifenti. One was Fulcardo Cunimundinghi, a rather handsome man on his late thirties, the only heir to all the lands south of Barga. Although his father Bishop Gherardo had been a careful land administrator, Fulcardo had an apparent tendency to simplicity of mind and bad luck. Poor decisions, most would say, had reduced the area of the Cunimundinghi to its present borders. Ever since the renovation of Corsena and the re-opening of the baths, Fulcardo had organised great celebrations in the Bagni, often forgetting not only about his still childless wife in Anchiano, but that those lands in Corsena did not belong to him. The debts piled up and more lands had been given in pawn, with Battista Burle in Lucca acting as a *fideiussore* for the two main *creditori*: the pope and the tenant Immanuel Malachi.

Riding next to him, a young woman. As they turned into the direction of Bagni, to ford the jolly waters of the Lima, Immanuel dropped his jaws. But he should have expected it. The woman was no one else but a splendidly dressed Maria Maddalena, his daughter.

According to the rumours that brewed on the next days, the landlord was quite satisfied with what he saw and happy with what he was reminded that still belonged to him. Maria Maddalena had snatched over the role of host, not acknowledging her father or anyone else. The whole family was hurried in and asked to obediently remain inside the manor, together with Béla. Meanwhile, with a splendid green tunic and a red robe and cowl, Maria sailed through the fresh alleys of Corsena with the bourgeois superiority that she was inclined to carry. The ideal companion that the brute could have hoped for. She had grown up finding easy ways to send to the Cunimundinghi hearsays on all affairs in the region: a sale of a heard of goats, a group of visitors in the baths, rich pilgrims paddling down the river, any deer brought from the forest, a pregnant girl, a precise report on calving, family feuds and any good gossip she thought that would interest the landlords. Fulcardo had been thankful to the girl, but it was only after this visit that a more serious notice on Maria Maddalena had been taken. She had been attentive, courteous, rigid with the villagers, precise on the reports, descriptive on the medicinal properties of the baths. And above all, she was exceptionally charming to Fulcardo.

With a piercing pain through his heart, Immanuel Malachi saw his daughter leaving Corsena riding together with the landlord.

'It is difficult to deal with Maria Maddalena', Immanuel sighed, giving an unrequested explanation to his family and to the old Magyar, who watched in silence. 'She is only fifteen, but a powerful presence.'

He stared down to the line of trees, where the playful waters silently slithered around the rocks of the Lima. A faint shriek from Turul broke from high above the cloudy valley. It had been a strange and exhausting day for Immanuel. The old man looked broken and worn. His beard was thinner and completely white now. His leathery skin squeezed his eyes even closer to his formidable nose.

'And I am tired, Béla,' he said looking at his old friend. 'Tired of trying to conduct my daughter into the pathways of righteousness while I still have twelve other children to rear, making everything within my reach to bring them up as honest men and women of these valleys.'

'Your children are a blessing, fönök' Béla said looking to the ground. 'It is just that Maria sometimes does not know her own pl—'

'It's a lot worse than that, Béla' interrupted Immanuel, with a disgusted expression. 'I have reasons to believe that Maria has lain together with this man'.

'Probably all of Corsena must suspect it,' said Béla.

'This is so wrong' said Immanuel. 'I have already told her that Fulcardo Cunimundinghi is a married man and that her indecent behaviour will only bring shame upon our family and risk leading to our banishment from Corsena. But she disagreed, of course. She said, Fulcardo fancied her and he could favour our family's position in this valley. And you know what else she said? That maybe Fulcardo Cunimundinghi would not be married forever'.

'What a stupid girl!' Béla spat, slapping his knee with revulsion. 'So typical of her arrogance. That is surely your daughter Maria Maddalena!'

Immanuel continued 'But then I insisted on the fact that as a landlord he is dangerously powerful and as a Cunimundinghi he is simple and of rude manners. I warned her that she would probably be used as a wench and tossed out of his lands when he was done and tired of her, for his wife Lucia is now with child, I told her. But apparently Maria Maddalena was not aware of this pregnancy. Do you know what she did then?'

Béla was quick to answer. 'She went out of the house and cursed the most horrendous blasphemes, stomping the ground and screaming, crying vengeance against Lucia Cunimundinghi, against your Christian God and everyone else she could think of.'

Immanuel was shocked. 'That's exactly what she did… how did you know that?'

The táltos smiled shyly 'We all heard it. The whole of Corsena knows that'.

'Of course,' said Immanuel, looking back at the river. 'Of course…'

Maria arrived home late that night.

Chifenti had been tending to a group of pilgrims which had come down the Serchio in a hurry, just before sunset. They brought terrifying news that swarmed the valley with fear: A horde of Saracen pirates had disembarked on the southern Ligurian shores.

Immanuel knew something about the people collectively known as Saracens. He had been born and raised in an land that followed the same faith. They had not been bad people to live with t all, but he knew they were certainly implacable foes. He was sure that once they'd be gone from Liguria, no grass would be growing where Saracen feet would be stepping on.

He had also learned to understand the reasoning that ruled politics in those lands. He knew that if papal troops were to come to Liguria to expel the invaders, the Roman throne would be demanding that all their debtors pay their commitments. Fulcardo Cunimundinghi would have to find some means to heal his obligations.

'Maria Maddalena, have you seen Attila's dagger?' Immanuel seemed unusually disturbed in the early morning.

'No, my father, you have never shown such a thing to me. I actually thought this was a product of your stories only,' Maria Maddalena said. 'But there is something else I would like to –'

'Well, then please check it to your brothers and sisters,' he grunted. 'The dagger is missing and it looks like it has been stolen. Times are bad enough with the pirates on the coast, and now this precious treasure missing. I am going to see Béla about this dagger'.

'Talk to Béla, then' she said with undisguised disdain. 'That old man has strange manners. I would not trust him too much. Only I know that.' She turned to her father and added with a bright smile 'Or maybe the village idiot. I am sure that he likes shiny things. Now I must go.'

Immanuel saw his daughter leaving with a satchel and saddlebag. A couple of Cunimundinghi horses were harnessed outside, waiting with an old groom that he assumed to be from the landlord's stables.

'Where are you going, child? I've just asked you to talk to your brothers about the...'

'It's Fulcardo's wife. Lucia of the Cunimundinghi's is with labour pains. I am going to assist with the birth.'

Immanuel frowned 'On your own? There are pirates on these mountains. Saracen pirates!'

She paid no heed. Immanuel continued 'Don't they have experienced midwives in Anchiano? Why do they need you?' She did not answer again, but her father carried on 'Well, in this case Béla should certainly go with you.'

'You should know better that we don't like men assisting in childbirth, father. Furthermore, I've already seen Béla this morning. He is not coming.' Maria said matter-of-factly as she mounted on the spare horse. 'I gave him honeyed blackberry wine with iron rust. He has not been well lately.'

With no other words she dug her heels into the horse's flank and galloped down to ford the Lima, followed behind by the groom.

Immanuel tried to shout words of caution at his daughter. When she was too far to hear his warnings, he hurried over to the baths and rushed into Béla's shed, to find the táltos in a miserable state of dehydration.

'Maria Maddalena tells me she gave you an iron drink. Are you with a loose bowel?'

'It is getting worse, fönök!' the old man moaned. 'Horrible cramps! I am afraid your daughter has given me something nasty!'

'Nonsense,' Immannuel said. 'If it's blackberry wine it will hold your bowels. It's the right concoction.'

'She's been giving it to me for a few days. But it could have been anything. Anything! The fruits of the *spino cervino*, or maybe foxgloves, or roots of the *rabarbaro*, or even the cuticles of *psyllium* seeds, I don't know! It just tasted like honey-sweetened wine to me.'

'Why would she do that?' asked Immanuel.

'The Cunimundinghi child, fönök!' groaned Béla. 'You have seen how Maria Maddalena has slipped into Fulcardo's life. I fear for mother and child. But I hope to be better when labour starts.'

Immanuel lost his breath. 'Maria has left! It seems that Lucia Cunimundinghi is about to give birth now.'

'Quick!' roared Béla. 'Get Divina, from the tavern in Chifenti to go and help. And to watch Maria!'

A flash of light crashed through the night on the path ahead of Divina. It furtively revealed, behind the long needles of icy-cold rain in front of her face, the winding lane disappearing into a ghostly maze of white branches and leafless trees. The light only splattered its whiteness for a blink of an eye, followed by utter darkness and a hollering thunder that exploded through the roar of the rain. Divina was soaked and cold, running through the torrential shower to get back into the safety of Chifenti. But much more than cold, she was exhausted and aching, panting from the desperate rush from the Cunimundinghi castle in Anchiano. Divina was scared. She had a very good reason to be so.

It had been a full, exhausting day and evening, if not a complete disastrous endeavour.

She had been helping Amadeo with daily chores at the tavern when a messenger from Immanuel announced that Béla, the old Magyar in Corsena, the best midwife in that part of the valley, was miserably ill. Therefore, Immanuel Malachi trusted that Divina, with good experience as a nun and midwife too, would assist and watch the young Maria Maddalena on the arts and secrets of midwifery to help on the birth of the Cunimundinghi heir in Anchiano. The messenger respectfully whispered that Béla had fair grounds to suspect the labour procedure could go astray under the supervision of Maria alone.

Divina left quickly, after being cautioned by Amadeo about the danger of pirate incursions into their valley. He gave her a horn to sound an alarm, if needed. Finally, young Ginevra warned her mother about Maria Maddalena, the *witch*.

The Cunimundinghi castle was strangely silent and solitary on top of its rock when Divina arrived. She climbed the steps up into the walls and was hurried through the large luxurious hall, passing by a group where Fulcardo Cunimundinghi, Lucchese relatives and a few servants prayed to Sant'Orso di Aosta. She smiled at hearing the homely name of the bear saint. The people smiled back. Divina was a small, greying but still vigorous and handsome woman. Most unusually, she wore a small crucifix around her neck, as a memento of her previous religious life, although crucifixes were not part of religious attire.

Divina was led away from the crowd, into a poorly lit lying-in room, where Lucia Cunimundinghi's ghostly sweaty image could be seen leaning back on the birthing stool. Her eyes were closed and she breathed heavily. A colossal sphere where her body was supposed to be indicated that the baby was not out yet. The landlady was watched by six women, including the formidable red-haired figure of Maria Maddalena. *The witch*, as her daughter Ginevra would say.

Maria was the only one who did not seem to acknowledge Divina's arrival, even after the announcement that Immanuel Malachi had sent her. Maria was seemingly busy oiling Lucia Cunimundinghi's vulva and perineum with some chestnut-coloured unguent.

'She is sleeping.' whispered one of the women, a young plump blonde with gorged blue-veined breasts eager to jump out of her corset. Divina reckoned that one would be the wet-nurse allocated to the coming baby. No landlady like Lucia Cunimundinghi would waste her body and breeding capacity with breast feeding. After delivery, she would be expected to have her breasts covered and bound with cabbage and sage leaves, to dry the milk.

The other women watched in tension. They were much older and deformed by the shadows of the flickering flames. One warty lady held a *cimaruta*, a spring of rue hanging with several charms, including a key, a moon and medals of Sant'Erasmo and Santa Margherita di Antiochia.

Divina asked 'Any contractions yet? I thought they had already started hours ago.'

'There's been more than twenty so far!' answered through rock-dry lips the eldest of the women, obviously annoyed with the youth and inexperience of the midwife in charge. Divina knew that older women were preferred for their experience but advised to stay away from touching and handling excessively mother and child. Naturally, it was well known that when women came to the age of no more monthly bleedings, they accumulated corporeal wastes and humours that were not flushed out, and this could cause illness or poison the baby. On seeing the horrified face of Divina, the old hag rehearsed a smile of sympathy and continued. 'I know! We've opened all the cabinets and drawers, we've untied all knots to release the child. At this stage we should certainly be trying to...'

Maria flung an air-splitting shush that quieted them all. On her defence, she simply stated, almost through a whisper, 'She is relaxing. I will get *it* out.' Her hand entered. It disappeared, sliding through the slick swollen lips between the spread trembling legs of Lucia Cunimundinghi.

Forgetting to verify what Maria's hand was actually supposed to be doing, Divina lost herself contemplating her landlady for the first time. She tried to extract the serene, resting face from the exhaustion, sweat and suffering. This prompted her to wipe Lucia's brow with a moist cloth she grabbed from one of the women. The room was stuffed with their intense breath and smoke from the coals, burning under a corner cauldron. She slowly blew on Lucia's face to refresh the drained woman. Divina tried but failed to locate any beauty in the Cunimundinghi lady. She had plain features, not touching the brutish, but by no means elegant. Perhaps something wrong with the way she was designed. Indeed, even at the dimness of the lying-in room, the exuberance of young Maria Maddalena was indeed annihilating the monotony of Lucia's appearance. The greasy eyelids were heavy and, as Divina delicately wiped away the transpiration droplets from the eyebrows, both of Lucia's eyes opened wide, almost jumping out of their sockets, as she howled with all her lungs in horrific pain.

'Now *it*'s coming out!' said Maria with a devilish smile.

Lucia was screaming and bucking. All the women held her firmly to the birthing stool.

Divina yelled through the nightmarish wail 'What have you done to her, Maria?'

For the first time, Maria turned to her, with a clear countenance and a refreshing smile. 'The baby was turned. Now it will come out easy. It will be over soon!'

On hearing that, Divina sighed, letting a breath of bitter air away from her heart. But Maria still added 'However, I think the child will not survive.'

Divina's stomach sank and twisted. Not only was the report disheartening, but Maria had presented it without wiping the grin off her face.

It all happened very quickly and Divina could not recall all facts. In one moment, the veiny head was appearing between the busting lips. In a second after, the baby boy was spurted out, falling in the hands of the midwives. He was already bawling powerfully with life from the top of his tiny lungs, as the women shrieked with joy. 'He's alive!'

Meanwhile a cascade of blood poured from Lucia's womb. Divina saw Maria quickly snatching the baby from the women's embrace, turning her body around and quickly severing the umbilical cord with a swift swing of what looked like a blade she produced out of her satchel. She fled from the room carrying the child with her, breaking through the father and servants outside, grunting 'We must save him, or he will die.' Her finger was stuck in the child's mouth.

The women were left alone, looking at each other. Still bleeding on the stool, Lucia was delirious, babbling, asking for the baby. Four women carried her to the bed, exhausted and still bloated, while a fifth assisted with more clean sheets. A generous stream of dripping blood followed Lucia from the stool up to the sheets. Divina jumped in to hinder the flow.

'Where did that girl go with the baby? Somebody please go and *watch her*!' she yelled.

Lucia was suddenly awake and articulate. 'Why does this Maria Maddalena need to be watched?' She pointed a tremulous finger to Divina. 'You. Why did you say someone should *watch* her?'

'I didn't say that. I thought it would be advisable if someone helped her.'

'No, I heard it very well', she moaned, 'You said *watch*.'

The oldest crone said very matter-of-factly. 'It's milk. She's gone out to bathe the child in milk!'

Divina fumed with anger. 'Superstitious nonsense!' she spat. 'But if bathed must the child be, why in the name of the Blessed Virgin Mary couldn't we have the milk in this room?'

None of those hags could have made a less stupid face. Lucia sighed deeply and fainted again.

Divina started to wonder if there would have been any reasonable ground for Maria Maddalena to suspect that the child would not survive. And what of the blade used on the umbilical cord? Did she see it properly as Maria turned around to cut it? Was it a curved blade… like a dagger? Or was it just imagery created by her fear and loathing for the young woman? *No time to think, Divina. Only act.*

The other women kept moving to help. More sheets were needed to stanch the insistent red flow. One of them prayed out loud on a cadence, a folk rhyme, as the old hard-lipped crone hurriedly bundled green stems of *millefoglio d'Achille*, yarrow, into a pack. It was wrapped in linen, crushed under her foot, tied to a string and carefully inserted into Lucia's bleeding vulva.

Divina did not trust the local concoctions. She knew that Béla had the right potions and remedies for these haemorrhages. Certainly his young assistant would have been properly replenished with it.

A commotion broke up outside the lying-in room. They could hear shouting and yelling. Someone crying. Startled, Divina left Lucia under the care of the other women for a few seconds, approaching the door just to see Maria Maddalena handling a bundled baby to a wide-eyed Fulcardo. A limp scrawny arm slipped out, dangling purple off the linen towel. Divina bit her lower lip so hard that blood gushed out.

'I baptised him for the Lord to take him to His kingdom, to join His Glory with all the Saints and Martyrs,' Maria Maddalena said to Fulcardo, before she embraced the landlord, keeping the dead baby between the two bodies.

The other people exited, leaving Fulcardo to his own grief. Only Divina wanted to cry, to yell *injustice, betrayal* and *murder*, and to skin that red-haired devil with her own nails. But now she just watched. The way Fulcardo Cunimundinghi's hands caressed the back of young Maria made Divina want to vomit. Witch, her heart cried.

Divina finally burst. 'My Lord, I heartily respect your mourning, but this girl has already managed to hand over to you a dead baby boy! This midwife you embrace so passionately is now leaving your wife bleeding to death!' Before finishing the sentence, Divina had already regretted having said that.

Fulcardo's red eyes shot at her. The women assisting Lucia squealed. Another folk prayer was immediately started. Maria Maddalena turned her head, still with her arms around Fulcardo's neck, and measured Divina from head to toes. The girl's thinned lips subtly drew a cynical smile, which quickly disappeared as she held Fulcardo's face with both of her hands, looked at him in the eyes and quickly kissed his lips. 'Never mind her', she said with a dismissive jerk of her chin, 'She is nervous and cannot handle the situation. They obviously need my help.'

She released the landlord and entered the dark lying-in room, brushing Divina to the side. But then, as she was half way into the darkness towards the fire where Lucia sat, she turned around and said with a shadowy grin 'Divina, if you really want to help, why don't you organise for the shroud, the pall or why don't you go down to the stables and talk to the carpenter about a wooden casket for the baby boy? As a nun, you should be familiar with all needs for a proper requiem, for an innocent, yet Christian soul. Even though you betrayed your sacred votes, I think we can all pretty much trust you for this simplest of tasks.'

'I...must...assist...' Divina babbled, pointing to the landlady spread on the bed. 'Lucia is bleeding... She may not...survive.'

Fulcardo turned to Maria. 'Please help Lucia', he sobbed.

'I will try,' Maria said, disappearing towards the opposite direction, and coming back with her satchel, adding 'But when our Father in Heaven wants one of us to join Him, there is nothing much to be done.'

She entered the lying-in room, joining Divina and the other midwifes once again. Maria quickly tested Lucia's forehead with the back of her hand, and pulled the blood-drenched plug from the womb. 'She is still bleeding', she said with an annoyed face, quickly reaching into her satchel and bringing out an exquisitely fashioned glass phial. 'Here Lucia, take this.' She lightly slapped the pale cheeks of the landlady to wake her up. 'Yes, please, swallow this; yes...this will surely make you better.'

And Lucia gulped down the liquid from Maria's glass phial.

The thick incessant rain erased any clear indication that, throughout the blinding darkness, a road extended ahead of Divina. Another thunder cracked with a flash of light right above her head. It was enough to illuminate the path, but not long-lasting to drive away the ghosts that hollered on her soul while she was immersed in total shadow. She knew they were not ghosts. It was the thick, flooded Serchio on her side, which furiously roared as it galloped down on the opposite direction, towards Lucca, bringing with it all the rain that fell into those valleys.

Every time after lightning bolt exploded, bathing the whole valley in quavering blue shadows, Divina had to readjust her eyes to the blackness of the world around her.

She had to stick to the path. And be swift.

Bad times to be travelling in the dark. Divina knew that, just behind those mountains, blood thirsty pirates had made a camp on the coast. The cani, dogs, were laying siege and destruction to castles, manors, cities and villages, bringing certain death to the Ligurian folk and an abominable faith to taint those shores. Divina had never seen a Saracen, but she knew of the dangerous threat this term represented. And people were speaking with horror of the *Musetto*. Never before had she heard about this Musetto, supposedly the leader of the pirates, a devil whose feet would make the earth quake as he walked. A monster that impaled men and women, sodomising them with his hot-iron rod.

Stories! These must have been no more than silly tales from the wicked imagination of Bernardo from the Rocks. Still, she did believe Bernardo when told them how he saw a few days before, from the top of the Panie mountains, the black smoke rising from the devastation of the Saracens in the Ligurian coast. The idea of falling prey to those monsters sickened her.

Her body was dead cold. She shivered and her legs were in pain, but Divina still hurried her pace through the cold rain that incessantly hammered on the hood or her coat. She needed to get back to the safety of Chifenti. Holding on to her small wooden crucifix, hanging around her neck, she recited to herself '*sed et si ambulavero in valle mortis non timebo malum quoniam tu mecum es virga tua et baculus tuus ipsa consolabuntur me*'. So different were those words in her memory from the language that people spoke. Still, she recited them with fervour in the heart. She would fear no evil, even though she would walk through the valley of death...

While she stumbled through the stony wet road, Divina's other hand touched the glass phial in the satchel. Maria Maddalena's phial. It was still safe and intact. She sighed, wondering if, by getting to Chifenti, she would still have the breath and the legs to make it to Corsena before Maria Maddalena returned. But maybe, back at the Cunimundinghi castle in Anchiano, the girl had already found out about the missing phial. She would be coming through the rainy night after Divina, like a falcon cuts through thin air. If Divina made it to the bagni, she would get an experienced impression from Immanuel and Béla on the contents of the phial. Immanuel would surely tell whether the vial had black comb, as Maria claimed. If not, the daughter of Immanuel Malachi would be unmasked. Fulcardo would learn of the heinous intentions of his favourite. But then again, if that was really a drug to stop the bleeding…well, Divina could still risk her suspicion. And she didn't think it was.

She could not erase from her mind the one image which was deeply and painfully engraved: the upside-down body of Lucia Cunimundinghi, hanging from the ceiling over a pool of blood.

Lucia's condition had never ameliorated since Maria Maddalena came back into the room with her saving concoctions. The bleeding continued, fluid and abundant, draining the colour of Lucia's skin and the heat out of her body. She still transpired abundantly and her eyes sank. Her cries of desperation were heard throughout the manor. She fought against death for several hours, calling for the name of Sant'Erasmo, to rescue her for that agony, from the fear of death. While the women tried all artifices to stanch the blood, making new plugs of yarrow, closing drawers and corking bottles, tying knots and reciting prayers in sequence, Fulcardo sat next to her, holding her hands. A genuinely sweating Maria Maddalena maintained a constant dribble of her phial potion into Lucia's mouth.

When unconscious Lucia's body lost its composure, Fulcardo desperately yelled for all to raise her feet. This should logically drive the blood to her head and stop the bleeding from her womb. All servants entered to help on this procedure. When she was finally fixed into an upside down position, with ropes pulling her knees towards the ceiling beam, a trickle of greenish liquid ran across her face. Her lifeless body swung over the bed.

Witchcraft! Poison! Murder! Those words were only screamed inside Divina's heart. She could not utter them. The silence of the room was only broken by sobs, as the household fell into a quiet grief. Fulcardo wept and left, with young Maria Maddalena on his heel. That was when Divina saw the phial on the bedside table. She quietly approached the other side of the bed, discreetly snatched the phial and sniffed at it. It was a sweet scent. Very sweet indeed. A herbal bouquet. She would have expected black comb to be musty. Not at all surprising, she thought.

Amid the movement to lowering the body of Lucia Cunimundinghi into a more decorous death posture, Divina had disappeared with the phial into the rainy night. When she had long passed the gates of Anchiano, on the way down to the Serchio road, she started to run. Faster than she had ever done before.

She raced for no more than a mile, until her muscles just refused to continue. She dragged herself through the rain, determinedly walking in spite of the torturing pain on the legs. Praying and holding on to her crucifix and to the accursed phial, Divina carried on across that blackest and wettest of nights. There would be still more than an hour walking through the storm to get to Chifenti, and stopping for a rest would be unthinkable. Maria Maddalena would be looking for her phial, even if at this stage she would be probably more interested in offering solace to Fulcardo Cunimundinghi. Sweet young comforting solace, to be found right between her –

Was that a horse she just heard?

The deafening rain still pounded on the valley, and the loud roar from the flooded Serchio continued, running wildly on Divina's side. But the clip-clop of hooves beating behind her was clear. She didn't hear it again. Still, it must have been a horse indeed.

Divina called.

Nothing answered. It could be just a runaway horse, scared off its shelter by the storm. Divina kept walking. She was not too far from the old abandoned hospital now, nearby the segment where the ferry crossed the river. It would be a comforting sight passing by, even when she did not need to reach the other bank.

But thinking better of it, it couldn't be any escaped horse just standing still. There was surely a rider. Someone who did not want to be seen or heard there, in that part of the road, at that time of the night.

Divina started running.

The hoof beats started again, she could hear them through her panting breath, and she struggled to run as fast as she could. She was now flying, with no pain on her legs to be concerned with. The hoof beats had now become a galloping thunder, getting agonisingly closer, catching up in a few breaths, so close that Divina could even smell it. Without slowing down, she looked back only to see the dark face of a horse puffing steam through desperate nostrils, not one arm of distance from her face.

Nobody, not a single soul in the entire valley of the Serchio heard the scream.

Divina was dead before it ever left her mouth.

One Day Too Late

In the fortified town of Johannispolis, around the magnificent basilica of San Paolo Fuori le Mura, Brother Buonaccorso was interrupted in his mid-day prayers in one of the chapels in San Aristo: it was a message to attend a visitor at the monastery patio. Rushing out of the church into the cypress-surrounded yard, all he saw was a luxurious carriage beyond the columns, with a page wearing the red and gold brocade, typical of the Crescentii palace in Nomenta. As neither the cart nor the page moved, Brother Buonaccorso hurried to fill a bucket from the trough and bring it to the sweaty horses.

'Leave these healthy beasts panting their lungs out, man of God! Come and help this old sick pheasant out of this cubicle,' a familiar voice said from inside the cart. Buonaccorso dropped the bucket and rushed to open the cart's tiny door, almost missing to recognise the skeletal figure inside.

'Beatissimo Padre!' Buonaccorso said with flooded eyes, bowing for respect and to hide the mixed memories raised into his heart. He tried to reach for the pope's hand, but for his surprise, no ring or gloves were to be found. Just the bony dry hands of an awfully thin John XVIII.

'Not any longer!' said the passenger with a smile of pain. 'The ring has been snatched off. Pope John XVIII has had his time. Now I am no more than your brother here in this monastery. I am Brother John.'

'How come you are no more the pope?' protested Buonaccorso, as he helped John Fasanus out of the carriage. 'You are here! Alive!'

'Look at me Buonaccorso', he said with an effort as he stood up in the sun. 'Is this the man you knew?' He saw the Pavese Leopard swallow and search for words. John carried on 'I have been very sick, Buonaccorso. Something grows in my liver.' Buonaccorso's eyes bulged in horror as John raised his shirt to expose a dark bloated side. 'Yes, they say the *cancer* is now going into the veins.'

'*Crab?*' Buonaccorso asked. 'You actually have a crab eating your insides?'

John giggled. He was leaning on his friend's arm to climb the stairs towards a side door to the basilica. 'No Buonaccorso! Not a crab with all its pincers. It is called a crab only because of the shape of this strange growth. My liver has turned into a rock and it does not stop bulging. The veins around it are all hard and thickened with this pestilence. I don't have more than a few months to live.'

'So they kicked you out of the Lateran because of your disease? The bastards!'

'No Buonaccorso! You got it wrong again. It was I who decided to leave. The crab is not contagious, the physicians guarantee it.'

'Perhaps they poisoned you?'

'Ha, this is no poisoning, Buonaccorso. My cousin, the lady Theodora of the Crescentii, now Prioress Theodora, has also come to see me immediately. She suspects her son John II Crescentius poisoned the Beatissimo Padre Sylvester II and now me. I don't know about my predecessor, but I have not been poisoned by Crescentius.' They both kneeled towards the Evangelist altar as they crossed the basilica's main nave. Buonaccorso helped John to stand up and the old man moaned 'I have no business in this basilica, my friend. Take me with you to San Aristo.'

Later at the refectory, after paying a visit to a most delighted abbot, followed by a round of the monastery with no less than a dozen obliging guides, both friends shared a cup of wine.

'I am tired, Buonaccorso. Not only my body is sick, but my heart is tired of it all. But by the grace and justice of God, I have been sent with this ailment to take me sooner than expected. And if it was for our failure in Pavia, that is indeed divine wisdom.'

Buonaccorso took a deep gulp of a refreshing wine, before saying 'Your piousness humbles me, Beatissimo Padre, but in what state have you left the...' Buonaccorso asked.

'Please do not call me that again!' hushed John, 'The pope has resigned! From this morning, I am no more than a monk. I have already told you, the abbot and to all those sycophants who followed me around this place like devil worshippers, with their slimy tongues stuck into a knot up my arse.'

'Sure, sure...Brother John, if you prefer.' Buonaccorso corrected. 'But I am still curious to know how a pope could resign. And in what state of conditions you have left the Lateran Palace.'

John smiled with gusto. 'Ah, my good soldier, I have been discussing this matter with my cousins the Crescentii for a few weeks already, ever since the physicians condemned me to a slow death. I could resign if I wanted. After all, I was the pope, the bishop of Rome, the successor to Peter, the Apostle of Christ! But it seems to be unbelievably more difficult for the pope's peers to accept that we may want to forward the function to a more willing and capable soul. They will all be watching me. The Crescentii will be scrutinising this monastery night and day, up to the moment when the Good Lord calls me to face judgement between heaven and hell. My cousins do not want me to be communicating with the emperor or with other families, especially our other cousins from Tusculum. For the Holy Pity of Christ, as if I bothered!'

'Do they have a replacement for you?'

'Yes, they will probably be announcing it tonight. You must know it. Thanks the Good Lord we did not raise that arrogant young Bishop John Theophylactus, the bishop of Porto. The divine light this time fell on the bishop of Albano. I have been briefing him over the last few days. His name is Pietro Boccaporca.'

Buonaccorso chuckled. 'Pietro Martino Boccaporca! I do not know him personally, but I have definitely heard of his silly name before. *Pig's Snout!*' He frowned more seriously and asked. 'A bishop called Peter. Will he keep the name of the Prince of the Apostles?'

John grinned again. 'Peter? Hell no! Boccaporca is too smart. He would not dare!'

During that service of vespers, it was announced that Pope John XVIII had resigned and that Pietro Pig's Snout had been elected to the throne of St. Peter. He chose the unfortunate name of not only one of the most wicked and vile pontiffs that the Lateran had seen, but also the same of the Patriarch of the Eastern Church in Constantinople, washing down the cloaca any hope of approximation between the ecclesiastical structures of Rome and Byzantius.

He was now Pope Sergius IV.

In the monastery of San Aristo, Brother John Fasanus could not attend the matins on the next morning. They found him being tormented by abominable pains inside his body. He was tended by his friend Brother Buonaccorso in the infirmary, where they spent hours talking.

'My loyal friend,' John said, 'I have something more serious to talk to you. I think you are wasting your time here.'

Buonaccorso protested 'Tending to the sick is a pious activity, a highly regarded...'

John cut him short. 'No, Buonaccorso, that is not what I mean. I talk about you wasting your life here in this nothingness. Look at yourself. You are still an able-bodied soldier. You are the Pavese Leopard, for the Sacred Sword of Saint Paul! Rather than selfishly spending the rest of your days as I do, looking only at my own tiny chances before the Divine Judgement, you should be living life to its fullest, deciding for your own destiny. So many places to go, so many battles to be won, so much to do, Buonaccorso. You should be fighting for justice, for goodness to prevail. Fight for Christ, for your people. Fight for a woman. Fight for love. The flame must be burning hot inside you Buonaccorso. You have not changed and I know your heart yearns for the intensity of life. Let the passion out. You should be finding yourself a good healthy wife and starting a family. Anything, but do find yourself a cause!'

'I have fought for several causes, Beatissimo...I mean, Brother John. And you have seen how much these just causes can deceive us. I still carry the burden of the dead in Pavia.'

'Rubbish!' spat John, twisting his face with pain. 'You know well that King Henry II is a perfect example of German lack of sensibility and inbred stupidity. He has committed many unspeakable acts under his rule, such as the massacre in Pavia. But he holds the crown and the power. What can we do then? Do you suggest we dig a hole in the ground and burry our heads like one of those Lybian *struzzi*? Of course not! Our life should have a purpose and it must include the constant pursue of justice, a search for the most valuable Christian ideals. And that should be with the emperor's help or without it. I never gave it up after Pavia. I continued with missionary work, I opened new bishoprics and confirmed the *pallium* on others, I guaranteed the possessions and privileges of several churches and abbeys, I created new saints for the wild peoples of the north, I tended to the sick and the dying during our plagues in Rome, I made friendships with enemies, I affronted kings and bishops in order to see justice made. I never gave it up. Never! Even though I now fade away with this illness and that stupid German king continues his pompous parade as the most blessed soul on earth. My Good Lord, I could bet my papal tiara that they will make Henry II a saint one day, with his own celebration date, churches, monasteries and feasts named after him. But God and the real Saints can see it all from heaven.'

'What do you suggest I do then?' said a puzzled Buonaccorso 'I cannot just leave the monastery if I decide to go into a battle from one minute to the other.'

'Of course you can!' John said, as he readjusted himself sitting on the bed, trying a more comfortable position. 'The abbot will gladly and obligingly accept if I personally request for your honourable dismissal. And then you should go and see the new pope. He has been briefed about you. I had long conversations with him over a special mission that I would confer only to you and another soldier.'

'Who is the other?' Buonaccorso asked with a cautious frown.

'You have to bring him with you to see Sergius IV, who's expecting to meet you both. Before you come to the pope, you must travel south to the Principality of Salerno, to the borders with the Byzantine states. You should look for the local garrison in Sapri and they will help you find this soldier. Yes, his fame for bravery has washed over those shores too. Just like the Pavese Leopard, they will all know him. This mercenary has lost himself into minor causes and keeps wasting his bravery away in local skirmishes.

'Tell me his name!' pleaded Buonaccorso.

'You know him well, my good soldier. It is Julian, of Mans.'

Three weeks later, Buonaccorso and Julian walked swiftly through the busy Lateran square as they entered Rome. As experienced soldiers, they contoured the colossal bronze mounted figure of Emperor Constantine by its right, leaving their ready-to-fight right arms on the side of the passers-by. They went straight to see the new pope, missing completely a stop to visit John Fasanus at the monastery.

On the marble-covered palace atrium, they found themselves in a colourful crowd of religieuses of many fashions, from monks to dignitaries, among palace custodes and filthy pilgrims who expected to get a peek of the Holy Father. They announced themselves to a visibly distrustful, but cordial custos, a palace guard, who left them to wait in a dusty scriptorium, visibly unused for a long time, with empty tables, chairs, rolled carpets and small cabinets piled against one wall. The same custos returned after a few minutes, this time with untroubled eyes, and took them to a large courtyard with a dry ornate fountain in the middle. They were kindly asked to wait a while more, sitting at a marble bench that faced beds of bright pink cyclamens overgrown with poorly kept shrubs of wild roses.

Both were silent. The call from their old friend John Fasanus had been sufficient to snatch Julian out of Sapri and bring him willingly to see the new pope. Fasanus had refused to tell Buonaccorso what it was about, but promised the Pavese Leopard that this would be the greatest mission ever granted to any Christian soldier.

Julian, now at twenty three, had acquired deep grave lines of anguish on his face. A handsome, but wooden expression that smiled with difficulty, surrounded by long silky strips of black hair. He was happy to see his soldier friend, who felt the tears on his shoulder after the long embrace of the meeting. Then, as they exchanged the news, Julian was quick to pack and bid farewell to the commander and soldiers at Sapri.

The journey to Rome did not take long, for it was hurried and quiet. Buonaccorso avoided too much talk about the 'good times' together, which had led to the disaster in Pavia. They just swapped brief words on the road and travellers, food, the inns and the pitiful state of health of John Fasanus. Not a word about Luna. Not a word about Clarissa.

After about two hours of waiting, listening to distant murmurs beyond the palace walls and to the thrushes rustling through the leaves under the shrubs, a robed deacon came hurriedly to call both visitors. 'Please follow me. I am the pontiff's factotum. The Beatissimo Padre will see you both at the pontifical office.'

Pope Sergius IV was a rather plump man, who spoke moving mostly his upper lip, exposing the front incisor teeth more often than his interlocutors would prefer. A protruding forehead and a thick flabby neck that connected his head to join directly with the narrow shoulders gave him an air of a wise farm animal. With an abundant fair beard, he certainly did not appear to be of Roman patrician origin. Julian saw in him the typical Lombard stock he had seen in northern Italy. And despite the porcine appearance, Sergius IV was an extremely sombre man. He watched the two soldiers entering the wide mosaic-floored hall, both visually relieved and nervous, after such a lengthy wait. They respectfully kneeled to kiss the ring over his glove, while receiving the grace of the apostolic blessing. Both soldiers were left on their knees as the Sergius looked beyond them, scanning the several people that stood in the back of the hall from side to side, nodding a few times with his big round head. Julian and Buonaccorso heard the shuffling of feet behind them and the swing of doors. The factotum, nomenclator, tesserarius, custodes and the entire papal household, maybe even a subtle member of the Crescentii, hurried to leave. Finally, a clang echoed through the office. Only God would witness their meeting with the new man in the post of Saint Peter.

'My predecessor John XVIII said I would find no better men than you two in all of Italy,' the pope started, ceremoniously. As both Julian and Buonaccorso humbly prepared to protest, Sergius raised a firm commanding hand, as if discreetly pointing to the witness of the angels and saints on the mosaics above, shutting them both up instantly. 'To the praise and glory of the Redeemer, our Lord Jesus Christ, you are to engage in the most secret and important mission ever taken up by a Christian soldier.' He watched both men draw a deep intake of breath. 'Julian of Mans, you were fighting for Prince Waimar in Salerno, protecting the coast from Saracen raids. You know well the evils that these devils may cause on Christian ground. The bloodshed of their filth mucks a great extension of known lands, from the kingdoms of Spain, through Lybia, across the Holy Land, all the way to the far lands of the East. They are in the islands of the interior sea and they are expanding their Mahommedhan faith. This has been a late concern of John Fasanus and I heartily and spiritually sympathise with the need to reverse the threat. I have humbly asked the Most Holy Redeemer that sponsors this basilica of ours for His divine light on my thoughts, for who am I but an ignorant peasant? Yet, no change of mind or spirit has He sent to me. It is a massive endeavour, that will cost nations, gold, bread and precious Christian blood, but aided through our Lord Jesus Christ's most holy wisdom, I try to gather strength now to assemble the powers of all Italian princes and margraves to unite and drive the Mahommedhans out of our seas.'

'It's an eternal fight Beatissimo Padre', Buonaccorso let slip out. He instantaneously lowered his gaze and waited, as regret for having interrupted the pontiff corroded his skin. Finally his eyes shot up again, to see the pope staring and him and opening a strange smile.

'Much more than an eternal fight, Buonaccorso, the Mohammedans are an enemy that will soon annihilate us from existence. Our blood will be turned into sand and blown away from knowledge, and no one else will be left. No more Christians, no more faith. We lose it and we leave God on His own. We cannot let this happen, since we enjoy the grace of having been redeemed by the precious blood of His Son, our Lord Jesus Christ.' The pope stood up and continued, slowly walking towards the men on their knees. 'God certainly needs His lambs around Him and, as the pastor of Christ, I have been burdened with the post to protect His herd. And do you know how we start? It is very simple: We simply have no choice.' Now he was standing in front of both. His rotund body towering above the soldiers. 'Three weeks ago we received the most dreadful news from my namesake, the Patriarch of Constantinople.' Both men looked up at him. His eyes were popping out of his face. 'It seems that a most un-Christian force, the mad caliph Al-Hakim, of Egypt, could be looking to seize the holiest of places. The very Church of the Holy Sepulchre, in Jerusalem!'

The pope watched them tremble. Eyebrows shooting up and tense shoulders. '*That* is what I want to see! I rejoice to witness God-fearing men shivering with excitement to engage into this mission to triumph against the pagans. There is no time, and Christianity relies on your bravery and faith to save its holiest of relics from peril and desecration. The enemies are coming and we must needs gather a proper army. If you accept this mission, you will be taking no more than twenty men with you, aided by nothing else but the mighty hand of Christ. Yes, only twenty soldiers! And you must set sail in no more than two days, to the Holy Land.'

The men had lost their colour. But Sergius did not wait for their acceptance of such a holy mission. A *no* just would not be considerable, considerate or considered. The pope called for his factotum to take both visitors to the elite Lateran century, where a tesserarius would help them select the men to follow in the ship. They were all to be in Porto at the break of two days. Upon arrival in the Holy Land, they should find their way into Jerusalem and join other Christians, locals and pilgrims, in defending the holy tomb of the Redeemer.

'My dearest apologies for such a rushed convocation and quick dispatch, but time is running against us.' the pope said. 'The great men of Christendom are ignoring the gravity of the moment, refusing to seize the opportunity to reinforce and unite the Holy Church around the blessed footprints of Jesus Christ. Neither the princes of Italy, or the emperor, nor the Roman families have acknowledged the threat of the pagans in Italy, and least in the Holy Land. It will be you, much greater men, who take upon this rather solitary burden.'

He solemnly blessed them, bid them farewell and, as the factotum was hurrying them out of the office, Buonaccorso humbly turned to the pope and delivered a last minute request, less as a condition, but more as an imploration. 'Will the Beatissimo Padre allow us to see and greet our old friend Brother John Fasanus in the monastery of San Aristo, in Johannispolis?'

'Of course you have my blessings' he pope said with a frank smile that showed his front teeth only, 'But you must fly! Not only have you little time for your most sacred burden, but I also hear that Brother John Fasanus is enduring his last earthly tribulations among mortals. *Deus vobiscum.*'

Moments later, as Julian still tended the tired horses at the patio of San Paolo Fuori le Mura, he heard a loud cry. Rushing to the side door of the basilica he found Buonaccorso on his knees, weeping.

'He's dead!' moaned the Pavese Leopard. 'He went this morning. The pheasant will be watching us from his flight above'.

They had a teary ride to Porto.

It was a glorious morning that nineteenth day of October of the year of our Lord of 1009 when, after being delayed for a few days by a ferocious gale, a roman ship disembarked twenty two armed Christians in the busy, exotic and most inconspicuous port city of Jaffa, in the Holy Land.

While trying to regain their movements in the firmness of land under a baking sun and a frenzied flock of seabirds, Julian and Buonaccorso struggled to battle through a multitude of merchants and slaves that surrounded the ship and exchanged energetic shouts with the captain, who did not seem to be in any fashion affected by that harassment.

The harsh sounds of those outlandish words and the cries of the birds hammered through Buonaccorso's ears, as he entered an intimidating sea of different people, dark and strange, with distinct shapes, features and colours of skin, dressed in exotic robes and drowned in a thick and smothering layer of the most peculiar fragrances and scents. While mesmerised by the glossy, darkened eyelids that many man seemed to display, perhaps out of fevers caused by local maladies, Buonaccorso lost sight of Julian.

The Pavese Leopard was subtly pushed and carried away by the flow of the colourful mob, finding himself taken to freer spaces, on doorways and corners where he felt his vulnerability, exposing the disparity of his appearance to the sharp awareness of the crowd.

He was approached several times and heard incomprehensible words, but it did not take too long for him to hear in good Lombard: 'Are you a Christian? Coming from Rome?'

What Buonaccorso initially could not have distinguished from two standing logs behind him, covered in rags and hair, were actually two old men. Their skin was dark, the sun having fried them to that colour.

'Are you Lombards?' he asked with suspicion, hopping a safe step back. 'Lepers? Are you lepers?'

'No, we are Tedeschi, from Bamberg', said one of them. 'No more than humble pilgrims of Christ into this land of the Devil.' The other man just smiled a toothless gum and nodded.

'I have only arrived' said a tense Buonaccorso, but more at ease for actually hearing his language. 'I was merely taking a stroll, but my ship is over in the pier.' He tried a shy smile to cheer the two Germans. 'We have soldiers. *Two decurie* of them. We must find our way to the Church of the Holy Sepulchre.'

'For what?' the same man asked with a nervous laugh. The other just kept smiling and nodding.

'We were sent by Pope Sergius IV.'

'A new pope? For what?' The man seemed tense.

'To protect the Holy Sepulchre against the pagans.' Buonaccorso said with some doubtful bemusement, as if this would not be obvious to any good Christian.

To his most shocked surprise, the man laughed, loud and theatrically, but stopped immediately and frowned with anger, raising a stiff dried twig of a finger towards the soldier's face. 'You are late!' he spat. 'Yesterday the church was razed to the ground. Go now! Go, soldier and pick up the pieces. The tomb of Jesus Christ is buried under ashes, rubble and the boots of two scores of Fatimid pagans!'

Buonaccorso almost squealed. He ran away, leaving the Germans from his sight as fast as he could, while the other man just kept nodding and smiling.

Livid with deception, the Pavese Leopard, delivered the heart-breaking news at the port. It made Julian fall on his knees. What had happened? *Was God distracted when He allowed the gale to keep that ship at sea? Why did He bring us here?* What could have been more important than the place that celebrated His Son's sacrifice for redeeming the sins of men?

One day! One day only would have made all the difference.

Had all papal troops arrived one day before, they could have easily stopped the Fatimid marauders from entirely tearing down the most important site in all of Christianity.

An interminable flock of seagulls kept hysterically screaming above Julian.

The Dagger of Attila

In the year or our Lord of 1016, a small crowd in Lucca watched the drowning of a person who had just been accused of sorcery. It happened on the old bridge of San Frediano. No written memories or records were kept of that.

Nobody can ever erase bad reminiscences, but an entire group can easily forget. With the passing of one generation, the incident had been entirely erased from memory.

'Here is how a witch is born:'
'On every fifteenth of June, the ghost of San Pellegrino gallops through the mountains and valleys on a blind horse, seeding faerie dust on the ground. Whenever the dust settles on ancient holy ground, it sprouts into the uovo malefico, the evil egg, the red fly agaric. These mushrooms will grow on a circular pattern, called faery rings for a good cause, as they usually harbour faeries, the small linchetti. Some know these small people as folletti or buffardelli. They are tiny prickly things. They will bring a pregnant cow to give birth into this fairy ring. The calf and placenta must fall within the circle of ovuli malefici. The cow will be so ravenous that she will try to eat the placenta, as cows do, but the linchetti must not allow it. They should give her the calf to eat instead. The linchetti then go into a village nearby and search through the privies, latrines and chamber pots, trying to find traces of hoiste, the bread that received Eucharistic Consecration. Once they find the debris of the Holy Body of Christ that has been excreted by a sinner deserving of absolution, they bring it back into the faery ring on a macabre ritual march, placing it on the cow's placenta. For the next four moons, the linchetti guard a vigil over the host-sprinkled placenta, protecting it from carrion feeders, especially from the horrible St. Jerome Flies, minuscule beetles with human arms and legs. On the fifth moon, a complete baby is formed from the placenta in the ring. A baby girl, for somehow it seems that most witches are women. As soon as the child starts to bellow with life, the linchetti feed it with the uovo malefico and take it to a foster home, so that human parents may find it and raise the baby witch without knowing the sin they are committing. The tiny imps will still surreptitiously watch over the child and protect it. So, we all know of the cemetery on the top of the Altar hill,

where quite often a ring of *ovuli malefici* is seen. Well, I tell you this is how Maria Tenebrosa was spawned. Immanuel and Elvira found the baby at their door a month before the real baby from Elvira was due. They took it in and, on the same night, Elvira gave birth to a dead child, which was thrown into the Lima. We all remember how Maria came into this world a month before...'

'Do we, Bernardo?' asked an indignant villager. 'With all respect, do we really remember any of this you tell us?'

Bernardo could only hold his laughter with a half-hidden smile behind tight lips.

'Bernardo, this is bloody irresponsible!' said Amadeo, the innkeeper. 'Most of these folk here now actually believe in your crap.'

There was sudden outburst of *I don't*s from several tables.

'Yes, it cannot be true that she lost her baby,' shouted one drunken pilgrim.

Amadeo continued 'The next person to learn of this will be Maria Maddalena of the Burle et Malachi. Then it will be like having to deal with Satanas himself.'

'There you go!' Bernardo grinned to Amadeo.

But before the shepherd could add another comment, Amadeo held him by his shirt collar and snarled on his face 'Tell them the truth! It's better for you, for me and for all of them.'

Most landlords would have been offended, but Bernardo just made an annoyed face and stood up to leave the tavern. 'Folks, these stories were nothing more than a big joke,' he said. 'You were right: I made them up! Maria Tenebrosa is just a horribly unfair young woman.'

But it was too late. By the time he left the tavern into a raging storm outside, unless for a few exceptions, most of them villagers had a clear explanation for why Maria was such an evil-filled woman.

Meanwhile, Amadeo wondered why it was taking so long for his Divina to get back home.

Turul shrieked high above the valley.

An unmistakably tiny point lost in the intense blue, with its majestic open wings paralysed in flight and a diamond-shaped tail. For Béla, the shadow of the lammergeyer was soothing. It placated his fears.

Béla was afraid of Lucca.

And afraid of that ride with the Devil.

Both horses were slowly dragging their pace through the dusty road down the Serchio. Ahead of the pair, an armed rider watched for the road. Behind them, two other riders to protect the rear. Times of piracy and death.

Each of the five horses had to traverse the Serchio at a time. The narrow ferry crossed where the abandoned hospital stood, opposite to Traghetto. Above Fornulo, the river had a few fords, but down towards Lucca it meant ferries or boats.

Never too deep, never too wide, the calm and copious waters of the Serchio harboured water demons that lived in deep currents and occasionally snatched reckless travellers out of their balance. The poor souls would take a good beating from these creatures and their drowned bodies would usually end up caught on the shallow rocks in Lucca, startling early women who came for their washing.

The ferryman Old Testa had a shameless loathing for Béla. Every time Immanuel assigned the táltos a task in Lucca, the loyal Magyar had to patiently endure a sore crossing of the Serchio under Old Testa's grunts and curses. But this time Old Testa was behaving. There were men-at-arms arranged by the landlord Cunimundinghi to ride with the táltos companion, the future landlady Maria Maddalena of the Burle et Malachi.

Master and apprentice waited for the remaining riders to be crossed. Maria kept slipping out teasing remarks, mocking the táltos for his poor riding skills, bad control of the language and for his utter lugubrious mood. Béla was more than displeased with the girl's presence on his mission to Lucca. He was certain that his apprentice had been the causer for his special designation to go and see her grandfather, Battista Burle.

Béla had been asked by Immanuel to go to the city and deposit into the banker's care and guard a granting document. A *launegildo*. An allowance ratified by Fulcardo Cunimundinghi granting to Amadeo, the innkeeper, and his daughter Ginevra a novel right to any villager in Chifenti: the free and eternal exploitation of a fairly large piece of land on the back of the inn. A land equivalent to thirty eight *heredia* – morns – or more specifically seventy six *jugera* – yokes. In this area, a ploughman had the equivalent of an area to be tilled with a yoke of oxen seventy six times, between ploughing and resting the animals. Such a document entailed the strictest attention and safeguard, after all it would increase the backyard of the inn thirty eight-fold, not all of it arable land, climbing up to the hills of Cunimundinghi land. And why had Fulcardo been so generous to Amadeo?

Every since the disappearance of Divina, a tragic scenario that grew ahead of Amadeo and their daughter Ginevra, the already busy widower entrepreneur Immanuel Ben-Malachi had fallen into self-disgrace. He shrouded himself with guilt, feeling accountable for having sent Divina to watch over the labour of Lucia Cunimundinghi. And if remorse corroding his heart did not seem to be enough, Immanuel also had to bear those inconvenient suggestions from Béla's delirious fears and suspicions. The táltos had dared to suggest that Maria Maddalena could have caused the death of not only Lucia Cunimundinghi and her new-born heir, but also the disappearance of Divina.

'Nonsense', grunted Immanuel to his old friend. 'You are throwing bones randomly, just like Turul does. Leave this filth for the vulture, Béla.'

On the night when Fulcardo lost his wife and unborn child, Maria Maddalena had been back at the Burle et Malachi house in Corsena before the sun rose. She grunted a few words on the deaths of the child and the Cunimundinghi woman before her father's stunned, hopeless eyes. She gulped down a cold goblet of spiced wine and fell deep asleep on her palliasse.

Amadeo, the innkeeper enquired about his wife to passers-by. By the time he was suffocated by apprehension and it was generally accepted that Divina was missing, the sun had long hidden behind the Apuani. Too late for a organising a searching party, too dark to hunt.

They combed the valley for six days. Divina, much more than shunned by her apostasy for abandoning the sacred orders, was loved by folk of the Serchio for her tender dedication to each traveller who crossed the door at the inn. Help for the hunt came in the shape of valiant volunteers, from as far as the village of San Bartolomeo Outside the Abbey, more than ten *leugae* to the south. Even the Rolandinghi family of Barga, up the river, heartily sent a battalion of farmers, brick masons and fishermen. So many people searching and never any sign of Divina. Every single bush across the lower hills was beaten. They turned the hay of every barn. Segugio hounds from the Cunimundinghi cry were set on the higher woods, trying to catch a whiff of Divina's scent but strangely, they always came back to the east river road. Hooks were thrown in to the darkest pools of the Serchio, hiding places of the *marabbecche*, water goblins and hags, but this time the iron snarls brought back only dark weeds and stones.

A *balivo* – bailiff – from Lucca arrived on the fourth day after the disappearance, thanks to a message from Immanuel and Battista Burle's city contacts. In spite of the uproar caused by the disappearance, the balivo did not accept to summon a *hutesium et clamor*, the hue and cry, for a true crime had not been determined, neither a perpetrator identified.

The balivo stayed at the inn, but on his last day in Chifenti he rode to Corsena, where Immanuel received him to report a missing dagger. The officer had also brought some documents to the Bukhari, sent by Battista Burle.

'Ah, the *chartula*! Thank you, bailiff. This is exactly what I wanted', said Immanuel with a troubled expression, letting away a cordial, but very brief smile. 'It's about time I settle this!' he said to himself, rolling the chartula carefully. He looked up to the tall balivo. 'What about the search? Any sign of Divina?'

'Nothing, I regret to say. I have already spoken to anyone I could in this stretch where she vanished, between Anchiano and Corsena. Even that idiot from Chifenti we managed to get a few words from.'

'Spatola? Did you hurt him?' Immanuel asked.

'Nothing more than a good beating, but the poor creature knows nothing. Anyway, it seems that the poor woman could have slipped and fallen into the flooded Serchio during that stormy night. Some fear bandits, who would have thrown her tiny body in the river after probably violating her, for no riches would have been found in her possession. But frankly, lazy bandits would not be out under the storm. Saracens from their camp in Liguria have raided villages and hamlets across the passes, sending hundreds of refugees to Camporgiano, but that is too far from here, and may God keep them away from these valleys. And I could not see any reason to justify their presence on the eastern bank in that part of the valley.'

'Poor Amadeo...' sighed Immanuel.

'Indeed,' confirmed the bailiff. 'Life is not going to be easy for him, especially with a young child under his care. He should surely find himself another wife. A big vigorous one this time, which could help on the heavy tavern duties and be able to bear him male heirs...'

Immanuel had lowered his eyes, imposing a proper grief posture on himself, as any good Christian would. They both waited for a dutiful instant of silence.

It was the bailiff who broke it, by clearing his throat and speaking with a freshened tone: 'And is there anyone else I should be speaking to, here in Corsena? About the missing dagger of yours… or the missing woman?'

Béla, thought Immanuel. He knew the old vulture had his own version of the facts. An insanely wicked fantasy, where Maria Maddalena could have been answerable not simply for the loss of Lucia and her child, but also for the disappearance of Divina. According to the táltos, Divina would promptly unveil the charlatanry of Maria if she was ever back at the Borgo. Surely this was the last chance for the bailiff to look at this disappearance from a new angle, to connect it to the family tragedy of the Cunimundinghi manor. Maybe Béla's derangement could in the end lead to new clues. He wouldn't have taken the dagger, no, but he certainly believed in his own version of Divina's disappearance. For the sake of universal fairness, over any eventual annoyance, embarrassment and disgrace that an involvement of Maria Maddalena in a possible demise of Divina could bring to his family, it would be quite just and truthful to bring the bailiff to the shed at the baths. To talk to Béla. Immanuel lowered his eyes again and felt the weight of a colossal boulder being amassed onto his shoulders as he answered 'No, balivo. There is no one else around who can enrich your knowledge of these most unfortunate occurrences.'

'I'm afraid this is it, then' said the bailiff with a frown. 'I am calling the search off. I must go back to Lucca in no time. Papal troops are expected to arrive on the next few days, going to front the Saracens in Liguria. Still, I will send messages to the communities down the Serchio, to stay on the lookout, and to the bankers in Lucca to watch for the dagger.'

He never noticed that Immanuel was looking away, to hide the tears.

The bailiff continued 'Believe me, during that swollen night when this woman vanished, the river was so furious that it covered the bridge of San Frediano. The waters of the Serchio brought a few mementos from these valleys. Bloated sheep and other beasts' carcasses washed up on the flooded banks in Lucca. Now we are smothered into stink and flies. Anyway, we may still find a body. Have a good day, Immanuel Malachi.'

No body was ever found.

'Divina ran away with the pirates, of course!' said Maria Maddalena, who sat at the large oaken table, on Fulcardo Cunimundinghi's side. Her eyes were blazing iron spheres. 'What else would you expect from an apostate?' she concluded.

'That's enough, Maria', Immanuel hissed through the few teeth that touched when he clenched his jaws. 'This is a painful insult to Divina and totally disrespectful to my friend Amadeo. Besides, how many times do I have to say that there are no pirates in this side of the Apuane?'

'You can think whatever you want, my father' she said. 'You are not made of these Tuscan stones! You are from another place and time. I know these valleys, I know these lands, I know the river and I know these people. Divina is no more than a cheap harlot.'

Immanuel stood up, trembling with anger, towering over his daughter and the Cunimundinghi landlord, whose head buried between the shoulders. 'Maria Maddalena!' he roared, 'I demand respect, not only because I am your father, but because I am maybe a hundred times a better Christian than you are! Look at yourself in a mirror with your eyes opened at least once in your life. Have you ever thought that all that you have become is thanks to your mother and I? I was twice as old as you are and travelled half of the known world when I brought you into God's gift of life. I brought you up, respecting Elvira's wishes, for you to be a physician, a midwife, to give continuation to the baths, to run the papal lands in Corsena. To be a pious soul and help the needed without asking back. Your mother wanted a daughter who could follow the generous example of our Lord Jesus Christ; the perfection of Saint Luke the physician; the zeal of Saint James and certainly the contemplation of Saint Mary Magdalene. We entrusted Béla with his craft to form your knowledge, but you abused us all!'

That was a gigantic Immanuel Ben-Malachi, not the frail convert that roamed the Serchio under the protection of the pope. Here was the physician who had travelled pestilent deserts and beaten death. Here was the hero who had crossed the sea to help a king gain his crown. That was the Bukhari, proud descendant of the lost tribe of Nephtali, steaming the words out of his mouth as his crooked finger pointed at Maria's nose. 'You are already fifteen, and a cheat! Folk in Corsena and Chifenti have withstood your cruelty and arrogance all these years. Enough! Now I ask, once and for all, that you shut your poisonous trap and let me deal with Fulcardo Cunimundinghi on my own. I certainly have not invited you to be sitting at this table with me. The matters I have with him do not concern you, so leave us for now, or you will regret this forever.'

Maria's eyes lost their shine. Their gray turned into granite. Her thumbs started massaging her own fingers, as caution told her to keep any words for herself or later. Fulcardo turned to Maria and begged with his eyes. She didn't lowered hers, but left the dining hall, towards the bedrooms.

When the echoes of his bellows had been muffled by an absolute silence, Immanuel sat down, looked at Fulcardo and, strangely, smiled.

'These are the documents,' he said coldly, pushing them across the table to Fulcardo.

The lord of Anchiano looked at them and chose one to read, for he could do it on his own. He was a large dark man, a bit unrefined of manners and thoughts but strikingly good looking for a man who had just lost his wife a few days before. His visitor patiently waited until he had finished reading the last document. Fulcardo paused for a while, thoughtful. He bit his upper lip, stared at the ceiling and finally asked Immanuel with a squint 'Are you really sure you want to do this?'

Immanuel sighed and patiently explained 'You are riding yourself of a huge debt in pawns, which is three times the value of that piece of land. Those slopes are not being productive and no difference will it make on your earnings in any taille. The launegildo is not conceding the land to the Rolandinghi or to any Lucchese family, so you do not have to worry about neighbours on your doorstep. The land will go to Amadeo, the innkeeper, and his daughter Ginevra. The lands of the Cunimundinghi are still immeasurable around these valleys. No fear will you have any more that Battista Burle passes your debts onto the care of another creditor family, which I certainly could, or to wake-up with unexpected collectors with a battalion of men-at-arms visiting you here in Anchiano.'

Fulcardo's eyes flicked quickly to the sides. 'But what about your daughter Maria? What would she think of this launegildo?'

Immanuel curled his lip 'What about my daughter? What are you asking me, man of God? Do I give a damn about my daughter's opinion on this affair which is nobody else's but yours and mine? And by the great Lord, Father above, she better have nothing to do with this matter. Nothing!' He stood up and walked around to where Fulcardo sat shrinking into his chair. His foaming face came close to the landlord's terrified. 'And if you don't agree with the launegildo now, I will never offer it to you again. Deal with your debts and with a bastard child, for I will never bless that fruit of yours that Maria carries in her womb!'

Fulcardo's face contorted with disgust. 'How dare you?' he squealed, standing tall and touching his nose with Immanuel's.

The old man did not move. His eyes were infused with blood. 'Oh, pull yourself together and be a real man at least once in your life, Fulcardo Cunimundinghi! A true man is much more than one that spreads maiden's legs while his wife dies from childbirth! If you honour your deeds and your title, do as I tell you! Put your name on this chartula and be happy to be rid of your debts!'

On that afternoon, Immanuel Malachi came back to Corsena with a chartula containing a launegildo signed by Fulcardo Cunimundinghi, ceding all lands of Chifenti behind the village, with no right to receive or charge any taille, to whomever Immanuel determined, namely the villager Amadeo, the innkeeper, and his daughter Ginevra. Other letters were signed by Immanuel, pardoning all of Fulcardo's debts to himself and to be witnessed by Battista Burle.

Immanuel did not go home, but headed towards the baths, to Béla's shed. He passed by the enormous vulture sitting outside. The round red eyelids opened wide to stare at him. 'Are you well, Béla?' he asked, entering the shed.

'My guts are much better than when Divina disappeared, fönök', the táltos answered bitterly 'but my heart is still in pain for the losses of life.'

'Can you go to Lucca for me one more time?'

Béla's legs lost their bones. He felt incredibly tired. 'But Lucca, fönök? Why Lucca? Why me? Send Giacomo instead! He is a good big boy, and he has gone to Lucca before.'

'Giacomo is still a child, Béla. I need you to go, one last time. We owe this to Amadeo, after sending his wife to Anchiano.'

Béla let his shoulders drop. 'Well, then what is the story this time?'

Immanuel explained it all, as the táltos just nodded.

Outside, massive wings beat vigorously as Turul took flight.

Early on the next day, Béla walked quickly past Chifenti. He did not have time to drop by the inn and greet Amadeo or to appreciate the fairy company of little Ginevra. He was to meet a group of riders from Anchiano, who would accompany him from the ferry crossing to Lucca. There, he would deposit the chartula Immanuel had given him under the care of Battista Burle. The document that would transfer a large piece of land from Fulcardo to Amadeo. A mission noble enough, he concluded. The last of his lifetime to the hideous city, and giving some closure to the whole affair of Divina's disappearance. So good was the thought of this being the last of his visits to Lucca that Béla did not give up when he saw that Maria Maddalena was among the riders to accompany him to the city.

In that same morning, something smelled foul.

Spatola was eating roasted chestnuts at the inn's yard. He sat on the floor, by the stables, when a sickening whiff pierced through his nose. The last chunk of chestnut he had just swallowed came unexpectedly back to the top of his tongue, bringing with it an acrid taste of vomit. He knew that wrong smell. He could recognise it from those colourful vegetable carts that came from Lucca. But people in Corsena and Chifenti did not appreciate it much. It was only Immanuel who bizarrely enjoyed that pungent herb, he knew it. At least the idiot this time was not him. As far as the herb was concerned, Carpo was as normal as all the villagers along the Serchio.

He got up and followed the smell, which was strangely strong. It got stronger and wronger as he passed around a fence and arrived at the river junction. He was tasting the water from the Serchio, when he quickly spat it out and started to run.

The táltos had taught him, a year before Maria Maddalena stepped in as apprentice, all about those horrible omens that the smell raised. He ran to Béla's shed to find it empty. Giacomo was selecting mulberry leaves nearby, sitting with Francesco and Piero.

'Béla?' said Giacomo with a disarming smile, 'I think he is gone to Lucca'.

The three boys were startled to see the village idiot disappearing into a mad run, towards the ford, on the way to Chifenti.

'You are not going to try to catch up with Béla, are you, Spatola?'

But he was already gone.

Béla looked up to the sky, verifying for Turul. He sighed with ease when he spotted the vulture miles above.

'Your eyes are as sharp as your buzzard's, Béla' said Maria Maddalena with a formidable smile 'but regrettably your mind is already corroded by your age.'

Béla looked at Maria with despise. She looked more beautiful than ever, towering, a splendid red hair and a rosy face. They rode side by side and he could see the shape of her body. The whole realisation hit him like a stone on the face and when he spoke, his words came with hot, spitting anger. 'You don't fool me, child. I know it all. I can see it all! You did not give Lucia Cunimundinghi the black comb syrup to hold the blood in, but the woodruff concoction with holy grass, to thin the blood out!'

'What? Holy grass? *Capelli della nonna?* You are indeed a madman, after all.' Maria was laughing with disgust. 'Ridiculous. And my father is another nitwit to leave such important, documents under your insane care. Both of you, no better than Spatola. Actually I think you two idiots should sit around with Spatola and scrape for leftovers on the back of that filthy inn'.

Béla continued. 'Yes, and the dagger, where is it? Where is Attila's dagger, Maria Maddalena? You have it, I know. Golden and murderous. Did you cut the umbilical chord with it? Did you? I told you not to use gold!'

'If I had the dagger with me, you old, sick man, I would cut your venomous tongue with it right now and feed it to your vulture' she snorted. 'I just cannot believe that Fulcardo would negotiate with you people.'

'*Us people?* You are made from the same shit that we are. You are no better just because you carry a Cunimundinghi child in your womb, Maria.'

'Shut up, you silly fool! Shut up now or I will throw you in the river!' she hissed.

'Just like you did to Divina?' asked Béla with poison.

'Hey, you, old man.' It was a voice from the escort rider coming behind. 'Do not bother the lady. We are here to escort you, and not to protect her from your foreign grunts. Keep quiet and do not say a word anymore. Lucca is still far and the sun is scorching.'

They continued in silence. Maria with a light grin on her face.

By mid-afternoon, when Lucca raised its towers in front of the riders, Béla felt the usual discomfort the city stirred in him. He would brave the buildings' menacing gaze one last time. He would cross the narrow fetid streets, dodge the suspicious Lucchese and reach that safe haven of Battista Burle's. He would deliver the chartula and wait for the confirmatory notes and testimonials from the banker. Then, he would be free to return and spent the end of his days in the comfort of Corsena, never again to face that city.

The horses slowly walked through the bridge of San Frediano. The hooves soundly hitting wood planks and stone, accounting for the repeated patching the bridge had suffered over the centuries. The river ran wide, dark green and hopefully not too deep on that north side of Lucca where San Frediano had dug its bed with a rake.

Spatola could not run any more. His legs were numb and his breathing dry and dusty. He finally saw the busy bridge of San Frediano ahead of him, as the road turned sharply to the south, crossing the Serchio onto Lucca. They were there: slowly reaching the middle of the bridge, four riders rode in a spaced line. Béla was there, for Spatola's relief. But for his terror, so was Maria Maddalena. The scent of the river got stronger.

Béla observed Maria, riding calmly in front of him. She stared at the waters. They all seemed to be looking at the river that firmly slithered underneath them. All the Lucchese and visitors traversing that long old bridge did it slowly, their eyes fixed on the water, including the horses, as if they had all been charmed by it. But the running water livened the táltos' senses.

He looked at the girl again. Why had she come all the way into the city with him? Would she want to interfere? What was she bringing with her? Not yet sixteen and she seemed to run the Cunimundinghi lands, so what was she doing accompanying an old man to the bank, with only her satchel?

Her satchel.

Béla swiftly dismounted and sped his pace to reach into Maria Maddalena's satchel, while all riders stared at the slow flow of the Serchio.

'I was right!' he yelled.

Maria turned around startled, just to see Béla standing next to her on the edge of the bridge, his horse left behind. The táltos was smiling, admiring a stone-incrusted golden dagger he held on his hands.

'Give me that right now!' Maria screamed.

'I was right all the time', Béla said more to himself than to Maria. 'You stole it. You killed the Cunimundinghi baby with it. And Lucia! And Divina! You were going to sell this beautiful dagger, which was not yours but your father's. It belonged not to your filthy hands, but to the great Attila's. Or maybe you would put it under pawn to pay for the Cunimundinghi's debts, so that the stupid man would not have to sell his lands to your father...' the táltos was so excited with his discovery and disgusted with that woman that emotion made him say those words in Magyarul.

Maria did not dismount. 'Help!' she yelled even louder. 'He stole the dagger! He is the thief who stole my father's dagger! Help!'

The escort riders dismounted and ran to the middle of the bridge. Old Béla was swift enough to stand with his feet on the edge board and reach his hand out with the dagger, over the dark murky water. 'You two come any closer and the dagger flies into the river.'

Maria was quick to understand what he meant and stopped the men before they reached Béla. She jumped out of her saddle. 'Give me that dagger, you fool of a vulture' she growled.

Béla giggled. 'No...never!' He stayed frozen in position, the precious dagger hanging from his fingers above the Serchio.

Maria turned around to the people who had been surprised by the commotion, shouting with her lungs '*Stregone! Borde! Stregone!* This man is a sorcerer! *Stregone! Borde! Sorcerer!* This foreigner has the dagger stolen from my father!'

'You *witch*!' Béla hissed. He nervously shouted to the crowd 'Pay no heed to her!' But nobody understood a word.

Maria Maddalena continued, as loud as she could, without taking her eyes from the old man standing on the edge of the bridge. 'He is a sorcerer! This filthy *stregone* gave me poison instead of remedies. He must have been the murderer of Lucia Cunimundinghi of Anchiano and her unbaptised child. He must have sold Divina of Chifenti to the Saracens!'

'Stregone!' someone else shouted behind her. Other cries of 'traitor' and 'sorcery' arose from the crowd that was gathering round the commotion. As they came nearer to Maria Maddalena, together with her escorts to close around the edge were Béla stood, she screamed 'Stay away! I will deal with him.' They all froze, but she leaped to the edge and grabbed onto Béla's fist, securing the dagger.

Maria was bigger and stronger than Béla. She slowly pulled his fist towards her, as her other hand held onto to the táltos free arm. They struggled for a couple of seconds, before the old man twisted his wrist and snatched it free from her grasp, bringing the dagger's blade to dive deep into his belly.

Spatola fell on his knees before he reached the bridge. He had just seen the old táltos, one of the few persons he had ever met that treated him decently, being stabbed.

Maria Maddalena did not wait or loosened her grip on the old man. She grabbed onto the blood-greased golden hilt and tried to pull it free off Béla. But the táltos kept it firmly interred into his guts. As Maria desperately tried to yank it out, she was horrified to see him smile languidly and firmly embrace her with his free arm, whispering in her ear with the most clear Tuscan words she had ever heard him say: 'Maria Maddalena I am indeed a sorcerer. I am a táltos! And I put a curse on you. You will live to be unhappy, to see this child you carry in your womb suffering the same death that I suffer now.'

'He is mad!' she screamed, terrorised. 'Get him off me!' The escorts and other man came to release the sorcerer from the young lady.

But he held on to her like a tick, the blooded hilt between their bodies. 'And if you wish to break this curse and save your child, Maria Maddalena' he slobbered into her ear, 'you will have to implore to the *Devil* himself! A *witch* can do that!'

She screamed and pushed him back. Béla's grasp slipped off, and he was thrown over the bridge's edge. They all saw the old man being flown and splashing into the water, disappearing behind a dark whirlpool of bubbles, with a golden dagger dug into his body.

Spatola squealed and ran down to the river's bank.

Above on the skies, something shrieked. Insistently.

Béla was deep inside a dark pool. He looked around and saw the dark green of the Serchio. The flavour of the water was dusty and foul. Why did it have to taste like decay? What was that? Perhaps a herb. Then, just ahead of him, something stood. Dark and fetid. Béla snatched the dagger off his body, and the dark thing went away, with a quick swirl of its legs, like a scared triton. Feeling the taste of his own blood in the water, the táltos touched the stony river bed and gathered his last burst of strength to stab it with the dagger. Attila's weapon stayed there, at the bottom of the Serchio, dug into the stones, to be forever forgotten under silt and weeds, to be covered one day by wood and stone, debris of the bridge that would sooner or later fall apart into pieces.

Béla stayed still in the bottom and allowed the water to fill his lungs. The taste was initially unbearable, but soon it turned sweeter and soft on the tongue. And the water was white. White as milk. It carefully involved him with a comforting warmth. He felt better and took impulse to reach the surface. It was not deep at all. He stood half immersed in the middle of a lake. On the banks around him, Béla saw the angels bathing.

At the bridge of San Frediano, the silent crowd watched the dark water of the Serchio that escaped away towards Pisa and the Ligurian Sea. There were bubbles coming from several spots, but the old man did not resurface.

Maria was on her knees. The dagger was gone.

The escorts came around with her horse and helped her to stand and mount. 'Come, Maria Maddalena, the old sorcerer is gone, probably just as well. We must be off to take the chartula to Battista Burle and tomorrow we should see the balivo to report Béla's crimes.'

She pulled the reins to turn the horse towards Lucca, leaving the crowd in the bridge. But just before reaching the bank, Maria rode closer to the edge, staring at the water. It was probably less than a second or two, but she saw it clearly and it made her hand instinctively embrace herself, the baby inside her: A dark shape had moved inside the Serchio. It stood in the bottom, looking up at her with eyes of fire.

Then, it smiled.

A Familiar Old Face

"Through the divine sanctuary
I will penetrate the divine Tomb,
and with deep reverence
will venerate that Rock.
And as I venerate that worthy Tomb,
surrounded by its conches
and columns surmounted by golden lilies,
I shall be overcome with joy."
Sophronius, Patriarch Of Jerusalem - 634-638 A.D

It had been hurting for a lifetime. Hell was indeed an eternity of pain and torture.

Initially, death had felt like a soothing slumber, but shortly the ache returned, pulsating, bulging, as if crushing his bones, all over his body, so intense that it awakened him up into a world of silence and utter darkness. As if he had been buried alive. It could have been years of punishment. Hunger and thirst thrived in hell and the eternal flames that licked over the sinners in damnation must have been the blazing pain that corroded his insides and pressed against his skin. There were no demons executing the torments. Just the torture of loneliness and agonising grief. Years of condemnation in burning blackness, eternal, unmovable silent shadows.

Shadows that were suddenly broken by voices.

They were distant, thinned by the darkness, bringing with it new and deeper explosions of pain. His chest was squeezed and his legs were flattened, the whole body being torn apart. The voices came nearer as he felt himself being shaken. There were hands gripping his ankles and an excruciating twinge in all of his joints.

Unseen demons were grabbing him for a more intense session of punishment. A burst of pain exploded on his nose. And suddenly, as a deceitful mockery that there could be forgiveness for the sinners, a blast of light blinded him. Light for the first time in the eternity of hell, toasting his eyes deep into his head, but surprisingly uplifting. His whole body somehow was filled with its brightness. And blocking the refreshing light, there was a face. It remained immovable, looking at him. He forced his eyes to adjust but failed at it. The face remained behind a cloud, dark, blocking the beam of light, its long hair being pulled towards him, undistinguishable into the darkness. It was a tired face, but doubtless reassuring. The face was smiling, and a word came out of it. Not a word that he could recognise, but probably from the language of angels, for it somehow denoted joy, contrasting with the perpetual pain he had endured. Then, as the face tried to disentangle him from the darkness and bring him into the light, Nicodemus recognised it. It had come to save him. The Holy Face of Jesus Christ, his Saviour.

Julian of Mans was taken to the area where the church of the Holy Sepulchre had stood up to two days before, but now only a smouldering pile of ruins and ashes. A few large solid pillars still remained tall, where a rotunda was likely to have been, the *Anastasis*. A cautious crowd observed from all sides, nobody daring to step over the ruins, as if the remains of the desecrated holy ground would contaminate them with evil. Buonaccorso and the other soldiers stood nearby. Many shed tears of disappointment.

'What is everyone doing just standing there? Shouldn't we be picking up the pieces, to reconstruct this temple?' Julian asked the man who had taken them through the streets of Jerusalem. A soldier translated the question.

The man laughed and shook his head in disbelief. 'Reconstruct? Why? If the men of Al-Hakim have brought it down, why would we want to undo what's done?'

'Bring up during the day what the devil has torn down at night. Good will eventually stand!' The powerful voice was Buonaccorso's, who had just approached from the other side of the ruins.

The local man laughed again and was leaving, when Julian asked 'Are you not a Christian? Where are the Christians around here?'

The man nodded respectfully and said he was a good Muslim. And that apart from the pilgrims that had arrived on that day, they were not going to see any local Christians.

'Were they all killed?' Buonaccorso asked.

'No, but they are afraid and defenceless. None of them were killed when the men came and burned the church.' He meant again to leave, but added, 'that is, except for the keeper of the temple, a man called Nicodemus.'

'What did they do with him?' Julian asked. 'Did they take him with them?'

The man yelled something to the crowd. A few men came forward and told him something, pointing to an area in the ruins. 'These men say he was crushed by a falling roof. His body must still be there.'

'So there is exactly where we start!' Julian said, rubbing his hands. 'It's already been two days and nobody has raised a hand to reconstruct this sacred place. Let's start it by giving this Nicodemus a proper Christian burial. This is our job here. To protect the sacredness of this place.'

The sun was high when the soldiers initiated the cleaning job, lifting beams, carrying bricks and rocks to pile them on the surrounds. A few pilgrims joined them on the chore, triggering a loud crossover of languages, chants and prayers. As the local Christians got hold of the hearsay, they came out of their hideaways, slowly appearing, first to observe, but then to shyly join on the strenuous task.

'He's here!' someone shouted. They had located the body of Nicodemus. Although he had been smothered by a pile of beams and tiles, at least they had uncovered his feet. Grabbing at his ankles, three men tried to pull him out of the heap, but the weight above him seemed to be excessive. Julian decided to concentrate on thinning the pile of bricks above the corpse. As he pulled a few tiles, he uncovered a hollow area, where he could see the head of the keeper, laying on the ground level, a couple of feet below.

Then, reaching down and retrieving a stone that balanced on the keeper's face, Julian shivered with happiness, as he saw Nicodemus coughing and shutting his eyes tight against the light that entered the dusty area and bathed his face.

'He's alive!' he shouted, and kept smiling as Nicodemus, who fought to adjust his vision to the light. Julian was waiting in joy to welcome the keeper back to the world of the living, but Nicodemus stared at him as if he had seen a heavenly ghost.

The screams were heard from their backs. The soldiers turned around to see a group of women running towards them, not long after the crowd started to mumble as the dust and blood-covered Nicodemus had been brought up by Julian from the rubble. The women cried and yelled Nicodemus's name, taking hold of his broken body and carrying him with them, quickly disappearing with it ahead of their wailing.

A younger woman stayed behind for a while longer. Helena was experiencing a miraculous episode of much wider significance than the stupid holy fire of the kouvouklion, which she suspected of being a hoax that her father was responsible for. Helena had never been a great believer of miracles, for they seemed to be less important than the secrets that were kept away from her. But now it was different. This was like Eleazaros ressurected from his tomb, being brought back into life by a miracle of Christ, the Saviour. Her own father, raised from the rubble, saved by angels that had defied the determinations of Al-Hakim. She smiled in tears, looking humbly at the soldiers with a thankful stare, kindly sheltered by her powerful eyebrows. But when Julian climbed up of the hollow in the rubble and stood tall against the setting sun, his shadow stretched out over the girl. With her vision blocked, Helena could only see his tall silhouette in front of the light, with his hair being blown by the hot Mediterranean breeze that spoiled that pleasant afternoon, and the sunrays shooting up from his shoulders like celestial wings. Humbled by the dazzling vision, she fell on her knees and thanked the saviour *seraph* of her father, before turning around and disappearing in a crowd that slowly oozed out of the alleys.

'What did she say?' An exhausted Buonaccorso asked the soldier who spoke Greek.

'She says that Julian is a *soter* – saviour.'

The long lines of the Pavese Leopard's sweated, leathery face changed into firm, horizontal creases, framing a frank smile to Julian. 'I think she likes you, boy!'

Julian did not return the warmth. 'I don't think so.'

In a basement in the north-western quarter of the city, candles were lit. An unconscious man was brought out of a warm water bath and laid in rags among the dim light. Cleaning the injuries, removing old blood and dust, washing the bruises, gently rubbing ointments, applying plasters and bandages, Helena helped the other women on bringing her father back into the world of the living.

While they carefully and gently tended for Nicodemus, with soft words and tender touches, a group of men stood behind. Like the shadows of bears projected against the wall, the solemn bishops observed without looking directly, running their fingers through their wise beards and mumbling remarks of disapproval and blame. *Emotional! Careless!* How could the keeper have been so injudicious by escaping during the attack? He could have unveiled their hiding.

But the keeper was unaware of that. Nicodemus just snored profoundly.

'Be in peace...' wished Helena in a whisper.

Prayers were silently muttered throughout the night.

In the morning, his right eye opened. '*Soter!*' He shouted in a jerk of his head.

The women came quickly around, advising restraint and praising Jesus and the Saints for his recovery. 'I saw Him! I saw His face!' Nicodemus insisted, yelling to Helena, trying to seat himself up, against too many attentive feminine hands that kept him on what they thought better as his resting position.

'You saw what?' the women asked.

'I saw the face of the Soter! The Holy Face of the Christ! It is He who brought me back from the dead!' Nicodemus spoke with a smile of satisfaction. Cloudy eyes which looked elsewhere, towards a place where he had felt on the arms of the Saviour. A number of frowns, and the bishops grunted more disapproval.

Helena giggled generously. 'Father. That was not the Christ who showed His holy face to you. It is just the man who found you in the rubble. He's a *Roman*,' she said, beaming, eyebrows gliding high, as the sooty falcons that slit the skies of Jerusalem.

Nicodemus looked at her with a sceptical face, before rolling his eyes and falling back like a rock. As he dived into slumber, he muttered 'The Holy face of the Christ...I saw His face...'

'She is a morsel!' Buonaccorso said with a mischievous smile. Julian ignored. The leopard continued 'Did you see her eyes? Those eyebrows! The colour of her skin, the long, straight nose, and she moves so well... And I do think she likes you, Julian!'

He kept throwing bricks and burnt pieces of wood from the high pile of rubble that accumulated right where the kouvouklion used to be. Each of those unrecognisable parts of the Holy Sepulchre rolled down with a cloud of dust, landing in front on Julian, who silently lifted them and handed to a line of soldiers that orderly stacked them along a side alley.

The Pavese soldier continued 'Helena is here at this ruined site too often, while her father heals. All because of you!' He wiped his brow, exposing the shiny leather of forehead in the middle of a dust-covered head.

'I don't think so, Buonaccorso,' said Julian, raising his face to stare at the Pavese leopard. 'She comes here to see us all. Helena seems to be interested in any of us Romans, as she seems to believe we all are.'

'Do you reckon?' Buonaccorso had also stopped.

Julian turned to the other soldier lining up behind him. 'What do you think?'

They all agreed that she made no distinctions.

Buonaccorso's reply came almost immediately 'So she could even be interested in…me?'

Julian laughed and said 'Of course, Buonaccorso! You are a terribly attractive old goat!'

Buonaccorso was paralysed for almost a minute. Then, he disappeared.

Julian chuckled again and continued to pass more bricks to the soldiers.

'They've been saying over the last few days that Helena's father thinks he saw the face of Jesus Christ!' said one of the soldiers standing right behind Julian. 'And do you know whose face this was?'

'Of course I do.' Julian said patiently. 'It was my own face. But Nicodemus is not well yet. He is delirious. Let him be cared for and we will go to meet him as soon as his health allows for visitors. He will recognise my face easily.' Julian bent down, ready to lift a large brick, when his effort was neutralised by a black leather boot that stood on it. A large foot.

'You know I never forget the face of a murderer, either!' said a rather familiar voice above him.

Affronted by that provocation, Julian looked up immediately and saw a tall man grinning at him. At a first glance Julian thought it could be any of the locals in the Holy Land. Just another dark-faced man. But confronted with the defying attitude and quite dreading the result, Julian started to put those features together: a fiery dark face with a pointed nose, a raptor's smirk, glittery well-greased black hair and a full beard that shone red in the sun.

Julian almost fell back when he realised the man had actually spoken his own native *langue d'oïl*. That was it! The man who floutingly kept his heavy foot on that brick of the utmost sanctuary of Christendom was nobody else but Foulques, the Black Falcon, Comte of Anjou.

'We seem to have a miracle here.' The Comte said, cordially extending his hand to help Julian up. 'Resurrected from the forest of Limoges, I suppose?'

Julian was livid with surprise. 'What do you mean?' he babbled.

'Bishop Avesgaud received your letter from a pilgrim who found it next to a grave in Limoges.'

Julian's eyes looked at a nothingness on the left side of Foulques. Soon it dawned on him. 'That letter!' He still looked elsewhere, with fluttering words. 'I had lost that letter!'

'It is now with your parents, who think you are dead, I'm afraid.' Foulques said with a smirk.

'How are they?' Julian asked desperately. 'Are they well?'

Foulques was not used to be on the answering side. He despised weakness and maintained a good distance from any sign of yielding. Observing the frantic Julian, he saw a repetition of the boy he had met in Angers and of his father Raoul, a few days later, hopeless about the loss of the son. Piercing his lips, the Comte walked around Julian, obliging him to follow behind.

The soldiers watched in silence the two men leaving through a western alley, speaking that far away language, much of it unknown to them.

'You know, Julian: they call me the Black Falcon!' Foulques said. His lips stretched wide in that devilish raptor grin. '*Nerra*, they are saying now. *Black*! That has certainly nothing to do with the tone of my skin, but with the lack of light in the depths of my soul. Although I am respected by my enemies and feared by my friends, I am considered an implacable foe and a cruel, ruthless lord. Never have I been judged by the piousness of my penitence. They call me a ravager, a rapist, murderer, pillager and even barbarian, but they never use any good attributes to describe me. Not *one* goodness is seen in me. Julian, there are many who call me the Devil! Can you believe in this?'

Julian swallowed an imaginary lump that suddenly choked him.

The Comte continued 'Those who call me iniquitous should know the sufferings and privations of this pilgrimage. It took me almost half a year to travel by land and river, through the new Christian lands of the Magyars all the way into Constantinople, the great city, a hundred times bigger than Angers, than Rome, or any city a mortal has ever seen. I was expiating my sins long before I was paying reverences to the true Seamless Robe of Jesus; to the Holy Mandylion that has a miraculous imprint of the face of the Christ; to the images of the Virgin and the Child, touching her face and suckling her breast, which were painted by Saint Luke himself; to the mantle that Elisha picked up from the ground when Elijah was lifted to heaven; to the garments of the Baptist, woven of camel hair; and to many bones and bodies of so many saints who have joined the podium of martyrdom in heaven. I crossed into this defenceless, hostile land of Mohammedans, where pilgrims are unprotected and the journey to Jerusalem is a trial of our endurance and piousness. This Holy Land, which kept me in prayer and penitence for weeks in sequence, through the chapels of Mount Tabor and the grottoes of Nazareth. I was humbled by the grandiosity of this sanctuary of which we only see the pillars now, so savagely destroyed; the saints and martyrs that honoured the Holy Sepulchre; the sacredness of the kouvouklion, the very place where our Lord was buried, birth of the Holy Fire, which glows but does not burn, fire that cures the worst illnesses, fire that makes the lame walk and the blind see; and I have been redeemed by the miraculous power of the Crown of Thorns, that inflicted so much pain and mockery on our saviour. On this Holy Soil I have learned some of the language and made myself at home with the sanctity of the place.'

'On my first visit to the Holy Sepulchre,' Foulques continued, 'not long after you mocked my hospitality in Angers, I found my inner peace after grieving for my first wife. I prayed for her, who had been purified from her abominable sins by the flames of heaven.' Foulques sighed profoundly, not looking at Julian any more. They had stopped on an unusually straight alley that opened wide towards the city wall. The hot desert air blew fresh on their faces. 'This is my second pilgrimage to the Holy Land and I come to redeem other sins. A good lord needs a heavy hand to keep peace and harmony in his land. Godliness will wash away any abuse in my past actions. Free from the burden of my transgressions, I left this place more than a week ago, and when I was in Acre I learned of its destruction. I decided to return to see it, but now look who I've found? The runaway Julian of Mans!'

And before Julian would explode with anxiety, Foulques finally said 'Your parents are alive and well, but devastated after the news of your death. And so is the bishop Avesgaud.'

Julian felt on his knees, sobbing. He covered his face.

Foulques looked at him with a head bend to the side. Rather with curiosity, but without a drop of compassion, 'Why are you so stupid, boy?'

'I don't really know!' Julian protested, still on his knees.

'Did you kill that man in the forest?' The voice of the Comte was icy.

'I did, I did...but it was an accident. I thought he was something else!' he moaned.

'I don't blame you. A repulsive creature, as I've been told.' Foulques said. He clicked his tongue and added 'What about the graves in Limoges? Did you kill there too?'

'Limoges? You mean in the forest?' Julian was trying to piece together those memories he'd kept hidden. 'No! That was an attack of marauders on a group of innocent pilgrims. They raped and maimed and murdered some of the pilgrims. It was horrendous...But yes, we managed to slay some of them. Do you want to know if I killed? Yes I did!'

Like a victorious warrior after battle, Foulques slowly stepped around the kneeling, defeated Julian. 'And where did you go? Where have you been all this time?'

'Luna.'

'*Luna? The* Luna in Liguria? I have seen the white marble castle on the Via Francigena.'

'The same.' Julian said, now putting himself together and standing up, looking defiantly at Foulques straight into his brown eagle eyes. 'I was under the hospitality of the Marchese of Tuscany, Oberto II.'

'And why did you leave?' Foulques asked, untouched by Julian's mood changes. 'What are you doing carrying pieces of broken stone in the desert?'

Julian looked at a point beyond the Comte. Somewhere near the wall that separated the sacredness of the city from the impurity of the world outside. 'I am running away from tragedy. Deception seems to follow me wherever I go.'

'Did you do any more killing in Luna too?' Foulques asked, scratching his dark red beard.

Julian thought of his last day in Luna and the discussion with Clarissa, up on the highest tower. 'Somehow I did.'

Foulques walked firmly back to the Holy Sepulchre.

Julian followed on his side. 'I am solely responsible for my errors. Nobody else bears the blame that I carry. And you, my Lord, you won't punish my parents because of my sins, will you?'

Foulques turned around in sudden fury, his face almost crashing against Julian's. 'Silly delinquent, who do you think I am? Do you think I am God?'

'Do you need any help, Julian?' a new voice shouted towards them, in Lombard.

Both swung around and saw Buonaccorso standing in readiness, with his hand on the hilt of his sword and the beautiful shape of Helena on his other side.

Foulques shook his head and smiled. Turning to Julian he said 'Tell your friend to stay away from that demon. She could be a well of lies and treachery. That soldier should also know that you need no help to defend yourself. Had you wanted, you could easily cut me down and save your parents from the terrors that you fear I'm about to impose on them.' He slowly stepped back and continued walking. 'But Julian, I am not God, nor any demon that you or my enemies could make of me.'

'Will you tell my parents of me?' Julian asked, following behind, with Buonaccorso on his track.

The Comte walked in silence and arrived at the place where he had met Julian moving the rubble. The sun shone burning on Foulques's dark face. 'You are not my concern, Julian. As long as you are not in the Anjou, you mean nothing to me. What I tell your parents in my lands is none of yours either.' He bent down to lift the same brick that he had stepped on when Julian was working. With an effort, he picked it up and released it on the ground, breaking the brick into smaller pieces and another cloud of dust. The Comte grabbed a sizeable crumb and gently kissed it. 'This here!' he showed Julian the piece of the brick. 'This sacred rock is my concern!' With a swing of his pilgrim cape, he gave his back to them and started leaving to the west again. 'My men and my ship await in Acre. I bid you a peaceful stay.'

Pope Sergius IV was interrupted in his prayers. His factotum cordially started to announce an important and unexpected visit.

'It is true. It has happened!' That was the womanish voice of Cardinal John Theophylactus, cutting through the cold air of the Lateran marble corridors. Resembling somewhat a mature woman, the handsome Theophylactus pushed himself into the papal office, ignoring the factotum, not even waiting for the fat pontiff to stand up from his prostrated condition. 'But the Beatissimo Padre should not do anything yet,' he continued. 'It could be too precipitated!'

Without uttering a word, Sergius pointed a fat finger to the door, with undisguised contempt for Theophylactus. 'Your presence in Rome spills over the limits of inconvenience. It baffles me that you have nothing of importance to do in your own bishopric.'

The handsome cardinal, initially puzzled by that gesture, finally had a light on his eyes, which was soon extinguished by a shadowy countenance of realisation. He reluctantly left the office saying on his tail. 'I'm the one who insisted to bring and accompany your visitor to Rome. He's just arrived from the Holy Land in Porto, yes, my bishopric. And he is bringing some very bad news. When the Beatissimo Padre is over with his prayers, maybe he should come and see his visitor. It's the Conte Folco d'Angiò.'

Pope Sergius met with Comte Foulques of Anjou in a lavishly decorated salon at the Lateran second floor. In addition to his full entourage, including scribes, factotum, tesserarius and a full display of army officers and custodes, there were a colourful collection of bishops and cardinals, most notably the member of the Tusculani family, including Cardinal John Theophylactus and, least notably, the tiny, plump dark skinned bishop ironically named Brunello, a cousin of John Crescentius, the patrician who still held the supreme authority in Rome. Now the archdeacon of the church, Brunello had been pushed into the highest Lateran circles by the increasingly concerned Crescentii, who regretted the ascension of their distant cousin, the Cardinal John Theophylactus. The Cardinal of Porto was now operating independently with his very threatening and opposed clan of Tusculum.

'Indeed, Beatissimo Padre, the Holy Sepulchre, where the body of our Lord Jesus Christ was laid to rest, the sanctuary which should forever exist in its full glory, has been totally destroyed by the impious Mohammedan hands of the mad caliph Al-Hakim's men.' said Foulques with a contrived contrition. An open-mouthed audience listened in tenebrous silence.

'What about our men?' the pope asked, curling his lip with a frowned face, justifying his name with a porcine caricature.

'You mean Julian of Mans, his Lombard friend and a score of soldiers?' A white smile ripped through the dark features of Foulques as he sniggered. 'They arrived in Jaffa one day too late, much helpless to prevent the destruction. The basilica was destroyed from top to foundations. These men are lost in a sea of ruins, carrying stones from one corner to the other, frantically trying to bring some order to the rubble.'

'They are carrying their own crosses, I suppose.' said the pope, more as a loud thought.

'Any relics left?' asked Cardinal Theophylactus, making all necks turn towards him.

Foulques recognised the feminine pitch on that voice and turned to face the suave features of the Cardinal who had escorted him from Porto. He endeavoured to answer Theophylactus. 'The Christian community must have saved the most sacred relics before the destruction. I saw no more than stones. Broken, but still holy.'

'Do you bring with you any of these holy stones?' Theophylactus insisted. 'Perhaps as a gift to the Beatissimo Padre?'

The little Bishop Brunello just shook his head in disapproval.

'No.' lied the comte, irritated with Theophylactus's perspicacity. Foulques managed to lead the narrative into a different subject. 'We pilgrims of the Christ have endured the affliction and the adversities of the journey, abandoning our temporal possessions to take up only our own crosses, to make ourselves His disciples and taking His route. We have been given the Holy Sepulchre by the Christ Himself, so that Pilgrims could find a safer road to the celestial kingdom.'

When the translator finished and the scribes scratched their last lines on the parchment, all the assistance nodded and turned their faces to see what the pontiff would do. Sergius pursed his lips and held the tip of his chin, which still protruded out of his thick swinish neck.

'Did you personally meet Julian of Mans and Buonaccorso, the Pavese Leopard?' the pope asked.

Foulques nodded and bowed quite theatrically. 'If that is what the Lombard soldier is called, I briefly met them both. They are safe with the Christian community. But the Mohammedans cannot be trusted to leave them alone.'

The pope stood up and talked more to himself than to the audience or to the visitor. 'This is certainly the most unexpected and grave matter. Both holy predecessors of mine, Sylvester II and John XVIII, had always been adamant about the protection of the Holy Sepulchre, but failed to follow up in such a holy mission. Now the church has been destroyed, under our times, under my time. We should unite efforts to restore it to its former glory and protect it from pagan hands. We should take on our own crosses and carry it following the steps of the Christ, protecting those who have left it all behind to obtain divine absolution by visiting the site where He was put to rest. They are mostly defenceless against the pagan enemy.'

Turning to Foulques, he asked 'So the mad caliph could renew the attack? Are the pilgrims ever going to be safe? Is there any hope for reconstruction?'

Before answering, the French Comte waited until the pontiff returned to his seat and made himself comfortable. With a raptor expression transforming his nose in a beak, Foulques looked deep into Sergius's eyes. 'The mad caliph is the Prince of Babylon, the Antichrist incarnated. He has sent a relatively small battalion to destroy the sanctuaries of Christianity in the Holy Land. Reconstruction of the Sepulchre of our Saviour has begun under the sweat of your soldiers. But it will sooner or later be halted again, under their blood. There are plenty of pilgrims. Good battle-trained soldiers, warriors and nobles from French, Italian English, Spanish, German and Nordic lands arriving in Jerusalem every day to secure absolution for their past violence. The journey to the Holy Sepulchre is a suitable penance for the sins of war and cruelty, for I am reborn on my penitence. But no matter how many more pilgrims arrive and go every day, they could not hold the armies of the mad caliph if he ever decided to send a serious force to march over the Holy City. Therefore princes and nobles from all of Christendom should mobilise generous donations and gifts of gold to aid in the reconstruction of the Holy Sepulchre and send their armies to free the Holy Land from the land of the

Mohammedans.' Foulques had no idea that this suggestion was about to shape the history of mankind from that moment on.

He finished his speech with a lesson of humility and piousness to all the assistance: 'And even when I have not stepped back on the soil of Anjou, I already plan to return one day to the Sepulchre of the Christ, if not with my sword, I will certainly be with my cross.' He bowed once more and added to the vicar of Rome, thinking of the rock of the Holy Sepulchre he had well hidden inside his vests. Now if you excuse me, I wish to be taken back to Porto. A ship waits for me to lower sail to the port town of Rupella, where I return to Anjou.'

Clearly satisfied with the report, Sergius IV only raised his hand and made the sign of the cross 'Deus vobiscum.'

'A soldier of Christ – miles Christi' the pope said to his small audience. Foulques had been sent back to Porto, but this time without Theophylactus, who stayed at the Lateran for the debate.

The pope sighed 'All of our men, Julian of Mans, Buonaccorso of Pavia, all soldiers of Christ in their most sacred mission, arriving in the Holy Land only to see in ruins the tomb of our Lord Jesus Christ. Such a shame!'

'Not too shameful, for they are on their own, and what news do we really get from those lands?' Theophylactus suggested.

A chuckle was heard. It was Brunello, the bishop of the Crescentii. The little plump cleric came from behind the other bishops and posted himself in front of the pope. 'It seems that the Cardinal Theophylactus forgets that omnipresence of God and His ability to see it all. If shameful it is, no matter how far, shameful it is before the eyes of the Lord.'

'True!' Said the pope, to the annoyance of Theophylactus. 'We should act now!'

'Act?' Theophylactus shouted, almost like a woman screaming. 'What can we do more than pray for our men?'

'We can appeal to all of Christendom!' The pope said with a wise and conclusive face, lifting his upper lip in a poor excuse for a smile. Coming to his side, the dark Brunello was subtly imitating his victorious grin towards Theophylactus. The pope continued. 'If we mobilise the princes and nobles of all Christendom, we can send an expeditio sacra to help our soldiers bear the cross and raise the tomb of the Christ once again to its full glory.'

Theophylactus just threw his hands up in helplessness and left the salon with wide and heavy steps.

The encyclical written by Sergius IV, appealing for the liberation and protection of the Holy Sepulchre, was exhaustively copied to reach even the most distant corners of Christendom. But Cardinal John Theophylactus was right: the script never fulfilled its noble purpose to sensitise nobles and princes across Christian nations to take their arms and march towards the Holy Land.

The Butchery of Partigliano

A red-haired young woman was returning home, after a trip of three days to Lucca.

'I heard about it, Maria Maddalena!' Fulcardo Cunimundinghi said, as he opened the door of the Anchiano Manor.

She was hesitant for a second. Although there were war movements in Lucca, with supplies arriving from all directions to stock the troops and people leaving the region in fear of violence reaching their grounds, Béla's death was certainly talked about during the two days she stayed in the city. It seemed to be general consensus that the stregone from Hungarian lands had received a well-deserved punishment for his devilries. But Maria was not sure what moods awaited her up the Serchio by the time news of Béla's demise arrived. The populace was likely to have different views, thoughts, and now, with cold sweat running down her face, she did not know what constructions were raised on Fulcardo's mind.

But when the lord Cunimundinghi stepped out to embrace her with passion, she just let her arms fall around him and cry 'It was horrible, Fulcardo, horrible! That nasty little man...' she sobbed on his shoulders.

'It's all over, my love,' he cooed. 'Now you can just rest.'

Maria pulled herself together. She brought Fulcardo to the dining hall and showed him the signed copies of the documents. The chartula with the launegildo ceding Chifenti to Amadeo and the letters of Immanuel pardoning Fulcardo's debts. 'Are you sure you want to go ahead with this?' she asked.

'We must!' he said, determined, 'and then we will be left in peace. Your father has given us his blessing if we agreed with the proposal. I am a man of honour and I will abide to it. But no more I will use the baths at Corsena, filling the pockets of your father, your grandfather in Lucca or the pope in Rome. No more will I raise my debts. One day I will just recover all the lost land, and Amadeo will be begging me to let him stay in Chifenti. Our son will inherit a large state, Maria.' and he tenderly caressed her belly.

Maria Maddalena felt deeply soothed by his presence. She opened a rarely seen forthright smile that illuminated the hall. Filled with joy, Fulcardo wet his lips and prepared Maria for more news. 'I have also arranged for a town crier and for a priestly blessing, for Saturday.'

Maria raised an eyebrow, waiting for the explanation, but her smile did not wane.

'Our marriage, of course. There is no reason to wait for longer. All we need is God's approval.'

In spite of having been found with Attila's dagger just before losing it; of missing the opportunity to give it in pawn or sell it, a unique chance to relieve Fulcardo of some of his debts; in spite of being falsely accused of murdering that senile stregone from distant lands; and regardless of the unpleasant encounter with an intimidating young man in the city, Maria Maddalena of the Burle et Malachi had never felt so happy in her entire life.

Maria purposely missed to mention Antelmino.

On arriving at the Burle House of Trade, three days before, Maria and the two escorts had brought their four mounts into the large patio, where other horses, mules, servants, pages and a couple of negroes obediently waited. It was probably one of the meetings of the Lucchese bankers. They convened once a week, discussing current trade matters, comparing rates and conducting transactions, deciding on minimum prices and ceilings. Mostly they met at Fraolmo Di Cunizio's, but more recently the moved to different venues – a house of trade – which made every banker host the reunion probably no more than four times a year.

Maria entered through the warehouse. Before her eyes got used to the darkness, there was a young man standing in front of her.

'So you must be Maria Maddalena of the Burle et Malachi! What an enchanting presence!' The voice was sibilant. The young man was not much older than Maria, probably on his seventeens. He was well built, but of low stature and very white skin, probably of the typical short Lombard stock. Rebellious locks of black hair tricked from under a wide-brimmed deer-hide hat. He smiled with a cynical mouth of yellow teeth, looking hungrily at her from head to toe. 'I hear you are to be my neighbour one day. A Cunimundinghi!'

Maria looked at him with revulsion. 'Forgive me, but I fail to recognise for which lord you work. I cannot recall your face among the household of any neighbours of the Cunimundinghi. Maybe you should stick to your place, outside with the other servants.'

He forced himself a giggle. 'What a smart young woman you are! Not only a delight to the eyes, you seem to be filled with fire.' He lowered his eyes to her body and said with poison 'And filled with something else too, by the look of it.' Maria's hands instinctively covered her slightly swollen belly.

'Tell me who you are, or I will start screaming,' she grunted.

But Maria only heard his next words after being yanked to a dark corner behind a pile of boxes and having the tip of a steel blade pinching the skin under her jaws. He held his dagger firmly, hurting her, pushing her head up to a height where she had to stand on her toes. His voice came wet and malicious, close to her ears. 'You don't play smart with me, young girl. I have slashed many faces for much less than that. You scream and I will leave, but my blade will be dug deep into your neck. No need to worry about me. All they will find is you and your unborn Cunimundinghi, dead in a pool of blood, but they will never know who did it.

'Who...are...you?' she managed to screech, as low as a whisper.

'I am the real man you should be marrying instead, stupid girl. Antelmino Di Gottefredo, at your service.'

Her terrified eyes were opened wide, paralysed, and no reaction came out in words. On realising his name had meant nothing to her, Antelmino lowered the dagger a bit and explained. 'Your grandfather and his old-fashioned competitors will not have me in their meeting. My house of trade is the fastest growing enterprise in this city. My lands will be soon touching the south border of the Cunimundinghi's. But the arrogance and envy of these old hogs have kept me out.'

'What do you want with me?' Maria moaned.

He grinned as his hands caressed her shape, feeling the firmness of her youth. His torso pressed hers against the large boxes, and his voice came close to her ears again, sucking in the saliva. 'I want you, girl. I want all of you for me, but I can wait a bit. You can think about it. Fulcardo Cunimundinghi quickly loses his lands, and mine will overwhelm it. He is not a real man for a smart woman that you are. Too smart, perhaps. Yes, I was at the bridge a while ago!'

The air went out of her lungs.

'I saw it all, my red-haired angel!' he continued. 'The poor old bastard took the dagger from your satchel! I know well who killed who!' he enjoyed to see the blood going away from her beautiful face, washed in sweat. 'I am sure the balivo would love to hear the true facts. But you are not going to lose your head, if you behave, Maria. I can wait until you are done with Fulcardo. How long should it take? Two or three years? What are your plans?' He felt her satchel and said. 'And talking about plans, let's see what documents you brought for Battista Burle...'

In this moment, the entrance door to the house opened and they could hear the bankers preparing to leave the meeting. Antelmino Di Gottefredo disappeared and left Maria there in the dark, drenched in sweat, trying to pull herself together and verifying for all the scrolls she had brought to be signed. Everything was still there.

On that afternoon, after conferring with the bishops Grimizzo and Rodilando, the bankers had been privately debating over their contribution to the efforts of war. Battista Burle sat on the least comfortable of his chairs, having given all the cushioned seats to his guests. With few exceptions, those Lucchese were inconspicuous bankers, modestly dressed and living in large town houses with humble exterior, but internally lined and furnished with the most comfortable and luxurious materials. It had only been recently, not a generation before, when the modesty shell cracked and a tower craze had taken over the richer families of the city. The Gualteri family had raised Lucca's highest tower, triggering a race among some families to build their own giants, reaching over nearer to the heights of heaven. Loyal friends, keepers of secrets and very careful strategists, the bankers privately enjoyed the simple pleasures of life, as good food, wines, soft fabrics around their skin and, occasionally, some discreet diversion with women.

With their goblets filled with Battista's best wine, the Lucchese bankers reached over to the large table to help themselves with thin slices of wild boar's fat and honeyed figs. The group was composed by some other convert families, such as the brothers Fraolmo and Sisemundo Di Cunizio; Salamone Natali; Giaccomo Guidiccioni; some very Lombard representatives, as Dino Gualteri; Bartolomeo Orsetti; Ildebrando Lucasio; the toothy Rafaello Rapondi; and the handsome Pietro di Filippo, called the 'Calandrino', from Sarzana.

'It is a calamity!' Pietro said, 'A disgrace!'

'We also have pawned lands which have been taken, young Pietro. You are not exclusive on your disgrace.' said the Fraolmo Di Cunizio, with his husked smoky voice. 'There is no doubt about the threat that the Saracens put against our patrimony every new day they continue their stay in Luni and raid the vicinities.'

He was followed by his brother Sisemundo, in an almost rehearsed-seemingly fashion, which the bankers were used to. 'We all seem to agree that we should be helping on the resistance effort against the Saracens, but how much are we willing to contribute with?'

'We can reduce a portion of the debts of all our current clients and debtors, from the church, including both Bishops Roldilando and Grimizzo, the pope, to all the nobles involved in the army.' said Dino Gualteri. He was a strange-looking old man, perhaps the most extravagant of them all, with his old angular face clean shaven and long blonde curls of hair falling over his shoulder. 'Maybe if we could agree to reduce one fifth of the total, they would heartily appreciate...'

'This will not be seen as a gesture of good will from our part' argued Battista Burle, sitting a bit further, with his hands crossed around his chest, but establishing the solidity of his remark with a deep bass voice. 'We must provide them with gold. Heavy, solid, shining, gold-coloured gold.'

'Battista is correct', Fraolmo said. 'The war is upon us. And the armies want guarantees. Whether we like it or not...'

'...we are part of it!' continued Sisemundo. 'Supplies are taken for granted, and the bankers will not be able to take credit. We can only demonstrate our true commitment by showing them the gold they will be looking for, after victory or defeat.'

'Because we fought hard to get where we are, and the wrong move now could jeopardise all our future.' Battista said.

Pietro leaned over the table and opened a fetching smile 'I will match the highest contribution.'

'As we are meeting here to come to a decision, nobody should be left behind with a lesser donation.' Fraolino suggested.

'We should all contribute equally.' finished Sisemundo.

Once an agreement was concluded on immediate mobilisation of their efforts of war, some of the bankers made small notes on their wax tablets. Their deliberations never required signed documents. Afterwards, they pondered about current trade affairs. Battista gave them an update on silk production and a few housekeeping issues were discussed. The meeting was ended with a new round of wine and a tray of fresh fruits. They left the comfort of Battista Burle's candle-scented dining hall to cross his carefully dusted warehouse towards the patio, where their horses and pages would take them back home. Bankers with a pain in the head just to think of the gold lost in that stupid, but necessary war.

When Battista accompanied them through the warehouse, he stopped midway, delightedly surprised to see a gorgeous red-haired young-woman sitting among the merchandise.

'Maria Maddalena!' he said with open arms, as she came to embrace him. 'Why have you come in these dangerous times? Is Fulcardo with you? Did you have escorts?'

She answered all his questions, hiding well her mix of fear and hatred from the previous encounter.

'I hear you are about to be a Cunimundinghi' he said with a wink.

She forced herself to smile.

When he brought her in to his dining hall, which was being tidied up by two servants, Maria casually asked 'Grandfather, who is Antelmino Di Gottefredo?'

He stood up erect, eyebrow raised and a face for very few friends. 'Why do you ask? Did you meet this young man outside?'

'Yes, he talked to me...'

'Stay away from Antelmino,' he said, pointing a fat finger to her nose. 'He is brewed out of shit. Behind a false curtain of benevolence, Antelmino and his father Gottefredo lend money to the vellutini outside of the walls. They charge exorbitant interests and collect their debts by means of violence. Beatings and slashed faces are common practice of Antelmino's thugs. Now father and son feel entitled to be part of our bankers' guild. They present themselves to our meetings every Wednesday, but thanks to God, none of us will accept them in. In the future, however, we will have to watch for those pigs.'

'Antelmino met me inside your warehouse.' Maria said, waiting for his reaction.

'For the head St. James!' Battista burst. 'My servants will certainly hear about this. Did he hurt you?'

'No,' she lied, dismissively.

Something else more important had to be delivered, much worse news. She cleared her throat 'Grandfather...it is Béla, the midwife...'

'Of course I know Béla. What is it with him?'

'He came with me... but he could not make it...there was an accident.'

Battista let the goblet fall on the floor, spilling bright red wine over the wooden boards.

In that first night back in Anchiano with Fulcardo, after they had made love, Maria Maddalena noticed the restlessness in her future husband.

'What bothers you, Fulcardo?' she said.

'It's the other news that came from Lucca...' he mumbled.

'What other news?' she asked, raising her tone. 'About the soldiers? Yes, I saw whole battalions on their way to Luna. But the battle is elsewhere, my love. Across the mountains!'

'It's not that...' he said, almost in a whisper.

'What it is then?' she demanded.

Fulcardo mumbled something.

'Louder!' Maria ordered, 'I cannot hear you!'

He pursed his lips and finally said 'They say that you stole a dagger from your father and killed Béla with it.'

'Who says that?' she roared.

'It's Bernardo from the Rocks. He always talks too much.'

'That shepherd? Am I being vilified by a *shepherd*?' she laughed forcedly. 'What does he know of what happened in Lucca?'

Fulcardo was going to explain how the news had spread, but instead he had to make sure of something. 'It is not true, Maria, is it?'

She sat herself up. 'How dare you doubt me? You miserable piece of a failed lord! Of course it is a filthy lie, spread by a venomous tongue. If the ignorant villagers will believe in this rubbish, well, that I could even expect from their impoverished spirit, but a man of your stature and position, doubting my honesty? And to think that I carry your heir within me! Shame on you!'

'I do believe you, Maria!' he begged.

'You better believe me, or you will have me no more, neither your child. And you better make this rat Bernardo pay for his lies.'

'I can go and see him sometime after the wedding...'

'We will go and teach him a lesson, immediately after the wedding.' she corrected.

'We are not sure where he is, Maria. For all we know, he seems to be found all over the place. Apparently Bernardo sits once in a while in his manor across the river just below us, at the village of Wald Ottavo, but as the shepherd that he likes to be, he is rarely found there.'

'We will take men-at-arms and search for him. We will beat every bush on this valley. I want to see him imploring us for forgiveness, or else I will hang his body on a high post along the Serchio. That will teach the folk something about liars.'

Fulcardo's hairline had almost disappeared behind his face, as if he had seen a ghost. 'Maria, we cannot do that. Bernardo delle Rocche is, after all, an Obertenghi. We cannot just enter their lands to chase him and bring him to justice. My family has lost too many lands to them. The western bank, all the way from La Cuna to Wald Ottavo.'

'Of course we can!' she rasped. 'Who's going to be there to stop us? And after all he is no more than a shepherd. With the Saracens at their door, the Obertenghi have more important things in hands right now, rather than protecting a lying peasant.'

Fulcardo dropped his shoulders. 'We'll go and look for him after the wedding, then.'

Father Martino had turned to a grave, greying, but compassionate man. He was often welcomed and sheltered in Anchiano when travelling between Controne and Lucca. Martino had been a friend of Fulcardo's father, the bishop, and in deference to this camaraderie, he respectfully attended to the heir of Anchiano, although he had seen little to justify any admiration.

On Friday, the sun rose rather warm for a cool autumn morning. Most of the woods still carried their leaves, heavy with dew, but a glorious golden tinge from the hornbeams and chestnut trees had already blessed those valleys. The land was still puffy and moist from the incessant rains and the air heavy with scents of harvest and ripened fruits. Peasants were occupied on chestnuts gathering from the covered ground. An aromatic smoke permeated the forest, from several stone-built *metati*, where the nuts were slowly roasted under a low fire on chestnut charcoal. On his steep descend towards the Lima fords, cheered by warblers that never exhausted from chirping and thrushes that busied themselves on the leafy ground, Martino could not miss to stop over and see Immanuel in Corsena.

He found the Bukhari in one of the newly built terraces, trimming his mulberry trees with some of his children. Immanuel was quick to greet him and bring the priest into the manor, for a sip of distilled wine.

'So you are not coming to Anchiano?' Martino asked.

Immanuel sighed and took a while to answer. 'It's different now, Father Martino. After the death of my good friend Béla and the news from Lucca, I do not see any purpose in approving this union.'

'Of course. Your friend, the Magyar... It had not occurred to me...' said the priest with embarrassment. 'And the woman Divina too. They never found any of them, did they?'

Immanuel shrugged his shoulders. 'They never did. Divina was a blessed soul. And Béla...well, I hope he is resting well wherever he is. You know, Béla was never a Christian, but a great man in his own way.'

Martino smiled warmly. 'There's plenty of space in heaven for the good people.' He meant to leave, but decided to confirm with Immanuel. 'Is that the only reason you do not go? After all it is your daughter's wedding.'

Immanuel put his goblet on the table and wiped his mouth with the sleeve before starting. 'I have a contract with Fulcardo Cunimundinghi, and that is enough for me. My other children and the friends from Corsena and Mutianum still need to be looked after. I feel no joy for Maria Maddalena's and her choices. Besides, she can take good care of herself.'

'But they do have your blessing, don't they?'

Immanuel curled his lips. 'Go and do what you have been asked to do, father Martino. My blessing has little bearing on this matter.'

'Maria Maddalena is young for a noble marriage in these lands. You heart's approval is essential for me to perform mine.' Martino insisted.

'They have already announced their union.' Immanuel said. 'To the very shame of poor Lucia's soul, everyone knows they've given each other the *verbum*. There is nothing we can do...except hope that this union is blessed by God.'

'I will do my best.' Martino said, bowing his head and leaving for Anchiano.

When Fulcardo Cunimundinghi and Maria Maddalena of the Burle et Malachi celebrated their wedlock, Anchiano had a spirited celebration with plenty of fresh wine and the best selection of wild meats from the Apennine that the valley had seen for decades. Few of the Lucchese guests were used to the strength and power of Immanuel's wine. Distinguished, but inebriated lords and ladies were spread unconscious across the ground, many being dragged out of their personal puddles of vomit. Battista Burle did come to see Maria, but he swiftly left to join Immanuel for a quiet evening in Corsena, much before the party moved into the couple's bedroom. Maria was undressed to a long silk gown, specially presented by her grandfather, made purely of product from Lucca. She slipped under the linens and pelts, while Fulcardo came after, pushed in by a noisy rabble. He stripped down to his hose and joined the bride. While the couple acknowledged their *verbum* through a public display of their wedlock consummation, holy water was sprinkled on them from a silver aspergillum. Father Martino held it with a renewed disdain for the tradition.

'Where is Bernardo delle Rocche?' Maria Maddalena demanded.

The villagers looked at her with a puzzled face, finally dropping their gaze to the ground.

It had taken no more than an hour to reach Wald Ottavo from the ferry crossing, and another half hour to climb up to the hamlet of Partigliano. The unannounced and flamboyant presence of Fulcardo Cunimundinghi and Maria Maddalena, clearly lords of other lands, was unexpected and certainly intimidating, especially because of the company of three men-at-arms. The tiny village of stone houses hung by the western valley side, looking above and between Wald Ottavo, that stood flat at the bottom, and the slopes that climbed quickly towards the rocky peaks of the Apuane. They could see the village of Ottavo below, with houses well hidden from the Via Francigena, beyond a sparse but vast area of willows and chestnut trees, which granted the region the Lombard name of *Wald* – forest. Not far from an abandoned church climbing on the hillside of Ottavo, Bernardo had one of his indistinguishable simple houses built behind a creek that happily trickled down its tales of the mountain tops. But Bernardo was not in Wald Ottavo, said the local minor lord Wido di Willo. A short, plump man with a wrinkle-ridded, freckled face and a generous, shaggy red beard, Wido di Willo was loyal to Bernardo delle Rocche. Reluctantly, he allowed the visitors to pursue Bernardo further up in Partigliano.

These villagers were not used to see travellers, except for Bernardo, a few monks and nuns, who would every so often travel through Wald Ottavo and Partigliano on their way to Pescaglia, and the family of Wido di Willo.

In Partigliano, an old but still strong man came out of a house, chewing something and sticking his fingers under his cow leather belt.

'Bernardo is not here.' He said with a touch of defiance. 'He has not been in Partigliano for three days. We sometimes do not see his face for a fortnight. Why don't you ask Wido di Willo down in Wald Ottavo? And may we know the names of the visitors he has just missed?'

'I am Fulcardo of the Cunim —'

'Tell us then where he is now!' Maria rasped with a powerful voice, completely interrupting her husband.

The old man chewed a bit more, looking defiantly at Maria. As he frowned against the sun, he seemed to have a constant grin on the face. He turned to look at the road going up the hill and pointed at it with his nose, rather than taking his hands of the belt. 'Bernardo left through there, that way up the mountain. He could be on the peaks, on other villages, he could be on the caves, he could be gone down across the passes, he could be in Pescaglia… Only the good Lord could know where he is.'

Fulcardo rode his horse around to his wife's.

'Pescaglia is a territory of the Rolandinghi' he whispered. 'We should definitely not try to chase Bernardo in their lands.'

Maria paid no heed. 'I don't like the manner in which this man speaks of the lord of these lands. Moreover, I cannot tolerate the arrogant attitude...' but her voice stopped and the words disappeared from her mouth. The village was all silent, looking at the track up the valley where the old man had pointed to, for a group of riders, six or seven of them, had just turned around the curve from behind the bushes. It was a group of riders nobody had ever seen before, not even in their most outlandish dreams.

They rode down their fine horses calmly, approaching at an easy pace. They were heavily packed, with large rolls and sacks tied to their ornate saddles and sheathed swords swinging next to their legs. Mostly they seemed to be dressed in long tunics or sheets wrapped around them, especially with some large colourful rags bundled around their heads, in the old style of ladies' wimples. Their exposed skin was unusually dark and they sported long black beards.

Fulcardo's men-at-arms slowly brought their horses to a safer distance next to his and his wife's. But the strange riders, now much closer, only acknowledged the movement with a serene smile. They had friendly faces and bowed their heads with respect. The front rider, wearing a bright honey-coloured rag on his head, pointed to the road down the valley and nodded with a shy, but bright grin, indicating that they would only pass along.

Maria Maddalena moved her horse to the side, so that the strange men could ride by. She wondered if these merchants were coming from Pescaglia. She was also starting to consider the chances that those men could be indeed Saracens that had crossed along the Apuane passes, when she was distracted by the old villager, who suddenly roared out with his loudest voice: '*Run! Run and hide, all of you!*'

It happened in the blink of an eye, and she was too slow to follow it all. As Maria saw the villagers panicking and screaming, a scrape of metal rasped next to her, and a round object knocked on the ground, rolling from under her horse. She turned to Fulcardo only to witness that he was still on his horse, but there was nothing where his head should have been.

When his lifeless body fell on the ground, Maria Maddalena was already screaming.

The Saracens continued to butcher the entire village. Maria kept screaming, and screaming again, as if the flames of hell itself were licking at her skin.

The Sinner of Ierosolyma

The sun had set behind the western city wall, bringing on its tail a formidable parade of colours, flaming banners that respectfully remained frozen in the sky as the faithful were called for the prayers within the walls. The cries of the *adhan* filled up the twilight of the Holy Land, while the blind *muezzin* carefully wove their chant onto the starry night that fell above.

In the Christian quarters of the city, the dark, Holy Face looked at Julian inquisitively.

The bulging eyes were tired. Thick, black, matted locks of sweaty hair were pulled to the sides, around a long, melancholic face, a bit curious indeed, but still indifferent to the man who had inspired it. The noble moustache spread across the sides, a feature that Julian had erased from his own face as soon as he saw it sculpted in wood.

Did it look like him? Julian hated to admit, but there wasn't any resemblance at all. When Nicodemus was fully recovered, he had reluctantly accepted that the Holy Face he had seen from under the rubble was Julian's. So impressed and thankful was the keeper for his saviour that he insisted on making a sculpture of that Holy Face to pay homage to his soter Julian. For this project, Nicodemus had chosen a valuable piece of the best walnut timber he could find in Jerusalem. The wood was hardened by the his drops of sweat, while carving a full bodied crucifix, a robed Christ wearing a long tunic, its thin long arms nailed to the cross that bore the weight of humankind's sins. The sculpture that took two years to be completed by the diligent Nicodemus was carved with the resemblance of Julian; the almighty saviour proudly painted with eggs and coal, red and brown ochre, rose from madder, burnt umber from Cyprus, yellow from buckthorn berries mixed with the cow urine, purple from Cretan seashells, green of Greece, blue from woad, and then successive coatings of hempseed oil to seal and varnish it. The three-dimensional Christ that was comfortably laid on its cross; the work of Nicodemus's life, a colossal statue. Nicodemus carved the figure almost two feet taller than Julian's actual height. It was made hollow to ease on the weight, but little difference it made, for the Christ was fixed on a massive cross of over fourteen feet by eight. A wonder of its age, the statue of the Holy Face was immediately repelled by the bishops.

'It's wrong! It's sensual!' they cried, 'It has no place among our worship! An abomination in the eyes of God. A round sculpture. Burn it, Nicodemus. Burn it!'

But the keeper did not destroy his masterpiece. The sculpture of the Holy Face was handed to Julian, who kept it inside his small room. He was lodged at the makeshift patriarchate in a Christian alley not far from the collapsed church. Three walls had to be broken to accommodate the crucifix in Julian's lodging. He set his gift snuggled against one of its corners. The Holy Face would be safe, as long as Julian slept next to it and took it away with him one day.

The reconstruction works of the Holy Sepulchre were not started yet, but the cleaning job had almost ended. Bronze, wood, bricks, stones and mortar had been allocated into different areas around the church, guarded by a zealous Christian community. The militia of Al-Hakim had temporarily eased on raids, especially after the arrival of those roman soldiers. With plans for a more impressive church, including a renewed aedicula with its intricate secret compartments and a series of chapels to commemorate the scenes of the passion, Nicodemus spend a good deal of his time discussing the new construction with the bishops.

Back in his lodgings, Julian could not look away from the crucified Christ, an exhausted face like his own. He had worked twice as much all day. Buonaccorso and some of the soldiers had headed down to the port in Jaffa, to see the Christian community and help recruit more pilgrims for the reconstruction of the church. Hopefully they would be back on the next day with reinforcements.

Finishing at sunset, Julian felt tired and broken, trying to convince himself that this was not even a fraction of the physical sufferings endured by the crucified Saviour. His door opened and Helena came in, looking at him with a pity-filled, worried expression, her sooty falcons opening their wings wide and meeting in the centre of her chestnut-coloured forehead. With soft movements of her body, she had a sensual fragrance of cleanness. 'You look awful, Julian. Smelling like a horse. You need a bath!' Helena extended her hand to Julian and he took it, warm, soft and a bit sweaty. She brought him out, into the night.

Julian could not fight his helplessness. Over those two years he had been approached by the impish Helena, now Buonaccorso's woman, who'd teased him to the point of desperation, but he could never believe the sincerity of her intentions. Like a hot ember, she was being passed from soldier to soldier, giving herself and her body openly to sin and only Buonaccorso seemed to take her seriously.

When in dire need to lie with a woman, Julian had tried to seek the services of any *vulgaris meretrix*. He had been with women since leaving Luna, basically in *lupanari* around Salerno. But in Jerusalem he found the brothels to be controlled by Muslim slave traders that established themselves in the heart of the Christian quarter. With Islam's forbiddance of prostitution in all forms, the Christian quarter seemed to provide a safe haven for the lucrative maintenance of sexual slaves, an activity which was apparently overviewed by the militia of Al-Hakim. On his first visit to that area, shyly avoiding direct looks from the passers-by, Julian was unfortunate enough to come across Nicodemus, who insisted on taking him away from that idea and delivered some advice.

'This is not a place for you, Julian. Don't be fooled by their luring appearance. They are filthy whores. They will give you their bodies for your riches, but they can also give you warts, chancres, Egyptian scabies. You could end up with acrid pudenda, pox, leprosy, fetid flows, and all kinds of German maladies. And none of such illnesses are worth the lack of passion of these sinners for their trade.' He walked Julian off the alley, holding him firmly by the elbow. 'Leave these unfortunate dens for old, spent men like me. Find yourself a good woman, Julian. I wish it could be my Helena. But then you know better my Helena...the poor Helena, so lost is her soul.'

And Julian knew how his body would be lost and how desirable Helena could be. And just how different she was from the woman he had loved before. Still, numbed by a blind craving, he followed the keeper's daughter into a laundry that was frequently used as a bath house. The fire was already on and the water steaming. She had it all prepared since the departure of Buonaccorso. Helena locked the door. Oblivious to any belief or memory, Julian let himself be undressed and bathed in warm water by her careful touch. He let himself be scrubbed, massaged, and made his desire obvious to her. He let himself undress her, revealing the copper shine her young beauty on its fullest. He let himself feel her, tender as a flower, and take her, hungry as a jackal.

A childish giggle woke him up.

Not a crow cawing from his window, but a demon from his dreams. An imp who guffawed from watching Julian ceding to the spell of temptation. But strangely, the imp's giggling seemed to be out of his dream, just spitting malice into his ears, waking him up. He was alone in his room. Just the Holy Face looked at him with pity and disapproval.

Trying to clear his mind from the memories, his bowels from the desire for more and his heart from ceding to invitation again, Julian dedicated his full attention to hard work. It was mid-afternoon when Buonaccorso arrived with more pilgrims, soldiers and able men to do construction work. The Pavese leopard had the sunniest of smiles.

'It looks like you are happy with your reinforcements, Buonaccorso.' Julian said, looking at the Norsemen that had accompanied him back to Jerusalem.

'Oh, much more than that!' Buonaccorso said, unhorsing with a swift leap. 'I am living the happiest days of my life.'

Julian raised an eyebrow. He waited for Buonaccorso to do the explanation.

'It happened yesterday morning, before I left for Jaffa, Julian. That is why I have not told you yet.'

'What is it?' begged Julian.

'I've asked Helena to be my wife and she accepted!' Buonaccorso said, grinning with all his teeth.

Julian had to re-swallow the rancid liquid column that suddenly filled his mouth, before managing to yell 'Congratulations, my friend! She is a lovely choice...'

That moment seemed to take forever to get out of his way. Besides being saddened, Julian was somehow surprised he did not feel he held any grudge against Buonaccorso for this. He pitied him and felt disgust for Helena who, in the end, he thought, had been no more than a false, smutty *fornicatrix*.

The keeper's daughter was soon greeting the arrivals, fresh and adorable, hugging Buonaccorso with passionate force. While trying to dodge the stares of Helena, who grinned maliciously at him, Julian watched his friend bathed in bliss, receiving the compliments from the other soldiers and calling for a celebration. When they left, Helena passed by the sceptical Julian and managed to whisper on his ear 'I will be with him, but I will still need you!' And she giggled, just like the wicked laughter that had awakened Julian that day.

Buonaccorso and Helena made their home next to the old patriarchate, now a one-storey reconstructed centre, housing some of the bishops' families, the keeper's and also a few soldiers that remained in Jerusalem. Those had overcome the shock of the Sepulchre desecration, staying to rebuild it and taking local wives.

Julian however, maintained a careful distance from Buonaccorso and Helena. While the reconstruction projects were carried on, Julian spent his time caring for the pilgrims. He ran, together with a few Christian families, the xenodochium. This was the hospital.

Rather than only providing health care for the sick in general, as would a Muslim *bimaristan*, with its specialised areas and a wide body of physicians, or a byzantine *nosocomia*, or any asylum, lazaret and leper house, the xenodochium was geared for a high turnover of visitors and short stays, for it cared and provided shelter for travellers and pilgrims.

There were many xenodochia along the pilgrimage routes, often maintained by religious houses. The Jerusalem hospital was special, as it was the final point of the route. Pilgrims arrived in all conditions, from dehydration to excellent muscular fitness, from complete exhaustion among sores and calluses, to ecstasy in rags and straps.

Initially, Julian watched the pilgrims weep upon arrival, seeing with their own eyes that the unbelievable news received as they approached the Holy Land were true: the Sepulchre of the Christ had been razed to the ground. But as soon as the relics were discreetly brought up by Nicodemus, Julian noticed a change. If any miracle could be attributed to the relics, it was the hope for continuation. Pilgrims rejoiced to celebrate the wood that undid the curse of the tree, or the thorns that pieced into the divine scalp, drawing blood of redemption. They were eager to walk the pavements of the Holy City and find the standing pillars among the rubble, remaining columns from the glorious Anastasis. Ignoring the devastation, they would approach the broken walls of the kouvouklion and touch the rock with the deepest reverence, leaving on it all their sins and, through that simple encounter between skin and stone, be showered with absolution, peace and a promise to be among the few worthy of entering the Kingdom of Heavens.

The makeshift xenodochium was being kept on a reconstructed shelter raised on the site of the destroyed monastery of St John the Baptist. It had previously functioned at a building destroyed by Al-Hakim a few years before. The hospital and library had taken pilgrims since its foundation. Now, as the Church of the Holy Sepulchre was slowly being re-built, pilgrims were lodged at the improvised structure.

Daily scores of pilgrims were received by Julian in the xenodochium. Arriving by boat, pilgrims from Italian lands communicated easily and complained much about their journey; Frenchmen proudly completed their long travel through land, from whom Julian kept a reserved distance; there were caravans of Bulgars and inconspicuous Greeks who mingled into the Christian community; there were tall, quiet Ethiopians with long faces and black skin; wild-looking peasants from the lands of Englaland; contrite and dedicated German pilgrims who travelled alone, arriving in near nakedness; a few short Magyars; scores of Libyans; Egyptians riding their camels and beautiful horses; Norsemen and Varangoi that came by river through the lands of the rhos; and even two or three white giants from the Island of Ice, beyond the seas of the North.

Julian did everything, from tending to sores, to directing construction of new divisions. Long before the sun was peeking its red baldness over the hills of Judea, he would venture into the cold stare of the morning stars and walk down the *via dolorosa* towards an increasingly luminous sky. He ordered grains, flour and bread from a number of storage houses near the eastern wall. Quantities were carefully specified to millers and bakers, and carts with sacks of buckwheat, barley, oats, rye and flours were later delivered at the hospital, with invoices to the donations-filled patriarchate. Then Julian would turn back, just in time to see the first towers of Jerusalem piercing their sandiness through the shadows, as he walked across the city, back to the western wall.

Passing by a small agglomerate of Jewish dwellings, outside the Gate of David, he would venture into a maze of market stalls hidden inside a thick cloud of aromatic smoke. Teapots boiled, *laffah* and *khubz* breads were slapped inside their smoky ovens to quickly bake and hundreds of skewered *kababs* hissed on charcoal fires. Packs of jackals were stoned by the merchants to keep a distance and return to their dens at that time of the morning. Julian would walk between hanging cages with colourful *babbaghah* birds, screeching and talking to each other in their strange Hindustani language. At the butcher stalls, he would examine hanging sheep carcasses and choose the freshest, go over to the fruit sellers and pick juicy plump grapes and select meaty figs, before sending the best deals into the hospital. The more pilgrims, donations and gifts arrived, the better he could supply the xenodochium. Occasionally, he would grab a chance to obtain cheap deliveries of sweet dates, freshly pressed oil, live poultry, milk and olives. And on a few opportunities, Julian took the luxury to buy a few spices and herbs for the hospital kitchen.

Besides food, Julian had to organise for constant new loads of fresh straw for the palliasses and always keep a generous supply of cheap black fabrics for the compulsory scarves and belts that Al-Hakim had imposed on Christians.

It was probably on the third year of Julian in Jerusalem when he returned to the hospital to find a disturbing scene.

Coming back from David's Gate, as every morning with the warming sun already shining on his face, he greeted Buonaccorso and the workers from the top of the western quarry and turned around the patriarchate to find a commotion at the entrance of the xenodochium: a crowd of pilgrims shouted curses and charged against a group of deacons who were trying to carry something huge out of the door. A large crucifix. It was Nicodemus's sculpture of the Holy Face.

In a few leaps, Julian flew into the crowd. Nicodemus, was there, trying to bar the deacons from bringing the statue out. He shouted at Julian. 'They want to burn it!'

With no weapon in hand, Julian was swift to scan around and notice a German pilgrim sporting exactly what he was looking for: a wooden hilt standing horizontally out of a baldric. As fast as a lion, Julian grabbed it and pulled the whole blade out, holding the straight sword pointed towards the deacons. The rasping sound of the blade scraping against the scabbard was enough to paralyse the crowd of pilgrims and deacons alike, except for the German who owned the sword. He just giggled.

'Drop the cross!' Julian ordered with a dark face. 'Leave it there!'

Frozen before the shine of the sharpened iron, one of the deacons carefully said 'We can talk. Lower the sword, please!'

'I will just lower the blade when you bring the crucifix back into my cell.' Julian growled.

'It's an abomination, Julian,' the deacon sighed. 'We cannot let this adoration go on.'

'What are you talking about?' Julian pleaded. 'What adoration? The crucifix is mine and we have agreed I would keep it in my cell, away from the pilgrims.'

Nicodemus dropped his gaze and suggested they all returned to Julian's cell. They carefully lowered the massive crucifix on the floor and the keeper explained. 'The pilgrims sneak inside here every morning as you leave for the market, Julian. They pray to the 'Holy Face' of the saviour. They touch the sculpture as a relic, expecting miracles.' Nicodemus almost smiled, feeling a sharp poke of pride as he thought of other miracles and relics he had been responsible for.

'Is this true?' Julian asked the deacons.

'That is why we came for it,' said Theophilus, one of the bishops. 'We cannot allow for this outrage. The sculpture is sinful and we will not let this scandal continue. On this sacred ground, there should be no abhorred adoration of sensuous images. Nicodemus made a mistake and so did we in allowing it to exist. The image will be incinerated to resolve the matter.'

Julian raised the sword again and touched the bearded chin of Theophilus with its tip. 'You touch this crucifix again and this blade will taste your blood.' The bishop lowered his eyes in disappointment. Julian left his cell and addressed a sudden silent crowd of pilgrims 'Anyone who dares to come and see that image on the cross will deal with my sword, which is much bigger than this one. This sculpture is *no* Holy Face. This is *my* portrait, made by the keeper of the church, Nicodemus. It is not a relic. It was finished no more than one year ago. Do not touch it, do not even look at it. This is *mine!*'

Julian returned to his cell, passing by the deacons who waited patiently. He retrieved his own Lucca-forged sword from under the palliasse and unsheathed it. The reflexes on the steel shone throughout the dark faces of the religious men. Comparing to the German's one-edged, his double edge felt did feel a bit heavier, but cruelly more lethal.

'You would have to put your lives on these blades to take the crucifix from me' Julian stated, with one sword on each hand. 'But you can tell me now if I should leave and take my cross or if you want me to stay and protect it from public view.'

Theophilus gestured for the other deacons to leave, but he indicated that Nicodemus should remain in the cell. When the three were left alone, Theophilus meant to sit on Julian's palliasse, but waited with eyebrows raised for his consent. Once given, he made himself comfortable and scratched his silvering beard. 'Julian, had we arrived earlier, we would have taken the cross and burned it. That would have solved the moral problem we have with this sculpture. Not that I particularly have any reservations, but a church council in Nicaea has decided on the inappropriateness of such style or sculpture, probably more than two hundred years ago. On the other hand, had we burned this cross, we would have lost the best hospitaller Jerusalem has had in its memory. It's been no more than three years since you came Julian, and the fire in your heart has temporarily replaced the Holy

Fire that healed those who sought healing. Not only have you the powerful touch to bring solace to the pilgrims that seek it, but you have a precious sense to establish priorities with our expenses and provide minimum conditions of comfort to the travellers. It is indisputable that your stay here is most welcome, heartily from our religious community and undeniably from the pilgrims' side.' He cleared his throat and continued. 'Now, having said that, I would beg you to stay at the xenodochium, but also to cover your cross, keep it inside your cell and never allow it to be exposed to the public, as long as it remains in the Holy Land.'

Julian nodded respectfully.

Outside his cell, the crowd had dispersed, except for the German pilgrim. He did not move, and just kept a grin on his bushy face, covered in lush brown hair. A strongly built red-skinned man with not a trace of a neck separating his chest from his chin, a sun-broken forehead and probably no more than three decades of age, he introduced himself as Jan Koogs, a Saxon. He had come with a group accompanying the men of a Duke Bernhard, with the blessing of an Archbishop Libentius, of Bremen.

'Apologies for stealing it from you', Julian said, listening courteously to the pilgrim's story.

'You can keep my *seax*.' Jan Koogs answered. 'I will be released of my sins and have no more need of an attack weapon.'

'Thank you, but I have no need of another sword.' said Julian. 'I have my own. And from now on I should better be carrying it every day, whether I stay here or not.'

'I would indeed if I were you.' the Saxon said, sheathing his seax with the single edged blade facing up. 'Knowing nothing of your feud with the priests, I find it nevertheless advisable for your protection. Although the sun and the sacred blessings of Jerusalem do attract my heart more intensely than my cloudy and quiet home of Koog, we are in a still very treacherous city. I am aware of your Roman soldier friends, but if you can ever make use of my blood, I will heartily be at your side. We are all here for redemption, and after such an arduous journey, the pilgrims need the soothing of body and soul. A good hospitaller as you is a blessing on this journey, Julian. We all agree this is the best of the xenodochia we have boarded since leaving our homes.'

While Julian humbly absorbed those words, the Saxon pointed at the Lucchese sword.

'You have a beautiful blade there, you move it swiftly, but still as if you were holding a heavy weapon. See my seax?' he said, unsheathing it once more and swinging it through the air. 'This is just an extension of my arm. I can scratch the flea bites behind my own scrotum with it,' he smiled. 'Julian, you held my seax as if you had done it with your sword. Now, if you master your long sword as just another finger in your hand, not any different than how I do it with my seax, you would be invincible in battle.'

'Invincible against the flea bites behind your scrotum?' Julian smirked.

'Those too! I'll teach you that.' Jan said. He bade him farewell and left.

Later on that afternoon, Nicodemus helped Julian wrap the crucifix with linen bandages, hemp, twine and leather. Just before the head was covered, Julian took one last look at the Holy Face. The bulging eyes of the brown Christ looked at him in sadness, before they were blinded by a dusty bandage.

For the following months, Jan Koogs and Julian practiced with their weapons under the raising pillars of the church.

'Your sword is awkward to use, difficult to control. It just doesn't feel right!' the Saxon said, tapping the blade flat with a stone, from the tip to the base, as he gripped the hilt with one hand. Next, he asked Julian to do the tapping with the same stone, but Jan was holding it now with two hands. 'The balance is most different, more harmonious when you hold it with two hands,' he said, as Julian finished the tapping. 'but in this case you should be hitting further with the tip, where the sweet spot is, for the way you hit now must be returning a hard shock into your hands. One day this hilt could burst into pieces inside your grip.' He stopped and tried different swings with one or the other hand. 'And what kind of pommel is that?' he asked, examining the large metal disk at the end of the hilt.

'This is actually a replacement pommel that I managed to insert in the hilt. The first one dropped out in a clash against Saracens near Salerno.'

'Nonsense!' Jan grunted. 'A pommel is not a counterweight, but a tuning device to make the handling of the blade more harmonic. This disk pommel is clumsy and obviously unnecessary. The grip vibrates too much with it' He pulled out his own seax and beat on the pommel with the back of the blade. The iron disk with a pin on the edge clinked on the ground.

'Now you have the extra length of the hilt functioning as a pommel.' Jan continued, as he easily swung the blade in a horizontal "8" wrapped around himself. 'It is a more balanced beauty now, but to be used with one hand only. Try it.'

Julian tried it, with lips pursed. He swung it fiercely and hit a wooden pole, digging a thick chip out. He tried again and again, until the pole parted. Looking back in amazement at Jan, Julian exclaimed 'It is not only lighter, but softer at the strike in my grasp!'

Jan chuckled in embarrassment for being so proud of his wisdom. 'That was the soft spot.' He said. 'You're hitting with it now! And to think that all these years you had been holding onto a bad sword…'

The Saxon taught Julian how to use the weapon in that new fashion, starting from repositioning the feet for a new balance, all the way to the blade, moving it so light and swiftly through the air and striking in preparedness to use the kick back as an impulse for the next strike, defending the blows with a deadly arch that would ensure no other would follow. They only stopped when Jan Koogs felt he could teach no more, and only a dangerous practice would follow with Julian's quick reflexes. As for the hospitaller, he knew he could slice all the walls of Jerusalem in the blink of an eye.

A goat's head looked at Julian with its square pupils in cloudy bulging eyes. Next to it, several other heads of goats and sheep waited for a slow roast process. The smell of cooking brains was not the most pleasant to Julian's nose, especially on that scorching summer day. As the vendors chanted their products with the power of elephants' trumpets, Julian held his breath as he passed by myriads of flies that contemplated and licked on skinned animal carcasses lined along the alley and through a corridor of steaming pots with their vapours escaping into his lungs. He sought refuge among the rather comfortable spice alley.

In the spice alley, Julian could be sheltered by the pungent oily smell of cinnamon and Malabar leaves. He could hide behind the strong sweet aroma of tiny, brown dried buds the Romans called *clavus* – nail pegs. Sometimes Julian would be attracted to the intriguing smells of fine dust raised by women beating their stone mortars and grinding dried Ethiopian berries called *bunn* and exotic seed pods called *hel*, used for hot curing brews. There were bags of caraway and cumin seeds, exhaling warm earthy aromas; sweet anise seeds for the local teas and refreshment; vividly coloured, but flavourless turmeric powders; preciously located boxes of nutmeg, attracting customers with their absorbing spicy sweet perfume; and linen pockets with saffron crocuses and tiny mustard seeds, giving away a faint but spicy burning aroma. Finally, the bags of sweet salt, a sandy brown grain extracted from a tall grass. It would melt at the touch, so sweet and addictive that most Christians suspected of its goodness.

The stalls displayed a collection of dry and fresh herbs, including fennels, inconspicuous ginger roots, deliciously fragrant garlic braids and pots of a plant that had always attracted Julian's curiosity, but he could never really explain why. It was a rather small green herb, similar to parsley, with white feathery flowers. Its smell, though, was significantly different from parsley. A bit too flowery and pungent, Julian had smelled and tasted it in local dishes. He did not think it was particularly vile, but he knew people like Buonaccorso could not find anything more rank and offensive.

'*Assalamu alaikum,*' the spice merchant greeted from behind his merchandise, his sudden floating smile taking Julian by surprise.

'*Wa 'alaikumus salam*' Julian answered, still intrigued by the smell of that herb.

'The rumi does not like the *koriannon*?' the merchant asked with a genuine concern.

'It does not particularly bother me' Julian said, warming up with a smile. 'But it does remind me of something else...'

'This is what you call *coriandrum,*' the merchant said, grabbing a pot and smelling the white flowers vigorously, so that a few petals seemed to enter his nostrils. 'We like it to flavour our foods, but many rumi pilgrims find it repulsive. Here!' he said, presenting a leave to Julian. 'Chew on it!'

Julian graciously declined it.

'They say that the koriannon is a herb from hell!' the merchant said, straightening his beard. 'Legend says that after three thousand years of fanning the embers in the darkness of hell, a *jinn*, a *diabolos*, came out some fresh air. And wherever the jinn touched the ground, the koriannon grew.'

Julian stepped back, disturbed by the merchant's words. His foot got caught in a bag of seeds, almost toppling him, but his head still brushed against a hanging bunch of coriander. He bid the merchant farewell and left in a hurry.

'And may God accompany you...' said the merchant with a grin, looking at the long-haired rumi that ran away along the alley like a scared gazelle.

The smell was on Julian's hair. He felt it deep and pungent. He sweated from the exhausting heat and the strangling stuffiness of the market. It became a stench that covered his tongue, sticking it to the palate, choking him with a strange tartness that made his lips heavy. His vision was confused by a cloudy curtain and his knees were about to cede when, through an explosion of pigeons that hurriedly flew out cooing, he found fresh air and the Gate of David ahead of him.

Walking quickly back to the hospital, he grabbed a wet lock of his long black hair that rested on his shoulder and put it under his nose. The stench of fresh coriander had stuck to it. Strangely, people in those alleys seemed to be in a hurry just as he was, but they ran on the opposite direction. It could be no more than the call of adhan for the noon prayers. He had to stand against a wall when a herd of sheep passed by in a hurry, bouncing their brown heads, all trying to run side by side, but no shepherd came to chase them. Bleating pathetically, their woolly pleasant smell was not sufficient to overpower the coriander from his hair. When the sheep freed the alley, Julian noticed the easily identifiable black rags of a Christian that had fallen asleep on the ground. Oddly enough, he had lain out in the sun. And there were noises. A high clamour of voices from around the corner, probably the xenodochium. But that was no chanting.

Julian only realised it when two people came quickly running by. The first was a pilgrim who ignored Julian with an expressionless face and disappeared into the alley. The second did not seem to be a local man, for he wore the uncommon *litham*, a veil covering the lower half of his face, more typical of the Mohammedan men from Egypt and Ifriqiya. Running behind the first one with a saif sword raised on his hand, he was startled, stopping the chase for a second when his angry eyes stared into Julian's puzzled face. The blade of the man's saif swung around and came down with a powerful strike to cut Julian in two, but clashing against the steel of Julian's Lucchese sword which had been swiftly and firmly drawn. Julian had to defend himself from a second, a third and a fourth blow, all with the strength and hatred to kill, before he managed to change the direction of the strikes and easily open a gash on the man's liver. When Julian stroke a second blow across the man's collar bone, he could clearly distinguish the screams in the xenodochium. It was a slaughter.

One week later and Julian's memory could hardly be put together to re-trace his steps as he charged into the hospital, harvesting his way through the militiamen in a blind fury, severing limbs and quickly trespassing them with his sword before drawing it for the next blow. A score of those invaders had cornered some of the most invalid pilgrims that remained in the xenodochium during the day and were mercilessly cutting down their prey.

The invaders turned back to the entrance, where the Christian with a long sword had broken a red gash into their flanks. Julian fell one by one, or by twos, as they came to him, leaving their victims and running in a rage, ready to smite the brave hospitaller.

Habituated to their surprise charges on the attacking side, they were good killers, but when dealing with fierce opposition, they revealed themselves to be poor defenders, individually or collectively, helpless against the weight of Julian's strength and the length of his sword.

Julian saw the terror on their eyes as they faced the first blow, just one second before receiving the next through their necks. The assassins finally figured that charging together as a group would give them the best chance, in spite of the narrow spaces in the xenodochium.

That was the second after Julian heard a shout from outside.

'By the Blood of Christ and the head of St. James!' The enthusiastic voice of Jan Koogs.

The Saxon broke into the hospital roaring, passing by Julian and charging against four attackers, nimbly deflecting their blows and cutting their throats with quick swings of his short seax. A bleeding and broken Julian went along, already cornering the militiamen at the back of the hospital, where they had initially been the executioners. By the time Buonaccorso arrived with his soldiers, Julian was fallen.

On that night, long past the muezzin had chanted for the nightfall prayer somewhere in the city, a few heavily loaded bullock carts slowly left Jerusalem by its eastern wall, conducted by both Christians and Muslims. Miles from the walls, at the edge of a ravine, they stopped.

'Dogs!' Buonaccorso said, looking at the cargo with disgust, spitting on the ground.

They started to unload the bodies from the carts. Thirty five militiamen that had been felled during that raid. Mostly by the hospitaller Julian of Mans. Those who were still alive were finished off by the Roman soldiers' lances.

As the corpses rolled down the ravine, sliding down the gravel, a pack of jackals was heard yelping with excitement somewhere down in the darkness. 'Quick!' one of the Muslims said. 'We must drop the bodies and leave this place as fast as we can.'

'Jackals are not a threat,' said Buonaccorso.

'When these beasts smell blood, they change. But worse, there are hyenas in the valleys north of here. A cackle of those stinking half-human, half-wolf demons could easily detect our scent and drink our bloods before we reach the safety of the city.'

A restless Buonaccorso was not sure if he fully understood that man, but he hurried to help pulling down the assassins and tossing them down the ravine, to the thrill of the jackals. He could smell the caked blood from the dead and something else which did not seem to be coming from the pack down in the darkness, and hopefully not from approaching hyenas. It was an unpleasant smell. Something spicy.

On the next day, there would be still a feast for jackals, hyenas, vultures, storks, crows, ravens and even the occasional leopard. And flies. Millions of them who would gorge on the carcasses of a tiny militia of the Caliph Al-Hakim bi-Amr Allah.

The men returned in a hurry, pulling their empty bullock carts towards the city. They had to still help finish burying the dead pilgrims, thirteen of them. Buonaccorso was sorry to hear about Julian. His friend had been seriously injured but, with the help of prayers, supervision and tender loving care of his friends, Julian would be brought back into full vigour sooner than expected.

The wounded hospitaller had a long rest. During his recovery he was often attacked by nightmares and soothed by good dreams.

While Buonaccorso cared for the disposal of the assassins, Jan Koogs and Nicodemus cleaned the xenodochium from the stains of death. Christian families minded the wounded and the dead pilgrims, recomposing, washing and dignifying the corpses with a shroud before burial. A heated argument exploded in one of the catacombs where a memorial service was being prayed for an old Franconian lord. His relatives who had travelled with him protested and demanded that the body be handed to them, to be disembowelled and boiled so that it could be easily de-fleshed and the bones carried for a burial at home. The altercation required Jan Koogs with his seax out, guaranteeing some dignity for the Franconian lord.

Most of the seriously injured were taken to the main bimaristan, where specialists attended to them at the emergency and trauma section. Julian, however, was stitched up in several places, immobilised, and taken to Buonaccorso's house, by insistence of the Pavese Leopard and his wife.

Julian dreamed of a dark-faced devil hidden behind a litham brandishing a curved sword, opening gashes in his flesh, streams of black blood oozing from his wounds. He dreamed of angels with needles and sheep gut threads piercing through the skin and lacing the sides together. He dreamed of the pain of a broken wrist and of marvelling at a beautiful mosaic ceiling during a painful reduction promptly performed by careful fists that held him. He dreamed of his hand being bandaged between two wooden planks, of the smell of eggs and seashells, which were patted around his dressing rags, while eyes of concern held a stare at him. His dreams were cloudy, often blurred by pain but increasingly distracted by a pleasant wave of gratification. Julian wasn't sure if those eyes watching him were an angel's, but he could easily notice they were sheltered by an intriguing pair of sooty falcons. He felt dizzy as his hard mattress swayed and the tall alleys of Jerusalem examined him from above, wobbling over his face. But once again with a hearth nearby, Julian felt himself warmed up by another body on top of his. He could feel no more straw under his back as he drank from a fountain of lips that poured the miracle wine into his own. Wet lips of honey that tenderly gripped his face, his nose and his tongue, distracting him from the pain of his bruises and cuts with a sensuous bliss before he felt himself plunging into a wet warmness that pulled him out of his body. A delicious agony, moist, hot, that covered him and ran away, just to be back around him with more power. A painful delight of flames that made his muscles tense and his wounds bleed, ache that burned his entrails until he boiled out in sweat, sizzling the skin as it oozed into the cuts. Although he pushed and trusted up, his whole body was still immobile, delicate fists holding his wrists and strong legs that clamped his thighs. The flames licked at his skin, uttering words that empowered him to an explosion in ecstasy, gasping for air, until his body relaxed and was wrapped by a refreshing feeling of achievement, a blessing that meant the conquest of pain through pleasure. Before releasing his last grasp on the lingering blissful tingle of this dream and to dive into another long spell of slumber, before closing his eyes just after being able to fly through the fog, Julian distinguished a clear image of dark figures standing next to him. Not the dark woven robes of the priests, but a black, hairy cover, stealing any light around it. They were all looking at him with yellow eyes of fire.

When Julian tried to scream, the nearest figure extended its palm to shut him up.

Julian tumbled into a heavy sleep, being vexed by nightmares in which dark figures with yellow eyes that giggled with scorn chased him. He tried in vain to get back to the comforting eyes of the Holy Face.

He woke up in delirium, that sinister laughter still lingering on his head. He opened his eyes and saw a faded leopard skin hanging on a wall. But he soon forgot about it all as he fell asleep again.

Ache unfolded over his skin. A vigorous rub woke him up. Among the shadows, he distinguished the beautiful dark face of Helena. She had a devilish smile.

'It's a balm from Ein Gedi. You will hurt, Julian. Your skin will burn, but the power of this balm will aid on the healing. And do not worry, my dear. I will not rub it there. For that special part, I will anoint you with clover oil, which will make you stand for longer. I'm ready to fuck you again.'

'Julian, you have had and endless row of visitors.' It was Buonaccorso's assuring voice, proud of his friend's popularity.

'Too many!' grunted Helena from the background. 'Julian can never heal properly with those interruptions of his rest.'

Buonaccorso chuckled. 'Look at my wife. So devoted to our guest that the mere presence of pilgrims by the door will annoy her! You have been delirious, Julian. And it was Helena who held you together, awake night and day to sooth your pain.'

Julian saw Helena behind Buonaccorso. She hid her face to conceal a grin.

'Come on, Julian, let's see if you can sit and stand, maybe walk,' Buonaccorso said. 'The physicians are positive of your readiness to start living again. Helena, help me here to hold this young man up.'

Julian could not allow his eyes to meet hers any more. Her touch still stirred his most immediate waves of heat, but much worse, now it had also awakened a dormant repulse, a wide and thick disgust behind which he felt protected from betrayal.

'Julian, I know what you and Helena have been up to!'

'Excuse me?' Julian could not believe the words he had just heard from Nicodemus. They had carefully walked out of Buonaccorso's house, visiting the scrubbed clean xenodochium. Jan Koogs had been minding the daily affairs. Pilgrims kept arriving and leaving, as usual.

'Julian, I know my daughter.' Nicodemus explained in a whisper as they left the building. 'You are only a man of flesh and blood, but Helena is a sinner, in desperate need of absolution. As the Magdalen has once been purged of her seven demons by the resurrected Christ, Helena needs her own soter to save her from damnation.'

'You don't expect me to be her saviour, do you?' Julian said between gritted teeth, verifying the sides. 'I have been washed in shame, sinning through lust as much as your daughter has.'

'Lust is indeed a sin, Julian, but its fulfilment feels as a blessing. Your quick recovery, after being butchered by those murderers, is owned partly to the physicians of the bimaristan...' He helped Julian to sit down on a low wall by the reconstruction site of the Holy Sepulchre, watching Buonaccorso and a battalion of masons from a distance. '...but also by fact that poor Buonaccorso, restless working on this sacred piece, was hardly at home, leaving Helena to cure you with her body, by hooking out your soul.' Julian tried to say something, but Nicodemus raised a silencing hand. 'You were immobilised, Julian. Your awareness was dormant, your defences beaten, but your most animal instincts were made alive. How could any man, but probably only a well-tanned ascetic survive such temptation?'

'I feel for Buonaccorso...' Julian said, more to himself than to the keeper.

'I *fear* for Buonaccorso!' Nicodemus corrected, shrugging. 'The moment he finds his wife is an *impudica, pecattrix*, a woman who's abandoned morals, he will kill her.' He drew his index finger across his neck. 'But not before tearing out of her tongue the names of all men who have helped him wear the cuckold horns on his head.'

Julian carefully considered Nicodemus's words. 'I certainly deserve punishment, for betraying the loyalty of my friend, but Helena does n–'

'Nonsense!' interrupted Nicodemus. 'You all deserve chastisement, but not death! And there are many fashions of retribution for a wrong. Do you know the story of Saint Mary of Egypt?' He waited for Julian to shake his head. 'They say that while in the desert, an ascetic monk called Zozimus managed to catch a stealthy wild old woman that agonised in the wilderness and he gave her his cloak to cover her nakedness. Mary then told him that in her youth she had been a sinner in Alexandria, committing the most shameful offences as adultery and incest. She came to Jerusalem buying her journey with her own body, corrupting the whole crew of her ship. But when right here, looking for new adventures on this very ground where we stand, she was stopped from entering the Church of the Holy Sepulchre by an angel. Alarmed with this intercession, Mary prayed outside for the Virgin Mary and the angel allowed her in. She heard from the angel inside the church that her sins of the flesh would be forgiven if she went across the Jordan. She went into the desert with three loaves of laffah bread, which lasted for seventeen years and when the bread was over she survived another thirty years without drinking or eating. Zozimus left the old woman in the desert and returned after a year, to give her the Holy Communion. However, he found her dead. The monk buried her with the help of a lion.'

'Do you expect Helena to retire to the desert for absolution, like St Mary or Zozimus?' Julian asked incredulous.

'I hate to admit it, but Helena is a lecherous woman. Probably not different than Mary of Egypt had been. I would never interfere in her life with Buonaccorso. Had they not been a married couple, I would be banning her to the desert, for a life of privation, chastity and penitence. Helena does not believe in prayer or in the sacredness of the footsteps of the Christ. She despises the relics and frowns upon the miracles. But exposed and naked only to the eyes of God, she will think otherwise. Living for years from locusts and honey, overwhelming bodily and spiritual suffering may grant her the ultimate reward of absolution of her sins.'

Julian realised the keeper was being serious. He raised an eyebrow. 'But Nicodemus, just being in the wilderness does not necessarily force the sinner to repent. Helena could just run away from the desert.'

Nicodemus tapped Julian on the knee and stood up. He gave his hand to help Julian stand and looked deep into the hospitaller's eyes. 'Julian, if I ever send my daughter to a life of asceticism, I will make sure that I take Helena to a place where she can only return from with the divine help of angels, rewarding her for the desired repentance.'

The Wife of Tempagnano

Behind a long jumbled line of confused rams, Bernardo from the Rocks pulled his donkey into the village of Tempagnano, dragging a loud cart that was not yet full of fleeces. Resting quietly on a flat valley less than a mile west of the neighbouring village of Wald Ottavo, Tempagnano had been reduced over the years to no more than a confused amalgamation of stone houses and an abandoned monastery.

Sister Caterina came with wine for Bernardo and brought the donkey down to a trough with clean water at a well-tended garden, a refreshing surprise inside the rotting walls of the cloister.

'The men haven't brought the off-season fleeces yet,' she said. 'In spite of the rains, it seems that they are unsoiled, probably in their best of conditions, ever. You will get a good value for them, Bernardo, it is excellent clip for this time of the year. I only sent the men out three days ago, when the weather improved.' Sister Caterina had a brilliant smile, watching the lord of those lands quench his thirst with boisterous gulps. Her cowl was flung back, allowing for her black mane to flow wild. Sister Caterina was past her fortieth year, but time had left no more than handsome lines across her face. A long and strong neck held out a proud head, where wisdom had shaped pleasing angles. She had matured with the grace of the mountains, ever renewed with the seasons and looking better at every year. The rough Tuscan men of the Apuane had a saying that Jesus always chose the best wives, and that Sister Caterina would have been the best choice for a mother of His children.

She took the donkey out and tied it to a small terrace. The sheep had already been herded into a paddock. Coming back in, Caterina was wiping her hands on her robe in an unpretentious manner that stretched the folds of the rough fabric around herself, wringing around the generous curves and volumes of a well-built torso, gifted with long and vigorous limbs. 'You may have to wait until tomorrow,' she said, 'but if you are going up the valley for the rams anyway, it's already worth the journey. And you can collect the clip on the way down.'

'That will be just fine, Sister Caterina.' Bernardo said, trying as always to brush off the lure that Caterina's magnificent presence constantly posed. 'These are good rams brought in from Bergamo. I purchased them in Lucca. It's time we improve our herds. And I still have one or two days to hand those rams to the shepherds up on the mountains before I return, then.'

'Are you taking any supplies to the hermits?' she asked.

'Not this time. I don't think I'll climb all the way up to the caves.' Sitting next to Caterina on at the bench in the abandoned cloister, he rested his hands on his knees. Frowning with the sunlight, he said. 'You know what?' he clicked his tongue. 'I hope God will thank me for that one day, because those filthy monkeys never raise a finger to acknowledge our alms. And quite honestly, without the help of shepherds and travellers, the poor bastards would not have the wits to produce a rotten fig.'

Sister Caterina laughed, as if clear water was showering Bernardo from a spring. 'You are a good man, Bernardo,' she said with a sweet smile, blinding him with the shine in her black eyes and resting her warm hand on his. 'I thank you for that, if it matters anything,' The sparkling warmth from her touch shot up from his hand up to his head, flushing him with a delicious redness.

'Sister Caterina,' Bernardo said, holding her hand with both of his. 'It matters a world to me. You are a good woman and ... But no,' he interrupted himself , 'you are actually too good! You are too good for this village, too good for these lands of mine. Look at you! A beautiful, lettered woman, caring for a group of brutes in lost merger of cottages, working the land, building, carrying, shearing. You should be living in a castle, treated as a queen, but instead you live in a land which is owned by a shepherd. What are you doing here? Why have you been left forgotten in this God-forsaken place? I would be humbled to have you as my wife, if I could only afford to dedicate myself to you.'

'And I would be the happiest wife in the world...' Caterina, said, taking her hand off his. The feeling was too delicious for the simple life she had chosen. 'Bernardo, my dear Bernardo. I do want to believe in all that flatter of yours...'

'It is heartily!' he interrupted.

'Fine, I believe it.' she said with liquid eyes. 'The only problem is that I am not meant to marry you, although I cannot think of a better husband. We have known each other for over 15 years. You come here once in a while bringing me your books, and your tenderness. You bring me your knowledge, your wits and your love and I value it with all my heart. You share my bed when you are here and you make me feel like a real wife, not like an eternal bride, feeling alive like no other woman could be in these or other lands. I know that you go and have get others' attentions elsewhere and it bothers me nothing, for I know well of manly needs. We have never asked each other questions. We have mutual acceptance by what we present ourselves to one another. And we have never spent any time together talking about who I am and who I have been once.'

'I have always respected your silence,' he said.

'And I am forever thankful for this.' She completed. 'But maybe it's time I tell you who I am.'

Bernardo fixed his gaze on her mountain-splitting black irises.

Her eyes shot up for a quick moment as if thinking of a forgotten dream. Then she concentrated on his gaze too. 'I was born in Pisa from a poor family, given early in my youth to the abbey of San Giovanni Battista, in Santa Maria Lei Giudice, a hamlet just in the south of...'

'I have been there!' Bernardo interrupted her again. 'I was there with a friend, when I came back to Tuscany, during the Anno Mille.'

'Well, this was before, much before, just for you to reckon how much older than you I am.'

'Sister Caterina, you are so well hidden in Tempagnano that even time has forgotten to age you.'

'Enough of interruptions, Bernardo. Let me finish what I started. When I was taken into the abbey, I was practically adopted by an old woman that lived there. She was older than anyone I have ever met and she had seen many generations of people come and go. She was older than the rocks that make these mountains, but more alive and fresher than the waters that cascade down these valleys. This old lady told us about the power she had held in Rome in her time, having the pleasure or displeasure of having held popes and patricians of Rome, kings and queens, on the palm of her hand. And all she had to do was to control them. And do you know how? She used her flesh! She taught me all about seduction and how to use it to do good.' She lowered her eyes for a second and continued, now without holding his gaze. 'Bernardo, I entered into a carnal relation with another young sister of the faith and soon we were both seducing several brides of Christ in the monastery. Not after too long we were discovered by some jealous nuns and our good abbess was obliged to open the doors for an investigation. How much of a basic mistake this enquiry was, they could not have calculated. It was a true feast of the flesh when those celibate priests, hungry for sensuality, came to interview us about our indecency. We had them one by one, until the day I found Brother Martino.'

Bernardo froze.

But Sister Caterina did not notice his livid face and just carried on. 'It shatters my heart to admit that I encountered true love and the love of my life in Brother Martino, that is now lost to me. He was a bright Roman monk who came to aid in the investigation, but who was naively seduced into perdition by a much younger temptress . . . me!' she giggled. 'Hunter became prey, as I delivered myself totally. I could have bled entirely and forever only to satisfy his eternal appetite for my love. And once we had given ourselves to one another, in flesh and spirit, in sweat and blood, in heart and soul, we felt wonderfully closer to God. Not arrogantly, no, Bernardo. We felt closer to Him for being humbly gratified to be blessed by our gift, and such miracle could only come from the eternal goodness that springs from His heart.'

Bernardo was still speechless. The coincidence was too much. Caterina and Martino, of course! So close and so separated from each other.

Caterina continued. 'But the heavenly delights last no more than the blink of an eye in this world. Martino and I were soon separated by the church that mothered us. Knowing that next time we would be together could be only in heaven, we exchanged promises of eternal love and kept our memories dear to our hearts, at least for this passing phase in the world of the living. Martino was sent to a place far away by the Lateran officials and I was smartly smuggled by the good abbess to this monastery of Sant'Agnese, here in Tempagnano. Over at San Giovanni Battista, the abbess listed me as a runaway, missing forever. In Tempagnano people hardly know what happens in Wald Ottavo, least on the other side of Lucca. I was safe. Still, after more than a year, I was visited by the abbess and got the news: The other young nun that started that spell of sensuality with me in San Giovanni, Sister Antonia, was taken to Rome and never heard of again. And under orders of the young German king, soldiers from Rome were sent in to the abbey of San Giovanni and smothered the old woman. Her name was Marozia. A name dreaded both by popes and emperors in her time.'

Caterina paused and inhaled for more, ignoring the fact that Bernardo had a very good reason to be with liquid eyes, much more than just for compassion towards her past.

'For years I lived with the poor sisters of this decaying monastery and, before the Anno Mille had arrived, insanity had already broken through these walls. Most of the nuns left because they believed the Beast was to be released. Sooner than later, I was left over with two elder sisters who returned from their hysterical wanderings after waiting too long for the end of times. That was when you came back to take over the land. We met during the Anno Mille, remember, Bernardo?'

He did not answer. He seemed to be paying attention to the manner in which his right hand fingers were playing with the fingers from the left hand.

'Bernardo,' she called, trying to catch his attention, 'have I insulted you? Are you disgusted at my past?'

He chuckled and shook his head. 'No, Sister Caterina, no...I am just thinking of the games that God plays on us. If it is cruelty or what...'

'Brief moments of bliss are worth living a whole life for,' she said with gusto.

'Some of them may not have to be that brief,' said Bernardo, finally looking at her.

'What do you mean? Are you referring to you and I?'

'No, my beloved Caterina,' he said with a warm smile, 'I am talking about Brother Martino.' He studied her puzzled face for a second, enjoying the expectation he had built. 'Hold on to yourself, Caterina. Keep your great heart in your chest, for I do know Brother Martino, and may God forgive me for never mentioning my past either. So many stories I tell, uncountable crafted tales, I could be for days doing my cantastorie act and still I have never told you about that friend. A simple word, a minor reference during our countless hours together could have changed three lives. Yours, his and mine. True love, Caterina, is unconditional, and all we want of the loved object is its happiness. Your happiness will overflow to my heart, for mine is forever connected to yours, no matter what happens.'

'Tell me what is going on!' she yelled, sweating profusely.

'Martino is now an ordained parishioner. He is alive and well, not far from here, caring for the parish of Santa Giulia, in Controne.'

Caterina stood up with a dizzy feeling. She managed to balance herself on her feet as she ran to the drinking trough and dipped her head into the gelid water, emerging with a yank of her head that splashed water in a comb-like fan from her hair.

'And where the *Hell* is Controne?' she asked, panting.

'Well, no more than a few miles up the valley, climbing straight north from Corsena. Father Martino was yesterday in Anchiano, granting a church blessing to the matrimonial union of Fulcardo Cunimundinghi with Maria Maddalena, daughter of Immanuel Malacchi, the widower of Elvira Burle, from Corsena.'

But Sister Caterina did not care who was getting married or who had died or was being born. She was thanking God for that day.

They talked until dusk. Bernardo updated her with all stories he could about Martino, never forgetting to insert here and there excerpts of the wicked tales of Maria Maddalena, the death of Lucia Cunimundinghi, the disappearance of Divina and the recent drowning of Béla, the shaman. Caterina acknowledged it all, but she could not hide the inquisitiveness about Martino and the airy light that her eyes fired when she heard of his generosity and compassion, his practical attitude and humorous spirit. Bernardo had to repeat probably all details of his trip South from the abbey of Saint Michael, accompanied by Brother Martino in the Anno Mille.

When Bernardo finally meant to leave, the air was cold outside the small church.

'Stay with me tonight.' Sister Caterina said.

On seeing his raised eyebrow, she completed with a smile of complicity 'I will not be breaking any extra vows tonight. Martino is still far, far away from me as he has been for these twenty six years. And love, Bernardo, true love, stays forever. Come with me. Do me more good.'

They made love with a wild intensity that night. Somehow Bernardo knew this was their last night together.

Early before the sun broke through the valley, Bernardo walked into the fog to find his donkey still on the terrace. The rams were behaving well, in spite of some solid clashes. A few villagers were already set for climbing up with him. They greeted Bernardo with respect. He came back to the church to kiss Caterina goodbye. She was standing at the door, savagely wrapped in her blanket, looking as glorious as ever.

'You take care of yourself up there, Bernardo delle Rocche. You are a very generous man, and the world would not be the same if anything was to happen to you,' she said, kissing him on the lips.

'I will be watching for any trouble.' Bernardo said, letting the thrill of her tenderness irradiate through his body. 'Weeks ago I have been across the passes and saw the smoke coming out of Luni. And by night, the town was under a red glow. It was a terrifying view. I offered my men to Alberto Azzo, who is recruiting mercenaries, but he has kindly declined. He says I should stick to the land, while he does the fighting. But nowadays, it seems that bands of Saracens are coming down for their raids towards these sides of the Apuane. Only God knows what happened to Divina.'

'The poor girl...' Sister Caterina said with eyes focused on emptiness. She turned to Bernardo, for he had to leave. 'I will be here for one more day. You can find your fleeces inside the church, if I'm not around. After tomorrow, I walk down towards Corsena.' she said with a grin. 'I am afraid of what will be, but I cannot wait to find him.'

'He waits for you, in this life or in heaven. I could wish you no better man than Martino. Good luck and take care of yourself, Sister Caterina!'

'Fare well!' she said, waving to him.

With a feeling of comfort and warmth, she watched him walk a few steps towards the donkey, almost disappearing in the fog, but turning around and coming back to her.

'One thing I forgot to ask you' he said, scratching his head. 'You mentioned that the old woman in the abbey was named Marozia?'

'That is very true. Supposedly, she was famous and powerful in her time.' Caterina answered assertively.

'Can you recall if she ever mentioned having a family, maybe children?'

'I remember everything about Marozia. She was very thorough in her stories, full of details and descriptions, just like yours. I remember the names and every single sordid note on her affairs and adventures. She had been married four times.'

'Was there ever a Guido, among these husbands?' he asked carefully.

'Of course there was!' she beamed. 'Guido of Lucca was her favourite man! We heard a lot about him.'

'That is impossible!' Bernardo protested. 'Caterina, you know how I am. I am a cantastorie such as my dad was, and his father before him. We are few among the Obertenghi who know about the history of our family. So the person you knew could not be Marozia. She should have been long dead! Marozia senatrix of Rome was the grandmother of my grandfather. From her marriage to Guido of Lucca, she bore Adalberto II, who was the Margrave of Tuscany, the grandfather of both Lord Oberto of Luni and my father.'

Caterina yelped with excitement. 'She must have been the one! The woman was one hundred years old! She had the same violet that you have in your eyes, but hers was stronger.'

'No...' Bernardo said, leaving again towards his cart, shaking the head with confusion. 'It can't be. It just cannot be...'

Sister Caterina, wrapped in her blanket, ran on bare feet and caught up with Bernardo near the cart. The village men looked elsewhere through the fog as the strange couple obviously had a few final words before the working day. She whispered in his ear 'It must be Bernardo! Marozia's blood is surely in you, given the wonderful way that you love me!'

Since then, Bernardo never tired of walking up to the mountains. His body was forever feeling lighter, and full of life. And that particular day, he carried a constant smile across his face.

Over in Partigliano, higher on the valley, Maria Maddalena tried to awake from a nightmare, but whatever reality she found out of her dreams only hurt her even more. Wrecked and throbbing with pain, her respiration was difficult, for screams would not come out and she could not breathe in. Only because she bore the weight of a man on her. And to make it much filthier, he was also inside her.

She prayed for it to be fast, to cease soon. She prayed to die. But it only went on for a lifetime. The man was hurting her, and he made it clear he was enjoying it, taking his time. Closing her eyes, she could only see the scene of Fulcardo's head rolling down the road, with his eyes wide open. And if she opened hers to try and wipe that vision from the mind, she saw the horrible face of that black-bearded pig.

Next to her were the bodies of two villagers, lucky enough to have died before. There was still some screaming, but she could not cover her ears. Her hands were being held.

The flames of hell receded somehow, with a heavier wait on her body and slobber tricking down her face. He was finished. Now he could go and she could die.

When the attacker was finally removed from her by the honey-turban man, she heard a few unintelligible words and was yanked on to her feet with a pang of excruciating pain on her scalp. Dragged by her hair, she had no voice to scream in horror, as she noticed it was the honey-turban who held her, walking towards his horse. The other riders all had a savaged village girl across their saddles already.

'God, where are you?' Maria Maddalena moaned. Why was He allowing those demons to carry her along for new sessions of torture in Hell? When she was tossed over the saddle, she gave up. She was already praying for the Devil's help.

Suddenly, a voice was heard. 'Leave this girl alone!'

And the torture stopped in that moment.

The man with the honey-colour turban had been searching through the houses. As it had been over those last days, that village was just as easy to take as any of those other nameless places they had been through. No weapons, no resistance. Christian villagers never withstood with much opposition, which was better than facing armies. Due to their isolation and relative safety in those valleys behind the white peaks, nobody ever seemed to suspect they could be visited by real fighters until it was too late. It always seemed that villagers found the visitors too odd and unreal, rather seeing them as friendly passers than invaders.

But regrettably, after rummaging over the little belongings of the villagers and the poor church that stood closed on a terrace, they had found nothing of interest that they could carry back to their leader Mugiàhid ibn abd Allah al Amiri. With their horses already packed with meager findings, it was time to return to Luna. They could bring one woman each, and if a better one was found on the way, they would replace her.

Having inspected the largest house, where only a surprisingly large amount of books was found, the honey-turban man came back outside, where most other riders were still using the women.

The red-haired girl, the one whose man was the first to feel the blade of his saif, was now being taken by one of his friends. She had been good and tight, but difficult to control. Mugiâhid was a patient man, and a man of taste. He could wait forever to have this well-built girl broken. But the honey-turban man himself was not willing to bring a fighting beast all the way. If she kept so reluctant to submit, he would have to slay her and get a more docile villager.

When his friend had collapsed on top of her, he kicked the exhausted man to the side and announced to all riders. 'It's time we go. There is nothing here. Bring with you whatever you find interesting, including the women. This red-haired one here is mine.'

She was resisting less, but still needed to be dragged. Not too good, for it looked like the girl would probably be no more than a lifeless body after some time. That was even worse than resistance.

When he tossed the girl over his saddle, he heard someone shouting at him.

A woman.

He had not seen that one. With a surprised and amused look on their faces, they realised a healthy mature woman had been missed.

'I said leave this girl alone!'

'What is she saying'? asked one of the men. They observed the woman from their horses.

'I think she is advising me not to take the red-haired one' the honey-turban man said, finishing his sentence with a snigger. A wave of laughter ran through the riders.

'Look at her roughly sewn robe.' One pointed out, as the woman kept shouting at them. 'I think she is a religion-woman. A true Christian. One of those that live in their temples.'

'Should we kill her?' asked another.

'Of course not.' said the honey-turban. 'Not yet. This is one of those ascetic women that renounce to men. We should show her what type of life she has been missing.'

'Be careful there!' one shouted. The religieuse had released her long wavy hair from her cowl, and she walked firmly towards the honey-turban man on his horse. He unsheathed his sword and waited, ready to strike.

'Cut her in two!' he heard one of the men.

'Not yet,' he said, 'not yet. Just look at her.' And he calmly observed as she reached her hand between his legs.

'She wants me! Look at her! She is indicating me to leave the red-haired girl and take her instead.' The woman was caressing his leg. She tried unsuccessfully to push the red-haired girl from the horse. The caresses became bolder, and she pulled the man's arms to feel her breast.

'She is a vigorous woman!' he shouted with glee. 'An old woman, but with all her teeth, and her body is firm as a virgin's. Maybe she is a virgin. You wouldn't find many at this age back home!' And they burst with laughter.

'Take her, then! She wants you! She will be a much better fuck than the young girl!' they shouted.

'I will take her now!' he said, dropping the red-haired girl from the horse. As she fell with her face on the ground, the others rode around with their *saifs* raised.

The woman cried in horror, asking them to leave the girl, to let her go, for she had a child inside her. Honey-turban considered for an agonising while. It was a renewed caress of the woman that made him say 'Let her go.'

An hour later, while Sister Caterina was being carried up the valley by the riders, Maria Maddalena slowly picked up her rags and started to think of how to return home, without a husband, but hopefully with any bit of dignity she could find.

Abbess Theodora

A scream was heard through the corridors of the Lateran Palace.

At the pope's chamber, Pietro Martino Boccaporca's was lying on the bed. His eyes looked up into his mosaic ceiling, where the Christ sat on a throne, breaking the bread and sided by six dedicated disciples, three on each side. The pope's eyes were rather bulged, immovable, and so were his lips, dried and curled, the upper lip practically joining his stubby snout. Between his still healthy teeth, a swollen tongue stood out. White and hard as a rock.

'The pope is dead!' cried the factotum, his servant. He ran through the corridors as fast as he could, slamming his fist on all doors to alarm the household of Sergius IV. 'Find the *camerarius* Brunello! We need Bishop Brunello.' He was looking for the pope's chamberlain to officially confirm the death of the pontiff and, as the archdeacon of the church, to conduct the process of succession to the throne of Rome. The factotum entered the camerarius apartment to find only a couple of sub deacons. 'Where is Brunello? He should be here!'

But they all seemed to be as puzzled.

The factotum panicked. 'Find Bishop Brunello! We must find him before Cardinal John Theophylactus learns about the pontiff's death and rides in from Porto!' he continued to yell, as he entered the main atrium of the palace. There, a sudden encounter with a small crowd of custodes, other men-at-arms and a few men lavishly dressed for war made him stop in terror.

'You are right!' grunted one of the men wearing fancy war attire. The factotum noticed he had a familiar face. He was almost as large to the sides as he was in height. That mountain of a man walked towards him in large, firm strides and continued in a calmer tone, almost sweetly 'So where is Bishop Brunello? We are all looking for him.'

The factotum was so confused by the situation that he could not precisely recognise that Roman patrician. He stuttered, but managed to say. 'I don't know. He's not to be found on his premises.'

'Then we don't really need you, do we?' said the large patrician. In less than a second, the factotum shot a quick glance at the crowd and finally recognised one of the warriors. It was the feminine face of Cardinal John Theophylactus, dressed up for battle.

Stricken by a heavy blow that exploded in his stomach, the factotum looked back in puzzle at the enormous man who had punched him and realised that he was Theophylactus's brother, Albericus III, Count of Tusculum. He was holding a short sword, with a red blade drenched in blood.

Holding his abdomen to protect it from more pain, the factotum felt the warm wetness cover his hands. His legs weakened and he fell on his knees, on a large puddle of blood in the centre of the Lateran's atrium. Before his vision darkened forever, he pleaded with his eyes to Theophylactus.

The Cardinal of Porto, very calmly, just observed the servant of the dead pope crashing his face on the polished marble floor. John Theophylactus turned around and shouted in a womanish voice 'Let's find that little olive-head Brunello!'

They tried, but they never found the camerarius Brunello, neither the papal insignia. Still, the Tusculani and their thugs had a good laugh when they received the news that, over in St. Peter's basilica, Brunello had been chosen by the Crescentii as the new pope, naming himself Gregory VI. On the same day the news were spreading through the city, a Tusculani party led by Albericus was breaking through the basilica on Vatican hill, but Gregory VI had already escaped from Rome, with the help of his cousins the Crescentii.

In less than a week, a parallel election took place in a side chapel at the Lateran, supervised by the enormous Albericus III, Count of Tusculum and his brother Romanus, a consul of Rome. Once the chosen one was named, they went to a chapel, standing imposingly in front of a respecting crowd of cardinals, deacons, soldiers and other patricians. This was a loyal group that guarded the most humble respect for Albericus's sword, a sharp blade that had sliced through a few guts over that last week. Now, the youngest sibling of Albericus and Romanus entered the chapel, dressed in the most simple papal attire that had been publicly witnessed for a long time. After twelve years fighting his way up through the high rings of the church, Cardinal John Theophylactus was exploding with pride and rage on this day he became a pope. As an anti-climax for the ambitious cleric, none of the papal insignia had been found. All had been taken by Gregory VI.

Wearing a simple, thin inner tunic and thick outer white cassock, John Theophylactus only held a woollen *pallium* as a signal of regalia, a cruel irony repeating itself since the day he had been ordained a bishop by Sylvester II. The head was uncovered, with his long hair accentuating the feminine features that intrigued so many. He walked decidedly to the chapel's altar, where a newly chosen factotum nervously stood, in a much less prominent position than a large wooden chair that had been placed in the centre: the *sedes stercoraria*, a defecating chair.

Theophylactus quickly sat on the chair with an elegant swivel of his vests, drawing up the fabrics and holding them by his waist, hidden between the solid armrests. But Theophylactus was not seated on the *sedes stercoraria* to defecate. The audience held its breath as the new factotum kneeled next to the chair and slipped his hand under the curtained compartment beneath the seat.

The factotum's fingers quickly found the cardinal's hairy scrotum, which hanged through the hole in the seat, a gross tactile sensation which made him quickly withdraw his arm from under that throne. He crossed himself and stood up, turning to the frozen audience and saying with a reassuring smile. '*Confirmatum est!*'

There was a loud sigh of relieve from the audience, making the giant Albericus turn to them in disgust. They trembled with fear, knowing that they could have all been incinerated if a stare of rage had the power to burn. The count turned to his brother Romanus and asked, while shaking both of his hands with all fingertips joined upwards '*Ma che cazzo! What did they expect?*'

Whether the large Tusculan noticed or not, the audience was happy that this unusual tradition had been instituted since the days of Popess Joan, and they were particularly comforted to know that his brother John Theophylactus, now Pope Benedict VIII, was indeed a man.

In that spring, Brunello was to be seen arriving with a small escort of men-at-arms in Acquisgranus, appealing for the support of the German emperor. The foggy-eyed, pock-marked faced Henry II, the same who had been crowned king of Italy in Pavia eight years before, listened to the plea of that small, dark cleric who presented his papal insignia and announced himself as Gregory VI. This visit was arriving only two days after the news of the death of Sergius IV. During the audience, the emperor sat next to his wife Kunigunde, who loyally held his hand a bit higher above the armrest, as if preparing the husband's hand to be ready for any gesture of deliverance.

While Brunello was being lodged in the imperial palace, Henry considered the prospect of this appeal from the Crescentti. This was the first time in over a century when Roman Patricians were directly appealing to the emperor. This Brunello was a member of the family, and the support of Henry against the Tusculani would get the most powerful of the Romans on his knees.

But the Tusculani never had to fight a final battle against the Crescentii for the dominance of Rome. While Henry still pondered about supporting Gregory VI, news arrived of the sudden death of the powerful John Crescentius, the son, only a week after the Sergius IV had died.

With a changed scenario, the Crescentii family slowly dwindled into oblivion, behind the massive emerging force of the Tusculani. The three brothers of Tusculum, Albericus, Romanus and the Pope Benedict VIII could not believe their luck when they heard from their informers inside the Crescentii palace in Nomenta that John Crescentius had perished after visiting a mysterious abbess in Johannispolis.

The German king Henry lost all interest in the claimant Gregory VI. He forced Brunello to a faraway monastery where the fugitive could spend the rest of his life in forgetfulness.

And the history of Rome could have changed forever had it not been for that sudden death of John Crescentius. The designations of God had made this demise feasible due to an unrelated meeting, many years before. It was the curious encounter between John Crescentius's mother, the beautiful Theodora, and an exotic visitor to the pope: the Bukhari Immanuel Ben-Malachi.

When Battista Burle left Corsena on that Sunday, Immanuel had been tidying Béla's shack, trying to identify his items, storing the pure materials and burning away some of the mixtures he could not identify. A thick, aromatic smoke rose over the valley, scaring away the bad sprites which fooled around along the Serchio and the Lima. Turul was nowhere to be found on the skies. Immanuel had not seen any sign of the lammergeyer since the last days of Béla. As he entered the shack again, he did not notice the elder woman that passed by the fire and came to the door.

'I've heard you didn't go to your daughter's wedding.'

Immanuel recognised that voice immediately. 'My lady!' he said with a burst of enthusiasm, the first he could gather to shower his heart with some bliss since the passing of Béla.

The slender, tall woman flung her cowl back and smiled magnificently, showing a rosy pair of cheeks between generous lines of age that time had carefully drawn around her splendour. Immanuel ran to hug his oldest friend, the only survivor of a time when he had first come to those lands: Abbess Theodora, formerly known as the Lady Theodora of the Crescentii.

'I'm so sorry about Béla...' she said, as his face was still buried just above her breast. 'Too many things happening at the same time.'

Immanuel accompanied her down to the manor and they drank a goblet or two of his distilled wine while watching the colours change down the Lima as the shadows of the Apuane advanced through the late afternoon.

'Do you still love your daughter?' Theodora asked, with her eyes still on the river.

'I hate Maria Maddalena for her abominable deeds. But this feeling will probably be evaporated, one day.' He chuckled to himself and continued, looking at the stone floor 'And I should be lucky I am not inside my *tagh tir*, so there will be no concentrated hatred leaking on the other side of the pipe.'

'Are you sure of the crimes Maria Maddalena is suspected of?' she asked.

Immanuel bit his lips and nodded, with his eyes furtively escaping to the sides.

'I admire your generosity,' Theodora said, taking another sip of that wine. 'I was never myself any tolerant with the man I detested: as you know well, my own son. And I have no regrets of my hatred and my crime. John killed the men I loved and I...'

'The *men* you loved?' interrupted Immanuel.

'Yes, my dear friend. You probably know well of my infatuation for Pope Sylvester II. But please, do understand that I never had any carnal commerce with the pontiff. He was a wonderful man who, like Jesus, just deserved to be loved! In flesh, I never betrayed my vow to be faithful to my husband. But as far as my son is concerned, that pitiless monster, he was capable of anything. When I accused my son John of poisoning Sylvester, my husband supported me. Well, John had his father smothered on the following night. For me it was too much. I was not that compassionate to ever forgive him for those murders.'

'My lady. Your love for the pope has never disgusted me,' Immanuel said. 'He's the man who put me in this piece of heaven and I have all respect for his blessed soul. And as far as I am concerned, it was after his death and your husband's when you retired to these lands of Lucca, granting us the pleasure to receive your visits and admire your beauty once in a while, wasn't it?' He opened the leather bottle and poured a bit more of his concoction in her goblet.

'Immanuel Ben-Malachi!' she said, warmly. 'The older you get the more charming you become.' She reached across the table and held his hand for a while, before hardening her face and continued 'I took the cowl and left Rome, coming to the monastery of San Giovanni Battista, in Santa Maria Lei Giudice. The name of my religious house never allowed me to forget the monster that ruled Rome during those years. And the location allowed me to make a few trips up the Serchio and visit some of the few friends I had, whose past were completely disassociated with Rome. And from these visits, you know well how I managed to commit that crime.'

'My lady, when was it? Four years ago? As you know it, news run through these valleys by no more than hearsay. I was in Lucca when I heard that your son John II Crescentius had fallen ill and died after visiting you in a convent outside of Rome. They say you were ill too, but that you survived.'

'Thanks to the good Béla.' she said, lowering her gaze.

Immanuel scraped his lower lip with his teeth. 'What was it?' he asked. 'Deadly nightshade? Monkshood?'

'Why both, of course!' Theodora said. 'Over the years I came over for my visits but never got the courage to ask. But one day I finally put the question to our shaman friend. Quite fortunately, he was happy to instruct me through the whole recipe and arranged for the ingredients.'

'Did he know what your intentions were?' asked Immanuel with a raised eyebrow.

'I told him exactly who I wanted to lay my revenge upon!' Theodora said. 'I boiled the roots of the flower that in Rome we call the devil's helmet, but you call it the monkshood. Mixed into your wine, it gave it a bitter aroma, but still pleasurable. The sisters in Johannispolis had already received from me a few bottles of your good wine and, although this appealing distraction was being kept in secrecy from Pope Sergius, my son John was quickly advised of the wondrous beverage. When I finally came to collect the roots, good Béla insisted that I also carried with me a special vial he carefully handed me. It contained a poison made from the *atropa*, the deadly nightshade. He guaranteed it would be the best antidote for the monkshood. The idea of taking one poison to stop the effects of another was preposterous and unacceptable, but I kindly thanked Béla for it. Well, I never intended to use an antidote, anyway. I rode to Rome with my leather bottle on very moment I heard of the death of Pope Sergius. I knew John wanted to continue his tyrannical rule by pushing his cousin Brunello into the papal seat.

'Brunello?' Immanuel asked.

'Do you remember a certain Gregory VI? No? Well, this was Brunello, who was elected by the Crescentii while the Tusculani put my curious cousin Theophylactus on the throne as Benedict VIII. But all changed when I sent message to my son that I would meet him for a bottle of wine in Johannispolis. He came cold and cautious, and only took his goblet after I decided to take mine. I was ready to die with my vengeance. After the second goblet, I did not feel my tongue or my face, all numb, and no words could come out any more. I saw John retching and covering the table top with vomit, before falling on his back, roaring for help. The cramps broke inside me with unforgiving brutality and the last thing I remember was resorting to the vial of deadly nightshade poison, not because I believed it could counteract the effects, but because I expected it to finish me off sooner. When I came to my senses, it was two days later. I had ridden Rome off a heartless princeps indeed, but I opened the path for a different kind of devil to take his place.'

There was a long silence. Immanuel took another full gulp from his goblet. The liquid seemed to try to make his head explode, before being passed down. Finally, he said 'My Lady. You are a very brave woman! I don't think I would have trusted Béla for the poison or the cure. I probably underestimated the old vulture.'

Miraculously, on that same moment, a powerful screech was heard above. Both the master of Corsena and the abbess of San Giovanni Battista looked up and spotted the mighty bird gliding high, a tiny moving spot against a quickly darkening sky. Immanuel and Theodora could hardly appreciate the power of Turul's eyesight, or the fact that the lammergeyer had, maybe an hour before, soared above the other side of the Serchio valley and witnessed the savage raping of Immanuel's daughter, Maria Maddalena.

Winged Omens

There were loud and boisterous pilgrims arriving late into the Jerusalem night. Two Neapolitans and a Florentine. Julian got up to shush them. They were reeking. 'Drunk pigs!' he said. 'Aren't you aware that wine is punished with death in this uncertain land? You could jeopardise all of our progress here.'

The Neapolitans lost their composure, but the Florentine laughed. 'Angry soldier!' he pointed at Julian, 'More of a soldier than a hospitaller. You need a woman! Why don't you visit the laundry, down this alley, and have some of the Lombard's wife's attention?'

'Helena?' Julian asked, visibly annoyed with the mention of that woman.

'Oh yes, Helena!' And the three giggled shrewdly, looking at each other and making gestures. The Florentine designed the sinuous curves of a feminine body with his hands. 'She can deal with you, soldier. Try her.' Another burst of laughter.

Julian shushed them again. It did not take long for the drunken pilgrims to be soundly snoring. Julian sneaked out into the empty alleys to verify on their suspicious story. He tried the patriarchate. A soldier stood on guard, confirming that Buonaccorso was inside his house, probably sleeping.

'And Helena, his wife?' Julian asked.

The soldier did not move his face. He was silent for a breath after Julian repeated his question, but his eyes escaped Julian's gaze to the sides.

'She's out, isn't she?' Julian groaned. 'And you let her do it!'

'She's a powerful woman,' the soldier pleaded. 'She knows how to make me quiet. A temptress she is, leading us all into sin.'

'Do I need to go to the laundry to verify if she's there?' Julian asked, trembling his jaws with rage.

'No, you do not,' the soldier said, facing the ground. 'Helena is there, and she has company.'

Julian looked up to the window from the room where Buonaccorso slept, the Pavese most certainly oblivious to all that treachery. Helpless to make a decision on whether to tell his friend of his wife's adventures, Julian returned to the hospital and could not sleep until the roosters announced another spring sun in the holy city. He thought of the Holy Face, gazing him with pity. A locust clung to its bandaged face.

Locusts. They appeared within one hour as the morning broke. Quite late in the season, they were small and numerous, and still buzzing their hard papery wings all over Jerusalem. Spotted brown, decided grasshoppers that invaded the gardens and crawled through the alleys. They entered windows and sneaked under doors. They woke up Julian late, when climbing over his face with their woody legs. The rancid smell of their entrails oozed through the alleys, as the inhabitants of the Holy City gladly squashed them with their sandals.

Julian quickly ran outside and verified that the thickness of the swarm was not too concerning. He was also glad to see that another swarm had come after the locusts: thousands of swifts that sailed like fish through the sky.

He came back into the hospital and left a few helpers to deal with the daily tasks. Walking decidedly towards the reconstruction site, he found Buonaccorso on good spirits, in spite of the locusts.

'Come and take a walk with me, Buonaccorso. We must talk.'

Stepping on crawling locusts, they went over to the city wall and climbed up to the battlements, immersing themselves into the swifts' flight.

'Are you a happy man, Buonaccorso?' Julian asked.

'Happier than ever. Why do you ask?'

'Does Helena make you happy?'

'Always, Julian. She is a sweetie. I could not be a luckier man.' He noticed Julian's nervousness. 'Why do you ask that, my friend? What is it with you?'

Julian sighed and tried to take some pleasure on squishing a large locust with his sandals. Looking at the line of visitors who entered the city, waving insects out of their faces, he turned abruptly to stare into Buonaccorso's eyes. He bit his lips and said to the Pavese leopard 'What would you do if Helena faltered in her loyalty to you?'

Buonaccorso shook his head in confusion. 'That's a strange question, Julian. How could I ever think of something like that?'

'I have reasons to believe that Helena is not being faithful to you.'

Buonaccorso stiffened. He walked away a few steps and came back hurriedly. 'Julian, why are you treating me in this despicable manner? Why do you disrespect my wife?' he pleaded in anguish. 'What is happening to you? Is it the locusts? Or is it the day? Yes, do you know what date is today? It's the fifteenth of May, Julian. It's been ten years!'

Julian dropped his head, with lips sealed, refusing to speak any other accusation. A battalion of nightmares exploded into his memory, as swifts swarmed the sky above.

'Think of it, Julian. It's you who's not well.' Buonaccorso said. 'Your demons of guilt still hunt and deceive you, my friend. If you never allowed yourself to be happy, then at least let me enjoy my piece of bliss during this life.' He left Julian on the wall.

Above Julian the swifts kept chasing the locusts. And like a couple of devilish eyebrows, a pair of sooty falcons happily cut through the swarm for their share of those morsels.

There were no more locusts or birds or Buonaccorsos or Helenas. There were only the demons of his past. Julian was flooded by images of the coronation day, ten years before. He could hardly believe how far behind it had been kept and how alive and painful the memories were.

Threatened by the furious Pavese mob outside the church of San Michele Maggiore, they were being temporarily sheltered by a wall of German armed men. These soldiers of King Henry kept retreating as they opened a safe passageway for the attendants of the coronation and mercilessly cut the Pavese down, but they also began to fall, one by one, under the force and numbers of the rabble. Following Buonaccorso, the papal and the king's entourage, Julian ran back to the royal palace, holding strongly the wrist of the Lady Railenda. They were hoping the troops stationed outside the wall had been alerted and Julian expected to see them anytime. Closer to the palace, a number of arrows coming from the Pavese whizzed by, hissing their flames before hitting the stony pavement. Not all of them missed a target: one deacon was felled by a shot through his neck, and one Milanese lady shrieked in terror as her household struggled to pull a broken arrow from her pierced forearm.

The king's crowd was in sheer panic when they entered the palace, slamming the doors behind them. Henry went to the back of the building and disappeared behind a thick barrier of his German soldiers. Buonaccorso got the pope's custodes to make a protective human wall before the stairs, while Julian brought the Lady Railenda next to the pontiff and his entourage, on the first floor.

'I am so sorry for bringing you here, my Lady!' said the pope with hopelessness. 'I did not expect this...I'm so sorry!' he insisted.

Railenda was mesmerised to hear that apology by John XVIII himself, among the thundering of troops inside the palace and the banging on the entrance doors. She chuckled and smiled warmly, with that enticing bright shine of her blue gems 'I'm sure we'll be talking about this incident over a bonfire soon. Let's just wait for the reinforcements and the Pavese will go home. Just do not worry about me, please.'

The doors exploded in, and the Pavese spilled into the atrium. Although the women shrieked with terror, the men were relieved to see that the reinforcement German troops had arrived, pressing the rabble from the rearguard. Julian saw an open fight breaking inside the palace, with approximately a hundred Pavese armed men surrounded by foreign soldiers.

Buonaccorso called for Julian to jump into the battle. However, the young soldier was quickly taking Railenda up the stairs, with other ladies. 'Leave the women right where they are, Julian,' Buonaccorso shouted. 'This fight will be over soon. The enemy is surrounded. We need you down here.'

But Julian kept climbing up. They came to the highest room in the palace and entered. A leisure room with a few chairs, a fireplace and a good view of the city. Julian peeked through the narrow window and saw that the battle was still boiling outside. A few flaming arrows spurted from the battleground, aiming for the highest windows of the palace.

'Close this door and lock it.' He advised the women. 'Keep quiet inside and stay away from the window. I am sending men to guard the door.'

'*What men?*' asked one of the ladies. 'I don't trust the Germans.' The other women agreed, including Railenda.

'I will send custodes of the pope's entourage, if that brings you peace,' Julian said.

Railenda approached Julian with a livid face, her eyes were tired and red, her face blushed by the escapade, but she was probably still more beautiful than he had ever seen her before. She kissed him on his cheeks. 'Thanks for being here with me, Julian! My son.'

'I will care for you, my mother.'

Before he could turn to rush down for the battle, there was a swish and a thump, and Railenda's eyes opened wide. Julian saw flames igniting on her hair, as her body collapsed on his arms. Sticking out of her back, a flaming arrow that had dug deep into her chest. The women screeched in horror and left the room in a rush, as Julian screamed for help, hugging the body of Railenda and hurriedly slapping the fire out from her head.

After the night of the carnage in Pavia, when the royal palace was destroyed and a large part of the Pavese population was slaughtered by German soldiers, Pope John XVIII returned to Rome with a beaten entourage. It included the scarred Buonaccorso and a singed Julian, who would leave the group in Luna, bringing with him the body of one of the few casualties on King Henry's side: the Lady Railenda of Lombardia, Marchesa of Toscana.

Jerusalem's skies were an inspiration for the plagues. Depending on the time of the year, different creatures made it busy with their flights. Locusts, bees, gnats, flies, aphids, mayflies, moths and cochineals attracted other myriads of swifts, terns, bee-eaters, starlings, swallows, rollers, martins, nightjars and always an intriguing pair of sooty falcons. As night was hurriedly raising its darkness around the holy land on that late summer evening, thousands of swifts drew their lines across the sky, diving to catch a cloud of moths that had risen from the desert. The Church of the Holy Sepulchre had been partially resurrected, raised to the height of its cupola's base, almost as tall as the columns that stood still inside the Anastasis. In the centre, a new aedicula had been raised, the kouvouklion, yet surrounded by an intricate web of scaffolding and beams that crossed the open cupola. An old man kneeled solitary on the stone floor.

'It's late already,' Julian said with concern, observing the old man from a distance. 'He should leave before it's too dark, and maybe come with me to the hospital.'

Buonaccorso raised his shoulders and let them drop. 'He's been there all afternoon. A solitary old man, he's arrived late this morning, from Jaffa. Although he looks as Jewish as all the tribes of Israel together, from his accent I could swear he is some wealthy Tuscan type.'

Carrying a torch, Julian approached the man, who still prayed in the Anastasis. He tried Lombard. 'The hour is late, my good man. I suggest we leave this area and take shelter in the hospital nearby. There you will have food and warmth.'

The old man calmly made the sign of the cross and groaned from the pain in his joints as he took Julian's hand to help himself up. Gracefully brushing his tunic from the dust, he wore a cordial smile. 'Thank you, my son. It is comforting to hear Lombard spoken in such remote land, but one would say: remote from what? Your speech, young man, is not entirely Lombard though, is it? French, maybe?'

'Well done! I am from the Maine, in France. My name is Julian.' They walked together out of the Anastasis, towards the area where Buonaccorso waited. 'We noticed you have arrived today. Do you come on your own? You seem to know well your way around, including recognising some of the accents of Christendom.'

'It is a pleasure to meet you. I am Cunerado Di Cunizio. I was a merchant from Lucca that decided to come to the Holy Land before the crepuscule of my life would not allow me.'

'Lucca?' said Julian with delighted 'but I have lived a few years nearby, in Luna.'

The old man froze and looked at him with a face as pale as the moon. '*Luna*? Did you say *Luna*?' He raised both of his hands. 'Oy how sad! Oy what a terrible thing! The reason I have prayed for longer in here is because of Luna.'

Julian grabbed the old man and held him by the shoulders, looking straight into his face. He was shouting 'What happened to Luna? Tell me, Cunerado Di Cunizio, what happened to Luna?'

'Saracens!' Cunerado said. He felt Julian's hands softening on his shoulder and saw the face losing its colour. 'I'm so sorry Julian. I heard about it as my ship left from Pisa. A large Saracen fleet had landed further north and invaded the land towards Luna. They have taken the town of Luni and killed the Bishop Filippo.'

Julian raised his eyes 'What about the castle? Is it taken? Or the Obertenghi. Are they safe?'

'I am sorry Julian.' Cunerado sighed 'I know no more of this. All I know is that the infamous pirate Musetto was heading the fleet.'

Julian released the old man. He turned to his friend 'Buonaccorso, I must go back to Luna.' He shook his head. 'I just could not keep on living without going.'

The Pavese Leopard held Julian's face with both hands, saying 'And I will go with you, my friend. Always loyal on your side.'

'What about Helena?' Julian said, not before clearing his throat.

'Helena goes with us, of course!'

Julian was quick to accompany Cunerado Di Cunizio to the xenodochium, where he told a stunned Jan Koogs of his plans to leave to Jaffa on the next morning and take the first ship to Rome.

'I will be minding the hospital for you,' said the German with conviction 'loyally waiting for your return.'

Julian ran into the night to find Nicodemus further down in the patriarchate. The keeper was devastated by the news of his departure. 'You are our saviour Julian. Soter!' he sobbed. 'Over and over you have proven your value, not only in defending us from evil, but in being a true hospitaller, a warm face and a caring hand that are sought after by pilgrims arriving into this strange land. Jerusalem needs you.'

'Nobody needs me, Nicodemus, really. I am but a nuisance that brings ill luck to those that open their hearts to me. But if there's a drop of decency that has not dried up inside my veins, this drop obliges me to do what I must. To run for the care of those who have cared for me. It may be too late, but I could never forgive myself if I did not move. Will you help me, then? I am leaving with Buonaccorso and Helena in the morning.'

'I'll have the horses for you and a cart for the crucifix as the sun breaks,' Nicodemus said with a defeated face. Julian hugged him for a long time.

The Holy Face had already been hidden from light for years. Now, it was a hard bundle of rags, undisguised into its cruel shape of a cross. Julian was not planning to unwrap it before he would be back in Italian soil, which could be in no less than two weeks, even if the winds were favourable. He wanted to show His Holy Face to Clarissa. Even though the similarities were inexistent, somehow he was proud of it. The suffering countenance of the Christ had little to remind Julian of the hard, woody, features he had developed in his own. What would Clarissa have thought? She would have laughed at it. She would certainly have no qualms on being cruel about it.

Had she ever been cruel to him?

He did not want to think of Clarissa. Of all those years when she never gave him a chance. Still, her beautiful ghost was assaulting him with violence on that moment, bringing to him the perfect recollection of the day when he left her behind in Luna.

She had brought him up to the tower. That solitary room, with nothing more than a palliasse with old straw, where Julian could see the white castle of Luna from above and enjoy a glorious view of the azure Ligurian Sea. He kept looking out through the small window because he was still crying. There had been two days since he had brought the body of the Lady Railenda back to Luna. Ashamed of his failure to protect Railenda, Julian had refused to accept the tragedy as fate, no matter how much the Obertenghi demonstrated their support for his bravery and understanding for their loss.

'Stop this!' Clarissa ordered. 'Look at me, Julian. For one moment, look at me. You have avoided me since you came back!'

'What do you expect?' he bellowed. 'I leave you for a festivity taking your mother by the hand and I return with her in a cart.'

'She was your mother too, Julian, you have said this many times.' Clarissa tried to look at his face. 'Julian we suffer with you on her loss. And we will suffer more if you leave us. We cannot lose another member of the family. Julian, we will miss you!'

'Can't you understand?' Julian sat on the palliasse and covered his face. 'It's the very reason why I left my family. The motivation to be away from the people I love. If I stay, we are going to lose another family member. I know that thing was right. The beast told me I would end up slaying them, father and mother!'

Clarissa took Julian's hands from his face and pulled them towards her, making him reluctantly stand. She held his face high, forcing him to look at her direction. Tired from shedding tears, the black of his eyes fought through a congestion of redness and surfaced to finally lay their mortified, unwilling gaze on Clarissa's face. There was a bothersome beauty that soothed him. As opposed to her wild nature, the long brown hair was neatly tamed, parted in the middle and revealing rainbow eyes that burnt with fire, on a perfectly shaped face, if not a bit too round. She held her neck standing proud, perched on an inconveniently well curved and developed body. Julian had suffered with yearning for every single day of that transformation of Clarissa into a shaped woman. Longer legs, plumper volumes and an ever determined face had disturbed him day and night since that day he brought the sandgrouse into their camp. Clarissa was now fifteen years-old, bearing a devastating beauty that attracted eyes across Lombardia, all the way to Rome, making the young and the old, nobles and servants, stare with craving and salivate with desire. The more magnificent she grew, the more aware Julian became of the impossibility of his chances. Her mouth was small and not wide, with a lower plump lip framed by an incredibly stubborn upper. They spoke with decision and authority 'Stay, Julian! Stay with those who love you.'

Julian held her shoulders 'Love? Do you love me, Clarissa? Do you?'

She held his face and pulled it towards hers.

Her lips embraced his with passion, and both bodies exploded in heat as they embraced each other. This was the kiss Julian had waited for years and it felt more formidable than he ever expected. The briefness of that eternity was too cruel to be interrupted, but Clarissa exercised power when Julian's body begged for hers. 'Stay, Julian, and we'll be together' she said with honest effort, holding him away from her.

Julian was panting. The passion of that kiss had blown him away off his legs. 'Clarissa, I cannot do it. I love you too much to hurt you, to make you unhappy.'

'You are too arrogant to understand us, aren't you?' she scorned.

'*Us*? Has there even been a *we*, Clarissa?'

'Julian, do you know how many times I have kissed in my life? How many men?'

'I don't want to know!' he groaned.

'You cannot even imagine, can you?' Clarissa dropped her wide shoulders. 'So blind you are by your fears that you make no idea of what love truly is.'

'My fear has good reasons to haunt me.'

'Then deal with it!' she said imperatively. 'I will be here, waiting for you.'

He opened the door to the stairs and rushed down.

'Please don't take too long!' she said in tears, but he had already disappeared down the stairs.

That was the last time Julian had seen Clarissa.

Day was about to break. While pilgrims still snored, some vocal Jerusalem roosters were sufficiently stirred by a flaming disk that had not even shown its face around the curve of the planet yet.

Julian had slept poorly, thinking too much of Clarissa, but he was up and ready to depart. And nothing had been heard from Buonaccorso. They needed to leave early to Jaffa and find a swift and reliable ship to take them to Rome. Outside the xenodochium, under the late night, Nicodemus was handing to Jan Koogs three harnessed horses, two mules and a bullock-cart.

'One for each,' the keeper said with melancholy looking at Julian, 'you, Buonaccorso, Helena and the cart for your cross. I will have a rider meet you in Jaffa to bring the horses back.'

'Do you know of Buonaccorso and Helena?' Julian asked, 'Shouldn't they be ready by now?'

Nicodemus made a face as if he had tasted something particularly bitter. 'I don't meddle with those two as much as possible, Julian. In fact, I'll be glad when Helena is gone. Maybe she can change, as she gets to see the world.'

Jan Koogs gasped and pretended he was not listening. Julian too did not think Helena could change. He preferred not to comment and went on his own up an alley to seek the couple in their house.

It was empty. Nobody there. The discoloured and dry leopard skin was thrown across the floor, at the entry door. Maybe they had left to the hospital by a different alley.

Julian returned to the xenodochium. As he darted by the old laundry, an unmistakable giggling coming from the other side of the wooden door made him freeze. He prayed that Helena was inside with nobody else but Buonaccorso.

He knocked on the door. 'Helena. Is that you? Is Buonaccorso there?'

No answer. The light inside the laundry was extinguished. Julian knocked stronger.

'Helena, I know you are there. Open the door now!' Again there was no response. When Julian threatened to burst the door, he finally heard her voice.

'Alright, just wait!' she said. She unbolted the door and opened, blocking the way in. 'What do you want?' Her voice gave away her drunken condition. A lose tunic had been hastily wrapped around her body. Still, Julian could not deny that her sweaty face was radiant, no less attractive than anytime he had seen her before.

'Where is Buonaccorso?' Julian asked. 'Isn't he there with you?'

'I don't know where that mad man could be,' she spat.

Showered by a quick stream of curses, Julian pushed her away and entered the room. He devised the figure calmly sitting in a corner. He could not tell if it was a pilgrim or a local Muslim, but certainly not Buonaccorso. Turning back to Helena, Julian said with spite 'You are a whore!'

She guffawed and embraced him indecently, groping him and dropping her tunic, as he tried to exit the laundry. Disentangling himself, Julian faced her with disgust 'What have you done? Who's this man? Where is Buonaccorso? Aren't you two coming with me?'

She cackled again. '*Going with you?* You two must be equally mad!' She picked up the tunic to cover her nudity. 'Buonaccorso came to me early in the evening, urging me to leave to Rome with him, with you, just like *that*! I refused this insanity. When he insisted and threatened to take me by force, I told him a few things!'

'A few *things*? What things?' Julian asked impatiently.

'Everything!' she said with a grin, biting her lower lip with a callous pleasure.

'Everything? *What* everything?' Julian's legs were starting to falter, but he still had a feeble hope it was not what he feared.

She ran a fingernail across the skin of his arm, smiling to herself 'You know what I told him, Julian. Things about me; things about men; things about men and I; things about you; things about you and I...' but she could not even finish, for Julian's palm exploded on her face. The man sitting inside the laundry did not move.

'You are a whore!' Julian foamed. He repeated the question slowly: 'Where – is – Buonaccorso?'

Helena's eyes could have ignited fire on an ocean. The sooty falcons of her eyebrows met in the centre, ready to strike. She held her sore face with fury. 'He ran away! I don't know where to. To hell, hopefully. Maybe you can chase him, but I would never run after a man like him. And as you can see,' she grinned again, already showing a red face from the slap, 'I have always something better to do. But you do know that.' She noticed then that Julian had disappeared.

He was flying towards David's Gate.

A few people circulated the alleys of the Christian quarters, with their bags, their sheep, their carts and donkeys, as roses of dawn expanded further west across the sky. Julian rushed through them all like lightning, to reach that western gate in time to get fresh information from the watchers, whether Buonaccorso had crossed it and when. If the Pavese Leopard had left the city, this would have been the most obvious way out.

'We have not seen the old Roman soldier.' one of the watchmen said. Camels grunted by the gate, as a crowd already gathered around the steaming stalls outside. A pungent smell of *koriannon* invaded Julian's nostrils. 'Try the other gates!' the watchman said.

Julian re-started his sprint, now back to the xenodochium. He would alert Jan Koogs, Nicodemus and others to be on the watch and hopefully find where Buonaccorso had gone. The stench of the herb was still infiltrated in his nose. Just before arriving at the hospital alley, Julian looked at the site where the Church of the Holy Sepulchre was being re-built. Buonaccorso could be there. He knew the

Pavese Leopard in a time of desperation would be praying at the rock of the sepulchre.

Julian climbed the steps towards the anastasis and prepared for the confrontation. He had to choose the right words. Apologies? Accusations? Could he claim weakness? Would he face the sword of Buonaccorso? He entered the open precinct and saw the small chapel in the middle. The kouvouklion, now feebly lit by the light of dawn. Nothing more than an elaborate construction of bricks that men would die and kill for. But there was no Buonaccorso to be found. Julian walked around the kouvouklion, knowing it could be his last time to see it, before taking the stairs down and keep searching for Buonaccorso.

A falcon chanted, high up on the church.

Not a common call for this time of the morning, it was clearly a sooty falcon. Julian stopped for a moment, midway down the stairway. The falcon chanted again, from somewhere on the top of the anastasis. Julian looked back and saw the massive columns, proud monuments standing tall, sticking out through the network of scaffolding and beams. He could not see the bird. The elaborate frames and boards hung from wall to wall, supporting a structure that one day would make the base for the construction of a new dome over the anastasis. Once again the falcon chanted, and this time Julian saw something that made his own legs disappear. Losing his balance, he tumbled backwards down the stairs, rolling and bruising his head and elbows, arriving at the base of the stairway in agony and pain, vomiting bile and crying for God's mercy. Even from where he was, he could still see Buonaccorso partially hidden by the scaffolding. The Pavese Leopard was dangling motionless from a rope under the highest beam.

The Saqlabi

It was late in that October evening, probably still one hour before Lauds, when Julian walked up to the top of the hill just to see the enormous disk of the moon about to refresh itself on the silvery Ligurian waters, delightful reward for having unfurled a gloriously clear blue night.

Below him, the wide plains softly climbed to his right onto the first Apennine hills and disappeared into a grey crevasse. Thousands of fires danced their flickering lights across the plain, filling up the dale and sinisterly surrounding the sad silhouette of the keep.

Luna had never looked so terribly beautiful before.

Although the sky was clear, the white castle was dark, towering lonely in the night. No soul seemed to be inside, not even the ghostly appearances that inflicted spread out fear on the Saracens. But around its injured walls, the pirates' fires could be spotted, all the way from the coast to the upper valley. Somewhere among those flames was the Musetto, the man Julian had come to help drive away from those lands. Julian fought his revulsion and tried to erase any thoughts of what the pirates could have done to those lands. The sweet memory of his shelter in Luna kept coming back to him, the hospitality of the lords, but mostly of course, the sadness of the losses, his farewell and the shining features of the ever blissful Clarissa.

His reminiscences were broken down by a magic synchronicity between two opposing universes. Exactly on the same instant when the silence of dawn was shattered by a *muezzin* in the Saracen field, with his cries of the *adhan*, calling for their prayer of dawn, right behind his back, on the valley to the south, a powerful choir started a *Responsorium hortationis*, softly but growing stronger.

'*Venite exultemus Domino*' Let us come and praise the Lord

'*H'ayya a'las's'alaah*' Make haste towards prayer.

It was back to haunt him. Julian was catapulted back to the Church of the Holy Sepulchre. Never had he thought – not in Liguria – that such conflicting cultures, both singing to their same God, both honest and true to the same Creator, would again pound heavily on his ears to flood up his mind with affliction and fire up his heart with haste.

'*quoniam Deus magnus Dominus et rex magnus super omnes deos*' For the Lord is a great God and a great king above all Gods.

'*Allaahu Akbar*' God is great.

The chants battled in his ears, duelling all the way from his churning stomach to a burning heart, until those invitatory words filled up his veins with a lust for battle, a desire to go down the hill and open way through the enemy with his sword and axe. To rescue the victims of the siege, protecting them from the wrong ways of the Saracens. A desire to retrieve Clarissa and give her what he had brought from the holy land. A yearn to fight for his cross.

Three hours later, the day was made warmer by rays of sunlight that started to peek through the Apennines. Julian had broken his fast and once again looked at his own face: the sculpted face of the brown Christ. The features of a suffered man, as broken and beaten as he had ever felt. He finished his moment of thought and contemplation and covered the wooden features on the cross, carefully wrapping it again in the linens. He kissed the bundle once more.

The Christian camp had received the arrival of that cross with renewed spirits. Julian had left it at the port in Pisa, on the small vessel that had brought him in from Porto. After a fast but impatient sea journey back to Italy, the dark-haired figure who had stood like a dragon at the prow for a week was relieved to be informed, at the Roman harbour, that even the pope himself was leaving to battle against the Saracens. Luna was still under siege, but not taken. Announcing himself as a returning soldier from the Holy Sepulchre, Julian had been received by an uninterested Benedict VIII in a minor hall of the Lateran palace. The pontiff was dressed in armour when Julian was brought into his presence. A sword which appeared to Julian to be too light and short was carelessly lying on the floor. Slowly ridding himself from the metal casing that gave him the appearance of a lobster with a woman's face, the handsome Benedict was helped by two valets, and constantly surrounded by two large, unfriendly noble men.

'So you tell me that the reconstruction plans are still under way? Even if that Pavese friend of yours is dead?' Benedict was now shamelessly dressed only in a hose, raising his arms for the valets to slip a linen tunic onto his naked torso.

'The works will continue, under the supervision of the Patriarchate and the keeper of the Holy Sepulchre,' Julian said, avoiding looking directly at the strange scene.

The pope tightened the laces of his collar. 'Then, that solves a problem. What about the Holy Fire? Any more miracles happened ever since?'

Julian cleared his throat. 'I have lived in Jerusalem for almost seven years, and never has the miracle expressed itself in all its past glory again. Nicodemus, the keeper, believed that once the *aedicula* of the rock was completely finished, the Holy Fire would be brought down from heavens again. The keeper himself participated on the reconstruction of parts of it.'

'Do you bring us any holy relics, to this *Sacrosanta lateranensis ecclesia*?' the pope asked without looking at Julian, but adjusting the folds of a cassock the valets were fitting onto his inner vests.

'Forgive my rudeness, Beatissimo Padre,' Julian said, lowering his head a bit 'but the only reason for me to leave Jerusalem was to come and fight the Saracens in Luna.'

The pope smacked his lips. 'Then you shall go!' He tied a belt around his waist and tapped his lean belly quite proudly. 'As I understand the tomb of the Christ is being well cared for, and no more need it has for the soldiers of this Mother Church. Our work there is fulfilled. As for your services to Rome, Julian of Mans, I will grant you a papal letter to be taken the Lords of Lucca and Luna. How about that? It will be with you this afternoon.' And he waved his hand for Julian to leave.

The smaller ship Julian took up the western coast would not venture further north than Pisa. He purchased a bony rouncey in the Tuscan port and galloped to Lucca, where the papal letter took him to the commander of the resistance, Alberto Azzo.

The busy Obertenghi was discussing plans with a few other nobles and he did not immediate recognise the long haired soldier that had ridden in, offering his services. But lifting his gaze to catch a glimpse of Julian's wooden face rehearsing a shy smile, Alberto ran to embrace his brother.

'And Clarissa?' Julian asked.

Alberto lowered his eyes but still held on strongly to Julian's arms. 'She still resists in Luna, with my father.'

On hearing that, Julian had difficulty in answering, so strong his jaws were clenched. 'We will bring them out, I promise you,' he finally said.

Julian was immediately given better armoury, an axe and one of Azzo's best war horses, a gray-coated destrier that Azzo had bought from a herd in Milano. As the army slowly moved northwest to the Ligurian coast, they were joined by a small Pisan contingent. The Genovese had been plagued by hunger and droughts in those years. They had a rather thin army to the northern limits of the invaded area.

Alberto sent an oxcart to Pisa, especially to retrieve Julian's cross that waited in the boat. Julian did try to tell them the story behind it, but all that was stuck in the soldiers' minds was the cross that had arrived from Jerusalem for their protection. The *Volto Santo*, they called that giant portrait of the Christ – Holy Face – no matter how much Julian intervened with the real facts behind its make. The fever around the Volto Santo at the camp had not subsided, and from tent to tent, many soldiers still marvelled at a miracle cross that was found in a beached boat, wrapped into a leopard skin. This legend would live for as long as they figured.

But Julian was impatient. 'We must free Luna,' he muttered to himself.

Outside the tent, he observed the soldiers with distant eyes. Even the young Antelmino di Gottefredo from Lucca was there, visibly unsatisfied with the length of the lance he had brought, going from tent to tent and bluntly asking to exchange for a longer one. Antelmino was loud about his plans to walk down to Luna and spear as many of those dogs – Saracens – that could fit through the length of the pole.

On a nearby tent, Alberto Azzo, the heir of Luna, awaited for further help, discussing attack strategies with his old rivals, the Pisan allies, while counting on re-enforcements from Rome. He was watched by his nineteen-years old son Albertazzo, an able fighter, eager to mount and ride down to face the enemy in Luna. Ready to help free his grandfather Oberto and his aunt Clarissa.

Many of Julian's old friends from Luna were there. They were all touched and grateful to see him back in their lands, but eager to organise for a charge. As soon as their contingent would be joined by the pope's, they would be more than thirteen thousand men, ready for the fight. But much more important than the support of the pope himself, who was coming to battle, they had the blessing of the Volto Santo, brought in by their 'little brother'.

The Saracens did not have to wait. They could renew the attack on the castle at any moment.

Would the pope be in time with his troops? They waited for a decision. Bored, scared men, killing their time, waiting for a chance to go back home or to put their lives in the hands of the Lord, in case they had to throw themselves into the claws of the terrible Musetto and his Saracen army. They were sleeping, stretching, gazing around, yawning, snoring, munching, grunting, protecting themselves from the sunlight, scratching, washing shields, sharpening axes, moulding wooden spears, grinding swords, boiling, roasting, gathering lumber, feeding fires, serving, tending, eating, spitting, pissing, shitting, digging, burying.

Waiting.

Julian put on his armour and a coat with a painted cross, donated by some soldiers who were fervently venerating his crucifix. He mounted his destrier and calmly took to the top of the hills, without ever contacting the command of the army. Soldiers hardly seemed to take notice of the dissociating rider, lonely withdrawing himself from their safe camp. His powerful steed was a massively-built battle beast, with the same colour as the smoke-stained walls of the castle. Destriers were rarely ever seen by any common soldier, and least in battles, except when used by the wealthy lords of castles such as Luna. Higher up on the hillcrest, Christian scouts issued warnings and came trotting to verify for the rider. As he watched the warriors approaching, Julian kicked in hard to ride down to the plains.

The hilltop was covered in lavender, an annoyance to some soldiers in the camp, for they all knew how soft men could get from the scent of that herb. Certainly not the best ground coverage to start a battle. Further down towards the castle, a few patches of gorse suddenly broke out before a long stretch of abandoned grapevines. The plants had been dry for a few years, and lining the northern edge of this field stretched a hedge of richly green olive trees. Beyond that, and before the southern barbican, the main gate of the castle that opened into a wide empty court, there were only a few houses and dry, dusty paddocks, everything already trampled by the pirates. Between Luna and the hills further down the coast, just a vast swampy area spread out as far as the eye could see.

Not long after the shouts of alert had been muted by distance, and well after he had covered two arrow flights from his fellow soldiers, Julian saw the dust rising from the Saracen lines alarmed with his suicidal ride: three riders approaching him.

The furious gallop of the brown slim horses could mean only one thing: Attack.

The silvery curved blades of the unsheathed *saifs* shone bright in the sun, heels kicking deep and frenetically into their mounts, the chargers faces not visible though the black head cloths that enfolded their features. Julian calculated the moves he would need to unsheathe his sword in time, or to swing the axe that was slotted into a leather strip on his saddle.

As the first rider was no more than forty feet from him, Julian looked at him in straight into those blood infused eyes, smiled, bowed his head and greeted.

'Assalamu alaikum.'

Mugiàhid was inspecting the looted pieces which had arrived on the previous day, from a nearby village.

As a Saqlabi ruler of Daniyya in faraway Spain, he was Mugiàhid ibn abd Allah al Amiri, known among the Italian Christians as the Musetto, the pirate. He commanded a great naval fleet which had already left its mark in Sardinia, promoted skirmishes in the surrounds of the powerful Pisa and even threatened the shores of the Sicily of another Saracen, the great Dja'far.

The Musetto was a fairly tall man, in contrast with most Saracens, for his Polish grandparents had been sold as slaves into the al-Andaluz caliphate to serve the caliph himself in Qurtuba. His father quickly scaled from the son of a *hachib*, clerk, into a soldier, commanding battalions on the province of Balansiyya. With the assassination of the caliph's regent in the Saracen, a frenzied disarray erupted in al-Andaluz, throwing army commanders into founding their own emirates. Mugiàhid was just over twenty years old and already a general at the time. He safeguarded the whole territory of Daniyya, including the Eastern islands Majorica and Manûrqa, to rule it alone.

The commander always gave himself the duties of selecting looted treasures for his own household, reserving a fraction for the harem, another for the sub commanders and a fourth part for the army. This would be passed onto the hands for Jewish merchants, to be send down in ships and sold in the Byzantine territories,

Calabria and Sicily. The value would be than returned into silver and gold pieces and distributed among the soldiers. They needed something else other than words or faith to keep their spirits up, for in Luna, swamp fevers were filling their camp with the stench of rot and death.

Mugìâhid had a reputation of rectitude and fairness, admired by officials, soldiers and all the hosts that followed the fleet, for his equanimity when it came to decisions and accountability for his division of war booty.

In the particular case of this latest treasure that he was examining, it was a poor collection of souvenirs that he would dedicate to the soldiers. Nothing here that his wife or his estate would value as much compared to his infantry's appraisal for the few coins he would be able to obtain from the merchants. The looted village was the typical case of just a poor amalgamation of huts, which mostly had been abandoned when the fleet had arrived in the shores of Luna. All that the raid could gather was a few silver cups and goblets, daggers, some images and crucifixes from the church, wooden panels with painted scenes from what Mugìâhid assumed it was the bible, candle holders, upholstered seats, carpets and small pieces of furniture. Tiny riches for maybe too much risk of wasting part of his army in such incursions. The cattle and horses had been distributed among the soldiers, just as the able women were.

On that day, Mugìâhid had made use of the best looking woman he had found, which still was not exceptional, at any rate. A robust fairheaded peasant with enormous breasts, her face severely beaten. A generous officer, he did not mind if women had already been raped by the soldiers, even though the physicians had already warned him about fevers and *lues*. Being a soldier, Mugìâhid never dispensed the idea of possessing the enemy's women, of letting out cumulated manhood, so common during battle times, and so much with a special flavour when it was outside of his harem.

Brushing away impure and distractive thoughts, Mugìâhid gave a final assessment of the booty. Effigies of crucified men; panels with headless people carrying their own heads in their hands, probably holy men; a man with arrows across his body, piously looking up to the heights; women on their knees pleading for their lives, begging for a soldier not to swing a sword through their necks. Mugìâhid despised the Christian prophets for their weaknesses.

He called in the accountants and instructed them to hand the items to the Jewish traders, which were just anchored a few miles away, on Ligurian waters. Gazing at last to a panel where a detail depicted a black demon with an enormous phallus violating a poor female soul that had been sent to Hell, the Christian version of the Islamic Jahannam, Mugìâhid once more exercised his abhorrence for the Christian faith.

Back at the harem tent, a huge blonde eunuch served a tray of fried saffron rice cakes to Mugìâhid, who leaned on the carpet, waiting to share the meal with his first wife. The commander had hardly started when the eunuch came back into the tent and announced an interruption.

'What is it?' Mugìâhid asked, jumping up on guard.

The Nordic giant just withdrew one of the tent's curtains and lead his master out, to face three of his mounted warriors accompanied by a fourth rider. A stranger. Hundreds of soldiers crowded around the visitor, who had the shape of a cross painted on his chest. Before the mounted men said anything, Mugiâhid approached the Christian stranger who, with a candid smile drawn across his face, bowed with elegance and wished Mugiâhid the peace of God.

'*Wa 'alaikumus salam*', answered Mugiâhid, if not flabbergasted, at least surprised to see such courage and elegance coming from one of the Christian soldiers.

'Who are you?' continued Mugiâhid, in the holy language of the Q'uran.

'My name is Julian, I am a soldier'.

'Are you a kafir?' asked the suspicious Mugiâhid, without paying attention to Julian's name, employing a provocative term, to unbelievers, idolaters from beyond the Levant or to the black peoples from the south of the great African desert.

'I believe that Allah is great, and the only One', continued the unruffled Julian in Arabic. 'There is no other god than God.' Then he wiped the grin from his face and took of the head cloth, dropping the long bundles of black hair around his shoulder. He looked at Mugiâhid straight into the eyes, declaring in a very low voice 'But I will not lie to you: I do believe that the messengers of God are Moses, Jesus and Mohammed, and may all Their names be blessed and peace be upon Them.'

Mugiâhid was delighted to be able to speak to someone else in what he considered the purest form of the language of God. Back in Daniyya, hardly, with any good believer, could he find the purity of Arabic that he had grown to learn from the Q'uran. The success of his slave grandfather, which became the Caliph's hachib, allowed him the privilege to grow under the tutelage of no one else than al-Mansur, the regent who overshadowed the Caliphs of Qurtuba, ruling al-Andaluz with an iron fist and protecting it from raids of Christian armies. A profoundly religious soldier, al-Mansur passed all deserving respect for the holy scriptures of the Q'uran to his pupil Mugiâhid, which one day would take his master's family name for his own emirate.

'What are you here for, stranger?' asked an admired Mugiâhid to a defiant Julian.

'For negotiation!'

Mugiâhid could not help but marvel at bravery. The visitor had plunged himself into the nest of the enemy, giving his life away into their mercy, just for the faint illusion of negotiating with a winning army. There rode a tall, strong young man, probably older than himself, certainly a soldier, for no one else in those lands would dare to brave the great 'Musetto'. The stony lines of his features denoted hardship. Maybe so severe that he would not be afraid to die. A man who respected religion, but that almost certainly had none himself. Those stern eyes under the long black hair gave him a strange, intimidating appearance. He invited Julian to dismount and break their fast in the tent.

'Do you want me to disarm?' asked Julian.

'You don't come across a sea of enemies just to be stupid, do you?' said Mugiâhid, and completed with a smile 'No need to disarm, no need to use your weapons, and certainly no need to try anything stupid.'

As they entered, Julian caught a glimpse of an enormous woman disappearing behind a curtain, accompanied by the blonde eunuch. Julian and the Saqlabi sat on carpets. Mugìâhid offered him the saffron rice cakes. Julian picked the closest to him, as the etiquette demands, and waited until the host spoke.

'Rider, I think highly of your courage and your respect for Islam, but I cannot put my mind to work on what exactly you are willing to negotiate.'

'I would like you to let me go into the keep, on my own' said Julian, plainly.

'Are you kidding?' asked the commander?

'Are we laughing?' rebated Julian.

'Do you have anything to offer in exchange?'

'Don't you think having your army untouched, the lives of your soldiers not wasted and have the whole keep of Luna opened for you to march into is a good compromise?'

'And what do you get in exchange?' asked a curious and amused Mugìâhid.

'Do you want to continue talking in questions only?' asked Julian, without hiding the sarcastic shape that his black eyebrows took.

'Why not?' hissed Mugìâhid, before exploding into laughter. Julian joined in the mirth and, after fading, they both sipped some beverage made of hot water and a powdered Ethiopian berry called *qahwa*.

'Quite simply,' explained Julian 'I want to go into the keep – on my own – and convince the lord and lady of Luna to leave their abode without putting up one more fight, thus saving their own lives and all of their soldiers' and servants'. As soon as they are all safe on the Christian side, south of the hills, you can enter the keep and we will not charge.'

Mugìâhid chuckled and helped himself with some cheese and strips of meat, squeezing it all together with olive oil into a ball. He waited until Julian had done the same from his side of the tray before continuing 'It's been eight weeks since we arrived. Swamp fever is slowly taking its toll on our ranks. My men are tired and afraid. They are also ready to die for the glory of Allah. But indeed it would do me good to show to my army that none of those ghosts on the keep are real. I'd love to demonstrate to them that even a loner as you can brave those masked people. But that is not the point. I'd actually like to know *how* exactly do you speak in the name of the papal army?'

'Actually, I was sent myself to Luna by the bishop of Rome, Benedict VIII.'

'Even if true, it does not mean you control the army'.

'I have a papal document in my saddle...' Julian had hardly uttered those words when the blond eunuch came into the tent from the front door, already holding the scroll, and presented it to Mugìâhid, before disappearing at the back of the tent. The commander read thoroughly through the manuscript and called some more people in. These were supposedly accountants, merchants, mullahs and officers. The group circulated the scroll back and forth, scrutinising it and whispering to each other in a strange mixture of languages, in what was probably Spanish. They continued for what seemed to be a quarter of an hour, before leaving Mugìâhid and Julian once again on their own.

'Looks real', consented Mugìâhid, 'but how can a rather brave and educated man like you be subject to such a despiteful, spoiled, dandy who calls himself the leader of the Christians?'

'Nevertheless a warrior, I have been told…' emended Julian, without contradicting the commander.

'Don't underestimate my knowledge, young man. Your effeminate pope is a hoax! He has been placed on the throne of Rome by his family, not by the people of Rome. Not even a cleric before they made him a bishop, but a layman, and certainly not at all a real soldier. A fighter of duels, with his own valets and stablemen.'

Julian was speechless for a moment, as the commander continued, carefully observing his visitor.

'You do not fight for your Tusculan puppet of a pope, nor for your crucified prophet. No, you do not risk your life for that…you seem to me to be better than these weaklings!'

Julian sipped some more of that intriguing *qahwa* berry broth, before trying to construct his thoughts. He had obviously underestimated the Musetto, as far as the finesse and education of the commander was concerned. The Musetto's own appearance was singled out from most of the Spanish Saracens. It was undeniable that his handsome mix of Saracen and some northern stock gave him a benevolent aura of magnanimity, not at all expected from the man that had conquered the whole island of Sardinia by the blade of his sword. The commander was well groomed, with dark, glossy ink of Saracen vanity on his eyelids and only a thin red moustache and goatee to elongate the wisdom of his features, perhaps a refined version of the comte Foulques. Still cautious, Julian was wondering if he had overestimated the stigma of malignity of the Saracen pirate.

He decided to make his quest transparent.

'In truth', he elaborated 'I seek the safety of a woman that…'

'I knew it!' burst Mugìâhid with a sudden boyish joy. The commander's eyes glimmered in the shade of the tent. 'Tell me about it! Details. I want details! How is she? Who is she?'

'It is Clarissa, the lady of Luna', said Julian, after clearing his throat, respectfully lowering his eyes and his voice.

'I hear she is not married', intervened Mugìâhid. 'Have you had marital commerce with her before?'

Julian smiled condescendly. 'No, if you mean as man and woman, no! I saw her last it was twelve years ago, when she was only twelve. I have tried to forget her, but she's been in my heart ever since.'

'You what? Twelve years ago?' asked a stupefied Mugìâhid.

'You probably would not understand…' said Julian.

'Oh yes, I do understand! I like young women too!' Mugiàhid boasted loudly, 'and this one must have been a unique morsel to be worth the wait…twelve years!'

Julian ignored the comments and proposed the entry into the castle. As he did it at a very low voice, the enormous eunuch entered the tent and whispered at Mugiàhid's ears.

'My first wife wants to tell me something', explained the commander with a forced smile.

Julian watched as the same imense woman approached from a back curtain, from a side where there seemed to be other women. A silken robed hippopotamus, her face covered with a dark green veil, the solidly black outlined eyes examining him with tiger velvet pupils. She sat down heavily next to Mugiàhid and talked to him at an inaudible tone. She kept firing those eyes at Julian, until the commander nodded and she clumsily began to stand up, with the help of all her hands, of Mugiàhid's and the eunuch's, who had magically appeared without a sign or a call. The commander waited until the immense woman had left their presence, to continue under a somewhat forced smile.

'My wife has been deeply sensitised by your pursuit. Consider yourself lucky, for this is a very jealous woman.'

'Your wife's concern fills me much with honour, as it does to my quest,' Julian said.

'Save your sweetness for the Lady of Luna, for you may see her soon, under a few conditions.'

Julian could not help but smile with relief at those words and make a silent prayer of thanks to the commander's wife.

'Open the door!' he bellowed at the gates. 'Down with the bridge! It is I, Julian of Mans.'

The mosquito-infested moat was now devoid of any birds or fish. The putrid fumes were nauseating, but he tried to concentrate and find the most appropriate words. 'I have a special consent from the Mugiàhid – the Musetto – who has given me his blessing to inspect what goes inside the walls. I am to see in what conditions live my beloved family, my loved ones.'

Ghostly round faces appeared on the parapets of the battered walls raising a murmur from the Saracen army watching from a distance.

Julian kept shouting 'Lord Oberto, my dear Lady Clarissa, are you there? Do you remember me?'

The ghoulish appearances increased in numbers, peering from the crenelles. Pale ashen faces with dark black holes for eyes and bloody wide-open mouths. Damned as they were for being sieged, they expressed it well as condemned souls to convey their suffering to the living. Julian could feel the silent tension on the Saracen army, staying alert but at a safe distance, almost half a mile behind him.

Julian was well aware of a number of arrows pointed at him from the loopholes. He also noted when a small stone was hurled at him from the battlements, wrapped into some leather or parchment. He reacted slowly to the projectile, watching it fall close to his mount. He unhorsed and picked it up from the debris-covered ground, very calmly. The parchment was freshly written in a fast but elegant text. Julian read the three questions twice, mounted the steed, approached the ramp where the movable side of the drawbridge should lean on and shouted loud, without hesitation: 'Hubert of Liege, six sandgrouse and Nobody of Arsehole!'

A woman's scream was heard inside, more ghostly faces appeared on the battlements and in an instant, metal and wood moved within, as the gate was being unlocked. The earth thundered when the bridge slammed down, raising a cloud of dust. The one slow and massive door dug a heavy track through the ground and it was pushed out. The Saracen army could hear the noisy gate at work, and see Julian and his horse disappear inside.

Many spearheads were pointed at him. The door was hurriedly shut and the bridge was drawn. In the darkness of the tunnel he tried to focus on the ghosts, all nervously pointing weapons at him. As he suspected, they were just people. Warriors wearing canvas sacs painted with yellow, with two big black dots for eyes and one large red circle for a mouth. A mute, terror-stricken countenance that indeed inspired a strange chill through the spine. Another masked person came running towards him from the light at the castle patio. By the way it ran, he saw it was a woman.

'Leave him!' she shouted, as she threw away the sac mask, revealing a glorious bundle of dark brown hair. When Julian saw her, his eyes filled up with tears and darkness. Friendly hands prevented him from hitting the ground as he fell from his horse.

Being God

You are back, my love!'

Julian heard the voice, while a blurred vision was slowly getting back to him. Soft hands were tenderly cupping his head, caressing his face. He was waking up in heaven.

'Clarissa', he managed to mumble as he tentatively focused on those eyes which flashed every possible colour. They were green, for sure, but looking closely, one would distinguish a thin dark grey ring on the edge of the iris, which quickly flicked to purple before exploding into a thick pool of richly emerald arrows, all pointed to an inner wheaten yellow circle. This golden ring turned brown just before flipping around the darkness of the pupil. Gazing into that darkness, Julian could catch the red light of the flames from Clarissa's blazing heart. The explosion of colours got closer and closer to his eyes, and his whole body shuddered as he felt moist lips touching his. Clarissa's tears were flooding the salty pools which Julian already had on his eyes. They stung with pleasure, the delightful moments of heaven.

As their lips parted, Julian came back to the world of mortals. He was alone with that magnificent presence in some clean cell. He had been stripped from his armour, lying only in his hose, on a comfortable and clean palliasse. He recognised the room up on the tower, where Clarissa took him for their last conversation. The room where she kissed him goodbye. And he could hardly believe the exuberance of Clarissa's beauty, long after she had passed the age for getting married.

'Clarissa, what are you doing? What have you done to your life?'

'Waiting' she managed to say between sobs. 'Waiting for this day. I told you I would.'

'How could you do that? Clarissa, you must be…twenty-seven by now!'

'I do not know what has been of you, dear Julian. But at least in my heart you have endured. No other man have I met that made me replace you as my destiny. Somehow I was certain of it, that you would be back. I will need to know what has been of you. Why are you here? You are surely not braving the Musetto to see this overripe twenty-seven-year-old hag.'

'The Musetto may be the devil, but still I would have braved God himself to see you, had you been even one hundred and seven years old.'

Clarissa smiled. 'There is no need for you to increase my happiness with your honeyed tongue. Your presence here already makes worth twelve years of wait.'

'Clarissa…my love. I apologise, but I cannot seem to stop the flow of sweet juices into my mouth. Twelve years is indeed nothing. There is no amount of time that is too much to pay for this. The touch of your hands on my face is already worth the sake of living.'

'I need more of this honey,' she said, and her lips snatched at his. There were more tender words and soft touches. They kissed passionately, never leaving each other's lips, a continuous flow between them as Clarissa climbed on top of him, trembling as she felt him rub against her thighs.

'My love, how long are you here with me for?' Clarissa asked as she quickly undressed and pulled down his hose.

From a dreamy haze of pleasure, Julian managed to hear her words and answer 'For the rest of our lives…' But he lost his senses as he almost choked when entering her in haste, the most incredibly tender and warm marvel, sending divine waves of comfort over his skin, angelic power lifting him floating above the straw. Embracing her soft skin, feeling the round curves of her waist, turning one of his hands down to grip her firm plump bottom, he drew lines with his nail on the ditch of her spine.

Bliss.

After such an ungrateful life, this is what awaited those who endured suffering. Those moments of being only one with the loved person were the blessings that the Christ had promised to those which are persecuted for righteousness sake. The real vision of the dreamed love, the sensation of being inside her, still touching her further and deeper as her love moistened him, as her words soothed his soul and boiled his blood, as her moaning set the cadence of their dance. That was the so promised Kingdom of Heaven! Yes, Julian was indeed savouring the milky sweetness of Paradise as he became one with Clarissa. Not only by where he entered her, or by their lips which explored each other's features. Their very skin was just one, as was their hair, entangled as were their arms and legs. Their eyes, never leaving each other, were one, as was the heat of their hearts, exchanged through bone and flesh for their bodies felt to be in flames. They were one as the moaning came fast and furious, until both souls were violently yanked out of their bodies by a blow of thunder, for a powerful ride out of the world of the living. In this prolonged instant of extreme blessedness and might, Julian and Clarissa were not just in heaven. They were ruling it.

They were God.

'Where is everybody?' asked an exhausted Julian, covered in cold sweat, but still entangled on his love.

'Everybody has left me alone with you, at my orders', answered a flabbergasted Clarissa, her milky eyes trying to recover from the explosion that had sent her pieces all scattered across the universe.

'And how long do we have together here…to make love again?'

'For the rest of our lives' Clarissa said, with a devilish smile, before covering Julian's face with kisses and engaging into a new session of caresses with the love of her life.

A city had been destroyed; lives had been lost by the hundreds; thousands more were waiting for battle, which certainly meant death for most; Clarissa's home, her family fortress was besieged by the most bloodthirsty pirates the Ligurian coast had seen in a century; the food supplies were already meagre and the resistance of the castle waning. But as Julian had said, those were the moments for what living was worth. Who cared about war when you could make love? Who cared about those deeds of the devil when beloved ones could be God Themselves?

They spent the night engaged into inexhaustible love. Each session was longer and more intense. But every time after they'd fall back on earth, Julian would talk about his plans to bring Clarissa, her father and the whole population safely out of the castle, and away from Saracen blades.

'I don't trust them', insisted Clarissa.

'We have no choice but to take this chance', said Julian. 'They seem to be reasonable, especially the Musetto'.

'Julian', said Clarissa holding his face with both hands, 'you have not changed. You are still the naïve boy that stole my heart. You may be impressed by the elegance of the Musetto, but you should see the unspeakable things we watched from our battlements. Most of the population has taken refuge inside our walls, but the ones whom the Saracens found hiding or scurrying about the land were brought to the front of the walls and made to suffer for all of us to see. Even those of us who turned our eyes away could not prevent their cries for mercy to reach our ears as the Saracens performed the most horrendous acts.'

'Clarissa, horrible things happen in wars', said Julian, holding her tight, feeling her body through every pore of his skin. It was invigorating. 'But I do not want any more of this horror at your doorstep. Please leave the castle as instructed by the Musetto. He gave me his guarantee'

'How could I? And leave my father here? And my people? No, I shall resist'

'But how much more can you all withstand?' Julian asked.

Clarissa bit her lip and closed her eyes. She finally conceded 'Probably no more than a week. We have a few horses and mules, that could feed us for a longer while, but then we will all be starving'.

'And do you expect swamp fever to drive them out of here meanwhile? Maybe it will kill you all before it gets the Saracens.'

She smiled 'Julian, we know a fair amount about swamp fever. Old Ignatius, our physician, knew the flowers and essences to keep the swamps free from *malaria* – the bad air. Unfortunately he's been slain by the pirates, taking the secret with himself, but all for their own doom. However, we also know that the castle walls are too high for these pestilent fumes to cross over. Old Ignatius always swore it came in the shape of those gnats and mosquitoes that thrive on the swamp but that do not come inside.'

'Whatever it is', Julian said, 'you cannot hope that the fever will drive the Musetto away. And his army is too big for that of your brother and the papal soldiers. There are at least two Mohammedans for every one of those Christians across the hills.'

'So will they dive into the pirates?' asked a suddenly smiling Clarissa, with a blinding shine on her eyes.

'Not until more soldiers are gathered by the pope', sighed Julian 'and by then, maybe more Saracens arrive in Luna. Come, Clarissa, let's put ourselves into composure and get down to see your father. We must talk to him.'

Julian savoured the high spirit of the woman, who stood up naked, the rising sun bringing a glorious scarlet glow to her robust slenderness and a divine shine to her hair, smiling candidly at him as she said 'you're not hoping to convince the old badger, are you?'

Lord Oberto, at fifty-three, would have been strong as an ox had he not become ill with the fever. The marchese had stood up long enough through those weeks of terror under siege, sparingly taking his food rations and generously passing most of his share to others. None were selected, for he heartily treated equally the lowest of servants, even wandering beggars, who were unlucky enough to be around when the Saracens landed, just as well as he would have done to his own daughter. Now, with a fragile gait, pale and hollow-eyed, he suffered from chilly tremors, and sometimes went delirious. Already for the third day, the fever did not seem to abate. Oberto had been the only person in the castle to have contracted the swamp fever, a common sickness that daily took its toll from the inhabitants of the region. Although he would not admit it, many believed that Oberto had climbed down the walls to sabotage the Saracens, or went through some secret passage into the free land, where he probably contacted the fever.

When he saw Julian being brought by the hand of his daughter, Oberto's eyes deepened behind sudden crystal puddles. With difficulty he stood up to embrace the visitor, hiding his emotion behind the usual verbal shield. 'My son, I am filled with joy to lay my eyes on you once again. I am even sweating because of that! No talk about my daughter, who has not spend a single day during these…twelve years?, without mentioning you. I hope you had a respectful night together!'

'Lord Oberto…' called Julian as they kissed on the faces.

'Son, please call me father!' said Oberto, tears generously flowing from his violet eyes. 'It's about time we settle this. I do not know what has been of you, neither had Clarissa – well not until last night, or this morning, I suppose!'

'Father, stop the irony. You know what we were doing all night!' said a radiant Clarissa.

That was the incredibly strong woman that Julian knew, the pride of lord Oberto.

'Spare me from these thoughts, Clarissa' her father smiled, and turned to Julian. 'See? I thought her springtime was long past, but she keeps blooming with the wildest imaginable flowers. I cannot put up with all the bees.' And he broke into a coughing spell. An obliging aide discreetly patted his brow with a wet cloth.

After a pause for the lord's chest, Julian cleared his throat and started 'Lord Oberto, I mean, father! The pirates are ready to let you all out. All alive. But you must surrender Luna.'

'Julian negotiated with the Musetto himself' added carefully an apprehensive Clarissa. She raised one eyebrow to wait for her father's reaction.

Oberto just lowered his violet eyes and smiled. He shook his head and asked. 'Really? Good people they must be. The Musetto himself promised you? And what does the Musetto get if he does not respect such promise? Do you go and give him a good beating, Julian? Or do you get the help of the pope? Will Benedict VIII come himself to slap all of the Saracens on their faces?'

'What do you expect?' Julian said, with a controlled tone. 'To endure here forever? To wait until the Musetto gives up?'

'Julian is probably right, father. You know we cannot withstand.' said Clarissa, with a forced conviction.

'Clarissa, my heart!' Oberto smiled with watery eyes. 'I don't have to tell you once more that you are probably the smartest person I have ever come across in this world, do I? No, perhaps this is the right moment for just a compliment. Then *think*, my dear. Your thoughts are blurred by your heart. Julian is here, yes, this is the happiest of our days, but we must survive. You two must survive.'

'Forgive me my interruption, but we know that!' begged Julian. 'Nevertheless they want this bastion and they will not give it up. I hate to admit that, but the Musetto's forces still overwhelm the Christian army. And there is nothing that makes me believe that we get reinforcement that soon. It may be hard, but you have to accept it: the white castle will be in Saracen hands, weather we avoid some more blood spillage or not.'

'So, what do you expect?' gasped the lord of Luna, 'These people would just let us all go? Christian forgiveness? We have seen enough of their merciful nature. Just ask Clarissa here, Julian. The city has been ravaged. The younger women of the valley have been taken to the boats to be traded as slaves, while most captured men and elderly women were executed right in front of our walls. I saw with my own eyes when they skinned alive poor Napoleone Genovesi and his old wife, while their daughters were repeatedly raped by their soldiers. When we left the battlements, refusing to witness such atrocity, their shrieks of horror permeated through our walls. Walls that the Saracen slingers have slow, but continually depredated with their stones. These slingers will be our doom, Julian. Where arrows cannot go, stones have a mortal precision. No ammunition will ever be in shortage here, for they use marble against marble.'

'My lord, we must go while there is still time. The wife of the Musetto intervened in our favour.' Julian said.

'The wife?' sneered Oberto 'Does he bring a wife to his raids?'

'He brings the whole harem, with eunuchs and everything!'

'Don't play silly, father!' said Clarissa. She turned to Julian 'My father knows well about the pirate encampment and all that the Musetto has brought. He's sneaked out into their troops at night: That is how he contacted this fever that ails his health at the most inconvenient time.'

Lord Oberto tried to chuckle, but all he did was cough. The man who once was large looked frail, sweating copiously. He was about to say something to Julian when a soldier broke into the salon, bringing a piece of leather. 'Lord Oberto, this message has been thrown in by one of the slingers.'

Julian read the message the Saracens had delivered in good written Latin. 'They're waiting,' he said. 'We should be leaving in pairs. It's safer for all the rest of you, as we can shut the castle gates until each person that leaves is out of danger, away onto the hills, by the Christian army. They can be patient and honourable, sticking to their promise. If they betray us, we do not lose the castle neither the people, and the gates will stay closed. The full withdrawal of all of us should take days. We buy time waiting for more armies and get everyone out in safety.'

Oberto and Clarissa looked at each other in surprise, but not one of them could come up with a better plan. Julian just added one more thing. 'But they want me out first. And alone.'

It took another two hours for Julian to reluctantly leave the castle. The destrier dragged its hoofs slowly as the gate was relocked behind and the bridge re-suspended. With a heavy chest and bitter flavour creeping up to his throat, Julian sighed, but still held hope. Things were going to be as settled between him and the Musetto. More specifically, the Musetto's first wife.

A silent Saracen army awaited on the distance, outside the court, already making way for his withdrawal. A rough sea of fabric, metal and dark, sweaty faces, where Julian did not expect to segregate the figures of the Musetto or his wife. The late summer sun blinded his vision as he crossed the path opened by the Saracens, up to the southern hills where Alberto Azzo's cavalrymen observed from the ridge.

Julian rode slowly, thinking of Oberto's revelation. The old marchese had delayed the whole operation to tell him about a meeting he had with an old woman in a place called Santa Maria Lei Giudice, before Clarissa was born.

'Dad, you do not really want to share that with Julian, do you?' Clarissa had pleaded, biting her lower lip with embarrassment.

'Of course I will, Clarissa. Do you want this information to dwindle and disappear between my decrepit memory and your silent reservation?'

Clarissa pleaded then to Julian 'It's an old wives' tale, don't mind it, Julian.'

'Oh that's true!' Oberto said, excited. 'She was an old witch! A true *strega*, who's fornicated with popes and cardinals, bearing many other angels and demons into our world. She was my great-grandmother, Julian. Have you ever heard of Marozia?' On noticing Julian's face of puzzlement, the marchese continued. 'Nobody knows of her any more, Julian. Her tale is gone from our folk's memory, but somehow my family has a talent for cantastorie and, whether I like it or not, I learned of her and I knew exactly who the old crone was when she called Railenda and I into the monastery. Her name was Mariozza, and she lived to see a hundred years of her time. One of her many husbands was Guido, the Margrave of Tuscany. From Guido she bore Adalberto II, my grandfather. Her half-sister was Theodora, named just like their mother. Theodora generated the Crescentii and the Tusculani, who are, as you know, the most powerful opponents of the emperor. But never mind that. Through other liaisons, Mariozza herself was the mother of Pope John XI, of that devil Albericus, Princeps of Rome and the grandmother of Pope John XII, whose fetid soul must be sizzling in hell. This Albericus put her in the dungeons of Rome and she was to be forgotten if not for my grandfather who charitably smuggled her into a convent just south of Lucca. The old hag survived her sons and grandsons, until the child Emperor Otto III learned of her whereabouts. We visited her one day before she was smothered by Roman soldiers who broke into the monastery.'

Julian swallowed a suddenly bitter lump, unable to react. Oberto continued 'This woman must have had a gift, and whether she wasted it for her own selfish good or not, she was indeed divinely talented. One would think there's devilry when a centenarian woman looks splendid, as if she was still less than half of her age. Mariozza must have called us because she knew death was coming to get her on the next day. She wanted to make one single and last act of generosity before delivering her soul to divine judgement. Pointing to Railenda's belly, the old woman predicted we would have a daughter. A baby to become a feisty girl, to inherit Mariozza's strength and determination, but who would use it in a generous, compassionate fashion. Mariozza pleaded that we gave our daughter freedom of choice in everything in life. More than begged, she demanded. To let our girl decide on anything that she wanted. To let her make her own choice on the friends she played with, what she ate or drank, where she went or lived and, especially, who she chose for her partnership in love. Her one and only man to be eternally loyal to. Sounds like an absurdity for a woman to be brought up with, but when Clarissa was pulled out bellowing like a siren, Railenda and I were enraptured by her spell. We discussed that strange episode and the powerful impression that Mariozza had left on us, that maybe the old woman had given the baby a genuine blessing. We have always been loving parents, Julian I can swear by that. Alberto and Berthe were raised with the heartiest warmth and the wisest advice, but still, irresponsibly or not, we allowed Clarissa to take charge of her life. She grew up to be a lioness, strong as a mountain, but the most generous soul that this marca has seen, and the most delightful arms to have around my neck whenever I came back to Luna'

Clarissa was shaking her head in a theatrical disapproval 'That's not me, surely.' Her eyes stung. She had never loved her father more intensely.

'Shut up Clarissa and let this old man finish,' Oberto said with soft eyes and an inconspicuous curl on the corner of his lips. Clarissa tittered quietly as her father continued 'Julian, it was Clarissa who made us invite you to join our group when we met that Hubert of Liege with his sandgrouse. It was Clarissa that insisted we brought you into our home and adopted you as our own. A risky venture, indeed, to adopt a foreigner we find in the woods, but your good nature constantly reassured us that Clarissa was right...'

'Clarissa was wrong!' protested Julian. 'I lost the Lady Railenda to...'

'Don't you dare speak of it again, Julian of Mans!' Oberto roared, standing his fragile frame up with difficulty, but still towering over Julian with his voice. 'Young man, you should be humble to accept fate and not be too arrogant to try to understand or judge God's actions, while you did everything to protect Railenda. My son, you have proven your value, a thousand times more than ever, by being here. By facing this full army of dogs and the Musetto himself, with only your sword, your bravery and your love for Clarissa, to negotiate the release of our people. How wrong could any of us be? Mariozza when she gave us the blessing, Clarissa when she chose you and all of us when we took you into our hearts?'

Julian could say nothing and just bowed his head humbly. Clarissa held his hand with bone crushing strength.

They conferred on the most advisable order of leaving the castle. Oberto was sceptical about the Musetto's generosity and insisted he would be the last, remaining inside until all others had gone. That could take two days. Although Clarissa protested, Julian was happy to see her as the first to depart, once he had reached the top of the hill. Among farewell tears, reassuring words, hugs and kisses, Julian was still staring at the pools in Clarissa's rainbow eyes when Oberto whispered in his ears 'Do not worry, my son. Clarissa will take care of you. And I will be with you one day. I do question God's actions too!'

Julian kissed his face. 'We will all be fine, my father.'

Hating God

On his way towards the Christian camp, Julian waited by the olive trees, a silent and windless spot, half way between the top of the hill and the white castle below him. He watched the movements in Luna, while far on the crest a wall of horses and Christian riders quietly trampled the lavender field, observing the developments in apparent readiness. In Luna, ahead of the main South gate, another cloud of dust was raised into the stale air when the Saracens reluctantly dragged their feet to re-open a passageway to allow the next pair of people to leave the besieged fortress to the safety of the Azzo's army. Julian heard some galloping coming from behind him. It was another massive single destrier, approaching downhill. Young Albertazzo rode it. His face was grave, but still friendly.

'Julian, you have braved the enemy and yet you have been left to live. But our men grow uneasy, and my father demands to know what you are doing here.'

'*Uneasy?*' Julian snorted. 'Why uneasy if they do not battle? Where the fuck is the pope and his army? You can tell your father that I have negotiated for the release of his father and sister, and all the people from Luna who are deprived from living decency in that castle.'

'You *what?*' Albertazzo gasped, incredulous. 'How can you trust these dogs? Julian, there were soldiers in our camp who think you are a traitor, by being taken into the enemy's camp,' he laughed nervously 'but now, as we see you coming out alive and fresh as an otter out of the brook, there are many who are suggesting it's the Volto Santo that is protecting you.'

Julian shushed him. A cart was being dragged out of the castle gate, pulled by a sack of bones vaguely resembling the shape of a mule. Both riders watched as the muted enemy horde waited along the avenue, the miserable creature bringing out two people of Luna. A man held the reigns and a woman sat next to him, with her head completely covered. They all knew that was the Lady of Luna. Julian finally let the air go out of his lungs.

'It's Clarissa!' Albertazzo shouted.

He galloped back to his father on the crest of the hills 'They are releasing Clarissa!'

But he missed to notice that a bubble grew on the eastern side of the Saracen crowd. Julian heard the shouts and saw a large black sphere emerge from the line of soldiers: the Musetto's wife. She was shrieking like a nightjar, nervously agitating her stubby arms. Julian froze and struggled to breathe, as three men approached the cart all of a sudden, halted the mule and pulled Clarissa out, dragging her towards the enormous woman. Julian hated God as he saw his precious treasure in the hands of the Mohameddans. Trying to keep his stomach in or he'd explode like a toad, fearing he would never set eyes on his love again, he prepared to charge. But strangely, there was something rather unbelievable in the whole scene. An unreality that made him doubt Clarissa could be slipping through his fingers just as they were finally each other's. While she struggled under the pirates' grasp, several ghostly heads were peering out of the battlements, and shouting indignities. As soon as Clarissa was brought forward to the Musetto's wife, the immense sow snatched the veil out of her face and a large murmur erupted out of the crowd. It confirmed to Julian that this victim was not Clarissa. They had Oberto Obizzo, Marchese de Toscana. Another shriek was heard and Julian saw the Saracens crowd moving in, like ants over honey, swarming over Oberto and his rider on the cart, making both vanish like stones in the sea.

Galloping towards the hillcrest, where Alberto Azzo watched petrified with his men, Julian screamed for their help. 'It's your father, Alberto. The filthy traitors have Oberto in their hands!'

'They won't hurt him,' Alberto said with a trembling voice, seeming to struggle to convince himself. 'They know he is a precious hostage, worth a fortune.'

Oberto could be anywhere in that sea of enemies. There was just a deafening clamour of the Saracen army, victorious and vicious.

'We must break into their flanks and rescue him.' Julian pleaded 'They have broken the agreement. Treachery!'

Alberto was grinding his teeth. 'We cannot go now, Julian. There's too many of them! We will be massacred.' He desperately tried to locate his father in the liquid mass of turbans and swords. 'The pope's army should be arriving any moment. They were seen to be a few miles...'

'The pope?' Julian gasped. 'There will be no mitre-sporting fop committing to protect your father, Alberto. I go with or without his help. *Fuck the pope!* and he galloped downhill towards the castle. When crossing through the grapevines, on reaching the olive trees, Julian was halted by a loud rattling noise, when a fierce attack by slingers battered on the marble walls of the castle, raising a taller curtain of dust over the marshy moat. This time, nausea exploded inside Julian without any mercy. He forever regretted the scene that he was made to watch.

While the slingers kept pounding their fatal marble stones on the beaten walls, the soldiers' ranks broke down and dispersed in the middle of the avenue, revealing ahead of the drawbridge a pair of nervous but strong horses that were being tormented by a few boisterous men. The racket and the maddening dust drove the beasts into a frenzy, trying to run away from one another, except for a certain burden they had attached between their tails: Oberto Obizzo. The naked marchese was being yanked up from the ground every time the beasts took off and stretched the ropes, just to drop again, roll and be dragged like a sack of carrion. Helpless to shut those pigs from their cheers, Julian prayed that Oberto had already been dead by that time, oblivious to the torture. Unfortunately, he knew it was not the case.

Closure happened faster than he could ever recall years later. The men grew more savage, screaming and poking, making the horses wilder, tugging the ropes helplessly as Oberto jerked up, screaming in pain. The cloud of dust that had soared over the boiling horde had a firm resolve to settle without dispersing. Julian turned to the hillcrest and shouted for Alberto with all his lungs. He was not heard, either because of the deafening screams from the Saracens, or due to a powerless paralysis stretching across the Christian riders watching that cruel quartering. And just before the dust drew its curtain between a besieged Luna and the world around them, Julian recognised a tall, slim figure stepping out of the crowd. The Musetto, trying to control the horses, too late against their helpless fury. The resolved pirate quickly pulled out his saif and raised it with both hands between the two horses.

Here's a decent, pious man that will cut down the ropes.

The curved blade flashed the sunlight as it came down once, twice, and the horses were let lose. Julian screamed with horror for a long time, as the dust got closer and erased the carnage scene from his view.

The screaming would not end. It lingered in the dusty air, lost in the enemy clamour, trying to frighten reality away, as if Julian could wake himself up from a dream where he would never see Oberto again. The scream came from all sides, as if was multiplied by two, three, four. Other voices, all screaming together with him.

When Julian noticed, he stopped, panting, filled with horror and rage, but the screams continued. Not horrified shrieks as his had been belched out, but hysterical laughs, coming from inside the olive trees, mocking at him. It could not be. Julian charged against one tree. He slashed through the hard branches and confirmed with his senses that there was nobody, nothing hiding in there. Nobody on the tree behind him either. A devilish distraction. He heard the crowd roaring from Luna and the rattling continuing against the walls. The dust had not settled and little could be devised from where he was. Turning back towards the southern hillcrest, he galloped enough to be clearly heard by Alberto, who was dismounted, crying, stomping his fists on the ground.

Julian raised his long Lucchese sword. 'Do you join me against the Mohammedans, Alberto?'

'I will flood the valley with their blood!' Alberto roared.

'So I go!' Julian moaned and dug his heels into the destrier plump flanks. The fuming beast was craving for battle. It galloped down towards the cloud-covered castle, in a mad rush, so vicious and grating that it could have ignited the hills into a raging fire.

He never heard Alberto's shouts that they were just not ready to strike yet.

The battle of Luna, in the Year 1016 of our Lord Jesus Christ, is memorable for its lack of memories and notable for the distorted notes it left in history. It was written by those who never saw it, and believed to have been won by those who never fought it. Forever their names, defeated and non-winner, will be repeated an association with the carnage in the boggy lands of Luna. And the true heroes of this battle, those who fought bravely under the Ligurian sun, are mostly buried under the paludal ruins of what used to be the most beautiful castle in Christendom. Or else, they are sometimes resurrected as the tale keeps being told by cantastorie, always passing it down, with one stretching of the truth, here and there, to the next generation.

Julian had ridden into a cloud of dust.

Alberto Azzo and the Christian army only saw him disappear into the sandy curtain. There was a deadly silence in the windless afternoon, but soon they could hear the shrieks of horror and pain that emerged from the hidden camp.

Julian's horse opened way through the pirates, allowing the dented but sharpened steel to strike with fury and violence on a murderous attack. The blinding rage made Julian dig into the heart of the Saracens, who found themselves being broken into by an extraordinary force. Dumbfounded and helpless, they could barely acknowledge the power of the Christian army, which had summoned that passionate demon, digging a horrendous gash through their very heart. The long black hair lashed ferociously around the rabid features of a mad man, as Julian never stopped cutting and wounding, spiking and maiming, chopping, mutilating and killing. The blade cut through flesh and bone like lard, opening mortal gashes or popping out limbs or heads. Once the dusty cloud thinned, Julian's killing frenzy was seen from the Christian side as a silvery spark, the shiny reflections of sword and axe, spinning and dancing through the sea of enemies' heads, until it faded in the crimson spray that it snatched at every strike. Those soldiers who were incredulous that the Julian of Mans could be still alive dropped to their knees and praised the Volto Santo, begging for Alberto Azzo to strike immediately in his support.

The Saracen army felt, for the first time, powerless. The front line of battle had closed around itself, creating a whirl of blades, which were only amounting to an unexpected jamming of cloth, boots and metal, but most dramatically, given the frantic anger triggered by that black haired demon's attack, to a deadly smothering of their own flanks. The enemy for them was not a mass or a battalion any more, but a single point of wrath which found its way into their body and was soon to reach the other side of the camp.

Although covered in blood, Julian was able to keep his foaming mount miraculously unharmed. As he crossed to the edge of the moat, he saw himself trapped between the fetid waters around the walls of Luna and the flabbergasted Saracen army, barely able to reorganise its lines. He shot a glance up to the ramparts and, disappointed that he had not caught a glimpse of the lady of the castle, he turned his steed around and dug the spurs hard on its sides. The firmness of the pain told the stallion to face and dive once again into the core of that menacing foe.

Upon seeing the furious charger with the Christian dashing towards them, scarlet sword and axe spiralling on its sides, some men had a last-moment reconsideration and preferred to save their skins by turning around and diving into the rocky ground. Few of them were able to escape Julian's blades or the lances of their disgusted fellows, who had no mercy on cowards.

On a desperate trial to annihilate the Christian demon, the Saracen archers and slingers aimed at the heart of the battle, trespassing more of their own as these approached the charging enemy. Mounted swordsmen tried to gain ground into the centre of the camp, where Julian was cropping heads, but only at the cost of infantry, which were crushed under the heavily charged beasts, or chopped down by furious cavaliers who were blinded by wrath and the desire to tear out the heart of that son of a hell's Christian whore.

The harvest had already been so intense that Julian's mount had to deal with a softer, uneven ground. No more could the horse step on firm soil, but it had to master its hoofs on the different surfaces of the enemies' bodies. Whether it was God Himself or one of Julian's guardian angels who made the Saracen arrows and stones fly by just to scratch his exposed skin or to bounce out of his armour, such divine force was allowing him to use his fuelled rage to, as he intended, wipe out those sickened devils from the land of Luna.

Julian's vision was red, not because of enemies' blood, but of his own, filling up his eyes from inside, with a never before experienced rage as that which drove him to destroy. Neither he nor the ocean of enemies, so desperate, disrupted and engaged into controlling the Christian demon, ever saw the cloud of smoke raised by the charging Christian army.

Flying down the hill, carried by the Christian cavalry, the traditional cries of *Benedictus, Sanctus Petrus, Sanctus Iohannes et Sanctus Martinus,* and *Sancta Maria, Redemptrix Gloriosa,* this time they were replaced by *SANCTUS VULTUS!*

The passionate clamour never made through the stifle crunch of Saracen armours, all facing the central point which was inflicting so much destruction into their heart.

It was only when the earth shook, as the charging cavalry exploded into the Saracen flanks, that Julian saw with surprise and relief that unexpected help had been provided. Alberto Azzo led them, digging a trench of blood into the midst of the Saracens, cropping them with his gyrating sword, foaming with anger as the Christian soldiers shrieked like badgers on breaking the enemy.

Now the pressure had suddenly eased on Julian, as the pirates turned around to repel the charge of the entire Christian horde, which was devouring their ranks. With hardly any blade charging against him, the long haired demon found himself freer to mercilessly pursue and cut down his hunt. He would hit hard on necks and shoulders, slicing helmets and piercing through chain, his blade digging deep into flesh and bone as the enemies howled in horror and pain. And whether consciously or not, he made his way towards the harem.

Minutes before, Mugiâhid had been thinking about the slain lord of Luna. The naivety of those barbarians would still surprise him from time to time. It was no wonder that the city had been taken so easily. Now that the infidel army had seen that there were no negotiation terms at all with the legions of the great Mugiâhid, they could turn around with their tails between his legs and ride back to their filthy Christian holes, leaving the territory to its worthy new owner.

He did have issues with betrayal though, the breaking of a given word, as he would have watched the whole withdrawal of Luna with a curious sense. However, he had been naïve enough too to trust the commitments proposed by his first wife. She had been ingenious, and cheated both the Christian and himself, but she did not get the lady of the castle as initially intended. But on the other hand, he had to admit that honour and truth should come in second, for those were times of war. For the dead, there was only heaven and hell. And if for the infidels there was only hell, so why spare them? The victim had come into their hungry fangs, so innocently that Mugiâhid even felt a drop of compassion when he noticed the horses would not have the strength to tear him apart. A victim of those games of war, the lord of Luna was quickly sliced in two by his saif. He had not even been back to start his lunch of pheasant cuts and olives when he was startled by the cries outside the tent. An attack!

As Mugiâhid jumped up for his armour, blades and shield, his aides informed of some mad man that had plunged alone into the besieging legion.

'And why haven't you befallen him already?' he asked, quickly mounting the steed and digging the spurs deep into the flesh. He was already on gallop when the aid answered.

'He is the one who is befalling us…'

Mugiâhid could not go too far. The confusion was such that all soldiers were trying to get to the same spot, right in front of the castle. The smothering of bodies formed a vast human barrier that the horse could not trespass. He shouted orders, but few were those that realised where the cries were coming from. Mugiâhid kept trying, kicking harder into his mount's groin, but the steed would not go forward, making little advance into the mass. It was during those brief moments of irritation and annoyance that he noticed the flash of silver dancing into the core of his army, and the ruby showers it splattered at every strike. There he was! The same demon he had received in his own tent. The long-black-haired Christian, swinging his blades with an abominable grace and ease, slaying and cropping heads as a farmer would have done with a sickle on wheat. Mugiâhid felt his skin drenched with anger.

Broken shields exploded in the distance and arrows whizzed by as the enraged commander cried for vengeance and tried to reach the Christian intruder. During the agonisingly slow advance, Mugiâhid's horse suddenly faltered, as a headless body lay flat, trampled on the ground. Looking down, he noticed with horror why there was no more dust, for the hoofs and boots were stepping into a lake of blood and piles of bodies. The harvest had already been through those grounds.

Looking ahead, Mugiâhid spotted the demon, much closer now, charging towards him. The black mane whipping wildly to the sides, the hard mouth foaming as fiery air gushed out at every strike of the sword. A cross on its chest was still visible through the red that oozed over the coat. His mount was as wild, driven by something more than just the pain of spurs. Mugiâhid saw, by the blind fury into the demon's eyes, that the rage was not driven by the so called Santiagos, or Santilarios. It was something much more primitive; more ancient than the Prophet, and may His name be blessed; more ancient than those Christian saints and even the Christ Himself; more ancient than the old patriarchs. Something dark and horrible, more ancient than God. For the first time ever, Mugiâhid felt what it was like for men to loose their bowels at the height of battle.

Now his own horse had to brave through a counter current of bodies, panic-stricken soldiers, all scurrying away from the destruction frenzy of the Christian demon. The experienced commander would have pierced each of the cowards with his own blade, but something made him spare those unfortunate souls. And looking ahead, his blood froze as he saw the Christian horseman getting nearer. Mugiâhid turned around to gain a gallop towards his tent, by the harem.

Just as he turned, the air went out of his lungs as he was blinded by the blast of the whole Christian cavalry, already breaking through the flanks of his army, destroying his men at no more than a few hundred feet from him. Where had they come from? Had they all been so blinded by the steel of the Christian demon that those thousand horsemen hid in shadows until they flared though his lines, howling as they slew Mohammedans by the clusters? That was a bad sign, only readable by someone with his experience.

Mugiâhid rushed to the harem.

With a wide corridor of his men trapped between the charging enemy and the moat of Luna, Mugiâhid had a safe, but not speedy parallel escape, fighting through currents of his own Saracens. They battled by the thousands, still plenty to crush the enemy. But an invigorated enemy, inspired by their warring demon, who strangely seemed invincible, dangerously corralling them back towards the moat and into the ruined village. It would not take long though, for more of his reinforcements would be marching up from the port. He swore to himself that his men should not be leaving any recognisable body parts of the Christian pigs.

Mugiâhid finally arrived at the unguarded harem tent. And there he changed his mind about the battle.

Julian had adjustments to make.

He finally made it to the harem, the largest tent, so isolated and strangely unguarded during the battle. He was preparing to dismount when the curtains flew open with a roar. Exploding out of it, like an enraged African unicorn, the giant white eunuch held firmly to a lance, crushing against Julian's horse, digging the spear deep into its chest. As the destrier screeched in pain, Julian hit the eunuch with his sword, but fell backwards, still mounted on the dead impaled steed. He quickly got up and looked at the eunuch. The Nordic monster stood at the place where he had lanced the horse, with a puzzled look as he examined his left side. Julian's sword had cleft through his shoulder, slicing down to his ribs. With his right hand, the giant tried to yank the hilt out of his chest, unsuccessfully. Julian approached and gently took the eunuch's hand off the hilt. The giant watched it silently. He rolled his eyes and collapsed backwards as Julian used his foot to push him out of the sword.

Another explosion startled Julian, but only to a point, for it was not unexpected. He had only time to swing his sword as fast as he could. It had been a hellish growl, and a round green shape had bounced violently out of the tent, brandishing a curved silvery blade. Still masked by her veil, the Musetto's first wife stopped still, avoiding Julian's sword. Once he had completed his swing, the woman advanced again, ready to slaughter the Christian pig, but he only stepped backwards, rather calmly. The enormous wife felt suddenly weak and her breasts unusually warm. Looking down, the blackness of her pupils disappeared behind her tiger eyes, as she noticed her silky green robe bathed by a red cascade, spilling from somewhere under her veil. The dagger flew away when her hands clutched to her neck, trying to block the slash.

Feeling his hate standing on top of every single hair, Julian felt a noxious herbal scent. As the Musetto's wife stood still, moaning and clasping at her slashed neck, Julian noticed that other Saracen warriors left the main battle and came towards him, some screaming savagely, some of them chased by Christians, but all of them swearing vengeance. He had less than one second before they brought down their metal on him, but enough to swing his sword once again. As the Lucchese blade cut through the air and flesh, the hippopotamus woman folded back in two when the lower front of her robe dropped and her belly opened into a large fat gash, as if the devil himself was suddenly smiling at Julian.

By the time Mugiâhid arrived at the harem, the clash had moved over to a different side and only slaughtered bodies laid spread on a thick pool of blood. His legs lost their bones when he saw the immense green corpse of his wife gutted in front of the collapsed tent. A strange smell of fresh coriander pestered the scene. Retching with sorrow and hate, he decided to end this quickly. It was time to go back into battle.

Horseless and on losing ground, he returned to the core of the fight in the hope to steal the mount of the first rider he could find, whether friend or foe. Luckily it was a Christian, whose body was parted in two by the sharp blade of his saif. Back on a horse, comfortable and powerful, he rode to his captains, shouting orders and determining the direction to go, which was very clear: Back to the ships.

Downfall

A group of riders hurried down a fertile valley by the eastern Apuane slopes, called *Hortus Novus*. They had ridden non-stop for two days, carefully keeping away from the villages they had raided a week before and circling the cruel peaks to avoid any surprise encounters with the advancing Christian front. Having lost two of their magnificent steeds, lean beasts bred for speed on the planes, they replaced them for sturdier local horses stolen from Rolandinghi lands.

They had spent a couple of frigid nights on the mountains, only warmed by the terrified bodies of those women they brought along. However, one of these village women stood out. She was stout of spirit and courageous, never moaning from pains or weeping along the way. Being the eldest, she was a fiery black-haired bride of the Christ, but seemed to be particularly fond of her encounters with those men, who hardly gave any consideration to the fact that she was keeping them from possessing the other women.

Their leader, wearing a honey-coloured turban, rode ahead as the valley opened lower, approaching the large white castle. Behind the walls of Luna, a large cloud of dust was rising.

'They're attacking!' he shouted, halting his horse.

The other riders approached hurriedly, with restless horses, as if the beasts sensed the nearness of the journey's end or maybe the scent of blood from the battle.

'Drop the women!' he ordered with gritted teeth, immediately elbowing the black-haired woman on the face, toppling her from his horse. Other bodies fell on the ground, with yelps of pain.

'Maybe we should pass them to the blade right now, so they will not run away.' suggested one of the riders.

'What makes you think we will not win this battle?' honey-turban asked, with an enraged grin. 'We *will* return and have more of these women. And if they are not here when we come back,' he continued, 'we will chase and crucify each one of them.' He looked at the old woman he had just punched out of his horse. 'Do you understand?' he shouted at her face. She stared at him blankly. With those same black eyes of hatred she had looked at him all the time, even when her body was seemingly enjoying his company.

They left on a gallop.

Coming down to the coastal plane and easternmost wall of Luna, they turned south and saw another line of Saracen riders galloping towards their direction. And much closer to them, another rider. A Christian, whose face lost its colour as he realised he had been surrounded.

Alberto Azzo was in grave peril. Isolated from his men, he was forced to head northeast, around the castle, closely chased by a group of furious enemies. He let out a curse when the passage ahead of him was suddenly blocked by another line of heavily armed riders. Outnumbered by Saracens on his heels and on his face, with the boggy waters of the moat to the west and the thorny trees of the sour apple to his right, Alberto had little choice but to confront them all and probably die. Die an honourable death that his father never believed in. After all, Oberto would say, *what good is honour when you're dead?*

The Saracens had slowed down. Opening the line to form a semicircle around Alberto, the pirates were calmly closing in, shutting the side of the moat, which could still be an escape route, but rather pressing him against the impenetrable wall of dry bushes. Alberto gyrated with his sweating steed, the red blade of his sword flashing under the high sun at every menacing swing. Two of the Saracens were giggling, savouring the terror of the prey before its slaughter.

'*Cani!*' Alberto shouted with despise. *You dogs!* They all flashed their teeth, certain to instil more fear on the helpless rider. And they probably did, however without expecting that the Christian soldier would, in the blink of an eye, and with a loud explosion of cracks and snaps, disappear with a suicidal leap with his ride inside the brambles.

His horse tried to keep its head and eyes above the branches, as Alberto frantically slashed through the dry wood. Thorns and rock-hard branches dug through the clothes and the skin of his legs, but mostly opened bloody gashes through the horse's front, from hoofs to face. The surprised Saracens where helpless outside that menacing patch of bushes, still considering if they would just wait for the Christian to slowly die, pinned to the woods, or if it would be worthwhile to venture into the trees and follow him along the sinuous path he had broken through.

Alberto could not control the terrorised animal, whose pain and fear made it leap against a dense thicket, where no more ground could be gained. Unable to move further or disentangle itself from the torturing branches, the pinned beast panted silently with its head up, bulging eyes and foaming mouth asking its rider for help. Alberto dismounted from the back, standing on the path he had broken through the trees. On a standing position, with his view covered by the grey of the dry shrubbery, he could not see if the riders were still outside, and with the horse still kicking about and breaking branches, he could not hear anything either. It was only by chance, before Alberto turned over to the ailing horse, that he saw the honey-turban pirate appearing though the path, flying in with fury, both hands holding his long saif above his head, ready to cut him down. Alberto just raised his newly-made Lucchese sword in an arch, already knowing that there would be no time to defend himself from the deadly strike. The honey-turban Saracen strangely lost the strength on his arms with a burst of pain, when the tip of Alberto's sword entered under his chin and came out above his nose, splitting his face in two. As the curved blade of the saif flipped up, loose in the air, the Saracen collapsed on the crushed branches in front of Alberto. The next rider came roaring and had to jump over the body of the honey-turban man, which was thrown against him. As he landed from his leap, he saw his belly skewered by Alberto's long sword, deep to the hilt. Azzo was grinding his teeth with rage as he pulled the blade out of the pirate and went over along the path to get the other dogs. On his race to find the Christian along the brambles, the third pirate who had dismounted and ventured inside was suddenly yanked back when a fold of his mantle got caught in a branch, making him topple over the fourth. Alberto found both on the floor. As he cut one down, the other tried in vain to escape crawling through the thicket. Reaching through the thorny branches, Alberto firmly pinned him to the ground. In this moment, a rattling sound cracked through the bushes. Arrows.

The remaining Saracens that had stayed on the horses had to choose for safety, abandoning the chase for the lonely rider and their mates in the thicket, as more arrows flew in from the walls of Luna. They rode back to the main battle, only to find that the Saracen army was retiring to the port, and they had been left behind, lined up for slaughter.

A loud cheer came from the walls, as Alberto was seen coming out of the bushes alive. He returned inside along his path, to find the horse still panting, but covered in blood with his belly up, twined on a bed of brambles and thorns. With sorrow and much pain in his heart, Alberto Azzo's swiftly slid his sword into the horse's neck.

While leaving, the marchese noticed that the honey-turban Saracen still moved on the muddy floor, under the corpse of another pirate. Somehow he was still breathing through the crack that had opened in his face. Alberto Azzo had not a drop of pity this time, leaving the Saracen to slowly die, in as much pain as the living could bear.

On the following days, looters would desecrate further the naked bodies of those Saracens, pinning them by the skin on the thorns and branches, on a grotesque banquet offered to the crows. The battle fought by Alberto Azzo, who single-handedly slashed down a band of Saracens in the thorny thicket of the sour apple trees, became soon the talk of Lucca and Pisa, gaining him the nickname of bad thorn: Marchese della Malaspina.

It would be after almost a century that the sour apples were again brought into Liguria, this time disembarking in Genoa, for cultivation under the experience of eastern men of knowledge. The Genovese called the green-juicy fruit of those trees, not at all even resembling an apple, by a name similar to the Persian word that the Eastern traders called it: *lemone*.

Once the stampede had been triggered by the Musetto'orders, the Saracen's abandoned the fight. They now ran for their life. On horse or on foot, the retiring army made the land tremble with their stomping.

Luna was in flames.

And Julian felt he would collapse into ashes.

He limped back past the harem. Dragging his sword, drawing a crooked line on the thick red muck of the ground, he had to get back into the castle, by the front gate of Luna. Walking with difficulty and exhaustion, he moved slowly and strangely untouched, against a heavy torrent of Saracens that flew towards the port. Crossing the sea of enemies towards his promised land, Julian's presence repelled the rushing stream of thousands of bodies that rushed by, opening a wide gap to avoid him.

Uninterested, he saw many of the pirates being cut down by Christian riders as they fled. Mounted men carrying the symbols of the church, howling in pleasure like demons, chasing and easily pinning the men of Daniyya to the ground, slashing them from behind or screaming in ecstasy to see a head flying with only one strike of their swords. Julian did not care if they spared the enemy or if they had slaughtered them all.

Julian did not care about anything else.

The stench of fresh coriander was so smothering that he had to stop and vomit. Evil was stuck to that ground. He knew it, but he did not care. The only thing to do now was to break into Luna and protect Clarissa from this wrong. To get her away from the pirates, away from the papal army, away from that bloody soil that reeked so acrid.

So blinded was Julian to what had been done in those mosquito-ridden plains that missed to see the tide of villagers and soldiers washing over piles of dead bodies to find any valuables, from gold, weapons, tin bracelets, fabrics, to a mouldy piece of bread. He missed to see a group of Pisans skinning a man who was found alive, or a young Lucchese with a deer-hide hat slipping in when the fight was over, defiling bodies with his dagger. He did not care. Julian saw the fat columns of smoke rising from behind the walls, but missed to see where the fire burned. He was also far away from a skirmish to the northeast of the castle, next to the moat, where a religieuse had attacked some Christian soldiers who were raping a passing group of peasant women. The soldiers were only stopped from further violation and from murdering the nun when Alberto Azzo intervened and killed their leader.

Julian came to the gate. On top of the castle walls there was a figure. This time it was not a blast-mouthed ghost, but a woman. She waved at him. And she was crying in horror.

Julian's tears stung his eyes. He roared for the bridge to be dropped. He roared again and again and again. He wouldn't stop until he could have that woman's warmth around him.

This time, the bridge did not pound on the front road, for the bodies lined by the moat made it thump silently on meat and bones. As Julian hurried to meet Clarissa, he missed to notice a lavishly-dressed group of riders that rushed by right behind him. Determined and daunting, they did not care to take note of Julian entering the castle, or even the fire that burned what was left of Luna. Trotting hurriedly and carrying colourful banners, they headed towards the village and the port, where the Saracens were re-grouping in their ships. Heading the cavalry was the thin figure of a tall greying man with strangely feminine features, wearing yellow and scarlet colours under his shining armour. Had he bothered to turn around, Julian would have recognised John Theophylactus, a now magnificent Pope Benedict VIII, covered in the glory of Holy War.

They cried at Luna's door. On each other's arms, Clarissa and Julian were one again. Not in heaven this time, but mutually climbing up the steps that could lead them out of hell. Comforting, hugging, squeezing, sobbing, rubbing faces and ears, intertwining arms and necks, touching and kissing, they savoured their tears and sweat. Relief for finding themselves alive and safe, but cries of anguish shed for the horror, for Oberto their father, for the cruelty, for the suffering, for the villagers, for the soldiers, for the dead.

For Luna.

Clarissa was losing her senses and, together with it, any strength she still held in her legs. It was only the sordidly delicious embrace from Julian that kept her standing. Seeing her father go and fall into the fangs of death had broken her. She was disconsolate and disgusted with destiny, but horribly relieved, happy and blessed to be with Julian.

She would never let him go again. *Never.*

Fires still raged, sending twirling columns of smoke up to the quick darkening sky.

Julian wailed and held on to Clarissa, firmly.

Although he had grown up to be hard and polished as the rocks of Luna and stand the adversities as firmly as the walls of Jerusalem, Julian was not cold-blooded. He had shed his share of tears after leaving his parents, or for the deaths of John Fasanus and Bonacorso. But not since the Lady Railenda had died in his hands had she wailed so inconsolably. 'I have done it, Clarissa! It's happened! I have done it!' he howled.

The pupils in her eyes swelled, hiding the rainbow behind their darkness. 'What have you done, Julian? You have won against these pirates! You won it for us, Julian!'

But he wept inconsolably, biting her shoulder as the sobs took away his breath. Words came out disconnected through his wailing and it was then that it all dawned on Clarissa. This time her legs could not hold Julian steady. She fell on the ground with him on top.

As the cries of the wounded filled the blood-stained air and the villagers and soldiers ravaged greedily, fighting as crows through the piles of the dead, riders nervously trotted by, raising dust and spluttering red mud around their path. Alberto Azzo was assisted by his son Albertazzo on command. Bleeding, covered in cuts and scratches from his face to feet after the struggle in the brambles, he was given a new horse and hurried to tend to his sister, who should be still somewhere in the castle. From a distance he already devised the wounded of Luna limping out of the gate as lost souls escaping by chance from damnation, ignoring on their way a young woman that sat in the middle of the bridge, mindless of anything else. She was serenely passing her fingers through the long black hair of a fallen warrior that rested his head on her lap.

'It's alright now,' she cooed. 'It's alright.'

...what has been my doom will be also yours.
The ones that you hold most dearly, father and mother...

Twisted Memories

The three cousins were wide awake. Old Albertazzo was pursing his lips while he listened to Lando's tales. They felt dry and pasty as his tongue. His head was rather heavy, telling him it would be wise to suspend the wine for that night. The contessa listened concentrated, always bearing her usual annoyed face. The pope snored, tightly wrapped into a mass of blankets and pelts. Bishop Liutprando's eyes were wide opened and unmovable, as if painted on his face.

'That was when I killed my first men,' Albertazzo said with a sigh. 'The siege of Luna…My first time and my last. I put so many through my blade that I refused to consider a head count. So much blood, and I have never thought of the battle of Luna since.'

Matilda snorted. She looked at her old cousin with despise. 'And after the battle you got lazy, then? You'd get someone else to stuff your enemies with rocks and toss them in the Serchio?'

Albertazzo ignored the comment and gestured with his face for Lando to continue.

Lando looked at the sleeping pope and turned to Matilda. Her furious eyes told him to carry on without any delays.

Lando continued, somehow relieved that the pope was sleeping. 'The battle of Luna is memorable for its lack of memories and notable for the notes it left in our history. It will be written by those who never saw it, as it was certainly won by those who never fought through it. That pope dressed up as a warrior survives in history as the deciding force that expelled the Musetto and his Mohammedan pirates from the Ligurian coast. Future generations will believe the rumours that Benedict VIII himself slew the wife of the ferocious Saracen from Daniyya in the battlefield.'

'Luna, the great white castle, is on its way to oblivion. Many pilgrims making to the hills of Il Poggio still wonder these days, why the famous tower, heroically retrieved from Saracen hands, is not to be seen even on clear days. It will not be the Lucchese, so busy with their trade, their silk and their money, who will be remembered for having won Luna from the Saracens, neither the Obertenghi, who are disassembling their old home.' he looked at Albertazzo, for the first time with an air of disregard. 'It is the Pisans, for what was left of Luna would one day, much after this story, move into their hands. The tower is being dismantled by our dear old cousin Marchese della Malaspina, and it will never stand erect again.'

'It's a *swamp*!' protested Albertazzo. 'It is sinking into the *malaria* infested waters as the hours pass.'

Lando rolled his eyes. 'Perhaps future generations will see the moon reflected on the stones of Luna when they admire the new cathedral and campanile in Pisa, for whom you sell your crumbling palace.'

'Tell me more about *Julian*,' the countess demanded, 'as I have no interest in the Pisans and their flamboyant dreams.'

Lando re-seated himself in a more formaly fashion. It was good to have Matilda interested, rather than in her furious moods.

'Julian of Mans would be on people's mouth for many other saintly deeds, but little will be written about his heroic achievement in Luna. He fought against his own memories of the battle. The prediction had been fulfilled and the very thought of closure would crush him with a God-defying guilt, closing his communication even with God.'

'But the threat was fulfilled,' Matilda said. 'There were no more debts to be paid, as the devil had crushed his vengeance on Julian. He could just retire with Clarissa in peace and build a proper bridge over the Serchio.'

The cantastorie narrowed his eyes. 'Oh you do underestimate them all, don't you?'

'Who?' asked Matilda, 'Julian? Or my cousin Clarissa?'

Lando smiled with satisfaction. '*All* of them, my dear noble cousin: Julian, our cousin Clarissa *and* the Devil! They never leave each other alone. Never!' And a shadow fell upon his face. 'The Devil doesn't give up, that old demon…'

Book 3: The Saint

Picking Up the Parts

Young man Antelmino Di Gottefredo, a watchful Lucchese bourgeois who had joined a group at the rear-guard of the papal army, had his dagger pinching the neck of a Tuscan religieuse. With his arms around her, Antelmino could feel the volume of her tense muscles fevering with a delectable heat. It lasted only but a few seconds, for that accursed Alberto Azzo came to kill the leader of his group and spoil the celebration. How could that so-called *nobleman* kill a good Christian soldier? Still, under the deadly blade of the heir of Luna, Antelmino was obliged to release the nun and watch her go with the other women. He cringed with rage for yielding to the despiteful triumph on her face.

With Azzo gone, Antelmino brushed off the incident by returning to the main battlefield and busying himself with his dagger, ripping through the corpses of the Saracens.

A few days later, the regulars of several taverns in Lucca saw Antelmino di Gottefredo casually showing up, sporting his deer-hide hat with some small spheres hanging from its wide brim. Drunk patrons, soldiers and pilgrims would approach for a closer look at those chicken giblets and burst with laughter as word of mouth pointed that the brave and victorious Antelmino di Gottefredo had twenty or more testicles of the Saracens attached to his hat. Days later the populace was avoiding the castrator of dogs – *Castracani*, as they were calling him – and most taverns forbid him to enter if he did not leave the accursed hat with those rotten spoils of battle reeking outside. Too proud to take it off, Antelmino refused. He carried on parading through the city with his bizarre trophy until it dried off and the citizens of Lucca got accustomed to the oddity.

When Antelmino the Castracani became old, losing the hat and all the vanity he once proudly held up high, his son Antelminello started wearing a new deer hide hat with dangling leathery bits, which one day also fell apart into crumbs. His great-grandson, young Ugo, found the flamboyant nickname and the association with the deeds of his ancestor no more than an embarrassment. The bandits from Santo Stefano di Tassignano decided to carry on their hats a sprig of black salsify – similarly called *castracane* by the locals –and they nailed it to their front door, declaring that the plant warded off evil eyes from the envious bankers of Lucca. Again, word of mouth will conquer memory. Thanks to Ugo, in another generation, our children will think the family was nicknamed after a plant.

Antelmino di Gottefredo was ready to return to Lucca after being triumphally victorious on the battlefields of Luna, knotting the last pair of stinky testicles from a dead *cane* to the brim of his hat. He knew the Lucchese would pay respect to him as a soldier now. He would be a few steps up on the ladder of power, and maybe better enabled to claim some of the prizes that his dead father had craved for. And if they did not submit to him this time, he would teach them a lesson.

True love, a passion that is mutually corresponded, is a state of bliss that grows and embraces, as a vine that spreads, clinging onto a creeper, bearing each other's arms, blurring and constantly reversing the roles of climber and pole. Like sizzling lover's legs, vine and creeper's roots will intermingle, guiding each other to the spots where growth will flourish, where they can be better nurtured by earth, and water. Their leaves spread out to the sun, to be nourished by Light, but also for mutual protection from the elements, guarding those intimate, unique flowers, most treasured blooms of mutual joy. Such flowers will blossom for a season or, depending on the strength of the stems, perpetually. In eternal love, vines often are no more than the silent spurts of pollination still burning in the air, frozen apexes of bliss that will forever cry out the complete devotion, affection, the warmth and lust that still is and will be.

Love can however befall, as vines so often do, into an asphyxiating grip, too strong to let the other plant thrive. Many can be the causes, but just one is the result. A vine topples, so the other loses its shaft, collapsing soon after.

Julian and Clarissa found the most extraordinary partners in each other. A couple, and much before they sent out the town criers, their hearts already knew that a couple they would forever stay. Lucky were they on those first days, for the inhabitants of Luna and the survivors of Luni had the esteem for Lady Clarissa, and her favourite had gained the hearts of the men-at-arms, the young and the old. Thus, as the soldiers and the populations which slowly returned to their ravaged land plundered the signs of the Saracens, some kind of order did reign in the ruined town and castle, even devoid of Julian, Clarissa, Alberto Azzo or Albertazzo in direct command. While the heir Alberto Azzo installed himself in what was left of the partially burned main hall, the young pair consumed the next three days after victory locked in the major tower of the castle, never leaving it, except for some light meals and a refreshingly sweet Lucchese mulberry juice, as red as the blood that pumped with passion inside them.

Even though lord and lady were taking great pleasure in their blissful moments at each other's mercy, they never seemed to lose their generosity. Formidable lovemaking, but it never hindered their devotion to each other and their own simple understanding of who God was. A God that started to show his magnanimous and freehearted side. A God that on the one hand allowed for Luna and Luni to be destroyed, but perhaps who would take Lord Oberto on His Side. A God that allowed their hearts to burn with rage and sorrow, but who seemed to bless the fire of their relationship. And hopefully a fair God, who would inspire them to cultivate their munificence, on conducting their vassals and lands with fairness and justice. This God with all His goodness and love, they thought, was hoped to be found in each other's arms.

For Julian, that encounter with love had freed him from the dark ghosts the past. Never before he had thought that life could be as pleasant and even more enjoyable than it had been prior to that ominous day in the woods of Mans. The most backbreaking burden, a boulder of fear, affliction and misery, the heaviest load of wrong had been lifted up from his shoulders by the corresponding affection he found with Clarissa. No more need had he seen for continuing his wanderings, for here was comfort. And Clarissa was the one who had opened that gate to light and freed him from the scourge. As for her, she had also encountered a nurturing source of strength and joy on the man who had beaten the invincible, done the undoable and mostly given himself to her. Body and soul.

On the sixth day after the victory, the bells tolled thrice. Julian and Clarissa attended the mass they had called for thanksgiving, celebrated at the ruined church of San Habet Deus, which had been immediately re-christened after bereaved of the maculae of Islam. For the profession of the faith, the creed was sung, rather than read as usual.

Yet, the land had not healed from the wounds of war. Alberto Azzo had indeed fulfilled his promise to flood the valley with Saracen blood. The horrid stench of death would still gust through the destroyed town, bringing the reminiscence of the carpet of corpses that still laid spread outside the gates. Disfigured, dark, bloated cadavers, bursting into gases or maggots, a field of fodder for ravens, crows, jays, dogs, foxes, rats, pigs and an appalling battalion of flies. Peasants kept searching through the fields of corpses, fighting the scavengers for their plunge at least for another fortnight. There was not a state of decomposition repulsive enough to keep them from the hope of finding any loot among those Saracen *cani*. Weeks later, a lush weed was already reclaiming their space, crawling over fabric and bones, for Luna would leave that field of human remains forever in peace.

As the destroyed city still held an empty bishopric, by orders of the Holy Father, who was already back in Rome, Bishop Grimizzo of Lucca sent to Luni his predecessor, the retired Rodilando, an old friend of the Obertenghi. The rival bishoprics of Lucca and Pisa just waited for the day when that stretch of the Ligurian coast could be incorporated into its yard. Tactfully, at this time, old Rodilando brought along the credence of the blessings from Benedict VIII and ordered that removal of treasures and relics from their hidden places in looted churches and monasteries. After kissing the altar and wishing peace for all, the bishop was to return without delay and accompany some more Saracen hostages all the way through Rome, where ransoms and discussions would be arranged between the See and the enemy fleet, still on the wait outside Anzio and Porto.

The town of Luni picked up the pieces and started to rebuild. But it would never thrive as in the glorious days before the siege. Not even enough survivors remained to populate the town. Soldiers would return to the fields, most without a family, only hoping to find a new one, and that their future lords would be promising leaders, of noble and tender heart. An uncomfortable amount of wandering peasants showed up at the broken gates of Luna, offering their loyalty and workmanship to Julian and Clarissa, in apparent exchange solely for the entitlement to carry on living. Designated by Alberto Azzo, the Lord and Lady of Luna dispensed the necessary time with each visitor reaching out for vassalage, allocating means and providing for the worthy. Artisans and merchants were also accepted to take shelter and tenancy on any unoccupied or unclaimed dwelling in town, with full tenure to be granted after ten years without petitioners.

The old Christian-Ligurian frescoes at the castle chapel were cleaned from the char and retouched to a vital composure. Julian and Clarissa vowed loyalty and eternal placement of their lives in each other's hearts before the altar of God. They wanted this intimate exchange to be personally blessed by Julian's friend, Father Martino, who took a few days to come, from the Parish of Controne, across the mountains. Upon Martino's arrival, Julian knelt to kiss his hands, but the priest helped him up, for it was his honour to embrace the hero of Luna. The warm embrace endured past the tears of relief and joy.

Love is the most important thing. That's what God is made of. The words of Martino were at his blessing of their sacrament felt truer than ever.

Life would change. For Julian, his disturbing encounter on the forest so many years before turned from a curse to just a bad memory.

The acceptance of death and loss became more bearable when the stench had dissipated. At this time, with the joy of freedom still fresh, the household of Luna realised they could not tolerate the idea of the marriage between Julian and Clarissa without a celebration. So much pride they took in both that they rebelled, convincing the couple to accept a banquet. Julian's condition for such occasion was a waiver to the public witnessing of consummation.

The swampy surrounds of Luna had been despoiled of game, and all dried meat in the region was from horses, poorly plundered after the battle, so traders were sent with carts to Lucca. The caravan was escorted by men-at-arms, for their war booty was to be bartered by wheat, farro, chestnuts, a vibrant variety of dried meats, fresh carcasses, giblets, salted or smoked game, sausages and even a good number of live beasts. Geese, chicken, ducks, partridges, pheasants, rabbits, a generous supply of thrushes, four scores of boars and their weaned litters, roe deer, goats, sheep and a three dozen cows. Full carts came back with the flocks and herds, more than enough for the celebration of the wedding. Clarissa engaged into selecting the meat for the celebrations, as Julian directed flocks and herds to the appropriate fields or to be released in the woods. Maybe one day in the future, he thought, the forest would be plentiful enough for hunting journeys, as he had done in his youth.

But perhaps better not think about those days, anyhow.

Luna was safe from the Saracens, but the roads were not less treacherous with victorious soldiers marching home under the blessing of the Christ.

It was more than three days after the battle when Sister Caterina came to Lucca. Resolute over her wounds and shamelessly proud of her heroism, she was the most severely beaten among those women from the Serchio valley who had been taken by the raiders. Once they were released by Alberto Azzo from the hands of Antelmino and his band, they entered the swampy waters of the moat to wash themselves from the Saracen filth. To cleanse their bodies from just a crust of the eternal, hellish memories of violence.

They walked silently and broken, taking shelter and food like beggars at village churches and pilgrim's hospitals along that coastal arm of the Via Francigena: San

Leonardo, near Massa Lunense, Hospitale Santi Pauli in Pietrasanta, Sanctae Mariae in Camp Majore and Sancti Michaelis in Albiano. Malnourished and humiliated by repeated violence onto their bodies, the women were again pestered by many boisterous soldiers returning from the battlegrounds, but always lucky and thanking God for eventually being left on their own. They took the *val Fredanna* detour, less conspicuous than the shorter way between the Lunigiana and Lucca. When the intimidating towers of Lucca were visible, as it meandered by the vellutini at Monte San Quirico, all the women but Caterina found wise not to seek any refuge inside the city walls. They could not bear the prospect of any more encounters with foreign, brutal men. As neither a life of begging for food in Lucca nor death from starvation were considered an option, quite resignedly, all they wanted was to return to their raided villages, pick up whichever pieces had been left behind since the Saracen raid and continue on with living.

Silent tears of gratitude were shed on the farewell to Caterina, who had given her body repeatedly, so that theirs could be spared from more wear. Those returning to Obertenghi lands would reclaim and conserve still their thin strips of ground and eventually re-marry, while the two that came back to Rolandinghi territory would find their raided villages abandoned and see themselves obliged to turn around and find a living as *puttane* among the vellutini in Lucca.

The city was not generous or appreciative to a hero nun venturing through its walls. The dozen or more xenodochia had been packed with travellers back from the siege and northern pilgrims waiting for better news before engaging on a return journey.

While carefully walking along the side of the cathedral square, Caterina saw a young pregnant woman being helped down from a bullock cart. It took her a while to recognise a face she had seen only a week before, but it seemed it had been in a different life.

The pain and suffering of rape and loss had dug deep lines into the dry countenance. The red-haired youth was conducted into the patio by a large, elder man, probably a local merchant, with his other hand carefully protecting her shoulder, more on a fatherly way than as a lover. Before entering the large house, something made Maria Maddalena of the Burle et Malachi turn her grey eyes to the passing pilgrims in the square. She saw a ghost. Standing right next to her bullock cart, was the woman who had saved her from more suffering, returning from the world of the dead and also recognising her. Maria's lips trembled and she ran towards Caterina, whose knees wobbled with emotion.

'I thought you were dead, gone by now!' grunted Maria, furtively throwing sudden fiery eyes to the sides. 'What are you doing here?'

Caterina was speechless with the young woman's challenging posture.

As a raptor ready to strike, Maria looked at the nun and continued, hissing between gritted teeth 'Have you told anybody? Who else knows about it?'

Caterina could not begin to formulate words.

The pounding continued from Maria Maddalena 'Don't you dare tell anyone. Just leave. Disappear from here and don't go back to that Wald Ottavo, if that's where you make your hiding.'

'I don't even know who you are.' Caterina finally said, dropping her shoulders and turning away.

'You will soon find out, if you go back!' Maria screeched.

She returned to the door, where Battista Burle had his jaws hanging. The banker asked his granddaughter something about that beggar and heard back no more than a yell 'Oh, never mind! She's a nobody!'

Maria spat three times on the ground before entering.

The large Battista was quick to make his granddaughter at ease at his home, calling for a warm foot bath and a goblet of wine. 'I'm glad you are safe!' he said, rubbing his hands, while Maria took the full goblet in a gulp. 'I've heard that Sigifredo was eager to take Anchiano from you as soon as he heard about Fulcardo's death. That is why I sent the message.'

'Thank you, Grandfather. The messengers were good to pass undistinguished by those Genovese brothers from Sesto and alert me of the danger in Anchiano.' Maria said, moving around the house with heavy steps, on a rather manly fashion on her grandfather's opinion, almost as if she was not pregnant.

'Tell me what happened then. There are rumours around...' Battista asked, wiping the sweat of his brow.

Maria Maddalena found a comfortable chair and raised a hand, impatiently waiting for the foot bath from an obsequious servant. She tittered at Battista's apprehension, taking another big gulp of her re-filled goblet before exclaiming triumphally 'The stupidity of that man! It must have been the city air, of boilers, dyers, tanners and blacksmiths that made my brother-in-law even more foolish than Fulcardo. Greed and haste undoubtedly blinded him to caution, for Sigifredo picked ten men, the worst scum of the vellutini and rode into my lands, expecting me to run away like a beaten dog.' Battista was trickling sweat from the tip of his nose. He kept one eye on Maria, while the other scanned the floor nervously. She continued 'We grabbed the riders just as soon as they entered my lands. Although we had lost some men-at-arms when Fulcardo was murdered in Partigliano, I did manage to gather fifty of the best fighters on horse to give Sigifredo a warm welcome. Those cowards were quick to surrender, but poor Sigifredo lost his composure and yelled at them, ordering them to kill me!' she laughed. 'That was an act of war!'

'What did you do, Maria?' Battista asked, rubbing his knuckles impatiently.

'We held the invaders with a blade under their chins and I ordered Sigifredo to leave those lands forever. He refused to go without his escort riders. I said I would start to slash throats if he did not run, so I demonstrated I was being serious. I walked behind a particularly repugnant prisoner that kneeled with his hands on his head, and I slit his throat. Grandfather, I know you will be shocked to hear it, but I felt good, powerful, by feeling the warm blood gushing over my hands and hearing the shrieks of Sigifredo as he disappeared down the track towards Lucca. I can defend my own lands! As for the remaining nine men, we cut the thumbs of their able hands, so they could forever remember how stupid it was to ride into Maria Maddalena of the Cunimundinghi's lands.' She placed her goblet on a small table near her seat. 'Is that the nature of the rumours you heard, grandfather?'

Battista had both eyes frozen on her, and his many-layered chin was dropped over his chest.

The cathedral of Lucca was particularly strict on those post-battle days, with money changers keeping beggars away to protect the sanctity of the well-off families who entered the duomo to thank heavens for protection. Nowhere else in the city could Caterina find any shelter or help, if not for a few crumbs from some kitchen doors and a couple of silver coins, charitably placed into her palm by a passing holy woman. Caterina's thankful black eyes met the supportive blue of her benefactor's. She would have been pleased to know those sympathetic eyes were Abbess Theodora's, of San Giovanni Battista, the same monastery in Santa Maria Lei Giudice where she had started her life as a religieuse. And the charming abbess would have been thrilled to find that the extraordinarily beautiful woman who was thrown out from a tavern in a fetid alley of Lucca after a painful and heroic week was one of the two young nuns of her house of God led astray by the poisonous tongue of the great Marozia. The two women paused for a while in respectful silence, appreciating themselves in each other's beauty, grace and vigour of their age, a gift granted to only a few. *The great Marozia, this other unknown woman with eyes so warm and kind, and perhaps I.* They did not speak a word, nor did they find out who they were, which could have changed the destinies of many about whom we still tell the story.

The kindness of one did not keep Caterina in Lucca. A burning heart begged her to go back to her land, where she would be ready to reconstruct her Tempagnano in case it had been taken also. *Screw that red-haired young woman and her threats.* Caterina hoped that Bernardo was alive and, quite perplexingly, she admitted to still yearn for that manly firmness to protect her from the evil that men do. It would be long before she could dream to venture down that western valley and make her way to a long lost love in Controne.

Inconspicuously, she walked back towards the north gate, slowly taking each step, fearing the harassment of wild battle men and ready to disappear from view towards the Serchio Valley. She held the cowl tight, covering her face as she crossed the crowded bridge of San Frediano, among soldiers with their shouts of victory, horses ridden by their Lucchese lords, farmers bringing carts of food into the city, vellutini children selling fattened dormice to famished soldiers or running away from irate gatekeepers, and pilgrims praising God for the defeat of the Saracens. Looking at the water a few feet below the bridge, running strongly towards her, Caterina thought she had seen something moving under the surface, when her arm was painfully clasped and she was yanked back. Her cowl was violently pulled backwards. A slobbering grin of a young man met her terrified black eyes.

'Help me here, my lady. Where were we again last time when we were ruthlessly interrupted?' his lips sizzled. Caterina had difficulties recognising the young man that kept a firm clench on her arm. His face was partly covered by a series of pendulous offal hanging from the brim of his hat, probably tripes or giblets, exhaling an offensive stench that suffocated her further into terror. But she did know that grasp. It was the man who had almost broken her arm, trying to rape her soon after they had been left behind by the Saracens. 'We have something unfinished to be resolved,' he said.

'Let me go, or I will scream!' Caterina ordered.

His clench tightened stronger in her arm. 'I do know how to deal with a rabid bitch in heat. Drown her in cold water, they say. You scream and I will push you from this bridge. I have seen it happen a couple of weeks ago. They do happen, these unfortunate accidents.'

'Leave her alone, Antelmino di Gottefredo!' A voice commanded from his back. Startled, Antelmino turned around to see purple eyes of fury and a known bushy face with long-matted hair groaning at him.

Still under Antelmino's grip, Caterina exploded in tears when she recognised Bernardo delle Rocche.

Antelmino snorted. 'Obertenghi excrement!' he spat. His right arm released Caterina and swung around to hit Bernardo, pushing the shepherd over the bridge's edge. Caterina screamed with horror as she saw Bernardo diving in the Serchio and disappearing under the bridge, but she also heard the thump of the violent kick on Antelmino's chin.

While the deer-hide hat was thrown spinning out of Antelmino's head, his whole body stretched in the air, falling with his back flat on the water. The boot on the chin had come from a man on a horse.

Caterina looked at the tall mounted figure, a greying olive skinned man, with hard but handsome lines on his face, quickly dismounting and falling on his hands and knees crawling down to the edge, lowering his head below the bridge and calling upon Bernardo. She lost her breath.

'Are you there, Bernardo?' the man shouted.

The voice came clear. 'Yes, Martino! I am alright. I am holding on to a pillar. Just throw me a rope.'

'What about that man that I just kicked in?'

'I held him for a while, but he fought his way out of my grip when he saw that stupid hat of his floating down with the current. He's sunk, the horrible bastard. You did a good job, Martino.'

A crowd had gathered to assist father Martino and to gently slap on the face of woman, who had just fainted as she looked at him.

Vellutini children were always warned by their parents to stay away from the Serchio, for they could be snatched and devoured by the horrendous marabbecche lurking in its dark depths. Everyone in Lucca knew that the vellutini had brought these water sprites with them from Sicily. Hungry creatures, unforgiving on fallen victims granted by the bridge of San Frediano. On the day that Bernardo and Antelmino fell from the bridge, creatures of the river that most God-fearing souls would doubt of their existence were alarmed by the two falling bodies. For their disappointment, one of the victims vanished up the surface when it was quickly pulled out of the water. Bernardo would for all his remaining days scare the people of the Serchio with tales of his near-death experience with the marabbecche when he was pushed into the river by that low-life crook Antelmino di Gottefredo. And the Castracani himself came with an ear-splitting splash and was washed down with the current. When the water sprites had their cold claws grasping his ankles, something happened that made this story continue as described earlier. A superior voice or command must have made them let the Castracani survive. He was seen a mile to the west, getting out of the river, with his soaked uncanny hat dripping from each testicle that hung around his face. And he was furious.

Hazelnuts, Farro and Heads

Among the many winners of the battle of Luna, the pope's army had reassembled to ride back to Rome. Victorious, Pope Benedict VIII sweated profusely. He argued with his brother Albericus about a certain trophy of war.

'We should take her to Rome and cover her with jewels and gold.' Albericus mused.

'That's an abomination!' shot the pope. 'We people of God only do those things for the saints, martyrs and their relics. We take the Saracen prisoners only to Rome.'

'So why did you cut her out to start with?' Albericus asked. 'Why did you held her up for all of us to see?'

The pope delicately cleared his throat with undisguised pride. He adjusted his long hair more like a lady would have done. 'Because I wanted it to stay in memory. I wanted them all to see how I had won that battle and remember it for history. I gave them the privilege to witness how I had executed the wife of the Musetto with my own sword.'

'But you didn't!' the fat Albericus chuckled. 'You only sawed her head off. And that's when she was already dead.'

'Well, that is *not* how people will remember me. Especially if you keep this loud trap of yours shut! Now get rid of that horrible head. Burn it!'

In Rome, after an exhausting discussion, the ambassador of the Saracen fleet could not come to an agreement with Pope Benedict VIII.

'Nonsense', dismissed the pope, before the envoy's arguments, 'there is no negotiation.' Benedict suddenly stood his handsome figure up and walked to the heavy oaken doors of the chapter. The emissary did not move. The corner of his eyes just followed carefully the motion of the pontiff closing the door. On reassuming his seat, Benedict VIII added with a patronising but articulate Latin 'We have learned to communicate with you. We are now using the language of the blade, the only reasoning that your people will answer to.'

'I do not think I understand what you mean…your Sanctity.", said the emissary, with a subtle sway of his head. The best method to avoid confrontations is to suddenly loose the capacity to grasp the language. His Latin was corrupted by Lombard and Ligurian, the usual he'd learned from trade with Genova.

'Oh yes, you do', smiled the pope, 'you do comprehend the idiom of swords, slings, axes, maces and picks. Your people are deathsmiths, skilled in the tongues of fire and they recognise the logic of flames. You respond to the speech of blood, hence you will be capable to read our sentences, for they will be shaped by rolling heads. Impaled bodies will be our arguments and, pain, your urge.'

'With all due respect,' swallowed the envoy, 'I find it lamentable that the Sacred Roman Empire is not being considerate…'

'We don't care what you think and that has nothing to do with the Empire!' slashed the pope.

'But, but…the manner in which the hostages are being kept…'

'Manner?' asked the pontiff indignantly, 'quite frankly, since the hostages were delivered by land by the Bishop Rodilando, we have not been using any manners. We are only following your rules of war.' He raised a hand and snapped his fingers, looking at the door. A custos who stood guard inside opened it. 'I've made it clear and you know what the demand is. Now go, for the hostages should not bear any more suffering.'

The envoy bowed hesitantly, but walked away quickly, as soon as he heard the irritated pontiff say 'Just go, you can refrain from kissing my ring.'

Benedict VIII sighed deeply and left the chapter, entering the basilica from the west apse. Except for the men-at-arms, few of the faithful and pilgrims paid any attention to him. He hurried to the altar and stretched out on the stone floor. Waiting until the coldness of the marble had numbed his face, he shut his eyes tight, clenched his teeth and tried again to transpire. 'Dear Lord Jesus Christ. I ask you not for my redemption, since I do not deserve it, but please forgive the sins of our Saracen hostages, those poor bastards, for they had not been exposed to any other conduct on the mysteries of the Father, the Son, and the Holy Spirit. Give them the entry into the so much sought after paradise, for soon they will see the face of hell here in the world of the living, when we roast them to death.'

'The envoy is back!' announced Albericus, erupting through the doors with a radiant smile, 'and I hear that he brings a coffer with him.' The pope's brother felt completely at ease to break into any of the pontiff's chambers.

'Already?' asked the pope surprised.

'Yes, call immediately for your factotum. We should entertain the envoy here in the chapter.'

'I would not think so. Just do it in the basilica, but tomorrow after Terces, so we can arrange for a suitable audience to witness it on a grandiose fashion.'

Albericus stood in front of him and grinned 'Great idea! Then, send the message.'

Benedict VIII never felt that it should be proper for the bishop of Rome to be sent to tasks like a patrician's servant. Even when it had indeed been his brother who had sat him on that throne. Behind closed doors, John Theophylactus could reveal his vulnerability when Albericus was around. Quite shyly, he dared to suggest 'And why do I have to do it…now?'

His brother stopped. With an obvious annoyance in his tone, and very pungent words, he asked. 'Great God's testicles! For what, or whom exactly should we wait? For the fucking emperor?'

'Don't blaspheme like that!' protested the pope.

'Well then do not behave like an imbecile,' said Albericus matter-of-factly, as he left the room 'I will send the message myself!'

The ambassador looked as if he had been enduring the fever for a week. All colour had gone from his features and streams of transpiration drew shinny lines on his feeble face. He looked at all the people watching his arrival. *Why would they be here? That will make things even worse for me.* After a number of trembling steps, he delivered the appropriate greetings and announced that the lord of Daniyya Mugiâhid ibn abd Allah al Amiri had sent the pope a package and a message.

The pope and his brother smiled to each other. The audience gave a big sigh and all heads turned to the door to see a large canvas bag being brought by two of the envoy's hired men.

'Where is the coffer?' said the pontiff, looking at the empty light that came through the door.

'Coffer, your Holiness?' asked the ambassador, with a genuine puzzled face. He swallowed and looked at all the audience before babbling 'I'm afraid there's no coffer involved in the message I bring.'

The pope gave a pleading look to Albericus, who was already conferring with one of his informants. An eternal uneasy silence fell on the nave as Benedict VIII waited for an approval to carry on. Albericus finally turned to the pontiff, with a smack of his lips. 'A problem with translation, words,' he explained with a confidence that overshadowed his embarrassment, 'could have been my mistake. It had always been a bag, and somewhere on its way, the message was changed to coffer.'

The ambassador acknowledged the explanation and waited for the motion to continue. He pulled out a silken scarf to wipe the sweat that shone on his forehead.

'So, what is the message?' asked the pope.

Approaching the pope with careful steps, the ambassador stepped on the first of five stairs that mounted the throne up and bowed, whispering quite loudly: 'Your holiness, forgive me, but I have been deprived of my dagger as I landed in papal lands. I am supposed to cut this bag open before the delivery of the message.'

'Guards!' shouted the pope hurriedly, with a rather sharp pitch to his voice, or else his brother would have done it. A custos pierced the bag with his lance, cutting it along the side. A number of brown pebble-looking spheres, nuts, started to pop out as the blade cut though the fabric, hitting the floor with a wooden sound, rolling away from the bag. Soon, the crackling noise was dominating the Lateran's hall. Hazelnuts. The ambassador lifted one side of the bag. A thick cascade of hazelnuts spilled from it, forming a noisy, wooden pool that spread quickly, covering his feet and happily reaching to the sides, where the flabbergasted guests were.

'Hazelnuts?' spat the disgusted pope. 'What in hell's name do they want with hazelnuts?'

'Pssst!' said his brother, pointing to the ambassador, who was opening the official message.

'In the name of Allah, the Beneficent, the Merciful. This letter is from Mugìâhid ibn abd Allah al Amiri, Saqlabi Lord of Daniyya. Come to a word common to you and us that we worship none but Allah and that we associate nothing in worship with Him, and that none of us shall take others as Lords beside Allah. Peace be upon him who follows the right path. I invite the bishop of Rome to release all the hostages, inhabitants and legitimate owners of the town of Luni, invaded two weeks ago by a horde of mercenaries and bandits from Lucca, Pisa and Genova, made prisoners by the bandits and hostages by the papal guard. They must be unharmed and given passage to the fleet of Daniyya. In addition…' he was cut short by the loud murmur of repugnance and revolt that grew from the crowd, mostly patricians who theatrically expressed their abhorrence as clearly as possible for the pope to see. 'In addition…' the ambassador continued, now with a despising look at the crowd, 'the Saqlabi Mugìâhid invites that 'all bandits temporarily settling in Luni leave the town immediately, evacuating the city, so that the legitimate inhabitants can go back to their homes. If you accept this suggestion, you will be safe, and Allah will double your reward.'

The ambassador ran his tongue over his lips nervously. 'But if such demands are not met with the urgency that it calls for, you will be committing a sin by misguiding your subjects. Ignore the wishes of Allah and the papal lands are going to see as many soldiers of Allah, the Only God, as hazelnuts that you see now coming out of this bag. This is what the Lord Mugìâhid tells you.'

'How do they dare?' cried the foaming pope. The crowd broke loose again. Shouts and curses were thrown upon the envoy, the fleet, and all the Saracen world. Women fainted, as did a few men. Some ran out of the church, probably thinking that the invasion was coming. Others tried to get at the envoy, but were contained by the custodes. The ambassador just stood there and bent his head. He could smell the sweaty stench that his body was producing.

A cheerful laughter pieced through the protest. Everyone stopped look at the throne. The pope was watching his brother, who held a vast belly that bounced with each whoop of laughter.

'Hazelnuts!' said Albericus, hilariously. 'What a great idea – hazelnuts!' and he left the church, still laughing. The crowd was mute, just listening to that powerful man who hooted his way out of the Lateran.

The Saracen fleet was turning its way back to Daniyya when a Roman vessel leaving Anzio was spotted by a scout single-banked dromon. The whole fleet was signalled to lower anchors again and drop the sails, waiting patiently as the small craft jerked its oars ahead to conquer the Tyrrhenian wind. The Roman boat was a comparatively poorly clinker-built dinghy, but there was the Saracen envoy, on board. He was lifted to the main dromon, a massive trireme directly commanded by Mugìâhid.

"Where is the dromon that took you to Anzio?' asked the Saqlabi.

'They kept it, my lord, those devils! The ship and all the crew.' said the ambassador. He excused himself, made the proper reverences and continued. 'Oh, my lord, here I come with no reply to your requests, but with a troop of envoys from the papal guard and another bag. Yes another bag!' He was very uneasy, as embarrassed as he could be.

Never looking at the envoy, Mugìâhid kept examining the Romans in the boat that rocked on the choppy sea against the solid hull of his dromon. He saw the bag between the soldiers.

'I don't suppose this bag is filled with pieces of our men', said the Saqlabi as he groomed his thin red beard.

'I am afraid not, my lord.'

'Let's see what is in it, then' and he clapped his hands.

The bag was lifted to the dromon and cut out. It shrunk quite fast as a river of brown grains flowed out of it. A cascade of farro spread over the deck. A roman soldier presented himself with the message. With an impressive Arabic, he read the message as well as most on that boat could never have done.

"In the name of God, Amen. His Holiness, the Pontiff Benedict VIII advises that if the pirate Musetto and his heathen army threaten the papal lands with more invasions, he should be reminded of his own shameful defeat, when his wife was slain by His Holiness, Himself, in the battle for the freedom of Luna. The Saracen army that is supposed to be as numerous as hazelnuts in that filthy bag is going to face as many Christian soldiers as grains of farro that you see now out of the same bag. Stay away! Do not touch our Christian lands.' Undersigned, blessed and sealed by the by His Holiness, the Pontiff Benedict VIII.' The soldier finished the speech and rolled the parchment nervously.

Mugìâhid shot his green eyes on the Roman soldier. But all he saw was a man who could well lose his bowels right then. The commander did not need or wanted to see such a miserable spectacle. He smiled softly to the soldier, who exhaled and dropped his shoulders. But Mugìâhid did not want to be caught unguarded, as a mother jackal that will teach her litter about hunting but gets knocked down by the ram. He had no diplomatic solution or strategic escapade to that game. And that was a lie, he knew about it. The pope had never been to Luna during the battle. Mugìâhid knew well the man who had killed his wife. That Devil Julian. The Saqlabi calculated all possible replies and alternatives, all the scenarios and the results, but at the end his thoughts were always invaded by a longhaired young man on horse. That same demon that had single-handedly destroyed his army, under the sign of the cross. He tried not to think of Julian, but the warrior kept diving into his thoughts with fury, the black mane, flowing wildly as the sword harvested heads along its path, intruding into any possible battle that he thought of.

A cold shiver froze his spine, and he felt his testicle closer to his body. *Must be this breeze*, he thought. Mugìâhid made a prayer to God, asking for guidance, for a sign. As he moved to better examine the Roman vessel, his sandals filled with farro. He smiled and turned back to the soldier. 'Your pope is a liar and a coward. He was never at Luna. But you, you seem to be a bright young man, my son!' he kept smiling 'And I am not going to hurt you.' Then he moved through the grains and leaned over the railing and continued, verifying the other Romans. 'You can read well and have the gift of languages. You are brave and bold and many in an army would have use for your talents. I actually think that I will keep you instead of lifting my tunic and bend over to Rome. Your pope can keep all the hostages.'

The soldier paled and tried to say something. His legs swayed and he felt a black curtain of unconsciousness trying to cover his vision. Suddenly, fast as a buck, he bolted to jump to the boat, but the Saracens of Mugiâhid were quicker to hold him. As he roared on their grasp, he heard the commander saying to his pirates: 'Kill the others.'

The boat with the dismembered bodies of all but one soldier was found, but the Lateran concluded that the message worked well, as the Saracens left those Ligurian waters not to return. Although they did not get the ransom they wanted, both Albericus and his brother, Pope Benedict VIII they decided not to burn the hostages. After a few months rotting in the dungeons of Sant'Angelo, they were all just decapitated.

The Theophylacts would always think of that great strategy, the bag of farro. And they laughed generously on the matter, a story that would be re-told through generations to come.

But the commander of the Saracen fleet, Mugiâhid ibn abd Allah al Amiri, never again thought of that insignificant bag of farro. He had soon forgotten all about that minor detail. But forever the Saqlabi would wake up in the middle of the night under a disturbingly chilling sweat, tormented by the Christian knight who would invariably break through his dreams. Nightmares where his whole city was beheaded by the demon with the long black hair.

The Bestiary

Clarissa sniggered. 'I'm so sorry to be laughing, Julian, but this does not have the slightest resemblance to you. Not at all! You have a handsome, strong countenance, but this figure is sad and weak. Not a trace of similarity.' She muffled another spell of giggles with her hands.

Julian scratched his head. 'You are right Clarissa. I've been fighting for a piece of wood. Fine, it's been exhaustively carved by the sweat of Nicodemus, but still, it will not give me a drop of the ocean of blessings that you bathe me with. When I think of it, I have not been battling for this cross. I brought it over the sea for you and, after all, my fight was always for you.'

Clarissa embraced Julian and kissed him passionately. When their lips reluctantly detached, she said with a grin 'You better have fought for me, my man, or I'll have you sleep your nights with this cross.'

Julian held her buttocks, feeling her firmness and enjoying the passion. He focused on the explosion of colours in her eyes. 'What do you want me to do with this *Volto Santo*?' he said, 'plant it out facing the sea to ward off pirate attacks?'

'Why not?' she said, running her fingers lightly along the lines of his face. 'This strong face means my life to me. The life I have chosen to live. But that holy face means a world to the people of Luni, who have lost their dear possessions and relatives during these months of siege. It means the force that they were blessed with to win this battle. I know it has a strong significance to you too, Julian, but of a time when I was not part of your life. Give it to the people and they will use their icon to help them rise up, and let's just live our memories together. I know who won this battle, and nothing will ever take my icon from me.'

'I will do it, then!' he said, opening a smile on his hard face. 'All that matters now is you and me, and any possible manner that I can find to share our love.' They renewed their kissing and Clarissa paused to cover that crucifix with a sheet before they made love.

When they rested on each other's arms, a servant shyly knocked on the door and announced the arrival of a Father Martino, from the Valley of the Lima, beyond the Apuane.

News were piling up on Father Martino's heart. The priest had learned that the Saracens had been expelled from Luna. The hearsay was that the army had been led by a Julian of Mans. That could only be him!

He left Controne and rode down to the Serchio, to find Bernardo delle Rocche in a desperate state, after losing many of his people to Saracen raids, especially near his home village of Wald Ottavo. The most bombastic news to Martino was that his long lost Caterina was alive and had been living in Tempagnano, not too far up on the valley. But the most shattering was that she had been lost for a week, since the raid of Partigliano.

They both rode to Lucca, where, on the bridge of San Frediano, an incident with Antelmino di Gottefredo re-united Martino and Caterina.

Now, at the insistence of both Martino and her long-friend Bernardo delle Rocche, Caterina was back in Luna, accompanied and sheltered by the best men of her life.

They stayed in what was left of the white castle for over two weeks, mostly on improvised tents, for guest rooms had been damaged by the fire.

Bernardo was warmly greeted by his second cousin Alberto Azzo, who had given the wedding couple a large featherbed that came all the way from Venice. It was made of duck feathers, more luxurious than anything Oberto and Railenda had used before. Alberto Azzo later introduced Bernardo to Clarissa, which he had not seen for sixteen years.

'You are a lucky man, Julian.' Bernardo said with glee, during their banquet. 'Not only you marry this most precious Ligurian jewel, but it also seems that your wife is my *cugina di secondo grado*. You are now my relative, Julian! No nobler privilege could you expect in these lands!' There was an explosion of laughter and more dishes were passed around for all to eat.

'Bernardo delle Rocche!' Alberto Azzo called from his seat, raising a hand to halt the goliards' music. 'Tell us now of your visit to the depths of the Serchio by the bridge of San Frediano. I'm sure my son Albertazzo will be very entertained.'

Bernardo suddenly frowned and trembled. 'Oh, this was a life threatening experience!' He waited for all guests to stop talking and listen. He took a loud gulp of wine and helped himself with some more before continuing 'I had seen poor sister Caterina being threatened by that pig Antelmino di Gottefredo right under my nose on the bridge.'

While Bernardo said that, Father Martino's gaze met Caterina's and he held her hand tight as they listened to it.

'I calmly dismounted and demanded the delinquent to let her go, but he was too quick for me. He pushed me with all his weight and I was soon plunging into the current. I can swim, so I was quick to resurface, and held on tight to a pillar. But two things intrigued me and made my spine cold as the ice of the Apuane. One was the impression that I had seen faces looking at me for those brief moments that I was inside the water,' he said, enjoying the dead silence across the hall 'and the other was the cold hands that slowly seemed to wrap their fingers around my ankles under the surface.'

Caterina shivered, but Martino asked, humorously 'The water is cold, Bernardo. How could you feel these hands?'

'You are right, Father Martino. The Serchio is very cold, but it is cold with life! A quick plunge, and the freshness and joy of those blessed waters will lively inject us with an inner force, as we know well how we can perceive and become aware of every part of our bodies!'

Clarissa whispered something on Julian's ear and he grinned. Bernardo continued 'But those hands that grabbed me were different. They were *dead* cold. The grip was saddening, slick and nauseous. It felt like life was being drawn out of me right through my ankles. So I dipped my face into the water and looked.'

He paused and noted that everyone's breath was being held in. Many in the audience were not used to his antics or even to his unusual appearance, his hair grown into a thick mat, sometimes breaking into locks. 'And by the blood of the martyrs in the holy podium,' he continued 'by the rake of San Frediano and the sword of San Michele the archangel, I will never forget what I saw.' All faces around the large table and the hall seemed to slowly approach closer to Bernardo. 'I could see probably half a dozen of them. Those that held my ankles disappeared with a swish behind a curtain of bubbles. I could not tell what they were. But the others were there in the darker depths, repugnant shapes serenely looking at me. They appeared to have human faces, but monstrous details. One clearly had the body of a goat and the face of a woman. The hair was long and it was moving with the current. Those were pale, expressionless faces, looking at me from their world of ghosts, where no heaven nor hell stirs their emotions. Another marabbecca that floated below the surface staring quietly at me was a large cat covered in golden scales. It had large women's breasts on its chest and a human head with long white hair. Her eyes were dead. And below her, many long shaped creatures that slithered on the river bottom. I could only see their dark shapes. A large body passed by, looking at me. It was a fish with the head of a boar, but without any scales, as the dolphin-headed mermaids that ride on a ship's wake. That was only a matter of an eye blink, for a large body splattered next to me and the ghosts all scurried away into the dark waters. I looked up and watched that idiot Antelmino, sinking towards me as I swam to the surface. I caught him by his collar, but he struggled with me when he noticed that stupid hat of him floating away. I let him go into his own destiny and looked underwater, where many of the marabbecche appeared from the depths, this time with a deadly grin on their faces, a smile of many rows of teeth, like manticores, moving their abominable shapes, laughing and swimming with their webbed feet and leathery fins, grabbing Antelmino by his ankles and wrists and pulling him down. The monstrous conglomerate of man and beasts disappeared from my view with the fast current.'

'Nevertheless,' Alberto Azzo finally broke into the narrative 'Antelmino is alive and well. He was seen entering Lucca again with that silly hat of his. So much about your creatures, Bernardo.' He smiled and raised a goblet towards his second cousin.

Bernardo raised his goblet back and drank it. 'I can only tell what I saw. How he got away I have not seen.'

'You have not changed, Bernardo' said Julian. 'Your absurd tales!' He turned to Clarissa, 'I told you he was a great cantastorie.'

'What makes you think they are not true, Julian?' asked Bernardo at ease. 'Don't you believe in devilish creatures?'

Albertazzo, the son, broke into the conversation. 'Whether it's true or not, I am frightened enough. I am not setting a foot inside that river for the rest of my life!' Another general burst of laughter broke through the hall, the music re-started and the guests carried on with their banter. Only three people were not laughing. One was Julian, who froze and stopped breathing when Bernardo asked the question. The other two were Clarissa, on Julian's side and Martino, sitting across, who immediately noticed that reaction.

Martino reached over to Bernardo, holding his hand and whispering 'Don't ask Julian about these things. He's got a tragic episode in his past…'

'Why? What episode?' Bernardo asked nervously. 'I don't want to hurt my friend's honour.'

'It's nothing, really. I tell you later.'

Bernardo insisted so much that Martino had to summarise the rudiments of Julian's tale of the forest while he ate. The shepherd listened to the whispers with his purple eyes lost inside a grey cloud, oblivious to the clattering of trays and bowls and the laughter and music that filled the hall. He finally said 'Why am I the only one who is called a liar when I tell of my crossroads with ghosts and demons? Everyone seems to believe Julian!'

'Just don't bring it up!' Martino hissed, annoyed. 'It's so inappropriate at this moment.'

'But I must.' Bernardo said, looking at nowhere. 'He should get over it. He is a God-damned lucky man, brave and strong, and he should not be afraid of ghosts. An *orco*? I've seen ogres. Dozens of them. I'll bring Julian to see them too!'

'No!' Father Martino almost yelled, but it was too late. Bernardo was already up and moving along the table to seat himself between Julian and Clarissa. 'Excuse this intromission, my lovely couple' Bernardo said, bringing a flagon of wine. 'Let me enjoy the contact with an old friend and newly discovered relative. Julian I hear you have been a keen hunter.' Julian pursed his lips, nodding sympathetically. 'You realise that even if you re-populate your lands, it will take years before you have good game in these lands after the Saracens, don't you? Well, but you are more than welcome to ride across the other side of these snowy peaks and hunt into my highlands. Do come and see for yourself the towering chestnut-coloured bears that could eat whole packs of horses...'

'No more bears, please Julian!' Clarissa said with an impish blink of her rainbow eyes. Julian giggled to himself, triggering a puzzled face on Bernardo. The cantastorie meant to continue, in spite of missing the humour between the couple.

Julian encouraged him 'Please, do carry on. I want to know all about the game up on the Apuane.'

Clarissa rolled her eyes and leaned back.

'Well, if you don't want bears, you should come and witness the stone-gray wolves of the Apuane, which can fillet a giant bear with their sharp teeth, so fierce, poisonous and terrifying that even the maggots will not eat a dead wolf cub. It will be left frozen, dried, or devoured by its siblings...'

As he spoke, Bernardo noticed with the corner of his eye that Julian had only slightly started to raise an eyebrow. The cantastorie continued now, more enthusiastic 'There are other reason-deceiving creatures, like the *l'onza*, a griffin that is part-cat and part-owl, with heavy paws that can grab the heaviest *urogallo* on the peak of its rutting season. But it is easy for an archer to shoot the l'onza when it takes to a tree for refuge. We also have the *genetta*, a tiny egg-eating leopard; the badger, a striped compact dog, with bad flavour and yielding nothing better than pelts for a child's first shoes. There is the *faina*, a brown cat of the beech forests that sucks the blood of its victims; and a hideous fur-covered lizard, the ermellino, which conceives through the mouth and gives birth through the ear, so wicked and corrupt that the male rapes its own offspring as soon as they are born; and the tiny *donnola*, untameable and brutal, the only beast capable of defeating a basilisk. As for the latter, I have never seen a basilisk on the mountains, as it is more of a river creature, but the presence of *donnole* on the highlands can only be justified by basilisks being around.'

The whole hall was silent again. Bernardo bit his lips with satisfaction, enjoying the attention to its fullest.

'There are creatures of all shapes and makes, some of them never seen by human eyes...'

'And what would those look like?' Martino asked.

'How in hell should I know? No one has seen any!' and a thunder of laughter broke into the hall.

Bernardo did not stop. 'There are birds for all meals, Julian! Food for peasants, but tasty as a gift from heavens. Tender, aromatic thrushes for breaking the fast; spiced magpies – with their stolen gold and silver – for a midday repast; and then, for evening supper; the pungent ravens, black creatures that love to perch on the old birches and spy on peasants' daughters bathing on the rivulets. Ravens, use their unnatural human voices to say the most scandalous indecencies and offenses to the startled maidens. Now, difficult to catch, not too flavourful and quite rich in worms and fetid gases, are the *astori*, or goose-hawks, the great eagles of Rome, the *poiana bastarda*, a lower kind of falcon and the *pellegrino*, a horrible tasting meat, but the best bird for falconry. Surely there are other types of griffins, akin to the *l'onza*, like the *avvoltoi*, the fat otarde and there's even a single lammergeyer, the bonecrusher, a true griffin that over the last few years has been dropping parts of its victims from the highest clouds. It's name, is Turul!'

Except for Father Martino, nobody knew what Bernardo was talking about, and nobody dared to ask. The cantastorie did not develop any more on Turul, but skipped to better known beasts. 'There are bad ominous beings as the nightly *succiacapre*, a ghostly creature of feathers only, with no body or meat inside. Succiacapre are hated for sneaking into farmsteads and sucking dry goats' teats, killing their kids from starvation. Their nocturnal churr attracts witches to spin their wheels, tormenting peace in the woods with the incessant whirl, which muffles their macabre cackling while they brew atrocities.'

Julian interrupted for a second. 'If there's no meat in the succiacapre, then there's no point in hunting them.'

'Quite right, Julian. But for your most pleasurable enjoyment, you will also find plenty of fat pigeons, and the all hunters' and peasants' favourites, as the quail, the rock partridge, the grey partridge and, up on the highest snows, the *pernice*, a bird with hares' feet.'

'Meaning that there should be plenty of hare on the mountains, to copulate with birds.' Julian concluded, with a touch of sarcasm.

'Surely there is. A cunning beast, the hare has both genders, with the balls and *cazzo* of a male and the flower of a female in the same animal. But this mountain hare lives above the line of crops and woods, which makes the hunt rather convenient for the landowners, as no peasants must be compensated for their losses. A mountain hare changes its colour faster than the eye can follow. When chased, it will turn from brown to white and back, to mingle with snow or rock, to disappear from here and re-appear there.' They all looked at where Bernardo had pointed, some half expecting to see a hare standing on the indicated spot. 'The hare is a challenge for the archer, or for the *levrieri*, who depend more on their sight, but not for the scent-specialised lymers. Now, related to the hare, but not game for the chase, are the *marmotte*, tiny hogs with delicious meat. They live in underground kingdoms in their thousands, all brothers and sisters, offspring of a big fat queen that is constantly delivering more pups and fed by its servants in the deepest chamber of their underground networks. There's also another hog that is very difficult and dangerous to catch. I think nobody knows the flavour of the *spinosa*, this solitary beast that carries an army of parasites on its back, all holding a long, sharp spear, ready to throw it at any enemies that threaten their carrier. It is said that the spinosa also holds a stone inside its head, a powerful pebble that can provide the cure against any poison. And talking about that, there's the tiny *mustiolo*, also called the *mus aranes*, spider mouse. But behold! It is not a true mouse neither a spider. It's a fox, so tiny, smaller than a man's thumb. Stinking like a fox, the mustiolo has sharp teeth, as poisonous as an aspis's, and it can kill and devour prey as large as a boar.'

'Boars? Now we're talking, Bernardo.' Julian slapped his knees, bringing Clarissa out of a slumber she had slipped into. 'Don't give me the meat of minuscule foxes or beasts covered with an army of lancers. Give me some good old true hunter's noble meat' he said.

'I'll give you, Julian. Our forests are thriving with boars. Dangerous and lustful animals, yes, I see you nodding, you know how vicious they can be. Well, the higher up on the mountain, the larger the boars. The blackest and most ferocious you will ever see. If you come to hunt them, you have to be prepared for another battle, against a devouring brute as big as a horse, its foaming mouth bristling with tusks and files, ready to kill the whole company in just one charge. A large boar cannot be stopped by arrow or spear. No dogs, whether *alani* or *mastini*, can deter its impetus. In the blink of an eye, ten or twenty men, their dogs and horses can have their guts spilled and dragged across the forest floor.' Bernardo noticed that some people clearly felt a slight discomfort, helping themselves with wine. Clarissa was sound asleep, leaning on Julian's lap.

'But the largest brutes ever to dwell on these forests were the *uri*. These colossal bulls could swipe away entire forests with the span of their horns.'

'Are these like the Sicilian bulls?' Julian asked.

Bernardo grinned. 'No Julian. The bufalu is like a mouse, when compared to the smallest of the uri. It is told that these uri were abundant in the times of our forefathers, but they have dwindled into oblivion, now hiding in the darkest corners of the woods. I only saw it once, when I was probably six or seven. Shepherds from the peaks came to inform my father that a large *uro* had been spotted in his lands. My old man was wise. He took no weapons, dogs or stable, but only me. We rode for a full day through the highest villages and woods, and just before the night fell, long after the sun had retrieved behind the Apuane passes, we crossed a dense forest of firs and came into a clearing. There we saw the uro, in the middle of it. If any of you have seen the giant white bulls of the swampy lands beyond Siena, you have seen little. The uro, my friends, was as large as a church, calmly grazing on the low grass. And the horns! I used to think that the cattle that some Lucchese merchants bring from Maremma had large horns... The uro had horns so long, opening wide and folding forwards, digging massive trenches in the land, that you could have cradled a sizeable horse between its tips. My father and I stood downwind. The giant raised its black head and looked at us. No weapons. He snorted a cloud of steam to denote his lack of concern, but we could sense his heat over our bodies. Had we been carrying any weapons or a cry of hounds, my father said, we could not have stood a chance to tell this story. Making the land tremble at every step, the uro calmly walked towards the silver wall of firs to the north and disappeared. And nobody has seen any more uri ever since.'

'Nonsense! Tell us of the deer, Bernardo. Let's hear about real game!' someone shouted across the table.

Bernardo savoured the demand and continued. 'Ah... if you are interested in the rich meats of grazing creatures, not all of them deer, you may see the *camoscio*, with strong flavour but the softest leather, an animal with sharp horns but that you can easily paralyse if you grab it by its beard. There is no horseman or hound that can offer a chase in camoscio territory. You will need no more than your mountaineering skills and your dexterity with the bow for a camoscio, Julian. Or else you can do as the northern Lombards do, driving them into a lake and harvesting each animal by the beard.' They all shook their heads, some in disapproval, but others just to agree. Bernardo changed the tone. 'Now, deer!' He took another sonorous gulp of wine. 'There are all kinds of deer on the mountains and its forests. The small *capriolo*, found year-round, sometimes freely hunted by my peasants, although they should know better not to. It doesn't have a bad flavour, but there is little merit on its chase. The capriolo is a loyal companion to its doe, as shy as a nubile lady, but as stupid as a Pisan banker...' he paused for the gales of laughter, 'We have the heavy, spotted daino, with its widespread shovel antlers, where the wood nymphs leave their *babies* for a nap while playing with satyrs. A buck daino barks and has generous quantities of meat that does not need to be salted. It should hold its head high and have flat broad palms on its antlers. This groaning beast offers little chase, for the heavy trophy and the large hips.'

When do you get to the *harts*, Bernardo?' a voice asked somewhere down the table.

'Be patient,' the cantastorie said with a smirk, 'as we finally, come to the most sought after fruit of the woods: the *hart*! This massive howling red deer, noble and ardent, is elusive and tireless, so a chase could take days and it is often lost when the hart cleverly crosses its path with those of hinds. For a hunter as skilled as you are meant to be, Julian, a good, sizeable hart should sustain a thick dark mane on its neck and it should carry at least a dozen tines to each of its antlers. The best trophies, hard and clean of their velvet, are found after the Feast of Santa Maria Maddalena and before the *Esaltazione della Santa Croce*, the Feast of the Holy Cross. And more than that, a hart with antlers so big is rare, for it is close to its natural death, which is unnatural. Those marvellous creatures do not die, if not by the violence of men or the greed of bears and wolves. The aging hart will search through the woods until it finds a white serpent and swallows it, following with a drink of water. The mixture of water and venom will rejuvenate the hart, which turns into a calf again. But Julian, you do know that if you follow the hart until it breaks down the chase, the reward will be enormous. A hart will cry like a woman when mortally wounded by a hunter's arrow, so a quick prayer should be offered to *Sant'Eustachio*, *Sant'Uberto*, the Virgin Mary and the Holy Spirit, and the beast drops dead with its legs up.'

'Very well, Bernardo,' said Alberto Azzo raising his goblet, 'this was an amusing introduction to our fantastic fauna, but on this day...'

'Wait, my cousin!' Bernardo interrupted. 'I am not done yet. There are two beings that I left for last.'

'And what would these be, Bernardo?' Alberto asked, not losing his good humour.

'The first is the *unicorno*.' Said the cantastorie, rather slowly, enjoying the general awe and the protests of some.

'Bernardo, a unicorn is just another beast that does not exist on our lands, as so many of those you have flamboyantly described to us now' said the constantly sceptical Martino, who had quietly put up with his friend's tales so far.

'Oh no, Martino, the preacher,' Bernardo said with solemn words, 'I hate to disagree, but you are indeed rather equivocated. Unicorns do exist, and they reside on these mountains towering above us, on God-forsaken areas so frigid and barren that no grass or moss manages to cover the face of the rocks. But behold, my good priest, for these unicorns are not the enormous, brutal, dark, hairy beasts that the classic tales describe, but a rather delicate, fair creature. Not lager than a doe, with cleaved hooves and a goat's beard, the elusive unicorn is the ultimate climber. It walks up vertical walls and it can stand upside down, resting on the ceiling of a cave. The long spiralling horn of the unicorn is a priced trophy for any lucky hunter, for when it touches foul water, it can make it clean. And drinking from a cup made from such horn can protect the drinker from poison. But attention here, for there's only one way to capture a unicorn and I will tell you how. This wondrous beast is lured by the sweet fragrance of virginity. Therefore, leaving a young maiden on the forest floor can attract a unicorn, which will carefully approach her, touch her breast and lay its head on her lap, falling asleep immediately under the spell of the maiden's natural purity. This is the time when a hunter can approach the beast and kill it.'

'Excuse me a moment, Bernardo delle Rocche' said Clarissa, who was suddenly awake. 'How do you expect a maiden to be waiting for this monster? On her own and in the forest?'

A voice came from a guest at the end of the table 'Just get rid of the ravens!' and they all guffawed with glee, as a pleasant conclusion to the tales.

'But I am not finished yet,' Bernardo insisted, raising a commanding and unmistakable Obertenghi hand, 'for there's one more beast on those mountains, and many of you have seen one. It's the only other creature capable of taming a unicorn.' They all held their breath in suspense. Bernardo ensured he had the control again, before revealing 'It's the *omo salvatico*!'

'The what?' asked a narrow-eyed Julian.

Bernardo chuckled, but answered courteously. 'The *uomo selvatico*, Julian, or *omo salvatico*, as we say it in the Apuane, but it could be called *om pelos, orco, pilosus, salvang,* from the Northern tales of the Lombards.

'Wild man, *wudewasa*!' admitted Martino, out of his experience among the anglo-saxons.

'Exactly!' Bernardo agreed, 'and in your lands, Julian, they call it *l'homme sauvage,* or simply, *ogre.*' Bernardo saw Julian livid with amazement and perhaps fear. 'Julian, many of us who have crossed the high passes of the Apuane have seen one or more *omini salvatici.* They are generally peaceful, quiet creatures, living in their solitary lives in caves and dens, in constantly prayer, so distant from our world that theirs have become a universe of absurdity. The omo salvatico is a hairy creature that wears no clothes, for its body is already covered in fur, protecting it from the icy cold winds. It cries and howls with agony when the days are sunny and rejoices with glee under miserable, rainy weather. Apart from a staff or mace, the omo salvatico has few utensils, if ever any and lives from meagre servings of wild berries, roots, leaves and crawling creatures of the caves. Peasants and shepherds fear this beastly figure, for under excessive privation, reason can be easily lost and the omo salvatico will pursue the milk from does, hinds and ewes, sucking straight from their teats. And the most dangerous thing that could happen when a hunter comes across an omo salvatico is to bring to its lair the scent of a woman. The creature can smell it for miles. The feminine smell can stir wild emotions in the beast, driving it to violence and indecency, and if not engaging into acts of bestiality, it will attack the hunter and often seize him like a rutting hart.'

Julian laughed nervously. 'You cannot be serious, Bernardo. Ogres only exist in stories that parents use to scare their children away from running into the woods.'

'Julian, its time I leave the word to others. I have said enough and most of your guests are rather bored. But nothing I have told is untrue. My lands are still thriving with game, and you are very welcome to come for a hunt anytime you want. I promise you will get to see your ogres and pity on their savageness. I will see that there's no reason for a hunter like you to be kept from running into the woods.'

Clarissa discreetly held Julian's hand and said 'I appreciate your invitation, but Julian does not need such challenges any more, no matter how many fabulous creatures he could see on the mountains. Depending on me, there's no more hunt. Julian stays forever with me.'

In a few weeks, when guests were all gone, Julian rode to Pisa, to recover his boat, which still had Buonaccorso's faded leopard skin in it. Everyone in Luna waited for the arrival of the famous boat that had carried the Volto Santo. He beached on the same spot where the carcass of the Leviathan had been stranded fourteen years before. Now that Bishop Filippo was gone and Luni was in ruins, Alberto Azzo had strongly suggested the erection of a chapel on the hill, where the cross would be housed forever, standing up with the Holy Face turned towards the sea. Saracen troops would never dare to approach those lands anymore.

While the chapel was being built, the cross with the Volto Santo was raised on the hillside, facing the Ligurian sea, bravely withstanding the harsh winds and the salty breeze. The local crows had found their favourite place to roost.

Later, the episcopate of Lucca determined the cross too precious a relic be left out on the hill, so far from the city. In spite of the protests of the remnant Lunensis population, the Volto Santo was solemnly seized and carried to the bishopric of Lucca, accompanied by Buonaccorso's cape. In the church of Saint Peter, also called *Domini et Salvatoris*, an excited Bishop Grimizzo deposited the leopard skin in a memorial to Buonaccorso.

M. S.

Bonacursus

Papiani Leopardi

Et contentionis benedictae eius ad tuendam et restaurandam

Ecclesiam Sancti Sepulchri Hieroslymae.

(To the memory of Buonaccorso, the Pavese Leopard, and his blessed dedication to the protection and the reconstruction of the church of the Holy Sepulchre in Jerusalem.)

Next to this slab, the proud bishop displayed the *Santo Simulacro*, or *Volto Santo*, the wooden sculpture carved by Nicodemus and miraculously transfigured after the face of the Holy Saviour. The image that helped Luna rid itself of the Saracen invaders was displayed as another attraction for the pilgrims, but it soon became the main repository of alms, surpassing the Cathedral and all other pilgrimage sites in Lucca.

In less than 50 years, a new cathedral was erected on top of the old duomo and a baptistery replaced the little church of Domini et Salvatoris. The statue of the Volto Santo was removed to a small pergola erected in the new Cathedral. The slab to Buonaccorso was lost under the rubble. His name was forever forgotten.

However, the fur cape made from spotted dogs' pelts from the Isle of Lagosta, in Dalmatia endured its final stage of deterioration, being displayed under the feet of the famous crucifix until it shredded into dust. Enough time to transform the leopard into a powerful symbol of the city of Lucca.

As for the Volto Santo, it would eventually consolidate the status of *acheiropoieta*, an icon not made by human hands, and it would gain a new story. A tale that would be sung by many cantastorie and read by so many scholars that the lore of Julian would also be torn into powder and swept away by the arrivals of every new generation of the people of Lucca.

The Castracani

Bishop Grimizzo was a small man. His seemingly frail, exhausted stature was bent down as he sat on his comfortable office, receiving the visitor. Tired, the bishop made sure the visitor saw his face contorting as if he was stung by a swell of pain on the neck whenever he stared him in the eyes. And he made no efforts to hide his disgusted amusement, for it was difficult to believe anyone in their sane mind would wear such a grisly hat.

'It is as I report, reverend bishop.' said the visitor, who did not have the courtesy to take his hat off. 'They have been living together throughout this last year, just as husband and wife. A sinful relationship, a clear defiance to the recommendations of Rome, blunt alienation from ecclesiastical conduct and a most inappropriate example, coming from our Lord's own house to *His* own herd.'

The bishop sighed. 'Antelmino di Gottefredo, who are you to throw the first stone? Your conduct is hardly a role model to be followed, starting by this repugnant hat of yours, which you do not care to take off, even when granted an audience with your bishop.'

Antelmino bit his lip and closed his eyes for a while. He took of his hat and placed it on the table, making the bishop cringe with disgust. 'Reverend Bishop,' he said humbly 'I am no more than a common sinner and the Divine Judgement will make me pay for my faults. But it's this parishioner Martino who entertains ambitions to be a shepherd of the Lord and to direct us towards the righteous conducts.'

'More than an ambition, Antelmino, it is a burden.' said the bishop, with a raised finger, almost distracting himself with his ring.

The Castracani was quick to answer. 'But not so much of a burden for father Martino, who exercises continence and chastity every night, warmed up between the legs of his whore, a nun!'

Grimizzo was getting tired of his visitor. Everyone in Lucca already knew that Antelmino held a bitter grudge against Martino from the day he had been kicked into the Serchio by the priest. 'What do you want me to do?' the bishop asked. 'Martino is well connected, being friends with the Obertenghi, including Bernardo delle Rocche, Alberto Azzo and Julian of Luna.'

Antelmino snorted. 'I'm well connected too,' he said.

'Really?' asked the amused bishop, nursing his ecclesiastical ring. 'You are not accepted in the league of merchants of Lucca. Your relation with your neighbours is based on fear and suspicion. You do not get along even with that bitter Maria Maddalena Cunimundinghi, and may the Lord bless the endurance of her good father.'

'Perhaps it does not sound as much, Reverend Bishop, but I have the total control over the vellutini around Lucca. I can suppress crime and provide protection in this city. Please do as I suggest: go to the monastery of San Giovanni Battista, in Santa Maria lei Giudice and talk to Abbess Theodora yourself, as the old cow refuses to accept an audience with me. You are an ecclesiastical superior and she cannot deny you the information. You will eventually find that Sister Caterina is a runaway from that monastery and the clerics of the Lateran could be very interested in her. So you must advise the Holy Pope of this corrupt priest and remove him from his woman and his church. The nun should be dealt with by the Lateran. As an enthusiast of clerical celibacy, the Beatissimo Padre will be no less than thankful to you.'

'I appreciate your visit, your alert and certainly your most conscious advice, Antelmino di Gottefredo,' said the bishop, rising from his chair with visible difficulty and extending his arm to conduct Antelmino to the exit. He waited for the visitor to retrieve his ghastly hat. 'But I will leave the decision for my conscience, Antelmino. The parishioner Martino of Controne is an extremely charitable and generous cleric, loved by the people along the valleys of the Serchio and the Lima. That is with the exception of two rather vocal landlords, of course, you and the Cunimundinghi Lady. But he is not in any of your lands and we may have to leave it to God Himself to do the judgement.'

Antelmino said nothing else.

In less than a week, Bishop Grimizzo was startled in the middle of the night by a strange man in his bedroom. The man beat the bishop unconscious and stole a few of his treasures, including his ecclesiastical ring. When the balivo of Lucca failed to find a culprit and retrieve the goods, giving up on the investigation, the defeated and wounded bishop had to resort to Antelmino di Gottefredo. The Castracani was quick to act on his contacts and returned in two days with the treasures, including the ring, and the body of a man who had been beaten to death during the struggle. The corpse was so defiled that the bishop could not recognise his attacker.

As soon as he was healed, Grimizzo took a day to visit the monastery in Santa Maria lei Giudice and, although the charming old abbess was reluctant to release the information, he managed to uncover the identity and history of Sister Caterina from other older nuns. On the same night of his return to Lucca, holding onto his ring more than ever before, he dispatched a letter to the pope, advising the bishop of Rome of Father Martino and Sister Caterina, and asking for instructions on procedures to be taken in order to end this scandal.

As for his own concubine and two children, Bishop Grimizzo would have to think what to do about them, for few people in Lucca knew of it.

The servant of Anchiano carefully told the visitor that it was the wishes of her lady that he should leave his hat outside before entering the manor. Maria Maddalena was in the main hall, carefully adjusting the folds of her dress and pompously waiting for that visitor. When Antelmino entered, she pretended to be reading some scrolls, totally uninterested in his repugnant presence. The visitor chose to seat himself and stare at her in amusement. 'What do you want?' Maria grunted without taking her eyes from the scrolls.

Antelmino grinned. 'I saw Arrigo playing outside. He's looking a fine young man. A perfect miniature of Fulcardo. What age is he? Almost three now?'

Maria dropped the scroll and looked into his eyes 'Leave my son out of your grime, Antelmino. Don't you ever dare to get any close to him. Now, why do I have to tolerate your unwelcome presence in my house?'

Antelmino did not wither his smile. He just cleared his throat and articulated quite delicately 'I have all the respect for you and your lands, but please do not mistake me for your deceased husband or for that stupid Sigifredo, or any others of the Cunimundinghi, especially the ones who have been silly enough to suggest they'd want your lands back. I am a man of class and distinction and I am here to come to an agreement, and not to impose anything, for who am I to...'

'Just say it' she cut, with lips as dry as if made of stone.

Antelmino almost smiled, before continuing. 'It occurred to me, Maria Maddalena, that the produce of the Cunimundinghi lands has been carried across the Serchio in a very clumsy craft at the Traghetto. I am sure you have lost some cargo and precious time in that small ferry. That is not a dignified manner to treat grains and silk, so important these days for the economy of our region.' He studied her indifference and continued with precise movements of his hands. 'My question is: why don't you use the eastern road of the Serchio to send your carts to Lucca? My lands are open to your transport, at no charge, you have always known that. You are well aware that I am currently having some my men clear my road from rocks and widening the spaces, making it as smooth as the western side where the pilgrims so inconveniently crowd.'

'Not men, Antelmino.' Maria said without changing the dry stoniness of her face. 'I have seen only women and children working on that road, but the manner in which you treat your servants is your problem only. So, you came here to tell me

414

I can freely transport my carts through your lands? And what do you want in return?' she scoffed, 'Admission into the bankers guild? Intermediation in silk trade?'

Antelmino lowered his eyes and smiled condescendingly 'No Maria Maddalena. I am only a small trader. I could never aspire to...'

'You are no trader, Antelmino. You are a just criminal! What is the deal then? You will pull a blade to my neck again? You want to take me by trade, rather than by force?'

Antelmino sneered and licked his lips. 'You mistake me, Maria Maddalena. I am a loving man, who would make a perfect husband for you.'

'You make me sick!' she said.

'But today, all I ask of you is to help me on a matter of personal interest. You do know a Roman parishioner named Martino, in Controne.'

'The one who kicked you into the river? Everyone knows about him!' Maria said, for the first time outlining a tentative smile, which Antelmino pretended not to notice.

'You also know that he lives in a sinful relationship with a woman. A nun.' he said, to which she confirmed with a hostile grunt. 'Well it happens that the Holy Father in Rome is engaged in ridding the clerics of the church from corrupt concubinage and marriage, but our Bishop Grimizzo in Lucca is being rather slow in acting upon the transgressors.'

'Would you like to see me supporting the separation and banishment of those two from these lands?' Maria asked.

Antelmino nodded. 'I know that Controne is not in Cunimundinghi land, but...'

'The pope holds many of my lands,' she intervened, 'including the northern bank of the Lima. I will recover them one day, when the *guadia* is paid for. But meanwhile, I can interfere directly with the pope, through the correspondence between the Lateran and the Burle House of Trade. So rather than doing a favour to you so that I can use your roads, I will act upon those sinners and, in return, you will kindly allow me to drive my carts through the east road to Lucca.'

Antelmino had not expected it to be that easy. Speechless for a moment, he bowed in appreciation. 'Maria Maddalena,' he finally said 'it feels as we have much more in common than one would reckon. Who knows if one day...'

'I know that never, not one day, will we have anything else in common than this agreement.' she said, standing up commandingly. That was her sign that the visit was over.

'I still think you should consider re-marrying, Maria Maddalena' he said, walking towards the door. 'For you are still young, and maybe the hardness of your face could still give way to the beauty that once was there.'

Maria Maddalena watched the door being closed and sat down, holding her face in agony. She cried while her fingers tried to snatch out her mask of hardness, but the enticing grey-eyed, red-haired girl was not behind it any more. Her power was no longer sustained by charm and it could easily be washed out by her fragility. Or by the memories of her defilement. She had to maintain the stony face and to erase those memories from the valley. And that included getting rid of the only witness: Sister Caterina, and forever.

Antelmino was at the end of a long straight track among a forest of black alders and he could see his rather modest manor at Santo Stefano di Tassignano at the end of the line of large oaks when a few riders passed by, coming from Lucca.

'Bishop Grimizzo!' Antelmino yelled. 'What a surprise!'

The bishop recognised the hat and reluctantly halted his horse, coming back to cordially greet the Castracani.

'Where do you go in such a hurry?' asked Antelmino.

'I ride to Prato, to meet a committee of the Holy Father. We are all heading to Goslar, where the emperor has offered his palace for a synod.'

'Goslar? I don't know where this is.' Antelmino shrugged. 'Sounds far...'

'Neither do I, but it is in German lands, not too far from Bremen. Arnoldo, the archbishop of Ravenna will lead us through the passes and forests. He is the emperor's half-brother.'

'Far enough, I guess,' Antelmino consented. 'That means you will be out for long? I have just been with Maria Maddalena Cunimundinghi and she was about to send you an advisory on...'

'It will have to wait, I'm afraid,' the bishop said with undisguised satisfaction. 'These trips can take a long time, as you probably know. But if this pertains to your grudge against Father Martino of Controne, rest assured that both the Holy Father and the emperor are deeply against clerics entertaining sensuous relations with a woman. That means I will probably have some new instructions when I come back. And if I was you, Antelmino di Gottefredo, I would stay away from that woman. They say that the deceased Benzo di Berardo, from Buggiano, a third cousin who wanted to take over Anchiano, was poisoned under her orders. And that was after Maria Maddalena chopped all the fingers of fifty men of the vellutini who tried to invade her lands.'

'A bit of an exaggeration, my bishop, but as you are well aware of, I do know how to take care of myself.'

Grimizzo rolled his eyes in nausea and said 'Now I must go, Antelmino. See you again!'

The Castracani watched the score of riders raising dust, as he cursed through greeted teeth. If the bishop was not in a hurry to correct that supercilious priest, he would have to organise for something more immediate. Martino could not remain unpunished.

Figures in the Fog

The Lady of Luna was on her horse, galloping towards the Southern hills, for a long-black-haired rider had just appeared across the crest. 'How was Lucca, my love?' she asked, grabbing Julian and kissing him powerfully as soon as their horses walked by each other. 'I have felt your heat next to me for three years already, and I suffer when you leave me for so long!'

'That was only five days of travel, Clarissa!' Julian laughed. 'I had barely more than a day in Lucca.'

'Tell me about it then!' Clarissa demanded, exultant.

'Bernardo was in Lucca. Seems to me that he is still looking for a wife.' He paused to enjoy hearing Clarissa laughing.

'He will never be happy with a city girl,' she said. 'He should be marrying a vigorous peasant woman, who will give him love and strong children; a woman that will survive the mountain climate without losing her wits and that can tolerate his delirious stories without telling him specifically what to do with them.'

'Well, Bernardo took me to the Di Cunizio house, so I could see old Cunerado, whom I had met in Jerusalem.'

'The pilgrim that warned you about the siege? And how was he?'

'Still healthy, and delighted to have completed his pilgrimage. He was in Jerusalem for three months after I returned. The hospital does carry on receiving pilgrims, under the instructions of Jan Koogs. Nicodemus is personally directing the reconstruction of the Holy Sepulchre, rather bitter after having taken his daughter to the desert.'

'What was her name again?' Clarissa asked.

'Helena. Apparently she was not seen again in Jerusalem.'

'The slut!' spat Clarissa. 'I hope she died from starvation or was attacked by wolves. The bitch got what she deserved!' Clarissa noticed that Julian swallowed a dry lump. She softened her face. 'I'm sorry, my love. I cannot be less jealous and enraged when I think of what that woman did to you and poor Buonaccorso.'

'It is fine, Clarissa.' Julian said, frowning. 'The memory is painful for me too. I entered the cathedral to visit Buonaccorso's plate. It looks beautiful, and there his memory will survive, but I had to fight a thick crowd of visitors and pilgrims that swarmed in to see the Volto Santo. And finding Buonaccorso's was not easy, among the dozens of slabs proclaiming pious donations of several Lucchese families towards the holy image, including the Di Cunizio.'

Clarissa rolled her eyes.

Julian continued. 'But I heard some bad news from the bishop Grimizzo, Clarissa. He has received a letter from the pope, censoring the Diocese of Lucca for allowing the concubinage and marriage of clerics such as with Martino and Caterina.'

'But that is absurd!' Clarissa yelled. 'No man can live without a woman. The church has forever advised for celibacy, but it is stupid. It's the same as forbidding one to eat, or to sleep, or to defecate, urinate! They cannot forbid men's passions or needs.'

'But it looks like this pope is making a good case of it.' Julian said. 'He seems to be heading towards complete forbiddance at all levels.'

'You have met this pope, Julian. Is he reasonable?'

Julian made a face of discomfort. 'I'm afraid he is not...'

'Oh God Almighty,' said Clarissa looking towards the blue Ligurian sky. 'Please look after those two and rid them from the stupidity of the church.' She turned to Julian 'And what will the good bishop do?'

'He said he will put the matter as a lower priority and delay any decisions.'

'Good man!' Clarissa said, smiling warmly.

'It was good to meet Bernardo!' said Julian.

'Does he still want you to come and hunt with him?' She saw Julian nodding with care. 'So are you ready to face the ghosts of a hunt?' she asked looking at his eyes.

'I think I am.'

'This summer?'

'I'm ready for this summer.' He said, with firm lips.

Clarissa extended her hand and Julian held it. They rode holding each other back to the ruined castle of Luna.

'I love when you hold my hand, Julian. I love you.'

'I love to know that you love me, Clarissa. To know that I have something to make you feel good. I love you too.'

At the end of July, they were meeting with Bernardo in a marble village, high on the mountains Southeast of Luna.

'Will you care for my husband when you venture across these passes, Bernardo?'

'I must confess that I wouldn't if we were not related, Clarissa.' Bernardo said, helping her back onto her horse. 'I certainly could make a good candidate to marry a young Obertenghi widow' he added. Clarissa giggled, leaning down to punch her cousin on the shoulder. 'However, I do not look for adventure inside the family. So I promise, my lady, that I will keep this man out of any wolves' jaws.'

Clarissa stared admiringly at her Julian, ready for the hunt, her eyes sparkling a rainbow of colours, shining with pride and already longing for her man. But whether conscientiously or not, all the company of chasseurs had to wait until the Lady of Luna would leave, for they had eyes only for her. Mounting on her tall destrier on a manly fashion, Clarissa reigned more magnificent than ever. Her vigorous figure was slim, tall, and powerful. A wild conductance that fascinated a few, but scared most. The long brown hair was not kept hidden, but fell in kind cascades, gently caressing a just slightly salient derrière, and long vigorous legs folded on the side of the massive horse. She bent down with a radiant smile to passionately kiss Julian one more farewell, granting to the full company a generous vision of a fabulous cleavage.

'Come back soon' she whispered to her husband.

'I'm already regretting leaving you for a second.' Julian answered whenever his lips parted from hers. 'And I already feel like a fool, for no man within his mental sanity would leave a woman like you alone.'

'Good bye, my love!' she said, straightening up and waving. Thirty seven men waved back. Clarissa rode down into an olive grove in that warm afternoon, back to Luna, accompanied by an escort of riders.

Standing out by that mountain hamlet, the company gathered at the manor. Next to a lively fireplace, hot stony disks hissed in steam as they were placed on top of each other. A plump servant lady laid a ladle of chestnut batter between each disk. The flattened hot chestnut cakes were served to the chasseurs with olive oil and *re-cotta* cheese.

'This is food of angels, unbeknownst to the city people.' Bernardo said to Julian. 'Lucchese nobility despises chestnut cakes and polenta even when there are severe shortages of food. Mountain people never starve.' He cut a few slices from a thick sheet of lard, drizzled some honey and rolled them with some soft flat cakes. Julian moaned with pleasure when he tried it. 'Never mind that it's Friday, Julian. This is from last Christmas's fat pigs, after eating all their acorns from the ground. The best quality pig fat you could find anywhere, Julian. It's spiced with herbs and cured in marble basins. Anyway, while we all enjoy these mountain delights, we should start our briefing before we cross the passes tomorrow.'

There were a dozen men from Bernardo's valleys and another two dozen from Luna, of the western valleys of the Apuane. Bernardo had brought a lymerer with three helpers, each one handling a *segugio*. These were hairy, affectionate scent hounds, with long droopy ears, a lively gait and a frame not as heavy as the French lymers and not as arched and slim as the grīghunds. In addition to those, a large Lombard from Wald Ottavo handled two vicious brown *mastini*. They were bulky molossers unlike the tall white alaunts with black patches of the North, but with shorter legs and a large wide head. The mastino's built was more than appropriate to bite the lips of an uro bull and only let go when one of the two was dead. But this was no hunt for an uro, but a bow and stable engagement. It involved a large group of men that funnelled the game of a particular area into a spot where the archers could get them before disappearing behind the line of arrows. A first for Julian, for he had been more involved with hound chases, either with a lymer or with grīghunds. They talked about travelling into separate groups on the next day, which would give them good training on horn communication. Bernardo warned them to keep away from and not to disturb any omo salvatico which they'd probably come across on the passes. The mere thought made Julian's hair stand on its base. After the warm meal and wine, they retired to bed early. As night fell, Julian could hear the howling of wolves, not far outside. The *segugi* were unquiet, apparently yelping with fear.

'These wolves could never have reared the gemelli Romolo and Remo,' Bernardo whispered through the muffling darkness from his palliasse. 'They have a poisonous bite, as they devour anything that moves, including the aspis...'

'I think that's enough, Bernardo' Julian grunted, a bit irritated. 'Just let us sleep. If you want to make noise, join the wolves outside.'

The fog seemed to flatten even the massive boulders of the Apuane. A solid mist that was only pierced by the distant cawing of the ravens. Daring alpine choughs flew and trilled around the company, attacking the knapsack of bread carried by one of the hound masters.

'*Maledetti gracchi!*' he rasped, frightening the black birds away with his staff, but for no longer than an instant, as they were soon back on his load.

White giants of rock appeared suddenly out of the whiteness, as the company slowly advanced through the meandering stony track. Leaving the manor at sunrise, the chasseurs rode for an hour through a forest of Turkey oaks, where small herds of black pigs foraged and crushed any precocious acorns they could still find. The oaks thinned away and gave ground to a thick darkness of beech and hornbeams, where Julian was haunted by memories of the forest in Limoges, a dirty grin of madness and a curtain of blood covering the breast of that girl. *What was her name? Louise. How would have life treated them had he been there to protect her? Would Louise have been a better wife than Clarissa? How dared he considered such comparison?* Fortunately, the sombre crossing was livened up by the distracting and constant clattering of Bernardo's endless tales.

When they surfaced from the forest, the cold fog silenced them all. Hooves stepped on mossy stones, and even the mastini held their ears and tails low, perhaps in fear of disturbing the quiet heights of the colossal peaks looming above, hidden beyond the clouds. The wet track was sided by a thick carpet of moist crocuses, tiny gentians and honey-coloured lilies, the *gigli di San Giovanni*, which flowered in late June, but up on the peaks they blossomed later. To the fog they were shy, firmly closed, just elongated shy buttons.

Further ahead, two square pillars of white marble greeted the travellers with their stoniness. 'These are probably the some of the marble quarries that have served Luna and its environs' Julian remarked, trying to break the deafening silence. 'I must look at a day when we re-build that castle.' But his voice was stiffened by the mist, hardly reaching Bernardo's ears, just one horse ahead of him. They were crossing an area of barren walls and giant steps, where stone had been cut out long before, leaving an abandoned icy hell, voiceless and solitary, mingling into the nothingness of the fog. In that blind zone, even the trilling of the choughs was mute. A solitary bird still remained, quietly balancing itself on the load of the lymerer, but none paid any more heed to it.

Just as they left the quarry, an appalling stench sneaked out of the mist. The dogs got uneasy and some of the men cursed. The putrid odour was now imbedded into the fog. A noxious acrid stink of faeces. More curses from the back of the line, and Bernardo shushed them. Ahead of the company, Julian saw, materialising from the haze, a stone warrior carved on a standing rock. A flat slab covered in lichens, standing straight up from a high meadow, still presenting the features of an ancient God or fantastic being of old, unknown peoples. It was short and not too wide. A thin neck separated a mushroom shaped head or helmet from the straight body. A few paces ahead, another flat slab carved into a warrior, or maybe a woman, with the same head shape, but neckless and with small lumps for breasts.

The hunters held their nostrils shut and looked down as the company paraded through the statues.

A deep voice croaked from above them. 'Horror unique animos, simul ipsa silentia terrent!'

Some of the men screamed in terror, crawling and uttering prayers. Dogs burst in yelping and barking. The horses became uneasy, as many men tried to hide under them. Bernardo whispered the translation to himself 'The horror and the silences terrified their souls.' He chuckled to Julian. 'How ironic!'

'Who is it?' asked Julian disturbed.

Another similar hellish voice broke just ahead of them 'Fac et aliquid operis, ut semper te diabolus inveniat occupatum!'

Bernardo translated. 'Make yourself busy, so that whenever the devil calls he may find you occupied.'

Meanwhile, the first voice repeated above 'Horror unique animos, simul ipsa silentia terrent,' followed again by a new round of 'Fac et aliquid operis, ut semper te diabolus inveniat occupatum! Horror unique animos, simul ipsa silentia terrent! Fac et aliquid operis, ut semper te diabolus inveniat occupatum!'

Some of the men started weeping. Bernardo groaned 'Oh you big baby girl pussies, just pull yourselves together! Don't you know who it is?'

'Who is that?' insisted Julian.

The voice approached from the front. 'Fac et aliquid operis, ut semper te diabolus inveniat occupatum! Fac et aliquid operis, ut semper te diabolus inveniat occupatum!' Some of the hunters in front ran back to hide behind Julian and Bernardo. The shepherd grinned and said 'Just watch, Julian.'

Out of the whiteness, a large black chicken jumped into the track. No, not a chicken, but with a black head and a dagger-shaped beak. It was a massive raven. It kept jumping towards them and croaked with a cavernous metallic voice *'Fac et aliquid operis, ut semper te diabolus inveniat occupatum!'* And the other raven responded with its own sentence and resonant voice from somewhere above on the rocks.

Bernardo was laughing out loud. 'Whoever taught this bird indeed must have made himself busy by constantly repeating the sentence to this stupid rook.'

'Can I set the dogs on them?' the lymerer asked.

'Don't be ridiculous!' Bernardo hissed. Don't waste our dogs with these creatures.

The raven approached them to a safe distance, and after looking at them all, opened its massive wings and flew back disappearing into the mist, endless repeating its phrase. Somewhere behind the fog, another raven made a disturbing noise of friction. While the company quickly re-gathered, the noise grew more intense and the raven dropped a few moans and sighs into the sequence. It did not stop until the whole company moved ahead. By the time they were distant already, the raven was screaming in delirium.

'It's probably Saint Jerome, or maybe Saint Anthony.' Bernardo said.

'What?' asked Julian, slightly annoyed with the scare. 'What the ravens were repeating? How do you know? And how would they learn that?' But Julian was shut silent when an eerie wide-eyed figure appeared out of the whiteness, quickly glancing at him and his horse, and crossing the track to disappear again into the silence. It was surely a human, naked, with a long beard and mane that mingled into his body hair. It was partially covered with moss and dried leaves that clung to its hairy skin, and wearing no more than a furry loincloth and a crown of leaves. But that man had disappeared as fast and quiet as he showed himself in the road.

'What was that?' Julian asked Bernardo in a whisper. 'Where did it go?'

'*Omo salvatico!*' said Bernardo, pressing his lips conclusively. 'That was one of the wild men we had talked about Julian. An *orco*. Ogre! And here's another one.' A fragile old man came limping towards them, whiter and furrier than the first one, his matted hair and beard grew to pass below his waist, or whatever he wore to hide his genitals. Clumps of decaying matter dropped from his beard. The old man stopped, standing in the middle of the track, legs trembling with cold, with an extended hand, begging for them in a whispered unintelligible language. Julian could smell the choking stench of that omo salvatico from a distance.

'Give them some of the bread.' Bernardo ordered the hunters.

'What about the dogs?' protested the lymerer, 'there won't be enough for the curée.'

Bernardo turned his horse around and faced the lymerer, who immediately lowered his gaze. 'Just give them the damned bread, will you?' said the Cantastorie. 'These are Holy Men! Hermits who spend their life in prayer and penance, so that sinners like you and I can live our mundane lives in total disarray and maybe still entertain hopes of ending up in the Garden of Eden one day.' The lymerer handed a small loaf to the wild man, who quickly disappeared behind the mist.

'They live in several caves just above our track.' Bernardo explained to Julian, as two more of those hairy apparitions silently approached from the rocks to get a few crumbs of bread.

'How many of these things are there around?' Julian asked, looking at their thin, flabby white skin, which gave them the appearance of cold walking cadavers.

'Who knows?' Bernardo shrugged. 'As many as there are caves that do not house a bear. If there's a grotto or a nook on these mountain passes and peaks, there's likely an omo salvatico living in it. They are just filthy lairs of human waste, where only prayer and mortification have any meaning at all to these men. Be it good luck or not, the fog brings them out of their holes. On glorious days, when the blue sea opens beyond the valleys, these creatures are hidden in their caves, eating no more than blind fish, crabs, all types of newts and any cave dwellers that's unfortunate to move around them. As fast as a spider, these wild men will jump onto anything that moves and ravenously devour a Godless critter, with no fire for food or comfort. They can see in the dark, their sense of smell can outlast any of these lymers, and they don't even appear to be affected by the poison of fire salamanders. They lick newts and green toads to escape from their mortifications. And because of solitary life in caves, their hearing is better than a bat's. They can be tormented by words that are spoken or uttered even miles away down the coast.'

'But are these wild men just... hermits? Holy men?' Julian asked, 'Like the Desert Fathers? I knew of them in Jerusalem, and many monks which were said to be living in caves, with the hyenas.'

'Yes Julian!' Bernardo said, as they rode along. 'Ascetics, probably not different from Saint Paul of Thebes and so many others that I learned about, but I doubt if theses ravens of the Apuane would bring them any bread and no desert lions would help on their burials either. They are inspired by models such as Saint Antony, who was beaten by demons with branches of quince in his cave and who fought temptation of silver and gold laid down by the Devil, but I don't think even Satan would venture into the God-forsaken place where we are. These wild men spend their existence in total abstinence from worldly pleasures; they crave to be the next Saint Onuphrius, who received his Holy Eucharist from the hands of an angel or a Saint Jerome, hoping to remove a thorn from the paw of some big beast.'

'Hard to believe such savage creatures are Holy men,' Julian said.

The company had left behind the two begging wild men with some stony pieces of dry bread, originally planned to be soaked in blood of any hunted beast and given to the dogs during the curée.

'Do they ever talk? Have you ever communicated with these creatures, Bernardo?'

Bernardo chuckled. 'Only if they want something from us and fear that they won't get it. I often bring these bastards supplies from my lands when I venture up here. More than bread, some expect me to bring them butter, cheese, even re-cotta. On the day of the final judgement, I will owe some explanation to my sin of indulging them with these luxuries, but to a certain extend I pity these creatures. Their exercise of asceticism can drive them into blunt insanity, after which they often pay a price, hitting their own hairy backs with birch twigs, renewing their fasting and increasing any fashion of mortification they may find themselves deserving of. They are harmless, mostly and I doubt that any of these hermits could have the resilience and obedience of a Saint John the Dwarf, who was given a plank of dry wood and ordered to water it. It happens that this poor dwarf had to walk all night to find water in the desert. He did it so every night for years, until the wood sprouted into a green tree that...oh, for Christ's blood! Look at that!'

One of the wild men was crouching on the track ahead of the company, sitting like a frog, with his back to them. He was completely bald and did not seem to have any other hair. He was defecating.

'Get out of here you miserable bastard!' Bernardo yelled. 'Look at what you have done!'

'I purge my mortal body of my sins coming out of my arse in this shit!' the wild man hissed at them with rage, slowly walking away with his skinny frog limbs, an arched bony back and a tongue of excrement still hanging from his rear. 'Sinners, murderers, fuckers! You are no better than this shit! Repent and take your punishment before it's late!'

'Leave us alone!' Bernardo said, much less enraged and pretending a certain indifference. 'Go back to your hole, clean yourself and pray for us.' The cantastorie made sure his horse did not step on the fetid mound and warned the rest of the company.

'Did you bring me milk?' the wild man asked, much less aggressively now. 'Do you have some milk? I need milk!' he drooled.

Bernardo did not look at him and kept his horse moving forward. 'Go clean up your mess. I'll bring you milk next time.'

The wild man broke down and cried, screaming out of his lungs, his bony fingers grabbing onto his hairless head as it howled in desperation 'If you do not bring me any, the milk in your ewes and cows will turn into oil!'

Bernardo said calmly to Julian, as they distanced themselves from the hermit 'We are lucky he is not throwing his faeces at us. I have experienced some of these ogres resorting to physical aggression and losing any composure of holiness. Ten years ago an omo salvatico called Epifanio attacked some peasants in my highlands. He bit the men and would probably have killed them if help had not timely arrived to scare him away. On the next day, two hermits showed down in a village denouncing that Epifanio had murdered and eaten another monk. We sat a hue and cry and before the night fell the dogs managed to drag Epifanio out of the bottom of a cave. He was so savagely slashed by the mastini that he died from his wounds before being taken to the balivo in Lucca.'

'How horrible!' Julian gasped. 'Very unholy!'

'And it does not end there. One of the mastini died days after the struggle in the cave. So I feared for the two peasants who had been attacked, that Epifanio had the disease of the rabbia and could have transmitted it as he bit them. So I collected the poor men from their fields and took them to two physicians in Corsena. One of the physicians, Immanuel Malachi, who you know, said there was nothing to be done. He told me that if the men had the *rabbia* already, we could only pray for salvation of their souls, but if not, they should just go home. But the other physician, who settled in Corsena together with Immanuel, was the old shaman from the Magyar lands. He was worried that the poison from Epifanio's bite would turn his victims into dogs, or wolves. A *luppo mannaro*!'

'A lycantrope?' Julian asked. 'And did they change into wolves?'

'Well, the shaman opened their wounds and touched them with the back side of a rooster, while massaging the bird. Supposedly the vent of the rooster sucks the venom of the rabbia out. It turned out that both the shaman and Immanuel claimed to be right as both of the victims of the attack are still alive.'

In this moment, the fog dispersed in an instant, and they saw the track ahead meandering down to a grassy valley covered in flowers and endless more dark green peaks below them. Their faces welcomed the warmth of a clear sky.

'No more ogres, Julian.' Bernardo smiled warmly. 'No omo salvatico will venture out in the sunlight. They hate it!'

Julian sighed with relief. 'I'm glad there's no more of them!'

'See, Julian?' said Bernardo. 'Ogres are a nuisance to everyone. Just get your thoughts past them and your heart and soul are at ease. Now we should be in the next village early enough to eat.'

But as Bernardo had just spoken, a voice soared onto the clear mountain sky, coming up from behind the rocky crest of the pass they had just crossed '*Go back to your white castle and your woman! Keep watching and praying that she may not come into temptation; her spirit is willing, but her flesh is weak.*'

'Who said that?' Julian roared, turning in rage. The whole company also turned around to check the peaks and the rocky pass above them. But nothing could be seen. Only rocks and a clear blue sky.

'Never mind the hermits, Julian.' said Bernardo, kicking the flanks of his horse 'Their tortured minds are filled with filth. Never mind them...'

The Genovese Brothers

Old ferryman Testa knew of their reputation, but he was not intimidated by the imposing stance of his two passengers. Both men had respectfully paid for the crossing, but their cold stare discouraged Old Testa to engage into any of his cantankerous antics. Tall and quite alike, the passengers appeared to be distinguishable only by the colour of their long beards and hair: one was outlandish blonde and the other was fiery red.

Lamberto and Lanfranco had come from different families, not even related, although they were generally thought to be siblings, even twins. They were often referred to as the Genovese Brothers. Both lived in the castle of Moriano, in Sesto, a hamlet on the eastern shore midway between Chifenti and Lucca. Their routine was little more than making almost daily excursions into the vellutini slums, silk boilers and dyers in Lucca, to sell supplies and collect their fees for protection. If anyone among the Sicilian migrants and families required protection from mysterious criminal raids, they would owe Lamberto and Lanfranco a considerable fee for their immunity. In those matters, the brothers worked closely with their neighbour and supplier of goods, the man who owned all land south of Sesto: Antelmino di Gottefredo, the Castracani.

Now they had been the usual silent, not exchanging a word since leaving the castle of Moriano that morning. That is, except for when riding by Diecimo and rendering to the seduction of roasted chestnut.

'What do you think, *baccan*?' said Lanfranco, or maybe Lamberto. They treated each other by the Genovese term for boss, a derivation from the orgy-indulgent *baccanti*. 'Should we grab a sextarius of chestnuts?

'Why not?' answered the other. 'The best chestnuts are from these mountains. You pay, baccan?' They devoured all their roasted delights before getting to the Traghetto. And there was no need to talk: they knew exactly what to do: to keep quiet and inconspicuous, walking all the way to the mountain hamlet of Controne. In the parish of Santa Giulia, they were to deliver an ultimatum to the parishioner – to leave those lands forever and present the nun Caterina to the ecclesiastical authorities in Lucca. And after the clear advice, they were to take their cudgels and beat the parishioner mercilessly.

On the previous day, one of the Genovese brothers asked the man who was generously paying them for the task 'And what if the thrashing is so ferocious that the parishioner dies?'

The Castracani chuckled and said: 'Then, that will be God's will, I guess. Martino's time will be over and the gates of Hell will be opening for him.'

When the ferry with the Genovese Brothers crossed the short width of the Serchio, another passenger waited with his horse on the rocky bank of the old hospital. While Lanfranco and Lamberto jumped out of the boat and helped pull their own mounts out, Old Testa grunted to the man waiting: 'Oh you again? Why don't you just stay where you are?'

'Shut up and just take me to the other side!' said the man 'I am in a hurry.'

Lamberto and Lanfranco followed the road to Chifenti and rode up the lush track next to ford the Lima at Corsena. They silently crossed the steaming village towards the baths and took the steep track into the chestnut forest to get up to Controne. Luckily, for the Genovese Brothers, the somewhat confidential character of the mission was benefited by the summer season, when the *metati* were empty, with roasting ended by early spring, and no peasants collected through the forest floor or beat the roasted harvest with their *mazzaranghe*. And it was no season for chestnut lumber to feed the *carbonaie* either. Therefore, except for a few children that concentrated their attention in setting traps for blackbirds and squirrels, Lanfranco and Lamberto saw nobody else on their ascend to Controne. And best of all, as the parish of Santa Giulia clung over the mountainside, lower than the village of Controne, they would get to the church before seeing anyone else.

'Welcome strangers! What do you seek here in Controne?'

On the first instant, both Lamberto and Lanfranco were startled by that fresh voice, and somehow disappointed to be surprised, when *they* were supposed to be the stalkers. They saw a woman standing firmly at the entrance of the church yard. She was vigorously built and certainly not young at all, for her black mane seemed to have no qualms in displaying silver strands, but her face was jovial and the smile sincere. Both men knew this handsome figure could only have been Caterina, the woman of Father Martino. And the next thought that occurred to them both was that the parishioner was a man of good taste.

'We are looking for Father Martino' said one of them.

'The parishioner has left on an urgent trip to Luna.' she said decidedly, and without waiting for a reaction, Caterina added 'What matters do you come for? Would you like to come in? I can treat you with a goblet of honeyed wine.'

Both men looked at each other. 'What do you think, baccan?'

They had fallen to her charm and they knew the day's journey had been wasted.

'To Luna? The ruined White Castle? And are you telling me that you actually saw father Martino and let him escape through your hooves at the ferry?' Antelmino di Gottefredo asked, incredulous. He was meeting with Lanfranco and Lamberto in a small blacksmith shed under a large oak tree, exactly half way between Sesto and Antelmino's own Santo Stefano di Tassignano. The Genovese Brothers were exercising a great deal of tolerance and patience to sustain the nervous fit of the Castracani without telling him precisely where to go.

'We did see a man taking the ferry, and yes, he could have been the parishioner.'

'And you talked to his whore?' Antelmino asked, between gritted teeth.

The Genovese brothers exchanged a silent gaze. One of them would have to cut short that nuisance. He stood up with the hands on his belt, where a cudgel was visibly hanging. 'We did talk to the nun Caterina, yes. She welcomed us very courtly and...'

Antelmino yelled 'I care shit how that harlot took you in, but now she knows…'

'Let me finish, Antelmino di Gottefredo!' Lamberto said. Or it could have been Lanfranco. They were both standing, towering above Antelmino, who immediately bit his lip in, and the large man continued 'You offered us a generous payment for a task that was not fulfilled. We took no silver from you on this issue and we deserve none. We are out. You can find your own means to do whatever you want with the parishioner. Now listen here, Antelmino,' he said, pointing a finger towards the Castracani's nose 'we owe you nothing and we will be glad to continue our common endeavours at the vellutini. So if you care for it and for that delicate skin of yours, do not raise your voice at us, or we will be using our cudgels to shove this stupid hat of yours up your coward arse.'

Antelmino swallowed a lump of pride. He closed his eyes for calm and sense before asking 'I understand. Just one more question. What business had Martino in Luna? Did she tell you?'

The man with the yellow beard spit on the floor and said, before leaving with the other 'Apparently there has been a tragedy in Luna.'

The Kill

A horn sounded through the forest. At the end of the night, the cold wind dug its way through the passes, bringing down the woody flares, which were filtered by the beeches and arrived tenderly on the archers' ears. Three long blasts of mellow waxed horn, indicating to Bernardo delle Rocche that the group of beaters to travel furthest had reached their starting point and they were ready to come down. He waited for the answer from the other four groups. When the woods finally let through three long blasts and four short ones, they knew all the groups were coming down.

The hunt had started.

On the previous day, after the unpleasant encounters with the hermits at the passes, the company of hunters arrived at another alpine village encrusted in a tidy terraced forest of chestnut trees. It was still early in the afternoon when they settled among the obliging villagers. Although the lands belonged by written rights to the Obertenghi, at least according to registration books in the notaries and in the bishopric of Lucca and Luni, little was owed to their lords, other than a yearly clip of wool, lodgings, hospitality, and the eventual help on a hunt or war. While they warmed up by the smooth aroma of chestnut polenta mingled with the smoke of chestnut coal, a rich meal of lamb and farro was served to the whole company.

'Bernardo, I am not used to stable and bow hunting.' Julian had said during the meal, making an effort not to be lulled into drowsiness by the mellow aroma of that alpine food. 'My previous experience with the organised hunts has been with a leash of sighthounds or brachets. We go after one beast, rather than wait for the whole herd to pass by us.'

'How naïve!' Bernardo chuckled and taped Julian on the shoulder. 'Well, my friend, you will see what you have been missing. Here in the Apuane, we wait for the game. And when it comes, we harvest the forest!'

Now the beaters had started. Gusts of wind were bringing the racket from the horns and cymbals and the occasional yelp of the segugi down to the archers. It could still be at least a quarter of an hour before the first animals crossed the funnelled corridor where the archers stood on guard. Julian, Bernardo and two other bowmen waited, each facing the higher valley, standing with the back to a tree. Initially, the two bowmen had stated their preference to be behind the trees and shoot only when the game had passed by, but Bernardo refused. Any beast lost or not properly felled would be chased by the mastini. The man from Wald Ottavo would be holding the leash and ready to release his beasts down the creek. No arrows should fly in his direction.

Julian had a new bow, a present from Bernardo, made from yew trees by the bowyers of Monte Gargano, where Saint Michael was seen to have slain the beast. The longbow was much larger than the weapons Julian had grown up with, reaching a span of sixteen hands from the tips of the limbs, dangerously brushing against his sword's scabbard. The string was waxed hemp, made in the Monastero de San Zorzo, in Genova. Bernardo had recently tried an alternative string of silk from Lucca. It was indeed stronger than gut or sinew, but not as resistant as hemp, in addition to being a strenuously expensive experiment. Julian had practiced with his new bow several times over the last two days, adjusting his aim to the new size, but he was not yet completely comfortable with it, probably more due to the inconsistency of the arrow make or the blunt arrowheads than the bow itself. Now, with proper sharpened steel broadheads, Julian had to trust the craft of the fletchers and accept that he had a precise mortal weapon on his hands. It had to be precise enough to pass through a galloping wild boar, which came ploughing through the forest floor, like a falling star shooting towards the archers.

'It's yours, Julian!' Bernardo yelled. 'A sow! The best meat of the forest!'

There were plenty of arrows stuck in the ground around each of the bowmen. Julian, however, preferred to use the arrows packed into his back quiver, even though it required his arms to reach further high over his shoulders. He would only resort to the ground arrows when his leather quiver was empty. While the sow continued its landslide, Julian's movements were smooth and obeyed a sequence that was not acknowledged by his thoughts. Hunting felt to have come from a much older blood-related heritage than just a learned skill. His eyes calculated the speed of the black monster coming down the valley. As his dominant left eye focused on the beast, his right hand firmly gripped the bow handle, while the left made a swift arch towards the quiver. The fingertips felt the trimmed goose feather fletchers and swiftly slipped between them in a soft caress, pressing firmly around the back tip of the arrow and pulling it out in another arch, as an extension of his limb. The arrow never stopped, but was smoothly slipped into the notch and pulled back as Julian tensed his muscles to keep the bow arm raised and firmly steady, drawing the string with the other. The tension was highest when the string touched his nose, when beast was just above the target, when the moment was right to release the fingers of the drawing hand. An explosion of power overwhelmed the twang of the release, all converted into straight flight, plunging directly into the flank of the sow.

The bowmen felt the skin of their faces blown away by the monstrous squeal broken out by the fallen animal.

'I missed it!' Julian hissed. 'I missed the God-forsaken neck. She is still alive!' he said, throwing the bow to the side and drawing his sword.

'Leave it Julian!' Bernardo cried. 'We'll shoot her!' but he knew it was too late. Julian was already waiting on guard, and the sow was ready to attack. 'Here she comes, Julian! It's now or never! Prepare for the Hellmouth!' Bernardo shouted, with a strange excitement in his words. The beast opened her jaws wide and hissed. She raised her head and looked straight into Julian's eyes, sprinting from the spot where she was shot, carrying more than half an arrow inside her as if nothing had affected her muscles, tendons or guts. Squealing as a demon, and presenting all of her large fangs to her victim, she charged against Julian, and all she could see was a silver circle of steel drawn in front of her and a blast of pain on her face. The sow did not realise she had lost not only her enemy but also the front half of her head. And in less than another second, her heart was cut in two by a plunge of Julian's sword with another swing of his arms.

'Bravo!' roared the three bowmen, but Bernardo was quick to add 'Julian, get back to your tree.'

Julian immediately swiped the blood from his blade on the sow's back and sheathed his sword, jumping back to the tree. Not only because of Bernardo's warning. It was the ground. It was shaking and rumbling.

The hinds came in herds. They were the fastest and the noblest of all does, leading the parade of beasts that cascaded down the gorge. In a desperate attempt to protect their calves from the threatening blare that surrounded them above on the valley, the panicked hinds huddled in their fast gallop and did little to avoid running towards the bowmen that shot them. This time Julian released the string at the right time. The hind collapsed while the other beasts just leaped over it. Julian released the air from his lungs. He could breathe, at last.

The archers felled another two and let dozens more go by, without a pursuit by the mastini. The dogs were being spared for more precious game. Strangely, no harts came down with those females. The rumbling continued. The yelping of the segugi was louder, being clearly distinguished from the cymbals and horns. A few *daino* does and their calves were let through, before a large pair of flattened antlers was seen coming down the woods. 'Here's a trophy!' Bernardo yelled. The fallow buck quickly increased in size, storming down towards his tree. It was his call and his shot. A fraction of a second of hesitation would make Bernardo miss the daino. But the arrow dove deep into the beast's ample chest. The shock was enough to topple the monster. It collapsed under its stampeding force, folding the massive body over its neck and head, sliding through the ground right towards the direction where the arrow had come from. While Julian yelled for Bernardo to seek protection, the shepherd's heart stopped beating as he saw the pair of shovelled antlers with sharp tines quickly advancing under the huge mass of the buck raised to vertical position, a killing device about to crush him against the tree. He could not walk out. There was no time. Even if he tried, the sliding antlers that were about to cut through the arrows in the ground like a sickle and would probably split his legs in half.

Yet, guardian angels are often ready at attention when least expected to be. Bernardo's was kind enough to allow him the time and space to leap to the side to avoid the heavy daino, which crashed on the tree. A shock so violent that the thick beech trunk was heard to crack, as did the antlers, which folded forwards, clashing against one another around it, like hands in prayer, showing to Bernardo this ancient bodily discipline to obey, when heart and soul raise their voices to divine powers.

The fallen daino was leaning dead on the trunk and all of Bernardo's arrows had been broken. He made sure he still had his bow on hand and ran to join Julian, while mentally making a prayer to thank his angel.

The mastini were restless. The clatter of the beaters was closer, but no more beasts appeared to be coming down the ravine. A small boar ran by with a few piglets, but the bowmen let them through. 'Where are they? Where's the rest?' Bernardo asked.

'Maybe this is it...' Julian suggested, almost slipping a smile through his lips.

'Certainly not!' Bernardo protested. 'We should see ten times more beasts than that!'

'We have heaps of meat for all the men to carry.' Julian said, without taking his eyes off the woods. 'A boar, three large hinds and a daino. Who needs more?'

'I can always distribute the game among the villages around' Bernardo said. 'But I cannot believe that the forest is so empty. 'Something must have happened.'

A few more animals came down. The archers easily felled two more hinds, four roe deer and a large boar, before the company of beaters appeared from the woods, chasing the last hind. She was going to escape by a western slope when a visibly annoyed Bernardo asked one of the bowmen to shoot her in the back. As the hind fell wounded, Bernardo turned around and gave to sign for the large Lombard to release the mastini.

'We should not deprive these good dogs from the pleasure of the chase', he said to Julian. 'Disappoint them now and expect them to fail you next time.'

All except one group of beaters, from the western slope, had arrived. Bernardo grew nervous. As the smell of blood drove the segugi and the mastini to stretch the leashes standing with excitement on their hind legs, the chasseurs indicated to Bernardo and Julian that the quarry had been plentiful, but much of it had been lost as they escaped through a gap on the western slope.

'Sound the horn!' Bernardo ordered. 'Let's find those lazy bastards! We have no hart among our kill because of them. We will start the butchering with the daino then. *A fucking daino with broken antlers!*

One short blast from the horn, three longs and a short one told the forest that the chase was over and the unmaking was about to start.

They waited for an answer.

From not too far away, four short blasts indicated that the final group was arriving. Bernardo exhaled the tension.

While the dogs watched with excitement, the big fallowbuck was turned on its back and the one of the men from Bernardo's team slit the skin of its throat with a narrow-bladed knife, extending the cut down the neck and opening the skin in two flaps. The chasseurs stood back and allowed the segugi to run and tear at the flesh of the neck for a while, as a reward for their obedience and understanding that their hard efforts meant in the end a fresh meal. They were then withdrawn for the turn of the mastini, which were unleashed separately, not to damage the lymers or each other during any confrontation as they slashed through the meat. Once the dogs were contained, the cut was slit further towards the rear end and to the limbs, around the leg joints and around the head. The skin was pulled away towards the spine, spread out as a sheet where the naked carcass was ready to be butchered.

'Where were you?' Bernardo roared, as the final group of four men appeared. 'Your delay and your gap ruined our stake!'

The men were visibly embarrassed by their failure, but something worse had stricken their faces. Bernardo noticed they were trembling. 'What in the devil has happened?' he asked.

'We lost one of our men!' the group leader said, shooting a quick glance at Julian.

The chasseurs stopped the butchering of the fallowbuck, as a general protest of dread broke through the woods. Bernardo let his shoulders drop and implored 'Oh merciful God! Tell me what happened! An accident? Did he fall from a ravine?'

The chasseur hesitantly turned to look at Julian and all the others from his group. They all nodded and lowered their eyes. Finally, he firmed his lips and said. 'We killed him.'

A pair of testicles was hanging on a stick forked at the top, the *forcella*, sided by loops of intestines, kidneys and a heart. Stuck in the ground, the forcella was no longer than Bernardo's own shepherd's crook. The noblest parts of the fallen daino were to be saved for Bernardo and Julian. The lungs were given to the hounds, with red-dripping pieces of bread that had been soaked in the pool of blood inside the opened skin. The dogs chomped on their prizes with joy, in complete oblivion to a murder which had just been revealed. As they devotedly crunched the segments of trachea which were carefully divided among them, hardly did they know that nobody could point precisely who the victim was.

'It was certainly not one of us!' Julian said, intrigued. 'My team is all here, complete with us and there's no suspicion of anyone else that could have come during these days.'

On hearing that, the chasseur got more distressed 'But we could swear he was a *Lunensis*!' he insisted, 'For the rest of us were all from Bernardo delle Rocche's lands in the Serchio valley.'

The alpine villagers also assured Bernardo that their group was complete.

'Who the fuck could it be then?' Bernardo burst, with the best of a hunter's vocabulary 'and why did you kill him?'

'We do not know who he was, my Lord. We assumed he was from Luna' the chasseur said humbly, but not missing to take a few quick glances at Julian. 'We had to stop him. The man just would not respect. He was being more than inappropriate.'

'What do you mean *inappropriate*?' Bernardi roared. 'How dare you have the right to kill in the name of appropriateness?' he asked. Julian stayed a step behind. As long as no man of his had been hurt, he had better leave this bitter matter for Bernardo to solve, but he would be handy for any support.

Nobody could come up with anything else to say. They just dropped their gazes to the leafy, bloody ground. All the rest of the company who had arrived in time just remained dead silent, pathetically pretending that nothing was happening.

Bernardo exploded 'If no man will have the *testicoli* to tell us what happened, then you are all murderers! We ride to Lucca and we will leave you with the balivo and his executioner. Your heads will be rolling in front of San Martino in less than a week!'

Finally, the best forest tracker in the group, a small man called Massimo, from the village of Colugniola, thinned his lips and stepped forward. 'I am not prepared to have a sword through my neck for that low vermin' he said with clenched fists 'I'll tell you what went on up by the forest rim.'

'Pour it out then, Massimo.' Bernardo ordered.

'However,' the tracker said raising a finger and shooting another furtive glance at Julian, 'I want a firm guarantee that the Lord Julian will bear to hear it all, so he'll be able to understand what drove us to execute that man.'

At the same time that Bernardo said *What?*, Julian jumped up and fronted Massimo up 'Me? Why me?' he asked with a lump up his throat. 'This is *none* of my direct business!'

Massimo cleared his throat. 'I am sorry to disagree with you publicly, Lord Julian, but we killed that man because of the horrendous things that man said about your wife. Yes my Lord, we killed him to defend the honour of the Lady Clarissa.'

The Road from Zena

In spite of the scorching sun, which was more implacable than the worst summers they were accustomed to bear, the ride from Zena had been rather pleasant so far. As they gained ground through the appreciated shadows of aged holm oaks and olive groves, the lord and the lady were delighted to be sprayed by the cool breeze of a turquoise Ligurian sea, a shining rainbow so different from the grey muddy ocean they had seen before, on a pilgrimage to the great abbey of Saint Michael. And no less entertaining than the colourful scenario of enlightened benevolence, was the talkative company of the old monk.

'This is enough walking for the morning' said the lord to the monk, as they rode up a steep hill that took their view away from the sea. 'Again I must insist you should use one of our mounts.' He pointed to the four men-at-arms and a couple of carrier mules that accompanied them.

The monk stopped, looked at the horses and smiled back with his toothless gums 'Thank you my lord' he said with that ever bizarre Genovese accent 'but I can do the walk. It makes me a better man!'

Lord and lady looked at each other, shrugged their shoulders and continued. They camped for a mid-day meal before the road meandered down towards the sea again. The *via Aemilia Scauri* was mostly wide and well paved, taking the best advantage of the terrain, a fortunate inheritance from Roman times which had endured eleven centuries.

The men-at-arms were clumsily trying to turn edible a fish they had purchased in Zena before sunrise. The noble couple were nauseated by the milky dripping sizzle of the roast fish, no matter how many coats of aromatic herbs it received. The monk heard the lord uttering harsh foreign words and figured it was a tone of dissatisfaction.

'My lord, it appears the *büdegassa* does not suit your appetite.'

'As a matter of fact, it doesn't!' the lord said with irritation. 'We were fooled by your merchants in Zena to pay dearly for this fish, but it smells as bad as it looks. That's worse than a *carpe*!'

The monk smiled in acquiescence 'The büdegassa is a valued fish for its sweetness and delicate flavour. But I can understand how foreigners could be intimidated by its monstrous appearance, so much that northern fisherman call it *diavolo de mar*.'

'*Sea devil?* I don't shy away from appearance or names,' the lord said, not less annoyed 'but it's the sickening stench of the cooked flesh. That indeed must smell like the devil!'

'I can share my Musetto with you, if the lord and the lady would prefer instead' the monk said, presenting to them a pungent-smelling bundle of meat.

'Musetto?' the lord asked standing up to examine the wrap on the monk's satchel. 'I have heard this name before.'

'This is a dolphin's stomach' said the monk, looking with amusement at the disgusted faces drawn by the noble couple. He explained that although dolphins were fish, appropriate for that Friday, their flesh tasted more like game, but to no help. The travellers kindly declined.

'But Musetto,' insisted the lord. 'Where is this name from?' He looked at his wife, who had the same inquisitive countenance.

The monk cleared his throat. 'The Musetto was the chief pirate from Daniyya.'

'That's the one!' the lord cheered. 'The Saracen who was in Luna?'

'The same,' the monk nodded. 'It was a few years ago when the Saracen ships swarmed the Ligurian sea, driving the dolphins to our shores, where they could be easily speared. Dolphin meat is tough but, in that year, the afflicted rabbles around our country had plenty to eat. The dried stomachs were packed in our storages in the monastery of San Zorzo, but no matter how much we convinced the ignorant peasants that the food was granted by God, they still kept calling it a gift of the Musetto.' He ripped one last piece of the leathery bundle and tucked the remaining volume into his satchel. 'That has been a few years already,' he said, almost unintelligibly, with the leathery piece moistening between his gums. 'Today dolphins are still caught once in a while. Their entrails are dried and given to the monasteries. A good desiccated stomach keeps for days, so we can take on our journeys and I know it goes even as far as the monastery San Comban de Bêubbi.

As they kept walking down, the lord did seem to be uninterested in the dolphin stomach, but not on the Saracen. 'Tell me of the siege in Luna. Who was it that expelled the Musetto from the white castle?'

The monk said, very casually, looking out towards the new stretch of a glorious sandy beach that appeared ahead of them: 'Why, it was the pope, our warrior Pope Benedict VIII, of course. Everyone knows about it.' He noticed the lord and the lady dropping their shoulders in disappointment.

The riding noble approached his horse to his wife's, to tenderly take her hand. They rode holding hands for a while.

An obviously foreign couple of evident noble lineage, given their high bearing and the craftsmanship of their fine but discreet attire. The man was fit for his age, carrying an excess of belly which made itself more obvious whenever he rode a horse. He had the long hair of nobility, grizzly and still quite generous, tied up on the top of his head like the old kings of his land, but only kept to the length that his powerful suzerain would have allowed to grow. The silver beard was shaggy and cut rather short, exactly to the length that his wife would allow it to grow. The lady was probably younger, but already past her mid years. However, no excesses in her shape revealed any accumulated time under her skin. She carried a cheerful mood on this trip, re-drawing the lines of suffering that had already dug deep trenches on her face. The hair was unresolved. Strands of brown, red and white revealed a past of fiery exuberance. They were both knowledgeable and talkative, communicating well with the old monk that had kindly joined their troupe on that day. They had not exchanged another word when the monk pointed out to where the beach met the cliffs. 'Look there. *Vitelli marini*, sea-veals!'

The travellers initially saw nothing, focusing their eyes better they disguised about a dozen bodies lying along the sand, resembling giant skins of wine basking in the cliff shadows. 'What are they?' asked the lady. 'Don't they have legs?'

'Of course not, said the monk. We call them veals, but they are actually fish, with flippers instead of limbs. The Romans call them *phocae*.'

'But fish do not come out of the water like those,' the lady said.

The monk turned to her and said firmly, as if offended by that stupid remark: 'But these do!' The company walked down the beach to see the dark lazy beasts. As they approached, the vitelli marini, which were indeed as big as cows, moved clumsily back to the water, struggling to drag their limbless fat bodies by wriggling and sliding over the sand, until they disappeared through the waves. 'Reeking stupid animals these are,' said the monk, 'a good fisherman could have speared the full dozen before they'd be lost in the water.

'Are they edible, these fish?' the lord asked.

'The hide is quite valuable,' the monk explained. 'A well-tanned pelt can fetch a few silver denarii in Rome. That's because a man travelling in a cloak of sea-veal hide can never be struck by lightning. It's also used for book covers. The bishop of Bêubbi, who is the abbot at San Comban, has his bible covered in sea-veal pelt.

They say the fur on the book cover rises and bristles when storms come about. The fat is useful, and the flesh is little appreciated among fishermen. Tough and gristly, it would be thrown back into the sea if not gratefully taken by those humble souls in need.'

Several fishing villages with slate-roofed shacks dotted the via Aemilia Scauri. The road turned south, bordering an ocean slowly losing its blue to reflect a silver sunlight directly on the travellers' squinting eyes. By the time they approached a small inhabited island at the southern point of a well-protected bay, the monk pointed to his destination. It was San Zoan monastery, hidden in the woods of the island of Sizestri Levante.

The monk suggested the travellers stayed overnight at his religious house. 'If you are riding to Luna,' he calculated, 'you won't find anywhere to stay before you reach the port of il Poggio, half the way from here. Do accept our hospitality for this evening and leave rested tomorrow morning. Our humble house of God does not know luxury, but it should be as welcoming as His heart.'

Lord and lady accepted the hospitality, as they had done since leaving their land far to the North. The men-at-arms camped in the continent, while a boat took the others to the island. The dinghy was lit by torches exhaling a fragrance that was pleasant to the visitors.

'I should not be surprised by the different customs of foreigners,' the old monk said, as the oarsman slowly brought the dinghy towards the island. 'We find the stink of this sea-veal oil rather offensive to our noses, but if you like it, then you won't mind the humble meal we are likely to have before retiring to sleep, as it is Friday and we should be eating fish – actually sea-veal pie!' he said shyly 'You know, we are those humble ones in need...'

The lord took another whiff from the smoke that flew from the torch and said 'I'm quite sure it will be far superior to that *diabolo*!'

'So what takes you to Luna?' asked the abbot rather casually, as he watched both visitors devour their *vitello marin* pie. All other monks sat at the table ate in silence and avoided staring at the visitors.

'We want to see the lord of the castle' the lord answered.

'The Marchese Oberto died a few years ago, when the Musetto came with his fleet' explained the abbot rather casually, but still carefully observing the visitors. 'And right now the new lord of the *marca* Alberto Azzo does not make his home in Luna.'

'But our visitors don't go for Alberto,' said the old monk that had brought them across. 'They go to see his brother-in-law, the Lord Zulian!'

'Julian!' corrected the visitor.

'Yes, Zulian!' confirmed the old monk.

'Oh, Zulian?' said the abbot, suddenly joyful and amused, 'I have met the lord Zulian, a goodhearted and kind man.' The abbot saw the faces of the visitors open a wide smile, but he missed to notice the tears suddenly flooding the lady's eyes. 'Zulian was the man who, alone on his horse, managed to expel the Musetto and his hordes from Luna!'

The visitor froze his smile suddenly 'But we just heard it was the Holy Father Benedict VIII, who came to battle from Rome' he said, still amused, looking at the old monk.

The abbot gave a quick glance towards the old monk. 'He knows *nothing*,' he said, with a touch of despise. 'That's the story everyone tells these days. But there are few who know what happened. It was Zulian!'

'We believe you!' the visitors said, cringing with satisfaction.

'Do you know the lord Zulian?' the abbot asked intrigued.

They both nodded and answered proudly 'Julian is our son!'

It looked like the rain was about to start pouring, but they were both happy to have made it to the white castle. While the mountains had been smothered in clouds, the towers could be seen from a while back after they stopped for a midday meal. They had brought a good supply of olives and dried fruits from the Monastery of San Zoan in Sizestri Levante and a few pastries with sea-veal meat that had lasted until they got to the town of il Poggio.

While the clouds embraced the whole coast with threatening rumbling, the noble couple hurried the pace towards their final destination. Just when the white castle was clearly visible in the horizon, they saw a beautiful woman standing on the road, holding her horse. The westbound wind blew a majestic mane of brown hair and clung her dress and cape to an elegant shape of youth. Behind her, a few other riders maintained a distance.

'I am Clarissa of Luna!' the woman on the road said, extending her hand and looking at those foreigners with a festival of colours in her eyes. 'Travellers leaving il Poggio this morning advised me of your visit. You two must be Raoul and Emma of Mans.' She opened a smile when the Lady Emma almost fell from her horse. 'Your son is my husband, Julian of Luni!'

'Oh God be praised!' sobbed Emma, as she ran to embrace that dreamlike woman; that palpable, warm and huggable proof that their son was alive and well cared for. Clarissa held the viscountess up as Emma shed a lake of tears that had been fed by nineteen years of anguish. Raoul joined them and cried with both.

'There is so much to be said and heard.' Clarissa said, riding between the couple as the first drops of rain started to fall. 'So much to be shared! But Julian will be back tomorrow night, or the day after. He is well. Just taking a few days on a hunt with a friend he met when he first came from Mans to these lands.' She pretended not to notice the glances the viscount exchanged with his wife as soon as hunting was mentioned. 'But you need to hear from him of his life ever since he left you. And I am sure you will want to know the reasons for leaving you too.'

'But meanwhile,' the viscount said, 'we will be delighted to hear what you have to tell us of your life with Julian.'

Clarissa smiled radiantly 'For me, that will be more than describing the world and heavens to you!'

And the showers opened from the clouds.

They talked on as the path meandered over the wet marshland, their voices getting louder, until they found themselves entering the castle gates, never even noticing how cold and heavy the rain had become.

'Our home has been terribly damaged since the siege of the Musetto.' Clarissa said. 'We have not found the means or the moment to renovate it deservingly yet. So as the guest rooms were mostly in the area destroyed during the recapturing of Luna, you will probably rest better by using my own bed. It is a large tick filled with duck feathers, much softer than any other woollen, straw or leaf mattress we have in Luna.'

'You should not bother, child!' said Emma. 'We are hardy people who can sleep on simple palliasses...'

'I don't bother. I just insist!' interrupted Clarissa with a kind smile. She took the couple by the hands and showed them to the main bedroom, where the rain pounded on the carpets blocking the windows. A servant came quickly with two candles for some light, as the hearth was already reduced to embers. Clarissa pointed to the water jar and bowl, woollen covers, pelts and pillows. 'These pillow-bearers are silken, a present from the Lucchese bankers. In case you find them overly smooth and unpleasant at the touch, you can use some canvas covers from the same chest as the pelts.' A number of curtains and hangings were rolled up the suspended canopy that hung over from the ceiling. 'I will keep the tester rolled up, for it will allow more heat from the fireplace. I'm also sending a servant to revive and steady the hearth, and bring you a jar of hot water. If you prefer, do feel free to release the hangings from the canopy.'

'Thank you so much, my dear.' Raoul said. 'Right now we are so exhausted that we could lie as we are. Worry no more about us and carry on with your duties. Emma and I can both skip supper and we will probably be fresh and rested as the sun rises.'

'Then, be at ease,' Clarissa suggested with a slight bow. 'The fire will be ready in a moment.' She gave instructions to the household and braved the rain to head to the stables.

Perhaps not a quarter of an hour later, as Clarissa saw to the needs of the two men-at-arms and their horses, a servant told her that the Lord Julian had just arrived. Clarissa ran back and noticed that Julian's horse, beaten and worn out, being taken to the stables. That's when she heard the screaming inside.

Filth

The chasseur Massimo started: 'We reached the forest rim and detached from the rest of the company after having walked for half an hour. While waiting for that horn signal, that disturbing man decided to casually recite to us the tales of a certain *black rider.*'

Bernardo and Julian listened attentively, while the others maintained their eyes down. A few pieces of venison were sizzling over a shy fire. Julian sweated profusely. 'I have never heard or seen such black rider!' he grunted.

'That was his point,' Massimo continued, 'He told us the black rider was a cunning foreigner who had been going to Luna for many years already. He would visit Luna in the absence of ...' he cleared his throat and looked at Julian, who reacted irritably.

'In the absence of whom?'

'Please don't be angry at me, Lord Julian! I am just telling you why we-'

'I am not!' Julian said, almost to himself, 'I am not pouring my anger at you, good man. I am only apprehensive about the insanity of this moment. Do carry on.'

Massimo assented. 'The man said the black rider would visit Luna during your absence, Lord Julian! He seemed to know the exact dates when you had left the castle and the black rider came in to take your place...'

'Take my place?' Julian was shaking his head.

'Yes, my lord. To take your place in bed, with the Lady Clarissa.'

Julian leaped up with eyes closed, tight-fisted. While only the muffled crackling of the wet lumber fire was all that was heard, he walked out leaving the group behind, the carcasses, the hunters, the farce. *What they were about to tell him was not true. Of course it was a sham. The dead man was insane, he provoked, he calumniated. Clarissa would never be untrue to him. She was not Helena. He was not Buonaccorso. But why? Why would this man come up with those lies? What would he achieve with venom, rather than a well-deserved dagger through his neck? Deserved. Done!* Julian walked back. 'Please continue, Massimo. Just finish the story.'

'When the man suggested the Lady Clarissa had been unfaithful, we demanded he retracted and apologised, but to no good. He laughed and told us that whatever he said made no difference to the truth. He mentioned that on that very hour the black rider was arriving in Luna to take the lady Clarissa at her own will.' Massimo paused while Julian gritted his teeth. The hunter continued 'On that moment, at least three of us unsheathed our daggers and pressed them against that man's neck, demanding the unsaying, the apology,' Massimo said, shaking his head and spitting on the leafy ground. 'But it seemed that a blade against the throat drove him to challenge death with the worst of his poison. He said the Lady Clarissa was a *fornicatrix*, a *vulgaris meretrix* whose sensual delights had to be satisfied by a stranger; that she laughed with her lovers while the Lord Julian obliviously wore the horns of the *cucco* on his head during his visits to Lucca or this hunting on the Apuane.' He waited for Julian to curse again and continued 'The man was insane! He wriggled under our blades, impossible to be held down. By this moment our rage overwhelmed our fists, pushing the daggers firmer and the blood was already flowing over his chest. When he noticed it, the mad man laughed and whispered more obscenities until his body fell limp...'

There was another silence. Some of the other hunters nodded, confirming Massimo's version of the facts. A thunder broke up high above the mountains.

'And where is this bastard?' Bernardo asked, trying to get everyone's attention out of Julian's reaction.

'When we realised he was dead, the hunting horns sounded across the woods for the start of the chase. We took time to decide what to do, that's why we were late. His body was left under the one single silver fir on the western edge of the valley. A giant among the smaller beeches. It could be seen from any point outside of the forest.'

'And if the body has been taken by wolves, or a bear...or by Turul?' Bernardo asked, pensive 'how can you prove your story?' he notice that Julian could be exploding into pieces at any moment.

Massimo shook his head. 'I have no shame on my participation on the death of that man. There are four of us who can bear witness to my words, and at least a thick pool of blood that lies down under that fir tree.'

Julian finally let the air come out of his lungs, breaking out 'I need my horse!'

'Where are you going, Julian?' Bernardo asked. 'The horses are far away. We should move together!'

Julian sweated coldly 'I must go Bernardo. I have to see this dead man. I should be in Luna, seeing that Clarissa is well.'

'Those were lies, Julian! Filthy lies from a madman!' an alarmed Bernardo implored 'You cannot let yourself be taken by it.'

'Sorry...' Julian said. 'Apologies for not staying. This was a mistake. A big mistake. I should have stayed.' And he left, walking towards the horses.

'We can all go Julian!' Bernardo insisted. 'We can leave the quarry behind. I can accompany you...'

'No!' Julian demanded. He had turned to him firmly. 'I thank you for this arrangement, Bernardo, but I have had bad experiences when I hunt. I must do this on my own. Good bye!'

The giant silver fir appeared through the rain on a rare moment when the mist seemed to dissipate, showing the naked rock of the mountains diving into the steep ocean of beeches. No human track cut through those woods. Julian's horse was carefully stepping through a wet rocky slope under a slippery sheet of dried leaves. The dark shelter of the forest was no barrier to the heavy drops that soaked the ground. Julian saw the signs of the hunters and followed them, until he reached the said fir tree, looming above him. He could see no cadaver lying against the massive trunk, but it must have been around the other side. He left the horse and climbed the next few steps until he emerged out of the forest, under the thick, protected canopy of the fir. And no sign of any corpse.

There was not a drop of blood to be seen. Only herbs grew on that side. Where was the pooled blood that Massimo had reported? No wolves, bears or vultures could have removed a corpse so cleanly or eaten it entirely so timely. The only possibility would be that he was looking at the wrong tree. But as if the angels or demons that lower the fog or bring down the rains had understood Julian's puzzlement, the mist was lifted for a moment and Julian could devise the forest line towards north and south. That was the only fir tree around.

No sign of death had survived that site. Julian sniffed the air, but only the pleasant scent of the rain washed down the sweet, resinous aroma of the fir. It was only when he started to climb down the rocks behind the tree that he caught a whiff of putrefaction. That herbal reek that he knew so well. The *koriannon*!

Julian knew the herb and had learned to dislike it. He would not expect the koriannon to be growing on those heights, in that zone. There was just the ominous feel about it. It was growing along the western side of the trunk, where supposedly the corpse had been laid against. With his stomach about to pop out of his mouth, Julian watched the growth pattern of the herb. The shape told him everything: He had to run!

Horse and man broke through branches, tripping over stones and lose ground as Julian chose the shortest, but perhaps the most inconvenient way to reach the Ligurian side of the Apennines. The short glimpses of the mountains had given him the knowledge of where the terrain led and the pass he should be reaching, but as the night fell, the ride was severely slowed down. When Julian felt he had again reached the top edge of the forest, high near the passes, the rain insistently fell on thick drops, blinding even the darkness away from him. His horse became uneasy. Nothing could be seen, except a spot of light that hung in front of Julian's eyes. A yellow glow in the distance, a fire burning bright somewhere ahead of him.

Under a hard-pouring rain, Julian dismounted the troubled horse and pulled the beast by hand, carefully advancing through alpine rocks and bush, using the unaffected fire as a target for his erroneous climb. The light grew ahead of him with his slow progress, flames withstanding the severity of the rain, probably in a metato - chestnut drying shed - or maybe a carbonaia that still burned inside its cooking core with beech or chestnut logs. But a closer look revealed a wide cave entrance. And Julian saw the profile of an animal standing near the fire. A goat.

A light coloured doe with long spiralling horns curved backwards, with the tip almost touching its tail. It stood there, trembling with the cold, or better, shaking as another animal that suckled on its teats, a small black, hairy beast, maybe a porcupine or a tiny suckling boar. It was only when Julian's horse nickered quite loud through the roaring rain that the startled goat turned to them, revealing that she had not two, but only a single horn, planted between its eyes. And on the next second, the goat leaped into the darkness, disappearing from view. Julian had little time to consider that strange beast, for the other dark thing that suckled on its teats suddenly raised itself from the ground and stood upon a full body, looking at Julian.

It was a man.

And in spite of the icy weather, he seemed to be comfortably naked.

The wild man was grinning at Julian. He ran back and forth, from one side of the cave entrance to the other, giggling as a rain-soaked Julian slowly approached.

'Did you bring me cheese?' the man asked.

Julian said 'No.'

The hairy man changed his expression to one of rage and screamed at Julian 'I can make my own! I don't need you.' And he calmed down, panting through the hair that covered his entire face. Now he whispered 'Nobody needs you! Not even your woman needs you!'

Julian unsheathed his sword. 'What devilry is this you say, insane man?' he asked already irritated. The wild man recoiled. Looking around, Julian saw a littered cave, lined with roots and stalactites on the ceiling and a layer of droppings on the floor, which could have been from goats, birds and the man's own. The rancid reek would have been insulting to any beast's lair. There were bones, from large and tiny animals, thorn brambles with lizard-looking creatures impaled on them, strange circular drawings with flowers on the walls, flickering in gold and silver reflecting the lively flames, and a colossal oxen skull hanging above them all, the tips of its horns reaching across the cave entrance. The cave meandered deeper into a hostile dark tunnel.

The wild man giggled again, nervously hopping around, not losing sight of the shiny blade pointing at him wherever he went.

'This morning, there was a dead man,' Julian said, following the unsettling creature with his sword. 'Under a large silver fir, two valleys to the southeast. He's disappeared. Do you know of him?'

'I know of all dead men!' the wild creature said, looking at Julian with his congested red eyes deeply dug into his hairy face. 'They are burning!' he said, slobbering, crumbling his giggles into a cackle. 'But this one? Who knows? The forest takes a body away in the blink of an eye. Spiders! Magpies! *Lupi manari* - werewolves! They will eat you before your heart stops beating!' he foamed. The saliva stuck to his beard and body hair, together with soil and plants and only the devil knows what else. Julian had to stand firmly on the ground to endure the thick shield of stench that involved that creature.

'You make no sense, do you?' Julian concluded. 'You are nothing more than a miserable soul, lost and forgotten in this God-forsaken shithole.'

The wild creature laughed and stooped suddenly. He crouched and concealed his head between his knees. 'I am nobody worthy, really. Just a sinner who's condemned to eternal damnation!' he looked up to Julian and hissed 'But you think you are the only living man on these heights, noble man? No,' his brown teeth ripped through a hairy smile, 'you are not! There are loggers and carbonai around these woods that take forbidden game from their lords, there are witches who come to collect flowers and dance on the high meadows,' he was already growling at Julian 'there are chestnut gatherers who bring their boys to the woods and use them as women for their filth; there is the black rider that hurries to the castle to mount the lady when the lord is out...'

Julian felt a sickening large boulder crushing over his heart 'What? What castle?' he demanded, almost cracking his jaws from the force of gritting 'What do you know about a black rider?' He kept his guard up.

'Oh, the white castle!' the wild man said and chuckled to himself. 'I can smell her.'

'You can smell who?' Julian felt the boulder rolling down to press against his stomach. Outside the storm rumbled incessantly.

'I can smell the lady! The scent of her heat! Yes, her cunt!' he drooled 'her precious lovely flower that opens to the black rider while her husband is hunting away!' his lips were foaming and his eyes rolling up. He sniffed the air. 'And even through the thick rain I can sniff it, her warmth, the sensuous desire, and the seed! A whiff of the black rider's seed, pouring out of her...'

Without any clear understanding of what he was doing, Julian roared and swung his sword with revulsion as soon as he noticed the wild man had been masturbating to his own poisonous words. The steel point ran close but very superficially, opening a wide gash on the wild man's chest. He screeched with hatred at Julian, raising his hairy arms forward, showing the long black fingernails and exposing his fanglike rotten teeth, but refrained from sprinting for the attack when the sword was back pointing at his face.

'Go away before I kill you!' Julian demanded. 'Go back to hell!'

The wild man spat on Julian's face and leaped back, disappearing in the black tunnel.

Julian ran back outside to wipe the sputum under the rain, to wash those filthy words from his mind, to cleanse the thoughts. Closing his eyes, his hand wiped down the face with the cold rain and he tried to breathe freely for a second. He was just not prepared to open them again and see a giant standing in front of him. And this time it was a towering bear.

Wide, tall and furry, it lowered its head and opened its jaws wide, ripping an earth-quaking roar through its long killer fangs, a howl that hit Julian straight on the face, making his suddenly standing sword tremble.

Julian was frozen. Whether it was the threatening raised sword or any plan of guardian angels, the bear came down to his paws and just walked around Julian, grunting and steaming, swinging its brown thick pelt to the sides as it moved. Its shoulders could have been as high as Julian's. A massive beast that ignored the fragile man with the metal blade and sprinted towards the cave. Julian just saw the giant brown body avoiding the dying fire and disappearing growling into the same hole where the wild man had gone. And an uncomfortable voice inside him suggested 'That was a bear! I wish Clarissa had been here to see that one...'

Clarissa!

A cracking thunder snapped nearby. A deafening blast of crushing stones and large trees bending their trunks, lingering on the night for a while. Julian couldn't tell if the roaring was still from the bear in the cave or if there was an endless human scream of horror that slowly died with the howl. He was just relieved to find his wide-eyed horse still whole, and ready to sprint. He needed that beast to cross the pass and fly back to Luna, as fast as an avenging angel.

'Fomes peccati!' Under the incessant pounding of the rain, the voice cawing *concupiscence*, reverberated on Julian's mind over the long cold night. Had it been one of those exasperating ravens or more of hermits' insanity, Julian couldn't guess, but the haunting fomentation of sin was uttered through the smothering darkness during those hours of slow progress, when nothing could be seen and only his horse's senses were to be trusted. He couldn't afford to fear attacks from bears or werewolves, and he did try, exhaustively, to brush off torturous reminiscences of betrayal that the dead hunter had planted, and that the omo salvatico had so shamelessly nurtured on his suspicions. *Filthy beast!* He was almost regretting having spared the hermit. A revolting mind that should never be allowed to spurt poison onto any other soul, deserving the same destiny as the ogre, so many years before.

A shadowy first light struggled to find its way through the dark grey clouds, helping a miserably wet and cold Julian to advance the pace. Slashed on the face with branches of hornbeams and beeches, as soon as the view was clear with lower vegetation, Julian dug his heels to ferociously avalanche down the Apuane. He skipped villages and cut short through lined chestnut forests, drawing his own tracks of mud as he slid into carefully tended terraced fields of green barley, of farro ready to harvest, and ploughed lots waiting for rye and spelt. His landslide cavalcade stirred herds and scared game, hauling creative curses from the few shepherds that had ventured out for minimum tasks on that accursed summer weather. An unplanned rush lead Julian to dead ends, to thickets of roses and blackberries, and often to the top of unsurpassable cliffs. Under that torment, he considered little of property or land usage, ignoring paths and breaking through peasants' livelihood. All Julian needed was to get to Luna and make certain that it was all a lie. To see his Clarissa and make it clear to the world than no man had come to lie with her, that the tale of the *black rider* was poison, that she was no whore, no liar. Not another deceiving Helena. And he, Julian of Mans, was no Buonaccorso. Clarissa was loyal to him, as she had always been. They would embrace and kiss passionately, and make love on their soft mattress...

Fomes peccati! The voice was louder and the memories heavier as he reached the coastal plains. The rivers had thickened from the incessant rain and a much wider swamp separated him from Luna. Should he ride across to use the coastal via Francigena or just cut through the swamps and head along straight to Luna? Julian was tired and hungry, not thinking. *How could the wild man know?* Julian thought as he kicked in for more speed. *But he did not know. He was not real, but a liar!*

I can smell her cunt.

The filthy beast! He was lying and he deserved to die. Again Julian regretted restraining his sword. Liars like that ogre deserved to die!

At mid-afternoon the rain had not eased. The path was heavy and the horse was exhausting its last remaining strength. Julian knew he was getting close to Luna, although he could not see its towers through the rain. Something inside his head told him to sniff the air. He got nothing but the smell of rain and smoke of chestnut coal from nearby houses. Not a hint of a man's seed. *By the Holy Face of Jesus Christ, what am I thinking? Clarissa is my wife. She loves me and we were made to be together. I was an honourable hospitaller in the Holy Land and I rode to Luna to rescue Clarissa from doom. From the rape of the Musetto. For twelve years she had been waiting for me...untouched...she loves me...*

Please, God, let it all be settled. It is a lie. Clarissa has always been loyal and true. There is no black rider or betrayal. Do not ridicule our love, please! So many moments have we shared together. So much has she become an inseparable part of me, my honey, my wine, my body. So many secrets shared... Clarissa is the only person that truly knows me. Is this why she can trick me? No, she would not do it. She cannot do it! She is not a whore!

He yelled for the gates to open and stormed into the patio. While tossing the reigns to an obsequious page, Julian could not avoid hearing a 'the Lady Clarissa has visitors' from the servant.

Visitors! The mention of the word triggered a blizzard of accusations on Julian's mind, blinding him with icy shards of jealousy, making his blood freeze and his legs tremble with fear from betrayal. The door to the main hall was kicked in with a roar and no sign of Clarissa was to be seen anywhere. The servants where all paralysed, looking at him with fear. Julian knew there was something wrong. A voice whispered in his ears that he was being made into a fool. That everyone except for him could see and have a good laugh from the horns of the cucco that were growing on his forehead. But he could straighten it up. He knew where to find the evildoers.

Swiftly, with wide steps he won the stairs to an inner terrace and carefully pushed the door of his room in.

Two layers of woollen carpets and a few pelts hung from the windows, blocking the wind and rain that forced its weight into the cosiness of the bedroom, homey warmth emanating from a well-behaved burning hearth. Clarissa was on their bed, sleeping. And Julian had to hold off a scream, for her arm was around a man who snored next to her.

THE BLACK RIDER!

While some voices inside his head burst into horselaughter, others kept screeching Whore! *Puttana! Maiala! Bagascia!* Filthy She-wolf! Louder and louder. *The fucking whore!*

Julian felt his head about to explode and all other sensation in his body disappeared, as if he was no more, except for the mockery crushing him. He was numb when his hands grabbed the hilt and swung the sword on a vertical arch, crashing across two necks that broke with a loud snap.

A thousand voices cheered!

He could only hear the swearing and the laughter when he raised the sword again and stroke once more. Blood was his revenge and it splattered on his face with anger. Only death could be punishment and well deserved. He would avenge Buonaccorso and all the lies they both had to bear. Finally he was doing it right. The laughter would stop.

But it did not stop. While two decapitated bodies lay on his bed, the woman he had once loved and called wife, with her lover on her side, the voices were laughing even louder.

And Julian started to scream.

That most horrid wail came out of Clarissa's lungs, as she desperately crossed the hall to reach the stairs. Her cry broke Julian's world in two.

On one side there were those now seemingly brief moments of intense love they had shared. The cosiness of each other's arms. Heat of bodies, touches, caresses, the shapes and volumes of passion under the Ligurian moon. The games of conquest, the joy of possessing and being possessed. A future they had dreamed together, as the happy lords of Luna. Dreams of the offspring they so much loved to endeavour into produce. The freedom to live away from the Saracen raids. The harmony of a fair treatment of the peasantry of Luna and the prosperity of the lands.

But such side of the world was just across a huge black hole, a ravenous gap of hell that was opening between Julian and that vanishing world of happiness, for Clarissa managed to utter a few words before collapsing only a few steps from her husband. To him it looked like she was still on that slice of life that was taking distance from his side. His world was now dark. It was a nightmare where he wanted to wake up from, or perhaps just dive into the darkness of the chasm that opened in front of him.

'WHY, JULIAN? WHY? THOSE ARE YOUR PARENTS! YOUR PARENTS!' was what his ears had heard, but the lack of blood in his head, the sudden cold numbness that took possession of him could only bring the blurred memories of the woods in Mans. The boar. The ogre....

You will live through misery and pain, and what has been my doom will be also yours. The ones that you hold most dearly, father and mother, Julian tried to cover his ears, but the howling was too fierce and loud, the ones that you hold most dearly, father and mother, will have their blood spilled by your own hands.

His right leg jerked out towards the room. For a split of a second he did have the hope that perhaps they could still be alive. *I have seen people survive after battle wounds.* But the rest of his body did not obey the heart. His left foot was like a rock and never moved. It was nailed to the stone floor by the dark truth that could not make him breathe. *I must have decapitated them.* He just stood, looking at Clarissa lying numb at his feet, her body so far from him. So far from the loneliest place in the world. From the mouth of hell.

My dear mother and father, his whole body trembled as he sobbed. I beheaded them! Murder! Oh please forgive me…But immediately he thought how could I be forgiven? And still, why ask for forgiveness? Is that the most important thing to be done? Why be so selfish so soon? AND WHAT IF IT HAD BEEN CLARISSA INDEED? Would it be any less horrid? He looked at the light that invaded the hall through the door. Light that exposed his selfish, blind misery to the world of the living. A number of servants were standing by the door, open-mouthed and horrified, their cautious and uncertain side-steps muffled by the cries of agony that stormed Julian. I DID NOT KNOW! he tried to shriek. No air came out of his throat. I was fooled! The DEVIL made me do it! He knew they would think that such an excuse was, if not pathetic, at least unimaginative. Again he was filled by these devious thoughts, this selfish arrogance. Oh my God, how could anybody be filthier than I was? He looked at his hands. They seemed unsoiled, but black with sin. Then he saw the droplets of blood on the fabric of his sleeves. Bloody as the juice of mulberries was also the curtain of sweat and tears that blurred his vision. MURDER! He noticed the stains of death that had sprinkled his chest. The air finally went out of him. Julian gasped, trying to breathe, but the strangling was too tight. I am covered with their blood!

'YOU ARE COVERED WITH THEIR BLOOD!'

As he heard the malicious observation, Julian thought the servants were accusing him with music. A lugubrious chant, with voices of others, long gone. Voices of their ancestors, who had also served the lords of Luna. Voices of the dead.

'MURDERER!' Now the chant was much louder. He looked at the populace at the door. They were still paralysed, not knowing how to proceed after their lord had committed such an abomination. But the cries were not coming from those lips. 'MURDERER, YOU WILL BURN!' pounded on his ears. A million voices crying out. Now he knew it. Those shrieks came from the dark gap that was leaving him stranded in a nightmare as the rest of his life kept going, very far, now hardly visible. The voices had no substance, but they hammered on his temples. 'MURDERER, MURDERER!' they roared. The chant was getting louder. Intermingled with the words, coiling subtly and viciously around the understandable language, were the cries of agony of all creatures that, as he was about to, had been sent to spend an eternity in hell. And Julian saw that they had broken loose.

The gap in front of him jolted up with an explosion, spewing a battalion of flying creatures, screaming with accusations and full of wrong. They howled and buzzed noisily around him. *MURDERER, MURDERER*, he heard them chanting through a horrendous scream. Some of those imps danced on the floor, simulating rage and indecency. Others tried to lick the blood on his clothes. They were misshapen, quick of movements and painfully spiteful. He could not devise them properly, so fast or repulsive they were, but it seemed that some had the bodies of cats and human faces. Sprites that flew with wings of birds, or bats. Julian knew immediately those were the demons of misery, agony, pain and torture. They were there to savour on his anguish. Tearing his clothes to suck on the blood that he had drawn from his mother and father. Laughing at his wicked act and dragging him with them.

I will not let them savour on my parent's blood, Julian thought, so he snatched his shirt off. As soon as he got rid of his hose and boots, the creatures lost interest on his attire, flying back to torment his undressed body. Demons of shame and remorse grabbing Julian by his arms, neck and hair. He felt their chilly grasp. *How cold, so very cold!* They licked his ears, with words of hatred and fear, they pinched hard on his skin until streams of black blood spurted out. '*Come and lick your mother's blood*' one of them whispered.

Julian fought back, but the army was too numerous. The beasts were clawing their talons and fangs in his skin, dragging him to the edge of the abyss. As he finally collapsed into their mercy, a hand grabbed his ankle. Not one of the gelid demons' paws, but a soft, warm and loving hand.

Clarissa.

She had woken up back to that nightmare and was feebly trying to save him from the gap. The demons, however, were much stronger and pulled Julian down to the chasm, dragging him with a final yank. His ankle slipped out of Clarissa's grip.

The servants saw their Lord of Luna, unclothed and maddened by his crime, plunge down from the terrace of his bedroom to the floor of Luna's castle hall. Before hitting the stone slabs, Julian still heard Clarissa's faint voice exhaling: 'Don't leave me...Julian...'

The Cleanest Whores in Town

'I see the dripping, but it's not as blood-red intense as the juice of mulberries!' said the boy.

'No, Domenico, it is not.' his father noted. 'The best wine to drip out of this contraption is almost as transparent as the water, but as powerful as a thunder.' He withdrew the goblet from the dripping pipe and, with an amused face, brought it near his son's nose. 'Can you feel the power?'

Domenico sniffed it, smiled, held the goblet and took a sip. He shut his eyes and waited for the thrill over his skin to subside. 'The aroma is very enticing, but it's the flavour that spreads throughout the whole body. I feel I could beat ten soldiers with one hand!'

'Now you see why we charge dearly for this wine and why we do not refine much of it,' his father said. 'An excess of this beverage could cause entire nations to be abusive. Well, I mean even more excessive than they are now.' He tapped Domenico on the head and they took the path back to the manor.

Immanuel Malachi was teaching his fourth son the arts of the using his *tagh tir*. They could distil from not only grapes' pomace, but also from fermented mulberries, now abundant with the expansion of silk production. While his oldest Giacomo was in Lucca learning the trades of grandfather Battista, the second son Francesco had taken over silk production, from the harvest of leaves to the maintenance of eggs, breeders, collection of cocoons, boiling and rolling the threads. His routine took him to the furthest orchards in Barga, all the way into the walls of Lucca, supervising boilers and dyers. Piero, the third, was set to run the baths, from the engineering of waters, plumbing, to health issues, cures, services to pilgrims and users, and the financial sanity of the thermal station in Corsena. Immanuel channelled fourteen year-old Domenico into any other activities the boy could manage from a fixed residence in Corsena, and that included winemaking. The younger children would be sorted out according to their talents and the activities' needs.

Immanuel rubbed the dust from his hands. Except for Medicine, of which his eldest Maria Maddalena had somehow learned on a disastrous endeavour, the aging Bukhari could rest assured that his legacy would be carried on by the new generations.

They stopped briefly at the baths, where the freckle-ridden Piero allowed them to quickly bathe in a pool of icy cold water, making Domenico immediately jump out of his torpor of mulberry wine. Walking home across the hillside, with the frolicking sound of the Lima running below the smoke-spewing windows, Immanuel heard the sound of crushing acorns. Out of the woods, the tall figure of Father Martino walked down the path from Controne.

'It is you that I came for,' Martino said, opening a warm smile.

'Then you are welcome to follow us home' Immanuel answered with his unmistakable eastern accent. When they arrived at the manor in Corsena, Domenico rushed in to bring them some refreshments.

'How is the lord of Luna?' Immanuel asked as they were comfortably seated. 'I heard about the tragedy.'

'Not well,' Martino sighed, with tired eyes. 'He is broken. Broken head and broken hearted for his stupid actions.' The parishioner raised his heavy eyebrows and pursed his lips, 'but he will come around it... he must come around it, somehow.'

'What a silly waste! I met him when the first shipments of silkworms came these lands. I have heard he has turned into a fine man...' said Immanuel.

'He has indeed. I have strongly advised them to leave that accursed place and maybe come to our lands. He needs to do penitence for his acts and that he can do well. The man was a hospitaller at the Church of the Holy Sepulchre, in the Holy land.' He noticed Immanuel's face of utter ignorance. 'The church that marks the place where the Christ was crucified!'

'Oh!' was all the Bukhari said.

'Maybe he could even consult the Holy Father for an appropriate designation, had he been back from Germany,' Martino wondered aloud. Immanuel just shrugged his shoulders. The refreshment arrived. One amphora of fresh mulberry juice and one small amphora with Immanuel's pomace wine.

'But the reason I come,' Martino continued, 'concerns not Julian of Luna, but Antelmino di Gottefredo, that one they call *Castracani.*'

'That man down South?' Immanuel asked. 'Nothing good comes out of him. A coward, they say. His father Gottefredo was close to ruin our silk production. Now, the son is worse. In addition to all of the bitterness my daughter has left for me to savour, I fear she could be on this man's wedding plans.'

'I know nothing of such plans, but he seems to be surely engaged into hurting me,' Martino said. 'While I rode to Luna for tending to Julian and his wife's spiritual needs, two strangers from these lands came for me in Controne. I actually saw them on the ferry and I know who they are: Lamberto and Lanfranco – the Genovese brothers, brutes from Sesto a Moriano.'

'Sturdily built men? Twins, one yellow bearded and one red?'

'The same' Martino confirmed. 'They were looking for my whereabouts. Caterina kindly welcomed both at the parish and gave them wine and chestnut cakes. It was quite obvious they had been sent by Antelmino, who holds a grudge against me.'

'And do you expect them to come for you again one day?' Immanuel asked.

'Anytime, I fear. If not those two, maybe others. And there is nothing I can do on my own, not even on papal land.'

'Hmm, I see your point.' Immanuel said. He could see the respectful height of Martino breaking down into a sweat of desperation. In spite of the pity he felt, there was a selfish tinge of pride for having a popular man like Martino of Controne to seek for his help. 'I will talk to Battista Burle. Controne is under his care. Meanwhile, we should alert the people of Corsena, Fornulo and Chifenti for strangers heading up to the mountain. Especially Chifenti, where the road exits Cunimundinghi land. We can post men in the town if I alert Battista and obtain his approval. I will also advise my daughter that this Antelmino has been sending his criminals across her lands.'

'I'm not sure Maria Maddalena will be moved by my plight.' Martino considered, with a sickly smile, 'She's another one who does not seem to have any special affection for me or Caterina.'

Immanuel chuckled. 'Worry not about how she sees you two. Maria has no special feelings for anyone. No wonder people call her names behind her back. Still, Antelmino is not entitled to send his villains for bashings in her lands, even when held under papal possession. It is blunt banditry as it happens in his lands, but surely not tolerated by Lucchese authorities. Maria will be furious if he does it again. As for you,' he pointed a callused finger at Martino, 'You should immediately advise those chestnut gatherers and carbonaii on the way up to Controne of the imminent danger of an attack and have always enabled men around yourself to protect you. This could be a small war.'

Indeed Antelmino di Gottefredo received his unexpected visit from Maria Maddalena Cunimundinghi. She rode into his manor at Santo Stefano di Tassignano with no less than a hundred men-at-arms.

'Very impressive, Maria Maddalena! A great display of might!' Antelmino said, coming out to his rather unkempt patio sheltered by oaks. 'Are you here to woo me?'

'Stupid man!' she cackled from her horse. 'What are you doing sending your villains through my land?'

Antelmino laughed loudly. 'Maria Maddalena, I hardly find this an appropriate forum for such a discussion, but it would sound to me that you are protecting a certain someone in Controne.'

'You can interpret it as you wish, if you bother to do some thinking, but do try to remember we had an agreement not long ago.' Her horse kept, at her dexterous command, vigorously marching around a fearless Antelmino. 'I will do something about that certain someone through my appropriate connections. Just wait, you fool! And keep your lawlessness out of my land! No wonder the via Francigena stirs away from your banditry!'

'You do realise the pope is in German lands, don't you?'

'Don't patronise me, Antelmino. I know well where the pope is. But when he returns, the issue will be properly addressed. Meanwhile, let me exercise some of my rare generosity and give you a piece of advice: do not take the reins into your filthy hands, or you will have war. Just revel in your shame, Antelmino.' And she was the one who laughed now. 'The Castracani! You can wear your spurious hat but you must live with the fact that you were kicked in the face by a pathetic priest and fell like a bloated frog into the river. It was long ago but we still laugh at the thought!' She spat on the ground three times, turned her horse away and said 'Good bye, Antelmino!'

The Castracani watched the men at arms follow her and shouted with all his lungs 'You are becoming uglier by the day when you get incensed, Maria Maddalena!'

It was on a late autumn morning when a lavishly harnessed horse rode into Fornulo from the North, bringing on its back a dust-covered cleric. The short stature man was the bishop of Lucca, looking for the manor of another small man: Immanuel Malachi.

'The committee of Pope Benedict VIII is riding down the Serchio. They should be here tomorrow morning,' Bishop Grimizzo advised, after a brief introduction. While Immanuel kindly listened, Domenico took the bishop's rouncey for water, brushing the beast's clod-ridden tail with a handful of straw. Inside the manor, the bishop explained 'We are on our way back from Goslar and I rushed to see you to ensure that His Holiness's sojourn in Bagni a Corsena will be a memorable one. The committee rode in a hurry to cross the Alpine passes before winter blocked us. The pontiff is tired and a pause of day or two in the baths would be more than beneficial for the Holy Father's health and troubled spirit.'

'Give me the exact number of people,' Immanuel demanded, quite tranquil, but extraordinarily flattered with the pope's choice of rest in his baths, 'and I will be ready for their arrival.' It was the first time in almost twenty years of the baths in Corsena, since the days when Sylvester II had decided to renovate them, that a pope would be relaxing in his brand new thermal facilities.

Grimizzo supplied all details on the numbers and identities of who exactly was riding South with Benedict VIII. Before leaving, the bishop added with a certain hesitation 'I should also let you know that in addition to consecrations and agreements with the emperor, the pontiff ratified his condemnation of concubinage and marriage of clerics.' Immanuel did not move an eyelash on hearing that. Grimizzo curled his lip in annoyance, cleared his throat and talked almost in a whisper 'Lately, I have been somehow obliged to alert the Holy Father of the parishioner Martino, of Controne, for his intimate association with a nun.'

'Would you like to talk to Martino in person? Controne is but a short ride up this mountain.'

'No!' said the tiny bishop firmly, with a drop of sweat suddenly materialising on his ample forehead. 'You can just let him know about this inconvenience. The parishioner will certainly find unsuitable to visit the baths and the environs while the Holy Father uses them.'

'Thank you for your thoughtfulness, Reverend Bishop.' Immanuel said, using the right treatment but with no more comments. He had noticed the bishop uneasiness, probably because Grimizzo wanted to avoid any direct confrontation with Martino on concubinage. As Immanuel himself was aware of the bishop's own woman and children, Martino was likely to know it too and use it if under attack. Immanuel could never understand the purpose of recommended celibacy. All priests he knew of generally had women and children. But regardless of the conceptual debate, Martino was a good man who probably had the adequate weapons to face the bishop, but not the pope. The Bukhari thought that there was a need for one element on this triangle to be equalised. He returned home to organise for the following day and send the message to Martino.

News spread faster than the plague. As swift as the water from the Lima travels down its four miles to run by Anchiano, Maria Maddalena of the Cunimundinghi learned that the pope would be making a leisure stop in her lands.

On that afternoon, Old Testa, cursing and grunting as always, carried two riders on his ferry. One was coming from Corsena, and the other from Anchiano. Both men were in a hurry and, as soon as they jumped from the ferry and pulled their horses onto the western bank, they galloped to Lucca, arriving roughly at the same time.

Big old Battista Burle was sitting covered in sweat in his dark office, receiving a couple of well-memorised, clear messages. Two different requests. And he was not happy with any of them.

The communication from Anchiano was on a typical demanding tone of his adored granddaughter Maria Maddalena. The lady of the rock was strongly suggesting the banker sent a welcoming note to the pontiff, who would be arriving on the next morning to use the bagni for the first time. The letter should contain a brief overview of their state of accounts but on rather more positive tone than their annual acknowledgements; in addition to a clear denunciation of the immoral and unacceptable liaison between the parishioner of Controne and a fugitive religieuse of the monastery of San Giovanni Battista, in Santa Maria lei Giudice. That was obviously one of those unexplainable games of his granddaughter's. An inconvenient denunciation of the good Martino, that Immanuel had, not too long before, asked Battista for protection.

The other message, from his son-in-law, strangely required that Battista sent to Corsena, on that same night, accompanied by his rider and another two or three men-at-arms, a bullock cart with the best looking whores from Lucca. Five or six young, vigorous women would suffice. Immanuel would care for their fees and lodging for two days.

Battista sighed with annoyance. He would have to do something, although both requests were a nuisance to his routine. After a brief meeting with young Giacomo, they both decided the old banker would find Peter, Hubert, John and Tempert, his notaries and procurators, to write a hurried but appropriate letter to the pontiff and include a subtle request from his favourite grandchild. On the other side of town, Battista's delighted grandson would personally choose the puttane and escort them on the bullock-cart to Corsena.

Giacomo was quite expedient on the task. He chose eight lovely, clean-looking young women.

The pontiff expected an audience with a disgraced couple at the bishop's palace in Lucca. He had just returned from his stay at Bagni a la Corsena on the previous day. Crestfallen, he had silently ridden down to the ford at the Lima. A cold, rainy morning, where the vapours of the baths mingled into the thick mist that smothered the valley. Probably the appropriate type of weather for entertaining thoughts of repentance. While the raindrops quietly spiralled down the thin branches of beech, the horses treaded carefully down the muddy slope and the pope tried to shake the memories of those days and nights out of his thoughts.

But how could he? The aromas escaping the windows along the track, chestnut polenta, freshly baked farro bread with olive oil and ewe's milk cheese, they tortured him with pleasant moods and forbidden longings. The desire to stay, forever, only to be tortured by disgrace as soon as he flew to the highest point of sensuality. Beauty and remorse, bliss and shame. A ride onto heaven before the inevitable plunge. And he craved for more of those blessings, no matter how much torture awaited thereafter. Knowledge, at last, for John Theophylactus was a new man.

Re-born for the second time, in less than four days. First, as a true man, out of a proud role model of righteousness and obedience. During that stay, John Theophylactus had looked back into life, seeing himself as a capon ostrich hiding his head inside the sands of his clerical vests, growing into a man's shape but ignoring its natural urges, climbing the pious steps of the episcopate while shunning away from sensual temptations.

He remembered being the beautiful eight-year old holding his father's fat fingers on the steps of the Lateran Basilica. That is when he watched a vibrant mob marching around the square, dragging the naked body of the dead pope and singing obscene songs about that Pope 'Malefacius', as they mockingly called Bonifacius. The excitement was so contagious that he slipped from the bishop's sweaty grasp, quickly squeezing through the custodes and joining the rabble before his brothers went on his chase. Albericus and Romanus only found their younger brother as the crowd dispersed, after the dismembered body of the pope was hanging from the colossal statue of Emperor Constantine. John Theophylactus had memories of that exciting morning ending up with some older boys taking him to an alley, groping him and exposing themselves. He had not yet reached the age that he could manage to evade the assaults of so many man and women who were enchanted by that faery appeal. As soon as Albericus and Romanus arrived, he remembers being trampled in a fight, blades, screams and gushes of blood. After John was safely handed to his father, Bishop Gregorius I, Count of Tusculum, he was beaten implacably, not because of the obscenities in the alley, but for joining a lynching mob that was desecrating the body of 'their' pope.

'But father,' reasoned a red-eyed John, after his bashing, 'they were all saying that Pope Malefatius was a monster, the murderer of popes before him.'

Bishop Gregorius sniffed loudly, cleared his throat and just shook his head in annoyance. 'Those people are like rats from the *cloaca*, my son. You cannot trust them. They exist to prey on our food and our lives. The holy man whose body now hangs on that square watches us from above, from the podium of the saints and martyrs, sitting next to Christ the Saviour and to the Almighty God. Pope Bonifacius was a virtuous man that dedicated his life to Jesus Christ, always caring for Rome and the true children of its church. The previous popes were puppets of the emperor, a foreigner who insists in ruling the lives of us Romans. And you,' he slapped John's face with uncontained strength, 'when following the steps of our saviour one day, you must be quick to determine who is the enemy, as he will be aided by the legions of hell. Smite him before he can prepare the battleground, and your gates to the stairways leading to heavens will remain opened.'

Instructed by his older brothers and cousins into battle and politics to one day take the position of his father as the bishop of Porto, John Theophylactus watched each pontiff's brief's stay on the throne of Rome, altering in loyalty with the Roman families or the emperor, but always and invariably with an ardent emphasis on celibacy for the high clergy, no matter how abusively they disobeyed those recommendations themselves. Early in his education, he became well aware of the popes' and bishops' sinful affairs and marital relations, a somewhat disgusting weakness that he hoped to unbend. He believed in consecration to God with an undivided heart, that the clergy should give themselves entirely to God and to the service of men. And he knew he could make them accept this blessing, this special task, with a joyous heart.

While his second cousin Crescentius Numentanus, was kept under siege in the Castel Sant'Angelo, John was safely protected from the emperor's troops in the family palace in Tusculum. He missed to witness the horror of another parade, this time organised by imperial troops, displaying the mutilated Pope John XVI, still alive and dressed up as an ass, a few days before Crescentius himself was slaughtered. Intriguingly enough, as each pope slated his predecessor's dealings, they all seemed to be working towards a common strengthening of the mother church, but mostly ignoring the call to be true pastors of the Christ and stewards of his holy words and sacraments. John then followed quiet and humbly the short years of Gregorius V, the German pope, while the tongues of his family lashed the pontiff for his foreign manners and unnatural liaisons with the young emperor. Once Gregorius had been fatally corroded by *lues*, the emperor determined a new foreign pope to the throne. That Antichrist Sylvester II had deprived John Theophylactus from the deservingly pomp and majesty during his ordination as the bishop of Porto. Although the damned pope was said to be a married man and a sorcerer, John investigated the pontiff thoroughly with his ever strengthening connections in the Lateran, but he never found any proof of the rumours, besides the pope's naïve infatuation for his cousin's wife, the Lady Theodora. Once Sylvester was dead, the next pope chosen by the Crescentii was said to be poisoned by the emperor's sympathisers but, quickly, another relative was chosen. It was that John Fasanus, who had always paid little heed to him. As a close collaborator of Sylvester, Fasanus also enjoyed knowledge, a good conversation and the company of women. But again John Theophylactus failed to find the pope yielding to temptation during his close scrutiny. When Fasanus retired to die in peace from his illness, it would have been John Theophylactus's very own time, but the Crescentti were still reluctant to place him on the papal throne. Sergius, the pig's snout, was a known celibate, but he lost the plot when he appealed to Christendom to mobilise their armies and save the Holy Sepulchre from infidel's hands. What foolishness! This lack of objectivity was the divine signal that destiny had to be forcibly changed. While his brothers Albericus and Romanus organised for a smooth passing of the pope, John made sure that the chamberlain Brunello never succeeded on the throne of Rome, no matter how much he claimed to be truly elected pope. Another divine strike of luck assured John Theophylactus the position when the malefic John Crescentius, the son, died suddenly of what was believed to be poisoning during a visit by an abbess. It was God that made John Theophylactus anointed Pope Benedict VIII, shutting up those who mocked his feminine ways, but sniggering when He forbade the angels in heaven to watch the ceremony in awe, for the papal regalia had been then taken away by Brunello. John Theophylactus's grandeur, he knew on that day he sat on the *sedes stercoraria*, was still to be fought for and gained over the next decade as Pope Benedict VIII.

Albericus and Romanus indulged in pleasures of the flesh, but Benedict VIII was heartily engaged on the strengthening of the papacy and Italy. He annihilated the ideas of sending Christian troops to the Holy Land; he made peace with the Henry IV by finally crowning him emperor; he allied with the Normans to crush the Byzantine in Sicily; he led his own papal troops and fleet to expel the Musetto from Luni. They were late for battle, but still victorious – and he was believed to have slain the Musetto's wife with his own sacred sword. John championed a war against simony, nepotism and especially incontinence, from the highest steps of the clergy, to the base of the church in the parishes.

A tired man, broken by a hurried ride from the North, the pope was not looking forward to return to a rotten Rome, where his brothers drained the blood of the church like ravenous werewolves. Moreover, he could not stand the antics of that spoiled brat Theophylactus, Albericus's son, shamefully named after him. Now Benedict VIII had relaxed under the warmth of the bagni in Corsena, inebriated by steam and aromas, balsams and ointments, by the touch of oily hands massaging his fingers, toes, thighs and lips. A shell of hardness slowly softened by hot water, the heat of bodies and another urge, from a man that grew inside him, a man that he had always proudly kept shut in the dark.

'You have true beauty!' one of them had said, while combing his long hair. 'Somewhat feminine to look at, if you allow my honesty, with delicate features, attractive, but still a man, and such a great one to make me a woman!'

Succubi! They were courteous and beautiful. They smelled of flowers and food. They came in from nowhere and disappeared as soon as he was smitten by regret. But they would soon be back, a different one, with touches and words that made him feel unique, undressing inside the baths and finally placing Benedict VIII on the throne of manhood. They had brought that lustful, devilish man out of the always continent John Theophylactus. How terribly delicious!

Between sessions of sensual caresses with local beauties in Bagni a la Corsena, while relaxing with a vigorous massage, the pontiff was interrupted by his factotum, announcing a visit of the local parishioner Martino, from the mountain hamlet of Controne. *The insolence*! Was it daring or just naïve of the priest to interrupt him? The factotum tactfully explained that this was the parishioner who had been mentioned by the bishop Grimizzo. He reminded the pontiff that Martino had taken a wife, supposedly a woman who had a liaison with the old Marozia.

Oh Jesus Christ, bound and mocked, flagellated, crucified and resurrected at the third day! Benedict sighed. Marozia? Do I want to unearth this stinking, rotting corpse that Christendom has already forgotten about? A disgraceful character of history, which is associated with my ancestors. Who am I to bring up the dead, like Pope Stephen did to Formosus, and spit on them? And who am I to condemn this man Martino, who is no more than just exercising this wonderful gift of God which is earthly love? How much better is the bishop to denounce this man? Grimizzo is probably married himself and with children and a future to worry about. Why are we fighting against God's creation? Or is nature a deed of the Devil? Maybe it is no more than remorse that is truly tossed upon our shoulders by the Enemy, while God offers us the blessings of nature.

Benedict VIII dressed up to see Martino. The parishioner humbly kneeled to kiss the pontiff's ring, before the pope took him to a terrace, where they sat down for some of Immanuel's special wine, watching the fog lowering down the red and gold cover of the valley. Martino seemed to be a perfectly reasonable, dedicated parishioner, and the pope could not refrain from admiring that man, who had taken the exercise of manhood out of the way of priesthood, not by defying it, but by not turning it into an obstacle at all. As the evening closed in early and they ceremoniously reviewed the work of the parish, Benedict cordially dismissed the parishioner and sent a grumpy message to Bishop Grimizzo, before plunging into another earthly dream of sensual delights.

When finally freed from those pleasures, a man in love with love and fighting the thorns of remorse, Benedict VIII forded the Lima and rode silently among a number of downcast pilgrims and beggars along the via Francigena. A cowled figure with his long silver hair adorning the edges of the hood, nobody looked at him, as if all were shunned by shame. But creatures under the dark green waters of the Serchio, which slowly moved on his right, opened wide round eyes on the quiet surface as the light rain kept trickling.

The pope came to an abandoned building and waited for the ferry. The drizzle seemed to be freezing into snowflakes. Grey broken walls, blackened by fire and age, stood out of a vast thicket of rosebushes and young beeches.

'What was this place?' he asked.

Grimizzo, who had kept to himself since the reprimand on the cheap denouncement of Martino, stepped his horse closer. 'This ruined place was a *xenodochium*, Beatissimo Padre. But it hasn't been used since immemorial times.'

'What was its name?' the pope asked.

'Who knows?' the bishop shrugged his shoulders. 'San Giacomo? Sant'Alessio di Roma? Santa Croce? Santa Fede di Agen? My apologies for the speculation, Beatissimo Padre, but it could be anything.'

Benedict did not mind the slight irritated tone of Grimizzo's answer. He was looking at the pilgrims standing on the side, waiting for the ferry to arrive and take the papal committee, before daring to step forward and pay for the crossing. Men and women, young and old. Shivering, they held onto their children or their crutches. Gelid rain water ran down the crevasses of their stony frowned faces, spilled by gutters from their leather hats and cowls. Wooden, dirty hands held their scarves up to their necks. He was wondering if any of those tough-skinned people, braving the cold and walking immeasurable distances to see a wooden crucifix in Lucca or to see treasures of the church in Rome, riches that would never touch their hands; if any of them had had such a lovely night, being gently kissed on the lips by a nymph, or lying themselves beside and inside the flesh of a warm goddess, smelling of flowery fragrances and ready to giggle or whisper the sweetest words at a touch. *Probably not. Had they slept comfortably at least? Had they had the luxury of a warm meal, as the herbal soups he had shared with the beauties of the bagni of Corsena?* He sighed deeply.

'Is the Beatissimo padre well?' Grimizzo asked.

The pope waved his hand, dismissing the thought. 'Where do these people spend the night?' he asked. 'In the baths?'

'Very few could afford that luxury. Some will pay for a dry palliasse at the tavern in Chifenti, but most will be happy with some clean straw in the stables or just huddle outside, under the dampness of the night.'

With a gloomy realisation laying its weight over him, Benedict just shook his head in dismay, while Grimizzo added 'They are hardy people, these pilgrims. They can bear it.'

Cursing between clenched teeth, young Testa pushed a loaded ferry onto the bank. Pilgrims coming back from Lucca got out and quickly followed the road north, towards Chifenti. Those who waited would have to wait longer, for the whole papal committee to cross with all its horses. Two horses and four men at a time, of the utmost importance. Testa had to control his tongue better than he had to manoeuvre the fully loaded raft. He hardly knew that Pope Benedict VIII was being reborn into a new man on that crossing, as the raft was pushed forward. The pontiff stared with sadness the huddled group under the implacable weather that announced winter. Behind them, stood the ruins of the hospital, cold, stony and just as wet as the pilgrims.

Later on that day, Testa would be ferrying a bullock cart with Giacomo dei Burle et Malachi. The young apprentice of Battista Burle waited on the western bank for the second trip, when eight freshly perfumed women giggled as Testa grunted his way with the pole. Back in Corsena, Immanuel Ben-Malachi hardly knew that a small gesture to please the pontiff committee and distract him from affairs with Martino of Controne would change the story of the Serchio forever.

The Interview

'Don't leave me, Julian...' Clarissa whispered.

Julian was spread on the straw, in the stables. The storm had been so intense that the lower grounds of the castle were flooded into a wide lake. It would be a few days before the walls were completely out of the water. Clarissa had treated his wounds with melissa and pot marigold balm. The injuries were cleaned and dressed with new bandages, a ritual Clarissa had repeated every other day over the last two weeks. Julian had knocked his head on the fall, breaking his nose and opening a gash on his forehead that initially seemed to refuse to mend. With Clarissa's constant care and whispers, healing decided to take its course. He ate and drank scarcely, always in silence and under the exhaustive insistence of his wife. Clarissa had repeatedly tried to pour broth into his mouth, to sooth the pain and swelling by applying *brugo*, heather from the mountains above, boiled in water and still warm. The wound was mending well a fortnight after the tragedy. Still, Julian had refused to open his eyes. Or to say a word.

'We sent out the men-at-arms on their way back to Mans, Julian.' Clarissa said, sitting at his side. At that stage, she did not expect much verbal response from him. 'They carry a letter carefully written by me, with the kind help of father Martino, explaining this most unfortunate accident. It carries the seal of Bishop Guido. They are aware they could be facing a terrible penalty for returning empty-handed, but they trust the understanding of your brother Raoul, who has been the Vicomte of Mans for a couple of years already.'

He turned his face away and refused to eat or drink for the rest of the day.

Corroded by shame, slashed by remorse and broken with sadness, Julian had handed his life and destiny into the strong, dark arms of the Devil. He had lost his battle. The ogre's promise had been fulfilled and there was nothing else to be undone or to mend. If those that Julian had once most loved had died from his own hands, he was not worthy of anyone's affection. He was not worthy of shedding a tear for his monstrous crime, nor of raising his eyes to Heaven and be stared upon by his victims. There was no other fate than burning in the eternal flames. For that, he just closed his eyes and waited.

Clarissa came back during the night. She lightly tapped on Julian's face with the silk, velvety touch of her hands. Julian could hear her voice, different, hoarse, calling for help from a dark place, calling him out of his dreams. Julian knew Clarissa was scared and badly needed his help. She did not want to be left alone in that forgotten den, dipped into full darkness, where the ground is soft and moves about, and our names stand out of whispers behind our back. A gloomy dungeon, with a smell of meat in putrefaction, where we don't want to walk down the stairs around us. A dark place where gelid little fingers touched her arms but scurried away as she blindly tried to grab them. And Julian knew Clarissa was not alone. It was not only the mischievous creatures with cold hands patting her more and more as they gradually lost their shyness. It was a much more powerful presence. A black creature, darker than darkness, towering above Clarissa, with long, twiggy fingers and eyes of fire. Julian knew this beast, tormenting him in his worst nightmares, leading him to evil deeds. He would not allow it to get any close to Clarissa. *Julian there's someone here!* she moaned from the darkness. Julian, *I can feel it!* She was almost screaming. And so was Julian, helpless, not knowing where to find her, impotent against that presence, lost in a bad dream. *Don't let it hurt you, Clarissa!* he managed to shout, after gathering all remains of force around him. But his voice was faint, evaporating into silence as soon as it left his mouth. Trying to run, Julian realised his legs were paralysed, dormant from his desistance to react, leaving him impotent, incapable to express the few honourable drops of sweat that remained on his skin.

An afflicted Clarissa called him, now almost howling with terror.

That was it. He had to wake up from this nightmare, from Clarissa's nightmare. Julian's body shivered as he dove out of that dream.

He opened his eyes to see a dark, hairy face grinning at him, with yellow eyes of fire.

Get out of here! Julian pleaded. Haven't you done enough?

The creature was pinning him to the ground, sitting on his belly. It seemed to widen its grin on hearing Julian, although its face was too dark to tell, too full of wrong and malice.

You've won! Julian spat. You got what you wanted, you fulfilled what you promised! Now go away!

It was really smiling, exactly when Julian could hear Clarissa's screams again. The hairy presence slowly lowered its large head and approached Julian's ear, licking it, leaving a foul whisper as it thinned out from Julian's view. Julian screamed, for his wrists were still being held.

He opened his eyes again, to find the warm sunlight coming through the stable door and the sweet desperation of Clarissa's face, dropping tears that burned as they splashed into a pool on his own eyes. Clarissa still had her firm grip on his fists, having just shaken him out of those nightmares.

Oh, my love...

The grip slowly loosened. Clarissa's hands softened with a mixture of relief and caution. Her fingers still firmly touched his wrists, not on a contained force, but on a shouting alert of passion. Lightly, their sweated skin came loose and she moved her fingers over to his palm, to delicately find the memory of his touch. Julian sobbed as he gave into the warmth of her embrace. The length and pain of his wail was not enough to fit any apologies that he would have found appropriate to her for the horror of his crime. And he had never found any. There were just sorrow and sadness.

They embraced at length, his face crying, buried on her right shoulder. Not a word was spoken, for no need there was for an audible exchange. Clarissa forced him backwards and looked at his face, which still cringed in shame. Her thumbs delicately rubbed his eyelids, wiping off tears of desperation, while her own eyes poured. They embraced again, now their heads to the left of each other.

'Where are they?' Julian finally managed to moan.

'We laid them to rest in the flowered graveyard of the Cathedral of San Habet Deus, next to my parents.' she said with a congested voice. 'That peaceful evergreen spot, where they receive warm sunlight and refreshing rains, the perfume of flowers and the shade of vines growing over willow arches. They are in good company, Julian.'

He held onto her to stand up. 'I must see them.'

'Easy, Julian,' she said, bringing him to a seated position. 'But you should wash yourself first, and I will take you with –'

'No!' he begged. 'I must do this on my own.'

Clarissa nodded in silence, while Julian sighed before the next effort to stand up. He turned all of a sudden to her and said 'It was back, Clarissa! It came to me in my dream! And I would wake out of it, but it was still there, haunting me with wrong. It came to tell me what I already know...'

'Hush, my love' she cooed, caressing his long hair.

'It whispered in my left ear that we will meet again one day,' Julian continued. 'And I know where this is, Clarissa. It can only be in hell!'

'Julian, your hair is pasty.' Clarissa said, totally ignoring the gravity of his words. 'What is it?' She looked at the brown and red stains in her hand. 'It's blood! You are bleeding. Let's clean your wounds and re-dress them.' They walked back towards the main door while Clarissa examined better the hair and the bandages. She gave a little yelp and pulled him faster towards the castle 'Julian, I should never have left you unattended on that straw floor.'

'Why? What happened?'

'The bleeding comes from your left ear. Something has taken a bite out of it.'

Julian did not return that night. The moon shone brighter than any night the people of Luna could have remembered. Clarissa set out to the town with an escort of riders. They entered calmly through the eastern gate, iron-clad hooves careful and lightly beating the stone pavement. Silently approaching the Cathedral cemetery, Clarissa saw that Julian was quietly weeping by a shiny white slab.

She left him to his own terms.

Julian returned to the ruined castle at the break of dawn, exhausted from so many tears and so much lament. With a bitter mouth of bile, he eagerly reached for water and gave himself to the comfortable arms of his wife. Delicate and diligently, Clarissa pulled him to their room, where she changed the bandages on his head and on the massive bite that had strangely appeared during the previous day, taking out almost half of his ear.

'That was the only condign act left to be done.' He sighed. 'Nothing more.'

'What do you mean nothing more?' Clarissa said, without taking her eyes out of the clean band of linen that she slowly wrapped around his head. 'There's plenty of condign acts to be done. You are not leaving me alone, Julian. We will stick together, always and forever, like two sides of a walnut core. We will leave this castle and give some new meaning to our life.'

'Leave Luna?' Julian asked incredulous. 'And go where? Do what?'

'It doesn't matter, Julian.' She had finished the wrapping. 'As long as we go somewhere and do something...'

His face did not move. It was still stony, with lips hard and dry. Although the swelling had reduced on his nose, it would stay crooked forever. But whereas his eyes did not relax, Clarissa could see that deep inside, those eyes were trying to remember how to smile.

Julian and Clarissa waited at the bishop's Palace, in Lucca, while Pope Benedict VIII was having a haircut.

'I still don't think you had to come here!' Clarissa said in a whisper, with the side of her mouth, very close to Julian's partly-bitten ear. He just sighed and said no more. Outside the palace, loud pilgrims talked and the cold hall absorbed their racket well. The pontiff's aid came to the *atrium*, holding his nose high as to avoid the rancid smell of pilgrimage that came from the entrance. He called out loud in a typical Roman version of Latin, reluctantly lowering his eyes towards the crestfallen lord of Luna and without even spending a glance towards Clarissa. 'The Beatissimo Padre is ready to see you.'

Julian kissed Clarissa gently and stood up, distractedly adjusting the folds of his rather simply woven shirt as he walked behind the hurried short steps of the aid towards the largest door in that hall. Both men disappeared behind a solid slam. The copper and oak resonance was still waking up the saints upon the coloured mosaics of the palace when the massive door was opened again and the papal aid stuck his head out, this time almost hiding behind it. He came just about crawling, walking on a much humbler position than a minute before. 'You are also cordially invited to see the Pontiff, Lady Clarissa' he mumbled, without daring to look at her.

When Clarissa entered the hall, she was welcomed with a kind smile and a nod, from a man that she did not expect to see on the throne. Clarissa was anticipating a flamboyant, vain rooster, with its long silver hair carefully folded over sumptuous vests, probably holding onto the hilt of a sword. Instead, the bald-shaven man had a tired face that floated high above a thin neck and a plain white cassock. Pope Benedict VIII certainly appeared different than the man Julian had described to her from his previous meetings. The pope's gaze was so honest that it felt too late when Clarissa caught herself smiling back.

Benedict watched the tall woman approaching in confident steps. Long legs and rather careless swaying of the hips were noticeable through the insistent clinginess of her gown. A firm chest fought its way out of the folds of a cloak that fell in waves below her neck. The hair, maybe black or dark brown, seemed to be quietly tamed under the wimple, and a beautiful face had not yet aged much, still conserving the roundness of a child's. But those eyes that shone through the hall as the rays of a stained glass window were what made the pontiff sigh with awe. *Did he desire that woman?* Not so much as he admired her magnificence, as he did likewise to the powerful man with long black hair and a crooked nose that knelt a few steps below him. Much more than envy, the pope breathed with a touch of melancholy but still with utter appreciation and respect for that union. When he saw Clarissa kneeling next to Julian, the pope advised 'Please, do take a seat.'

'If my husband will kneel down, I will be with him.'

Benedict fought against the temptation to make a couple of unnecessary remarks that occurred to him for a second or two, before directing the word to Julian. 'My son, I was rather non-attentive to you when we met for the first time, in Rome.' He heard or saw no reply and continued. 'You came from the Holy Land, bringing with you the Holy Face of Our Saviour, and still you told me nothing of it.'

There was a loud clang from a darker corner that reverberated through the walls, when Bishop Grimizzo accidentally dropped a German brass goblet he had been fumbling with. The bishop mumbled a discreet apology.

Julian cleared his throat and spoke to the pope without raising his eyes. 'Beatissimo Padre, the crucifix was a present given to me by the keeper of the Holy Sepulchre, a man called Nicodemus. The sculpture was considered inappropriate by the clergymen of Jerusalem, who only tolerate flat depictions of the Christ. It was I who saved it from destruction by my promise to carry it away when I left.

This crucifix is no more than an image made as a gift to me for saving that man's life. It is no relic at all, certainly never deserving of your attention in a time of Saracen siege in Italian lands. However, if there is one more item to include in my humble request for your forgiveness though, it should be for the blasphemy of the use of my resemblance by the dedicated sculptor to carve the face of the Christ.'

The pope nodded quietly in condescension, before suggesting 'I suppose such words of honesty should not be uttered again, for the tranquillity of our Bishop Grimizzo.'

Julian continued 'It appears that the belief in the miraculous power of this Holy Face cannot be shaken by the truth behind that statue. I have tried many times to convince –'

'Then you have done enough, Julian of Mans' interrupted the pontiff, with a raised voice and a forced grin. Clarissa lowered her head further to conceal a bitten lip. Benedict lifted the worn skullcap that covered his baldness and ran a thin, feminine hand over the coarseness of the hurriedly shaven skin. 'I am tired, Julian,' he continued, 'This has been a long trip and an uncomfortably hurried return. An educating experience it was, certainly pleasurable, but moreover it has been revealing. I do not look forward to the troubles that await me in Rome, but my heart and my body do need a rest. Rather than lose ourselves in matters that have been resolved, we should talk about your burden.'

'Yes, Beatissimo Padre,' Julian said, for the first time raising his black eyes towards the pontiff, 'I came to ask for penitence, as my punishment was the very perpetration of my crime and the resulting loss. You probably know the nature of my gravest sins.'

'I do,' the pope said, refraining from curling his lips, 'for the parishioner of Controne has spoken to me of this tragedy. But how could you? Certainly you must have had the *devil* in your heart to savagely kill a sleeping couple, regardless whether you thought it was a cheating wife with a lover.'

Clarissa did not move. Anything she did, any movement, any sound, would have been out of place.

'I am quite sure I was well-guided by the devil.' Julian sighed.

'Watch your tongue, Julian of Mans!' the pope said, raising his voice with a shadow of anger in his eyes. 'We are discussing murder, not heresy. Unless you want to confess that you have had dealings with Satanas.' In his dark corner, Bishop Grimizzo almost dropped the goblet again.

Julian swallowed some bitter saliva. 'Forgive this poor choice of words to express my loss of conscience, Beatissimo Padre.' He felt that Clarissa could have broken his rib if she had dared to elbow him.

'I can forgive your language, but not your crime. This task, Julian, I don't have to tell you, is up to God!' the pope said, raising his long index finger towards the ceiling. He stood up and slowly walked around Julian. 'I do have a good memory and I can link a silkworm to a moth. Julian, you have been an exceptional hospitaller in the Holy Land, this is what I hear. A brave defender of Salerno and a champion of the Holy Sepulchre. An implacable foe of the Saracens, when it came to protect the most holy of sanctuaries of the Holy Land or to expel the infidel dogs of the

Musetto. A warrior that I envied but never was. A champion of Christ who opened the way for my name in the history of Luni.' Benedict wiped the sides of his lower lip with his thumb and forefinger, before returning to his seat. 'You slaughter your parents in a fit of rage, a man whose heart had been pierced by an arrow of betrayal. How much can a man do for love? Death does not restore love,' he giggled 'and who am I but a man who's only been dedicated to the love of God?' his gaze went from Julian to nowhere, as if savouring a long lost memory. He sighed. 'A man that has not known material love...' mumbling, '...physical love...' almost in a whisper, with his eyes shining as if an explosion of stars had broken inside him, '...the caresses of a woman...the sweetness...the softness...'

Pope Benedict woke up from his fantasy with the stare of Julian and Clarissa. He cleared his throat and stood up energetically. 'I have looked back into my life, Julian. Climbing the steps of the cross as an apostle of Jesus Christ has often taken me away from the footprints of Saint Peter and I found myself on the podium of Pride, so distant and so detached from His herd. Behind this big oaken door, Julian, across the atrium, you can look outside and you will see them. Pilgrims from all over Christendom. The true followers of the Christ. That's God's herd! They are dirty, and hungry, and cold. They are giving themselves away into the caring arms of God. But much better than me, you know them, Julian, don't you?'

'I have cared for pilgrims, that is true.' Julian nodded.

'Then do it! If you want penitence, dedicate your life to others. Don't do it for yourself, for your crime, or as your punishment. Just exercise your generosity and use the warrior in you to protect, not to kill. Be again a champion. Be the hospitaller that a man like me could never be.'

Julian and Clarissa had their heads raised. They were looking flabbergasted at the pope. No mortification, or penalties. No payments, but just an advice.

'Grimizzo!' the pope called.

The bishop emerged promptly from the corner. In spite of the cold in the palace, his forehead sported some drops of sweat.

'The ruined xenodochium we saw yesterday.' The pope said. 'Whose land is that on?'

'I will be surprised if that doesn't belong to the Episcopate of Lucca.' Bishop Grimizzo said. 'We must look at the registers and make sure the Cunimundinghi do not claim it for their own?'

'Of course, our old Bishop Gherardo presented his own family with many parcels of land...' the Tusculan pope said, nearly curling his upper lip.

'Yes, they own vast areas of the eastern bank, up to the Apennines, Grimizzo said. 'Maria Maddalena is the widow *del fu* Fulcardo. She is young, but already quite a powerful woman. Her grandfather is the merchant Battista Burle, who looks after papal accounts. We were to see him this afternoon, but the Beatissimo Padre has cancelled this audition too.'

'Then do organise for the reconstruction of the xenodochium,' said the pope, standing up again, now on a conclusive stance. 'I don't need to see that banker, but he holds the means to make a xenodochium for those pilgrims that need a station, a shelter before they come into Lucca,' he declared. Then he turned to Julian, 'Julian of Mans, you will be the hospitaller. 'That's your penance, if you want to submit to God's will! You are to leave all your possessions in Luni, and of course you should bring your good wife, if she wants to leave home too. And you will care for the pilgrims that come to and from Lucca and Rome, running a xenodochium, or better, a domus hospitalis pauperum, as people say these days, on the Via Francigena, by the river Serchio, in the parish of Controne.'

Grimizzo again cleared his throat. 'That xenodochium is not any more on Controne's land, which stops in Chifenti. The xenodochium belongs to Anchiano.'

The pope was losing his patience. 'Well, then make it part of Controne!' He turned again to the couple and said solemnly 'Raise, hospitaller. Raise and look at the different man that I am. Like me, you are re-born today. If you want to look at redemption, go and serve God, and He will look into forgiveness.'

The couple kissed the papal ring and left.

Clarissa was ecstatic, holding tight to Julian's arm, ready to explode, but she had to contain herself before reaching the front door. Julian's face was expressionless still. The pope's blow of generosity came as a surprise and told him something about rescue from hell. It the atrium, they both bowed their head respectfully to an elegantly dressed red-haired young woman, who made a tremendous effort to acknowledge the civility. Outside, Clarissa threw herself into his arms.

'Hospitallers, Julian! How come we never thought of that? We will have the best hospital on the via Francigena! Moreover, we will be close to Martino and Caterina!'

Julian embraced her. He tried to smile, but his heart was still too heavy for that.

In the bishop's hall, the pope's aid returned from the atrium and whispered something in the pontiff's ear.

'What does this Maria Maddalena want with me?' Benedict groaned. After a few more whispers, he finally said with the wave of a hand. 'I have no idea who Sister Caterina is! If she is the woman that allegedly lives with Martino of Controne, I did not meet her. I am not interested and I am sure that she is a perfectly presentable woman, to divide a home with such a bright, active parishioner. I had a pleasurable time in Corsena, including when I sat down with Martino. I have looked at Battista Burle's state of accounts and I am satisfied with it. The baths have been gainful and now I want to see more comfort and care provided to those thousands that come to Lucca and cannot afford it. I have made the best out of a good man's penitence for a heinous crime.' He stood up and left, climbing the steps towards the bedrooms. From the top of the staircase, Pope Benedict VIII took his skullcap off and ran his hand again over the trimmed scalp. He shouted to the aid that still waited in the hall 'Tell this Maria Maddalena that we have no dealings to converse about. The pope is weary, tell her, and he must make his way into Rome. She has the pope's Apostolical Blessings to return empty-handed to wherever she came from.'

'You should all appreciate that the Beatissimo Padre gave me his personal blessings when he called to see me in Rome.' Maria Maddalena of the Cunimundinghi said, with her chin so high that it was all that some people could see.

Uncomfortable with the knowledge of the truth, Bishop Grimizzo lowered his eyes.

'I'm unsure of what that means,' Bernardo delle Rocche said. 'Does that make you more deserving of some flattery before our eyes?'

Julian and Clarissa were surprised to see Bernardo fronting that powerful young woman, who owned that castle and most of the frost-covered land they saw above and below them. Bernardo was an Obertenghi indeed, but he was there at the invitation of that rather handsome but arrogant redhead, whose father was the fragile foreigner with the thin beard that Julian had accompanied to Il Poggio years before. Bernardo had described her as a witch, but a courteous Maria Maddalena started by devoting ceremonious attention towards Clarissa, the Lady of Luna. Not much later, on learning that the couple was renouncing their riches and the fortress in the lands of Luni to be hospitallers down the road, she was quick to drop the tone and carry on with no more than long stares at the couple from the heights of her nostrils. Clarissa sat beside Julian while Bernardo discussed the hospital with Maria Maddalena, Martino of Controne and Bishop Grimizzo, who looked older and more caustic by the day.

When Maria was about to open her lips to explain the honour of the pontiff's blessing, Bernardo was quick to intervene: 'Anyway, although I am not obliged to, I will ensure that my people participate on the building of the hospital, not only those in the Traghetto, but from the Rocca of Mutiano, Oneto, La Cuna, Diecimo, all the way to Colle di Manch and Tempagnano, down from Wald Ottavo. However, the hospital sits on your lands Maria Maddalena. So it is *your* people, from Menabla, Chifenti, Luliano, to Bertagna and Anchiano, who should be much engaged up to their necks.'

Maria clenched her jaws to keep control. She exhaled after a while, just to say 'Bernardo, you need not to tell me where my loyalties should sit. That is for *me* to decide.' She grabbed an iron bowl of water that stood on the table and poured it into another empty bowl. Unexplainably, to all visitors, she kept doing that, pouring water slowly, from one bowl to another.

'There are fines, you know' Bernardo shrugged, brushing off that bizarre image from his thoughts. Martino and the bishop carefully nodded.

'I know much better than anyone!' she said, without stopping her exercise and then, looking at Grimizzo, 'Those from my lands who do not contribute into road maintenance pay the stipulated twelve *denarii* penalty per head by the statutes of the bishopric.'

The lady of Anchiano sounded serious, and they all considered the weight of such penalties on the peasants, knowing that she would charge them, easily. A true granddaughter of Battista Burle. Twelve denarii was a full solido, the most effective penalty the bishopric could have devised for obliging the villagers to clean and maintain their roads and even hospitals. There was silence for a moment, somehow triumphantly for Maria Maddalena of the Cunimundinghi.

It was mid-afternoon in Anchiano and a cold breeze blew through the draperies, allowing for some light onto the thick oaken table where they sat around. The castle of Anchiano stood tall and lonely on the top of the rock, overseeing the vast mulberry orchards, olive groves and harvested fields of farro that extended across that flat valley, all the way to the woods of the Serchio. That winter had frozen the ground a few times, but not too deeply, and little snow had fallen since December.

The bishop meant to wrap up the meeting. Grimizzo was tired and cold. He felt uncomfortable under the same roof as that menacing woman, of which so many rumours he had heard about. Poisonings, executions, murder, witchcraft. He took a gulp of wine and slammed the goblet soundly on the table. 'So when are we to have the villagers gather in the old xenodochium to renovate the building under the direction of Julian of Mans?'

'Why not by the twenty-fifth of March, the Feast of the Incarnation?' Bernardo suggested, quite careless. 'Springtime will be at our door. We can start the New Year working on the xenodochium.'

'Not at the start of spring,' Maria was quick to intervene. 'All villages will be busy by then. Road maintenance is usually done for a week before.' Her knowledge of the rigidity of town life along the Serchio was certainly more precise than Bernardo's.

'Let's do it two weeks before the Feast of the Incarnation then.' Bernardo suggested. With enough people and good weather, we can clean the terrain and raise the walls in one week.'

They all nodded, including the stone-lipped Maria Maddalena, which just lowered her eyelids in agreement. She dropped the bowls on the table and stood up, on a clear gesture to take her guests to the door 'It will be cold indeed, but two weeks to the feast of the Anunciation of the Blessed Virgin Mary it is then. The hospital should be ready in a fortnight if all come down to help. It could be functioning on the New Year, the day we celebrate the Annunciation of the Arcangel Gabriel, *the day that the porter of light fell from the sky.*'

While retrieving their horses at the foot of the rock, Bernardo waited until they were left alone by the farriers and stablemen of Anchiano to say 'I'll not be surprised if the witch hides this decision and her people will not come down to assist on the day, just out of ignorance. Then she'll be touring the land to collect some fines.'

'I don't think so,' Martino said. 'With many of the Cunimundinghi eyeing Maria's lands, she needs the might of her men-at-arms to protect herself. Her personal magnificence would not be sufficient to sustain her if she betrayed her own people.'

They kicked their heels in, but not without sparing a last glance up to the castle and notice, on the single tower standing taller than the walls, out of the highest window, two heads peering out.

'Who's that other one watching us with Maria?' Clarissa asked. 'Is that a child?'

'That's probably Arrigo, her son' said Bishop Grimizzo, 'the only heir of Bishop Gherardo's line of the Cunimundinghi to inherit Anchiano, when all the children of Fulcardo's only brother Sigifredo are in Lucca.'

'And you know what they say about Arrigo?' Bernardo asked.

'No.' Julian and Clarissa said together, shrugging their shoulders. His eyes were still dark with grief, but hers were flashing with avidness to hear his tale.

Bernardo gave one of those grins of satisfaction before starting a story. 'Rumour has it that, among many other wicked deeds, Maria Maddalena of the Cunimundinghi was the murderer of an old foreign midwife that lived in Corsena. The old man drowned in the Serchio after an altercation with her, under the Bridge of San Frediano, on the same place where I plunged with Antelmino di Gottefredo. They say that Béla cursed her unborn child before he fell into the dark waters. He dared her to beg the Devil himself to lift the curse.'

They all touched their own foreheads and hearts, shoulder to shoulder, marking a sign of the cross. Except for Julian and Clarissa.

On reaching the river path, where Bishop Grimizzo would turn southwest and brave the shorter road to Lucca with a good number of escorts, the bishop seemed to be in the worst of his moods, before splitting from Martino, Bernardo, Julian and Clarissa.

'I expect to see the xenodochium ready to take on the first pilgrims that walk these paths in springtime,' the bishop said. 'Two weeks is not much, but there is little needed to make a hospital. I shall be here right after the Feast of the Incarnation or, as Maria Maddalena well said and you did not notice, *the day the porter of light fell from heavens.*'

They all made a blank face, as if asking the bishop for an explanation.

But it was Martino who enlightened them. 'This woman is indeed smart. She knows more than one suspects. *The day the porter of light fell from the sky.* Can' you tell? *The Morning Star – Lucifer!*'

They all crossed themselves, except for Julian and Clarissa, who were too frozen to move. When they had already turned north towards Chifenti, Bernardo kept saying. 'I told you she was a witch. She is a witch!'

On that eleventh day of March from the year of our Lord One Thousand and Twenty, crowds filled the Serchio route of the Via Francigena, or *Via Clodia* as many of the inhabitants of the Caferonia preferred to call it. They were not going to Rome, neither to Lucca, but to the old hospital of Chifenti, and they came from as far as Menabla, hidden from the Lima valley into the Apennines, or Tempagnano, at the feet of the Apuane. One individual per household, as it was traditionally required. Old Testa had never been more cantankerous than on that cold day when he transported hundreds of them across the Serchio. His son, the not less bitter-hearted and hostile Young Testa, took over at mid-morning.

After a well-slept but anxious night in Controne, Julian and Clarissa had strolled down the chestnut forest and crossed the Lima before sunrise, ready to instruct the newly arrived on the clean-up task. From Chifenti, they were accompanied by a few peasants and a well-meaning simpleton, shy and tame. They all called him Spatola.

On this first day the people of the Serchio pulled out stones from the ground, wrenched vines, removed trees and chopped grass and bush with the limited tools that few had bought. They carried their own meagre rations and it did not take all day to finish all that could have been done.

From the second day, with pickaxes, spades, ropes, mattocks and rakes, they managed to clear the area around the building and place the stones in an organised disposition to be re-used for the walls. The building had a long rectangular shape, of over sixty feet by thirty. One of its ends had a rounded shape, which had probably been used as a chapel. Most walls did not survive above a height of two to three feet, but parts of the back wall stood to full height of two floors, above sixteen feet up to the roof line.

The villages also sent cartloads with food supplies and lime, for the mortar mix. They had to pray for good weather with the materials they had.

Clarissa found a clean area to organise a kitchen, the ample square end of the rectangle, which took priority over the following days. Masons, loggers and carpenters came next, plus cartloads of marble slabs, and soon the flooring for the kitchen was finished, courtesy of Bernardo delle Rocche.

Layers of stone spiralled on top of each other, growing quickly into walls, but not so much to the expected rate, for lime mortar would not dry in wet weather, and least under rain, when it gobbed out like raw dough under the weight of the stones. By the time the walls had reached half the projected height, two days of rain stalled the laying of stone bricks.

The quality of mortar used in that country had horrified the Bukhari Immanuel from the days when he was first told lime and clay was all he had to build the baths. He knew there was an essential ingredient missing, which would make it water and weather resistant, but maybe they would find him incurably crazy if he suggested it. Given the rush in which the hospital was done, he didn't bother.

Firm beams were positioned across the building, to provide support for a second level. Walls were reinforced with wooden and brick columns. Besides one larger opening for a window next to the front door, one in the kitchen and one next to the back, a few smaller openings were placed over the top of the walls above the upper floor. The structure for a roof was completed for a wooden type. However, Bernardo insisted they would be tiling the roof with the traditional flat stones, which few houses along the river could have afforded.

At this stage, past the two planned weeks of reconstruction, the hospital was already in full use, night and day, as workers and pilgrims ate from food prepared in the kitchen and many already spent the night between the safety of those new walls and the scant roof that started to build above them.

The upper floor was not completed except above the kitchen, on a bedroom for Clarissa and Julian; and on the rounded end of the building, as storage for straw. It left a large central hall with a high ceiling and plenty of air to breathe over a mass of pilgrims that could be lodged in that post. A solid set of stairs led up to the bedroom, but only a common ladder to the upper straw boards. With the approval of Martino of Controne, the chapel was not to be rebuilt inside the large building, but a new chapel would be erected on the side, in a future endeavour. Although severely sharp over the front wall, the roof behind the building sloped gently and extended further over a terrace for beasts of burden. The hospital was the fastest construction the Serchio had ever seen.

For those who loved Julian, they saw him softening his features and diving into the daily work. Not that he smiled easily, but some warmth in his heart was once again perceptible, by his friendly touch, welcoming eyes and encouraging words. Those were blessed times that would have been remembered for long, in spite of a couple of upsets.

One was the frequent transit of men-at-arms from Anchiano. They were daily sent by Maria Maddalena to the villages for verification of attendance. The twelve denarii were charged from each family of more than two that had not sent a healthy member. There was anguish and outrage, with frequent beatings, and lootings and even destruction. The troops were always accompanied by a riding page that took the little Arrigo on his saddle, not yet four-years-old. All villagers watched in silence the parading of that child, fearing a grim future that awaited them when it was announced that the heir of those lands was being sent to a raid to learn how to deal with the rabble.

The other upset was the death of Old Testa. The ferrymen had quickly dwindled during the intense traffic of those days, physically and verbally. He started by tiring easily, walking with difficulty back to his shed and being replaced by a fiery Young Testa. The skeletal figure of Old Testa was still there at the bank of the Serchio every morning, defying and intimidating the villagers with the same old questions and demanding payment, even when he was told, day-after-day, that those trips were not to be charged. But when the cursing and grumbling ceased and Testa only moved the raft with trembling hands holding the pole, they all knew there was something wrong with the old grouch.

The houses of the Traghetto were an extension of Mutianum, where the local priest Diloguardi came from to perform the unction of God with the consecrated oil. Old Testa was laid on the floor in his shed, while the priest rubbed his oiled fingers on every organ correspondent to the senses he recited: 'Through this holy unction and His own most tender mercy may the Lord pardon you whatever sins or faults you have committed by hearing, smell, taste, touch, walking, carnal delectation.'

Young Testa watched it from a dark corner, mumbling with little sympathy for the priest's or anyone else's words 'You fucking, wicked, men of God, calling my father a sinner, when true iniquity is across the damned river. All, those bastards, foreign devils, building an accursed den for the miserable pilgrims, mostly outlandish beggars without a rusty denarius to spare, working my father out to death, those fucking pricks...'

The hospital was named Santa Croce – the Holy Cross – anointed by the bishop of Lucca and the parishioner of Controne in a ceremony two weeks after the Feast of the Incarnation. It would charge no fee to care for the pilgrims, being sustained by the diocese of Lucca, maintained by the lands on both sides of the Serchio, as far as north as Fornulo and Chifenti and as far South as Wald Ottavo.

The xenodochium of Santa Croce became a favourite stopover within a route that gained fame over its rival Ligurian stretch. Gentle care, a warm shelter, a frank welcome and great food made the reputation of few other hospitals but Santa Croce. Julian's name was spoken from starting pilgrimage points far away over the Alps, while Clarissa's refreshing aura was made famous. Her fame was carried along all pilgrimage routes of Christendom , from Urbe Compostella across to the Holy Land. In a few years, the inhabitants of the Serchio village could swear that all rainbows in the region started from the hospital.

No matter whether they used the hospital as a stopover or not, pilgrims were still required to hand a fee of one denarius to cross the river to the western side, where no more tolls would be charged through the lands of Bernardo until they reached the vellutini and gates of Lucca. Young Testa was frequently visited by a few riders from Lucca and he would grudgingly forward the collected toll to the bishopric.

The alternative to cross the Serchio at the xenodochium of Santa Croce would be to follow the eastern road south, risking the danger of marauders and path tolls that were often imposed by Anchiano or by Antelmino di Gottefredo's lands, both before and after the castle of Moriano. So the obvious choice for crossing the river established well the western road as the main route for the Via Clodia, leaving its eastern counterpart into greater oblivion and negligence.

Julian and Clarissa used some of their own funds, all deposited under the care of Battista Burle and the Di Cunizio brothers from Lucca, to build a storage house in the back and an extra shed to be used as a stable. The chapel itself was never erected during those years that the hospital was cared for by the couple. And neither the name of Santa Croce picked up. The xenodochium of Chifenti, as it was sometimes called, was better known as the house of Julian, the Hospitaller.

A Clapper in the Storm

In the year of our Lord of One Thousand and Twenty Four, the Italian peninsula was devastated by a very wet autumn season, mercilessly followed by a ferocious winter. While many crops failed to bestow their precious grain, toppling with rot on the muddy ground, timber for fire swelled with moisture and coal supplies hissed at failed attempts to light them. The only plentiful harvest of that year was kindly granted to the Angel of the Lord, whose scythe cropped thousands out of cold, famine, diseases and the inevitable violence triggered by living life as defenceless, cornered, wounded beasts.

The valley of the Serchio was not particularly affected by snow, being instead hammered with incessant deluges that made stretches of the roads impassable for the pilgrims and isolated several villages along the river. It was during one of these freezing nights that a storm was pouring over the crowded xenodochium south of Chifenti. The generous building accumulated an extraordinary number of travellers seeking refuge under its protective roof. There were itinerant monks, stationary rings of shy nuns, cripples seeking miracles before holy images in the city, rich families that could have afforded a more comfortable stay in a tavern, poor migrants fleeing the winter, young men from the mountains on their way to try better luck with menial jobs in Lucca and local peasants of Cunimundinghi land which had been caught by the storm between deliveries of their produce to Anchiano. Not only shelter they would get, but warmth and food. The wise direction of Clarissa and Julian included overburdening their pantry and sheds with supplies, strict supervision of all food storage and a very warm, but basic runny soup. Breaches and gaps around doors and windows could not be filled, for a circulation of air was necessary to spew out the smoke from the xenodochium's three hearths and kitchen fire. A high window by the gable functioned as a smoke outlet. The Roman custom of placing tubes on top of fireplaces as a draft exit for smoke had not been used in that land for a few centuries already.

The pilgrims smothered under pelts and woollen blankets, laid over a reasonably dry palliasse. Clarissa maintained a rigid regimen for transit and the turning of straw to prevent excessive moisture and rot. Extra bales were strategically placed to avoid direct drafts on the huddling bodies that tried to sleep in that painfully cold night.

Outside, the storm fell mercilessly over the forest's lining of dry leaves, raising a crackling rumble that lingered in the thin needles of air that resisted the downpour, mingling well into the loud roar of the swollen Serchio. Gusts of wind slammed the rain on the window boards, overwhelming the pilgrims' sleep with a constant beating, and damping the crackling of the kitchen fire that still blazed under a soup with some *farro* and a diced old rooster.

And far away, under the storm's holler, a blood-chilling wail of pain and desperation arose out of the night. A petrifying human moan that begged for help, raising many startled heads out of their uneasy sleep.

'Witches!' one of the pilgrims whispered quite loudly, making more heads rise out of their covers. 'They will call our names, those demons. Shut your ears!'

Julian and Clarissa came down from their room above the kitchen. Clarissa was saying 'There's someone asking for assistance, probably across the river.' Julian was tying a cape around his neck.

'Don't go!' the same pilgrim alerted them, 'They are witches. They will call your names from behind you! Don't look back, or they'll take you into the forest!'

Clarissa said 'Sounds like you have been listening to the tales of Bernardo from the Rocks. But did you hear that lament? It's just a poor soul, probably freezing to death under the cold rain.'

An argument broke out, with many pilgrims rising from their pelts and blankets, supporting the warning, while few said it was nonsense. They were all cut out by the chilling lament that rose out of the storm again.

Julian opened the door. While a fight broke between an excited pilgrim that was genuinely afraid of the witches and two of the hospital wardens, Julian tried to devise who was yelling for help, but the rain was too thick. The cry rose into the storm again, definitely from across the river. A few rays of moonlight pierced the clouds, exposing a man on the western bank. Laid on the ground, he would indeed freeze to death.

Julian turned back to the hospital 'I must go, Clarissa,' he said briefly. 'It seems the people in the Traghetto passively listen to his appeal but will turn their backs and let that man die. I cannot leave this miserable soul out under the storm.' Clarissa bitterly acquiesced, lowering her eyes, understanding that nothing would stop Julian from one more penance and knowing that the boat ride across the swollen river could be a lethal challenge. She just hugged her husband, making a quick prayer for his safety. But before Julian turned outside again, his sleeve was held by a small crippled woman who had been listening.

'Don't go, Hospitaller! Please!' Her face was livid. All the blood gone from the petrified features.

Julian was gentle detaching each of her fingers off his sleeve 'It's not a witch, I could see. It's a poor soul in need of shelter. I will get my boat and...'

'You don't understand, Hospitaller. It is not just the wailing. There's something else. Maybe most of you did not hear it. Please don't go!'

'For the love of Christ how could I not go?' Julian reasoned, 'Then, should we just watch him die?'

'Can't you hear the noise now?' the crippled woman said, 'The rattling! He has got a *tarabaccola*!'

'A *tarabaccola*? And what is that?' Julian asked.

The woman shook her head, dismayed that Julian did not know. 'Tell him, woman!' someone yelled.

'It's a metal piece hanging from a wooden plate,' she explained 'It's a clapper, Hospitaller. This filthy creature must rattle the tarabaccola to clearly advise any other soul where he is. Those who hear the rattling will know they should keep the distance from his God-inflicted contagion. This sinner is a leper!'

All hell broke loose in the hospital.

While a heated discussion followed in the xenodochium, the leper cried for help again. A thin wail, almost a moan, muffled by the storm and the quarrel among the pilgrims. This time however, all those who watched the western bank outside saw Young Testa coming out into the rain, hurrying towards the man.

'Yes Testa! Help him out! Bring him over here!' Julian shouted, excited. The ferryman wasted no time in grabbing the pole he used for the ferry in calm stream days, raising high above his head and bringing it down on the leper with all his strength. While darkness thickened, Julian immediately hated his own naivety for believing Testa would have been out under the cold rain to meliorate the crisis. The Hospitaller shouted into the darkness for the ferryman to stop. A mischievous cloud allowed a ray of moonlight through, exposing Testa viciously beating the leper like a mountaineer breaking chestnuts with his *mazzaranga*.

'Leave him!' a pilgrim shouted from the hospital, 'God's already punishing this man for his sins!' At those words, which may never ever endured the storm to his side of the river, Testa finally halted, panting with rage. Cursing incessantly, he threw the pole to the side and returned to his shed.

Julian was in the storage shed, splicing all the ropes he could find. Clarissa mobilised a group of large men to help him drag his rowboat out and push it into the swollen river. Once freed in the boat, with the rope looped around his waist, Julian had little dominance over the current. While he rowed strongly, the vessel was inevitably pulled downstream, losing itself from view of the hospital and the Traghetto. On a brief but failed attempt to moor the boat near a thicket that was partly submerged, Julian appreciated the gravity of the speed the current was taking.

And the rope was getting frightening short at the hospital's end.

Very little there is to do or hope when one finds himself powerless under a massive force of nature that can destroy anything on its path. Especially when, on the next whirlpool or hills of water raising around rocks and trunks, Julian would likely roll down over such force and crash in the middle of the path, before being washed away. The odds of a fortunate outcome could only be worsened in that dark night. Or worse, the boat would be carried down over the surface while Julian would be yanked back by the rope being retrieved on the hospital bank and pulled into the water against the current. He would sink like an anchor under the force of the stream. *How stupid...*

Julian held on to a thin willow branch at the margin.

At the hospital end, there was a final yank at the rope as it reached its short end, held now by just one of the wardens. 'Don't let it go!' Clarissa cried. 'Let's pull him back and he can try again.' They started to retrieve the rope, eight people altogether. It was well stretched and certainly being pushed away by the current, but definitely not as a sinking weight. There was surely a boat in the other end. What made Clarissa's blood sink down to her stomach was the fact that when the boat appeared out of the darkness, the rope was tied to its prow. Julian was not in it. She fell on her knees, ready to retch.

'I made it!' Julian yelled from the other side. They all heard him. Clarissa laid on the wet stony bank, allowing the cold rain to beat her face, bringing her back into life after one more scare. Julian was running along the sheds of the Traghetto, towards the leper and the ferry. The raft was firmly tied to the bank, well withstanding the impulse of the rebellious currents.

Julian found the man stretched on a puddle of muddy freezing water, battered by the rain, still holding his clapper in one hand an empty bowl of alms in the other. The Hospitaller touched the leper's cape and heard a moan. The man was shivering. *Alive!*

He went to the ferry, waving at the group on the eastern bank. Behind them, the warm lights of the hospital feebly battled the darkness. 'Throw me one end of the rope.' He shouted. They were probably no more than twenty paces across the river from him. They threw it a few times but it fell short of Julian's reach. Trying again, now hurling it upstream, with a branch tied at the end, Julian managed to hook it out with the ferry pole.

While he tied the rope firmly to the ferry, they were shouting something else at him. Julian tried to figure what it was, but only the voice of Clarissa stood out crying 'It's Testa! Behind you!'

Turning around, Julian had little time to defend himself from the ferry pole, which came swinging full towards his head.

I forbid you to ever enter a church, a monastery, a fair, a mill, a market or an assembly of people. I forbid you to leave your house unless dressed in you recognizable garb and also shod. I forbid you to wash your hands or to launder anything or to drink at any stream or fountain, unless using your own barrel or dipper. I forbid you to touch anything you buy or barter for, until it becomes your own. I forbid you to enter any tavern; and if you wish for wine, whether you buy it or it is given to you, have it funneled into your keg. I forbid you to share house with any woman but your wife. I command you, if accosted by anyone while travelling on a road, to set yourself downwind before you answer. I forbid you to enter any narrow passage, lest a passerby bumps into you. I forbid you, wherever you go, to touch the rim or the rope of a well without donning your gloves. I forbid you to touch any child or give them anything. I forbid you to drink or eat from any vessel but your own.

The Office of Exclusion
Edmond Martène - De Antiquis Ecclesiae Ritibus, 'Ordo I'
qtd. in Martinus Cawley, 'The Life of Alice the Leper
and the Silver Age of Villers,'

Blood streamed from Julian's half ear, thinning out into the water that taped his long hair to the shoulders. He was holding the ferry pole now, getting off his muddy knees, with a severe stony face of clear disapproval. 'Testa, you fool,' he groaned, 'you must hit me much harder and faster if you want to topple me off my feet.'

The ferryman walked backwards, looking in terror at both Julian and the leper. His eyes grew in disbelief as Julian meant to drop the pole and help the leper up. 'You cannot...' Testa said, with a trembling chin.

'I will!' Julian answered, leaping forward to hold him by the collar, hissing on his face. 'Now if you insist to interfere, you will taste the timber of this pole on your tongue, Testa, obviously going in from your bottom. Understood?'

'It's an abomination!' Testa shouted, the vein on his forehead almost burning as he screamed at Julian, 'You are defiling the ferry! You are corrupting it all!'

'Go away,' Julian said, shoving Testa back on his feet.

'Fucking foreigner!' the ferryman spat, 'I always knew it. We have too many of your lot! Only a fucking foreigner – you – would end it all for these lands. That's it, Hospitaller: I'm gone! You may take the ferry and crash it down the river, taking with you the leper and his disgrace downstream to the marabbecche. As for me, I won't touch this ferry again, ever!' and he turned back to his shed, the largest but not the best kept shed in the Traghetto.

And that was the last time they ever saw Young Testa in those parts of the Serchio.

Julian carried the leper to the ferry. 'My tarabaccola and my bowl!' the leper moaned, extending bandaged hands with a hideously deformed shape. Julian laid him on the ferry and quickly retrieved the leper's most valuable objects from the riverbank. One which would alert and protect the world from his corrupt warp and the other which allowed the world to help him subsist in existence until death ended his misery.

On the opposite bank, those watching Julian took the other end of the rope and moved as much upstream as they could. When Julian untied the ferry and gave the sign, they pulled the rope vigorously and, in spite of the ferocious current, the ferry quite easily made the arch to the eastern bank.

Clarissa had no time for savouring Julian's safety or for inspecting the wound on his ear. Carrying the leper, so light and weak on his arms, Julian felt the rain thinning out, but the largest challenge in saving that man from freezing to death stood at the hospital door. A crowd. The pilgrims and guests at the xenodochium were silently waiting to see how close Julian would get, carrying that hooded man with a veiled face. And they were ready to fight.

'The leper does not enter here.' A voice said in the crowd.

'Out of the way!' dismissed Julian, with the shivering man flat on his arms. 'This poor soul needs help or he will die.'

'What? Are you a Hospitaller or just the village idiot?' asked one of the disgusted pilgrims. 'Let God decide! But we know this is a xenodochium, and no lazar house!' They were forming a human wall behind the opened door. 'You can help this creature by the river bank and let him go. There are a dozen xenodochia in Lucca, if they are stupid enough to accept lepers. There's talk about the construction of a *Domus infectorum Sancti Laçari* on the road to Porcari, but this wretch should better find his place among the *leprosaria* in Rome, or in Genova, away from here. Hospitaller, hear us well: We will not allow you to defile this shelter with that sickness.' He was a fairly large man. Arms crossed in defiance and legs firmly planted. Behind him, most of the pilgrims supported the banishment. Monks and nuns stood on that barrier. None of them contemplated the idea of sharing that safe haven with that repellent creature.

'Nonsense!' said Julian. 'This is my house and I should be entitled to bring in the guests that I choose. For the love of God...'

'God? How dare you defy the designations of God, Hospitaller?' one of the monks asked. 'God has chosen to punish this man for his sins and you have the bile to debate it?'

'Take that hood out!' the crippled woman suggested. 'Look at the leper's face under the veil and think again if you want to bring him inside.' She laughed bitterly.

Julian looked at the single hole on the hooded man's dark veil, the terrified eye deep behind it, trembling so close to his face, so close to falling forever into darkness.

Before he could say anything, Clarissa intervened, stepping menacingly towards the human wall. 'Out of the way, you scum!' her noble blood was now doing the talk. 'This is my house and it was I that allowed you in! The night is high and we all need sleep and warmth.' She spoke with firmness and command, beauty and supremacy towering over the defying crowd. 'Now if you want shelter from the rain and cold, to keep away from the forest witches, stay quiet inside and shut your mouths about anyone else who sleeps in here,' she extended her clawed hands towards them, opening a funnel through the pilgrims' wall towards the door. 'And if you have a problem with that,' she continued, as she entered through the trench, 'I will personally drag you out and call Maria Tenebrosa, our forest witch. She will fly through the woods, faster than a falcon. And you will hear your names, one by one. And we will hear Maria Tenebrosa gladly eating the flesh of those that she calls, feeding their bones to the river...'

When they had all stepped to the sides, some livid with fear, others fuming with humiliation, Clarissa turned to Julian and peacefully asked 'Bring him in, Julian. Into our room. Keep him away from this ignorant rabble.' As Julian passed carrying the leper on his arms, Clarissa rattled the clapper in front of the pilgrims' faces. The crowd stepped back further. The crippled woman spat.

'We need to get you warm!' Julian said, as they hurriedly entered the small bedroom. In addition to a number of wooden chests and the couple's mattress, the space held no more than a small fire that still burned firmly inside a copper pan. Julian was quick to ask Clarissa to get more blankets and he told the leper 'We will rid you of your clothes.'

'No, please...I don't want you to witness this...' the man moaned with a hiss, stretched on the floor straw. Suddenly his voice rose to a command. 'Actually, I don't want to see *myself*.'

'You're under my care now.' Julian said, holding the man firmly and standing him up. The leper could hardly keep on his feet from the violent shivering. 'What is your name?' Julian asked.

The leper coughed violently. Julian imagined he could have been laughing. 'I have no name. I am not even alive. You are a good man, but make no mistakes: I have lost my name the day I died without meeting death. I am a leper, that's my name. A walking eyesore. Stay away and you will not be affected by my curse. Hear my tarabaccola!' His trembling hand, ruined and in tatters, stretched out and felt the straw, searching for his clapper,.

'Let me help you out of this freezing death and we will tend to your wounds.'

'No...' the leper moaned. He whispered other things, not understandable, maybe curses, but it was too late. Julian raised the dark veil that covered the man's face.

The one eye that was opened, the one recognisable humanity that still lingered in that stony mass of thickened skin, calmly lowered its eyelid in shame. Julian said nothing, while Clarissa, returning with rugs to dry the man, dropped her chin, paralysed at the door. The bulky rock that covered the leper's face softened, moving into shapes of sadness and, somewhere inside its crevasses, salty tears burned the exposed flesh that bulged under his scaly skin.

Julian broke the silence with an expedient tone 'Hand me the rugs, Clarissa. We need to get him out of these wet clothes before they kill him.'

They could not rub vigorously to wipe him dry, for the scaly skin seemed to be excessively moist, breakable, too delicate to the touch. While Clarissa carefully patted every bit of skin revealed, Julian continued to slowly and respectfully undress the man.

When the quivering figure stood naked, shoeless, balancing on his shortened feet while Julian and Clarissa unwrapped his hand bandages, the man brought out a hidden force from within to speak, murmuring with a bitter smile of sarcasm behind his stone-thickened lips: 'Are you satisfied now? See how much more repellent I can be? Yes look at this monstrosity! See? No manhood, no fingers! No fingers needed to hold a dick when I piss. Look at me! This is not a man you are caring for.'

'I have seen many people with your sad ailment.' Julian said, as Clarissa covered the man's nakedness with a dry rug. 'That was in the Holy Land. Pilgrims who sought for a miracle that was never granted. But behold. Leprosy in the East is not excluded from everyday life as we do to lepers in our lands.' Julian quickly spread an ointment of pot marigold on what was left of the man's hands and feet. 'You are still freezing! Your body is cold.'

Someone shouted from downstairs 'Do not bring the plague of this sinner here among us!'

Julian looked at his bed for a long time. The comfortable, soft, crackling mattress stuffed with dried beech leaves, cosily covered with a thick layer of pelts and blankets. He could not brush the image off his thoughts. He exchanged a gaze with his wife, on a brief moment of mutual understanding and sad realisations. Clarissa bit her lip and lowered her eyes in acquiescence. Julian understood she had reluctantly but generously given him freedom to exercise the size of his heart.

'Please sit at my bed and have some soup.' Julian said.

Clarissa went downstairs and returned with a bowl of the broth. The leper feebly held it and took a few sips. In a couple of minutes, bowl and a small cube of rooster meat rolled down the floor when the man fell unconscious on Julian's lap.

'He is going to die, Clarissa! He is so cold.' Julian was desperately trying to revive the man, gently tapping the thickened face. 'Wake up! Please stay awake!'

'He needs to be warmed up!' Clarissa said with a face of doubt. Julian embraced the man and leaned down, rubbing him energetically but not too hard on the skin. Clarissa covered both with layers of wool blankets and pelts. She prepared a palliasse and fed the fire in the pan. The pleasant, yellowish smoke of relatively moist beech and chestnut danced in thick sinuous lines to form a ceiling in their room, escaping with the draft that came through the stairs by a well placed gable window.

'Please wake up. Stay warm! God, keep this man alive!'

The leper moaned.

'Yes!' Julian encouraged. 'Please stay awake. C'mon! Stay awake. Tell me something, tell me about you!' Julian patiently continued the rubbing, sweating desperately, covering the man as much as he could with his own body heat.

The leper moaned again.

I am Theodoro del fu Sanjacopo, from Bologna. I am perhaps twenty two or twenty three years old, not really sure, for I have lost my past life and pay no heed to time or to the current days. And why? It's probably because I was born in the year that Satanas was bound to break his chains and return to this world of sinners. After all I come from a wealthy family of landowners and coppersmiths, always loyal to the Church of Saint Peter in Bologna and the miraculous power of the stolen relics of Saints Vitale and Agricola.

It all started when I was fourteen, when my father Sanjacopo del fu Geremia succumbed to an endless spell of nose bleeds. Although the best physicians in Bologna applied their most powerful concoctions, the nose kept fragile, runny, bleeding constantly. Moreover, a skin ailment seemed to irradiate from it, covering the entirety of his face. Coincidently, our neighbour Lamberto del fu Liuccio, another coppersmith who controlled a number of foundries and a house of trade, was also cursed with a similar plague. I remember hurting my fingers and hands much more frequently those days, and the healing process of a wound was frequently interrupted by renewed damage. It had not even dawned to the family that we had all the same ailment as my father, until the physicians of both my father and his neighbour Lamberto exchanged information about their patients.

And then, one day, our house was invaded by masked men. Terrifying memories. I just wish I could forget the pain, those men pitiless beating us all with wooden sticks and breaking all of the family's valuables. But how could I forget, if such thrashings have happened to me ever since, as you have just recently witnessed. Those men broke my mother's teeth when they could not tolerate her screams of protest as they undressed her and my sisters. We were all laid facing the floor, naked, while they poked us with their sticks. We were asked who we had been fornicating with. The question was so preposterous that we responded with a baffled silence, which triggered another vicious attack. My sisters had lost consciousness by the time they stopped the brutal beating. My father was quick to say that he and my mother had carnal commerce, but the children were naturally virgins.

'This is for us to find out.' those monsters said.

We were taken to a dungeon under a house next to the church of Saint Peter the Apostle. My whole family was thrown in a small cold cell, dark, fetid, moist, with soiled straw which must have been there for a long string of past prisoners. While my father shouted protests about the obvious misunderstanding and my mother tended to my sisters' wounds, we were given black robes with cowls and a veil. That's when we suspected we were being considered plagued. Hardly did we know that forever we would be obliged to hide under that attire to alert the rest of the living world of our inappropriateness. And to our greatest surprise, we found that Lamberto del fu Liuccio and his family were on the cell next to us. They had suffered similar humiliations and ruin, with little notion of what was happening and the reason for that wrong.

On the next day they took us to a storeroom in the dungeons, where we were again beaten for answers concerning our carnal commerce. We were shocked to realise many of our captors were religieux and I just could not understand why they were so interested in an activity that I had never even engaged into, and supposedly neither had they. The women bled in pain after having been probed with iron tools. Devilish devices for which I still pray to God that He sends them into the vaginas of our torturers' mothers, lovers, sisters and daughters, maiming them for life, forbidding that caste to share its acrid venomous blood into future generations. I had not even been beaten yet when my father had his legs broken and bled profusely due to the delicate scaling of his skin. By the time he was about to spill out with any lies they wanted him to confess, the door to the storeroom opened and we were delighted to see the familiar figure of Bishop Frogerio.

We implored for his benevolent assistance in that terrible wrong which had befallen us, after all, the episcopate of Bologna was our largest customer in the metal forgeries. The calm bishop sat down and listened with constantly blinking eyes and a bitter smile on his face. He finally motioned for us to halt and gently explained that they had no fault or blame on that wrong. Cold-blooded and not once lowering his gaze to our naked beaten bodies, that deceitful pig of a bishop had the God-granted rashness to look into our sore eyes and blame us, reverting all the fault for their violence on us! God, he said, was punishing us very likely because we must have engaged into intimate associations with lepers, or demons or, most likely, Jews. Bishop Frogerio assured us he would be putting a stop on the burden of those city officials to extract precious information from our private life. He expected us to give our confessions freely on the next day, with names of associate families. It was of utmost importance that they found who was infecting our families with the leprosy, to cut that evil from its roots. After we were tossed back into our cell, the cold stones of the wall were not dense enough to spare us from the screams of horror and pain of Lamberto del fu Liuccio's family, having an afternoon session with the concerned city officials in that storeroom of tortures.

The night was high when Sanjacopo del fu Geremia and Lamberto del fu Liuccio discussed through the hole in the wall our possibilities. Lamberto advised us that new relatives, in-laws, had been taken in and tortured too. The bishop seemed to seize the opportunity of the plague and free the episcopate of its debts with both families. And they wanted more names. A golden chance to take justified possession of more properties if they could incriminate other families, especially Jews, who were equally involved in our families' type of activities. His relatives reported that both our houses had been looted clean by the city officials and the remaining straw, mattresses and cheaper furniture burned out on the street. Sanjacopo and Lamberto knew they were forever condemned by fate and decided to confess on the next day. The story was silly, if not childish, but sufficiently ingenious too keep the wrath of God only to our families. It would not give away any justifiable consent for the bishop to destroy more homes and lives, whether they were Jews or not, for both our families knew that three generations before they too had been Jews.

Maybe you have already heard our tale these days, for all of Bologna knows it. It tells that one day, Sanjacopo del fu Geremia was on the back patio of his house, helping his wife gut a few chickens. He had just diced a rooster when his neighbour Lamberto del fu Liuccio saw the tray with the bits of the rooster and said, looking at the nearby tower of the church, that not even Saint Peter could make that rooster crow again, even if he denied Christ a thousand times. Sanjacopo laughed at that remark and said that not even Jesus Christ Himself could command that rooster back to life any more. At that, the diced rooster immediately crowed, whole and feathered, and flew off Sanjacopo's tray, frenetically running out of his backyard. On that same day, both men were afflicted with the disease as God's penalty for their blasphemous sacrilege.

Pure lies, but the bishop seemed contented with the prodigy. They could not find the rooster, but the disease in both families was the living evidence of that miracle. We were all not only punished by God with our leprosy for mocking the Divine Powers, but we lost all our possessions and paid the episcopate and the city with our manual labour. Our families were enslaved into renovation of the church and construction of others. As Bologna did not have its own Lazar house, we were allowed to live in the yards of Saint Peter the Apostle, lodged in an underground cubicle with a grilled window on the ceiling and attend mass from a gallery build inside the church's wall. Visitors were taken to walk over our grilled ceiling to witness the lepers involved in the miracle of the rooster. They threw us crumbs, sometimes spit and urine, but hardly alms. We were all made to work mostly at night, when the citizens of Bologna did not have to be displeased with our presence in the open.

My sisters were the first to die, not too long apart. Although we were always refused to let be seen by a proper physician, we know the girls had never shown any of the stains of leprosy. They died immaculate by the plague, but from pure exhaustion, not enduring much the life of working animals, thanks to the God's mercy on their soul. Meanwhile, leprosy slowly savoured the corrosion of my skin, it killed some of Lamberto's family and it showed on my parents the deformations it promised to inflict on my own body one day. After seven years, we were all horrendously disfigured. I had lost my name. I did not resemble a Theodoro that once had lived, not to my parents, not to myself.

We began to avoid revealing our repellent appearance to each other. My father died one week after my mother was spared from this existence. That's when I ran away. I stationed myself in the environs of Milano, begging for alms. A day could only be survived without a vicious beating by carrying my tarabaccola. And it was a month ago, fleeing a brutal death that never bothered to take me with its scythe, when a group of lepers told me they would be coming to Lucca, asking the Volto Santo for a miraculous cure. I considered this nonsense for a week before heading south too. I stayed mostly on the western bank as I walked down this valley, away from people. The cold rain hammered on me for two days, until I found myself weak and exhausted, unable to continue, exactly at the point where the pilgrimage route crosses to the western side, right across a hospital of which pilgrims had told me a good soul would look at me. They were right.

Julian did not say anything.
'Are you awake, Hospitaller?' Theodoro del fu Sanjacopo asked. He was still shivering, even though the hospitaller Julian had stayed warmly wrapped around his back, with pelts and blankets.
Julian made no answer. He was sleeping profoundly.

Clarissa woke up in the middle of her dreams. The utter darkness only allowed the fire in the pan to hiss its last sparks for help. Both Julian and the leper were sleeping. She poked the embers with a few fresh sticks of chestnut and walked down the stairs to verify the pilgrims. Through the calm darkness she could discern that most were soundly asleep under a rough sea of pelts, with the exception of two wardens who minded the fires and a faint whisper that crept through the hilly blankets: nuns in prayer. The cold draft that went up the stairs told Clarissa that the unforgiving temperatures still lingered in the night outside. She went back to her palliasse. Julian still slept deeply on their mattress. She tried to fall into a rest, on that cold floor, the straw doing little to separate her from the winteriness of that night. Thinking of the tasks and chores for the next day, Clarissa's thoughts were inevitably dragged back to her warm and soft mattress. She tried not to regret her decision. She had humbly accepted that the leper should take the most comfortable bed arrangement, meaning their dear mattress, the only place where she and Julian could exchange the physical love they still entertained for each other, more than ever before. Their mattress, the only place where Julian was no more a hospitaller, but instead her saviour, her lord, her rider. But now he had brought his hospitaller role into their room, into the nest of their intimacy, all for a greater penitence for his crime. It was sad for them as a couple, she thought, but admirable for Julian as a cleanser for his soul. She would arrange for a replacement of the mattress when the leper was gone. When the weather calmed down.

When the leper was gone?

It suddenly dawned on her that the man may not have been alive, for she only heard Julian's snoring. And in a split of a second before she opened her eyes to a bright light, she already noticed that the temperature in the room had suddenly become very warm. Clarissa jumped up, looking for fire.

But what she saw made her think it was only a dream. The room was flooded with light. With her chin dropped, the gradual realisation that her vision could be real and that she was fully awake made her legs boneless, and she fell flat on her bottom. Seated on her palliasse on the floor, Clarissa raised her gaze to the gloriously tall and beautiful woman that sat on the mattress, smiling at her and gently caressing Julian's shoulder as he snored pleasantly.

Clarissa's eyes were flooding with tears. Not a bitter outpour of jealousy, for not even a pinch of selfish, possessive concern had crossed her heart when she saw that woman. Those were tears of comfort and relief. She knew well her beloved Julian was being cared for and protected by that magnificent woman. Not only because of a clearly visible a pair of wings grew from behind her shoulders, but her blinding beauty transcended any feeling of possession, property, emanating only generosity, goodness.

And the leper…he was not there anymore.

Clarissa opened her mouth to talk, half expecting not to hear her own words. 'Are you an angel?' she asked, not loathing herself for the sudden helplessness, for the embarrassment of the confusion, but actually taking delight on the sensation of suddenly feeling like a child lost in a good dream. 'And where is that man, the leper?'

'Theodoro is gone,' the giant woman said, irradiating a clear whiteness never before seen, a warm, peaceful luminescence that filled the room with the light of a sunny morning. 'Do not worry. It was his time to go.' Her voice was grave and firm, truthful, much more solid than the young features of her hands and face. Clarissa tried to keep herself together. She could not hold back the tears from seeing that wonderful creature, even though the angel's wings were hidden behind her white luminescence. That woman that could have been made of the most polished, whitest marble, a breathing sculpture with wide spiralling locks of hair, of the same malleable milky stone, held back behind her ears by rays of light that emanated from the top of her ample forehead. Although her eyebrows were ostensibly wise and imposing, she had a childish face, with full cheeks and a delicate, rounded nose. A thin, but protuberant upper lip stubbornly covered the lower one, leaving it hidden, except for a central lump that mischievously peeked out. Her small chin popped out of her round jaws, and she held a head proud above the solid, long neck.

'But, who are you?' Clarissa dared to ask, with trembling lips.

The silvery presence smiled fondly, making the light even brighter. 'I am Ish,' she said, with a sweet, but still powerful and echoing voice. 'I came to free Julian from his burden.'

Clarissa fell back, her shoulders on the wall. 'God be praised!' she exhaled in a sob. 'So he needs not pay for his crimes anymore?'

The woman moved her legs and hips to face Clarissa more directly, still sitting erect on the mattress. The sculpted stone folds of her mantle settled delicately, with the lightness of feathers. Her wings made a slight move, revealing to Clarissa the magnificent colours that hid behind the light. Ish tapped on the place next to her, where the leper had lain, 'Please come and sit here,' she suggested. 'Softer than the floor!'

Clarissa obeyed, as if commanded, but trembling and still sobbing with inadequacy and humility for being so human and inappropriate. But now that they were both seated on the side of the mattress, both touching Julian with a hand, both feeling the warmth and the heart of that man, Clarissa felt herself growing to a dimension never dreamed. She was forming a triangle with her man and a giant creature that had descended from her heights to present herself to them, eye to eye, to make her bigger.

She was face to face with an angel.

With her totally white, polished marble eyes, Ish looked at Clarissa 'You may call it penance, but that is only a choice out of confusion and sorrow,' she said. 'Penitence does not require penance. But generosity comes out of the heart, regardless of wrongs perpetrated. Julian was born with kindness and it keeps growing in him. I am here to let you know that Julian's errors have long been forgiven. He was led into it by deceit.'

'Then, there is really a Devil?' Clarissa was quick to ask.

Ish closed her eyes with a courteous grin and gracefully shook her head, throwing her spiralling locks forth and behind her shoulders. 'Men believe in a devil! Then, there is one!'

'But men believe in angels too,' Clarissa pleaded, 'and in saints, and in miracles, and in God!'

'In this case, they do exist!' Ish said, looking at Clarissa with a curious look, almost a smile.

'So why do you tell me that Julian is forgiven?' Clarissa asked. 'Why not tell him directly? Just present yourself to him.'

Ish laughed, emanating an almost blinding light and thick rays of luminescence from her forehead. She said 'Julian is too modest to share such an experience. He would keep it to himself. But his generosity should be as visible as yours. While you are noted for your goodness, Julian is famous for his crimes and his penitence. *Forget penance!*' she said delicately, raising a luminous forefinger, on a beautiful, firm hand. 'Look deeper into goodness rather than into paybacks. It is you I want to tell that, for Julian is too stubborn to accept. He will listen to you, not me. Julian is going too far on his penance. You two can do it all without mortification, without paying a painful earthly price. Did Julian have to go as far as offering his own bed to a leper? Did you have to agree with that? Julian does it for his penitence, while you do it for your love of him. From now on, only practice charity because you feel good about it.' She leaned back but held on to her knees, almost childlike, softly raising her uncommonly large feet from the floor. 'But I know Julian! He would not spread the word. He should be seen as a role model, rather than be an undiscovered hero.'

'But I am only his wife!' Clarissa reasoned, with pleading eyebrows. 'I would believe him if he told me. I can believe you when I see and talk to you! Others won't, if they only listen to me.'

Ish stood up. Not only she was taller than any human being that Clarissa had ever seen, but her wings were more gigantic than ever now. With a rainbow of colours across their width, the wings were not made of light rays as the beams that sprang from her forehead. They had real volume and real feathers. The marginal coverts around the top edge were metallic green, sliding into a bright gold, laced with blue and black rims in the inner side of the coverts, and a row of long primary and secondary feathers in the lower edge, bright red and the same shiny blue rims. The back of the wings was little visible, for she kept them erect, touching each other, but not completely extended. They appeared to be as white and marbled as the rest of her make.

'Don't go!' Clarissa implored, suddenly nearing desperation. She wanted to savour every view, every moment, every angle of that encounter with Ish. 'Please stay with us!'

'The message has been understood, hasn't it?' Ish said with her soothing solemn voice. 'But if you want me to stay, I will keep both of you company.'

'It will mean a world for Julian and I!' Clarissa moaned, as she felt suddenly tired, but in peace. Ish touched her shoulder and helped her to get into Julian's embrace. The angel covered Clarissa with some more blankets and sat still by her side, looking at her with those milky white eyes, a blindness which could penetrate through skin and explore all of Clarissa's heart.

'Do I have my own angel too?' Clarissa asked, yawning slumberous.

'You must be assuming I am Julian's own!' Ish said with a merry question tune to her words. She leaned to plant a kiss on both Clarissa and Julian, who were then deeply asleep. And regardless whether the dawn rooster crowed only three hours after that moment, this was their best sleep, ever.

The rooster crowed, loud and strident. Heads shot up in the hospital.

Clarissa opened her eyes! Not surprisingly, the angel was gone. She still had Julian's arms around her. When other roosters responded, far away across the river, she heard the crowing in the hospital again, very harsh, resonating from somewhere within those walls.

Clarissa cursed and giggled. 'There is a damned bird inside this house.' She kissed Julian on his lips. He was stretching, trying to sit up.

'But we have killed our last chickens yesterday.' Julian said, scratching the back of his head. Our rooster is diced!' He stopped to admire Clarissa's fresh beauty, the rainbow brightness that started to show in her eyes within the dusk.

'And the rooster is mostly eaten, my love!' said Clarissa, leaning to embrace him. 'Now let's see if you can quench my hunger, for I want to eat you.'

Julian tightened his embrace. His lips accepted the moisture of hers and other caresses with glee. They rolled on the mattress, and entangled their legs.

'THERE'S A ROOSTER IN THE CAULDRON!' a scream came from downstairs, followed by a strident sequence of squawking, yelling, cursing and cackling that made both hospitallers jump out of their mattress.

'The leper!' Julian yelled. He had suddenly realised Theodoro was gone. While downstairs the world seemed to be turning its guts inside out, the events from the previous night were quickly falling in order into his mind. Even his ear was hurting from the pole blow. 'Where is he, Clarissa? Where is the leper?'

Clarissa held his face close to hers 'Julian, now you have to trust me with what I will tell you.' She didn't wait for his confirmation and continued 'Theodoro, the leper, has been taken care of. There is so much I must tell you about last night, but let's resolve this revolution downstairs and I will tell you later.'

When the front door was opened, letting in a shy morning light of a warmer, dry day, the rooster flew out like a shooting star, leaving only a few feathers softly swaying in the air, while all pilgrims and guests watched in amazement the signs of the prodigy. One of the hospital wardens came with the cauldron, to show it to Clarissa and Julian. 'It's only water and vegetables. The meat is gone.' said the warden.

'The chicken could have been taken by one of the guests at night, a greedy one.' Julian suggested, curling his lip in annoyance. Many guests were now crowding behind him to listen to that conversation.

'No my lord,' the warden said, treating Julian as if he was still the Lord of Luna. 'I was sitting by the cauldron all night. Even when I slept, anyone meddling with it would have had to pass by me, and they would have received a fabulous slap. This rooster that crowed today was inside the cauldron, I swear it. It scared me dead to hear it so close, especially after such a good dream.'

There was a sudden silence, all eyes slightly rolling up, digging memories of a pleasant night. Clarissa's hand searched for Julian's and found a firm grasp that sent hot shivers through her body.

'I do remember having a pleasant dream too' a rich man from Modena said. 'The sweetest, most peaceful dream ever. With the leper! The leper that the Hospitaller took up.' As the words came out of his mouth, all other people started to protest, saying that they had also dreamed with the leper, a good dream, but they were shut frozen by Clarissa's commanding hand, raised for all to see and wait to hear the rest of the tale. The man continued 'The leper forgave the Hospitaller from his crimes, whatever they were, and walked down the stairs, I just know that. But now the leper was an angel, so beautiful and tall, white and bright as the moon that shone on the last feast of Saint Quiricus.'

While tears ran down Clarissa's face as she almost crushed Julian's hands, many others were weeping or falling on their knees in prayer. 'The long feathers on his wings were coloured like a rainbow, and it stepped carefully among us, telling me secretly what had happened. After that, I just slept my best night of sleep, ever.'

'This is the same dream that I had!' a child yelled. And a roar of general glee burst out of the hospital. 'Mine too!' they were shouting and crying.

Except for Julian who had just had a fantastic sleep, everyone's hair was standing on its base. They knew they had witnessed a miracle, praising heavens and raising their arms, probably to attract onto themselves a shower of blessings expected to be poured from heavens on such occasions of miraculous feats.

Clarissa pulled herself together and verified Julian's feet, glad to see that he was wearing warm boots. The hospital was a den of exaltation and she could see where this encomium was leading to. A few people had fainted from heat waves going through their bodies, while one of the young religieuse had entered into a state of ecstasy. Lauds were being rushed in by the monks and nuns. *Benedicite, omnia opera Domini, Domino; laudate et superexaltate eum in saecula. Benedicite, caeli, Domino, benedicite, angeli Domini, Domino...*

Clarissa rushed to the bedroom and came back with a few rugs, discreetly siding Julian and whispering between firm lips 'Let's leave Julian! Just come with me, we go outside and climb up the hill behind the stables. We go to the Altar.'

Outside, day was clearing through a refreshing haze and they could see a flat, much more behaved, but still swollen river. The ferry was gone. Julian and Clarissa contoured the building and came across a few pilgrims at the storage shed. They were pleading with a warden to let them in to verify if the rooster was hiding in there. Clarissa gave the warden the authority to allow them into the shed for a quick search. So eager they were to find a material proof of that prodigy that they missed to notice the Hospitaller's wife rushing into the track that steeply climbed the bushy cliff behind the stables, pulling a slightly reluctant Julian by the hand.

'Clarissa, tell me what's happening! What has been of the leper?' he reasoned, pushing the wet branches of beech from his face and stepping wide to avoid broad patches of rosebush thorns. She climbed further into the woods, pulling him into the protection of the wet canopy that covered the cliff, until they could not be seen by anyone down at the hospital or across the river. There, in a dark patch of the track that led to the 'Altar', no more than two hundred paces from the xenodochium, Clarissa embraced Julian passionately.

'Do you feel good this morning, my love?' she asked, when their lips parted.

'Better than ever, if it wasn't for my concern over the leper. He has disappeared and I fear that he could have been thrown down the –'

'Fear nothing!' Clarissa whispered, shutting his lips locked with one finger. Her eyes fired colours even through the darkness of the woods, in an early winter morning. She almost exploded to tell him. 'The leper did this to us, Julian! I saw the angel and she talked to me! Julian, we may never believe that it could ever happen to one of us, but it is indeed a miracle!'

'She? What?' he yelled, tremulous, holding himself onto a thin black stalk of a young beech tree. He thought he would lose the wonderful morning vigour, slipping away as his stomach tried to hurl itself out of his mouth.

'Shush!' Clarissa hasted him, and they climbed higher and deeper into the bush. Soon, they could no more hear the commotion in the xenodochium, nor even the sounds of the river. As they calmly walked up the wet track, so beaten by those days' rain, Clarissa reported to a flabbergasted Julian every single word she had exchanged with Ish. By the time the winter morning sun had welcomed both to the top of the mountain with its reassuring warmth, they were reaching a clearing called *the Altar* and Julian was only starting to try to come to terms with a message delivered by an angel.

'You have tried to convince me of the devil all of these years. Now it's your turn to believe me if I told you of an angel.' Clarissa said, her lips warmly close to his. She caressed his long hair, biting her lower lips, looking at his, which opened into a grin. Julian tightened his embrace, reassuring Clarissa of his support to her tale. She smiled back at him and said 'I want you to believe it, Julian.'

'I'm almost convinced, my love!' he said and kissed her with a passionate vitality.

Under a patch of warm light, they were lying on her rugs, over a thick layer of dried grass that had lain down from the constant rain. The cold moisture was soaking into the rugs, but Julian and Clarissa were not affected by it. Such an intense heat emanated from their bodies, too intense to be quenched by the wet grass, so much that they could not wait to finish what was unfinished that morning. And while the bleating of sheep could be heard across from another ridge, where the mountain village of Bertagna stood, the birch forest around the Altar kept the sounds of Julian and Clarissa's intimacy to that clearing only. Nobody heard any music of their lovemaking during all that day.

Except for the angels.

In the xenodochium, while the fervent pilgrims had pushed the monks to already weave the Lauds into Primes and Terces, to thank God for the blessings of a miraculous day, the crippled woman cried inconsolably. A nun brought some newly prepared broth to comfort her.

'I loathed the leper!' the woman wailed, pushing the bowl to the side. Her body felt unusually hot. Not feverish, but ready to inadequately explode. She hid herself under a blanket. 'How would I know that a filthy, low creature, a proof of God's discontent with sinners, was in reality an angel in disguise? I despised him. I spat on him. An angel of the Lord! The Hospitaller was forgiven for his sins, but I was not!' and she dug her face into a pelt, bawling with pain.

The nun was also feeling a strange heat irradiating throughout her body. She felt tender impulses of sensuality that were quite tameable and channelled into sheer generosity and compassion. She touched the crippled woman's shoulder with kindness 'You will be forgiven at the day of judgement if you –'

'Too fucking late!' the woman yelled, grabbing the nun by the cowl and violently yanking the religieuse to face her legs. She pulled her crooked, limp foot from the covers. 'Look at my leg! Look at this limping paw of mine! I cannot walk! I don't want to wait to heavens or to a final judgement. What if I am not approved? I want my cure *now*! The leper is cured, the Hospitaller is a saint, but I am still a fucking cripple!'

'A saint?' someone asked from the other side of the hall. 'Where's the Hospitaller?' They had all stopped their prayers. A burning heat was emanating from their crowded bodies.

'He's left a few hours ago,' a warden said. The hospital was a dead silence. One could see steam rising from the crowd.

'North or South?' they asked. 'Did he cross the river?'

'I don't know. I did not see…' the warden lied. 'The ferry is gone.'

The silence slowly turned into a very low hum of whispers, where the word *saint* was being constantly singled out. The buzz swell into a murmur. They felt the heat, the sensual waves that put so many to shame, but so many others to hold their partner's hand and dream of a peaceful and intimate time for later.

A few pilgrims ventured outside, bathed by the warm sunlight that hit them at Terces, verifying whether Julian and Clarissa were to be seen along the road or across on the Traghetto. Others stepped out to find some privacy in the stables.

That's when the crippled woman broke into a frenetic screaming 'Touch me Julian! Touch me Saint Julian! Heal me! Forgive me, Saint Julian!'

The uproar that exploded in the hospital sent many of the pilgrims to immediately spread the word: They had been there. It was a miracle. They had seen the leper and the angel. And Julian, the Hospitaller, was a saint!

I saw in his hand a long spear of gold, and at the iron's point there seemed to be a little fire. He appeared to me to be thrusting it at times into my heart, and to pierce my very entrails;…when he drew it out, he seemed to draw them out also, and to leave me all on fire with a great love of God. The pain was so great, that it made me moan; and yet so surpassing was the sweetness of this excessive pain, that I could not wish to be rid of it. The soul is satisfied now with nothing less than God. The pain is not bodily, but spiritual; though the body has its share in it. It is a caressing of love so sweet which now takes place between the soul and God, that I pray God of His goodness to make him experience it who may think that I am lying.

(Saint Theresa of Avila's description of her encounter with an angel)

When angels had revealed themselves to men and women, the sweet pain, the craving, the deliverance, the ecstasy, the lovemaking, the communion with God.

'Clarissa' Julian called in a whisper. She moved the long hair from her face and opened her eyes, blinding Julian with a brilliant festival of colours. He could see the sparks of her flaming heart burning deep inside the dark pupil, surrounded by a walnut edge with a golden crown lain on a bed of fresh green grass of spring, rimmed by purple and blue ripples that soon foamed into the grey of the moonlight on marble. *The lady of Luna*! Julian had never felt so happy. Their warm bodies were touching, sharing their generous heat, tingling still from their last explosion. Her hand touched his face, contouring nose, lips, chin…

'Yes Julian.' She broke the delicious silence of mutual understanding.

'You never told me what Ish looked like,' he said.

Clarissa chuckled. 'You obviously noticed that!' She had raised her torso, leaning on one elbow and still making lines with her fingers on Julian's features. 'But somehow I knew you were going to find out.' She kissed him on the lips and asked 'Why don't you tell me what you saw?'

Julian frowned with a smile 'What I saw? When?'

'Just now!' she said with an irresistible grin.

'When…I…exploded?' Julian hesitated to ask.

'When we exploded!' she hissed, with a mischievous grin.

'Good Lord!' Julian exclaimed. He sat himself next to her and cleared his throat 'Let me see: I only saw her face briefly, when she looked back a few times. A girl. She was smiling at us! Yes, she was flying over the valley and we were mounted on her back. You and I!'

'I was in front of you. You embraced me from behind.' Clarissa completed, with eyes already stinging with tears.

'That's exactly what I felt, what I saw, what I did!' Julian exclaimed with excitement. He noticed her eyes shining like a treasure of precious stones, springing tears that ran down her face and softly joined below her chin. He continued 'We could see the Serchio meandering far below, and we were as high as the snowy peaks. She was huge, a giant. Marble white, but strangely light and warm, comforting, with massive wings and feathers as long as my legs. They were white feathers where we could see, on the back of the wings, but as soon as she beat them, we could see a rainbow of colours underneath the wings.'

'Anything on her head? A halo?' Clarissa hinted, already cringing herself with excitement..

Julian thought for a second 'Yes, but not a halo. Rays of light beaming out of her forehead.'

'Hair?' Clarissa asked, just to make sure.

'Spiralling locks, light as the wind, as if marble from the Apuane had been made malleable. The locks were blown backwards by the wind which chilled our skin and she emanated a strong light that intensified our explosion. Clarissa, this was the longest outburst of ecstasy and the most realistic I could never even dream of.'

Clarissa embraced him for a long time. 'You know I saw that too, don't you?' she asked.

'I think I do,' he gulped.

'Not only on the first time. But on the others that followed too!' she grinned again, kissing him. Clarissa did not want to part lips from that heavenly exchange, but she still had to add 'And Julian, it was not only the sequential lovemaking we have enjoyed this morning. I have never felt so powerful, so safe and protected, so divine. I was one with you. It was the intensity of the pleasure, the durable explosion of delight that made us part of this angel. Julian, I love you more than ever.'

'Clarissa, I would be nothing without you. With you, I am invincible. I am God. We are God!'

They were God, and getting ready for another explosive flight in heaven.

'We haven't had that much since...' Clarissa suggested playful. They were walking down the track from the Altar. The warm sun was reluctantly leaving them, past the ninth hour of the day.

'Since a long time, Clarissa.' Julian calculated. He hurried his pace to catch up with her.

'I almost feel like boasting about it. How many times was that? Six?' she asked, extending her hand to hold his.

'No my love. Don't tell anyone. This is for us only. And I don't think it was six. It must have been five only!'

They embraced again. They did not want to leave that place.

'Do you think that's what Mary felt when she saw the angel?' Clarissa asked. Her face felt the warmth of his shoulder.

'You mean the Angel of the Annunciation?' he considered.

'Yes. Do you think Mary felt these bodily waves of sensual heat after she saw the Angel Gabriel? One of those visions and a night with Joseph would well explain her pregnancy afterwards.'

Julian laughed. 'Well, I hope you don't suggest that to anyone outside these woods. This is a blasphemous thought. Maybe when the angel visited Zecharia, the old billygoat did have to go for some intensive humping, but I don't know whether the Baptist's birth was supposed to be from immaculate conception or not. But Mary... well, that one's supposed to be a virgin. She was made with child by the Holy Spirit.'

Clarissa pursed her lips 'Well, she was the only one to tell the story. And Joseph, well, he'd be quiet about whatever she told people, as long as he could have it again.'

'Good Lord, Clarissa!' Julian laughed, 'Don't you ever dare to say that again in public!'

She dropped her shoulders, warming up her eyes. 'I will be careful, my love. It's just that I don't see angels that often.'

'Maybe we can try to see her again when we get home tonight.' Julian grinned, with all his teeth showing.

'Certainly, Julian. Number six, or seven?'

They walked together, so close, so intense the need to be touching to be feeling each other, to share that heavenly power again, and again. Forever.

It was Julian who broke the silence much later down the track. 'Do you think this intensity will bring us a child?'

Clarissa smiled to the ground, but did not look at him. 'I don't think so. We have made anything possible that a couple could do to conceive a child. It never came. It may never come. We have been so generous to others and to us. No place for a child, I guess. Probably not on the divine plans.

'We are so dedicated to each other...' Julian wondered with a frown 'so generous and yet so selfish.'

Clarissa waved her hand to brush the remark off 'Nonsense. If we are dedicated to each other, so intensely, that love is what allows us to be generous. We are indeed meant to have each other until death.'

'What if I die tomorrow?' Julian said, raising both eyebrows.

'It was worthy, and I would die together with you.' Clarissa said immediately.

'Oh, it's so easy to say that!' he said, with a chuckle.

They were walking down the narrow track that snaked through the woods on the steep slope of those hills, diving into the bottom of the valley and approaching the xenodochium. Clarissa shot her arm to stop Julian from walking any further as soon as she heard the furore, crouching behind the bushes, listening, a few paces from the stables back wall. A couple of young pilgrims were leaving woods nearby, hurriedly tidying themselves up. Other pilgrims were seen running back and forth the road, on foot and on horse. An oxcart was arriving from Chifenti, welcomed with exaltation and cheers. Their noise and the shouting were so loud that Julian and Clarissa could distinguish a crowd on the opposite margin, at the Traghetto, aroused by the hospital mob.

Clarissa paled. 'My God, we better get out of here!' she whispered.

'What is going on?' Julian asked nervously, 'I just hear and see the turmoil, but is that all because of the leper?'

She pulled him by the hand, backing up on that track, back towards the Altar. 'We cannot be here. These people are drowning in their own ecstasy. We must return and maybe find a shortcut directly down to Chifenti before it gets dark. Perhaps Amadeo can help us spend the night in peace.'

'What is going on?' Julian asked, patient as ever, always supportive and trusting Clarissa's commands. 'The leper is gone! They should be glad his is no more.'

'That is exactly the problem. The leper is gone, because of you. Because of your generosity. They say you are a saint, Julian. That is what they are saying. You are a saint!'

That day saw the birth of the legend of Saints Julian and Clarissa, the Hospitallers. Their story, to be read and to be told, would live to endure the years and still be newly written and re-written about.

Book 4: Auserculus

The Warrior Dies

It was a beautiful blue day on the Serchio. One of those days when nobody thinks of the devil.

'You are the saint, they say, aren't you?' the old religieuse asked the boatman, quite amused. Julian just smiled and shook his head. The slim woman measured him with wise blue eyes, not yet deep-set into a handsome rosy face, so alive and disarming that Julian nearly forgot to cordially help her seat herself comfortably into the unsteady boat. The Serchio ran silent and firmly beneath them, concealing *marabbecche* that softly ran their fingers alongside the planks. With nobody else to row over to the eastern bank, Julian released the boat and quickly grabbed the oars. They both sat in silence, with Julian concentrating on rowing, but shooting furtive glances at the nun, who almost grinned with amusement, never taking the cosiness of her turquoise blue eyes from him. A cold gust of wind made her tighten the cowl around her face. She had a beautifully-shaped head, far from bony, elegantly decorated with motifs of fine lines, with meaty cheeks and perhaps just too many good teeth to reflect a whole life of frugality in a monastery. Julian could notice across the distance that the meeting had finished in the hospital, and people were now dispersing. He would have passengers to row back to the Traghetto.

'Thank you,' she said, holding his hand until she was firmly on land. She handed him a denarius.

'There is no charge for crossing the Serchio on the boat, since the ferryman has left us last winter,' Julian explained, still taking the coin. 'But I do accept your donation for the hospital costs, which build up by the day.'

The nun wrapped her long fingers around Julian's fist, holding it tight around the silver piece 'You are indeed a good man!' she said with an enchanting smile. 'Care for the travellers with that fiery heart. Your reputation has reached us across the South, in Santa Maria lei Giudice.'

Another man on the river bank extended his hand and helped her onto the path. He had a thick silver mane of matted hair. Even if she had taken notice of his violet eyes or talked to him, still she would never have known he was a distant relative or her dead husband and of the boatman's wife. The nun's eyes were set elsewhere, now puzzled by a somewhat familiar face that was watching her from the road up to Chifenti.

Further north, it wouldn't be a difficult task to ford the Lima river, but definitely not an advisable exercise for a wheeled wagon. Piero of the Burle et Malachi had been patiently waiting for his father, holding his red-haired head up at attention, ready with a bullock cart, waiting at the base of the stairs of St. Peter's church in

Fornulo. The unmistakable fragile silhouette of Immanuel appeared across the shimmer of the Lima. Once his father had forder the river, Piero extended a callused hand to help him up the wagon.

'Where is Father Martino and Sister Caterina?' Piero asked. 'Weren't they heading with us to Corsena too?'

'They stayed behind, probably waiting for someone, so we walked back ahead of them,' Immanuel said, wringing the wet edges of his shirt off that gelid Lima water.

'Should we wait for them?' his son asked.

'No, not really. They could take much longer. Besides, they are strong, healthy old people. They can always take the short cut up to Controne, instead of taking the path from Corsena. Let's go. I'm hungry.'

Piero flicked the reins. The oxen slowly raised their hooves to start the short journey back to Corsena.

'This Maria Maddalena seems rather uncomfortable with your presence around.' Martino said to Caterina as soon as they left the meeting in the hospital. Ahead of them, Immanuel Ben-Malachi and Amadeo of the tavern were already walking back to Chifenti. The day was still clear and bright, with high white clouds not yet threatening to change colours. Sheltered on both sides by the valley, a cold wind blew from the south, announcing a definitive end of that summer. Julian was just leaving the Traghetto, with a passenger on his boat.

Caterina never made any comment to Martino's remark. Among other reasons, she had stopped walking, staring at the religieuse that elegantly sat on the boat with Julian. A familiar face.

Bernardo Delle Rocche was on the stony bank of the Serchio. He approached the boat and extended a helping hand to the old nun, but she barely thanked him or bothered to watch the loose stones that she stepped on. Her eyes were fixed on Caterina.

'Do you head towards Chifenti, sister?' Martino asked with a cordial bow, before she reached them.

Without taking her eyes from Caterina's stare, the old nun answered 'I go to Corsena.'

'Then, if you care for our company, we may walk with you.' Martino said.

The old woman was so concentrated on Caterina that Martino's kind offer was lost in the air. The mutual stare between them was too obvious to be a coincidence.

'Do I know you?' she asked, reaching for the younger woman's hands.

Caterina felt the comforting warmth of that grip, the same reassurance that she had felt when that religieuse had come to her aid. Nevertheless, she still had to swallow a lump to be able to speak. 'You gave me a couple of denarii when I found myself lost in Lucca eight years ago.' Bathed by the tenderness of that woman's ever brightening smile, Caterina introduced herself, 'My name is Caterina. And this is Martino, parishioner of Controne.'

They exchanged an amicable embrace and courteous kisses on the faces. Caterina and the old woman held onto each other's embrace for an eternity.

'I am Abbess Theodora, of San Giovanni Battista, in Santa Maria lei Giudice.'

On hearing the name of the monastery she had fled from, Caterina felt the heavy corpse of old Marozia falling down from heaven and crushing upon her head, while the earth moved under her feet, from the trampling of emperor armies and papal soldiers coming to get her. She began to lose the tone of her legs and her eyes were just starting to roll up.

The abbess was quicker to see it than Martino, who was stunned by the mention of his first investigative mission, when he had discovered love with Caterina and Antonia, and too distracted to notice the slackening of his wife's grip. Theodora just reached over to squeeze Caterina's hands and yanked her up, capturing her suddenly alert gaze with peaceful eyes of assurance. Martino held onto normalcy, but saw his woman awaking from a shiver. He could tell she had been shaken by the memory of that place.

The abbess maintained her serenity. Her voice came soothingly low. 'I took the cowl in San Giovanni late in my life, years after the death of Marozia Maricuccia, a powerful oblate guest whom and I am sure you have heard of.' She spoke matter-of-factly, as if exchanging mundane news with a friend while drinking wine in the courts of Rome, 'You know, my dead husband was a grandson of Marozia's sister, Theodora, whom I was named after.'

Caterina was stunned. Her muteness was broken by the shelter and trust she felt with that woman, and words escaped out of her mouth before reason told her not to. 'Good abbess, I did meet Marozia. I was in San Giovanni Battista in my youth, and I left it certainly before your time, as old Marozia still lived then.' Martino had dropped his chin. He knew this was only the second time Caterina was confessing to this secret period of her life in more than thirty years.

Theodora did not seem to be much surprised 'Well then we should talk about her one day. I'd be very interested in knowing more of Marozia.' She cleared her throat and looked at the path north, with her hands distractedly adjusting the folds of her mantle 'Anyway, we better keep walking now, or my old legs will decide to retire for the day.'

They slowly followed the path into the lose forest of young beech trees, which allowed some warmth of the afternoon sun to dry the stones. As soon as the silence became too uncomfortable for the three of them, Theodora clicked her tongue and said 'So you must be the same Martino that was indicated to take over the bishopric of Lucca when old Grimizzo died.'

A beam of sunlight shóne over Martino's dark roman lines when he merrily wobbled his head, nodding and negating at the same time. 'Indeed, I met the Beatissimo Padre Benedict VIII years ago, on his return journey from Germany. When Grimizzo died, the pope did nominate me to run the diocese, but he must have been exceptionally equivocated. That position is not for the smallness of me as I am not for the greatness of that chair. I live better on these green valleys with my herd of the faithful, much more than I would in a palace, getting fat and resting my tired feet on the coldness of shining marble stones. I declined the designation and it was accepted. Our good Bishop Johannes is now on a rank that does all justice to his ambitions.'

Theodora eyes seemed to darken. She thinned her lips and continued to look at the path ahead. 'Sure, this *German* bishop, that nobody in Lucca cannot even understand a word he barks. Not a surprise second choice of this emperor-loving pope, I suppose. But given the family this pontiff comes from and the history of his rule, I'm surprised Benedict has made such a conscientious choice on *you* to start with.'

'I probably know where your opinion originates, but you'd be astonished to learn how much the pontiff has changed to a more humble person, they say.'

'No, he hasn't!' she grunted, almost in a rasping way, calling in an uncomfortable silence that walked with them for a long while, until they got to the village of Chifenti. When the path divided between the Lima ford to Fornulo and the dark road east that sided the Lima, Theodora opened her eyes wide, with renewed bright blueness, wisely capturing both Martino and Caterina, making the pair immediately forget about her bitterness. 'I believe there's still a decent bridge in Corsena, correct? Which would probably be a better choice for an old woman like me than fording this river in Chifenti, is that right?'

Caterina chuckled, suddenly more comfortable with a change of subject. 'The river carries away the bridge with it on a yearly basis,' she said. 'But in Corsena, for the very sake of the movement for the baths, they replace the planks and logs every time a flood destroys what was done by men. It is indeed a safer and more comfortable option then getting your legs wet by fording it here or there.'

'Moreover, we can walk with you to Corsena,' Martino said, 'as a direct path will take Caterina and I from the baths directly to Controne, up on the mountain.' Theodora opened a pleased smile on hearing that. Martino continued 'Who do you seek in Corsena, if we may ask?'

'The baths master, Immanuel Ben-Malachi. He's an old friend.'

'Why, Immanuel is a good man that we know him well!' Martino said. 'We will accompany you to his manor. We were just meeting with his daughter, in that Hospital of Santa Croce. She is Maria Maddalena of the Cunimundinghi. Lady of all these lands on our right side.'

Theodora raised an eyebrow, but her lips were still grinning. 'I know of Immanuel's daughter and her reputation, but I have not returned to Corsena since after the passing of Béla, the old midwife that Immanuel brought from Magyar lands. Therefore, I never yet met this famous woman of Anchiano that she became. On another side, I have been visited by the lord of the lands just south of hers, the infamous Castracani.'

Caterina looked nauseated. Martino said nothing and Theodora felt she had said too much. Once again, an uncomfortable silence materialised on their side and followed the three, with its light steps and an amused curiosity.

The tunnel in the woods soon filled with hoof beats of riders galloping back from the higher Lima valley. Although they passed by in a hurry, they all lowered their heads to Martino, except the first rider. A child.

Caterina had shivers of disgust. Martino held her hand, in an understandable manner that meant she should probably make the greatest effort to refrain from making any derogatory remarks on Maria Maddalena's son.

When the steam-choked trees of Corsena could already be devised, they crossed the slippery planks set over mossy stone piers of the Lima. Theodora made a short prayer thanking providence for the handrail that was fixed to the beam. 'Wouldn't it be reasonable to make a bridge across the Serchio too? That poor man Julian is a living saint. He should be minding the hospital, not rowing pilgrims across the water.'

'There should be one,' Martino confirmed, 'it is a deep and treacherous river.'

'Besides,' intervened Caterina, 'the marabbecche of the river are always hungry for the poor souls who dare to ford it –'

'Caterina, you do sound like Bernardo delle Rocche or the vellutini with these foolish stories.' Martino interrupted, looking half amused and half annoyed at his beautiful wife. 'There are *no* water goblins in this river,' he continued, '...or in any other, for that matter. The fact, Abbess Theodora,' he turned to the older woman 'fact is that we need a solid structure and this is the reason why we convened at the Hospital of Santa Croce today. We decided to build a bridge.'

'Oh what a coincidence! That is wonderful then.' The abbess said, rubbing her hands, partly because of the cold air, partly because of satisfaction with the news, and partly as a conclusive gesture, for she knew well the way they were close to Immanuel's mansion and she wanted no company for her visit. 'I hope to be living on the day when the first soul crosses this bridge. But now, dear friends, you have been a blessed guidance during this walk, and I thank you for your lovely company.' While they now kissed her on the faces, Theodora dared to add 'But I still have a few words to put you at ease.'

They frowned, standing and waiting for her last deliverance.

Theodora closed her eyes for a second and continued. 'So, if you allow me to express a strong opinion about that Antelmino di Gottefredo that we discussed before, what a repulsive pig he is.' She noticed that both Caterina and Martino seemed to agree, by their guiltless exchange of glances. Theodora added, looking at Caterina 'this man was interested in your story many years ago, Caterina, whether you were the so-called fugitive nun from San Giovanni Battista. I told him nothing, but Bishop Grimizzo found out through force of authority. Now the bishop is dead, and only Antelmino and the pope are aware of your secret with the old Marozia. Soon, it will only be Antelmino, the Castracani. I know he has a grudge against you, but I cannot deal with that one.'

'Can you deal with the pope then?' Caterina asked.

Theodora clenched her jaws and that same shadow fell over her eyes. She waited a moment, before answering 'That man will not be alive for long.'

'He's changed, Theodora!' Immanuel insisted.

'What kind of devil in you makes you think such bloodthirsty animal has changed?' the abbess asked, filling up another goblet with Immanuel's mulberry wine. 'The pope is a monster indeed and there is nothing you can say to change my mind.' She took an enviable gulp.

'He was here in Corsena, using our baths, as I told you,' Immanuel said, rhythmically moving his arms together while he pronounced each syllable, as if instructing one of his children on the careful use of his *tagh-tir*. 'I served the pontiff some of the most formidable prostitutes from Lucca, and a different man emerged out of his wet nights and days.'

Theodora gasped, and rested her goblet on Immanuel's table. 'By the severed head of the Baptist!' she screeched and laughed blissfully, 'Immanuel, you still keep surprising me, no matter how much I reckon I know you.' She waited until she could catch her breath. 'But why did you do that? Nobody would think that the ladylike Benedict VIII was the man to be tempted by the pleasures of the feminine flesh.'

Immanuel answered quite humbly 'My lady, I could hardly forget the young bishop who interviewed me with Sylvester II twenty four years ago.' He noticed Theodora sighing with pain at the mention of Sylvester and the shine of her eyes wandering away into a world of pleasant memories. 'And if he remembers who I was,' he continued, 'Benedict did not bother to see me. I simply kept the pope occupied to distract his attention from Father Martino of Controne, whose wife Caterina was being sought after. I just took the instructions of Bishop Grimizzo to provide the pope with a memorable stay in the baths. After all, it was Rome who paid for the reconstruction.'

Theodora's blue eyes shone against her rosy cheeks. Her lips thinned to a beautiful grin as she leaned over to say 'Indeed, a wise distraction! And in your opinion, my dear Immanuel, does a memorable stay relate to carnal pleasures?'

The old Bukhari took a long, bulky gulp from his wine, making his face contort as the fluid burned down his throat. Theodora was at least a decade his elder, but still a vigorous woman who could be attractive to many a men. Her cowl was flung back and although she had all mostly white over her blonde hair, it was all nicely arranged into elegant rolls of braids.

'I am but a lonely widower, Theodora,' Immanuel confessed. 'I know nothing of the luxuries appreciated by popes, especially those who are not interested in discussing arithmetic with me. But I am perfectly aware that any a man craves for bodily delights.'

'And you think a few nights between the warm thighs of a Lucchese girl could have changed John Theophylactus into a good man?' Theodora asked, now leaning back and straightening her posture across the table. She waited for no answer. 'No, Immanuel. Take my horrible son, for example, who visited most of the wombs from both sides of the Tevere, and still he was worse and more flooded with venom than a serpent. The warmth of a woman never stopped him from killing Sylvester and my husband.'

'How do you know it was him?' Immanuel asked, with eyebrows disappearing behind his ample forehead.

Theodora face darkened. 'If it wasn't my son John, that's only because his Tusculani cousins could have beaten him to it, including this accursed pope of ours.'

Immanuel pondered a bit and scratched his head. 'I firmly believe the pope has changed. He's designated Julian and Clarissa, two saintly souls, to revive the Hospital of Santa Croce. He's also considered Martino, a good man for our people, to be the successor of Grimizzo.'

'You will not change my mind, Immanuel,' she said, still with hardened features. 'In those years, when you had just entered this country, Benedict VIII made an enemy in me. A mortal one. Today I fully understand I am but a faint nobody if compared to the armies he claims to have crushed, or even the Museto's wife, whom he claims to have decapitated. But between the him and I, we still haven't fought our last battle.'

Immanuel frowned humorously and lifted his chin, making his thin beard stick forwards. 'You can fight your own battles, my lady, and seduce me with your presence, but I will not teach you again how to boil the roots of the monkshood.'

Her face softened and a fond smile opened. She leaned over again to hold his hand across the table. 'No, my dear friend. We are here to enjoy the company of each other. Not to discuss recipes.' She tilted her head to look at a window opening and bit her lip. 'It is late and I will not be able to return this evening. Will it be too disconcerting if I ask for your hospitality, Immanuel?'

'Of course not, my lady!' he said, squeezing her hand. 'I have already made arrangements for a room where you can stay overnight.'

'Thank you, my dear!' the abbess said, looking down. 'Actually...' she suggested...and stood up, walking around the manor's hall and looking outside. She returned to sit next to Immanuel. Holding his hands again, she continued. 'Actually, I am too an old, lonely woman. And I too dream and still crave for those delights that I have not experimented for so many years.' She giggled to the floor, suddenly embarrassed. 'Would you mind,' she made a struggle to continue, 'if we made a different type of arrangement for my overnight?' She was looking into his eyes when she finished.

Immanuel was abruptly pale as a ghost. And all of a sudden, he flushed, as if fire had been lit underneath his buttocks. Then, he was pale again. And he finally flushed once more, smiled disconcertedly at his self-consciousness. 'I'm...I'm...I'm...I'm –'

'You're?' she giggled, her rosy cheeks reflecting light upon his eyes, her smiling lips so close to his.

'I'm sure we can arrange for a memorable overnight, my lady!' he finally said.

She smiled with delight, but Immanuel still intervened with a wise finger raised. His gaze dropped to the ground. 'However, my lady, I must make a confession.'

'Please don't...' she said. 'Let's just get –'

'I have had thirteen children with my wife Elvira,' he said, ignoring her plead, 'and it was thirteen times only that we engaged into carnal commerce. You know, Elvira had always said that the Devil lives in man's testicles.' His voice lowered. 'And I have known no other woman.'

Theodora was glowing with compassion, or perhaps passion. 'I don't believe in a devil, Immanuel, but in any case, I want you to prove to me that she was right.'

His moustache flicked to the side as he grinned.

Pope Benedict VIII, the warrior pope, was dead.

On the night before, the pontiff had about finished an interesting meal, with cold cuts of wild boar glazed in honey and sausages, with a generous serving of the best Roman wine. Under the discomfort of a slight indisposition, sweating with pain in the stomach, the pope conveniently retired to the cosiness of his chamber. His personal attendant, an old mute nun, newly appointed from a northern monastery, prepared a warm digestive soup of black cabbage and grains for him. The nausea eased and, as he started to doze off, the nun slipped a small piece of parchment with a written note:

The Lady Theodora of the Crescentii will be delighted when she is informed of your death.

John Theophylactus tried to scream, but he felt too tired even for that effort. He needed a deep intake of breath before reacting with force. He tried, but the air would not enter. And his hands would not move, for the nun was firmly holding his wrists. Stronger than him, she was resting her body on his face.

When the pope stopped the struggle, the nun readjusted his tongue into his mouth, his eyeballs back into the orbits and his facial expression back to restfulness. A few hours later, she left the chamber in a hurry to call for help.

While most of the Lateran Palace officials swiftly dragged their sandals, rushing to prepare the body of the deceased pontiff for the funeral pomp, a layman was being hustled through the marbled corridors to be presented to a selected group of cardinals. It was Romanus, an older sibling of Benedict VIII. He was to undergo the same procedures that his brother had passed through to rise to the throne of St. Peter. When John Theophylactus had been ordained a priest, made into a bishop and elected for a cardinal vest, the span of this normally lengthy process had been reduced to no more than two years, thanks to the pressure of the Roman patricians such as the oldest brother Albericus of Tusculum. Now, for the stiff and rather wide Romanus, a merchant with little knowledge of the nature of affairs of his brother's church, the urgency required a direr route. It would only cost Albericus a thicker layer of his treasure, for even the pope has a price. Romanus of Tusculum was ordained a priest and made into a pope in one day.

And although he was not the nineteenth pope to take the name of John, he was known as John XIX.

A Bridge and a Price

On the opposite margin of the Lima, Amadeo waved at Piero and Immanuel.

'Such a good young man Piero is' the taverner said to his daughter, who waved also.

'Too bad the resemblance to his hag sister reminds us all of her wickedness.' Ginevra said, quickly lowering her hand and extending it to her father 'Come! We have a tavern to run.'

But the fat, sooty hand that took hers was not Amadeo's. It was Spatola's.

The three walked back to the tavern, side by side. While the widower Amadeo was losing some of his vigour to mind the inn, the young and strong Ginevra took over many of the tasks and, as a good wench, she was old enough to entice desire and occasionally managed to obtain a few extraordinary denarii from the customers she chose to be the lucky donors.

Spatola was just happy to be holding her hand.

'How was the meeting?' she asked.

Amadeo shook his head 'As good as a meeting with Maria Maddalena of the Cunimundinghi could go.'

'Did she mention taking our lands from us again?'

'As always.' Amadeo sighed. 'Even though we were discussing a different matter, the witch never misses an opportunity to threaten us with a cancellation of the launegildo from her dead Fulcardo.'

Spatola just looked blank. With his mouth half-open, he spoke little, being happy enough to be tolerated by the most beautiful woman he had ever seen. But he never ceased to squeeze Ginevra's hand every time she mentioned Maria Maddalena.

'The witch gets more wicked by the day,' she said. 'There are rumours she rummages the river stones under the full moon, and I have just heard that she was seen dancing among the flowers on the *Prato Fiorito*.'

Amadeo scoffed and looked northwest, searching a hidden peak behind the clouds. '*Prato Fiorito*? The mountain is too far from her lands. She would not dare cross the Lima and walk by all those villages on her own. Ginevra, this sounds like one of those stories of Bernardo delle Rocche.'

His daughter's face suddenly lighted up. 'Bernardo was there?'

Amadeo did not notice her excitement and nodded. 'He was. One of the two people who least feared Maria Maddalena, the other being Clarissa.'

They arrived at the tavern, in the centre of the village. A group of pilgrims packed their horses outside. The door was opened and the noise of some drunken customers could already be heard. Ginevra was still thinking of what her father said. 'That's why I like them both!' she exclaimed. 'Bernardo and Clarissa are brave enough to defy that woman who killed my mother.' And she entered the inn.

Amadeo was about to reprimand his daughter again for the dangerous insolence, but it was too late. Ginevra was already busying herself in the kitchen and nobody seemed to have heard her. After all, he also believed Divina had been murdered by Maria Maddalena. He gave a last glance to Spatola to verify if the village idiot had captured that dangerous statement. But the innkeeper soon realised that Spatola was too busy looking at his own hand. Amadeo just never realised this was the hand that was carelessly released by Ginevra as soon as she heard mention of the name of Bernardo.

Not much later, Ginevra was asking 'Father, why do you feed this accursed offspring of the Devil?'

Amadeo was holding her wrists in the tavern's kitchen. His daughter had been ready to storm out into the eating area. He thought he could see steam coming out of her forehead. 'He's only a child, Ginevra. How old is he? Seven? Eight?

'I don't even know why these men bring him in!' she shrieked. 'These are not lands of the Cunimundinghi. This snotty-nosed Arrigo should be fed by his mother. Not by us. He is *not* welcome here. Not at all.'

'The people of Anchiano are no worse than we are, Ginevra.' Amadeo said. 'Maria Maddalena's men-at-arms are ordered to travel with little Arrigo through her lands. And the brat specifically commands them to stop here for a meal. These men are helpless to deny it, or they will hear from his mother when they return to Anchiano. Do not worry, Ginevra. I will charge them twice the price for this piglet.' He felt her tension cede and finally released her wrists.

When the boy Arrigo was had finally left with the armed men, Ginevra approached her father, who busied himself scraping a couple of wooden trays. 'How much did he pay you?' she asked.

'The boy carries no silver.' Amadeo answered, without raising his eyes.

The girl defiantly put her hands on the round of her hips and raised an incredulous eyebrow. 'And you did not charge it from the men-at-arms?'

Amadeo dropped the board and the knife on the table. He faced his daughter impatiently. 'These men have little to pay me with.' He rasped. 'When they get back to Anchiano, Maria Maddalena will not reimburse them, even if all they did was to cover for another extravagance of the boy. How could I charge them?'

Ginevra spat with despise. 'Father, you are a fool. Had you been a rich banker you could be paying for the excesses of that son of the devil. Do you realise this boy will grow into a horrible landlord?' She left the kitchen, but Amadeo could still hear her grunts 'At least Caterina can understand me. She knows he is an accursed child. We know it. Next time Arrigo comes in here I will poison that little shit.'

A well-groomed horse trotted Maria Maddalena down the eastern Serchio bank. Still a handsome woman, she had dry lines that hardened her face, evidence of adversities and mysteries that few were acquainted with: violence on her body; disrespect to her grandeur; and brutality that was brought out of her aspiring chest for no less than the noble purpose of protecting her own destiny. The once enchanting grey of her eyes scarcely shone any more, being constantly shaded by concealment, secrets piling over her shoulders and that would be deeply buried and rotten with her corpse when time would come.

On the western path across the pools of the Serchio, Maria observed pilgrims and a couple of carts driving towards the Traghetto, crossing their way against that fool Bernardo Delle Rocche. But her gaze was inevitably attracted to those pools. An eel stuck its fleshy lips out of the water, as if peering at her for a second, creating circles of ripples that grew from inside each other, mouths that kept opening to swallow her, dragging her to gelid water dens that hid demons and ghosts. The dead of the Serchio, she thought, observing her from its dark depths, probably wise and old, maybe hungry to see her suffer, perhaps ravenous to fulfil the ominous curse uttered by Béla, on those seconds that life quickly evaporated from his stabbed body. She could not get it out of her thoughts.

Bah, nonsense! She brushed those feelings off. Arrigo was surely safe with her best men-at-arms. He would grow strong and powerful, lord of her lands and people, to be the greatest man of that valley. A true son to his deserving, hard-working mother.

Two miles down the road from the hospital, Maria Maddalena did not need to lead her horse to take a homely left turn around a cliff, when the lonely rock and castle of Anchiano arose above the mulberry trees. Passing by an old abandoned metato, she was glad to see herself on the road back home.

Had Maria forced her ride to continue its pace straight southward on that river road down to Sesto di Moriano, on the same route as much of her produce had done since the flood took the ferry away, she would have had the displeasure to be halted by a series of toll collectors from Antelmino di Gottefredo. The departure of that accursed young Testa and the disappearance of the ferry had limited the crossing at the Traghetto to a small row boat.

And it was that pathetic Julian of the hospital who conducted pilgrims across the river, but only little cargo could be rowed on that tiny vessel. This obliged Maria to send Anchiano's bullock carts down the eastern bank and pay high tolls once they trampled on Antelmino's road. And if she wanted to ferry the river down in Sesto it would be even more expensive, for those delinquents Lamberto & Lanfranco extorted several denarii per cart and wagon crossing, regardless of the traveller's territorial or ecclesiastical power. So Maria had finally organised for a complicated system of messages, carts and a pace of donkeys to depart from Lucca and collect bags that were patiently crossed on Julian's boat at the Traghetto. This complex mobilisation system was slightly cheaper than going through Antelmino's land, but sooner than one would expect, the Castracani came back with a special offer for Maria Maddalena: she would pay the tolls for only one in every five loads of goods sent through his path of land, and in exchange he would have free access to move up to Chifenti and have a closer ear to the whereabouts of the petulant priest Martino of Controne.

Maria had a profound dislike for that choice granted to her southern neighbour, but she knew that this would soon be over. There would be a bridge, and she would freely send her riches to Lucca over Bernardo delle Rocche's stretch of the Via Francigena. This would give her total control of the sales of her goods and Antelmino would lose his freedom to enter her territory. The Castracani needed to be crushed, and she could wait a lifetime to see him destroyed.

The path spiralled around the rock and placed her before the massive gates of her castle. An aide rushed in to take her horse, informing that Arrigo had not yet returned with the men-at-arms. Maria went inside and asked for a bowl of water and an empty one. Sitting by the window that overlooked her flat lush valley all the way to the tree line of the Serchio, while pouring water from one bowl to another and waiting for Arrigo, she considered the morning's decision to build a bridge. Her contribution would not be a cheap exercise, but certainly worthwhile. But there was something else she had to be careful about. And how to convince anyone about this cost? She knew it. She knew so deadly right that the bridge would not stand without a costly toll paid to the river.

Not without human sacrifice.

Bernardo delle Rocche had just delivered the news to Julian, as they crossed the Serchio to the Traghetto. There would be a bridge and Julian could retire from the rowing.

'It's no burden on me,' Julian said, truly embarrassed for feeling like a nuisance.

Bernardo laughed and slapped Julian on the shoulder. 'Oh, you poor tormented soul, you must be wishing to be Saint Peter himself, tortured and nailed to the cross upside down while the soldiers piss on his face. You don't need that, Julian. You're a saint already!' The shepherd turned suddenly serious and said 'Julian, don't get lost in this self-gratifying torment. Your rowing is indeed heartily appreciated, but once we have a bridge, we can use your generosity for other things, such as helping your beautiful wife, who's now overburdened in the hospital. And this damned boat of yours can be pushed down the current, to meet the waves on the sea one day.'

Julian docked the boat and waited until Bernardo was out. 'And how did you find Clarissa? Is she looking too tired?'

Bernardo sighed. 'No Julian. Clarissa works hard and never stopped to see us provided for during our meeting this morning. But actually she looks more radiant than ever, this cousin of mine. I find it indeed a pleasure just to be seen by her beautiful eyes. You are a blessed couple. The more I see you the more I believe that indeed an angel must have visited you two in the shape of that leper.' He straightened himself up and said before leaving 'this is why you should be looking forward to have this bridge made. So you can enjoy the company of your own angel.' He jumped out onto the bank.

Julian smiled humbly. 'I can't wait for that to happen, Bernardo. I really cannot wait!' and rowed slowly back to the hospital bank.

Bernardo collected his ride at a small stable in the Traghetto. He was not going to stay at the Rocca or at La Cune or at his favourite Wald Ottavo. He was trotting south, straight through towards Lucca. Excited with the new endeavours, Bernardo would arrive in the city before sunset, in time to see the bankers about the bridge. That would include Maria Maddalena's grandfather Battista Burle. Initially, Bernardo considered not involving any of his funds cared for by the Trade House of Burle for the planned bridge, but thinking better, Battista was a known honest repository of trust. The old man was still as healthy as ever, so it would be wiser to have him aware of Bernardo's involvement, for the financial commitment of his granddaughter was supposed to mirror his. Each landowner on each side of the river should equally contribute. Once the bankers were warned of the project of the bridge at the Traghetto, they should seek for the right engineering for such a construction.

Bernardo rode by a few wagons, carts and pilgrims heading North, on their way to take a boat ride with the always patient Julian. He looked across the river and saw an elegant figure on a horse, riding south too. Quite sadly, Maria Maddalena of the Cunimundinghi posed for an inexistent audience, if not for him or anyone else who rode across the river. Bernardo was tempted to shout out a mockery of her posture, but he just giggled and said nothing.

He could never trust that woman. Yes, she had agreed with the bridge and the necessary investment, but probably only because this would be a less expensive venture than continuing to pay the insulting tolls to Antelmino di Gottefredo. But everyone knew Maria Maddalena was a treacherous, ambitious creature. The horrific reports from her brother-in-law Sigifredo were probably not lying about her throat slashing courage. And the missing fingers of several men around the veluttini were painful witness of her anger. And who could guarantee she had not murdered the old shaman of Corsena? How suspicious was her participation on the conveniently failed birth of Fulcardo's first son and the death of his first wife. So was Fulcardo really slaughtered by the Saracens? Maybe he should investigate that one day. There were people who survived the slaughter in Partigliano. They would know what happened. And finally, there was the disappearance of Divina, of Chifenti, the midwife that vanished in those days of the siege in Luna.

But lately, Bernardo was just pleased to trigger general laughter when he'd been referring to Maria Maddalena as Maria Tenebrosa.

'So a bridge we will have, my love.' Julian exclaimed, entering the hospital through some hungry pilgrims waiting for a meal. His arms hung limp around his body.

'I'll tell you about it,' Clarissa said, sticking her head from out of the kitchen, 'but first, you must eat something, or you'll drop dead from exhaustion.' The sight of her radiance and the tone of diligence lifted Julian's spirit. It renewed him every time he sat eyes on her eternal youth and vigour. Clarissa fetched a bowl of green farro broth, the newest and earliest harvested from that year. Before her casual majesty, the hungry pilgrims opened a corridor for her passage, carrying the bowl through to the boatman. 'Eat, and rest, my love. I don't want this boat to kill you one day. I've already sent for a warden to take over the boat while you pause for a breather.'

Julian ate ravenously and went to his chamber for a nap. While lying on their comfortable palliasse, Clarissa came to sit on his side, in a somewhat angelical fashion. 'The meeting was quick,' she said. 'When we all and mostly expected that pest Maria Maddalena to oppose anyone, she was quick to agree in an equal investment, between herself, Bernardo and the episcopate of Lucca.'

Julian yawned. 'I don't think the bishop will give us any single denarius,' he said. 'As a good *Tedesco*, Bishop Johannes is as frugal as an omo salvatico. So parsimonious that following the generous years of Grimizzo, Rodilando and Gerardo, he is set on the reconstructing the bishopric's treasures, and that will mean no hand-outs.'

Clarissa thought for a while, biting her lower lip. 'So if the church won't help, do you think Maria will share half of the cost for the bridge with Bernardo?'

Julian laughed. 'That depends on how furiously she hates Antelmino di Gottefredo and how much he is bleeding her gold for the use of the eastern road. Especially now that all those silk cocoons must be taken with urgency to the boilers in Lucca, I have little space on the boat to cope with her volume of bags. She will inevitably resort to the eastern roads and bend over to pay Antelmino's tolls after

all. Bernardo better get an agreement right now, when it hurts most to the witch.'
He continued giggling. 'I feel bad about taking pleasure in her misery, but I cannot
help!'

Clarissa was just deliciously amassed by the immensity of her happiness to see
Julian smiling again. So blessed to see her husband awaken from his misery that she
forgot to mention a detail of the meeting. Something they all only thought about
much later. It was a brief comment that Maria Maddalena made in a whisper, pretty
much just to herself. She said that no matter what, the bridge would not stand
without a price. Builders wanted gold, but the river wanted more.

An Engineer is Named

'Arrigo is dead.'

Julian said it in an indifferent tone when he entered the tavern. 'I just heard the
news from Lucca.' A dozen faces looked at him, but nobody was more excited than
Ginevra, who came running from the kitchen.

'Someone finally killed the little monster?' she asked, holding her fists tight as if
waiting for an explosion of happiness.

Julian was puzzled for a second, before waking up to the confusion. 'Oh, no!
Not Arrigo from Maria Maddalena. No, there's nothing wrong with the boy, as far
as I know. I am talking about the Emperor Arrigo II.' There was a general murmur
of respect from some foreign pilgrims, including a few that had recently learned
that Julian was a living saint. But one would struggle to find a local Chifenti villager
aware of whom the emperor was or wondering whether that distant German figure
affected any of their daily tribulations at all.

Ginevra dropped both arms once she heard Julian's explanation. Her
disappointment was greater than the excitement for her initial understanding. Of
course she was confused because Julian, like anyone in that region, was using
Arrigo, the Italian name for Henry, the emperor.

This was blasting news for Julian, as twenty years before he had accompanied
the Lady Railenda, Buonaccorso and the Pope John Fasanus to Pavia, to personally
meet the airy, vain king and watch him take the Iron Crown of the Lombards. Even
though Henry became famous across Italy for having ordered the massacre of Pavia
on the dreadful night of his coronation, Arrigo had still been a popular name since
those days. A few years later, Emperor Henry II would be made a saint by Pope
Clement II, who was coincidently a German too.

'What does it mean for us, Julian?' Amadeo was alarmed by Julian's presence in
Chifenti. 'Will we have war?' He had not seen the boatman that often in the tavern
since the "miracle" of the leper.

'I don't think.' Julian said aloud. 'But this emperor had always been an ascetic.
The man has left no heirs, apparently by his own choice of celibacy.'

Amadeo shook his head, brushing off such a preposterous idea. Even if this was
a lifestyle option of such an important figure as the emperor, the initiative seemed
silly to him. The taverner still asked 'So who will be the next emperor then?'

Julian answered quickly 'How would I know?'

Months later Julian would learn that an assembly of German princes was summoned to elect a new king. The choice was for Conrad, a distant relative of Henry II, and likewise, a descendant of Henry I, the Fowler. This Conrad had started from a relatively modest environment, growing into the most powerful of the princes. He was crowned king of the Germans in 1024, king of Italy a year later, and the pope crowned him Roman emperor in 1027. He reigned as Conrad II.

Julian accompanied Amadeo to the kitchen, to fetch himself a goblet of wine.

'Is that why you came to Chifenti, Julian?' Amadeo asked, while searching for an amphora of better quality wine. 'To tell us of the emperor's death?'

Julian laughed. 'No, Amadeo. Excuse the distraction, but I came to tell you of much better news. And therefore, to prepare you for talking to the people of Chifenti.' Amadeo and Ginevra jumped to hold on to his arm, both with hungry faces, as dogs wriggling their quarters, begging for a friendly scrub on the head. The Hospitaller was quick to deliver the news. 'Bernardo has found an engineer to build our bridge. He is arriving from Rome next week. You should be ready to mobilise strong and talented men of Chifenti, carpenters and masons, to contribute on the construction, starting on the coming spring. I just think you should better be prepared with your men before Maria Maddalena decides to demand anything at all from Chifenti.'

They were both ecstatic with Julian's kindness. 'Thank you so much for your engagement, Julian,' Amadeo said, filling another goblet for himself too, 'but Maria Maddalena should know well that she does not have any authority—'

'Have you seen the devil about this issue?' Ginevra interrupted.

Julian almost gagged with the wine. 'Excuse me?'

'Ginevra!' Amadeo cut. 'Please do not use this language so openly! Maria Maddalena may have ears all over the place.' He turned to Julian with a forced smile 'Excuse my daughter, Julian. She was referring to Maria Maddalena. Have you consulted with her on this matter?'

'Oh, you know Maria...' Julian said. 'I can heartily sympathise with Ginevra's feelings. No matter how much Maria Maddalena will gain from the construction of this bridge, that woman will still torment us all about her contribution, financial aid and contingent of men. Bernardo has some promises from her but we never know what else she could come up with. I just find advisable to be prepared with your contribution before she amasses you with demands.'

'And I sincerely appreciate your kindness' Amadeo said. 'I will send a message to Bernardo Delle Rocche that I will be prompt to select and make my men available as soon as the engineer comes to this region.'

'Wise decision, Amadeo.' Julian said. He emptied the goblet and added 'But the best part is the name of the engineer. You will not believe his name.'

The taverner and his daughter stopped with their utensils in the air, waiting for Julian to tell them. When the boatman said the name, they all laughed so hard that Amadeo had wine coming out of his nose. Soon, he was running into the dining hall and delivering the big joke.

The guffaws could be heard as far up as on the mountains as Controne.

'Is that your name? Your actual name, christened at the sacred baptismal pool?' Lanfranco asked, frowning with scepticism. Or maybe it was Lamberto that did it.

'Yes,' confirmed the resigned Roman. 'The idea came from my parents, as you would expect. I know that it stirs some type of mockery, but I'm used to it.'

The hairy-faced giants muffled some inconvenient giggles behind their hands, as it would probably be indelicate and offensive to such a scholar from Rome to be scorned by two brutes. Lanfranco and Lamberto were both relieved to have finally found their man. It had been almost a week of exhaustive wait in Pisa, discreetly making casual conversation with hospitallers, taverners, stablemen, farriers, church clerks, pilgrims, men-at-arms and the *custodes portae*, the gatekeepers. When they were finally advised that the Roman engineer had arrived, they purposely gave the impression to have lost all interest. And while the visitor dined that evening, the two men observed him in the tavern. They made mental notes on his appearance. A rather short and solid structure, but not fat at all. He had very white freckled skin and wore a clean, white head cover, sporting a proud dark mane of well-groomed curls cascading from the side. A thin, straight nose ran down from between small green eyes, probably too separated apart, a typical sign of airy selfishness. And whether it was a coincidence or not, on the next morning, moments after the engineer found out that his horse had been stolen, the Genovese brothers of Sesto di Moriano drove their mule cart by the stables, where the Roman desperately argued with the Pisan stable master.

'Hey, Roman!' one of the two large men on the cart barked. 'We hear your horse has been stolen. You were heading to Lucca, right? We'll be happy to take you there.'

'?' the engineer could not even start to comprehend those news travelling so fast. 'How do you know? How could... ? No, I cannot... Do you know who I am? I have been called by the bishop!' He pointed to the stablemaster, who he had been arguing with 'This man only wants to pay me less than three – '

'You can argue forever, Roman,' said one of the Genovese brothers 'but in this part of Christendom we are not sponsored by the pope's luxuries. We only pay for them. Take whatever this good man offers you and hop on our cart if you want a free ride.'

The engineer hesitated for a while, before making his white face flush red and accepting the few coins the stable master had offered for the stolen horse, but not without spewing a rather creative spell of Roman swearwords, of which he later made a prayer to apologise for.

Lamberto and Lanfranco talked to the Roman all the way up through the hills of Santa Maria lei Giudice. When the flat wide valley opened in front of them and the towers of the city stood out of an autumn monochrome, the Roman asked. 'This is Lucca then?'

The hairy-faced giants confirmed and exchanged a glance. It was the signal to change the subject. 'So tell us: what exactly are you planning for the construction of such bridge?' the red-bearded Genovese brother asked.

'Wood!' the engineer said with satisfaction. His eyes shone distantly, dreamingly, on each side of his head. 'The best way to build bridges these days, like the great Caesars did a thousand years ago.'

'Tell us about it!' incited the blonde-bearded.

'It's quite simple!' the engineer said, proudly, 'We all know the complex and intricate work of stone bridges and that is exactly why we have few of them. Only glorious cities such as Rome can justify them. But the Roman armies built wooden bridges to cross over to many savage lands. It requires much less headaches than the complex engineering of stone bridges. We just drive timber pilings into the riverbed and build the road on top of them. It is a very durable solution too.'

Lanfranco said 'We can't wait to see it finished'.

Or maybe it was Lamberto.

Antelmino di Gottefredo took his hat off and sat down to laugh, while he scratched his uncovered head.

'I cannot believe that name.' He said, wiping tears and noisily scuffing his lice-ridden scalp. 'What a fucking silly idea to name a child on such fashion!'

'That is his real name, apparently,' said one of the Genovese brothers.

The three men were talking at Antelmino's property in Santo Stefano di Tassignano. This time, extraordinarily the Castracani had offered them seats and a refreshment, although one could doubt if that wine was still good to drink. The Genovese brothers described in all details their conversations with the Roman engineer and his plans for the bridge upriver.

'Should we encourage him to leave our valley as soon as he can?' asked one of them.

'No!' Antelmino said, with lowered eyebrows. He put his hat back on. 'Not at all! Let these people burn their riches and efforts in a wooden bridge. If it is indeed a contraption similar to the bridge of San Frediano, I hate to admit it, but this is a terribly fragile construction that could catch fire and burn within an hour. These unfortunate accidents always happen, you know.'

'We'll just observe, then.'

'Yes, Lanfran—' Antelmino started to say, but not too sure if that was Lanfranco or Lamberto, almost losing his enthusiasm. But he continued, energetically, 'So let them all lose their precious silver and gold in this foolishness. Didn't you two drop him at Fraolmo & Sisesmundo di Cunnizio? I'm sure that fat pig Battista Burle is also involved with those converts, given the backloads of silk cocoons that travel down the river. We will watch these rich bastards losing their treasure by the day.'

Lamberto looked at his goblet, still filled to the half, and decided it was not worthwhile to drink that wine, even though it had been offered for free. 'That's decided. We will just watch him, then.'

Antelmino saw them to their horses. When his visitors were about to kick in, the Castracani asked with a bit of a frowned face. 'It's rather embarrassing, but I must ask: which one of you is Lamberto and which one is Lanfranco?'

'I'm Lamberto.'

'And I'm Lanfranco'.
But the Castracani would soon forget about that.

They drove the timber pilings quite easily into the green sloped western bank. As for the long rocky shore of the eastern bank, just a few score of paces north of the Hospital of Santa Croce, more than two years were spent on driving those beams into the soil.

The engineer had his enthusiasm renewed when the Genovese brothers dropped him in Lucca. The bankers treated him to some local delicacies and pleasures that made him forget the bitter experience of Pisa. 'It's the Pisans...' they would say with a chuckle, 'what can you do?'

After an audience with the bishop, which lifted his spirits higher, the engineer arrived in Wald Ottavo. He spent a few days with the locals, looking at the whole terrain. Indeed, the cross section where the ferry had been and where Julian exercised his muscles to row across the Serchio was the most suitable for the construction of a bridge. They visited the landlords and several communities to select their best workers, arranging for the villagers' release from the local councils. Bernardo delle Rocche and the Roman engineer were spotted all around the valley, consulting with fishermen and hunters. They saw the sour Maria Maddalena, who bit her lips while she poured water from a jug to another. The intimidating woman never seemed to express her true opinion about the bridge. They saw Amadeo, Immanuel, Martino, Wido di Willo, and they spent hours discussing strategies with Julian, sitting in the hospital's table and being well fed by an ever accommodating Clarissa. Even the shy Spatola, who knew a fair amount about the shores of the Serchio, took those men to selected spots which would be worth looking at. And the people of the Serchio valley, curious passers-by realising who the Roman engineer was, would stop and look with a smile at the man they had heard about, a name that would make them break into frank laughter every time it was mentioned.

The engineer made his plan and presented it to a selected audience in the bankers' guild in Lucca. The reaction was enthusiastic, and they started immediately. Everything would go according to plan if it wasn't for the river itself, which was never consulted.

Maria knew that well.

The ground knew it. It would just not cede. Hard black rock that could not be split in two by wood. The men brought giant trees down from the Apennine, but by the time they were ready and sharpened to stab the land, when the massive stones were winched up their pile drivers and released on the end of the beams, it just shook the ground and crushed the wood. The engineer watched it all, shattered by disappointment. There was only one solution, he concluded: to dig.

Two years it took to dig and drive those beams into the eastern bank. Not because of the hardness of the ground, or because of any actions by Antelmino di Gottefredo. The Castracani was just sitting back and enjoying the delay. It was actually Bernardo delle Rocche that caused it.

On a particular summer drought, when it was easier to reach further into the riverbed, a number of isolated puddles dried out, so while many fish died from asphyxia as algae took over the warm waters, insects had their feast on the dead matter, as newts and frogs moved over to fresher pools. And one eel, a single unfortunate victim that had been trapped in that dying pool, panting with its lips out for scorching days and nights in a row, gathered its last remaining forces and ventured itself out of the fetid water over a full moon night. After a few minutes of wiggling and snaking, it found nothing.

A bittern boomed not too far. *Die from a powerful stroke of a sharp beak, die from dehydration, or die from exhaustion.* The third alternative seemed to be the less hopeless. The eel continued its wiggling and hoping, until it lost its ground and fell into nothing but a very deep hole with some fresh, clean water in the bottom. It saw the break of a new day and a few human faces looking at it.

The workers came early in the morning to continue to deepen the hole they had hardly dug through the rocks. At the end of the previous day, they had finally found some softer ground and some water that pooled up to cover the bottom. But in that morning, there was not only water. A fish was looking at them.

Superstitious creatures, none of the workers in the Serchio dared to dig further and risk killing the eel. They decided to consult with the engineer. The Roman was awake and praying in his comfortable chamber up on the Rocca, where they had strategically set him up to overlook the whole construction site.

'A fish?' he grunted. 'You are stopping the works for a *fish*?' He got up from bed and splashed some cold water from a bowl over his freckled face. With a dripping chin, he grunted even louder. 'You little shits! We have been asked to do this job by the bishop himself! Kill the fucking fish with your spade and get on with the work.'

Bernardo delle Rocche could not hold his tongue when he heard about it on the next day. He was in Amadeo's tavern. On hearing that an eel had halted the work for a few hours, he was quick to yell 'No wonder!' And in a second, when everyone's eyes where bulging with expectations, waiting for his next words, he let it out: 'They found it! It's the Hellmouth!'

On hearing those words, using just the power of their bottom muscles, most pilgrims that were at the tavern moved a place away from that man, with his thick-matted silver hair. Father Martino, who had gone down to see Bernardo, just shook his head with a familiar annoyance. But that did not stop the shepherd from continuing. It incited him to tell a tale that would ruin many lives along the Serchio.

'A gaping mouth, wasn't it what they saw?' Bernardo said, in the best of his cantastorie style. 'A fish that comes from a hole in the ground. There's no other creature that bears such diabolic nature. If those workers had looked better, they would see the suffering of condemned souls inside it. A passage between a world of sinners and an unwanted land of condemnation. A doorway into a realm of suffering where destined souls fry before being daily devoured by demons. A mouth into hell!'

Martino tried to intervene, but Bernardo was louder. 'Could they hear the screams?' he said with pleasure, livid with the terrorised eyes from the bodies that now squeezed against the wall, 'the moaning, the imploration? Or the roars of dragons; and the grunts and shrieks of all shapes of beasts? Didn't any of them hop out? The hellmouth has been reported to spew myriads of devils that will drag many sinners into immediate damnation—'

'That's enough, Bernardo!' Martino cut like an axe, imposing his austere figure in front of the shepherd. 'Can't you see the damage you will cause?' And he silently watched half a dozen pilgrims flee through the front door. 'See?' he asked Bernardo, pointing at the dust that had been raised outside, 'you believe they will keep quiet about this?'

'Don't make a big scene out of this, Martino.' Bernardo said, flicking his hands up. 'It's no more than a scary story.' These people like to hear them.

'Exactly!' Martino said, showing Bernardo his closed fist.

The parishioner was right. All villagers refused to work on the eastern bank on the next day. And they did not show up for work on the following day either. The engineer was edging desperation, and sent for Bernardo, who had just left for the mountains. The Obertenghi came down as fast as he could and enquired many of the families of the masons and carpenters who were avoiding the construction site. They were in hiding, fearing devils or God's punishment for having uncovered, interfered with or killed the hellmouth. Distraughtly realising the extension of the damage his vain storytelling had triggered, Bernardo went down to the riverbank, to verify the hole that had been covered ever since. With bare hands, he franticly dug through the fresh gravel, only to stop when he found two stinking halves of an eel. Slimy rotten halves with a stench that would scare an ogre out of its den, and that he zealously carried for a few days, visiting all the villages where disappeared workers could have gone. From Montefegatesi to Colle di Manch, Bernardo implored those families to tell their relatives that the fish was harmless and that it was only a silly story he had told. Meanwhile, Antelmino di Gottefredo thrived in the news from the Serchio.

Much worse fate suffered those workers from the Cunimundinghi lands of Maria Maddalena. The reprisal for their hiding was fierce, with beatings and dispossessions. A few men gave themselves in, agreeing to go back if their families could still remain in the land. Across the valley, Bernardo was informed about the fines and tried to secretly provide some compensation to those affected families in Maria's lands. But more public slashes followed, floggings often witnessed by little Arrigo, laughing delighted at every new cry snatched out with skin and blood. Clarissa ran to Anchiano and asked to see Maria Maddalena, imploring her to stop the beatings.

'Stupid woman,' Maria said to her visitor, quite unceremoniously 'can't you see that this is all for the good of the bridge? These ignorant men know nothing about the devil. They will work if I tell them to do so. The faster that accursed bridge is built, the sooner your stupid husband can cease to be a slave of the rabbles.'

Maria's head banged back with a solid wooden knock on the wall, for she never saw Clarissa's hand flying at her neck. She could only understand what had happened by the time she felt the older woman pinning her up with one hand against that hard rocky wall. 'Don't you ever offend my husband, you sad, bitter woman!'

Maria held tightly onto Clarissa's forearm and tried to scream 'Arrigo...' but just a faint whisper escaped through her squeezed throat.

Clarissa ripped a grin of rage 'You call that little shit of yours and I will pin him up with my free hand.' Maria's eyes were popping out, one with fury, and the other with fear. She was losing her colour of anger and entering into a purplish tinge. 'Will you stop the beatings?' Clarissa insisted. 'Leave the workers and their families alone. They will return to the bridge.'

'I will leave them!' she hissed, her hands relaxing and dropping from Clarissa's arm. 'I promise I will leave them alone!'

Clarissa released her. Maria gasped and coughed dramatically. 'I will leave them...' she repeated now, with her actual voice coming out of her purple lips. 'I will leave them alone...' she said clearly. Clarissa was still looking at her, with eyes of fire, flames that hid any other colour from that gaze. Maria did not respond to it. The Hospitaller's older majesty was humiliating enough. Maria was a younger and richer woman, who should not be intimidated in that manner. *What was wrong, for the Devil's sake?* She fumbled around the wooden planks of the large door of Anchiano, finding the latch and tremulously opening it.

'Go,' she said to Clarissa. 'You are not welcome in Anchiano. I don't ever want to see you here.'

Clarissa did not move. 'I wish I could say the same,' she said 'but unfortunately I know I will still have the displeasure to see plenty of you. I just ask you that you consider treating people with respect, peasants and all. And that is especially for my husband, and you will never have to be humiliated again.' And she left the manor.

'Just watch your back, from now on!' Maria hissed.

Clarissa graciously turned the upper half of her body around to look back at Maria Maddalena. 'Don't you think when someone is ready to strike me from behind they will be looking into your eyes? Think of you own neck, Maria Tenebrosa. It could be in my hands again.'

The door was slammed.

After the engineer launched solid threats to abandon the project, Bernardo made a few agreements that would cost him dear silver and gold, but which maintained the Roman in a brighter mood. Re-committed to the bridge, it was now more as a personal endeavour responding to a higher call, but a monetary investment. Once the recruitment was renewed, the workers eventually returned to the site. With the close watch by a much more contained Bernardo delle Rocche, they picked and dug through the rocky shore to reasonably fix a double series of pilings, all the way into the area where the bank descended abruptly into the river. This time, a road was hurriedly built over those piles that had already been fixed. It extended smoothly across the stony riverbank for over thirty paces before stopping as the pilings entered the river. From the western bank, the road descended quickly from the Traghetto ridge for ten paces and ended unfinished, like the open jaws of an aspis frozen while in a deadly strike. The empty gap in between the incomplete segments of the bridge extended across the deep core of the Serchio for over a score of paces. So far, building the bridge had been an easy task.

Long poles were thrown between the incomplete embankments, where they would assemble the massive pile drivers that were to be set onto the bottom. By the end of the summer, they finished pre-fabricating the pyramid-shaped driver and managed to re-built it in the gap. The heavy frame settled successfully in the dark, muddy bottom, and a colossal pillar was ready to be driven into the hard riverbed.

But the weather changed overnight.

Nobody could prevent the force of the flooded Serchio taking away the wooden pyramid and literally disappearing with its remains.

Maria Maddalena was sorry to see her investment in time and gold disappear with a storm. She knew the people of the Serchio were not ready to learn what was missing for the successful completion of the bridge.

More poles where stretched across the gap and soon a second pyramid was built and placed in the river. They lifted a new stone which was specially moulded for the pile driver and released it repeatedly over the end of the wooden pillar. The progress was slow, for under the muddy bottom, the soil was hard rock.

The engineer knew it was no fast affair, which particularly needed his resilience of character. Therefore, more than ever, he would face all adversities to conclude it. Every day he was the first to arrive and the last to leave. And it was in one of those early autumn mornings, when he left the Rocca under stars that had not been seen for many a night, and walked down the wet track through recently harvested farro terraces, that he heard his name being called.

It always felt strangely unreal to hear other people use his name, which incited a deep disgust in his entrails, and a jolly laughter in the heart of others. *Who was it?* He turned back to see a large figure appearing from behind the shadow of a cypress. It looked to the engineer like one of those bearded giants that had kindly brought him from Pisa to Lucca. It just stood there, in the dark.

The Roman squinted with his already small eyes and tried to remember the names... 'Lanfranco? Lamberto?' he called to the standing figure.

Another person left from behind the other cypress across the path. Large and silent, like the first. It could only be those brothers. The engineer was not too certain, but he thought they were brothers indeed. 'I'm glad it's you two,' he said, dropping his shoulders with a nervous smile 'For a moment, I was even afraid.' One of the men advanced quickly and the engineer felt and explosion of pain on his thin, delicate nose, which took him off the path, to return with his whole body back on the ground.

He shrieked in pain. 'It's me!' he screamed. 'Don't you remember? You picked me up in Lucca.'

'Of course we do,' said one of the giants. 'We would never forget a name like yours.' And with a powerful kick he dug his foot violently into the engineer's stomach. The darkness of the morning suddenly became totally black for the Roman, with green fiery explosions inside his head. But the horrendous feeling was halted by a new kick, now up on his ribs. He could hear the bones cracking and the pain assaulting again, attacking like an army of hell.

'Go away from here, do you understand?' a voice said, behind the boulder of pain that compressed every part of his body. He tried to roll on the wet ground, but he felt like all bones would be crashing if he did any more. A tick clot of blood was forming inside his mouth. The distant voice said something again '*Leave this bridge, unfinished as it is! Go back to Rome!*' And he closed his eyes.

A rooster crowed. Had he slept much? It was still dark. Probably he had slept for a few seconds only, for he could hear the voices of the bearded brothers from Sesto di Moriano in the harvested fields, not too far from him:

'*Baccan*, have you found a stick?' One of the voices asked in the darkness.

'No, *baccan*. Nothing.'

'Don't bother then. Look here! I have got two good ones. I think they'll be firm enough.'

To his horror, the engineer understood that those men were coming back to him, this time with sticks. They stood one on each side.

'Leave' *WHACK!* 'this' *WHACK!* 'place' *WHACK!* 'now!' *WHACK!*

'Do' *WHACK!* 'not' *WHACK!* 'come' *WHACK!* 'back!' *WHACK!*

'Never!' *WHACK! WHACK! WHACK! WHACK! WHACK!*... and one of the sticks broke with a loud snap. Lamberto rolled the body of the engineer, who whimpered quietly. Still alive.

'Listen here' Lanfranco, said. 'We'll let you live, now. Make good use of the rest of your life, leaving these lands and praying to God that he forgives your cowardice for being such a cry-baby.'

Once the engineer had disappeared without leaving any traces or reasons, the Lucchese bankers were fast to receive reliable information that the coward was back in Rome.

'Kill him!' Maria barked. 'He ran away from his battle. Arrange to kill the coward! You can do that.'

Old Battista Burle just raised his hand to halt his granddaughter from carrying on. The banker was just too tired for reprimands or even explanations. A wool and leather head cover protected his bald skull from the wind entering through the one office window. Sitting on his favourite chair, his obese body pointed out to him that the fire in the hearth by his side needed a revival, but his mind tried to concentrate on the granddaughter that boiled with anger in front of him.

'We don't do that. Ruffians do it, Maria Maddalena. Bu we don't!' he said with a deep, semi-choked voice. He moved a couple of parchment rolls from the middle of the desk and left only the clay tablet, as if to prepare for calculations. 'Besides, we may not need him to finish it. Those pile drivers are still there. Finishing the gap that remains will be an easy job. And cheap! That engineer was not paid for his task work. Payment would only be effectuated upon completion of the bridge.'

Maria just shook her head. She had not bothered to sit. 'We still need the bridge. Profits from our latest harvests have been lost on the moroseness of that imbecile Julian, the Hospitaller, or on insulting tolls for the Genovese brothers or that filthy Castracani. What a dirty man!' She was talking now almost to herself. 'Antelmino sees himself as a suitable husband for me! That pig.' She laughed nervously, 'and at the same time he lusts for the whore of Controne, Father Martino's wife. He's even promised me lower charges for his roads if I could arrange a night with her.'

'Now there is a logic explanation.' Battista said, dismissing the iniquity remarks but touching the side of his nose with a raised finger, to capture Maria's attention. 'There are indeed suggestions, rumours, that the engineer was intimidated into abandoning the project by Antelmino di Gottefredo or by the Genovese brothers.'

'I knew it!' Maria shrieked, and started walking from side to side in the crowded office, among the heaps of materials. 'It had to be those pigs!'

Battista suddenly stood up, surprisingly fast for his weight. 'Maybe I should not have mentioned it...Now Maria, please do not involve yourself with these people. Antelmino is a treacherous coward—'

'And don't I know that, grandfather? From a long date?' She spoke as if she was twice as old. 'But you also know how much of a foe I can be in a battle.'

'You have proven yourself brave indeed, against Sigifredo,' Battista said slowly, crafting words that would not offend his granddaughter, 'and in so many other occasions,' and he cleared his throat 'but those men do not use bravery. They use deceit. And especially the Genovese brothers. I know them. They are not cowards like Antelmino, fearing nothing and nobody. Just be very aware of them.'

Maria was fuming red, as if she would explode in an instant. She took a deep breath and said 'I will deal with them one day. Maybe they are just what the river needs.'

Battista raised an eyebrow. '?'

'You know well what the river needs, grandfather...' She said, waiting for Battista to change his incredulous expression. But he didn't. 'The river wants blood. Sacrifice! Or else it will not allow us to complete the bridge.'

'Maria Maddalena!' Battista curled his lip with disgust, 'Where did you learn this nonsense? Is this all that old Béla could leave to you?'

Maria exhaled and sat down. She leaned over the table and met Battista's gaze, close to his face. 'You know it is true, grandfather. Béla knew about demons. It is as true as your father's tale of the ghost and the tower that leaned to the ground.'

Battista lowered his gaze. 'What will your father think, Maria?'

Maria leaned back and laughed. 'My father is a fool!'

On that night, another storm kept many of the Lucchese indoors. In the Hospital of Santa Croce, once the weather cleared, Julian went outside to verify the damage. His boat was still tied to the hungry ends of the unfinished bridge, but the pile drivers had been taken away by the enraged river.

Over River and Under River

On a cool spring morning of the year of our Lord One Thousand and Twenty Eight, Maria Maddalena of the Cunimundinghi stood on one of the unfinished edges of bridge.

At twenty seven, there was little resemblance to the beautiful redhead that had conquered the heart of the deceased Lord Ruggiero. Maria had surely grown even taller, maybe half a head above the average men in the region, reassuring the majesty that she took upon her wide shoulders. Time outside and acidity inside had dug deep lines of bitterness on her handsome, hard face. Her hair was almost completely silvery now, with only a few copper strands left to shine. She would appear to the inexperienced eye as a fairly sad figure, reminding many of her compunctious mother Elvira, but that was only the isolated outline of Maria on her own, independent from any other life form around her. As soon as as living creature was perceived around her, as soon as any drop of dew would detach itself from the grass, the cantankerous, niggardly Maria Maddalena would reveal itself out of her shell.

She had paused on her way from the Burle et Malachi manor in Corsena, where she often spend one night per week to verify the yields on mulberry leaves and silk. Her son Arrigo would not accompany her in these journeys to Corsena. The boy would be cared for at Anchiano.

Reminiscing about the failures of the past, the unfairness of destiny and the new tasks ahead, Maria was looking through the thick mist that raised from the river, standing tall alone on top of the unfinished bridge, wrapped in her winter cloak as an eerie statue in the fog.

Silently beneath the mist, the Serchio ran swiftly through the wooden pillars, dangerously engorged with the rains that had poured down on the mountain slopes. Just on those days, a child had been swept into the current, viciously grabbed by the river and never given back. The Serchio had not been happy.

Maria could hear the muffled sound of joyful voices from the hospital and the rocking of the boat against wood, somewhere behind on the bank. No pilgrims were heard to be coming up and down the other side and, strangely, no birds where yet singing.

A few beams of the half bridge ventured through the fog, reaching the other side across the deadly current, on a rather delicate-looking trestle that wobbled with the water movement, without any proper paving successfully lined over them. Four years had passed, a few drownings had been forgotten and several trials had been attempted to join the sides, but the river refused to be so easily defeated. The thickest currents got used to snatching pillars and trestles away and destroying by night what was achieved by day.

Dismantling by night the work of the day.

So obvious to Maria Maddalena, this irony of destiny. She knew exactly what the solution for the problem was. She had learned it from the stories of her father, who had come from a world away and seen many wonders. She had learned it from Béla, the táltos, who knew about nature and about things people cannot see in nature. The spirits of the river, whoever they were, if water goblins or mystical fish, if ghosts or the Devil himself, would not allow the people of that valley to finish the bridge without receiving proper acknowledgment.

Maria Maddalena needed to secure the future for Arrigo. She wanted to see the prosperous land of the Cunimundinghi supplying Lucca with grains, wool, fruits and silk, without having to depend on the filthy Antelmino and his land. Without yielding to his wickedness or to the avarice of the Genovese brothers. She needed to bring more pilgrims and visitors into the baths, securing an attractive income for her estate.

Maria Maddalena needed a bridge.

She was convinced that no other feat of engineering or collective impetus would help them see the edges joined one day. If there was any manner in which to persuade the people, it would be a different story, but she knew there was only one answer to the problem. The river wanted blood. The Serchio wanted sacrifice.

She heard soft steps behind, coming towards her. Appearing in the mist, Maria saw the still remarkable figure of Sister Caterina, arriving on a hesitant pace, with a shy, but gracious smile on the side of her lips. Maria acknowledged the nun with a slight bow of her head, but with nothing affable on her countenance. She always felt that Sister Caterina was a terrible inconvenience to her personal comfort. Somehow, the strength of that nun was a constant reminder of Maria's weaknesses. Sister Caterina was, after all, the most concrete and palpable link and witness of Maria Maddalena with her tragic past.

'What are you doing here?' Maria asked abruptly.

Caterina looked at her with an amused smile. 'I should never catch myself surprised with your rudeness any more, but somehow I still expect everyone to have a soul. If you want to know, I just left the hospital, where I was helping Clarissa and Julian. Now, I am on my way back to Controne. I will stop in Chifenti to offer some help to Ginevra, my dear Ginevra...' she almost lost herself in sweet thoughts of the motherless young woman she had learned to love as a daughter. But soon she realised she was not talking to a friendly face. 'I couldn't help but notice through the mist that someone was watching the river,' she continued, looking at Maria, who skipped her gaze. Caterina's age was almost double of Maria's, but they both looked contemporaneous. The nun had silvery strikes on her black mane, still flowing wild, and the lines of age had gracefully dug interesting and flattering curves around her pleasant and full lips and her smiling black eyes.

The thick fog still insisted on laying itself in the bottom of the valley. Both women were engulfed into it, but the mist was repelled by Caterina's aura, and took refuge around the younger woman. The undeniable majesty and beauty of the elder further irritated Maria Maddalena.

'Going back to your man?' Maria asked, uninterested.

'Yes!' Caterina said, beaming. 'I have been away for two days already, and I miss him as if it was a lifetime.'

'It is a wicked lifestyle that you have indeed chosen.' Maria said, curling her lip. 'But there is still salvation before the day of the Final Judgement.'

'Tell me about it.' Sister Caterina said, cynically amused.

'I will be very blunt, old nun. As you seem to have no problems in spreading your legs to that old priest Martino, why couldn't you satisfy the urges of my neighbour Antelmino Di Gottefredo? He has desired you for so many years. Perhaps he would help us fund this bridge or open the road down to Lucca.'

Caterina was livid with shock. 'By the spilled blood of the Christ, you must be joking with me!' she gasped.

'Joking? I hardly find any amusement on it,' insisted Maria, 'you don't want to convince me that you did not enjoy your time with the Saracens from that morning in Partigliano, do you?'

'*Maria Tenebrosa!* How could you?' groaned Caterina, just about to explode. 'After all that you have been through. After all that I had to bear to save you from further desecration and to spare the child in your womb. After all of that, you are indeed the soulless monster that everyone says!'

Maria said nothing, but both of her arms rocketed with all her strength towards Caterina's chest. The woman was flung backwards, falling over the edge. Her back broke the first wooden beam it encountered and her head hit the next, changing the direction in which her body spun, before diving and disappearing into the thick current.

A dead silence reigned immediately, except for the boat that still rocked in the bank, the mute voices that came from the hospital and the heartbeat that pounded on Maria's ears. She could see nobody. Nobody had seen or heard anything.

It was done. The river was granted its much needed blood. Goblins, sprites, nymphs and water witches were satisfied. Marabbecche! The bridge would be finished.

And Maria's past was no more. She could now erase those memories forever.

She hurried her pace towards Anchiano. Walking quietly by the hospital, she heard the same muffled voices form the interior and swiftly accelerated her steps, sliding quickly across the front of Traghetto, which also seemed to be asleep.

Sooner or later they would find Caterina's body, Maria thought. *And better be later than sooner.* Better be when she would be surprised by the news in the comfort of the Anchiano manor. And maybe, just maybe and hopefully, the water goblins and river spirits would take her with them to the darkest depths of the Serchio and a body would never be found. Just like it had been with Béla and Divina.

The fog was dispersing. Less than two miles down the road, after the left rocky bank dug deep into the river, making it run northwest on a curve that stretches into a long and wide marshy, reed-covered strip, and where the entrance to Anchiano left the river road, Maria was ready to walk up the hill to her manor when she heard a moan.

A human moan.

Her soul froze. It was coming from the tall grass at the bank. There were no bitterns booming or frogs croaking. No paludicolous creature could have done it. *It sounded definitely human.* Looking to the sides, verifying the three stretches of the road, Maria saw nobody coming or going.

She carefully climbed down towards the water. Entering the boggy soil under the tall grass, she disappeared behind the reeds and watched for the river. A space had to be opened through the long stalky leaves with her hands before she ventured with every next stride, raising a myriad of gnats and flies that were attracted by her sweat. Her feet started to sink deeper into water, stepping over the fallen grass. When her hands opened a window through the last thicket before the water, a bittern flew up with a scream, startled, almost hitting Maria on her face. With water half way up to her thighs, she watched the bird fly away and observed the river carefully. The current flew fast and angry. Nobody was seen. Nothing found.

Just before turning around she noticed a clear spot in between the reeds nearby, where the current did not move the shallow water. A small eel swam next to the surface, with its mouth emerged. It was staring at her face. Looking around, Maria saw more of those. Eels grasping for air, with their fat lips panting out of the water. They were all staring at her with their nailhead eyes.

'*Maledetti anguille!*' she cursed them and turned around to leave that mosquito-ridden marsh. But a strong and cold hand grasped around her ankle.

'H...' the person lying on the tall grass tried to say.

It was Caterina. Alive and agonising.

Before Maria panicked, a shout came from the road – 'Hello there!' – making her stomach churn.

'Someone there? Is that you, Maria Maddalena of the Cunimundinghi?'

She stood up stretched, looking above the grass. It was a cart. The driver waved at her.

'Do you need any help?' the driver asked.

And Maria's own entrails almost loosened out completely when she saw behind the driver, another man in the cart. Perhaps the worst and best possible person to be there, smiling, with his rotten teeth shaded by the wide-brimmed deer hide hat. Antelmino Di Gottefreddo. The Castracani.

Maria Maddalena had the time for an intake of breath to think. She could not afford to push Caterina back into the current, with those men watching the river down the road. No time to admit the truth, but to think of a lie.

She could bring the wounded Caterina up to her home in Anchiano for vital help. Nobody better than herself to tend to the wounds and watch for Caterina's best recovery. And when that accursed nun could finally breathe properly, and talk, she would accuse Maria of attempted murder.

The other option was to hand the nun to that shit Antelmino. Maria knew well that, among few others, wickedness was the greatest attribute of the Castracani. He could easily take her home and keep her in silence, for himself, forever. And so would Maria herself be further tied into her neighbour's strangling grip.

No, the lies had to cover a vast area of possibilities.

And there was a third option.

'Please help this woman here!' she cried to the men in the cart, trying to stand tall with her head above the grass. 'I think she is dying!' Maria's voice was in pain, full of desperation. 'Please help me take her out of the water!' And she lowered herself to grab Sister Caterina. Her hands clenched across the nun's neck, firmly pushing it down. Caterina's black eyes burst open with shock, suddenly looking at the desperate Maria Maddalena from underwater.

The men came down to the reeds and found their way to help Maria. They never saw the struggle.

Caterina's eyes were soon looking at nothing else.

Lamb soup and warm milk. Freshly baked bread, a hen's giblets and chestnut polenta. In the dining hall, some remaining pieces of coal still cracked as they burned red in a thick bed of ashes, raising the warmth of the blackened room to a level much above comfort. Vapours and smoke, especially the heat of human activity, were building up in the hospital. Apart from Sister Caterina, that had already left earlier, the pilgrims had stayed sheltered until quite late that morning. No lower windows had yet been opened to allow fresher air to enter. With eyes itching from her sweat, Clarissa pushed open the windows for a breath of cool, spring air.

The wind that hit her face was certainly fresh, but heavy with an unusual herbal scent. Nauseating to her stomach.

With a raised eyebrow, Julian discreetly opened the door to verify what went on outside. The fog was dissipating, but the stench still embraced him.

Nobody on the road. Nobody on the Via Francigena. Traghetto was still.

The bridge stood still like a ribcage, broken and silent over the hurried waters of the Serchio.

It was a quiet day.

Spatola was having a pleasant morning. He left Chifenti with a light pace, towards the nice sheltering whiteness of the fog, which was raising itself to reveal all of the Serchio's beauty.

It must have been already the hora tertia, the third hour of the day, when the bells tolled somewhere up the valley. There were two or three different sounds, but Spatola immediately recognised one of them. Although the pitch was low, with a rather short duration, the pace was not quick, with a long, heavy interval between the clangs. It must have been the large bronze bells that had been ordered for the constructing duomo in Barga, used for many other churches of that parish. This was the trigger for other bells down the valley to toll, on a melodic encounter with the beautiful harmony of the Lucchese towers, which travelled up the valley of the Serchio. Many bells started their chant immediately behind him, up on the Lima. The hurried and joyous pace of the soft bell of San Pietro, low in tin, with a vivacious and long-lived pitch; San Salvatore and San Frediano further up; Santo Stefano; San Chirico and Spatola's favourite – a deep soft wail that soared above them all, mellow and full of sadness, but beautiful and still somehow uplifting, the voice of the angels from far away on the mountain – It was the Ottone, the cry of Santa Giulia in Controne.

A recent fad on bell-making was the utilisation of yellow bronze, an alloy which was imported all the way from Acquisgranus - Aachen. It had not been a decade before when Immanuel Malachi had purchased a fairly large bell for Father Martino in Controne, made with this magical mixture of copper and calamine, obtained from the mines found right under the seat of the Roman Empire. In Lombardy and Rome, this increasingly popular material was generally coined *L'Ottone*, brought in from the same land as the emperors with that name.

Spatola savoured the warm song of the Ottone. After the last stroke of the clapper, when the chant was yet no more than a fading moan soaring up onto heavens, the towers of Anchiano and Diecimo down the river were still clanging their tin-rich bells, cold and hard, as if an insistent blacksmith from Lucca had decided to shape his steel up on the valleys.

The village idiot continued his jovial pace next to the Serchio. Like most mornings of his nothing less than uncomplicated routine, Spatola would walk down the river and try to cross to the Via Francigena for alms. And more recently, with the functioning hospital at the ferry cross, he would slip into the kitchen and help Clarissa and Julian in whichever duties they could put him in charge of. That would render him warmth of hearts and a place at the table. He knew the hospital was this piece of heaven where a simpleton like him was treated rather as an angel than as a beast, a miracle that he could never obtain at Chifenti or elsewhere. Why did he stick to Chifenti then? Why remain impassibly stubborn, living in that same village and bear so frequent bullying by so many? The answer was clear: it could be found during occasional early mornings, at the backyard of the tavern, sparing Spatola a smile and sharing a few chestnuts with him. The owner of the tavern, Ginevra Di Amadeo.

At nineteen, besides the small stature, Ginevra had little on her skin that reminded anyone of the fragile figure of Divina, her mother. A hard worker with strong arms and muscular legs, her youth and vigour was for many travellers and pilgrims the best justification to avoid the charity at the hospital and spend a coin with a palliasse at the tavern. With undisciplined dark hair, and brilliant sheens of copper furtively seen even below her neck line, Ginevra was doubtlessly dark as her father and with the same tact for the strangers. With her proud posture and large brown eyes, she was quick of wit, generous with laughter on customer compliments or their incautious, yet harmless jostles. But she would be ready to drop a heavy fist after any more reckless gropes. To most of the travellers, Ginevra was the most vibrant wench one could find on that stretch of the Via Francigena. To Spatola, Ginevra was lovely as ripe berries and aromatic as chestnuts.

He had his brief moments with her, earlier that morning, looking quietly at the elegant chickens that Amadeo had brought in from Livorno. The partridge-feathered hens had the colour of Ginevra's rebellious hair. While the rooster balanced his generous wattles and rubbery white earlobes, the hens were scratching across the tidy backyard of the tavern and discretely waiting for their first serious meal, when any leftovers of breakfast, too offensive to be saved for another day, would be tossed across the kitchen window. Spatola had the privilege of those two minutes with Ginevra, away from the customers who treated her with no respect and spared him no heart. He munched on roasted chestnuts and kept staring at her. Ginevra had a warm smile on her lips as she observed the chickens. She embraced her legs to protect herself from the chill of the morning. He had never seen her more beautiful and vibrant. Spatola was certain Ginevra was made *and* tasted of berries and chestnuts.

Chifenti had been left behind, and now the unfinished bridge appeared through the thinning fog on his right side. Further down, the square block of the hospital on the left, now sending up with the breeze a faint whisper of voices and merriment through the gurgling murmur of the Serchio. Spatola could have gone inside the hospital if he wanted, but that morning had a special taste in the air. Besides, the road was as empty as it never had been at the third hour. He continued his easy stride down the path, following the direction of the water. A pair of ducks flew hurried up the valley, ignoring the village idiot that never tired from watching their flight. As the road turned around the long rocky bank that pushed the river against the other side, just below the still deserted Via Francigena, Spatola noticed some people further down on his side of the road. And what he saw made him feel his heart sink, for it would inhabit his bad dreams for many nights to come.

'Who's that?' Antelmino asked startled, dropping the legs of Caterina, as they carried her body to the cart.

They looked at the paralysed small-headed figure of Spatola up on the road.

'It's the idiot from Chifenti' Maria said with undisguised apprehension. 'We should better talk to him, or we may have problems with the villagers.'

'Hey, idiot, come over here and help us, boy.' Antelmino shouted, imperiously.

They saw no reaction. The cart driver tried a more tactful approach. 'Boy, please help us here. There has been an accident!'

Again, the figure did not move, and kept staring at them, open mouthed. Antelmino helped raise the heavy body to the cart and turned over to walk up to where Spatola stood. 'I will get him!' he said, reaching over to the sheathed dagger on his belt. It was in this blink of an eye that Spatola also turned around and started running for his life, towards the hospital.

Antelmino meant to follow him, but Maria Maddalena yelled 'Let him be! You will never catch up with the idiot when he's already running. Let's take this woman up to Anchiano, so that she can be properly dressed for the death rites, and handed to any family that comes to claim her.

The Castracani grinned and returned to the cart. Almost thirty years old, Antelmino di Gottefredo was still an agile and surprisingly strong man for his age. In spite of his blue eyes being too close to his thin nose, he would have been a rather handsome figure if he stood taller than his usual suspicious hunched posture and if his face had not been ravaged by pock mark-like craters.

'Maria Maddalena,' he said, 'you know well that this whore had no family. She lived with that priest from Controne.'

'You seem to be well acquainted with her, Antelmino, now help us here, unless you want to take her with you. You never had a chance to have Sister Caterina in your bed, did you? She must be easy now, I suppose.'

Antelmino stood outside of the cart, staring at Maria, who took control of the reins. 'Maria Maddalena, my repulse towards you is only broken by a spike of admiration, for little people have I met that would read my thoughts as you do. You are the real witch who should have been drowned in the Serchio under the bridge of San Frediano, so many years ago, and not that foreign old shit. And here,' he laughed and spit on the ground, 'here only the Devil will know how you came to find this woman drowning in the Serchio. You have a world of account to do about this corpse after that idiot boy reaches the hospital or Chifenti. And a lot more clarification to me, if you survive this ordeal.' He slapped the hind of the donkey and the animal started a slow pace, pulling now a cart with Maria and the driver in the back, holding the body of Caterina.

Antelmino was left behind, shouting to Maria 'I will walk back home. I don't think I will have the displeasure to come across anyone else drowning in these waters.'

Julian was somehow not too surprised when he saw Spatola breaking into the hospital and screaming as if his fingernails had been pulled off. Was it the silence, the quiet day that suggested of trouble? Was it rank stench of that herb that was carried on with the fog? Julian should have guessed. The idiot was squealing like a slaughtered pig. Many of the pilgrims jumped back, scared, dropping plates and spilling the lamb soup. Others laughed with scorn at the noticeable idiocy on the flat face that seemed so frightened and lost. Clarissa let go her affairs at the kitchen and rushed to lend Spatola's brow a friendly hand, to sooth and calm him as he continued yelling an unintelligible sentence, held still by some of the pilgrims, among the general commotion created at the hospital hall. And it was Julian that spilled all the freshly warmed milk on the floor when he finally understood what Spatola had said. Very clearly, the poor boy was terrorised with whatever he had seen, screaming from the top of what was left of his lungs 'They've killed Sister Caterina!'

Caterina's Revenge

'Go away!' Maria Maddalena shouted from the walls of Anchiano. 'Return to your homes and to your obligations, lazy peasants, or I will have you run by my men-at-arms!'

'We just want to have justice for Sister Caterina!' a voice rose from the crowd.

'*Who* said that?' Maria roared.

Silence was the answer. There were probably a hundred who had gathered outside of her gates. It was getting close to the *hora nona*, the ninth hour of the day and they had come from as far as Corsena and Wald Ottavo. The news had been spread up and down those valleys, as quick as the fog disappeared. They all knew that Sister Caterina was dead and, according to the idiot of Chifenti, she had been made dead by the hands of Maria Maddalena of the Cunimundinghi and Antelmino di Gottefredo. The lady of Anchiano had taken Sister Caterina's body and locked herself with it inside the walls of the manor, on the top of the rock. She watched with concern the gathering of the rabble, but never allowing her skin to sweat out any fragility, standing behind the battlements next to two or her most fierce-looking men-at-arms, servants whom she had hired among the vellutini of Lucca.

'If you want justice,' she shouted at the crowd, 'raise your prayers to the heights of heaven, for it is only God that can answer for His acts. But if you do not accept the destiny that He's reserved for us, then don't make it *my* problem.'

'Spatola said you have killed the nun,' another voice rose from the mob and it was followed by a general murmur of approval.

Maria scowled. '*Spatola*? Are you referring to the village idiot of Chifenti?' She cackled with laughter. 'You sad poor things...being led by a nitwit! I had overestimated you then, by thinking you no more than peasants, ignorant farmers, but you are probably no better than the idiot Spatola, who needs a good beating for his lies. A herd of fools who should be hung on a cage at the city centre for the amusement of passers-by.'

'Maria, tell us what happened then,' a woman's voice shouted. 'Clear the truth for us, if you know of it.'

Maria Maddalena recognised the voice of her own sister Mira. The Lady of Anchiano scanned through the heads, hats, scarves, dimples, staffs and pitchforks until she spotted the dark face of the young woman on the crowd, surrounded by other brothers.

'Mira, Domenico, Malachia, Tomaso and Matteo!' she clapped her hands theatrically. 'The Burle et Malachi offspring leave their duties behind and mix with the riffraff for a skirmish with their Overlady. How disappointed I am... I hope my father knows of your whereabouts.'

'Our father wanted us to come and find out the facts with you, Maria Maddalena, to meet the truth hearing from your mouth.' Malachia said.

Maria Maddalena was privately glad for those words from her brother. Now much more ensured of her safety, she waited for a few seconds and finally said, as from a pulpit to a crowd of the faithful. 'Do you want to see the truth? Do you want to see the justice of God? Then look around you. Look back down the road to the river. To these ill-tempered waters that we so badly want to lay a bridge across. But what have we achieved so far? Nothing! The Serchio does not allow us to build this bridge! We are not worthy of it, are we?' She scanned again the crowd, the sun-browned faces that listened with silence. 'No wonder,' she continued, 'if you look at the lewd habits of our people. The Serchio keeps taking away the bridge and it will continue to be snapping lives from our folk too.' She pointed down to something inside the walls, 'and now it's this unfortunate wicked woman, whose lifestyle has gone astray from the exemplary ways of our Lord Jesus Christ's. Before her, there was the poor kid from the Traghetto, and only God knows if he had been baptised in Christ. But how many has the Serchio taken away before? Isn't the Serchio acting under a more supreme command then just the seasons? If you don't believe in that, you are doubting the actions of God. Is there anyone among you who is sceptical of the almighty power of God?'

'Do not twist this around, Maria Maddalena. Just let us know what happened.'

It was Malachia again. That little shit was not helping at all.

'Malachia, my brother, I owe you no explanation, neither to anyone here. It surprises me to see my kin among this rabble. This gathering brings up connotations of rebellion, and we all know that only the sword and lance can pierce through the bubble of an upheaval.' She walked to one of the men-at-arms and grabbed his sword. 'Who wants to feel the sharpness of this steel under their chin?'

They repeated their dead silent answer.

Maria handed the sword back and continued, walking back and forth along length of the front battlements of Anchiano. 'I was strolling down the road from

Corsena, when I heard someone moaning from the riverbank. Naturally concerned, I faced the reeds and dug my way through, to find this regrettable creature gasping for air, breathing water across her last moments. That was when Antelmino di Gottefredo drove by on his cart, and do not ask me what he does when he wonders to the north of his lands. But that is not the point, anyway. Antelmino and his cartman helped me pull the body out of the river. The idiot from Chifenti saw us in this moment and ran away immediately, concluding the worse on his tiny shithead and spreading out lies. I will see to it that he is rightly punished for his insolence.'

'Are you innocent of Sister Caterina's death. Maria Maddalena?'

'Of course I am, Malachia. How she fell into the water or how the river grabbed her, I don't know and I hardly care, but thanks to me we have a body to be properly dressed for a funeral, if she deserves a Christian one, or else it would be stranded, bloated and maggot-ridden in the marshes of Lucca, or worse, Pisa.' There was a general humming, and Maria concluded 'And if I am not telling you the truth, may God strike me right now, from the heights of heaven.'

The majority of the folk turned their heads up to the sky, but all they saw was an immense, benevolent blue.

'Hand us Sister Caterina back, then.' someone said. 'We will take her to Santa Giulia in Controne for her funeral rites.'

'What? Hand her to you?' she said. 'And *who* are you to demand that? This woman had no family in my lands, but she was found here. To the best of my knowledge she has no kin in other lands either. I will make her remains available to the diocese of Lucca, and if no one is sent to claim her, I shall find a proper place for her burial.'

'No!' the crowd shouted in unison. 'Hand her to us. To Father Martino. To Controne!'

'Silence!' Maria demanded, louder. 'Forget this matter, for I will deal with her burial if it comes to the need.' She disappeared behind a merlon, looking down to the ground of Anchiano, inside the wall and across the closed gate that separated it from the mob below: a few soldiers, Arrigo her son, distractedly cleaning his fingernails with a dagger, and the terrorised cartman of Antelmino. She could not refrain from grinning when she said it out loud, so they could hear her outside. 'Now I have here an issue to be solved. I must release the cartman of Antelmino di Gottefredo to return to his lord.' And she stuck her head through the crenel, so they all could see the sheer madness on her face. 'You will let him through, untouched.'

A man-at-arms carefully approached Maria behind the battlements and whispered. 'My Lady, they will lynch him.'

'They will *not*.' She answered quietly, looking at the incensed faces below. 'And if they attack him, we will know how just angry they are. It will be a good reason to slay a good number of them as a well-learned lesson.'

The man-at-arms was speechless, but not as terrorised as the cartman himself, who had fallen on his knees, moaning quietly 'Please let me stay… please let me stay.'

'Nobody gets out without Sister Caterina!' the crowd shouted. A loud cheer was heard. Staffs and tools were raised and shaken, claiming for the body of their nun.

'Fools!' Maria spat, rabid from her heights. 'Can't you see that this is our opportunity to appease the voracity of the Serchio? Can you understand that the Serchio wants blood for our bridge?'

At this moment, a score of riders galloped across the vineyards, coming from the Serchio. The crowd shivered. Heading the dusty cloud, a fine, tall, fawn-brown stallion, setting the pace and stomping the road with fury. The rider carried a lance, leading other helmeted men-at-arms with picks, swords and arches seen through the glittering dust. The wild matted mane of grey hair was not tamed by a helmet, but he was more than prepared for war. Fires of rage burnt in his violet eyes. Bernardo From The Rocks. And he carried a *francesca* axe across his lap.

The crowd sighed.

'Maria Maddalena, open the gate.' Bernardo said.

She laughed. 'Bernardo Delle Rocche, I am very impressed. A soldier? When it comes to a pair of woman's legs, you prove to be a more efficient man than just a lice-ridden shepherd.'

Bernardo narrowed his eyebrows. 'It's a concept you are not familiar with, Maria Maddalena. It's called *loyalty*.'

'Then maybe, if you are interested in concepts, you should be made aware of the notion of property. You are in my lands, uninvited and sporting weaponry of war. This is an inexcusable offense and I advise you to kindly apologise and take the road that you came from.'

'Not without Sister Caterina!' he grunted.

Maria shook her head, as if to brush sarcastic thoughts off it. 'Bernardo, you don't want me to make public your past history with Sister Caterina, do you?'

With nervous steps of his beast, Bernardo rode around in a circle and said. 'I make no secrets about my love for Sister Caterina, and there is no shame which will ever make me hide it.' And he pointed at her with his rather short sword 'But you, Maria Maddalena, you do keep you past hidden…and your secret of Partigliano will not be buried with this good woman.'

All the villagers who were standing in front of the gate of Anchiano saw the blood rise to Maria Maddalena's face. She spat three times on the ground next to her feet. 'You low, filthy hermit!' she shrieked. 'If it is war you want I will give you war!'

The mob boiled as Bernardo continued. 'We will empty the village and take those willing out of harm's way. You are in no castle to protect yourself, Maria Maddalena. We will not shoot the first arrow, but by God and by Santa Caterina I swear: we can bring you out of your hole, holding you by the tail.'

Maria turned to the man-at-arms and hissed 'Prepare the archers, bring them all around…' she lost her words as the man-at-arms started squirming. 'What? What is it that makes you quiver as a coward?'

The man-at-arms straightened up and said with the side of his mouth 'They are too many, my Lady. We cannot win on a straight face-to-face confrontation.'

Maria heard that and immediately verified the mob down the wall. They were loud, too excited with the manoeuvring of the riders and never got hold of what the man-at-arms had said. She turned to him with eyes as large as grey marble balls and said between gritted teeth. 'Are you a real man or a rat? Get your men and have them pierce with their arrows as many necks as they…'

'Enough!' a voice interrupted them all.

It was deep and grave. A powerful command with a pitch so low, as if it had come from a giant bronze bell lining the surface of the Apuane mountains.

'Enough with these devilries!' the voice rose again.

They all turned to the road below the walls and saw the figures of two riders which had just arrived. They were now hurriedly approaching around the rock on their sweating beasts, which could no more than do a quick pace. They slipped through the riders of Bernardo, who quietly let them pass and entered through a funnel opened by the crowd, leading to the entrance of Anchiano. Maria Maddalena was leaning over the wall, watching them come to her gate. On the smaller, black mule was Julian, the Hospitaller. On Julian's own horse, a grey-coloured mare, tired as it could, but still imperious on its gait, rode the long tall figure of Father Martino.'

'I had enough of it all, Maria Maddalena!' Martino continued, with his earth-shaking baritone staring at Maria with bewildering gravity. His dark eyes were deep-set on his rather well-carved head, standing like a log with the cowl flung back. 'I came to take my beloved Caterina with me' he stated with disarming poignancy. 'There will be no blood spilled, neither outside these walls, nor inside your house.' He looked at his friend Bernardo, which respectfully bowed his head in sympathy. 'The riders will leave and no arrow shall be shot, neither a splinter may be snatched from your gates. Bernardo will turn around and head to his lands with his men as soon as you peacefully hand me the body of Caterina.'

Maria tried to say something, but her voice did not make it to the air.

Martino unhorsed and walked calmly, with wide firm strides to the gate. His eyes never left the marble white face of Maria Maddalena. Finally, looking up to the lady of Anchiano, he said with a low grunt, slowly trembling out between his still strong and white teeth: 'Open this gate and *give me my Caterina!*'

Maria Maddalena's head seemed about to explode. Finally, she let out a sigh and allowed her eyelids to drop with exhaustion. Her head disappeared from the top of the crenel and her voice was heard inside. 'It's a mistake, hear me. I'll give her to you. You can do anything you want with this woman, but it's a mistake!'

When Martino turned his back onto Anchiano, he was carefully embracing the cold body of Caterina on his horse. With a firm face and stone-dried lips, he bore the pain from the wail broken out by the villagers in seeing their dear Sister Caterina beaten down to a lifeless body. And he did not shed a single tear. There would be a lifetime of tears, but only when he would be alone with his beloved and with God.

As the mournful parade disappeared from her sight, with Bernardo and Julian gone and the mob dispersing, leaving the front gate and going back to their villages, Maria seemed to wake from the commanding spell of Martino's voice. On seeing some of the crowd still there, under her wall, she filled her lungs and shouted 'It's a mistake! The Serchio claimed her life! The river wanted her sacrifice to grant us the bridge! She belongs into those waters. She should be put underneath the bridge. It's a mistake!'

On hearing those words, one of the pilgrims who had accompanied the rabble turned to Maria, disgusted. 'You horrible woman. How can you say that? There is word that Sister Caterina was as good as a saint!'

Maria gasped with a guffaw. She started giggling, shaking her whole body, finally falling into frantic laughter, as if she had heard the best joke of her life, making her eyes drop to the sides of her face. 'A saint? Another one?' she scowled, finally catching some breath. She leaned over the ramparts, eyes open wide in an eerie grin. 'Well, that is even *better*! Saintly relics for the river. It will be an honour, and certainly more than a satisfactory bargain for a bridge!'

She screamed even louder now, provoking, to all of those who were still around Anchiano. 'Take Caterina's relics to the Serchio, and we will have a bridge!'

But Martino was already too far to hear that.

There were those who heard Maria and gave some thought to it.

And there were others who were still hopeful, who kept staring at the sky.

Father Martino's eyes were looking at the stars. He could not sleep. It had been a full day, after another sleepless night, such an unyielding farewell to Caterina.

Julian had stayed at the hospital. He would come later, together with Clarissa, for the burial. Martino carried on fording the Lima. His hard face had softened as he slowly climbed the steep path to Controne. A warmer countenance, but of pain and discouragement for the loss of his dear love, became more real at every step of his horse.

The visit of the balivo from Lucca was the expected waste of time, if not painful. But the church had been busy with visitors who came to pay their respect to so good a soul that had blessed them with her compassion. Sobbing with desolation, some mourners were prostrating before the coffin, hoping to be blessed by the saintly woman, while others demanded justice, at least an investigation on the unexpected drowning.

Ginevra was disconsolate for losing a mother figure for the second time. After a full day next to the body of Caterina, she was finally taken down to Chifenti by Bernardo, who convinced her to rest.

The general disgust made the air heavier with suspicion and fear, for Controne was still in the lands of the Cunimundinghi. So many and varied were the demands of mourners and so intense the outpouring of grief that by the time they put Caterina to rest in a peaceful spot under a gracious chestnut tree, Martino had already ran out of tears.

The priest found some peace as the people drifted away, leaving him alone next to a freshly dug mound. When the stars were already piercing through the moonless Tuscan sky, Martino lied down next to the tree and spent the night together with his beloved.

An adorable morning came up, defying mourning. Martino retired to the parish house to spend his strange, lonely day busying himself on menial tasks, trying to believe that those few years with Caterina had been a blessing added to his life, and that now he should carry on by himself, as he had always done before the day when she re-appeared on the bridge of San Frediano.

Many more travellers came to see the grave. From Montefegatesi to Tempagnano, they visited for a personal farewell. Several pilgrims had taken a detour from the Via Francigena, told by the locals that a true saint had just been buried in the parish of Santa Giulia in Controne.

On that third night, Martino's body was in pain, feeling old and broken as never before. Caterina did not need his company, he thought, after all, she was everywhere. It was he, who craved for her presence around to sooth him. He yearned for her warmth and sweetness to make his muscles relax and certainly, that would not be achieved by sleeping next to her grave. In heaven, she would have all the power to be next to him. Whether there was any ecclesiastical base for that concept, he did not care, but he certainly believed in it when he fell in bed and had the most comforting rest and deep sleep he had had in a long time.

Martino's belief on Caterina's mystical presence, if not saintly or divine, was even stronger when, during the next night, he was strangely awoken as the monastery bells of the Serchio tolled the matins. There were unnatural noises outside the church, bothering the quiet gusts of wind he was used to. Nobody was expected to be circulating at church during those late hours, not even shepherds on an early journey. Wolves could not be either, or the lambs would be bleating for their lives. He got up to verify and faced the dark chill of the valley, stepping carefully into the night. Hearing better, probably behind the church, he distinguished the grainy sounds of metal blades being trusted on the soil. Shovels at work.

Grave robbers?

Three men diligently and incautiously digging. Three men whose souls left their bodies for a second, frozen with fear when, like a rabid werewolf materialised from the darkness, Father Martino flew on top of them with a raging roar.

Fortunate indeed were those two who slipped away from his grasp, mingling into the shadows of the cemetery, disappearing in the distance, still carrying their screams of terror tied to their tails. The unlucky third was having his jaws and nose broken by the granite-hard knuckles that kept hammering on his face.

Father Martino recognised a common delinquent he had seen before, roaming around Fornulo and Chifenti. He kept beating him until the robber's limbs had lost any tone.

'Monsters! *What* did you want by digging there?' Martino shouted on the broken face, holding the thief like a heavy boneless scarecrow.

There was no answer. The cloudy eyes were not even focused at him.

Martino beat him more, repeatedly, and two more teeth were lost on the cemetery ground, among few that were still left.

'What did you want by digging there?' he insisted.

'Relics...' a feeble moan came out of the mass of blood.

'Who sent you for this?'

No answer. Just closed eyes.

Another tooth.

'We were sent by no one, father.' The thief said suddenly, through bubbles of blood, raising a weak hand between his face and the priest's fist. 'It was our idea that we could sell Sister Caterina's bones for those who want the bridge finished.'

Martino heard that with a sudden tension in his body. He held it for a while with clenched jaws, praying to God that he would not kill that man out of desolation for having lost Caterina. Finally his eyelids fell, unlocking the keys to the air that strangled his heart and to all his muscles, which relaxed with reluctance.

'Tell your damned friends or anyone who is interested in relics that Sister Caterina is in heaven. And so will her bones be in heaven too!'

The robber managed to nod with a slow blink of his terrified eyes.

Martino carried him like a bag of grain to the edge of the church yard. 'Don't you ever let me see you again in Controne, or I will tear your throat out with my own hands.' He grunted, before tossing the robber far down on the pebbled road. The man shrieked at the fall and disappeared on a limping run.

Out into the chilly dusk came the early morning farmers in Corsena, Fornulo and Chifenti. They were ready to conduct their herds to the grazing areas above on the valleys. But on taking a glance to the northeast, they were surprised to encounter the warm glowing of dawn flickering at that time of the night.

And it was not the sun.

Behind the woods to the north, on the parish of Controne, a fire burnt.

Father Martino watched with pride his beloved Caterina being factually elevated to the skies. Sparkles and embers of his love were happily flying up to heights above the reach of any mortal. The smoke soared with fury, mingling into the heavy grim ceiling that had built up over the last couple of hours. The parishoner's blackened face was streaked by tears of sadness, joy and soot.

Chifenti and Corsena still saw the smoke continuing to rise from the furious fire for a good portion of the morning. When the last woods were burning, by the sixth hour of the day, Caterina had already been distributed throughout the clouds of Tuscany.

And by the look of the clouds, Caterina did not seem to be very happy.

The storm exploded when the day had its darkest moment, exactly by the time the sun should have been midway through its journey across the valley. An implacable amount of water poured down on the Apuane and the Apennines for days and nights without stopping. The rivers grew strong and angry, washing down the valleys and marauding the banks, taking with them anything they could. The Via Francigena was impassable for days, and the Serchio rose fat and vicious, reaching all the way to the door of the hospital. Julian and Clarissa were sheer fortunate to have enough supplies to maintain their pilgrims there for a few days.

And when the rain ceased and the waters receded, a new scenario was seen in that stretch of the Serchio. There was no more bridge. No sign of it.

The Devil's Spawn

On the northern edge of Lucca, the Bridge of San Frediano expanded long and firmly over the wide extension of the Serchio. *Well-planted and smooth*, Maria Maddalena thought, *just as my bridge should have been.* The hoof beats on the planks were louder than the general murmur of the morning crowd that opened way for the cart. An able rider, Arrigo was not holding the reins this time, for he could not take his eyes of his gift. At fourteen, he was growing to have a large frame like his mother's, a sharp and unemotional mind in the financial dealings of Anchiano and a freckle-ridden face that still reminded Maria of the little lonely child he had been, without a father and without company worthy of his level.

They were returning from a night spent at Battista Burle's, when Arrigo finally received, what had been custom-designed and carefully crafted by the best blacksmiths and goldsmiths in Lucca and paid by a voluminous sum of gold from Maria Maddalena's treasury chest: a copy of Attila's dagger.

While Arrigo scrapped his thumb across the new steel sharpened blade, a correction of the original dagger that was agreed upon all involved in the project, Maria held the reins and looked at the Serchio over the jetsam side of the bridge.

Somewhere in those depths, marabbecche were laughing at her, playing with the original dagger of Attila, hiding among Béla's bones and looking at the child she had born into the world. The child accursed by Béla.

Maria brushed off those thoughts, as the cart came onto the embankment and followed on the Via Francigena towards the valley. 'We could have returned through the lands of Tassignano,' she said to Arrigo on her side, 'but that Antelmino is just too powerful these days since we lost our bridge. Our unfinished bridge. And my coffers could not bear another toll raise, which a man of his level could easily do, just by seeing us driving through.' She looked at her son, who would not stop staring at that blade. 'Are you listening to what I'm saying, Arrigo?'

The boy looked at her, without changing his expression. 'Sure...' and he turned his attention back to his new toy.

By the sixth mile, when the valley menacingly started to narrow over the Via Francigena and the road parted, they took the right path, where other carts were coming from. And it proved to be the wrong decision to go through the ferry of Sesto, by the castle of Moriano.

'What do you mean we have to pay again?' Maria shouted, towering over the ferryman. I have paid for my passage yesterday, and now I am returning. The use of the ferry is paid for when I go to Lucca. Now when I return to my lands, with my cart, my son, my mule, my horses and my man-at-arms, this is already accounted for.'

The ferryman opened his palms in front of his chest, as if to stop a boulder from rolling over. 'My lady,' he said, with a nervous laugh, 'the lords of Moriano have demanded it. Nobody crosses to Sesto without paying for the ferry.'

'I do understand that, you poor stupid thing,' Maria said, ignoring the ferryman's halt, flicking the reins and making the mule pull the cart onto the ferry. 'But I am returning from already having paid. Just take us over and, if you have any problems,' she pointed to the man-at-arms that had accompanied them to Lucca, 'you may prefer to talk to him.'

The ferryman had no alternative but to accept their presence aboard and dig his pole into the riverbed for pushing them across.

When his passengers left the ferry, he did not hesitate to abandon it and run up the hill to the castle of Moriano.

The road north from Sesto was always a disgrace. A dark, unkempt winding path that bordered cliffs and often slid down, plunging riders and carts towards the Serchio. Lamberto and Lanfranco allowed little time for the people of Sesto to spend on repairs, probably just enough to have their ally Antelmino use it for his carts when investigating his Northern neighbours. The most common feeling of pilgrims and travellers on that stretch of road was to observe the good quality path coming down from the hills across the river and wish they had taken the western bank. But when it opened into the lands of the Cunimundinghi, the path straightened and reflected the rigid discipline maintained in the lands of Maria Maddalena.

Driving through orchards of mulberry trees and vineyards, the Lady of Anchiano could already devise her castle on the rock when they heard the riders approaching. She looked over her shoulder to see Lanfranco and Lamberto galloping after them. 'Those two bastards are coming to debate the ferry toll! Go stop them and tell them to crawl back to their lands!' she shouted to her man-at-arms. While the man turned his horse around, Arrigo did little to acknowledge the move.

Maria yelled at the mule, to quicken the pace while the man-at-arms kicked in to meet the Genovese brothers. But looking over her shoulder, Maria screamed with shock when she saw her man-at-arms leaning back as he approached them, and finally dropping from his horse like a sack of stones. 'Arrows!' she cried. 'Those criminals! They will catch up with us much before we get to Anchiano!'

Her son did not lift his gaze.

Soon they had been stopped by Lamberto and Lanfranco, who were dismounting and standing in front of the mule cart.

'What have you done do to my escort back there?' Maria shrieked. 'Did you kill him?'

The Genovese brothers just stood smiling, each combing in his own beard with the fingers. One yellow and one red.

'The witch and her son!' Lanfranco said with a grin, in a tone loud enough for Maria and Arrigo to listen. 'Do you think she could have been the passenger that crossed the ferry without adequately paying, baccan?'

'Well, baccan, they did say she was carrying a prick with her in the cart.' Lamberto said with a giggle. Arrigo did not raise his eyes to look at them. 'But I wouldn't expect a landlady to behave so lowly.'

Maria ignored and continued the shrieking. 'You will pay for this! You do not come into my land and kill my men—'

'First of all, if I may say' Lanfranco said, 'we don't kill anyone. It's God that does!' the bearded giant looked up to the skies and crossed himself. 'All we did was to pass our arrow through your man.'

'We saw it all! Arrigo is my witness!' Maria said imperiously, standing on the cart.

The men laughed. 'Who saw it?' one of them said. 'Your child? Witness of a nitwit? Have you bred another village idiot, Maria Maddalena?'

Arrigo did not move his head.

'He does not react!' red beard said, with eyes wide open. 'Too busy with his— what is that? A dagger?'

'Looks like a dagger indeed,' yellow beard said, 'Do you want me to get it, baccan?'

'By all means.' Red beard said, as yellow beard moved to the cart, 'The prick could hurt himself with that toy.'

'Don't touch him!' Maria roared.

The grinning yellow beard approached Arrigo 'Now just hand me this blade, will you? Or else I will kick your ear with my boot—' The Genovese ended his sentence with a howl of horror and pain, when Arrigo swung his arm as fast as a lightning bolt. It startled the mule, which sprung to a gallop, flinging Maria back, to lose control of the cart. Arrigo had jumped out, with dagger in hand, ready to defend himself from the other giant, who had a sword in hand and was ready to cut him in two. The yellow bearded one screamed, while blood poured through the fingers that covered his face. He stepped back and lost his footing, falling off the path and rolling down into the wooded ravine.

The mule galloped towards Anchiano, almost reaching the curve off the river path, with Maria desperately trying to recover the reins. The cart ran on one wheel when it hit a stone, entering the curve by the metato. This was when Maria realised Arrigo was no longer in the cart, but left behind with those menacing men. And it was too late to look back, for the cart already entered the orchard path to Anchiano. Maria recovered the reins by the time the beast was climbing around the rock. She roared for her men-at-arms on the battlements and pulled the reins to turn around and rescue Arrigo. The mule hesitated to go back but a neck-breaking yank of Maria definitely told it who was in control.

The furious runaway was a desperate eternity for the Cunimundinghi lady. Her fifteen-year old son was in the hands of two bloodthirsty brutes. She considered praying. If needed, she had always been ready to see the devil himself to save her boy from harm.

From a distance she devised the three horses and one body stretched across the path, relieved to see that it was too large to be Arrigo's. It was the red-bearded, but she was not sure whether it was Lanfranco's or Lamberto's. And there was no sign of her son.

'Arrigo!' she screamed to the world, standing on the cart, with the men-at-arms arriving hurriedly behind her.

'I am here, mother...' an exhausted voice came down from the ravine.

Maria almost lost her senses. Her legs were weak, but she got out of the cart and peeked down through the woods. She saw Arrigo just a few paces down on the leaf-covered floor, on his knees and covered in blood. 'This is a good dagger! Attila's dagger!' he said, smiling for the first time since he got his gift. Next to him was the body of the yellow-bearded Genovese brother, butchered like a wild boar.

Maria smiled.

The balivo respectfully kissed the Episcopal ring. He was coming back from the valley of the Serchio, after a week of investigations upon the deaths of Lamberto and Lanfranco, the lords of Moriano.

'*Und?*' Bishop Johannes asked, with a touch of impatience.

'It was definitely self-defence, most reverend bishop.' The balivo said with a trembling voice.

The bishop considered it for a while. He looked at his parish clerk who stood by. If anything could be read from that face, it was suspicion.

'Are you sure of that?' the bishop proceeded, with his strong German accent. 'Can we carry on with the re-possession of Anchiano and consider Maria Maddalena of the Cunimundinghi and her son Arrigo an innocent party?'

'Most certainly, m-most reverend bishop!' the balivo said, looking at the marble floor of the bishop's palace.

The German bishop paused for another long moment and looked at the parish clerk again. This time, the clerk gave him a slight nod. Johannes asked one more question. 'Do we have to worry about your integrity, my good balivo? Have you come to these conclusions based on the facts, under the eyes of God? And no gold has been withdrawn from the chests of the Cunimundinghi, or the Burle et Malachi?'

The eyes of the balivo quickly glanced at the bishop. 'No!' he answered, looking back at the floor as he did. 'You need not worry, and by the spilled blood of the Christ, if any gold has left their chests, it has not gone to mine!' he lied.

The bishop dismissed the balivo. He was not happy, but rather satisfied with the outcome. Prosecuting Maria Maddalena of the Cunimundinghi would have given Johannes a skull-crushing headache with the city bankers. When the parish clerk closed the door behind the balivo and calmly returned to his superior, Bishop Johannes asked 'Do you think this man's conclusion has been purchased with gold, *myn capellan?*

'Only God could know the truth, *myn Bischoff,* about the deaths of those men and about the honesty of our balivo.'

'You are right,' said the bishop. 'But with the deaths of the heirless Genovese brothers, God has given Moriano back to His church. That is probably a higher purpose, rightly designed and likely under all fairness. But for now,' he raised the tone of his voice, on a commanding fashion, 'I want you to go to visit all the sites in this river, between the villages of Sesto and Chifenti. We have committed to a build a bridge in Chifenti in those days we came for this bishopric, but it was never finished. Maybe the village of Sesto would have a better geography to set up the bridge. Meanwhile, the ferry will be controlled by the closest neighbour of Sesto. That is Antelmino di Gottefredo.'

The parish clerk bowed his head lightly. 'I will start immediately, *myn Bischoff*.'

Behind the groups of pilgrims that still sat in the hospital hall that morning, Arrigo was distractedly leaning against the wall, looking at nowhere, oblivious to all the stares directed at him. It was widely known how Arrigo had slaughtered the Genovese brothers during their chase in Anchiano lands. But Clarissa was not afraid of him, neither of his mother's threats. The Hospitaller woman had told Maria that she would still be welcome to respectfully enter the hospital, particularly if they were meeting about the bridge. And even though Spatola would be terrified of his presence, the fearsome Arrigo was also decently treated.

Old Immanuel could not take his eyes off that youth, so distant, so hard to believe that Arrigo was his first grandson. He had something important to suggest about a new bridge, but he had completely forgotten about it at the sight of Arrigo.

The taverner Amadeo, from Chifenti, tried to control his hatred for the young man, searching for a fine balance between indifference and the minimum respect. He always tried to keep the *devil's spawn*, as his daughter called Arrigo, as far away from Chifenti, from his tavern, from Ginevra, as it could possibly be.

Bernardo delle Rocche sympathised with his friend, the taverner. He was perfectly aware that Maria's ferocious son was quickly turning into a man, a despicable one. A threat as a landlord and as a neighbour. He would need to prepare his villagers to start watching Arrigo's steps across the river.

The parishioner of Controne, Father Martino, was the only one around that table that did not spend a glance towards Arrigo. He had little to think about that spawn of the witch. Martino quietly prayed to be taken by Caterina as soon as possible, and for the eternal damnation of Maria Maddalena and her rancid offspring.

Julian, the Hospitaller, the boatman, just sat back at ease. He looked uncommitted at Arrigo, trying to decipher what purpose that young man would have, what future role he would play in those lands. Arrigo would have found that stare defying, if it had not been for that man they called a saint, so it was just unsettling.

Maria Maddalena did not see a bored youth ignoring a meeting that would decide for a bridge. She only saw the future lord of all those lands, a brave commandant who would control the bridge, recover the hospital to the Cunimundinghi, recover Chifenti, Corsena and conquer more of neighbouring lands. The hero she needed to crush that Antelmino di Gottefredo, a man whose claws were tightening over her, with his control of the eastern roads, ferry tolls and knowledge of her connection to the deaths of Béla and Caterina.

The eighth person who sat on that table for the meeting was Anton, the parish clerk of San Martino, in Lucca. He looked at the youth across the hall, knowing well the butchery he had been capable of in the allegedly self-defence murder of the Genovese brothers. Something familiar in that face. A strange sweetness that he had seen before. Maybe it was a hint of his mother's eyes.

And it was while Anton kept staring at the lady of Anchiano, trying to dig through his memory any reminiscence of those gray eyes, when Maria said 'We must have a bridge here! A proper one! A bridge to carry us over the river, and not through the river. It should take pilgrims and horses and carts higher above any flood level and it should outlast the last of our descendants. I am ready to open my silver chests for it, if we have the equal support of the Obertenghi – she rarely acknowledged Bernardo as a landlord – and the bishopric.'

The table was silently impressed with Maria's willingness on that communal task. Like an Apennine shepherd dog, Bernardo was shaking his matted-covered head. 'You do know, Maria, that I would commit to it, so why the pomp?'

Maria was ready to look at the parish clerk as an answer when, Anton himself, well aware of his foreign accent, cleared his throat and proposed to talk. 'You should all know that Bishop Johannes is currently engaged into a frugal year for the episcopate, re-filling the chests of our Lucchese churches. The expenses of his predecessors with personal vanity and donations to relatives over the last few years have been just too abusive to the maintenance of the House of God.'

Maria curled her lip. It was also a subtle reference to her lands, granted to Fulcardo by his father, the bishop Gerardo. 'You mean Bishop Johannes will not commit?' she asked.

Anton almost picked up the memory when he saw her disgust, but it evaded him. 'That is not too precisely what I tried to say, my lady.'

Maria cursed between clenched teeth. This could be just another strategy devised by the river demons when they did not get their serving of blood.

Bernardo was not happy either, although seeing Maria upset could always lift his spirits. He was ready to discuss alternatives when the clerk interrupted.

'You may think that my presence here is solely for the purpose of non-commitment, but the most reverent Bishop Johannes and I are also well aware of the attractiveness of Corsena as a public bath. Rather than a bridge for taking local produce to Lucca, or carrying pilgrims up and down the Via Francigena, we should consider that this is the main gateway into Corsena. The baths!' he said with enthusiasm, 'We should not forget that those lands belong to the bishop of Rome!'

'True!' Immanuel confirmed. 'The pope had a lovely time when he was here...what?...ten years ago. We all remember that!'

Maria did not find it amusing. 'That pope is dead!' she barked. There was something in her face that was familiar to the parish clerk, but he still could tell what it was.

'Indeed he is dead,' Anton said, 'but we all remember that stopover in the baths. That was when the pope brought the cannon Johannes from Fulda, as a suggestion from the emperor. And as you all know, Johannes is now our bishop and I came with him in that occasion.'

Martino had suddenly woken up to the conversation, asking quite hesitantly 'Is the ...n-nature of Benedict VIII's stay in Corsena specifically known amongst the clergy?'

The parish clerk cleared his throat again and stuttered 'The pope was resting in the baths and he had a memorable time. That is, as far as we all know...'

Amadeo grinned with malice. The taverner pointed his finger to Anton's face until the clerk had his attention. 'But you do know what the pope was up to, don't you? It's just that you Tedeschi prefer to ignore, as if it never was.'

Anton smiled with tight lips, as if receiving a flattering compliment. 'I did come from Germany, but I am not a Tedesco. I was christened Anton, and I am a Magyar, from the land of King Stephen.' He did not notice Immanuel's eyes turning into a liquid bright. The clerk continued 'I was a pilgrim in these lands in my youth. And I do remember meeting an old Magyar on the road here.'

'Béla!' many of them said.

'He's dead now.' Immanuel groaned.

'That's it: Béla!' Anton said, smacking his lips with satisfaction. 'We were then taking to Lucca a deformed child we found on the road, when this Béla interrupted us. He told me that he was a local, a táltos - shaman, believe it or not. He begged me to deliver that creature at a bank in Lucca. The House of Battista Burle, a man that I now still have many dealings with on the episcopate treasury.'

'Béla is dead now.' Immanuel repeated, and a brief silence followed, when many of the stares found their focus on Maria Maddalena.

The lady of Anchiano adjusted herself on the bench and was quick to change the subject 'So are you certain that this stretch of the river is a more suitable site to construct the bridge than Sesto?'

Anton was strangely driven to savour the look of that powerful woman. 'Indeed I do. Not only the terrain makes it more suitable, but the western road is better kept and safer than the eastern road up to Anchiano. Only the good God knows of the intimidating thugs I came across in the dark roads from Sesto yesterday afternoon!'

Arrigo heard this, but did not move his head, nor any muscled of his face twitched to form a smile. His eyes just shone with pride.

At the end of the meeting, Julian had agreed to go and see the pope in Rome with Anton.

Maria hesitated for a while, watching all those people leaving the hospital. She gave an obvious glance to Arrigo, to wait for her in the stables.

'Father...' she called Immanuel, as he was ready to leave with Amadeo.

'What do you want?' the Bukhari said with impatience. She walked a few paces, distant enough from where Amadeo stood waiting. Immanuel followed, an aged tiny figure, trailing the steps of his stately, estranged daughter.

'You do know what else has been missing from the construction of this bridge, don't you?' she hissed between clenched teeth, 'It will never be completed without it'.

'What?' he asked in a loud voice. 'I don't know what you are talking about.'

Maria clenched her teeth and hissed. 'Blood! The river needs blood! You know it!'

Immanuel ran his tongue over his lips. 'What are you talking about, mad woman?'

'You *know* it!' she said. 'You were there! They would have sacrificed you for that building! Béla knew what was right.'

The Bukhari paled 'How *dare* you quote Béla? What do you want? My help? Me? Will you order your son to slay one of us for this sacrifice?' He looked at her expression of disgust and understood that there could never be further understanding between them. 'Maria Maddalena. You are scaring even me, your own father. For your own sake and for the stability of Anchiano, maybe you should be aware that there is a fine line between fear and hatred.' He turned away and walked over to Amadeo, asking the taverner 'Where can we get some...mm, what's the name...rice?'

Maria stomped back to the stables, wiping her tears before Arrigo could see her.

'Arrigo,' she said while they rode back to Anchiano, 'I want to visit all the villages of our land.'

'Why is that, mother? I know these villages well. Anything I can help you with?'

'Do you know all the midwives?'

The Lord of the Flies

Anno Domini 1032

'Julian? A hospitaller in Santa Croce? Where is this hospital?' the pope raised his lower lip almost up to his nose, 'I must confess that I have never heard of you before.' John XIX was a large man unbelievably fitting quite snugly between the firm wooden armrests of his chair. With a typical Roman face, with strong, handsome features and a commanding nose, he was a more masculine and much larger version of his deceased brother, Benedict VIII. His eyes however were not firm, but shaky, probably no more than lost in his ignorance during that visit from those two men. John XIX sat in the chapter of the Lateran basilica, while receiving a visit of Anton, the parish clerk of San Martino in Lucca, who was an envoy of Bishop Johannes, and the hospitaller of Santa Croce, Julian of Luna. The Bishop of Rome turned to the only other person in the chapter who appeared to be of any prominence: another fat, lavishly-dressed man, large as a door, who stood up ahead of a court of clerks and custodes. 'What about you, Albericus?' asked the pope.

The pope's brother analysed the two men. The hospitaller was thin, but strong, humbly dressed in a strange combination of clean but uncoloured tunic and shirt which made it hard to distinguish him as a noble, for the quality and workmanship of the fabrics or as a peasant, for the lack of colours or adornment. Moreover, he wore his silver-streaked black hair unusually falling over his shoulders, much longer than any noble would dare, more like a chieftain or a village councillor. His face was hard, with a crooked nose probably from physical engagement, and respectful eyebrows and eyes that would not move when staring at him. A bit of a touch of defiance on the Count of Tusculum's opinion, but certainly an honest man, with eyes of trustworthiness and loyalty. The other was a tidy foreign clerk, difficult to read, as any of those northern barbarians with the high cheeks making their eyes squint. He was not sporting a stole, so obviously he was no more than a subdeacon, but his preparedness, manners and the richness of the silk velvet that covered his satchel indicated access to higher levels of the clergy. He was probably a smart man. Albericus could read them no more and turned to the pope. 'During that autumn when the Holy Father Benedict VIII returned from his synod in Germany,' referring to their own brother by his title, 'he rested for a few days in one of our thermal stations, the Baths of Corsena.'

Although John XIX had an apparently exhausted face, he raised his eyes to a nowhere, picking up the memory from a big nothingness. The reminiscence opened a childish smile on his old face 'Indeed! That was when he came back so exhausted, so changed from the man we knew...'

'Exactly,' said Albericus. 'It was reportedly a memorable repose for the Beatissimo Padre.' He approached the table in front of the pope and produced a *codex* of parchment, opening in a page that he seemed to know exactly where it was. 'The acta refers to the goodness and commiseration of Pope Benedict VIII on his providence of penance for a heinous crime, a parricide, allegedly accidental, by our visitor here, *Julian of Luni.*'

'Oh!' the pope's shoulders jumped, triggering a reverberation of fabrics over his body.

His brother gave them the necessary pause to absorb it all, but quite appropriately ignored John's excessive reaction, before continuing to read the acta 'the Beatissimo Padre ordered the reconstruction of an abandoned hospital by the place named...Chifenti.' he looked at the visitors and closed the codex. 'Is this also where you want your bridge to be?'

Julian was not sure if he should direct the word to the powerful and well-known Albericus, or to the pope, who seemed to be a lower head next to his brother's majesty on that audition. He decided for the first option. 'Indeed the hospital was rehabilitated, thanks to a suggestion of the Beatissimo Padre for my penance,' he said. And running his tongue along his lips, he took a breath of air before declaring 'As for the horrendous crime that covers me in shame, I have never made any secrets about it. My penance continues as I live, but it only gives me joy to care for the needed. Nothing that could be set upon me, atonement or punishment, could match the pain of my grievance, a weight that I must bear till the end of my days.'

'Very noble indeed' Albericus said, with no smile or frown, hardly allowing the visitors to detect any sarcasm. 'But I understand you two come to Rome for a plea.'

'Indeed, My Lord' said Anton, the parish clerk, stepping ahead with a well-studied posture and a good memory for names. 'We respectfully kneel to the Beatissimo Padre to request the support of the Holy Mother Church to finance the bridge over the Serchio. Julian comes in the name of the people of the Serchio, by the hospital of Santa Croce at the Via Francigena; of the Obertenghi, of the very loyal Margraves of Tuscany; and of the Cunimundinghi, descendants of Ingefredo di Cunimondo, namely the lords of Anchiano, Uzzano, Bozzano and Buggiano. I humbly represent the bishopric of Lucca, equally committed to the construction, but helpless to find a single denario to be dedicated to the bridge.'

Both men were silent for a while, before Albericus approached the pope and exchanged a few whispers with the tired-looking pontiff. The count scratched his generous silver beard and spoke again, with his loud, boisterous voice.

'It's rather daring of Bishop Johannes, a German protégé of the dead emperor, to appeal to the House of Tusculum for finances.'

'With all respect, my lord,' Anton said calmly, 'the most reverend bishop is a loyal servant to the Mother Church, and he only appeals to the *Holy See* because the lands across the Serchio and the Lima belong to *Her*. This bridge could be a gateway to the baths of Corsena. Bishop Johannes does not ask for loans from the Lateran, but for the approval of the investment in the baths. Only with the blessing of the Beatissimo Padre would the good bishop resort to loans from honest Lucchese bankers. The use of the baths has slowly but consistently contributed to pay for the debts of the Lateran, but a bridge can facilitate transport and access, boosting the use of the thermal station and paying up the debts in a shorter period.'

Albericus nodded slowly. He wanted to discuss that at length with the pope, before giving any answer. 'Do you have a statement of accounts of our loans with the Lucchese bankers?' he asked.

Anton was quick to present a few rolls of parchment.

'The Beatissimo Padre will study the details with his *tesserarius*,' Albericus said and 'and we should re-convene in three days –'

'If you allow me an interruption,' Julian stepped in, startling the Tusculan count and the pope with that somewhat insolence, 'I should still make another appeal for His Holiness's divine authority to convince our bridge architect to return to his project.'

'Architect?' Albericus asked, raising an eyebrow.

'Yes, an engineer.' Julian said, almost matter-of-factly. The pope smiled languidly, still with a tired face. Julian continued 'He had almost finished our previous bridge, a wooden one, which was taken by a flood. But this engineer left us with an unfinished deal, long before the bridge was finalised. The poor man was certainly a diligent constructor, and probably correct, but he was chased out by two rogues from the castle of Moriano.'

'Why would they do that?' asked the pope.

'Because they were quite happily charging insulting tolls for their ferry down the river.' said Julian.

'So would these men accept the bridge now?' Albericus asked.

'They're dead!' Julian answered with a neutral expression. 'They were both killed in a local dispute with their neighbours the Cunimundinghi.'

'And what about their lands and castle...?' Albericus asked again, approaching his forehead closer to Julian.

'Now it's all with the bishopric' Anton answered, gleaming with pride.

Albericus exhaled, but he was not still at ease. We walked towards the clerks and swung back 'This engineer. Why do you beg us to call him? Who is he? What is his name?'

Anton stepped ahead 'He is a Roman and we believe that a higher call, such as from the Holy Father's blessed tongue, could convince him to return to the project.'

Julian continued, controlling himself not to show an inconvenient smirk that was haunting his face. 'Maybe you have heard of his name?'

'And what is his name?' both the pope and the count asked in unison.

The meeting ended on a high note, after the explosion of laughter from that small usual crowd in the Lateran's chapter. Albericus promised to find the engineer and have all the means to convince him to re-engage. John XIX wiped his tears from the outburst of guffaws and casually mentioned 'Maybe I'd like to go to these famous baths once...'

He hardly knew how important such a visit would be for the Devil's plans.

Nothing was more convincing to the engineer than that highest call from the Apostle of Christ. Within a couple of weeks, wearing a newly bought silk cape, the Roman was triumphantly marching up the Serchio road again, this time accompanied by a team of Lucchese bankers.

The engineer contained his excitement. He was somewhat irritated with the delays of that rather slow, loud, and humorous group of travellers. They were curious and justifiably intrigued with the loans requested by the bishopric to build a new bridge, and more with the particular interest expressed even by the pope himself. So they had made it a special event. There were no recollections in Lucca of any previous occasion when the most prominent representatives of the bankers' guild had left the city altogether for such an excursion. With few exceptions, they were mostly office men, little used to the mundane amusement provided by the same roads that united their commercial networks. Even before arriving in Sesto, they had already replaced some of the mules, sending for more subservient beasts from their stables back in Lucca. They had also repeatedly paused to swap cargoes, in seemingly futile and slow operations, and even paid an unscheduled visit to a busy Sicilian cartwright by the vellutini, just past the bridge of San Frediano. During their midday meal in Sesto, the bankers entertained some speculation about the feasibility of an alternative site for the bridge, right under the nose of Moriano, where the ferry was still conducting most of the movement between both banks. Back on the road, while the extravagant Dino Gualteri kept complaining about the protuberant pommel in his saddle that kept pressing against his balls, Fraolmo and Sisemundo Di Cunizio were enquiring every single passing pilgrim about the nearest location they could buy some roasted chestnuts. Bartolomeo Orsetti and Rafaello Rapondi demanded an arguable stop at Wald Ottavo, where they crossed the little forest to confer with the hirsute Wido do Willo. They enquired about Bernardo delle Rocche, one of the patrons of the bridge, but the shepherd was up on the mountains those days.

The bankers were all positively impressed with the tidiness of the mulberry orchards across the river in lands of Anchiano and the countless baskets of cocoons that swayed on the back of mules all the way from Corsena.

They finally arrived in Mutianum late in the afternoon and walked over to the Traghetto, where a considerate Julian waited for them with a good supply of wine. While some refreshed their necks with Serchio water brought in a bucket by an accompanying servant, Julian rowed others comfortably to the eastern bank. Old friends, such as Pietro di Filippo, the Calandrino, were glad to note the vitality in the Hospitaller. Even after the loss and pain that Julian had endured in Luna, it still did not make an old, broken man out of him. And when Clarissa briefly appeared to greet them from the hospital, that group of wise men sighed with a touch of envy and pleasure for witnessing such a view. A sigh of mutual agreement and deep understanding on how a good woman could defy the passing of time and take her partner along for that challenge.

The engineer, oblivious to the impact that Clarissa had produced on the bankers, ignored Julian's courteous welcome and interrupted the bankers to carefully explain 'Now the most important factor in this new endeavour is the location. The new bridge will be about half a mile north of where the wooden bridge had been constructed.'

Fraolmo Di Cunizio noticed the snub and attacked with a question. 'And the best reason for that—' he started.

'— is exactly what?' continued Sisemundo, as expected by all who knew the fraternal synchronicity of the Di Cunizio. The enquiry was obvious, for the area pointed by the engineer was not near as flattened as the stony bank where the first bridge had once stood.

'We need a firm base for the foundation piers.' the engineer gestured with his hands. 'Those rocky ridges that surface out of the river are solid. They will be the ideal support for the abutments. Of course we'll still need to dig around them for the best possible footing. But in this manner we will not need to deviate the river.'

The Di Cunizio brothers looked at the engineer and at the appointed site for a brief pause, while the cold waters giggled around the stones at their feet. Sisemundo was the first to say something, with a touch of embarrassment for sounding dull. 'But look at that wide gap between the last ridge and the western bank.'

Fraolmo was quick to pick his thoughts 'Isn't that just too broad for an arch?'

The engineer shook his head with a sneer. Condescendingly closing his eyes, he produced his best amicable smile 'I suppose none of you have been to Rome, have you?' his tongue swiftly ran along his lips with satisfaction and, before allowing any of the bankers to answer, he carried on 'The Pantheon! Wonder of wonders of my Roman ancestors, proving that there is no limit to the clear span of an arch, as long as the *voussoirs* – the *cunei* – are adequately and precisely placed, all the way to the keystone. The wider the span, the higher the rise.'

The effect was not what he expected. Rather than blown away with awe, the bankers ran their lower lips under their teeth and distractedly picked their nails clean with a seemingly lack of interest.

Rafaello Rapondi was the oldest of the group. A simply-dressed man who would not measure any efforts to disguise his wealth, he tried to purse his lips over his protruding large teeth and looked at the stony ground for a moment, before raising his gaze thoughtfully and saying quite casually 'Listen here...' and he frowned, 'what was your name again?'

The guffaws smothered the engineer's voice when he repeated his name. Smiling with those invasive teeth, the old banker Rafaello calmly waited for the appropriate tempo until the commotion had been reduced to a scarce titter and added 'I suppose you haven't dealt with Lucchese bankers before, have you?' The engineer only opened his startled mouth to react, when Rafaello continued 'As bankers, our activities vary, and we have investments in this project in many different ways. Take me, for example. I am one of those who is lending money to Our Mother Church, while Giacomo here, sitting on that bag of rice, has direct investment on this road, not only because of his family's silk that is produced in this valley, but also for the loans to his sister Maria Maddalena of the Cunimundinghi. The Di Cunizio brothers, over there, are financing the Obertenghi side, while Pietro di Filippo, the one they call Calandrino, cares for the interests of Julian of Luna. But we agree that an investment must have a guaranteed return. We all agree, when it comes to us being a group of basically honest, fairly intelligent, let's say *average*, but most of all, God-fearing men. Yes! We do obey God's commandments, the Holy Sacraments and we look at the humility of His son Jesus Christ as a role model.'

Rafaello found a rocky edge to seat himself, while the engineer tried to understand what he was talking about. In spite of all the bankers, the men-at-arms and Julian being around there, Rafaello looked to sides as if alone with the engineer and continued in a confessional tone 'But let me tell you of something that we bankers particularly do which may contravene the ways of a good Christian. A peccadillo that is probably seen with disapproval by the divine eyes of our Lord.' At this change of subject by the banker, the engineer suddenly found himself choked, muted with fear, with a lump across his throat, and his eyes struggling to stay in their orbits. The banker carried on 'It's the sacrifice of fasting!' he made a pause and shot a quick glance of annoyance at Pietro di Filippo, who muffled a giggle. The other bankers just waited in silence, scattered along the bank, unpretentiously looking at the slow currents and waving flies from their faces.

'The problem, my dear Roman,' Rafaello continued, 'is that in the eyes of God, we should be abstaining from all types of viands at the Friday repasts, restricting our frugal meals to the blandness of fish. But look at this river,' he opened his arms wide, almost embracing the valley, 'this very Serchio which runs here is so rich in all kinds of water creatures...and I am not talking about the ghosts and marabbecche. If you want to learn about the water goblins, talk to the Obertenghi that owns this land on the western side, for Bernardo delle Rocche knows them all. I am actually referring to the trout and pikes, chubs, tench, carps, bleak, *rovelle*, eels, gobies, bullheads and *vaironi*! The rich flavours of freshwater fish that delight our tongues on every Friday. Surely we cannot be fooling God, Our Omnipresent Father, by pretending that a sumptuous banquet of fish is anything but an excess. Especially when we get a chance to savour our favourites! And the best reason for enjoying fasting is the earthy meat of lampreys, the perfumed rosy flesh of crayfish and the subtle sweetness of crabs!'

The engineer opened a yellow grin, relieved with the harmlessness of Rafaello Rapondi's story.

But the banker was not finished. 'Oh, so generous indeed is the Serchio and so plentiful are all of its creatures to us, but very little do we offer in exchange for our secret pleasurable Friday meals. What do we really do?' he shrugged his shoulders. 'We mostly ignore these gifts of God...' he said, staring coldly at the engineer,

'...except...' he bared his well-cared teeth '...when we give something back! We feed them! See? We come for them at night...silently...by boat... and we drop in the river a large body of meat, fresh with blood and filled with entrails. We must make sure it is tied to a heavy stone, to guarantee that the Serchio can have it for a complete, plentiful repast. And how the river loves it! The smell of death attracts the hordes of blood-sucking lampreys, and scavenging crayfish and crabs, which appear from the dark rocky riverbed and attack the carcass, tearing the flesh with their pincers and allowing for the larger fish to have their serving. Over the next few days, the only leftovers will be slowly sinking in the bottom slime, and there is no balivo in this world who will be able to recognise the body: a white clean skeleton. You do know who gets a chance to become food for crayfish, don't you?'

Trying to babble an answer, the engineer was a sweating, frozen, white cadaver. But Rafaello did not wait for the answer. The banker raised a commanding finger and said 'That will be anyone who fucks with us, my friend. Anyone who fucks with us...'

A pair of mallards quickly flew over the water, quacking excitedly to each other as they disappeared over the river curve, while all the bankers nodded, quietly confirming Rafaello Rapondi's threat.

'Still...' the engineer finally managed to say, clearing his throat, 'if I have been called by the bishop of Rome himself, it must be a mission with a divine —'

'God knows all about it!' Rafaello interrupted, standing up and signalling for the group to re-convene. 'And we pray to Him that you will fulfil your commitments. As for our good hospitallers here, they are the reason why this bridge will stand up and also why you get your silver and gold. But it is *our money*, understand? We do pray that you finish what you have been paid to do and God knows about it! We're praying and fasting, every week, and God knows that we don't want anybody to fuck with us.'

God was being good with the engineer, for providing with such an expedient start and a fast pace in the construction. With a blue Tuscan sky helping along months of benevolent temperatures, the harmony between so many different parties, functions and regions involved in the construction was smoother than any of the sceptics could ever expect. High abutments were raised in no time on the dry riverbed and, in place of what then had been a series of inconspicuous rocky ridges on the wide eastern bank of the Serchio. Where the only crests of naked rock that would still emerge through furious waters in times of flooding, there were now colossal towers of stone. They were finely cut out of the caves and quarries in lands of the Obertenghi and the Rolandinghi, and glued together with a certain mortar mix that the bankers forced the engineer to use, after a debate and trials on mortar quality which would trigger a consequence out of hell.

Ironically, it had all started with a final attempt of Immanuel Ben-Malachi to prove his theories on the quality of mortar. The old Bukhari first shared his thoughts with Amadeo, who ignored him, thinking him just an eccentric foreigner. Next, Immanuel confided with his sons, who cautiously heard him with a reverent scepticism, but quietly retired for their chores, leaving the father on his own. Then, it was time for the landlord of Corsena to walk down towards the hospital of Santa Croce and share his thoughts with Julian. The Hospitaller listened carefully to Immanuel's tales of the age-and-weather-defying mortar used in his native lands. This time, the idea triggered the curiosity in Julian, who later conferred with Bernardo delle Rocche, and soon they were both consulting the bankers, who had divided opinions on the old Bukhari's suggestion. Unfortunately, the material that Immanuel requested was quite expensive. It was old Battista Burle who said during a banker's meeting: 'That Roman engineer has ordered these cartloads of ashes from Napoli, supposedly to make a firmer mortar. He says it could withstand the force of the water. Still, that does not stop Immanuel Ben-Malachi from being on the right track. Forget the fact that the man is my son-in-law. His knowledge goes far beyond the thinness of his beard. Let's give him his bag of rice and a month, not to make expensive Saracen sweets or medicine, but to prove that he can make better mortar than the Roman.'

The result of using rice to make a firm, water-resistant mortar proved a disappointment to Immanuel. Experimenting by the old shed where Béla used to make his shack, now a chicken coop, the Bukhari planned to build two walls: one with the mix he recalled from his homeland and one with the mortar mix suggested and prepared by the engineer, so there would be no cheating. The engineer came to the shed with a fiery grin on his face. He walked by the tagh-tir, but not without pausing for a minute to analyse it with a malicious curiosity. Struggling not to ask a question about the unexplainable copper contraption, he maintained his height and explained to Immanuel the secret to make the mortar, while he folded the mixture in. It was the traditional lime added to sand and water, plus a mixture of broken ceramics and the referred ashes brought from Puteoli, near Napoli. With the help of several witnesses, he bricked the wall up. When the engineer confidently walked out of Corsena, Immanuel waited for all the curious bystanders to leave before proceeding to boil the rice. Sadly, it never boiled to become the sticky material that he expected. The hard grains turned into soft grains, but they did not stick. Immanuel knew it wouldn't work, but he still gave it a go. Adding it all with the same formula that the engineer had prepared, the old physician sighed while he diligently built the wall.

A week of sunny weather gave the mortar the necessary dryness, and Immanuel returned to verify the work, carrying mallet, chisel and little confidence in his heart. Going to the first wall, made by the engineer, it took him considerable strength and a few hits to drive the chisel into the mortar and dislocate the first brick. Not a disaster, he thought. Certainly much superior to the mortar used in the baths of Corsena or at Julian's hospital. But when he moved to his own wall, built with the same mortar added with rice, his heart sank with humiliation as the brick easily popped out. This was nowhere near the quality of the mortar made of sticky rice they used in Bukhara to line the canals, or the public waterways, and to make walls that stood centuries in the desert, to build battlements that withstood attacks from armies of elephants, to build bridges. This was just crap.

Before dropping his tools in helplessness, he tried to dislocate another brick. Placing the blade between the stone and the dried layer of mortar, he lifted the mallet not too much, just bringing it down to a delicate hit –

An explosion almost blew the little Bukhari out of his feet.

It did not take place on the chisel or on the brick, which clicked out as easily as the first did right in front of his face. It happened behind him, where one could discern through the cloud of dust a disconnected scatter of cackling chickens running in zigzag towards the woods. They left behind a destroyed coop, broken in half, as if a giant had just stepped its colossal feet over it. Before Immanuel recognised what had caused that, he saw a shadow coming from above. The flapping of giant wings made him duck for cover and he saw a huge honey-coloured creature with black wings landing its massive feathered body in the destroyed coop. The severe yellow eyes looked at the Bukhari for a second, before losing any further interest in the little man. The white head with long black moustache dove inside the straw and pulled up a massive bone. Turul had dropped it but it did not crack open. The bone only managed to split the shed in two.

Before Immanuel could savour the view of that magnificent creature that he had not seen for so long, the lammergeyer lifted his wings and took to the heights again. It carried the colossal bone under its talons, probably ravenous for bone marrow and ready to drop it on a harder surface, maybe up on the peaks. As Turul soared beyond eyesight, the old Bukhari investigated the damage left on the ground. In addition to the smashed ceiling, parted walls and broken baskets that were meant to be used as nests, there were two dead chickens and a considerable amount of eggs that had been crushed. That's when Immanuel felt one side of his brain elbowing the other side. He ran to his children and asked them for a new favour.

In the end of the stipulated month, Immanuel invited Julian, Bernardo delle Rocche, Father Martino, the Roman engineer and many other witnesses to use the chisel in both his freshly built wall and the original wall, now already dried for three weeks.

Immanuel's wall was only a week old, but still, the difference was brutal.

The new wall was firmer and the mortar harder. It had glued the stone together in a manner which made it difficult to break it with reasonable ramming of the chisel. It took some sweat to actually crack the stone out.

'So what's the secret with the rice?' asked the exhausted engineer, dropping the tools on the ground and wiping his brow. He was disappointed to have lost the trial with his mix, but cringing with curiosity to learn the secret.

'No, it's not made of anything as expensive and difficult to obtain as rice!' said Immanuel, with undisguised excitement. 'It's eggs!' he said, watching everyone make a stupid face, 'I mixed egg whites into the mortar. And it turns mortar into stone!'

Dozens of men from the region quarried white limestone and brought it in carts over to the site. There were countless broken wheels, exhausted oxen and a thickening of the traffic and flow of people through the several boats that now crossed the Serchio to and from the Traghetto. Cartloads and baskets full of eggs came from markets in the region and also from Lucca, Livorno, Pisa, Florence, and as far as Genoa.

The starter of the recipe, Immanuel Ben-Malachi, watched the cargo with a glint on his eyes. He could not get over the whiteness of those thousands of eggs. 'What colour would you expect them to be?' Domenico asked.

Immanuel shrugged his shoulders 'I had never seen a white eggshell before I came here. In Bukhara, chicken eggs were always brown or blue.' This was enough for all the locals, including his children, to think that the man was definitely becoming senile.

The wariest description for the stale smell of broken eggs under the heat of that Tuscan summer would be *pungent*. Unlike the subtle brimstonish scent of some of the waters of Corsena, which soon evaporated with their steam, this rank stench built up to soar above the valley, attracting a novel number of seagulls, herons, buzzards, and even the great Turul, fooled by its sense of smell, spotted quite often gliding against the blue. And flies. Hordes of flies emerged out of nowhere like black buzzing shadows, and invaded chambers, stables, kitchens and anyone's mouth, who would keep it open for too long. The stench and the pests disturbed the populace of Traghetto, Mutianum, Chifenti, Fornulo, La Cuna and many villages along the valley. They all whinged that it made the livestock uneasy, that it caused the milk to curdle, that it caused the sheep's bottoms to burst with maggots, and that it burned the farro in the bottom of the pans.

But it was Father Rocco, the old priest of Cerreto, who created trouble. His chapel was inserted in a small cluster of houses between the Traghetto and La Cuna, on the hillsides right above the bridge. Father Rocco was one of the few literate clerics to be found on those lands of the Obertenghi. He had been a quiet man for as long as anyone could remember, but the stench seemed to wake up a ferocious angel inside him.

'This fetid presence,' he roared to the faithful, 'these fumes of fire and brimstone invoke us the deserving chastisement of God upon the sinners of Sodom and Gomorrah!' To an ever growing crowd of locals and pilgrims that could not fit into the church and withstood the myriads of flies outside, the old priest blasted from his simple wooden pulpit that the Devil was at work 'The days of judgement are not around the river bend! They are rising from this accursed bridge! Repent now, for the Enemy is choking us with Its filth!' The discourse spread fear and rage, often against the engineer's. The Roman was starting to be seen with hostility by the peasants as he walked to the bridge every morning. He was even pissed on by Father Rocco himself when passing by the wall below the church cemetery.

The consensus was finally to remove the Roman from his lodging at the Rocca castle and transfer him to a small room in Chifenti.

But others had their rage against Father Rocco. Julian was upset with the visible disturbance the ominous words had laid on the workers. Bernardo had not been around for a few days, so the Hospitaller tried to go reason with the old priest. But old Rocco refused to halt the rant, spitting obscenities and blaming Julian for the disruption.

'Oh, you murderer! They say you are a saint but I can smell your breath! It's the breath of the devil! You are waking it from the infernal fires. The mouth of hell will be opening and vomiting their demons and flies to drag you sinners. You will burn while watching the abominations perpetrated on your murdered parents.'

Julian did not wait to hear the rest.

In three days, with all pilgrims in the hospital debating the rants of the rabid priest, Julian walked up to Cerreto again, but this time Father Rocco escaped through the back of the church, disappearing like a wounded hare behind blooming rose bushes and green terraces of farro.

Rumours of the priest's announcement of the Devil's return had reached the tired ears of Father Martino. Cantakerous since the death of his Caterina, he made himself walk down the valley to the building site, take a boat ride across the Serchio and climb up the winding path to the Cerreto. This time, a few peasants protected the church door, preventing Martino from entering. 'Padre Rocco is not in,' one of them said, rather nervously, 'and we are not to let anyone inside.'

'That is preposterous!' Martino grunted. Boiling red, he walked down the extra mile to Diecimo, to discuss the matter with the local parishioner, a young cleric who would be eager to hear his complaints.

Meanwhile, someone else was furious too.

'That old pig Rocco will spoil it all!' Maria Maddalena said to herself, but loud enough for Arrigo to hear it. It was just after the midday meal, and he was sitting in the hall in Anchiano, refreshed by the cold stone floor, cutting stripes of tanned leather with his dagger. The coolness of Anchiano's interior kept the myriads of flies away.

'Do you want me to see to it?' Arrigo asked, with a touch of authentic concern in his eyes.

Maria thought for a while. 'No!' she decided. 'You go down to the bridge and keep those lazy beasts doing their job and make sure you get the names of every villager, from wherever they are, who have stopped the work since Father Rocco started his spell.'

Arrigo stood up in a jump. His dagger flipped in the air and fell back firmly in his grip. 'I can do that.' He said, with a glint in his eyes. 'Will you go and see the priest?' he asked his mother. 'He was talking about the devil, wasn't he? Maybe he can assist you with whatever you wanted with every God-damned midwife in our land. They did not seem to be able to help you with your needs.'

Maria Maddalena clenched her jaws as a shadow fell upon her face. She closed her eyes, waiting for her features to relax sufficiently. 'Son, I just wish I could share my wisdom with you, but there is more to be achieved before I can rest at peace and teach you all I know. I found that our midwives know nothing of a higher craft, and there's little they can assist me with. If the Devil is indeed about to rise from the fires of hell, it should not be up to that shit priest in the Cerreto to stop it. I will go and talk to this Father Rocco. If he is wise, he will understand my concerns about the bridge, but I'm afraid he isn't an enlightened soul.'

They rode down to the river and took the path north, towards the hospital. With the stench of old eggs and a dark cloud of flies, the structure of the bridge soared above the wide riverbank further up on the valley. Maria and Arrigo were relieved to notice that stones were still being carried in and workers swarmed around the construction site, apparently oblivious to the warnings of the priest. Large semi-circular wooden frames were being mounted between the pillars, like giant sunken watermills peeking out of the river. Those were the frames where the voussoirs for the stone arches would be laid upon, all the way to the placement of the keystone, on the top of the arch. Once the keystone was inserted, it would hold the arch together and the frame could be removed.

While Arrigo continued the path towards the bridge, his mother ignored the hospital and left her horse cared for on the eastern bank, crossing the river in one of the many boats that were ready to carry pilgrims across. As Maria prepared to take the path that winded through the chanting of some rather cheerful peasants up the hill, she heard a thundering snap, a cracking sound coming from the bridge.

The beams snapped loudly and the structure collapsed. Arrigo roared to a passing carter to hold his horse as he ran towards the broken arch. The semi-circular frame, not yet finished, had imploded onto itself just as he was arriving, and a number of workers shouted through the cloud of dust that was raised. Flies buzzed frantically. One man screamed in horror, drawing his hand from a fallen beam with a bloody stump where a finger was expected to be. The Cunimundinghi youth found the frantic engineer, who screamed orders to his subordinates.

'It was the idiot!' the engineer protested.

'The nitwit from Chifenti? Spatola?' Arrigo asked, incredulous, drawing a smirk in spite of the protests of pain somewhere behind the engineer. 'What has Spatola done this time?'

'He ran away.' The engineer answered, off guard. 'He was holding the beam, this idiot, but he dropped it as soon as someone pointed to...' the Roman looked at Arrigo with undisguised suspicion and his words disappeared. Behind him, the man with the squashed finger howled in pain while he was been contained by fellow workers.

'But why was Spatola working here?' Arrigo asked. 'He's an idiot...'

The engineer sighed, relieved that Arrigo had missed the unfinished sentence. 'That boy is the strongest man in this region. He can lift a beam and hold on to it forever. We have never seen such firm grip. He listens to and understands instructions, often better than these Tuscan peasants of yours,' the Roman said, with little regard to the men around him, 'The idiot is always happy to assist. Probably, it makes his God-forsaken heart cheerful when helping. Quite frankly, I was never bothered to use him until just now. This disaster will throw the construction probably a couple of weeks to a month back. The bankers will feed the fish with my guts for that.'

Arrigo bit his lower lip. 'I'll kill Spatola then!' he said, and turned back to get his horse.

'No, please don't do it!' the engineer begged.

Arrigo frowned, in puzzlement 'Why not?'

'Because...because...' he looked around the other workers, but they had little to say when Arrigo was present. The engineer would have had no qualms about Arrigo ridding that region of the idiot, better a dead Spatola than him being used as crayfish fodder. But he would have to use Spatola's strength and grip to expedite the re-construction of that arch, to fix what had been undone. '...Because we need him!' he finally snapped, 'Spatola! Yes, we need Spatola to help us advance the works. He is the best gripper we have. He will help us carry these beams up to where they should be.'

The young Cunimundinghi considered it and kept going towards his horse. 'I'll fetch him then!' And he left on gallop towards Chifenti.

The engineer turned to the workers and said to the group. 'Thank you for not telling Arrigo that his approach was the cause for the idiot to drop the beam. I had never seen someone so scared.'

'Arrigo would have killed Spatola if he knew...' One of them said.

The Roman nodded and said 'Let's hope he doesn't slay the idiot while he brings him back. We need the nitwit.' He looked at them all, clapped his hands and shouted. 'C'mon! Back on the labour. We must clean up this mess before we re-start!'

While Arrigo was tying the hands of a well-beaten Spatola to his horse's saddle, his mother was on the eastern bank of the Serchio, ready to take a boat back, when Father Martino walked by, accompanied by the young parishioner of Diecimo and the priest of Mutianum.

'Maria Maddalena!' the young cleric called, to the annoyance of Martino, who would have preferred to ignore her. 'We are on our way to see Father Rocco, in Cerreto. Did you know he has been preaching against the construction of the bridge?'

'Of course I do,' Maria answered, looking at the clerics from her unattainable noble heights, 'the old chough has been a nuisance every since these idiots started using eggs in the bridge. I went to see Father Rocco now, but he has escaped through the back door of the church, hiding behind the bushes like an old rat. If you were planning to see him, I wouldn't bother. You won't find him.'

The clerics thanked her for the advice but diligently headed up the hillside towards the small church of the Cerreto. Quite disappointed, they found an empty church, confirming what Maria Maddalena had predicted.

But Rocco, the priest of Cerreto, never came back. Vanished from that valley, leaving no traces, nor sending any messages from wherever he had gone. Nobody knew anything, although some suggested he left corroded by fear, for not bearing the stench of fire and brimstone. Others said he walked up to the peaks to join the hermits, rotting in the caves as an omo salvatico himself, or devoured by wolves that had thrived in that plentiful season. And there were many, like Father Martino, that believed the priest's disappearance was surely another wicked act of Maria Maddalena of the Cunimundinghi.

She laughed when a balivo was sent in from Lucca to question her in Anchiano. 'If I had killed that stupid man,' Maria shamelessly told the flabbergasted balivo, 'I would have bled and gutted him right under the pillars of the bridge. Everyone knows that the bridge will not succeed without sacrifice. Sooner or later, it will stop, and there will be no prayer, nor saint that will carry on with the construction if we don't do the right thing.'

But the bridge did stop. That was on the night they saw the ghost of San Pellegrino.

Before Father Rocco's disappearance from the Cerreto, his blusters were watched by many pilgrims that enthusiastically dragged themselves over that stretch of the Via Francigena. One of them was a Benedictine monk on his way north, back to his House of God, the Abbey of Cluny. While spending the night in a cloister in Lucca, Raoul Glaber – *the Bald* – was told about the bridge on the Serchio and the bad omens recently raised by the local priest. With a fire always aching to burn in his zealous heart, Raoul decided to change his route from the coastal Via Francigena to the Serchio stretch, northwards through the Caferonia. He found his way up to the Cerreto, joining a thick crowd of peasants who fried under the unusually spring sun and the drone of flies, pilgrims and other curious passersby, to witness the explosive revelations of the old man. Although the first obstacle was to understand the local accent spoken in the Serchio, Raoul was not too impressed by the simplistic oratory of the priest. He was however blown away by the obviousness and the ominous presence of the stench and the battalions of flies. Those tiny black demons that would inadvertently end their quick soarings to maliciously land and rub their little hairy hands onto anyone's sweaty skin, ears, eyes, nostrils and lips.

Still tormented by the insects, which seemed to take a particular taste to dive and lick moist surfaces, the monk left the crowd at the Cerreto sermon before it was even finished. He came down to the bridgeworks and found the engineer, who was shouting orders and waving the flies from his face as violently as he could.

'It's a higher call,' Glaber heard the engineer proudly tell him, 'The pope himself has asked me to finish this task. Pay no heed to that ignorant priest in the Cerreto. He is an uneducated animal that cannot fathom progress. God willing, I will have this bridge finished by next year. One Thousand and Thirty-Third year of Our Lord, the year the Bridge of Chifenti was built.'

Raoul Glaber was certain there was something to it. Rushing back to cooler Cluny, away from the heat of that fly-ridden valley, he spent nights awake in study, inconveniently visiting all libraries in monasteries along the Via Francigena. His name was known in many monasteries throughout Christendom. His writings had already been famous and deadly when he explained how the Church of The Holy Sepulchre had been destroyed by the incitement of the Jews. The fiery discourse of the past was the best door opener for the monk.

And now, another idea was forming into his mind, reinforced by every coincidence revealed at his visits to the books.

et adprehendit draconem serpentem antiquum qui est diabolus

et Satanas et ligavit eum per annos mille

Of course, the Book of Revelations could never suggest the Devil was going to be unbound and free on the Year One Thousand of our Lord. Those profecies for the Anno Mille were never substantiated. Anyone with a bit of mathematical sense would understand that the date for the breaking of chains by Satanas was one thousand years after the death of Jesus Christ our Lord:

Anno Domini MXXXIII

Then, from the Gospel of Luke, Glaber verified:

Et erat ejiciens dæmonium, et illud erat mutum.

Et cum ejecisset dæmonium, locutus est mutus, et admiratæ sunt turbæ.

Quidam autem ex eis dixerunt: In Beelzebub principe dæmoniorum ejicit dæmonia.

There were references to Beelzebub in the books of Mark, Matthew and Kings. Back in Cluny, Glaber consulted the Gospels of Nicodemus, where Beelzebub was mentioned at the *Descensus ad Infernos* and in an old Greek text where King Solomon receives a ring with God's seal and orders a legion of demons to build his temple, especially the prince of all demons:

Βεελζεβούβ

Glaber knew there were more connections. As the monks of Cluny spent a good deal of their time transcribing and translating sacred books, he came across a Hebrew translation of the original Greek Πράξεις Πιλάτου, the Acts of Pilate.

בעל זבוב

The Hebrew word Beelzebub – Lord of the Dung Pile – was a mockery of Beelzebul – Lord of Heaven. It was clear and loud as the drone of insects that came out of the ground during that hot spring, to announce the obvious. Beelzebub was the Lord of the Flies!

Ovulo Malefico

'I've heard rumours that you have seen the devil! Have you really?'

Julian was blown away by that question. Even the daring Bernardo delle Rocche, who walked on his side quietly waving flies, had the impression that a gale-force wind had stretched his friend's face backwards. The Hospitaller would never expect the pope to enquire about his personal life and much less to be demonstrating blunt excitement with that idea. They were walking with the very slow papal entourage from the hospital to the bridge. The papal horse, a large chestnut charger that had some difficulty in crossing the river on a boat, was being pulled behind by an aide. John XIX would spend a few days in the baths of Corsena. It was about time he took a break from the confusion he had triggered in Rome.

After a disastrous spell of faux-pas, granting erroneous titles to undeserving clerics, declaring patriarchal dignity to the wrong bishops and endowing excessive powers to questionable friends of the mother Church of Rome, Pope John XIX was being sent to the baths in Corsena by his brother, the Count Albericus. Besides spending time away from the indignation triggered by the pope through the Roman see, Romanus of Tusculum was assured by Albericus that a breath of new air and the relaxation of the baths would open his heart to the words of God, perhaps for a more enlightened conduction of His herd. The Count instructed the bath administrators to treat Romanus as well as they had cared for their brother John Theophylactus in the past.

Being a layman who had lived away from ecclesiastical matters during all his life, the man who had been made a pope was enjoying the journey, in spite of the thick heat that drenched his vests with sweat and the myriads of flies that tried to repose on his face. A brief stay in Lucca had given him some more insights on the politics of the Serchio, including on the crimes of the man who had come to Rome asking for support to that bridge: Julian, the Hospitaller. He found a collective belief that a man like Julian could only have been guided by the devil to perpetrate such horrors.

'I have had daydreams, and I was very scared.' answered Julian, rather carefully, for no matter how much he perceived the seemingly enthusiasm of John XIX, he was after all addressing the head of the Church, and any involvement with the devil could be immediately punished with reasonable justification.

'But Julian, my good man, if the air here smells so strongly of fire and brimstone, it's undeniable that there is an insight into Hell, as everyone is talking about,' the pope insisted, 'Haven't you heard of Glaber's predictions? Tell me then, how is it? You have had the experience. How does the Lord of the Flies appear to you? Like an ordinary angel?'

Julian grinned to himself and raised his eyes to the sky, searching for the true angel he had seen in a special moment. But except for the moving black dots that buzzed around his face, there were not even birds flying that afternoon at the end of July. 'Beatissimo Padre, I have had bad dreams with ghosts and demons, like any good Christian has. They are dark apparitions that invade us with their malice. As you know, I did not make myself to wake up of from one of these dreams in time.'

'*Incubi?*' the pope asked, meaning using the Latin term used for *bad dreams*. The word was gradually turning into a synonym for a demon in male form. Good Christians knew that bad dreams were caused by visits from demons. St. Augustine had described these demons as *satyr* or *faun-like*. That's when Julian saw an opportunity to talk about something else.

'That's right, Beatissimo Padre. I had an *incubo*. But in my language of Mans, we didn't have a specific word for a bad dream as Latin does. We call it a bad dream a sleep with a *mære*.'

'Is that a demon?' asked the pope.

Bernardo nearly moaned when Julian's elbow dug between his ribs. It took the shepherd a second to understand that he should jump in. 'Yes, the mære is a nocturnal creature that silently crawls through our doors and windows, entering our chambers and sitting on our chests. It rides us and watches us weep while we have bad dreams. Some people call it a *vellea*. It is not a sprite of ethereal nature, but a real demon with hairy arms and iron shoes on all its limbs.' Bernardo had enthusiastically drawn himself between the pope and the Hospitaller. 'The mære's weight' he continued 'presses on our chest and belly, as the demon jumps on top of us. And it's no wonder that we call it *pesaruola* and our Ligurian neighbours use the word *pesón*, meaning a heavy weight, to describe a bad dream. The mære may even try to choke us from breathing.'

Julian was glad the pontiff had bitten the bait. The conversation would drift out of his crime and his demons. He noticed that the pope's eyes were wide open and the lips mutely begging for words about this fascinating subject, almost drooling for more on the Enemy of Christ. That was the moment to shut it off. 'But that was a long time ago. I do not remember it, Beatissimo Padre. I have crushed these moments out of my memory.'

'Oh!' the pope said, with clear disappointment, but his attention quickly turned to the nervous man with curly hair who pompously stood a few paces ahead: the Roman engineer.

They had stopped by stretch of the road to Chifenti where it bordered the banks over a re-enforced stone terrace, widening towards the left and the approach embankment, entering the yet unfinished bridge. The path raised itself courageously on a steep slope over the first arches, with solid spandrels already filled and compacted. A smooth stone pavement had been beaten in and the parapet walls were starting to be raised. The bridge path kept on soaring to a humbling height, where it ended abruptly before the peak of the main arch. That was where a massive semi-circular wooden frame had been raised. It stretched over the main body of the Serchio, to sustain the most critical voussoirs of that bridge, all carefully crafted and precisely cut by the best masons, personally selected by the engineer himself. For him, John XIX's visit would be the highest moment of the bridge's construction. The confirmation of his mission as a higher call, a mandate directly from God.

The excited pope salivated with the prospect of calling aloud the engineer's name in front of such a numerous crowd of workers, reverently lined up along the bridge's parapet. He extended his hand to offer his ring, while the engineer paid respect to his authority.

'It is with honour and humility,' the engineer said, 'that we receive the blessed visit of the Apostle of Christ in this majestic piece. The Bridge of Chifenti will be a glorious achievement of the Beatissimo Padre's apostolic commitment to the holy pilgrimage route of the Via Francigena, to the Roman Relics and the Volto Santo of Lucca, to the very pious inhabitants of this great city, the parishes, churches and monasteries of the valley of the Serchio, the Caferonia, Barga, San Pellegrino. It will aggrandise and exalt the name of the –'

'What have you heard from the priest that disappeared?' The pope interrupted.

The engineer blinked nervously 'The *priest?*'

'There was a priest around here who was predicting a new coming of the Beast,' the pope explained, 'in account of these fumes.'

'That's eggs, Beatissimo Padre,' said the engineer, laughing relaxed, as if kindly explaining to a child. 'We use eggs – *uova* – to be mixed in the mortar. There's nothing about devils. Those were hysterical illusions of an old man. They were eggs...' but he looked at the pope, who did not appreciate the dismissal, and concluded, this time with less conviction, probably ready to blame the foreigner Immanuel 'Egg whites makes the mortar firmer...supposedly.'

Romanus of Tusculum was not a man who appreciated to be patronised. He paused for a moment with jaws clenched, while the engineer felt his own veins freezing from the heart out. Finally, the pope smacked his lips in impatience. 'Uova... I smell evil, though. Let's hope it's not *malefic eggs* you are using' he said, mentioning the name used for the feared fly agaric mushroom and, turning back towards the road, the pope walked to his horse, grunting 'How far is this Corsena? I think I need a bath.'

He mounted his chestnut charger with some difficulty and kicked in with the full weight of his heels. The horse felt the pain on its ribs and jumped to accelerate into a gallop, but its mouth was jerked back into a halt position. The pope was gasping and coughing. John XIX leaned on the horse's neck and tried to spit convulsively, while a few aids rushed around to assist him.

'I am fine!' he said, raising and spitting out with disgust whatever residue of saliva he felt he still had on his tongue. 'It was only a fly! Yes, let's move. Let's carry on to the baths. The pope is fine. I have just swallowed a fucking fly!'

Later, when the papal cavalcade left Chifenti, it was followed by an inconvenient number of curious peasants and workers that were dispensed from their tasks in the bridge for that day. They filled the gallery path along the woods bordering the Lima, to cross it about less than a mile further, in Corsena.

Back in the centre of Chifenti, a small crowd started to disperse. Ginevra rushed back to the tavern, graciously swaying her shapes to the sides as she trotted with ease, but Amadeo stayed behind. He was staring at a much younger man.

'I don't like the way you look at my daughter.' The taverner said, with his best brawl-separating baritone.

Arrigo exhaled with a whistle, humorously surprised. 'Thank you for sharing your taste with me, old man. Do you suppose I'm interested in what you like and what you don't?' and he looked back at the tavern, where Ginevra had already disappeared behind a door. He was left alone with Amadeo.

'You should be, for your own sake,' Amadeo said, 'for if you get close as if to touch Ginevra, your experience will not be as rewarding and easy as beating a village idiot.'

'Taverner, you forget who I am. Why would the Lord of Anchiano want to touch a smutty peasant? A wench!'

'Probably because both your grandfather and your father have done likewise. But do not get me wrong, Arrigo. I never forget who you are. I know you carry your dagger somewhere within the folds of your vests, and I will always be prepared for you. As a good coward, stay away from me and you will be glad you have done so.'

Arrigo rolled his eyes and exploded with laughter. 'I cannot decide if you are suffering from stupidity or bravery.' he said.

'Yes, I am a free man, boy. Chifenti is a free town. Here the shit that comes out of your arse is just as brown as any of ours. You may beat to the ground a strong, but stupid man like Spatola, but you will not have me as simple. Now if you just want to turn around, take the road South and return to your mother...'

'I will, taverner, but only after a goblet of your best wine.'

'No, Arrigo, No! Not today. We are closed, and we are busy with your uncles and aunts, who are serving the pontiff's kitchen –'

He was interrupted by a rider that came at full gallop from the South, using one of the local horses. They quickly recognised the handsome figure of Giacomo, of the Burle et Malachi.

'The papal parade is gone.' Amadeo said. 'But your brothers and sisters are fording the river right here, between Chifenti and Fornulo. It's more convenient to serve the baths from —'

'Thank you Amadeo, but I do not come for the pope or for my siblings. I come for Maria Maddalena, my sister,' and turning to Arrigo, he asked quite brusquely 'Where's your mother?'

'She never came to this reception. She was going to —'

'Take me to her, then.' Giacomo said, swallowing some of the flavour of the thick heat in his mouth, 'It's urgent.'

Uncle and nephew opened a tunnel of dust into the cloud of flies as they galloped towards Anchiano, where Maria Maddalena heard the story from that brother that she hardly saw since moving to Cunimundinghi lands.

'It is true, Maria!' a sweat-covered Giacomo said while recovering from the effort. He drank a goblet of wine and thanked the good God for the coolness of the castle in that late afternoon. 'It was our grandfather that sent me here to advise you as soon as possible.'

'Of what?' Maria asked, her face a rough stony sculpture of impatience.

'The pope has been poisoned with evil words from many forked tongues in Lucca. That bastard Antelmino di Gottefredo has shown his dirty face on the bishop's Palace, suggesting to the pontiff that you have engaged into heresy.'

Maria's petrified expression did not change. 'That is true, but what proof does he have?'

'What do you mean it's true?' Giacomo asked, almost gagging with his wine.

'Never mind, Giacomo. Just tell me all of it.'

Her brother obeyed. 'The pope seemed interested in devilries, apparently due to recent letters from a monk in France. Letters informing us that the coming of the Devil will be next year, as if it wasn't enough the damage done in the Anno Mille. Anyway, the pope liked the taste of Antelmino's poison, so the balivo was brought in for an interview. The stupid man confirmed you had been recently around the country, meeting with midwives and enquiring about evil eyes, amulets, invocations. There were talks of your encounter with the Genovese brothers and soon someone mentioned your ambush on your brother-in-law Sigifredo of the Cunimundinghi. Apparently it did not take longer for envious people to associate you with the ill fate of Sister Caterina, that woman who lived with Father Martino, or with the unfortunate demise of Fulcardo's first wife Lucia and her unborn child.'

'Where were you then to defend me?' Maria asked, closing her fists tight over the table.

'We were not there, don't be ridiculous, or else we would have stopped this nonsense.'

'And how do you know about it?' she asked, with an incredulous eyebrow slightly raised over her stony features.

Giacomo dropped his shoulders 'There was actually one individual who would not accept any of that was true,' he smiled shyly. 'It was Anton, the parish clerk.'

'The Tedesco?' Arrigo asked.

'He is not German,' Giacomo cordially corrected his nephew, explaining 'He is a Magyar. Like Béla was. The man who came from the East with your grandfather Immanuel.'

Maria felt the customary uneasiness that clogged her throat anytime the name of Béla was raised. She rasped 'Forget Béla! Just continue, brother!'

Giacomo looked at her with a surprised fear and hesitated for a second before carrying on 'To his utmost disadvantage, and the surprise of the bishop and all the papal entourage, Anton demanded an end to the calumny, and insisted that the pontiff retired from those venomous interviews. He came to warn us of the pope's disposition to enquire you for alleged crimes and heresy. And earlier this morning, news was that Anton had fallen into disgrace before John XIX, who firmly believed that heresy was rampant in these lands.' He dropped the empty goblet on the table. 'At least grandfather will be happy you were not there at the bridge site to receive the pope.'

'I was planning to pay my respects to him tomorrow,' Maria said more to herself than telling her brother, 'a personal visit, as I would deserve, not mixed with the rabble.'

'So I strongly suggest you do not show your face in Corsena, at this stage,' said Giacomo.

'No,' she wondered, her eyes vaguely changing the focus from nowhere to nowhere else, 'I will definitely have to change my plans.' She paused for a second and stood up with a jump, holding Giacomo by the arm and pulling him out of his bench. 'You should be going now, brother, as your horse should be rested by now and twilight will allow you to find your way for a few hours still.'

'What?' said Giacomo, disgusted with his sister's determination to rush him out. 'I shouldn't expect to be welcomed as a guest for the night, should I?'

'You can stay in Corsena, with our father,' Maria said, 'if you do not want to ride back to Lucca tonight.'

She was ready to shut the door behind him when he held it firmly and asked 'Maria Maddalena, tell me true if you are really recommending human sacrifice for this bridge.'

Maria sneered and shook her head. '*Of course* I am! We all know that a sacrifice must be made for this construction. How could we, children of Immanuel Ben-Malachi deny it?'

Giacomo digested her words with pursed lips. Then, just before weakening his hold on the door that she was still pressing against him, he asked 'What about the devil? Why would you want to summon him?'

'That's between him and I!' she said, and put all her weight on the heavy door, that clanged loudly as it locked behind Giacomo. He would have to walk down the gate and stairs, to fetch his horse in the stables. High on the terrace of Anchiano, he paused to look down towards the ample gray orchards of dry olive and mulberry trees that slowly darkened with the sunset. And he was slightly annoyed with the flies, which were still active at that time of the evening.

Arrigo leaned out the window to watch Giacomo leaving on gallop. He turned inside to find his mother at the table, already pouring water from a rusty iron jar into another one. 'What do you want me to do?' he asked with a grin.

She poured the water back from the second jar to the first 'Can you get into the baths?' she continued, without taking her eyes of the water, pouring back and forth.

He laughed 'I can get anywhere I want. Besides, the baths belong to my grandfather. He wouldn't keep me out. '

She bit her lip with excitement 'Will you bring your mother a strand of hair of the pontiff?'

'I'm afraid he's a bald man, mother.'

She stopped for a while, stretching her neck like an alerted doe, bringing her brain away from the crystal clear water that had been poured into one of the jars.

Arrigo noticed her disconcert and suggested, looking distractedly at the floor 'I could dig my dagger deep into his heart, if that's needed...'

'Stupid kid!' she roared, slamming the table with the palm of her hand. 'I'm doing all of this only for you and you want to spoil it with murder? Sometimes I wonder if this is all in vain, you cretin.' Arrigo straightened his face while she continued with the pouring and added almost in a whisper 'Forget your foolishness and take this water into the baths. See that it is poured into the pope's basin.'

'Is it poisoned?' asked Arrigo.

'It's only water.' She said firmly. 'Now, get a pouch to put this water and go! But before that, give me your dagger here for a moment.'

Immanuel himself was ensuring that the pope enjoyed quality care during his visit to the baths. The Bukhari watched every step of the service, only expecting to leave as soon as the bishop of Rome fell into intimacy. As bathmaster, he coordinated his children working in the central kitchen, set up to prepare elaborate dishes with the best game collected over the previous weeks; he controlled the spouts to the pool at the main bath chamber, assuring that the tepid bath was not too hot and keeping a constant renewal of the water; and he verified for the right balance of herbs and salts to be added to the water for a refreshing feeling.

A beautiful Lucchese girl turned away her nose as she helped the pontiff rid himself of his several layers of clerical vests. Every new garment of grimy fabric that was detached from Romanus's large body revealed a renewed stench collected during the hardships of travel, especially after an early summer in Rome. To Immanuel, the idea that any of these people would be concerned about the odour of eggs in the bridge must have been nothing but a mockery. When the last piece of soiled drapery was carefully pulled out from the white, humid, rash-ridden skin, in this case a waxy brown plate that must have been a delicate white canvas when first worn, it revealed a pestilent reek that would have beaten a dead heard. Immanuel prepared to leave the chamber and vomit, if needed. His mind quickly ran over the idea of scrubbing the walls to rid the chamber of the putrid smell when the visitor would be gone.

Holding himself with arms slightly stretched, descending the slippery stone steps to the square pool, Romanus was little impressed by the sensuous attendant that poured the salts and dried herbs into his bath. The mixture lifted a flowery steam that was not yet sufficiently potent to mask his bodily stink. The pope raised a careless hand to refuse a rubbing with a dried gourd, which had been politely offered by the young attendant.

'We have softer marine sponges, if the Beatissimo Padre prefers,' said Immanuel, rather concerned that the pope was somehow impatient 'it will be tender on your skin, and our beautiful masseuse can rub the grime off your back with the utmost —'

The pope's discourse rolled over Immanuel's obsequious offer 'Good man, let me be and immerse my body into these soothing waters, for I am uneasy and I need resting before the next days. I have been told that the regional upriver parishes celebrate San Pellegrino tonight. It would have been appropriate to bless the feast adequately, but I'm afraid I need this rest more than they need my presence.'

'Most certainly, Beatissimo Padre,' said Immanuel, preparing himself to step out of the chamber, 'should I leave you alone with our kind attendant?'

'Nah,' quacked the pope, 'do stay here, bathmaster, please. An old layman like me needs the company and wisdom of an old layman such as you.'

With a helpless expression, Immanuel bowed, waiting for the pope to continue. The girl had discretely retired to the annex room, where a table had been served for the pope's meal. John XIX was submerged to his neck into a pool that was not much wider than his floating width. He turned his large white body around to get equal temperature coverage, as if bleaching a piece of ham in a small copper pan. 'Bring me something to drink.'

Immanuel jumped to the serving table on the room next door, where several finely cut cold meats waited, including duck, venison, lamb and half a piglet. They were next to a tray of braised thrushes and a roasted partridge, local cheese, several cups of oil and wooden bowls of dried fruits. Although the local food was not highly esteemed by the Lucchese citizens, Immanuel still insisted that his children made available a pile of warm chestnut pancakes intermingled with hot flat stones and a copper pot with steaming chestnut polenta. One never knew if the pope would try them or even enjoy it. Around the table's edge, there were several flacons and goatskins of wine and small amphorae with different herbal infusions. The Bukhari swiftly grabbed a goblet and had it in no time at the pontiff's reach 'Here's a sample of the local wine, from grapes of the Cunimundinghi. I hope it is of the Beatissimo Padre's approval.'

'It's passable,' the pope said, curling his lip after drinking the whole goblet in a gulp. 'I need to get this fly through, the bastard. You know, I swallowed a fly today, by the bridge. The miserable insect must be still walking inside me.'

'I'm sure it's already dead,' Immanuel said with a soothing ease, confident in his knowledge of anatomy and physiology. 'If the Beatissimo Padre wants, we have a very strong wine that I make, crafted from mulberry pomace.'

The pope ignored his comment and lowered his body deeper into the water dipping his chin into the warm bath. Like a grumpy hippopotamus, he grunted 'I think there is something lurking in these lands!'

'?' Immanuel took a few seconds to wipe the stupid expression from his face. His little blue eyes shone bright when he smiled loudly 'Ah! You mean the flies? Well, they don't bother us here, as the Beatissimo Padre can notice,' he said, while reaching his hand towards the only small window in the bath chamber. Before the mesmerised pope could interrupt him, the Bukhari explained, getting hold of a wooden cup that sat by the window sill 'We do not get flies into the premises because I poison them with a special mixture. I just cut some mushrooms and dunk them into —'

'That's not what I meant, old man!' the pope rasped, impatiently. Immanuel froze, while John continued 'I'm referring to devilries! Demoniac activities. Blunt heresy that has been practiced by the locals. People like that Hospitaller and the Lady of Anchiano. It does seem that Satanas is breaking its chains and he will come out of hell right through these lands. It has been said and it has been written. A thousand years ago!'

Immanuel was stunned, chin and shoulders dropped. He had slammed the cup on the table, but still held the wooden *aspergillum*, which he had been sprinkling the room with, hanging from the tip of his fingers and dripping the milky insecticide concoction on the floor. 'Did...did the Beatissimo Padre mention the Lady of Anchiano?' he babbled.

'I know she is your daughter, bathmaster, but I won't hold it against you,' the pope said, as he waved his hands in the water, watching the ripples created on the surface. 'Your daughter is guilty up to her ears of wickedness. She will not escape an accusation of heresy. It's up to God to forgive her when she's at heaven's gates. And only the good Jesus knows who else will be bundled with her. The Hospitaller? The parish clerk in Lucca? No doubt this is a filthy land you have chosen to settle in, but it's time we have it cleansed.'

It was in this moment that the old Bukhari noticed the girl entering the bath chamber, discoloured as if she had seen the devil, sweating profusely and shaking her arms while carrying a bowl of water. She approached the bathtub from behind the pope and discreetly poured the water in it.

'Thank you, my dear!' Romanus said. 'That's quite refreshing.'

Immanuel was still watching that strange moment. The girl trembled as if her bones were going to detach from each other. He could see the goose bumps behind her fleshy young arms. When she entered the annex chamber, Immanuel caught a glimpse of someone else inside. A man, lurking behind the shadows, smirking a feline set of teeth. It was certainly not one of his sons who had been bringing the food. The figure slipped swiftly out of view, disappearing through the back door. Immanuel tried to run out after him, but the pontiff's voice arose over his thoughts. 'I think I could have one of that special wine of yours, bathmaster.'

'What? Which? Sure! Yes, the special mulberry wine. Immediately, Beatissimo Padre,' said Immanuel, walking backwards into the annex chamber. He hopped in and grabbed the attendant by her arm, asking with a swooshing whisper 'Who was that? What did he give to you? That was Arrigo, my grandson, wasn't he?'

The girl exploded into tears, as silently as she could 'How am I supposed to know who it was? The man had a dagger on my neck and handed me an amphora. I don't know your grandson and I don't know any Arrigo. I am from Lucca, my lord. Have you forgotten you are paying me to be here?'

Immanuel released her arm 'Of course... you are a whore...'

'Where is my wine, bathmaster?' the pope shouted from his bath.

'In a moment, Beatissimo Padre!' Immanuel shouted and, back in a sizzling whisper 'What was that he gave to you?'

'The man said it was only water, my lord.' She wiped her tears with the back of her hands. Now hiccups had taken care of her words. 'But – he – pressed – that – dag – ger – of – his – ag – gainst – my neck, saying he – would – kill – me if – I – did – not – pour – it in – to the pope's bath. What could I do?' Her hiccup-broken whisper had melted into a whimper.

Immanuel gambled on the waiting time the pope would endure, still asking 'And did he do anything else to the food? Or the wines?'

'No, my lord,' she answered with a bit of hesitation. 'I don't think –'

'This is unprecedented!' the pink fleshy figure of pope suddenly appeared on the door, with a wide clean sheet hurriedly wrapped around his wet, steaming body. By the horizontal folds on his face, he was visibly displeased. 'Where is my damned wine?'

'It's here my lord, I mean, Beatissimo Padre,' Immanuel answered promptly, slithering around the table to grab the goatskin with the mulberry wine. He filled a goblet and handed it to the pontiff. 'Now, if the Beatissimo Padre wants to be careful, this is a very strong beverage that should be taken in small —'

But it was too late. The pope drank the whole goblet in one gulp.

There was not even an instant of reckoning. The explosion occurred as immediately as the concoction tried to burn its way into the pope's oesophagus. His eyes bulged out like boiled eggs as his face bloated red and veiny like an inflated goat's stomach. Gasping desperately, he gushed over the dishes whichever amount of wine his body was able to recover from the throat. Coughing and desperate for a soothing sensation, the pope gave away on his visual chastity and dropped his sheet, reaching to the table, grabbing a wooden cup with milk and drinking it all at once. But now, the difference was that he savoured the velvety feeling of the milk caressing his insides, refreshing his throat and bringing him back to the direction towards normality. By the time he placed the cup back with a loud knock, he had not seen Immanuel walking backwards against the wall, hitting it and dragging his back down, all the way to a sitting position on the floor. The girl promptly tried to help him stand up, but the bathmaster seemed to be in tears.

'This was absolutely delicious, this milk,' the pope exclaimed, 'What was it? Such a nutty, tangy flavour...what are those bits left in the cup?'

But Immanuel was speechless, sitting on the floor, looking at an inexistent point beyond nothing. The pope shook his head in disapproval and grabbed the sheet from the floor to cover his fat, wet nudity. Turning to the girl, Romanus said 'This man has probably drunk too much of this mulberry wine. My bath is over, so I have no more need of his services, but he better be well and alert tomorrow. Now, will you show me to my bedchamber?'

When they left, Immanuel crawled to the table and, with a painful effort to conquer that vertigo, he put himself up again. After not daring to look at the cup for an agonising moment, he saw it. And it was empty. And it was his fault! Battalions of outcomes fought fiercely against one another to fill the blanks in his mind. He needed a drink.

Taking a full goblet of mulberry wine, he drank it profusely, and it rolled down as smooth and cool as an otter taking a plunge in the Lima.

In the end, he thought, he would be comforted by the fact that instead of his daughter being tried for heresy, he would be condemned for murdering the pope. Poisoning the Apostle of Christ with the mushrooms they called *uovo malefico* - the evil egg.

As for the fly, Immanuel was pretty sure it would be dead.

The Mære and the Ghost

The night had rolled over the valley like a big black bear settling to hibernate, smothering its inhabitants with unbearable heat. And such an awfully hot night was that night of San Pellegrino. It was a new moon and nobody saw it, but it is said that even the stones were sweating and the trees moved closer to the rivers to get some cooling around their roots.

In Chifenti, Ginevra had lain with nobody, but retired to the chamber above the kitchen, where her palliasse had always been set opposite to Amadeo's. Below them, on the main hall, a few wealthier guests took their corners and some straw, as always, while most were allowed to use the stables. A thick, warm cloud of body odour permeated through the walls and choked many out of their sleep. There were no fires or flames on to give any indication whether the hall was still there. No snoring either. Mosquitos had been silent, cooling themselves by the riverbanks, while fleas had halted their biting. Most of those restless people had their eyes opened, facing an infinite darkness. As dark as what Chaos could have been.

The men were distracting themselves with considerations on how Ginevra could be battling the heat. Would she have her legs uncovered? Maybe up to her thighs? Would her flesh be sweaty, glistening under the moonlight? Well, there are no silver reflexes during new moon, unfortunately. Ginevra would be away in the darkness, unreachable, a solid blackness that allowed no distinction of depth or distance. One could be facing a wall or the sky. They were only sure of their whereabouts by the echo of their sounds, the brushy movements of bodies trying to find their sleep or sighing with discomfort and exasperation.

And a lashing scream outside.

It started with a low, guttural whisper, a rumbling that many thought was coming from their own stomachs, but it quickly grew into a low chant, a smooth roar that was now clearly somewhere outside. And as everyone's skin crawled with the realisation that the mooing was real and getting close, and by then it was already a scream of horror.

The scream repeated itself several times, with different voices, screeches and howls, not only in the tavern and in the stables, but probably inside every house and inhabited shed in Chifenti. In the tavern, there were bodies trying to run in the darkness, thumps and crashes, bangs of pain, with shelves flipping and tables turning over. While the noise of confusion still lingered on the mucky darkness, before Ginevra and Amadeo could tact their way around to finding their tinderboxes, they all heard the hoof beats outside. Probably coming from the South, maybe the hospital, the bridge, or Anchiano. But who could be galloping across the night at such a desperate speed? The ground trembled as it approached in its frenzied stampede.

Amadeo and Ginevra found their tinderbox, but no matter how much they tried, they couldn't kindle a fire. Some of the folks downstairs dared to raise their faces to where they knew the window openings were, but looking outside and saw more blackness. Only the warm air could be felt, being pushed away, displaced by the furious presence of the horses on stampede, a savage steam that blew inside, as the tavern rumbled when they galloped by.

The tavern had been built on the confluence of the path that led eastwards alongside the Lima and the main alley of Chifenti, which forded the river almost at its mouth. While the hoofbeats thundered the ground, Amadeo and Ginevra reached over the small window high on the wall of their chamber. Nothing could be seen, but sheer blackness. However, the fury of the horses could be felt through their bones. And although their ears refused to believe, muffled by the thumping and puffing, there was a suggestion of sniggering. Quick voices outside, laughing as the horses passed by, softly disappearing with the distance, as they entered the alley, fading into a sudden raise of splashing when the cavalcade forded the Lima.

'Who was that?' Ginevra dared to ask, breaking the silence that had frozen the population of the tavern.

'Castrated, tortured, executed and damned if I know…' Amadeo said, finally managing to kindle a fire. He descended with Ginevra into the hall to restore some order into the disorder. Through the backdoor, they paid a visit to the back shed, where the terrified stablemaster had some control over the uncontrolled fear spread through the poorer guests. As soon as more candles were started downstairs, the prospect of finding what had happened outside was so frightening to the guests in that they covered the windows. Nobody wanted to dare step out into the road. Amadeo decided he would look. Ginevra bravely went along, clinging to her father's arm. With a lit torch, they walked out, carefully considering every step ahead. The rivers resonated calmly in the distance. Verifying for the hoofprints, they confirmed the suspicion that the horses had gone through the path and forded the river towards Fornulo.

'They're all gone,' said Amadeo, conclusively.

They entered and calmed everyone else. The door was firmly bolted back into place. But this time nobody could accept to spend the rest of the night in sheer darkness, so a candle was left with a flame on. People comforted each other.

'Good night.'

'May God answer our prayers and protect us all.'

The night dragged on and little else was heard. Neither the snoring, the buzzing of mosquitoes nor the scratching on flea bites, for the exhausted people of Chifenti had given up on their night fears and fallen into deep slumber. As always, there were a few who had a lighter mode of sleep. Ginevra was one of them, who had her eyes wide open as quick as she heard the soft hoof beats of one or two horses walking outside. Amadeo snored loudly and turned around when she lit her tinder. She raised the candle to the high window and climbed on a small chest to peek outside. Too dark. She could only hear the pace of a horse walking by, getting closer, but nothing else could be seen, except other faint glows of candles on windows alongside the curvy alley.

It had to be a horse that was left behind, or sent back by the first riders, whoever they were, Ginevra thought. She heard a noise coming from the hall and saw a glare from downstairs. One of the guests must have lit a torch down there. 'Put it off!' she shushed, walking down the steps, 'it's only a horse, or a rider. You do not want him to come in here now as we sleep!'

The guest was trembling with fear, but he managed to roll the torch in his hands, so it burned entirely. 'I will not put it out, by the blood of the Christ crucified. I must see who it is that defies darkness and rides alone in the night. It is here, just outside, the horse is walking by us.'

Ginevra bit her lower lip for a second and added 'Let's go, then.'

Everyone else was sleeping. Ginevra unbolted the door and the guest pulled it open. They both held on to the torch as if it was a rope to rescue them out of hell. Stepping cautiously outside, they came huddled pushing the torch ahead of them, expecting that the horse would be startled by the sudden glare of the fire. But there was only darkness by the tavern.

clip clop clip clop clip clop...

The horse would be walking a few steps in right in front of the tavern, but they still could not devise it beyond the blackness, especially with the torch blinding the vision of both. The rider should have seen them already, so there was no need to call. The rider would be riding towards them.

clip clop clip clop clip clop...

One more step forward, together, and one more. Their skin was cold as ice, as if an immeasurable frigid presence had descended upon that village. They raised the torch higher, displacing it from their view, expecting to see the one horse in the alley. It took a moment to adjust their eyes to the illuminated darkness.

But they were so wrong.

The whites of hundreds of blind eyes flashed at them. It was a full, packed herd, with scores of white horses, thin to the bone, silently walking by. The beasts were touching shoulder to shoulder, making no sound at all, as if gliding over the path, hiding the one horse in the middle that was pacing soundly over the dusty road.

CLIP CLOP CLIP CLOP CLIP CLOP...

Where was it?

Torch raised higher. In the middle of the packed heard, a dark grey lonely movement stood out from the forest of lifeless eyes, bony heads, mute withers, hips and croups that drifted through Chifenti. A pair of thin shoulders dropped from what appeared to be a white helmet. Unexplainably, the herd thinned out as the rider got closer. There were increasingly less of those silent blind horses and most had vanished in the instant the naked white body materialised from the darkness before the glare of the torch. A rather fat, sagging upper body, bluish uncoloured and old, with thin legs and long limp arms hanging on its side. The head was bald, fat on the neck and rather pointed on the top. His frowned expression seemed to be focused ahead, towards the path going south, ignoring the two people who had braved the night outside the tavern. He rode naked, on an unharnessed white horse.

Ginevra bit her hand in order not to scream. The guest holding the torch shook so much on his legs that they started to bend down. He collapsed on the ground and dropped the torch, scuffling to stand up and jump back inside through the door. Ginevra caught the torch from the ground and raised it again. When her eyes once again adapted to the darkness, she saw a renewed thick herd of thin horses gliding over the path, leaving the village heading south.

But stopped in the middle of the flow was the rider on his horse. He was mounted backwards, with a pair of mad eyes staring at Ginevra. He was holding onto his genitals and he was grinning.

'Can you feel the heat?' he hissed.

She ran to the door and slammed it shut, bolting it and trying not to think of what made the blood in her veins freeze. And the best way of dragging that image away was screaming as loud as she could.

Weeks after this episode, when the autumn rains had finally ripped through, keeping the flies away, Bernardo delle Rocche walked along the road heading north from the bridge, to confer with Amadeo in Chifenti. He noticed the unusual quantity of faery rings alongside the dark, wide path. Large circular patterns of toadstools, the *uovo malefico*, spread along the mile between the bridge and the ford to Fornulo.

By the time Bernardo got to the tavern, he was so eager to talk to the pilgrims about San Pellegrino, that he almost forgot the other reasons why he was there: One was Ginevra, and the other was Maria Maddalena.

On the night of San Pellegrino, Pope John XIX had a dream.

He was sweating profusely, with little comfort to be found lying on in the freshly made mattress of beech leaves. The good Immanuel had had the care to use a thread that had been passed through the crushed leaves of wormwood to sew the mattress. The aromatic scent did not please the pope though, or little it did to sooth his ample body for the night. Pelts and linen sheets, too hot for the touch to his burning skin, had been thrown around the bed chamber. He could not relax or fall asleep, probably tormented by the thoughts of flames, which would burn heresy out of that place. Although he had lost some of his energy during the hot bath, he managed to be reasonably expedient with the attendant. It was a fast relief, where she did have to help him with the necessary patience and dedication.

While the sweat-dripping pope rolled his body around, leaving an ample stain on the mattress during his first night in Corsena, the still waters of the very low Serchio rippled with a sudden movement and a puff. A pair of lips had emerged, bulging and panting, with two long barbels around the nostrils and four more under the lower lip. Nobody would ever see it anyway, for the night was blacker than chaos. The head came out further for an instant, with desperate eyes on its side, as if it needed to get away from that warm water, but it soon dived again, sliding its back down on a curve like a miniature version of the Leviathan. It would only surface again under the bridge that was being built, the stone monster standing out in segments like an unfinished dragon.

Vast areas of scaffolding held the arched frames and a mini village had been built around the pillars. Several carpenters and stone masons were removed from their homes to occupy those lodgings. They had been trying to sleep for hours, fighting the heat and rolling around the straw to cool as much of their bodies as they could. Some had found their way for a quick bath into the warm waters of the Serchio, probably at its lowest point in memory. It was past midnight when a chill fell upon the riverbank, allowing them to finally fall profoundly asleep, at the same time that some much larger nostrils emerged from the river surface.

The pope could see them vividly in his dream. Large heads with bulgy blind eyes, screeching mutely as they slithered out of the water. He tried to brush them off his mind, but they clung to it like slugs. He was not at the riverbank, but four miles up the current, agonising in his bedchamber in Corsena. Still, he could watch them, colossal leeches, dragging their long soft bodies across the pebbles and the masonry, leaving dozens of tortuous trails of slime over the bank. They clung to the stone terraces and climbed swiftly, pulling their bodies up to the road like a wet lizard's tongue disappearing behind its dry lips.

The pope's skin sizzled in heat, choking his breath, while he watched the creatures raise, growing long thin limbs and hooves on all legs and stretching longer into the shapes of horses. But there was a smaller creature with much bigger malice that he could not see. He knew it was there, shaking the water out of its back, throwing alert glances to the sides, scratching itself with tiny claws, walking on fours and on twos. He could not see its face, but he could hear it giggling.

Romanus of Tusculum was a man of little religious education. Although he was literate and had been dedicating his time and attentions to the seat of Rome for the twelve years of his brother's papacy, he had never bothered to read any religious excerpts. His knowledge of the Word of God was entirely based on loud readings of his aides. The letters from Raoul Glaber arrived as he was leaving to Lucca. *So it was true. Beelzebub, the Lord of the Flies, was brewing in the Serchio.* More than a coincidence, the pope thought, it was a providential designation. He started to believe his participation on the throne of Peter was indeed a divine mission. And that his own presence in that infernal area, where fire, brimstone and legions of flies came from under a bridge, heresy brewed in a castle and evil oozed in a hospital, was the obvious sign that a great wrong should come out of it.

Screeching savagely, the creature leaped on its four limbs towards the road. On the second it reached the horses, they exploded into the stampede that ran up the path and passed through Chifenti a few minutes later. The exhausted workers sleeping under the bridge had little time or disposition to find out what the noise on the road was. But the pope watched it all, striving to inhale some fresh, cool air into his burning body. He could not. The air was still hot and heavy, now smelling and tasting like a herb of some foreign flavour. And it was so thick it could not enter through to his lungs anymore.

Romanus of Tusculum opened his eyes moaning desperately, glad to see that a candle still burned by his side, but horrified to find that a little man, no bigger than a dog and with long brown hair growing below the waistline was sitting on his chest. And he had both of his hands around the pope's throat.

Nobody saw him arriving. They didn't even hear the horse. By the time they had all felt the unnatural night heat and they had seen the glare above their huts, the woods were already crackling and snapping from the fire that burned high, and a sinister laughter cackled through the night.

'Burn, Hellmouth burn!'

As the flames engulfed the bridge, the larger beams started to snap. The local populace could see it and they were coming to help.

It hadn't taken too long after the screams of horror from the vision of that naked man riding by Chifenti. He had vanished into the darkness, but there were soon a good number or torches glaring from Fornulo. The riders forded the Lima and entered Chifenti, shouting desperately to the villagers. 'The pope! The pope has disappeared! We need all abled men for a *hutesium et clamor* - a hue and cry!'

Amadeo came out promptly from the tavern. Ginevra and a number of pilgrims followed him.

'A ghost was seen here this hour.' He alerted the men-at-arms, obviously from the pontifical entourage. 'Maybe he has taken the Beatissimo Padre.'

'We all have seen ghosts tonight, taverner,' the Roman custodes said. 'Nightmares. For us all! But the pope has vanished from his chamber and is nowhere to be found in Corsena. Villagers have heard a horse coming towards this direction.'

'We heard the gallops earlier too,' Amadeo explained, 'but scores of beasts, and heading northwards. Later my daughter could hear a walk or canter. One horse returning. She went out but they saw a full herd of ghost horses —'

'That is true!' A pilgrim intervened. 'I saw him there, the ghost of San Pellegrino!'

And a louder scream broke above the whole confusion of villagers getting out of their houses 'The Bridge! The bridge is burning! My bridge is burning!' They watched the Roman engineer running by with all his fingers dug into his face, howling in desperation and heading towards the path south. His silhouette quickly faded into the dark road, but above him, diamonds shone a yellow light, as if demons were watching awake on the canopy. The people of Chifenti were quick to understand that those were the few spaces on the thick canopy of beeches that allowed them to see the valley down the river, lit by a hellish fire that consumed the bridge.

And then, they all heard the thunder. The bridge was crumbling.

'Kill him!' someone shouted. 'Throw him into the flames!' They were holding a man who they thought was responsible for the fire.

The flames now burned lower, spread out wider over the workers' shacks, with tall black structures standing out above them, like columns of hell, stubborn remains of the pillars of the charred bridge. The construction workers had contained the bulged-eye madman they had found standing naked on the edge of the broken embankment, laughing hysterically at the flames that licked high, raising dangerously close to his face.

'Burn Satanas!' he was shouting, oblivious to the blows he received or the hands that held him, 'Burn for another thousand years in your chains! Leave us alone, Beelzebub and take your legions back into your arsehole!'

Nobody knew him. They had grabbed and felled the madman onto the ground, kicking him mercilessly while he laughed harder at every new blow. He was dragged towards the crowd that arrived from Chifenti, headed by the engineer, who was sporting his darkest mood ever.

One of the workers hurried to meet the engineer 'We caught the culprit! We did not see him starting the fire. It was just too late when we noticed it.'

The engineer could have eaten his lower lip. Shoving the worker from his way, he advanced towards the group, who stood on the bridge path that disappeared into the still roaring fire. They opened space for him in a semicircle and lowered their torches to show their trophy: a bald, naked old man was lying on the ground, bruised and blackened with soot. He was striped with white, pinkish bands of skin, opened folds of his slack body that had not been covered by the smoke. Trembling, he still giggled through a pool of blood in his mouth. And in spite of the blows he had received, an erection could make itself visible under his sagging belly.

The engineer groaned to the workers 'Give me a dagger and I will gut this pig alive!'

There were a few murmurs and someone produced a long hatchet. The man on the ground shivered like a stunned frog and cackled even louder. 'It's too late!' he shrieked, 'The bridge is gone! The Hellmouth is shut for another thousand years!' he sniggered, spluttering blood from his broken lips. The engineer roared with anger, raising the hatchet with both hands, ready to split the man's skull, when a sharp object poked his shoulder blade.

'Do not do it!'

The Roman did not lower the hatchet. He just turned around mesmerised, to find a mounted *custodes* wearing the Lateran red and yellow, and holding a long spear that pointed at him. Other men-at-arms stood behind, on horses and on foot, and a whole crowd of people from the hospital and from Chifenti.

'Well, I am glad you are here!' shouted the engineer, lowering the axe. 'Just in time!' he pointed to the flaccid body on the ground. 'This madman is possessed by the devil. He has caused this fire, destroying a masterpiece of engineering that has been commissioned by the pope. You should know it well that the Beatissimo Padre was at this site just yesterday. Now if you don't put your lance through this criminal and roast him alive for the pope to see, I will chop him into pieces right now. Yes, I have been appointed by the Beatissimo Padre himself to built this —'

'Shut up' ordered the custodes. 'This man is Pope John XIX.'

The engineer just had to give a quick glance to the naked figure on the ground to recognise it and start fighting the vertigo and nausea that had suddenly avalanched over him, the guards approached and carefully tried to carry the pope, who was crying and giggling. They needed four guards to awkwardly drag the toneless body of Romanus across the path, passing by the engineer, who was now on his knees, all the way to the other crestfallen riders that waited.

The pope was taken to Corsena and cared for by a sweat-drenched Immanuel. With no improvement on his delirious state, they put him in a cart back to Lucca, crossing the Serchio by boat just below the smothering remains of the bridge he had burned. His eyes were opened and cloudy, looking at nothing.

'It's evil… Destroy it… It's the more evil than you could even begin to imagine.' He would babble sometimes.

In the Lucchese bishopric, treated by the most knowledgeable physicians, John XIX did not show any signs of improvement from his soporific delirium. Messages from Albericus, who had been alerted of the incidents, ordered that the pope should be sent in no time and properly escorted back to Rome. But when the Count of Tusculum saw the state of mental limbo in which his brother had fallen into, he knew it was time to quietly prepare for the succession of the throne of St. Peter.

The descendants of Domenico of the Burle et Malachi say that John XIX was poisoned by the fly agaric which had been dunked in milk, accidentally drunk by the pope. But not to Maria Maddalena, who was certain the outburst of madness was the accursed water on the pope's bath, water poured from iron to iron that she had stabbed with the golden dagger. For the populace of the Serchio, everyone knew that the bishop of Rome had swollen a fly while visiting the bridge. It was obvious that the diabolic insect had inserted itself into the pope's brain, causing him to be attacked by demons. However, several sceptics from Chifenti were insistent it was the ghost of San Pellegrino that had terrified the Beatissimo Padre into madness. They had seen the ghost, naked as a toad, riding a blind horse through the night. That image would drive any Christian into insanity.

But for most of Christendom, which learned about a pontiff's death so late after happening, it was no more than a pope's death. And the events that would soon happen in the bridge, at the break of the Thousand and Thirty Third year of our Lord, would prove forever to the population of the Serchio that John XIX was thrown into insanity by the Devil himself.

As for the Roman engineer, whose name was never to be forgotten by those who had heard it, he was forgotten into time for not finishing the bridge. Beaten and damned by the Shepherd of the Lord, he left those lands, dragging his scarred bare feet over the dust and stones, whispering prayers of forgiveness and never to be found or to be heard of again. As a new constructor was to leave his name on the bridge that would be finished, every new generation that came thereafter forgot what exactly was the name of the one who had started it.

Sedes Stercoraria

As if specially designed for the coming of the Beast, heaven and hell concocted one of Italy's coldest winters in memory, not coincidently after the wettest autumn, which by no chance followed the hottest summer.

In Rome, almost a foot of snow covered the ground. For the first time in almost a decade, the city looked clean. Filth was hidden under the white coating of winter. The Tevere was frozen and markets were closed. Pilgrims, beggars and the homeless had taken refuge in the city's churches, hospitals and monasteries, praying for protection against the Beast on that coming Christmas, believed by many to be their last. Streets were empty and silent, only broken by the cawing of hooded crows scavenging for dejecta.

On the Tusculan heights, a large man dragged his boots alone in a frozen garden, making a double track on the white path.

'Where is that imbecile?' stormed Albericus as he burst open the front doors of his son's palace. He stomped his frozen boots through the stairs, to stand in the well-lit centre of the hall, legs firmly planted on the marble floor and bellowing with all the power of his wide lungs.

'Where-is-he?'

Like a blast of frightened mice, a number of servants scattered around in all directions. After peering out to verify the his master's potential for hazard, the butler approached with a shy and extremely cautious pace, but something else had caught the Tusculan Count attention – one of the upper room's door was being carefully, but not very silently, shut.

Albericus dashed to his son's dormitory, but the door had just been quickly locked from inside. He did not bother about demanding that they opened it, for his immense stature and the weight of a fat ox would be enough to bring the door down. The first kick shook the whole palace, but hinges and lock resisted it well. The door was still firmly closed.

'Wait, wait!' shouted a voice from inside, 'I'm opening it!'

The door squeaked open to reveal a shy smile of a young woman. Looking incredibly fresh and livid from a morning bath, she had her long brown hair tied on a precarious knot behind her head. Bright brown eyes were embarrassedly shooting to the sides, searching for a comfortable target to rest upon. One delicate hand maintained a woollen blanket wrapped around her body. Before entering, as she still held the door semi-opened, Albericus visually inspected her from head to toe and calculated how that adorable figure must have looked bare-naked beneath that heavy fabric. Trying to ease her awkwardness, the count relaxed his posture and forced a sympathetic smile, which, to such an attractive morsel, came smooth and gentle. Enchanted by Albericus's controlled and somehow elegant attitude, she finally let the door go and stepped aside. The count entered the room and once more exploded into rage, for he did not like what he saw.

The room was musky warm, ranking of wine and sin. Lying on the bed, sleeping like a mastiff and entangled in linens and pelts was Theophylactus, his son, totally naked. The young man's body was painted in red and green, and his bony face all smeared up with lipstick. A puddle of dried vomit was connected to his gapping mouth by a string that vibrated at every clattering snore. Beside and across him, in an entanglement of thighs, legs, arms and long bundles of hair, two women also slept, with their spectacular naked bodies relaxed into some rather inelegant positions. Legs were crookedly thrown to the sides, showing clearly, naïvely and quite bluntly their majestic pudenda. Green paint handprints decorated symmetrically the round buttocks of one of the girls.

'What the in the hell happened here?' his shout thundered through the palace.

'We…had a…party, last night, Messer', explained the girl who answered the door, with an apologetic but lovely leer on her face.

I know what happened here, you silly cow, thought Albericus, but he spared the girl from that harsh comment, for the energetic Count was already forecasting some other plans with the beauty later on that day. Again, without much effort, he produced an amicable smile and delicately asked the girl to get dressed, fetch some water and call the servants for help.

'But don't leave this house. Stay around', he said with a wink 'I want to see you later today'.

Without any attempt to cover the nudity of his son, and so irritated that he paid no attention to the women's bodies, he disentangled Theophylactus from their legs and dragged him out of bed. As Albericus waited, he looked at the undignified body of his son, scattered across the floor in front of him. He was starting to wonder if Theophylactus was actually the best option for the post. *It doesn't really matter*, he thought, *he is the only choice*.

One of the women in bed woke up and rolled over, trying to set her puzzled eyes on that noisy man who had invaded the room. Albericus spat with despise when he finally saw her face. 'You!'

She tasted the foul bitterness of her own tongue and ignored the count, turning around again and pulling a bear pelt to cover part of her nakedness.

Albericus advanced and grabbed her by the hair 'If you want to be a whore,' he whispered with gritted teeth on her ear, 'Go ahead, fornicate with every creature alive, and sleep with your own damned dogs. But please leave your brother out of this excrescence which you've made of your life!'

She was snoring soundly when the count finished the sentence.

The butler at last appeared with a jug of luke-warm lavender-scented water and a set of towels. Albericus threw his massive hands up 'No, not this' explained the count patiently, 'I want a pail of very cold water; water from the troughs outside. We've got to wake up this man!'

Theophylactus opened his eyes wide at the first generous slap his father gave him. The smack did burn on his cheek, but actually awoke him for much more pain. The sensation of the heaviest of mallets, pounding mercilessly the inside of his head.

'You cretin' started the count. 'Do I have to tell you that a *baccanalle* like this mess in here is not appropriate for a man of your cast? And least for the post you're about to receive. All the servants must have seen your sister here!'

'I did not fornicate with my sister'.

The count sighed dramatically 'What difference does it...'

But Theophylactus intervened with a crooked smirk on his face '...we did *other things*!'

At this moment, the sober girl who'd opened the door was already dressed, helping the butler in with a bucket of cold dirty water he had fetched from the stables. Incensed with fury, refraining from just about strangling that delinquent that was his own son, Albericus seized Theophylactus by the neck and, as he saw the pail, quickly dragged him and dipped the head inside the water, keeping it there for a desperate while. The count just watched his son's painted limbs fidgeting about, like a grasshopper, trapped in a child's hand. After what he reckoned as being a reasonable and safe time underwater to get the young man back into his senses, he let it go.

Theophylactus gasped out, stunned. Panting heavily, he shot an odious look of blood-engorged bulging eyes at his father. 'You bastard!' he snarled, after vomiting enough to fill the pail 'You should be respecting me now' and he arrogantly extended the back of his hand towards the count.

'I am not going to kiss your ring' observed Albericus calmly as he held Theophylactus wrist and threw it down. 'You are still nothing! You are nobody, until tomorrow comes. Meanwhile, just do what I tell you.' He held his son by the arm and pulled the young man out of the room, completing 'and you can shove this silly ring up your arse – you will be wearing the proper ring tomorrow, when you finally become the pope.'

Twenty-year old Theophylactus ascended to St. Peter's chair just before Christmas celebrations in the year 1032. He took the name of Benedict IX. His father, Count Albericus III of Tusculum, was worried. They had climbed as high as they could get. Now, the time was as delicate as ever for the family. There was no affording a fall against the emperor.

We cannot fail now, thought Albericus gravely, as his son grinned maliciously when a page touched his scrotum at the sedes stercoraria, during the papal inauguration in the Lateran.

If you follow the steps of your uncles and do as I say, our family will prevail.

'*Confirmatum est. Habemus papam!*' the page declared. And the Cardinals cheered.

LUCCA, almost half a century after

'That's it!' the pope said, raising his stubby fingers on the air. 'I will not have any more of these lies.'

'Excuse me?' Lando delle Rocche asked, with a touch of annoyance and a faint glow of fear in his heart.

'Yes, that is what you heard! Lies! And I will not tolerate any more of it,' said Pope Gregory. He jumped from his chair and raised a hand for a *vassalus*.

In mesmerised silence, the cantastorie watched the pope leaving the hall while a vassalus bowed his head to a level lower than the pontiff's. And as for his cousin the contessa, Lando had the impression that she was about to boil inside, ready to explode, like a toad that has been pinched with salt.

Old Albertazzo broke the quietness with a snort. 'Will the Beatissimo Padre just leave then? With the story unfinished? The man is only telling us the story that we all asked him to. If you cannot deal with the truth –'

'Keep quiet, old man!' barked the contessa. She raised a commanding finger to Lando. 'The Beatissimo Padre has had enough of your filthy lies,' she hissed, short from foaming. And so have I, but I will give you one more chance to tell me the truth.' Meanwhile, the vassalus slammed the big door shut after the pope left.

Lando laughed nervously. 'The Beatissimo Padre is only respecting some of the old traditions of the Mother Church.'

'Such as protecting the sanctity of the names of his predecessors,' said Albertazzo, 'as if their faults would stain the grandeur of the office they occupy, and most importantly, turning away from the truth.'

The contessa leaned back fanning her face in a staged restedness, but her shooting eyes did not betray her, neither the bulge under her chin, swollen with rage like a fat gourd. Lando just lowered his head, fearing what Matilda could do.

She ground her teeth before being able to growl 'By insulting the pope, you insult me, you insult Bishop Liutprando and you insult all Christendom, including you two oafs, if you dare to call yourselves Christians.' She closed her fan with a snap and threw it to the side. 'Right now I could care little whether you are my cousins, as your blasphemies could put you to burn. I'd personally dispose your guts to the fish in the Serchio, but I do need to know the rest of this story. So sit quiet, old man, or I will send you away, and you, Lando, keep to the story and no more suggestions of clerical lewdness.'

Bishop Liutprando had no words for the moment. Lando couldn't help but open a shy smile of aquiescense.

'Do you understand me?' the contessa shut his smirk.

'I do, Contessa Matilda,' he said with a theatrical bow. And he knew that nothing would make him change his story. Dangerous or not, he just could not tell a different version from the truth.

When a downcast Julian finished rowing the last member of the papal committee across the Serchio, he made the final recommendations for those on horse who could not cross, to ride down though the crooked eastern bank path.

The sky had turned grey and going towards black. At least a swollen river would wash away some of the smouldering remains of their dream. It was painful to look up the valley and see the pillars of the broken bridge standing out of the black debris. He sighed deeply and entered the hospital, just to hear Clarissa's voice inside.

'Are you mad as well?' she was asking angry, 'Have you all eaten a fly too?'

Julian knew this was not with him. He hurried to find a visibly distressed Clarissa facing a table where some villagers from Chifenti, Traghetto and Anchiano sat huddled. Amadeo of the tavern and Bernardo delle Rocche were sitting there among them.

Amadeo stood up as soon as he saw Julian. 'Maria Tenebrosa is right, Julian. We can say anything about her wickedness, but Maria Maddalena of the Cunimundinghi was always right from the beginning. She knows about the arts of the enemy. We have not succeeded in raising this bridge and no matter even if we have the support of the Mother Church of Rome, the failure takes over, sooner or later. It's clear now: the river needs its blood to allow us to take the bridge.

Julian held Clarissa's trembling hand and faced Amadeo 'What are you talking about?'

The taverner lowered his gaze 'Sacrifice, Julian. That's what is needed.'

A deadly silence froze the hospital hall.

Julian tried to capture anyone's eyes, but they all held their gazes low. He looked at Bernardo, who seemed to be distracted with devising how many positions an empty goblet could find on the table. 'Bernardo!' Julian called. Under the shelter of his matted grey mane, the shepherd flashed his violet gaze on Julian for the blink of an eye and came back to the goblet. Julian insisted 'What do you make of this insanity? Do you support this? Sacrifice is murder!'

Bernardo played so much with the goblet that it slipped from his grasp and popped to an unreachable corner of the table. He cleared his throat and said, without meeting Julian's stare: 'The woman in Anchiano could be right, Julian. This bridge is accursed. We will never have it. She's been suggesting blood for years. We should have used the pope. That bastard would have made the perfect foundation sacrifice.'

'You are all mad!' Julian said. 'What do you know about devils? You're all mad!'

Book 5: The Bridge of Borgo a Mozzano

The Altar

Many were those days when the Serchio was covered in ice. During that relentless winter, lone travellers would venture on across the white shell to reach the warmth of the hospital. Like a broken ribcage of a rotting giant, the unfinished pillars of the bridge stuck out of the ice cap. Lonely arched piles of stone, sheltering pigeons and silently watching the slow movement of the ice and its passengers, a frozen dragon, waiting for the people of the Serchio to make a decision.

A decision to succeed on finishing the bridge. A choice that could fall onto death.

Julian entered the woods and calmly started his ascend to the hill whose original name has long been forgotten, standing tall right between the hospital, Chifenti and the another hill, where the village of Bertagna observed. Sheltered by the higher Apennines, this deserted mound was capped with a cemetery on the clearing of what had once been a vineyard. An eerie cold and forgotten place they called 'Altar'. Julian had been there before. The place where he and Clarissa had *felt* the angel. And he wanted to feel Ish again.

The barren spaces between the naked trunks offered him innumerable choices for a white, silent path. Winter days were usually reinvigorating for Julian. He would be walking out before dawn, filling his lungs with icy fresh air, watching the crystals of dew taking shine as the sun revealed the splendour of the valley. He would seize the best out of everything, infecting those he cared for, making life more bearable to swallow.

On that morning though, Julian was inexplicably sad. The vaults of clouds just did not have the right hue of grey. The wintry stillness was muffled by the gusty whistle that blew around his ears. The chalky frost was not glowing and an implacable temperature was lashing the skin. His right shoulder ached, as if misery was chewing on his bones. His fingers where numb and a strange taste of acrid wine made his stomach twist around itself.

Half the way up to the summit, he turned back to view the Traghetto. Melancholic roofs were bent down to the rage of the weather. No living soul was venturing out. A dog barked somewhere behind an alley. The squeak of a window shutter escaped from the gentle silence of the breeze. A muffled voice shouted at children in some domestic shed. Julian thought he heard a faint roaring noise, but it could have been just the ice cap of the river readjusting itself to new volumes of the current underneath. The individual paths down to the river stretched across the western bank, forming a chain of dark shapes, like an arched back of a black skeleton, its arms reaching out for help.

For help Julian was going to the Altar.

Years had passed since he had settled his life around the hospital, just below that hallowed ground. Who knew the tales of saints and witches, warriors and chiefs, monks, hermits, lovers and sacrifices that had been forgotten about the old cemetery? Bernardo delle Rocche could tell some of them and made others up. Not a live soul could then remember the last to be put to rest on that pinnacle, for it had actually been since the great flood, two centuries before. In those times, a group of villagers, inflamed by the local parishioner, climbed the hill and destroyed the old flat statues of pagan gods, who stood still like tombstones, proclaiming the memory of the deceased. Hardly had the last crumb of stone been broken when the rain started. After a couple of weeks, entire villages been washed away by the Serchio. And to remind the people of Chifenti of the forces in charge of the torrential rain, mudslides had brought ripe corpses down the hill, leaving ghastly jumbled remains of the deceased hanging around the woods, as the populace squeezed for shelter at the edge of the village.

For help Julian was going to the Altar.

He needed to put a definitive stop to that nonsense, which in one way or another, he felt he needed to share the blame. It was he who had idealised the bridge. It was he who had first talked about the bridge. It was his so-called saintly reputation who had convinced the people of Anchiano, Mutianum, Traghetto, Chifenti, Fornulo and Corsena of the need for a bridge. And after all, he felt that it was he who was leading a group of people to build a bridge. And now they seemed to be ready to accept sacrifice, maybe even to commit murder.

But it was *not* him leading them. Julian was a Saint, although he did not believe it. He would give his life to save anybody's, as he had already proven, to earth and to heavens. There was just no more hate or indictment in his heart to point the finger to the true responsible for such a monstrosity. From that moment, he wanted to take it in his own hands and nobody else's.

Julian finally reached the Altar, that peaceful clearing in the thin woods capping the hill. There were no devisable tombstones, or crosses, or any sign of a grave at all. There were just the black eyes of a few birches, now mistrustfully guarding the graveyard. A thick moist carpet of brown leaves had some of its folds sticking out of the gelid snow. It was a cold, windy and lonely place. That's where Julian had gone for help and where he would make the next most dreadful decision of his life.

Julian knew that Immanuel Ben Malachi had never hidden his past from anybody. Rather than deny it, endeavouring to be perceived as a local that he would never be, he made the most of his origins and the great adventure to his destiny. It was told that many times after the evening meal, in the earlier days of baths, he would congregate with his children around the table and tell stories, emulating the best antics of Bernardo delle Rocche, with flickering lanterns flashing a yellow mantle on his face. The little man would grow with his shadows, bigger as the tales took shape and developed into quests. He'd raise his eyebrows in an arch, bringing them back, diving down into the centre of his forehead, as he recounted his tales of sordid luck when he roamed through distant lands. The children were proud of their father and his adventures. Those were the times when Maria Maddalena was a girl, her gray eyes attentively watching the gestures of the man who was one of the only living heroes around those curves of the Serchio: her father Immanuel. The stories were so remarkable that it seems Maria particularly never forgot one of them: the one which spoke of being buried alive.

What exactly was the taste of life that had curdled Maria's soul, Julian could comprehend. Perhaps just out of random nature, her bitterness grew to a point of hazing childhood memories, as if she had forgotten them all. Of crimes, she was culpable of many, but what sin had she been swept by? Maybe *superbia* – better translated as *arrogance*, as an alternative to *pride* – was probably the case, for it was one of the red-headed girl's specialities. *Superbia* was considered as the worse of the sins, ever since the Book of Proverbs. Apart from her recent venture into wilful heresy, Maria had already accumulated a number of peccadilloes and crimes that could be sorted through an official Cardinal list, fulfilling every level. Such talent would surely put her as one of the most perverse personalities on those Tuscan lands. She could be accountable for arrogance, wickedness, avarice, perversion, gossip, pestering, lying, despise, blackmail, falsehood, dishonesty, cruelty, defamation, theft, indifference, felony, violence and murder.

Now it seemed to Julian that the powerful Lady of Anchiano, who had climbed high on the ladders of nobility, wanted to share this privilege of perpetrating evil with as many people as she could possibly convince. No matter how much the people of the Serchio kept their thoughts to themselves, it was inevitable that poisonous words about live entombments in the bridge had even reached the ears of the Lucchese. While neither Battista Burle made himself publically believe the rumours nor the parish clerk Antonio, who had always seen the best in that strange woman, Bishop Giovanni was careful about the Lady of Anchiano, especially after the madness of John XIX, dismissing the gossip and ignoring further stories, as long as the church was safe and that she remained a loyal faithful.

Julian knew that Giacomo opposed those notions but stayed silent at the Burle House of Trade, while in Corsena, among the other siblings who silently acquiesced to the only solution to carry on with the bridge's work, Domenico vocally supported Immanuel against Maria Maddalena's proposals.

The routine for Maria was a constant harassment of Mira, Cara and Muscatta, who blindly supported their sister's absurdities, all in the name of a finished bridge to facilitate access to Corsena and to allegedly keep a decent union within the emerging family. As for Maria, she had become a frequent presence in the hospital, the tavern in Chifenti and the baths in Corsena, on daily rides along that route. While putting a smile on her hard face, lighting up those grey eyes and being somewhat careful about stepping on people with lower merits than herself, she could never fool Julian and Clarissa, who knew there was an empty space in her chest.

Julian saw little of Spatula, always kept distant and hidden, and Ginevra was vocal about Maria's presence in Chifenti as nauseating as Arrigo's. The taverner's daughter had lately complained about the young Cunimundinghi harassing her some favours, but Maria's constant presence kept him at bay, which made Amadeo quite happy about it.

But Julian and Clarissa knew Maria Maddalena. The nature of the devil. The human nature.

Clarissa was not at ease. She couldn't stop worrying about her husband, out on the hill, alone under that freezing drizzle. If that was not the ghastliest of winters that the Serchio had ever seen, it surely felt as the worst of days. Activity in the hospital was dramatically intensified with the weather, but so was the volunteering. She was able to keep up with demand with the help of Mira and Cara from Corsena, and a battalion of wives, moving around like headless geese, seemingly aimless but with expedition, bringing pots and pans back and forth to thaw the frozen soul of the travellers. With an eye on the weather, Clarissa recruited a couple of brutes to help her fetch more logs, worthy a day's fire. As soon as she had the firewood being unloaded into the hospital, she filled a skin with wine, another with hot boiling broth, which she knew would spoil the hide, rolled a leg of lamb into some parchment and set out for the Altar.

As she left the hospital, little tiny sparks of the whitest down filled the air. She hastened her pace, which made her teeth ache as the midday air filled her mouth.

Oh, God, please keep him warm…Please, protect him. As she prayed for her beloved she did not take special notice of the strange herbal smell that came down with the gelid wind from the Altar.

Julian was not aware of the cold. Not that his body wasn't being hardly beaten by the chill of the snow. His lips were swollen dry, cracking open in bloody thrushes, the hair on the back of his frozen hands was standing up and a foggy, icy gelatine seemed to haze his vision. A faint wind blew around his red ears, but so ferociously cold that it hardened the thick long tongues of black hair that fell around his shoulders. The air was glistening with crystals, floating in different directions and accumulating as white chalk over his hairline. Nevertheless, he was dangerously in peace with the elements. The Hospitaller had all senses funnelled into something he had hardly done for years: a prayer.

Whereas many people pray with their heads, making it a mind exercise, Julian prayed with his heart, making it a work of love. He wanted just an answer, the faintest spark of light into that people. He was searching for the proper direction to unroll the hank, so that it would not get bigger and heavier. God had to be powerful, and He had to be righteous! There should be a way out of that cave, a well that was getting darker and deeper.

So much was Julian unaware of his surroundings that he never noticed a pair of black eyes watching him. Those were eyes that had already seen much more than any living soul could ever claim to. They were set on the sides of a raven's head, a creature seldom seen at those heights or latitudes. The fat bird silently perched on a lower branch at the rim of the clearing. It was studying the man in prayer, waiting for that flash of sensitivity that few could experience, making possible a communion between the world of the living and the world of the dead and the unborn.

Julian's heart was bursting with prayer and devotion. The Hospitaller was nearing that moment. He could feel the soaring sensation. He would catch his angel.

His spirit was about to float and his heart would speak. Only his physical being would be present on that clearing then, which made the raven concerned. It could be excessively dangerous. The black bird decided to show up as human. To get rid of that noxious outfit and take what been its usual form. It had to be careful, though. Would it choose the right shape? Depending on how much would Julian remember of their previous encounters, he could not be mislead into error.

A ferocious guff of wind punched its way through the clearing, breaking the calmness of the gelid air. Julian was numb, in communion with God. Giving up his senses, he let himself been taken away by the darkness that embraced his thoughts, hoping to become part of God. The raven realised the urge and was just about to reveal itself when it noticed, through the thick drapes of gelid mist, that the Hospitaller had lost its senses and fallen asleep into the frozenness. His body being tenderly covered by the snowfall.

It started with music in his heart. Than it was a tingling of chimes that travelled through his body and stopped at his head. After a few rounds, the rhythm metamorphosed into Clarissa's voice, far and diffuse. Julian had never heard such a soothing tingling. As the call repeated itself, it became clear that it was indeed from Clarissa, for his name. But he did not want to leave that position. He was so comfortable that it felt as if he floated, devoid of body. The call came again, loud and near, startling the Hospitaller and breaking the wholeness of that peace. It made him open his eyes and at once he realised the severity of the snow.

He had slept, comfortably stretched on his side, on the soft carpet of ice flakes. But now the cold hit him like a boulder. He stood up painfully, shaking the snow from his mantle.

'Thanks the Lord, for you are alive!' exclaimed Clarissa alleviated, as she approached the centre of the clearing. 'You silly old goat! Look at you. Who do you think you are?' She handed him the skin with the broth.

'Forgive me if I made you worried'. He gasped as the first gush of the hot liquid left a burning track from the tongue down to his stomach. The heat then started to spread, like a vine of fire crawling and invading every chilled muscle of his body.

'You don't have to apologise, my love. Do it, but for yourself. It is cold and unprotected here. You are not doing any good for you, and that also hurts me!' She smiled as a nice blush came back to his pale and still strong face. 'Here, take the wine now. I got some lamb too, very cold already.'

'My dear Clarissa, you have left your duties... what is of the hospital? It is kind enough that you've come all this way to give me food and wine, but this skin is going to be spoiled by the broth, and there are still so many travellers trying to shelter from the cold. Besides, I don't think we have a good opportunity to spend time making love here today.'

Clarissa's eyes shone brightly, making the snow colourful with its rainbow. 'Well, I could stay here, for they don't need me down there. Today we have Mira and Cara from Corsena, Marta, Domitila, Catarina and Rosa from Anchiano, Carlo, Giovanni, Cristina and Giulietta from the Traghetto, Adelmo, Fantina and all the group from –'

'*Of course,*' interrupted Julian with a sorrowful sarcasm, now his breathing suddenly spewing vapours of concern and indignation on the freezing air. 'The people of the Serchio will help the *Saint's wife*, but they will not listen to the *Saint himself*, not even if to put reason in their minds and hearts.'

'What can we do, Julian? Nobody, not even Maria Maddalena will admit to it, but it is brewing.' Clarissa hug him strongly. Body warmth and heart passion to comfort her husband.

Julian delicately disengaged himself from her embrace. 'That's the reason I want to stay here, by myself.' His voice was faint. He moved his eyes around the glade, 'I am in search of some enlightenment.'

Clarissa inspected the surroundings with sad but understanding eyes, sighing 'If I never knew who you are, or what this clearing looked like when we were here once, I would think that such a dreadful place would only be an inspiration for *endarkenment*'.

Julian was opening a grin when they heard the neigh from across the dale, on the eastern hillside.

'Blood of Jesus!' said Julian, 'what on God's world are they doing up there?'

From that distance, it looked like they were all dressed up quite lavishly. Carriers with bundles on their heads broke through the bushes, creating a straight path on the snowy hill. The man on the horse was the most striking contrast to the monotony of wintery leafless branches. Rich colourful mantles shone like feathers of a peacock, or the talking birds from the East, which the Saracens called *babbaghah*. The horse was carefully choosing its steps on the slippery snow, the steep slope livened by noise and colour.

Julian and Clarissa were not sure if the caravan had seen them yet, or even, given the way they were not using any known path, whether those people knew at all that Chifenti was just across the next rise.

'Hello, here!' Julian's sudden and loud call startled his wife but also indicated that some of his strength had returned.

None of the carriers looked up at the shout, but the rider waived. The wind brought a jolly chuckle across the gorge to the observing couple. Julian proceeded with clear and loud instructions. 'Follow this valley straight to the river. Then stay on the path south to the hospital. There you will be able to cross the ice to the Traghetto and Mutianum, where there's a better road to Lucca. You will find food and shelter the first village, or at the hospital...' He babbled those last words with distraction, for something bizarre had caught his attention. 'Clarissa, can you see the carriers?'

'Their size...' Clarissa shaded her eyes with her hand, 'Are they children? Oh sweet God, Julian, how can they bear such a big load?'

'It must not be. They do not move like children...' he saw the rider shouting orders to the carriers ahead, who turned immediately west, towards the river trail. The language was bizarre, more like a series of hums.

With a small, but sharp chill of concern, Julian turned to his wife.

'You better go back, my dear. Looks like your full house is getting some more visitors.' He kissed her gently on her forehead. 'I will stay here. I just want some peace to be able to pray more.'

Clarissa was going to try one last plead to get Julian to come down the hill with her, but she saw the shine on her husband's black eyes. They were reflecting the sun, which had just sneaked out from a breach through the heavy clouds. She kissed him on the lips and set out to her obligations.

The Hospitaller closed his eyes and called for God. He did not see what the raven on the birch witnessed. Across the glade, the bird was casually fluffing his heavy feathers with the gross beak, but deviously observing the rider splitting from the rest of the group, riding up towards the Altar. To meet the *Saint*.

And Julian looked up to the sky, which was strangely opening into a bright blue, a tone that the Tuscan lands had not seen for many a fortnight during that horrible winter.

Seth

'You are a *what?*' Julian knew exactly what he had heard, but he could hardly believe somebody was actually resurrecting that term. As soon as he asked, he was filled with regret for the inflection of mockery that accompanied his what.

'A *businessman*, my friend' responded the rider still grinning, apparently oblivious to Julian's sarcasm. He threw himself from the saddle with amazing grace for a man of his bulk. 'It's a rather new term... Well, in reality it just hasn't been used since the times when the Caesars were actually Romans.'

He patted the neck of his ride with vigour. It was probably the most formidable horse Julian had ever seen. The white stallion stood like a marble sculpture, gleaming and steaming, proud of its strength and impervious to its rider's generous size. It had the elegance of the steeds from the Saracens, but much more overpowering, like a giant destrier, with the built and volume of the best workhorses he had seen at the Maine. The heavy rider had a well-groomed silver beard, with a long friendly moustache covering his upper lip. His big blue eyes were frank and full of light, with heavy eye pouches pulling down a strip of red flesh showing below, contrasting with the dark ink that highlighted the contour of the eyes, in a foreign fashion of Saracen kind. Julian could recognise the clothes of a merchant, actually what would have been any tradesman best merchandise. His tunic had the finest work of wool, gleaming with the sudden benevolent weather. Sleeves and edges lined with the shiny silk fabrics, with seemingly eastern motives. A Genovese barret topped his ample forehead. He held his cap as he elegantly bowed to Julian.

'Or else, if you prefer, you may call me a *Man of Affairs.*'

As they were speaking a jam of languages that spiced up the Old Latin in the Lombard lands, the rider was utilising the word *Negotiator* – businessman. It derived from the Latin term *neg ocium*, which literally means a denial of sloth. Equally, the term *Affari* - affairs - meant *something to be done.*

Julian was no longer listening to the rider. The unusual presence of that magnificent figure on the Altar, a desert place where not even the folk of Chifenti or Bertagna ever roamed, the unnatural sequence of events, made he immediately tumble into an exciting torrent of speculations. The weather, the horse, the children, those extraordinary clothes. Losing his composure, he tripped as he eagerly rushed to the merchant, holding both of the visitor's hands, almost half-kneeling in front of the big old man.

'Did... anybody sent you to see me?'

To Julian's disappointment, the rider burst into a contagious laugh, holding his belly as it bounced. 'Doesn't the good Lord open all the paths for our ways?'

The Hospitaller stepped back. He blinked nervously before explaining more clearly his enquiry. 'What I mean is: are you here specifically to meet me?'

'Does it look like I am here on this hill to meet anybody else?' The merchant looked around theatrically, as if searching for someone.

Julian was puzzled. 'So, *why* are you here?'

'Well then, why are *you* here?' rebated the merchant, mocking a serious expression and poking Julian's chest with his ring-covered finger.

Julian gave up. After a brief pause, he raised one eyebrow. 'Is this a game of *questions only*?'

The merchant was quick 'Why? Do you want to play?'

They both exploded into honest laughter, echoing their joy through the quiet valleys. After so many dark weeks of silence, a sore period for Julian's plans, nothing felt better than that spillage of bliss under protection of a clear spring sky. They secretly enjoyed that strange moment of bondage, two men cackling in the middle of a lonely frozen cemetery, lost on the cold peaks by the Tuscan Apennines.

It was the merchant who cut the giggling, with a less melodramatic pitch, sounding almost forthright. 'I did see a lady here with you...'

'Clarissa, my wife,' cut Julian immediately, recovering his composure. 'We run a hospital by this side of the river. She ran back to attend your...uh, servants?'

'Oh, she never had to...they can take care of themselves.'

'Their size,' Julian was being careful, afraid of insulting the foreigner, 'they wouldn't be juvenile, would they?'

'Oh, not at all,' his face took a serious, *businesslike* expression. 'But it doesn't surprise me you may have mistaken them for brood. My good aides are actually a different breed of people,' he extended his arm back, without looking at it, opening his hand, fat stretched fingers pointing to five different directions. 'They come from a faraway country.'

Again, that vagueness sounded too obvious for Julian. 'Really? I never knew...' but he decided not to extend into what the merchant made secretive. It would be best to find out if that man could help him or not. If he couldn't be of any use he would excuse himself and resume prayer. 'I am Julian,' he bent courteously 'but I don't think you told me your name.'

The merchant dragged his right foot across the snow, revealing the brown leaves beneath it. He had a fancy leather shoe, with its tip curled up, pointing back to his shanks, one that Julian had only seen on the eastern lands. He kept looking down. 'Well, my dear Julian, believe it or not, people call me different names everywhere I go.'

'What is your original name then?'

'Coming from a businessman, which folk will often perceive as untrustworthy, you will have to take my word that, at this point, I cannot even recall what I was called, to start with.' He studied Julian reaction, which was imperceptible, except for an eyebrow craving to be raised. Lining up his belts, the man opened his blue eyes as wide as he could 'For you Julian, maybe you can call me Seth. It's an Egyptian name, if you want to know, but I am not Egyptian.'

'Are you from the Holy Land?'

'Not from the Holy Land that you must be thinking, but it is certainly holy where I was born!'

Julian was about to open his mouth when the merchant continued 'but we're not here to talk about my life. We are here for business. What can I do for you?'

Before answering, Julian looked up to the blue skies, his eyes soaked in tears. A smile broke out of his face and he whispered to the azure 'Thank you!'

The raven watched the two men talking for more than an hour. As most corvi, it had excellent vision, appropriate for spotting prey or carrion when flying, but lacked a good long distance hearing. Its ears were more accustomed to their clumsy loud call, not to the distant words of men. There were few of those words that it heard clearly, and little would have one made out of it, especially as they all came jumbled, as if from just one voice.

...bridge?... show it... glade... down across... next to... hospital... pilgrims... Lucca... Traghetto... Bagni... idea... support... good start... why not?... fire... collapse... superstitious... foundations... monstrous... hopeless... talk to them... engineering... can do it... my men... faster... imagine... about you?... me?... you... me?... thought... had me... had you... lost you... always... me... yours... deal?... who... you?... afraid... deal... bridge... cross... soul... you...deal?... you are... for me... for others... need it... deal!

The raven, however, knew one of them. It understood it.

And then, they were shaking hands.

See, I have no weapons, touch my hand...I see, you come in peace too. Not that the Hospitaller and the merchant actually exchanged those words, but they were practising a sacrament of mutual understanding and trust, that strange ritual of shaking hands, which had been widespread throughout Europe, especially among the freemen. Lords and vassals were still affirming their vows to their appropriate rankings and causes by the kiss on the noble's sword, a remnant of the touching each other's testicles as done in biblical times. Merchants and burgesses just shook hands.

'Will you descend with me to the riverside? I'm sure we will find a place in our hospital –'

'Thank you for your kindness, Julian, but you should better go to your wife. She needs help. I bring fairness to this peak,' he said without a hint of mockery on his face. 'The weather down in the river is not that forgiving. And for any matter, I will be around here, waiting for you.'

'Will you help me Seth?'

'I just hope it's not too late when you make a decision to let me start it. Remember, you still have to convince the folk.'

'I know, and that's why I still need some time.'

'Farewell, Julian.'

The raven watched Julian heading back to the hospital. With a loud croak, it took off from the birch and flew ungraciously down the hill.

'How can you put up with this crap?' murmured Maria Maddalena to no one in particular, but loud enough to allow host Clarissa to hear it. 'What is this wine made of? Cow dung?' The hospital hall was full.

'Actually,' started Mira, 'I think it tastes splendidly.'

Clarissa made a casual remark, unaffected, without stopping her serving duties. 'You are welcome to leave, if you don't like it, Maria Maddalena.'

Maria stood insulted 'I have a responsibility over the welfare of these lands,' she proclaimed in a crescendo now, almost on a public speech tone. 'Travellers deserve much better than crumbs in my lands.'

'So these lands belong to the witch now, do they?' said a voice out of the dining crowd.

Maria turned around fast as lightning, as if she had a sword to pin it through that insolent's neck. But there were just too many people, all eating, everybody looking at their food. It could have been any of them. If she could just tell where the voice came from. She watched for a few seconds until, quite innocently, her sister Mira intervened.

'Shut up, Carlo!' Mira said indignantly, 'Maria Maddalena's husband Fulcardo was granted all of these lands by the bishopric of Lucca. Now, it's just that another bishop has taken it away for the hospital. It's only a matter of time before the lands are back on Cunimundinghi hands.'

Carlo, a boatman from Fornulo, swore at Mira between his clenched teeth, but whitened with fear of what was to come one day. All the locals saw the lines on Maria's face hardening further. They did not need much creativity to construct the words she must have been thinking of while she measured Carlo from head to toes: *So, I think this little shit is going to be our offering to the bridge.*

Satisfied with the denouncement, Maria Maddalena sighed arrogantly and pretended to forget about the boatman. She drank a sip of her father's mulberry wine and turned to Clarissa, without necessarily addressing her. 'I have discussed my suggestion of a bridge with the bishop, the Obertenghi, even the Corvaresi and the Porcaresi.' Maria said 'and they do agree that its immediate completion is crucial for the future of our communities. Nevertheless, it is quite obvious, even to the thickest head amongst yourselves, that the responsible for the bridge's planning and construction was rather incompetent.'

'Of course he must have been' completed the sisters Mira and Cara, in unison. 'He's not worked in it since before the fall.'

Maria continued, 'We do know that sacrifices must be made for lifetime achievements, but it looks like our home *saint* will not accept what Abraham did, for his own...'

She was cut by a loud thump, when Clarissa put her tureen on the table, where diners quickly took care of it. 'I feel sorry for you two, Mira and Cara. So naïve and so imbecile.' She then pointed a stiff finger to Maria Madallena. 'But you, *hag*, you will step on any child's head just to prove your niggard points and proceed with your execrable schemes.'

'Be careful, Clarissa.' Maria had a strange smile on her face. 'The Lord might think that the relics of a Saint or his family will hold better the bridge pillars in place!'

'So which *Lord* is exactly this one you're thinking about?'

A strange shadow fell on Maria's brow. 'How dare do you —'

The door was kicked in. An intrusive gelid wind swept through the chamber as a large figure clad in furs and mantles slammed the door into its place, quieting the howl of the windy night outside. As the creature kicked its boots on the wall to get rid of the chunky snow and mud, it pulled down the cloak to reveal a shaggy bearded face, a matted long mane of gray hair, rosy cheeks from the cold and passionate violet eyes. Everybody recognised the wild, but friendly features of Bernardo Delle Rocche, the shepherd landlord of the Western bank.

Bernardo's unusual presence put everybody back on their seats as it cooled down the heated humours. He looked around the room, swivelling his dripping red nose, like a hedgehog trying to sniff worms. Bernardo Delle Rocche made everybody at ease when he spoke, letting the cantastorie side of the Obertenghi out. Instruction for a man like Bernardo, even if from his time at a monastery, was seen as at least odd, especially by the highest classes in the fields and several priests along the valley. His excellent relation with the peasants, his enviable wealth and, above all, his success in survival passed unnoticed to landlords such as Maria Maddalena, who could only see his strange ways and aversion to a harsher treatment of the peasantry as a weakness.

'Pardon my intrusiveness…' he said in a very un-shepherdly manner. All eyes were geared to that rosy matted head sticking out of a mountain of fur. 'It is…I was told…asked…I came…' The silence made him a bit nervous. Apathetic faces just made the wind outside roar with more fury. He swallowed the stringy paste that his dried saliva had become and announced: 'There's been a death.'

Maria jumped up, spilling all her mulberry wine on the table. Mira seemed to ignore the announcement and quickly reached for her apron to try and absorb some of it, for the precious liquor should not be vainly wasted.

'Excellent! Who is it? *Who is it?* The news was so stupendous for Maria that she could not even disguise her satisfaction.

Bernardo Delle Rocche looked down and tried to open his mouth. He took another breath and kept switching his gaze from Maria' eyes to the shadows on the wall behind her, but nothing came out.

'Go on, oh silly man, spit it out!'

In face of such indelicacy from the big woman, he gulped and said it, facing her fiery eyes 'It's your father, Maria Madallena. I am heartily sorry to inform you that my friend Immanuel Ben Malachi is dead.'

Julian was just approaching the perimeter of the hospital. As the merchant had forecasted, down by the river the weather was worse. He was dragging his feet across the carpet of snow and leaves, absorbed on the new horizons that the merchant had opened. Night, wind and snow were closing around him when the cheery sound of a giggle stopped him. Scanning around, just the trees silently looked away.

And a pale grinning mask that popped up, the wide smile of a boy's face, which appeared from behind a rocky hedge on the back of the hospital, chilling in its revelation as a face in the woods could be.

'Who was that man up on the Altar with you?' asked the boy unceremoniously.

Julian was so startled that he had to take a breath. 'Where you *sneaking* on me?' he scolded.

'I was watching you from a birch at the rim of the Altar'. The boy was dressed in woollen thighs and a felt coat, with shoulder blades decorated with brilliant stones. The outfit reminded Julian of the Hibernian travellers he had seen in his youth. He had the most handsome black eyes and a frolic smile framing his teeth. Fairly young, he would not be more than eight or nine.

'You *were* sneaking on me!' said the Hospitaller 'Shame on you!' and kept walking. He jumped the hedge and still turned to the boy, who was disappointedly left behind 'Where is your home? Anchiano? Chifenti? Or are you with the pilgrims in the hospital? It is too late and cold for a squirrel like you to be outside.'

'And it's too dreadful for a *Saint* like you to deal such important matters with a *stranger*' shouted the boy.

The intrusiveness of the boy annoyed Julian, who turned back and marched all the way to the hedge and faced the boy, standing tall and grave. 'What important matters, son? A bridge?'

'No, Julian' whispered the boy with an accomplice wink, pointing at Julian's face. 'Not the bridge. It's your soul!' and he touched the Hospitaller's forehead with his childish finger.

Julian legs felt suddenly limp. Suddenly he had a blank on his mind, as if he could not recall what he had done on the last hours, since leaving the hospital. His memory as bleak as the dunes of the Holy Land. 'Who are you?' he demanded. 'Some kind of devil? Are you in the hospital with others birds of your plumage? I do not think I know you from here…'

'You do know me. But that was many, many years ago.'

'Good!' laughed Julian, nervously 'very good adult talk. But you…you were not even around when it was *many, many years ago*. In those times you must have been only a love story'.

'In fact, it was a story of fear'.

Julian froze. He had only then realised that they were holding a conversation in the *langue d'oïl* of Julian's native land.

'What do you mean by fear?' shouted Julian. 'Where do I know you from?'

'Never mind that… sometimes it does not need to be explained. This reasoning is much incomprehensible to the crude wits of men, and neither can I be clear about my purposes with you, but I owe you this one…'

Julian was shaking his head. 'I am not dreaming, therefore you must be a demon, sent from hell to confuse me.'

'*Saint* Julian, the Hospitaller! You are already misguided. Shouldn't you be able to recognise the devil at this stage of your unique life?'

An eerie screech broke the surreal nature of their meeting, as if a pig was being bled right inside the hospital. It was followed by a desperate wail of dreadfulness and shouting. To Julian it was obvious where it came from.

'The hospital. I must go.' He turned to the boy but there was nobody there any more. Far inside the woods, at the edge of the visible tree line, he saw the figure of a boy running away, hoping frantically between the trunks as if the ground was burning hot.

All of a sudden, things became clear to Julian. He shouted to the boy in such a low voice that he would be the only one to hear it: '*You*…. So it was *you*…'

But how could it be? That had been so many years ago.

'*You*! How could you do that?' Maria was shouting. 'How could you do that?' Julian had ran to the hospital, only to find Maria Madallena outside, raging against the night, swearing and cursing at the wind, for nobody else could be seen with her. Hiding behind the northern wall, he did not allow the Cunimundinghi lady to see him. She punched the invisible, stroke the air and kicked the solid rocky ground. 'You son of the harlot's fetid cunt! Insensible shit eating pig! Why did it have to be him? How can you do that to me? Bastard!'

Merciful Jesus, she must be really a witch, thought Julian, hidden in the shadows, keeping a distance from that outburst of fury. Yet, the Hospitaller was looking at a Maria that could not have been further from being *Tenebrosa*. Her face had an overwhelming sadness that surpassed the acidity of that obscene attitude. For the first time in years, Julian saw her as simply Maria Maddalena, a poor crumbling spirit, cornered by her own intrigues and hiding secrets that no living soul could ever know.

Heartbroken or not, she kept furiously investing at the hollow darkness 'Piss on my devotion! Shit on your acknowledgement! I do not deserve that! *He* does not deserve that!'

The snow had stopped and the wind calmed down. A beam of light invaded the ground as the hospital door opened and was quickly shut down again, but not before a number of faces peered out to inspect Maria's anger. Meanwhile, Julian almost gasped from his hiding when a very large dog dashed by him and leaped playfully towards Maria.

As large as a wolf, the Hospitaller reckoned, but with not a drop of wolfish savagery on its mischievous gait. The dog wagged its whole body with excitement, ready to tease her with a nibble and run away as if it had known her all its life. Maria had stopped the uproar when she saw the dog. It was blacker than a wolf, at least much darker than the pelts they had seen. Unlike wolves, which have cold yellow or amber irises, the dog had black expressive eyes. The most handsome black eyes and a frolic smile framing its teeth, while the tongue hung out, panting in expectation.

Panting heavily too, Maria tried to pull herself together, looking around the desolate path, north and south, reflecting over the sudden silence and verifying for spectators. Nobody in sight, but the dog, which seemed quite happy to see her. And given the angry, desperate hardness on Maria's face, the dog soon realised the woman was not in the mood for flippancy.

Slowing down to a shy pace, it laid sad ears along its neck and a submissive tail curved in between the short steps. Maria brushed him of her gaze. She held a sequential sob and cursed once again, feeling the air whistle coldly around her covered ears.

Ignoring the black beast that shivered under the freezing wind while staring amusingly at her, she walked down to the bank, stepping over the ice. Julian watched her for a long time. The dog still sat while the woman stood on the whiteness of the Serchio's crust, looking at that bridge. That damned bridge. Silent broken pillars, painful thorns of hell sticking out of the ice.

Finally, Maria Maddalena exhaled and dropped her shoulders, turning back to the hospital. Walking around the southern side of the building, she grabbed the reigns of the mule and stepped on the cart. The startled mule steamed through its nostrils, quite eager to trot across that snowy path back to Anchiano as briefly as possible. When the cart rounded the hospital back into the road, Maria hesitated for a moment and halted the mule. She looked back and saw the black dog, which was still sitting, ears alert watching her with an inexplicable melancholy. And to Julian surprise, still looking back, the stone lady of Anchiano leaned over to slap her knee. 'Come!' she motioned. The dog yelped and leaped with joy, following the grim but still large silhouette on the cart towards the manor.

Julian emerged out of the shadows and ran to the hospital, just to find another chaos inside.

'Gracious God!' exclaimed Clarissa, throughout the turmoil of voices and shrieks. 'I had even forgotten about you!' She was trying to hold on to Mira. Cara was uncontrollable, with limbs shuddering and vomiting copiously. Julian saw Muscata crying over her soup, spilled on the table, and some of the women trying to comfort her. 'Help us here with these pour souls. They've just heard the worst news about their father'.

'Immanuel is dead?' he asked. When Clarissa nodded, Julian started to understand why Maria was shouting at the world.

Of course!

Maria Maddalena was facing the idea of burying her own father under the bridge's foundations.

The Dragons of Christmas Eve

Dawn was breaking through the Pennines. A clear purple aura behind the peaks revealed the magnificence of the day to come. Julian had his thick woollen cloak sitting in front of him, across the saddle. After such an unusual day and turbulent night, the warm air was not being seen as a surprise, even though there would be still three months before spring should arrive with its splendour. The chirping of thrushes amalgamated with the chime of hundreds of streams, formed as snow patches dissolved into the ground. The Serchio rumbled in the distance, carrying huge flakes of its frozen crust under the still hard shell along the meandering course. If the temperature rise continued, there would be thaw and flood in a few days, for sure. And then, thought Julian, maybe the whole bridge will be gone.

Unless the merchant was telling the truth.

The mule walked her own pace. She knew where to go, without any guidance from the Hospitaller's reins. It had been the most exhaustiing night that Julian had been through since the leper's crossing. Mira and Cara had to be controlled and dispatched with the younger sister Muscata to Corsena. Bernardo Delle Rocche promptly offered to accompany the ladies to their deceased father's house. Julian, however, could not refrain from offering his comfort and console, so he escorted them to the manor and helped the family bear the painful hours still to come across the night. The rush gave him no time to share the events of the 'Altar' with Clarissa. It never occurred to him though, that none of the Seth's servants were seen at the hospital.

Sad, but serene, the situation at the Burle et Malachi house in Corsena was already being well conducted by some of the brothers when Julian had arrived with the sisters. Hours before, when the cold winds had abated, servants had been dispatched to Lucca to seize the other brothers.

Immanuel had died in his sleep.

Never complaining about sickness or old age, the old Bukhari spent the last years of his life crowning his accomplishments of three decades. One would have to look at the hidden ruins behind rosebushes in the ancient baths of Corsena in the Anno Mille and the village that had grown around the new baths thirty years later to marvel at the diligence of that strange newcomer.

The man who had brought the silk to Lucca was adequately honoured for his courageous enterprise. Shattered by seeing his dear son-in-law go away before him, old Battista Burle sent with Giacomo a large measure of locally embroidered silk sheet, which they elegantly wrapped Immanuel's body with. This was slipped into a long linen envelope, which was tied at the head and the feet. And very few of those villagers from Corsena, Fornulo, Chifenti and so many other areas, who came to give Immanuel their heartily farewell, had ever seen a real coffin made of wood, quickly built with local chestnut planks.

Julian had prepared to leave as soon as the heavy steps of Maria Madallena shook the house. She ignored him and entered into the back room, ready to take complete control. As tolerant as he could make himself be, Julian could not endure the passiveness of all other brothers and sisters, obeying to her demands and ludicrousness, as timid sheep herded by a ferocious dog. And it was too late to realise he had been staring at her all of this time.

'What are you looking at, Hospitaller?' she barked viciously, taking heavy steps across the manor hall to face him almost nose to nose.

Julian stood expressionless and said nothing for a good while, before lightly smacking his lips 'It's a pity, I think.'

Maria foamed 'Don't waste your saintly commiseration with us, Hospitaller. Considering your crimes, you should better use your soft sympathy to line a pebbly ground instead, to kneel and ask God for the forgiveness He should never grant you.' Her voice was powerful, attracting the other Burle et Malachi brothers and sisters, who quickly gathered around the commotion.

Julian calmed them with a steady hand, without taking his eyes from Maria's. 'I am leaving,' he said, 'but just watch your sister here and her ideas about that bridge down the river.'

Maria cackled. 'Do not mistake me, Julian. Unlike you, I have never murdered my parents. And if you fear that I can have my father to be buried under that bridge, you overestimate the value of that old fool's bones. His thin blood will not quench the Serchio's thirst. But when we are considering a holy man, *Saint* Julian,' she sneered, 'that would be indeed an appropriate offering.' The brothers tried to push her back to the back room, but they were frozen by her raised hand. Now she spoke to all present in the hall 'Remember a few years ago when those fools in Camaldoli allowed their holy man to escape before they could guarantee that his body and bones remained in their monastery? Coincidently, that Romualdo was their hospitaller too. Stupid sods! They let him escape and they say he went to die somewhere in Spoletto, leaving not even a digit bone as a relic to the Camaldolese. Watch your back, Julian, for we will not let you escape if you try –'

Julian was out of the house before she had finished her speech. Had he stayed longer, he would have opened his arms and offered himself for her to scrape the meat off his bones. He knew this would trigger a fit in the witch, but he did not want to cause an even greater commotion on that day of mourning for Immanuel.

As he descended towards the ford at the Lima, Maria's new found friend greeted him with a jolly tail wag. The black pair of eyes accompanied him with a handsome smile on its face, all the way until he disappeared across the Lima, on the path to Chifenti.

Now, as the first warmth of sunlight fell on him to soothe his body, he shook off the apprehensions and incidents of that long night, trying to recapitulate all about that strange merchant and their deal. He had not told anyone about it, but he still remembered each word of how that dialogue started:

'Tell, me Seth: do you understand anything about engineering?'

'As a matter of fact, Julian, I don't! But I can find somebody who does. What seems to be the problem?'

'My problem is the bridge we are trying to build.'

'A bridge? Well, no bridges are problems…they are solutions!'

'Exactly. Let me show this one to you. We may be able to see it at the edge of the glade. See, if you look down across those branches you will distinguish the unfinished arches sticking out of the river.'

The merchant looked for a while and nodded slowly 'I see…'

'The whole idea', continued Julian, 'was that the bridge would be next to the hospital, providing pilgrims and travellers with easy access between both eastern and western sides of the Serchio river, Chifenti, Mutianum and of course, the Bagni a Corsena. This would make Chifenti an important centre for the pilgrims on the Via Francigena. It would benefit the local market, increase value of the local lands and individual production and services and facilitate access of miserable souls into our hospital.'

'Julian, you are a businessman as well'. Said the merchant with a smile of satisfaction and wiggling eyebrows of approval.

'I am not sure about that but, as I was saying, the support to build the bridge was unanimous among both banks of the river, even from different, very unfriendly parties, plus the bishopric in Lucca, bankers and most of the landowners around here.'

'Then, there should be no obstacles to its completion...' deducted Seth, touching the side of his nose.

'The problem is the bridge seems to be cursed. We have witnessed it falling into pieces from a series of incidents that have reduced it to ruins. Our engineer has fled twice, the second time nobody knows where to. And now the only solution seems to be an absurdity seeded into the local folk by the lady of these lands, the widow of the lord of the Cunimundinghi, from Anchiano. She believes that a relevant sacrifice should be placed under one of the pillars or walled within. The worst part is that the villagers are believing her now. And I hear that they are even talking about murder.'

'That is absolutely unnecessary,' the merchant intervened.

'Excuse me?' Julian asked startled. 'Did you say necessary?'

'No! I say UNnecessay!' Seth said, quite carelessly humorous about it. 'Sacrifices need to be made, but different ones.' He held Julian by the arm and walked slowly across the white clearance 'Julian, I can arrange for this bridge to be ready by springtime next year.'

'Are you mocking me?' Julian asked.

'Just because I smile?'

'No. Because you talk nonsense. How can you suggest the bridge could be over and done in a few months?'

'Julian, I have never been so serious. I have the contacts and the means to finish it.'

'And what do you want for that?' Julian asked, quite suspicious.

'It's only a simple condition...' the merchant said, with his smile more frank and wide as ever.

But that was it. Julian could not remember the rest. He knew they had a deal, but the details or the payment were not clear in his recollections. It felt incomplete, like waking up from a dream and telling it to himself, but not being able to re-tell it later to anyone else.

He decided to ride up to the Altar, to re-trace his steps and exercise the memory. It was a long steep path from Chifenti, but on that mid-winter morning freshness, the ride was a rather pleasant exercise, at least for him, and not necessarily for the mule. Getting to the old pagan cemetery, Julian soon realised he was looking at a different clearance, with melting snow opening patches for brown grass and the trees around looking at the sun, rather than staring at him.

There was nothing to refresh his memory there.

He rode down the steeper path to the hospital and, this time, as soon as he passed by the rocky hedge behind the stables, some fleeting, vaporous memory drifted by and he barely caught it.

A boy.

The boy, indeed he could remember that. They had talked about the deal, whatever it had been, and the boy had touched his forehead. The magical boy with black eyes, who made him forget it all.

Arriving in the hospital, he came upon the usual number of travellers, most of them leaving the building during the midday to profit from the fair weather and maybe arrive at their destination for the Christmas mass. They were covered in pelts, rugs and large leather capes, breathing foggily through their quiet words and marching into the icy landscape to find the next hospital. Their swaying figures were soon reduced into trollish silhouettes against the whiteness of the land. There were peasants from Liguria, a troupe of Veronese cripples, a pair of blind German traveling hermits, French monks, a family from Menabla and an unfortunate mute man whose humanity had been completely snatched out from his face, probably by fire. Some were hoping to find solace and miracles among the relics, treasures and holy places in Lucca and Rome. Others were returning with their spiritual triumphs gleaming in their hearts or their physical disappointments hidden behind shadowy faces. Many of those pilgrims had witnessed the incidents of the evening, probably not much different than any other night they had spent in hospitals along their journeys. They saluted Julian with a comforting smile, sharing his exhaustion, but probably not envying the Hospitaller's responsibilities with his wife to clean up after their stopover. Julian entered the hospital and was greeted by the familiar balmy breath of their hall. A warm combination of soot, sweat, straw and lanoline, which overwhelmed any aroma of soups or foods that Clarissa could have been cooking or already served.

But true warmth irradiated down his body from Clarissa's rainbow greeting, a gentle kiss on his lips and a light hand on his face. 'How are they doing?' she asked, after their lips parted, without hiding a sad shadow of concern in her powerful eyebrows.

'The boys know Maria is capable of anything, so I think they will guard well the tomb' he said, but with eyes elsewhere, distracted by a second thought, and not unnoticed by his wife.

'What's bothering you?' she asked.

'The merchant up on the Altar.'

Her eyes suddenly opened wide green 'Yes, the merchant!' she flicked quick glances to the side, at the pilgrims who were leaving and others that were arriving. 'We never talked about him since the events from last night. What happened?'

Julian sighed. 'It's Christmas eve, Clarissa. Let me help you with the duties and I'll tell you about it this evening. There will be no mass celebrated in the Ceretto, anyway. And we will not be going to Chifenti.'

Clarissa was glad for that. Many of the helpers had gone back to Corsena and now she was left alone with two wardens only.

First they concentrated on the building tasks, shovelling snow and mud, opening paths that would bring less dirt to the hospital. They gathered the rancid, used straw and tossed it on the sty, washed up the hall, scraped the trestle tables and the floors and dropped new dry straw from the storage above. Then, they went outside to pick logs from the shed and move newer wood from the log piles to replace those taken from the shed. They fed the horses, pigs, goats and cows. They searched the chicken coop and killed two old hens that were not likely to return to lay when springtime came. Back inside, they fed the fires and hearths and they tended to wounds of some travellers, bought some extra grain from passing carts, plucked the hens, boiled some *farro*, added the pieces to the broth and fed the hearty soup to a good number of new incomers.

When the night had fallen, as early and dark blue as a benevolent winter wanted, a sweet smoky air was soothing the guests in the hospital. But the cold wind was back and furious. Walking to Chifenti was going to be an arduous challenge for those who wanted to attend mass. Upstairs in their chamber, Julian leaned back on his mattress, forgetting the strange events of those days as he quietly watched his wife bathing. Clarissa was kneeling in front of two pans. One that protected the fire that still heated the room, and another with warm water, where she dunked the bath cloth in. Copper shone on a silky curtain of her long brown hair, which occasionally revealed to Julian glimpses of his beloved treasure, a dance of flames reflected on her curves and volumes. The fire flickered in the pan, shining golden curvaceous shapes on Clarissa's body, brilliant from the wet rubbing that she softly gave herself. Julian admired the youth that still disguised her age. A young tenderness that gently covered the strong muscles of a hard-working diligent hospitaller. She stood up tall and naked, looking at Julian with a mischievous curve on the corner of her lips. She rolled a large linen sheet as a cape around her shoulders and extended her hand to Julian. 'Come. I will bathe you too.'

Much before she had finished that last task, they were already in communion with each other.

Under the layers of pelts and blankets, their naked bodies were still warm from their athletic love session. Clarissa held him close to her and whispered in his ear. 'You are so silent.'

Julian was catching his breath, looking at the shadows that the renewed flames in the pan still threw against the wall. Making love to Clarissa was always a journey through heaven, a reward that strengthened his beliefs in goodness and in heavens, and the best reason to start a new day with renewed enthusiasm. But when he exploded this time, arching his back under a whirlwind of sensuous images, touches, smells, sounds and flavours, snatching his soul away for a brief moment, he was disturbed by uninspiring flashes of that forest clearance, the fleeting memories of the merchant and the alleged deal. And while he stretched himself in delirious pain, paralysed in ecstasy from the utmost physical expression of love, deep in the back of his fantasies, a passing image corroded his pleasure. A burst of darkness with yellow eyes of fire looking at him.

Julian finally seemed to have heard what Clarissa had said while she tenderly embraced him from behind. Looking at the stone wall in front of his eyes, he explained his silence, describing everything that happened and was discussed in that meeting with Seth, up to the point that he could not remember the rest. He also told her about the strange boy that he came across before arriving back in the hospital.

'That's all?' Clarissa asked

'Yes, and I fear that I have indeed made a deal.'

'To pay for the construction of the bridge?'

'Yes, but I just cannot think of what it was.' Julian said bitterly, 'And I know that it was ever since the boy touched my head, I have had that idiotic sensation of forgetfulness. For a moment I had thought that the merchant Seth was some sort of Godsend angel...'

Julian felt Clarissa giving a quiet chuckle. She moved his hair and kissed the back of his neck. 'We have seen the angel, Julian. She had wings.'

'True, but everything seemed to be in accordance to my prayers, to stop the insanity about the foundations, the sacrifice.'

Clarissa raised her head and held it meditatively, leaning her elbow behind Julian's head. 'Maybe Seth was just there to confuse you,' she said, 'maybe it was the boy who was the true angel who came to brush those memories of your thoughts.'

'Maybe...' Julian considered, 'but he did not have wings either.'

'Maybe it was for the better,' Clarissa concluded. 'Whatever it was that happened on the altar, you don't remember. So just forget it. If you cannot think of it, there is no deal. Next time Seth shows his charming smile around this valley, tell him to be clearer.'

Julian sighed. He was quiet for a long time, listening to the howling of the wind outside. 'Hold me, Clarissa,' he asked softly, but with pain in his voice, 'hold me close to you.'

She wrapped her arms tenderly around him, comforting his body from the cold incertitudes that travelled under his skin, warming him for a peaceful night.

They slept profoundly, embraced cosily under the pelts.

But only to be awakened by a hospital warden who climbed to their chamber and shook Julian out of his ease. 'What is it?' Julian asked, blinking, trying not to look at the trembling light of the candle that the warden held in front of him. Outside, the wind whistled and booed around every single salience of the hospital.

'We don't know, Julian,' said the warden trembling on his feet, 'but everyone down there is very nervous. It sounds like there are voices outside. We can hear them. Devilish voices that are laughing and singing, scorning at us. We feel their heavy footsteps, running around the building, poking at the door and the windows.'

Julian got up on a jump 'In this cold night? We should bring them in.'

The warden opened his eyes wide. 'No, Julian. No!' his skin had turned greyish white, 'Can't you understand it? It would be wrong. It *feels* wrong.'

'But the night has turned freezing! We must help them.' He started to dress up in a thick fur coat.

Wide awake and still under the pelts, Clarissa asked 'Why don't we just open the door? We are a hospital, if you have forgotten about it.'

'*Witches*, Clarissa!' the warden hissed. 'That's what the voices sound like! We don't want to let witches inside!' And looking at the puzzled face of the hospitaller couple, he continued. 'Those voices! They sound wrong. We can hear them and the songs they sing. Words of abominations and insult,' and he swallowed a lump in his throat before admitting 'and the worst of all is that it sounds like they those voices outside...are children's.'

Julian kicked the door opened. The giggling immediately stopped.

The night ceremoniously wooed the beam of light from the hospital doorway, fighting against the darkness across the road and embracing Julian's back as he stepped out to look around. Although the weather had gone bitterly cold again, few clouds covered the starred sky. The silvery surface of the frozen river could be devised on the distance. No witches, or children. But standing far away, waving at them from the river bank, a human figure stood black and at ease.

Julian dropped his shoulders in relief and turned to Clarissa, who stood among a legion of faces under the doorframe. 'It's Seth, the merchant.' But he seemed to be the only one comforted by the realisation. They all seemed to be terrorised, including Clarissa.

'Julian, it's not!' her voice trembled.

'Sure it is him. He must be freezing. I'll see if he wants to come in' Julian said, advancing through the snow, without waiting to hear Clarissa's words of caution. He walked through the squeaking snow and approached Seth, who was not moving forward to greet him. The merchant had a grin on his face, but his countenance was not of a smile.

'You should join us in the hospital. We could heat some soup for you.' Julian said before he finally stood in front of the merchant.

Seth ignored the comment. 'They say that you have lost your memory,' he said, drily enough to make his grin look like carved wood. And before Julian could ask who he had meant by *they*, the merchant continued 'We have a *deal*, Julian, and I don't care if you remember it or not. But it isn't by forgetting about a deal that you will nullify it.' He held Julian's shoulder amicably, but with incredibly firm fingers. Regardless whether the Hospitaller wanted or not, Seth pulled him for a walk across the frozen river.

Clarissa saw Julian leaving the hospital to see the merchant.

'Who's that man?' one of the wide-eyed pilgrims asked. Clarissa did not hear the question. She was watching Julian's every step towards something that froze her there at the hospital door, unable to decide what to do, if anything could be done to help her husband.

Julian had reached the merchant and said something that could not be heard.

'They say that you have lost your memory' a loud voice answered.

Some people fell back inside the hospital through the door, for it was not just one voice. Unlike Julian's words, which came from far on the Serchio's frozen bank, these words were loud and clear for them, not only coming from the river bank, but from the darkness around the hospital. They could hear several voices saying the words at the same time. Children's voices.

'We have a *deal*, Julian, and I don't care if you remember it or not. But it isn't by forgetting about a deal that you will nullify it.'

'*Who is saying that?*' was the question the pilgrims were all whispering. Clarissa could feel them quivering with fear behind her. She squinted to see through the darkness, the children who were simultaneously repeating the powerful voice of that merchant. But every time she tried to look, the winter darkness closed in, maliciously concealing any hint of who could be playing that mockery.

'Witches!' someone hissed.

'Psst!' the warden said, 'let's hear what they say!'

'Julian, on that meeting we had up on this mountain behind you, you asked me to finish that bridge for you,' the voices continued, from the snowy cover of the ice and from the dark surroundings, 'and look at her: broken, ugly, never meant to unite these banks. You're a man of this big wide world, Julian, and so am I. You know I can do it for you and I have promised that. But you, Hospitaller, you have pledged to pay me somehow.'

Clarissa could hear it too, but she was not listening to Seth's words any more, no matter how much the children in the darkness made it a unison. She was lost in despair, watching them walking further across the icy cap of the Serchio. Although the merchant seemed to have a hungry darkness to his silhouette, a blackness that stole the starlight reflected on the snow, Clarissa could see his shadow. And both of her hands flew towards her mouth to shut it from screaming when she devised the large shape of his wings.

Julian was starting to connect together lost pieces of memory as Seth described their meeting.

'...You're a man of this big wide world, Julian. Your crooked nose and your half ear are witnesses of some painful past. You know I can do it for you and I promised to. But you, Hospitaller, you have promised me something too.'

'Seth, I was led to believe you were someone else...'

'There are no excuses for your actions, Julian. Do not blame others for what you do or cause.'

'But I told you the reasons: the locals want the bridge finished and I was only trying to find an alternative way to prevent them from desecrating a body in eternal rest, or to avoid murder or —'

'Yeah, yeah, yeah I know it all, Julian,' the merchant said, waving a dismissing hand and looking at the small crowd of pilgrims that stood outside the hospital door, so far behind Julian, 'just do not put any other reasons behind you. That's a selfish attitude, so typical of your decisions.'

Julian tried to protest, but he was overwhelmed by the darkness that was taking over their surroundings. He could remember that Seth had blue eyes when they'd met in that clearing. But now the merchant seemed to have changed, but Julian could not tell what the glint appeared to be. It made the tiny hairs in the back of his neck prickle.

'The delivery date, of a complete and finished bridge, broad enough to allow for the widest and heaviest cart to cross the Serchio, is in the spring equinox. But I am a generous man, Julian. I will give the new bridge to the people of the Serchio a few days ahead. For it is not on the Twenty First of March, as your church does not know how to count days of the year properly, but on the Fifteenth, the real equinox, when spring day length will match the length of winter darkness. That is, if you like, on the feast of Saint Longinus then, for the holy man who speared the side of your Jesus Christ, the Son of God, so he could bleed to death.' Seth continued now with a deeper toned speech, and Julian noticed that his words were multiplied by loud voices coming from far away, probably from the hospital. And a rustling sound on the top of it, with thumping, making the atmosphere darker. 'Julian, an agreement has been made. Keep that in mind, and never forget your part of the deal!' And now Julian could hardly see anything at all. Just a growing stain of blackness in front of him, and what appeared to be two huge dark towers soaring behind the merchant's shoulders. Seth grunted so low now that the ice could be heard cracking 'The first soul to cross the finished bridge is *mine*, for eternity.'

If Julian had the time to capture the statement, he had none to appreciate its power, for a savage scream cut through the darkness, and someone else's body was flung in front of him, crashing against Seth's and suddenly bringing back the night light, refreshingly reflected on the whiteness of the snow. The person in front of him was Clarissa. She had her back to him and she held onto something. Seth was gone, but there were many things on the snow. And they were moving.

'It's an angel!' someone whispered. 'See? Aren't those wings?'
An old German monk prayed on his knees, while his young acolyte growled 'Black as the night, this angel. The fallen dragon. The morning star: *Lucifer*!'
'*Psst!* Listen to what he has to say to the Hospitaller. It's about that bridge.'
'The delivery date, of a complete and finished bridge, broad enough to allow for the widest and heaviest cart to cross the Serchio, is in the spring equinox. But I am a generous man, Julian. I will give the new bridge to the people of the Serchio a few days ahead...' Seth's voice was becoming as loud as a roar, no matter how much further he walked from the hospital. The guests could only see the black shadow moving and eating away the light.
'Julian is a living saint!' the warden reminded them. 'No dragon will tempt him into sin or damnation.'
The German monks continued, now all together "Let the Holy Cross be my light; let Saint Michael be my warrior; let not the dragon be my guide; step back Satanas; never tempt me with vain things; what you offer me is evil; you drink the poison yourself; get back to your lonely den of punishment."
Meanwhile, Clarissa was climbing down the ladder from the upper storage. With a large pitchfork in her hand, she calmly pushed the crowd away from the doorway and stepped out into the freezing night. Taking her first breath in before running forward, she was overwhelmed by the smell of fresh coriander. In this moment, a group of small figures silently hopped onto her way, appearing from the dark sides where the hospital interior light did not reach. Those were certainly not children, by the menacing manner in which they extended their claws towards her, but they

kept repeating the words of Seth as he spoke to Julian so many paces far on the frozen river.

'...man who speared the side of your Jesus Christ, the Son of God, so he could bleed to death.'

Shrieks of horror were heard from the pilgrim crowd. Gripping firmly to the pitchfork, Clarissa advanced against the living barrier of those children-sized figures. The outside darkness tried to blacken her out, but strangely Clarissa had a shade of light. As the darkness clung hard to her shoulders like a sucking tick, as large as the sky, desperately trying to put its hands in front of her face and cover her eyes, she could easily see her way ahead, from the luminescent shadow she produced. It was her own shadow, she could tell it. Her shape, moving exactly like her, but which lightened the snow as if daylight was only being protected by her stature. She advanced towards the figures and they quickly withdrew their little hands, running away in terror from her steps. One of them hopped desperately by the light and she incidentally saw the little man's hairy head, but totally absent of a face.

Clarissa advanced with fury and renewed vigour. While the little helpers of Seth were left behind, still calmly repeating the words of the merchant to Julian, she was now running like a warrior, gaining ground over the packed snow and quickly approaching the pair on the frozen river. She saw Seth, large and dark, wings opening wide and tall, as he looked at Julian with dead yellow eyes of fire. She missed to see that her radiant shadow on the ground, sliding over the ice as she ran against the wind, had stretched from the sides of where her shoulders would be, like long wings of an eagle, with a rainbow of colours on the fringes.

'The first soul to cross the finished bridge is *mine*, for eternity.'

She flew onto Seth like a lioness, bellowing a shattering war cry, a power built up over forty four years, diving the pitchfork into his chest on a killing strike. But rather than feeling the impact of bone and muscle, instead of hearing the shrieks of the wounded dragon, the pitchfork only slipped through a confusion of coiled bodies and slime, the night starlight returned to reflect on Serchio's ice and Clarissa heard no more than the slick sound of scaleless black serpents disentangling from a heavy knot and the thumping of each of them popping on the ice.

Panting heavily, she was still growling, scanning the silent ice cap, searching for the Merchant, who had disappeared on her strike. And there was nothing else, but the whiteness of the frozen Serchio, and dozens of black eels, slithering helplessly on the ice, grunting and puffing their last desperate breaths before freezing under the heartless winter wind that started to blow again.

Clarissa turned back to a wide-eyed Julian, who seemed to be as frozen as the river.

'Do you know who that was?' she asked with irritation.

Julian begged with a trembling chin 'I'm so sorry Clarissa. I'm so sorry!' The sight of his scared face, livid as a boy's, made Clarissa want to cry.

She dropped the pitchfork and fell on his arms.

'It cannot be!' Maria Maddalena said, sitting at the table, with the dog at her feet. She felt a sudden bout of pain in her bones. Her son had heard the news on that Christmas morning and rode to Chifenti, to enquire along the way about the incidents of the previous night

'They all heard it. And they all saw him.' Arrigo said. He was trimming his nails with the tip of his dagger.

'The *Devil*? Talking to the *Saint*? Making deals with that stupid, weak man?' Maria's eyes were lost in a desperate nothingness. 'It cannot be. I should have been the one. I SHOULD HAVE BEEN THE ONE!' she slammed the table with her fist, bursting the skin of her knuckles.

Arrigo kept concentrating on his nails. 'Well, you've got your bridge on the promise. Don't you want to be independent from Antelmino? Either you do a deal with the Castracani or with the Devil, although I think we should better associate with the former than the latter.'

'You don't understand, Arrigo my son,' Maria said with her gritted teeth, contained with a shield of forced patience, especially after noticing her knuckles were bleeding, 'if the Devil has indeed appeared to the Hospitaller, I should have been the one to be there.'

Arrigo made a puzzled face and looked at his mother. 'They all saw Julian and the Devil, and Clarissa sending it back into hell. They said there were scores of frozen eels scattered over the ice cap. The pilgrims took them all with them.'

'For *what* ?' Maria asked, raising her head and gaze to Arrigo.

Arrigo chuckled. 'Supposedly they want to eat the serpent to triumph over the Devil, who came to them when they did not attend mass on Christmas Eve.'

'Ignorant, miserable animals. They will not defeat the Devil,' Maria growled to herself, not out loud, 'God will not listen to their prayers. That Hospitaller bitch will never overcome the Devil. If I only had a chance...'

'There is a chance, mother, if you are stupid enough to be the first to cross the bridge on the day the bridge is delivered, ready to be crossed.'

Maria Maddalena of the Burle et Malachi froze. She was silent and paralysed for a long pause, when her heart seemed to stop beating, allowing for her thoughts to be put into a sensible order. As soon as it started beating again, her heart was rattling like a thunder. She was sweating, swept by chills over her skin. The mighty Lady of Anchiano stood up trembling and approached the window with difficulty. She moved the heavy tapestry to the side and felt the cold morning wind on her face.

'What is it, mother? You are white as a cloud!'

Breathing deeply, she pursed her lips and finally produced one of her rare, but forced smiles 'You would not understand it, Arrigo. But do trust me: anything I do is always for your well-being.'

Clarissa had refused to allow the use of her hospital or surrounds to cook or roast any of the eels. The pilgrims took the frozen fish with themselves to their next destination, where it was appreciated as an unexpected out-of-the-season delicacy. Many of them would find it a worthwhile exercise, for a whole year had gone by thereafter and the Devil had not broken out of his chains or appeared out of any

Hellmouth into their lives. Several of these pilgrims would carry on for the years after and endeavour to find an eel to be symbolically eaten on Christmas Eve.

The newcomer pilgrims were downstairs. They could only talk about the stories they had heard about the previous night's events, but Julian was quick to deny them. The hospital wardens and helpers were ordered to remain silent about it, for as long as the rumours remained in the air.

Now, while all ate their supper, Julian was retired into the seclusion of his chamber, lying in bed, leaning on his side. Clarissa was mirroring him. They had had their gazes on each other for hours, perhaps, on a somewhat pleasurable exercise that reminded them of their mutual gazing on their first days together, so many years before, on their journey from France.

'I could look into your eyes forever, Clarissa.'

'You will, Julian, but tell me before, what is happening.'

He shrugged his shoulders. 'I don't know.'

'What will happen? Do you think that was all for real?' she asked, still mirroring him.

'If we suddenly see this bridge being reconstructed, Clarissa, we will know.'

'And then, if they finish, who will be the first one to cross it? We cannot allow anyone to do it. What would be the point of a bridge?'

'I don't know, Clarissa. I don't know and I don't know.'

She smiled condescendingly. 'Then sleep, my love. We must rest.'

He moved now and kissed her 'I love you Clarissa.'

'I love you too,' she said, before starting to undress.

That evening had turned unusually hot, and more bizarrely for being in the middle of winter. The following days and weeks would be noted for a warmer weather only over that stretch of the Serchio valley. That early spring was bringing flowers up, buds on the trees and leaves hurriedly unfolding into lushness. Birds were singing and busy, catching bees and insects that appeared again out of their holes, out of nowhere. Although the river was thawed, there were no floods or raised water levels. Winter was still freezing and firm up on the Apuane and the Apennines. The strange fact was noticed by the few pilgrims who faced the Via Francigena after such an impetuous early winter. When the news arrived in Lucca, the bishop was more than concerned. The ominous phenomenon did seem to confirm the rumours that the devil had appeared on Christmas Eve, and that Julian was behind it all.

He would have to do something about it.

They're Coming…

A thin layer of clouds sheltered the valley from the stars. And as if unusualness wasn't enough usual during that strange winter, that moonless night was unusually quiet. No nocturnal creature was being heard in along the valley. When crickets would normally chirp throughout the high hours of the spring night, this time they were still, observing the northward movement of the clouds against the southward flow of the river. Voices from the villages where hushed by the shadows. As people hurried between the houses, leaving the tavern, a friend's or a loved one, the dogs only watched, not daring to bark their territorial warnings.

The Serchio too, was muffled into silence. The peaceful black flow reflected the low clouds that slid up the valley. The water murkily oozed in silence, slipping through the stony edges of the bridge. In the reeds next to a pair of rocks, a bittern was startled by a puff which spattered it with a cool mist. Looking down to the blackish water, the bittern saw the panting mouth of a catfish. The fat lips designed a white ring which pulsated, as the long slimy whiskers extended to the sides, as if begging for help. The catfish, unusual in that river, pushed its head further out of the water. Wide cloudy eyes mirroring the bittern, which fled away silently, gliding over the more frolicking currents down the stream. The fish head looked to the sides and stood out of the surface, on an unnaturally human neck. It shook the water out of its whiskers and jumped out of the river, onto one of the rocks. The dark unctuous creature cursed some blasphemies on a foreign tongue and stood up on its very human legs. It was not much more than one palm tall. Its tiny body had a naked torso with a rather inflated belly; the arms, ended in long talon fingers that were scratching its hairy buttocks; above the shoulders, a leathery cowl was drawn up, exposing the catfish head. The long soft whiskers still touched the stone when the minuscule beast stood up, drawing strange words of moisture on the rocky facet as the face moved to the sides.

A movement in the reeds caught its attention, as the creature saw another pair of tiny hands pulling the grass to the sides. A long beak approached from the dark tuft and spoke foul words to the catfish-head beast. It came completely out of the reeds and continued its strange filthy whispering. It was a snipe, or else a woodcock, but it had tiny human arms instead of wings, and human legs ending in webbed feet. As it spoke, it kept its long snout between the legs of the catfish-head creature, which listened with great impatience, as it looked up to the unfinished bridge. Both imps turned back to the reeds and entered the clump, cursing as they moved the canes away from their path.

The stump of a hag entered the village of Chifenti from the north road. Not taller than two feet high, she was probably wider than that. Large black eyes the size of chestnuts were deeply dug into her blue face. A cadaveric bloated disk, framed by straight white hair, all tucked in to the cowl that she wore laced around the neck. For all else, the hag was bare naked. Her enormous pot belly was brilliant red, almost bursting with fullness and it had milky eggs-size boils distributed through its whole surface. Her bluish bare feet advanced decidedly. She knew what she had to do. Not even the arse that kept making faces at her was distracting enough to annoy her. It was the creature that marched in front, almost as tall as a short man. All, green, bony thin, with a dry mossy skin, it balanced itself on frail stretched legs, which supported a chisel shaped body, long hanging arms with droopy fingers and a pair of dried bat wings, folded on its shoulder blades. The large head was a confusing muddle of fangs, folds and horns. Huge conic shaped calluses accompanied down the spinal column all the way to its most annoying feature: the arse. Under a hound-like tail, protruding between two small red human-like eyes, teeth and a tongue would be jutting out between the moving buttocks, spitting curses and tossing mockery at all those pathetic creatures that it could see, walking down to the same direction as it was.

Above the valley, the carpet of clouds moved slowly onto itself. A silent gust pierced down the hanging mist, revealing the swift flutter of brown feathers from the wings of a yellow-eyed mouse. Gliding over the village, it descended in spirals, scratching its hairy tummy with long clawed toes, until its disproportionate raptor-eyes spotted the movement of other tiny creatures moving to the edges of the Serchio. With a draughty giggle, if half closed its wings and stooped down to the converging point.

To the skeleton of the bridge.

They were all gathering at both edges of the river, a carnival of monstrosities coming down the alleys, hundreds of spiny, slimy and scaled creatures, crusted shapes that walked, skipped, crawled, hopped, slithered and dragged themselves to where they had been called upon. Gloomy anthropoids with sharp horns jutting out of their foreheads: Wingless bats, spiny toads, long–tongued moles. Pikes and carps walking on their own boots, and tiny sticklebacks wearing iron helmets hauled themselves through the rocky road with the help of ghostly tiny human limbs. Several shapes of humanoid imps, with man-like arms and legs, as cats, badgers, piglets, hedgehogs, woodcocks, herons, limpkins, coots, partridges, lizards, newts and foxes joined into an army of revulsion which had been called to that area for an easy task.

Out of the black Serchio waters that mirrored the night, eel-headed goblins shook the moisture out of their hairy arms and climbed to the road. Spoon-billed beavers combed their fur to rid themselves of moths and crabs that pestered them, before marching ahead. Hundreds of gnomes grunted to each other, many with faces more resembling those of rails and salamanders. A large group of fish and waterfowl was rather noisy. All dressed up in religious and monastic attire, playing mockery postures of intercourse and cracking up in hysterical laughter. Tailed frogs waked on their hind legs, some wearing battle attire, some wearing a type of orgy veil.

From the murky skies, indecently crooked owls and nightjars, goatsuckers and swifts glided down silently, as flying newts and stoats flapped their reptile-like wings to break their unbird-like bodies from splattering onto some rock, below at the river banks. A long-armed turtle was being carried between the strong legs of a small ape. An incredibly bloated grey squirrel rode on a broom, flying on the fashion that witches were believed to do, with the stalks ahead and the stick to the back. Out of the wooded areas, hordes of hybrid choughs with hummingbirds buzzed down to the swarming alleys of Mutianum. A badger walked on its hind legs, wearing the mitre of a bishop.

They were meeting.

Meeting to see the one who had called them all.

Although the parade of monstrosities was noisy, coming from all roads that stretched from the bridge, nobody heard them appearing, nobody saw them passing. Barga was silent, Chifenti was sleeping, Anchiano, Traghetto and Mutianum ignored the legions breaking loose outside of their doors. Livestock and wild animals were quiet, ignoring the silent passage of shapes so inappropriate and repugnant that they could hardly appreciate their presence.

The creatures started to gather on the edges of the bridge. Four legged midgets, shark tailed egrets, humanoid dragonflies. There were many of such imps which resembled just human parts. Upside down heads on feet, limbed bellies, figures with several faces distributed throughout their repulsive bodies. Armoured eggs and marching mushrooms opened way through bird-faced spiders, magpies and ravens wearing conch helmets. A moth-winged toad landed on the knees of an enormous carp. Looking at each other, from both sides of the bridge, the two spiny crowds of devils waited.

Noisily grunting and screaming, laughing and cursing, swearing, barking and chanting, they pushed more and more, as many others kept arriving. Some were smothered and hauled over the edge, and some fell into the frigid water, just to get out again, climbing the pillars and uttering the filthiest words to those that had pushed them. A dark goblin covered itself with a cape, only with its white, long-snouted mole face sticking out. It carried a shield, with a dry toad nailed to it. It was whispering indecencies to a human legged woodpecker, which immediately turned to the white-faced goblin unceremoniously and pinched away one of its eyes. As the goblin screamed with pain and others laughed with mischievous joy, a much bigger dark shape started to materialise on the space between the two crowded edges.

It stole away all light from the night. It just accumulated a colossal blackness, hanging above the water, right on the space where the arch of the bridge should have been. As its darkness got deeper and deeper, the legion of demons quieted down, including the goblin that had its eye snatched out. The darkness started to take shape. A shape that many had never seen, but something that all the devils knew what to expect. An ancient shape of fear. They had all been summoned there because of it. Something to be done, they knew. And right as it started to define the very shape of evil, they could all see, from both opposite sides, the two yellow eyes of dark fire staring at them.

And it told them what to do.

That was the first night of the devils on the Serchio.

For the following seven weeks, the valley would drag its way through endless cold blind nights of fear, unquietness and nightmares.

It started with the Serchio, which warmed up on that very night the demons came, raising a thick white mist that covered the valley into constant blindness. A foul fog that muffled life around the valley, from Diecimo to Fornulo.

Open windows in the morning could only view whiteness. Open doors out to the alleys could only see the unknown. Voices became whispers, as the people could not devise who could be making those noises just a few feet ahead of them. If there was anyone at all. Dragging feet, dogs sniffing or chicken foraging for a stray beetle. Those sounds came from the mist in a distorted way. Muffled and crooked. The valley was as silent as it had ever been.

The bridge, so far away into the thickness of the mist, was forgotten for a while. The inhabitants of Chifenti, Traghetto, Mutianum and other villages stayed at home. No visitors, pilgrims or passer-by's were seen, and the bells never rang in the churches. Some locals, with shrunken hearts by the absence of noise, on a sudden outburst of fear and devotion, lit their candles to saints of old, offering them prayers for the insistent mist to go away, so they could continue with their lives.

This was also the night when three men-at-arms were dispatched from the bishopric of Lucca, to go ride up the Via Francigena through the valley of the Serchio and fetch Julian of Mans at the Hospital of Santa Croce. The rumours of witchcraft and associations with the devil were too strong for Bishop Giovanni to ignore it. Although the bishop did not put much faith on actual devil summons, and very much supported by his parish clerk Antonio to ignore it, they had both enough pressure from Antelmino di Gottefredo to investigate the screaming rumours that had washed up in the city, to deal with the matter accordingly and start by interrogating Julian with the appropriate strictness. The bankers in Lucca seemed to have little interest in sending anyone to go to the Hospitaller, so Antelmino offered assistance, including his own men-at-arms to fetch Julian.

Someone in Diecimo did see the riders entering the fog thick on their way to Mutianum.

And neither the men nor the horses were ever seen again.

People could sense the wrong outside. It could be breathed as they went out of their houses. It could be felt as *maere* escaped from the construction site and sat on the belly of sleepers, giving them bad dreams and a heavy stomach. Initially, the inhabitants knew nothing concrete about the devils, as the progress on the bridge was not to be seen for the first few weeks. However, they could feel the wrong in the air they breathed. They could taste the foulness in the rather warm water that was being drunk. Indeed, they were all aware of the deal, but few believed, at the end that anything was to be done. Even those few who had seen the Devil thought he would be too lazy to engage into his part.

They were afraid, though. Afraid of the devilry which could be heard from their windows. Afraid to go out and verify what exactly was being brewed out there, which caused the nausea, the mist and the fear. It was a harsh period, for the limited resources were made spoiled quickly by the mischief of the stray imps. Fresh eggs, which were being laid by local hens aroused by spring temperatures, soon got rotten by inexplicable reasons. Leavened bread did not grow, sour milk did not clot and turned noxious. Dogs would sudden appear in the morning with their hair shaved or covered in oil. Horses had their tails braided with each other. Goats were found blanketed in a crust of burdock and beggars lice, although the prickly and sticky pods were not seen in that region. Objects such as shearers, spoons and knifes were frequently lost, hidden on impossible places, where people could never think of having laid them. Wine became bitter and turned foul. And everyone's humour got as dark as it could get.

The night breeze was especially fetid. It smelled of decay, but it did not attract any gulls or crows towards the river during the day. The air just drove away most wildlife from the surroundings of the valley. People felt it in themselves, but not many dared to speak of it to each other, but rather silently accepting the fear. Excuses were quickly produced to justify a denial even for a quick stroll across the alleys when darkness had fallen. And knowledge of the mist lead passers to somehow avoid the way down the valley. There were less visitors, except for those strayed ones who came during the day hours. Many pilgrims using the Via Francigena had coincidently taken the coastal route to make it quick, in and out of Rome. When night rolled over, still in its winter rush, only the devils remained. Laughter and shrieks were heard through the nocturnal gusty wind, turning the skin of the people inside out and freezing their souls with horror. And still, with the fetid breeze and the gusty wind, the mist stayed.

And no one talked about what could really be causing it.

Many could not sleep, especially in the hospital, where panic sometimes engulfed the few newcomers. Julian and Clarissa tried hard to counsel and comfort those in agony. Some were not aware of the deal, but they were still fully under the fear and spell of the wrong that went outside during the dark.

And one day, after more than a fortnight since the frigid fears had started to distil in the warm dark waters of the Serchio, the fog was gone.

'Julian, come outside to see this!' Clarissa shouted from the door.

A beautiful winter sun shone its pink glaze as the morning rose in the silent valley, revealing to the mesmerised people who came out of the hospital and to those who watched from the Traghetto something new on the bridge. There was surely construction going on.

A complex and mysterious scaffolding system ingeniously crafted around the pillars of the bridge. A wooden staircase built for each span, spiralling around the pillars and strangling them as they abruptly ended in their collapsed edges. As Julian and Clarissa walked closer, they noticed that railing was composed of metal spears in all different shapes and fashions, some axes, some lances, mostly battle gear. Secondary staircases twirled around the first, these latter much smaller than the former, which were also so tiny that hardly children would be able to use them. The two braided complexes, on both sides of the river, of stairs and corridors, bridges and lifts, pulleys, beams and cables stretched high, from each span of the unfinished bridge, meeting at a point high above the river, exactly where the future bridge's arches should be doing the same, as it had been envisioned by many. It was a much more elaborate structure than the giant wooden arched frame that had previously been set for the main arch, and much more delicate.

But that devilish network of walkways and ladders did not hang there, just leaning on thin air, supported on the sides only. No, the whole mesh was seated on an enormous egg-shaped tree trunk. More like a gigantic shell made of tree bark, the size of a travelling chart. This horizontal oval structure seemed to have grown from two parallel tall trees, their long dry trunks each firmly planted on two canoes that floated on the water, allowing the swift current, now cold as usual in winter, to run by. The whole grid of structures swayed slowly as the canoes struggled to maintain the weight of the trees, the egg and the scaffolding up in place. The roots were firmly coiled around the boats, gripping firmly to the canoes' gunwales, while the branches at a certain height grew into the strange elliptical wooden structured that sustained the tallest part of the scaffolding. A big crack could be seen in the egg, with parts of the barky shell missing, but nothing could be seen inside. Just darkness.

On that late January morning, in the houses along the valley, breads were left unbaked, or burned to charcoal. The cows were not milked, the chicken not fed and the horses did not get their water. Buckets were left down in the wells, and the wine was not drawn from the barrels. The silage was not moved, and straws were not replenished. Even at the hospital, Clarissa found herself left on her own, for everybody else had walked closer to see what had been woven around the remains of the bridge.

Julian was standing on the riverbank, watching with all the others. They were crowding around both edges of the Serchio. He could hear shrieks of panic from the opposite bank on the Traghetto and on the path further north, recognising the timbre of Mira of the Burle et Malachi, who would not miss an event such as that. Facing a scenario of such bizarre, she threw her hands up on the air and fell on her knees, reciting the *Pater noster* in loud voice, as many others did the same. Soon, a jumbled choir of prayer was heard from both banks.

'What do you think it is?' asked Bernardo Delle Rocche, as he approached Julian.

'Oh, good morning, Bernardo! So soon here?' said Julian, surprised to see the hairy figure of the shepherd in the small crowd.

'The air was different last night' Bernardo said, as his eyes scanned the surroundings. 'I knew there was going to be a change, and as the night started packing to go away, I decided to come down to Mutianum and the Traghetto, even if there had been no changes. I must confess that it was not a surprise that when the dawn broke I saw the mist had gone. But then, I was not prepared for *this*!'

'Bizarre, isn't it?' said Julian, almost to himself, his voice lost on the heavy choir of prayers which was thickening. He kept looking at the hole in that enormous egg on the trees. 'I am afraid of even trying to figure out who did it, or what did it'.

'It looks like everything is too small for a bridge worker to use. Have you realised the size of those stairs?' asked the almost incredulous Bernardo.

'Well, he did have small workers. Clarissa and I saw the little men before that silly deal.'

'Yes, the *deal*, Julian. The *deal*! What if He finishes the bridge? Who's going to be the first one to cross it?'

Julian was about to open its mouth, to say something, when he had the impression of some movement going on inside the egg. Some changes in the darkness of the crack. He pointed it out to Bernardo. The shepherd saw nothing. Maybe it had been only Julian's impression. He had been so accustomed to the blindness of the mist for that past fortnight that now vision on a long distance seemed to be rather blurred. He continued then, 'Anyway, even if there was a deal, we don't really know if this man that we saw, Seth, had anything to do with it, correct?'

'Julian, look at me seriously: how can you say that? Everyone has the same story of what they saw.'

'I don't know, Bernardo. *I just don't know!*' Julian said hopelessly. 'I find it difficult to accept this whole absurdity'.

'Do you think it is any easier for me? Of for any of these people here?' Bernardo hissed with annoyance. 'Look at them, Julian. Look at them! Look at this bridge. Who else but the *Devil Himself* could be responsible for this?'

But Julian was not looking at the people in prayer. His soul was frozen when again he saw something move through that hole. He had the clear impression that a dark face peered out. Mean green eyes which blinked for a while and then disappeared.

'Oh Holy Man, save us from this evil,' cried a woman from Chifenti, falling on her knees next to Julian and grabbing onto his ankles. The Hospitaller was so much startled that he jumped back, dragging the woman together with him. 'It is corrupted!' she screamed, 'our river is corrupted!'

'*Saint Julian*, our *Holy Man*, please rid us from this wrong.' cried the others, who started to drag themselves on their knees towards Julian, including Mira herself. 'Saint Julian, bring us the Angel of Repentance to defeat this corruption in the name of the Holy Cross and grant us eternal salvation!' Some of the younger men around the group reached in to yank their wives out of the praying crowd, slapping them for their scene, but others fell or their knees too, pleading to Julian to clean the valley. The chorus for Julian started on the other side too. He could hear shouts of *Saint, Holy Man* and his name, and see the people waving desperately at him. He was being pushed back by his assailers, grabbed at the legs, shoes, sleeves and neck, on a smothering scene that made Bernardo laugh nervously, before realising the potential tragedy that could be building up and going to help his friend out of the mob.

But everything froze as a loud floundering noise broke out of the egg in the middle of the bridge. Heads turned to look at the elliptical structure balancing on the dead trees on the canoes, as the flatus like reverberation shut the prayers and the clamour which was building up around Julian. For an eternal brief moment, nothing else happened, until a black bubble started to grow out of the hole in the egg. Julian stepped back at the sight of the boil, which pulsated, swelling and shrinking, as it grew heavy, bending down as a colossal clot of blood.

Bernardo felt his heart trying to escape through his neck: 'By the ulcers of Job', the shepherd exclaimed, 'This is indeed the end of days!'

And just as if death itself had broken free of its placenta, the black bubble burst open, oozing a cascade of back matter, a dark catarrh that sprung out of the egg, missing the canoe below and raising a greyish and fetid vapour as it poured into the water. The growing mist immediately blew away a stench of rot, hammering the watching crowd on their noses all the way to curd their souls. The warm fetor was so thick and intense that instantly corrupted both banks of the Serchio, driving the people to a frenzy of panic and fear, running back to their homes or seeking refuge at the first open doors they could find.

As the roads emptied, the Serchio quickly warmed up. Julian and Bernardo ran to the hospital and helped other fear-stricken villagers in, before making sure the roads appeared safe, everyone was in, and locking the door behind them.

Only one person was seen remaining at the river bank. Before the fog once again blanketed the valley into complete whiteness, Maria Maddalena still watched the wonder in the bridge. She was smiling.

Soulgrinders

Bernardo and Clarissa tried to establish some sanity within the refugees in the hospital, no more than two scores, crying, praying, fighting and begging for food and water. Julian kept watch for the rest of the day, noticing that the mist was back, already crawling itself into the alleys, soon invading the whole valley again together with the stink it emanated. They all spent a long exhausting day and a vicious night of fear into the limited space of the hospital. Children and women cried and some desperate souls prayed, but they were constantly silenced by other villagers, alert for any sound of activity at the bridge, not too far away. Nothing was heard of any construction noises, although rustling and scratching could be heard once in a while. The animals were silent during the whole day, and at night no wind, crickets or owls made themselves heard.

The sun was not yet awake when the first creature made its way out of the coop, braving the thick mist of the night and perching on the fence behind the hospital. It flapped its wings, took a deep breath of the stinky mist and, although it was almost knocked down by the noxious gas, blew it out on a glorious crowing.

'Sounds like our rooster does not mind the fog, my dear,' Clarissa said, as she raised herself painfully from their mattress. Other women downstairs stood up to tend the fire. Julian and Bernardo unlocked the door and ventured outside. The stench was a lot milder now, and so was the mist. They walked up to Chifenti, talking to each other and passing by the bridge, which looked unchanged, behind a thick cloud of fog that involved it.

Windows in Chifenti were opened as they passed, hearing several '*who's there?*' by reassured villagers that had also stayed a full day and night locked indoors. They could however feel the warmth of the mist. Once verifying that all had been as normal as it could have, Julian and Bernardo took the path back to the hospital. As the road south approached the river bank, they could not see the water, and not yet the bridgeworks, still covered by that thick layer of mist. They could hear however the rather joyful flow of the river through the muffling mist. Both men paced slowly down the road and as they got to a thicker layer of the mist, nothing could be seen, except for the choking warmth that was emanated from the waters. And a few feet below them, a shuffling of bushes made them freeze. They saw the head of someone climbing up the bank through the thick brambles between the beech trees. Someone wearing a blue and white chequered tunic.

'Hey!' called Bernardo, 'Spatola, is that you?'

'He has got a name. You know that, Bernardo!'

'Never mind', dismissed the shepherd, as Carpo raised his apathetic eyes to them and climbed the path where they were. He looked at them with his usual empty expression.

'What are you doing down there, Carpo?' Julian asked.

'Looking.'

'How *long* have you been there?' Bernardo asked, more impatient.

'Very long, I think…'

'*How* long?' Bernardo insisted.

'All night.'

'You must be cold, creature. You never left since that…*bubble* broke out?'

'I did, but I left shelter, Amadeo's tavern, before the night fell.'

'He let you out?' Julian asked.

'I escaped,' said Carpo with a straight face, No emotion whatsoever, be it pride or shame on his act.

'Did you see anything going on at the bridge during the night?' Bernardo asked. He interposed himself between Carpo and Julian.

'No. I could not see the bridge. Fog'

'So you saw nothing?'

'No, I saw many things!'

'What things?'

'Many things.'

'Spatola, tell us more!' insisted Bernardo.

'Big things and small things.' And after looking at the annoyance drawn on Bernardo's face, he continued, 'Walking back and forth from the river... Devils, I think'.

'Oh Christ in the Holy Cross!' Bernardo said, closing his mouth with the hand, 'Look at your legs!'

'Ginevra, go fetch some fresh water! Spatola is back!' shouted an apprehensive Amadeo, from the tavern hall. 'And get something for his wounds. He has been badly hurt!'

Ginevra hurried to the well, ignoring the pain on her joints that she had gained after a poorly-slept night in the kitchen. Many villagers had sought refuge in the tavern, and the dark hours had been some of the most laborious for her, with unwanted guests demanding unreasonable comforts.

The mist was very thin. Ginevra smelled the frigid air that came from below, as the bucket was thrown into the dark stony pit. *Not foul any more*, she thought gladly, cranking the heavy windlass and thinking of the poor Carpo, out all night and coming back hurt. What would have happened?

Ginevra reckoned they had very limited purified lamb fat left. Pity that Immanuel was dead, for he had been their greatest source of remedies and herbs for tending wounds. Now, they hoped for an eventual travelling pettifogger from the north, or the long journey to be at the mercy and quackery of some doubtful barbers from Lucca, for medicinal knowledge in that stretch of the Serchio was solely under control of Maria Maddalena. And hardly for anybody would Ginevra dare and go to the hag for help. Except maybe for one person.

She turned into the tavern hall and almost dropped the bucket for, into the clearance that the crowd was opening for a table where Spatola had been laid, not only were Amadeo and Julian helping the boy, but surprisingly, and for her greatest joy, there he stood, as a victorious angel that had come to bring comfort to all of them: Bernardo Delle Rocche.

Ginevra also noticed the frank smile that split open on Carpo's face as he saw her floating skirts turn into the hall with her strong arms carrying the bucket of water, he well knew, Ginevra had brought *only* for him. But she missed the quick fading of his grin into a disappointment that would be blended with the emptiness of his usual features, as the village idiot sensed so easily the adoration that Ginevra had for Bernardo, the shepherd. Bernardo's presence surely made her cheeks go rosier, her lips meatier, it made her apron much lighter to move around her curves and her eyes twinkle like the Tuscan sky on an early winter night. And she was very aware of another young man across the hall, quietly leaning on the back wall and nibbling through the length of a straw, watching her quite well.

A horrified crowd stepped back as the men around the table raised Carpo's tunic to reveal a series of burning sores on his thighs. They were not bleeding, for they looked as if cauterised, but the skin was already oozing with clear yellow humours from the boils that were still brewing on the surface.

'What are *these*? Ginevra asked.

'We are not sure, yet', Julian said with a grave face, 'but these wounds must be cared for.'

'We hardly have any lamb fat left', stuttered Ginevra, as she tried to look at anywhere but Bernardo's face.

'Never mind that', the shepherd quickly said, 'do you have any Mary's blossom oil?'

'Mary…*blossom*?', Ginevra tried to think hard, now completely hypnotised by the rough charm of Bernardo, who delicately curved one side of his lips up, and looked at her with honey on his eyes.

He rapidly came up with another name of that flower 'Marigold!'

'Ah, Marigold! Definitely we do not have that one', she said authoritatively and swallowed hard before adding 'however, should I try to find it with… Maria Maddalena?'

'No!' he yelled, making Ginevra freeze. But her legs promptly went soft again as Bernardo completed with a devious grin 'If the witch lets you out alive, she will still probably give you a concoction that will most likely dispatch poor Spatola too sooner to his angel siblings!'

'Ooh, I heard that!' hissed the man across the hall, to himself, snapping the straw with a bite. Except for Ginevra, nobody paid heed or noticed it. When people concentrate on the plight of human pain, all else can be left ignored.

'What about lavender?' Bernardo continued, 'Do you have any?'

'Yes!' jumped Ginevra, vibrantly, forgetting about the young man across the hall, 'plenty of lavender'.

'And in the hospital,' completed Julian 'dried lavender and oil, I should have thought of that. Clarissa uses that for the pilgrims' sores.'

'Perfect then,' instructed Bernardo. 'If someone can fetch the oil at the hospital, we should gather all leaves and crush them here in a pestle…' But Ginevra didn't even care about listening to the rest. She was already rushing to the hospital, braving the thin white mist that still haunted the alleys of the Chifenti. She was relieved to see Julian following her. Nothing could be guaranteed in terms of safety of travellers in that road going south from Chifenti, for one would necessarily walk by the unfinished bridge.

The young man biting a straw across the room had his eyes on everything. How the idiot watched the promptness in which Ginevra had jumped at any questions or suggestions from Bernardo. So intense and noticeable was her worship for the shepherd that Ginevra surely paid little heed to the evident darkness that filled up the idiot's eyes. He finally turned his stare to Bernardo, hardening his facial muscles and thinning his lips, bringing his forehead down, on a thick fold of skin to almost cover his now blood-injected eyes.

The crowd around the table, so eager and easy to observe human misfortune, soon was bored by the idiot's lack of reaction to the strange wounds up to his thighs. They dispersed back onto their tables while others ventured outside, trying to return home through the misty morning.

The young man that watched from a distance saw Bernardo returning from the kitchen with Amadeo, with lavender, rosemary and olive oil, and also some spiced wine to soften the pain which the idiot did not seem to feel. Before leaving the long table where he had been laid, the idiot had clear hatred depicted on his face.

The young man that watched from a distance understood everything. 'How convenient!', Arrigo thought, smiling to himself, as he pushed his back away from the wall and let the straw fall on the floor.

As the men took Carpo's tunic to the hospital, to be washed from the blood and skin, he was laid down to rest on new straw, in the back of the stables, where a well-protected oven could offer him some solace from the cold weather. The idiot was also given some pelts for blanketing and an hour later his wounds were carefully washed by Ginevra.

'Who did that to you, Carpo?' Ginevra asked when she saw herself alone with him.

'Don't know…'

'But you must have seen someone'

'I saw many of them!' he answered without ever changing the flat expression.

'And *who* were they?'

'Don't know…small things…they were working on the bridge…and they came when they saw me. They were ugly and small…like animals…Must have been *devils*.'

Ginevra just wiped the lymph that oozed from some boils, as if nothing had been said. A frozen lump of panic went up through her throat as she heard those words. She knew that the innocence of Carpo would never let any space for deceit.

The idiot had not once been known to lie. He never changed his word, even when receiving a good beating. Everyone in that valley knew that Spatola could not just invent a story. So Ginevra tried hard to think that this was his first time pretending, but even if this was the case, whatever happened on the riverbank, must have been wicked enough to twist the idiot's frank nature.

When the wounds seemed to be fairly drained, she engaged into rubbing his thighs with the lavender oil. Carpo's eyes were fixed on the whiteness that could be seen through the jumbled tiles on the ceiling. His face never changed from its emptiness as her hands moved closer to the crotch, to delicately cover with the oil some of his deepest wounds. His manhood however, was not so indifferent to her strokes. Ginevra quickly withdrew her hands.

'Oh Mother of Christ! What is happening, Carpo?'

'Touch me Ginevra…please' he said, still looking at the ceiling.

'Stop this! I cannot.' she said nervously spilling a snigger, using his nickname for the first time ever. 'You are a boy…Spatola!'

'*Man*! I am a man, older than you.' His voice was soft but firm. His eyes moved slowly, from one tile to another. 'I can pay for it…one day.'

'Forget it,' she stood up hastily, throwing another pelt to cover his lap. 'It is not the payment…' and she hurried out of the stable, leaving Carpo on his own, still looking at the ceiling.

Outside, she saw Arrigo, observing what was going on inside the stable through the crevices of the wood.

'What are you doing here?' she asked the young man with his face stuck to the wall. 'Leave! This is our ground! You have no right to be here.'

But Arrigo only giggled as he watched Spatola inside the stables.

Bernardo was surprisingly panting as he was still half the way up the hill. The mist was suffocating compared to the clean air that he was used on the crests of the mountains. Crossing that accursed river on a boat was also a tense moment. But now he saw himself emerging out of the foggy blanket that muffled the valley, relieved to inhale a fresh winter breeze. Below him, the strange thicket of cloud that involved the Traghetto, keeping it silent and hidden. Above him, the blinding white of the Apuane broke the clear mid-day severe blue sky. Its transparency and purity, the coolness and the aromas of the mountain, the sound of a bell and goats bleating somewhere filled him with vigour to continue the march. He was home. But just after arriving at his manor at the Rocca, he looked up northeast, across the valley, on the first wooded peaks as high as he was. He needed to go back and pursue father Martino in Controne. If someone had to deal with the Devil, then a man of sense should face the Beast. A man that did not believe in it.

The whole affair of the bridge had become a puzzling invasion of real nonsense into the absurdity of Bernardo's lore. Indeed, the shepherd had shyly and quietly refrained from telling fantastic stories since his friend, the upright Julian, had confirmed the rumours about the non-less bizarre episode of the deal. The supposed apparition of the Devil himself had been witnessed by many others. And after a fortnight of stink and mist, when the valley had been immersed into a fog that had kept him up above the valley, Bernardo went down to verify himself what had been of the villages. The display on the bridge and the fetid black ooze were right out of his own repertoire, making him shiver with a strange excitement. Moreover, the injures on Spatola's skin, together with his innocent story, such grim event, drove the shepherd to suspect that maybe in such cases, in these very extreme cases, where reality could be challenging his imagination, he would need help. And with Julian and Clarissa up to their necks in the muck of their hospital, the only other person left which Bernardo could extract some common sense from would only be Father Martino. That could offer a challenge, to drive the old cantankerous priest from constant bitterness for having lost his beloved.

The unnatural fog that muffled the valley did not extend to the upper portion of the Serchio. Climbing from Fornulo and looking down to the point where the cold waters were swollen by the fog, Bernardo firmed his strides against the stones of the path which rounded the mountain. Behind him, the shepherd missed the flutter towards the quiet clouds that were hiding the river. An uncommon flutter from a dotted cloud that materialised from the heights and mingled into the fog.

As Ginevra turned out of the kitchen, carrying Carpo's tunic already washed and beaten, she was startled to the sound of a fat hairy moth, popping under her foot.

'Disgusting shit!' she heard a voice say, and looked around through the dim afternoon mist to locate its source. The slim figure of a young man appeared materialised through the fog on her right, coming from the trees on the south side. The sight of his perfect smile made her heart sink. She almost dropped the tunic on the floor, as Arrigo continued, 'They are all over the place, these moths. Like a fucking plague.'

'Not much different from you, Arrigo', she dismissed and carefully turned away, calmly trying to continue her walk towards the stables. But suddenly Ginevra realised that each step she took forward was likely going to squish another moth. Thousands of those fat hairy insects silently buzzed their silk wings, literally covering the ground behind the tavern.

'Ooooh…still a nasty wench!' he hissed, as the popping of moth juice filled the air while he approached her with a false calm but full awareness of his surroundings, clenching his teeth on a forced smile. 'Nasty as the yellow shit that squirts from these moths.'

'Stay away from me', she warned.

'Saving yourself for the idiot?' Arrigo asked without losing his grin. 'Maybe Spatola is finally a partner that is up to your level. You would probably be delighted under his slobber. He likes your touch, I have noticed.'

'You are so wicked, Arrigo, you surpass your mother. Indeed the hag is an evil woman, and you must have been shaped only from her sick entrails' she spat. Ginevra's fists were ready to dive into his eyes.

'Talking about mothers', he continued serenely, appearing unshaken by her insult, 'Where is yours? Ran away with a moor? Does she write to you from the harem?'

'That wicked mother of yours probably knows much better where she was seen alive last, you son-of-a-murderer!'

'Careful, wench. You don't want to be arrested for false accusations against the lady of these lands, do you?' Arrigo said softly. He was used to such explosions of emotion among the villagers, but never showing to be affected by any.

'Thank you for the warning, you animal,' she smirked cynically, but plainly aware that Arrigo was a dangerous man. 'I should be already used to your manners into cowardice. Just remember that these lands are ours, and now, please leave.'

'Not before we set a deal for Spatola, you insolent slut!' he said, losing his grin and quickly grabbing her wrist.

'Don't you touch me!' Ginevra growled and swung her forearm, but not enough to loosen his grip. 'What do you want, you little shit?' she challenged, 'haven't we people of the Serchio had enough deals?'

'You seem to feel to be too good for me, although you're older than my mother,' Arrigo said, looking into her eyes and tightening the grasp, making Ginevra cringe with pain. 'Now, maybe the idiot back there in the stables is good enough for your skin'. He watched her eyes open wide, trying to understand what he was coming up with. 'The unfortunate idiot wants you. He needs you. And poor thing, this Spatola: he's been spilling his deformed seed on the stables floor. All for you, old wench!'

'Let me go!' she yelled, now with both her arms being held by Arrigo. Carpo's tunic was already on the ground, covering a few moths. The loud bustling from the tavern muffled her plea, for anyone who would be at the kitchen.

'I will pay you, wench,' he continued, with blood injected eyes and thin lips of hate, 'I pay you as much as you want, to open your legs for Spatola.'

'Oh, Jesus Christ our Saviour! You are such a monster. Haven't you understood yet, you little shit?' Ginevra spat, now finally freeing her arms from Arrigo's painful grasp. 'You have no control over me. I open my legs to whomever I want.' She moved her face close to his, lips foaming with fury, carrying a victorious smirk on them. 'Yes, Arrigo, and I do it to many, many others. I am so good at it. And they all love it. Just ask them: I am good! I am the best one!'

'What is going on out there?' It was the voice of Amadeo, coming from the kitchen. The taverner came out just in time to see Ginevra picking up the blue and white chequered tunic from the ground and the figure of Arrigo disappearing in the mist. Ginevra saw Amadeo halting frozen, completely forgetting that he had just heard his daughter being threatened by the Cunimundinghi. He was looking at the ground, at the thousands of heavy fat moths that kept humming their wings for their afternoon rest. 'Jesus Christ Crucified!' he murmured in awe, 'Where the hell did these things come from?'

Clarissa did not get too disturbed about the moths.

'These are things we have to accept,' she said. 'They are here, these moths. So what? Life goes on!' she mentioned to her audience at the full hospital eatery, while she busily conducted her duties. 'And maybe...' she paused, resting a large casserole on the heavy table, 'maybe the bugs have nothing, nothing at all to do with *that*' She said with a frown. Clarissa hated to mention the deal or the bridge. Ever since the episode of the supposed apparition, when news galloped through the aisles of Mutianum and Chifenti, giving the people an update on the dealings of her husband and the devil, Clarissa had refused to talk about him or his deeds. Unlike the villagers, she preferred to carry on with normal daily routine, rather than wait for the end of times.

'To do with *what* exactly, Clarissa?' It was the clear metallic voice of Maria Maddalena. The tall woman stood at the door, as if waiting to be invited into the hospital. She was grinning.

Clarissa sighed with exhaustion. The days were already too difficult with the general fear the fog had spread. Enough people were already crowding at the hospital. The presence of that Maria Tenebrosa was not a refreshing sight. She raised one eyebrow. 'Are you expecting to be invited in, Maria? We have soup for few, but too many souls in need. If you insist, I may have to…'

'Never mind the charity, Clarissa. I don't need your watery broth.' Maria cut with a hiss, entering the hospital as if it was her house. 'Have you seen what is going on in the bridge?' she asked with a smirk.

'I have heard of what went on there, Maria.' She said with a forced fortuity, picking up the casserole back and leaving to the kitchen. She added just before disappearing 'Why do you ask if I have seen it?'

'Well, you seem to live with the man,' Maria laughed forcibly, making the ears of all guests buzz with vibration, 'the *saint* who has arranged for these devilish deeds in my lands.' She said as she marched through the hall, following Clarissa into the kitchen. But at the door passage she was surprisingly halted by Clarissa's furious gaze, pointing to the line below the frame.

'Now you do not cross into my kitchen, Maria Maddalena.' Her voice was full and thunderous. Clarissa was once again the Lady of Luna, in all her majesty, making the whole hospital silent to hear the avenging angel which threatened to smite the witch down with her sword. 'You may have acquired the rights of the Cunimundinghi,' she continued, walking towards Maria. 'Your son may command the gendarmerie, and although not invited into my hospital, you may enter the guests' facilities without being a nuisance to anybody.' Maria was already walking backwards, with Clarissa spitting fire at her. 'But in my kitchen, you do not set your filthy hexed hoofed feet, or I will drown you in the fetid waters of the Serchio, with my own hands and you will get a taste of what poor Béla and Caterina suffered because of your shameless lies.

Maria spat 'You will regret these words, you pathetic woman. And do mark mine. *Nobody* accuses me like that!' She reached the front door, perhaps furious for her display of weakness, in front of all guests in the hospital, including many of the locals. And as she turned around, she almost fell back as she saw Julian's stern face gazing at her, just outside the hospital.

'What do you want here, Maria Maddalena?' Julian said. 'By the tone of the conversation it seems to be quite clear that you are not welcome at this stage.'

Maria's dog was also waiting outside, sniffing every single moth it could, but never biting them. Seeing herself still at the door and taking advantage that she was still holding everyone's attention, Maria's voice came as loud as a hammer on an anvil 'Oh, here is the *saint*! Our own holy man, who brings Satanas and his legions into our valley!' But what the guests saw was just Maria's face disappearing behind the heavy oaken door, swung by Clarissa with all her might, slamming just inches from Maria's face, outside.

Julian could not hold a grin. 'Are you looking for me, Maria?'

'What is it that you have agreed?' she asked brusquely, not used to answer questions, and rather surprised to see Julian there, with Ginevra.

'None of your business' Julian dismissed and advanced to push the door in.

'All of my business.' voiced Maria, stomping on the ground, missing the moths, but giving Julian the impression that she made the land move. 'These are my lands!'

'The hospital is free from your ownership.' Julian said calmly.

'But not the bridge!' she cut.

'Partly true,' said Julian, already annoyed with himself for letting Maria run the discussion, as always. 'What do you want to know? Ask the right questions and you get the right answers.' He allowed for Ginevra to quickly slip in through the door.

Maria was indignant. 'Who do you think you are for such insolence? Am I here to play games with you?'

'Try me' smiled Julian, very aware that his composure was innerving to her.

'Who did you make a deal with?' she roared.

'Wrong question. I do not know the answer'.

'What are these things at the bridge?' she screamed louder.

'Wrong question again! I do not know the answer either.'

'Then did you make a deal with someone to build the bridge?' she controlled her voice.

'Ha! We are finally learning to ask the right questions:' Julian celebrated with his hands up.

'Did you or did you not?' She stomped again, this time exploding a fat moth, into a cloud of dust and yellow lymph.

'I made a deal' Julian said austerely.

'Who with?' Maria asked.

'Wrong question! You've asked that one already.' He rubbed his hands, discretely observing Maria's exhausted features. No matter the dominance she preferred to display, Maria frailty transpired easily. She already resembled a very old and tired woman, but still far from any merit of pity. 'Maria, if you don't mind, may I just enter? It is cold here outside, and I do not like these moths.'

'Wait!' she ordered. 'When do you expect to receive the bridge completed?'

'On the day of San Longinus, Maria. Just as the sun rises, we all get the bridge.' He pushed the door in and did not wait for Maria to follow.

'And what does *He* get?' Maria asked, almost pleading, '*Who* does He get?' but only to hear Julian wishing her a good day before shutting the door firmly behind him.

Julian felt the dead silence in the eatery. A stillness of fear and admiration, so intense that he thought the gurgling sound of Maria's blood, boiling up to her temples, could be heard from the breeze outside.

The door blew in violently.

From the blinding exterior, revealed among a myriad of fluttering moths, a shadow stood at the entrance: the dreadful figure of the Cunimundinghi widow in her full display of wrath.

'Julian of Mans you insolent parricide' roared Maria, trembling the skin around her thin lips with rage, her voice hitting Julian on his face, embodied with depth and sputter. 'Do not take me for a cheap bloodless peasant. You should think much better, much more carefully, before making the big mistake of shutting the door on my face, you little...'

Julian just swung his left hand and the door was once again slammed, thudding mutely, an inch from Maria's face.

Father Martino had been a lucky man, thought Bernardo.

The shepherd was thinking about sister Caterina, an extraordinary woman that he had loved himself, but whose life was destined to be side-by-side with Martino. She was dearly missed not only by her men, but also by many families, from Partigliano to Controne, who had received her care and attention. The thought of her sunny features made Bernardo at ease, almost forgetting the bizarre happenings of those days. Caterina had a disorderly way about everything, often sitting like a man and even talking with the language of man. She had treated her man Martino with a public display of affection, but never, thought Bernardo, never looking vulgar. Caterina had been one of those few creatures, indeed like Clarissa, who could have made obvious to the world, but especially to him, the ultimate proof of the existence of a divine power of God. And the pain for her loss had dug ugly trenches in the face of Father Martino.

Controne had not been entirely affected by the spring weather which had washed upon the Serchio. The mountain top still had some thick patches of snow sitting on the wet ground of chestnut leaves. Martino and Bernardo were outside the church, looking above the woods down to the clouds of steam raised by the baths on the Lima valley below. Bernardo had told the parishioner every detail that he knew about the events of the bridge, for Martino had not been down to see it yet.

'Bernardo, I had heard the rumours and I preferred to ignore,' Martino said, with a hoarse voice, as he watched the shapes taken by the clouds down below. 'But then, when the spring weather came out of time and the fog was lifted, it raised my own suspicions too. And now the villagers are describing a hellish scenario down by the bridge and what you tell me does sound like one of your stories.' He turned to Bernardo 'I would surely send you back to your lands with some penitence to pay if it wasn't for the truth I can detect in your eyes.'

'Don't trust my eyes, Martino. Trust your own. Let's go down to the bridge and you will witness this devilry yourself.'

'We will, my friend. And I will show you that there are no devilries to be afraid of. I have seen many things in my life that have been attributed to the devil. They are all human and harmless. But we go tomorrow. It is late now and you should stay in the parish until we leave in the early hours.'

They were fording the Lima at sunrise, from Fornulo, horrified to see the amount of moths on the trees and on the ground. Walking swiftly through a moth-ridden Chifenti, they did not want to stir attention and have anyone follow them. The walk down to the bridge, especially under that particularly pleasant weather, did not take too long. As they got closer, the scenario was hazed by the fog, still concealing the entire pillars of the bridge and the scaffoldings that had been raised over the last weeks.

'Nothing! I can see nothing...' wondered Martino, standing by the eastern embankment. Floating two paces in front of him, there was a wall of mist. Nothing could be seen beyond it, but a few paces of the paved path raising itself towards the bridge. 'Whatever it is in there, we will soon find out. I'm not afraid of anything these days.' He said with a curve of his lips and a shine in his eyes that almost gave his wooden features a well-humoured countenance.

'I should better just run down to the hospital and fetch Julian before you start it.' Bernardo suggested with undisguised nervousness. He was regretting not having brought a *francesca* or any other weapon.

This time, the shepherd noticed that Martino was really smiling 'If indeed our Hospitaller had a deal with the devil, we will get no help from someone who seems to be up to his neck into this dirt. Let's leave Julian be before we clean this mess up.'

Bernardo was speechless when he heard the parishioner adding 'Do you come with me?' and stepping into the mist before even receiving an answer.

Bernardo tried to protest, but it was too late. Martino had disappeared. Too desperate to think, the shepherd took a deep breath and followed the parishioner into the fog.

Martino was only a few paces ahead. He was standing on the edge of the embankment, where the scaffolding structure began. The woodwork was complex, with boards and planks and twigs and metal plates, ropes and bars, chains and leather straps, all nailed, tied, pinned, inlaid and plaited together, in a colossal confusion of materials so well connected that it sustained well its own massive bulk across and over the pillars. The stairs and footpaths that climbed over and around the contraption were not only too small for a normal person to walk over, but they were crooked and confused, ending abruptly behind a corner, diving into hidden trapdoors or into the wooden wall, where another one had not even started.

'It's...so tiny, so inhuman.' Martino said, almost in a whisper. The dead silence reigned fat and comfortably inside the fog.

Bernardo tapped the parishioner's shoulders from behind and stuttered to start his own whispering 'However small it could be, remember that it has hurt Spatola. Maybe we should just leave. Let's go back, Martino. It's not wise to-'

'Nonsense!' Martino intervened with a somewhat humorous tone. 'If there's a devil in here, he will have to deal with me!' He stepped over the structure.

The wood creaked and a faint crushing sound was head underneath, but it kept firm under the priest's weight. He gave another step, avoiding a tight rope between two poles and a tiny ladder of thin wood that seemed to go around the whole surface seen under that fog. He heard another creak and more crushing, but again felt his foot finding solid base underneath.

'It's easy,' Martino said, turning to Bernardo with relief on his voice. 'The structure is firm enough to sustain a fully grown man. I will go to the middle and make sure whoever is doing this poor taste mockery will be properly cast out of — ' but he did not finish his sentence, as the structure where he was standing on ceded with a loud crack and he slipped down through a hole, down to his waist.

'MARTINO!' Bernardo shouted, reaching out with his hands, but too far to grab the priest. Martino had luckily hit firmer ground inside that confusion of planks. His upper body was sticking out of the hole. He turned around, looking embarrassingly inappropriate 'Now I cannot get my body out of here.'

Bernardo stepped on with his right foot and extended his hand 'I will help you there, let me just —'

'No, Bernardo, no!' Martino interrupted, 'Just stay there! If you're not careful we'll be both stuck here. All I need to do now is to lift some boards around me and...what was that?' he said, looking around in haste.

'What?' Bernardo asked. 'I didn't see anything.'

'No, listen...'

They heard some shuffling inside the boards. Steps and grits, and something that sounded like...whispering. Bernardo had no time to think when the eyes of Martino seemed to bulge out in sheer horror.

'There's something in my legs!' the priest said, just a second before he was immediately yanked in with a violent blow, snapping the boards around him and disappearing into the dark hollow.

Helpless and incapable of stepping ahead, Bernardo bellowed for Martino's name, while the priest's screams could be heard through a sequence of snapping sounds and slamming doors inside that mass of wood and metal, a sound that slowly seemed to move further away from the shepherd, towards the middle of the bridge. But the priest's screams could still be heard 'OH MY GOD! OH MY GOD! PLEASE HELP ME! CATERINA! TAKE ME WITH YOU, CATERINA! TAKE ME AWAY FROM HERE!'

The movement through the structure was quick, as it seemed to break and crash with violence through any internal obstacle, but it faded away and became silent in no time. No more words or howls were heard from Martino.

Bernardo kept crying for Martino's name, unable to step further out of the stones on the embankment, unable to move to help his friend. He did not stop calling until his voice faltered under his own cascade of tears. He finally dropped his shoulders and ran back to the road, towards the Hospital of Santa Croce, to look for his other friend.

But his cries had already been heard all the way to Traghetto and to the hospital. He was running and crying like a lost boy, when he saw a people coming towards him. He hoped it would be Julian, but another loud sound drew his attention to the bridge: the same floundering noise they had heard when the black bubble broke out of the enormous egg structure. This time he stopped running and looked back to see that the fog had dissipated exactly in the area where the egg was suspended, on the tallest arch. And after the bubbling noise subsided, a new cascade spewed out of the egg into the river. Bernardo fell on his knees and howled out in anguish, for this time the liquid that poured into the Serchio was viscous and brilliant red.

The cascade was brief, but it seemed to stir the appetite of the fish, or whatever voracious creatures dwelled in the river, boiling avidly under the red stain that quickly dispersed down the current. But Bernardo's horror had not ended for, as the fog closed in once more, he caught a glimpse of several large pieces of leather hanging from the scaffolding spikes around the egg, like wet clothes left out to hang. And his stomach tried to jump out through his mouth on realising that some were empty horse hides, but others looked like hollow human skins.

Volunteers for Damnation

Weeks struggled to squeeze through a heavy sitting time of sorrow and fear. While the fog came and went, briefly exposing a growing collection of ghastly trophies hanging on the spears, dripping down into the Serchio, looking at the bridge became undesirable, with locals learning how to avoid its sight, even when they walked by. Pilgrims had an instinctive distaste for the subject. The bridge seemed unnatural and so much of a sign of the end of times. Its vision just hurried them into their sites of prayer and contemplation. They did not dare to stare at the bridge and they did not mention it.

The days passed darker, lonelier and colder. Folk along the Serchio were nauseous, with sadness and anger growing inside their hearts and guts, like eel-sized parasites, fed by desperation and helplessness. And in several cases, it was fomented by night visits sent by the bridge construction crew. While many villagers and peasants just stayed indoors, hoping and praying for the end of that nightmare and quick deliverance and mercy in the final judgement, there were two locals who took to travel frequently along the eastern road of the Serchio. These were Arrigo and his mother Maria Maddalena, of the Cunimundinghi.

Bernardo was inconsolable and, to Ginevra's utmost desperation during those times of uncertainty, he disappeared from view in his most recluse manors up on the Apuane.

'It's time you get her!' Arrigo hissed, catching Spatola by surprise as he strolled through Chifenti, holding the idiot firmly by the shoulder. 'The old shepherd is gone. She needs you now Spatola. Ginevra is in dire need of a man like you between her legs!'

The idiot grabbed onto Arrigo's wrist and firmly pulled it out of his shoulder, no matter how much the Cunimundinghi tried to prevent it.

'I'm your friend now,' insisted the young lord of Anchiano with a new-found sweetness to his voice, 'never mind when I was too young and played rough with you. I understand you now, Spatola. I know what you want and what you need. And it's Ginevra that you should have.'

With jaws tightly clenched, Carpo still held Arrigo's hand firmly away from him, with cautious eyes in his blank face. But the young Cunimundinghi continued 'I can understand you anger and frustration, my friend. I am the only one that truly considers your feelings, that truly knows you. I'm your only friend.'

'LEAVE HIM ALONE!' They both turned their heads to see Ginevra roaring from the tavern door. She was covered in sweat, as usual, from the hard work to attend all patrons. But she was standing in alert, ready to strike.

Arrigo just smiled, raised his free arm and opened his other hand, showing clearly that he was the one being held. Carpo dropped his gaze and released the young man's wrist. Ginevra grunted and disappeared into the tavern.

'Look at the wench!' Arrigo continued, 'Howling at you like a she-wolf. That bitch needs to be held down while she gets what she deserves. Just keep the shepherd away from her and she'll forget about him.'

Carpo just stood there, expressionless.

The darkness of that early year of Our Lord of One Thousand and Thirty Three, in the lower valley of the Serchio, just south of the Caferonia, still felt somehow sunny and refreshingly uplifting for one of the inhabitants. She had not been depressed or waiting for the end of days, although she was, like so many masses of Christians, waiting for the coming of the Beast. Maria Maddalena of the Cunimundinghi had been exceptionally courteous to all, from her household in Anchiano to the villagers and peasants, but quite especially pleasant, to the best of her limitations, to Julian, the Hospitaller.

'I don't trust the sincerity of this witch.' Clarissa would tell Julian, while he quietly nodded and never gave in to Maria's niceties. He maintained a neutrality of mood, welcoming her assistance when rarely offered, but not bowing to her newly-brewed honey.

Maria Maddalena had been particularly happy about two major developments around her life. The first was the disappearance of Father Martino. The priest had been a link to the woman Caterina, a witness of her humiliating past. With the loss of Martino, no more memories could be raised about that time of darkness. They were slowly all leaving, taking with them knowledge, alibis and reminiscences that stained her own glorious elevation to nobility. Divina, Béla, Caterina, her own father Immanuel, and now the Parishioner of Controne. She was counting on three more events to fulfil the success of her ascension and continuity for her son Arrigo. One would be to clear the world of that savage Obertenghi landlord Bernardo delle Rocche. The shepherd had known Caterina before Maria became aware of the nun's existence. She knew he was also an active reminder of her past, but since the day that the parishioner Martino had disappeared from this world for not having taken the Devil seriously, Bernardo had not shown his hairy face around those lands. Next would be to eliminate the filthy Antelmino di Gottefredo, who had her in his hands, extorting exorbitant tolls for her produce and savouring knowledge of her links with Béla and Caterina's deaths. But for that she would need a complete bridge. Once the bridge was functioning, she could strengthen the ties of Anchiano with Lucca and weaken the gold chests of the Castracani. She would smother the hospital and soon control the bridge. The following natural steps would be to recover Chifenti and look at claiming Obertenghi lands across the river. But the first event that she eagerly waited for was the day of deliverance of a complete bridge. The feast of Saint Longinus. That is the day when she would be the earliest person on the embankment and, as the sun shone its first rays on the newly built-stonework, she would be the first to cross the bridge.

Maria Maddalena had a very pragmatic approach to life and death. Not that she had no appreciation for the rewards of heaven and punishment in hell. She did have faith in the ominous existence of both and on judgement before God, which also included belief in the power of the Devil, as well as in the curse which Béla had whispered in her ears. Never thinking that it would be ever possible to undo the curse unless by Béla's wicked design, she had now the hope and firm certainty that everything in life had a purpose, and that her chance to meet the Devil and deliver herself to him, imploring for the Arrigo's salvation.

Damnation could be a reasonable price for a happy and successful life for herself and for the continuation of her line.

In those first months of the Year of our Lord of One Thousand and Thirty Three, Antelmino had little notion of how big the empire of his dynasty would turn out to be one day. He was tense about the bridge, surreptitiously visiting the region on foot, and spying on everyone's activity, especially on his neighbours, the Cunimundinghi. He was sorry to hear about father Martino's tragic disappearance, for he wanted to be the one personally delivering a hard boot on that man's face before dropping him into hell. But one could not have it all, so he was glad that the insolent parishioner had been slaughtered, as the rumours had it.

Now Antelmino respected the bridge as an inevitable future to deal with. He needed to study the ground and the movements of the lecherous Lady of Anchiano and her intractable son. Antelmino trusted nobody and preferred to make the visits to that stretch of the Serchio on his own. And the other landowners that he would specifically be alert for, were the Hospitaller, the owner of Chifenti and the two other women in that region who should learn their right position under a real man's cock: the Hospitaller's wife, and the wench from Chifenti.

And one day, not too long before the bridge's handover, Antelmino would find himself lucky. He would finally take control of an opportunity that would change his life forever.

The Hospital of Santa Croce received the repeated visits of the few religious men and women that did not leave the region upon news of the ominous coming of the beast. Some had fled when the suggestions of Raoul Glaber's washed over Italy. But a new contingent fled when the rumours of a deal with the Devil down by the broken bridge had been spread across every village and farmstead. Julian was patient, carefully bearing enquiries and complaints from the quiet old Vannozzo from Chifenti, the blind priest Bartolomeo from Fornulo, the cantankerous Francesco from Menabla, the albino Father Nerozzo from Saint Peter in Corsena, the very distressed Father Diloguardi from Mutianum, and Father Lorenzo from

Bertagna, up on the mountains behind the hospital. Abbess Lodovica and the few sisters that remained at San Salvatore, even the parishioner of Diecimo and some monks from Pescaglia came to Julian. The only still resident priest that did not go was the chaplain of Anchiano, who was told by a stern Maria Maddalena to leave the matters be, for that nonsense could only be a superstitious rumour.

Such pestering from the God-approved authorities in matters of heaven and hell, demanding answers about Father Martino that could not be given and explanations that would make no Christian sense, left both Clarissa and Julian with little time to be dedicated to each other. Except for the moments in their chamber, sharing their comfortable mattress, their daily routine allowed them no chances to consider and less to confide the thoughts and emotions of the day.

Under the silent watch of night, when all pilgrims and guests had dined, it was the Hospitallers' best opportunity to hold each other's hands and exchange their very own protecting, comfortable gaze. That was when Julian and Clarissa could feel the warmth inside, the flames from their mutual love, a chance to be powerful and intense, to deliver themselves submissive and lovingly, to be the owners of their own heaven.

Still, they could not pretend that nothing was happening outside.

'Do you want to talk about it, Julian?' Clarissa whispered, for the lights and flames were out, except for the hearth by their palliasse and for the candles downstairs, in the hall.

'Not really, Clarissa, but maybe I should.'

'What are you thinking about, then?'

'The *deal*, of course. It looks like we will have a bridge indeed. Every time the fog dissipates we see more of a construction. And who's going to be the first one to cross it?'

'Maybe nobody,' Clarissa suggested. 'Maybe we should raise a large wall around each embankment.'

Julian made a clicking sound with his tongue. 'That would not work, you know that. Someone would be fool enough to trespass it and cross the bridge.'

'If they are stupid enough and bold enough to dare trespass, maybe they deserve damnation then.' said Clarissa.

Julian held her hand, warm and delicately. 'Clarissa, I can only think of one solution to prevent anyone from crossing this bridge on the day it's delivered.'

'And what would that be?' Clarissa asked, instinctively withdrawing her hand.

'I will be the first one to cross!'

Clarissa was silent for a long time. She finally cleared her throat and said 'Julian, I think I didn't hear too clearly what you have just said a while ago. Maybe I misheard it, so can you please tell me again what the solution would be?'

'I know it's not easy to understand, Clarissa, but when you think —'

'*Just tell me again* what you said, Julian.' Interrupted Clarissa, 'I have a problem in understanding or maybe in believing my hearing.'

'Clarissa, my love, you heard what I said. I will be the first one to cross the bridge.'

She clenched her jaws and let a long uptake of air slowly escape from her lungs. 'Tell me more,' she demanded.

'Clarissa, I'm giving away my soul in exchange of anyone else's. I am not doing it for my willingness to burn in hell, but for sparing someone else from this fate. Whether they call me a saint or not, it's irrelevant for I do not become what people decide. But angels are watching us, we both know that. And it is these same angels that will protect me. They know my heart, they know you're in there, so they know the reason I am doing it, and they cannot ignore my selflessness. *God cannot ignore this sacrifice.*'

Clarissa said nothing. She just moved her body away and got up, looking for the tinderbox. She calmly started a flame and fed it to a lantern. Julian watched passively, while she approached their bed and sat comfortably beside him, adjusting her long hair to the side with a delicate movement of her fingers and bringing the lantern closer to their faces.

'Julian, just look at me,' she said, 'look at me, closer into my eyes.' The Hospitaller leaned on his elbow and made a good-natured effort to keep steady in his thoughts, without losing himself into heavens while staring at her rainbow of colours. Clarissa continued 'Julian of Mans, Lord of Luna and Hospitaller of Santa Croce. Either you are a formidable imbecile, which I think may not be the case, for I don't think I'm giving my life and love to such a fool, or you are sick out of your mind, which is likely to be true. Whatever preposterous absurdity that you have just uttered a while ago was, I just ask you to be aware and believe me: it was nonsense! It was pigeon shit, to be scrapped off and thrown away. It was fish shit, that just murks crystal-clear water. There is no sacrifice, there is only stupidity. Julian, if you go, I will not let you. If you try harder, I promise you will never see me again.'

Julian held her hand tight, smiling, but shaking his head in denial 'Clarissa, try to think of it, you don't understand –'

'No, Julian. It's *you* that do not understand. The explanation is quite simple. It's *love*! I love you for the loving man that you are, for your amazing generosity and your willingness to be good. But I love you enough and quite selfishly to not allow you to do it. Very simply, if you try to cross that bridge you will never see me again.'

'I will Clarissa. I will chase you, wherever you are.'

'You will not find me.'

'I will.'

They had an unforgettable night.

Clarissa was furious and she rode Julian ferociously. And while exploding into thousand pieces scattered throughout heaven, she visited the angels and talked to them.

When she finally exhaled from the explosive wave that carried her through the most beautiful lands, letting her body fall into rest, into a comfortable bed of feathers and petals, her heart was at peace and her lips had a smile.

It was one thousand years since the death of the Son of God. This year the fallen angel, the Light-Bearer, finally broke his chains. Lucifer was at large.

A young nun was scared. She had only arrived in the Eternal City and its first images overwhelmed her with their powerful messages of chaos. She had left the far away security of her house of prayer with her sisters in God and they camped for uncountable days, accompanied by hordes of pilgrims seeking ultimate salvation in the heart of the church. They had crossed foreign countries, lands that had been ravaged by wandering mobs, burned farmlands and abandoned parishes; they had carefully walked through the hostile stares of peasants, not used to such movement; she had hid her young face behind the darkness of her cowl, preventing strangers from contemplating her pristineness, for which only the Son of God was worthy.

Now, the nun couldn't help but vomit at the first whiff of cartloads of bloated corpses being dumped out of the city gates. Rome's frenzied streets were the Hellmouth materialised, opening its fat lips and spewing out all suffering and punishment from its entrails. Brutal accumulation of wretched souls seeking asylum next to the throne of Saint Peter had infested the waterways with pestilences that soiled the streets buildings and waterways, killing the pilgrims and locals by the hundreds, to a point where catacombs or graveyards' wardens where not accepting any more cadavers. The nun knew deep in her heart that this was a clear sign of Satan's work, she knew he was there, trying to topple the true Christ from his cross. And all other pilgrims agreed on that.

Lost in the overrun alleys under the loud buzz of the city, trying to communicate in vain on a foreign language, the nuns struggled to walk in an unintelligible direction, stepping over drunken bodies, dodging beggars and ragged women who were frantically imploring for food and carrying the cadaveric frail bodies of their malnourished offspring. Everything new to the young nun, everything more poignant and pungent than she had ever dreamed of for that city of God. Her heart broke into as many grains as a mountain of sand could have, witnessing pickpockets assaulting the elder, children swarming over dejecta from taverns and fighting for scraps of food, and diseased bodies being tossed out of their homes to die under the winter chill. Vile, raw cruelty that dragged up choking bile from her stomach, creeping up to the nose, entangling with the drone in her ears and forming a lump of nausea that was blurring her vision, especially when the group found itself stuck at the end of an alley, smothered in a cul-the-sac and cornered by a troupe of ravenous drifters. Hearing the sisters crying and praying in utter desperation, the young nun still had a glimpse of a very thin man with a furious grin exposing his sinful shame to her eyes. She was preparing to give all her senses into the saints and martyrs' hands, when the rustling sound of a latch was heard and a hand grabbed her robes, pulling her into cold darkness.

Wooden scents dissipated into those of sweat, oil and incense, permeating the silent interior of that heavenly church where the flames burned out of cups of oil, rather than on tallow candles. As the nuns were somehow hastily pushed towards the altar, where a monk gave them a few pieces of stale bread and a bowl of water, the young nun viewed with marvel the rays of light that entered from the high alabaster windows, illuminating the columns that ascended onto the nave, headed by lions and angels, cherubs that would protect the true faithful from the dragon, with the heavenly power of their swords.

They passed the bowl, drinking the foul tasting liquid, and the nuns praised the angels for their providence and shelter, for allowing them to spend their remaining days before the final judgement in a house of God. The young nun was strangely given a larger piece, of which she was happy to share again with her sisters. Under the continuous murmurs that muffled the night, they slept in peace, protected by the large cross where an exhausted Jesus had dropped his head.

Late, when the sun stood high on the south, the doors were opened by ceremonious monks, bringing in an explosion of light and a parade of thurifers, swinging their fumigant censers and casting a thick, blinding cloud, blessing that temple with the aroma of frankincense, myrrh, juniper and roses. Out of this cloud sailed a glorious figure, slow and decisive, robbed in shiny vests and covered in gold and silver, wearing a tall conic hat that was covered in shiny stones of all colours. With tears running down her healthy cheeks, the young nun knew that this blissful privilege could only be a heavenly gift of their dedication to the love of Jesus Christ.

The papal mitre raised shining and tall, with all its treasures ahead of her. Only after a moment could she adjust her eyes against the light to see the divine figure that stood angelically on its pontifical majesty. He was a young man. A Jesus incarnate, with a tender smile and loving eyes that met her unworthy gaze, before she immediately dropped to her knees, and lied flat on the floor, undeserving of this blessing, unfit for his beauty, embarrassed of her smallness, ashamed of her tears. And she heard sweet words from his heavenly voice just above her. Unintelligible but universally comforting, from the tenderness of his voice and the beauty of the Latin resonance. And her body shuddered with emotion as his hands touched her shoulder, calling her to raise her sinner's eyes towards his cloud, towards the divinity of his height. She held onto his warm hand and kissed the shiny stones of his large golden ring. With a heart full of devotion, she kissed his fingers while they tenderly traced the contour of her lips.

'Ecce tetigit hoc labia tua et auferetur iniquitas tua et peccatum tuum mundabitur.'

The heavenly language. *See, this has touched your lips; your guilt is taken away and your sin atoned for.* She could not make anything of them, but a sense of love and redemption. Still with that divine hand on hers, with those fingers touching her face, she needed to inhale its scents, to feel its smoothness, the healed wounds of the cross, to taste its moisture, to be part of it.

'Surrexi ut aperirem dilecto meo manus meae stillaverunt murra digiti mei pleni murra probatissima.'

I arose to open for my lover, and my hands dripped with myrrh, my fingers with flowing myrrh, on the handles of the lock.

Her eyes were closed in her ascension tasting the honey of his skin, but missing his hand through her slippery grasp as the pope turned around and slowly vanished into the luminous cloud of incense.

As the young nun inhaled deeply to catch her breath and her heart fought the angst of being culled out to stay in the world of the living, gentle hands held her arms and helped her to her feet. She was whispered soft words on her ears, while being conducted towards the luminous cloud. Her legs trembled as she forced herself once again into her knees and felt an explosion of glory in her heart. She was saved. Her dedication had paid. Satanas would not seize her.

The hands helped her up and onto a tall cart, a rich ark of treasures, the chosen ones, a vehicle that glided high above the sinners, crushing with its massive wheels the iniquity, the poverty, the greed, the madness and the filth of the end of days. It took her into the expansions of light, carrying her up the Lateran hill, that great and high mountain, where the great city, the holy Jerusalem, descended out of Heaven from God. The papal palace stood splendidly for her, like a stone most precious, clear as crystal, and she knew it had its twelve gates through its high walls, and at the gates twelve angels and names written thereon, which were the names of the twelve tribes of the children of Israel.

Inside the glorious palace she heard the music and laughter from the angels and saints, and there were scents of myrrh and frankincense and ripened fruits and wine. And the pope descended to take her hands once again, young and beautiful, a tender smile with the touch of petals on his skin. The cool air around her head, uncovered for the first time since her dedication to the cross, made her face flush, but she broke with a smile of blessedness when he flung her cowl backwards. Her delicate body heated in white flames of love, overwhelmed under his reassuring embrace, as he sang words of honey, lifting her carefully in his arms and gliding through a patio of dried cyclamens and roses, a winter Eden where she planned to return for the eternal spring that lied ahead. Limp with sanctity, she allowed her lips to implore for his goodness and generosity, which he gracefully shared, touching them with his and allowing those streams of holy blood, crystal clear and fresh with affection to flow between them.

If only any other soul could be so blessed as to appreciate a tiny proportion of the passion, of the ascension to paradise on the pope's arms, the young nun would be eternally happy for that generosity of God.

They entered a warmer room, lit by flickering flames in oil cups, scented with copper, milk and musk, where music permeated through the curtains and shame was no more among the other angels. He rested her upon a silk-covered *triclinium* and rid himself from the regalia, naked as the Son of God, pure as the Creation of God. She was naked with her husband, and they felt no shame.

'Statura tua adsimilata est palmae et ubera tua botris. Dixi ascendam in palmam adprehendam fructus eius et erunt ubera tua sicut botri vineae et odor oris tui sicut malorum. guttur tuum sicut vinum optimum dignum dilecto meo ad potandum labiisque et dentibus illius ruminandum.'

Your stature is like that of the palm, and your breasts like clusters of fruit. I will climb the palm tree; I will take hold of its fruit. May your breasts be like the clusters of the vine, the fragrance of your breath like apples, and your mouth like the best wine.

His sacred hand slowly and tenderly acknowledged her treasures and anointed her inviolability. Opening her eyes through the cloudy delights, she noticed the glistening bodies of other angels exercising heavenly love around them. And she knew she had that love, built up of fire over her lifetime, ready to be delivered to her object of adoration, in an explosion that would make all those angels in heaven stop and watch, singing hymns to her glory.

In a long and sensual sigh of release, her body arched in sweat, ceding the shyness, releasing the muscles, preparing for the ultimate deliverance. She opened herself to him and moaned passionately on seeing the joy on his face. The petals of her flower wet in dew, tingling with music, yielding to grace, finally opening for the eternal springtime. This was her utmost reward for the ultimate sacrifice.

When the fiery plunge drove through flesh and moisture, she was flooded with oceans of perfume, rivers of sweetness and lightning bolts, uncontrollable forces so furious that exploded inside her, screams of angels and flights of doves, powerfully driving her fingernails on his skin, dragging them towards her, opening trenches of red, like the sacred blood that flew from the reed scars of the smitten Christ. It was now, through the immaculate womb of the Virgin, when she was finally united with God, bursting in light and glory, screaming with the full fiery joy of her lungs and oblivious to any mundaneness of His creations on earth, ignoring even the screams of the pope.

'Not yet! *Not yet!* I am *not* finished!' he roared.

But the divine fire still burned her body, stretching it to the infinite extensions of heaven, the flavours of honey and pomegranates still lingering in her mouth. Her muscles flickered, thrilled with the power to be the lover of Men, to be the mother of Men, slowly cooled by the chill breezes that blew as the storm of love signalled to move away. The effect would be sweet and soothing, if it wasn't for the stone-heavy fist that crushed with a burst of pain in her jaw.

'Move, you limp cow! *Move!* I told you I was *not* done!'

Tasting blood in her mouth and with sheer horror in her eyes, the young nun saw Benedict IX raising his fist once more and bringing it back on her face on a formidable arch, again with an explosion of pain as tooth broke against tooth and bone cut through flesh.

She tried to breathe in, but the shock had frozen her lungs. Paralysed with fear, with strings of blood hanging down her chin, she felt the pope leaving her and looked around the dimness with revulsion, a filthy den, an orgy where she had been lured into. Opening her arms wide and finally gathering the strength, she screamed for God's help.

Two older men came to her aid, lifting her from the triclinium. Both were naked. They tumbled her down on an *accubita* and held her head against a pillow. She could not move, fight back or breathe, for a firm, large hand held her face. They were quick to hold her legs apart and break inside, burning like a hot poker. She understood the filth in their cackling as infernal bouts of throbbing pain exploded behind her. Inside her.

The young nun could only open her eyes to her side and detect, behind a curtain of tears and mass of sweating bodies, that young man, that monster wearing the papal mitre, committing an abominable carnal sin with another deacon. Her soul drifted away from the soreness and mortification on her body, her eyes focused better on the demon that was now drooling and grunting like a pig, as he dropped his mitre and raised a gaze of blood-injected eyes of fury towards her.

She did not ask why, nor tried to understand the reason. She just knew that her lifetime devotion to the painful steps to the true Cross had not been sufficiently heartily. And now, she began to accept that her violation by Satanas himself was only the beginning of her punishment.

The Metato

On that cold morning of the thirteenth of March, a thousand years after the death and resurrection of Jesus Christ, when the few churches in Italy that had not been abandoned by fear of the end of days were celebrating the feast of Saint Euphrasia, the shepherd Bernardo delle Rocche had some issues to adjust, not with his distant cousin, but with a different type of devil. He wanted revenge on that thing, whatever had built that bridge. On whomever had taken away the life of Father Martino.

Fuck the bridge! I will burn that bastard into ashes.

Bernardo had silently rowed across the Serchio north of the bridge, not far from the village of Chifenti, where the river gained body from the cool crystal waters of the Lima. In that stretch, the current moved slow, but decisively, with no cascading drops or rocky obstacles. A boat could easily be left on its own and the currents would take care of it. It would drift firmly downstream, through the newly built pillars, under the complex scaffolding structure. The egg-like structure had already been gone, but the bridge, if there was indeed one there, was still completely hidden by a thick mass of wooden scaffolding. So if the boat had a mast, a long tall mast, it would get stuck under the construction. And if it was burning hot in flames, it could start a colossal blaze and reduce the bridge and all its demons to ashes.

During his reclusion in the castle of the Rocca, watching the eventual appearances of the damned bridge through the fog, Bernardo was visited by some of his underlords. He asked them all about what would happen to their lands if the bridge was a non-event. They all confirmed that life would be as it had ever been.

Now he had only one day to do it. But he would make it in half. He would drag the floating log pile silently to a point not too far upstream. He would set it on fire still before dark and not too far from the bridge. And before the night was high, the bridge would be gone. And there would be nothing to be delivered to anyone on the day of St. Longinus.

And the best of all, no one's soul would burn in hell either.

Bernardo pulled the boat over to anchor it on the narrow rocky bank. He would start immediately, collecting twigs and piling the boat with wood. But that was not his own land and he should not clear it unauthorised. That riverbank belonged to Amadeo.

Bernardo would have to climb up to the path and see the taverner for a permit to cut some trees. It would be convenient to step into Chifenti for a moment, for maybe he could find Spatola and convince the idiot to help him with the logs. And much more, he could have a chance to see the lovely Ginevra. Something had been suggesting the shepherd that in spite of the age difference, the young tavern wench was rather exalted towards him. It made him crave for her presence and company, more than he could ever remember feeling towards female company. Perhaps he was getting older and needed a wife. With a swing of his matted locks, he shook the thoughts of desire out of his hairy head and started the climb.

The terrain soared high, almost vertically, through a wooded slope of beeches, right under the eastern path, which curved maybe twenty paces above the water, between Chifenti and the hospital, much further to the south. Snow had already melted, and the forest floor was covered in wet leaves and thorny berry bushes. Bernardo held on to the smaller beech trunks that had sprouted on the previous spring and pulled his weight upwards. Looking around, he saw many dead trees which could probably be used for the bonfire. He climbed carefully, to a vertical stone wall, a terrace that held the road curve. Grabbing onto the top of the wall, he managed to slip his foot into a crevasse and lifted himself to see the road, and a pair of hairy feet in front of his face.

Bernardo looked up. Above the dirty, scarred shanks, he devised a blue chequered tunic, and sighed with relief.

'It's you, Spatola!' he said with glee, extending a hand 'I'm glad you're so prompt when I need you. Give me a hand here and we will go to the tavern so I can–'

But he was stopped by a crunch, an explosion of pain on his head, which made everything dark and all thoughts meaningless.

Spatola watched Bernardo's body falling from the wall and rolling down the hill side, just to stop at some young beeches. Looking at the large rock on his own hands, Spatola saw the blood and appreciated the power that his blow had carried. He hurled the rock against Bernardo, downhill, just missing the shepherd's face. He wanted to climb down and finish what he had started, but pilgrims had shown over the road, leaving Chifenti.

Spatola could not waste time trying to think. He just ran.

The doors of Anchiano whined when opened, and Arrigo rode out slowly, spiralling down around the rock and enjoying the sunshine.

Arrigo was seventeen now. Of strong built and large hands, he was not as tall as one would expect from a son of Maria Maddalena, for he inherited mostly his father's height. That was about all he had taken from the Cunimundinghi blood. Everything else seemed to recall his mother. His grey eyes were dull, but alive with their speed. His lips were thick, which would have matched well a frank smile, but they were not yet adjusted to his carefully-constructed countenances. With the red hair and the freckles across his stubby nose, he had a childish face which had grown wider as he aged and certainly lost its grace. But today, he looked altogether pleasant. He was even smiling as the sun shone on his face. To start with, it was agreeable enough to ride away from the coldness of the manor, from the bitterness of his mother, who had been so gloomy of late. He could tell she was brewing something, but he could not conceive what it was.

But mostly, Arrigo had decided to act on his own. He was prepared to have a full day and he hoped it would be a profitable one. He was ready to ride through his lands and raise a movement that would be giving a new beginning to the history of the Cunimundinghi. When the stony path down to the village ended, he kicked his heels in and started a gallop towards the road to his triumph. Towards his destiny.

His plans only changed after a couple of minutes, as soon as he entered the Serchio road and saw the village idiot of Chifenti running like a terrified hart.

'Whoa, Spatola! Whoa!' he shouted, jumping off his horse and holding on tightly to the idiot's arm. 'What happened? Tell me. Who's after you? The devil?'

Carpo was a strong man. He could have easily taken Arrigo along if he wanted. But gasping for air, he tried to say something, and the sounds came out completely unintelligible, as he panted and tried to talk at the same time.

'Take your time, Spatola. Calm down and tell me what bothers you. I'm your friend and I can wait till you catch your breath.'

'It's Bernardo,' Spatola finally said. 'I finally hit him. And I think I killed him.'

Arrigo had to refrain from shouting in ecstasy. He held a smile back and just grinned reassuringly to Spatola, pulling him to the side of the path, next to a small construction that stood by the crossroad. 'The shepherd? Bernardo delle Rocche? This is good, Spatola. This is very good. You finally got rid of that filthy bastard. You wouldn't want his greasy shepherd hands on your precious Ginevra, would you?'

Spatola was speechless. He just stood there, panting and looking at Arrigo with his usual expressionless face.

'Where did you hit that man, Spatola?'

'North of this road. On the hillside down to the river, just outside the main curve east towards Chifenti.'

'Anyone seen you doing this?'

'No.' He said. And after a moment, he trembled his lips and confessed. 'I'm afraid. He saw me. The bastard saw me. Now if anyone knows it was me, they will kill me. They will burn me alive.'

'No!' Arrigo whispered. 'They won't know. They will never know. Bernardo had an accident and dropped down the hillside. You will be safe to have your Ginevra, my good Spatola!'

The idiot said nothing, neither moved any facial muscle.

Arrigo pulled Spatola to the construction's only door. 'Spatola, I think you should stay in hiding while I verify if there was nobody that saw this...incident.' The young Cunimundinghi lord opened it with a strong yank. It was an old *metato*, used for smoking hides or for drying and toasting any chestnuts of Cunimundinghi lands that had not been processed already. The building was empty and the drying racks were disassembled outside, so from inside nobody would be able to reach the only window, high on the wall. 'You will be safe here' he said to Spatola, pulling him inside. 'I will keep the door closed and nobody will dare to open it in my lands, without my permit. Meanwhile, tell me where Bernardo is.'

And Spatola told him everything.

The tavern was not too busy. At mid-morning, the scant crowd included two shepherds from Montefegatesi who had walked down from the mountain to exchange some cheese for oil and chestnut, a young English pilgrim on his way from Rome, helplessly trying to get his negro to translate a complaint about the quality of the ale, a local fisherman who needed some spiced wine to soothe his cold, and an old lonely man from Fornulo, distractedly drinking wine at that tavern, his daily routine being just an excuse to contemplate the beauty and vigour of the taverner's daughter.

Arrigo stormed in with a white, shocked face. He could not see Ginevra. Dodging the tables and guests with long strides, he went straight to Amadeo.

'Where's Ginevra?'

Amadeo spat on the floor. 'What the hell do you want with her?'

'I don't want anything with that girl,' Arrigo said, without changing his lines of concern, 'I just wanted to tell her that Bernardo delle Rocche has been attacked.'

'*What?*' Ginevra yelled, coming from the kitchen. 'Attacked? By whom? *You?*'

Arrigo opened his usual cynical grin and hissed 'He's still alive. You can hear from his own cantastorie lips who the attacker was. But maybe if you keep accusing me you will get there too late and he may not be saved.'

They harnessed a mule to a cart and drove to the curve where Arrigo had indicated. Ginevra screamed with horror when she saw Bernardo's body down the hill, with his face covered in blood. With Arrigo's most dedicated assistance, they jumped down from the wall and carried Bernardo up the slope, struggling to hoist his limp body to the path. The shepherd moaned in pain when his body was laid in the cart. Ginevra wept and desperately tried to wipe the blood from his face. 'What happened, Bernardo? Please tell me what happened?'

'The bridge...' he sighed, in a faint whisper.

'What's with the bridge?' Ginevra yelled.

Bernardo tried to focus his eyes, but he only saw whiteness. His head was pierced by excruciating pain when he attempted to move his jaws. He tried then to talk only with his lips, puffing, a tiny voice coming out of them, 'It must be burned down...'

Arrigo was impatient and almost yelled at the shepherd. He held his impetus and delicately suggested 'Just ask him who was his attacker.'

Ginevra acquiesced 'Bernardo, tell me who did this to you. Tell me, please! Was it them, at the bridge?'

Bernardo tried to smile, but the sudden bulge in his eyes clearly indicated he was suffering with pain. Ginevra shushed him, putting a finger delicately across his lips 'No need to say anything now. We will see to it later.'

Stupid woman, Arrigo thought, almost loudly, throwing both of his hands on his head. That was not how he had planned things. Everything had been working according to his plans on that morning. His new plans, anyway. The day had changed completely when he saw Spatola running down the river road. A moment after he approached the idiot, he knew he would have many people under his control. Forget his men-at-arms. He could get his help later. He could always storm the bridge and burn down all of Chifenti when he wanted. But now, Arrigo craved for some amusement. He had been back to Anchiano for a quick update to his mother, and now he had passed by the spot where Bernardo was. He did not want to go down the hill before alerting Amadeo and Ginevra. It had all gone according to his plans.

Now he wanted to single out Ginevra. And he had a few plans for her. But if Bernardo said nothing else, he would have to intervene. And maybe by force.

When Amadeo flicked the reigns, Bernardo held on to Ginevra's fingers. She jumped onto the moving cart with him. Arrigo just watched her carrying his head towards her bosom. The young lord of Anchiano was starting to fume with annoyance as the cart left in a hurry, when he saw Ginevra suddenly talking to Bernardo. She looked at Arrigo, back to Bernardo and Arrigo again. He mounted his horse and rode after the cart.

'What is it, Ginevra?'

She was white as a ghost. 'It was Spatola! Bernardo said that Spatola attacked him.'

Arrigo sighed and almost smiled. He hurried the ride to catch up with the cart, already entering Chifenti. 'Do not worry, Ginevra' he said, 'we should care for Bernardo now and I will find Spatola. We will see the idiot hanging from a tree for that.'

'Look at all of this mess!' Arrigo said with disgust, as Bernardo's wound was washed. The shepherd was laying unconscious across one of the tables. 'The idiot must have crushed his head. I think he cannot make it. But my mother should be able to help with those wounds,' and on seeing their sudden stiffness, with necks stretched up in attention like frightened deer, he completed 'She is the best healer in this region, you all know.'

Ginevra walked around the table and looked at Arrigo, very close into his eyes. 'Are you serious? Would she help us? I mean, would she tend for Bernardo's wound?'

Arrigo shrugged his shoulders. 'Bernardo will certainly die without her care. I don't even know if she can save him, but I'm sure she could try...for a price, of course.'

With a grunt of rage, Amadeo advanced over the table to hit Arrigo 'You little sh—' but Ginevra held him firmly. Arrigo smiled, now with his old grin of cynicism.

'It's all up to you,' he said with tranquillity, 'I'm not the one who's in love with this shepherd. As far as I'm concerned, the maggots can eat his brain. You can just raise suspicion of my intentions and argue forever while this man's wounds rot away. Or you can ride as fast as the wind to Anchiano for proper help. My mother has been advised already. She will be prompt to help.'

The taverner opened his eyes wide. 'You mean *what*? How would Maria Maddalena know about Bernardo?'

Arrigo was suddenly mute, biting his lip for a moment, eyes moving like flies around the tavern hall. That had been so careless, so silly to slip out too much information. Now it would be wise to fix it immediately, and maybe ruin his plans. 'I knew it had been the idiot,' he consented, 'He told me about the attack when I met him running aimlessly down the road by Anchiano. Now the creature is locked. Do not worry.'

'I worry only for Bernardo,' Ginevra confessed, lowering her eyes.

'Then take my horse and fly to Anchiano.' The young Cunimundinghi suggested, eyebrows raised with obviousness. 'It's the fastest courser in these lands. And if you convince my mother to come for Bernardo,' he said shrugging his shoulders, 'give her the same courser and she will be here the fastest, if there's any hope for this shepherd at all.'

Ginevra and Amadeo looked at each other for a moment. Finally the taverner pulled her to the side and said in a whisper 'You go, Ginevra. I could not do it. It would be too humiliating for me to beg to the witch.'

When Arrigo saw Ginevra preparing to go, he almost slipped out his grin. But he watched her kick in the courser's flanks and burn the path with its gallop. Arrigo turned to Amadeo and said 'Now I want to borrow your mule. I will follow her and make sure all is well.'

Maria Maddalena was sitting at her largest oaken chair. From head to toe, she was measuring Ginevra, who stood in her hall, uninvited to seat and eat. With wild brown hair and fiery brown eyes, barefoot and with delicate lines on her face, Ginevra had those hateful curves and that perfect stature that men loved to look at and drool. Maria found it horrible to admit, but that tavern wench, who was no more than eight or nine years her younger, could appear young enough to come across as her daughter. Or was it Maria herself that looked old enough to be Ginevra's mother? The Cunimundinghi lady curved her lip in a grin which accused precisely where Arrigo had gotten his from. She knew of Ginevra's mother, and nobody else knew. But better not think of Divina. Now her adversary was younger and smarter. She could still remember the day that girl was born. She was watching that blood-covered tripe coming out of Divina's womb. It had given Maria an ill sensation, and she immediately hated the child ever since. She had waited forever for this day of triumph, and now it was unfolding, ahead of her eyes. Arrigo was right. She would have Ginevra in her hands. Once the taverners were out of her lands, begging on the streets of Lucca or Rome, that beauty would be consumed in the blink of an eye.

'I understand you like that old man probably more than your position should allow for.' Maria said, with a curl of her upper lip.

'But I don't understand what you mean,' said Ginevra. 'I just need your help. Bernardo is your neighbour, an Obertenghi. He's been attacked and we fear he will not survive. You have a moral duty as the Lady of —'

'Don't throw any moralities on my feet, *wench*!' Maria cut, with her raised voice echoing around the hall. 'I have no interest in Bernardo delle Rocche, and least for his well-being. Bernardo has always been a poisonous liar, and whether he's a jester or a shepherd, it just demonstrates that he should not be owning any land.' With a sweet flavour of enjoyment in her tongue, she watched Ginevra's face filling up with purple rage. And before her visitor could yell out anything, she continued 'However, I am interested in what concerns you and your father. You own what has once been mine.'

'Maria *Tenebrosa*!' Ginevra finally said, controlling an irate tremor that irradiated through her limbs. 'You are very good in making people hate you. That is such a waste of your medicinal talent, when you could use your healing power for love and compassion. I can understand that there is no sense in arguing with you. You are indeed a low, dirty, treacherous witch.'

'Watch it, wench. I could kill you with my own hands.'

'I know you could, but you *won't*.' Ginevra hissed, 'You are icy cruel, but too greedy to do it. Why waste an opportunity to publicly steal what belongs to my father by the use of our compassion? It is land that has never been yours, for the widower Fulcardo of the Cunimundinghi, the bishop's son, conceded it to my father before you jumped into marriage with him, Maria of the Burle et Malachi! You want the lands of Chifenti? You can have them back – I give you my word – but only when you can prove to us that Bernardo delle Rocche is alive and well. Use your talent now, *bitch*!'

Maria stayed still, seated and fists closed, her fingernails almost digging through the flesh of her palms. She bit her lips and her eyebrows lowered for a moment, as if preparing a deadly strike. Then, her grey eyes soared, wondering into nothing, and her features relaxed. 'Your word then? Chifenti will be mine if I heal Bernardo?'

'It depends on you. I would give anything to save a life. And to save Bernardo's, I would give mine. But of course you will never appreciate to any degree the power of human compassion. Land, Maria, is *nothing*. You can have it and die alone and unhappy with it, but you must give us Bernardo back! Now go, before it's too late. And take *my horse*!'

From the battlements of Anchiano, high on the rock, Ginevra watched Maria Maddalena leaving at a mad gallop on Arrigo's courser, tailed by her huge black dog, racing happily along that path across the gnarled, brown landscape of late winter. Ginevra despised the urge that the Lady of Anchiano had taken through that alley of long drops of cypress green. A rush not for saving a life, but for the sake of increasing her wealth. With that display of haste, she trusted that Maria would use of her best talent as a healer, wisdom of her father and knowledge from Béla to save Bernardo. If Maria Maddalena of the Cunimundinghi could not save him, Ginevra had little faith that any prayers would.

Moments later, another rider galloped on the same rode, in the opposite direction, towards the castle. From the gait of that pace, more of a fast canter, and the built of the beast, he was riding a mule. Ginevra recognised her father's own mule and walked down the spiralling path, to meet with Arrigo.

'How's Bernardo?' she asked, when they met by the village at the foot of the rock.

'I just told my mother as I came across her on the way that Bernardo's not changed. He is not awake. Maybe you want a ride back to Chifenti?'

'Yes' she said, but not too sure, scanning around the buildings and the village, looking for the stables.

'You will find no good horses at this time.' Arrigo said. 'They're all tending the fields, breaking the ground. Ride with me.' And he extended his hand to her.

Ginevra hesitated, but resolved to take it. At that point, Maria was riding as fast as she could to Chifenti. If they forced the mule carrying both, they could be there within the hour. She mounted and held on to Arrigo, rather disgusted to having done so.

With a whimper of disapproval from the combined weight of her riders and the pain from Arrigo's heels, the mule obediently started its fast canter. Throughout that initial bumpy ride across the plain of Anchiano, Ginevra tried to pay attention to the wealth that occasional floods had granted to those lands. Near the castle and village, there were peasants breaking the land with a plough. Rows of olive trees passed by, revealing to the coming spring a new canopy of silvering buds, and later the still naked mulberry trees patiently waited for warmer times, when a battalion of workers would harvest their greenery to feed the worms that weaved gold. As the road approaches the Serchio's eastern path, the rocky hills to the north closed in by the junction, just across an old metato that was not frequently used. The mule was slowing down, and Ginevra had no time to ask why. Before she started to appreciate the frailty of her situation, her thoughts disappeared into thin air when Arrigo's elbow crunched across her face and everything became dark as she flew from the mule and hit the muddy ground.

'You don't feed the rats, do you?' Maria reasoned with Amadeo, as he watched her wiping the blood off Bernardo's wound and matted hair. 'That's because you know the rats will eat your children if they know they're in control. It's the same with the idiot. This is all because of your foolishness. You have fed that idiot during all these years, and now he attacks a landowner. We should have hung that little monster in a cage on the market in Lucca long ago, when I handed it to those pilgrims across the river. That idiot, the clerk Anton...' but she swallowed what she was to say next, for a sudden thought of the parish clerk of the cathedral reminded her that, naïvely or not, he had been the most supportive person she had ever met, except for her stupid sisters and for her grandfather Battista Burle. She extended a hand down the table to pat the head of her large black dog that would not leave her side.

Amadeo was silent, standing among the small crowd that watched as Maria used a sharp blade to shear the matted locks off Bernardo's head. The shepherd was not awake, but his eyes had a scary whiteness which was not ominous of a good prognosis. Amadeo was giving little thought to the action at all. He had been warned by Maria, as soon as she arrived, that Ginevra had promised to hand their lands in Chifenti over to Anchiano in case she managed to save Bernardo. That was a serious demand, and an extremely careless commitment of his daughter. He did not dare to stop Maria from treating an Obertenghi, but he was trying to figure out what to do next, to avoid losing his lands to the witch.

'That's why it's a mistake to grant land to people like you.' she continued. 'That *launegildo* was a terrible mistake, rather typical of my husband's idiocy. You people do not know the difference between master and slave, between the chosen and the unlucky. Look at that,' she said, pointing a red-blooded finger at the surprised face of the negro that watched next to his English master, 'negroes in the same room. You will never sit above the animals, Amadeo.'

The taverner swallowed his pride and left for the kitchen. Maria, meanwhile, was overly irritated with the fact that she had to save a life of a man she despised in order to recover what once had been hers. She carefully opened the cuts and bruises and wiped off any earth or smaller residues of soil or stones that she found. Bernardo moaned with pain. 'Shut up, you pig! Just sleep!' she said, shoving into his mouth a cloth drenched with mandrake juice, mulberry wine produced by her father's own *tagh tir* contraption, and poppy juice. Bernardo gasped and tried to take it out with his hands, but quite immediately his eyes were rolling upwards and he was snoring aloud.

'Eggs! I need eggs!' Maria barked.

'Hens' or geese's?' Amadeo yelled from the kitchen.

'Whatever. Just give me a couple of fresh eggs.'

'It's not even springtime yet,' he grunted, 'most hens are not back into lay. The few eggs we get are being consumed. I'll go verify in the coop, but I do not expect we'll find anything at this time.'

'Well, then if he dies we know why it was.' Maria said with a low tone of voice, almost to herself. The small crowd stood quiet, watching her procedures.

'What are you looking at?' she yelled at them. 'Disband!'

They were quick to disappear through the front door, while Amadeo came back from the coop with two eggs. 'That should do,' Maria said quietly. She separated the yolks into a goblet and beat the whites in a bowl, to which she added a few spoons of pine tree oil and a full vial of rose petal oil, that she had taken from her large satchel. She smeared the mixture over the wound, waited until it was dry and put some more on top, repeating the process over and over. After the procedure, Bernardo's head was as glossy as a giant blob of amber with a large furry ball inside.

'Now,' she finally talked, grabbing the goblet with the two yolks, 'we wait.'

'What about cauterising? Are you not burning the wound?' Amadeo asked without hiding the alarm on his face.

Maria just looked at him with an expression of mocked pity and said nothing. They waited for a few minutes while she stared at the brilliance of the yolks in the goblet.

'Where's Ginevra?' Amadeo asked all of a sudden, almost awaking from his preoccupation with the trade of land for Bernardo's life.

Maria ignored his question 'Can we see the bridge from here?'

'No. You have to go back the road south for a couple of hundred paces' Amadeo said with irritation, 'Now *where is my daughter?*'

Maria left through the front door, carrying the goblet with her and followed by the dog. She answered from outside. 'The wench should be here anytime. Arrigo is bringing her in that mule of yours. Now come, Altobello.'

'Altobello?' The taverner asked to himself in an incredulous whisper 'She calls the dog *Altobello*?'

Maria walked over under the network of dry branches that shaded the path until the bridge could be seen through the thin canopy. She looked down towards the river. The slope was too steep to go down. That was probably where Bernardo had been attacked. *How pathetic! One idiot crushing the head of another.* She laughed. Destiny was letting in all demonstrations of being good to her. In two days, she would see the devil and guarantee all power for her beloved son, Arrigo, and for Anchiano. The devil would listen to her. She would undo Béla's curse and laugh at old vulture, deep in the darkness of that river. And if the devil wanted her soul, she cared little. She would ask God for forgiveness in the last minute.

Grinning with satisfaction, Maria Maddalena mixed the yolks with her index finger, while singing a song. Then she poured part of the yolk mixture onto the ground very slowly, watching the yellow ropes stretching with the faint breeze. Altobello did not dare to sniff it. And still with the grin of triumph on her face, Maria spit into the goblet three times and drank it all.

In this moment, the land below them bulged over a cavernous sigh, as if it was just awakening from a long sleep and not too happy about it. Altobello yelped in fear.

'Go on, Spatola. She's yours now. Take her. *Take her!*'

Waking up from an immeasurable moment of darkness, struggling to open her eyes through an entanglement of hair, coal-black soil, and jolts of excruciating pain coming from her face, her neck, arms, wrists and knees, the voice of Arrigo was the first intelligible sound that made sense to Ginevra. And it surely indicated that the nightmare was just beginning.

Ginevra was immobilised on her knees, but toppled over to the ground. She could feel the weight of Arrigo sitting on her head, and her folded arms behind her back, held by the young Cunimundinghi, so painfully pulled backwards that she felt he could just snatch them of her shoulders with a light yank. From the cold draft she could feel on her bottom and her legs, she knew she was uncovered. She tried to scream out for help, but no voice could yet be gathered from her breathing.

'Like a nice, tame, submissive bitch, Spatola. Take her! She's no good for anybody, this bitch, but for you.' Arrigo's voice was ravenous with joy, almost shrieking. 'Don't you like how she looks, Spatola? Ready for you, isn't she?'

'No Spatola!' Ginevra finally managed to cry. 'Please don't do it! This is not you. This devil is Arrigo, and you are *not* him!' but she was shut up, strangled further from the pressure of Arrigo's thighs around her face and the pain of her shoulder blades being pulled further back, ready to break out.

'Shut up, wench.' Arrigo growled, trying to kick her face with his heel. He missed it and only kicked his other heel. 'You are good for nothing, you little whore. You are not worthy of anybody but this idiot here. Let's marry you with Spatola!'

Spatola was covered in sweat. Trembling from head to toes, he had kneeled down behind Ginevra and even raised his blue chequered tunic.

'Yes, Spatola!' Arrigo cackled, drooling with rage, 'I can see that you like her! Show this sow how you can make other little monsters in her.'

Ginevra froze with a jolt of her whole body when she felt a pair of cold, sweaty hands holding her hips carefully. 'No Spatola! Don't do it!' She managed to shout, through the dusty ground that was pressed against her face. 'It's me, Ginevra! Please don't do it! You would never hurt me...Carpo! CARPO!'

Arrigo saw that Spatola hesitated. 'Go on, idiot,' he roared, 'Take her now! Hasn't she humiliated you sufficiently? She is only trying to convince you that you are not good enough for her. Will you let her go on unpunished, fucking any dog that comes across the tavern but snubbing you? Go on, *fuck her*!'

Spatola sweated more, trembling his jaws and chattering his few teeth, looking at Ginevra's exposed bottom with an anger never before seen on his expressionless face.

'Oh, what is it Spatola?' Arrigo whined, with mocked pity. 'She is making you become again no more than a boy? Lost your manhood, Spatola? You are not a man near Ginevra?'

'Carpo, go away!' Ginevra cried from between Arrigo's thighs. 'Don't hurt me Carpo. You would never hurt me!'

'Shut up, Ginevra.'

That was Carpo saying with an icy cold voice. Both Ginevra and Arrigo stopped for a moment, surprised at the commanding tone. Arrigo was the first to react after this, yelling with excitement 'Yes Spatola! Give it to her. Tell this wench who is her man!'

But Ginevra struggled against his weight, crying 'Carpo, go away! Leave while you can! You will *not* hurt me, Carpo!'

'*Shut up, Ginevra!*' Carpo cried, raising both of his heavy arms high and bringing them down on her back, exploding his fists against her kidneys. Ginevra did not have the strength to scream in pain. She just collapsed on the ground as Carpo now punched her buttocks and her thighs. Arrigo had stood up in excitement, screeching to Spatola to keep beating her, leaping around both and opportunely kicking Ginevra as Spatola's rage still impelled him to continue.

Ginevra was unconscious again when Arrigo noticed that he was the only one digging his boots into the limp body, while Spatola was frozen as a stone, looking at what he had done. And the idiot was just too quick when he disappeared through the door.

Arrigo meant to follow Spatola out of the metato, as the idiot disappeared behind the curve, heading north. But still cool-blooded and keeping his composure, the young lord Cunimundinghi looked at Ginevra, beaten, laying on the ground, moaning in pain. There was a brief moment to consider what the most urgent thing to do was. He could take his courser that remained outside and follow Spatola. The idiot was already known to have attacked Bernardo delle Rocche, therefore a publicly known criminal. Then, he could easily be blamed for the murder of Ginevra too. Arrigo only had to take care of Ginevra now, to go and later find Spatola. He would hang Spatola's neck from a tree before the idiot could spill out his own version of the facts, which would be very unlikely anyway, given the idiot's usual silence when under pressure. That would be the easy part. The difficult would be to find the idiot, who could hide like a badger.

That was it. Arrigo knew what needed to be done to clean up the situation.

Looking around to verify that no peasants were coming his way, Arrigo leaped inside the metato again. He kneeled behind Ginevra and held her under her arms, raising her torso onto his lap. He felt the curve of her breasts, the warmth of her volumes, before pulling his dagger out. His copy of Attila's dagger shone in the dark interior of the metato. It had been newly sharpened, with a thin blade that still showed the dry scuff marks from the stone. That blade would cut through her neck as if it was going through a soft mushroom cap. Holding Ginevra by her chin, he placed the blade under her neck, ready to slit it, only considering how he would accuse Spatola of slitting Ginevra's throat, if the idiot carried no knife.

'Arrigo, you are a low, shit coward,' Ginevra suddenly moaned. 'You are never going to be a real man.'

The lord Cunimundinghi giggled and relaxed the blade. The titter became a frank laughter and Arrigo sheathed the dagger, standing up and dropping Ginevra back on the coal-covered floor. Still laughing, he got outside and placed the door back in place, for those drying sheds would never be built with hinges. He used the poles of the drying rack to barricade it, leaning them firmly against the door. Ginevra would not be able to leave. He could take care of her later. That was an opportune change of plans for him. Now the best strategy was to find Spatola and accuse him of Ginevra's disappearance too. Once Spatola was dead, Arrigo would be able to prove he was right, by finding the body of Ginevra hidden somewhere in the woods, raped and beaten to death by the idiot.

He took the mule and kicked in, heading north on its fast canter, never noticing that someone else had watched him leave. In that moment, the land seemed to bulge for a second, rumbling like a colossal stomach swallowing its own belch.

Someone had heard an altercation, and immediately hid behind the dried bushes across the road, just across the old metato by the entrance to Anchiano. Ears that were shut to the thrushes and blackbirds that moved the dead leaves, but which listened to the excited screams of one, and pleads of another. Eyes focused through the leaves of sea-buckthorn to observe the village idiot of Chifenti coming out of the door like a scared piglet and disappearing towards the north road, and that later watched Arrigo, the young Lord Cunimundinghi of Anchiano, blocking the door with old poles and taking a mule on a race after Spatola. The Lord Cunimundinghi was up to some devilry.

And when the earth burped with a sudden bloat, that person knew it was much more than devilries. Hell was about to open up.

Ginevra rolled around, to lie on her belly. There was no spot on her body that did not seem to be broken with pain. Arrigo was gone, she heard the mule trot away, and she needed to find a position to breath better. Her ribs ached cruelly, making it difficult to bring any intake of air in. She dragged her body, feeling so heavy across the ground, and seated herself against the wall.

There was still a beam of light going in through the high window, but little else entered through the door edges, for it was larger than the frame, and she knew Arrigo had blocked it from outside. In spite of the bursting pain in her neck and shoulders, she looked up and noticed that the window was too high to reach. Nothing else in that room, which she could tell was a metato. What was she doing there, for the Holy Blood of Jesus Christ? What had she done? She had only tried to save the poor Bernardo, offering herself to talk to the witch, giving away all her possessions in exchange for Bernardo's life, trusting Arrigo and his mother. Now she had almost been raped by Spatola, she had been beaten to a pulp, she was covered in chestnut soot, her tunic had been ripped to her waist, she was about to face a horribly freezing night in that lonely building and she could only expect Arrigo to return later with his dagger in her neck again.

Where was her guardian angel then? She wondered if guardian angels would be sitting next to her, stubbornly crossing their arms and cold-bloodedly watching her suffering, refusing to help if she did not start to pray.

That's when she heard noises outside, someone taking off the poles that blocked the door.

'Help me here!' she yelled with shortness of breath. 'I'm hurt! Please help me out of here!' She tried to stand up, but her body seemed to be too heavy and painful to be lifted from that sitting position. The door was finally pulled out and light entered quite generously, bringing an immediate scent of the river, running far behind them. Ginevra exhaled in relief. Freedom did have a sweet taste.

Her liberator entered. Ginevra could not see the shadowed face against the light, but she did notice that wide brimmed hat with small spheres hanging around its rim.

'Oh, gracious God! Look who we have here!' Antelmino said, taking off his coat and revealing the protruding hilt of a dagger by his waist. He had a wide grin that appeared even through the darkness that covered his face.

Ravenous Creatures

Wido di Willo combed his long, red beard with his fat fingers, looking down to the forest.

'I don't like this,' he muttered.

Only the playful sounds of the creek could be heard, as some of the men of Wald Ottavo watched him in silence. They were frightened. The land had never moved before in their lifetime, at least never as if it had been alive. It felt like a gigantic worm trying to find its way under the village of Ottavo. Now, as afternoon was dragging the brief winter sun further behind their backs in the Apuane, he had just received a message from an inhabitant of Mutianum.

Wido turned his barrel-shaped body to the villagers and said 'These news are the worse that we could have expected. Bernardo delle Rocche has been attacked.'

'Was it Antelmino, the Castracani?' asked one of the villagers, while others still whispered in awe.

'Apparently not. This is what baffles me. They say it was the idiot of Chifenti. I doubt it. I know that cretin. He worked for the construction of the second bridge. The man is a creature strong enough to hold a marble column of St Martin, but he couldn't hurt an ant. With the disappearance of the parishioner of Controne, and now this attack on Bernardo, I fear that we are dealing with more devilries of that accursed bridge. Now it seems that hell is ready to blow up under our feet. It is indeed the year of the beast, as we refused to believe. But even if not, we can still lose our landlord, and that bastard the Castracani will be eyeing our lands. A bridge will make it easier for him to invade us.'

'Should we do something about it?' a villager asked.

Wido curled his broken lips, making them visible even through his thick moustache. 'Yes, we should,' he said decisively, punching the palm of one hand with his other fist. 'Let the men of God mind the devil, and the people of Chifenti that forgive us, but we will set fire to those slums of demons that arch across the Serchio. That is what Bernardo wanted, that is what will rid us from that Hellmouth!'

There was a murmur of approval.

Wido bared his teeth and said 'As our priest has left, we should march to Diecimo to be blessed by the parishioner. We will start tonight!'

While they all moved excitedly back to their houses to arm, a loud howling was heard, not too far above on the mountains.

Father Diloguardi, of Mutianum, was cold. Hiding behind a square column, crawled in a corner of the altar, he felt abandoned, scared. He looked at his lord on the altar, the crucified Christ in wood, facing an empty nave with his teary eyes, oblivious to the fear of that orphaned priest, alone in the dark church.

He shed bitter tears of regret. How could he not have left when old Father Rocco, from the Cerreto warned them about the bridge? Weren't the flies sufficiently portentous? Or the letters of warning that circulated for half a year? What about the disappearance of father Rocco? And the madness of the pope? Father Diloguardi should have known. So stupid to ignore it all, to snub the exodus of the local priests. He should have left long ago, on pilgrimage to Rome, to be protected.

Most of the population of Mutianum had left from the day the devils came. His church was forlorn, empty, only filled by the winds, which did not bring any news. And now, the earth had just rumbled. Father Diloguardi knew that his God had forsaken him. Christ had long been gone, turned into wood, scared away from that church by the grotesque lionheads that stuck out of each column, by the devilish dwarves that hopped along the rain gutters outside.

A wolf howled nearby.

Father Diloguardi held on to his silver cross so tight that it opened a gash in his palm. He watched the blood flow, cursing between clenched teeth and praying for the intervention of the saints. He knew that even the saints and their prayers would not stop them before they came out, the Hellmouth.

'I have not seen Carpo here.' Clarissa said to Arrigo. The Lady of Luna had calmly walked him out of her hospital as soon as he broke into the hall, requiring information on Spatola's whereabouts.

'Anyone's seen the idiot of Chifenti? He came this way! Where is he?' he had enquired.

One of the wardens had raised his head from the kitchen, but a calming hand from Clarissa on his shoulder stopped him from reacting. She walked Arrigo back to the mule and handed it to him.

'This mule belongs to Amadeo. Take it back to him,' she said.

The puzzled Lord of Anchiano was somehow overwhelmed by her stature, her determination and serenity. He mounted on the mule, with an apparent shameless obedience.

Clarissa looked down the road towards Anchiano and up the path towards the bridge. Empty. Just the naked trees moving to that afternoon winter breeze. 'It looks like the wind will be picking up,' she said, casually, watching the bridge showing a bit of itself through its disguising mist. It did look like the scaffolding was a lot thinner around a very tall arch. And her attention was drawn for an instant where here vision seemed to see things moving in those structures. But it must have been an illusion. She turned to Arrigo and said conclusively 'No... definitely not here.'

Arrigo spat on the ground. 'Watch out for the idiot. He's attacked the shepherd, and only the Good Jesus knows what he has done to Ginevra.'

'Ginevra?' asked Clarissa, genuinely surprised, certainly more intrigued than on her previous airy tone. 'Why would you think Carpo could have done anything to her? Ginevra did ride by here, on your horse. Then, it was you who rode by on Amadeo's mule. Later, we saw your horse carrying Maria, your mother, towards Chifenti. We trust that she is caring for Bernardo. My Julian is there with them –'

'Your Julian has no dealings to be in Chifenti.' He said.

'Rather than trying to tell a free man what he should or should not do,' Clarissa mended with calm, 'why don't you tell us what has been of Ginevra?'

Arrigo almost stuttered, but he was quick to answer 'Why should I know where she is? She left Anchiano on foot. The wench did not want to wait for me.'

'We have not seen her past here, though.'

Arrigo lowered a suspecting eyebrow. 'You seem to be so aware of the transit of travellers along this path. Then you surely must have known that the idiot passed by after he attacked the shepherd this morning.'

'Indeed, he ran to towards Anchiano,' she said, 'but that is the last we have seen of him.' Clarissa was about to turn around and enter the hospital, as Arrigo was already mounted. But then she looked at him pensively, raising her index finger to the side of her nose 'Maybe we should ask the peasants around Anchiano. I am sure they have seen who arrived and who left the rock.'

Arrigo kicked hard in, struggling to make the mule march in a narrow circle around Clarissa. He needed a few seconds to put his thoughts in place before uttering a word. His plans were simple and there was no allowance for anyone to complicate them. That bitch was making him nervous. Finally, he said 'I'll find the idiot. He is an abomination that has been tolerated for too long. Now that he has committed a serious crime, you should all be blamed for it. That little beast would not have survived if you did not feed him with scraps. But not to worry anymore: I will turn him into food for the crayfish.'

Clarissa looked at him almost on a Spatola fashion, without any expression on her face. Except for the fire in her eyes. 'We will find the truth about it. Just don't hurt Carpo. I promise that you will regret it if you touch him.'

Arrigo laughed. 'If you knew how small you were, woman, you would never dare to make such a threat against me.' He left on a fast canter towards Chifenti.

Clarissa returned to the hospital. There were only a few hungry pilgrims who would stay for the night. A warden was already heating the stones to make the chestnut pancakes. He was carefully selecting chestnut leaves to line the stones and preventing the wet dough from sticking to the surface. Clarissa verified her pots and amphorae, in a kitchen that was pleasantly scented by sprigs of rosemary, bushes of thyme and *santoreggia* – winter savoury – hanging from beams under her bedchamber. There was plenty of fresh *re-cotta* curd in a large canvas bag and, given the low number of pilgrims in those times, there would be enough olive oil to last another two to three weeks. She counted the sausages and wild boar dry cuts, which were safely protected hanging from the back wall, acquiring generous smokiness around the hearth. Returning to the main hall, she suggested the other warden climb the ladder to the straw storage and renew some of the palliasses. Meanwhile, she left through the back door and verified for any onlookers before entering the storage shed. Eight goats were tied at the door, with a short rope around their necks. Clarissa gracefully walked around the tawny, long coated animals, which curiously rattled their wide curved horns as they all tried to reach over to her tunic. Behind the goats, there were a few *mazzaranghe*, the curved stick with a flat wooden sphere at the end, used to break the roasted shells of chestnuts. Against the wall there were sacks of *farro*, stacks of wine barrels, olive oil amphorae, chestnut trunks, rakes, hoes and tools to make barrels, as a large unassembled *segantini* saw, chisels, pincers, hatchets, pegs, wooden hammers, and a pile of loose staves, wooden hoops and unfinished barrels, missing their heads or top chine hoops, with their staves opened wide, like Rafaello Rapondi's teeth. On the other side harnesses hung from the main beam, curtaining an anvil, blacksmith tools, a broken bellows and a small cart with woollen pelts. But the back half of the shed was filled with straw. A large pile of different makes of straw, reaching up to the ceiling. Clarissa climbed through the lower slope of the pile, hearing the squeaking of field mice scattering away. She pulled up a large bundle and Spatola's face came out, covered in dust, expressionless.

'He's gone.' Clarissa said, with little sympathy in her face, but warmth of trust in her eyes. Spatola did not react. 'Now, Carpo,' she said 'tell me exactly what happened.'

His eyes opened wide and he shot a quick glance to the door, where the goats calmly watched.

Clarissa narrowed her eyes. 'Do not even think of running out,' she said drily. 'I will be after you like an eagle.'

His lips trembled for a moment, not preparing Clarissa for what came after. With the power of his lungs, he bellowed a painful wail and dug himself deeper into the straw, yelling 'No, no, no, no! It was my fault! It was all my fault! I hurt her! I should go to hell. I must go to hell! I WILL GO TO HELL!'

Across the river, far above on the hills, beyond the Castle of Rocca, a cavernous howl was heard.

Arrigo stopped on the road. Did he hear a human wail? Or was that one of the wolves yelping? Blood sucking beasts that strangely seemed to have descended from their cold forests up on the Apuane. The mule was very uneasy. Wolves were a bad presence. Arrigo looked across the river but there was little to be seen, for he was right on the eastern embankment of the bridge, soaring up into the fog. Upstream, the woods looked calm and the cold river moved dark and slowly. Except for a dead cow. Its bloated grey body with stretched legs floated down the current, quite swiftly disappearing into the fog. Arrigo wondered what disease or accident would have killed it when he heard a commotion inside the fog. There were giggles, whispers and grunts. Gurgling voices repeating incoherent words and screeches of laughter and arguments. While his hair stood up and he carefully listened to whatever was being uttered in the fog, he watched for the downstream current. The dead cow never seemed to make it outside of that fog. And while thinking of what could have happened to that corpse as it got tangled into the bridge's scaffolding, a sequence of splashes was heard. Things were falling from the bowels of the bridge into the water. He hoped they were not falling stones, for the bridge should be ready for delivery in two days. And in this moment, something happened beyond his perception, but it made the mule jump up high in the air, making Arrigo lose his balance and fall on the ground, flat on his back.

Arrigo felt that he lost his senses for a while. Feeling the hard surface on his back and head, he opened his eyes and saw the canopy above him. Moving the head towards the right, he watched the mule hurriedly trotting towards Chifenti. He would have to walk.

While getting up, his eyes distractedly shot a glance to the left and found out that something was standing there, looking at him.

The scare was so sudden that Arrigo tripped backwards and rolled on his back again. He got up in alert, pulling his dagger out, ready to strike, when he noticed that the creature was rather small. It was a bird, apparently. Not much bigger than a chicken, it looked at him with an unmistakable air of curiosity. It moved his head from one side to the other, almost as if alternating the eyes which he would watch Arrigo. The body was tawny, with a rather long neck and a very long beak, in the shape of a spoon. Arrigo had seen spoonbills before, especially wading by the Lucchese swamps, but he thought tht they were white, and he had never noticed how odd they could appear from close range. He would not have known that they had those hairy, almost human-like feet and a naked rat's tail that was almost twice as long as the body and beak together.

What a stupid-looking creature. What a scare. Arrigo sheathed his dagger and made it to the spoonbill with firm strides, not waiting or preparing the creature for the kick. His boot came on a full swing, getting the spoonbill right in the middle of its fragile body. With a squeak of pain, the bird was shot in an arch, disappearing into the fog. Arrigo heard more squeaking from inside the mist, but it soon dissolved into silence.

He walked back to Chifenti, with the howling across the river becoming louder now.

'Wowawawolw?' Bernardo tried to ask, but he noticed his lips were not even moving. When he tried to open his mouth, he felt an excruciating pressure crushing against his head, as if his jaws had been tied to his scalp. The pain made him limp again.

'He's waking up' Julian said lividly. He turned to Amadeo 'The important thing now is to keep him still. Maria said so.'

'Beats me how you trust that witch.' Amadeo said, with a curled lip of disgust. Outside, the wolves were howling nearer, making Bernardo twitch.

The shepherd tried once again, trying to move only his lips *'Wassarawolf?'*

'Yes, Bernardo,' said Julian. 'There seem to be wolves coming down across your lands. Now, if you want to stay quiet, we will be with you here at the tavern for the night. Cannot trust the wolves to go back to the hospital now.'

'Sfhazula! Eewassa eerioz zat hiz me!'

'Yes, we know it was Spatola that hit you. You told us just before you lost conscience this morning. Now you should keep quiet. Maria Maddalena of the Cunimundinghi has applied a curing potion to the wound on your head. She's left now, with Arrigo, heading back to Anchiano. You should keep –'

'Maria?' Bernardo said in alert, perfectly clear and articulated, no matter how badly it hurt on his head to say that, *That fucking witch must have sewn a poisonous thorn inside my head. I will turn into a pigeon!*

'Do not worry, Bernardo.' Julian said, touching the shepherd's forehead and bringing him to a rest, 'Maria has pledged to save your life. It was Ginevra that guaranteed it.'

'Hinefhra?' Bernardo said, opening his eyes for the first time, *'Wa-a szupiz girl...'* He only saw Julian and Amadeo. *'Wherez she? I wannaheefer a khish...'*

Julian and Bernardo exchanged a worried glance. 'We don't know,' said the Hospitaller. 'She went to Anchiano and talked to Maria indeed, but nothing has been heard of her since. We're hoping she stayed at the hospital for the night.'

'Ze wolfhes...' Bernardo sighed, 'I hoef shees shafe fhom ze wolfhes...'

In a cold Wald Ottavo, twilight was ready to set its colours up on the sky and Wido di Willo was ready to set fire to the bridge. His only son, Willo di Wido, a young man not unlike his shape and colour, had arrived from the villages higher on the hill, bringing bags of chestnut flour to be distributed along the lower valley. He was coming from an empty metato behind their house, where he had shoved the donkey with pigs, goats and chickens.

'There's wolves coming down, father,' he said, while cutting for himself a generous slice of spiced pork belly. 'The villagers are shutting themselves in, and I almost had to push the cart over the donkey as I drove down from Partigliano. Now how do you expect to leave our village with these blood-sucking beasts roaming about the valley?'

Wido blinked with certainty 'We'll be marching in a large group of men. We will have torches and we will be loud. Wolves would never attack such an unlikely prey.'

'Just be careful, father,' his son advised, with a paternal tone, handing him a piece of that well-cured cold cut.

'I'm always careful!' Wido said with good humour, chewing the dried meat as the fat pleasantly melted in his mouth. As a farmer, a hunter and a leader of his village, Wido was rather satisfied with their decision to help their lord. If they were helpless to assist on Bernardo's recovery, they would at least make sure that the most threatening menace to their lands was cut off from an easy invasion. Antelmino would be stopped. Bernardo had confessed his will to burn the bridge to ashes. Wido was certain that this was because of Antelmino, and he thought they still could do it. He would march with his men to Diecimo for a proper consecration of their mission, onto Mutianum, walk to the bridge and quite unceremoniously raise an inferno of flames that would crack the mortar and stone, making the giant collapse into the riverbed.

He collected some oil into a goatskin, covered himself with a thick fleece cape, grabbed hold of a good torch and a long pole, and felt his lips tingling, ravenous to burn the arse of those demons.

Kissing his son goodbye, he stepped out straight into the main road that ran through Wald Ottavo. In this moment, a woman's scream somewhere in the village almost distracted him from the enormous gray shape that growled in front of him.

The dog-like monster had fire-set eyes of amber, baring his poisonous teeth as it snarled with rage. Wido knew immediately that no bridge would be burned that night.

The Devil knew well how to protect Himself.

'WOLVES!' Wido shouted with the strength of his lungs to the whole village. The monster was distracted by this yell for a second but, recovering its point of attention, it renewed its rage even more. With no delay to kill, it leaped towards Wido, as the round man dropped the torch and goatskin, swinging his pole with both of his hands, as if attacking with a mazzaranga. It hit the wolf like a gourd on the side of the head, deflecting the strike for an instant, but long enough for him to step back into the house.

Holding the door shut with his son Willo, Wido prepared for a long night.

'Oh shit!' he grunted.

In Mutianum, Father Diloguardi had been kneeling behind the altar. He pressed his hands against his ears as hard as he could, but the screams outside the church perforated his skull, their terror being heard deep inside his head.

Hours before that, he already knew they would be coming.

It had been late afternoon and by then many candles had been lit as the monsters arrived. Yelping and snarling outside, they roamed around the church, sniffing loud and hungry as they slipped their wet muzzles under the well-latched door, starving for the blood that still oozed from Father Diloguardi's hand. The wolves could detect the scent of fear in his clothes. They sensed the victim, shivering, helpless, Godless. He knew that they knew.

Looking at the hard lines on the face of the wooden Christ at the altar cross, Father Diloguardi let himself fall into the deepest well of desolation. He rolled over the cold stone floor as if possessed, probably his best try at mortification of the body, any possible strategy to draw attention for the owner of that holy house. But the Christ was under just too much pain to care about an unpretentious mortal soul in utter fear.

They howled outside, agitatedly scratching the door with their large paws. Father Diloguardi could hear them trying to climb on the church walls. He expected those demons to stick their heads through the vertical windows on the facade, or to raise the roof tiles just to enter and desecrate that house of God. And what was God doing? In His unfathomable omnipresence and His infinite love, God was watching it all unfolding right in front of His divine eyes, *and not moving a fucking finger!* Father Diloguardi fought against that hatred for God, growing in his heart like boiling water bubbles. Loathing for that impassiveness, as God calmly watched him breaking up in sobs, weeping on a foetal position, alone and unguarded on the corner of that altar.

'God please, protect me!' he moaned in desperation.

Diloguardi – *"God protect him"* – a name in the Pistoiese fashion of ominously naming babies, had always hoped, much rather than believed, to be personally watched by the Creator of everything. Vain hope after all. Like so many others equally week of heart, Diloguardi had evaporated any hope long before he retired from a normal life as a young man to take the service of that same God. *Now, that God was bluntly forsaking him, that's what He was doing, the bastard...*

It was silent again outside. The wolves were gone.

But God was still waiting for the next team of jesters to take the stage.

Voices. Human voices outside, men, women and children. They started by knocking at the church door. The shouted for help, pleading in a foreign language, most likely pilgrims on their way back or to Lucca, frantic souls begging for shelter, looking for sanctuary. Father Diloguardi could hear their voices rising to a tone of desperation, screaming, while brutally trying to push the door in. He tried to shut his ears, to make the sound go away. Beggars! They were no more than careless *beggars* caught out of shelter. And now they wanted to put him at risk. Why wouldn't they try the villagers' houses? Was everyone else so selfish that they wouldn't open the door? No, *he* would not open that door too.

They stopped knocking outside. But their screaming increased, now everyone, and in sheer horror.

Father Diloguardi tried to brush it out of his mind. He touched the wound on his hand. Mortification, inflicted by the holy cross. Would that lead him to salvation? Self denial to overcome his physical weakness, to grow in virtue. Did he have enough strength to get up, walk across the nave, unlatch the door and let them in? *Oh God, why couldn't they stop that screaming?* But he just could not move. Shutting his ears again, he yelled out loud, disconnectedly, shouting curses at the voices outside, those deceiving voices that were forcing him to open the gates. To let them in. Demons in disguise.

Drowning in shame, he crawled into the darkness behind a column. He shut his eyes and ears, and sang songs of his childhood. Songs of his mother, of freshly baked bread and olive oil, which quickly changed into indecent rhymes, of the bishop and the courtesan, of the milkmaid and the donkey. His body stretched and he uttered blasphemies and profanities. And while babbling and rolling his eyes in a heroic attempt to make those screams go away from his head, he jolted when his face felt the warm breath of milk and a child voice whispered right into his ears '*Now get out and see what you did, murderer!*'

Father Diloguardi sat up, alert, but there was nobody next to him. Where was that child? Still from behind the protection of the altar, he scanned through the dark central nave. Only a faint light came through the narrow windows up on the facade.

Silence.

He scrambled to stand up, when a playful tittering was clearly heard from the southern nave.

'Who's there?' he said, grabbing onto a candle.

Silence.

Slowly, taking very careful and silent strides, he walked over to the darker southern nave. Nobody. He stepped with caution on that cold floor, walking around each of the columns and assuring himself that there was no one else there but him.

Upon getting to the end of the nave, he realised just how close he was to that locked door. It was silent outside. Not even a suggestion of all the screaming that had tormented his soul just moments before. He approached the door and carefully touched the wood. Solid, smooth and cold. Putting his ear against it, he felt the winter stillness hanging out there, and who knows, maybe with a light breeze and the night prepared to close in.

Father Diloguardi felt rather silly, but he could not refrain from knocking at the door. His own church door, from inside.

And again, silence was the only response.

He held onto the heavy latch beam and carefully lifted it, avoiding any creaks or scrapes, and gently laying it against the wall.

The heavy door moaned when he pulled it in. Diloguardi felt the thin band of twilight greyness stripe him from head to toe, but kept his foot down, preventing the door from opening too much. The narrow slit allowed him to see good part of the stony door sash and a limited angle of the southern road, empty and silent. Father Diloguardi held on to the door and pulled it further, never noticing that his left fingers were touching a sticky surface. He was in that instant too distracted with a column of vomit that jolted out of his mouth and by locking in tightly an inept pair of weak legs, trying to contain his bowels from losing themselves at the church entrance.

Oh my God, you're so fucking cruel!

The pilgrims had been scattered throughout the church stairs and the road north. In pieces. Father Diloguardi wretched again on witnessing those poor souls splattered against the walls of the village, on the church door. The crimson scenario of ferocious butchery was a silent display of the Hellmouth's fury. He clenched his teeth and scanned the scene again, this time with anger. And he was struck by the presence of only one live creature remaining on that centre of Mutianum. A large bird, probably a stork, or a massive heron, poking through the entrails of a corpse with its strange shoe-shaped bill. It raised its large grey head and looked quite severely at the priest, carrying a piece of human flesh on its beak. Or no. It was a lizard, hanging from that creature's beak.

Again, something giggling inside the church.

Father Diloguardi turned around quickly, and in spite of the dark interior, this time the corner of his eyes snatched a glimpse of a figure running across the altar and disappearing in the blackness of the southern nave. Strangely enough, although it must have been a child that had ran around, he had the bizarre impression that it had the shape of a pig.

Growl.

Behind him, outside.

The priest turned to look out again. But the wolf was already flying with fangs wide open, straight into his neck.

Ginevra watched in horror as Antelmino carefully replaced the door into the frame, from the inside. That pig was surely planning something that was not supposed to be noticed from anyone on the road. And how much worse could it be for her than being raped by Arrigo or Spatola? That little strength she had been able to gather to sit herself up seemed to wane away, as Antelmino made sure the door looked firmly into place and turned to her again.

'Now, tell me, my dear,' he asked with a grin, 'which one of those two left an impression on you as a better fuck? The idiot or the brat?'

Ginevra tried a smile. That didn't hurt. 'Why do you ask? Are you interested in any of them?'

Antelmino swung his boot full into her left shoulder, making her crumple to the floor. The blinding blast of pain put her on a delirious state of unconsciousness for a moment. Scrambling for sustenance with her hands over the sooty ground, she raised herself up to a seated position again, with her knees bent and together, and her feet firmly planted.

Antelmino watched the efforts with his devious grin. 'Do you want to keep being smart when you talk to a superior man like me?'

Ginevra swallowed the coal dust she had in her tongue before trying to say anything. 'I am sorry.' she finally said, softening her voice but keeping it firm. 'I am just upset that they beat me. That's all. I should not take it upon you.'

'Now here's an intelligent wench,' Antelmino said. 'If you treat me with respect, I will be respectful to you too. Simple, isn't it? Now let's see how clean you are.' He extended his foot and carefully introduced it between her shanks, moving it to the right, dragging her left leg to the side, and doing the same to her right leg, dragging it to the opposite side. Ginevra found herself sitting with her legs wide open and an extremely alert Antelmino di Gottefredo standing between them.

'They were not men enough,' she said, looking shyly to the sides.

'Excuse me?' Antelmino lost his smile.

'They did not take me. The idiot had one of his fits and just beat me mercilessly, leaving this metato like a castrated piglet...'

'Yes, he is indeed a piglet,' Antelmino said, giggling more agitatedly, 'I saw him running up the road towards Chifenti, like a piglet who's lost his balls.'

Ginevra smiled. 'Indeed, he had no balls, but neither had the Lord Cunimundinghi, who watched the idiot beat me incessantly and did *nothing* to protect me. And after the little monster left, he was not man enough to show me how a woman should be properly treated. He went after the idiot, without even touching me.' She slowly raised the shreds of her ripped tunic, exposing well her thighs. 'You are not like them, are you?'

Antelmino chewed on his dry saliva. He babbled something, trying to say 'No', as his heartbeat almost made his chest explode.

Ginevra opened an appetising smirk. Her lips still bled, but that was not important for the moment. She caressed her thighs softly. 'Maybe you can remind me now how it is to feel like a woman. I haven't entertained a real man in me for so long —'

Antelmino fell on his knees between her legs. He threw his hat to the side, holding on to her thighs, avidly caressing them. 'I'm gonna make you cry, wench. I'll split you in two. You'll be crying like a little girl. You will be begging me to get out of you!' he drooled.

Ginevra met his gaze. His chin was trembling with anticipation.

'Let me feel your skin!' she ordered in a whisper, biting her lower lip.

The overwrought Castracani raised his tunic from his belt and pulled it up to his torso and head. In a second, while dealing with the fabrics around his elbows and face to undress, he felt a light movement on the sheath of his dagger and an excruciating flare of pain in his groins, as if it had caught on fire. He screeched in agony, while trying to get rid of that tube of clothes around his arms and head.

'*Ti faccio vedere come piange una raggazza!*' Ginevra groaned, as she twisted the dagger around its axis, poking deeply, with the blade interred into a red wet stain that quickly grew around Antelmino's groin — *I will show you how a girl cries!*

While Antelmino fell back, screaming loud in sheer torture, still squirming and blinded, with a cocoon of his own tunic immobilising his arms, and with the hilt of the dagger sticking out of his lower pelvis, Ginevra quickly managed to get onto her feet. She pulled out the dagger, making the blood drip generously. 'That's how you do, it, Antelmino di Gottefreddo, Very well done! That's *exactly* how a girl cries,' she hissed, 'And now I'm going to show you how you become a *real Castracani*!

He screamed again as she stabbed him deeply, right between his legs, pulling the blade out on a long arch, bringing out shreds of hose fabric, skin and an splatter of blood, which drew a red line from her forehead to her chin. She stepped over his wriggling body and pushed the door out into the early evening twilight.

While Antelmino roared inside, Ginevra found the strength to overcome her own pains in all bones and joints. She had to put the door back into place, fixing it with the long poles lying outside. She made sure the Castracani would need some inhuman effort to move the door out of his way. Grabbing the dagger firmly, she tried not to concentrate on Antelmino's bellows and looked at the road towards Anchiano. That would be a short walk. But she took the longer road back home, towards Chifenti.

Limping, walking with difficulty, weeping from pain and leaving the metato behind, Antelmino's screams of horror still echoed inside Ginevra's head, so much that she had the impression that his screams were coming from across the Serchio.

Fears of the Dark

They had just left the tavern in Chifenti. With tireless tail-wagging Altobello following them, mother and son had gone on foot, so they could talk calmly over the day's events and achievements. Arrigo pulled the courser by the reigns, carefully describing how the violent Spatola had slipped through his grasp. At that stage, he wisely omitted to report to his mother some of his deeds involving Ginevra. He feared that the rather rough treatment he had dedicated to the wench could give her an acceptable reason to back down on the agreement about Chifenti. That was probably *not* worth telling his mother, who had just left Bernardo in a sleeping state, with a fairly optimistic prognosis. It felt like life was arranging itself around his interests. Arrigo would deal with Ginevra later, as soon as he could bleed Spatola with his dagger. Exciting and strange things were happening in those hours.

Bodies were floating down the Serchio's silvery current at twilight. Arrigo and Maria Maddalena stopped at the path, far away, to watch the silent procession of bloated corpses. Goats, sheep, cows, deer, and a man, which Arrigo laughed generously at the sight. There were also a few unrecognisable dead things, mostly small, but some inexplicably large, too confusing for the Lord and Lady of Anchiano to mention to each other.

Half the way between Chifenti and the hospital, while hearing the wolves howling across the river, just behind a small curve of the path, they came face to face with Julian, on his way to see Bernardo. Both Maria and Arrigo had tried to pretend they were not noticing him, looking ahead and avoiding his gaze. Altobello leaped to greet Julian, a wet friendly muzzle on the Hospitaller's hands.

'Good evening,' said Julian, with a well-humoured tone, catching them unguarded, roughing Altobello's ears but looking at Maria and Arrigo. The startled

Cunimundinghi couldn't help but hate themselves for not avoiding his sudden gaze and acknowledging the greeting with a humiliating nod. Julian seemed thrilled with their discomfort. 'What news do you have of Bernardo?' he asked, as they had continued their walk.

Maria turned around, measuring the Hospitaller from her unattainable heights as if he was the most repulsive creature on earth. 'Why don't you ask the taverner? Isn't there where you're going?' And she turned around, hurriedly catching the pace with Arrigo and the horse. Altobello followed her, as if this was a game.

Julian kept moving, little affected by their hostile mood. However, on looking down towards the river, his face hardened as the floating corpses made his stomach churn. He thought of his decision for the delivery day. He needed a few minutes to assert himself that it was the right one.

Maria and Arrigo were silent for a while, until they instinctively stopped at the bridge's paved embankment. The attraction was too strong. Curiosity could kill, it had been said.

From under their feet, the stone pavement soared onto the bridge. But in a few paces, as it raised itself from the bank, it disappeared in the smothering fog. Altobello's ears were alert, but his tail had stopped.

'It's the day after tomorrow...' Maria wandered.

'The delivery?' Arrigo asked.

'Of course it is.' She looked at her son with impatience, 'What else could it be?'

'Someone will walk across, I'm sure somebody will do it!' said Arrigo, showing his teeth in pleasure.

Maria bared hers in displeasure, visibly exasperated by Arrigo's interest. 'Leave this matter be! Do *not* come any close to the bridge then. I *forbid* you!'

Arrigo looked at his mother in dismay. 'It sounds as you do believe after all that it is the Devil that is building it, mother.'

Maria laughed, angrily. Straightening her face, she snarled 'Of course it is the Devil! And straight out of hell, you simpleton! That is the very reason that I order you to stay in Anchiano the morning after tomorrow. Let me deal with it. This is *my* field!'

He shrugged his shoulders 'I am not afraid of any devil.'

Altobello growled at the fog, drawing attention with his ears back against his neck, triggering an agitated sequence of short howls, yelps and whines, coming from the somewhere over the bridge. Maria cried 'These must be wolves! *Run!*' Arrigo's courser reared up. With its eyes bulged in fear, the beast pulled its reigns free from Arrigo's grasp and raced away towards the southern road.

While Maria's black dog stood firm on the embankment, growling menacingly, with shoulder and neck hairs erect as an urchin, both mother and son were running. 'To the hospital!' she said, looking desperately at the building that stood half a mile away down the road.

Arrigo ran ahead of his mother. When he saw himself alone, he paused to wait for her.

'No! Do not wait for me!' she yelled, panting. 'You never understand, do you? This is all for you, Arrigo. It's all about you! Just go and leave me behind.' She looked to the Serchio, flowing out of the fog. And there it was already: running alongside on the bank there was a large gray wolf, ears dropped back and looking restless at her.

Those mountain monsters had crossed the Serchio, thanks to that accursed bridge and probably at the cost of Altobello's guardianship. She felt a stitch of pain in her heart, not irradiating from her legs, but out of sadness, bringing out pleasant moments of that dog's companionship.

Her Altobello was lost, surely, but her Arrigo would not be. Maria just had to make it to safety, for he still needed her protection. Running faster than her exhaustion could catch her, she felt no more pain in the legs. Seeing the hospital shaking closer ahead of her eyes, she watched Arrigo going in and waiting for her at the door. Now she only needed to make it before that wolf – she looked towards the river bank again – and there was a whole pack of wolves silently running. This time, towards her direction.

South of the hospital, Ginevra was dragging herself away from a rocky outcrop that blocked Antelmino's screams from reaching her ears. On hearing the galloping, she managed to leap out of the path, expecting Arrigo to be coming back for her. But only his courser passed by, with an empty saddle. God be praised, she thought. *Something must have happened to that devil.*

But her flame of enthusiasm lasted little, extinguishing as she heard screams coming from the path ahead. It sounded like Maria Maddalena, yelling at her son.

Ginevra limped through the bushes edging the path and watched, with a heavy heart, a healthy and alive Arrigo running towards the hospital door. The young Cunimundinghi stopped by the building's entrance and waited for his mother, who followed on a stampede, pushing the son through with her impetus, slamming the door behind them.

This could represent the bleakest scenario for Ginevra, as now she felt the need to avoid the hospital and drag her way straight through almost two more miles to get home, in Chifenti. But on that young evening of Saint Euphrasia's Feast, darkness ahead of her fate just became darker when she watched with dismay a pack of wolves crushing their fangs on the hospital door as soon as Maria Maddalena disappeared through it.

Ginevra jumped deeper into the ditch by the road, trying to hide herself under those not too dense bushes. Given her short distance from the hospital, it would be too late for her to try to escape further away and too risky to be seen running. She silently slithered her body under the wet ground dead foliage, covering herself with the soil, hoping that the wolves would not smell the blood in her wounds. She could hear the clear growling of those creatures, barking and whining with excitement as they tried the entrances and surrounded the building with their devilish yelps. There was a sudden silence, when Ginevra hoped that the wolves had gone up the mountain, away from her path, but they were soon yelping again, this time around the desperate bleating of a goat. The growling increased, a menacing clamour, sounding like a fight, making her skin congeal under the cold soil and the pain in her body disappear as if having been no more than a minor annoyance. And soon, the yelps came closer, approaching fast the ditch by the path where she was hiding, and so did the bleating of the goat, coming towards her with a terrifying speed. Ginevra prepared her courage and fists to hit full the first muzzle that uncovered her. And she knew this would only be for the sake of a pathetic heroic death, which in the end not even the saints in heaven would ever learn about. And for sure there would be no escape.

While her eyes were distracted by a circle of *prugnoli* mushrooms that edged not too far from where her face was buried, the bleating from the path above died away, and so did the wolves' barking and howling. The silence around that area suggested to Ginevra that they were gone. She shot a sudden glance at those mushrooms again. Standing still, whitish and deliciously scented. Strangely, somehow she had gotten the chilling impression that those prugnoli had been staring at her.

She had to leave. Standing up carefully, she shook the leaves from her arms and walked to the path. No sign of life, except for a dark track of blood along the road, which hadn't been there before. The wolves had gone south, probably dragging that goat with them. Ginevra turned north and continued her fast walk, limping and somehow reviving all the pains she had on her joints. For an instant, she regretted having locked Antelmino so well. The wolves could tear him apart, as far as she was concerned.

She walked silent by the hospital. The lone building sounded equally mute and empty of life. She wanted to cry out for Julian's help, for Clarissa's care, but she knew that the deceiving Arrigo was in there and, if they met this time, she would not have the opportunity to cut his balls off. Ginevra kept going, ignoring the hospital, exhausted but decided. Minutes later without looking back, she limped by the bridge's embankment. She looked at the fog that covered the bridge.

Bridge of the devil!

Everyone had wanted that bridge so much and now it was opening the gates of hell into earth.

Something came out of the fog. Large and black. And it was snarling at her.

With her legs trembling, Ginevra recognised Altobello, Maria Maddalena's dog. Black eyes focused, it approached menacingly, with flexed limbs, its body low above the stoned path, ready to sprint. Ginevra just could not understand why such a friendly dog had turned hostile all of a sudden. The bridge should probably explain.

But Ginevra of Amadeo was not defeated yet. She turned around to run. But this time she could not move a step, for a dozen amber eyes had been staring fixed at her.

The wolves were silent, baring their teeth and carrying those large grey heads with their ears pulled backwards, at the same level as their spines and tails. Hackles on their shoulders were erect, and they were no more than a leap's distance from Ginevra.

Inside the hospital Clarissa's eyes widened when a terrorised Arrigo of the Cunimundinghi broke all of a sudden into her hall, snatching the door open. And to complete the surprise, Maria Maddalena entered soon after him. But nothing had prepared Clarissa for the violence of the wolves outside, trying to bite that same solid door off its firm hold. The wardens jumped up to restrain the doors.

That's when Clarissa had a chill freeze over her body: *Spatola.*

She rushed to open the back door, but she was pushed off by the warden.

'Leave it, Lady Clarissa! There are wolves outside!'

Clarissa couldn't allow herself to accept that Spatola had good chances to be found in his hiding and devoured by those wolves. But she considered the presence of Arrigo, a deadlier foe than any mountain beast. With him in the hall now, there was no opportunity to inform anyone of her concealed guest. Once she was sure that Arrigo was busy enough with the front door, she discreetly whispered to the warden about the village idiot of Chifenti in the back shed. The warden raised his eyebrows in awe and clear understanding of the sensitivity and urgency of the matter. Looking at Maria and Arrigo, both holding the front door against the wolves' trusts, he turned around with a hand forced against his door and another pulling the handle, careful and firmly opening it.

A chilling draft entered as both Clarissa and the warden peeked through the narrow opening, across the area between the hospital building and the back sheds. They saw no wolves, but did not dare to step out, as someone just stood in the darkness outside that door. It was very quick. A plump old woman, standing naked on her long legs. She was holding her large breasts with a mischievous face and, as soon as her incensed eyes fell on them, peeking from inside, she flexed her legs and crouched as a frog, giggling with a guttural voice.

The warden slammed the door back and looked at Clarissa, who had lost any colour in her face. He could not quite believe what he had witnessed, but Clarissa's panic-stricken features were clear proof of what his eyes had seen. After exchanging their appalled glances, they both looked at the door again. The warden opened it wide this time, and the woman was not there, but a large grey wolf ran by, dragging a blood-covered goat in its jaws.

'*Close the door!*' Maria screamed.

A second wolf came running towards them. The warden pushed the door back just in time to bar its leap, cracking the wood when the monster crushed against it.

'There's a witch here!' shouted the warden. But suddenly noticing that Maria had turned at him with blood-infused eyes, he corrected himself 'I mean...outside!'

Clarissa swallowed a lump before confirming 'She's out there, with the wolves.'

In a moment, they heard no more howls or snarling. The doors were no longer touched. A few candles flickered in the dark interior of the hospital, as no more than half a dozen guests were huddled against one corner, squirming with fear. Clarissa stayed with a warden by the back door, praying that Julian was safe somewhere in Chifenti, while the other warden stayed with Arrigo by the front door. Maria Maddalena went to the kitchen to find herself something to eat.

It was a night of silent tolerance, as much as fear. Hardly anyone had much sleep until the doors were finally opened at sunrise. And that is when Clarissa went outside to wait for her husband and verify what had happened with Spatula.

That night was infernal.

When rumours came to Chifenti that the wolves had crossed the Serchio by nightfall, the villagers kept their doors firmly shut. In the tavern, Amadeo had sent all the patrons out by mid late morning, when Maria Maddalena had arrived. Now, on a clean palliasse, Bernardo's head throbbed with pain. Julian and Amadeo prayed for Clarissa and Ginevra, while keeping the shepherd refreshed and soothed between delirious dreams. For hours he blabbed out curses and tried to move his jaws to describe the legions of devils flying out of the bridge before their final night.

The first scream that startled them during the night came clearly from a house across the road. Amadeo quickly opened the tavern door, seeing a few diffuse shadowy figures, large and small, swiftly scattering disappearing into the darkness around him. He shouted at his neighbours. They responded by shouting back that all was fine, except for some birds that had invaded their house through their smoke window, attacking the old woman of the house. They had managed to kill a couple of those stinky creatures before the other crow-like invaders fled.

Julian and Amadeo were tormented by more cries and sounds from outside, grunts slipping under the door, howls coming through the walls, croaks and squeals moving on the roof. Shaking like a green shoot of beech under an April rainstorm, Amadeo prayed for his protection and for Ginevra's, wherever she could be taking shelter, hopefully in Anchiano, better in the hospital. He wept for her name, haunted by memories of the night of San Pelegrino, when the saint's ghost was seen just outside his tavern.

Julian tried to distract the taverner, by asking for his assistance in soothing Bernardo's headache. While Amadeo poured some more wine, they heard rustling sound of tiles being moved on the roof above.

'*Whaeesit?*' Bernardo mumbled.

Amadeo rushed to grab onto a staff he normally used to handle unmanageable patrons who did not want to move when having their last skin of wine. Julian lit one more candle and carefully walked with it, to stand under the spot on the roof where the sound came from.

'Don't look up right underneath it, Julian.' said Amadeo, stepping away, 'You are a saint, for sure, but tiles are as heavy as tiles are. They can still fall on your face.'

As soon as he mentioned that, the noise moved to the area immediately above him. Looking up, Amadeo saw one tile being flipped up behind the straw lining, disappearing into the night. He leaped to the side, just escaping from being hit by a silvery long shape that was dropped through the opening, almost hitting him on his shoulder.

What appeared to be a sharp metal blade did not plunge straight into the ground, but it rather hit it with a blunt splattering thump. Amadeo and Julian approached their candleholders and looked closer. They had to blink and open their eyes again to believe in what they were seeing.

'It's a chub!' said Amadeo with disgust. 'A *chub*! What devil in this world would drop a *fish* from someone's roof?' He was about to giggle when another large shape splattered heavy on top of the chub. A much greater, greenish, slimy fish.

Julian shook his head in complete disbelief. 'A demon with a very good grip, to be able to raise a slippery tench that far.'

More dead fish were dropped in a flashing cascade. Several chubs, *rovelle* and *vairone*, in a silvery dead rope, slipping wet through the hole while a maddened laughter cackled outside. Amadeo gagged in horror and fell backwards as some of the fish scuttled away around the floor, walking with little thin legs under them. Julian grabbed the staff from his grasp and tucked one of the walking fish with its tip. The fish fell dead to the side, with the belly opened. Inside it was a large mouse, which had been walking with the fish on its top as a disguise. The mouse looked at Julian with an eerie tiny human face and screeched in rage, before scurrying away into the dark corners. On the roof, the fish cascade had turned into a rope of excrement. They could hear someone whooping and laughing, as shit slipped like diarrhoea through the hole in the roof, splashing on the pile of fish below.

Julian jumped up on a table and shoved the staff deep through the roof hole. A monstrous roar of pain was blown through the hole and the staff was violently yanked out, pulling Julian together with it. When it was finally released, it made Julian's feet fall straight through the pile of shit and fish on the ground. The roar continued, more enraged than before, and a black arm entered through the hole, its open claws grabbing more of the tiles and pulling them up. Julian was quick to swing the staff and hit that hand as hard as he could. Another screech of pain and the hand disappeared back into the night.

Then, something shining appeared through the hole. Amadeo raised his candle, trembling, and his legs faltered as they saw the eye. Big as a human skull and honey-coloured, peeking at them with a slotted pupil that thinned as soon as the flame was raised. It was staring at Julian, and it was furious, but it was not sufficiently intimidating to stop him from poking the staff with all the strength he could gather into it. The entire tavern shook with the scream, as pole was sucked out, disappearing after the eye. Julian and Amadeo heard the staff cracking and watched helpless that dark hole increasing as the scream persisted, when the tiles were furiously beaten and disappeared into the night, as if blown by a windstorm. One of the ceramic tiles flew into Amadeo's face, opening a gash across his nose and cheek, while others fell upon Bernardo. They ducked for cover while the roof collapsed and vanished away. Amadeo contracted all of his muscles, waiting for the final blow.

And suddenly there was a silence.

A mute interval of apprehension in the night, which continued in silence for an agonising moment.

And a faint knock was heard on the door.

Amadeo quickly stood up to attend to it, missing the loud sniffing that could be heard from under the door.

Julian shouted 'Do *not* open, Amadeo, it could be a trap!'

But it was too late. The taverner opened the door wide.

In addition to the large black dog that appeared to be Altobello, Amadeo saw Ginevra standing there, trembling, beaten, hurt and bleeding. When she saw her father, her eyes finally rolled up and she just collapsed into his arms.

The Soup

The sun rose over a quiet valley.

From Lucca to the Caferonia, the wide length of Serchio seemed to be particularly quiet, except for that short segment just down from the Lima: that foggy area where a bridge was to be build. A muffled swarm could be heard irradiating from the mist at the break of day.

When the door of the Hospital of Santa Croce was opened, Clarissa gave little attention to that distant buzz. While her noble guests from Anchiano scurried away to their lands without even thanking her for the shelter, she quietly hurried to the straw shed. The four goats had been snatched out from their ropes, disappearing behind red, muddy tracks. She did not expect to see any piece of those poor beasts left behind. The shed interior was a gory tinge of blood. Moving to the back of the construction she saw Spatola's foot sticking out of the straw.

He was snoring deeply.

Clarissa laughed in relief. When she woke him up, he had no recollections whatsoever of wolves. He had just slept from late afternoon, throughout the whole night.

With an unbundled nest of straw sticking out of his hair, Spatola listened to her account without a smile or a nod.

'Aren't you happy you've survived the night, Carpo?' said Clarissa.

'Makes no difference,' he said, expressionlessly as a plank. 'I will go to hell, anyway.'

Ginevra had Bernardo's head on her lap. 'You stink of eggs,' she said with a sad smile.

He looked miserable. His head was shorn, swollen and glazed with egg whites. But for him, in spite of the blinding clarity that came through the roofless tavern, somehow his position relieved the pain from his wound, his jaws and his neck. Probably it had something to do more with the warmth of her hands, or the comforting proximity of her breasts than the adjustment of his head angle. It just felt incredibly soothing to be in her arms, and now his memory was engaged into calculating how long it had been since he had enjoyed the warmth of a woman. *Embarrassingly long.*

Amadeo cared for the cuts and bruises on his face, using some duck fat and marigold that had been left over from Spatola's rescue. He had the help of Julian to dress some of Ginevra bruises.

When Ginevra had suddenly appeared outside of his door that night, Amadeo quickly hauled her into the tavern and, quite shyly, the dog Altobello followed, stepping in too. Then, whatever the creature was that had been devastating their roof, seemed to have been gone. But before closing the door, Amadeo looked into the darkness outside and saw the icy sparkle of dozens of eyes, staring at him from a distance. Nevertheless, from the arrival of Ginevra, the attacks in the village ceased and Chifenti dragged itself through a long, but relatively peaceful night.

Julian shovelled the fish and the excrement out, while Ginevra told them that the wolves seemed to have been afraid of Altobello. With threatening growls and howls, they had followed her all the way from the bridge. Her progress had been slow, she was thirsty, hungry, weak, and soon she could do no more than drag herself on all fours along the path. The wolves yelped in excitement, but Altobello had patiently stood by her side. At every glance the dog spared to the pack, they would shoot away with their tails down.

And as the night progressed into the late winter dawn, Amadeo tried to adjust himself to the uncomfortable pang of fatherly jealousy on noticing that once his daughter had cared little for her own good. Instead, she was dedicating her time entirely to Bernardo delle Rocche.

Julian left early at sunrise, but just as he closed the door behind him, he was called by the tavern neighbours who had been attacked by the crows. They took him to their door, they pointed to a large, fetid piece of tissue from a dead animal, tossed outside. He thought it looked like viscera from a sheep. They told him that the two birds they had managed to kill had quickly deteriorated into ashes overnight.

While a pilgrim arrived from the hospital, bringing calming news of Clarissa's safety, other villagers in Chifenti called Julian. It was comforting for them to have the saint around. Some had lost animals from their herds. Others were cleaning up their houses, keeping doors opened, wiping out their floors from all kinds of dejecta that had been dropped in, discussing the devilish invasion of the wolves and the strange things that happened. A solid old man who was an olive presser told them of a horse-sized goldfinch that he had seen behind the trees in the late afternoon. A potter's wife who lived by the southern part of the village reported witnessing a very small pilgrim running along the road down to the bridge just before the sun rose. She had been sickened by the impression that the pilgrim had the face of a duck. The local miller could swear that he had seen a headless pig laughing in his backyard, with no more than a round metal shield covering the empty space of its neck. Someone asked how he could know the pig was laughing when it had no head. In this moment, they were alerted by the people of Fornulo. A death was reported by the mouth of the Lima.

It was Carlo, the boatman from Fornulo. The wolves had not crossed the Lima, sparing Fornulo, Corsena and the villages further north and up the mountains from their vicious attacks. The conclusion was that Carlo must have been caught at night, while fishing for early pike near the southern bank.

They cried in horror on seeing his body entangled on the branch of a large willow tree. But Carlo was not hanging. He was rolled around the branch. The wolves had snatched his entrails out. His back had been bent backwards, and his feet entered through the sides of his spine, showing his toes at the gaping ribs which protruded ahead.

Julian had to hold his own stomach from popping out. 'Wolves don't do that!' he spat.

The path south was striped with blood. Goats had been dragged towards Anchiano and Moriano. Nobody would expect the wolves to be attacking by daylight, but still Maria and Arrigo hurried to get to the safety of their castle. A clamour was heard across the river. They could tell that Mutianum had been badly hit by the wolves. When mother and son turned away from the Serchio road, they walked in silence by the old metato. Arrigo sped up his pace and pointed excited to the rock in Anchiano, talking almost disconnectedly. Soon, a few peasants and villagers from Anchiano left their fields and came to greet them, expressing their relief in knowing their lady and lord were safe, but preparing them for the bad news: Arrigo's courser had been gutted by the wolves. Its half-devoured parts were scattered over a circle of half a mile around the castle.

Maria did not allow her son to get himself distracted with those matters in that critical moment of returning home. She held onto his arm and pulled him along, as they both walked up the spiralling path to the castle under the curious eyes of the locals, who were cleaning up the road from the horse's remains. Only when the heavy doors closed behind them she turned to him, dry as a rock. 'Do you think I am stupid enough not to notice the old metato with a barricaded door from outside? What has happened here, Arrigo?'

He was hopelessly silent, dodging his gaze from any point that he looked at.

Maria's open hand exploded on his face, almost breaking his neck. Arrigo lost his balance for a while, holding onto his hit side. 'Don't hit me again!' he roared, pulling his dagger out.

Maria looked at the shining blade with dismay and they exchanged a quick glance. She dropped her shoulders.

'Put that blade away. I paid a lot of money for it, you imbecile,' said she, through grinding teeth.

Arrigo too, sighed in acquiescence and sheathed the dagger. 'I will tell you what happened, when we eat' he said, 'I must take away that flavour of peasant food from my mouth.' And he added 'but don't you ever hit me again like that. It's bad enough to lose my courser on this day.'

A female servant brought olives, a cold wood pigeon and a teal that had been roasted on the previous day. They washed it down with some wine. Meanwhile, she plucked some mistle thrushes to roast on a spit.

Maria never lost her livid face of disbelief while her son told her a fairly accurate account of the events of the previous day. Incidentally, he skipped only the bits about his desire to physically possess Ginevra.

'You never seem to run out of surprises,' said she 'but unfortunately there are only a few of them that would increase my happiness or pride. Right now, you make me nauseous with your lowness. Arrigo, you don't have to hide the facts from me. I know what a pig looks like. I have seen the Saracens close and I know what they smell like. You are stinking of rape, and you should be ashamed of that. *Rape*!' she cackled, with a face almost as red as a chicken comb, 'What do *you* know about rape? If you only knew...' she laughed, nervously, 'A young noble like you risking his whole future for a dirty little wench, who's much older than you. And I am here sacrificing myself, trying to make a decent, powerful man out of you. Everything I have done in my life was to give you a future. I'm ready to go to hell to ensure your happiness and salvation. But why? Why do I do all of this? At this stage, it is only because you are the continuation of my line and your father's. You are a Cunimundinghi and you better start behaving like one, so I will not regret what I am about to do.'

Arrigo raised an eyebrow 'What are you going to do?'

Maria lowered her eyelids in a patience gathering intake of breath. She shook her head. 'Never mind. Just go and silence that woman. Make it quietly and come back quickly, so I can arrange that nobody will ever know about it. Next, you must find that idiot, while I will investigate if anyone ever saw you entering that metato with the wench.'

Arrigo grabbed a roasted mistle thrush before leaving in a hurry.

Considering the damage inflicted in just one night across some of the villages on the eastern side of the Apuane mountains, it was later calculated that hundreds, or probably thousands of ravenous wolves had marched down to that slaughter on Saint Euphrasia's night.

On the following day, villagers and peasants spent most of the morning occupied with picking up destroyed livestock, re-counting the herds, discussing the odd monstrosities observed or experienced as the night fell and, saddest of all, mourning their dead.

They learned that in Pescaglia and Coloniogla, many were the families that had been destroyed by being caught so early in the afternoon. Men working the fields, women with their mazzaranghe, breaking down roasted chestnuts into flour, children setting traps for blackbirds, none of them ever had the time to hide in their homes once the howling had started.

In La Cuna, when night was high and the wolves had been gone, the villagers saw a hooded stranger with a lantern calmly climbing the steps of their small church. At every level the stranger stopped, raised his tunic and laid an egg. Before sunrise, a villager opened its door and saw a flock of woodcocks and curlews at those stairs. The birds were humming and sticking their long beaks into those eggs, drinking all the contents. They left early and only the thin, empty shells remained.

In many villages, some people just disappeared and they were never found. In Bertagna, a family saw an outlandish dwarf wearing deer antlers on his head, eating the chickens in their farm. When chasing the dwarf with his pitchfork, the farmer was toppled and mauled by a cete of badgers.

In Diecimo, everyone was accounted for on the next day, but the corpse of a large creature was found in the morning. The monstrosity had a human face, quite unrecognisable from so much damage it had received, but the most appalling feature was it very long body, with about a dozen arms and legs. A villager leader pointed out that the creature was a string of five or six human corpses, one sticking the head into the stomach of another. The macabre travesty was completed by brooms and shovels sticking out of the creature's many arseholes. The horrified villagers did not want one more second of the sight of that abomination. As per the parishioner order, they set fire to it.

And in Mutianum, gore was so extensive that no one could tell how many had been the pilgrims caught defenceless by the pack. All the villagers invariably assured one another that they never heard the screaming of the pilgrims for help, asking why the priest had not opened the church. They had encountered the door opened, and each of the villagers fell on their knees when they saw Diloguardi's head spiked on the top of the altar cross.

'Ginevra is gone…' Arrigo said, slamming the door behind him. He was as white as a clear day cloud.

Maria stood up, with jaws clenched. 'You let her escape?'

'It's worse than that, mother…' he trembled his chin. 'There was someone else in the metato.'

'A witness?' she raised both of her hands in helplessness. 'Now *that's* all we needed!'

'Not just a witness, but someone who needs help, and badly.'

Maria just kept her gaze and waited for more explanation.

'You better come with me now. It is Antelmino di Gottefredo that I found locked inside that shed. And he is badly wounded. I think he has been castrated.'

In Lucca, riders had arrived from the Serchio, bringing news of the slaughter. Pilgrims at the gate were advised not to use the Serchio stretch of the Via Francigena, but take the Lunigiana segment instead.

'Wolves don't do that!' said the parish clerk Anton, slamming his fist on the table. 'That priest Diloguardi was decapitated and his head was carefully displayed on the altar. This desecration is obviously done by some bandits. We should send men-at-arms and put these criminals through the sword.'

Bishop Giovanni picked his lower lip pensively. 'We do not know what is going on in this area. It has been months, already and our men never came back. Many priests have deserted the region. They all talk about the devil and that bridge…'

'Yes, indeed,' confirmed Anton, impatiently 'that the bridge is being built by an army from hell, but nobody has seen it yet.'

'Nevertheless, they report the bridge is practically ready,' said the bishop, raising an explanatory finger, 'and that the delivery date is tomorrow, the feast of Saint Longinus.'

Anton gasped '*Who*'s delivering it? *Der Teufel*? Why would the King of Darkness chose this very spot among so many others in Christendom to appear?'

'Just one of many devils, Anton. What do we know about it?'

'We will not find anything else if we keep closing our eyes and ears to what is happening upriver,'

'Times are dare, Anton. There are news of widespread disease and mutiny in Rome. The pope is said to be lost in sensuous orgies with pilgrims and religieuses. Our church has probably never been thrown is such a pit of disgrace. We cannot ignore this devilish threat, I agree, but I suggest that at the moment we concentrate our prayers on the deliverance of those poor souls from evil.'

Anton slammed the table again. 'Prayers will not save them. We must find who's raiding those villages. Give me some men-at-arms and I will go now.'

Bishop Giovanni lowered his eyes 'I have no desire to face the devil with my men. I cannot do it. I will not do it. I will wait until the bridge is ready. Then we can investigate.'

'I will go on my own then' said the clerk, kneeling before the bishop.

Giovanni held onto Anton's head and gave him a kiss. 'I envy your courage, Anton but I fear for your safety. If I forbid you, I'm afraid that I will lose you anyway. You are curious and fearless, so I better give you my most heartily blessing. Take any two men-at-arms that are willing to face the devil, and go see the old Battista Burle before you leave. He may add some help.'

Anton found the banker in his office, finishing a dish of coot cooked in a casserole. Battista offered some of the fishy flavoured bird to Anton, who kindly declined and went straight into the subject.

Battista heard it all in silence, just pausing to gobble some more wine at intervals. Finally, he said 'That area has been isolated for too long. I have not seen my grandchildren for months. But all of us merchants have lost control of the bridge's construction when that insane pope burned the previous one. And now, these rumours of Satanas building the bridge have disturbed my good sleep, and no matter how much I have advised my granddaughter to stay away from it, I still cannot trust her. You would not imagine what she is capable of, my dear Anton.'

'She is a good woman, I know her.'

'No, you don't know her at all,' Battista chuckled for a second, and returned to the original tone, 'I will send two men-at-arms with you and your escorts. Go and protect Maria Maddalena from harm. Bring her to reason and please avoid any confrontations with Arrigo. That boy has a fiery heart, not yet tamed in good Christian ways. And please, do not take the western road, not too safe these days. I will have you provided with some coins for the ferry at Moriano. If Antelmino di Gottefredo has a problem with that, ignore it and tell him about me. Just follow on towards Anchiano, that I can deal with the Castracani.'

By the time the five riders reached the ferry, the ice storm had already started.

'What do we do with him?' Arrigo asked. He was standing outside the metato with his mother, two servants and a bullock cart. They had already been inside, where Maria made a rough examination on a more than delirious Antelmino.

'He still have his eggs in place,' she said, 'but the whole area has been badly minced somehow. Who would have done that?'

'Ginevra?' said Arrigo, shrugging his shoulders.

'Whatever the answer is, *you* will deal later with that. But first we must figure what to do with this man we have here. Do we want him dead or alive?'

Arrigo raised an eyebrow 'Is he not going to survive?'

'Oh, he's survived the night. Bad vases do not break that easily. But there could be other illnesses from such a wound. He could always fade on the second night, who knows?'

'I think you should care for him,' said Arrigo. 'I admire Antelmino in many ways. He has always been courteous to me. He can serve us better alive than dead.'

Maria paused for a second with jaws clenched. Then she nodded to herself, accepting the suggestion. They called the servants and immediately a roaring Antelmino di Gottefredo was being carried into the bullock cart.

'Quiet, stupid man.' Maria grunted. 'Consider yourself lucky. I am the best person in these lands that could have found you for your care.'

Antelmino extended his hand and grabbed her by the cloak, pulling her towards his face, hissing 'Do not tell anyone about this, Maria Maddalena. Never!'

'Shut up, Antelmino,' Maria said, snatching his hand from her cloak with a disgusted expression. 'You've got a disaster between your legs that will give you more to worry over the next few weeks than whether anyone else knows about it or not.' She looked up to the blackening sky early in that afternoon and completed, to all of them. 'Move it! Slash these oxen hard, for a storm is coming and it could catch us before we get to safety.'

After a sleepless night, tripping on a foot after another, Julian came exhausted from Chifenti, quite late in the morning, accompanied by a large number of pilgrims that had walked all the way from Barga. Before he entered the hospital, he still walked across the bank and shouted to the people of the Traghetto, asking them how they had fared with the night. A boatman quickly rowed across the silent Serchio and complained to the saint – as if he was the cause of it all – that it had been bad enough. Most livestock in the settlement had been gone, taken by wolves and other misshapen creatures that roamed the village at night, but as opposed to Mutianum, just a few minutes to the south, no death had affected them. When he rowed back, Julian dropped his shoulders and crouched at the river margin, throwing pebbles at the calm but decided currents and looking at the outline of the bridge behind the fog. A dragon with an arched back, waiting to reveal itself on the next day.

Clarissa came to meet Julian by the riverbank, with a comforting hug and a kiss for a soldier, returning from war. Returning to war.

At the touch of her hands, his skin seemed to expand and burn with a soothing white fire of peace and comfort. 'It's so good to see you well and safe, Clarissa,' he said, closing his eyes and holding her hands tighter against his face. 'I craved so much to be back here, to feel your touch.'

'You must rest, my love,' she said, holding his face. 'Let's get inside, for a storm is shaping.' They walked slowly. Julian did not bother to look up to the blackening sky. They walked together, sending mutual warmth through the hands that they firmly held onto. Clarissa made a brief summary of the previous day and night. But in contrast to that night, now the hospital was very full. Most pilgrims that arrived from the North decided to stay and not risk the storm. Moreover, there were curious villagers from the region that wanted to be there for the next day. The rumour was out, that the devil would be waiting on the other side.

Julian let himself drop like a cold corpse onto his mattress. He was snoring at the blink of an eye. There were dreams of nothing, while he just kept falling into the deepest pit of slumber. Only the warmth of Clarissa's presence was able to bring him out of it when she fed the hearth with more logs than usual. He opened his eyes for that enjoyable moment when he watched her profile looking at the dancing flames, unaware of his gaze, drawing a subtle smile of satisfaction on her lips. He quickly closed his eyes when she stood to cover him with more pelts and drop a light kiss in his cheek, before leaving. The biting cold weather permeated through the walls and it was dark outside already. He could hear no wolves this time. The beasts had been intimidated by the brutal weather, he thought. But in reality, it would be learned later, the wolves that remained in the valley were mostly frozen to death.

He slipped into slumber again.

It was the glorious aroma of *zuppa di farro* soaring from the kitchen that convinced Julian to, quite vigorously, leave the comfortable hospitality of his pelts. Much more complex than the earthy, grainy smell of a normal emmer soup, this was a rich, smooth combination of all the game to be found foraging in the forest in early spring, permeating the walls with a warm coating of comfort. Julian descended the steps, slowly into the kitchen, immersing himself into a warm pool of scented smoke. In addition to the soup that boiled in a large iron pot, he noticed with satisfaction the long piles of steaming-hot flat stones, compressing cakes between chestnut leaves, and that all the sausages had been gone from their hanging hooks. There were opened barrels of wine, olive oil, cheese, and the scrapings of mushrooms. In the hall, a graceful and tireless Clarissa moved diligently with the wardens amid a silent but lively crowd, a bright exchange of cheerful gazes from rose-cheeked guests that gorged themselves with the richest meal ever served at the hospital of Santa Croce.

Clarissa greeted Julian with a warm hand on his face 'There's more soup coming,' she said, with a half smile, raising an eyebrow. 'Now that you're rested, I want you to eat well tonight.' Julian was squeezed among the pilgrims for a place to sit. The soup delighted him. Never before had it been that generous in flavours and ingredients, bringing a reassuring cosiness to the hall. He looked at those faces, happy with each other, almost unaware of the freezing storm outside those walls castigating the valley, or totally oblivious to the terrifying creatures of the previous night, the nocturnal dangers that raided those villages, threatened their livestock and lives, causing so much pain and destruction. Now it was an invigorating, almost blinding sense of safety. There were no worries or fears to what could await for them over that freezing night, but rather a warm exchange of liquid gazes, friendly smiles, hands touching, helpfulness. Children held on to their parents' fingers with pride irradiating from their faces and couples retired for a quiet corner in the straw.

Clarissa was upstairs. She had pulled her mattress out to puff it up, fluffing it, holding the fabric close to her face, enjoying the perfume of the beech leaves insinuating itself through the reassuring scent of Julian. Her eyes were fixed on the floor, the wide wooden box filled with straw where the mattress laid upon. They had been living in that hospital for almost seventeen years now, and she wondered if Julian had ever lifted their mattress during that time. Not a shadow of doubt that he was a most helpful and willing hand, but she suspected he had never bothered to look under their bed. Somehow the task of changing straw and refilling the mattress with new dried leaves every autumn had always been hers. She was wondering if Julian would know what had been hidden under their bed, when she heard his steps going up the stairs.

Julian had been distributing a flat cake of chestnut flour to each empty plate. The thankful guests were eating it with the remaining soup, olive oil and re-cotta cheese. While they savoured that treat, he climbed over to the straw storage and pushed a generous pile of more bedding for the needy pilgrims. He looked over through the high window and saw the freezing needles of rain dropping with force. Sticking his hand out, he touched the layer of ice that glazed the stone. There was no manner in which a wolf or any other devilish creature would be out. They were safe at the hospital that night.

And it would all be over on the next day.

The warmth of the room below him could be felt in his heart. In the hospital of Santa Croce, dozens of pilgrims were happy, on their way to Lucca or Rome, searching for their cures or for answers to their prayers and spiritual needs. Others were on their way back to their homes, heart-filled, ready and eager to carry on with life after an extraordinary and rewarding journey following the steps of the Cross. Their numbers and warm-heartedness composed the fabulous heat that compensated for the insufficient hearths. The air smelled of new straw and food, and of people indeed, but not of wounds or infections, not of poverty or misery. Julian could hear no moaning or complaining. No wounds had been dressed and no children seemed to whine or cry. He climbed the ladder down to the floor and went to the kitchen, as the pilgrims accommodated themselves into the straw for a warm, loving sleep.

Julian could see the beautiful shapes of Clarissa's shadow moving gracefully over the wall up on their chamber. The eagle, the lion and the bull, altogether. His angel, his sphinx. He stepped up the ladder and saw her standing with her back to him, holding their mattress, probably preparing their room, but she quickly threw it down on the palliasse. She turned her torso around slowly, a smooth curve to look at him and open an inviting smile. Julian could not but notice the great lines that she was made of, and that reminded him of how much of a lucky man he was to have that angel watching over him. He felt his whole face and body tingling at her sight.

'This was the best soup ever!' said Julian, with a renewed face.

Clarissa savoured the satisfaction in his lips. Actually, strangely enough, there was a delicious volume to them. She could notice a return of those lips that, after the tragedy in Luna, had gone thin and stony, even when he smiled. Now they were meaty and young, and when he drew that passionate beam, they made those delicious flames caress her inside.

'I wanted this to be the best one ever,' said she, almost biting her own lips.

'No thoughts to rationing it, or the next day?' Julian said, approaching her, holding her waist and touching his body to hers.

'We all know what's happening tomorrow, and everything will be so different thereafter,' said Clarissa, her hands lacing around his neck, slithering under his hair. 'Only *love* will remain.'

'I don't want to talk about *tomorrow*,' said Julian, pulling her closer. His lips were brushing against hers already.

'Neither do I,' she moaned, 'not even if I had the choice to.' Clarissa felt her legs going soft. She was sweating, and desperately needed his warm hands to spread that coolness over her skin.

'Are you sure the guests will be alright during the night?' he asked, his lips now touching hers, making them move together with his words.

Clarissa pulled him tighter and said 'Angels are watching over us,' before finally opening herself for his lips. The silky kiss spread a silvery flow between them, which would have taken both like a flash flood into the sea of heaven, but she had one last thing to say.

'Julian...' she whispered, panting from the flames inside, holding his face away from her.

'What is it my love?' That smile although sweet and touched with sadness, was definitely the young, meat-lipped Julian again.

'Go cover the doorway and love me all night, as if this was our last night together.'

His lips caressed hers again. 'It's not our last night together.'

Reluctantly, she pushed him away from her but still held onto his shoulders 'Don't argue with me, Julian. We all know it will not be the same after tomorrow, but I really don't want to talk about it. I just want our love to be lingering in this world, always. And right now all I need is for you to walk two steps away from me and cover that doorway. And come back to undress me, because I am burning inside.'

It took no time for Julian to cover that entrance to their chamber. And for the rest of the night, for their bodies did not seem to separate, ever.

Pons Diaboli

An icy night kept the people of the Serchio indoors. Fires were carefully tended; all pelts and extra straw were used; bodies huddled closer and more intimately, little else than love, affection, optimism and lust was sparked from that warmth. The sensuous delights were never sinful, but enjoyable. Plenitude caressed their skins with bliss, as if the valley had been protected by angels.

Those who blamed the devils for the explosion of sensuality had misplaced the priorities of hell. On that very last night of construction, the infernal legions were busy, finalising the bridge, allowing for the crossing, tending to the wolves that came down from the mountains, helplessly trying those beasts from the ice storm.

The cold had a heavenly presence in the valley. Clarissa knew it had been coming. She thanked the angels for that long night of eternal delight, and she knew so precisely in her heart that the same angels were now battling hard at protecting the village, protecting their entitlement to Paradise, answering to her prayers and preventing any soul to be condemned under such a meaningless deal. Clarissa was certain that angelic power had sent the icy rain, for those few who wanted to be the first across the bridge stayed tucked into irresistible warmth, protected by cosiness, sleeping past the break of dawn. Had anyone stayed out, they would have been frozen to death, as it happened to some of the wolves on the western bank. Nevertheless, dead members of the pack did not break their demoniac resolve. A cold carcass could only stir their rage, as they ferociously fought to snatch lumps of their own fallen, weakened beasts, which were not resilient enough to survive the icy rain and whose flesh was not sufficiently poisonous to kill their own kind.

Clarissa woke up. Although the day was dark, her body could feel the sun had been out for probably an hour and, much worse, that she was late in waking. And for her desperation, Julian was not at her side any more.

She crossed a vast cluster of bodies that still huddled to steal some warmth from one another and tried the front door. It was stuck; did not move.

'It's frozen from outside.' A warden said, peeking out of a mound of straw.

'But Julian has left!' Clarissa said. 'How could he have gone?'

'Try the back door then,' said the warden, standing up and shaking the straw off his pelts. 'If the icy rain came from the west, the back door must be free.'

Clarissa rushed past the pilgrims and opened the back door. She was met by a crushing gelid blow that snatched any feeling out of her skin. There were fresh footprints on the icy mud. Julian's.

Out into the cold, Clarissa's feet cracked the frosted soil and the glaze of ice that layered over dead leaves. She walked across the thicket of beeches that separated the hospital from the eastern embankment, to enter the road and find a completely frozen river, thick and crusty, but this time, not with a heavy cloud of fog sitting over the scaffolding. This time, a giant silver dragon lazily arched its shiny, slim spine across the icy gap.

The bridge was ready.

The grey slopes of the Apennines dropped sharply and unceremoniously onto the Serchio bank, almost on the same careless manner that the hills of the Rocca and Cerreto delicately squeezed the valley from the western side. Winter haze forbade Clarissa to discern anything further north than the Altar's line or even the Rocca castle itself, but now there was something else that would change the horizon forever. The Bridge of Chifenti. It climbed majestically, perfect, higher than anyone could have pictured: the tall main arch carefully avoiding the thicker stream of the Serchio, now a jumbled mass of thick ice chips, mute and dormant under the frozen morning. Clarissa could see the Traghetto across the river. The houses looked deserted. Frozen stone boxes which were shut, probably from the inside, and the Via Francigena was empty. No birds or sounds of life, no smoke from the chimneys.

A deadly chill ran through her body. She had not heard any wolves during the night, but it would be horrible to imagine that the village had been devastated by them.

Turning her gaze further north, to her side of the bridge, Clarissa saw a group of people on the embankment. She could not yet detect who they were and what they were doing, but surely Julian must have been one of them. She rejoiced with the fact that there seemed to be nobody on the other side. Yes, the whole western bank was deserted. A great scenario for that early morning, with no devil or demon to receive the soul of the first to cross the bridge. *Stupid, superstitious nonsense that drove them all into sheer madness*. She even giggled with her personal mind triumph of reason over fantasy.

Walking quickly over the frozen road, getting closer to the bridge's delicate approach embankment, Clarissa's giggles turned into guffaws of laughter as she was able to devise the pathetic scene: Julian helplessly trying to grab to the low parapet that opened like a lily at the bridge's end, and Maria Maddalena trying to crawl almost with her belly on the ground, but none could move more than an arm's length. Clarissa knew than that her angels had worked well again overnight, by having sent the storm. The bridge was covered with a hard glimmering, splendid layer of ice.

Glazed, slippery as oil, not even a seagull would be able to walk up across it, from either side. And even if anyone or anything could have approached the top of the arch on that day, the person would slide down on the icy slippery slope, so fast and heavy, that a crash would surely be waiting across the stony surface of the Via Francigena.

In addition to Julian and Maria Maddalena, Spatola stood helpless at the approach embankment, with Altobello, lost but curiously watching the pitiable struggle of the pair trying to walk the bridge. The dog came to greet Clarissa with a jolly sprint.

In that moment, she saw the birds appearing from the haze, and the screams that came with them.

Arrigo was late. He had to find that village idiot and hold him accountable for the violence on Ginevra.

Like a shattered gargoyle in a cathedral workshop, Antelmino snored deeply inside a crate with some straw. He had been sedated by potions, and his wound dressed with Maria Maddalena's secret ointments. Arrigo slept next to him by the hearth in the main hall. However, he woke up much later than he wanted. At that time, Spatola would still be out on the run, opening his wide slobbering mouth about that afternoon of Ginevra's abduction. The only way to shut him up was to get him away from others before any more damage was done to Arrigo's reputation. He would not allow the idiot to expose his minor weaknesses to the world outside. Ginevra did not need a witness if she ever dared to accuse him of violence against her.

Scrambling through the table, waking the servants in the kitchen, verifying the main room, looking for his mother, Arrigo realised she was not in the manor. Maria had left much earlier.

But how?

The freezing rain had encased the manor on the rock of Anchiano inside a thick shell of ice. Those were the times when Arrigo would consider the rumours that his mother was indeed a witch.

He used a rope to safely climb down the stairs towards the village around the rock and get a horse. A widely awake stablemaster strongly advised him to change the horseshoes and take another mount in case his own horse faltered and injured itself slipping across the ice. Arrigo was reluctant to accept the suggestion, but the stablemaster insisted that, given the ice that had covered the region, this would be the safest, earliest and most guaranteed fashion to arrive in Chifenti. While impatiently waiting for the farrier to remove the old shoes, trim the hooves, carve around the frogs, and nail some crimped horseshoes onto another of his coursers, Arrigo wondered if the whole delay was being done on purpose. If those people were trying to protect the idiot.

'Are you aware of what I am about to do in Chifenti?' Arrigo asked the farrier.

'No, my lord.' the farrier answered without looking at the Cunimundinghi, as he smoothly hammered another long-headed nail into the courser's hoof. 'I only know you are in a hurry. That is why I am cold shoeing. It's the best compromise between safety and immediacy. We have no time to feed the forge, although hot shoeing would give you a better fit.'

'By the time it's done, the ice will be already melted.' grunted Arrigo. He was going to carry on complaining, but a shuffling noise coming from the hay barn next door distracted his attention. The stablemaster and the farrier were too concentrated on the horses' welfare to notice it.

'My lord, you should make sure the hooves are cleaned from snowballs by the time you get into Chifenti,' the farrier advised, 'for too much ice and mud could accumulate under the sole.' But Arrigo was not paying attention. He was trying to keep standing when all blood drained from his face, as a large bale of straw took flight, carried by a winged creature that surely must have come out of a demon's nightmare.

Wido di Willo was out with bow and arrow. Carrying a long lance and a sheathed sword, he carefully walked down the icy ground and knocked on other doors in Wald Ottavo to collect some of his peasants and thicken his ranks. He wanted a party to clean up the area from the wolves. While few men appeared in that morning with their lances, bows, lit torches and pitchforks, someone screamed with horror in a house across the creek. They quickly crossed the ice and came to a woman who yelled disconnectedly. Wido tried to calm her and she took them to the sheepfold, a small pen where they had sheltered some of the herd from the icy night. The men saw all sheep huddled in a fenced corner outside but noticed that there was movement in the shed. Wido got hold of a torch and prepared to enter, but his legs did not move when he saw what was inside. 'Christ's blood!' he said, trembling, forgetting all about the wolves.

It was rolling the straw into a large bale. Mostly it was a huge serpent, with leathery wings clinging to its back. The creature's head and torso were womanish, covered in wavy brown hair. She groaned with the effort of rolling the largest bale possible. He serpent body, spotted with circular red marks, wriggled and coiled through the straw, fixing itself into a firm base to move the weight around.

'Someone shoot it!' Wido yelled, but nobody seemed to be able to move. The creature rolled the bale towards the door. The men of Wald Ottavo only saw the large wall of dried straw blocking the entrance of the pen, and suddenly the hands of the creature, crushing it into a smaller bale. It popped out with the beast wriggling its serpent tail behind it, making all men squeal with fear. Raising its human torso, it looked around with lively eyes. Its arms embraced the straw bale and the creature stretched its wide brown wings, ready to take flight. But the bale was still too large and heavy. With a powerfukl and noisy beat of powerful wings, it only dragged the bale across the snow, down the slope towards the creek. As it furiously broke the bale in two, an arrow hissed through the cold air and plunged deep into its back, right between the wings.

'Got it!' Wido said, with a fizzle of satisfaction.

The beast was quick to look at him with rage, showing long slashing fangs through its growling grin, but it soon combusted into an odorous flame, losing its shape and melting quickly through the snow, leaving only the herbal smell of coriander hanging around the creek. The men of Wald Ottavo watched the vile scene when new shrieks were heard from the sky. Out of the haze, several hellish creatures flew by, coming down the valley with wrong shapes and fabulous wings, many carrying their straw bales. The screaming was loud, and it was already late when they noticed their lord of Ottavo, blood gushing down his long beard, impaled into a beast's tail. A bipedal winged dragon shook Wido's dead body off its arrow-pointed tail and descended towards the creek, where the serpent woman had been shot. It grabbed the bale easily with its talons, looked around the villagers, licked its own tail, red with Wido's blood, and hissed 'I will be in your nightmares forever', before taking flight with the straw.

Amadeo walked down the road from Chifenti, accompanied by a large crowd from the village. Ginevra followed, for Bernardo insisted in seeing what historical events would unfold at the bridge.

Chifenti had just been raided. Not by bandits, not by wolves. They just did not know exactly what it had been. Amadeo knew that the only thing which had been taken was straw. Dry straw was kept for bedding, for both humans and animals. He had seen the wretched creatures coming out of their barns: griffins and harpies, aberrations of the mind that rolled the straw into bales and carried it out, taking flight down the river. Heading towards the bridge.

The screeching and screaming was unbearable. Unlike the sweet, smooth cries from old Turul, these were slammed down loud and strident, spat out with rage and malice, as the flying creatures approached the bridge carrying their straw. Clarissa held on tight to Julian as they all watched the terrifying flock of winged demons approaching in flight and dropping their straw along the paved road on the bridge, filling a gap between the parapets. As soon as those barbaric creatures saw themselves free from the burden, they either flew back to wherever they had come from, perhaps in search of more straw, or gathered around the western approach embankment, perching gargoyle-like on the parapets of the bridge, folding their leathering wings high above their shoulders and roaring in satisfaction. Facing the embankment, with those gaping mouths lined with needle barbs drooling as they shrieked, they watched a new force take shape and grow amidst them.

'The straw is for us to cross over' Maria Maddalena concluded. She had a light smile on her face. Altobello was trying to hide under her legs.

'I wouldn't be so sure.' Julian said. 'These things have not quieted down yet.'

Spatola tried to climb across the bridge, sprinting over the straw, but it all came back, sliding down with his weight. 'Get out of there, you idiot!' Maria growled. She raised a heavy hand, ready to strike him, when Clarissa interfered, holding her hand before it hit Spatola.

'Leave him!' she ordered.

'Take your filthy hands off me, you shameless leper lover!' Maria hissed. Her hand was heavy as stone and made Clarissa feel dead tired all of a sudden.

'Leave her, Clarissa.' Julian pleaded. 'She is not worthy any of our worries.'

Clarissa released it with guiltless relief, without looking at Maria Maddalena. She feared that if she had looked into the rage-infused eyes of the Cunimundinghi landlady, she would see the last reflection of their beloved Caterina and so many others that had disappeared from their lands. She had to erase from her mind the temptation to grab Maria's neck and squeeze it until her eyes popped out.

'How can you be so bitter, Maria Maddalena?' Clarissa asked. 'What in your life has made of you such a repulsive...' but she never ended the phrase, for they saw the fire coming down the bridge.

It had started in the western embankment, hidden from their eyes. A powerful presence took shape and volume among the harpies. It grew taller and dark, powerful, old and full of rage, with yellow eyes of fire, quickly consuming the straw around it in a hellish blaze. The fire hurriedly spread out across the length of the bridge, crackling up in tall flames, dancing wildly within the parapets and instantly reaching all the way to the eastern embankment.

Amadeo and the people of the Lima were carefully shuffling and taking small steps on the ice, walking south in that frosty morning. When they first saw the finished Bridge of Chifenti, they slipped on the frozen surface and many like the wounded Bernardo fell on their knees. The frozen dragon's spine arched in a blaze, with bright flames that ferociously stretched along its back, hissing and flickering like dorsal plates of embers on an ancient beast, reaching across the river and raising a thick curtain of smoke that divided the valley. While the bridge burned and sweated, the flying demons, excited by the fire, took flight and traced malicious circles above the smoke, screeching louder and disappearing in the darkness where the smoke dissipated into heavy clouds.

Clarissa figured: this time the demons were undoing by day what the angels had so elegantly crafted by night. As the frozen glaze of the bridge thawed under the burning straw, a slow stream of boiling water slid down towards the embankments. Julian, Clarissa, Maria Maddalena, Spatola and now many of the people arriving from Chifenti opened the way to the sides, so the slush of burnt straw, water and small islands of fire could flow through and leave the path clear. Julian re-lit his torch as the strength of the winds increased and the darkness encased them. They could not see or imagine the unnatural shape that had materialised on the western embankment, for the dragon's back was raised between them.

'There *it* is!' shouted the voice of Bernardo delle Rocche. He was approaching from the north, while some pilgrims were coming with wardens from the hospital in the south. Surely that conflagration had been heard even inside the thick walls of the xenodochium. '*It* is standing there on the western bank,' Bernardo yelled, 'waiting for you. *It* is there!'

Julian stepped back. The finished bridge, the deal, the fire, the demons, everything seemed vague and distant compared to the spectre he feared to be beyond the dragon's back. Waiting for him.

'Who is it, Julian?' Clarissa asked.

'It's him!' Maria Maddalena cried triumphantly through the winds.

Julian tried to shush the Cunimundinghi lady, but she was spellbound by the apparition. He held Clarissa's hand and they walked down to see the bridge from the side. On the top of the dragon's back, a gap had opened in the fire. It was slowly widening as the ice melted, bringing the straw down towards the embankments on both sides.

The flying beasts had already vanished, but on the western embankment, they saw the dark shape.

Clarissa's hand was almost crushed by Julian's grasp. Her husband had lost his breath as the shape across the bridge had materialised straight out of his most tormented nightmares. A sight so terrifying that it sent many of the villagers scrambling back to Chifenti in panic and confusion. It was large and invasive as a giant, emitting shadows over the flames and sucking all the light emanated from that fire. It had a muscular body, tall as the height of ten men, stretching out its long limbs and exercising its joints as it seemed to have awakened from an eternity hibernating in hell. Above its short neck, almost nested between strong brawny shoulders, was a large round head, dark as the blackest moon, with a disproportionately small face encrusted on its front. A delicate countenance, with subtle lines, almost feminine, drawing an enticing smile along its small lips, but with unmistakable eyes of dead yellow fire, small windows of hell carved in the middle of that large dark head.

'That's *It*!' Julian managed to babble.

Clarissa looked at Julian and noticed that all colour had gone from his skin. She held onto his hand and pulled closer to her heart. 'Is that the one who you had seen?' she asked, as the shape across the river seemed to look at them and stretch its smile, while raising its fists.

'That's the one,' Julian said, 'and it has never seemed so big before.'

'Come, Julian!'

Clarissa was paralysed, pulling Julian towards her. She had said it, but the creature on the bridge had said it too. Both words had come out of the dark shape, together, concomitantly as she had spoken them. It was no more than a whisper, but clear and loud for them all to hear. A rather feminine tone, smooth and full of perfume. A perfume of herbs. And coriander it was.

Julian disentangled himself from Clarissa's grasp. 'I must go,' he said, with a bitter taste rising to his mouth. 'So sorry, my love, but I must finish with this nonsense.'

Clarissa dropped her jaws for a while she desperately tried to hold on to Julian. His arms were slippery with sweat and once he pulled himself free, she changed directions, turned towards the hospital and started to run.

'Don't even think of it, Clarissa!' the dark creature rumbled, making Clarissa stop. Its voice was now loud and commanding as a thunder above the valley, opening a hungry gap lined with rows of long, curved swordlike teeth in its mouth. 'Or I will chew you alive, just as I did to that weakling Rocco.'

People were starting to scream and run. Bernardo was paralysed, looking at that figure on the bridge, as if something that none of his darkest stories had been able to embrace. Clarissa turned her head back and saw the creature's teeth, sticking out of its dark gap as the *saif* swords that had raided Luna so many years before. While the flames around it weakened, the shape stretched its arms wide as if to embrace the valley with its horrible glory and opened its fists for the first time. Clarissa shuddered on witnessing those talon-like fingers slowly opening wide, particularly one of the claws, long as a praying mantis's, like a massive black blade, ready to snatch back and break its prey in two.

Once it saw that Clarissa had stopped her run, the dark face turned to Julian. *'Come to me! Do your part!'* it roared.

Altobello barked menacingly. Clarissa was paralysed. Julian slowly approached the embankment with his torch lit, but then he noticed that someone else had already started walking along the bridge. It was Maria Maddalena. She had done it quickly, now almost approaching the highest point of the dragon's back.

Julian lost his air. *There's no more time*, he thought.

'No, I can run faster!' Spatola's voice was heard, with clarity.

The Hospitaller shook his head with disgust, too tormented to be able to come up with words. 'No, Spatola!' he managed to yell. 'That is not for you! You do not deserve it. It is *my soul* it wants!'

'Let it take me, Messere Hospitaller.' Spatola begged. His face was more expressive than ever and strangely, his hand bled profusely. He started climbing up the bridge 'I do *not* have a soul anyway,' he shouted to Julian, 'and even if I had, it would not deserve to go anywhere but −'

'Nonsense!' cried Julian, holding on to the idiot's arm. 'You *do* have a soul Carpo. You are not *some beast* as they have always said.'

They both paused and looked at each other, while the wind whistled ferociously through their ears and only Altobello barked with the same power. Maria had disappeared from the top of the bridge. They could just hear the hungry moans of carnality being slobbered from the other side as the dark shape saw Maria approaching.

Altobello barked even louder. Julian caught himself looking at the dog. He felt Spatola's bloodied hand reaching to his own hand that held the torch. They both knew what to do.

Maria Maddalena was very close to finally getting to *reason* with the devil.

Moments before, she had seen the merchant walking along the western bank. A flamboyantly dressed old man, brilliant with colours and silk, exactly as the pilgrims from the xenodochium of Santa Croce had described Seth on that Christmas Eve. Although he was far across the frozen river, she could tell he was looking at her, and smiled with a mutual understanding of that great moment.

As the bridge was being cleared from the ice with the fire ignited by fantastic creatures, the skies became darker and the winds increased their force. She heard Bernardo delle Rocche among the crowd behind, pointing out that *it was there, standing on the western bank.*

'It's him!' she cried triumphantly through the winds.

She felt Julian's grasp on her shoulder, trying to allure her to something else, but it did not matter. Nothing else mattered. She was close, very close to peace.

Julian let her go. With a dreamlike, blurry view of her surroundings, Maria Maddalena watched the Hospitaller pull his wife away from the embankment and point to the other side. *Weaklings.* With a sudden bout of appreciation of her rather selfish, greedy nature, she was filled with a generous sentiment of pity for those weak creatures. They would never be able to have a drop of her courage to cross the bridge.

She took a deep breath, filling her lungs with a strange herbal scent, and started by giving the first step forward to cross the Bridge of Chifenti.

And so did the hairy black wolf Altobello, which was quick to leap ahead of her and stand menacingly in front of his very own Lady of Anchiano, legs wide open apart and barking repeatedly at her, clearly preventing her from going any further.

'Oh my dear Altobello,' she said with a sigh, her eyes filling up with tears. 'It's so sweet how you want to protect me.' She dropped to her knees and embraced the shaggy dog. This was her moment and she could certainly say farewell to a creature that loved her. Altobello rubbed his head tenderly between her neck and her shoulder. The dog felt her cold hands around his head, ruffling his ears in a soft cuddle. He was passing its own warmth to Maria when he jolted with a yelp, scared away by a cavernous shriek that the woman brought from the darkest pit of her soul.

'Get him, Altobello!' she screamed, pointing towards a figure walking up the bridge. 'Get that beast out of the way!' she said with rage. 'Bring him here right now!'

Altobello was quick to obey, running up the bridge and grabbing on to the tunic. The blue-checkered fabric was torn to shreds when the dog tried to stop Spatola from moving further. But the dog knew how to stop the idiot more efficiently. His jaws clenched around Spatola's hand, digging its fangs deep into the flesh. Spatola stopped and looked at it as if the dog hanging from his hand was a passing nonsense. He ignored the pain and tried to continue.

But the dog was stronger than he ever dreamed of.

'Let me go, wolf.' Spatola said calmly. 'It's my punishment to burn in hell. At least allow me the dignity to walk myself into the devil's embrace.' But the dog was already pulling him, slow and firmly towards the embankment. Spatola tried to firm his feet on the wet stone but it was too slippery. The dog was stronger.

Meanwhile, as both dog and idiot were busied in their struggle, beast dragging beast back to the embankment, Maria Maddalena swiftly walked by, starting her quick ascend across the bridge. She hurried her pace, carefully firming her feet over the small rounded stones that had been craftily inserted across the pavement. Even in her trancelike ascend, across the back of the dragon, she couldn't but notice the quality of the workmanship, better than anything she had seen in the best bridges of Lucca or Pisa. Pleased with the devil's work, Maria Maddalena filled her chest with pride and marched over the top of the bridge without even looking back. Seth was on the other side, waiting for her with an open smile drawn across his face, showing a long row of gleaming white teeth. She would feel his warm embrace and gracefully receive the compliments for her courage, she, who was the only one brave enough to have done it. She was ready to be rewarded with a lift on the curse over her son. Arrigo would be free to thrive and rule the lands of the Cunimundinghi for many years to come. And the rewards could be extended over many more riches, uncountable treasures that the devil could offer for their corporeal existence.

Her smile opened up so loosely that a gasp of laughter came out. For the first time, perhaps in many years over a trail of bitterness and hatred, Maria Maddalena was frankly laughing.

Her pace started to pick up and she held her tunic higher above her heels, running freely from the weight of her wet clothes, down the slope straight towards Seth. He had his arms opened, ready for a hug. His smile had increased to a wide gap and the teeth were shining as steel, pointed, sharp as a row of daggers. His arms seemed longer, with massive claws that folded in as a blade in the ends snapping opened to catch her in a few seconds as she would finally complete the first crossing of the Bridge of Chifenti. In a few more paces she would dive into his embrace – if it was not for a swooshing ball of fire that came from the top of the bridge, flying past by her and plunging into the arms of Seth.

Maria stopped frozen, just a few strides from Seth. She watched his eyes grow with rage as two yellow pits of fire melting with the flames, immediately as his immense arms and claws clasped with a spine breaking snap around that burning projectile. Only now she started to appreciate Seth was not the merchant that had a few seconds before appeared in front of her eyes. Now it was a massive, dark shape, glistening with rage, as it picked the flaming form and screeched up to the whole valley, with the power of all the suffering souls in hell. Closing its long talons around that the body that still burned, with a loud crack the demon pulled it apart in two.

The blue light that exploded out of it blinded Maria immediately.

Carpo had spent the whole night awake. Forgotten in the shed behind the hospital, he had crossed his arms and refused to enter and join the pilgrims. Clarissa brought him a few bowls of soup, which he slurped in the blink of an eye, but he preferred to be left alone, spread on the straw and chewing on scrapes of dried pork that she had kindly left on his side.

With open eyes quickly drying with the frost, the hours passed as he tried to remember the moments in the darkness exactly when the bells should have tolled, had any brave and dedicated soul remained in those empty churches, parishes and monasteries following the religious hours that had formerly punctuated the night. He imagined them tolling just for him, every three hours, sharp and clear, heavy and grave, for this very last time. They were still there, he knew, but lazy and inanimate, each of his friends, of different alloys and sizes, coming from a variety of towers across the valley, above and below.

At some point, he felt that the bells were floating above that stretch of the valley outside, looking at him with pity and disappointment. Carpo braced himself not because of the cold, but of the shame for his weakness of the previous day. The freezing rain did little to change his mind, for no matter how the sharp iciness tried to tear his skin apart, that somehow heavenly light outside kept a strange warmth that emanated from his heart. His conscience made every possible effort to cool it down though.

Finally, when counting the drops of ice that still broke from the branches outside, and on hearing the first blackbird weave its elaborate trill across the woods, he knew that in a few hours the sun would be poking its rosy clarity out of the horizon, somewhere still far away, behind the Appeninnes.

He left for the bridge.

Dark and icy, the stone bridge was completely exposed for the first time. With five flawlessly round spans stepping across the river bank, it was a work of perfection. A huge gap reached across the main body of the river, the fourth span, with eighty five cubits of extension. It raised dramatically from the third pillar onto a gigantic arch, with the keystone, the most vital piece that sustained all the weight of the dragon's back, hanging from a height of fifty cubits above the ice. The path rose smoothly from the eastern embankment, catching up with the impressive height at the top of the main arch to abruptly dive down on a steeper descend to the western bank.

Carpo's eyes were well used to the darkness. He scanned the Traghetto and found no sign of life. The bridge stood frozen glazed, mocking him even before he tried to climb its slippery path to find his deserved destiny. Above the valley, the sky was slowly clearing into a lighter purple of clouds, but little sign of the Devil could be seen across the bridge.

He sat down on the short icy wall that held the road above the river bank and waited, watching the silence spread itself over the frozen shield covering the Serchio. Far behind him, blackbirds and thrushes seemed to get more talkative on the woods announcing to the valley that a new day of spring was quickly approaching: the Day of Saint Longinus, which everyone else never wanted to arrive.

His thick-skinned feet were hanging a few inches above the frosty river stones of the bank. After a few minutes of watching over the nothingness, he heard a faint shuffling in front of him. A tiny beetle was leaving a thicket of frozen reeds, investigating every cranny that it would find along its way over the stones. It seemed to be sniffing its path over the bank, quivering with the cold, swift but clumsy over the icy surface. Carpo changed position to look closer, but the creature jumped with a snatch, almost biting his face. He only then realised it was not a beetle, but a minuscule mouse-like creature of not more than an inch. It was probably the legendary *mustiolo* that Bernardo had spoken of. The *mus-aranes*, spider mouse. Carpo scrabbled over the icy surface to keep away from that beast, for he knew that the voracious creature with a poisonous bite could eat a whole man. He kept a respectful distance and observed. The mustiolo raised itself on its hind legs and looked at Spatola. No, it did not look with any type of eyes, for the creature had none. It just sniffed the air with its tiny snout, gyrating its tip with curiosity. Carpo knew it was looking at him and that it could smell the sham from his sweat.

Shame on you, Spatola!

Someone approached. He turned around to see the figure of a tall woman covered in pelts and rugs, steadily approaching through the snow. It was Maria Maddalena. Accompanied by the affable Altobello, she marched over the frozen ground as if to face an army of a thousand enemies. Again, Spatola clutched through the ice to stand up in preparedness before she came across him on her path. Throwing a quick glance to where that mustiolo had been, trying to find if indeed that creature had said something to him, he saw a large amount of crabs walking to the sides, scuttling over the rocks with their eyes standing alert, all looking at him. Did they have despise in their faces too?

'Get out of the way, you monster,' Maria barked as she approached, 'animals are not allowed on the bridge.'

Spatola looked back at the crabs but they were not there. Only the rocks remained as a witness of those visions. He stepped aside for Maria to face the bridge and was quite surprised to see her trying to firm her hand on the frozen parapet and walk up the path. A light of amusement flickered inside his stomach when her foot majestically slipped on the surface and kicked up high above her head, bringing her whole body down in a memorable fall.

'Wipe that filthy grin off your snout, you miserable creature,' was the first thing she could manage to say after pulling herself together.

Spatola filled his lungs and said 'I will cross this bridge before everyone else does it, witch!'

She lunged at him but slipped on the ice, sliding across the road on her back and landing at the root of a beech tree.

When Julian arrived, Spatola was struggling to hang onto the left side parapet and Maria to the right side.

In a few minutes the birds came out of the clouds and Spatola ducked for cover, yelling with horror, as the bridge was covered in straw. On noticing that even the Hospitaller was willing to cross the bridge, Spatola tried to run over the bed of straw, but his weight brought him down on a smooth slide towards the feet of Maria Maddalena.

'Get out of there, you idiot!' Maria growled. Spatola protected himself when she raised a heavy hand, ready to strike him, but he heard Clarissa's voice coming out of nowhere.

'Leave him!'

The strike never came down, as Clarissa was holding Maria's hand. While the Lady of Anchiano cursed at Clarissa, Spatola saw the flames erupting over the bridge. It was the gateway to hell. He was just shaking too much to stand up, and least to enter it.

And for his utmost desperation, the villagers arrived from Chifenti, including Bernardo delle Rocche and Ginevra. It was too much for his humiliation. He could not even look at the shepherd, who sported a large bandage wrapped around his head or Ginevra, who he had beaten so heartlessly in that chestnut shed.

Still on his hands and knees, he quickly turned his gaze down to the ground. Patches of burning straw washed by, sliding from the melting cap of the bridge, bringing water, flames and smoke with it. Spatola could hear the crowd screeching with horror, when a small patch of hay slid by with some bulbs in it. He could not tell if those were old discarded onions or vaguely similar to that, so fast they went past, but he had the clear impression that they were all laughing at him.

You're doomed, Spatola!

The deep, unassailable voice came with a bitter taste from his stomach. He raised his head and saw faces expressing mockery and disgust at him, in every stone and tree that he looked at.

Turning around, he saw Maria Maddalena distracted while she embraced her dog. And a clear path to cross the bridge.

Spatola ran, knowing that this would be for the last time in his life.

Let me crush you for what you've done, Spatola!

He heard the voice calling for him, and never felt when Altobello pulled him by the shirt. It was only when the dog's teeth where dug into his hand when he realised there was going to be one more battle to win through. Altobelo's paws were firmer on the wet stone than Spatola's own feet. While the dog dragged him down with unnatural strength, Spatola could do little than watch Maria running by, climbing towards the top of the bridge.

He gave in and walked back with Altobello.

When Julian came to meet them, Spatola felt himself renewed. They saw Maria almost reaching the top. Spatola insisted in going, begging Julian to deliver his soul into the devil's arms, that is, if he actually had one.

'Nonsense!' cried Julian, holding on to the idiot's arm, while Altobello barked savagely at something on the other side of the bridge. 'You *do* have a soul, Carpo,' Julian continued, 'you are not *some beast* as they have always said.'

In this moment, Julian's voice disappeared behind an echo of *some beast – beast – beast – beast…* Spatola glanced at Altobello, growling at the path raising towards the back of the dragon, and back to Julian. The Hospitaller had a clear look of understanding in his black eyes.

It's cruel, Spatola, we know that we cannot surpass Maria. But it must be done.

Not a word was exchanged between them. Spatola only reached over his hand and grasped Julian's, which held the torch. The fire came down in an arch and flames spread around Altobello like a spark on dry pine needles. The dog yelped with terror as the flames engulfed him. He raced up the bridge like a shooting star. Maria had already disappeared from view. And it was only a couple of seconds after Altobello vanished from the bridge's peak in that early morning of the Feast of Saint Longinus that everyone watching from the eastern bank of the Serchio was blown back by an explosion of blue light when the devil embraced the first one to cross his Bridge of Chifenti.

The Chaos of the Deep

The few witnesses who dared to look drew a fairly exact conclusion of what the winged dark shape could have been. The powerful image would be engraved forever in their minds. Now some of those who were standing on that day by the newly built Bridge of Chifenti would always re-count that the devil was filled with deceit and rage, that it broke the dog in two with its blade claws, throwing both pieces so vigorously against the ground that it opened a hole, so deep and endless that it was a direct passage into hell. And that is where it entered, for no more was seen of that apparition.

Others sustain that the dog disappeared into a blue beam of light that exploded from the collision, shooting its angelic soul into heaven, as it pierced the highest clouds with that divine light. They could swear the dog had been an angel all of the time, defeating the devil in that battle, which found no choice, but to dig a pit and disappear straight to hell.

Bernardo delle Rocche's head still hurt as if a nail was dug into it. Upon arrival at the bridge's site in that early morning, he had cared little for Spatola, as he realised this would be his once-in-a-lifetime chance to see Maria Maddalena embracing the devil. Regardless of the absurdity of her unmistakable initiative to cross the bridge, he did not bother to try to understand. The shepherd had only yearned to see Maria succeed. Yelling with delight, he had moved through the other shocked villagers and pilgrims on the bank, who prayed for the assistance of all saints. He went further to the southern side of the bridge, to better see the Lady of Anchiano meeting her destiny. And he had seen it clearly, beyond any imaginary vision of his wildest stories, he had devised the dark shape rising, eyes glowing with yellow fire, a muscular body powerfully growing in presence and slowly erecting a massive pair of long black-feathered wings above its shoulders. It opened long strong arms with fists closed, slowly opening them with long talons, one particularly much longer, as the forelimbs of a titanic praying mantis. And Bernardo had yearned to watch that claw snapping over the Maria Maddalena's neck. But it was with dismay that he had seen a shooting ball of fire sailing like a comet along the bridge path quickly catching up with Maria. He snatched a fast glance to his side of the embankment and was gutted to realise that it was Spatola and Julian that had set fire to that dog. One saint and one idiot. They had spoiled it all.

Bernardo lost his air when the flaming dog crushed against the dark presence at the end of the bridge, just a couple of seconds before Maria Maddalena would have done it. The shepherd could swear on his most sacred treasure that he clearly saw those long crablike claws snatching over the dog on a spine-breaking snap. That was just when the blue explosion blew them off their feet.

Julian and Spatola saw nothing of it, for their view had been blocked for the very width of the bridge, towering high between the two of them and the western bank. However, both were quick to turn around and look back when a horse approached from the south on a wild gallop over the ice.

Arrigo of the Cunimundinghi was quickly advancing towards them, and the young lord of Anchiano had a dark shadow of murder across his face.

Spatola moaned with pain. He could see that the devil had something worse in store for him. In a few seconds he saw himself cornered between Arrigo's horse, which Julian tried in vain to control, the two parapets and the path running along the bridge. Spatola chose the last one. He ran up as fast as he could.

Arrigo wasted no time with Julian's interference. Ignoring the Hospitaller efforts to detain him, he dug both heels into his mount's flanks and started the ascension to pursue the fleeing idiot. While Carpo advanced swiftly with his bare feet firmly gripping to the paved path, the horse had an initial struggle to steady its strides with the crimped horseshoes. Gaining ground quickly, Arrigo smiled from his height on that magnificent bridge and laughed out loud with the ease of the chase. Rider and horse caught up with Spatola at the highest point.

A big silence descended over the eastern bank, except for the metal scratching and ticking on stone. The villagers watched the terrorised Spatola being encircled by a dexterous horse ridden by the feared young Lord of Anchiano.

'I got you now, you slippery pig!' Arrigo hissed from his horse.

He made to dismount and Spatola was about to squeal when a feeble voice came from the western embankment.

'Arrigo, is that you there?'

'*Mother?*' For the first time Arrigo realised that his mother had been nowhere to be seen when he passed by the hospital and arrived at the bridge. Blinded by his pursuit to Spatola, he had forgotten about her. He could see the strong woman now on her knees, down by the end of the bridge.

With a last glance of rage upon Spatola and spitting on the idiot's face, Arrigo opted to force his horse down to the western embankment.

The horse approached with reluctance. 'Mother, what happened?' Arrigo asked.

Maria Maddalena was scrabbling to stand up. 'I cannot see!' she yelled with impatience. But her voice was cracked, broken, exposing an almost pitiful fragility that he had never witnessed before. 'That light has blinded me!' Feeling her way over the path, she found the parapet and grabbed onto the edge to pull herself up. 'I cannot see, Arrigo,' she said, leaning against the wall, with eyes lost in a vast nothingness that unfolded in front of her. She heard the slow approach of the horse. 'The dog came through before me. Yes, Altobello! He crossed before me. And then that light…it blinded me!'

Arrigo did not hurry the pace. When the horse got too uneasy for his master, he slapped the beast on the face. That only made it neigh with annoyance and walk backwards.

Maria reached over with her arms helplessly through the nothingness. 'Arrigo help me here,' she begged, on hearing that her son was still mounted.

With a grand swing of his leg, he finally got off and let the horse go. 'Fucking, stupid beast!' he cursed. 'We should find better horses, mother.'

He approached her without even meeting her hands, still stretched, only inches from touching his face. 'What happened to you, anyway?' he asked, inspecting her from head to toes and the ground just a couple of steps from them: a gaping hole with a thin column of steam escaping from it.

Maria tried to recover her breath. 'I was to be the first to cross the bridge.'

'*For what*, mother?' he gasped.

She hesitated for a while, with red, swollen eyes moving around, trying to find a solid view to rest upon. 'Arrigo, I just wanted to lift a curse that has been put on you on the day that Béla died.'

'And who the fuck is Béla, in case you don't mind me asking?'

'I've told you that, already a thousand times, Arrigo. Béla was the man who came with my father from the Magyar lands. He was the local midwife that kept a filthy vulture around his shed. He put this curse on you when he took Attila's dagger with him into the river.'

'A foreign midwife? What's so special about that? You don't expect me to memorise all these names of the rabble, do you?'

Maria let the comment go 'He told me I would have to beg the Devil to let you live your life as –'

'He told you *that*?' Arrigo yelled. 'To see *the Devil*? And that is why you came to do this crossing?' He giggled, shaking his shoulders for a few seconds, and while his mother grunted in disbelief, he finally fell into sheer laughter. Maria held onto the parapet firmly and explained to him how her plans had been laid to ruins by the dog, how Altobello had outrun her…

Meanwhile, an uninterested Arrigo approached the hole on the western embankment, which still fumed with a strange herbal, nauseous scent. A stench of corruption, not of something dead, but of something infectious and destructive, a corroding fragrance of wrong. Arrigo said nothing as he walked around the dark, seemingly bottomless gap, wide enough for a grown man to fall through. Raising his tunic, he pulled down his hose and pissed in it.

Spatola watched the Lady of Anchiano yelling at her son as he urinated down a hole on the embankment. But something else stirred his attention on the river just below him. It sounded like a giant donkey braying, trapped under the ice. The warping sound made him look over the parapet. He saw sheets of water running wide, the melted snow covering the crackling thin shell of ice. The fissures extended aimlessly across the surface, quickly zigzagging through the crust, popping and banging as they met thicker layers where the ice went deeper into the river. Spatola saw the whole crust bulging and heard another giant bray. Then the crust exploded, right under the bridge.

Looking down from the parapet, Arrigo saw the ice shell popping up in shreds, as a dense cloud of steam raised itself from the river, exhaling a perfumed, herbal, rancid smell of fresh coriander. The cracks extended further down and up the current, and in a few seconds the whole river was shedding its icy shell onto the steaming current.

'What is happening?' Maria asked when her son slipped away from her grasp. Her eyes were tight shut. 'What is this sound? Where are you, Arrigo?'

'Nothing much,' he said uninterested, taking her arm again. 'It is just the river that is melting.'

'What about this smell?' she asked, uneasy as before.

'Vile, isn't it?' he said.

'It's the Devil!' Maria said, halting. She held onto Arrigo's arm with a painful expression on her tired face. 'I know the Devil is still around! I can smell Him! That dog was just not enough for Him.'

Arrigo grabbed onto her wrist instead. 'Keep walking mother, you are going mad.'

They continued their ascension back to the top of the bridge.

Spatola was still there when they walked by. 'Get away from this bridge, idiot,' Arrigo barked. 'I'll deal with you later.'

'What? *Spatola*?' Maria asked, startled again. 'This rat is still around? Then just take me back to Anchiano and come back to shut him up immediately, Arrigo.'

Spatola was looking at the two, in utter disbelief. Maria Maddalena, blinded, disabled, defeated, but still belching out commands as if a goddess, sitting on the rock of Anchiano with powers to cast lightning bolts at humans. And Arrigo, a treacherous young man, filled with rage in his eyes, more interested in petty revenge against an unfortunate soul than in his wounded mother. Feeling a sudden explosion of compassion and courage, Spatola finally said: 'Carpo.'

Maria tried to open her eyes but only squinted. 'What was *that*?'

'Carpo!' He said firmly. 'My name is Carpo.'

Giggling for the first time since she had been blinded by light, Maria Maddalena said 'You don't even have a soul, idiot. How can you expect to have a name?' She had hardly noticed that Arrigo was not holding her arm anymore.

He was on Carpo. His face sombre and close, and his body pressing Carpo's against the parapet. 'I will cut you down like a pig, so you never raise your voice again.'

Carpo had not been quick to react. When he least expected, he could feel Arrigo's breath of rage steaming over his face as he was crushed against the parapet by the young man's impetus. A strange, deep pain glowed inside him as Arrigo seemed to struggle to bring his arm up. Carpo looked down and saw Arrigo's arm covered in blood. Only then he realised that the lord Cunimundinghi had dug the blade of a dagger inside him. Arrigo grunted as he pressed it deeper, slowly managing to bring it up against Carpo's ribs.

The young Cunimundinghi grinned, seeing Spatola's eyes bloating up to the size of goose eggs. Holding on tight to the hilt, as he did not want to repeat his mother's mistake, Arrigo poked his copy of Attila's dagger deeper, still waiting for Spatola to moan, howl or cry. But the silent idiot did little to push his arm back of try to withdraw the blade from under his ribs. Instead, Spatola put his arms around Arrigo and embraced him, pulling him against his own body with all his strength.

'Let me go!' Arrigo ordered, irritated by the idiot's reaction, but he felt no release, just a slow and steady tightening. 'Let me go!' he repeated now with a pitch of desperation.

'What is happening, Arrigo?' Maria called. She was no more than three steps from him, fumbling helplessly through the air.

Spatola stepped back, lifting Arrigo from the ground, hugging and carrying the lord Cunimundinghi, still with the dagger blade interred into his belly.

'LET ME GO!' Arrigo screamed in sheer terror.

But Spatola only hit the southern parapet with his back, leaning and arching his body backwards, taking Arrigo up with him. The Lord Cunimundinghi shrieked with horror as his legs were raised up while his face got closer to Spatola's. Screaming louder, and joined by the desperate wail of his mother, who could only hear his plight, he saw the smile on the idiot's face before the weight over the parapet was too much for Spatola's feet: they let go from the pavement.

From the hole that the devil had opened, a wet booming echoed faintly.

But on the other side of the bridge, no one was not aware of this sound. They watched Maria Maddalena pleading for her son, while Arrigo yelped helpless under Spatola's embrace. And they all jumped in horror as they saw them fall.

Still clinging like conjoined twins, the two bodies flipped over the parapet and dropped from the bridge's highest point, straight down, accompanied by Arrigo's most frantic screams, disappearing with a gulp as they plunged like a dead boulder into the steaming waters of the Serchio.

While Maria screamed in desperation, Bernardo delle Rocche smiled.

But neither Arrigo nor Spatola surfaced, so the Obertenghi shepherd forced himself to leap ahead and hold Julian, or the Hospitaller would have climbed down the bank and jumped into the river to rescue them.

'Oh stupid man!' Bernardo grunted, while rolling on the ground, struggling to contain Julian. 'They are gone. They are *gone*!' he said.

The Hospitaller still resisted, but the shorter Bernardo gathered unrecognisable forces to contain the stronger man and, with a calmer voice, said 'Leave it Julian. They have left us. But not you, Julian. We need you here with us. We need you here.'

Julian felt the pain of helplessness defeating his forces. He finally gave in. But before Bernardo said anything, their attention was drawn to the bridge, to a perverse force that launched itself out and to the sudden darkening sky closing itself above the valley.

Clarissa heard the scream, suddenly muted out by the plunge. Had it been Arrigo, who she had seen riding past her? Had he been in a hurry to rescue his mother from that crossing? Clarissa had been for less than a minute in the hospital, stepping hurriedly through the frightened pilgrims and now leaving the building. She could not see what had happened, and neither did she recognise the eerie sad wailing that lingered in the air from the distance, making the tiny hairs in the back of her neck stand up. Coming out through the door, Clarissa firmed her grip on the hilt and looked at the blade. The wavy lines across the steel shone back the bluish tinges of the morning, but as the surface of the blade faced her, it mirrored the rainbow sparkles that her eyes emitted. Puzzled by the effect, Clarissa even noticed on the reflection a blur of bright colours above her head coming from behind her shoulders. She lowered the blade and looked back, seeing nothing of colours or tones behind her, except the dull hospital building, covered in a layer of ice, now quickly melting from the hot breath that the Serchio exhaled.

The sword felt light, almost like an extension of her arm. She cut through the air with it, and felt complete, plain and sovereign in power. Somehow she felt that her grasp would never let it go.

In another second, her legs softened when she heard a dreadful drone coming from the bridge. Everyone had started screaming, and something much worse too, screaming with them.

Courage, Clarissa, a milky voice echoed inside her. She clenched her jaws and started running. She knew that there was nothing - no matter what could happen - nothing that would stop her Julian from self-sacrifice.

The ground boomed, bloated out and farted, defecating a demon on the same instant that Arrigo disappeared with Spatola in the Serchio waters. On the first moment there had been a face: amphibian, mucous, dark and wide, curiously sniffing the air outside the hole as Arrigo was still screaming on the bridge. But on the next second, when the bodies hit the water, the slick, thick body of a gigantic eel protruded from the hole on the western embankment, sliding out on a rush, a massive explosion of infinite muscle and slime, slithering up the bridge. The monster's length bulged as it poked out of hole, endlessly long and fatty, headed by a blackened face, grim with tiny black eyes of ancient blindness and a wide gaping mouth adorned with long wet whiskers and barbels, whips of flesh licking the parapets as it rushed up the bridge. It viciously stretched along the path, heading towards the highest arch, where the Lady of Anchiano fumbled through the quickly darkening air.

Desperate in her clear sense of loneliness, conscious that Arrigo had just disappeared from her side, the wailing Maria Maddalena felt the stones of the bridge suddenly heating under her knees. Her ears captured the sensation of a foul large mass of slime skidding along the stones, and behind her neck, a reeking breath of offense neared in a frantic speed.

Maria turned around and, although not being able to see, she gaped straight into eel's maw, spread wide open ahead of her. She never got a glimpse of the long jagged teeth, sticking out like *saif* sword blades. Nor the uncountable critters that scurried around the gums, large flea-like creatures, hairy and wet, some with human features. Many of these parasites were floating on the boiling saliva, which oozed out of the eel's fat lips. They dropped on the pavement like dead pigeons and scampered to all directions. Maria never bothered about the imps that grabbed onto her tunic and started climbing up, for her senses were focused on the lament that insinuated itself from the eel's innards. And the sound exploded out from the eel's maw, a burp containing voices of hordes crying for mercy, a scream of millions of damned souls in pain.

The power of that screeching blew Maria back, tumbling halfway over the bridge towards the embankment. Blisters popped with boiling sera on her' frying skin, and she felt her own bones shrinking with the torment, the pain, the violence and the rage in that diseased breath. She could not even scream, declare repentance or beg for mercy, but she could tell that was a gateway into hell.

Still on the ground, Julian felt the wrong filling up the air. He was yanked up by Bernardo, who pointed speechless to the top of the bridge. A large black shape hovered behind Maria Maddalena. They could not recognise any features until a jagged aperture opened wide. Then they realised the shape was only the head.

'What is *that*?' Bernardo shouted, as the winds accelerated, bringing in more darkness into the valley. 'Is that a giant boar?'

But before Julian even tried to answer, they heard the deafening drone.

All the voices from hell cried in pain at once, blowing them both backwards like a massive wave had exploded on their faces. Bernardo was washed back with leaves and dirt against the roots of some large beech trees beyond the road. Julian managed to hang on, not too far away. 'Oh Christ, Almighty, crucified on the Holy Cross!' Bernardo shouted, through the howling winds, 'Please save that woman from this!'

The eel lifted its head, detaching itself with a wet smack from the stone pavement. The movement brought the tips of its barbels and whiskers forward, maliciously licking their thin tracks of slime over the stones. High it raised its head, like a furious cobra. A towering giant, looking with its tiny black eyes at Maria, far down the pavement, or Julian, much further away. It opened its mouth slowly and retched when the voices howled out again, thrashing and convulsing, jolting its whole body in a wave of regurgitation, from the body still inserted in the hole, towards its gaping ragged mouth. But this time those lips opened even wider, and the eel spasmed, vomiting a solid cascade of limbs, bodies and heads, pouring out of its mouth like a stinking flood from a broken cloaca.

The dead.

The avalanche of limp cadavers was spewed in slimy gushes, piling up on top of each other on the bridge's road. So voluminous was the column of human vomit that the dropping bodies filled the space between the parapets, slowly oozing along the road, a moving human lake rolling down the slope towards Maria Maddalena.

Trying to find her own self through the pain that torn her body apart, Maria could not grasp what exactly had fallen upon her when she was swamped by the repugnant tide of corpses, sliding around, rolling on top of her. She was smothered by their weight. Flaccid, cold, wet cadavers, loosely bringing their heavy limbs with a fetid scent of death over her face. She dug herself out and gasped for air. Finally, she screamed.

And with her, all the bodies jolted and screamed together.

Old heads of suffering and torture rose from the sea of corpses, as if the dead mass was boiling with life again. Sick, suffering faces, fearful and screaming from lungs filled with fluid. Maria tried to stand above the slippery knot around her, but cold hands held onto her.

On the bank, Julian was standing and started walking towards the bridge.

'Maria! Someone must help her,' he said to himself.

'NO!' Bernardo roared and leaped again to contain the Hospitaller.

The heads of the dead still screamed with horror, thousands of them. They were all looking back towards the gigantic fish, which slowly lowered its grim head, resting it on the tip of that pile of corpses. The jaws opened again, retching, cavernous and wide, but this time with a different howl pulsing from its entrails. And when it came, it started with more cadavers hurled out. But the cascade of death was soon replaced by more convulsions and a fiery explosion.

Julian had Bernardo delle Rocche grabbing him by his sleeves, holding him back. But when he saw those furious flames, his legs failed and he collapsed onto his knees. Bernardo watched the catharsis in terror and no words could be put together in his mouth. He saw those bodies desperately trying to move. A mass of condemned souls, rolling over to the parapets and diving into the river in hope to escape forever from the asylums of hell. Those who had been slobbered further down to the embankments were able to stand up and engage into a frantic run. All that Bernardo could do was to hide himself behind the paralysed Julian, as dozens of dead bodies with faces plagued by terror ran by, some slipping and falling onto their own slime, but most trying to disappear into the woods.

For Hell was coming for them.

ne cumaþ þa næfre of þæra wyrma seaðe
ond of þæs dracan ceolan þe is Satan nemned.
Þær æt his ceolan is þæt fyr gebet,
þæt eall helle mægen on his wylme
for þæs fyres hæto forweorðeð

'*[they] never come out of the pit of snakes, and of the throat of the dragon which is called Satan. There in his throat is the fire attended to, so that the entire host is destroyed in his burning because of the fire's heat*' Vercelli Homilies, 4.46-8

Hi þær in farað
unware weorude, oþþæt se wida ceafl
gefylled bið; þonne færinga
ymbe þa herehuþe hlemmeð togædre
grimme goman. Swa biþ gumena gehwam,
se þe oftost his unwærlice
on þas lænan tid lif bisceawað,
læteð hine beswican þurh swetne stenc,
leasne willan, þæt he biþ leahtrum fah
wið wuldorcyning. Him se awyrgda ongean
æfter hinsiþe helle ontyneð,
þam þe leaslice lices wynne
ofer ferhtgereaht fremedon on unræd.
þonne se fæcna in þam fæstenne
gebroht hafað, bealwes cræftig,
æt þam edwylme þa þe him on cleofiað,
gyltum gehrodene, ond ær georne his
in hira lifdagum larum hyrdon,
þonne he þa grimman goman bihlemmeð
æfter feorhcwale fæste togædre,
helle hlinduru; nagon hwyrft ne swice,
utsiþ æfre, þa þær in cumað,
þon ma þe þa fiscas faraðlacende
of þæs hwæles fenge hweorfan motan

They enter in there, an unwary troop, until the wide jaw is filled; then suddenly, around the prey the savage jaws crash together. So it is with any man- who most often regards his life heedlessly in this transitory time, allows himself to be deceived by the sweet smell, a false desire, so that he is stained with sinsagainst the king of glory. Towards them the accursed one opens hell after their departure from here, those who have falsely and ill-advisedly advanced the pleasures of the body over the rights of the spirit. When the traitor, crafty in his treachery, has brought into that prison, into that whirlpool of fire, those who ling to him, covered with sins, who previously eagerly obeyed his teachings in the days of their life, then he crashes together securely those grim jaws after the death of the living, the barred doors of hell. There is no right to a way out or an escape or a

Behind the flames, from the deep cavern in the eel's throat, the clashing of metal and phantasmagorical chants were heard for a moment. Then, as the monster knotted and unknotted its viscous black length along the bridge, vicious and deformed, a new column of bodies erupted out of the ragged mouth, from within the flames, this time as if hell was regurgitating its own spiny faecal mass. This long roll of crusty figures soon opened itself into an expanding swarm of beasts. A wide front of spiny monstrous arms, claws, talons, carapaced limbs, horns and rusty blades thrashing against one another, where glimpses of red gaping throats, glaring saw toothed grins or ravenous fangs were quickly flashed through the swelling darkness. A gloating horde of demons, every unimaginable monstrosity unleashed from the depths of hell, howling with malice and rage, armed with hooks and ropes, spears and poles, cascading from the sides of the bridge and running down the path, biting, clawing, strangling, impaling all corpses they could reach, and dragging them back to Hellmouth for another eternity of enslavement and pain.

Maria's face disappeared under the trampling crowd of the dead trying to flee from the swarm. Cries of horror and howls of pain filled whichever space was still vacant from the demons' raw debauchery, occupying those blackened skies with the brutality of their grunts and squeals.

The embodiment of beasts took all unnatural shapes and obscene sizes. From a vast number of tiny violent creatures to unforgiving monstrosities the size of elephants. They screeched in triumph while mercilessly hooking and skewering the fleeing dead, still as the Hellmouth vomited more hordes of demons. There were blackened strong shapes with yellow eyes of fire, long serpents with many rows of fangs and basilisks with thin wings and massive hooked bills, helping them prey more efficiently on the dead. The frantic souls were being caught on the roads running away from the bridge, hunted in the woods and speared out of the Serchio current. Enormous griffins were collecting the fleeing dead and crushing their ribs as if they were wicker dolls picked up from the floor. There were venomous foxes and hairless red apes, long-legged ravens, armies of cuckoos and a few lewd, vicious baboons. They were unnatural, nightmarish creatures, all distorted with hatred, with deep fiery eyes, aroused with the pleasure to inflict pain. Rats and badgers bit their ways into bodies cavities, entering them with fury, to the victims utmost revulsion and agony. Blood was black, old with death, but always running thin in the veins of the condemned souls, to guarantee an eternity of pain and rebirth into agony.

When bodies were broken, crushed, torn apart by the ravenous creatures, there was no merciful death to take the dead away to a better place. Those miserable souls were still alive in death, eternally suffering from the most painful formats of torture. That swarm of hungry demons made their purge from Hellmouth a fruitless exercise. The dead were all being seized, one by one, to suffer as they had been forever before, forever after, in hell.

The catharsis was well extended into the river. Water boiled, while strange shapes appeared on the surface, slithering around the floating dead, occasionally snatching a head with a quick splash of silvery long fangs. Other corpses howled out in anguish, begging to be taken out. Several demons held on to the bridge's pillars and hooked the dead with poles and long nails. The blunt, rusty blades entered through their skins. They were lifted and sewn to each other through a long rope passing from their back through their stomachs. In an instant, there were heavy ropes of screaming, piled cadavers hanging from the bridge, while hosts of smaller imps climbed over them and twisted their features around the ropes into demented positions.

Islands of bodies were formed, down the slow current, tortured corpses that mounted on top of each other, gasping for breath, but brutally beaten by dark flying devils, to sink into the river, agonising and helpless. And there were demons observing from the banks and on the bridge, with putrid greenish muscles showing through the skin, holding long poles and maintaining the condemned souls submerged in the water that boiled with suffering, being minced by submerged beasts. Those who managed to climb out were pushed back from the bridge, head down screaming in terror, crashing on top of others, or impaled by the demons' lances. And there were large black beasts that scrambled out of the water, keeping their balance and screeching with desperation, trying to firm their hooves and paws on the floating bodies, a horse, a bull, a hydra, a bear, and a chimera, with their decaying heads biting the foul air, all black with death, pushing the live corpses deeper into the river. Some of the demons were defecating more souls onto the sea of bodies, as if on the moment one damned soul died in torment, it would be immediately re-born for a new eternity of torture.

Julian and Bernardo watched those hordes of bestiality out, collecting the dead purges of Hellmouth, but both wondered what would stop those demons from dragging a new victim into their fiery realm, except for the fact that not a single condemned soul seemed to be able to escape. Ginevra and the villagers of Chifenti had mostly fled from the first conflagration, running back to the village much before the eel slithered along the bridge. Julian was trying to make its way through that explosion of cold cadavers in sheer panic and the hellish hosts hunting them. His eyes were fixed on the area near the embankment where Maria Maddalena had disappeared, smothered by the stampede. Using Julian as a shield, Bernardo gripped hard onto the Hospitaller, holding him back from approaching the chaos.

As the dark air was thickened by blood-chilling cries of corpses assailed by a crusted mass of demons, it wasn't bravery that kept Bernardo's eyes opened or his hands from covering his face. Although terrified, the shepherd was as stirred by curiosity as he had ever been. He could feel the heat of the flames blowing from that fish's gaping maw, so far away up on the bridge. Its plague-ridden herbal scent made him nauseous and the feeling of anguish and the loss of any will to live told him of an unimaginable source of evil. He could feel the sickening swoosh of flying demons hover above. His skin was grated by the ravenous stares of dark, fleeting shapes, perhaps goats or cats, furious beasts dragging corpses next to him. Restraining the thrashing cadavers, with firm claws, they would stop by Bernardo and slobber on his ears, touching him with malice, while their talons tightened around the corpses' throats. The shepherd could feel the eternal suffering from those touches, causing more anguish than pain, while the beasts whispered threats in his ear:

'Soon, you'll be with us!'

What kept sanity inside his terrorised heart was the hope that he could tell his story one day, the utmost wish of a cantastorie – being to hell and back. He wanted to memorise every moment of that morning of the day of Saint Longinus, when the Devil waited across the Bridge of Chifenti, releasing Behemoth, the true Leviathan. Not an inert sea monster that rotted away on a desert beach, but a monstrous creature which spewed the legions of condemned souls from hell into this world.

And coming after, hunting the dead, Bernardo saw all demons and beasts and princes of hell that he had surreptitiously learned from the forbidden books, selected readings that novices and oblates loved to pilfer in the libraries of San Michele and Saint-Michel. The most abominable creatures trotted down the bridge into the eastern bank of the Serchio, skewering the dead with their picks and arrows, strangling and dragging them with hooks and ropes, burning them with torches, and clawing them from the air.

He would tell one day that he saw the raven-headed Baal-Hamon, the owl-faced Andras riding a black wolf, the greedy Mammon, wearing the papal regalia in an obscene manner, and impaling more bodies than he could in his bishop's staff. And that the dead roared in horror when Baal Pegor raped them sequentially with his incandescent priapus. And the two horses that came out of the flames from the Hellmouth, one ghostly white and the other dripping blood red, ridden by Beleth and Berith, reaping with their swords, as the ghastly rolling heads kept screaming in pain. Bernardo wanted to be able to one day describe the scales and gills of Obizuth, a round female demon who skidded on the slime from the dead, so obese and lethargic that it could hardly move much to catch any soul. But to compensate her stupor, the tall Abaddon raised himself with violent flaps of his long wings, permanently showing a wide skeleton grin as he laughed in shrieks, precisely clawing the escaped by their heads, even though he looked at nowhere with the empty hollows of his eye-sockets. And so many humanoid pigs, squirrels and rats, snipes, woodpeckers, ducks and herons, in mini battalions, all dressed as warriors, in iron helmets and rusty armour, scuttling about, giggling as they jumped on the back of fugitive souls, biting fingers and ears off, opening gashes that oozed with black dead blood on their grey skin. And he wanted to survive, to swear one day that he did see among the demons, emerging from the Hellmouth and sitting on a two headed dragon, Satan himself, fat and bald, with a bushy beard and wearing the bloody rags of the crucified Christ, with serpents coming out of his ears, all gulping down condemned mortal souls that screamed with terror as smaller demons pushed them towards the devourer.

'Bernardo delle Rocche' a voice whispered next to him. Bernardo realised that he was not holding onto Julian. The Hospitaller had disappeared through the darkness and instead the shepherd was holding onto a dark demon. The tall beast was grabbing both of his hands. It had a black, fiery hair, not alight, but flickering shadows of black flames. Bernardo could only tell he was looking at him because of the demon's yellow eyes of burning embers. 'Ginevra has already been taken.' It said, with a voice full of plague. 'She is being sodomised by Lucifer Himself. And she is enjoying it, that harlot. You'll be able to be there in time to watch her howling while we slaughter her!'

The shepherd shut his ears as firmly as he could and threw himself on the ground, unable to react, with a voiceless, frozen howl on his face, the terrified screams coming straight from his heart.

Darkness was so ferocious that no more than a pearly lustre could be seen of the bridge's stones. Only the burning mouth, gaping wide on top of the bridge, illumed the valley, like a massive cave entrance curtained by flames. Along the bridge, the sheen of slimy corpses reflected the burning eyes of demons around them. Creatures that stole all light from around them.

Julian was getting closer to the bridge, but every step that he gave put him deeper inside a battle scene.

But no! Not a battle. This was a hunting scene. It was a slaughter.

Julian walked slow, but firmly, while grey bodies of the already dead were dragged by creatures he preferred not to look at. A large four-armed woman with a very dark blue skin ran by in front of him, carrying a cleaver and viciously hacking any of the dead that she could find, even those brought in by other demons. She carried their screaming heads in a garland around her neck. When she saw Julian, she released a lolling tongue and looked at him with fiery eyes of hatred. Behind his shoulders, malicious voices licked on his half ear and bawled that he would die for his sins.

Julian tried to ignore those threats, carefully extending his foot ahead for another risky step. Other demons that he encountered ahead were lion-headed, black as the night, carrying straight daggers with which they tortured the dead, skinning them in death; or ghostly white figures, with eagles' talons and jackal heads, pushing the dead over the bridge's parapets to watch them crush their heads on the stony banks. There were winged dogs and a gritty dwarf with a ring-like protuberance on his head and four wings spread out behind his back. It hissed at Julian and leaped, flying straight towards his face.

Julian ducked and pushed the heavy dwarf over his head. The beast crushed against the ground with a yelp. This attracted the attention of more demons, which initially had been oblivious to the Hospitaller. Now they were quick to surround him.

Julian found himself with a large warrior standing in front of his way. Covered from face to feet with plates of rusty iron, the creature wore a metal mask shaped like a *mastino* dog head. On the warrior's stomach, Julian noticed a door and latch, shut around an area which looked an incandescent furnace. Faint howls of agony came through that metal door. The beast looked down at Julian from its height with eyes of fury. It spoke to him, and the iron masked moved as if made of skin. The mastiff lips raised themselves to reveal shiny steel fangs. The words were paused, as if voicing the wish of someone else.

'*To the land of no return. To the afar off. To the regions of corruption.*'

'Move, go back to your hole!' Julian ordered.

But the monster did not move. Its face kept uttering those words. *I force the gate, the bold I shatter, I strike the threshold, I raise the dead, devourers of the living…*'

Julian made to push him away, but on the instant the Hospitaller's fingers touched the demon's metal arm, Julian felt the worst wrong ever to abate upon him. The misery of that touch brought the screams not only of whatever was being incinerated in that stomach. It revived all the screams of those people that had been killed by Julian's blades and arrows, in battle, in rage or in accident. They cried inside his head, and Julian recognised each one, especially the pleadings of his parents, Raoul and Emma.

A wave of pain rapidly expanded all over his skin. He felt desiccated by the revival of that violence, and his muscles seemed to dry and stretch thinner. And that sudden incapacity of his to gain forgiveness from voices that he was sure they would forever haunt him made him drop his shoulders and chin. He was prepared to beg to die.

But somehow the touch exerted something on the monster, an exhaustion of evil, fatigue from torment, for it too weakened and moved aside.

Julian was slow to realise the way was opened. And something caught his attention amidst the glistening shapes of countless corpses that were being herded back to the flaming Hellmouth: the desperate figure of a blind woman, frantically trying to figure where she was being led to.

'Maria Maddalena!' Julian cried.

Instinctively she turned her head towards him and implored for help. But Julian received little of her attention, for a much louder wail rose from outside of the bridge. Louder and thicker than all the drone of devils and the throng of corpses being massacred through an endless death, it was a fresh cry, young, howling out with the catastrophic realisation that this torture would be destiny, that pain would be eternal. Maria Leaped over the corpses and demons, trying to fight her way towards the top of the bridge, where the flames came from. Where that wail of her son, Arrigo of the Cunimundinghi, was coming from.

'He's alive!' Maria yelled, exultant.

Naked, wet, not as dull grey as the corpses that continued to be slaughtered, but purple and swollen as a fresh wound, Arrigo's body was being hoisted from the water, not too far from the spot where he had fallen with Carpo. His skin was stretched like a cow's hide, suspended and pulled from all sides by hooks and nails attached to chains and ropes, held by several demons on the parapets of the bridge. They pulled and chanted, screeching and arguing, hissing their forked tongues, while Arrigo's face was distorted by that torture, and he howled even louder in excruciating pain.

'Arrigo, my son, come to me' Maria shouted, trying not to think what kind of torment would snatch those bellows out of her son's lungs.

Julian grabbed a hold of her arm and contained her as they passed through the cold, slippery mob that was quickly herded back into the burning Hellmouth. He saw a number of deformed creatures bringing Arrigo over to the parapet, the crusty lengths of their fingers wrapped around his face.

'There he is!' Julian said. 'I'll go and get him.' But he noticed something on Arrigo's deformed face that made him hesitate. It was swollen purple, turning grey, with a big black gaping mouth and deep, cloudy eyes, lost in shadows, devoid of life. It was easy to figure that Arrigo was not of his world any more. He was one of the dead.

'MOTHER!' Arrigo roared again, disengaging himself from the hooks and shackles, ripping his back, tearing his skin apart. Flaps of skin turned inside out as a sleeve around his hands. The little blood that ran from the gashes was thin and black. He started to run down the bridge against the dark hordes returning to the Hellmouth. But this time the zealous demons that had fished him out of the river seemed to allow him to escape. They jeered and cheered virulently, as the naked, bloated body made its way towards his mother.

With a dull splatter, like the fat stomach of a cow being dropped to the ground, mother and son met in a bouncing embrace, where she never had a chance to look at his face.

'Get me away from here, mother. *They*'re hurting me!' he whined.

'Oh Arrigo, you're so freezing cold, let's go home,' Maria grunted. 'Where's your horse?'

Julian had little to say in that sad spectacle. He wanted to hold on to Maria's shoulders and shake her out of that illusion, to find a gentle way to break it to her. But those considerations vanished and his own body was washed gelid by a flush of chilled blood when a wall of darkness, a shadow larger than thirteen demons, blacker than the deepest pit, rose gigantic behind them, hindering the monster eel's fiery mouth from view.

With a heavy leonine head and a furious mane, it looked down at Julian with dead yellow flames in his eyes. A gaze of despise and a pestilent breath steaming out of its nostrils drove the Hospitaller sick with horror.

That was his worst enemy, always. Fear impersonated.

A pair of enormous black sharp talons clasped around Arrigo's chest with a quick snap, ripping Maria's clothes with violence when they closed. Arrigo tried to scream for help, but his voice was squeezed, reduced to a faint wheeze.

'Help me mother… It is taking me to their gates…'

The claws snatched Arrigo away as the towering shadow turned around and calmly walked towards the Hellmouth, joining the last remnants of demons returning to the gates. Julian saw the massive black wings folded, raising high above its shoulders and the long hairy tail. Each of those beast's steps, with its colossal eagle-like talons in place of feet, was equivalent to many paces of a normal sized man. And he saw Maria Maddalena being dragged together like a ragdoll, as her wrist was clutched in Arrigo's dead grasp too.

She'd be burned alive through those fiery jaws.

The Hospitaller ran up towards the Hellmouth to help the entrapped woman. It was easier to gain ground with the flow of a now much thinner throng of demons. Catching up with the winged shadow before it reached the flames, Julian leaped around to stand in front of it, feeling the burning heat of the eel's jaws on his back. He shot a quick glance over his shoulder and his eye was slashed by the roaring incandescence. The cavernous mouth was lined with several rows of long sharp teeth, standing blades that the demons leaped over but pushed their prey through.

With a quick slap of its talons, the beast brushed Julian aside. He was thrown violently against a light-skinned creature that was on its way to the Hellmouth. It had a strong, human body, but the head of what appeared to be a goat, with no eyes, and a long dolphin-like snout. Infuriated by the shock, the dolphin-goat creature, which was dragging two bodies by their feet, raised its rusty metal spear and hurled it at Julian's neck. The Hospitaller was quick to grab the spear in time and yank it out of the creature's hand with the hurl. He wasted no time and turned back with the spear towards the big black beast at the eel's mouth.

The monster had raised Arrigo above Hell's jaws, pulling Maria together with it, hanging dangerously close to the flames, Mother and son were still yelling at one another, imploring not to be left alone.

'Leave her be, Arrigo!' Julian shouted grabbing onto Arrigo's wrist, not surprised at himself for talking to a ghost, but trying desperately to move the cold, dead fingers that clutched Maria's wrist like an iron shackle. The beast noticed the intervention and reached over with its other hand. Julian moaned in pain when those talons snatched at his chest. He released Arrigo's wrist on the moment he felt his own ribcage breaking under the claws' embrace. Two of the talons had dug their sharp points deep under his ribs and he felt the warmth of his own blood embracing him as his vests got drenched.

The beast's eyes narrowed as it examined Julian. It seemed to grin. Not a smile of friendliness or irony, but a barring of teeth, as black as they could be, lining those leonine jaws that clasped like soulbreakers as it spoke. 'Do you think you scare me with your fearless stance? You are nothing, defenceless. I will pull you apart in the underground,' it roared gravely. 'Your parents will be there to watch your suffering.'

'You cannot kill me' Julian shouted at it. 'There is no more deal. Move away to your hole and do not come back. And take your infernal hosts with you.'

Julian felt a freezing breath of cold, stale air coming from the beast's nostrils. 'I would even laugh if I wasn't so eager to cause you slow pain and let you see the suffering of those who you love. I can kill you as I will, at my will. The gateways are opened and I came to take you by force. I will watch you die as you burn in hopelessness, growing you hatred towards your omni-impotent God.' It squeezed Julian further, and more than ribs seemed to snap with an explosion of pain.

When black stains of nothingness expanded in front of his vision as the pain irradiated in deadly bouts from his chest, Julian had completely forgotten about Maria Maddalena. The crushing pain made it difficult to breathe, impossible to think. He dropped his head to the side, ready to close his eyes and sleep. He could not bear it anymore. He was letting it go.

'No, you don't even exist.' he murmured, rather quietly, just to himself and his eyelids slowly started to close down.

This time the creature inhaled deeply, before releasing an earth-shaking snort that seemed to be its own version of a laugh. 'In this world, I *do!*' it said. 'In fact, I am the Prince of This World' it thundered. 'I am Perfection before the touch of God.'

Its other hand dropped Arrigo and Maria like two sacs on the floor, having lost the interest on that mother and son. Now its free talons were slowly closing around Julian's head, ready to pluck it out like a dove.

'I am Chaos!' it finally said with triumph.

The Arrow of Marduk

Julian waited for the final embrace of those black fingers. His thoughts were suddenly rested, staled into a patch of warm rainbow lights, a comfortable place where he only saw Clarissa smiling at him. He was thinking of nothing else, and he knew there would be no pain when his skull would be certainly closed into total darkness and slowly crushed. It just took a while for him to realise that the quaking shriek uttered by the beast was not a howl of elation.

He saw very little of the blade cutting through the beast. The giant demon dropped him in a panicked struggle to fight back, but it was too late. With a crushing explosion of pain on his chest, Julian fell on the top of the slippery eel's bloated flesh and slid to its side, almost bouncing on the parapet and dropping to the water. However, his hand was able to find a space on the stone wall to grip onto, so he reclined on the parapet and tried to understand what battle had broken ahead of the Hellmouth.

The dark clouds over the bridge even parted away in a circle to the eruption of screams uttered by the beast. Behind the black, shattered wings that grew from the demon's shoulders, Julian could only see a struggle of the massive limbs and tail, huge serpents of blackness that desperately fought against a source of light that emanated from the other side. There were glimpses of feathers, coloured flashes of blue, scarlet and gold, but mainly a polished surface of brilliant white, malleable and moving faster than the eye could see. That milky embodiment branded a shiny blue blade, tirelessly swinging in wide arcs, reflecting more light around the beast and mercilessly striking through its weakening darkness.

As the battle unfolded a few paces from Julian's face, the slimy monster eel on his side wriggled and spasmed uneasy. Its massive body began to turn around and coil in a long spiral, as if sick and ready to vomit or defecate. Exhaling a stronger herbal stench, the giant volume of the fish expanded and pushed against Julian several times, but the Hospitaller firmly held onto the parapet. On the struggle ahead, the dark winged demon kept shrieking and helplessly trying to defend itself from its attacker, but with a speedy loss of its giantness, it was quick to abandon the fight. With a swift turn, it leapt into the Hellmouth, disappearing from view behind the flames in the toothed tunnel.

The darkness left by its presence a second before, so thick and powerful, still hung around in front of the eel's face for a brief instant. Julian could see no sign of Maria, but the eel was even more uneasy, now wheezing deeply, convulsing as if ready to vomit again. And the demon's shadow had not dissipated completely when Julian finally saw Clarissa crossing through it.

With a determined gait, left fist ahead in readiness to strike, and right hand holding Julian's sword of Damascene steel, a long mirror of bright blue above her head, she took no time to swing it in a wide arc and –

'No Clarissa!' Julian screamed.

-- she brought the sword down with all strength and power that steel had ever tasted, sliding the long blade through the head of Hellmouth.

Bernardo delle Rocche saw it all.

Curled into a foetal position, with his face pressed against the cold ground, he endured the screams of the hunt, the smell of dead blood, the grating of metal and the breaking of bones. He could sense in all of his pores, the pain, the slaughter and torture of the condemned souls unfolding around him. And permeated among so many howls and voices of the dead, tireless insisting for mercy, but slowly making their way to a distant point, perhaps to the top of the bridge, Maria's live screams stood out quite chilling and he finally dared to open his eyes again.

The scenery was no less devastating. Many of the demons were now returning to the bridge carrying their prey in pieces, or impaled in their spears, or dragging them by chains or pulling them by their own guts. Grey cadavers of dead matter, who had a glimpse of freedom from pain, running away from repeated death. Useless hope, for they were suffering new tortures, realising that they were being dragged back to hell to continue their eternal ordeal.

Bernardo heard a strange sound of violence next to him. He turned his face to see a desperate cadaver being sodomised by what looked like a flea, as massive as a horse. The poor soul, which Bernardo could not exactly tell if it had been a man or a woman, screamed mutely and looked at nothing. It had no tongue or eyes, for the giant flea mounted on its back was also eating those, while ravenously pumping a misshapen feature into the corpse.

'Stop it!' Bernardo grunted, disgusted as he had never been before. The necrophagic beast noticed him and quickly turned its head to Bernardo, dropping the remaining eye that it was about to eat. But its body continued the movement.

'STOP IT!' The shepherd repeated.

It certainly worked, for the beast stood up and violently yanked the corpse away from its body and tossed it like an empty skin behind its boneless shoulder. But in a second, those hairy claws were clasping on the sides of Bernardo's face and the multi-faceted eyes looked at him with a despised expression of hunger.

Bernardo could feel the skin of his cheeks tearing apart as the beast pulled his head towards its mouth. Its jaws snapped like an iron clasp, ready to bite through Bernardo's head like a melon.

The blue silvery light that flashed above the shepherd's face for a blink of an eye cut the top of the flea's head. While it popped opened like an empty gourd, the claws eased on Bernardo's cheeks. The monster collapsed and Bernardo fell on top of its dead articulated body, which immediately dissolved into of a myriad of mite-looking critters. Thousands of multi-legged devilish miniatures, scuttling away towards the bridge, all screaming their little voices in horror, just like the condemned souls had done.

Bleeding profusely from his face, Bernardo rolled his body only in time to see Clarissa looking at him, holding an unusually long sword, similar to what he had seen with Julian on the hunt after the siege of Luna.

But he must have been delirious, for behind Clarissa, he had the clear impression of catching a glimpse of a towering statue of the whitest marble. A magnificent woman, milky white with wings that had more colours than the rainbow. She held a sword and looked at him exactly in the same fashion as Clarissa did ahead of her.

Bernardo rubbed his eyes and tried to re-focus, but at that stage, none of the two were there anymore.

Leaning on his elbows and looking ahead towards the bridge, he saw where Clarissa had gone. The legions of hell flocked into the Hellmouth, bringing the last escapees of eternal torment into the toothed maw. A determined Clarissa walked up the bridge. Holding onto Julian's sword, swinging it heavily every time she came close to another sizeable threat, however they were speedier to find refuge back into the Hellmouth.

But then Bernardo saw the most breath-taking of them all.

If all of the grotesque shapes that had swarmed the eastern bank of the Serchio, all of the monstrous creatures that surged from the Hellmouth, all of the devils that flew around the valley to liberate the ice-encased bridge, if all of these abominations could amalgamate into one single being of pure wrong, the result would not be as terrifying as what stood on the bridge. A giant of a shadow, an impersonation of everything that could be fiendish, it held Julian in one hand and what looked to be Arrigo of the Cunimundinghi in another. And so tall and powerful it was, that hanging onto Arrigo's hand was his mother Maria Maddalena and she did not touch the bridge's floor.

Clarissa stroke the beast when it had dropped Arrigo and Maria from his grasp. The eel was quick to snatch hold of Arrigo's dead body, who had a frozen howl of terror still carved on his face, and throw back its head, swallowing the young lord Cunimundinghi with a single gulp.

And the winged giant was just ready to pull Julian apart when the Damascene steel sword made by Caligero disappeared into its repulsive dark flesh. With an ear-splitting shriek, the shadowy figure raised its wings to the sides and violently turned its huge leonine head to face its attacker. But rather than just tip Clarissa from the bridge with a light slap with the back of its talons, it viciously attacked her as it would do to an equal opponent.

The entanglement of black muscle and silvery flashes, the continuous growth of endless coils of the Hellmouth behind and the explosion of light and shadows on the battle that followed were difficult to follow from the road, where Bernardo laid immovable from fear. In the blink of an eye, he would see the warring Clarissa inside the tornado of darkness. Although dwarfed by the leonine monster, she avoided its bird-like talons and stabbed the hard flesh tirelessly with her long sword, like a mighty amazon leading an entire army. But as the lonely Clarissa faced the giant, the shepherd caught glimpses of a fabulous flash of colours from the massive wings of a colossal milky woman, who now powerfully defended herself from the destructive strikes of the shadow.

And surely Bernardo thought he must have been dreaming, affected by divine illusions after that earlier outpour of hellish displays, for in addition to this spectacular winged female, a third party seemed to be arising to join the combat. Materialising from the blue light that the two women emanated, a magnificent ethereal creature, much more gigantic than Clarissa and her winged reflection, emerged so powerful that Bernardo could see the yellow eyes on the demon's face growing with fear.

The shepherd would forever remember it as the most extraordinary creature ever witnessed by human eyes. Even though he had but a few brief moments and a poor angle to observe that apparition, those features would be eternally engraved in his memory. He could not see its human face, but the colourful cone-shaped crown, only for a second, when its massive golden wings were briefly spread apart. Standing on four long, firm limbs, its chest and neck seemed to be covered in a thick mane of the same gold. The fantastic being erected itself on its two hind hooves, spread its wings wide and quickly strung an arrow of pure white fire into a boat-sized arc of the same brightness. Holding the arrow back firmly with its paw, it only let it go and disappeared completely as Clarissa dug her sword deep into the shadow's chest.

On that moment, the demon did not collapse or burst, but it shrunk to a size smaller even than Clarissa. Bernardo saw little of it as turned around to disappear through a curtain of dark haze that it left hanging on its shrinkage, probably disappearing swiftly into the Hellmouth.

Having eaten all the demons and condemned souls back into its throat, the monstrous eel was still stretched across the western slope, but Clarissa did not wait. With those angelic reflexions gone, she stood alone on her side of the vanishing dark haze, raising her sword again, and ready to strike. Bernardo watched her leap through the curtain. And shining through it, the blue, silvery brightness of the Damascene steel blade, making a wide arc and crushing against the Hellmouth.

There was a mute thud, which sucked in all the sound from the valley. The dark clouds that hung close above the Serchio were violently drawn in to this instantaneous second of muteness, cleaning the entire area from shadows and clearing it from sounds. And this brief moment of nothingness was followed by a tremendous expansion of light. A blob that started bright grey and expanded bluish, turning purple, when an explosion of emerald rays, shattering like arrows, slowly being reduced to a golden crown of rays, which contained in its central core the red flames of its burning heart. It quickly brought all the colours back to it into a white, milky amalgamation and shot straight up. A white marble beam, disappearing into the blueness of the sky, while sparks of rainbow luminosity bloomed out of it, flakes of light that delicately fell into the waters below, melting away into the current.

Bernardo was not blinded by this outburst, but pleasurably attracted to that light. Reluctant to turn his gaze away from the immense sky that opened above him, he had to adjust his vision to the bridge.

How different it seemed all of a sudden.

Not a dragon, but a slim kitten. An arched stone structure, peaceful and quite delicately reaching across a wide stony bank and a dark green current of amused waters, whose soft giggling announced the coming of spring. A masterpiece of engineering and beauty. There were no more signs of an eel or demons or a flaming gateway into hell. No more rush of bodies or monsters in battle. There was only Julian, the Hospitaller, adjusting himself with difficulty on the parapet, his robes covered in scarlet, and Maria Maddalena of the Cunimundinghi on the ground, sobbing, trying to stand on her feet. On the opposite bank, a rider approached on gallop. It was Anton, the parish clerk.

But Bernardo could see no sign of Clarissa.

Julian was not blinded by the light. While the coloured blob exploded as Clarissa stroke the Hellmouth, the comforting warmth emanated by that sequence of colours expanded over the stony surface of the bridge and wrapped itself around him, straightening him safely on the parapet, soothing the pain around his chest, assuring him that it was over, that everything would be alright.

He saw the trembling body of the eel disintegrating into clear air and the bloom of rainbow flakes flowering from the clash. In the blink of an eye, like a stigma growing from within the coloured petals, a milky column raised high from its centre, disappearing into the sky before the eyes could follow it.

And everything was clean. The bridge stood shining under the spring morning sky.

While Julian tried to put himself together, seating on the parapet, strangely with no more pain from his crushed ribs, he touched himself around through the blood soaked vest and found no pain of wounds and broken bones.

Maria Maddalena was silently weeping, a few paces down towards the eastern bank.

'He's gone,' she sobbed. 'My Arrigo is gone…'

Julian looked back and saw the shiny surface of the bridge leaning down towards the western embankment. Empty. Clarissa was nowhere to be seen.

Clarissa!

She was not there, neither on the other side. Further down the road, a rider approached on gallop, but it wasn't her either.

Please Clarissa!

Sweating profusely, Julian could smell his own fear. He tried to control his breath and looked over the parapet, watching the Serchio that slowly rolled southwards. The last flakes of light were dissolving their colours, rainbow stains that quickly faded into the dark green current.

Do NOT leave me alone, Clarissa!

He could feel his teeth crushing from the force of his bite.

The parish clerk Anton shouted at him from one side of the bridge, and so did Bernardo from the other side. But the Hospitaller could not hear or bother. He had only one thing to do. Raising his leg on a wide step was enough to bring him up, standing on the parapet, he looked down for a second and hurled his whole body over.

Diving like a kingfisher, Julian disappeared, swiftly and gracefully with a sharp plunge into the dark waters.

And this was the last that was ever seen of Julian the Hospitaller around that valley of the Serchio.

Ponte Della Maddalena

On those days after the Feast of Saint Longinus in the year One Thousand and Thirty Three, Antelmino di Gottefredo woke up from a delirious slumber of pain and nightmares. He found himself recovering from a mutilating injury in an empty, cold castle.

The Castracani walked down the stairs around the rock to the stables in Anchiano and demanded a horse. Moaning in pain, he tried to mount, but given the unfortunate location of his wound he could not even sit on the saddle. He ended up being laid on a cart and taken to his manor in Tassignano by a terrified stableman, who expected to deal later with the Lady Maria Maddalena.

Over the next weeks, his wound expelled vast quantities of reeking liquid and solid materials, while Antelmino lived in a delirious limbo between life and death. When the slashed skin decided to heal, he found himself once again forgotten in his chamber, while his household was taken over by his son Antelminello.

Feeling old and tired, Antelmino lost all the fury he had in his blood, dropping any will for revenge and wishing for forgetfulness. While the son Antelminello grew ravenous for blood, Antelmino never told him how his injury came to be. He also never went back to the metato near Anchiano to retrieve his old deerhide hat. His son dropped the search and arranged to make a similar one for himself, using goats' testicles for the ghastly adornments.

The Castracani's body grew immensely fat and his voice became thinner, in few years strangely resembling the timbre of an old woman's.

Antelmino disappeared from Lucca, hiding in Tassignano, partly for the shame, the difficulty in locomotion, and partly for his son Antelminello, who found the monstrous figure of his father an embarrassment and did little to provide him with the comforts of life.

One morning Antelmino finally realised he was alone. He had just woken up on the floor, under the table. He had eaten and drunk himself to an offensive state of obese monstrosity. But now, as debilitated and deformed as he was, there was no manner in which he could put himself in a seated position.

That is it: I have been abandoned.

Much more than desperate for help, he felt annoyed. So if his son wanted revenge, he would have it. If for a little bit of dignity he had to tell his son that he had been gored by Ginevra of Chifenti, then he would say it, so Antelminello could go and gut her too.

At least Antelmino could negotiate, he though, some comforts to live with his size of body.

He cried for his son. Nobody came.

He tried again, and again.

As the day outside got hotter and an inconvenient myriad of flies seemed to be attracted to the residues around his body, Antelmino cried and cried louder for his son. He finally fell into an exhausted slumber at night, on the same spot where he had woken up. In the next morning, all soiled from his gastronomic abuse, he felt weaker and screamed louder for Antelminello. There were more flies around him, defying the few tremors that he could attempt to make to slap them. He screamed madly for help, so much that his screeching faded into a wheeze and his mouth got tired of exercising.

In the late afternoon, he could feel the flies coming inside his lips, but he was too tired to do something about it.

Antelminello opened the door two weeks later, releasing a battalion of flies from the manor. The nervous servants met him in the patio and told him that the old master had screamed for several days, before finally silencing. Antelminello gave them a reward for having done as they were told and a threatening alert about any spread of the word. He sent the servants in to clean it up, while he adjusted his new hat.

As for what went on in the Bridge of Chifenti, Bernardo delle Rocche was the cantastorie who had seen it all. Torn between the anguishing moments of wait, helplessly expecting to see Julian resurfacing from the gelid waters of the Serchio with Clarissa on his arms, and the desperate need to know that Ginevra was well and safe back in Chifenti, Bernardo was frozen, but his mind was running wild.

He was quickly rushing all those images and fears and sensations and absurdities that sprouted from that bridge on that morning of Saint Longinus. He had to witness it all. *Have I missed nothing? Will I remember everything? Will anyone believe anything?* His face and his head were not in pain anymore. He touched the skin and felt the scars on his cheeks, on his head. Healed, as if from old wounds of a different life.

The river was silently moving, except for a few trickles of melted snow and ice here and there, trying to run away from the sunshine that rose bright and warm.

The only other sound in that silent, calm valley was the weeping of Maria Maddalena.

Although Bernardo badly wanted to be disappointed to find that horrible woman *alive* after the chaos that had broken on the bridge, he was only saddened to feel a sting of pity for her broken stance.

Brushing it off his thoughts, he stood up and looked at the river. Julian should have appeared, if not there, at least down the current, gasping out of the surface from his long dive, reaching out to the rocks and reeds, bringing a water-drenched Clarissa with him.

But nothing.

The cantastorie felt desperately lonely.

He feared that Julian would not be returning, and perhaps neither Clarissa. All of those memories would be hurriedly vanishing if Julian would not be around anymore. The moments they had spent together but never talked about. From the day he had met him south of Poitiers, on his journey back home, the raid in the forest, the adventures in Lucca, the wedding, the hunt. Nobody else was left with those memories but him. Even though the cantastorie carefully nursed their memories of old tales, sharing them, sowing them wherever an eager pair of ears wished to hear them, it was rarely that these memories involved accounts of themselves. Hardly any of the storytellers had a tale of their own.

More than losing his best friend, Bernardo was losing the main character in his stories.

The Serchio carried on running, silently. Bernardo observed the parish clerk on the bridge, laying a friendly hand on Maria's shoulder. Bernardo wanted that warmth. Watching that kind gesture made him feel even more profoundly abandoned. He inhaled with a spasm, on a sudden sob of desperation. He craved a human touch, more than he had ever needed.

Ginevra! he thought, freezing his blood.

Bernardo ran. Faster than his own feet could, he flew back the entire mile through the tunnelled road back to Chifenti. The demons had to be lying to him. Ginevra had to be safe. Not stopping until he entered the village, Bernardo was gutted to see all doors opened, houses deserted, chickens and dogs eating from trays and bags that had been left scattered across the grounds.

His breathing had not slowed down when he rushed to the tavern, only to find it empty too. Not a sign of Ginevra or Amadeo.

Now he was panting, wheezing. He verified the stables, the haystack, hoping that she had hidden from those demons. All was empty.

'GINEVRA!' he cried, in utter desolation. Nauseous with vertigo, he returned to the tavern and headed outside, sensing a black abyss threatening to open wide in front of his feet, a dark, fetid crack that would swallow him, with promises of pain and misery. Leaving the tavern, he saw the deserted road and fell on his knees. 'GINEVRA!' His voice was the only sound that broke through the village air. He embraced the ground and punched it with his fists, sobbing 'Ginevra, don't leave me here. Not you too…'

A hinge creaked sharply as the door of the small stony church of San Frediano was pushed opened by an old, thin, trembling hand. The pointed bearded chin of old Father Vannozzo peeked out. With alert eyes as big as chicken eggs he scanned through the village and stopped at the tavern. Clearing his throat, he called with a fragile, but commanding voice 'Bernardo Delle Rocche! Is that you or a demon that haunts us?'

Bernardo raised his head startled. His eyes took a moment to adjust the focus to the church, not too far, by the village entrance. Father Vannozzo narrow frame wore a cloak which hung above his thin shins as if from a one-hooked hanger. His head seemed to be wider than his shoulders. The silver beard sprouted out in all directions from the prominent chin, and a set of bulging eyes clearly revealed the priest's anxiety. The old man did not hesitate or wait longer for an answer. He swiftly turned around and entered the church again and pulling the door closed.

'Wait, old priest!' Bernardo finally said, standing up and running towards the church. 'It's me, it's *me*!'

The door creaked open again, and this time it was Amadeo. Other villagers appeared through the door too, out in the sunlight.

'No more demons, Bernardo?' Amadeo asked, raising a hand to his brows, protecting his eyes from the sunshine.

'They're gone!' said Bernardo, cutting the air with his hand towards the south. 'They're all gone!'

Amadeo nodded and extended his hand into the door. Out of the darkness came Ginevra, holding his hand. She was trembling, but opened a sunny smile on seeing Bernardo. The cantastorie ran to her arms.

The witch Maria Maddalena of the Cunimundinghi did not want to leave the bridge. Blinded by an explosion of light, she missed to see the fate of her son, but she feared that Arrigo had been lost forever to the Serchio. And worse, with every indication that he would be eternally suffering in hell.

She laid there on the cold stone, crying all the tears that those eyes had never shed in her thirty two years of age. The parish clerk Anton was the only person throughout the valley on that day who took pity on the sobbing figure that sat on that bridge. Holding warmly to her shoulders, he tried to comfort her with tender words, to help her up, but she would not listen, she would not try. Rushing to the hospital Anton managed to fetch her a bowl of milk. Strangely, her eyesight slowly returned to normal later on that day, as did her strength, which had been stolen away by the exposure to Hellmouth.

For many days, while Maria insisted in remaining at the bridge, perhaps waiting for a miracle to bring her son back, Anton stayed at the hospital of Santa Croce, now an abandoned house where he feared the owners would not be returning. He brought her food and water and he covered her for the night. Eventually she returned with him to Anchiano.

And in spite of her melancholy, rather miraculously she bore three more children fathered by the Magyar.

Maria ordered a small sanctuary to be built in memory of her son at the bridge's site, but the chapel was forever known as the Santuario della Maddalena. Years later, the locals would give her name.to the bridge.

And by never mentioning again her bargain with Ginevra, the Lady of Anchiano made an effort to display small portions of generosity. But she was living in a distant universe, apart from the children that she brought into the world with the dedicated Anton. While she maintained a gaseous gaze on her eternally shocked face, her children were mostly raised under the supervision of their father, Anton. Decades later, all the lands of Anchiano would be lost to other descendants of Bishop Gherardo. His youngest daughter Pallia, would still hold Anchiano for a few years before being overwhelmed by the children of Antelmino's son, Antelminello.

Maria's children made their lives in Lucca, staying away from Anchiano and the burden associated with those lands east of the Serchio. They were called the Magiari.

Their mother never had a chance to see them grow prosperous. She was lost as they were still very young. It was indeed a strange thing that occurred during one her daily visits to the sanctuary she had built at the bridge. Few people could figure what had happened after all.

On her exhaustively repeated routine at the bridge, Maria Maddalena would weave fervorous prayers for the soul of her good son Arrigo. Locals guessed she pleaded for his salvation, others for resurrection, but another group speculated that she begged to join him in afterlife. Then, she would walk up the bridge to its highest point, lean on the parapet and stare at the green waters for hours. Passers-by shook their heads and smiled in warm sympathy for that ember of hope that still glowed inside her.

It was in her fortieth year of life, on a beautiful summer day, under a wide and bright sky, when traffic at the bridge was at its highest. There were groups of pilgrims crossing in both directions, a rich family riding back to Barga and an oxcart that took barrels of silk cocoons to the city boilers, while several other carts with wine and olives waited for their turn in both banks. Fishermen carried one or two trouts and baskets full of *rovelle* along the rocky shore. And while few birds wheeled high on the sky, Maria Maddalena, as always, leaned on the parapet, staring silently at the currents, where ducks dabbled noisily, foraging on the shallows.

Nobody saw it happening. They only heard the loud crunch, like a blind axe beating against an old dry log. And in the same moment, Maria was rolling down the bridge slope towards the eastern embankment.

She was dead, with her head completely crushed.

Next to where she fell, they found a massive bone. It was a partially gnawed-clean femur of an ox. Nobody had seen it lying there when they crossed the bridge. Some people suggested it was the bone that killed Maria, perhaps falling from the sky, tossed by God.

The Commissioner

Old Albertazzo was profoundly asleep on his bench when he was shaken awake by Lando Delle Rocche.

'Wake up, you old thorn,' said the cantastorie, 'there is a bright sun up on the skies, and perhaps it is time we leave. Everyone is gone, including the mute goose Liutprando. There has been a messenger, and plenty of shuffling of feet and men at arms running about.

Albertazzo looked at him with unfocused eyes. While trying to straighten himself up on the bench, the old man grunted, chewed on his toothless gums and farted.

Lando could not help but laugh. 'I'm too boring for your one hundred years of memories. All I get is reproach from Matilda and from you a hellish fart. I guess you're too old for nightime stories anyway.'

'Just pass me that wine, will you?' Albertazzo asked with a tremulous finger pointing at a jar. Lando was quick to hand him the strong wine. He knew that after a good goblet in the morning, his cousin would not be looking as aged as he was.

The Marchese dalla Malaspina drank from his goblet with a passionate dedication, and closed his eyes for a moment, in a nearly sinful enjoyment of the irradiation of pleasant feelings over his body. 'I agree,' Albertazzo finally said. 'There is nothing good to come out of Matilda after her knowledge of this story. We should leave immediately. I will call for my men, who are stationed over at the city market.'

'The Beatissimo Padre has sent us a message!' announced Contessa Matilda of Canossa, breaking through the dining hall. Although she had been piously dressed with a brown linen robe and cowl, the plated furs of *ermellini* that rimmed the robe were a clear and undeniable statement of her power. Bishop Liutprando followed her with his parchment and quill.

'We were just… we were about to leave, my dear *Grancontessa*,' said Lando with a touch more than the required deference, but not without showing some hesitation in his voice. 'We have abused your hospitality for so long and even our dear Marchese Albertazzo here perhaps needs to –'

'Rubbish!' interrupted the contessa without even paying a glance to her cousins. She walked decisively to her large chair. 'Never mind the old man. He's always been a bad thorn, and a bad thorn he will always be. But I still need to know a few things.'

'Does Gregory have any questions in his message?' asked Albertazzo, finally standing up, and with not a drop of amusement on his face.

'I will tell you about the message in a moment,' dismissed Matilda with a wave of her hand. 'But for now, just tell me, any of you two, whatever has happened to those relics they found in the Serchio?'

'*Ma che cazzo?*' Lando asked with the tips of his fingers in one hand all together pointing up. 'Haven't I told you yet? A couple from the Holy Land took the skeletons away.'

The contessa stared at Lando for a few seconds, just with a trembling movement of her jaws, as if she wanted to eat him alive. 'Never mind your language in my own house, shepherd. You will regret that one day. For now, tell me about the skeletons and the people who found them. So they pulled both Julian and Clarissa out of the Serchio?'

'Well, ever since their disappearance, nobody had ever found the bodies. There had been so many years and the river was always cruel, taking others, pilgrims lost in the storm, uncautious children, women washing clothes, but all the bodies would surface sooner or later. Not those two. Julian and Clarissa had been lost forever.

'So when those pilgrims arrived from the Holy Land, they called for my father. Those were times when Bernardo was already a widower, very old, with his children mostly in Lucca, Barga, Pistoia and Genoa, except me, but I was too young then. My father missed his wife dearly. He never failed to talk to Ginevra, as if she was always on his side.

'After finding that the couple had come from Jerusalem to take Julian's bones with them, he allowed them to rake the river from his side, and conferred with Pallia of the deceased Sigifredo to allow them to extend the search from the hospital side.

'And they raked the river for days, much longer after my father had been given up. And as I told you, it was on the moment when the pilgrim and his wife exchanged their stories of Julian with my father, the bones were found. There were two skeletons, Grancontessa.'

'Julian and Clarissa?' Matilda asked, leaning her body forward.

But the cantastorie never answered that. He just continued 'The bones were cleaned from the mud and algae, and carefully conditioned into a small cedar wood casket with little adornments. When the pilgrim couple came to say their farewell to Bernardo at the Rocca, the man had plump red cheeks popping out of his old face and a healthy smile. Their bright eyes were burning livid with satisfaction. And they asked Bernardo for a favour, since he was a man of studies. My father listened carefully to what the man had to say. Then, his wife opened a bundle and handed him a roll of goatskin parchment. Bernardo went for his chests and returned with a good crow feather quill and a vial of Norseman hawthorn ink. Opening the roll, Bernardo thought carefully before dipping the quill in the vial. And he wrote:

Hic iacent SS Iulianus et Clarissa Hospitalieri
Beata Memoria
Amantium hospitalariorum
Qui vivi et mortui
Amore iuncti.
(Here are the remains of Saints Julian and Clarissa, Loving hospitallers, Strong and generous creatures, Joined together by love, In life and in death)

'They waited patiently until it dried. Then the wife opened the casket and wrapped the bones with the parchment.

'What were their names?' Matilda asked, 'those pilgrims.'

Lando answered very quickly 'The man was Jan, and his wife was Helena.'

'Jan and Helena' Matilda repeated, 'and you said they knew Julian from Jerusalem…'

'And they would be heading to Amalfi or Salerno' Lando completed, 'but those years have gone by and we have never heard of them again.'

'So there's nothing else you can tell me about them?' the contessa asked.

'There's one thing that my father told me,' Land said. 'He walked with the pilgrims to the edge of town and asked the one last question: "What makes you so sure that these two are Julian and Clarissa, for two other people disappeared into the river on that same spot, that same day?"

'The pilgrim's beard and moustache moved to make a shape of a smile. "Because those two were hugging dearly onto each other!"'

'The wife seemed to understand what her husband had said. She laid a warm hand over his shoulder. The pilgrim flicked the reigns and the cart slowly moved down the road, turning their backs to the Bridge of Chifenti.'

After a brief moment of silence, Albertazzo grunted and moved his thin legs to stand up, plainly readying himseld to leave. 'I could listen to much more, my cousin Lando, but the hour is late and I should –'

Matilda cleared her throat discreetly and announced 'Perhaps both of you should know the contents of the Beatissimo Padre's message.'

Lando's face turned into a smile. 'I thought you were never going to tell us!'

Bishop Liutprando stood up and, for a moment, the expected him to talk. But he only handed another roll to Matilda.

'His Holiness commands that – listen to that you too, Albertazzo' she yelled to her old cousin, who had not demonstrated any interest in the message. 'He commands that none of the lies told by Lando delle Rocche in this palace about the hospitaller Julian, of Santa Croce, or about the coming of the devil, or about the Crescenti or Tusculani popes and their predecessors and successors, ever be repeated to a living Christian again.'

Lando laughed.

Albertazzo spat, eyes wide with incredulity. 'These were not lies, Matilda.'

'Let-me-finish!'she roared. 'The holy pope has allowed for the change of name of this bridge, which will take my name, as the commissioner of this renovation. No Chifenti, no Maddalena and no Devil. Your lies shall never be uttered again.'

'Renovation?' Alberto cackled, 'the bridge is as firm and complete as it has ever been. You are only wasting your time and silver trying to cover the hole that was opened by the devil. And you have not even fulfilled that task yet.'

'These are commands by the pope himself!' Matilda rasped, almost hysterical.

Lando was serious again. '*Why*? What does Gregory intend to gain with my silence? To safeguard the good name of the papacy? Benedict XIX was indeed a monster, and so many before him, we all know that. Or better: most of us have forgotten about that. If Gregory wants to clean up the reputation of the throne of Saint Peter, he should do it by his own acts, and not by attempting to silence history. Matilda, you can try and spend all your silver and gold to change that bridge, and you can show your sword to keep us quiet, but that will never change the truth.'

'Your stories will be forgotten, Lando delle Rocche.' Now it was Matilda's turn to laugh. 'One day history will know that the Bridge of Chifenti was commissioned by Matilda, Contessa of Tuscany.'

'It's not worth arguing, Lando,' said Albertazzo, shaking his lowered head. 'We should be on our way.'

'Good bye, Matilda del fu Bonifacio'. Lando said, calling her by the patronymic form. 'You are just sitting up too high on your chair, blinded by the shine of your star. You will never understand the cantastorie! Never.' He waved her a hand and left, carrying his francesca and with Albertazzo holding onto his arm.

On the palace stables, Albertazzo had some help from Lando to mount his large destrier.

'You head to Luna now?' Lando asked.

Albertazzo looked at the Contessa's palace with suspicious eyes. 'For now I do, but I don't trust that woman. In our decaying Luna I am still too vulnerable to her troops. Perhaps I should fare further. An old man does not need his roots any more. I can spend my next hundred years in a life of adventure. And so should you Lando.' He roughed the head of the cantastorie amicably. 'Stay away from Matilda. Beware of anyone in Lucca. That ugly toad can always appear less deadly than she really is.'

'Thank you, old cousin, but I have my own francesca to defend myself and not many foes will dare to defy me. I will spend some time in the city, drinking to forget, finding a nice pair of legs to warm mine, perhaps in the market, or maybe at Santa Maria Ursimanni…'

Albertazzo's dry lips opened into a toothless smile. 'Oh, had I been twenty years younger…'

'You'd still be in your seventies, you old bad thorn!' Lando said, extending his hand to Albertazzo. 'Farewell, my cousin. I hope to see you again.'

The old man held onto the hand firmly and swiftly inclined to plant a kiss on his cousin's head. 'You will, Lando. We are Obertenghi. We will meet again one day, and every day after. And we will talk about all of these stories.'

Letter received by Pope Gergory VII at the Lateran Palace, Rome:

In the name of God, Amen.

I pray that the Beatissimo Padre Gregory, with the Blessings of the Angels and Saints, fares well with His demanding tasks as the keeper of the keys of the Holy See.

And I pray that the power of God and the hand of Saint Peter will protect the Beatissimo Padre from sorrow, as this letter is filled with remorse. Nevertheless, it is my duty to make the Beatissimo Padre aware of the misfortunes that have occurred over the last few weeks.

As for your most humble servant and the most pious lamb of your herd, I have endeavoured to convince the cantastorie Lando, descendant of the once noble Obertenghi of the Rocca, to take a vow of silence on his malicious version of the events that led to the building of the bridge of Chifenti and the seizing of the bones of the hospitallers of the Santa Croce. I regret to inform the Beatissimo Padre that my most virtuous appeals were ignored, and Lando left my hospitality with mockery on his tone, accompanied by the Marchese Albertazzo della Malaspina, who kept the same defiance on his gait.

It is with greater regret that I must inform the Beatissimo Padre that on the morrow after Lando of the Obertenghi left the palace, his body was found lifeless on the banks of the river Serchio, with a barbaric francesca axe dug into his chest. May God have mercy on his wicked soul. To this day, there is no information of the assassin, but we will soon find the culprit, perhaps among the slums outside the city. This tragic occurrence at least conforms to the divine designations dictated by the Beatissimo Padre, that none of the lies told by Lando of the Obertenghi during his stay at the palace should ever be repeated to a living soul. As a loyal servant of God, I will be certain to ensure the vows of silence are taken by any of his descendants.

As for the Marchese dalla Malaspina, we do not believe that any malicious words will reach us from his mouth. The marchese has forsaken Luna, Milan and Este, having taken ample vows of silence and refuge in the abbey of Vangadizza, in Verona. May God forgive his soul one day, a day that should not be taking too long to arrive.

These are indeed grave tidings, and I pray that in Heaven I will understand the mysteries and challenges that God puts ahead of us to make his will fulfilled. I also pray that such words have not caused more discomfort to the Beatissimo Padre than the very disquiet of the story of Julian, the Hospitaller. But has this been the case, I re-iterate my invitation, eternally extended to the Apostle of Christ to sooth your mortified body at the Baths of Corsena at the Val di Lima.

With the renewal of the bridge, commissioned by your most loyal servant, any malice bent by the words of Lando of the Obertenghi should be forever expurged from the valley of the Serchio and never again reach our most pious ears.

Asking for your apostolic blessing, from your faithful servant,

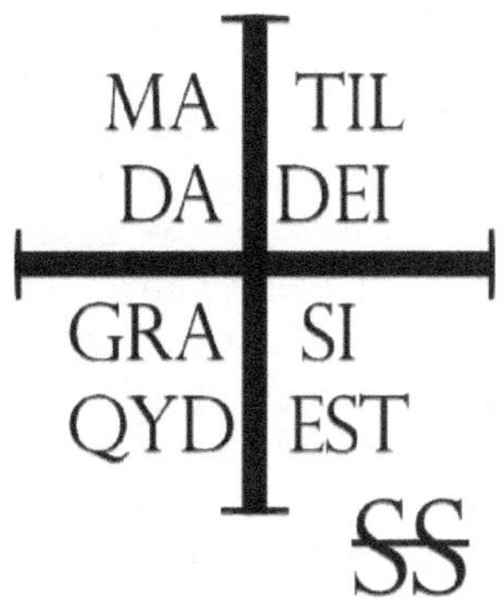

Epilogue: What the Other Cantastorie Tell

The gelid waters gladly accepted Julian in with a freezing crunch when he plunged into the Serchio. He was embraced by the icy current, which squeezed all the air out of his lungs in a curtain of bubbles that rose fast, as his numb hands hit the murky bottom. There was no pain to be felt from the impact, only the feeling of loneliness, of being dunked into a different world, dark as the darkest night, cold as the highest peak. He saw a light above him, the surface, which separated the depths from the world he wanted to take Clarissa back to. Something pulled at his legs. He though immediately of marabecchi and other water goblins, or an escaped soul that still hid from the demons under the silt. But in a second he realised his feet had been caught snarled into some flood-washed branch lying in the bottom. Inexperienced underwater, Julian only wanted to touch that river bottom and find Clarissa. He was pulled untangled by the current, tumbling down over silt and rocks, but opening his arms to catch anything with a human feel.

With no more air in his chest, he tried to breathe, but choked with cold water. Coughing it out only made it worse, as his lungs were flooded deeper with that icy feeling. It made him number and heavier, with an overwhelming squeeze around his head as if a boulder was sitting on it. He felt a sudden and desperate need to move himself out of the glacial world and gasp that water out. The surface was not too far above him. He could try and reach it, force his legs, beat them like a duck.

But Julian had to find Clarissa before breaching for air.

He was weaker, slow, but he managed to reach over the bottom with his hands and started moving, pushing himself forward with his legs. The bitter cold pressed around his head eased up as numbness took control of his body. But he had a sensation that he was getting closer to finding her, a certain warmth detected in the current. Yes, it must have been Clarissa, he thought, for not only he began to physically sense that warmth, but his nose, which had been stinging with icy water, suddenly eased up and he could smell that milky scent of hers. Clarissa was close to him. The water became much warmer and comforting, and its colour quickly changed to an opaque but smooth milky white. The warmth was healing, a blessed embrace that nurtured all his senses and he felt more alive than ever. He smiled and slowly reached over with his hands towards a green spark of light that travelled through the milk towards him. And as it got warmer and more inviting, a rainbow of coloured arrows shot through the whiteness, feeling him and filling him with a relieving happiness that made his eyes salty. He felt her hands holding his.

'I *found* you Clarissa!'

It was time to surface. She pulled him up and they breached out together, both standing on that lake, with their waists dipped into the calm whiteness.

'No,' she smiled, 'as always, it was *I* who found you!'

The Hospitaller never got tired from hearing those tales by the cantastorie, lying on the soft grass, with his head resting on Clarissa's lap, at the shade of a willow tree. On the lake in front of them, the others bathed and played.

The Family Tree of the Theophylactii, the Obertenghi, the Crescentii and the Tusculani during the Papal "Pornocracy"

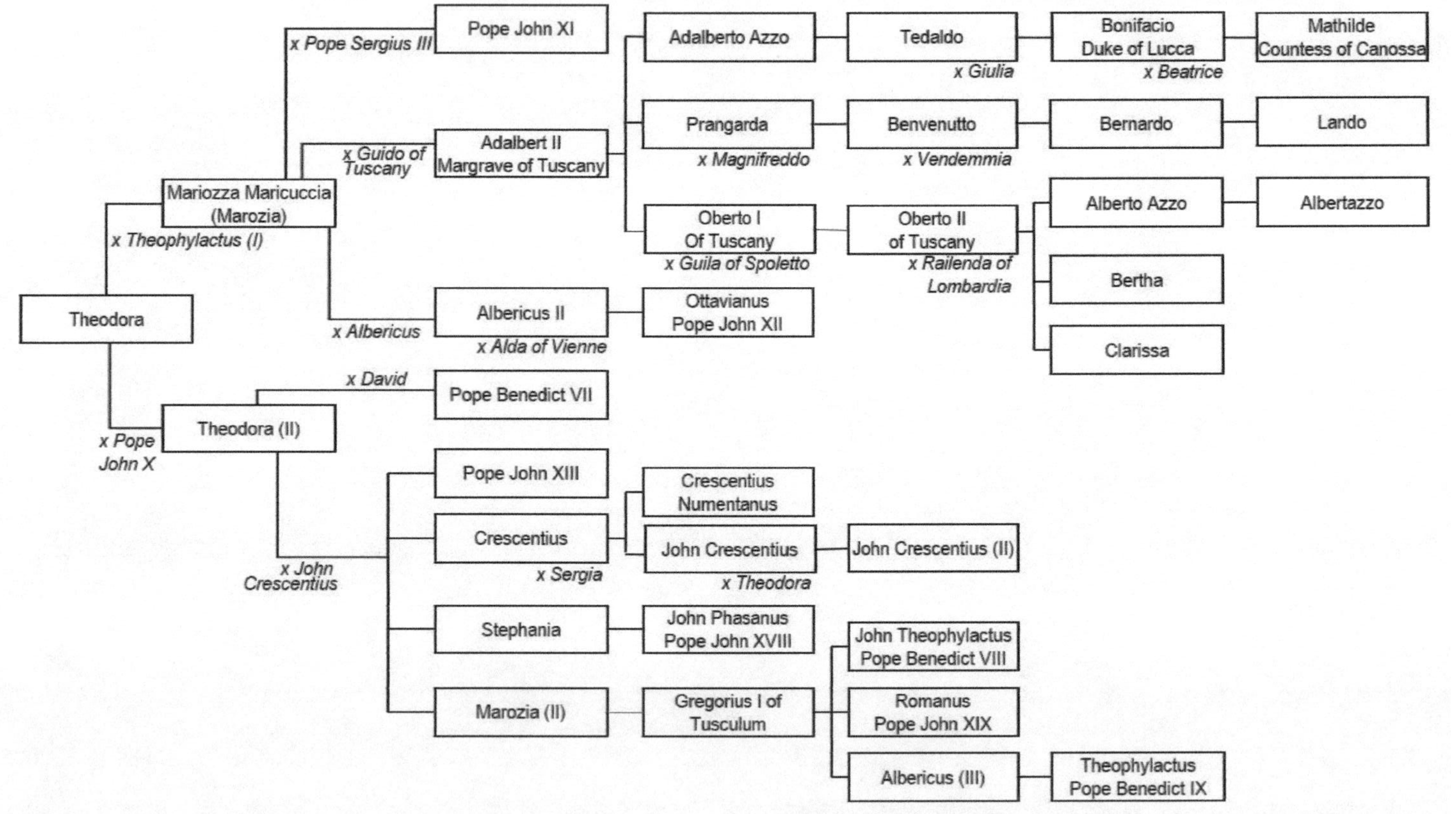

The Family Tree of the Cunimundinghi, later the Suffredinghi and the Rolandinghi from the Serchio Valley and Lucca

A small glossary, with some of the many words and expressions in diverse languages and dialects used in this story:

* *abakos*: abacus
* *accubita*: furniture couch for reclining upon at meals
* *Adhan*: the call for Islamic prayers
* *Aedicula*: shrine in the Church of the Holy Sepulchre encasing the tomb where the body of Christ is said to have been lain to rest
* *alani* (plur): molosser dogs; *alaunt* (sing.)
* *allevillamento*: a land transfer
* *Anastasis*: rotunda of the Church of the Holy Sepulchre
* *Anguilla*: eel; *anguille* (plur.)
* *Anno Mille*: the thousandth year of the Christian Era, A.D.1000
* *apodeipnon*: complines, the prayer after supper
* *aspergillum*: liturgical implement used to sprinkle holy water
* *Assalamu alaikum*: "peace be upon you", greeting, to which one answers in cordial retribution "*Wa 'alaikumus salam*"
* *astori*: goshawks
* *atrium*: large open air or skylight-covered space surrounded by a building
* *avvoltoi*: vultures
* *babbaghah*: parrot
* *bagni*: the baths
* *bailli, balivo*: bailiff
* *Basileus Autokrator*: title for the emperor of Byzantium/Eastern Roman Empire
* *Beatissimo Padre*: Most Blessed Father, a form of address to the pope.
* *befane*: Italian witches
* *bimaristan*: a hospital
* *bischoff*: bishop
* *borde*: sorcerer (Tuscan dialect)
* *borgo*: village
* *büdegassa*: monk fish, anglerfish
* *calandrino*: diminutive of 'calandro', a passerine bird known as lark or pipit
* *camerarius*: chamberlain
* *camoscio*: chamois
* *cappa*: mantle, a papal vest

* *capriolo*: roe deer
* *carbonai*: coal makers; *carbonaia*: a coalmill, a logpile to burn into coals
* *castro*: castle
* *cazzo*: a penis, swearword
* *chartula*: a document, a declaration
* *cimaruta*: sprig of rue, a charm to protect from evil eyes
* *complines*: night prayers, the last canonical hour of the day
* *comte*: count
* *contessa*: countess
* *corvi*: crows, ravens
* *creditori*: creditors
* *crux pectoralis*: a cross that hangs from a necklace resting on the chest
* *cugina* di secondo grado: second degree cousin (fem.)
* *cunei*: wedge-shaped stones in arch; *cuneo* (sing.)
* *custos*: guard; *custodes* (plur.)
* *daino*: fallow deer
* *decuria*: a command of ten guards
* *del fu*: "of the deceased", a form to refer to someone by the deceased father's name
* *denario*: silver coin of Roman currency, still used in the Middle Ages
* *diabolos, diavolo*: devil
* *diavolo de mar*: sea devil, one of the many names of the anglerfish, monkfish
* *dietas*: a deliberative assembly of the states of the Roman Empire in the Middle Ages
* *donnola*: least weasel; *donnole* (plur.)
* *dromon*: byzantine boat propelled by oars and sails
* *duomo*: cathedral
* *Ebreo*: Hebrew
* *Eleazaros*: Lazarus
* *ermellino*: stoat, ermine; *ermellini* (plur.)
* *excitatoria*: arousing or stirring texts
* *extramuri*: outside the city walls
* *factotum*: a general servant, the butler
* *faina*: beech marten
* *faraone*: guinea fowl

• *farro*: a type of wheat. In Tuscany, it refers to emmer
• *ferendæ sentential*: officially-pronounced sentence
• *fideiussore*: guarantors
• *folaga*: coot; *folaghe* (plur.)
• *forcella*: a "y"-shaped stick
• *francesca*: throwing axe used by several Germanic tribes
• *gemelli*: twins
• *genetta*: genet
• *Giudeo*: Jew. *Giudei* (plur.)
• *glirarium*: containers where peasants keep and breed dormice for food
• *gracchi*: choughs, a type of bird
• *grīghund*: greyhound
• *guadia*: pawn
• *habemus papam*: we have a pope
• *hachib*: an officer in the califate of Al-A Andaluz equivalent to the vizier.
• *hemicranias*: migraines
• *heredia*: a *heredium* is a measure of land, equivalent to two yokes, approximately 5040 m²
• *hutesium et clamor*: hue and cry
• *impudica*: shameless
• *intramuri*: within the city walls
• *Iouda*: Jew
• *jinn*: supernatural creature in Islamic mythology (genie)
• *jizya*: tax imposed on non-Muslim citizens of Islamic states
• *jugera* (plur.): a *jugerum* is a measure of land equivalent to how much a single "jugum," or yoke of oxen was capable of plough in one day, approximately 2520 m²
• *kafir*: infidel, non-Muslim
• *khubz*: round bread
• *koriannon*: coriander
• *Kouvouklion*: see "edicule"
• *Kyrie eleison*: Christian prayer: "Lord have mercy"
• *l'onza*: lynx
• *laffah*: flatbread
• *launeguildo*: a land transfer
• *levrieri*: hare dogs, sighthounds
• *lidérc*: a devilish, supernatural being of Hungarian Folklore
• *litham*: veil, headscarf used by Muslim women

• *Longobards*: Lombards, a Germanic tribe that settled across northern Italy
• *Lucchese*: the inhabitants of Lucca
• *lues venerea*: venereal disease
• *Lunensis*: native of Luni
• *lupanar*: a brothel
• *lymerer*: in medieval hunting, the caretaker and conductor of lymers, the scenthounds
• *ma che cazzo?*: the best translation (not literal) for this expression is perhaps "what the fuck?"
• *Magyar*: Hungarian
• *Magyarul*: the Hungarian language
• *maledetto*: damned; *maledetti* (plural)
• *manicae*: armguards in warfare
• *marabecchi*: (Sicilian) water goblins of the Serchio river; *marabecca* (sing.)
• *marca*: a march, a margravate
• *marchese, marchesa*: marquess, marchioness, the margraves, nobility titles referring to the lord and lady of a *marca*
• *marmotte*: marmot
• *mastini*: mastiffs
• *mazzaranga*: tool to crush roasted chestnuts; mazzaranghe (plur.)
• *meretrix*: prostitute
• Messere: My Lord, a respectful form of address
• *metato*: a shed used for drying/roasting chestnuts; metati (plur.)
• *mustiolo*, mus aranes: the Etruscan shrew
• *Narrenturm*: a tower in the city where people with mental disabilities are suspended kept for 'treatment' or public ridicule
• *nepos*: nephew
• *nomenclator*: the announcer of guests, a personal assistant to fulfil a schedule
• *nosocomia*: hospitals
• *omo salvatico*: Wildman, wodewose; *omini salvatici* (plur.)
• *orco*: ogre
• *ordinations*: ordinations
• *ördög*: a demonic being of Hungarian mythology, identified with the Devil
• *otarde*: bustards
• *pallium*: woollen cloak worn by clerics; *pallia* (plur.)

- ***parastás***: a vigil held for the deceased in the eastern christian church
- ***peccatrix***: sinner (fem.)
- ***pellegrino***: pilgrim, peregrine falcon
- ***poiana bastarda***: buzzard
- ***protoscrinarius***: chief notary of the pope
- ***prugnoli***: mushrooms of the species Calocybe gambosa, also known as St George's mushrooms
- ***psyllium***: mucilage
- ***puttana***: whore
- ***qahwa***: coffee
- ***rabarbaro***: rhubarb
- ***raccoglitore***: the cleaners of cesspits & latrines in the city
- ***reredorter***: communal toilets in monasteries
- ***rovelle*** (plur.): roach, a freshwater fish
- ***rumi***: an Arabic term used for Romans, Europeans
- ***Sacrosanta Lateranensis Ecclesia***: Sacred Holy Church of the Lateran
- ***saif***: curved Saracen sword, better known today as scimitar
- ***sandgrouse***: a pigeon-sized bird
- ***santoreggia***: winter savoury
- ***Saqlabi***: dynasty of slave/serf-descendant rulers of the small Spanish principalities of taifas
- ***scriptorium***: an office
- ***seax***: short sword/hatched typically used by the Saxons
- ***sedes stercoraria***: defecating chair, said to be used to verify the gender of a newly chosen pope
- ***segantini*** saw: a framed bandsaw used for making barrels
- ***segugio***: scent hound; ***segugi*** (plur.)
- ***seraph***: an angelical/celestial being; ***seraphim*** (plur.)
- ***Sirocco***: the south-east hot wind
- ***soberbia***: the sin of pride
- ***soldo***: local currency; ***soldi*** (plur.)
- ***solido***: a gold coin issued by Rome, equivalent to 12 denarii
- ***soter***: saviour
- ***spino cervino***: buckthorn
- ***spinosa***: porcupine
- ***strappado***: a fashion of torture in which the victim's hands are first tied behind their back and suspended in the air by a rope attached to wrists
- ***strega***, ***streghe***: witch, witches
- ***stregone***: sorcerer
- ***succiacapre***: nightjar
- ***táltos***: a shaman of Hungarian tribes
- ***tasso***: badger
- ***Tedesco***: German; ***Tedeschi*** (plur.)
- ***terces***: the third hour of the day, midmorning prayers
- ***terme***: the thermal baths
- ***tesserarius***: a military commander, the treasure keeper of the pope
- ***Teufel***: devil
- ***Theotokos***: God-bearer, or the one who gives birth to God. Mother of God.
- ***Tramontana***: the north wind
- ***túlvilág***: the world where dead souls rest, in Hungarian mythology
- ***uovo malefico***: the fly agaric mushroom, Amanita muscaria
- ***uro***: the auerochs; ***uri*** (plur.)
- ***urogallo***: capercaillie
- ***vade retro***: "go back", step back"
- ***vairone***: a small Italian freshwater fish
- ***Varangoi***: Nordic army serving the Byzantine Emperor, the Varangian guards
- ***vellutini***: "little velvets", the nickname given to the population gathered outside of the walls in Lucca, mainly Sicilians
- ***verbum***: an unquestionable, biding, verbal declaration of wedlock that a couple would make to each other, validating the union and requiring no witnessing or priest
- ***via dolorosa***: the path that Jesus walked on the way to his crucifixion
- ***vitelli marini***: monk seals
- ***voussoirs***: a wedge-shaped stone used to construct an arch
- ***wisent***: the European bison
- ***xenodochium***: a hospital for pilgrims
- ***zuppa di farro***: emmer soup